OXFORD WORLD'S CLASSICS

THE GOLDEN BOUGH

SIR JAMES GEORGE FRAZER was born in Glasgow in 1854 and educated at the local university and at Trinity College, Cambridge, where he was Fellow from 1879. Initially attracted to philosophy, he embarked in the mid-1880s on a sustained programme of research into the early history of mankind, and into the relationship between ancient cultures and those of the contemporary non-Western world. The comparative observations thus afforded gave rise to *Totemism* (1887), followed by the multi-volume *The Golden Bough* (1890) which became an instant classic. He was to amplify the second of these works in two further editions of increasing grandeur, but in the meantime turned his mind to other matters. *Pausanias's Description of Greece* (1897) was the fruit of two arduous journeys throughout the Greek mainland, undertaken on foot or on horse-back. *Totemism* provided the basis for the later *Totemism and Exogamy* (1910), and Frazer also wrote on fire myths and the worship of the dead. In 1896 he married Lilly Grove, a French authority on the ethnology of the dance. It was largely due to her unceasing efforts that Frazer's work became widely known in France, in Germany, and in Italy. After periods of residence in Cambridge, London, and in Liverpool where he was briefly profes-sor, the Frazers roamed the Continent in the post-war years. Deteriorating eyesight led to his blindness in 1930, but even after-wards, with the help of amanuenses, Frazer remained unstinting in his output as his influence on writers and artists, as well as on the burgeoning science of anthropology, continued to grow. He died in May 1941, to be followed a few hours later by his wife.

ROBERT FRASER lectures at Royal Holloway and Bedford New College in the University of London. He has taught in Africa, the Middle East, and Latin America as well as at the universities of Cambridge, London, and Leeds. He is the author of *The Making of the Golden Bough: The Origins and Growth of an Argument* (1990) and edited *Sir James Frazer and the Literary Imagination: Essays in Affinity and Influence* (1990).

T0130605

OXFORD WORLD'S CLASSICS

*For over 100 years Oxford World's Classics have brought
readers closer to the world's great literature. Now with over 700
titles—from the 4,000-year-old myths of Mesopotamia to the
twentieth century's greatest novels—the series makes available
lesser-known as well as celebrated writing.*

*The pocket-sized hardbacks of the early years contained
introductions by Virginia Woolf, T. S. Eliot, Graham Greene,
and other literary figures which enriched the experience of reading.
Today the series is recognized for its fine scholarship and
reliability in texts that span world literature, drama and poetry,
religion, philosophy and politics. Each edition includes perceptive
commentary and essential background information to meet the
changing needs of readers.*

OXFORD WORLD'S CLASSICS

SIR JAMES GEORGE FRAZER

The Golden Bough
A Study in Magic and Religion

A NEW ABRIDGEMENT
FROM THE SECOND AND THIRD EDITIONS

Edited with an Introduction and Notes by
ROBERT FRASER

OXFORD
UNIVERSITY PRESS

OXFORD
UNIVERSITY PRESS

Great Clarendon Street, Oxford OX2 6DP

Oxford University Press is a department of the University of Oxford.
It furthers the University's objective of excellence in research, scholarship,
and education by publishing worldwide in

Oxford New York

Auckland Bangkok Buenos Aires Cape Town Chennai
Dar es Salaam Delhi Hong Kong Istanbul Karachi Kolkata
Kuala Lumpur Madrid Melbourne Mexico City Mumbai Nairobi
São Paulo Shanghai Singapore Taipei Tokyo Toronto

Oxford is a registered trade mark of Oxford University Press
in the UK and in certain other countries

Published in the United States
by Oxford University Press Inc., New York

Editorial matter © Robert Fraser 1994

The moral rights of the author have been asserted

Database right Oxford University Press (maker)

First published as a World's Classics paperback 1994
Reissued as an Oxford World's Classics paperback 1998
Reissued 2009

British Library Cataloguing in Publication Data

Data available

Library of Congress Cataloging in Publication Data

Frazer, James George, Sir, 1854–1941.
The golden bough: a study in magic and religion / Sir James George Frazer;
a new abridgement from the second and third editions;
edited with an introduction by Robert Fraser.
p. cm.—(Oxford world's classics)
Includes bibliographical references (p. xliv–xlvi) and index.
1. Mythology. 2. Religion, Primitive. 3. Magic. 4. Superstition.
I. Fraser, Robert, 1947– . II. Title. III. Series.
BL310.F7 1993 291—dc20 93–36189

ISBN 978–0–19–953882–9

Printed in Great Britain by
Clays Ltd, Elcograf S.p.A.

CONTENTS

THE GOLDEN BOUGH

BOOK I: THE KING OF THE WOOD

BOOK II: KILLING THE GOD

ACKNOWLEDGEMENTS

I am indebted to the British Library for permission to quote from manuscripts in their Frazer collection and to Alan McCormick of the Castle Museum, Nottingham, for permission to reproduce his map of Nemi. Others to whom warm acknowledgements are due, either for general encouragement or for particular points of information, are Warwick Gould, Jeremy Maule, Roger Paulin, Ralph Pite, and Deirdre Toomey. Lastly, for putting up with the editor whilst engrossed in his fascinating task, no words are sufficient to convey his gratitude to his wife Catherine and his son Benjo.

INTRODUCTION

I

FEW books have been bought by so many as *The Golden Bough*. Few have been perused so perfunctorily, or been so blithely misunderstood. It is one of the great classics of the world, a foundation stone of the modern sensibility, and yet we do not know it. We do not like to read our great books, yet they read us, every day of our lives. It is not we who have made the literature of the twentieth century. It is the literature that has made us. If we wish to know ourselves better, it is to the literature that we must turn.

Our grandparents, in some ways more diligent readers than ourselves, had a different problem. For them, from the very beginning, Frazer's book possessed a shady reputation. 'If it's anything like what you make it out to be, it's neither a safe nor a proper book to have knocking about here.' So the head librarian to the young Sean O'Casey, who in a moment of adolescent curiosity had requested it in Dublin. In its time *The Golden Bough* was the sort of book to read beneath the bed-sheets by the light of a torch. When the first edition appeared in 1890, a little *frisson* seems to have gone round the literary world. People sent one another letters, phrased in an urgent whisper. The speed and extremity of this reaction is even now not surprising. For *The Golden Bough* is a dangerous book which retains its ability to disconcert. As then, so now, it is a work whose essence lies in its challenge to received cultural attitudes. Authors who place such a challenge are seldom likely to find uncritical favour amongst any readership. If the *status quo* is conservative, they are called liberals. If it fancies itself as liberal, they are called reactionaries. The effect of such gratuitous labelling is, however, often to tempt readers less easily gulled to read the forbidden text.

One of Frazer's subjects in this book is that strange phenomenon, well known to Victorian society but named after an obscure Tongalese custom, called a taboo. Frazer was interested in this subject, amongst other reasons, because he was aware that books are often taboo, just as words and even thoughts sometimes are. He was also well aware that in certain companies religion is a tabooed subject, either amongst those who take their religion for granted or else those who dismiss it too lightly. Frazer was neither. Instead he was a man deeply fascinated by religion, who could not bring himself to subscribe to any doctrinal beliefs. In the late nineteenth century such people were often called free-thinkers. For Frazer the fittest response to such a dilemma was to shed light in obscure places: to investigate the sources of religion and, thereby, the root causes of taboo.

Taboos are fences around cultures, guide-posts to provinciality, definitions of belonging and of place. All of us hold such taboos dear because they inform us, whether through inclusion or else through exclusion, of who we are. Therefore no taboo is more sacrosanct than that which ensures our difference, and no idea more scarifying than the levelling notion of our kinship with those whose taboos are otherwise. Frazer knew this, and he knew the power of infringement. Victorian society was full of taboos that informed its members as to who they were. Christian society too was full of taboos reassuring its adherents that they were in possession of a unique and revealed faith. Victorians did not like to be told that there were other societies whose taboos were as rooted as their own, or that this taboo-building capacity was something that all human beings hold in common and which, by means of the very devices intended to enforce difference, render all men akin. Victorian Christians did not like to be told that other people have religions, that many of these religions are sacrifical. Nor did they relish being instructed that sacrifice could sometimes be explained as mere magic, or that magic might lie at the tap-root of much they themselves held dear. All of this Frazer implied. The equivalences set up between things so apparently unlike were taboos; to find them, in 1890 or thereabouts, you read *The Golden Bough*.

In the later twentieth century anthropology and criticism have become much obsessed by the idea of *l'autre*, the other. It was a concept which for Frazer was so obvious as to be of little real interest. In the late twentieth century we take our sameness for granted, and furtively probe for difference. The late Victorians by contrast took their otherness for granted, and probed forbidden areas of parity. Hence Frazer was much less interested in otherness than he was in sameness. It was a preoccupation that got him into trouble, since most Victorians were assured of their own otherness, and were even quite proud of it. The notion that, to quote one of Frazer's own formulations, all humans possessed an 'essential similarity', was at one level very threatening to the Victorian mind. Hence the notoriety of Frazer's comparative study of culture and belief when first published in 1890. Hence the reaction of the head librarian to Sean O'Casey's passionate request.

II

Frazer's subject is the comparative study of culture, a subject which he knew about because he had deep cultural roots of his own and had investigated widely the cultural contexts of others. He was thus interested in the idea of bringing experience and investigation, life and reading, into the same discursive zone. To see how this became possible, we need to know something about him.

At the turn of the year of 1854 James George Frazer was born in a tiny flat in Brandon Place, Glasgow, a city to which he always remained devoted and where, a few streets away, his father practised as a pharmacist. New Year's Day was thus always to be his birthday, a fact which may or may not have influenced his later assiduous speculations as to New Year's rites in many lands, including Scotland, where he thought the feast must originally have fallen on 1 November, the beginning of the Celtic Year, Hallowe'en thus being the original New Year's Eve on which ghosts and demons were driven out to ensure fair prosperity over the following few months. In the comfortable, pious household of the Frazers such primordial rites must, however, have seemed far distant. The father was industrious, punctilious, thrifty (he wrote a brief treatise on pens); the mother, Katherine Frazer, née Bogle, romantic, excessive, and given to ample dissertations upon her family history. The Bogles, she claimed, had had dealings with the royal House of Stewart. The surname Bogle too turns up with a fair amount of regularity in Caribbean history, since Robin Bogle, in the eighteenth century, had emigrated to the West Indies where he started a sugar plantation. One of his namesakes, a certain Moses Bogle, turns up later as a ringleader in the Morant Bay rising in Jamaica in 1865; combined with that other iconic name of Caribbean history, 'L'Ouverture', the name survived until recently as part-title of one of London's most flourishing black presses. The Bogles were thus travellers: one of Robin's brothers, George Bogle, found his way to India where he so endeared himself to Warren Hastings that he was sent over the Himalayas where he visited the Teshu Lama, one of the first Englishmen ever to step on Tibetan soil. His account of this episode, reprinted in Frazer's lifetime at the behest of the Frazer family, was one source for Frazer's theory of the carrier or scapegoat; and an ornate necklace, a present from the Teshu Lama to his eighteenth-century ancestor, was kept as an heirloom in the house of one of Frazer's numerous Bogle aunts.

Rumour of distant times and places thus ran through Frazer's childhood home, together with more recent reminiscences of the part played
by the family in Scottish ecclesiastical history. It was Frazer's maternal
uncle Ninian Bannatyne who, when Thomas Chalmers had stormed out
of the Assembly of the Church of Scotland in Edinburgh in 1843 to form
the so-called Free Church of Scotland, had stalked behind him as second
in the column. Into the wilderness they had gone, sacrificing stipend and
status, an example of moral courage and independence of mind that
Frazer seems always to have held dear. The Reverend Bannatyne lived
on in Old Cummock and as a boy Frazer used to visit him: he
remembered him as frail, kindly, and precise and, jejune as Frazer must
have been, this observation at close quarters of faith, and the consequences
of faith, is something that he retained through later years when his
sympathies ran riot away from the religion which as a boy he had known
and cherished. In obedience to the tenets of the Free Church, the family
were frugal, diligent in religious observance, but never morbid. Family
prayers every evening, church several times on Sunday, a Sabbath
rigorously maintained. Contrary to our current prejudices, such an
upbringing was the opposite of oppressive. Fun of a rather rumbustious
sort was always, apparently, breaking out. One of the most memorable
photographs of the Young Frazer in Ackerman's biography was taken at
the family holiday home on the Gareloch above Glasgow, and shows him
crawling out of an ivy-framed hole as if caught out in an amorous prank.
A later photograph, taken at Cambridge, shows him looking Sherlock
Holmes-like in a laboratory with a Watson-like scientist-friend who is
pretending to drink acid out of a straw. When covered in honours later
in life, Frazer's face assumed a somewhat solemn cast, but the humour
is always there in his books. On rarer occasions it even broke out in his
social life: he had a marvellous, almost invisible way of putting preten-
tious people down. In conversation this irreverence and tact were often
misunderstood by people of a more literal turn of mind. Frazer was never
literal nor, despite a widespread impression to the contrary, was he ever
dour.

Daniel Frazer's business was sufficiently flourishing for James to be
sent to several private schools before matriculating, according to the then
widespread Scottish custom, at the local university, that is, at Glasgow.
At school he received a thorough grounding in Latin and Greek, which
stood him in good stead when he took to academic life. At the university
he received an education much broader than he would have enjoyed
south of the border, studying philosophy under John Veitch, Latin under

George Gilbert Ramsay, and physics under William Thomson, later Lord Kelvin. These studies set the foundations of his life's work. The course-work in philosophy introduced him sequentially to the great figures of the Scottish epistemological tradition, with its marked grain of scepticism, most notably to David Hume, whose *Treatise of Human Nature*, with its investigation of the sources of human credulity, was to form the ground-plan of the treatment of human belief in *The Golden Bough*. Latin and Greek gave him access to a wide range of classical sources which he would later use to lend historical depth to his argument (indeed *The Golden Bough* itself begins with a classical problem). Science gave him methodology, clarity, and a basis in inductive logic which he would later use to great effect. Later nineteenth-century physics, tutored by Kelvin, Frazer's own professor, was deeply pessimistic about the future in discernible ways, which Frazer too imbibed. A certain philosophical pessimism, a darkening of the clouds around the dying sun, infiltrates the fading moments of *The Golden Bough*. This too Frazer learned from Kelvin and from Glasgow.

The family were inclined towards business, but Frazer wanted to be a scholar. In those days a degree in a Scottish university was not always deemed sufficient. Splendidly though Frazer had already been prepared, therefore, he was sent south of the border where it was felt desirable that he should attend one of the ancient English universities. Oxford recommended itself, and as a future anthropologist he might have learned much there: Oxford had Edward Burnett Tylor, the Quaker iconoclast whose *Primitive Culture* was to lure Frazer into the ethnographic fold. It had Friedrich Max Müller, whose theories as to the origins of language, much though Frazer came to dissent from them, clearly ran parallel to those he himself would later propose as to the origins of culture. It was soon to have Andrew Lang, a fellow Scot much interested in folklore whose attitude to Frazer in later years wavered between adoring disciplehood and petulant, irksome querulousness (Frazer, as always with his critics, forgave him). But Oxford also had the Tractarians and their offspring—Catholics or, worst still, Anglo-catholics—and Calvinist Daniel Frazer did not want any of it. So to Trinity, Cambridge, James went instead to apply himself assiduously to the classics—all of Herodotus in Greek, all of Virgil in Latin—until three-and-a-half years later he came out with his expected First, and a life of uncontroversial scholarship was his almost for the asking.

But Frazer seldom took the easy path, even if his early steps look conventional. The way to an academic career lay via a college fellowship.

Frazer duly set to work and produced a trim and witty account of Plato's dialogues. While doing so he also took the train to London a few days a week and sat for his Bar examinations, probably to appease his father who must have been doubtful that his son could make a living from mere scholarship. But Frazer got his fellowship and thus stayed on, his mind a lumber-room of learning, his book-shelves groaning with volumes. (A few years later he had to be moved out of the Great Court because the weight of his accumulated erudition threatened literally to sink him through the floor into the set of rooms beneath. According to Lady Frazer, the floor was bending inwards like a sail.)

In this benign, traditional society Frazer lived as a resident fellow for twenty years until marriage obliged him to move out. He was a man who understood rules, and this partiality for convention, or for what sentimentally we might call tradition, seems to have equipped him splendidly to comprehend the conventions of other societies. He knew that rules are founded on rituals which in turn enshrine magical beliefs. Rules are held to be sacrosanct, not because people are stuffy, but because the beliefs they embody are essential to a society's conception of man, the universe, and his place within it. Frazer believed, at one level quite passionately, that acts have consequences, and this was a conviction in which his subjects shadow him. If an aborigine stood on a hill in central Australia greeting the dawn with a lighted candle, this was because he was assured that the sun would more effectively rise as a consequence. And while we might think his concern naïve or absurd, our no-less ardent attachment to other such customs obliges us at least to understand him. The world is founded on cause and effect. When a given cause arises, none of us can at that moment discern the consequences. Our shortsightedness, however, does not inhibit us from acting on assumptions founded on the most sanguine form of determinism. All actions based on calculation are, therefore, acts of faith.

All of this Frazer knew instinctively, but he needed a framework in which to say it. Initially, in the wake of his still-unpublished dissertation, he seems to have wanted to turn himself into a professional philosopher. There are philosophical jottings in various notebooks, interleaved with speculations as to early law to which Frazer had been introduced by the writings of Henry Maine and John Ferguson M'Lennan. There are also meditations on the origin of language. At one point he even seems to have been on the trail of an elementary form of semiological linguistics ('Language', he scribbled in pencil at the back of a hastily compiled bibliography headed 'Books to read', 'is a system of signs'). But in Easter

1883, at a loss as to what to do for vacation, he accepted an invitation by the psychologist James Ward to accompany him on a walking tour of Spain, where amongst other things Ward lent him a copy of Tylor's *Primitive Culture*. The effect was instantaneous. Tylor's thematic account of superstitions the world over, his conviction that much in modern behaviour consists of a series of survivals from ages gone by, his explicit and sceptical account of the theology of the Mass as a sort of latter-day magic, gripped Frazer from the very beginning. On his return to Cambridge he set about more systematic reading, still searching for a theme. That autumn another vital meeting occurred, with William Robertson Smith, Lord's Almoner's Reader in Arabic, who had recently been expelled from his Old Testament Chair at the Free Church Academy in Aberdeen for his advocacy of critical methods in studying the Bible and, without a college to call his own, was putting up at Trinity until a fellowship became available elsewhere. Smith had just been appointed editor of the ninth edition of the *Encyclopaedia Britannica* for which he commissioned some classical contributions from Frazer, together with two seminal articles on 'Totem' and 'Taboo'. Both articles were eventually to lead to books: 'Totem' to the tiny *Totemism* of 1887, later expanded into the vast *Totemism and Exogamy* in 1910; 'Taboo' to *The Golden Bough*.

III

It was the second of these books that Frazer started to write in 1889. But before he did so there was much preparation to be done. Frazer had already steeped himself in the classics and had imbibed the historical bases of law, but this was not enough. From the beginning he seems to have had in mind a single study which would incorporate the whole of man's early culture and beliefs, set out not, as Tylor had done it, thematically, but in the form of a narrative. He therefore needed two things: a wide framework of reference in cultures, and a nexus on which to hang it. With the first of these in mind he sat down to read through as many accounts as he could of non-western societies: accounts in ethnographic journals, in the memoirs of colonial administrators, the observations of missionaries. In 1887 he had the idea of amplifying these by sending out a questionnaire to workers in the field requesting information on certain specified matters: marriage customs, rules of succession, myth and ritual. The answers were instructive, and by means of this method Frazer formed a close professional association with many workers in the field, some of whom, like Canon Roscoe in Uganda and Baldwin Spencer in Australia, would have a quite crucial effect upon his thinking.

But the nexus was still lacking. At one stage taboos concerning various kinds of marriage or sexual union seem to have been a likely common strand, but soon these speculations dissolved to be replaced by other and more promising ones until, in the March of 1889, the inspirational and galvanic moment occurred when *The Golden Bough* in its essence lay before his mind.

The elements that cohered to form the germ of the work were various. In the sixth book of Virgil's *Aeneid* Aeneas, after fleeing from Troy, is on his way to Italy where he will found the dynasty of kings that will rule the city of Rome. On the way, however, his father Anchises dies, and Aeneas pays a visit to the grotto of the Sybil at Cumae on what is now the Bay of Naples to ask whether she will gain him admittance to the Underworld to visit him. The Sybil is doubtful: few, she says, have been that way and lived to tell the tale but, if he is determined, then he must take some manner of protection with him. There then follows a passage which in William Pitt's translation of 1743 runs thus:

> But since you long to pass the realms beneath,
> The dreadful realms of darkness and of death,
> Twice the dire Stygian stream to measure o'er,
> And twice the black tartarean gulf explore:
> First, take my counsel, then securely go;
> A mighty tree, that bears a golden bough,
> Grows in a vale surrounded by a grove,
> And sacred to the queen of Stygian Jove.
> Her nether world no mortals can behold,
> Till from the bole they strip the blooming gold.

> > *(Aeneid*, vi. 133–9)

It was these lines, and in this translation, that had come to the attention of Turner in 1834, and around them he had composed a picture which stands as a frontispiece to Frazer's book. It depicts the legendary Lake Avernus at the mouth of the underworld. In the middleground the mythical Shades dance in a circle. Beyond stretches the immemorial Italian landscape crested by pines, while at the very last moment Turner added the Sybil herself in the foreground holding up the bough. She seems to have been something of an afterthought, since several years after the picture was acquired its owner found, to his dismay, that she was coming away from the canvas, having been hastily painted on paper and then simply stuck on to the surface. When Turner heard of it he rushed round and painted her in again where still she stands, a sickle in her right hand, the eponymous bough in her left.

What manner of branch Virgil's bough was we can never be sure. Frazer thought it was mistletoe, with which Virgil compares it, but in that case the simile is circular. But Frazer's interpretation of the picture and of the Virgil passage on which it is based is finally indebted less to botanical identification than to another passage in classical literature which Turner did not know. In the fourth century AD, commenting on Virgil's lines, the scholar Servius had written:

Those who write about the mysteries of Prosperine hold this branch to be mystical, but rumour states otherwise: that after killing the King Thoas in Taurica, Orestes . . . fled with his sister Iphigenia, and near Aricia re-established the effigy of Diana, in whose temple the rite was transformed. There was a certain tree whose branch none might disturb, except that a prerogative was granted to runaway slaves that whosoever broke this branch might challenge the fugitive priest to single combat, and so become priest himself in commemoration of the original flight.

Now this passage was a lot odder. Iphigenia had been transported to Taurica (the present-day Crimea) after her father Agamemnon had supposedly caused her to be sacrificed so as to secure fair sailing for the Trojan expedition. Later, her brother Orestes had taken refuge there after killing his mother Clytemnestra who had murdered his father Agamemnon in revenge for Iphigenia's death. All this was well known, but that the destination of the flight was Aricia, a small town about twelve miles from Rome along the Appian Way, that they had set up there an effigy of Diana (whose priestess, in Taurica, Iphigenia had become), and that the rule of succession to the priesthood of the newly established cult proceeded in the manner described, was bizarre in the extreme, and almost equally suggestive.

It was on to this passage that Frazer latched in 1889, all the more eagerly because Aricia had recently been in the news. In 1885 the British ambassador to Rome, a keen amateur archaeologist, had excavated a site about five miles south-east of Aricia at the foot of an escarpment beneath the tiny town of Nemi (see map). The dig had confirmed the connection with Diana, various statuettes of whom were found; it had discovered, however, no evidence of a priest or of the somewhat grisly rite of succession which Servius expounds. Various other factors might well contribute to incredulity on that score. Whoever had heard of a kingship

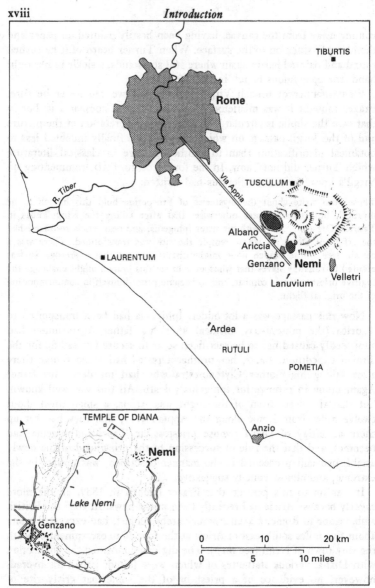

Nemi and its surrounding area, showing towns and peoples of the Latin League.
Inset: location of the Temple of Diana. (After A. G. MacCormick)

confined to slaves and runaways? What kind of kingdom was it that could be focused on a tree?

But that the cult had existed Frazer could be sure. In 1889 he had been perusing the first book of the travels of Pausanias, a doctor from Asia Minor who is one of our main informants on the ancient Greek sites, and whose work he was thinking of translating and editing. At one point Pausanias visits the sanctuary of Aesculapius, the Greek god of medicine, at Epidaurus in the Peloponnese. Various monuments stood in the shrine, one of which was of especial interest:

Apart from the others stands an ancient tablet with an inscription stating that Hippolytus dedicated twenty horses to the god. The people of Aricia tell a tale which agrees with the inscription on this tablet. They say that Hippolytus, done to death by the curses of Theseus, was raised from the dead by Aesculapius, and that being come to life again, he refused to forgive his father, and disregarding his entreaties went to Aricia in Italy. There he reigned and there he dedicated to Artemis a precinct, where down to my time the priesthood of the goddess is the prize of victory in a single combat. The competition is not open to free men, but only slaves who have run away from their masters.

(Pausanias, ii. 27. 4)

Here, if you like, was confirmation of the rite, but what caused Frazer to sit up and pay attention was the phrase 'down to my time'. Pausanias was writing in the second century AD. If what he said was true it was startling confirmation that the cult itself was no mere myth, even if Hippolytus, the focus of the above passage, was just that. Hippolytus is relevant because at some level the cult itself seems to have involved horses, which feature in his name (from Greek *hippos*), and by which he was torn to pieces. One of the quaintest features of the shrine at Nemi was that horses for some reason were excluded from it, but that the shrine existed Frazer could be sure. With Pausanias's help he could also be sure that, no mere atavistic memory, it had flourished right through the classical period, through the reigns of Julius Caesar and Caligula, both of whom watered there, and within earshot of the villas of the polite patricians who, in the most affluent days of the empire, flocked there to disport themselves on the shores of Lake Nemi.

All of this might seem a footnote to classical literature, and a pretty minor one at that, but it was not for this reason that Frazer valued it. In March of 1889 he was scouring the tightly packed volumes of John Pinkerton's *General Collection of the Best and Most Interesting Voyages and Travels* (1808–14), when he came upon a reference to the kingdom of Malabar in southern India. There, it seemed, according to Alexander

Hamilton who visited Malabar in the eighteenth century, the raja or king had previously been obliged to step down every twelve years, until the rite of succession had been commuted to a combat at arms in which, defended by his bodyguards, the king was theoretically forced to defend his kingdom against all comers. Here was a rite rather like the Arician one, but a great deal more recent. Did the Arician rite and the Malabar one draw on similar habits of mind? If so, here was a platform on which Frazer could build up his structure concerning early societies, the way they organized the affairs, and the philosophies of life that sustained them.

It is important to realize, however, that Frazer's subject is no more southern India than it is ancient Rome. Both of these simply exist for him as exempla of something much broader and deeper: the intellectual principles upon which early men conducted their corporate lives. Frazer's work might seem to be a compendium of ritual and custom. In fact it is something very different: a book on the human mind and the connections habitually made by it. If Frazer had begun his research life as a philosopher, his migration to anthropology in 1883 was not as drastic as it may now seem. From studying the nature of human thought he had simply turned aside to examine its history. It was because the human mind, across a variety of cultures and times, and especially when trained upon the religious and the magical, showed certain constancies that generalization of the sort that fascinated Frazer became possible. It was to examine the refinements of such universal thought-processes, and their different ways of expressing themselves in a variety of places and periods, that he wrote his book.

IV

Before long he was sufficiently confident to approach a publisher. To George Macmillan, on 8 November 1889, he wrote:

I shall soon have completed a study in the history of primitive religion ... The resemblance of the savage customs and ideas to the fundamental doctrines of Christianity is striking. But I make no reference to this parallelism, leaving my readers to draw their own conclusions, one way or another. (B.L. Add. Ms. 55134)

Macmillan accepted and the text, enough to fill two generously spaced volumes, was soon at the printers: R. & R. Clark of Edinburgh. Conscious of being on the trail of a book with some popular appeal, Frazer plied Macmillan with letters. No aspect of the book was to be left to chance: the cover had to be green and carry an elegant Art Nouveau design based on the mistletoe motif; the typeface must be bold and clear; a reproduction of Turner's painting was to be included as a frontispiece. Frazer was in a hurry; he wanted to go off to Greece to continue his work on Pausanias. So by March the proofs were read and dispatched and Frazer was off on a strenuous itinerary of walking, writing, and observing—his author's copies had to be posted to Athens. Frazer had to come back to England before he found that he had written that unusual thing: a scholarly best-seller.

The success was not unprovided for. Frazer had wanted a book which the layman could read. He had an urgent theme, he expressed himself well, he raised far-reaching questions without first raising hackles; he caught the mood and curiosity of the hour. Besides, *The Golden Bough* was to some extent written like a pot-boiler or detective story. Like Conan-Doyle, he kept back the solution until the end. It was a kind of whodunnit: 'I find it very difficult to summarize the gist of the book', he wrote to Macmillan, 'without disclosing what I may call the plot.'

This plot ran on two levels. It was first a disentanglement of the knotted skein around the ritual of Nemi, but it was much more than that: an exposition of a deeply embedded pattern of belief observable in many cultures at different periods of history. This ancient cosmology or metaphysic may be summarized thus. Each year nature dies. People too weaken and then expire. These events are connected, and the force that connects them is magic. Magicians are people who know about these processes; their usefulness is that they intervene. Sometimes the magicians themselves are kings, but in any case kings, in whom much of the energy of the community is invested, are able to orchestrate the process. But kings too sicken and die, and in so doing imperil the whole. There is a force of energy within them which, if diminished by illness or death, will diminish everyone along with it. The force, however, transcends them and is transferable from individual to individual. If, when the period of their weakness is upon them, kings can be forced to relinquish their power, it can then be handed on to a different human vessel who will ensure its survival.

Frazer scoured history for examples of kings who were obliged to relinquish their authority at the end of a fixed term or else to defend their power in some kind of trial of strength. An example of the latter was the priest of Nemi, with whom he begins his account, obliged to defend his power against all comers. But he had other examples, some of the more promising of which came from India or Africa. Sometimes, it seemed to Frazer, the king went quietly; at other times he was, not surprisingly, reluctant and forced others to die in his stead in a kind of surrogate sacrifice. Sometimes (and this is where uncomfortable parallels with Christianity came in), the substitute was the king's son. At others a buffoon or slave was selected who enjoyed the king's privileges temporarily before his life was summarily snuffed out. At such times it was often convenient for this individual to double as a scapegoat (as Christ, it seemed to Frazer, was a scapegoat).

Later, the original purpose of the rite was entirely forgotten and men and women played out the role of sacrificial gods and goddesses with very little sense of what they were about. This was the stage of what, from the second edition of 1900 on, Frazer called religion as opposed to magic. Later still, death was converted into a ritual humiliation until at length the process, once so grisly, degenerated into a series of ossified and purposeless mumming plays, the folklore of the modern or industrial age. At the root of it all, still dimly discernible, lay a desire to master the forces of nature by controlling them, ensuring that the life force flowed from ruler to ruler, generation to generation.

Thus summarized, two things become obvious about Frazer's story-line. It is strongly dependent on a rather abstract notion of energy as an immanent force like electricity that somehow informs the universe and binds it together; it is thus dependent on seeing the whole human organism in terms of the science of, say, Faraday. It is also, unconnec-tedly, itself rather mystical and capable in its turn of provoking strong mystical feelings among readers who are often swept along by a sugges-tion of things half remembered and brought to life. How much of this Frazer intended is hard to say: had it been pointed out to him that the continuing success of his narrative one hundred years after its inception was due to half-buried intimations stemming from residual mysticism, it is not clear that he would have been pleased.

The potential for misunderstanding was present from the beginning, and in order to forestall it Frazer inserted into the second edition a triple scheme of evolutionary development intended to clear the mind. It was all, he now argued, a question of cultural phases. Men want, say, rain. They begin by performing a rain-dance, which often does not work. This is the Age of Magic. Then, baulked of success, they do the next best thing and fall on their knees to pray. This is the Age of Religion. When the prayers do not work, they set about investigating the precise causes of the natural world, and on the basis of their new understanding attempt to alter things for the better. This is the Age of Science which, Frazer argued, we now inhabit. Magic and science have this in common: that they are techniques of intervention, while religion is an abjuring of all responsibility in favour of the gods. The closeness of intent shared by magic and science should not, however, blind us to the fact that the second is informed while the first is not. All recourses to magic in later ages are relapses. Faced with such relapses, which indubitably occur, the proper attitude of science can only be to regard them as phenomena themselves fit for examination. To confuse the process by indulging the phenomena investigated, as contemporary occultists too often did, was, Frazer argued, both an adulteration of the scientific method and an anachronism. It was, to use a metaphor which he borrowed from Carlyle's *French Revolution*, to tread upon a sheet of ice which too readily would give way, precipitating the trespasser into the lightless abysses beneath.

With these distinctions clear in our minds, it is possible to paraphrase Frazer's argument. After a brief description of the shrine at Nemi and the rites associated with it, he proceeds to enunciate the grand principles upon which all magical (and later religious) principles are based. Having illustrated these principles, he then proceeds to show how the kingship is to be explained as the supremacy of those whose manipulation of magical practices is most impressive and conclusive. This leads him to a discussion of kingship in general and thence to the devices by which the power and kudos of the king is sustained. Of these the most important is a peculiar mystical charge surrounding the regal person operating rather like an alternating electrical current. This he calls 'taboo', a word whose meaning for Frazer is somewhat more complicated than that which we ascribe to it. For Frazer, taboos were ways of insulating certain persons and activities from harmful social contact. Some of these persons and activities are deemed holy; others, abhorrent. Frazer's point is that, in the mind of early man, these two states are not rigorously separated: thus the emperor of Japan was secluded from the world, but so were homicides. 'Taboo', like the Latin world *sacer* which Frazer regarded as a conceptual synomym for it, therefore meant both sacred and profane. The ambiguity of the concept and the attitudes bred by it serve to explain much that follows.

Frazer's account continues with a lengthy dissertation on the mortality of kings and human gods, contained, in the early editions of *The Golden Bough*, in one extended chapter. After considering the mortality of the gods, he turns to those special kinds of human god called kings, and illustrates how they do not simply die but are sometimes forced to relinquish their lives in order to safeguard the divine pulse within them, which is then transferred to their successors. Such practices are, strictly speaking, forms of magic, but Frazer next turns his attention to the deposits left by such practices in religious systems. Of these he has two main extended examples: the religious cults of the ancient Near East—of Phoenicia, Phrygia, and Egypt—and the religious myths of the ancient Greeks. He then turns to that peculiar kind of semi-divinity known as a scapegoat, and shows how individuals who in ancient communities are at intervals obliged to carry away the sins of the people often fuse with the divine essence as already perceived. Such orgies of cleansing were, Frazer thought, regular features of the ancient and non-western world; within recorded memory they had been embodied in annual Saturnalia celebrations such as may once have preceded the Christian Lent.

The reference to the magical foundations of Christian rites brings him within the vicinity of Christian theology. It is at this stage that, in the second edition of 1900, Frazer incorporated a large section preparatory to his climactic discussion of Jesus Christ as the ultimate scapegoat, a discussion later demoted to an appendix, then finally cut (see Section V below). In all versions of the work, however, Frazer continues with a dissertation on one particular dying god, the Norse deity Balder. According to the Icelandic sagas Balder was slain by a sprig of mistletoe, and then cremated on a flaming ship. He therefore serves as a pretext through which Frazer examines seasonal fires and finally the nature of the 'Golden Bough', the mistletoe, itself, with a discussion of which he closes.

V

Thus set out, Frazer's thesis seems fairly self-contained, but there are doubts and ambiguities within it. From the very beginning, for example, he seems to have been genuinely tormented by the issue of religion. In a very early notebook, dating from about 1885, we find him worrying about that old chestnut, the relation between religion and morals. Why were the manners of any given age so often out of kilter with its declared beliefs? Frazer found the answer to this question in a kind of ossification that set in to religious systems once their heyday was past. The theology of any given society represents a past age of social development; when men progress further, a disparity between belief and custom opens up, and reformers arise to bring them into line, by modifying the belief so as to reconcile it with the best of modern practice. When the religion is handed down by word of mouth (as it is in many non-literate societies and was, by and large, even among the Greeks and the Romans) this is easy because the force of written precedent will not weigh against them. When, as in India, the Arab world, or Christendom, the religion is enshrined in a book, the task is much more difficult because the opponents can always cite chapter and verse in support of their conservatism. This is the point which western society, Frazer believed, had reached in his own age, of which 'conflicts between thought and religion . . . form so marked a feature':

In our own age as the progress of knowledge has been immense, so the breach between religion and science has widened; hence the number of people who are seen to be busily employed in endeavouring to fill up this breach. Nor is it between religion and science alone that men are beginning to become conscious of the breach. Between religion (that is, of course, the book religion) and morality they begin to see a gulf opening. That this gulf should be narrower, in other words that the difference between should be less than the difference between religion and science is due to the fact that an advance in morals is necessarily subsequent to an advance in knowledge . . . Hence we see the disadvantages of a book religion.

(B.L. Add. Ms. 45, 442)

In any age, therefore, there were on the one hand rebels, those who tried to reform religion or else do away with it, and on the other integrationalists or consolidators who attempted to reconcile belief and practice by some less drastic method. It is to the first, revolutionary category that Frazer thought of himself as belonging. All religions breed counter-religions; book-religions breed counter-books. The fossilized religion of the early Greeks had its answer in Socrates and through him the works of Plato; the fossilized religion of the early Hebrews, the pedantry of the Scribes and the Pharisees, had its answer in Christ, and through him the New Testament. The book religion of his own day, Victorian Christianity in its various forms, also required a counter-book. There is a strong case for saying that this book, whether consciously or unconsciously, was *The Golden Bough*.

Frazer seems to have groped towards these possibilities somewhat timidly at first; and towards the end of his life the timidity well-nigh overwhelmed him. The 1890 edition of *The Golden Bough*, as Frazer's letter to his publishers avows, is a cautious, though already a disturbing book. But in 1900 Frazer took his courage in both hands and produced what in effect and in structure was a sort of counter-Bible. The second edition hence begins where the first had begun: in an Edenic Grove with a tempter on the prowl; but proceeds upwards through a great arch until, at the climax to the second volume, 'The Crucifixion of Christ' is reached. Having demolished the orthodox theology on which the act of Christian atonement is based (or, what amounts to the same thing, demonstrated its equivalence to *all* other supposed acts of atonement), Frazer then proceeds with an elaboration of the motif until, in the closing paragraphs of the work, a sort of sceptical apocalypse is reached. In the third edition of 1906–15, this counter-Biblical typology grows still more ornate: so we have a Passover sequence; an Immaculate Conception sequence; a Nativity sequence; a Baptism sequence; a sequence on fires followed by a Resurrection sequence—all of which are embedded within the text. To identify them is part of the fun of reading.

But, having dealt his great blow, Frazer was then seized with panic. Had he gone too far? Was the disparagement of the uniqueness of the Christian revelation perhaps too bold? These nagging doubts were reinforced by an attack launched on his crucifixion theory by Andrew Lang in the pages of the *Fortnightly Review*. Hastily Frazer rethought his position and in 1913, when rewriting the section of his work that has to do with the atonement, transplanted 'The Crucifixion of Christ' to an apologetic appendix where it was admitted as being 'in a high degree speculative and uncertain'. And in 1922, when collaborating with his wife on an abridgement of the work for the wider reading public, he cut it out altogether, rendering the argument of the 1900 edition innocuous, its shape less than recognizable. Many of the other counter-Biblical episodes go as well. In *The White Goddess* (1956) it was Robert Graves's contention that such cat-and-mousery is unworthy of critical scholarship, and a symptom of cowardice:

Sir James Frazer was able to keep his beautiful rooms at Trinity College, Cambridge, until his death by carefully and methodically sailing all round his dangerous subject, as if charting the coastline of a forbidden island without actually committing himself to the declaration that it existed. What he was saying-not-saying—was that Christian legend, dogma and ritual are refinements of a great body of primitive and even barbarous beliefs, and that almost the only original element in Christianity is the personality of Jesus.

This indictment is over-flattering to Frazer's college, the only stake in which he retained at the end of his life was a large room in which he kept his library. About the retention of 'the personality of Jesus' as the lone core of Christianity Graves was, however, more accurate; one of the texts constantly cited in Frazer's early notebooks is Renan's *Vie de Jésus*

(1869) which for Frazer's own generation had been as effective a counter-gospel as Strauss's *Das Leben Jesu* (1835–6) had been for the previous generation of free-thinkers, such as George Eliot, who had translated it. But such counter-gospels require Old Testaments, Acts of the Apostles, Revelations to flesh them out if they are to attain the status of fully fledged counter-Bibles. If *The Golden Bough* is indeed that, then in the abridgement of 1922 the Frazers kept the frame but threw out the Gospel. In the present abridgement, it is retained.

VI

Hence in Frazer the quiet iconoclast we meet a spectacle quite common in the late Victorian period: a Protestant-inspired exegetical honesty turning against itself. Earlier in the century, and especially in Germany, a painstaking examination of Holy Writ had led to two results: a recognition of its textual instability and of the radical similarity between Judaeo-Christian traditions and those of pagan religions. In Frazer's work this enterprise is carried to its logical extreme, the Christian focus dissolving to give way to a cultural and moral relativism disorientating to those who take their certainties too seriously. That such relativism carried dangers Frazer cannot help but be aware; at times the plethora of example threatens to swamp the theme, but then Frazer draws back, gathers in his evidence, and take stock of the proceedings. The tension in the work between spiralling example and a centripetal tendency to argue an overwhelming case is something which *The Golden Bough* never quite resolves.

To later anthropologists it seemed perverse to separate magic and religion from other aspects of society, as if the myth and ritual and of a given people could somehow be set apart from their fishing skills or methods of exchange. To this generation, led by Frazer's protégé Bronisław Malinowski, it seemed that Frazer lacked a holistic appreciation, not of mankind but of individual, local cultures. The decline in Frazer's reputation in professional circles since his death has much to do with this particular objection. But as the functionalist school of social anthropology itself falls astern we can perhaps see how its strictures, valid in their own terms, ignored the climate of receptivity to which books like *The Golden Bough* were addressed. Frazer's readers were less interested in the ethnographic tabulation of the rites, customs, and economy of particular societies than they were in the broad trans-cultural sweep. For, whatever else we may think of them, late Victorians readers had hearty theoretical appetites. Schooled in the historicism of their age, and in the comprehensive attempts to make sense of man's social and mental development already proposed by scientific popularizers like Herbert Spencer and George Henry Lewes, their inclination was for vistas that would enable them to make sense of themselves as part of an unfolding scheme. And if Frazer cared neurotically about the details, few who read him were so fastidious. For his first readers Frazer offered the facilities not so much of a field camp as of a headquarters with an extensive and reliable network of communications. Frazer neither was, nor claimed to be, a first-hand observer: what he offered instead was a panorama of mankind's mental development which stimulated the historical curiosity while opening up large views towards a horizon shrouded in mist, though amenable to the compass.

The bearings of Frazer's own compass, checked at regular intervals, were more complicated than they may now seem. The assumptions underlying *The Golden Bough* are, for example, both materialist and idealist: materialist in that the motivation behind all ritual, whether 'magical' or 'religious', is interpreted as a struggle for physical survival; idealist in that, in Frazer's epistemology—derived from his academic upbringing in Scotland—thought is invariably seen as preceding practice, doctrine as preceding ritual. It is thus, with very uneven success, that Frazer strives to reconcile a Darwinian belief in life as a combat in which the fittest survive (and what else is the hand-to-hand duel at the lakeside shrine at Nemi but this?) with a Humean conviction that all belief, rational or otherwise, stems from associations of ideas abstracted within the mind. The fight at Nemi, and the analogies he records were, Frazer thought, no such abstractions, but historical events. But that the necessity for such events was based on the presence in the minds of the participants of philosophical tenets which, however befuddled, were capable of subsequent analysis is, finally, the very essence of his case.

His essential tenet, set out near to the beginning, is that human behaviour is based on the association of ideas, a phenomenon first identified by David Hartley and later classified by David Hume into three categories: association by contiguity (this is next to that); by resemblance (this is like that); and by cause and effect (this produces that). The ramifications of this Enlightenment view in the nineteenth century were widespread. For Frazer, who had imbibed this model in Scotland where an unbroken philosophical tradition stretched back to Hume, these divisions were the foundation of all magic which was either contagious (I cast a spell on something which pertains to you—your hair, for example, or your fingernails), or homoeopathic (I cast a spell on something which resembles you—a wax effigy or doll). Frazer spends some time establishing these types, which may to us appear too absolute. More recently, however, with an explicit acknowledgement to Frazer but little sense of the epistemological tradition that lies beyond him, an equivalent divide has been diagnosed in our use of language, which the linguist Roman Jakobson (who read *The Golden Bough* in German) has divided into functions of metonymy (calling attention to affinities of adjacency) and metaphor (articulating affinities of resemblance). That such a view should have found its way into modern semiotics is testimony to its resilience.

Frazer's is thus a book with strongly etched and well-attested premisses. Much of the earlier part, covering a full two volumes of the great third edition, is devoted to outlining these, on which foundation the rest of the structure is reared. The pyramid that results is not so much amplificatory as rhetorical. On occasions one is even reminded of the advocate it was once Frazer's intention to become. At the bar of the court he stands, his wig tight about him, his gown a little dowdy, mustering the evidence. Mankind, the rambling and devious historical species, is in the dock, and, a little stunned by the weight of exhibits though undeniably impressed by his forensic charm, sit the readers, held by that severe but subtly twinkling eye.

For Frazer, as for his readership, anthropology was meaningless unless it instructed one as to the general nature of the species *anthropos* or man. The key to that understanding was the comparative method, which earlier in the century had already been used in the study of language and of law. Some indication of the relevance it seemed to possess to the study of *anthropos* may be gleaned from Frazer's synopsis of an introductory lecture on 'The Scope and Method of Mental Anthropology', delivered at Trinity College on 4 November 1921:

Anthropology a modern science. Physical Anthropology and Mental Anthropology. No absolutely primitive race known to us. Application of the Comparative Method to the study of lower races: analogy with comparative anatomy. Mental or social anthropology a science of origins ... Importance of the study of uncivilized races for the early evolution of human thought. The method is inductive. Necessity of the exact observation of living savages. Observation and comparison to be kept strictly apart and carried out simultaneously by different classes of workers.

Notice, first, that anthropology is defined as a scientific: as the carrying through into the accurate depiction of human society of that project of

disinterested observation defined once and for all in the writings of
Francis Bacon. Notice secondly the substitution for the (to us more
familiar) term Social Anthropology of the highly revealing term Mental
Anthropology. For Frazer anthropology is the study of thought: not so
much of what men now think (though that is not irrelevant to it) as the
study of what men have thought, the stages through which the thinking
process has passed. Just as it was, or had been, vital to the physical
anthropologist to see human types evolving each from each; just as it had
become mandatory for the archaeologist to classify the deposits he dug
up as belonging to the Stone, Iron, or Bronze ages; just as it had become
conventional for the student of prehistory to regard all early societies as
having passed through hunting, pastoral, and agricultural phases; so it
behoved the 'Mental Anthropologist' to seek out equivalent phases in the
history of human thought. Throughout the 1890s and beyond there was
a fairly vigorous debate among students of early society as to what these
stages might have been, and in what order they had occurred. By 1900
Frazer himself thought that he had identified the order of succession
as magic, followed by religion, followed by science. That such stages in
the development of human thought corresponded to successive ages
in the evolution of particular societies few at the time seem to have
doubted; but equally the superimposition of these ages, like the superimposition of geological or archaeological strata, implied—as Tylor had
argued—coexistence. Dig down wherever you are, and at some level or
other the Age of Magic would be waiting for you. Such persistence into
later ages of characteristics of earlier ones had been called by Tylor
'survivals', and it was to the survival into the classical or modern ages of
phenomena characteristic of earlier ages of man that Frazer paid particular attention in *The Golden Bough*.

In order to hunt down such survivals it was sometimes necessary to
travel far and wide but, as Frazer's programme also strongly implies, the
observation and the collation were distinct activities. There were thus
'descriptive ethnologists' and 'comparative ethnologists', the task of the
former being to supply the latter with information to be interpreted or
woven into a significant pattern. Some indication of the scope of each of
these activities may be sought in an obituary notice which Frazer wrote
after the death of one of his most diligent respondents: the naturalist
Baldwin Spencer who, for twenty years, had supplied information
concerning the Australian aborigines. For Frazer, the books which
Spencer wrote with his collaborator Francis Gillen were valuable precisely because of the bare factuality of their style:

The openness of a mind unwarped by preconceived notions and foreign conclusions, which is one of Spencer's formal characteristics, is conspicuous in all his writings and contributes largely to their scientific value. Not a few scientific descriptions of primitive people are to a certain extent vitiated by the comparison which the observer institutes with the customs and beliefs of other ages and other parts of the world—comparisons which, while they serve to display the extent, too often reveal the superficiality, of the author's reading, and in any case are best left to be drawn by the comparative ethnologist, whose function is at once different from and complementary to that of the descriptive ethnologist. From all such ill-judged exercises into alien fields the writings of Spencer are absolutely free.

For the modern reader that passage may appear to be rife with a particular form of wishful thinking. Spencer is portrayed as a *tabula rasa*, a blank eye, a retina merely receptive and innocent of all preconception, as if one's impressions really could be sorted out from one's pre-existent ideas. Thus far Frazer's aspirations on Spencer's behalf fly in the face of the Lockean empiricism both had inherited. But the fact is that Frazer needs Spencer to be transparent, needs him to be the neutral eye in order to transmit back to him, Frazer of Staircase 'E', Great Court, the unadulterated rays emanating from a distant and moving object. The vices that Spencer has avoided may thus become Frazer's virtues. Spencer's writings are blessedly unvitiated by 'comparisons . . . with the customs of other ages and parts of the world' precisely so that Frazer's own writings may be informed by these very things.

The comparative method, and the techniques of information-gathering associated with it, are now facets of the history of anthropology, but the subsequent history of the subject is instructive. Shortly after the close of the First World War the division between observer and interpreter broke down when the next generation of social anthrologists, led by Malinowski, insisted that all anthropologists worthy of the name got their shoes dirty by researching in the field. To this generation it seemed that at last the observing and the interpreting eye had fused, to the everlasting benefit of science.

That measure of improvement, that sanguine sense of a necessary momentum, seem to us naïve—for two connected reasons. The first is this: that no eye, however detached, can possibly attain the complete objectivity which Frazer required of his informants and which his successors strove personally to put into effect. The second is that, of all forms of observation the most imperilled by personal imposition is that in which the eye occupies the field of its observation, since the inquisitive occupant of any social space will of necessity send out ripples of disturbance caused by his very presence and by the persistence of his inquiry.

Thus, it has come to seem to us, all anthropological accounting of whatever kind partakes of a variety of personal testimony. The recognition of such mitigating factors in the operation of the anthropological intelligence has had the recent effect of placing in extreme highlight those facets of the subject which correspond to a species of writing. Anthropology may aspire towards the condition of science. It is, however, whether it likes it or not, inevitably a branch of literature. When the implications of such an inference have been absorbed, the effect is to drive us back to the founding fathers of the subject, such as Frazer, for whom all discourse was a form of literature, and literature itself no badge of shame even for (perhaps especially for) the would-be empiricist. It is no accident that in expounding this train of consequences I have already had reason to adapt a sentence of Walter Pater who, in the years immediately before the publication of the first *Golden Bough*, had devoted some attention both to the boundaries between, and the grey-areas across, disciplines. In 1888, in an essay on 'Style' (collected in *Appreciations*), he had this to say about the distinction between what he called 'the literature of fact' and 'the literature of the sense of fact':

The line between fact and something quite different from external fact is, indeed, hard to draw. In Pascal, for instance, in the persuasive writers generally, how difficult to define the point where, from time to time, argument which, if it is to be worth anything at all, must consist of facts or groups of facts, becomes a pleading—a theorem no longer, but essentially an appeal to the reader to catch the writer's spirit, to think with him, if one can or will—an expression no longer of fact but of his sense of it, his peculiar intuition of the world, prospective, or discerned below the faulty conditions of the present, in either case changed somewhat from the actual world. In science, on the other hand, in history so far as it conforms to the scientific rule, we have a literary domain where the imagination may be thought to be always an intruder. And as, in all science, the functions of literature reduce themselves eventually to the transcribing of fact, so all the excellences of literary form in regard to science are reducible to various kinds of painstaking; this good quality being involved in all 'skilled work' whatever, in the drafting of an act of parliament, as in sewing. Yet here again, the writer's sense of fact, in history especially, and in all those complex subjects which do but lie on the borders of science, will still take the place of fact, in various degrees. Your historian, for instance, with absolutely truthful intention, amid the the multitude of facts presented to him must needs select, and in selecting assert something of his own humour, something that comes not of the world but of a vision within. So, Gibbon moulds his unwieldy material to a preconceived view. Livy, Tacitus, Michelet, moving full of poignant sensibility amid the records of the past, each after his own sense modifies—who can tell where and to what degree?—and becomes something else than a transcriber . . .

Pater's essay was published in book form by Frazer's publisher in the same year as the first *Golden Bough*. With how uncanny a touch does he put his finger on precisely those writers who had played so large a role in the make-up of Frazer's being: Pascal, Livy, Tacitus, Michelet. To hold the whole of man's history in the mind's eye, transmit the spectrum of human cultural experience through a single pane of richly coloured glass—this is what Frazer had learned from the masters of classical and neo-classical historiography, and this is the perspective which as readers he invites us to adopt, both to the entirety of his written structure and to each and every part of it.

The method by which Frazer achieved such refraction of matter into sensibility is his style, which has often been misunderstood. Ackerman, his biographer, refers to it somewhat dismissively as 'literary' without realizing that its literariness is part of the point. For if Frazer's methods of research, his evolutionary convictions and empirical edge, belong to the nineteenth century, his style is from another stable altogether. His critical essays, his polite imitations of Addison's 'Roger de Coverley' give the clue: it is to the balance and perspicacity of the eighteenth century that he aspires. His wit, for example is of a distinctively Gibbonian order, exposing the absurdities of human credulity in paragraphs which emulate a detachment ever-so slightly etched with scorn. Here he is on the rivalry of the Christians and the followers of Attis over the priority in devising resurrection festivals in the Spring:

In point of fact it appears from the testimony of an anonymous Christian, who wrote in the fourth century of our era, that Christians and pagans alike were struck by the remarkable coincidence between the death and resurrection of their respective deities, and that the coincidence formed a theme of bitter controversy between the adherents of the rival religions, the pagans contending that the resurrection of Christ was a spurious imitation of the resurrection of Attis, and the Christians asserting with equal warmth that the resurrection of Attis was a diabolical counterfeit of the resurrection of Christ. In these unseemly bickerings the heathen took what to a superficial observer might seem strong ground by arguing that their god was the older and therefore presumably the original, not the counterfeit, since as a general rule an original is older than its copy. This feeble argument the Christians easily rebutted. They admitted, indeed, that in point of time Christ was the junior deity, but they triumphantly demonstrated his real seniority by falling back on the subtlety of Satan, who on so important an occasion had surpassed himself by inverting the usual order of nature. (pp. 363–4)

The whole effect of this passage lies in the seriousness of demeanour, which is appreciated as serious until the subtle twinkling of the ironic eye is discerned beneath it. The adjective 'remarkable', for example, has the flat force of something 'fit-to-be-observed' until the remarkableness of the coincidence is found to be such patent evidence of chicanery. The case for the followers of Attis is seemingly undermined by the adjective 'superficial' until, following through the logic of the construction, you realize that this particular superficiality has the unquestionable strength of a tautology. Then the tautology is written off as 'feeble', which in the logical sense it can never be, a tautology being always true even when, especially when, it is trite. This achieved, the adverb 'triumphantly', the seemingly conclusive epithet 'real', simply enhance an impression of absurdity into which the Christian case ineptly falls, even in the act of acknowledging the power of Satan to deceive the faithful and the disinterested observer alike. Then back to tautology again, the 'usual' order of nature being just that, 'usual'. Thus we reach sanity at last across the sandbanks of antique casuistry, the result being a confirmation of the folly, not of the Attis cult nor of the Christ cult, but of religious adherents everywhere, especially when inspired by what the eighteenth century liked to call 'enthusiasm'.

But wit is only one aspect of Frazer's style. More largely it is a matter of what Pater calls 'humour', meaning a 'peculiar intuition of the world', a sensibility infusing everything, even the most harrowing. As one telling instance we might take Frazer's account of the climax of the Toxcatl feast in pre-colonial Mexico which, as he disarmingly notes, 'corresponded in date as well as character to the Christian festival of the death and resurrection of the Redeemer'. He is describing the moment when the boy-victim, who, for twenty days has enjoyed the privileges of 'the god of gods' Tezcatlipoco, is obliged finally to succumb to the knife:

On the last day the young man, attended by his wives and pages, embarked in a canoe covered with a royal canopy and was ferried across the lake to a spot where a little hill rose from the edge of the water. It was called the Mountain of Parting, because here his wives bade him a last farewell. Then, accompanied only by his pages, he repaired to a small and lonely temple by the wayside. Like the Mexican temples in general, it was built in the form of a pyramid; and as the young man ascended the stairs he broke at every step one of the flutes on which he had played in the days of his glory. On reaching the summit he was seized and held down by the priests on his back upon a block of stone, while one of them cut open his breast, thrust his hand into the wound, and wrenching out his heart held it up in sacrifice to the sun. The body of the dead god was not, like the bodies of common victims, sent rolling down the steps of the temple, but was carried down to the foot, where the head was cut of and spitted on a pike. Such was the regular end of the man who personated the greatest god of the Mexican pantheon. (p. 609)

The theoretical vantage-point from which the episode is viewed is that of Euhemerism: the doctrine that godhead is an afflatus visited upon mortal beings who have at one time or another enacted the part of a God. Thus the dignified yet frightened young man—dignified because frightened, frightened underneath his dignity—does not so much play the part because he is a god as grow into godhead by virtue of his enacting it. In the eyes of the worshippers and celebrants, therefore, he is, and must perforce be viewed as divine before, at, and beyond the moment of his slaying. As he ascends the steep flight of steps towards the altar (one can almost see it: the slow, drugged yet pious gait, the inexorable half-reluctant, half-joyous commitment of his advance, step after step in the still morning air), it is as a god regretting the fragility of his manhood, or a man regretting the fragility of his godhead. In any case the simple and relentless gesture of breaking a flute on every stair perfectly conveys the simplicity and inevitability of a renunciation which is simultaneously a form of apotheosis. There is a sharp movement up and then down as in reaching the summit he collapses into the waiting arms of the priests, a rapid conflation of spiritual possibilities and limitations, a quick-as-lightning reflex by the ministrants, the brandishing of the boy's still beating heart by one of whom is an action both of obeisance and of triumph. But as always Frazer's almost imperceptible intervention is reserved for the last sentence which honours while disclosing the temporary suspension of belief on which the rite is founded. The sacrifice is a waste—Frazer's 'regular' here being both descriptive and ironic—yet for all that he has 'personated the god', not impersonated him. His end is both fitting and noble.

It will be observed how crucially such writing depends upon a constant, darting repositioning of the reader in relation to the man, the god, and the priests. We are witnesses to the rite. Fitfully we are celebrants too and throughout, with a controlled seepage of feeling as subtle as it is pervasive, we are ourselves the victim. A revealing practical exercise might be to contrast this passage with the New Mexican sacrifice at the culmination of D. H. Lawrence's story 'The Woman Who Rode Away', partly based, like his novel *The Plumed Serpent*, upon a reading of episodes in this same chapter. Lawrence has his human victim staring up into the eyes of the priests, the eldest of whom seems instinct with qualities which the author seems as incapable of recognizing as he is of naming:

Only the eyes of that oldest man were not anxious. Black, and fixed, and as if sightless, they watched the sun, seeing beyond the sun. And in their black, empty concentration there was a power, power intensely abstract and remote, deep, deep to the heart of the earth, and the heart of the sun. In absolute motionlessness he watched till the red sun should send his ray through the column of ice. Then the old man would strike, and strike home, accomplish the sacrifice and achieve the power.

The confusion between cthonic and solar potency here is but one facet of a redundant intellectual fug which blunts everything except Lawrence's own befuddled mysticism. Frazer's virtues by contrast are those of a perfect clarity, a clarity all the more impressive for burning through the author's own declared prejudices. He does everything that Lawrence tries and fails to do. By refusing to say what he means, he says everything; by renouncing comment or palapable emotion he commends the episode to our attention, making it the focus for that shifting field of attitude and readerly response on which his work as a whole depends.

The effect of such focusing is to leave his theories in tatters. God or man, frightened or noble, the human subject of this ghastly yet solemn ritual fits nowhere into Frazer's schemes. He is neither hunter nor nomad, stone-age man nor bronze-age man, magician nor priest, nor yet scientist. He is simply what he is: a young man climbing a flight of steps on a May morning: everywhere and nowhere, everything and yet nothing. The effect is achieved partly through a manipulation of tense which modulates between what the French would call the iterative imperfect, and the past historic. As viewed, the incident is singular since dependent upon a given moment in time, yet repetitive: the 'regular' close of a tradition of which we cannot, and do not want to see the far end. Confounding all evolutionary schemes, the action is timeless, primitive and yet modern.

VII

With these aspects of his achievement in view, Frazer has frequently been seen as a harbinger of modernism. This has a certain justice; yet the uncertainties of Lawrence's prose have much to tell us about the nature of Frazer's influence on the literature of this century. For the writers of the years immediately following the First World War he seemed to offer a way back to intimations of a religious or magical kind. W. B. Yeats, for example, read him with an eye to the folklore of the peasantry, as a lens through which the beliefs of his own Irish countrymen could be given both context and depth. In the Twenties T. S. Eliot read the sections on Adonis, Attis, Osiris and briefly deployed the idea of pagan baptismal rites in *The Waste Land* (especially in the section 'Death by Water'). Wyndham Lewis's *The Childermass* is apparently indebted to the volume of the third edition known as *The Scapegoat*. In none of these attempts was Frazer remotely interested. When towards the end of his life his amanuensis Robert Angus Downie read him extracts from *The Waste Land*, he apparently fell asleep.

Again, in old age Frazer often has a dead-set jaw and unsmiling countenance that remind the modern viewer irresistibly of Freud, and it was Freud who took up some of his most daring hints as to the origins of religion, and in *Totem and Taboo* extended them in directions which would probably have given Frazer indigestion if not apoplexy. For Freud again the widespread belief in contagious magic was reminiscent of the delusions of neurotics; it is not entirely certain, however, that Frazer would have known what he meant. He might very well have been more interested in the widespread deployment of rituals and myths identical or analogous to those he mentions by artists originating from the cultures concerned. That Igor Stravinsky composed a ballet in 1913 called *The Rite of Spring* and depicting a female sacrifice to the Russian deity Yarilo is remarkable confirmation of the power of a rite that Frazer depicts, though no tribute to his influence. The same may be said of the frequent structural use of Yoruba or Igbo ritual by recent African writers.

Thus to call Frazer a proto-modernist is both just and richly mistaken. What separates him finally from the modern movement is the severity of a humour determined to be taken in by nothing, and opposed to all forms of mystification. The splicing of echoes from different religious cultures is, for example, fundamental to Eliot's method in *The Waste Land*, but Frazer's ambivalence over these matters is not of the Eliotic kind, nor like Eliot is he disposed towards faith or despairing of the future. What holds his work together is a delicate, ever-so-slightly sardonic poise, a sceptical musing, a wise and trenchant passiveness. Even in his scepticism he is not extreme, expressing in his final pages a sense of the appeal of the religious seemingly at odds with his programme. In both the second and third editions he ends his deconstruction of the religious with the salutation 'Ave Maria', but though the bells of St Peter's sound over his closing paragraphs, he is not inclined to follow them. Frazer is a mild man, and much as we may wish to turn him into a sort of rationalist ogre, behind the unsmiling countenance played a quicksilver wit, even a puckishness, displayed clearly in early photographs and forever bubbling beneath the lucid surface of his prose. It is the contradiction between scholarly deliberateness and subversive humour that provides much of the attraction of his book, an attraction which is forever erupting in the most surprising places: in footnotes or paragraphs where his prime concern is festivals for the exorcism of the dead. To us it may seem as if the contradictions in his literary personality are almost wilfully extreme; so extreme that if we are not very careful we ignore one half of the equation and so misconstrue him completely.

Black humour; scholarship; religious nostalgia; doubt: what can all these creatures be doing in the same menagerie of the mind? But flourish together they do and, though with polite stringency they may sometimes turn and rend one another, the general effect is one of a consort of attitudes. Of all the scientific writers of the late nineteenth century Frazer is among the most fluent, but his fluency sometimes sweeps past, and into, peculiar corners, precarious and craggy river bends. In reading him one is aware of kinships he would have been loath to acknowledge: to Pater, even to Wilde; but beneath the *fin-de-siècle* smoothness there is something else that anchors and sustains it: a toughness that comes from his reading in the seventeenth and eighteenth centuries: Sir Thomas Browne (*Urne-Buriall* particularly); Milton (whose works as a young man he apparently searched for impressive-sounding locutions); Gibbon; Swift; Hume. Like Pater he will feel his way sentiently through a seeming contradiction; but then like Hume he will argue it out patiently, with tortuous and spellbinding logic.

Nothing more clearly demonstrates his contrariness than his attitude to his subject-matter, the many and varied peoples of whom he writes. There is an apocryphal story of his once dining with William James in Rome and, on being asked whether he had encountered any of the tribes on whom he had waxed so prolix, replying with anecdotal disdain: 'Good God, no!' There is no truth in the story whatsoever. There is another prevailing impression that he believed himself to exist mentally at the apex of a pyramid from where, in descending ranks, mankind sloped down to the fabled primitive. Like many statements intended simply to derogate this is both true and utterly false. Frazer, let it be said, was the product of his time (as those who raise the objection are products of theirs). It was a time beset with jingoism, with the Raj at its height, with, at the time he started writing, Africa newly divided. When Lord Lugard created the colony called Nigeria, Frazer was 47; it is a sobering thought.

But no man gives everything to his age. If Frazer's scepticism is allowed in one direction, it must be allowed in others. If he could implicitly take on the monstrous regiment of the faithful (who, though fatally weakened, in the 1890s still had the upper hand, and nowhere more so than in Cambridge), he could also counter assumptions that ran deep in most of his contemporaries. As impressive as the subversiveness of his wit (more impressive in the circumstances) is the subversivenes of his imagination. Frazer was an ethnographer, yes, but unlike many, including some of his officially more-liberal disciples (Malinowski, for example, who, when performing field-work in the Trobriand Islands, kept Conrad's *Heart of Darkness* in his back pocket), he was also an inhabitor of skins—including that of a frightened Mexican boy on one distant May morning.

Because Frazer was a product of the nineteenth century we think of him, confusedly, as an imperialist and a romantic. He was at bottom neither, believing fixedly in a kinship of the intellect that transcended cultures, and above all in the primacy of thought. Magic was this: schematized thought; and ritual was thought-in-practice. His aborigines, like his Romans, come with a completely worked out, if fallible, system of epistemology and ontology, even of technology. They had views, so do we; they got things wrong; but which of us, in the last resort, is wiser? In one of his chapters on taboo Frazer reports a conversation between an unknown missionary and group of Australian tribesmen. The missionary is endeavouring to persuade the aborigines of the superiority of the Christian doctrine of the soul. A conversation ensues which may be set out as follows:

MISSIONARY: 'I am not one as you think, but two.'
(*laughter*)
MISSIONARY: 'You may laugh as much as you like. I tell you that I am two in one; this great body that you see is one; within that there is another little one that is not visible. The great body dies, and is buried, but the little body flies away when the great one dies.'
ABORIGINES: 'Yes, yes. We also are two, we also have a little body within the breast.' (p. 154)

Footnoting this dialogue Frazer sagely comments: 'In this edifying catechism there is little to choose between the savagery of the white man and the savagery of the black.' The purport of this remark is not only to bring the whole of mankind together into one imaginative pool, but also to question the very notion of 'savagery' or, supposing there to be such a thing, our conviction that we do not possess it. Curiously and carefully, *The Golden Bough* is a book that calls the bluff of its own readers.

NOTE ON THE TEXT

The Golden Bough is one of the hothouse plants of the Victorian age. Frazer's friend, the poet and classicist A. E. Housman, once compared it to a banyan tree. In any case, it grew and grew and grew. The first edition of 1890 had two volumes, the second of 1900 three. The third, written between 1906 and 1915, occupies a decent-sized shelf, possessing twelve volumes if one includes the index, to all of which in 1936, towards the end of his long life, Frazer added a supplement, bringing the whole to the inauspicious number of thirteen.

It was clearly unreasonable to expect the general reading public, for whom the book was originally intended, to read in its entirety what had by then become a reference work of considerable proportions. At some time or another, if the book were to retain its widepread appeal, pruning of a fairly drastic sort was going to be necessary. Accordingly, in April 1922, Lady Frazer sat down in the Albermarle Club, Mayfair, to make a one-volume abridgement. On the second of the month she wrote to Macmillan:

Thankyou for sending me the whole GB sheets. I began same night at my Club where I often stay in the afternoons. *So far* the task has been easy and I am through, roughly speaking, Vol 1. On the whole I think it will make a good book & clear up J.G.'s theories. Of course (& I neglected to mention it when you kindly saw me), J.G. will have to write an *entirely* new Preface & for that I allow 30 pages or so. *Nearer* the time of completion I will ask you to badger him, poor Fellow! to get it done, if necessary to hurry him to get it done in time as, at present his Polynesians absorb him greatly. (B.L. Add. Ms. 55140)

Her technique of abridgement was simple. Armed with an immense pot of gum and some scissors, she cut out snippets of the full text which she then mounted flat on fresh sheets of paper. A minor adjustment of the method was introduced when, realizing that she was being forced to sacrifice everything on the verso of passages already selected, she continued in the fashion of an amateur philatelist, hinging the extracts at one side. Even so, the task was onerous, and she asked Frazer to help her.

But Frazer was constitutionally incapable of abridging anything. When the third edition had been in course of preparation in 1903 he had compared himself to a mother elephant, and the edition itself to her offspring. The object now was to reduce this elephant calf to a piglet.

Instead, elephantiasis once more set in. Be that as it may, from some unspecified point on the Frazers would seem to have worked at it jointly. Thus the task was completed in three weeks, since on 22 April Lady Frazer again writes to Macmillan: 'I wish to report that today we are posting to Clarks the *last* vol. of *Golden Bough* minor—i.e. prepared for the press.' Latterly, it appears, Frazer himself had been throwing his full energy into the work. He certainly read the proofs which, with a dispatch that puts modern publishers to shame, were ready exactly one month later. 'It reads smoothly', he wrote on 22 May, 'and I think that the argument gains in clearness and force from being disentangled from many examples and digressions.'

The exact extent of his participation in the hastily undertaken abridgement of 1922 remains, therefore, unclear. The result is certainly lacking in certain respects. It dates from a time when Frazer's fame had spread, when his conclusions were beginning to permeate scholarship in many fields, and when considerable curiosity had been stimulated among the general reading public who desired to know, in as pithy a form as possible, the essence of his case. His best work, however, was long past him, and he no longer had a stomach for the fight. The abridgement of 1922 possesses, therefore, the advantages of caution. It is cogent, fluent, clear about its principles and competent in illustrating them. But it goes to extreme lengths sometimes not to offend. Gone are the risky paragraphs concerning the crucifixion of Christ, gone are the speculations concerning matriarchy, the deliciously irreverent passages on sacred prostitution. Instead, Frazer elaborates the principle of taboo at laborious length, and entertains us to a lengthy discussion of tree worship in Northern Europe, a safe enough subject at any time.

But seventy years later we do not need protecting, and those aspects of the work which are likely to interest us are precisely those which the Frazers felt might cause offence. My plan has been as follows. Starting from the full twelve-volume set, I have reduced much of the preparatory discussion of magic types from the first volume of the work, that is, the portion that Lady Frazer abridged single-handed, on the grounds that, once the principles are spelled out, the rest of the book illustrates them sufficiently. In place I have brought back the passages on sexuality in the ancient world, as well as those leading up to the discussion of the crucifixion in the place where they appeared in the second edition of 1900: at the climax of the discussion of the Saturnalia and of ritual substitution in general. I have somewhat curtailed such sections as those discussing tree-worship. But I have drawn more fully than the Frazers felt able to do on the mesmeric descriptions of cultic religion in the Middle East contained in the fifth part of the third edition, *Adonis, Attis, Osiris: Studies in the History of Oriental Religion*. This volume, originally issued as a separate work in 1905, contains some of the most vivid of Frazer's prose, some of which disappears in the 1922 abridgement. It has been my purpose to restore it, along with those passages in which the disquieting force of the relativistic argument is most sharply drawn. Frazer is a versatile writer of considerable literary resourse, a fact which some of his detractors—even, let it be said, some of his defenders—have been slow to recognize. It has been my intention to convince readers of this fact, which Frazer's well-meaning stewardship of his own work occasionally serves to disguise.

The last change that I have instituted is also in the nature of a restoration, and concerns the division of the text. The first edition of 1900 is arranged in four great chapters, curves or arches that support the keystone of the argument. In the second edition of 1900 this arrangement is retained but filled out to fit three squat volumes. When planning the great third edition in the early years of the century, however, Frazer completely recast the whole, adopting instead an arrangement into seven 'parts', some of which themselves stretch to two volumes, making twelve volumes in all. In 1922 the Frazers threw this all into the melting-pot, cutting their abridged text into sixty-nine shortish chapters running end to end. The result has the merit that individual short chapters can be referred to in isolation from the rest, but the whole strikes me as shapeless. I have therefore returned to Frazer's original plan of four great divisions. These are now called 'Books' rather than chapters or parts. Hence Book I ('The King of the Wood') contains material from Parts 1 and 2 of the third edition; Book II ('Killing the God') material from Parts 3, 4, and 5; Book III ('The Scapegoat') material from Part 6; and Book IV ('The Golden Bough') from Part 7. The result is not necessarily an improvement, but it is an alternative. No words are used other than those Frazer supplied. His footnotes have been dropped, as have his sectional headings; his marginal glosses, however, have been retained. Throughout the guiding motive has been to enhance the onward thrust of the story. Where Frazer articulates theoretical principles (such as those of magic, taboo, or expulsion rites) as a preliminary to the next stage of the argument, my inclination has been to allow him to state them, and then pass on, reducing his prolific documentation of instances and subordinate types.

The Golden Bough is the product of one of the most dangerous and fretful periods of human intellectual history, the period that gave rise to our own age. The present edition attempts to restore a feeling of period, to highlight aspects which possess the cutting edge of the nineteenth century *fin de siècle* when the work was conceived, and in the spirit of which it was written. It is as a miniature of a literary classic that this abridgement, therefore, is offered up, rather than as a work of reference. For those who wish to pursue the matter further there is always, it should be stressed, the full twelve-volume set. As the inherent literary values of anthropological discourse make themselves clearer, it is to this, I believe, that readers will increasingly turn.

SELECT BIBLIOGRAPHY

1. THE EDITIONS OF THE GOLDEN BOUGH

First edition, 2 vols. (London: Macmillan, 1890).

Second edition, 3 vols. (London: Macmillan, 1900).

Third edition, 12 vols. (London: Macmillan, 1906–15). To this a supplement, *Aftermath*, was added in 1936.

Abridged edition, 1 vol. (London: Macmillan, 1922). This is thought to have been compiled largely by Lady Frazer with Frazer's assistance (see Note on the Text above).

2. OTHER WORKS BY FRAZER

For details of his massive output, see 'A Chronology' below. An appreciation of the matrix of ideas from which *The Golden Bough* emerged is much enhanced by a reading of, especially, *Folk-lore in the Old Testament* (for Frazer's growing immersion, from 1905 on, in Biblical scholarship); *The Belief in Immortality and the Worship of the Dead* (for his growing conviction from about 1911 of the strength of the Euhemerist theory and the importance for early civilizations of the placation of the dead); and *Psyche's Task* (on the historical and social advantages of superstition).

3. BIOGRAPHICAL

ACKERMAN, ROBERT, *J. G. Frazer: His Life and Work* (Cambridge: Cambridge University Press, 1987).

DOWNIE, ROBERT ANGUS, *James George Frazer: The Portrait of a Scholar* (London: Watts & Co, 1940).

——*Frazer and The Golden Bough* (London: Gollancz, 1970).

4. THE BACKGROUND

ACKERMAN, ROBERT, 'Frazer on Myth and Ritual', *Journal of the History of Ideas*, 36 (1975), 115–34.

EVANS-PRITCHARD, E. E., *Social Anthropology* (New York: The Free Press, 1951).

——*Theories of Primitive Religion* (Oxford; Oxford University Press, 1965).

——*A History of Anthropological Thought*, ed. André Singer (London: Faber, 1981), esp. pp. 132–52.

FRASER, ROBERT, *The Making of the Golden Bough; The Origins and Growth of an Argument* (London: Macmillan, 1990).

HARRIS, MARVIN, *The Rise of Anthropological Theory* (New York: Crowell, 1968).

HYMAN, STANLEY EDWARD, *The Tangled Bank: Darwin, Marx, Frazer and Freud as Imaginative Writers* (New York: Atheneum, 1962).

KIRK, G. S., *Myth: Its Meaning and Function in Ancient and Other Cultures* (Cambridge; Cambridge University Press; and Berkeley, Calif.: University of California Press, 1970).

LOWEI, ROBERT H., *The History of Ethnological Theory* (New York: Rhinehart, 1937).

STOCKING, GEORGE W., *Race, Culture and Evolution* (New York: The Free Press, 1968).

——*Functionalism Historicized: Essays in British Social Anthropology*, History of Anthropology, no. 2 (Wisconsin: University of Wisconsin Press, 1984).

——*Victorian Anthropology* (New York: The Free Press, 1987).

5. ASSESSMENTS

Beginning with the seminal and trenchant comments of Wittgenstein, Frazer's work has provoked violent reactions, for and against. The following is a fair selection of both:

BENEDICT, RUTH, 'Anthropology and the Humanities', *American Anthropologist*, 50: 4, Part 1 (Oct.–Dec. 1948), 585–93.

DOUGLAS, MARY, 'Judgements on James Frazer', *Daedalus*, 107 (Fall, 1978), 151–64.

JARVIE, I. C., *The Revolution in Anthropology* (London: Routledge & Kegan Paul, 1964).

——'Academic Fashions and Grandfather-Killing—In Defence of Frazer', *Encounter*, 26 (Apr. 1966), 53–5.

——'The Problem of the Rationality of Magic', *British Journal of Sociology*, 18 (Mar. 1967), 55–74.

LEACH, EDMUND, 'Golden Bough or Gilded Twig?', *Daedalus*, 90 (1961), 371–99.

——'On the Founding Fathers: Frazer and Malinowski', *Encounter*, 25 (1965), 24–36; repr. in *Current Anthropology*, 7 (1966), 560–7.

MACCORMACK, SABINE, 'Magic and the Human Mind: A Reconsideration of Frazer's *The Golden Bough*', *Arethusa*, 17 (Fall, 1984), 151–76.

WITTGENSTEIN, LUDWIG *Remarks on Frazer's 'The Golden Bough'*, ed. Rush Rhees (Refford, Notts.: Brynmill Press, 1979).

6. THE INFLUENCE

Frazer has influenced writers, composers, classicists, painters, and even the occasional anthropologist. Much work remains to be done on this facet of his achievement but the following will give some indication of the spread:

ACKERMAN, ROBERT, *The Myth and Ritual School: J. G. Frazer and the Cambridge Ritualists* (New York: Garland, 1991).

BEARD, MARY, 'Frazer, Leach, and Virgil: The Popularity (and Unpopularity) of *The Golden Bough*', *Comparative Studies in Society and History* (Cambridge University Press), 34: 2 (Apr. 1992), 203–24.

FRASER, ROBERT (ed.), *Sir James Frazer and the Literary Imagination; Essays in Affinity and Influence* (London: Macmillan, 1990); contains essays on Yeats, Eliot, Wyndham Lewis, Lawrence, and modern British fiction.

HODGART, MATTHEW, 'In the Shade of the Golden Bough', *Twentieth Century*, 157 (1955), 111–19.

TRILLING, LIONEL, 'On the Teaching of Modern Literature', in *Beyond Culture* (New York: Viking, 1965), 15–18.

VICKERY, JOHN, *The Literary Impact of the Golden Bough* (Princeton, NJ: Princeton University Press, 1973).

A CHRONOLOGY OF
SIR JAMES GEORGE FRAZER (1854–1941)

1843   Great Disruption of the Church of Scotland. Ninian Bannatyne, Frazer's great-uncle, storms out of the Assembly Hall in Edinburgh at second in a column whom he leads into ecclesiastical exile to help found the Free Church of Scotland, in whose austere doctrines Frazer would gratefully be raised.

1854   James George Fraser born in Brandon Place, Glasgow, of Daniel Frazer, pharmacist and Katherine Frazer, née Bogle, whose forebears included George Bogle of Daldowie, who in 1774 had been Warren Hasting's envoy to Tibet.

mid-1860s   Daniel Frazer acquires a property at Helensburgh on the Gareloch, where the young James will spend most holidays until early middle age. At Larchfield Academy, Helensburgh, he imbibes under Alexander Mackenzie the headmaster the rudiments of Latin and Greek. On Sundays he listens to the church bells echoing across the lake, a sound that later reminds him of 'the bells of Nemi'.

1869   Matriculates at Glasgow University, at which he studies Latin under George Gilbert Ramsay, rhetoric under John Veitch, and physics under the great Lord Kelvin (Sir William Thomson), originator of the Second Law of Thermodynamics.

1874   Matriculates at Trinity College, Cambridge, from which in 1878 he graduates with first-class honours in the Classics tripos.

1878   Enters the Middle Temple whence, in January 1882, he is called to the bar, but never practises.

1879   On the basis of a dissertation on Plato, is elected on 10 October to a Title Alpha Fellowship at Trinity. His fellowship is thrice renewed, in 1885, 1890, and 1895.

1886   Commences magisterial translation and edition of Pausanias's *Description of Greece*.

1887   Sends out questionnaire to missionaries, doctors, and administrators throughout the empire, requesting information on the customs and beliefs of the local inhabitants. *Totemism*, his first ethnographic monograph, published in Edinburgh by Adam and Charles Black. Sidetracked from Pausanias by a suggestive passage in Book One, and by certain eighteenth-century travellers' accounts of southern India, commences work on *The Golden Bough*.

1890   First edition of *The Golden Bough*, in two volumes, published by Macmillan. Frazer immediately embarks for Greece, where he travels extensively in preparation for his resumed work on Pausanias, visiting Athens, Sparta, Corinth, Ithome, Olympia, Helicon, Thebes, Aegion, Delphi.

1895   Further travels in Greece, partly on horseback, partly on foot. Visits the Valley of the Styx where he hears sounds 'as if hell-hounds were baying at the strangers who dared approach the infernal water'.

1896–7   Marries Lilly Grove, a French widow, who had come to Cambridge requesting advice on the ethnology of dance. From now on Frazer lives with her and her two growing daughters. Complains, apparently, of noise levels. Pausanias's *Description of Greece* published in six volumes, one of translation, five of commentary.

1900   Second edition of *The Golden Bough* in three volumes. Chapter on 'The Crucifixion of Christ' savagely attacked by Andrew Lang in *The Fortnightly Review*. Spends Christmas in Rome, where he meets William James.

1904–5   Commences the study of Hebrew under tutelage of Robert H. Kennett, his fellow students being Jane Ellen Harrison, Francis Cornford, and A. B. Cook. Delivers 'Lectures on the History of the Kingship', the basis of the eventual second volume of Part One of *The Golden Bough*, third edition (*The Magic Art and the Evolution of Kings*).

1909   *Psyche's Task*, a defence of the social usefulness of superstition.

1910   Appointed to Chair of Social Anthropology in the University of Liverpool. Disgruntled by lack of emolument, and disheartened by large industrial city, flees back to Cambridge. *Totemism and Exogamy* published in four volumes, tabulating kinship systems world-wide.

1906–15   Third edition of *The Golden Bough*, in twelve volumes, with vastly extended exempla and revised theory of Midsummer Fires. 'The Crucifixion of Christ' placed decorously in an appendix. Departs for the Continent.

1913   Volume I of *The Belief in Immortality and the Worship of the Dead*, covering Australasia and Melanesia. Vol. II covering Polynesia and Vol. III covering Micronesia are published in 1922 and 1924 respectively.

1914   Knighted.

1914–18   Spends the Great War in London, in a tiny flat in the Middle Temple, to which his nominal membership of the bar entitles him.

1918   *Folk-lore in the Old Testament*, in three volumes, applying the sceptical method of *The Golden Bough* and Frazer's newly acquired Hebrew scholarship to the text of holy writ.

1921   *Apollodorus: The Library* in two volumes, for the Loeb Library.

1926   *The Worship of Nature*.

1927   *The Gorgon's Head and other Literary Pieces; Man, God, and Immortality*.

1929   Edition and translation of the *Fasti* of Ovid in six volumes. This had been commissioned for the Loeb Library, but had grown beyond all bounds. Later (1931) Frazer shortened it to the extent required by the Loeb Library, who then published it.

1930　*Myths of the Origin of Fire*. His Trinity fellowship dissertation is eventually published as *The Growth of Plato's Ideal Theory*. Is struck blind while making a speech at the annual dinner of the Royal Literary Fund, his eyes 'filling with blood'. From now on will need the services of various amanuenses, notably of Robert Angus Downie, a fellow Glaswegian.

1931　*Garnered Sheaves.*

1933　*Condorcet on the Progress of the Human Mind. The Fear of the Dead in Primitive Religion*, vol. 1; further volumes were published in 1934 and 1936.

1935　*Creation and Evolution in Primitive Cosmogonies and Other Pieces.*

1936　*Aftermath: A Supplement to The Golden Bough.*

1937　*Totemica: A Supplement to Totemism and Exogamy.*

1938　*Anthologia Anthropologica*, extracts from Frazer's notebooks compiled by Downie. A second volume appeared the following year.

1941　Dies, 7 May, to be followed several hours later by the redoubtable Lady Frazer. They are buried side by side in St Giles's Cemetery, Cambridge.

THE GOLDEN BOUGH

To my friend

WILLIAM ROBERTSON SMITH

in gratitude and admiration

From every warlike city
  That boasts the Latian name,
Foredoomed to dogs and vultures,
  That gallant army came;
From Setia's purple vineyards,
  From Norba's ancient wall,
From the white streets of Tusculum,
  The proudest of them all;
From where the Witch's fortress
  O'erhangs the dark blue seas,
From the still glassy lake that sleeps
  Beneath Aricia's trees—
Those trees in whose grim shadow
  The ghastly priest doth reign,
The priest who slew the slayer,
  And shall himself be slain—

Thomas Babington Macaulay,
'The Battle of Lake Regillus'.

BOOK I

THE KING OF THE WOOD

CHAPTER 1

THE KING OF THE WOOD

i

WHO does not know Turner's picture of the Golden Bough? The lake of Nemi. The scene, suffused with the golden glow of imagination in which the divine mind of Turner steeped and transfigured even the fairest natural landscape, is a dream-like vision of the little woodland lake of Nemi—'Diana's Mirror', as it was called by the ancients. No one who has seen that calm water, lapped in a green hollow of the Alban hills, can ever forget it. The two characteristic Italian villages which slumber on its banks, and the equally Italian palace whose terraced gardens descend steeply to the lake, hardly break the stillness and even the solitariness of the scene. Dian herself might still linger by this lonely shore, still haunt these woodlands wild.*

In antiquity this sylvan landscape was the scene of a strange Its tragic memories. and recurring tragedy. In order to understand it aright we must try to form in our minds an accurate picture of the place where it happened; for, as we shall see later on, a subtle link subsisted between the natural beauty of the spot and the dark crimes which under the mask of religion were often perpetrated there, crimes which after the lapse of so many ages still lend a touch of melancholy to these quiet woods and waters, like a chill breath of autumn on one of those bright September days 'while not a leaf seems faded.'

The Alban hills are a fine bold group of volcanic moun- The Alban hills. tains which rise abruptly from the Campagna in full view of Rome, forming the last spur sent out by the Apennines towards the sea. Two of the extinct craters are now filled by two beautiful waters, the Alban lake and its lesser sister the lake of Nemi. Both lie far below the monastery-crowned top of Monte Cavo, the summit of the range, but yet so high above the plain that standing on the rim of the larger crater at Castel Gandolfo, where the Popes had their summer palace, you look down on the one hand into the Alban lake, and on the other away across the Campagna to where, on the western horizon, the sea flashes like a broad sheet of burnished gold in the sun.

The lake of Nemi is still as of old embowered in woods, where in spring the wild flowers blow as fresh as no doubt they did two thousand springs ago. It lies so deep down in the old crater that the calm surface of its clear water is seldom ruffled by the wind. On all sides but one the banks, thickly mantled with luxuriant vegetation, descend steeply to the water's edge. Only on the north a stretch of flat ground intervenes between the lake and the foot of the hills. This was the scene of the tragedy. Here, in the very heart of the wooded hills, under the abrupt declivity now crested by the village of Nemi, the sylvan goddess Diana had an old and famous sanctuary, the resort of pilgrims from all parts of Latium. It was known as the sacred grove of Diana Nemorensis, that is, Diana of the Wood, or, perhaps more exactly, Diana of the Woodland Glade. Sometimes the lake and grove were called, after the nearest town, the lake and grove of Aricia. But the town, the modern Ariccia, lay three miles away at the foot of the mountains, and separated from the lake by a long and steep descent. A spacious terrace or platform contained the sanctuary.* On the north and east it was bounded by great retaining walls which cut into the hillsides and served to support them. Semicircular niches sunk in the walls and faced with columns formed a series of chapels, which in modern times have yielded a rich harvest of votive offerings. On the side of the lake the terrace rested on a mighty wall, over seven hundred feet long by thirty feet high, built in triangular buttresses, like those which we see in front of the piers of bridges to break floating ice. At present this terrace-wall stands back some hundred yards from the lake; in other days its buttresses may have been lapped by the water.

The great wealth and popularity of the sanctuary in antiquity are attested by ancient writers as well as by the remains which have come to light in modern times. Ovid has described the walls hung with fillets and commemorative tablets; and the abundance of cheap votive offerings and copper coins, which the site has yielded in our own day, speaks volumes for the piety and numbers, if not for the opulence and liberality, of the worshippers. Swarms of beggars used to stream forth daily from the slums of Aricia and take their stand on the long slope up which the labouring horses dragged well-to-do pilgrims to the shrine; and according to the response which their whines and importunities met with they blew kisses or hissed curses after the carriages as they swept rapidly down hill again. Here Julius Caesar built himself a costly villa, but pulled it down because it was not to his mind. Here Caligula had two magnificent barges or rather floating palaces, launched for him on the lake.* Vespasian had a monument dedicated to his honour in the grove by the senate and people of Aricia: Trajan condescended to fill the chief magistracy of the town; and Hadrian indulged his taste for architecture by restoring a structure which had been erected in the precinct by a prince of the royal house of Parthia.

In spite of a few villas peeping out here and there from among the trees, Nemi seems to have remained in some sense an image of what Italy had been in the far-off days when the land was still sparsely peopled with tribes of savage hunters or wandering herdsmen, when the beechwoods and oakwoods, with their deciduous foliage, reddening in autumn and bare in winter, had not yet begun, under the hand of man, to yield to the evergreens of the south, the laurel, the olive, the cypress, and the oleander, still less to those intruders of a later age, which nowadays we are apt to think of as characteristically Italian, the lemon and the orange. _{Nemi an image of Italy in the olden time.}

However, it was not merely in its natural surroundings that this ancient shrine of the sylvan goddess continued to be a type or miniature of the past. Down to the decline of Rome a custom was observed there which seems to transport us at once from civilisation to savagery. In the sacred grove there grew a certain tree round which at any time of the day, and probably far into the night, a grim figure might be seen to prowl. In his hand he carried a drawn sword, and he kept peering warily about him as if at every instant he expected to be set upon by an enemy. He was a priest and a murderer; and the man for whom he looked was sooner or later to murder him and hold the priesthood in his stead. Such was the rule of the sanctuary. A candidate for the priesthood could only succeed to office by slaying the priest, and having slain him, he retained office till he was himself slain by a stronger or a craftier. _{Rule of succession to the priesthood of Diana at Nemi.}

The post which he held by this precarious tenure carried with it the title of king; but surely no crowned head ever lay uneasier, or was visited by more evil dreams, than his. For year _{The priest who slew the slayer.}

in year out, in summer and winter, in fair weather and in foul, he had to keep his lonely watch, and whenever he snatched a troubled slumber it was at the peril of his life. The least relaxation of his vigilance, the smallest abatement of his strength of limb or skill of fence, put him in jeopardy; grey hairs might seal his death-warrant. The dreamy blue of Italian skies, the dappled shade of summer woods, and the sparkle of waves in the sun, can have accorded but ill with that stern and sinister figure. Rather we picture to ourselves the scene as it may have been witnessed by a belated wayfarer on one of those wild autumn nights when the dead leaves are falling thick, and the winds seem to sing the dirge of the dying year. It is a sombre picture, set to melancholy music—the background of forest shewing black and jagged against a lowering and stormy sky, the sighing of the wind in the branches, the rustle of the withered leaves under foot, the lapping of the cold water on the shore, and in the foreground, pacing to and fro, now in twilight and now in gloom, a dark figure with a glitter of steel at the shoulder whenever the pale moon, riding clear of the cloud-rack, peers down at him through the matted boughs.

Possibility of explaining the rule of succession by the comparative method. The strange rule of this priesthood has no parallel in classical antiquity, and cannot be explained from it. To find an explanation we must go farther afield. No one will probably deny that such a custom savours of a barbarous age, and, surviving into imperial times, stands out in striking isolation from the polished Italian society of the day, like a primaeval rock rising from a smooth-shaven lawn. It is the very rudeness and barbarity of the custom which allow us a hope of explaining it. For recent researches into the early history of man have revealed the essential similarity with which, under many superficial differences, the human mind has elaborated its first crude philosophy of life. Accordingly, if we can shew that a barbarous custom, like that of the priesthood of Nemi, has existed elsewhere; if we can detect the motives which led to its institution; if we can prove that these motives have operated widely, perhaps universally, in human society, producing in varied circumstances a variety of institutions specifically different but generically alike; if we can shew, lastly, that these very motives, with some of their derivative institutions, were actually at work in classical antiquity; then we may fairly infer that at a remoter age the same motives gave birth to the priesthood of Nemi. Such an inference, in default of direct evidence as to how the priesthood did actually arise, can never amount to demonstration. But it will be more or less probable according to the degree of completeness with which it fulfils the conditions I have indicated. The object of this book is, by meeting these conditions, to offer a fairly probable explanation of the priesthood of Nemi.*

I begin by setting forth the few facts and legends which have come down to us on the subject. According to one story the worship of Diana at Nemi was instituted by Orestes, who, after killing Thoas, King of the Tauric Chersonese (the Crimea), fled with his sister to Italy, bringing with him the image of the Tauric Diana hidden in a faggot of sticks. After his death his bones were transported from Aricia to Rome and buried in front of the temple of Saturn, on the Capitoline slope, beside the temple of Concord. The bloody ritual which legend ascribed to the Tauric Diana is familiar to classical readers; it is said that every stranger who landed on the shore was sacrificed on her altar. But transported to Italy, the rite assumed a milder form. Within the sanctuary at Nemi grew a certain tree of which no branch might be broken. Only a runaway slave was allowed to break off, if he could, one of its boughs. Success in the attempt entitled him to fight the priest in single combat, and if he slew him he reigned in his stead with the title of King of the Wood (*Rex Nemorensis*). According to the public opinion of the ancients the fateful branch was that Golden Bough which, at the Sibyl's bidding, Aeneas plucked before he essayed the perilous journey to the world of the dead. The flight of the slave represented, it was said, the flight of Orestes; his combat with the priest was a reminiscence of the human sacrifices once offered to the Tauric Diana. This rule of succession by the sword was observed down to imperial times; for amongst his other freaks Caligula, thinking that the priest of Nemi had held office too long, hired a more stalwart ruffian to slay him; and a Greek traveller, who visited Italy in the age of the Antonines, remarks that down to his time the priesthood was still the prize of victory in a single combat.*

Of the worship of Diana at Nemi some leading features can still be made out. It appears that she was conceived of especially as a huntress, and further as blessing men and women with

Legend of the origin of the Nemi worship: Orestes and the Tauric Diana.

The King of the Wood.

Chief features of the worship of Diana at Nemi.

Importance of fire in her ritual.

Diana as Vesta.

Diana's festival on August 13 converted by the Christian Church into the festival of the Assumption of the Virgin on August 15.

Egeria, water-nymph and wife of Numa.

Virbius, the male companion of Diana.

offspring, and granting expectant mothers an easy delivery. Again, fire seems to have played a foremost part in her ritual. For during her annual festival, held on the thirteenth of August, at the hottest time of the year, her grove shone with a multitude of torches, whose ruddy glare was reflected by the lake. Further, the title of Vesta borne by Diana at Nemi points clearly to the maintenance of a perpetual holy fire in her sanctuary. Here the sacred fire would seem to have been tended by Vestal Virgins, for the head of a Vestal in terra-cotta was found on the spot, and the worship of a perpetual fire, cared for by holy maidens, appears to have been common in Latium from the earliest to the latest times. At her annual festival, which was celebrated all over Italy young people went through a purificatory ceremony in her honour; wine was brought forth, and the feast consisted of a kid, cakes served piping hot on plates of leaves, and apples still hanging in clusters on the boughs. The Christian Church appears to have sanctified this great festival of the virgin goddess by adroitly converting it into the festival of the Assumption of the Blessed Virgin on the fifteenth of August.*

But Diana did not reign alone in her grove at Nemi. Two lesser divinities shared her forest sanctuary. One was Egeria, the nymph of the clear water which, bubbling from the basaltic rocks, used to fall in graceful cascades into the lake at the place called Le Mole, because here were established the mills of the modern village of Nemi. The purling of the stream as it ran over the pebbles is mentioned by Ovid, who tells us that he had often drunk of its water.* Women with child used to sacrifice to Egeria, because she was believed, like Diana, to be able to grant them an easy delivery. Tradition ran that the nymph had been the wife or mistress of the wise king Numa, that he had consorted with her in the secrecy of the sacred grove, and that the laws which he gave the Romans had been inspired by communion with her divinity. The other of the minor deities at Nemi was Virbius. Legend had it that Virbius was the young Greek hero Hippolytus, chaste and fair, who spent all his days in the greenwood chasing wild beasts with the virgin huntress Artemis (the Greek counterpart of Diana) for his only comrade. Proud of her divine society, he spurned the love of women,* and this proved his bane. For Aphrodite, stung by his scorn, inspired his stepmother Phaedra with love of him; and when he disdained her wicked advances she falsely accused him to his father Theseus. The slander was believed, and Theseus prayed to his sire Poseidon to avenge the imagined wrong. So while Hippolytus drove in a chariot by the shore of the Saronic Gulf, the sea-god sent a fierce bull forth from the waves. The terrified horses bolted, threw Hippolytus from the chariot, and dragged him at their hoofs to death. But Diana, for the love she bore Hippolytus, persuaded the leech Aesculapius to bring her fair young hunter back to life by his simples. Jupiter, indignant that a mortal man should return from the gates of death, thrust down the meddling leech himself to Hades. But Diana hid her favourite from the angry god in a thick cloud, disguised his features by adding years to his life, and then bore him far away to the dells of Nemi, where she entrusted him to the nymph Egeria, to live there, unknown and solitary, under the name of Virbius, in the depth of the Italian forest. There he reigned a king, and there he dedicated a precinct to Diana. He had a comely son, Virbius, who, undaunted by his father's fate, drove a team of fiery steeds to join the Latins in the war against Aeneas and the Trojans. Horses were excluded from the Arician grove and sanctuary because horses had killed Hippolytus. It was unlawful to touch his image. Some thought that he was the sun.

It needs no elaborate demonstration to convince us that the stories told to account for Diana's worship at Nemi are unhistorical. Clearly they belong to that large class of myths which are made up to explain the origin of a religious ritual and have no other foundation than the resemblance, real or imaginary, which may be traced between it and some foreign ritual.* The incongruity of these Nemi myths is indeed transparent, since the foundation of the worship is traced now to Orestes and now to Hippolytus, according as this or that feature of the ritual has to be accounted for. The real value of such tales is that they serve to illustrate the nature of the worship by providing a standard with which to compare it; and further, that they bear witness indirectly to its venerable age by shewing that the true origin was lost in the mists of a fabulous antiquity. We cannot suppose that so barbarous a rule as that of the Arician priesthood was deliberately instituted by a league of civilised

The legends of Nemi invented to explain the ritual.

communities, such as the Latin cities undoubtedly were. It must have been handed down from a time beyond the memory of man, when Italy was still in a far ruder state than any known to us in the historical period. The credit of the tradition is rather shaken than confirmed by another story which ascribes the foundation of the sanctuary to a certain Manius Egerius, who gave rise to the saying, 'There are many Manii at Aricia.'

ii

Origin of the Arician myths of Orestes and Hippolytus.

I have said that the Arician legends of Orestes and Hippolytus, though worthless as history, have a certain value in so far as they may help us to understand the worship at Nemi better by comparing it with the ritual and myths of other sanctuaries. We must ask ourselves, Why did the authors of these legends pitch upon Orestes and Hippolytus in order to explain Virbius and the King of the Wood? In regard to Orestes, the answer is obvious. He and the image of the Tauric Diana, which could only be appeased with human blood, were dragged in to render intelligible the murderous rule of succession to the Arician priesthood. In regard to Hippolytus the case is not so plain. The manner of his death suggests readily enough a reason for the exclusion of horses from the grove; but this by itself seems hardly enough to account for the identification. We must try to probe deeper by examining the worship as well as the legend or myth of Hippolytus.

Worship of Hippolytus at Troezen.

He had a famous sanctuary at his ancestral home of Troezen, situated on that beautiful, almost landlocked bay, where groves of oranges and lemons, with tall cypresses soaring like dark spires above the garden of the Hesperides, now clothe the strip of fertile shore at the foot of the rugged mountains. Across the blue water of the tranquil bay, which it shelters from the open sea, rises Poseidon's sacred island, its peaks veiled in the sombre green of the pines. On this fair coast Hippolytus was worshipped. Within his sanctuary stood a temple with an ancient image. His service was performed by a priest who held office for life: every year a sacrificial festival was held in his honour; and his untimely fate was yearly mourned, with weeping and doleful chants, by unwedded maids, who also dedicated locks of their hair in his temple before marriage. His grave existed at Troezen, though the people would not shew it. It has been suggested, with great plausibility, that in the handsome Hippolytus, beloved of Artemis, cut off in his youthful prime, and yearly mourned by damsels, we have one of those mortal lovers of a goddess who appear so often in ancient religion, and of whom Adonis is the most familiar type.* The rivalry of Artemis and Phaedra for the affection of Hippolytus reproduces, it is said, under different names, the rivalry of Aphrodite and Proserpine for the love of Adonis, for Phaedra is merely a double of Aphrodite. Certainly in the *Hippolytus* of Euripides the tragedy of the hero's death is traced directly to the anger of Aphrodite at his contempt for her power, and Phaedra is nothing but a tool of the goddess. Moreover, within the precinct of Hippolytus at Troezen there stood a temple of Peeping Aphrodite, which was so named, we are told, because from this spot the amorous Phaedra used to watch Hippolytus at his manly sports.* Clearly the name would be still more appropriate if it was Aphrodite herself who peeped.

Hippolytus a mythical being of the Adonis type.

Another point in the myth of Hippolytus which deserves attention is the frequent recurrence of horses in it. His name signifies either 'horse-loosed' or 'horse-looser'; he consecrated twenty horses to Aesculapius at Epidaurus; he was killed by horses; and horses were sacred to his grandsire Poseidon, who had an ancient sanctuary in the wooded island across the bay. Thus Hippolytus was associated with the horse in many ways, and this association may have been used to explain more features of the Arician ritual than the mere exclusion of the animal from the sacred grove. To this point we shall return.

Hippolytus in relation to horses.

The custom observed by Troezenian girls of offering tresses of their hair to Hippolytus before their wedding brings him into a relation with marriage, which at first sight seems out of keeping with his reputation as a confirmed bachelor. However we may explain it, a custom of this sort appears to have prevailed widely both in Greece and the East. Argive maidens, grown to womanhood, dedicated their tresses to Athena before marriage. At the entrance to the temple of Artemis in Delos the grave of two maidens was shewn under an olive-tree. It was said that long ago they had come as pilgrims from a far northern land with offerings to Apollo, and dying in the sacred isle were buried there. The Delian virgins before marriage used to cut off

Hair offered before marriage to Hippolytus and others.

18 — The King of the Wood

Syrian practice; sacrifice of chastity regarded as a substitute for the sacrifice of hair.

a lock of their hair, wind it on a spindle, and lay it on the maidens' grave. In the sanctuary of the great Phoenician goddess Astarte at Byblus* the practice was different. Here, at the annual mourning for the dead Adonis, the women had to shave their heads, and such of them as refused to do so were bound to prostitute themselves to strangers and to sacrifice to the goddess with the wages of their shame. Though Lucian, who mentions the custom, does not say so, there are some grounds for thinking that the women in question were generally maidens, of whom this act of devotion was required as a preliminary to marriage. In any case, it is clear that the goddess accepted the sacrifice of chastity as a substitute for the sacrifice of hair. Why? By many people, as we shall afterwards see, the hair is regarded as in a special sense the seat of strength; and at puberty it might well be thought to contain a double portion of vital energy, since at that season it is the outward sign and manifestation of the newly-acquired power of reproducing the species. Thus the substitution permitted at Byblus becomes intelligible: the women gave of their fecundity to the goddess, whether they offered their hair or their chastity.

Hippolytus and Artemis.

But how, it may be asked, does all this apply to Hippolytus? Why attempt to fertilise the grave of a bachelor who paid all his devotions to a barren virgin? What seed could take root and spring up in so stony a soil? The question implies the popular modern notion of Diana or Artemis as the pattern of a straight-laced maiden lady with a taste for hunting. No notion could well be further from the truth. To the ancients, on the contrary, she was the ideal and embodiment of the wild life of nature—the life of plants, of animals, and of men—in all its exuberant fertility and profusion. The truth is, that the word *parthenos* applied to Artemis, which we commonly translate virgin, means no more than an unmarried woman, and in early days the two things were by no means the same. With the growth of a purer morality among men a stricter code of ethics is imposed by them upon their gods; the stories of the cruelty, deceit, and lust of these divine beings are glossed lightly over or flatly rejected as blasphemies, and the old ruffians are set to guard the laws which before they broke. In regard to Artemis, even the ambiguous *parthenos* seems to have been merely a popular epithet, not an official title. At Ephesus, the most celebrated of

Artemis a goddess of the wild life of nature.

all the seats of her worship,* her universal motherhood was set forth unmistakably in her sacred image. Copies of it have come down to us which agree in their main features, though they differ from each other in some details. They represent the goddess with a multitude of protruding breasts; the heads of animals of many kinds, both wild and tame, spring from the front of her body in a series of bands that extend from the breasts to the feet; bees, roses, and sometimes butterflies, decorate her sides from the hips downward. It would be hard to devise a more expressive symbol of exuberant fertility, of prolific maternity, than these remarkable images.

The Ephesian Artemis.

To return now to Troezen, we shall probably be doing no injustice either to Hippolytus or to Artemis if we suppose that the relation between them was once of a tenderer nature than appears in classical literature. We may conjecture that if he spurned the love of women, it was because he enjoyed the love of a goddess. On the principles of early religion, she who fertilises nature must herself be fertile, and to be that she must necessarily have a male consort. If I am right, Hippolytus was the consort of Artemis at Troezen, and the shorn tresses offered to him by the Troezenian youths and maidens before marriage were designed to strengthen his union with the goddess, and so to promote the fruitfulness of the earth, of cattle, and of mankind. In the story of the tragic death of the youthful Hippolytus we may discern an analogy with similar tales of other fair but mortal youths who paid with their lives for the brief rapture of the love of an immortal goddess. These hapless lovers were probably not always mere myths, and the legends which traced their spilt blood in the purple bloom of the violet, the scarlet stain of the anemone, or the crimson flush of the rose were no idle poetic emblems of youth and beauty fleeting as the summer flowers. Such fables contain a deeper philosophy of the relation of the life of man to the life of nature—a sad philosophy which gave birth to a tragic practice.

Hippolytus the male consort of Artemis.

iii

We can now perhaps understand why the ancients identified Hippolytus, the consort of Artemis, with Virbius, who, according to Servius, stood to Diana as Adonis to Venus, or Attis to

Virbius the male consort of Diana.

the Mother of the Gods. For Diana, like Artemis, was a goddess of fertility in general, and of childbirth in particular. As such she, like her Greek counterpart, needed a male partner. That partner, if Servius is right, was Virbius. In his character of the founder of the sacred grove and first king of Nemi, Virbius is clearly the mythical predecessor or archetype of the line of priests who served Diana under the title of Kings of the Wood, and who came, like him, one after the other, to a violent end. It is natural, therefore, to conjecture that they stood to the goddess of the grove in the same relation in which Virbius stood to her; in short, that the mortal King of the Wood had for his queen the woodland Diana herself. If the sacred tree which he guarded with his life was supposed, as seems probable, to be her special embodiment, her priest may not only have worshipped it as his goddess but embraced it as his wife. There is at least nothing absurd in the supposition, since even in the time of Pliny a noble Roman used thus to treat a beautiful beech-tree in another sacred grove of Diana on the Alban hills. He embraced it, he kissed it, he lay under its shadow, he poured wine on its trunk. Apparently he took the tree for the goddess. The custom of physically marrying men and women to trees is still practised in India and other parts of the East. Why should it not have obtained in ancient Latium?

Summary of results.

Reviewing the evidence as a whole, we may conclude that the worship of Diana in her sacred grove at Nemi was of great importance and immemorial antiquity; that she was revered as the goddess of woodlands and of wild creatures, probably also of domestic cattle and of the fruits of the earth; that she was believed to bless men and women with offspring and to aid mothers in childbed; that her holy fire, tended by chaste virgins, burned perpetually in a round temple within the precinct; that associated with her was a water-nymph Egeria who discharged one of Diana's own functions by succouring women in travail, and who was popularly supposed to have mated with an old Roman king in the sacred grove; further, that Diana of the Wood herself had a male companion Virbius by name, who was to her what Adonis was to Venus, or Attis to Cybele; and, lastly, that this mythical Virbius was represented in historical times by a line of priests known as Kings of the Wood, who regularly perished by the swords of their successors, and whose lives were in a manner bound up with a certain tree in the grove, because so long as that tree was uninjured they were safe from attack.

Clearly these conclusions do not of themselves suffice to explain the peculiar rule of succession to the priesthood. But perhaps the survey of a wider field may lead us to think that they contain in germ the solution of the problem. To that wider survey we must now address ourselves. It will be long and laborious, but may possess something of the interest and charm of a voyage of discovery, in which we shall visit many strange foreign lands, with strange foreign peoples, and still stranger customs. The wind is in the shrouds: we shake out our sails to it, and leave the coast of Italy behind us for a time.

A wide survey required to solve the problem of Nemi.

CHAPTER 2

PRIESTLY KINGS

The two questions to be answered.

THE questions which we have set ourselves to answer are mainly two: first, why had Diana's priest at Nemi, the King of the Wood, to slay his predecessor? second, why before doing so had he to pluck the branch of a certain tree which the public opinion of the ancients identified with Virgil's Golden Bough? The first point on which we fasten is the priest's title. Why was he called the King of the Wood? Why was his office spoken of as a kingdom?

Priestly kings in ancient Italy and Greece.

The union of a royal title with priestly duties was common in ancient Italy and Greece. At Rome and in other cities of Latium there was a priest called the Sacrificial King or King of the Sacred Rites, and his wife bore the title of Queen of the Sacred Rites. In republican Athens the second annual magistrate of the state was called the King, and his wife the Queen; the functions of both were religious. Many other Greek democracies had titular kings, whose duties, so far as they are known, seem to have been priestly, and to have centred round the Common Hearth of the state. For example, in Cos the King sacrificed to Hestia, the goddess of the hearth, the equivalent of the Italian Vesta; and he received the hide and one leg of the victim as his perquisite. In Chios, if any herdsman or shepherd drove his cows, his sheep, or his swine to pasture in a sacred grove, the first person who witnessed the transgression was bound to denounce the transgressor to the kings, under pain of incurring the wrath of the god and, what was perhaps even worse, of having to pay a fine to the offended deity. In the same island the king was charged with the duty of pronouncing the public curses, a spiritual weapon of which much use was made by the ancients. Some Greek states had several of these titular kings, who held office simultaneously. At Rome the tradition was that the Sacrificial King had been appointed after the abolition of the monarchy in order to offer the sacrifices which before had been offered by the kings. A similar view as to the origin of the

Traditional origin of these priestly kings.

priestly kings appears to have prevailed in Greece. In itself the opinion is not improbable, and it is borne out by the example of Sparta, almost the only purely Greek state which retained the kingly form of government in historical times. For in Sparta all state sacrifices were offered by the kings as descendants of the god. One of the two Spartan kings held the priesthood of Zeus Lacedaemon, the other the priesthood of Heavenly Zeus. Sometimes the descendants of the old kings were allowed to retain this shadowy royalty after the real power had departed from them. Thus at Ephesus the descendants of the Ionian kings, who traced their pedigree to Codrus of Athens, kept the title of king and certain privileges, such as the right to occupy a seat of honour at the games, to wear a purple robe and carry a staff instead of a sceptre, and to preside at the rites of Eleusinian Demeter. So at Cyrene, when the monarchy was abolished, the deposed King Battus was assigned certain domains and allowed to retain some priestly functions.

This combination of priestly functions with royal authority is familiar to every one. Asia Minor, for example, was the seat of various great religious capitals peopled by thousands of sacred slaves, and ruled by pontiffs who wielded at once temporal and spiritual authority, like the popes of mediaeval Rome. Such priest-ridden cities were Zela and Pessinus.* Teutonic kings, again, in the old heathen days seem to have stood in the position, and to have exercised the powers, of high priests. The Emperors of China offer public sacrifices, the details of which are regulated by the ritual books. The King of Madagascar was high-priest of the realm. At the great festival of the new year, when a bullock was sacrificed for the good of the kingdom, the king stood over the sacrifice to offer prayer and thanksgiving, while his attendants slaughtered the animal. In the monarchical states which still maintain their independence among the Gallas* of Eastern Africa, the king sacrifices on the mountain tops and regulates the immolation of human victims. Among the Matabeles* the king is high-priest. Every year he offers sacrifices at the great and the little dance, and also at the festival of the new fruits, which ends the dances. On these occasions he prays to the spirits of his forefathers and likewise to his own spirit; for it is from these higher powers that he expects every blessing.

Priestly kings in various parts of the world.

But when we have said that the ancient kings were commonly priests also, we are far from having exhausted the religious aspect of their office. In those days the divinity that hedges a king was no empty form of speech, but the expression of a sober belief. Kings were revered, in many cases not merely as priests, that is, as intercessors between man and god, but as themselves gods, able to bestow upon their subjects and worshippers those blessings which are commonly supposed to be beyond the reach of mortals, and are sought, if at all, only by prayer and sacrifice offered to superhuman and invisible beings. Thus kings are often expected to give rain and sunshine in due season, to make the crops grow, and so on. Strange as this expectation appears to us, it is quite of a piece with early modes of thought. A savage hardly conceives the distinction commonly drawn by more advanced peoples between the natural and the supernatural. To him the world is to a great extent worked by supernatural agents, that is, by personal beings acting on impulses and motives like his own, liable like him to be moved by appeals to their pity, their hopes, and their fears. In a world so conceived he sees no limit to his power of influencing the course of nature to his own advantage. Prayers, promises, or threats may secure him fine weather and an abundant crop from the gods; and if a god should happen, as he sometimes believes, to become incarnate in his own person, then he need appeal to no higher being; he, the savage, possesses in himself all the powers necessary to further his own well-being and that of his fellow-men.

This is one way in which the idea of a man-god is reached. But there is another. Along with the view of the world as pervaded by spiritual forces, savage man has a different, and probably still older, conception in which we may detect a germ of the modern notion of natural law or the view of nature as a series of events occurring in an invariable order without the intervention of personal agency. The germ of which I speak is involved in that sympathetic magic, as it may be called, which plays a large part in most systems of superstition. In early society the king is frequently a magician as well as a priest; indeed he appears to have often attained to power by virtue of his supposed proficiency in the black or white art. Hence in order to understand the evolution of the kingship and the sacred

character with which the office has commonly been invested in
the eyes of savage or barbarous peoples, it is essential to have
some acquaintance with the principles of magic and to form
some conception of the extraordinary hold which that ancient
system of superstition has had on the human mind in all ages
and all countries. Accordingly I propose to examine the subject
in some detail.

CHAPTER 3

MAGIC AND RELIGION

i

The two principles of Sympathetic Magic are the Law of Similarity and the Law of Contact or Contagion.

IF we analyse the principles of thought on which magic is based, they will probably be found to resolve themselves into two: first, that like produces like, or that an effect resembles its cause; and, second, that things which have once been in contact with each other continue to act on each other at a distance after the physical contact has been severed. The former principle may be called the Law of Similarity, the latter the Law of Contact or Contagion. From the first of these principles, namely the Law of Similarity, the magician infers that he can produce any effect he desires merely by imitating it: from the second he infers that whatever he does to a material object will affect equally the person with whom the object was once in contact, whether it formed part of his body or not. Charms based on the Law of Similarity may be called Homoeopathic or Imitative Magic. Charms based on the Law of Contact or Contagion may be called Contagious Magic. To denote the first of these branches of magic the term Homoeopathic is perhaps preferable, for the alternative term Imitative or Mimetic suggests, if it does not imply, a conscious agent who imitates, thereby limiting the scope of magic too narrowly. For the same principles which the magician applies in the practice of his art are implicitly believed by him to regulate the operations of inanimate nature; in other words, he tacitly assumes that the Laws of Similarity and Contact are of universal application and are not limited to human actions. In short, magic is a spurious system of natural law as well as a fallacious guide of conduct; it is a false science as well as an abortive art. Regarded as a system of natural law, that is, as a statement of the rules which determine the sequence of events throughout the world, it may be called Theoretical Magic: regarded as a set of precepts which human beings observe in order to compass their ends, it may be called Practical Magic. At the same time it is to be borne in mind that the primitive magician knows magic only on its practical side; he never analyses the mental processes on which his practice is based, never reflects on the abstract principles involved in his actions. In short, to him magic is always an art, never a science; the very idea of science is lacking in his undeveloped mind. It is for the philosophic student to trace the train of thought which underlies the magician's practice; to draw out the few simple threads of which the tangled skein is composed; to disengage the abstract principles from their concrete applications; in short, to discern the spurious science behind the bastard art.

If my analysis of the magician's logic is correct, its two great principles turn out to be merely two different misapplications of the association of ideas.* Homoeopathic magic is founded on the association of ideas by similarity: contagious magic is founded on the association of ideas by contiguity. Homoeopathic magic commits the mistake of assuming that things which resemble each other are the same: contagious magic commits the mistake of assuming that things which have once been in contact with each other are always in contact. But in practice the two branches are often combined; or, to be more exact, while homoeopathic or imitative magic may be practised by itself, contagious magic will generally be found to involve an application of the homoeopathic or imitative principle. Both trains of thought are in fact extremely simple and elementary. It could hardly be otherwise, since they are familiar in the concrete, though certainly not in the abstract, to the crude intelligence not only of the savage, but of ignorant and dull-witted people everywhere. Both branches of magic, the homoeopathic and the contagious, may conveniently be comprehended under the general name of Sympathetic Magic, since both assume that things act on each other at a distance through a secret sympathy, the impulse being transmitted from one to the other by means of what we may conceive as a kind of invisible ether, not unlike that which is postulated by modern science for a precisely similar purpose, namely, to explain how things can physically affect each other through a space which appears to be empty.

It may be convenient to tabulate as follows the branches of magic according to the laws of thought which underlie them:

The two principles are misapplications of the association of ideas.

Sympathetic Magic
(*Law of Sympathy*)

Homoeopathic Magic   Contagious Magic*
(*Law of Similarity*)   (*Law of Contact*)

I will now illustrate these two great branches of sympathetic magic by examples, beginning with homoeopathic magic.

ii

Homoe-
opathic
Magic.

Perhaps the most familiar application of the principle that like produces like is the attempt which has been made by many peoples in many ages to injure or destroy an enemy by injuring or destroying an image of him, in the belief that, just as the image suffers, so does the man, and that when it perishes he must die. A few instances out of many may be given to prove at once the wide diffusion of the practice over the world and its remarkable persistence through the ages. For thousands of years ago it was known to the sorcerers of ancient India, Babylon, and Egypt, as well as of Greece and Rome, and at this day it is still resorted to by cunning and malignant savages in Australia, Africa, and Scotland. Thus the North American Indians, we are told, believe that by drawing the figure of a person in sand, ashes, or clay, or by considering any object as his body, and then pricking it with a sharp stick or doing it any other injury, they inflict a corresponding injury on the person represented. For example, when an Ojebway Indian desires to work evil on any one, he makes a little wooden image of his enemy and runs a needle into its head or heart, or he shoots an arrow into it, believing that wherever the needle pierces or the arrow strikes the image, his foe will the same instant be seized with a sharp pain in the corresponding part of his body; but if he intends to kill the person outright, he burns or buries the puppet, uttering certain magic words as he does so.* The Peruvian Indians moulded images of fat mixed with grain to imitate the persons whom they disliked or feared, and then burned the effigy on the road where the intended victim was to pass. This they called burning his soul.

If homoeopathic or imitative magic, working by means of images, has commonly been practised for the spiteful purpose of putting obnoxious people out of the world, it has also, though far more rarely, been employed with the benevolent intention of helping others into it. In other words, it has been used to facilitate childbirth and to procure offspring for barren women. Thus among the Bataks of Sumatra a barren woman, who would become a mother, will make a wooden image of a child and hold it in her lap, believing that this will lead to the fulfilment of her wish. Among some of the Dyaks of Borneo, when a woman is in hard labour, a wizard is called in, who essays to facilitate the delivery in a rational manner by manipulating the body of the sufferer. Meantime another wizard outside the room exerts himself to attain the same end by means which we should regard as wholly irrational. He, in fact, pretends to be the expectant mother; a large stone attached to his stomach by a cloth wrapt round his body represents the child in the womb, and, following the directions shouted to him by his colleague on the real scene of operations, he moves this make-believe baby about on his body in exact imitation of the movements of the real baby till the infant is born.

Another beneficent use of homoeopathic magic is to heal or prevent sickness. The ancient Hindoos performed an elaborate ceremony, based on homoeopathic magic, for the cure of jaundice. Its main drift was to banish the yellow colour to yellow creatures and yellow things, such as the sun, to which it properly belongs, and to procure for the patient a healthy red colour from a living, vigorous source, namely a red bull. With this intention, a priest recited the following spell: 'Up to the sun shall go thy heart-ache and thy jaundice: in the colour of the red bull do we envelop thee! We envelop thee in red tints, unto long life. May this person go unscathed and be free of yellow colour! The cows whose divinity is Rohini, they who, moreover, are themselves red (*rohinih*)—in their every form and every strength we do envelop thee. Into the parrots, into the thrush, do we put thy jaundice, and, furthermore, into the yellow wagtail do we put thy jaundice.' While he uttered these words, the priest, in order to infuse the rosy hue of health into the sallow patient, gave him water to sip which was mixed with the hair of a red bull; he poured water over the animal's back and made the sick man drink it; he seated him on the skin of a red bull and tied a piece of the skin to him. Then in order to improve his colour by thoroughly eradicating the yellow taint, he proceeded thus. He first daubed him from head to foot with a yellow porridge made of turmeric or curcuma (a yellow plant), set him on a bed, tied three yellow birds, to wit a parrot, a thrush, and a yellow wagtail, by means of a yellow string to the foot of the bed; then pouring water over the patient, he washed off the yellow porridge, and with it no doubt the jaundice, from him to the birds. After that, by way of giving a final bloom to his complexion, he took some hairs of a red bull, wrapt them in gold leaf, and glued them to the patient's skin.

One of the great merits of homoeopathic magic is that it enables the cure to be performed on the person of the doctor instead of on that of his victim, who is thus relieved of all trouble and inconvenience, while he sees his medical man writhe in anguish before him. For example, the peasants of Perche, in France, labour under the impression that a prolonged fit of vomiting is brought about by the patient's stomach becoming unhooked, as they call it, and so falling down. Accordingly, a practitioner is called in to restore the organ to its proper place. After hearing the symptoms he at once throws himself into the most horrible contortions, for the purpose of unhooking his own stomach. Having succeeded in the effort, he next hooks it up again in another series of contortions and grimaces, while the patient experiences a corresponding relief. Fee five francs. In like manner a Dyak medicine-man, who has been fetched in a case of illness, will lie down and pretend to be dead. He is accordingly treated like a corpse, is bound up in mats, taken out of the house, and deposited on the ground. After about an hour the other medicine-men loose the pretended dead man and bring him to life; and as he recovers, the sick person is supposed to recover too.

Further, homoeopathic and in general sympathetic magic plays a great part in the measures taken by the rude hunter or fisherman to secure an abundant supply of food. On the principle that like produces like, many things are done by him and his friends in deliberate imitation of the result which he seeks to attain; and, on the other hand, many things are scrupulously avoided because they bear some more or less fanciful resemblance to others which would really be disastrous.

Nowhere is the theory of sympathetic magic more systematically carried into practice for the maintenance of the food supply than in the barren regions of Central Australia.* Here the tribes are divided into a number of totem clans, each of which is charged with the duty of multiplying their totem for the good of the community by means of magical ceremonies. Most of the totems are edible animals and plants, and the general result supposed to be accomplished by these ceremonies is that of supplying the tribe with food and other necessaries. Often the rites consist of an imitation of the effect which the people desire to produce; in other words, their magic is homoeopathic or imitative. Thus among the Warramunga the headman of the white cockatoo totem seeks to multiply white cockatoos by holding an effigy of the bird and mimicking its harsh cry. Among the Arunta the men of the witchetty grub totem perform ceremonies for multiplying the grub which the other members of the tribe use as food. One of the ceremonies is a pantomime representing the fully developed insect in the act of emerging from the chrysalis. A long narrow structure of branches is set up to imitate the chrysalis case of the grub. In this structure a number of men, who have the grub for their totem, sit and sing of the creature in its various stages. Then they shuffle out of it in a squatting posture, and as they do so they sing of the insect emerging from the chrysalis. This is supposed to multiply the numbers of the grubs. Again, in order to multiply emus, which are an important article of food, the men of the emu totem paint on the ground the sacred design of their totem, especially the parts of the emu which they like best to eat, namely, the fat and the eggs. Round this painting the men sit and sing. Afterwards performers, wearing headdresses to represent the long neck and small head of the emu, mimic the appearance of the bird as it stands aimlessly peering about in all directions.

It is to be observed that the system of sympathetic magic is not merely composed of positive precepts; it comprises a very large number of negative precepts, that is, prohibitions. It tells you not merely what to do, but also what to leave undone. The positive precepts are charms: the negative precepts are taboos. In fact the whole doctrine of taboo, or at all events a large part of it, would seem to be only a special application of sympathetic magic, with its two great laws of similarity and contact. Though these laws are certainly not formulated in so many words nor even conceived in the abstract by the savage, they are nevertheless implicitly believed by him to regulate the course of nature quite independently of human will. He thinks that if he acts in a certain way, certain consequences will inevitably follow in virtue of one or other of these laws; and if the consequences of a particular act appear to him likely to prove disagreeable or dangerous, he is naturally careful not to act in that way lest he should incur them. In other words, he abstains from doing that which, in accordance with his mistaken notions of cause and effect, he falsely believes would injure him; in short, he subjects himself to a taboo. Thus taboo is so far a negative application of practical magic. Positive magic or sorcery says, 'Do this in order that so and so may happen.' Negative magic or taboo says, 'Do not do this, lest so and so should happen.' The aim of positive magic or sorcery is to produce a desired event; the aim of negative magic or taboo is to avoid an undesirable one. But both consequences, the desirable and the undesirable, are supposed to be brought about in accordance with the laws of similarity and contact. And just as the desired consequence is not really effected by the observance of a magical ceremony, so the dreaded consequence does not really result from the violation of a taboo. If the supposed evil necessarily followed a breach of taboo, the taboo would not be a taboo but a precept of morality or common sense. It is not a taboo to say, 'Do not put your hand in the fire'; it is a rule of common sense, because the forbidden action entails a real, not an imaginary evil. In short, those negative precepts which we call taboo are just as vain and futile as those positive precepts which we call sorcery. The two things are merely opposite sides or poles of one great disastrous fallacy, a mistaken conception of the association of ideas. Of that fallacy, sorcery is the positive, and taboo the negative pole. If we give the general name of magic to the whole erroneous system, both theoretical and practical, then taboo may be defined as the negative side of practical magic. To put this in tabular form:

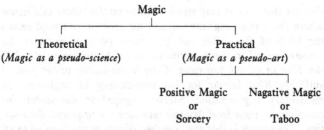

I have made these remarks on taboo and its relations to magic because I am about to give some instances of taboos observed by hunters, fishermen, and others, and I wished to show that they fall under the head of Sympathetic Magic, being only particular applications of that general theory. Thus, among the Esquimaux boys are forbidden to play cat's cradle, because if they did so their fingers might in later life become entangled in the harpoon-line. Here the taboo is obviously an application of the law of similarity, which is the basis of homoeopathic magic: as the child's fingers are entangled by the string in playing cat's cradle, so they will be entangled by the harpoon-line when he is a man and hunts whales. Again, among the Huzuls of the Carpathian Mountains the wife of a hunter may not spin while her husband is eating, or the game will turn and wind like the spindle, and the hunter will be unable to hit it. Here again the taboo is clearly derived from the law of similarity. So, too, in most parts of ancient Italy women were forbidden by law to spin on the highroads as they walked, or even to carry their spindles openly, because any such action was believed to injure the crops. Probably the notion was that the twirling of the spindle would twirl the corn-stalks and prevent them from growing straight. For a like reason in Bilaspore, a district of India, when the chief men of a village meet in council, no one present should twirl a spindle; for they think that if such a thing were to happen, the discussion, like the spindle, would move in a circle and never be wound up. In some of the East Indian islands any one who comes to the house of a hunter must walk straight in; he may not loiter at the door, for were he to do so, the game would in like manner stop in front of the hunter's snares and then turn back, instead of being caught in the trap. For a similar reason it is a rule with the Toradjas of Central

Celebes that no one may stand or loiter on the ladder of a house where there is a pregnant woman, for such delay would retard the birth of the child; and in various parts of Sumatra the woman herself in these circumstances is forbidden to stand at the door or on the top rung of the house-ladder under pain of suffering hard labour for her imprudence in neglecting so elementary a precaution. Malays engaged in the search for camphor eat their food dry and take care not to pound their salt fine. The reason is that the camphor occurs in the form of small grains deposited in the cracks of the trunk of the camphor-tree. Accordingly it seems plain to the Malay that if, while seeking for camphor, he were to eat his salt finely ground, the camphor would be found also in fine grains; whereas by eating his salt coarse he ensures that the grains of the camphor will also be large. Camphor hunters in Borneo use the leathery sheath of the leaf-stalk of the Penang palm as a plate for food, and during the whole of the expedition they will never wash the plate, for fear that the camphor might dissolve and disappear from the crevices of the tree. Apparently they think that to wash their plates would be to wash out the camphor crystals from the trees in which they are imbedded. The chief product of some parts of Laos, a province of Siam, is lac. This is a resinous gum exuded by a red insect on the young branches of trees, to which the little creatures have to be attached by hand. All who engage in the business of gathering the gum abstain from washing themselves and especially from cleansing their heads, lest by removing the parasites from their hair they should detach the other insects from the boughs. Again, a Blackfoot Indian who has set a trap for eagles, and is watching it, would not eat rosebuds on any account; for he argues that if he did so, and an eagle alighted near the trap, the rosebuds in his own stomach would make the bird itch, with the result that instead of swallowing the bait the eagle would merely sit and scratch himself. Following this train of thought the eagle hunter also refrains from using an awl when he is looking after his snares; for surely if he were to scratch with an awl, the eagles would scratch him. The same disastrous consequence would follow if his wives and children at home used an awl while he is out after eagles, and accordingly they are forbidden to handle the tool in his absence for fear of putting him in bodily danger.

The reader may have observed that in some of the fore-going examples of taboos the magical influence is supposed to operate at considerable distances. This belief in the sympathetic influence exerted on each other by persons or things at a distance is of the essence of magic. Whatever doubts science may entertain as to the possibility of action at a distance, magic has none; faith in telepathy is one of its first principles. A modern advocate of the influence of mind upon mind at a distance would have no difficulty in convincing a savage*, the savage believed in it long ago, and what is more, he acted on his belief with a logical consistency such as his civilised brother in the faith has not yet, so far as I am aware, exhibited in his conduct. For the savage is convinced not only that magical ceremonies affect persons and things afar off, but that the simplest acts of daily life may do so too. Hence on important occasions the behaviour of friends and relations at a distance is often regulated by a more or less elaborate code of rules, the neglect of which by the one set of persons would, it is supposed, entail misfortune or even death on the absent ones. In particular when a party of men are out hunting or fighting, their kinsfolk at home are often expected to do certain things or to abstain from doing certain others, for the sake of ensuring the safety and success of the distant hunters or warriors.

Many of the indigenous tribes of Sarawak are firmly per-suaded that were the wives to commit adultery while their husbands are searching for camphor in the jungle, the camphor obtained by the men would evaporate. Husbands can discover, by certain knots in the tree, when their wives are unfaithful; and it is said that in former days many women were killed by jealous husbands on no better evidence than that of these knots. Further, the wives dare not touch a comb while their husbands are away collecting the camphor; for if they did so, the interstices between the fibres of the tree, instead of being filled with the precious crystals, would be empty like the spaces between the teeth of a comb. In the Kei Islands, to the south-west of New Guinea, as soon as a vessel that is about to sail for a distant port has been launched, the part of the beach on which it lay is covered as speedily as possible with palm branches, and becomes sacred. No one may thenceforth cross

that spot till the ship comes home. To cross it sooner would
cause the vessel to perish. Moreover, all the time that the
voyage lasts three or four young girls, specially chosen for the
duty, are supposed to remain in sympathetic connexion with
the mariners and to contribute by their behaviour to the safety
and success of the voyage. On no account, except for the most
necessary purpose, may they quit the room that has been
assigned to them. More than that, so long as the vessel is
believed to be at sea they must remain absolutely motionless,
crouched on their mats with their hands clasped between their
knees. They may not turn their heads to the left or to the right
or make any other movement whatsoever. If they did, it would
cause the boat to pitch and toss; and they may not eat any sticky
stuff, such as rice boiled in coco-nut milk, for the stickiness of
the food would clog the passage of the boat through the water.
When the sailors are supposed to have reached their destination,
the strictness of these rules is somewhat relaxed; but during the
whole time that the voyage lasts the girls are forbidden to eat
fish which have sharp bones or stings, such as the sting-ray, lest
their friends at sea should be involved in sharp, stinging
trouble.

Among the Tshi-speaking peoples of the Gold Coast* the
wives of men who are away with the army paint themselves
white, and adorn their persons with beads and charms. On the
day when a battle is expected to take place, they run about
armed with guns, or sticks carved to look like guns, and taking
green paw-paws (fruits shaped somewhat like a melon), they
hack them with knives, as if they were chopping off the heads
of the foe. The pantomime is no doubt merely an imitative
charm, to enable the men to do to the enemy as the women do
to the paw-paws. In the West African town of Framin, while
the Ashantee war was raging some years ago, Mr. Fitzgerald
Marriott saw a dance performed by women whose husbands had
gone as carriers to the war. They were painted white and wore
nothing but a short petticoat. At their head was a shrivelled old
sorceress in a very short white petticoat, her black hair arranged
in a sort of long projecting horn, and her black face, breasts,
arms, and legs profusely adorned with white circles and cres-
cents. All carried long white brushes made of buffalo or horse
tails, and as they danced they sang, 'Our husbands have gone

to Ashanteeland; may they sweep their enemies off the face of the earth!'

iii

Thus far we have been considering chiefly that branch of sympathetic magic which may be called homoeopathic or imitative. Its leading principle, as we have seen, is that like produces like, or, in other words, that an effect resembles its cause. The other great branch of sympathetic magic, which I have called Contagious Magic, proceeds upon the notion that things which have once been conjoined must remain ever afterwards, even when quite dissevered from each other, in such a sympathetic relation that whatever is done to the one must similarly affect the other. Thus the logical basis of Contagious Magic, like that of Homoeopathic Magic, is a mistaken association of ideas; its physical basis, if we may speak of such a thing, like the physical basis of Homoeopathic Magic, is a material medium of some sort which, like the ether of modern physics, is assumed to unite distant objects and to convey impressions from one to the other. The most familiar example of Contagious Magic is the magical sympathy which is supposed to exist between a man and any severed portion of his person, as his hair or nails; so that whoever gets possession of human hair or nails may work his will, at any distance, upon the person from whom they were cut. This superstition is world-wide; instances of it in regard to hair and nails will be noticed later on in this work. *[margin: Contagious Magic.]*

Among the Australian tribes it was a common practice to knock out one or more of a boy's front teeth at those ceremonies of initiation to which every male member had to submit before he could enjoy the rights and privileges of a full-grown man. The reason of the practice is obscure; all that concerns us here is the belief that a sympathetic relation continued to exist between the lad and his teeth after the latter had been extracted from his gums. Thus among some of the tribes about the River Darling, in New South Wales, the extracted tooth was placed under the bark of a tree near a river or water-hole; if the bark grew over the tooth, or if the tooth fell into the water, all was well; but if it were exposed and the ants ran over it, the natives believed that the boy would suffer from a disease of the mouth.

Among the Murring and other tribes of New South Wales the extracted tooth was at first taken care of by an old man, and then passed from one headman to another, until it had gone all round the community, when it came back to the lad's father, and finally to the lad himself. But however it was thus conveyed from hand to hand, it might on no account be placed in a bag containing magical substances, for to do so would, they believed, put the owner of the tooth in great danger. The late Dr Howitt* once acted as custodian of the teeth which had been extracted from some novices at a ceremony of initiation, and the old men earnestly besought him not to carry them in a bag in which they knew that he had some quartz crystals. They declared that if he did so the magic of the crystals would pass into the teeth, and so injure the boys. Nearly a year after Dr Howitt's return from the ceremony he was visited by one of the principal men of the Murring tribe, who had travelled some two hundred and fifty miles from his home to fetch back the teeth. This man explained that he had been sent for them because one of the boys had fallen into ill health, and it was believed that the teeth had received some injury which had affected him. He was assured that the teeth had been kept in a box apart from any substances, like quartz crystals, which could influence them; and he returned home bearing the teeth with him carefully wrapt up and concealed.

The Basutos* are careful to conceal their extracted teeth, lest these should fall into the hands of certain mythical beings who haunt graves, and who could harm the owner of the tooth by working magic on it. In Sussex some fifty years ago a maidservant remonstrated strongly against the throwing away of children's cast teeth, affirming that should they be found and gnawed by any animal, the child's new tooth would be, for all the world, like the teeth of the animal that had bitten the old one. In proof of this she named old Master Simmons, who had a very large pig's tooth in his upper jaw, a personal defect that he always averred was caused by his mother, who threw away one of his cast teeth by accident into the hog's trough. A similar belief has led to practices intended, on the principles of homoeopathic magic, to replace old teeth by new and better ones. Thus in many parts of the world it is customary to put extracted teeth in some place where they will be found by a mouse or a rat, in the hope that, through the sympathy which continues to subsist between them and their former owner, his other teeth may acquire the same firmness and excellence as the teeth of these rodents. For example, in Germany it is said to be an almost universal maxim among the people that when you have had a tooth taken out you should insert it in a mouse's hole. To do so with a child's milk-tooth which has fallen out will prevent the child from having toothache. Or you should go behind the stove and throw your tooth backwards over your head, saying, 'Mouse, give me your iron tooth; I will give you my bone tooth.' After that your other teeth will remain good. Far away from Europe, at Raratonga, in the Pacific, when a child's tooth was extracted, the following prayer used to be recited:

> 'Big rat! little rat!
> Here is my old tooth.
> Pray give me a new one.'

Then the tooth was thrown on the thatch of the house, because rats make their nests in the decayed thatch. The reason assigned for invoking the rats on these occasions was that rats' teeth were the strongest known to the natives.

Other parts which are commonly believed to remain in a sympathetic union with the body, after the physical connexion has been severed, are the navel-string and the afterbirth, including the placenta. So intimate, indeed, is the union conceived to be, that the fortunes of the individual for good or evil throughout life are often supposed to be bound up with one or other of these portions of his person, so that if his navel-string or afterbirth is preserved and properly treated, he will be prosperous; whereas if it be injured or lost, he will suffer accordingly. Thus certain tribes of Western Australia believe that a man swims well or ill, according as his mother at his birth threw the navel-string into water or not. Among the natives on the Pennefather River in Queensland it is believed that a part of the child's spirit (*cho-i*) stays in the afterbirth. Hence the grandmother takes the afterbirth away and buries it in the sand. She marks the spot by a number of twigs which she sticks in the ground in a circle, tying their tops together so that the structure resembles a cone. When Anjea, the being who causes conception in women by putting mud babies into their wombs, comes along and sees the place, he takes out the spirit and carries it away to one of his haunts, such as a tree, a hole in a rock, or a lagoon, where it may remain for years. But some time or other he will put the spirit again into a baby, and it will be born once more into the world. In Ponape, one of the Caroline Islands,* the navel-string is placed in a shell and then disposed of in such a way as shall best adapt the child for the career which the parents have chosen for him; for example, if they wish to make him a good climber, they will hang the navel-string on a tree. The Kei islanders* regard the navel-string as the brother or sister of the child, according to the sex of the infant. They put it in a pot with ashes, and set it in the branches of a tree, that it may keep a watchful eye on the fortunes of its comrade. Among the Bataks of Sumatra, as among many other peoples of the Indian Archipelago, the placenta passes for the child's younger brother or sister, the sex being determined by the sex of the child, and it is buried under the house. According to the Bataks it is bound up with the child's welfare, and seems, in fact, to be the seat of the transferable soul, of which we shall hear something later on. The Karo Bataks even affirm that of a man's two souls it is the true soul that lives with the placenta under the house; that is the soul, they say, which begets children.

Even in Europe many people still believe that a person's destiny is more or less bound up with that of his navel-string or afterbirth. Thus in Rhenish Bavaria the navel-string is kept for a while wrapt up in a piece of old linen, and then cut or pricked to pieces according as the child is a boy or a girl, in order that he or she may grow up to be a skilful workman or a good sempstress. In Berlin the midwife commonly delivers the dried navel-string to the father with a strict injunction to preserve it carefully, for so long as it is kept the child will live and thrive and be free from sickness. In Beauce and Perche the people are careful to throw the navel-string neither into water nor into fire, believing that if that were done the child would be drowned or burned.

A curious application of the doctrine of contagious magic is the relation commonly believed to exist between a wounded man and the agent of the wound, so that whatever is subsequently done by or to the agent must correspondingly affect the patient either for good or evil. Thus Pliny tells us that if you have wounded a man and are sorry for it, you have only to spit on the hand that gave the wound, and the pain of the sufferer will be instantly alleviated.* In Melanesia, if a man's friends get possession of the arrow which wounded him, they keep it in a damp place or in cool leaves, for then the inflammation will be trifling and will soon subside. Meantime the enemy who shot the arrow is hard at work to aggravate the wound by all the means in his power. For this purpose he and his friends drink hot and burning juices and chew irritating leaves, for this will clearly inflame and irritate the wound. Further, they keep the bow near the fire to make the wound which it has inflicted hot; and for the same reason they put the arrow-head, if it has been recovered, into the fire. Moreover, they are careful to keep the bow-string taut and to twang it occasionally, for this will cause the wounded man to suffer from tension of the nerves and spasms of tetanus. 'It is constantly received and avouched', says Bacon, 'that the anointing of the weapon that maketh the wound will heal the wound itself. In this experiment, upon the relation of men of credit (though myself, as yet, am not fully inclined to believe it), you shall note the points following: first, the ointment wherewith this is done is made of divers ingredients, whereof the strangest and hardest to come by are the moss upon the skull of a dead man unburied, and the facts of a boar and a bear killed in the act of generation.'* The precious ointment compounded out of these and other ingredients was applied, as the philosopher explains, not to the wound but to the weapon, and that even though the injured man was at a great distance and knew nothing about it. The experiment, he tells us, had been tried of wiping the ointment off the weapon without the knowledge of the person hurt, with the result that he was presently in a great rage of pain until the weapon was anointed again. Moreover, 'it is affirmed that if you cannot get the weapon, yet if you put an instrument of iron or wood resembling the weapon into the wound, whereby it bleedeth, the anointing of that instrument will serve and work the effect'. Remedies of the sort which Bacon deemed worthy of his attention are still in vogue in the eastern counties of England. Thus in Suffolk if a man cuts himself with a bill-hook or a scythe he always takes care to keep the weapon bright, and oils it to prevent the wound from festering. If he runs a thorn or, as he calls it, a bush into his hand, he oils or greases the extracted thorn. A man came to a doctor with an inflamed hand, having run a thorn into it while he was hedging. On being told that the hand was festering, he remarked, 'That didn't ought to, for I greased the bush well arter I pulled it out.' If a horse wounds its foot by treading on a nail, a Suffolk groom will invariably preserve the nail, clean it, and grease it every day, to prevent the foot from festering. Similarly Cambridge-shire labourers think that if a horse has run a nail into its foot, it is necessary to grease the nail with lard or oil and put it away in some safe place, or the horse will not recover. A few years ago a veterinary surgeon was sent for to attend a horse which had ripped its side open on the hinge of a farm gatepost. On arriving at the farm he found that nothing had been done to the wounded horse, but that a man was busy trying to prise the hinge out of the gatepost in order that it might be greased and put away, which, in the opinion of the Cambridge wiseacres, would conduce to the recovery of the animal.* Similarly Essex rustics opine that, if a man has been stabbed with a knife, it is essential to his recovery that the knife should be greased and laid across the bed on which the sufferer is lying. So in Bavaria you are directed to anoint a linen rag with grease and tie it on the edge of the axe that cut you, taking care to keep the sharp edge upwards. As the grease on the axe dries, your wound heals. Similarly in the Harz Mountains they say that if you cut yourself, you ought to smear the knife or the scissors with fat and put the instrument away in a dry place in the name of the Father, of the Son, and of the Holy Ghost. As the knife dries, the wound heals. Other people, however, in Germany say that you should stick the knife in some damp place in the ground, and that your hurt will heal as the knife rusts. Others again, in Bavaria, recommend you to smear the axe or whatever it is with blood and put it under the eaves.

The train of reasoning which thus commends itself to English and German rustics, in common with the savages of Melanesia and America, is carried a step farther by the aborigines of Central Australia, who conceive that under certain circumstances the near relations of a wounded man must grease themselves, restrict their diet, and regulate their behaviour in other ways in order to ensure his recovery. Thus when a lad has been circumcised and the wound is not yet healed, his mother may not eat opossum, or a certain kind of lizard, or carpet snake, or any kind of fat, for otherwise she would retard the healing of the boy's wound. Every day she greases her digging-sticks and never lets them out of her sight; at night she sleeps with them close to her head. No one is allowed to touch them. Every day also she rubs her body all over with grease, as in some way this is believed to help her son's recovery. Another refinement of the same principle is due to the ingenuity of the German peasant. It is said that when one of his pigs or sheep breaks its leg, a farmer of Rhenish Bavaria or Hesse will bind up the leg of a chair with bandages and splints in due form. For some days thereafter no one may sit on that chair, move it, or knock up against it; for to do so would pain the injured pig or sheep and hinder the cure. In this last case it is clear that we have passed wholly out of the region of contagious magic and into the region of homoeopathic or imitative magic; the chair-leg, which is treated instead of the beast's leg, in no sense belongs to the animal, and the application of bandages to it is a mere simulation of the treatment which a more rational surgery would bestow on the real patient.

Again, magic may be wrought on a man sympathetically, not only through his clothes and severed parts of himself, but also through the impressions left by his body in sand or earth. In particular, it is a world-wide superstition that by injuring footprints you injure the feet that made them. Thus the natives of South-eastern Australia think that they can lame a man by placing sharp pieces of quartz, glass, bone, or charcoal in his footprints. Rheumatic pains are often attributed by them to this cause. Seeing a Tatungolung man very lame, Mr Howitt asked him what was the matter. He said, 'Some fellow has put *bottle* in my foot.' He was suffering from rheumatism, but believed that an enemy had found his foot-track and had buried in it a piece of broken bottle, the magical influence of which had entered his foot.

Similar practices prevail in various parts of Europe. Thus in Mecklenburg it is thought that if you drive a nail into a man's footprint he will fall lame; sometimes it is required that the nail

should be taken from a coffin. A like mode of injuring an enemy
is resorted to in some parts of France. It is said that there was
an old woman who used to frequent Stow in Suffolk, and she
was a witch. If, while she walked, any one went after her and
stuck a nail or a knife into her footprint in the dust, the dame
could not stir a step till it was withdrawn. Among the South
Slavs a girl will dig up the earth from the footprints of the man
she loves and put it in a flower-pot. Then she plants in the pot
a marigold, a flower that is thought to be fadeless. And as its
golden blossom grows and blooms and never fades, so shall her
sweetheart's love grow and bloom, and never, never fade. Thus
the love-spell acts on the man through the earth he trod on. An
old Danish mode of concluding a treaty was based on the same
idea of the sympathetic connexion between a man and his
footprints: the convenanting parties sprinkled each other's
footprints with their own blood, thus giving a pledge of fidelity.
In ancient Greece superstitions of the same sort seem to have
been current, for it was thought that if a horse stepped on the
track of a wolf he was seized with numbness; and a maxim
ascribed to Pythagoras forbade people to pierce a man's footprints with a nail or a knife.

The same superstition is turned to account by hunters in
many parts of the world for the purpose of running down the
game. Thus a German huntsman will stick a nail taken from a
coffin into the fresh spoor of the quarry, believing that this will
hinder the animal from escaping. The aborigines of Victoria put
hot embers in the tracks of the animals they were pursuing.
Hottentot hunters throw into the air a handful of sand taken
from the footprints of the game, believing that this will bring
the animal down. Thompson Indians used to lay charms on the
tracks of wounded deer; after that they deemed it superfluous
to pursue the animal any farther that day, for being thus
charmed it could not travel far and would soon die. Similarly,
Ojebway Indians placed 'medicine' on the track of the first deer
or bear they met with, supposing that this would soon bring the
animal into sight, even if it were two or three days' journey off;
for this charm had power to compress a journey of several days
into a few hours.

iv

Wherever sympathetic magic occurs in its pure unadulterated form, it assumes that in nature one event follows another necessarily and invariably without the intervention of any spiritual or personal agency. Thus its fundamental conception is identical with that of modern science; underlying the whole system is a faith, implicit but real and firm, in the order and uniformity of nature. The magician does not doubt that the same causes will always produce the same effects, that the performance of the proper ceremony, accompanied by the appropriate spell, will inevitably be attended by the desired results, unless, indeed, his incantations should chance to be thwarted and foiled by the more potent charms of another sorcerer. He supplicates no higher power: he sues the favour of no fickle and wayward being: he abases himself before no awful deity. Yet his power, great as he believes it to be, is by no means arbitrary and unlimited. He can wield it only so long as he strictly conforms to the rules of his art, or to what may be called the laws of nature as conceived by him. To neglect these rules, to break these laws in the smallest particular is to incur failure, and may even expose the unskilful practitioner himself to the utmost peril. If he claims a sovereignty over nature, it is a constitutional sovereignty rigorously limited in its scope and exercised in exact conformity with ancient usage. Thus the analogy between the magical and the scientific conceptions of the world is close. In both of them the succession of events is perfectly regular and certain, being determined by immutable laws, the operation of which can be foreseen and calculated precisely; the elements of caprice, of chance, and of accident are banished from the course of nature. Both of them open up a seemingly boundless vista of possibilities to him who knows the causes of things and can touch the secret springs that set in motion the vast and intricate mechanism of the world. Hence the strong attraction which magic and science alike have exercised on the human mind; hence the powerful stimulus that both have given to the pursuit of knowledge.

The fatal flaw of magic lies not in its general assumption of a sequence of events determined by law, but in its total

Magic like science postulates the order and uniformity of nature; hence the attraction both of magic and of science, which open up a boundless vista to those who can penetrate to the secret springs of nature.

The fatal
flaw of magic
lies not in its
general as-
sumption of
the uniform-
ity of nature,
but in its
misapprehen-
sion of the
particular
laws which
govern the se-
quence of
natural
events.

misconception of the nature of the particular laws which govern that sequence. If we analyse the various cases of sympathetic magic, we shall find that they are all mistaken applications of one or other of two great fundamental laws of thought, namely, the association of ideas by similarity and the association of ideas by contiguity in space or time. A mistaken association of similar ideas produces homoeopathic or imitative magic: a mistaken association of contiguous ideas produces contagious magic. The principles of association are excellent in themselves, and indeed absolutely essential to the working of the human mind. Legit-imately applied they yield science; illegitimately applied they yield magic, the bastard sister of science. It is therefore a truism, almost a tautology, to say that all magic is necessarily false and barren; for were it ever to become true and fruitful, it would no longer be magic but science. From the earliest times man has been engaged in a search for general rules whereby to turn the order of natural phenomena to his own advantage, and in the long search he has scraped together a great hoard of such maxims, some of them golden and some of them mere dross. The true or golden rules constitute the body of applied science which we call the arts; the false are magic.

Relation of
magic to reli-
gion.

If magic is thus next of kin to science, we have still to enquire how it stands related to religion. But the view we take of that relation will necessarily be coloured by the idea which we have formed of the nature of religion itself; hence a writer may reasonably be expected to define his conception of religion before he proceeds to investigate its relation to magic. There is probably no subject in the world about which opinions differ so much as the nature of religion, and to frame a definition of it which would satisfy every one must obviously be impossible.

Religion
defined: it is
a propitiation
or concilia-
tion of super-
human
powers which
are believed
to control na-
ture and
man. Thus
religion com-
prises

All that a writer can do is, first, to say clearly what he means by religion, and afterwards to employ the word consistently in that sense throughout his work. By religion, then, I understand a propitiation or conciliation of powers superior to man which are believed to direct and control the course of nature and of human life. Thus defined, religion consists of two elements, a theoretical and a practical, namely, a belief in powers higher than man and an attempt to propitiate or please them. Of the two, belief clearly comes first, since we must believe in the existence of a divine being before we can attempt to please him.

But unless the belief leads to a corresponding practice, it is not a religion but merely a theology. In other words, no man is religious who does not govern his conduct in some measure by the fear or love of God. On the other hand, mere practice, divested of all religious belief, is also not religion. Two men may behave in exactly the same way, and yet one of them may be religious and the other not. If the one acts from the love or fear of God, he is religious; if the other acts from the love or fear of man, he is moral or immoral according as his behaviour comports or conflicts with the general good. Hence belief and practice or, in theological language, faith and works are equally essential to religion, which cannot exist without both of them. But it is not necessary that religious practice should always take the form of a ritual; that is, it need not consist in the offering of sacrifice, the recitation of prayers, and other outward ceremonies. Its aim is to please the deity, and if the deity is one who delights in charity and mercy and purity more than in oblations of blood, the chanting of hymns, and the fumes of incense, his worshippers will best please him, not by prostrating themselves before him, by intoning his praises, and by filling his temples with costly gifts, but by being pure and merciful and charitable towards men, for in so doing they will imitate, so far as human infirmity allows, the perfections of the divine nature.

[marginal note: two elements, a theoretical and a practical, or faith and works, and it does not exist without both. But religious practice need not consist in ritual; it may consist in ethical conduct, if that is believed to be well-pleasing to the deity.]

But if religion involves, first, a belief in superhuman beings who rule the world, and, second, an attempt to win their favour, it clearly assumes that the course of nature is to some extent elastic or variable, and that we can persuade or induce the mighty beings who control it to deflect, for our benefit, the current of events from the channel in which they would otherwise flow. Now this implied elasticity or variability of nature is directly opposed to the principles of magic as well as of science, both of which assume that the processes of nature are rigid and invariable in their operation, and that they can as little be turned from their course by persuasion and entreaty as by threats and intimidation. The distinction between the two conflicting views of the universe turns on their answer to the crucial question, Are the forces which govern the world conscious and personal, or unconscious and impersonal? Religion, as a conciliation of the superhuman powers, assumes the former

[marginal note: By assuming the order of nature to be elastic or variable religion is opposed in principle alike to magic and to science, both of which assume the order of nature to be rigid and invariable.]

member of the alternative. For all conciliation implies that the being conciliated is a conscious or personal agent, that his conduct is in some measure uncertain, and that he can be prevailed upon to vary it in the desired direction by a judicious appeal to his interests, his appetites, or his emotions. Conciliation is never employed towards things which are regarded as inanimate, nor towards persons whose behaviour in the particular circumstances is known to be determined with absolute certainty. Thus in so far as religion assumes the world to be directed by conscious agents who may be turned from their purpose by persuasion, it stands in fundamental antagonism to magic as well as to science, both of which take for granted that the course of nature is determined, not by the passions or caprice of personal beings, but by the operation of immutable laws acting mechanically. In magic, indeed, the assumption is only implicit, but in science it is explicit. It is true that magic often deals with spirits, which are personal agents of the kind assumed by religion; but whenever it does so in its proper form, it treats them exactly in the same fashion as it treats inanimate agents, that is, it constrains or coerces instead of conciliating or propitiating them as religion would do. Thus it assumes that all personal beings, whether human or divine, are in the last resort subject to those impersonal forces which control all things, but which nevertheless can be turned to account by any one who knows how to manipulate them by the appropriate ceremonies and spells. In ancient Egypt, for example, the magicians claimed the power of compelling even the highest gods to do their bidding, and actually threatened them with destruction in case of disobedience. Sometimes, without going quite so far as that, the wizard declared that he would scatter the bones of Osiris* or reveal his sacred legend, if the god proved contumacious. Similarly in India at the present day the great Hindoo trinity itself of Brahma, Vishnu, and Siva is subject to the sorcerers, who, by means of their spells, exercise such an ascendency over the mightiest deities, that these are bound submissively to execute on earth below, or in heaven above, whatever commands their masters the magicians may please to issue. There is a saying everywhere current in India: 'The whole universe is subject to the gods; the gods are subject to the spells (*mantras*); the spells to the Brahmans; therefore the Brahmans are our gods.'

Claim of Egyptian and Indian magicians to control the gods.

This radical conflict of principle between magic and religion sufficiently explains the relentless hostility with which in history the priest has often pursued the magician. The haughty self-sufficiency of the magician, his arrogant demeanour towards the higher powers, and his unabashed claim to exercise a sway like theirs could not but revolt the priest, to whom, with his awful sense of the divine majesty, and his humble prostration in presence of it, such claims and such a demeanour must have appeared an impious and blasphemous usurpation of prerogatives that belong to God alone. And sometimes, we may suspect, lower motives concurred to whet the edge of the priest's hostility. He professed to be the proper medium, the true intercessor between God and man, and no doubt his interests as well as his feelings were often injured by a rival practitioner, who preached a surer and smoother road to fortune than the rugged and slippery path of divine favour. Hostility of religion to magic in history.

Yet this antagonism, familiar as it is to us, seems to have made its appearance comparatively late in the history of religion. At an earlier stage the functions of priest and sorcerer were often combined or, to speak perhaps more correctly, were not yet differentiated from each other. To serve his purpose man wooed the good-will of gods or spirits by prayer and sacrifice, while at the same time he had recourse to ceremonies and forms of words which he hoped would of themselves bring about the desired result without the help of god or devil. In short, he performed religious and magical rites simultaneously; he uttered prayers and incantations almost in the same breath, knowing or recking little of the theoretical inconsistency of his behaviour, so long as by hook or crook he contrived to get what he wanted. So far as the Melanesians are concerned, the general confusion cannot be better described than in the words of Dr R. H. Codrington: 'That invisible power which is believed by the natives to cause all such effects as transcend their conception of the regular course of nature, and to reside in spiritual beings, whether in the spiritual part of living men or in the ghosts of the dead, being imparted by them to their names and to various things that belong to them, such as stones, snakes, and indeed objects of all sorts, is that generally known as *mana*.* Without some understanding of this it is impossible to understand the religious beliefs and practices of the Melanesians; and This hostility comparatively late: at an earlier time magic co-operated, and was partly confused, with religion.

this again is the active force in all they do and believe to be done in magic, white or black. By means of this men are able to control or direct the forces of nature, to make rain or sunshine, wind or calm, to cause sickness or remove it, to know what is far off in time and space, to bring good luck and prosperity, or to blast and curse.' 'By whatever name it is called, it is the belief in this supernatural power, and in the efficacy of the various means by which spirits and ghosts can be induced to exercise it for the benefit of men, that is the foundation of the rites and practices which can be called religious; and it is from the same belief that everything which may be called Magic and Witchcraft draws its origin. Wizards, doctors, weather-mongers, prophets, diviners, dreamers, all alike, everywhere in the islands, work by this power. There are many of these who may be said to exercise their art as a profession; they get their property and influence in this way. Every considerable village or settlement is sure to have some one who can control the weather and the waves, some one who knows how to treat sickness, some one who can work mischief with various charms. There may be one whose skill extends to all these branches; but generally one man knows how to do one thing and one another. This various knowledge is handed down from father to son, from uncle to sister's son, in the same way as is the knowledge of the rites and methods of sacrifice and prayer; and very often the same man who knows the sacrifice knows also the making of the weather, and of charms for many purposes besides. But as there is no order of priests, there is also no order of magicians or medicine-men. Almost every man of consideration knows how to approach some ghost or spirit, and has some secret of occult practices.'

Confusion of magic and religion in ancient India.

　　The same confusion of magic and religion has survived among peoples that have risen to higher levels of culture. It was rife in ancient India and ancient Egypt; it is by no means extinct among European peasantry at the present day. With regard to ancient India we are told by an eminent Sanscrit scholar that 'the sacrificial ritual at the earliest period of which we have detailed information is pervaded with practices that breathe the spirit of the most primitive magic'. Again, the same writer observes that 'the ritual of the very sacrifices for which the metrical prayers were composed is described in the other Vedic texts as saturated from beginning to end with magical practices which were to be carried out by the sacrificial priests'. Some good authorities hold that the very name of Brahman is derived from *brahman*, 'a magical spell'; so that, if they are right, the Brahman would seem to have been a magician before he was a priest. We are told that in France 'the majority of the peasants still believe that the priest possesses a secret and irresistible power over the elements. By reciting certain prayers which he alone knows and has the right to utter, yet for the utterance of which he must afterwards demand absolution, he can, on an occasion of pressing danger, arrest or reverse for a moment the action of the eternal laws of the physical world. The winds, the storms, the hail, and the rain are at his command and obey his will. The fire also is subject to him, and the flames of a conflagration are extinguished at his word.' For example, French peasants used to be, perhaps are still, persuaded that the priests could celebrate, with certain special rites, a 'Mass of the Holy Spirit', of which the efficacy was so miraculous that it never met with any opposition from the divine will; God was forced to grant whatever was asked of Him in this form, however rash and importunate might be the petition.* Again, Gascon peasants believe that to revenge themselves on their enemies bad men will sometimes induce a priest to say a mass called the Mass of Saint Sécaire. Very few priests know this mass, and three-fourths of those who do know it would not say it for love or money. None but wicked priests dare to perform the gruesome ceremony, and you may be quite sure that they will have a very heavy account to render for it at the last day. No curate or bishop, not even the archbishop of Auch, can pardon them; that right belongs to the pope of Rome alone. The Mass of Saint Sécaire may be said only in a ruined or deserted church, where owls mope and hoot, where bats flit in the gloaming, where gypsies lodge of nights, and where toads squat under the desecrated altar. Thither the bad priest comes by night with his light o'love, and at the first stroke of eleven he begins to mumble the mass backwards, and ends just as the clocks are knelling the midnight hour. His leman acts as clerk. The host he blesses is black and has three points; he consecrates no wine, but instead he drinks the water of a well into which the body of an unbaptized infant has been flung. He makes the sign of

Marginal notes:
Confusion of magic and religion in modern Europe.

Mass of the Holy Spirit.

Mass of Saint Sécaire.

the cross, but it is on the ground and with his left foot. And many other things he does which no good Christian could look upon without being struck blind and deaf and dumb for the rest of his life. But the man for whom the mass is said withers away little by little, and nobody can say what is the matter with him; even the doctors can make nothing of it. They do not know that he is slowly dying of the Mass of Saint Sécaire.

The early confusion of magic with religion was probably preceded by a still earlier phase of thought, when magic existed without religion.

Yet though magic is thus found to fuse and amalgamate with religion in many ages and in many lands, there are some grounds for thinking that this fusion is not primitive, and that there was a time when man trusted to magic alone for the satisfaction of such wants as transcended his immediate animal cravings. In the first place a consideration of the fundamental notions of magic and religion may incline us to surmise that magic is older than religion in the history of humanity. We have seen that on the one hand magic is nothing but a mistaken application of the very simplest and most elementary processes of the mind, namely the association of ideas by virtue of resemblance or contiguity; and that on the other hand religion assumes the operation of conscious or personal agents, superior to man, behind the visible screen of nature. Obviously the conception of personal agents is more complex than a simple recognition of the similarity or contiguity of ideas; and a theory which assumes that the course of nature is determined by conscious agents is more abstruse and recondite, and requires for its apprehension a far higher degree of intelligence and reflection, than the view that things succeed each other simply by reason of their contiguity or resemblance. Thus, if magic be deduced immediately from elementary processes of reasoning, it becomes probable that magic arose before religion in the evolution of our race, and that man essayed to bend nature to his wishes by the sheer force of spells and enchantments before he strove to coax and mollify a coy, capricious, or irascible deity by the soft insinuation of prayer and sacrifice.

Among the Australian aborigines magic is universal, but religion almost unknown.

The conclusion which we have thus reached deductively from a consideration of the fundamental ideas of religion and magic is confirmed inductively by the observation that among the aborigines of Australia, the rudest savages as to whom we possess accurate information*, magic is universally practised, whereas religion in the sense of a propitiation or conciliation of the higher powers seems to be nearly unknown. Roughly speaking, all men in Australia are magicians, but not one is a priest; everybody fancies he can influence his fellows or the course of nature by sympathetic magic, but nobody dreams of propitiating gods by prayer and sacrifice.

But if in the most backward state of human society now known to us we find magic thus conspicuously present and religion conspicuously absent, may we not reasonably conjecture that the civilised races of the world have also at some period of their history passed through a similar intellectual phase, that they attempted to force the great powers of nature to do their pleasure before they thought of courting their favour by offerings and prayer—in short that, just as on the material side of human culture there has everywhere been an Age of Stone, so on the intellectual side there has everywhere been an Age of Magic? There are reasons for answering this question in the affirmative. When we survey the existing races of mankind from Greenland to Tierra del Fuego, or from Scotland to Singapore, we observe that they are distinguished one from the other by a great variety of religions, and that these distinctions are not, so to speak, merely coterminous with the broad distinctions of race, but descend into the minuter sub-divisions of states and commonwealths, nay, that they honeycomb the town, the village, and even the family, so that the surface of society all over the world is cracked and seamed, sapped and mined with rents and fissures and yawning crevasses opened up by the disintegrating influence of religious dissension. Yet when we have penetrated through these differences, which affect mainly the intelligent and thoughtful part of the community, we shall find underlying them all a solid stratum of intellectual agreement among the dull, the weak, the ignorant, and the superstitious, who constitute, unfortunately, the vast majority of mankind. One of the great achievements of the nineteenth century was to run shafts down into this low mental stratum in many parts of the world, and thus to discover its substantial identity everywhere. It is beneath our feet—and not very far beneath them—here in Europe at the present day, and it crops up on the surface in the heart of the Australian wilderness and wherever the advent of a higher civilisation has not crushed it under ground. This universal faith, this truly Catholic creed, is

Magic is probably older than religion, and faith in it is still universal among the ignorant and superstitious.

a belief in the efficacy of magic. While religious systems differ not only in different countries, but in the same country in different ages, the system of sympathetic magic remains everywhere and at all times substantially alike in its principles and practice. Among the ignorant and superstitious classes of modern Europe it is very much what it was thousands of years ago in Egypt and India, and what it now is among the lowest savages surviving in the remotest corners of the world. If the test of truth lay in a show of hands or a counting of heads, the system of magic might appeal, with far more reason than the Catholic Church, to the proud motto, '*Quod semper, quod ubique, quod ab omnibus*',* as the sure and certain credential of its own infallibility.

Latent superstition a danger to civilisation.

It is not our business here to consider what bearing the permanent existence of such a solid layer of savagery beneath the surface of society, and unaffected by the superficial changes of religion and culture, has upon the future of humanity. The dispassionate observer, whose studies have led him to plumb its depths, can hardly regard it otherwise than as a standing menace to civilisation. We seem to move on a thin crust which may at any moment be rent by the subterranean forces slumbering below. From time to time a hollow murmur underground or a sudden spirt of flame into the air tells of what is going on beneath our feet. Now and then the polite world is startled by a paragraph in a newspaper which tells how in Scotland an image has been found stuck full of pins for the purpose of killing an obnoxious laird or minister, how a woman has been slowly roasted to death as a witch in Ireland,* or how a girl has been murdered and chopped up in Russia to make those candles of human tallow by whose light thieves hope to pursue their midnight trade unseen. But whether the influences that make for further progress, or those that threaten to undo what has already been accomplished, will ultimately prevail; whether the impulsive energy of the minority or the dead weight of the majority of mankind will prove the stronger force to carry us up to higher heights or to sink us into lower depths, are questions rather for the sage, the moralist, and the statesman, whose eagle vision scans the future, than for the humble student of the present and the past. Here we are only concerned to ask how far the uniformity, the universality, and the permanence of a belief in magic, compared with the endless variety and the shifting character of religious creeds, raises a presumption that the former represents a ruder and earlier phase of the human mind, through which all the races of mankind have passed or are passing on their way to religion and science.

If an Age of Religion has thus everywhere, as I venture to surmise, been preceded by an Age of Magic, it is natural that we should enquire what causes have led mankind, or rather a portion of them, to abandon magic as a principle of faith and practice and to betake themselves to religion instead. When we reflect upon the multitude, the variety, and the complexity of the facts to be explained, and the scantiness of our information regarding them, we shall be ready to acknowledge that a full and satisfactory solution of so profound a problem is hardly to be hoped for, and that the most we can do in the present state of our knowledge is to hazard a more or less plausible conjecture. With all due diffidence, then, I would suggest that a tardy recognition of the inherent falsehood and barrenness of magic set the more thoughtful part of mankind to cast about for a truer theory of nature and a more fruitful method of turning her resources to account. The shrewder intelligences must in time have come to perceive that magical ceremonies and incantations did not really effect the results which they were designed to produce, and which the majority of their simpler fellows still believed that they did actually produce. This great discovery of the inefficacy of magic must have wrought a radical though probably slow revolution in the minds of those who had the sagacity to make it. The discovery amounted to this, that men for the first time recognised their inability to manipulate at pleasure certain natural forces which hitherto they had believed to be completely within their control. It was a confession of human ignorance and weakness. Man saw that he had taken for causes what were no causes, and that all his efforts to work by means of these imaginary causes had been vain. His painful toil had been wasted, his curious ingenuity had been squandered to no purpose. He had been pulling at strings to which nothing was attached; he had been marching, as he thought, straight to the goal, while in reality he had only been treading in a narrow circle.* Not that the effects which he had striven so hard to produce did not continue to manifest themselves. They were still produced, but not by him. The rain still fell on the thirsty

The change from magic to religion may have been brought about by the discovery of the inefficacy of magic.

ground: the sun still pursued his daily, and the moon her nightly journey across the sky. All things indeed went on as before, yet all seemed different to him from whose eyes the old scales had fallen. For he could no longer cherish the pleasing illusion that it was he who guided the earth and the heaven in their courses, and that they would cease to perform their great revolutions were he to take his feeble hand from the wheel. In the death of his enemies and his friends he no longer saw a proof of the resistless potency of his own or of hostile enchantments; he now knew that friends and foes alike had succumbed to a force stronger than any that he could wield, and in obedience to a destiny which he was powerless to control.

Recognising their own inability to control nature, men came to think that it was controlled by supernatural beings.

Thus cut adrift from his ancient moorings and left to toss on a troubled sea of doubt and uncertainty, his old happy confidence in himself and his powers rudely shaken, our primitive philosopher must have been sadly perplexed and agitated till he came to rest, as in a quiet haven after a tempestuous voyage, in a new system of faith and practice, which seemed to offer a solution of his harassing doubts and a substitute, however precarious, for that sovereignty over nature which he had reluctantly abdicated. If the great world went on its way without the help of him or his fellows, it must surely be because there were other beings, like himself, but far stronger, who, unseen themselves, directed its course and brought about all the varied series of events which he had hitherto believed to be dependent on his own magic. It was they, as he now believed, and not he himself, who made the stormy wind to blow, the lightning to flash, and the thunder to roll. To these mighty beings, whose handiwork he traced in all the gorgeous and varied pageantry of nature, man now addressed himself, humbly confessing his dependence on their invisible power, and beseeching them of their mercy to furnish him with all good things, to defend him from the perils and dangers by which our mortal life is compassed about on every hand, and finally to bring his immortal spirit, freed from the burden of the body, to some happier world, beyond the reach of pain and sorrow, where he might rest with them and with the spirits of good men in joy and felicity for ever.

The change from magic

In this, or some such way as this, the deeper minds may be conceived to have made the great transition from magic to religion. But even in them the change can hardly ever have been sudden; probably it proceeded very slowly, and required long ages for its more or less perfect accomplishment. For the recognition of man's powerlessness to influence the course of nature on a grand scale must have been gradual; he cannot have been shorn of the whole of his fancied dominion at a blow. Step by step he must have been driven back from his proud position; foot by foot he must have yielded, with a sigh, the ground which he had once viewed as his own. Now it would be the wind, now the rain, now the sunshine, now the thunder, that he confessed himself unable to wield at will; and as province after province of nature thus fell from his grasp, till what had once seemed a kingdom threatened to shrink into a prison, man must have been more and more profoundly impressed with a sense of his own helplessness and the might of the invisible beings by whom he believed himself to be surrounded. Thus religion, beginning as a slight and partial acknowledgment of powers superior to man, tends with the growth of knowledge to deepen into a confession of man's entire and absolute dependence on the divine; his old free bearing is exchanged for an attitude of lowliest prostration before the mysterious powers of the unseen, and his highest virtue is to submit his will to theirs: *In la sua volontade è nostra pace.** But this deepening sense of religion, this more perfect submission to the divine will in all things, affects only those higher intelligences who have breadth of view enough to comprehend the vastness of the universe and the littleness of man. Small minds cannot grasp great ideas; to their narrow comprehension, their purblind vision, nothing seems really great and important but themselves. Such minds hardly rise into religion at all. They are, indeed, drilled by their betters into an outward conformity with its precepts and a verbal profession of its tenets; but at heart they cling to their old magical superstitions, which may be discountenanced and forbidden, but cannot be eradicated by religion, so long as they have their roots deep down in the mental framework and constitution of the great majority of mankind.

A vestige of the transition from magic to religion may perhaps be discerned in the belief, shared by many peoples, that the gods themselves are adepts in magic, guarding their persons by talismans and working their will by spells and incantations.

to religion must have been gradual.

The belief that the gods are magicians may mark the transition

from magic
to religion.

Thus the Egyptian gods, we are told, could as little dispense with the help of magic as could men; like men they wore amulets to protect themselves, and used spells to overcome each other. Above all the rest Isis was skilled in sorcery and famous for her incantations. In Babylonia the great god Ea was reputed to be the inventor of magic, and his son Marduk, the chief deity of Babylon, inherited the art from his father. In the Vedic religion the gods are often represented as attaining their ends by magical means; in particular the god Brhaspati, 'the creator of all prayers', is regarded as 'the heavenly embodiment of the priesthood, in so far as the priesthood is invested with the power, and charged with the task, of influencing the course of things by prayers and spells'; in short, he is 'the possessor of the magical power of the holy word'. So too in Norse mythology Odin is said to have owed his supremacy and his dominion over nature to his knowledge of the runes or magical names of all things in earth and heaven.

The fallacy
of magic is
not easy to
detect, be-
cause nature
herself gener-
ally pro-
duces, sooner
or later, the
effects which
the magician
fancies he
produces by
his art.

The reader may well be tempted to ask, How was it that intelligent men did not sooner detect the fallacy of magic? How could they continue to cherish expectations that were invariably doomed to disappointment? With what heart persist in playing venerable antics that led to nothing, and mumbling solemn balderdash that remained without effect? Why cling to beliefs which were so flatly contradicted by experience? How dare to repeat experiments that had failed so often? The answer seems to be that the fallacy was far from easy to detect, the failure by no means obvious, since in many, perhaps in most cases, the desired event did actually follow, at a longer or shorter interval, the performance of the rite which was designed to bring it about; and a mind of more than common acuteness was needed to perceive that, even in these cases, the rite was not necessarily the cause of the event. A ceremony intended to make the wind blow or the rain fall, or to work the death of an enemy, will always be followed, sooner or later, by the occurrence it is meant to bring to pass; and primitive man may be excused for regarding the occurrence as a direct result of the ceremony, and the best possible proof of its efficacy. Similarly, rites observed in the morning to help the sun to rise, and in spring to wake the dreaming earth from her winter sleep, will invariably appear to be crowned with success, at least within the temperate zones;

for in these regions the sun lights his golden lamp in the east every morning, and year by year the vernal earth decks herself afresh with a rich mantle of green. Hence the practical savage, with his conservative instincts, might well turn a deaf ear to the subtleties of the theoretical doubter, the philosophic radical, who presumed to hint that sunrise and spring might not, after all, be direct consequences of the punctual performance of certain daily or yearly ceremonies, and that the sun might perhaps continue to rise and trees to blossom though the ceremonies were occasionally intermitted, or even discontinued altogether. These sceptical doubts would naturally be repelled by the other with scorn and indignation as airy reveries subversive of the faith and manifestly contradicted by experience. 'Can anything be plainer', he might say, 'than that I light my twopenny candle on earth and that the sun then kindles his great fire in heaven? I should be glad to know whether, when I have put on my green robe in spring, the trees do not afterwards do the same? These are facts patent to everybody, and on them I take my stand. I am a plain practical man, not one of your theorists and splitters of hairs and choppers of logic. Theories and speculation and all that may be very well in their way, and I have not the least objection to your indulging in them, provided, of course, you do not put them in practice. But give me leave to stick to facts; then I know where I am. The fallacy of this reasoning is obvious to us, because it happens to deal with facts about which we have long made up our minds. But let an argument of precisely the same calibre be applied to matters which are still under debate. If such reasonings could pass muster among ourselves, need we wonder that they long escaped detection by the savage?

CHAPTER 4

HUMAN GODS

The conception of gods has been slowly evolved.

In a society where every man is supposed to be endowed more or less with powers which we should call supernatural, it is plain that the distinction between gods and men is somewhat blurred, or rather has scarcely emerged. The conception of gods as superhuman beings endowed with powers to which man possesses nothing comparable in degree and hardly even in kind, has been slowly evolved in the course of history. By primitive peoples the supernatural agents are not regarded as greatly, if at all, superior to man; for they may be frightened and coerced by him into doing his will. At this stage of thought the world is viewed as a great democracy; all beings in it, whether natural or supernatural, are supposed to stand on a footing of tolerable equality. But with the growth of his knowledge man learns to realise more clearly the vastness of nature and his own littleness and feebleness in presence of it. The recognition of his helplessness does not, however, carry with it a corresponding belief in the impotence of those supernatural beings with which his imagination peoples the universe. On the contrary, it enhances his conception of their power. For the idea of the world as a system of impersonal forces acting in accordance with fixed and invariable laws has not yet fully dawned or darkened upon him. The germ of the idea he certainly has, and he acts upon it, not only in magic art, but in much of the business of daily life. But the idea remains undeveloped, and so far as he attempts to explain the world he lives in, he pictures it as the manifestation of conscious will and personal agency. If then he feels himself to be so frail and slight, how vast and powerful must he deem the beings who control the gigantic machinery of nature! Thus as his old sense of equality with the gods slowly vanishes, he resigns at the same time the hope of directing the course of nature by his own unaided resources, that is, by magic, and looks more and more to the gods as the sole repositories of those supernatural powers

As religion grows, magic declines into a black art.

which he once claimed to share with them. With the advance of knowledge, therefore, prayer and sacrifice assume the leading place in religious ritual; and magic, which once ranked with them as a legitimate equal, is gradually relegated to the background and sinks to the level of a black art. It is now regarded as an encroachment, at once vain and impious, on the domain of the gods, and as such encounters the steady opposition of the priests, whose reputation and influence rise or fall with those of their gods. Hence, when at a late period the distinction between religion and superstition has emerged, we find that sacrifice and prayer are the resource of the pious and enlightened portion of the community, while magic is the refuge of the superstitious and ignorant. But when, still later, the conception of the elemental forces as personal agents is giving way to the recognition of natural law; then magic, based as it implicitly is on the idea of a necessary and invariable sequence of cause and effect, independent of personal will, reappears from the obscurity and discredit into which it had fallen, and by investigating the causal sequences in nature, directly prepares the way for science. Alchemy leads up to chemistry.

The notion of a man-god, or of a human being endowed with divine or supernatural powers, belongs essentially to that earlier period of religious history in which gods and men are still viewed as beings of much the same order, and before they are divided by the impassable gulf which, to later thought, opens out between them. Strange, therefore, as may seem to us the idea of a god incarnate in human form, it has nothing very startling for early man, who sees in a man-god or a god-man only a higher degree of the same supernatural powers which he arrogates in perfect good faith to himself. Nor does he draw any very sharp distinction between a god and a powerful sorcerer. His gods are often merely invisible magicians who behind the veil of nature work the same sort of charms and incantations which the human magician works in a visible and bodily form among his fellows. And as the gods are commonly believed to exhibit themselves in the likeness of men to their worshippers, it is easy for the magician, with his supposed miraculous powers, to acquire the reputation of being an incarnate deity. Thus beginning as little more than a simple conjurer, the

The conception of a man-god or deity incarnate in human form belongs to an early stage of religious history.

medicine-man or magician tends to blossom out into a full-blown god and king in one.

With these explanations and cautions I will now adduce some examples of gods who have been believed by their worshippers to be incarnate in living human beings, whether men or women. The persons in whom a deity is thought to reveal himself are by no means always kings or descendants of kings; the supposed incarnation may take place even in men of the humblest rank. In India, for example, one human god started in life as a cotton-bleacher and another as the son of a carpenter. I shall therefore not draw my examples exclusively from royal personages, as I wish to illustrate the general principle of the deification of living men, in other words, the incarnation of a deity in human form.

Temporary incarnation of gods.

The belief in temporary incarnation or inspiration is world-wide. Certain persons are supposed to be possessed from time to time by a spirit or deity; while the possession lasts, their own personality lies in abeyance, the presence of the spirit is revealed by convulsive shiverings and shakings of the man's whole body, by wild gestures and excited looks, all of which are referred, not to the man himself, but to the spirit which has entered into him; and in this abnormal state all his utterances are accepted as the voice of the god or spirit dwelling in him and speaking through him. Thus, for example, in the Sandwich Islands,* the king, personating the god, uttered the responses of the oracle from his concealment in a frame of wicker-work. But in the southern islands of the Pacific the god 'frequently entered the priest, who, inflated as it were with the divinity, ceased to act or speak as a voluntary agent, but moved and spoke as entirely under supernatural influence. In this respect there was a striking resemblance between the rude oracles of the Polynesians, and those of the celebrated nations of ancient Greece. As soon as the god was supposed to have entered the priest, the latter became violently agitated, and worked himself up to the highest pitch of apparent frenzy, the muscles of the limbs seemed convulsed, the body swelled, the countenance became terrific, the features distorted, and the eyes wild and strained. In this state he often rolled on the earth, foaming at the mouth, as if labouring under the influence of the divinity by whom he was possessed, and, in shrill cries, and violent and often indistinct sounds, revealed the will of the god. The priests, who were attending, and versed in the mysteries, received, and reported to the people, the declarations which had been thus received. When the priest had uttered the response of the oracle, the violent paroxysm gradually subsided, and comparative composure ensued. The god did not, however, always leave him as soon as the communication had been made. Sometimes the same *taura*, or priest, continued for two or three days possessed by the spirit or deity; a piece of a native cloth, of a peculiar kind, worn round one arm, was an indication of inspiration, or of the indwelling of the god with the individual who wore it. The acts of the man during this period were considered as those of the god, and hence the greatest attention was paid to his expressions, and the whole of his deportment. . . . When *uruhia*, (under the inspiration of the spirit,) the priest was always considered as sacred as the god, and was called, during this period, *atua*, god, though at other times only denominated *taura* or priest.'

But examples of such temporary inspiration are so common in every part of the world and are now so familiar through books on ethnology that it is needless to multiply illustrations of the general principle. It may be well, however, to refer to two particular modes of producing temporary inspiration, because they are perhaps less known than some others, and because we shall have occasion to refer to them later on. One of these modes of producing inspiration is by sucking the fresh blood of a sacrificed victim. In the temple of Apollo Diradiotes at Argos, a lamb was sacrificed by night once a month; a woman, who had to observe a rule of chastity, tasted the blood of the lamb, and thus being inspired by the god she prophesied or divined. At Aegira in Achaia the priestess of Earth drank the fresh blood of a bull before she descended into the cave to prophesy. Similarly among the Kuruvikkarans, a class of bird-catchers and beggars in Southern India, the goddess Kali is believed to descend upon the priest, and he gives oracular replies after sucking the blood which streams from the cut throat of a goat. At a festival of the Alfoors of Minahassa, in Northern Celebes, after a pig has been killed, the priest rushes furiously at it, thrusts his head into the carcase, and drinks of the blood. Then he is dragged away from it by force and set on a chair, whereupon he begins to prophesy

how the rice-crop will turn out that year. A second time he runs
at the carcase and drinks of the blood; a second time he is
forced into the chair and continues his predictions. It is thought
that there is a spirit in him which possesses the power of
prophecy.

The other mode of producing temporary inspiration, to which
I shall here refer, consists in the use of a sacred tree or plant.
Thus in the Hindoo Koosh a fire is kindled with twigs of the
sacred cedar; and the Dainyal or sibyl, with a cloth over her
head, inhales the thick pungent smoke till she is seized with
convulsions and falls senseless to the ground. Soon she rises and
raises a shrill chant, which is caught up and loudly repeated by
her audience. So Apollo's prophetess ate the sacred laurel and
was fumigated with it before she prophesied. The Bacchanals
ate ivy, and their inspired fury was by some believed to be due
to the exciting and intoxicating properties of the plant. In
Uganda the priest, in order to be inspired by his god, smokes a
pipe of tobacco fiercely till he works himself into a frenzy; the
loud excited tones in which he then talks are recognised as the
voice of the god speaking through him. In Madura, an island
off the north coast of Java, each spirit has its regular medium,
who is oftener a woman than a man. To prepare herself for the
reception of the spirit she inhales the fumes of incense, sitting
with her head over a smoking censer. Gradually she falls into a
sort of trance accompanied by shrieks, grimaces, and violent
spasms. The spirit is now supposed to have entered into her,
and when she grows calmer her words are regarded as oracular,
being the utterances of the indwelling spirit, while her own soul
is temporarily absent.

The person temporarily inspired is believed to acquire, not
merely divine knowledge, but also, at least occasionally, divine
power. In Cambodia, when an epidemic breaks out, the inhabitants of several villages unite and go with a band of music at
their head to look for the man whom the local god is supposed
to have chosen for his temporary incarnation. When found, the
man is conducted to the altar of the god, where the mystery of
incarnation takes place. Then the man becomes an object of
veneration to his fellows, who implore him to protect the village
against the plague. A certain image of Apollo, which stood in a
sacred cave at Hylae near Magnesia, was thought to impart

superhuman strength. Sacred men, inspired by it, leaped down
precipices, tore up huge trees by the roots, and carried them on
their backs along the narrowest defiles. The feats performed by
inspired dervishes belong to the same class.

Thus far we have seen that the savage, failing to discern the
limits of his ability to control nature, ascribes to himself and to
all men certain powers which we should now call supernatural.
Further, we have seen that, over and above this general super-
naturalism, some persons are supposed to be inspired for short
periods by a divine spirit, and thus temporarily to enjoy the
knowledge and power of the indwelling deity. From beliefs like
these it is an easy step to the conviction that certain men are
permanently possessed by a deity, or in some other undefined
way are endued with so high a degree of supernatural power as
to be ranked as gods and to receive the homage of prayer and
sacrifice. Sometimes these human gods are restricted to purely
supernatural or spiritual functions. Sometimes they exercise
supreme political power in addition. In the latter case they are
kings as well as gods, and the government is a theocracy. Thus
in the Marquesas* or Washington Islands there was a class of
men who were deified in their lifetime. They were supposed to
wield a supernatural power over the elements: they could give
abundant harvests or smite the ground with barrenness; and
they could inflict disease or death. Human sacrifices were
offered to them to avert their wrath. There were not many of
them, at the most one or two in each island. They lived in
mystic seclusion. Their powers were sometimes, but not always,
hereditary. A missionary has described one of these human gods
from personal observation. The god was a very old man who
lived in a large house within an enclosure. In the house was a
kind of altar, and on the beams of the house and on the trees
round it were hung human skeletons, head down. No one
entered the enclosure except the persons dedicated to the
service of the god; only on days when human victims were
sacrificed might ordinary people penetrate into the precinct.
This human god received more sacrifices than all the other
gods; often he would sit on a sort of scaffold in front of his
house and call for two or three human victims at a time. They
were always brought, for the terror he inspired was extreme. He
was invoked all over the island, and offerings were sent to him

*Human gods,
or men per-
manently pos-
sessed by a
deity.*

from every side. Again, of the South Sea Islands in general we are told that each island had a man who represented or personified the divinity. Such men were called gods, and their substance was confounded with that of the deity. The man-god was sometimes the king himself; oftener he was a priest or subordinate chief.

The ancient Egyptians, far from restricting their adoration to cats and dogs and such small deer, very liberally extended it to men. One of these human deities resided at the village of Anabis, and burnt sacrifices were offered to him on the altars; after which, says Porphyry, he would eat his dinner just as if he were an ordinary mortal. The ancient Germans believed that there was something holy in women, and accordingly consulted them as oracles. Their sacred women, we are told, looked on the eddying rivers and listened to the murmur or the roar of the water, and from the sight and sound foretold what would come to pass. But often the veneration of the men went further, and they worshipped women as true and living goddesses. For example, in the reign of Vespasian a certain Veleda, of the tribe of the Bructeri, was commonly held to be a deity, and in that character reigned over her people, her sway being acknowledged far and wide. She lived in a tower on the river Lippe, a tributary of the Rhine. When the people of Cologne sent to make a treaty with her, the ambassadors were not admitted to her presence; the negotiations were conducted through a minister, who acted as the mouthpiece of her divinity and reported her oracular utterances. The example shows how easily among our rude forefathers the ideas of divinity and royalty coalesced. It is said that among the Getae down to the beginning of our era there was always a man who personified a god and was called God by the people. He dwelt on a sacred mountain and acted as adviser to the king.

According to the early Portuguese historian, Dos Santos, the Zimbas, or Muzimbas, a people of South-eastern Africa, 'do not adore idols or recognise any god, but instead they venerate and honour their king, whom they regard as a divinity, and they say he is the greatest and best in the world. And the said king says of himself that he alone is god of the earth, for which reason if it rains when he does not wish it to do so, or is too hot, he shoots arrows at the sky for not obeying him.' The Mashona of

Southern Africa informed their bishop that they had once had a god, but that the Matabeles had driven him away.* 'This last was in reference to a curious custom in some villages of keeping a man they called their god. He seemed to be consulted by the people and had presents given to him. There was one at a village belonging to a chief Magondi, in the old days. We were asked not to fire off any guns near the village, or we should frighten him away.' This Mashona god was formerly bound to render an annual tribute to the king of the Matabele in the shape of four black oxen and one dance. A missionary has seen and described the deity discharging the latter part of his duty in front of the royal hut. For three mortal hours, without a break, to the banging of a tambourine, the click of castanettes, and the drone of a monotonous song, the swarthy god engaged in a frenzied dance, crouching on his hams like a tailor, sweating like a pig, and bounding about with an agility which testified to the strength and elasticity of his divine legs.

The Baganda* of Central Africa believed in a god of Lake Nyanza, who sometimes took up his abode in a man or woman. The incarnate god was much feared by all the people, including the king and the chiefs. When the mystery of incarnation had taken place, the man, or rather the god, removed about a mile and a half from the margin of the lake, and there awaited the appearance of the new moon before he engaged in his sacred duties. From the moment that the crescent moon appeared faintly in the sky, the king and all his subjects were at the command of the divine man, or *Lubare* (god), as he was called, who reigned supreme not only in matters of faith and ritual, but also in questions of war and state policy. He was consulted as an oracle; by his word he could inflict or heal sickness, withhold rain, and cause famine. Large presents were made him when his advice was sought. The chief of Urua, a large region to the west of Lake Tanganyika, 'arrogates to himself divine honours and power and pretends to abstain from food for days without feeling its necessity; and, indeed, declares that as a god he is altogether above requiring food and only eats, drinks, and smokes for the pleasure it affords him'. Among the Gallas, when a woman grows tired of the cares of housekeeping, she begins to talk incoherently and to demean herself extravagantly. This is a sign of the descent of the holy spirit Callo upon her.

Immediately her husband prostrates himself and adores her; she ceases to bear the humble title of wife and is called 'Lord'; domestic duties have no further claim on her, and her will is a divine law.

The king of Loango* is honoured by his people 'as though he were a god; and he is called Sambee and Pango, which mean god. They believe that he can let them have rain when he likes; and once a year, in December, which is the time they want rain, the people come to beg of him to grant it to them.' On this occasion the king, standing on his throne, shoots an arrow into the air, which is supposed to bring on rain. Much the same is said of the king of Mombasa.* Down to a few years ago, when his spiritual reign on earth was brought to an abrupt end by the carnal weapons of English marines and bluejackets, the king of Benin was the chief object of worship in his dominions. 'He occupies a higher post here than the Pope does in Catholic Europe; for he is not only God's vicegerent upon earth, but a god himself, whose subjects both obey and adore him as such, although I believe their adoration to arise rather from fear than love.' The king of Iddah told the English officers of the Niger Expedition, 'God made me after his own image; I am all the same as God; and he appointed me a king.'

A peculiarly bloodthirsty monarch of Burma, by name Badonsachen, whose very countenance reflected the inbred ferocity of his nature, and under whose reign more victims perished by the executioner than by the common enemy, conceived the notion that he was something more than mortal, and that this high distinction had been granted him as a reward for his numerous good works. Accordingly he laid aside the title of king and aimed at making himself a god. With this view, and in imitation of Buddha, who, before being advanced to the rank of a divinity, had quitted his royal palace and seraglio and retired from the world, Badonsachen withdrew from his palace to an immense pagoda, the largest in the empire, which he had been engaged in constructing for many years. Here he held conferences with the most learned monks, in which he sought to persuade them that the five thousand years assigned for the observance of the law of Buddha were now elapsed, and that he himself was the god who was destined to appear after that period, and to abolish the old law by substituting his own. But to his great mortification many of the monks undertook to demonstrate the contrary; and this disappointment, combined with his love of power and his impatience under the restraints of an ascetic life, quickly disabused him of his imaginary godhead, and drove him back to his palace and his harem. The king of Siam 'is venerated equally with a divinity. His subjects ought not to look him in the face; they prostrate themselves before him when he passes, and appear before him on their knees, their elbows resting on the ground.' There is a special language devoted to his sacred person and attributes, and it must be used by all who speak to or of him. Even the natives have difficulty in mastering this peculiar vocabulary. The hairs of the monarch's head, the soles of his feet, the breath of his body, indeed every single detail of his person, both outward and inward, have particular names. When he eats or drinks, sleeps or walks, a special word indicates that these acts are being performed by the sovereign, and such words cannot possibly be applied to the acts of any other person whatever. There is no word in the Siamese language by which any creature of higher rank or greater dignity than a monarch can be described; and the missionaries, when they speak of God, are forced to use the native word for king.

But perhaps no country in the world has been so prolific of human gods as India; nowhere has the divine grace been poured out in a more liberal measure on all classes of society from kings down to milkmen. Thus amongst the Todas, a pastoral people of the Neilgherry Hills of Southern India, the dairy is a sanctuary, and the milkman who attends to it has been described as a god. On being asked whether the Todas salute the sun, one of these divine milkmen replied, 'Those poor fellows do so, but I,' tapping his chest, 'I, a god! why should I salute the sun?' Every one, even his own father, prostrates himself before the milkman, and no one would dare to refuse him anything. No human being, except another milkman, may touch him; and he gives oracles to all who consult him, speaking with the voice of a god.

Further, in India 'every king is regarded as little short of a present god'. The Hindoo law-book of Manu* goes farther and says that 'even an infant king must not be despised from an idea that he is a mere mortal; for he is a great deity in human form'.

Human gods in India.

There is said to have been a sect in Orissa some years ago who worshipped the late Queen Victoria in her lifetime as their chief divinity. At Benares not many years ago a celebrated deity was incarnate in the person of a Hindoo gentleman who rejoiced in the euphonious name of Swami Bhaskaranandaji Saraswati, and looked uncommonly like the late Cardinal Manning* only more ingenuous. His eyes beamed with kindly human interest, and he took what is described as an innocent pleasure in the divine honours paid him by his confiding worshippers.

A Hindoo sect, which has many representatives in Bombay and Central India, holds that its spiritual chiefs or Maharajas, as they are called, are representatives or even actual incarnations on earth of the god Krishna. And as Krishna looks down from heaven with most favour on such as minister to the wants of his successors and vicars on earth, a peculiar rite called Self-devotion has been instituted, whereby his faithful worshippers make over their bodies, their souls, and, what is perhaps still more important, their worldly substance to his adorable incarnations; and women are taught to believe that the highest bliss for themselves and their families is to be attained by yielding themselves to the embraces of those beings in whom the divine nature mysteriously coexists with the form and even the appetites of true humanity.

Pretenders to divinity among Christians. Christianity itself has not uniformly escaped the taint of these unhappy delusions; indeed it has often been sullied by the extravagances of vain pretenders to a divinity equal to or even surpassing that of its great Founder. In the second century Montanus the Phrygian claimed to be the incarnate Trinity, uniting in his single person God the Father, God the Son, and God the Holy Ghost. Nor is this an isolated case, the exorbitant pretension of a single ill-balanced mind. From the earliest times down to the present day many sects have believed that Christ, nay God himself, is incarnate in every fully initiated Christian, and they have carried this belief to its logical conclusion by adoring each other. Tertullian records that this was done by his fellow-Christians at Carthage in the second century; the disciples of St Columba worshipped him as an embodiment of Christ; and in the eighth century Elipandus of Toledo spoke of Christ as 'a god among gods', meaning that all believers were gods just as truly as Jesus himself. The adoration of each other was customary among the Albigenses* and is noticed hundreds of times in the records of the Inquisition at Toulouse in the early part of the fourteenth century.

In the thirteenth century there arose a sect called the Brethren and Sisters of the Free Spirit, who held that by long and assiduous contemplation any man might be united to the deity in an ineffable manner and become one with the source and parent of all things, and that he who had thus ascended to God and been absorbed in his beatific essence, actually formed part of the Godhead, was the Son of God in the same sense and manner with Christ himself, and enjoyed thereby a glorious immunity from the trammels of all laws human and divine. Inwardly transported by this blissful persuasion, though outwardly presenting in their aspect and manners a shocking air of lunacy and distraction, the sectaries roamed from place to place, attired in the most fantastic apparel and begging their bread with wild shouts and clamour, spurning indignantly every kind of honest labour and industry as an obstacle to divine contemplation and to the ascent of the soul towards the Father of spirits. In all their excursions they were followed by women with whom they lived on terms of the closest familiarity. Those of them who conceived they had made the greatest proficiency in the higher spiritual life dispensed with the use of clothes altogether in their assemblies, looking upon decency and modesty as marks of inward corruption, characteristics of a soul that still grovelled under the dominion of the flesh and had not yet been elevated into communion with the divine spirit, its centre and source. Sometimes their progress towards this mystic communion was accelerated by the Inquisition, and they expired in the flames, not merely with unclouded serenity, but with the most triumphant feelings of cheerfulness and joy.

About the year 1830 there appeared, in one of the States of the American Union bordering on Kentucky, an impostor who declared that he was the Son of God, the Saviour of mankind, and that he had reappeared on earth to recall the impious, the unbelieving, and sinners to their duty. He protested that if they did not mend their ways within a certain time, he would give the signal, and in a moment the world would crumble to ruins. These extravagant pretensions were received with favour even by persons of wealth and position in society. At last a German

Modern incarnation of Jesus Christ.

humbly besought the new Messiah to announce the dreadful catastrophe to his fellow-countrymen in the German language, as they did not understand English, and it seemed a pity that they should be damned merely on that account. The would-be Saviour in reply confessed with great candour that he did not know German. 'What!' retorted the German, 'you the Son of God, and don't speak all languages, and don't even know German? Come, come; you are a knave, a hypocrite, and a madman. Bedlam is the place for you.' The spectators laughed, and went away ashamed of their credulity.

Transmigra-
tions of
human deities.
Sometimes, at the death of the human incarnation, the divine spirit transmigrates into another man. The Buddhist Tartars believe in a great number of living Buddhas, who officiate as Grand Lamas at the head of the most important monasteries. When one of these Grand Lamas dies his disciples do not sorrow, for they know that he will soon reappear, being born in the form of an infant. Their only anxiety is to discover the place of his birth. If at this time they see a rainbow they take it as a sign sent them by the departed Lama to guide them to his cradle. Sometimes the divine infant himself reveals his identity. 'I am the Grand Lama,' he says, 'the living Buddha of such and such a temple. Take me to my old monastery. I am its immortal head.' In whatever way the birthplace of the Buddha is revealed, whether by the Buddha's own avowal or by the sign in the sky, tents are struck, and the joyful pilgrims, often headed by the king or one of the most illustrious of the royal family, set forth to find and bring home the infant god. Generally he is born in Tibet, the holy land, and to reach him the caravan has often to traverse the most frightful deserts. When at last they find the child they fall down and worship him. Before, however, he is acknowledged as the Grand Lama whom they seek he must satisfy them of his identity. He is asked the name of the monastery of which he claims to be the head, how far off it is, and how many monks live in it; he must also describe the habits of the deceased Grand Lama and the manner of his death. Then various articles, as prayer-books, tea-pots, and cups, are placed before him, and he has to point out those used by himself in his previous life. If he does so without a mistake his claims are admitted, and he is conducted in triumph to the monastery. At the head of all the Lamas is the Dalai Lama of Lhasa, the Rome

of Tibet. He is regarded as a living god, and at death his divine and immortal spirit is born again in a child. According to some accounts the mode of discovering the Dalai Lama is similar to the method, already described, of discovering an ordinary Grand Lama. Other accounts speak of an election by drawing lots from a golden jar. Wherever he is born, the trees and plants put forth green leaves: at his bidding flowers bloom and springs of water rise; and his presence diffuses heavenly blessings.

But he is by no means the only man who poses as a god in these regions. A register of all the incarnate gods in the Chinese empire is kept in the *Li fan yüan* or Colonial Office at Peking. The number of gods who have thus taken out a licence is one hundred and sixty. Tibet is blessed with thirty of them, Northern Mongolia rejoices in nineteen, and Southern Mongolia basks in the sunshine of no less than fifty-seven. The Chinese government, with a paternal solicitude for the welfare of its subjects, forbids the gods on the register to be reborn anywhere but in Tibet. They fear lest the birth of a god in Mongolia should have serious political consequences by stirring the dormant patriotism and warlike spirit of the Mongols, who might rally round an ambitious native deity of royal lineage and seek to win for him, at the point of the sword, a temporal as well as a spiritual kingdom. But besides these public or licensed gods there are a great many little private gods, or unlicensed practitioners of divinity, who work miracles and bless their people in holes and corners; and of late years the Chinese government has winked at the rebirth of these pettifogging deities outside of Tibet. However, once they are born, the government keeps its eye on them as well as on the regular practitioners, and if any of them misbehaves he is promptly degraded, banished to a distant monastery, and strictly forbidden ever to be born again in the flesh.

From our survey of the religious position occupied by the king in rude societies we may infer that the claim to divine and supernatural powers put forward by the monarchs of great historical empires like those of Egypt, Mexico, and Peru, was not the simple outcome of inflated vanity or the empty expression of a grovelling adulation; it was merely a survival and extension of the old savage apotheosis of living kings. Thus, for example, as children of the Sun the Incas of Peru were revered like gods; they could do no wrong, and no one dreamed of offending against the person, honour, or property of the monarch or of any of the royal race. Hence, too, the Incas did not, like most people, look on sickness as an evil. They considered it a messenger sent from their father the Sun to call them to come and rest with him in heaven. Therefore the usual words in which an Inca announced his approaching end were these: 'My father calls me to come and rest with him.' They would not oppose their father's will by offering sacrifice for recovery, but openly declared that he had called them to his rest. Issuing from the sultry valleys upon the lofty tableland of the Colombian Andes, the Spanish conquerors were astonished to find, in contrast to the savage hordes they had left in the sweltering jungles below, a people enjoying a fair degree of civilisation, practising agriculture, and living under a government which Humboldt has compared to the theocracies of Tibet and Japan. These were the Chibchas, Muyscas, or Mozcas, divided into two kingdoms, with capitals at Bogota and Tunja, but united apparently in spiritual allegiance to the high pontiff of Sogamozo or Iraca. By a long and ascetic novitiate, this ghostly ruler was reputed to have acquired such sanctity that the waters and the rain obeyed him, and the weather depended on his will. The Mexican kings at their accession took an oath that they would make the sun to shine, the clouds to give rain, the rivers to flow, and the earth to bring forth fruits in abundance. We are told that Montezuma, the last king of Mexico, was worshipped by his people as a god.

The early Babylonian kings, from the time of Sargon I till the fourth dynasty of Ur or later, claimed to be gods in their lifetime. The monarchs of the fourth dynasty of Ur in particular had temples built in their honour; they set up their statues in various sanctuaries and commanded the people to sacrifice to them; the eighth month was especially dedicated to the kings, and sacrifices were offered to them at the new moon and on the fifteenth of each month. Again, the Parthian monarchs of the Arsacid house styled themselves brothers of the sun and moon and were worshipped as deities. It was esteemed sacrilege to strike even a private member of the Arsacid family in a brawl.

Divinity of
Egyptian
kings.

The kings of Egypt were deified in their lifetime, sacrifices were offered to them, and their worship was celebrated in special temples and by special priests. Indeed the worship of the kings sometimes cast that of the gods into the shade. Thus in the reign of Merenra a high official declared that he had built many holy places in order that the spirits of the king, the ever-living Merenra, might be invoked 'more than all the gods.' 'It has never been doubted that the king claimed actual divinity; he was the "great god," the "golden Horus," and son of Ra. He claimed authority not only over Egypt, but over "all lands and nations," "the whole world in its length and its breadth, the east and the west," "the entire compass of the great circuit of the sun," "the sky and what is in it, the earth and all that is upon it," "every creature that walks upon two or upon four legs, all that fly or flutter, the whole world offers her productions to him." Whatever in fact might be asserted of the Sun-god, was dogmatically predicable of the king of Egypt. His titles were directly derived from those of the Sun-god.' 'In the course of his existence,' we are told, 'the king of Egypt exhausted all the possible conceptions of divinity which the Egyptians had framed for themselves. A superhuman god by his birth and by his royal office, he became the deified man after his death. Thus all that was known of the divine was summed up in him.'

We have now completed our sketch, for it is no more than a sketch, of the evolution of that sacred kingship which attained its highest form, its most absolute expression, in the monarchies of Peru and Egypt. Historically, the institution appears to have originated in the order of public magicians or medicine-men; logically it rests on a mistaken deduction from the association of ideas. Men mistook the order of their ideas for the order of nature, and hence imagined that the control which they have, or seem to have, over their thoughts, permitted them to exercise a corresponding control over things. The men who for one reason or another, because of the strength or the weakness of their natural parts, were supposed to possess these magical powers in the highest degree, were gradually marked off from their fellows and became a separate class, who were destined to exercise a most far-reaching influence on the political, religious, and intellectual evolution of mankind. Social progress, as we know, consists mainly in a successive differentiation of functions, or, in simpler language, a division of labour. The work which in primitive society is done by all alike and by all equally ill, or nearly so, is gradually distributed among different classes

Evolution of sacred kings out of magicians.

of workers and executed more and more perfectly; and so far as the products, material or immaterial, of this specialised labour are shared by all, the whole community benefits by the increasing specialisation. Now magicians or medicine-men appear to constitute the oldest artificial or professional class in the evolution of society. For sorcerers are found in every savage tribe known to us; and among the lowest savages, such as the Australian aborigines, they are the only professional class that exists. As time goes on, and the process of differentiation continues, the order of medicine-men is itself subdivided into such classes as the healers of disease, the makers of rain, and so forth; while the most powerful member of the order wins for himself a position as chief and gradually develops into a sacred king, his old magical functions falling more and more into the background and being exchanged for priestly or even divine duties, in proportion as magic is slowly ousted by religion. Still later, a partition is effected between the civil and the religious aspect of the kingship, the temporal power being committed to one man and the spiritual to another. Meanwhile the magicians, who may be repressed but cannot be extirpated by the predominance of religion, still addict themselves to their old occult arts in preference to the newer ritual of sacrifice and prayer; and in time the more sagacious of their number perceive the fallacy of magic and hit upon a more effectual mode of manipulating the forces of nature for the good of man; in short, they abandon sorcery for science. I am far from affirming that the course of development has everywhere rigidly followed these lines: it has doubtless varied greatly in different societies. I merely mean to indicate in the broadest outline what I conceive to have been its general trend. Regarded from the industrial point of view the evolution has been from uniformity to diversity of function: regarded from the political point of view, it has been from democracy to despotism. With the later history of monarchy, especially with the decay of despotism and its displacement by forms of government better adapted to the higher needs of humanity, we are not concerned in this enquiry: our theme is the growth, not the decay, of a great and, in its time, beneficent institution.

CHAPTER 5

DEPARTMENTAL KINGS OF NATURE

THE preceding investigation has proved that the same union of sacred functions with a royal title which meets us in the King of the Wood at Nemi, the Sacrificial King at Rome, and the magistrate called the King at Athens, occurs frequently outside the limits of classical antiquity and is a common feature of societies at all stages from barbarism to civilisation. Further, it appears that the royal priest is often a king, not only in name but in fact, swaying the sceptre as well as the crosier. All this confirms the traditional view of the origin of the titular and priestly kings in the republics of ancient Greece and Italy. At least by shewing that the combination of spiritual and temporal power, of which Graeco-Italian tradition preserved the memory, has actually existed in many places, we have obviated any suspicion of improbability that might have attached to the tradition. Therefore we may now fairly ask, May not the King of the Wood have had an origin like that which a probable tradition assigns to the Sacrificial King of Rome and the titular King of Athens? In other words, may not his predecessors in office have been a line of kings whom a republican revolution stripped of their political power, leaving them only their religious functions and the shadow of a crown? There are at least two reasons for answering this question in the negative. One reason is drawn from the abode of the priest of Nemi; the other from his title, the King of the Wood. If his predecessors had been kings in the ordinary sense, he would surely have been found residing, like the fallen kings of Rome and Athens, in the city of which the sceptre had passed from him. This city must have been Aricia, for there was none nearer. But Aricia was three miles off from his forest sanctuary by the lake shore. If he reigned, it was not in the city, but in the greenwood. Again his title, King of the Wood, hardly allows us to suppose that he had ever been a king in the common sense of the word. More likely he was a king of nature, and of a special side of nature, namely, the woods from which he took his title. If we could find instances of what we may call departmental kings of nature, that is of persons supposed to rule over particular elements or aspects of nature, they would probably present a closer analogy to the King of the Wood than the divine kings we have been hitherto considering, whose control of nature is general rather than special. Instances of such departmental kings are not wanting.

Kings of rain in Africa.

On a hill at Bomma near the mouth of the Congo dwells Namvulu Vumu, King of the Rain and Storm. Of some of the tribes on the Upper Nile we are told that they have no kings in the common sense; the only persons whom they acknowledge as such are the Kings of the Rain. *Mata Kodou*, who are credited with the power of giving rain at the proper time, that is in the rainy season. Before the rains begin to fall at the end of March the country is a parched and arid desert; and the cattle, which form the people's chief wealth, perish for lack of grass. So, when the end of March draws on, each householder betakes himself to the King of the Rain and offers him a cow that he may make the blessed waters of heaven to drip on the brown and withered pastures. If no shower falls, the people assemble and demand that the king shall give them rain; and if the sky still continues cloudless, they rip up his belly, in which he is believed to keep the storms. Amongst the Bari tribe one of these Rain Kings made rain by sprinkling water on the ground out of a handbell.

Priesthood of the Alfai.

Among tribes on the outskirts of Abyssinia a similar office exists and has been thus described by an observer. 'The priesthood of the Alfai, as he is called by the Barea and Kunama, is a remarkable one; he is believed to be able to make rain. This office formerly existed among the Algeds and appears to be still common to the Nuba negroes. The Alfai of the Barea, who is also consulted by the northern Kunama, lives near Tembadere on a mountain alone with his family. The people bring him tribute in the form of clothes and fruits, and cultivate for him a large field of his own. He is a kind of king, and his office passes by inheritance to his brother or sister's son. He is supposed to conjure down rain and to drive away the locusts. But if he disappoints the people's expectation and a great drought arises in the land, the Alfai is stoned to death, and his nearest relations are obliged to cast the first stone at him. When we passed through the country, the office of Alfai was still held by an old man; but I heard that rain-making had proved too dangerous for him and that he had renounced his office.'

In the backwoods of Cambodia live two mysterious sovereigns known as the King of the Fire and the King of the Water. Their fame is spread all over the south of the great Indo-Chinese peninsula; but only a faint echo of it has reached the West. Down to a few years ago no European, so far as is known, had ever seen either of them; and their very existence might have passed for a fable, were it not that till lately communications were regularly maintained between them and the King of Cambodia, who year by year exchanged presents with them. The Cambodian gifts were passed from tribe to tribe till they reached their destination; for no Cambodian would essay the long and perilous journey. Their royal functions are of a purely mystic or spiritual order; they have no political authority; they are simple peasants, living by the sweat of their brow and the offerings of the faithful. According to one account they live in absolute solitude, never meeting each other and never seeing a human face. They inhabit successively seven towers perched upon seven mountains, and every year they pass from one tower to another. People come furtively and cast within their reach what is needful for their subsistence. The kingship lasts seven years, the time necessary to inhabit all the towers successively; but many die before their time is out. The offices are hereditary in one or (according to others) two royal families, who enjoy high consideration, have revenues assigned to them, and are exempt from the necessity of tilling the ground. But naturally the dignity is not coveted, and when a vacancy occurs, all eligible men (they must be strong and have children) flee and hide themselves. Another account, admitting the reluctance of the hereditary candidates to accept the crown, does not countenance the report of their hermit-like seclusion in the seven towers. For it represents the people as prostrating themselves before the mystic kings whenever they appear in public, it being thought that a terrible hurricane would burst over the country if this mark of homage were omitted. Probably, however, these are mere fables such as commonly shed a glamour of romance over the distant and unknown. A French officer, who had an

Kings of Fire and Water in Cambodia.

interview with the redoubtable Fire King in February 1891, found him stretched on a bamboo couch, diligently smoking a long copper pipe, and surrounded by people who paid him no great deference. In spite of his mystic vocation the sorcerer had no charm or talisman about him, and was in no way distinguishable from his fellows except by his tall stature. Another writer reports that the two kings are much feared, because they are supposed to possess the evil eye; hence every one avoids them, and the potentates considerately cough to announce their approach and to allow people to get out of their way. They enjoy extraordinary privileges and immunities, but their authority does not extend beyond the few villages of their neighbourhood. Like many other sacred kings, of whom we shall read in the sequel, the Kings of Fire and Water are not allowed to die a natural death, for that would lower their reputation. Accordingly when one of them is seriously ill, the elders hold a consultation and if they think he cannot recover they stab him to death. His body is burned and the ashes are piously collected and publicly honoured for five years. Part of them is given to the widow, and she keeps them in an urn, which she must carry on her back when she goes to weep on her husband's grave.

Supernatural powers of the Kings of Fire and Water.

We are told that the Fire King, the more important of the two, whose supernatural powers have never been questioned, officiates at marriages, festivals, and sacrifices in honour of the *Yan* or spirit. On these occasions a special place is set apart for him; and the path by which he approaches is spread with white cotton cloths. A reason for confining the royal dignity to the same family is that this family is in possession of certain famous talismans which would lose their virtue or disappear if they passed out of the family. These talismans are three: the fruit of a creeper called *Cui*, gathered ages ago at the time of the last deluge, but still fresh and green; a rattan, also very old but bearing flowers that never fade; and lastly, a sword containing a *Yan* or spirit, who guards it constantly and works miracles with it. The spirit is said to be that of a slave, whose blood chanced to fall upon the blade while it was being forged, and who died a voluntary death to expiate his involuntary offence. By means of the two former talismans the Water King can raise a flood that would drown the whole earth. If the Fire King draws the magic sword a few inches from its sheath, the sun is hidden and men and beasts fall into a profound sleep; were he to draw it quite out of the scabbard, the world would come to an end. To this wondrous brand sacrifices of buffaloes, pigs, fowls, and ducks are offered for rain. It is kept swathed in cotton and silk; and amongst the annual presents sent by the King of Cambodia were rich stuffs to wrap the sacred sword.

Contrary to the common usage of the country, which is to bury the dead, the bodies of both these mystic monarchs are burnt, but their nails and some of their teeth and bones are religiously preserved as amulets. It is while the corpse is being consumed on the pyre that the kinsmen of the deceased magician flee to the forest and hide themselves for fear of being elevated to the invidious dignity which he has just vacated. The people go and search for them, and the first whose lurking place they discover is made King of Fire or Water.

These, then, are examples of what I have called departmental kings of nature. But it is a far cry to Italy from the forests of Cambodia and the sources of the Nile. And though Kings of Rain, Water, and Fire have been found, we have still to discover a King of the Wood to match the Arician priest who bore that title. Perhaps we shall find him nearer home.

CHAPTER 6

THE WORSHIP OF TREES

i

IN the religious history of the Aryan race in Europe the worship
of trees has played an important part. Nothing could be more

Great forests
of ancient Eu-
rope. natural. For at the dawn of history Europe was covered with
immense primaeval forests, in which the scattered clearings
must have appeared like islets in an ocean of green. Down to
the first century before our era the Hercynian forest stretched
eastward from the Rhine for a distance at once vast and
unknown; Germans whom Caesar questioned had travelled for
two months through it without reaching the end. Four centuries
later it was visited by the Emperor Julian, and the solitude, the
gloom, the silence of the forest appear to have made a deep
impression on his sensitive nature. He declared that he knew
nothing like it in the Roman empire. In the reign of Henry II
the citizens of London still hunted the wild bull and the boar
in the woods of Hampstead. Even under the later Plantagenets
the royal forests were sixty-eight in number. In the forest of
Arden it was said that down to modern times a squirrel might
leap from tree to tree for nearly the whole length of Warwickshire. The excavation of ancient pile-villages in the valley of the
Po has shewn that long before the rise and probably the
foundation of Rome the north of Italy was covered with dense
woods of elms, chestnuts, and especially of oaks. As late as the
fourth century before our era Rome was divided from central
Etruria by the dreaded Ciminian forest, which Livy compares
to the woods of Germany. No merchant, if we may trust the
Roman historian, had ever penetrated its pathless solitudes: and
it was deemed a most daring feat when a Roman general, after
sending two scouts to explore its intricacies, led his army into
the forest and, making his way to a ridge of the wooded
mountains, looked down on the rich Etrurian fields spread out
below.

From an examination of the Teutonic words for 'temple'
Grimm has made it probable that amongst the Germans the

oldest sanctuaries were natural woods.* However this may be, tree-worship is well attested for all the great European families of the Aryan stock. Amongst the Celts the oak-worship of the Druids is familiar to every one, and their old word for a sanctuary seems to be identical in origin and meaning with the Latin *nemus*, a grove or woodland glade, which still survives in the name of Nemi. Sacred groves were common among the ancient Germans, and tree-worship is hardly extinct amongst their descendants at the present day. How serious that worship was in former times may be gathered from the ferocious penalty appointed by the old German laws for such as dared to peel the bark of a standing tree. The culprit's navel was to be cut out and nailed to the part of the tree which he had peeled, and he was to be driven round and round the tree till all his guts were wound about its trunk. The intention of the punishment clearly was to replace the dead bark by a living substitute taken from the culprit; it was a life for a life, the life of a man for the life of a tree.

Proofs of the prevalence of tree-worship in ancient Greece and Italy are abundant. In the sanctuary of Aesculapius at Cos, for example, it was forbidden to cut down the cypress-trees under a penalty of a thousand drachms. But nowhere, perhaps, in the ancient world was this antique form of religion better preserved than in the heart of the great metropolis itself. In the Forum, the busy centre of Roman life, the sacred fig-tree of Romulus was worshipped down to the days of the empire, and the withering of its trunk was enough to spread consternation through the city. Again, on the slope of the Palatine Hill grew a cornel-tree which was esteemed one of the most sacred objects in Rome. Whenever the tree appeared to a passerby to be drooping, he set up a hue and cry which was echoed by the people in the street, and soon a crowd might be seen running helter-skelter from all sides with buckets of water, as if (says Plutarch) they were hastening to put out a fire.

Among the tribes of the Finnish-Ugrian stock in Europe the heathen worship was performed for the most part in sacred groves, which were always enclosed with a fence. Such a grove often consisted merely of a glade or clearing with a few trees dotted about, upon which in former times the skins of the sacrificial victims were hung. The central point of the grove, at

Tree-worship practised by all the Aryan races in Europe.

Tree-worship among the Finnish-Ugrian peoples.

least among the tribes of the Volga, was the sacred tree, beside which everything else sank into insignificance. Before it the worshippers assembled and the priest offered his prayers, at its roots the victim was sacrificed, and its boughs sometimes served as a pulpit. No wood might be hewn and no branch broken in the grove, and women were generally forbidden to enter it.

But it is necessary to examine in some detail the notions on which the worship of trees and plants is based. To the savage the world in general is animate, and trees and plants are no exception to the rule. He thinks that they have souls like his own, and he treats them accordingly. 'They say', writes the ancient vegetarian Porphyry, 'that primitive men led an unhappy life, for their superstition did not stop at animals but extended even to plants. For why should the slaughter of an ox or a sheep be a greater wrong than the felling of a fir or an oak, seeing that a soul is implanted in these trees also?' Similarly, the Hidatsa Indians of North America believe that every natural object has its spirit, or to speak more properly, its shade. To these shades some consideration or respect is due, but not equally to all. For example, the shade of the cottonwood, the greatest tree in the valley of the Upper Missouri, is supposed to possess an intelligence which, if properly approached, may help the Indians in certain undertakings; but the shades of shrubs and grasses are of little account. When the Missouri, swollen by a freshet in spring, carries away part of its banks and sweeps some tall tree into its current, it is said that the spirit of the tree cries while the roots still cling to the land and until the trunk falls with a splash into the stream. Formerly the Indians considered it wrong to fell one of these giants, and when large logs were needed they made use only of trees which had fallen of themselves. Till lately some of the more credulous old men declared that many of the misfortunes of their people were caused by this modern disregard for the rights of the living cottonwood. The Iroquois believed that each species of tree, shrub, plant, and herb had its own spirit, and to these spirits it was their custom to return thanks.

The conception of trees and plants as animated beings naturally results in treating them as male and female, who can be married to each other in a real, and not merely a figurative or poetical sense of the word. The notion is not purely fanciful,

Trees are regarded by the savage as animate.

Trees married to each other.

for plants like animals have their sexes and reproduce their kind by the union of the male and female elements. But whereas in all the higher animals the organs of the two sexes are regularly separated between different individuals, in most plants they exist together in every individual of the species. This rule, however, is by no means universal, and in many species the male plant is distinct from the female. The distinction appears to have been observed by some savages, for we are told that the Maoris 'are acquainted with the sex of trees, etc., and have distinct names for the male and female of some trees'. The ancients knew the difference between the male and the female date-palm, and fertilised them artificially by shaking the pollen of the male tree over the flowers of the female. The fertilisation took place in spring. Among the heathen of Harran the month during which the palms were fertilised bore the name of the Date Month, and at this time they celebrated the marriage festival of all the gods and goddesses. Different from this true and fruitful marriage of the palm are the false and barren marriages of plants which play a part in Hindoo superstition. For example, if a Hindoo has planted a grove of mangos, neither he nor his wife may taste of the fruit until he has formally married one of the trees, as a bridegroom, to a tree of a different sort, commonly a tamarind-tree, which grows near it in the grove. If there is no tamarind to act as bride, a jasmine will serve the turn. The expenses of such a marriage are often considerable, for the more Brahmans are feasted at it, the greater the glory of the owner of the grove. A family has been known to sell its golden and silver trinkets, and to borrow all the money they could in order to marry a mango-tree to a jasmine with due pomp and ceremony.

Artificial fertilisation of the date-palm.

Marriages of trees in India.

In most, if not all, of these cases the spirit is viewed as incorporate in the tree. But, according to another and probably later opinion, the tree is not the body, but merely the abode of the tree-spirit, which can quit it and return to it at pleasure. The inhabitants of Siaoo, an island of the Sangi group in the East Indies, believe in certain sylvan spirits who dwell in forests or in great solitary trees. At full moon the spirit comes forth from his lurking-place and roams about. He has a big head, very long arms and legs, and a ponderous body. In order to propitiate the wood-spirits people bring offerings of food, fowls,

Trees sometimes conceived not as the body but merely as the abode of spirits.

goats, and so forth to the places which they are supposed to haunt. The people of Nias think that, when a tree dies, its liberated spirit becomes a demon, which can kill a coco-nut palm by merely lighting on its branches, and can cause the death of all the children in a house by perching on one of the posts that support it. Further, they are of opinion that certain trees are at all times inhabited by roving demons who, if the trees were damaged, would be set free to go about on errands of mischief. Hence the people respect these trees, and are careful not to cut them down. On the Tanga coast of East Africa mischievous sprites reside in great trees, especially in the fantastically shaped baobabs. Sometimes they appear in the shape of ugly black beings, but as a rule they enter unseen into people's bodies, from which, after causing much sickness and misery, they have to be cast out by the sorcerer.

Transition of tree-spirit into anthropomorphic deity of the woods.

When a tree comes to be viewed, no longer as the body of the tree-spirit, but simply as its abode which it can quit at pleasure, an important advance has been made in religious thought. Animism is passing into polytheism. In other words, instead of regarding each tree as a living and conscious being, man now sees in it merely a lifeless, inert mass, tenanted for a longer or shorter time by a supernatural being who, as he can pass freely from tree to tree, thereby enjoys a certain right of possession or lordship over the trees, and, ceasing to be a tree-soul, becomes a forest god. As soon as the tree-spirit is thus in a measure disengaged from each particular tree, he begins to change his shape and assume the body of a man, in virtue of a general tendency of early thought to clothe all abstract spiritual beings in concrete human form. Hence in classical art the sylvan deities are depicted in human shape, their woodland character being denoted by a branch or some equally obvious symbol. But this change of shape does not affect the essential character of the tree-spirit. The powers which he exercised as a tree-soul incorporate in a tree, he still continues to wield as a god of trees. When the missionary Jerome of Prague was persuading the heathen Lithuanians to fell their sacred groves, a multitude of women besought the Prince of Lithuania to stop him, saying that with the woods he was destroying the house of god from which they had been wont to get rain and sunshine. The Mundaris in Assam think that if a tree in the sacred grove is

Trees supposed to give rain and sunshine.

felled the sylvan gods evince their displeasure by withholding rain. In Cambodia each village or province has its sacred tree, the abode of a spirit. If the rains are late the people sacrifice to the tree. In time of drought the elders of the Wakamba in East Africa assemble and take a calabash of cider and a goat to a baobab-tree, where they kill the goat but do not eat it. When Ovambo women go out to sow corn they take with them in the basket of seed two green branches of a particular kind of tree (*Peltophorum africanum* Sond.), one of which they plant in the field along with the first seed sown. The branch is believed to have the power of attracting rain; hence in one of the native dialects the tree goes by the name of the 'rain-bush'. To extort rain from the tree-spirit a branch is sometimes dipped in water. In such cases the spirit is doubtless supposed to be immanent in the branch, and the water thus applied to the spirit produces rain by a sort of sympathetic magic.

Again, tree-spirits make the crops to grow. Amongst the Mundaris every village has its sacred grove, and 'the grove deities are held responsible for the crops, and are especially honoured at all the great agricultural festivals'. Before harvest the Wabondëi of east Africa sacrifice a goat to the spirit that lives in baobab-trees; the blood is poured into a hole at the foot of one of the trees. If the sacrifice were omitted the spirit would send disease and death among the people. The Gallas dance in couples round sacred trees, praying for a good harvest. Every couple consists of a man and woman, who are linked together by a stick, of which each holds one end. Under their arms they carry green corn or grass. Swedish peasants stick a leafy branch in each furrow of their corn-fields, believing that this will ensure an abundant crop. *[margin: Tree-spirits supposed to make the crops grow.]*

Again, the tree-spirit makes the herds to multiply and blesses women with offspring. In the Tuhoe tribe of Maoris 'the power of making women fruitful is ascribed to trees. These trees are associated with the navel-strings of definite mythical ancestors, as indeed the navel-strings of all children used to be hung upon them down to quite recent times. A barren woman had to embrace such a tree with her arms, and she received a male or a female child according as she embraced the east or the west side'. The common European custom of placing a green bush *[margin: Tree-spirits grant offspring or an easy delivery to women.]*

on May Day before or on the house of a beloved maiden probably originated in the belief of the fertilising power of the tree-spirit. In some parts of Bavaria such bushes are set up also at the houses of newly-married pairs, and the practice is only omitted if the wife is near her confinement; for in that case they say that the husband has 'set up a May-bush for himself'. Among the South Slavonians a barren woman, who desires to have a child, places a new chemise upon a fruitful tree on the eve of St George's Day. Next morning before sunrise she examines the garment, and if she finds that some living creature has crept on it, she hopes that her wish will be fulfilled within the year. Then she puts on the chemise, confident that she will be as fruitful as the tree on which the garment has passed the night. Among the Kara-Kirghiz barren women roll themselves on the ground under a solitary apple-tree, in order to obtain offspring. Some of the hill-tribes of India have a custom of marrying the bride and bridegroom to two trees before they are married to each other. For example, among the Mundas the bride touches with red lead a *mahwá*-tree, clasps it in her arms, and is tied to it; and the bridegroom goes through a like ceremony with a mango-tree. The intention of the custom may perhaps be to communicate to the newly-wedded pair the vigorous reproductive power of the trees.

ii

May-trees in Europe.

From the foregoing review of the beneficent qualities commonly ascribed to tree-spirits. It is easy to understand why customs like the May-tree or May-pole have prevailed so widely and figured so prominently in the popular festivals of European peasants. In spring or early summer or even on Midsummer Day, it was and still is in many parts of Europe the custom to go out to the woods, cut down a tree and bring it into the village, where it is set up amid general rejoicings; or the people cut branches in the woods, and fasten them on every house. The intention of these customs is to bring home to the village, and to each house, the blessings which the tree-spirit has in its power to bestow. Hence the custom in some places of planting a May-tree before every house, or of carrying the village May-tree from door to door, that every household may receive its share of the blessing. Out of the mass of evidence on this subject a few examples may be selected.

Sir Henry Piers, in his *Description of Westmeath*, writing in 1682 says: 'On May-eve, every family sets up before their door a green bush, strewed over with yellow flowers, which the meadows yield plentifully. In countries where timber is plentiful, they erect tall slender trees, which stand high, and they continue almost the whole year; so as a stranger would go nigh to imagine that they were all signs of ale-sellers, and that all houses were ale-houses.' In Northamptonshire a young tree ten or twelve feet high used to be planted before each house on May Day so as to appear growing; flowers were thrown over it and strewn about the door. 'Among ancient customs still retained by the Cornish, may be reckoned that of decking their doors and porches on the first of May with green boughs of sycamore and hawthorn, and of planting trees, or rather stumps of trees, before their houses.' In the north of England it was formerly the custom for young people to rise a little after midnight on the morning of the first of May, and go out with music and the blowing of horns into the woods, where they broke branches and adorned them with nosegays and crowns of flowers. This done, they returned about sunrise and fastened the flower-decked branches over the doors and windows of their houses. At Abingdon in Berkshire young people formerly went about in groups on May morning, singing a carol of which the following are two of the verses:

May-trees and May-bushes in England.

May garlands in England.

> 'We've been rambling all the night,
>   And sometime of this day;
> And now returning back again,
>   We bring a garland gay.
>
> A garland gay we bring you here;
>   And at your door we stand;
> It is a sprout well budded out,
>   The work of our Lord's hand.'

In some villages of the Vosges Mountains on the first Sunday of May young girls go in bands from house to house, singing a song in praise of May, in which mention is made of the 'bread and meal that come in May'. If money is given them, they fasten a green bough to the door; if it is refused, they wish the

May customs it France, Germany, and Greece.

family many children and no bread to feed them. In the French department of Mayenne, boys who bore the name of *Maillotins* used to go about from farm to farm on the first of May singing carols, for which they received money or a drink; they planted a small tree or a branch of a tree. Among the Germans of Moravia on the third Sunday before Easter, which goes by the name of *Laetare* Sunday, it is customary in some places for young girls to carry a small fir-tree about from door to door, while they sing songs, for which they receive presents. The tree is tricked out with many-coloured ribbons, and sometimes with flowers and dyed egg-shells, and its branches are twined together so as to form what is called a crown. In Corfu the children go about singing May songs on the first of May. The boys carry small cypresses adorned with ribbons, flowers, and the fruits of the season. They receive a glass of wine at each house. The girls carry nosegays. One of them is dressed up like an angel, with gilt wings, and scatters flowers.

Village May-poles in England.

It would be needless to illustrate at length the custom, which has prevailed in various parts of Europe, such as England, France, and Germany, of setting up a village May-tree or May-pole on May Day. A few examples will suffice. The puritanical writer Phillip Stubbes in his *Anatomie of Abuses*, first published at London in 1583, has described with manifest disgust how they used to bring in the May-pole in the days of good Queen Bess. His description affords us a vivid glimpse of merry England in the olden time. 'Against May, Whitsonday, or other time, all the yung men and maides, olde men and wives, run gadding over night to the woods, groves, hils, and mountains, where they spend all the night in plesant pastimes; and in the morning they return, bringing with them birch and branches of trees, to deck their assemblies withall. And no mervaile, for there is a great Lord present amongst them, as superintendent and Lord over their pastimes and sportes, namely, Sathan, prince of hel. But the cheifest jewel they bring from thence is their May-pole, which they bring home with

Bringing in the May-pole.

great veneration, as thus. They have twentie or fortie yoke of oxen, every oxe having a sweet nose-gay of flouers placed on the tip of his hornes, and these oxen drawe home this May-pole (this stinkyng ydol, rather), which is covered all over with floures and hearbs, bound round about with strings, from the top to the bottom, and sometime painted with variable colours, with two or three hundred men, women and children following it with great devotion. And thus beeing reared up, with handkercheefs and flags hovering on the top, they straw the ground rounde about, binde green boughes about it, set up sommer haules, bowers, and arbors hard by it. And then fall they to daunce about it, like as the heathen people did at the dedication of the Idols, whereof this is a perfect pattern, or rather the thing itself. I have heard it credibly reported (and that *viva voce*) by men of great gravitie and reputation, that of fortie, threescore, or a hundred maides going to the wood over night, there have scaresly the third part of them returned home againe undefiled.'

Villages of Upper Bavaria renew their May-pole once every three, four, or five years. It is a fir-tree fetched from the forest, and amid all the wreaths, flags, and inscriptions with which it is bedecked, an essential part is the bunch of dark green foliage left at the top 'as a memento that in it we have to do, not with a dead pole, but with a living tree from the greenwood'. We can hardly doubt that originally the practice everywhere was to set up a new May-tree every year. As the object of the custom was to bring in the fructifying spirit of vegetation, newly awakened in spring, the end would have been defeated if, instead of a living tree, green and sappy, an old withered one had been erected year after year or allowed to stand permanently. When, however, the meaning of the custom had been forgotten, and the May-tree was regarded simply as a centre for holiday merry-making, people saw no reason for felling a fresh tree every year, and preferred to let the same tree stand permanent-ly, only decking it with fresh flowers on May Day. But even when the May-pole had thus become a fixture, the need of giving it the appearance of being a green tree, not a dead pole, was sometimes felt. Thus at Weverham in Cheshire 'are two May-poles, which are decorated on this day (May Day) with all due attention to the ancient solemnity; the sides are hung with garlands, and the top terminated by a birch or other tall slender tree with its leaves on; the bark being peeled, and the stem spliced to the pole, so as to give the appearance of one tree from the summit.' Thus the renewal of the May-tree is like the renewal of the Harvest-May; each is intended to secure a fresh portion of the fertilising spirit of vegetation, and to preserve it throughout the year. But whereas the efficacy of the Harvest-May is restricted to promoting the growth of the crops, that of the May-tree or May-branch extends also, as we have seen,

to women and cattle. Lastly, it is worth noting that the old May-tree is sometimes burned at the end of the year. Thus in the district of Prague young people break pieces of the public May-tree and place them behind the holy pictures in their rooms, where they remain till next May Day, and are then burned on the hearth. In Würtemberg the bushes which are set up on the houses on Palm Sunday are sometimes left there for a year and then burnt.

So much for the tree-spirit conceived as incorporate or immanent in the tree. We have now to shew that the tree-spirit is often conceived and represented as detached from the tree and clothed in human form, and even as embodied in living men or women. The evidence for this anthropomorphic representation of the tree-spirit is largely to be found in the popular customs of European peasantry. At Thann, in Alsace, a girl

called the Little May Rose, dressed in white, carries a small May-tree, which is gay with garlands and ribbons. Her companions collect gifts from door to door, singing a song:

> 'Little May Rose turn round three times,
> Let us look at you round and round!
> Rose of the May, come to the greenwood away,
> We will be merry all.
> So we go from the May to the roses.'

In the course of the song a wish is expressed that those who give nothing may lose their fowls by the marten, that their vine may bear no clusters, their tree no nuts, their field no corn; the produce of the year is supposed to depend on the gifts offered to these May singers. Here and in the cases mentioned above, where children go about with green boughs or garlands on May Day singing and collecting money, the meaning is that with the spirit of vegetation they bring plenty and good luck to the house, and they expect to be paid for the service. In Russian Lithuania, on the first of May, they used to set up a green tree before the village. Then the rustic swains chose the prettiest girl, crowned her, swathed her in birch branches and set her beside the May-tree, where they danced, sang, and shouted 'O May! O May!' In Brie (Isle de France) a May-tree is set up in the midst of the village; its top is crowned with flowers; lower down it is twined with leaves and twigs, still lower with huge green branches. The girls dance round it, and at the same time a lad wrapt in leaves and called Father May is led about. In the small towns of the Franken Wald mountains in Northern Bavaria, on the second of May, a *Walber* tree is erected before a tavern, and a man dances round it, enveloped in straw from head to foot in such a way that the ears of corn unite above his head to form a crown. He is called the *Walber*, and used to be led in procession through the streets, which were adorned with sprigs of birch.

Thus far we have seen that the tree-spirit or the spirit of vegetation in general is represented either in vegetable form alone, as by a tree, bough, or flower; or in vegetable and human form simultaneously, as by a tree, bough, or flower in combination with a puppet or a living person. It remains to shew that the representation of him by a tree, bough, or flower is sometimes entirely dropped, while the representation of him by a living person remains. In this case the representative character of the person is generally marked by dressing him or her in leaves or flowers; sometimes too it is indicated by the name he or she bears.

Thus in some parts of Russia on St George's Day (the twenty-third of April) a youth is dressed out, like our Jack-in-the-Green, with leaves and flowers. The Slovenes call him the Green George. Holding a lighted torch in one hand and a pie in the other, he goes out to the corn-fields, followed by girls singing appropriate songs. A circle of brushwood is then lighted, in the middle of which is set the pie. All who take part in the ceremony then sit down around the fire and divide the pie among them. In this custom the Green George dressed in leaves and flowers is plainly identical with the similarly disguised Green George who is associated with a tree in the Carinthian, Transylvanian, and Roumanian customs observed on the same day. Again, we saw that in Russia at Whitsuntide a birch-tree is dressed in woman's clothes and set up in the house. Clearly equivalent to this is the custom observed on Whit-Monday by Russian girls in the district of Pinsk. They

Marginal notes:

The *Walber*.

Tree-spirit or vegetation-spirit represented by a person alone.

Green George in Russia.

Whitsuntide customs in Russia.

choose the prettiest of their number, envelop her in a mass of foliage taken from the birch-trees and maples, and carry her about through the village. In a district of Little Russia they take round a 'poplar', represented by a girl wearing bright flowers in her hair. At Whitsuntide in Holland poor women used to go about begging with a little girl called Whitsuntide Flower (*Pinxterbloem*, perhaps a kind of iris); she was decked with flowers and sat in a waggon. In North Brabant she wears the flowers from which she takes her name and a song is sung:

'Whitsuntide Flower,
Turn yourself once round.'

May customs in France.

All over Provence on the first of May pretty little girls are dressed in white, decked with crowns and wreaths of roses, and set on seats or platforms strewn with flowers in the streets, while their companions go about begging coppers for the Mayos or Mayes, as they are called, from the passers-by. In some parts of the Ardennes on May Day a small girl, clad in white and wearing a chaplet of flowers on her head, used to go from house to house with her playmates, collecting contributions and singing that it was May, the month of May, the pretty month of May, that the wheat was tall, the hawthorn in bloom, and the lark carolling in the sky.

Leaf-clad representative of vegetation sometimes called a King or Queen.

Often the leaf-clad person who represents the spirit of vegetation is known as the king or the queen; thus, for example, he or she is called the May King, Whitsuntide King, Queen of May, and so on. These titles, as Mannhardt observes, imply that the spirit incorporate in vegetation is a ruler, whose creative power extends far and wide.

At Hildesheim, in Hanover, five or six young fellows go about on the afternoon of Whit-Monday cracking long whips in measured time and collecting eggs from the houses. The chief person of the band is the Leaf King, a lad swathed so completely in birchen twigs that nothing of him can be seen but his feet. A huge head-dress of birchen twigs adds to his apparent stature. In his hand he carries a long crook, with which he tries to catch stray dogs and children. At Grossvargula, near Langensalza, in the eighteenth century a Grass King used to be led about in procession at Whitsuntide. He was encased in a pyramid of poplar branches, the top of which was adorned with a royal

The Leaf King.

The Grass King.

crown of branches and flowers. He rode on horseback with the leafy pyramid over him, so that its lower end touched the ground, and an opening was left in it only for his face. Surrounded by a cavalcade of young fellows, he rode in procession to the town hall, the parsonage, and so on, where they all got a drink of beer. Then under the seven lindens of the neighbouring Sommerberg, the Grass King was stripped of his green casing; the crown was handed to the Mayor, and the branches were stuck in the flax fields in order to make the flax grow tall.

Often the spirit of vegetation in spring is represented by a queen instead of a king. In the neighbourhood of Libchowic (Bohemia), on the fourth Sunday in Lent, girls dressed in white and wearing the first spring flowers, as violets and daisies, in their hair, lead about the village a girl who is called the Queen and is crowned with flowers. During the procession, which is conducted with great solemnity, none of the girls may stand still, but must keep whirling round continually and singing. In every house the Queen announces the arrival of spring and wishes the inmates good luck and blessings, for which she receives presents. In German Hungary the girls choose the prettiest girl to be their Whitsuntide Queen, fasten a tower-ing wreath on her brow, and carry her singing through the streets. At every house they stop, sing old ballads, and receive presents. In the south-east of Ireland on May Day the pret-tiest girl used to be chosen Queen of the district for twelve months. She was crowned with wild flowers; feasting, dancing, and rustic sports followed, and were closed by a grand proces-sion in the evening. During her year of office she presided over rural gatherings of young people at dances and merry-mak-ings. If she married before next May Day, her authority was at an end, but her successor was not elected till that day came round. {.marginal} May-Queens and Whitsun-tide Queens.

Again the spirit of vegetation is sometimes represented by a king and queen, a lord and lady, or a bridegroom and bride. Here again the parallelism holds between the anthropomorphic and the vegetable representation of the tree-spirit, for we have seen above that trees are sometimes married to each other. At Halford in south Warwickshire the children go from house to house on May Day, walking two and two in procession and {.marginal} Spirit of vegetation represented simultaneous-ly by a King and Queen or a Bride-groom and Bride.

headed by a King and Queen. Two boys carry a May-pole some six or seven feet high, which is covered with flowers and greenery. Fastened to it near the top are two cross-bars at right angles to each other. These are also decked with flowers, and from the ends of the bars hang hoops similarly adorned. At the houses the children sing May songs and receive money, which is used to provide tea for them at the school-house in the afternoon. In a Bohemian village near Königgrätz on Whit-Monday the children play the king's game, at which a king and queen march about under a canopy, the queen wearing a garland, and the youngest girl carrying two wreaths on a plate behind them. They are attended by boys and girls called groomsmen and bridesmaids, and they go from house to house collecting gifts. In a parish of Denmark it used to be the custom at Whitsuntide to dress up a little girl as the Whitsun-bride (*pinse-bruden*) and a little boy as her groom. She was decked in all the finery of a grown-up bride, and wore a crown of the freshest flowers of spring on her head. Her groom was as gay as flowers, ribbons, and knots could make him. The other children adorned themselves as best they could with the yellow flowers of the trollius and caltha. Then they went in great state from farmhouse to farmhouse, two little girls walking at the head of the procession as bridesmaids, and six or eight outriders galloping ahead on hobby-horses to announce their coming. Contributions of eggs, butter, loaves, cream, coffee, sugar, and tallow-candles were received and conveyed away in baskets. When they had made the round of the farms, some of the farmers' wives helped to arrange the wedding feast, and the children danced merrily in clogs on the stamped clay floor till the sun rose and the birds began to sing. All this is now a thing of the past. Only the old folks still remember the little Whitsun-bride and her mimic pomp. In Sweden the ceremonies associated elsewhere with May Day or Whitsuntide commonly take place at Midsummer. Accordingly we find that in some parts of the Swedish province of Blekinge they still choose a Midsummer's Bride, to whom the 'church coronet' is occasionally lent. The girl selects for herself a Bridegroom, and a collection is made for the pair, who for the time being are looked on as man and wife. The other youths also choose each his bride.

Marginal notes:

Whitsuntide King and Queen.

Whitsuntide Bridegroom and Bride in Denmark.

Midsummer Bridegroom and Bride in Sweden and Norway.

Often the marriage of the spirit of vegetation in spring, though not directly represented, is implied by naming the human representative of the spirit, 'the Bride', and dressing her in wedding attire. Thus in some villages of Altmark at Whitsuntide, while the boys go about carrying a May-tree or leading a boy enveloped in leaves and flowers, the girls lead about the May Bride, a girl dressed as a bride with a great nosegay in her hair. They go from house to house, the May Bride singing a song in which she asks for a present, and tells the inmates of each house that if they give her something they will themselves have something the whole year through; but if they give her nothing they will themselves have nothing. In some parts of Westphalia two girls lead a flower-crowned girl called the Whitsuntide Bride from door to door, singing a song in which they ask for eggs. At Waggum in Brunswick, when service is over on Whitsunday, the village girls assemble, dressed in white or bright colours, decked with flowers, and wearing chaplets of spring flowers in their hair. One of them represents the May Bride, and carries a crown of flowers on a staff as a sign of her dignity. As usual the children go about from cottage to cottage singing and begging for eggs, sausages, cakes, or money. In other parts of Brunswick it is a boy clothed all in birch leaves who personates the May Bride. In Bresse in the month of May a girl called *la Mariée* is tricked out with ribbons and nosegays and is led about by a gallant. She is preceded by a lad carrying a green May-tree, and appropriate verses are sung.

CHAPTER 7

THE SACRED MARRIAGE

i

The marriage of the King and Queen of May intended to promote the growth of vegetation by homoeopathic magic.

FROM the preceding examination of spring and summer festivals we may infer that our rude forefathers personified the powers of vegetation as male and female, and attempted, on the principle of homoeopathic or imitative magic, to quicken the growth of trees and plants by representing the marriage of the sylvan deities in the persons of a King and Queen of May, a Whitsun Bridegroom and Bride, and so forth. Such representations were accordingly no mere symbolic or allegorical dramas, pastoral plays designed to amuse or instruct a rustic audience. They were charms intended to make the woods to grow green, the fresh grass to sprout, the corn to shoot, and the flowers to blow. And it was natural to suppose that the more closely the mock marriage of the leaf-clad or flower-decked mummers aped the real marriage of the woodland sprites, the more effective would be the charm. Accordingly we may assume with a high degree of probability that the profligacy which notoriously attended these ceremonies was at one time not an accidental excess but an essential part of the rites, and that in the opinion of those who performed them the marriage of trees and plants could not be fertile without the real union of the human sexes. At the present day it might perhaps be vain to look in civilised Europe for customs of this sort observed for the explicit purpose of promoting the growth of vegetation. But ruder races in other parts of the world have consciously employed the intercourse of the sexes as a means to ensure the fruitfulness of the earth; and some rites which are still, or were till lately, kept up in Europe can be reasonably explained only as stunted relics of a similar practice. The following facts will make this plain.

Intercourse of the sexes practised in order to make the crops grow.

For four days before they committed the seed to the earth the Pipiles of Central America kept apart from their wives 'in order that on the night before planting they might indulge their passions to the fullest extent; certain persons are even said to have been appointed to perform the sexual act at the very moment when the first seeds were deposited in the ground.' The use of their wives at that time was indeed enjoined upon the people by the priests as a religious duty, in default of which it was not lawful to sow the seed. The only possible explanation of this custom seems to be that the Indians confused the process by which human beings reproduce their kind with the process by which plants discharge the same function, and fancied that by resorting to the former they were simultaneously forwarding the latter. In some parts of Java, at the season when the bloom will soon be on the rice, the husbandman and his wife visit their fields by night and there engage in sexual intercourse for the purpose of promoting the growth of the crop. In the Leti, Sarmata, and some other groups of islands which lie between the western end of New Guinea and the northern part of Australia, the heathen population regard the sun as the male principle by whom the earth or female principle is fertilised. They call him Upu-lera or Mr Sun, and represent him under the form of a lamp made of coco-nut leaves, which may be seen hanging everywhere in their houses and in the sacred fig-tree. Under the tree lies a large flat stone, which serves as a sacrificial table. On it the heads of slain foes were and are still placed in some of the islands. Once a year, at the beginning of the rainy season, Mr Sun comes down into the holy fig-tree to fertilise the earth, and to facilitate his descent a ladder with seven rungs is considerately placed at his disposal. It is set up under the tree and is adorned with carved figures of the birds whose shrill clarion heralds the approach of the sun in the East. On this occasion pigs and dogs are sacrificed in profusion; men and women alike indulge in a saturnalia; and the mystic union of the sun and the earth is dramatically represented in public, amid song and dance, by the real union of the sexes under the tree. The object of the festival, we are told, is to procure rain, plenty of food and drink, abundance of cattle and children and riches from Grandfather Sun. They pray that he may make every she-goat to cast two or three young, the people to multiply, the dead pigs to be replaced by living pigs, the empty rice-baskets to be filled, and so on. And to induce him to grant their requests they offer him pork and rice and liquor, and invite him to fall to. Among the Tangkhuls of Manipur*, before the rice is sown and when it is reaped, the boys and girls have a tug-of-war with a tough rope of twisted creeper. Great jars of beer are set ready, and the strictness of their ordinary morality is broken by a night of unbridled licence. It would be unjust to treat these orgies as a mere outburst of unbridled passion; no doubt they are deliberately and solemnly organised as essential to the fertility of the earth and the welfare of man.

In Uganda parents of twins are supposed to fertilise the plantains.

The Baganda of Central Africa believe so strongly in the intimate relation between the intercourse of the sexes and the fertility of the ground that among them a barren wife is generally sent away because she is supposed to prevent her husband's garden from bearing fruit. On the contrary, a couple who have given proof of extraordinary fertility by becoming the parents of twins are believed by the Baganda to be endowed with a corresponding power of increasing the fruitfulness of the plantain-trees, which furnish them with their staple food. Some little time after the birth of the twins a ceremony is performed, the object of which clearly is to transmit the reproductive virtue of the parents to the plantains. The mother lies down on her back in the thick grass near the house and places a flower of the plantain between her legs; then her husband comes and knocks the flower away with his genital member.

Continence practised in order to make the crops grow.

To the student who cares to track the devious course of the human mind in its gropings after truth, it is of some interest to observe that the same theoretical belief in the sympathetic influence of the sexes on vegetation, which has led some peoples to indulge their passions as a means of fertilising the earth, has led others to seek the same end by directly opposite means. From the moment that they sowed the maize till the time that they reaped it, the Indians of Nicaragua lived chastely, keeping apart from their wives and sleeping in a separate place. They ate no salt, and drank neither cocoa nor *chicha*, the fermented liquor made from maize; in short the season was for them, as the Spanish historians observes, a time of abstinence. To this day some of the Indian tribes of Central America practise continence for the purpose of thereby promoting the growth of the crops. Thus we are told that before sowing the maize the Kekchi Indians sleep apart from their wives, and eat no flesh for five days, while among the Lanquineros and Cajaboneros the period of abstinence from these carnal pleasures extends to thirteen days.

Again, the sympathetic relation supposed to exist between the commerce of the sexes and the fertility of the earth manifests itself in the belief that illicit love tends, directly or indirectly, to mar that fertility and to blight the crops. Such a belief prevails, for example, among the Karens of Burma. They imagine that adultery or fornication has a powerful influence to injure the harvest. Hence if the crops have been bad for a year or two, and no rain falls, the villagers set down the dearth to secret sins of this kind, and say that the God of heaven and earth is angry with them on that account; and they all unite in making an offering to appease him. Further, whenever adultery or fornication is detected, the elders decide that the sinners must buy a hog and kill it. Then the woman takes one foot of the hog, and the man takes another, and they scrape out furrows in the ground with each foot, and fill the furrows with the blood of the hog. Next they scratch the ground with their hands and pray: 'God of heaven and earth, God of the mountains and hills, I have destroyed the productiveness of the country. Do not be angry with me, do not hate me; but have mercy on me, and compassionate me. Now I repair the mountains, now I heal the hills, and the streams and the lands. May there be no failure of crops, may there be no unsuccessful labours, or unfortunate efforts in my country. Let them be dissipated to the foot of the horizon. Make thy paddy fruitful, thy rice abundant. Make the vegetables to flourish. If we cultivate but little, still grant that we may obtain a little.' After each has prayed thus, they return to the house and say they have repaired the earth. The Battas of Sumatra think that if an unmarried woman is big with child, it is necessary to give her in marriage at once, even to a man of lower rank; for otherwise the people will be infested by tigers, and the crops in the field will not yield an abundant return. The crime of incest, in their opinion, would blast the whole harvest if the wrong were not speedily repaired. Epidemics and other calamities that affect the whole people are almost always traced by them to incest, by which is to be understood any marriage that conflicts with their customs.

In some parts of Africa, also, it is believed that breaches of sexual morality disturb the course of nature, particularly by blighting the fruits of the earth. Thus the negroes of Loango suppose that the intercourse of a man with an immature girl is

Illicit love supposed to blight the fruits of the earth.

punished by God with drought and consequent famine, until the culprits atone for their sin by dancing naked before the king and an assembly of the people, who throw hot gravel and bits of glass at the pair. For example, in the year 1898, it was discovered that a long drought was caused by the misconduct of three girls, who were with child before they had passed through what is called the paint-house, that is, before they had been painted red and secluded for a time in token that they had attained to the age of puberty. The people were very angry and tried to punish or even kill the girls. Amongst the Bavili of Loango, it is believed that if a man breaks the marriage law by marrying a woman of his mother's clan, God will in like manner punish the crime by withholding the rains in their due season. Similar notions of the blighting influence of sexual crime appear to be entertained by the Nandi of British East Africa, for amongst them a girl who has been gotten with child by a warrior, may never look inside of a granary for fear of spoiling the corn. Among the Basutos likewise 'while the corn is exposed to view, all defiled persons are carefully kept from it. If the aid of a man in this state is necessary for carrying home the harvest, he remains at some distance while the sacks are filled, and only approaches to place them upon the draught oxen. He withdraws as soon as the load is deposited at the dwelling, and under no pretext can he assist in pouring the corn into the baskets in which it is preserved.' The nature of the defilement which thus disqualifies a man for handling the corn is not mentioned, but probably it would include unchastity. The Toradjas of Central Celebes ingeniously employ the incest of animals as a rain-charm. For they believe that the anger of the gods at incest or bestiality manifests itself in the form of violent storms, heavy rain, or long drought. Accordingly they think that it is always in their power to enrage the gods by committing incest and so to procure rain when it is needed. However, they abstain from perpetrating the crime among themselves, first, because it would be necessary to put the culprits to death, and second, because the storms thus raised would be so furious that they would do more harm than good. But they fancy that the incest, real or simulated, of animals is a lighter offence, which by discomposing, without exasperating, the higher powers will disturb the balance of nature just enough to improve the

Breaches of sexual morality supposed to prevent rain, and so to blight the fruits of the earth in Africa.

Incest of animals employed as a rain-charm in Africa.

weather. A ceremony of this sort was witnessed by a missionary. Rain was wanted, and the headman of the village had to see that it fell. He took his measures accordingly. Attended by a crowd he carried a cock and a little sow to the river. Here the animals were killed, laid side by side in an intimate embrace, and wrapped tightly up in a piece of cotton. Then the headman engaged in prayer. 'O gods above and gods below,' said he, 'if you have pity on us, and will that we eat food this year, give rain. If you will not give rain, well we have here buried a cock and a sow in an intimate embrace.' By which he meant to say, 'Be angry at this abomination which we have committed, and manifest your anger in storms.'

It would seem that the ancient Greeks and Romans enter- Blighting ef-
tained similar notions as to the wasting effect of incest. Accord- fect at-
ing to Sophocles the land of Thebes suffered from blight, from tributed to
pestilence, and from the sterility both of women and of cattle incest by the
under the reign of Oedipus, who had unwittingly slain his ancient
father and wedded his mother, and the Delphic oracle declared Greeks and
that the only way to restore the prosperity of the country was Irish.
to banish the sinner from it, as if his mere presence withered plants, animals, and women.* No doubt the poet and his hearers set down these public calamities in great part to the guilt of parricide, which rested on Oedipus; but they can hardly have failed to lay much also of the evil at the door of his incest with his mother. Again, in ancient Italy, under the Emperor Claudius, a Roman noble was accused of incest with his sister. He committed suicide, his sister was banished, and the emperor ordered that certain ancient ceremonies traditionally derived from the laws of King Servius Tullius should be performed, and that expiation should be made by the pontiffs at the sacred grove of Diana, probably the famous Arician grove, which has furnished the starting-point of our enquiry. As Diana appears to have been a goddess of fertility in general and of the fruitfulness of women in particular, the atonement made at her sanctuary for incest may perhaps be accepted as evidence that the Romans, like other peoples, attributed to sexual immorality a tendency to blast the fruits both of the earth and of the womb.

Thus the belief that incest or sexual crime in general has power to blast the fruits of the earth is widespread and probably goes back to a very remote antiquity; it may long have preceded

Belief in the blighting effect of incest may have helped to institute the forbidden degrees.

the rise of agriculture. We may conjecture that in its origin the belief was magical rather than religious; in other words, that the blight was at first supposed to be a direct consequence of the act itself rather than a punishment inflicted on the criminal by gods or spirits. Conceived as an unnatural union of the sexes, incest might be thought to subvert the regular processes of reproduction, and so to prevent the earth from yielding its fruits and to hinder animals and men from propagating their kinds. At a later time the anger of spiritual beings would naturally be invoked in order to give a religious sanction to the old taboo. If this was so, it is possible that something of the horror which incest has excited among most, though by no means all, races of men, sprang from this ancient superstition and has been transmitted as an instinct in many nations long after the imaginary ground of it had been forgotten. Certainly a course of conduct which was supposed to endanger or destroy the general supply of food and therefore to strike a blow at the very life of the whole people, could not but present itself to the savage imagination as a crime of the blackest dye, fraught with the most fatal consequences to the public weal. How far such a superstition may in the beginning have operated to prevent the union of near kin, in other words, to institute the system of prohibited degrees which still prevails among the great majority of mankind, both savage and civilised, is a question which deserves to be considered by the historians of marriage.

Explanation of the seeming contradiction in the foregoing customs.

If we ask why it is that similar beliefs should logically lead, among different peoples, to such opposite modes of conduct as strict chastity and more or less open debauchery, the reason, as it presents itself to the primitive mind, is perhaps not very far to seek. If rude man identifies himself, in a manner, with nature; if he fails to distinguish the impulses and processes in himself from the methods which nature adopts to ensure the reproduction of plants and animals, he may leap to one of two conclusions. Either he may infer that by yielding to his appetites he will thereby assist in the multiplication of plants and animals; or he may imagine that the vigour which he refuses to expend in reproducing his own kind, will form as it were a store of energy whereby other creatures, whether vegetable or animal, will somehow benefit in propagating their species.

To readers bred in a religion which is saturated with the ascetic idealism of the East, the explanation which I have given of the rule of continence observed under certain circumstances by rude or savage peoples may seem far-fetched and improbable. They may think that moral purity, which is so intimately associated in their minds with the observance of such a rule, furnishes a sufficient explanation of it; they may hold with Milton* that chastity in itself is a noble virtue, and that the restraint which it imposes on one of the strongest impulses of our animal nature marks out those who can submit to it as men raised above the common herd, and therefore worthy to receive the seal of the divine approbation. However natural this mode of thought may seem to us, it is utterly foreign and indeed incomprehensible to the savage. If he resists on occasion the sexual instinct, it is from no high idealism, no ethereal aspiration after moral purity, but for the sake of some ulterior yet perfectly definite and concrete object, to gain which he is prepared to sacrifice the immediate gratification of his senses. That this is or may be so, the examples I have cited are amply sufficient to prove. They shew that where the instinct of self-preservation, which manifests itself chiefly in the search for food, conflicts or appears to conflict with the instinct which conduces to the propagation of the species, the former instinct, as the primary and more fundamental, is capable of overmastering the latter. In short, the savage is willing to restrain his sexual propensity for the sake of food. Another object for the sake of which he consents to exercise the same self-restraint is victory in war. Not only the warrior in the field but his friends at home will often bridle their sensual appetites from a belief that by so doing they will the more easily overcome their enemies. The fallacy of such a belief, like the belief that the chastity of the sower conduces to the growth of the seed, is plain enough to us; yet perhaps the self-restraint which these and the like beliefs, vain and false as they are, have imposed on mankind, has not been without its utility in bracing and strengthening the breed. For strength of character in the race as in the individual consists mainly in the power of sacrificing the present to the future, of disregarding the immediate temptations of ephemeral pleasure for more distant and lasting sources of satisfaction. The more the power is exercised the higher and

Indirect benefit of some of these superstitious customs. The ascetic view of chastity not understood by the savage.

stronger becomes the character; till the height of heroism is reached in men who renounce the pleasures of life and even life itself for the sake of keeping or winning for others, perhaps in distant ages, the blessings of freedom and truth.*

ii

Dramatic marriages of gods and goddesses as a charm to promote vegetation.

We have seen that according to a widespread belief, which is not without a foundation in fact, plants reproduce their kinds through the sexual union of male and female elements, and that on the principle of homoeopathic or imitative magic this reproduction can be stimulated by the real or mock marriage of men and women, who masquerade for the time being as spirits of vegetation. Such magical dramas have played a great part in the popular festivals of Europe, and based as they are on a very crude conception of natural law, it is clear that they must have been handed down from a remote antiquity. We shall hardly, therefore, err in assuming that they date from a time when the forefathers of the civilised nations of Europe were still barbarians, herding their cattle and cultivating patches of corn in the clearings of the vast forests, which then covered the greater part of the continent, from the Mediterranean to the Arctic Ocean. But if these old spells and enchantments for the growth of leaves and blossoms, of grass and flowers and fruit, have lingered down to our own time in the shape of pastoral plays and popular merry-makings, is it not reasonable to suppose that they survived in less attenuated forms some two thousand years ago among the civilised peoples of antiquity? Or, to put it otherwise, is it not likely that in certain festivals of the ancients we may be able to detect the equivalents of our May Day, Whitsuntide, and Midsummer celebrations, with this difference, that in those days the ceremonies had not yet dwindled into mere shows and pageants, but were still religious or magical rites, in which the actors consciously supported the high parts of gods and goddesses? Now in the first chapter of this book we found reason to believe that the priest who bore the title of King of the Wood at Nemi had for his mate the goddess of the grove, Diana herself. May not he and she, as King and Queen of the Wood, have been serious counterparts of the merry mummers who play the King and Queen of May, the Whitsuntide Bridegroom and Bride in modern Europe? and may not their union have been yearly celebrated in a *theogamy* or divine marriage? Such dramatic weddings of gods and goddesses, as we shall see presently, were carried out as solemn religious rites in many parts of the ancient world; hence there is no intrinsic improbability in the supposition that the sacred grove at Nemi may have been the scene of an annual ceremony of this sort. Direct evidence that it was so there is none, but analogy pleads in favour of the view, as I shall now endeavour to shew.

Diana was essentially a goddess of the woodlands, as Ceres was a goddess of the corn and Bacchus a god of the vine. Her sanctuaries were commonly in groves, indeed every grove was sacred to her, and she is often associated with the forest god Silvanus in dedications. But Diana was not always a mere goddess of trees. Like her Greek sister Artemis, she appears to have developed into a personification of the teeming life of nature, both animal and vegetable. As mistress of the greenwood she would naturally be thought to own the beasts, whether wild or tame, that ranged through it, lurking for their prey in its gloomy depths, munching the fresh leaves and shoots among the boughs, or cropping the herbage in the open glades and dells. Thus she might come to be the patron goddess both of hunters and herdsmen, just as Silvanus was the god not only of woods, but of cattle. Similarly in Finland the wild beasts of the forest were regarded as the herds of the woodland God Tapio and of his stately and beautiful wife. No man might slay one of these animals without the gracious permission of their divine owners. Hence the hunter prayed to the sylvan deities, and vowed rich offerings to them if they would drive the game across his path. And cattle also seem to have enjoyed the protection of those spirits of the woods, both when they were in their stalls and while they strayed in the forest. So in the belief of Russian peasants the spirit Leschiy rules both the wood and all the creatures in it. The bear is to him what the dog is to man; and the migrations of the squirrels, the field-mice, and other denizens of the woods are carried out in obedience to his behests. Success in the chase depends on his favour, and to assure himself of the spirit's help the huntsman lays an offering, generally of bread and salt, on the trunk of a tree in the forest. In White Russia every herdsman must present a cow to Leschiy

Diana a goddess of the woodlands.

Diana not a mere goddess of trees, but, like Artemis, a personification of the teeming life of nature, both animal and vegetable.

A deity of the woods is naturally the patron of the beasts in the woods, both game and cattle.

in summer, and in the Government of Archangel some herds-men have won his favour so far that he even feeds and tends their herds for them. Similarly the forest-god of the Lapps ruled over all the beasts of the forest; they were viewed as his herds, and good or bad luck in hunting depended on his will.

Conceived as the moon, Diana was also a god-dess of crops and of child-birth.

But Diana was not merely a patroness of wild beasts a mistress of woods and hills, of lonely glades and sounding rivers; conceived as the moon, and especially, it would seem, as the yellow harvest moon, she filled the farmer's grange with goodly fruits, and heard the prayers of women in travail. In her sacred grove at Nemi, as we have seen, she was especially worshipped as a goddess of childbirth, who bestowed offspring on men and women.

As a goddess of fertility Diana had herself to be fertile, and for that pur-pose needed a male part-ner.

Now on the principle that the goddess of fertility must herself be fertile, it behoved Diana to have a male partner. Her mate, if the testimony of Servius may be trusted, was that Virbius who had his representative, or perhaps rather his embodiment, in the King of the Wood at Nemi. The aim of their union would be to promote the fruitfulness of the earth, of animals, and of mankind; and it might naturally be thought that this object would be more surely attained if the sacred nuptials were celebrated every year, the parts of the divine bride and bride-groom being played either by their images or by living persons. No ancient writer mentions that this was done in the grove at Nemi; but our knowledge of the Arician ritual is so scanty that the want of information on this head can hardly count as a fatal objection to the theory. That theory, in the absence of direct evidence, must necessarily be based on the analogy of similar customs practised elsewhere.

Marriages of the gods in Babylonia and Assyria.

At Babylon the imposing sanctuary of Bel rose like a pyramid above the city in a series of eight towers or stories, planted one on the top of the other. On the highest tower, reached by an ascent which wound about all the rest, there stood a spacious temple, and in the temple a great bed, magnificently draped and cushioned, with a golden table beside it. In the temple no image was to be seen, and no human being passed the night there, save a single woman, whom, according to the Chaldean priests, the god chose from among all the women of Babylon. They said that the deity himself came into the temple at night and slept in the great bed; and the woman, as a consort of the god, might have no intercourse with mortal man.

At Thebes in Egypt a woman slept in the temple of Ammon as the consort of the god, and, like the human wife of Bel at Babylon, she was said to have no commerce with a man. In Egyptian texts she is often mentioned as 'the divine consort', and usually she was no less a personage than the Queen of Egypt herself. For, according to the Egyptians, their monarchs were actually begotten by the god Ammon, who assumed for the time being the form of the reigning king, and in that disguise had intercourse with the queen. The divine procreation is carved and painted in great detail on the walls of two of the oldest temples in Egypt, those of Deir el Bahari and Luxor; and the inscriptions attached to the paintings leave no doubt as to the meaning of the scenes.

Marriage of the god Ammon to the Queen of Egypt.

At Athens the god of the vine, Dionysus, was annually married to the Queen, and it appears that the consummation of the divine union, as well as the espousals, was enacted at the ceremony; but whether the part of the god was played by a man or an image we do not know. We learn from Aristotle that the ceremony took place, not at the sanctuary in the marshes, but in the old official residence of the King, known as the Cattle-stall, which stood near the Prytaneum or Town-hall on the north-eastern slope of the Acropolis. But whatever the date of the wedding, its object can hardly have been any other than that of ensuring the fertility of the vines and other fruit-trees, of which Dionysus was the god. Thus both in form and in meaning the ceremony would answer to the nuptials of the King and Queen of May.

Marriage of Dionysus to the Queen at Athens.

If at Athens, and probably elsewhere, the vine-god was married to a queen in order that the vines might be loaded with clusters of grapes, there is reason to think that a marriage of a different kind, intended to make the fields wave with yellow corn, was annually celebrated not many miles off, beyond the low hills that bound the plain of Athens on the west. In the great mysteries solemnised at Eleusis in the month of September the union of the sky-god Zeus with the corn-goddess Demeter appears to have been represented by the union of the hierophant with the priestess of Demeter, who acted the parts of god and goddess. But their intercourse was only dramatic or

Marriage of Zeus with Demeter at Eleusis.

symbolical, for the hierophant had temporarily deprived himself
of his virility by an application of hemlock.* The torches having
been extinguished, the pair descended into a murky place, while
the throng of worshippers awaited in anxious suspense the
result of the mystic congress, on which they believed their own
salvation to depend. After a time the hierophant reappeared,
and in a blaze of light silently exhibited to the assembly a
reaped ear of corn, the fruit of the divine marriage. Then in
a loud voice he proclaimed, 'Queen Brimo has brought forth a
sacred boy Brimos', by which he meant, 'The Mighty One has
brought forth the Mighty.' The corn-mother in fact had given
birth to her child, the corn, and her travail-pangs were enacted
in the sacred drama. This revelation of the reaped corn appears
to have been the crowning act of the mysteries. Thus through
the glamour shed round these rites by the poetry and philosophy of later ages there still looms, like a distant landscape
through a sunlit haze, a simple rustic festival designed to cover
the wide Eleusinian plain with a plenteous harvest by wedding
the goddess of the corn to the sky-god, who fertilised the bare
earth with genial showers.

Marriage of
Zeus and
Hera at Pla-
taea.

But Zeus was not always the sky-god, nor did he always
marry the corn-goddess. If in antiquity a traveller, quitting
Eleusis and passing through miles of olive-groves and corn-
fields, had climbed the pine-clad mountains of Cithaeron and
descended through the forest on their northern slope to Plataea,
he might have chanced to find the people of that little Boeotian
town celebrating a different marriage of the great god to a
different goddess. The ceremony is described by a Greek
antiquary whose note-book has fortunately preserved for us not
a few rural customs of ancient Greece, of which the knowledge
would otherwise have perished.*

Every few years the people of Plataea held a festival which
they called the Little Daedala. On the day of the festival they
went out into an ancient oak forest, the trees of which were of
gigantic girth. There they set some boiled meat on the ground,
and watched the birds that gathered round it. When a raven was
observed to carry off a piece of the meat and perch on an oak,
the people followed it and cut down the tree. With the wood of
the tree they made an image, dressed it as a bride, and placed
it on a bullock-cart with a bridesmaid beside it. It seems then

to have been drawn to the banks of the river Asopus and back to the town, attended by a piping and dancing crowd. After the festival the image was put away and kept till the celebration of the Great Daedala, which fell only once in sixty years, and was held by all the people of Boeotia. On this occasion all the images, fourteen in number, that had accumulated from the celebrations of the Little Daedala were dragged on wains in procession to the river Asopus, and then to the top of Mount Cithaeron. There an altar had been constructed of square blocks of wood fitted together, with brushwood heaped over it. Animals were sacrificed by being burned on the altar, and the altar itself, together with the images, was consumed by the flames. The blaze, we are told, rose to a prodigious height and was seen for many miles. To explain the origin of the festival a story ran that once upon a time Hera had quarrelled with Zeus and left him in high dudgeon. To lure her back Zeus gave out that he was about to marry the nymph Plataea, daughter of the river Asopus. He had a fine oak cut down, shaped and dressed as a bride, and conveyed on a bullock-cart. Transported with rage and jealousy, Hera flew to the cart, and tearing off the veil of the pretended bride, discovered the deceit that had been practised on her. Her rage now turned to laughter, and she became reconciled to her husband Zeus.

Thus the custom of marrying gods either to images or to human beings was widespread among the nations of antiquity. The ideas on which such a custom is based are too crude to allow us to doubt that the civilised Babylonians, Egyptians, and Greeks inherited it from their barbarous or savage forefathers. This presumption is strengthened when we find rites of a similar kind in vogue among the lower races. Thus, for example, we are told that once upon a time the Wotyaks of the Malmyz district in Russia were distressed by a series of bad harvests. They did not know what to do, but at last concluded that their powerful but mischievous god Keremet must be angry at being unmarried. So a deputation of elders visited the Wotyaks of Cura and came to an understanding with them on the subject. Then they returned home, laid in a large stock of brandy, and having made ready a gaily decked waggon and horses, they drove in procession with bells ringing, as they do when they are fetching home a bride, to the sacred grove at Cura. There they

The custom of marrying gods to images or to living persons is found also among uncivilised peoples. Custom of the Wotyaks.

ate and drank merrily all night, and next morning they cut a square piece of turf in the grove and took it home with them. After this, though it fared well with the people of Malmyz, it fared ill with the people of Cura; for in Malmyz the bread was good, but in Cura it was bad. Hence the men of Cura who had consented to the marriage were blamed and roughly handled by their indignant fellow-villagers. 'What they meant by this marriage ceremony', says the writer who reports it, 'it is not easy to imagine. Perhaps, as Bechterew thinks, they meant to marry Keremet to the kindly and fruitful Mukylčin, the Earth-wife, in order that she might influence him for good.' This carrying of turf, like a bride, in a waggon from a sacred grove resembles the Plataean custom of carting an oak log as a bride from an ancient oak forest; and we have seen ground for thinking that the Plataean ceremony, like its Wotyak counter-part, was intended as a charm to secure fertility. When wells are dug in Bengal, a wooden image of a god is made and married to the goddess of water.

Custom of the Peruvian Indians.

Often the bride destined for the god is not a log or a clod, but a living woman of flesh and blood. The Indians of a village in Peru have been known to marry a beautiful girl, about fourteen years of age, to a stone shaped like a human being, which they regarded as a god (*huaca*). All the villagers took part in the marriage ceremony, which lasted three days, and was attended with much revelry. The girl thereafter remained a virgin and sacrified to the idol for the people. They shewed her the utmost reverence and deemed her divine. The Blackfoot Indians of North America used to worship the Sun as their chief god, and they held a festival every year in his honour. Four days before the new moon of August the tribe halted on its march, and all hunting was suspended. Bodies of mounted men were on duty day and night to carry out the orders of the high priest of the Sun. He enjoined the people to fast and to take vapour baths during the four days before the new moon. Moreover, with the help of his council, he chose the Vestal who was to represent the Moon and to be married to the Sun at the festival. She might be either a virgin or a woman who had had but one husband. Any girl or woman found to have discharged the sacred duties without fulfilling the prescribed conditions was put to death. On the third day of preparation, after the last

Marriage of a woman to the Sun among the Blackfoot Indians.

purification had been observed, they built a round temple of the Sun. Posts were driven into the ground in a circle; these were connected with cross-pieces, and the whole was covered with leaves. In the middle stood the sacred pole, supporting the roof. A bundle of many small branches of sacred wood, wrapped in a splendid buffalo robe, crowned the summit of the temple. The entrance was on the east, and within the sanctuary stood an altar on which rested the head of a buffalo. Beside the altar was the place reserved for the Vestal. Here, on a bed prepared for her, she slept 'the sleep of war', as it was called. Her other duties consisted in maintaining a sacred fire of fragrant herbs, in presenting a lighted pipe to her husband the Sun, and in telling the high priest the dream she dreamed during 'the sleep of war'. On learning it the priest had it proclaimed to the whole nation to the beat of drum. Every year about the middle of March, when the season for fishing with the drag-net began, the Algonquins and Hurons married their nets to two young girls, aged six or seven. At the wedding feast the net was placed between the two maidens, and was exhorted to take courage and catch many fish. The reason for choosing the brides so young was to make sure that they were virgins.

Marriage of girls to fishing nets among the Hurons and Algonquins.

The Oraons of Bengal worship the Earth as a goddess, and annually celebrate her marriage with the Sun-god Dharmē at the time when the *sāl* tree is in blossom. The ceremony is as follows. All bathe, then the men repair to the sacred grove (*sarnā*), while the women assemble at the house of the village priest. After sacrificing some fowls to the Sun-god and the demon of the grove, the men eat and drink. 'The priest is then carried back to the village on the shoulders of a strong man. Near the village the women meet the men and wash their feet. With beating of drums and singing, dancing, and jumping, all proceed to the priest's house, which has been decorated with leaves and flowers. Then the usual form of marriage is performed between the priest and his wife, symbolizing the supposed union between Sun and Earth. After the ceremony all eat and drink and make merry; they dance and sing obscene songs, and finally indulge in the vilest orgies. The object is to move the mother earth to become fruitful.'

Sacred Marriage of the Sun-god and Earth-goddess among the Oraons.

CHAPTER 8

THE KINGS OF ROME

i

Egeria at
Nemi a
nymph of
water and of
the oak, per-
haps a form
of Diana.

FROM the foregoing survey of custom and legend we may infer that the sacred marriage of the powers both of vegetation and of water has been celebrated by many peoples for the sake of promoting the fertility of the earth, on which the life of animals and men ultimately depends, and that in such rites the part of the divine bridegroom or bride is often sustained by a man or woman. The evidence may, therefore, lend some countenance to the conjecture that in the sacred grove at Nemi, where the powers of vegetation and of water manifested themselves in the fair forms of shady woods, tumbling cascades, and glassy lake, a marriage like that of our King and Queen of May was annually celebrated between the mortal King of the Wood and the immortal Queen of the Wood, Diana. In this connexion an important figure in the grove was the water-nymph Egeria, who was worshipped by pregnant women because she, like Diana, could grant them an easy delivery. From this it seems fairly safe to conclude that, like many other springs, the water of Egeria was credited with a power of facilitating conception as well as delivery. The votive offerings found on the spot, which clearly refer to the begetting of children, may possibly have been dedicated to Egeria rather than to Diana, or perhaps we should rather say that the water-nymph Egeria is only another form of the great nature-goddess Diana herself, the mistress of sounding rivers as well as of umbrageous woods, who had her home by the lake and her mirror in its calm waters, and whose Greek counterpart Artemis loved to haunt meres and springs. The identification of Egeria with Diana is confirmed by a statement of Plutarch that Egeria was one of the oak-nymphs whom the Romans believed to preside over every green oak-grove; for while Diana was a goddess of the woodlands in general she appears to have been intimately associated with oaks in particular, especially at her sacred grove of Nemi. Perhaps, then, Egeria was the fairy of a spring that flowed from the roots of a sacred oak. Such a spring is said to have gushed from the foot of the great oak at Dodona, and from its murmurous flow the priestess drew oracles. Among the Greeks a draught of water from certain sacred springs or wells was supposed to confer prophetic powers. This would explain the more than mortal wisdom with which, according to tradition, Egeria inspired her royal husband or lover Numa. When we remember how very often in early society the king is held responsible for the fall of rain and the fruitfulness of the earth, it seems hardly rash to conjecture that in the legend of the nuptials of Numa and Egeria we have a reminiscence of a sacred marriage which the old Roman kings regularly contracted with a goddess of vegetation and water for the purpose of enabling him to discharge his divine or magical functions. In such a rite the part of the goddess might be played either by an image or a woman, and if by a woman, probably by the Queen. If there is any truth in this conjecture, we may suppose that the King and Queen of Rome masqueraded as god and goddess at their marriage, exactly as the King and Queen of Egypt appear to have done. The legend of Numa and Egeria points to a sacred grove rather than to a house as the scene of the nuptial union, which, like the marriage of the King and Queen of May, or of the vine-god and the Queen of Athens, may have been annually celebrated as a charm to ensure the fertility not only of the earth but of man and beast. Now, according to some accounts, the scene of the marriage was no other than the sacred grove of Nemi, and on quite independent grounds we have been led to suppose that in that same grove the King of the Wood was wedded to Diana. The convergence of the two distinct lines of enquiry suggests that the legendary union of the Roman king with Egeria may have been a reflection or duplicate of the union of the King of the Wood with Egeria or her double Diana. This does not imply that the Roman kings ever served as Kings of the Wood in the Arician grove, but only that they may originally have been invested with a sacred character of the same general kind, and may have held office on similar terms. To be more explicit, it is possible that they reigned, not by right of birth, but in virtue of their supposed divinity as representatives or embodiments of a god, and that as such they mated with a goddess, and had to prove their fitness from time to time to discharge their divine

The legend of the nuptials of Numa and Egeria may be a reminiscence of a sacred marriage which the kings of Rome contracted with a goddess of water and of vegetation.

functions by engaging in a severe bodily struggle, which may often have proved fatal to them, leaving the crown to their victorious adversary. Our knowledge of the Roman kingship is far too scanty to allow us to affirm any one of these propositions with confidence; but at least there are some scattered hints or indications of a similarity in all these respects between the priests of Nemi and the kings of Rome, or perhaps rather between their remote predecessors in the dark ages which preceded the dawn of legend.

ii

The Roman king seems to have personated Jupiter and worn his costume.

In the first place, then, it would seem that the Roman king personated no less a deity than Jupiter himself. For down to imperial times victorious generals celebrating a triumph, and magistrates presiding at the games in the Circus, wore the costume of Jupiter, which was borrowed for the occasion from his great temple on the Capitol; and it has been held with a high degree of probability both by ancients and moderns that in so doing they copied the traditional attire and insignia of the Roman kings. They rode a chariot drawn by four laurel-crowned horses through the city, where every one else went on foot; they wore purple robes embroidered or spangled with gold; in the right hand they bore a branch of laurel and in the left hand an ivory sceptre topped with an eagle; a wreath of laurel crowned their brows; their face was reddened with vermilion; and over their head a slave held a heavy crown of massy gold fashioned in the likeness of oak leaves. In this attire the assimilation of the man to the god comes out above all in the eagle-topped sceptre, the oaken crown, and the reddened face. For the eagle was the bird of Jove, the oak was his sacred tree, and the face of his image standing in his four-horse chariot on the Capitol was in like manner regularly dyed red on festivals; indeed, so important was it deemed to keep the divine features properly rouged that one of the first duties of the censors was to contract for having this done. The Greeks sometimes painted red the face or the whole body of the wine-god Dionysus. These customs may have been a substitute for an older practice of feeding a god by smearing the face, and especially the lips, of his idol with the blood of a sacrificial victim. Many examples of such a practice might be adduced from the religion of barbarous peoples. As the triumphal procession always ended in the temple of Jupiter on the Capitol, it was peculiarly appropriate that the head of the victor should be graced by a crown of oak leaves, for not only was every oak consecrated to Jupiter, but the Capitoline temple of the god was said to have been built by Romulus beside a sacred oak, venerated by shepherds, to which the king attached the spoils won by him from the enemy's general in battle. We are expressly told that the oak crown was sacred to Capitoline Jupiter; a passage of Ovid proves that it was regarded as the god's special emblem. Writing in exile on the shores of the Black Sea, the poet sends the book which he has just composed to Rome to be published there; he personifies the volume and imagines it passing along the Sacred Way and up to the door of the emperor's stately palace on the Palatine hill. Above the portal hung shining arms and a crown of oak leaves. At the sight the poet starts: 'Is this, quoth I, the house of Jove? For sure to my prophetic soul the oaken crown was reason good to think it so.'*

The oak crown as an emblem of Jupiter and of the Roman emperors.

According to a tradition which we have no reason to reject, Rome was founded by settlers from Alba Longa, a city situated on the slope of the Alban hills, overlooking the lake and the Campagna. Hence if the Roman kings claimed to be representatives or embodiments of Jupiter, the god of the sky, of the thunder, and of the oak, it is natural to suppose that the kings of Alba, from whom the founder of Rome traced his descent, may have set up the same claim before them. Now the Alban dynasty bore the name of Silvii or Wood, and it can hardly be without significance that in the vision of the historic glories of Rome revealed to Aeneas in the underworld, Virgil, an antiquary as well as a poet, should represent all the line of Silvii as crowned with oak. A chaplet of oak leaves would thus seem to have been part of the insignia of the old kings of Alba Longa as of their successors the kings of Rome; in both cases it marked the monarch as the human representative of the oak-god. With regard to Silvius, the first king of the Alban dynasty, we are told that he got his name because he had been born or brought up in the forest, and that when he came to man's estate he contested the kingdom with his kinsman Julus, whose name, as

The kings of Alba seem also to have claimed to represent Jupiter.

The Silvii and the Julii.

some of the ancients themselves perceived, means the Little
Jupiter. The people decided in favour of Silvius, but his rival
Julus was consoled for the loss of the crown by being invested
with religious authority and the office of chief pontiff, or
perhaps rather of Flamen Dialis, the highest dignity after the
kingship. From this Julus or Little Jupiter, the noble house of
the Julii, and hence the first emperors of Rome, believed
themselves to be sprung.

The Alban
kings seem
to have been
expected to
make
thunder and
rain for the
good of their
subjects.

But in ceding the pontificate to their rivals, it would seem
that the reigning dynasty of the Silvii or Woods by no means
renounced their own claim to personate the god of the oak and
the thunder; for the Roman annals record that one of them,
Romulus, Remulus, or Amulius Silvius by name, set up for
being a god in his own person, the equal or superior of Jupiter.
To support his pretensions and overawe his subjects, he constructed machines whereby he mimicked the clap of thunder
and the flash of lightning. Diodorus relates that in the season
of fruitage, when thunder is loud and frequent, the king
commanded his soldiers to drown the roar of heaven's artillery
by clashing their swords against their shields. But he paid the
penalty of his impiety, for he perished, he and his house, struck
by a thunderbolt in the midst of a dreadful storm. Swollen by
the rain, the Alban lake rose in flood and drowned his palace.
But still, says an ancient historian, when the water is low and
the surface unruffled by a breeze, you may see the ruins of the
palace at the bottom of the clear lake. Taken along with the
similar story of Salmoneus, king of Elis, this legend points to a
real custom observed by the early kings of Greece and Italy,
who like their fellows in Africa down to modern times may have
been expected to produce rain and thunder for the good of the
crops. The priestly king Numa passed for an adept in the art of
drawing down lightning from the sky. Mock thunder, we know,
has been made by various peoples as a rain-charm in modern
times; why should it not have been made by kings in antiquity?

Thus, if the kings of Alba and Rome imitated Jupiter as god
of the oak by wearing a crown of oak leaves, they seem also to
have copied him in his character of a weather-god by pretending
to make thunder and lightning. And if they did so, it is probable
that, like Jupiter in heaven and many kings on earth, they also
acted as public rain-makers, wringing showers from the dark

sky by their enchantments whenever the parched earth cried out for the refreshing moisture. At Rome the sluices of heaven were opened by means of a sacred stone, and the ceremony appears to have formed part of the ritual of Jupiter Elicius, the god who elicits from the clouds the flashing lightning and the dripping rain. And who so well fitted to perform the ceremony as the king, the living representative of the sky-god?

The conclusion which we have reached as to the kings of Rome and Alba probably holds good of all the kings of ancient Latium: each of them, we may suppose, represented or embodied the local Jupiter. For we can hardly doubt that of old every Latin town or settlement had its own Jupiter, as every town and almost every church in modern Italy has its own Madonna; and like the Baal of the Semites the local Jupiter was commonly worshipped on high places. Wooded heights, round which the rain-clouds gather, were indeed the natural sanctuaries for a god of the sky, the rain, and the oak. At Rome he occupied one summit of the Capitoline hill, while the other summit was assigned to his wife Juno, whose temple, with the long flight of stairs leading up to it, has for ages been appropriately replaced by the church of St Mary 'in the altar of the sky'* (*in Araceli*). *Many local Jupiters in Latium.* *Capitoline Jupiter and Juno.*

As the oak crown was sacred to Jupiter and Juno on the Capitol, so we may suppose it was on the Alban Mount, from which the Capitoline worship was derived. Thus the oak-god would have his oak-goddess in the sacred oak grove. So at Dodona the oak-god Zeus was coupled with Dione, whose very name is only a dialectically different form of Juno; and so on the top of Mount Cithaeron he was periodically wedded to an oaken image of Hera. It is probable, though it cannot be positively proved, that the sacred marriage of Jupiter and Juno was annually celebrated by all the peoples of the Latin stock in the month which they named after the goddess, the midsummer month of June. Now on the first of June the Roman pontiffs performed certain rites in the grove of Helernus beside the Tiber, and on the same day, and perhaps in the same place, a nymph of the grove, by name Carna, received offerings of lard and bean-porridge. She was said to be a huntress, chaste and coy, who gave the slip to her lovers in the depths of the wood, but was caught by Janus. Some took her to be Diana herself. If she were indeed a form of that goddess, her union with Janus, *Sacred marriage of Jupiter and Juno.* *Janus and Carna.*

that is, Dianus, would be appropriate; and as she had a chapel on the Caelian hill, which was once covered with oak-woods, she may have been, like Egeria, an oak-nymph. Further, Janus, or Dianus, and Diana, were originally mere doubles of Jupiter and Juno, with whom they coincide in name and to some extent in function. Hence it appears to be not impossible that the rite celebrated by the pontiffs on the first of June in the sacred grove of Helernus was the marriage of Jupiter and Juno under the forms of Janus and Diana.

At the sacred marriage of Jupiter and Juno in later times the parts of the deities may have been acted by the Flamen Dialis and the Flaminica.

If at any time of the year the Romans celebrated the sacred marriage of Jupiter and Juno, as the Greeks commonly celebrated the corresponding marriage of Zeus and Hera, we may suppose that under the Republic the ceremony was either performed over images of the divine pair or acted by the Flamen Dialis and his wife the Flaminica. For the Flamen Dialis was the priest of Jove; indeed, ancient and modern writers have regarded him, with much probability, as a living image of Jupiter, a human embodiment of the sky-god. In earlier times the Roman king, as representative of Jupiter, would naturally play the part of the heavenly bridegroom at the sacred marriage, while his queen would figure as the heavenly bride, just as in Egypt the king and queen masqueraded in the character of deities, and as at Athens the queen annually wedded the vine-god Dionysus. That the Roman king and queen should act the parts of Jupiter and Juno would seem all the more natural because these deities themselves bore the title of King and Queen. Even if the office of Flamen Dialis existed under the kings, as it appears to have done, the double representation of Jupiter by the king and the flamen need not have seemed extraordinary to the Romans of the time. The

The Flamen and Flaminica may have been the deputies of the king and queen.

same sort of duplication, as we saw, appears to have taken place at Alba, when the Julii were allowed to represent the supreme god in the character of Little Jupiters, while the royal dynasty of the Silvii continued to wield the divine thunder and lightning. And long ages afterwards, history repeating itself, another member of the Julian house, the first emperor of Rome, was deified in his lifetime under the title of Jupiter, while a flamen was appointed to do for him what the Flamen Dialis did for the heavenly Jove. It is said that Numa, the typical priestly king, at first himself discharged the functions of Flamen Dialis, but afterwards appointed a separate priest of Jupiter with that title, in order that the kings, untrammeled by the burdensome religious observances attached to the priesthood, might be free to lead their armies to battle. The tradition may be substantially correct; for analogy shews that the functions of a priestly king are too harassing and too incongruous to be permanently united in the same hands, and that sooner or later the holder of the office seeks to rid himself of part of his burden by deputing to others, according to his temper and tastes, either his civil or his religious duties. Hence we may take it as probable that the fighting kings of Rome, tired of parading as Jupiter and of observing all the elaborate ritual, all the tedious restrictions which the character of godhead entailed on them, were glad to relegate these pious mummeries to a substitute, in whose hands they left the crosier at home while they went forth to wield the sharp Roman sword abroad. This would explain why the traditions of the later kings, from Tullus Hostilius onwards, exhibit so few traces of sacred or priestly functions adhering to their office. Among the ceremonies which they henceforward performed by deputy may have been the rite of the sacred marriage.

CHAPTER 9

THE SUCCESSION TO THE KINGDOM

What was the rule of succession to the Latin kingship?

On the other hand none of the Roman kings was immediately succeeded by his son, but three were succeeded by their sons-in-law, who were foreigners.

This suggests that the kingship was transmitted in the female line and was held by foreigners who married the royal princesses.

BUT we have still to ask, What was the rule of succession to the kingdom among the old Latin tribes? According to tradition there were in all eight kings of Rome, and with regard to the five last of them, at all events, we can hardly doubt that they actually sat on the throne, and that the traditional history of their reigns is, in its main outlines, correct. Now it is very remarkable that though the first king of Rome, Romulus, is said to have been descended from the royal house of Alba, in which the kingship is represented as hereditary in the male line, not one of the Roman kings was immediately succeeded by his son on the throne. Yet several left sons or grandsons behind them. On the other hand, one of them was descended from a former king through his mother, not through his father, and three of the kings, namely Tatius, the elder Tarquin, and Servius Tullius, were succeeded by their sons-in-law, who were all either foreigners or of foreign descent. This suggests that the right to the kingship was transmitted in the female line, and was actually exercised by foreigners who married the royal princesses. To put it in technical language, the succession to the kingship at Rome and probably in Latium generally would seem to have been determined by certain rules which have moulded early society in many parts of the world, namely exogamy, *beena* marriage, and female kinship or mother-kin. Exogamy is the rule which obliges a man to marry a woman of a different clan from his own; *beena* marriage is the rule that he must leave the home of his birth and live with his wife's people; and female kinship or mother-kin is the system of tracing relationship and transmitting the family name through women instead of through men.* If these principles regulated descent of the kingship among the ancient Latins, the state of things in this respect would be somewhat as follows. The political and religious centre of each community would be the perpetual fire on the king's hearth tended by Vestal Virgins of the royal clan. The king would be a man of another clan, perhaps of another town or even of another race, who had married a daughter of his predecessor and received the kingdom with her. The children whom he had by her would inherit their mother's name, not his; the daughters would remain at home; the sons, when they grew up, would go away into the world, marry, and settle in their wives' country, whether as kings or commoners. Of the daughters who stayed at home, some or all would be dedicated as Vestal Virgins for a longer or shorter time to the service of the fire on the hearth, and one of them would in time become the consort of her father's successor.

This hypothesis has the advantage of explaining in a simple and natural way some obscure features in the traditional history of the Latin kingship. Thus the legends which tell how Latin kings were born of virgin mothers and divine fathers become at least more intelligible. For, stripped of their fabulous element, tales of this sort mean no more than that a woman has been gotten with child by a man unknown; and this uncertainty as to fatherhood is more easily compatible with a system of kinship which ignores paternity than with one which makes it all important. If at the birth of the Latin kings their fathers were really unknown, the fact points either to a general looseness of life in the royal family or to a special relaxation of moral rules on certain occasions, when men and women reverted for a season to the licence of an earlier age. Such Saturnalias are not uncommon at some stages of social evolution. In our own country traces of them long survived in the practices of May Day and Whitsuntide, if not of Christmas. Children born of the more or less promiscuous intercourse which characterises festivals of this kind would naturally be fathered on the god to whom the particular festival was dedicated.

In this connexion it may not be without significance that a festival of jollity and drunkenness was celebrated by the plebeians and slaves at Rome on Midsummer Day, and that the festival was specially associated with the fire-born King Servius Tullius, being held in honour of Fortuna, the goddess who loved Servius as Egeria loved Numa. The popular merrymakings at this season included footraces and boat-races; the Tiber was gay with flower-wreathed boats, in which young folk sat quaffing wine. The festival appears to have been a sort of

This hypothesis explains some obscure features in the traditional history of the Latin kings, such as the stories of their miraculous birth.

The Latin kings perhaps begotten at a Saturnalia.

The Roman festival of Midsummer was a kind of Saturnalia, and was specially associated with the fire-born King Servius Tullius.

Midsummer Saturnalia answering to the real Saturnalia which fell at Midwinter. In modern Europe, as we shall learn later on, the great Midsummer festival has been above all a festival of lovers and of fire; one of its principal features is the pairing of sweethearts, who leap over the bonfires hand in hand or throw flowers across the flames to each other. And many omens of love and marriage are drawn from the flowers which bloom at this mystic season. It is the time of the roses and of love. Yet the innocence and beauty of such festivals in modern times ought not to blind us to the likelihood that in earlier days they were marked by coarser features, which were probably of the essence of the rites. Indeed, among the rude Esthonian peasantry these features seem to have lingered down to our own generation, if not to the present day. One other feature in the Roman celebration of Midsummer deserves to be specially noticed. The custom of rowing in flower-decked boats on the river on this day proves that it was to some extent a water festival; and, as we shall learn later on, water has always, down to modern times, played a conspicuous part in the rites of Midsummer Day, which explains why the Church in throwing its cloak over the old heathen festival, chose to dedicate it to St John the Baptist.

But the uncertainty as to the paternity of the Roman kings may only mean that in later times the names of their fathers were forgotten.

The hypothesis that the Latin kings may have been begotten at an annual festival of love is necessarily a mere conjecture, though the traditional birth of Numa on the festival of the Parilia, when shepherds leaped across the spring bonfires, as lovers leap across the Midsummer fires, may perhaps be thought to lend it a faint colour of probability. But it is quite possible that the uncertainty as to their fathers may not have arisen till long after the death of the kings, when their figures began to melt away into the cloudland of fable, assuming fantastic shapes and gorgeous colouring as they passed from earth to heaven. If they were alien immigrants, strangers and pilgrims in the land they ruled over, it would be natural enough that the people should forget their lineage, and forgetting it should provide them with another, which made up in lustre what it lacked in truth. The final apotheosis, which represented the kings as not merely sprung from gods but as themselves deities incarnate, would be much facilitated if in their lifetime, as we have seen reason to think, they had actually laid claim to divinity.

If among the Latins the women of royal blood always stayed at home and received as their consorts men of another stock, and often of another country, who reigned as kings in virtue of their marriage with a native princess, we can understand not only why foreigners wore the crown at Rome, but also why foreign names occur in the list of the Alban kings. In a state of society where nobility is reckoned only through women—in other words, where descent through the mother is everything, and descent through the father is nothing—no objection will be felt to uniting girls of the highest rank to men of humble birth, even to aliens or slaves, provided that in themselves the men appear to be suitable mates. What really matters is that the royal stock, on which the prosperity and even the existence of the people is supposed to depend, should be perpetuated in a vigorous and efficient form, and for this purpose it is necessary that the women of the royal family should bear children to men who are physically and mentally fit, according to the standard of early society, to discharge the important duty of procreation. Thus the personal qualities of the kings at this stage of social evolution are deemed of vital importance. If they, like their consorts, are of royal and divine descent, so much the better; but it is not essential that they should be so.

Where descent is traced through women only, girls of the highest rank may be married to men of humble birth, even to aliens and slaves.

The hypothesis which we have been led to frame of the rule of succession to the Latin kingship will be confirmed by analogy if we can shew that elsewhere, under a system of female kinship, the paternity of the kings is a matter of indifference—nay, that men who are born slaves may, like Servius Tullius, marry royal princesses and be raised to the throne. Now this is true of the Tshi-speaking peoples of the Gold Coast in West Africa.* Thus in Ashantee, where the kingdom descends in the female line to the king's brothers and afterwards to the sons of his sister in preference to his own sons, the sisters of the reigning monarch are free to marry or intrigue with whom they please, provided only that their husband or lover be a very strong and handsome man, in order that the kings whom he begets may be men of finer presence than their subjects. It matters not how low may be the rank and position of the king's father. If the king's sisters, however, have no sons, the throne will pass to the king's own son, and failing a son, to the chief vassal or the chief slave. But in the Fantee country the principal slave succeeds to

In Ashantee, where the kingdom descends through women, the rank of the king's father is not regarded.

the exclusion of the son. So little regard is paid by these people to the lineage, especially the paternal lineage, of their kings. Yet Ashantee has attained a barbaric civilisation as high perhaps as that of any negro state, and probably not at all inferior to that of the petty Latin kingdoms at the dawn of history.

Traces of female descent of the kingship in ancient Greece.

At Athens, as at Rome, we find traces of succession to the throne by marriage with a royal princess; for two of the most ancient kings of Athens, namely Cecrops and Amphictyon, are said to have married the daughters of their predecessors. This tradition is confirmed by the evidence, which I shall adduce presently, that at Athens male kinship was preceded by female kinship.

With this rule of descent of the kingship males rule over different kingdoms in successive generations.

Further, if I am right in supposing that in ancient Latium the royal families kept their daughters at home and sent forth their sons to marry princesses and reign among their wives' people, it will follow that the male descendants would reign in successive generations over different kingdoms. Now this seems to have happened both in ancient Greece and in ancient Sweden; from which we may legitimately infer that it was a custom practised by more than one branch of the Aryan stock in Europe. Take, for instance, the great house of Aeacus, the

Migrations of the male descendants of Aeacus.

grandfather of Achilles and Ajax. Aeacus himself reigned in Aegina, but his descendants, as has been justly observed, 'from the beginning went forth to other lands'. His son Telamon migrated to the island of Salamis, married the king's daughter, and reigned over the country. Telamon's son Teucer, in his turn, migrated to Cyprus, wedded the king's daughter, and succeeded his father-in-law on the throne. Again, Peleus, another son of Aeacus, quitted his native land and went away to Phthia in Thessaly, where he received the hand of the king's

These migrations not understood in later times.

daughter, and with her a third of the kingdom. Various reasons are assigned by ancient Greek writers for these migrations of the princes. A common one is that the king's son had been banished for murder. This would explain very well why he fled his own land, but it is no reason at all why he should become king of another. We may suspect that such reasons are afterthoughts devised by writers who, accustomed to the rule that a son should succeed to his father's property and kingdom, were hard put to it to account for so many traditions of kings' sons who quitted the land of their birth to reign over a foreign kingdom. In Scandinavian tradition we meet with traces of similar customs. For we read of daughters' husbands who received a share of the kingdoms of their royal fathers-in-law, even when these fathers-in-law had sons of their own; in particular, during the five generations which preceded Harold the Fair-haired, male members of the Ynglingar family, which is said to have come from Sweden, are reported in the *Heimskringla* or *Sagas of the Norwegian Kings* to have obtained at least six provinces in Norway by marriage with the daughters of the local kings.

Traces of similar migrations in Scandinavian tradition.

Thus it would seem that among some Aryan peoples, at a certain stage of their social evolution, it has been customary to regard women and not men as the channels in which royal blood flows, and to bestow the kingdom in each successive generation on a man of another family, and often of another country, who marries one of the princesses and reigns over his wife's people. A common type of popular tale, which relates how an adventurer, coming to a strange land, wins the hand of the king's daughter and with her the half or the whole of the kingdom, may well be a reminiscence of a real custom.

A reminiscence of the transmission of the kingship through women is preserved in popular tales.

Where usages and ideas of this sort prevail, it is obvious that the kingship is merely an appanage of marriage with a woman of the blood royal. The old Danish historian Saxo Grammaticus puts this view of the kingship very clearly in the mouth of Hermutrude, a legendary queen of Scotland, and her statement is all the more significant because, as we shall see presently, it reflects the actual practice of the Pictish kings. 'Indeed she was a queen,' says Hermutrude, 'and but that her sex gainsaid it, might be deemed a king; nay (and this is yet truer), whomsoever she thought worthy of her bed was at once a king, and she yielded her kingdom with herself. Thus her sceptre and her hand went together.' Wherever a custom of this sort is observed, a man may clearly acquire the kingdom just as well by marrying the widow as the daughter of his predecessor. This is what Aegisthus did at Mycenae, and what Hamlet's uncle Feng and Hamlet's successor Wiglet did in Denmark; all three slew their predecessors, married their widows, and then sat peacefully on the throne.*

Where such customs prevail, the kingship is an appanage of marriage with a princess.

Bede tells us that down to his own time, in the early part of the eighth century, whenever a doubt arose as to the succession, the Picts chose their king from the female rather than the male line.* The statement is amply confirmed by historical evidence. For we possess a list of the Pictish kings and their fathers which was drawn up in the reign of Cenaed, King of the Scots, towards the end of the tenth century; and for the period from the year 583 to the year 840 the register is authenticated by the Irish Annals of Tigernach and Ulster. Now, it is significant that in this list the fathers of the kings are never themselves kings; in other words, no king was succeeded on the throne by his son. Further, if we may judge by their names, the fathers of the Pictish kings were not Picts but foreigners—men of Irish, Cymric, or English race. The inference from these facts seems to be that among the Picts the royal family was exogamous, and that the crown descended in the female line; in other words, that the princesses married men of another clan or even of another race, and that their issue by these strangers sat on the throne, whether they succeeded in a prescribed order according to birth, or whether they were elected from among the sons of princesses, as the words of Bede might be taken to imply.

Succession to the throne determined by a race.

Sometimes apparently the right to the hand of the princess and to the throne has been determined by a race. The Alitemnian Libyans awarded the kingdom to the fleetest runner. Amongst the old Prussians, candidates for nobility raced on horseback to the king, and the one who reached him first was ennobled. According to tradition the earliest games at Olympia were held by Endymion, who set his sons to run a race for the kingdom. His tomb was said to be at the point of the racecourse from which the runners started. The famous story of Pelops and Hippodamia is perhaps only another version of the legend that the first races at Olympia were run for no less a prize than a kingdom.

Greek traditions of princesses whose hands were won in a race.

Custom of racing for a bride among the Kirghiz and Calmucks.

These traditions may very well reflect a real custom of racing for a bride, for such a custom appears to have prevailed among various peoples, though in practice it has degenerated into a mere form or pretence. Thus 'there is one race, called the "Love Chase", which may be considered a part of the form of marriage among the Kirghiz.* In this the bride, armed with a formidable whip, mounts a fleet horse, and is pursued by all the young men who make any pretensions to her hand. She will be given as a prize to the one who catches her, but she has the right, besides urging on her horse to the utmost, to use her whip, often with no mean force, to keep off those lovers who are unwelcome to her, and she will probably favour the one whom she has already chosen in her heart. As, however, by Kirghiz custom, a suitor to the hand of a maiden is obliged to give a certain *kalym*, or purchase-money, and an agreement must be made with the father for the amount of dowry which he gives his daughter, the "Love Chase" is a mere matter of form.' Similarly 'the ceremony of marriage among the Calmucks is performed on horseback. A girl is first mounted, who rides off in full speed. Her lover pursues; and if he overtakes her, she becomes his wife, and the marriage is consummated on the spot, after which she returns with him to his tent. But it sometimes happens that the woman does not wish to marry the person by whom she is pursued, in which case she will not suffer him to overtake her; and we were assured that no instance occurs of a Calmuck girl being thus caught unless she has a partiality for her pursuer. If she dislikes him she rides, to use the language of English sportsmen, "neck or nothing", until she has completely escaped, or until the pursuer's horse is tired out, leaving her at liberty to return, to be afterwards chased by some more favoured admirer.' The race for the bride is found also among the Koryaks of north-eastern Asia. It takes place in a large tent, round which many separate compartments called *pologs* are arranged in a continuous circle. The girl gets a start and is clear of the marriage if she can run through all the compartments without being caught by the bridegroom. The women of the encampment place every obstacle in the man's way, tripping him up, belabouring him with switches, and so forth, so that he has little chance of succeeding unless the girl wishes it and waits for him. Among some of the rude indigenous tribes of the Malay Peninsula 'marriage is preceded by a singular ceremony. An old man presents the future couple to the assembled guests, and, followed by their families, he leads them to a great circle, round which the girl sets off to run as fast as she can. If the young man succeeds in overtaking her, she becomes his mate; otherwise he loses all rights, which happens especially when he is not so fortunate as to please his bride.' Another writer tells us that among these savages, when there is a river at hand, the race takes place on the water, the bride paddling away in one

Custom of racing for a bride among the Calmucks and some tribes of the Malay Peninsula.

canoe and pursued by the bridegroom in another. Before the wedding procession starts for the bridegroom's hut, a Caffre bride is allowed to make one last bid for freedom, and a young man is told off to catch her. Should he fail to do so, she is theoretically allowed to return to her father, and the whole performance has to be repeated; but the flight of the bride is usually a pretence.

Thus it appears that the right to marry a girl, and especially a princess, has often been conferred as a prize in an athletic contest. There would be no reason, therefore, for surprise if the Roman kings, before bestowing their daughters in marriage, should have resorted to this ancient mode of testing the personal qualities of their future sons-in-law and successors. If my theory is correct, the Roman king and queen personated Jupiter and his divine consort, and in the character of these divinities went through the annual ceremony of a sacred marriage for the purpose of causing the crops to grow and men and cattle to be fruitful and multiply. Thus they did what in more northern lands we may suppose the King and Queen of May were believed to do in days of old. Now the right to play the part of the King of May and to wed the Queen of May has sometimes been determined by an athletic contest, particularly by a race. This may have been a relic of an old marriage custom of the sort we have examined, a custom designed to test the fitness of a candidate for matrimony. Such a test might reasonably be applied with peculiar rigour to the king in order to ensure that no personal defect should incapacitate him for the performance of those sacred rites and ceremonies on which, even more than on the despatch of his civil and military duties, the safety and prosperity of the community were believed to depend. And it would be natural to require of him that from time to time he should submit himself afresh to the same ordeal for the sake of publicly demonstrating that he was still equal to the discharge of his high calling. A relic of that test perhaps survived in the ceremony known as the Flight of the King (*regifugium*), which continued to be annually observed at Rome down to imperial times. On the twenty-fourth day of February a sacrifice used to be offered in the Comitium, and when it was over the King of the Sacred Rites fled from the Forum.* We may conjecture that the Flight of the King was originally a race for an annual kingship, which may have been awarded as a prize to the fleetest runner. At the end of the year the king might run again for a second term of office; and so on, until he was defeated and deposed or perhaps slain. In this way what had once been a race would tend to assume the character of a flight and a pursuit. The king would be given a start; he ran and his competitors ran after him, and if he were overtaken he had to yield the crown and perhaps his life to the lightest of foot among them. In time a man of masterful character might succeed in seating himself permanently on the throne and reducing the annual race or flight to the empty form which it seems always to have been within historical times. The rite was sometimes interpreted as a commemoration of the expulsion of the kings from Rome; but this appears to have been a mere afterthought devised to explain a ceremony of which the old meaning was forgotten. It is far more likely that in acting thus the King of the Sacred Rites was merely keeping up an ancient custom which in the regal period had been annually observed by his predecessors the kings. What the original intention of the rite may have been must probably always remain more or less a matter of conjecture. The present explanation is suggested with a full sense of the difficulty and obscurity in which the subject is involved. Thus, if my theory is correct, the yearly flight of the Roman king was a relic of a time when the kingship was an annual office awarded, along with the hand of a princess, to the victorious athlete or gladiator, who thereafter figured along with his bride as a god and goddess at a sacred marriage designed to ensure the fertility of the earth by homoeopathic magic.

If I am right in supposing that in very early times the old Latin kings personated a god and were regularly put to death in that character, we can better understand the mysterious or violent ends to which so many of them are said to have come. Too much stress should not, however, be laid on such legends, for in a turbulent state of society kings, like commoners, are apt to be knocked on the head for much sounder reasons than a claim to divinity. Still, it is worth while to note that Romulus is said to have vanished mysteriously like Aeneas, or to have been cut to pieces by the patricians whom he had offended, and that the seventh of July, the day on which he perished, was a festival which bore some resemblance to the Saturnalia. For on that day

The violent ends of the Roman kings.

Death of Romulus on the seventh of July, [cont'd]

the *Nonae Caprotinae*, at a festival resembling the Saturnalia.

the female slaves were allowed to take certain remarkable liberties. They dressed up as free women in the attire of matrons and maids, and in this guise they went forth from the city, scoffed and jeered at all whom they met, and engaged among themselves in a fight, striking and throwing stones at each other.

Violent ends of Tatius, Tullus Hostilius, and other Roman kings.

Another Roman king who perished by violence was Tatius, the Sabine colleague of Romulus. It is said that he was at Lavinium offering a public sacrifice to the ancestral gods, when some men to whom he had given umbrage despatched him with the sacrificial knives and spits which they had snatched from the altar. The occasion and the manner of his death suggest that the slaughter may have been a sacrifice rather than an assassination. Again, Tullus Hostilius, the successor of Numa, was commonly said to have been killed by lightning, but many held that he was murdered at the instigation of Ancus Marcius, who reigned after him. Speaking of the more or less mythical Numa, the type of the priestly king, Plutarch observes that 'his fame was enhanced by the fortunes of the later kings. For of the five who reigned after him the last was deposed and ended his life in exile, and of the remaining four not one died a natural death; for three of them were assassinated and Tullus Hostilius was consumed by thunderbolts.' This implies that King Ancus Marcius, as well as Tarquin the Elder and Servius Tullius, perished by the hand of an assassin. No other ancient historian, so far as I know, records this of Ancus Marcius, though one of them says that the king 'was carried off by an untimely death'. Tarquin the Elder was slain by two murderers whom the sons of his predecessor, Ancus Marcius, had hired to do the deed. Lastly, Servius Tullius came by his end in circumstances which recall the combat for the priesthood of Diana at Nemi. He was attacked by his successor and killed by his orders, though not by his hand.

The succession to the Latin kingship may sometimes have been decided by single combat.

These legends of the violent ends of the Roman kings suggest that the contest by which they gained the throne may sometimes have been a mortal combat rather than a race. If that were so, the analogy which we have traced between Rome and Nemi would be still closer. At both places the sacred kings, the living representatives of the godhead, would thus be liable to suffer deposition and death at the hand of any resolute man who could prove his divine right to the holy office by the strong arm and the sharp sword. A parallel to what I conceive to have been the rule of the old Latin kingship is furnished by a West African custom of to-day. When the Maluango or king of Loango, who is deemed the representative of God on earth, has been elected, he has to take his stand at *Nkumbi*, a large tree near the entrance to his sacred ground. Here, encouraged by one of his ministers, he must fight all rivals who present themselves to dispute his right to the throne. This is one of the many instances in which the rites and legends of ancient Italy are illustrated by the practice of modern Africa. Similarly among the Banyoro* of Central Africa, whose king had to take his life with his own hand whenever his health and strength began to fail, the succession to the throne was determined by a mortal combat among the claimants, who fought till only one of them was left alive. Even in England a relic of a similar custom survived till lately in the coronation ceremony, at which a champion used to throw down his glove and challenge to mortal combat all who disputed the king's right to the crown. The ceremony was witnessed by Pepys at the coronation of Charles the Second.*

Combats for the kingdom in Africa.

CHAPTER 10

THE BURDEN OF ROYALTY

i

Life of divine kings and priests regulated by minute rules.

AT a certain stage of early society the king or priest is often thought to be endowed with supernatural powers or to be an incarnation of a deity, and consistently with this belief the course of nature is supposed to be more or less under his control, and he is held responsible for bad weather, failure of the crops, and similar calamities. To some extent it appears to be assumed that the king's power over nature, like that over his subjects and slaves, is exerted through definite acts of will; and therefore if drought, famine, pestilence, or storms arise, the people attribute the misfortune to the negligence or guilt of their king, and punish him accordingly with stripes and bonds, or, if he remains obdurate, with deposition and death. Sometimes, however, the course of nature, while regarded as dependent on the king, is supposed to be partly independent of his will. His person is considered, if we may express it so, as the dynamical centre of the universe, from which lines of force radiate to all quarters of the heaven; so that any motion of his—the turning of his head, the lifting of his hand—instantaneously affects and may seriously disturb some part of nature. He is the point of support on which hangs the balance of the world, and the slightest irregularity on his part may overthrow the delicate equipoise. The greatest care must, therefore, be taken both by and of him; and his whole life, down to its minutest details, must be so regulated that no act of his, voluntary or involuntary, may disarrange or upset the established order of nature. Of this class of monarchs the Mikado* or Dairi, the spiritual emperor of Japan, is or rather used to be a typical example. He is an incarnation of the sun goddess, the deity who rules the universe, gods and men included; once a year all the gods wait upon him and spend a month at his court. During that month, the name of which means 'without gods', no one frequents the temples, for they are believed to be deserted. The Mikado receives from his people and assumes in his official

The Mikado or Dairi of Japan.

proclamations and decrees the title of 'manifest or incarnate deity' (*Akitsu Kami*) and he claims a general authority over the gods of Japan. For example, in an official decree of the year 646 the emperor is described as 'the incarnate god who governs the universe'.

The following description of the Mikado's mode of life was written about two hundred years ago:

Rules of life formerly ob-served by the Mikado.

'Even to this day the princes descended of this family, more particularly those who sit on the throne, are looked upon as persons most holy in themselves, and as Popes by birth. And, in order to preserve these advantageous notions in the minds of their subjects, they are obliged to take an uncommon care of their sacred persons, and to do such things, which, examined according to the customs of other nations, would be thought ridiculous and impertinent. It will not be improper to give a few instances of it. He thinks that it would be very prejudicial to his dignity and holiness to touch the ground with his feet; for this reason, when he intends to go anywhere, he must be carried thither on men's shoulders. Much less will they suffer that he should expose his sacred person to the open air, and the sun is not thought worthy to shine on his head. There is such a holiness ascribed to all the parts of his body that he dares to cut off neither his hair, nor his beard, nor his nails. However, lest he should grow too dirty, they may clean him in the night when he is asleep; because, they say, that which is taken from his body at that time, hath been stolen from him, and that such a theft doth not prejudice his holiness or dignity. In ancient times, he was obliged to sit on the throne for some hours every morning, with the imperial crown on his head, but to sit altogether like a statue, without stirring either hands or feet, head or eyes, nor indeed any part of his body, because, by this means, it was thought that he could preserve peace and tran-quillity in his empire; for if, unfortunately, he turned himself on one side or the other, or if he looked a good while towards any part of his dominions, it was apprehended that war, famine, fire, or some other great misfortune was near at hand to desolate the country. But it having been afterwards discovered, that the imperial crown was the palladium, which by its immobility could preserve peace in the empire, it was thought expedient to deliver his imperial person, consecrated only to idleness and pleasures, from this burthensome duty, and therefore the crown is at present placed on the throne for some hours every morning. His victuals must be dressed every time in new pots, and served at table in new dishes: both are very clean and neat, but made only of common clay; that without any considerable expense they may be laid aside, or broke, after they have served once. They are generally broke, for fear they should come into the hands of laymen, for they believe religiously, that if any layman should presume to eat his food out of these sacred dishes, it would swell and inflame his mouth and throat. The like ill effect is dreaded from the Dairi's sacred habits; for they believe that if a layman should wear them, without the Emperor's express leave or command, they would occasion swellings and pains in all parts of his body.' To the same effect an earlier account of the Mikado says: 'It was considered as a shameful degradation for him even to touch the ground with his foot. The sun and moon were not even permitted to shine upon his head. None of the superfluities of the body were ever taken from him, neither his hair, his beard nor his nails were cut. Whatever he eat was dressed in new vessels.'*

Similar priestly or rather divine kings are found, at a lower level of barbarism, on the west coast of Africa. At Shark Point near Cape Padron,* in Lower Guinea, lives the priestly king Kukulu, alone in a wood. He may not touch a woman nor leave his house; indeed he may not even quit his chair, in which he is obliged to sleep sitting, for if he lay down no wind would arise and navigation would be stopped. He regulates storms, and in general maintains a wholesome and equable state of the atmosphere. On Mount Agu in Togo, a German possession in West Africa,* there lives a fetish or spirit called Bagba, who is of great importance for the whole of the surrounding country. The power of giving or withholding rain is ascribed to him, and he is lord of the winds, including the Harmattan, the dry, hot wind which blows from the interior. His priest dwells in a house on the highest peak of the mountain, where he keeps the winds bottled up in huge jars. Applications for rain, too, are made to him, and he does a good business in amulets, which consist of the teeth and claws of leopards. Yet though his power is great and he is indeed the real chief of the land, the rule of the fetish forbids him ever to leave the mountain, and he must spend the

Rules of life observed by kings and priests in Africa and America.

whole of his life on its summit. Only once a year may he come down to make purchases in the market; but even then he may not set foot in the hut of any mortal man, and must return to his place of exile the same day. The business of government in the villages is conducted by subordinate chiefs, who are appointed by him. In the West African kingdom of Congo there was a supreme pontiff called Chitomé or Chitombé, whom the negroes regarded as a god on earth and all-powerful in heaven. Hence before they would taste the new crops they offered him the first-fruits, fearing that manifold misfortunes would befall them if they broke this rule. When he left his residence to visit other places within his jurisdiction, all married people had to observe strict continence the whole time he was out; for it was supposed that any act of incontinence would prove fatal to him. And if he were to die a natural death, they thought that the world would perish, and the earth, which he alone sustained by his power and merit, would immediately be annihilated. Similarly in Humbe, a kingdom of Angola, the incontinence of young people under the age of puberty used to be a capital crime, because it was believed to entail the death of the king within the year. Of late the death penalty has been commuted for a fine of ten oxen inflicted on each of the culprits. This commutation has attracted thousands of dissolute youth to Humbe from the neighbouring tribes, among whom the old penalty is still rigorously exacted. Amongst the semi-barbarous nations of the New World, at the date of the Spanish conquest, there were found hierarchies or theocracies like those of Japan; in particular, the high pontiff of the Zapotecs in Southern Mexico appears to have presented a close parallel to the Mikado. A powerful rival to the king himself, this spiritual lord governed Yopaa, one of the chief cities of the kingdom, with absolute dominion. It is impossible, we are told, to overrate the reverence in which he was held. He was looked on as a god whom the earth was not worthy to hold nor the sun to shine upon. He profaned his sanctity if he even touched the ground with his foot. The officers who bore his palanquin on their shoulders were members of the highest families; he hardly deigned to look on anything around him; and all who met him fell with their faces to the earth, fearing that death would overtake them if they saw even his shadow. A rule of continence was regularly imposed on the Zapotec priests, especially upon the high pontiff; but 'on certain days in each year, which were generally celebrated with feasts and dances, it was customary for the high priest to become drunk. While in this state, seeming to belong neither to heaven nor to earth, one of the most beautiful of the virgins consecrated to the service of the gods was brought to him.' If the child she bore him was a son, he was brought up as a prince of the blood, and the eldest son succeeded his father on the pontifical throne. The supernatural powers attributed to this pontiff are not specified, but probably they resembled those of the Mikado and Chitomé.

The rules of life imposed on kings in early society are intended to preserve their lives for the good of their people.

Wherever, as in Japan and West Africa, it is supposed that the order of nature, and even the existence of the world, is bound up with the life of the king or priest, it is clear that he must be regarded by his subjects as a source both of infinite blessing and of infinite danger. On the one hand, the people have to thank him for the rain and sunshine which foster the fruits of the earth, for the wind which brings ships to their coasts, and even for the solid ground beneath their feet. But what he gives he can refuse; and so close is the dependence of nature on his person, so delicate the balance of the system of forces whereof he is the centre, that the least irregularity on his part may set up a tremor which shall shake the earth to its foundations. And if nature may be disturbed by the slightest involuntary act of the king, it is easy to conceive the convulsion which his death might provoke. The natural death of the Chitomé, as we have seen, was thought to entail the destruction of all things. Clearly, therefore, out of a regard for their own safety, which might be imperilled by any rash act of the king, and still more by his death, the people will exact of their king or priest a strict conformity to those rules, the observance of which is deemed necessary for his own preservation, and consequently for the preservation of his people and the world. The idea that early kingdoms are despotisms in which the people exist only for the sovereign, is wholly inapplicable to the monarchies we are considering. On the contrary, the sovereign in them exists only for his subjects; his life is only valuable so long as he discharges the duties of his position by ordering the course of nature for his people's benefit. So soon as he fails to do so, the care, the devotion, the religious homage which they had hitherto lavished on him cease and are changed into hatred and contempt; he is dismissed ignominiously, and may be thankful if he escapes with his life. Worshipped as a god one day, he is killed as a criminal the next. But in this changed behaviour of the people there is nothing capricious or inconsistent. On the contrary, their conduct is entirely of a piece. If their king is their god, he is or should be also their preserver; and if he will not preserve them, he must make room for another who will. So long, however, as he answers their expectations, there is no limit to the care which they take of him, and which they compel him to take of himself. A king of this sort lives hedged in by a ceremonious etiquette, a network of prohibitions and observances, of which the intention is not to contribute to his dignity, much less to his comfort, but to restrain him from conduct which, by disturbing the harmony of nature, might involve himself, his people, and the universe in one common catastrophe. Far from adding to his comfort, these observances, by trammelling his every act, annihilate his freedom and often render the very life, which it is their object to preserve, a burden and sorrow to him.

Of the supernaturally endowed kings of Loango it is said that the more powerful a king is, the more taboos is he bound to observe; they regulate all his actions, his walking and his standing, his eating and drinking, his sleeping and waking. To these restraints the heir to the throne is subject from infancy; but as he advances in life the number of abstinences and ceremonies which he must observe increases, 'until at the moment that he ascends the throne he is lost in the ocean of rites and taboos'. In the crater of an extinct volcano, enclosed on all sides by grassy slopes, lie the scattered huts and yam-fields of Riabba, the capital of the native king of Fernando Po. This mysterious being lives in the lowest depths of the crater, surrounded by a harem of forty women, and covered, it is said, with old silver coins. Naked savage as he is, he yet exercises far more influence in the island than the Spanish governor at Santa Isabel. In him the conservative spirit of the Boobies or aboriginal inhabitants of the island is, as it were, incorporate. He has never seen a white man and, according to the firm conviction of all the Boobies, the sight of a pale face would cause his instant death. He cannot bear to look upon the sea; indeed it is

Taboos observed by African kings.

said that he may never see it even in the distance, and that therefore he wears away his life with shackles on his legs in the dim twilight of his hut. Certain it is that he has never set foot on the beach. With the exception of his musket and knife, he uses nothing that comes from the whites; European cloth never touches his person, and he scorns tobacco, rum, and even salt.

Taboos observed by African kings.

Among the Ewe-speaking peoples of the Slave Coast,* in West Africa, 'the king is at the same time high priest. In this quality he was, particularly in former times, unapproachable by his subjects. Only by night was he allowed to quit his dwelling in order to bathe and so forth. None but his representative, the so-called "visible king," with three chosen elders might converse with him, and even they had to sit on an ox-hide with their backs turned to him. He might not see any European nor any horse, nor might he look upon the sea, for which reason he was not allowed to quit his capital even for a few moments. These rules have been disregarded in recent times.' The king of Dahomey himself is subject to the prohibition of beholding the sea, and so are the kings of Loango and Great Ardra in Guinea. The sea is the fetish of the Eyeos, to the north-west of Dahomey, and they and their king are threatened with death by their priests if ever they dare to look on it. It is believed that the king of Cayor in Senegal would infallibly die within the year if he were to cross a river or an arm of the sea. In Mashonaland down to recent times the chiefs would not cross certain rivers, particularly the Rurikwi and the Nyadiri; and the custom was still strictly observed by at least one chief within the last few years. 'On no account will the chief cross the river. If it is absolutely necessary for him to do so, he is blindfolded and carried across with shouting and singing. Should he walk across, he will go blind or die and certainly lose the chieftainship.' So among the Mahafalys and Sakalavas in the south of Madagascar some kings are forbidden to sail on the sea or to cross certain rivers. The horror of the sea is not peculiar to kings. The Basutos are said to share it instinctively, though they have never seen salt water, and live hundreds of miles from the Indian Ocean. The Egyptian priests loathed the sea, and called it the foam of Typhon; they were forbidden to set salt on their table, and they would not speak to pilots because they got their living by the sea; hence too they would not eat fish, and the hiero-

Prohibition to see the sea.

Horror of the sea.

glyphic symbol for hatred was a fish. When the Indians of the Peruvian Andes were sent by the Spaniards to work in the hot valleys of the coast, the vast ocean which they saw before them as they descended the Cordillera was dreaded by them as a cause of disease; hence they prayed to it that they might not fall ill. This they all did without exception, even the little children. Similarly the inland people of Lampong in Sumatra are said to pay a kind of adoration to the sea, and to make it an offering of cakes and sweetmeats when they behold it for the first time, deprecating its power of doing them mischief.

Among the Sakalavas of southern Madagascar the chief is regarded as a sacred being, but 'he is held in leash by a crowd of restrictions, which regulate his behaviour like that of the emperor of China. He can undertake nothing whatever unless the sorcerers have declared the omens favourable: he may not eat warm food: on certain days he may not quit his hut; and so on.' Among some of the hill tribes of Assam both the headman and his wife have to observe many taboos in respect of food; thus they may not eat buffalo, pork, dog, fowl, or tomatoes. The headman must be chaste, the husband of one wife, and he must separate himself from her on the eve of a general or public observance of taboo. In one group of tribes the headman is forbidden to eat in a strange village, and under no provocation whatever may he utter a word of abuse. Apparently the people imagine that the violation of any of these taboos by a headman would bring down misfortune on the whole village. Taboos observed by chiefs among the Sakalavas and the hill tribes of Assam.

The ancient kings of Ireland, as well as the kings of the four provinces of Leinster, Munster, Connaught, and Ulster, were subject to certain quaint prohibitions or taboos, on the due observance of which the prosperity of the people and the country, as well as their own, was supposed to depend. Thus, for example, the sun might not rise on the king of Ireland in his bed at Tara, the old capital of Erin; he was forbidden to alight on Wednesday at Magh Breagh, to traverse Magh Cuillinn after sunset, to incite his horse at Fan-Chomair, to go in a ship upon the water the Monday after Bealltaine (May day), and to leave the track of his army upon Ath Maighne the Tuesday after All-Hallows. The king of Leinster might not go round Tuath Laighean left-hand-wise on Wednesday, nor sleep between the Dothair (Dodder) and the Duibhlinn with his head Taboos observed by Irish kings.

inclining to one side, nor encamp for nine days on the plains of Cualann, nor travel the road of Duibhlinn on Monday, nor ride a dirty black-heeled horse across Magh Maistean. The king of Munster was prohibited from enjoying the feast of Loch Lein from one Monday to another; from banqueting by night in the beginning of harvest before Geim at Leitreacha; from encamping for nine days upon the Siuir; and from holding a border meeting at Gabhran. The king of Connaught might not conclude a treaty respecting his ancient palace of Cruachan after making peace on All-Hallows Day, nor go in a speckled garment on a grey speckled steed to the heath of Dal Chais, nor repair to an assembly of women at Seaghais, nor sit in autumn on the sepulchral mounds of the wife of Maine, nor contend in running with the rider of a grey one-eyed horse at Ath Gallta between two posts. The king of Ulster was forbidden to attend the horse fair at Rath Line among the youths of Dal Araidhe, to listen to the fluttering of the flocks of birds of Linn Saileach after sunset, to celebrate the feast of the bull of Daire-mic-Daire, to go into Magh Cobha in the month of March, and to drink of the water of Bo Neimhidh between two darknesses. If the kings of Ireland strictly observed these and many other customs, which were enjoined by immemorial usage, it was believed that they would never meet with mischance or misfortune, and would live for ninety years without experiencing the decay of old age; that no epidemic or mortality would occur during their reigns; and that the seasons would be favourable and the earth yield its fruit in abundance; whereas, if they set the ancient usages at naught, the country would be visited with plague, famine and bad weather.

Taboos observed by Egyptian kings.

The kings of Egypt were worshipped as gods, and the routine of their daily life was regulated in every detail by precise and unvarying rules. 'The life of the kings of Egypt,' says Diodorus, 'was not like that of other monarchs who are irresponsible and may do just what they choose; on the contrary, everything was fixed for them by law, not only their official duties, but even the details of their daily life . . . The hours both of day and night were arranged at which the king had to do, not what he pleased, but what was prescribed for him . . . For not only were the times appointed at which he should transact public business or sit in judgment; but the very hours for his walking and bathing and sleeping with his wife, and, in short, performing every act of life were all settled. Custom enjoined a simple diet; the only flesh he might eat was veal and goose, and he might only drink a prescribed quantity of wine.'* However, there is reason to think that these rules were observed, not by the ancient Pharaohs, but by the priestly kings who reigned at Thebes and in Ethiopia at the close of the twentieth dynasty. Among the Karen-nis of Upper Burma a chief attains his position, not by hereditary right, but on account of his habit of abstaining from rice and liquor. The mother, too, of a candidate for the chieftainship must have eschewed these things and lived solely on yams and potatoes so long as she was with child. During that time she may not eat any meat nor drink water from a common well. And if her son is to be qualified for the office of chief he must continue to observe these habits.

Of the taboos imposed on priests we may see a striking example in the rules of life prescribed for the Flamen Dialis at Rome, who has been interpreted as a living image of Jupiter, or a human embodiment of the sky-spirit. They were such as the following: The Flamen Dialis might not ride or even touch a horse, nor see an army under arms, nor wear a ring which was not broken, nor have a knot on any part of his garments; no fire except a sacred fire might be taken out of his house; he might not touch wheaten flour or leavened bread; he might not touch or even name a goat, a dog, raw meat, beans, and ivy; he might not walk under a vine; the feet of his bed had to be daubed with mud; his hair could be cut only by a free man and with a bronze knife, and his hair and nails when cut had to be buried under a lucky tree; he might not touch a dead body nor enter a place where one was burned; he might not see work being done on holy days; he might not be uncovered in the open air; if a man in bonds were taken into his house, the captive had to be unbound and the cords had to be drawn up through a hole in the roof and so let down into the street. His wife, the Flaminica, had to observe nearly the same rules, and others of her own besides. She might not ascend more than three steps of the kind of staircase called Greek; at a certain festival she might not comb her hair; the leather of her shoes might not be made from a beast that had died a natural death, but only from one that

Taboos observed by the Flamen Dialis at Rome.

had been slain or sacrificed; if she heard thunder she was tabooed till she had offered an expiatory sacrifice.

Among the Grebo people of Sierra Leone there is a pontiff who bears the title of Bodia and has been compared, on somewhat slender grounds, to the high priest of the Jews. He is appointed in accordance with the behest of an oracle. At an elaborate ceremony of installation he is anointed, a ring is put on his ankle as a badge of office, and the doorposts of his house are sprinkled with the blood of a sacrificed goat. He has charge of the public talismans and idols, which he feeds with rice and oil every new moon; and he sacrifices on behalf of the town to the dead and to demons. Nominally his power is very great, but in practice it is very limited; for he dare not defy public opinion, and he is held responsible, even with his life, for any adversity that befalls the country. It is expected of him that he should cause the earth to bring forth abundantly, the people to be healthy, war to be driven far away, and witchcraft to be kept in abeyance. His life is trammelled by the observance of certain restrictions or taboos. Thus he may not sleep in any house but his own official residence, which is called the 'anointed house' with reference to the ceremony of anointing him at inauguration. He may not drink water on the highway. He may not eat while a corpse is in the town, and he may not mourn for the dead. If he dies while in office, he must be buried at dead of night; few may hear of his burial, and none may mourn for him when his death is made public. Should he have fallen a victim to the poison ordeal by drinking a decoction of sassywood, as it is called, he must be buried under a running stream of water.

Among the Todas of Southern India the holy milkman (*palol*), who acts as priest of the sacred dairy, is subject to a variety of irksome and burdensome restrictions during the whole time of his incumbency, which may last many years. Thus he must live at the sacred dairy and may never visit his home or any ordinary village. He must be celibate; if he is married he must leave his wife. On no account may any ordinary person touch the holy milkman or the holy dairy; such a touch would so defile his holiness that he would forfeit his office. It is only on two days a week, namely Mondays and Thursdays, that a mere layman may even approach the milkman; on other days if he has any business with him, he must stand at a distance (some say a quarter of a mile) and shout his message across the intervening space. Further, the holy milkman never cuts his hair or pares his nails so long as he holds office; he never crosses a river by a bridge, but wades through a ford and only certain fords; if a death occurs in his clan, he may not attend any of the funeral ceremonies, unless he first resigns his office and descends from the exalted rank of milkman to that of a mere common mortal. Indeed it appears that in old days he had to resign the seals, or rather the pails, of office whenever any member of his clan departed this life. However these heavy restraints are laid in their entirety only on milkmen of the very highest class. Among the Todas there are milkmen and milkmen; and some of them get off more lightly in consideration of their humbler station in life. Still, apart from the dignity they enjoy, the lot even of these other milkmen is not altogether a happy one. Thus, for example, at a place called Kanodrs there is a dairy-temple of a conical form. The milkman who has charge of it must be celibate during the tenure of his office: he must sleep in the calves' house, a very flimsy structure with an open door and a fire-place that gives little heat: he may wear only one very scanty garment: he must take his meals sitting on the outer wall which surrounds the dairy: in eating he may not put his hand to his lips, but must throw the food into his mouth; and in drinking he may not put to his lips the leaf which serves as a cup, he must tilt his head back and pour the liquid into his mouth in a jet from above. With the exception of a single layman, who is allowed to bear the milkman company, but who is also bound to celibacy and has a bed rigged up for him in the calves' house, no other person is allowed to go near this very sacred dairy under any pretext whatever. No wonder that some years ago the dairy was unoccupied and the office of milkman stood vacant. 'At the present time', says Dr Rivers, 'a dairyman is appointed about once a year and holds office for thirty or forty days only. So far as I could ascertain, the failure to occupy the dairy constantly is due to the very considerable hardships and restrictions which have to be endured by the holder of the office of dairyman, and the time is probably not far distant when this dairy, one of the most sacred among the Todas, will cease altogether to be used.'

ii

The effect of these burdensome rules was to divorce the temporal from the spiritual authority.

The burdensome observances attached to the royal or priestly office produced their natural effect. Either men refused to accept the office, which hence tended to fall into abeyance; or accepting it, they sank under its weight into spiritless creatures, cloistered recluses, from whose nerveless fingers the reins of government slipped into the firmer grasp of men who were often content to wield the reality of sovereignty without its name. In some countries this rift in the supreme power deepened into a total and permanent separation of the spiritual and temporal powers, the old royal house retaining their purely religious functions, while the civil government passed into the hands of a younger and more vigorous race.

Reluctance to accept sovereignty with its vexatious restrictions.

To take examples. In a previous part of this work we say that in Cambodia it is often necessary to force the kingships of Fire and Water upon the reluctant successors.* In some parts of West Africa, when the king dies, a family council is secretly held to determine his successor. He on whom the choice falls is suddenly seized, bound, and thrown into the fetish-house, where he is kept in durance till he consents to accept the crown. Sometimes the heir finds means of evading the honour which it is sought to thrust upon him; a ferocious chief has been known to go about constantly armed, resolute to resist by force any attempt to set him on the throne. The savage Timmes of Sierra Leone, who elect their king, reserve to themselves the right of beating him on the eve of his coronation; and they avail themselves of this constitutional privilege with such hearty goodwill that sometimes the unhappy monarch does not long survive his elevation to the throne. Hence when the leading chiefs have a spite at a man and wish to rid themselves of him, they elect him king. Formerly, before a man was proclaimed king of Sierra Leone, it used to be the custom to load him with chains and thrash him. Then the fetters were knocked off, the kingly robe was placed on him, and he received in his hands the symbol of royal dignity, which was nothing but the axe of the executioner. It is not therefore surprising to read that in Sierra Leone, where such customs have prevailed, 'except among the Mandingoes and Suzees, few kings are natives of the countries they govern. So different are their ideas from ours, that very few are solicitous of the honour, and competition is very seldom heard of.' Another writer on Sierra Leone tells us that 'the honour of reigning, so much coveted in Europe, is very frequently rejected in Africa, on account of the expense attached to it, which sometimes greatly exceeds the revenues of the crown'. A reluctance to accept the sovereignty in the Ethiopian kingdom of Gingiro was simulated, if not really felt, as we learn from the old Jesuit missionaries. 'They wrap up the dead king's body in costly garments, and killing a cow, put it into the hide; then all those who hope to succeed him, being his sons or others of the royal blood, flying from the honour they covet, abscond and hide themselves in the woods. This done, the electors, who are all great sorcerers, agree among themselves who shall be king, and go out to seek him, when entering the woods by means of their enchantments, they say, a large bird called *liber*, as big as an eagle, comes down with mighty cries over the place where he is hid, and they find him encompass'd by lyons, tygers, snakes, and other creatures gather'd about him by witchcraft. The elect, as fierce as those beasts, rushes out upon those who seek him, wounding and sometimes kiling some of them, to prevent being seiz'd. They take all in good part, defending themselves the best they can, till they have seiz'd him. Thus they carry him away by force, he still struggling and seeming to refuse taking upon him the burthen of government, all which is mere cheat and hypocrisy.'

The Mikados of Japan seem early to have resorted to the expedient of transferring the honours and burdens of supreme power to their infant children; and the rise of the Tycoons* long the temporal sovereigns of the country, is traced to the abdication of a certain Mikado in favour of his three-year-old son. The sovereignty having been wrested by a usurper from the infant prince, the cause o the Mikado was championed by Yoritomo, a man of spirit and conduct, who overthrew the usurper and restored to the Mikado the shadow, while he retained for himself the substance, of power. He bequeathed to his descendants the dignity he had won, and thus became the founder of the line of Tycoons. Down to the latter half of the sixteenth century the Tycoons were active and efficient rulers; but the same fate overtook them which had befallen the

Sovereign powers divided between a temporal and a spiritual head.

Mikados. Immeshed in the same inextricable web of custom and law, they degenerated into mere puppets, hardly stirring from their palaces and occpuied in a perpetual round of empty ceremonies, while the real business of government was managed by the council of state. In Tonquin* the monarchy ran a similar course. Living like his predecessors in effeminacy and sloth, the king was driven from the throne by an ambitious adventurer named Mack, who from a fisherman had risen to be Grand Mandarin. But the king's brother Tring put down the usurper and restored the king, retaining, however, for himself and his descendants the dignity of general of all the forces. Thenceforward the king or *dovas*, though invested with the title and pomp of sovereignty, ceased to govern,. While they lived secluded in their palaces, all real political power was wielded by the hereditary generals or *chovas*. The present king of Sikhim, 'like most of his predecessors in the kingship, is a mere puppet in the hands of his crafty priests, who have made a sort of priest-king of him. They encourage him by every means in their power to leave the government to them, whilst he devotes all his time to the degrading rites of devil-workship, and the ceaseless mutteing of meaningless jargon, of which the Tibetan form of Buddhism chiefly consists. They declare that he is a saint by birth, that he is the direct descendant of the greatest king of Tibet, the canonised Srongtsan Gampo, who was a contemporary of Mahomed in the seventh century AD and who first introduced Buddhism to Tibet.' 'This saintly lineage, which secures for the king's person popular homage amounting to worship, is probably, however, a mere invention of the priests to glorify their puppet-prince for their own sordid ends. Such devices are common in the East.' The custom regularly observed by the Tahitian kings of abdicating on the birth of a son, who was immediatley proclaimed sovereign and received his father's homage, may perhaps have originated, like the similar custom occasionally practised by the Mikados, in a wish to shift to other shoulders the irksome burden of royalty; for in Tahiti as elsewhere the sovereign was subjected to a system of vexatious restrictions. In Mangaia, another Polynesian island, religious and civil authority were lodged in separate hands, spiritual functions being discharged by a line of hereditary kings, while the temporal government was entrusted from time to time to a victorious war-chief, whose investiture, however, had to be completed by the king. To the latter were assigned the best lands, and he received daily offerings of the choicest food. The Mikado and Tycoon of Japan had their counterparts in the Roko Tui and Vunivalu of Fiji. The Roko Tui was the Reverend or Sacred King. The Vunivalu was the Root of War or War King. In one kingdom a certain Thakombau, who was the War King, kept all power in his own hands, but in a neighbouring kingdom the real ruler was the Sacred King. Similarly in Tonga, besides the civil king or *How*, whose right to the throne was partly hereditary and partly derived from his warlike reputation and the number of his fighting men, there was a great divine chief called *Tooitonga* or 'Chief of Tonga', who ranked above the king and the other chiefs in virtue of his supposed descent from one of the chief gods. Once a year the first-fruits of the ground were offered to him at a solemn ceremony, and it was believed that if these offerings were not made the vengeance of the gods would fall in a signal manner on the people. Peculiar forms of speech, such as were applied to no one else, were used in speaking of him, and everything that he chanced to touch became sacred or tabooed. When he and the king met, the monarch had to sit down on the ground in token of respect until his holiness had passed by. Yet though he enjoyed the highest veneration by reason of his divine origin, this sacred personage possessed no political authority, and if he ventured to meddle with affairs of state it was at the risk of receiving a rebuff from the king, to whom the real power belonged, and who finally succeeded in ridding himself of his spiritual rival. The king of the Getae* regularly shared his power with a priest, whom his subjects called a god. This divine man led a solitary life in a cave on a holy mountain, seeing few people but the king and his attendants. His counsels added much to the king's influence with his subjects, who believed that he was thereby enabled to impart to them the commands and admonitions of the gods. At Athens the kings degenerated into little more than sacred functionaries, and it is said that the institution of the new office of Polemarch or War Lord was rendered necessary by their growing effeminacy.

In some parts of western Africa two kings reign side by side, a fetish or religious king and a civil king, but the fetish king is really supreme. He controls the weather and so forth, and can put a stop to everything. When he lays his red staff on the ground, no one may pass that way. This division of power between a sacred and a secular ruler is to be met with wherever the true negro culture has been left unmolested, but where the negro form of society has been disturbed, as in Dahomey and Ashantee, there is a tendency to consolidate the two powers in a single king.* Thus, for example, there used to be a fetish king at New Calabar who ranked above the ordinary king in all native matters, whether religious or civil, and always walked in front of him on public occasions, attended by a slave who held an umbrella over his head. His opinion carried great weight. The office and the causes which led to its extinction are thus described by a missionary who spent many years in Calabar: 'The worship of the people is now given especially to their various *idems*, one of which, called Ndem Efik, is a sort of tutelary deity of the country. An individual was appointed to take charge of this object of worship, who bore the name of King Calabar; and likely, in bypast times, possessed the power indicated by the title, being both king and priest. He had as a tribute the skins of all leopards killed, and should a slave take refuge in his shrine he belonged to Ndem Efik. The office, however, imposed certain restrictions on its occupant. He, for instance, could not partake of food in the presence of any one, and he was prohibited from engaging in traffic. On account of these and other disabilities, when the last holder of the office died, a poor old man of the Cobham family, no successor, was found for him, and the priesthood has become extinct.' One of the practical inconveniences of such an office is that the house of the fetish king enjoys the right of sanctuary, and so tends to become little better than a rookery of bad characters. Thus on the Grain Coast of West Africa the fetish king or Bodia, as he is called, 'exercises the functions of a high-priest, and is regarded as protector of the whole nation. He lives in a house provided for him by the people, and takes care of the national fetiches. He enjoys some immunities in virtue of his office, but is subject to certain restrictions which more than counterbalance his privileges. His house is a sanctum to which culprits may betake themselves without the danger of being removed by any one except by the Bodia himself.' One of these Bodias resigned office because of the sort of people who quartered themselves on him, the cost of feeding them, and the squabbles they had among themselves. He led a cat-and-dog life with them for three years. Then there came a man with homicidal mania varied by epileptic fits; and soon afterwards the spiritual shepherd retired into private life, but not before he had lost an ear and sustained other bodily injury in a personal conflict with this very black sheep.

At Porto Novo* there used to be, in addition to the ordinary monarch, a King of the Night, who reigned during the hours of darkness from sunset to sunrise. He might not shew himself in the street after the sun was up. His duty was to patrol the streets with his satellites and to arrest all whom he found abroad after a certain hour. Each band of his catchpoles was led by a man who went about concealed from head to foot under a conical casing of straw and blew blasts on a shell which caused every one that heard it to shudder. The King of the Night never met the ordinary king except on the first and last days of their respective reign; for each of them invested the other with office and paid him the last honours at death. With this King of the Night at Porto Novo we may compare a certain king of Hawaii who was so very sacred that no man might see him, even accidentally, by day under pain of death; he only shewed himself by night. The King of the Night.

In some parts of the East Indian island of Timor we meet with a partition of power like that which is represented by the civil king and the fetish king of western Africa. Some of the Timorese tribes recognise two rajahs, the ordinary or civil rajah, who governs the people, and the fetish or taboo rajah (*radja pomali*), who is charged with the control of everything that concerns the earth and its products. This latter ruler has the right of declaring anything taboo; his permission must be obtained before new land may be brought under cultivation, and he must perform certain necessary ceremonies when the work is being carried out. If drought or blight threatens the crops, his help is invoked to save them. Though he ranks below the civil rajah, he exercises a momentous influence on the course of events, for his secular colleague is bound to consult him in all important matters. In some of the neighbouring islands, such as Rotti and eastern Flores, a spiritual ruler of the same sort is Civil rajahs and taboo rajahs in the East Indies.

recognised under various native names, which all mean 'lord of the ground'. Similarly in the Mekeo district of British New Guinea there is a double chieftainship. The people are divided into two groups according to families, and each of the groups has its chief. One of the two is the war chief, the other is the taboo (*afu*) chief. The office of the latter is hereditary; his duty is to impose a taboo on any of the crops, such as the coco-nuts and areca nuts, whenever he thinks it desirable to prohibit their use. In his office we may perhaps detect the beginning of a priestly dynasty, but as yet his functions appear to be more magical than religious, being concerned with the control of the harvests rather than with the propitiation of higher powers. The members of another family are bound to see to it that the taboo imposed by the chief is strictly observed. For this purpose some fourteen or fifteen men of the family form a sort of constabulary. Every evening they go round the village armed with clubs and disguised with masks or leaves. All the time they are in office they are forbidden to live with their wives and even to look at a woman. Hence women may not quit their houses while the men are going their rounds. Further, the constables on duty are prohibited from chewing betel nut and drinking coco-nut water, lest the areca and coco-nut should not grow. When there is a good show of nuts, the taboo chief proclaims that on a certain day the restriction will come to an end. In Ponape, one of the Caroline Islands, the kingship is elective within the limits of the blood royal, which runs in the female line, so that the sovereignty passes backwards and forwards between families which we, reckoning descent in the male line, should regard as distinct. The chosen monarch must be in possession of certain secrets. He must know the places where the sacred stones are kept, on which he has to seat himself. He must understand the holy words and prayers of the liturgy, and after his election he must recite them at the place of the sacred stones. But he enjoys only the honours of his office; the real powers of government are in the hands of his prime-minister or vizier.

CHAPTER 11

THE PERILS OF THE SOUL

i

THE foregoing examples have taught us that the office of a sacred king or priest is often hedged in by a series of burdensome restrictions or taboos, of which a principal purpose appears to be to preserve the life of the divine man for the good of his people. But if the object of the taboos is to save his life, the question arises, How is their observance supposed to effect this end? To understand this we must know the nature of the danger which threatens the king's life, and which it is the intention of these curious restrictions to guard against. We must, therefore, ask: What does early man understand by death? To what causes does he attribute it? And how does he think it may be guarded against?

What is the primitive conception of death?

As the savage commonly explains the processes of inanimate nature by supposing that they are produced by living beings working in or behind the phenomena, so he explains the phenomena of life itself. If an animal lives and moves, it can only be, he thinks, because there is a little animal inside which moves it: if a man lives and moves, it can only be because he has a little man or animal inside who moves him. The animal inside the animal, the man inside the man, is the soul. And as the activity of an animal or man is explained by the presence of the soul, so the repose of sleep or death is explained by its absence; sleep or trance being the temporary, death being the permanent absence of the soul. Hence if death be the permanent absence of the soul, the way to guard against it is either to prevent the soul from leaving the body, or, if it does depart, to ensure that it shall return. The precautions adopted by savages to secure one or other of these ends take the form of certain prohibitions or taboos, which are nothing but rules intended to ensure either the continued presence or the return of the soul. In short, they are life-preservers or life-guards. These general statements will now be illustrated by examples.

The soul as a mannikin.

Addressing some Australian blacks, a European missionary*
said, 'I am not one, as you think, but two.' Upon this they
laughed. 'You may laugh as much as you like,' continued the
missionary, 'I tell you that I am two in one; this great body that
you see is one; within that there is another little one which is
not visible. The great body dies, and is buried, but the little
body flies away when the great one dies.' To this some of the
blacks replied, 'Yes, yes. We also are two, we also have a little
body within the breast.' On being asked where the little body
went after death, some said it went behind the bush, others said
it went into the sea, and some said they did not know. The
Hurons* thought that the soul had a head and body, arms and
legs; in short, that it was a complete little model of the man
himself. The Esquimaux believe that 'the soul exhibits the same
shape as the body it belongs to, but is of a more subtle and
ethereal nature'. So exact is the resemblance of the mannikin to
the man, in other words, of the soul to the body, that, as there
are fat bodies and thin bodies, so there are fat souls and thin
souls; as there are heavy bodies and light bodies, long bodies
and short bodies, so there are heavy souls and light souls, long
souls and short souls. The people of Nias* think that every
man, before he is born, is asked how long or how heavy a soul
he would like, and a soul of the desired weight or length is
measured out to him. The heaviest soul ever given out weighs
about ten grammes. The length of a man's life is proportioned
to the length of his soul; children who die young had short souls.

ii

Attempts to
prevent the
soul from es-
caping from
the body.

The soul is commonly supposed to escape by the natural
openings of the body, especially the mouth and nostrils. Hence
in Celebes they sometimes fasten fish-hooks to a sick man's
nose, navel, and feet, so that if his soul should try to escape it
may be hooked and held fast. One of the implements of a
Haida* medicine-man is a hollow bone, in which he bottles up
departing souls, and so restores them to their owners. When any
one yawns in their presence the Hindoos always snap their
thumbs, believing that this will hinder the soul from issuing
through the open mouth. The Itonamas of South America seal
up the eyes, nose, and mouth of a dying person, in case his

ghost should get out and carry off others. In Southern Celebes, to hinder the escape of a woman's soul in childbed, the nurse ties a band as tightly as possible round the body of the expectant mother. And lest the soul of a babe should escape and be lost as soon as it is born, the Alfoors of Celebes, when a birth is about to take place, are careful to close every opening in the house, even the keyhole; and they stop up every chink and cranny in the walls. Also they tie up the mouths of all animals inside and outside the house, for fear one of them might swallow the child's soul. For a similar reason all persons present in the house, even the mother herself, are obliged to keep their mouths shut the whole time the birth is taking place. When the question was put, Why they did not hold their noses also, lest the child's soul should get into one of them? the answer was that breath being exhaled as well as inhaled through the nostrils, the soul would be expelled before it could have time to settle down.

Often the soul is conceived as a bird ready to take flight. This conception has probably left traces in most languages, and it lingers as a metaphor in poetry. The Malays carry out the conception of the bird-soul in a number of odd ways. If the soul is a bird on the wing, it may be attracted by rice, and so either prevented from flying away or lured back again from its perilous flight. Thus in Java when a child is placed on the ground for the first time (a moment which uncultured people seem to regard as especially dangerous), it is put in a hen-coop and the mother makes a clucking sound, as if she were calling hens. And in Sintang, a district of Borneo, when a person, whether man, woman, or child, has fallen out of a house or off a tree, and has been brought home, his wife or other kinswoman goes as speedily as possible to the spot where the accident happened, and there strews rice, which has been coloured yellow, while she utters the words, 'Cluck! cluck! soul! So-and-so is in his house again. Cluck! cluck! soul!' Then she gathers up the rice in a basket, carries it to the sufferer, and drops the grains from her hand on his head, saying again, 'Cluck! cluck! soul!' Here the intention clearly is to decoy back the loitering bird-soul and replace it in the head of its owner.

The soul of a sleeper is supposed to wander away from his body and actually to visit the places, to see the persons, and to perform the acts of which he dreams. Now the absence of the soul in sleep has its dangers, for if from any cause the soul should be permanently detained away from the body, the person thus deprived of the vital principle must die. There is a German belief that the soul escapes from a sleeper's mouth in the form of a white mouse or a little bird, and that to prevent the return of the bird or animal would be fatal to the sleeper. It may meet the soul of a person just deceased and be carried off by it; hence in the Aru Islands the inmates of a house will not sleep the night after a death has taken place in it, because the soul of the deceased is supposed to be still in the house and they fear to meet it in a dream. Again, the soul of the sleeper may be prevented by an accident or by physical force from returning to his body. When a Dyak dreams of falling into the water, he supposes that this accident has really befallen his spirit, and he sends for a wizard, who fishes for the spirit with a hand-net in a basin of water till he catches it and restores it to its owner. The Santals tell how a man fell asleep, and growing very thirsty, his soul, in the form of a lizard, left his body and entered a pitcher of water to drink. Just then the owner of the pitcher happened to cover it; so the soul could not return to the body and the man died. While his friends were preparing to burn the body some one uncovered the pitcher to get water. The lizard thus escaped and returned to the body, which immediately revived; so the man rose up and asked his friends why they were weeping. They told him they thought he was dead and were about to burn his body. He said he had been down a well to get water, but had found it hard to get out and had just returned. So they saw it all.

It is a common rule with primitive people not to waken a sleeper, because his soul is away and might not have time to get back; so if the man wakened without his soul, he would fall sick. If it is absolutely necessary to rouse a sleeper, it must be done very gradually, to allow the soul time to return. A Fijian in Matuku, suddenly wakened from a nap by somebody treading on his foot, has been heard bawling after his soul and imploring it to return. He had just been dreaming that he was far away in Tonga, and great was his alarm on suddenly wakening to find his body in Matuku. Death stared him in the face unless his soul could be induced to speed at once across the sea and reanimate its deserted tenement. The man would probably have died of fright if a missionary had not been at hand to allay his terror. In Bombay it is thought equivalent to murder to change the aspect of a sleeper, as by painting his face in fantastic colours or giving moustaches to a sleeping woman. For when the soul returns it will not know its own body, and the person will die.

But in order that a man's soul should quit his body, it is not necessary that he should be asleep. It may quit him in his waking hours, and then sickness, insanity, or death will be the result. Thus a man of the Wurunjeri tribe in Australia lay at his last gasp because his spirit had departed from him. A medicine-man went in pursuit and caught the spirit by the middle just as it was about to plunge into the sunset glow, which is the light cast by the souls of the dead as they pass in and out of the under-world, where the sun goes to rest. Having captured the vagrant spirit, the doctor brought it back under his opossum rug, laid himself down on the dying man, and put the soul back into him, so that after a time he revived.

Some of the Congo tribes believe that when a man is ill, his soul has left his body and is wandering at large. The aid of the sorcerer is then called in to capture the vagrant spirit and restore it to the invalid. Generally the physician declares that he has successfully chased the soul into the branch of a tree. The whole town thereupon turns out and accompanies the doctor to the tree, where the strongest men are deputed to break off the branch in which the soul of the sick man is supposed to be lodged. This they do and carry the branch back to the town, insinuating by their gestures that the burden is heavy and hard to bear. When the branch has been brought to the sick man's hut, he is placed in an upright position by its side, and the sorcerer performs the enchantments by which the soul is believed to be restored to its owner.

The departure of the soul is not always voluntary. It may be extracted from the body against its will by ghosts, demons, or sorcerers. Hence, when a funeral is passing the house, the Karens* tie their children with a special kind of string to a particular part of the house, lest the souls of the children should leave their bodies and go into the corpse which is passing. The children are kept tied in this way until the corpse is out of sight.

The wandering souls may be detained by ghosts.

And after the corpse has been laid in the grave, but before the earth has been shovelled in, the mourners and friends range themselves round the grave, each with a bamboo split lengthwise in one hand and a little stick in the other; each man thrusts his bamboo into the grave, and drawing the stick along the groove of the bamboo points out to his soul that in this way it may easily climb up out of the tomb. While the earth is being shovelled in, the bamboos are kept out of the way, lest the souls should be in them, and so should be inadvertently buried with the earth as it is being thrown into the grave; and when the people leave the spot they carry away the bamboos, begging their souls to come with them. Further, on returning from the grave each Karen provides himself with three little hooks made of branches of trees, and calling his spirit to follow him, at short intervals, as he returns, he makes a motion as if hooking it, and then thrusts the hook into the ground. This is done to prevent the soul of the living from staying behind with the soul of the dead. When the Karo-Bataks* have buried somebody and are filling in the grave, a sorceress runs about beating the air with a stick. This she does in order to drive away the souls of the survivors, for if one of these souls happened to slip into the grave and to be covered up with earth, its owner would die.

Often the abduction of a man's soul is set down to demons. Thus fits and convulsions are generally ascribed by the Chinese to the agency of certain mischievous spirits who love to draw men's souls out of their bodies. At Amoy* the spirits who serve babies and children in this way rejoice in the high-sounding titles of 'celestial agencies bestriding galloping horses' and 'literary graduates residing half-way up in the sky'. When an infant is writhing in convulsions, the frightened mother hastens to the roof of the house, and, waving about a bamboo pole to which one of the child's garments is attached, cries out several times, 'My child So-and-so, come back, return home!' Meantime, another inmate of the house bangs away at a gong in the hope of attracting the attention of the strayed soul, which is supposed to recognise the familiar garment and to slip into it. The garment containing the soul is then placed on or beside the child, and if the child does not die recovery is sure to follow, sooner or later. Similarly some Indians catch a man's lost soul in his boots and restore it to his body by putting his feet into them.

In the Moluccas when a man is unwell it is thought that some devil has carried away his soul to the tree, mountain, or hill where he (the devil) resides. A sorcerer having pointed out the devil's abode, the friends of the patient carry thither cooked rice, fruit, fish, raw eggs, a hen, a chicken, a silken robe, gold, armlets, and so forth. Having set out the food in order they pray, saying: 'We come to offer to you, O devil, this offering of food, clothes, gold, and so on; take it and release the soul of the patient for whom we pray. Let it return to his body, and he who now is sick shall be made whole.' Then they eat a little and let the hen loose as a ransom for the soul of the patient; also they put down the raw eggs; but the silken robe, the gold, and the armlets they take home with them. As soon as they are come to the house they place a flat bowl containing the offerings which have been brought back at the sick man's head, and say to him: 'Now is your soul released, and you shall fare well and live to grey hairs on the earth.'

Again, souls may be extracted from their bodies or detained on their wanderings not only by ghosts and demons but also by men, especially by sorcerers. In Fiji, if a criminal refused to confess, the chief sent for a scarf with which 'to catch away the soul of the rogue'. At the sight or even at the mention of the scarf the culprit generally made a clean breast. For if he did not, the scarf would be waved over his head till his soul was caught in it, when it would be carefully folded up and nailed to the end of a chief's canoe; and for want of his soul the criminal would pine and die. The sorcerers of Danger Island* used to set snares for souls. The snares were made of stout cinet, about fifteen to thirty feet long, with loops on either side of different sizes, to suit the different sizes of souls; for fat souls there were large loops, for thin souls there were small ones. When a man was sick against whom the sorcerers had a grudge, they set up these soul-snares near his house and watched for the flight of his soul. If in the shape of a bird or an insect it was caught in the snare, the man would infallibly die. In some parts of West Africa, indeed, wizards are continually setting traps to catch souls that wander from their bodies in sleep; and when they have caught one, they tie it up over the fire, and as it shrivels in the heat the owner sickens. This is done, not out of any grudge towards the sufferer, but purely as a matter of business. The wizard does not care whose soul he has captured, and will readily restore it to its owner, if only he is paid for doing so. Some sorcerers keep regular asylums for strayed souls, and anybody who has lost or mislaid his own soul can always have another one from the asylum on payment of the usual fee. No blame whatever attaches to men who keep these private asylums or set traps for passing souls; it is their profession, and in the exercise of it they are actuated by no harsh or unkindly feelings. But there are also wretches who from pure spite or for the sake of lucre set and bait traps with the deliberate purpose of catching the soul of a particular man; and in the bottom of the pot, hidden by the bait, are knives and sharp hooks which tear and rend the poor soul, either killing it outright or mauling it so as to impair the health of its owner when it succeeds in escaping and returning to him.

iii

A person's soul conceived as the shadow.

But the spiritual dangers I have enumerated are not the only ones which beset the savage. Often he regards his shadow or reflection as his soul, or at all events as a vital part of himself, and as such it is necessarily a source of danger to him. For if it is trampled upon, struck, or stabbed, he will feel the injury as if it were done to his person; and if it is detached from him entirely (as he believes that it may be) he will die. In the island of Wetar* there are magicians who can make a man ill by stabbing his shadow with a pike or hacking it with a sword. After Sankara had destroyed the Buddhists in India, it is said that he journeyed to Nepaul, where he had some difference of opinion with the Grand Lama. To prove his supernatural powers, he soared into the air. But as he mounted up, the Grand Lama, perceiving his shadow swaying and wavering on the ground, struck his knife into it and down fell Sankara and broke his neck.

In the Banks Islands* there are some stones of a remarkably long shape which go by the name of 'eating ghosts', because certain powerful and dangerous ghosts are believed to lodge in them. If a man's shadow falls on one of these stones, the ghost will draw his soul out from him, so that he will die. Such stones, therefore, are set in a house to guard it; and a messenger sent to a house by the absent owner will call out the name of the sender, lest the watchful ghost in the stone should fancy that he came with evil intent and should do him a mischief. At a funeral in China, when the lid is about to be placed on the coffin, most of the bystanders, with the exception of the nearest kin, retire a few steps or even retreat to another room, for a person's health is believed to be endangered by allowing his shadow to be enclosed in a coffin. And when the coffin is about to be lowered into the grave most of the spectators recoil to a little distance lest their shadows should fall into the grave and harm should thus be done to their persons. The geomancer and his assistants stand on the side of the grave which is turned away from the sun; and the grave-diggers and coffin-bearers attach their shadows firmly to their persons by tying a strip of cloth tightly round their waists. Conversely, if the shadow is a vital part of a man or an animal, it may under certain circumstances be as hazardous to be touched by it as it would be to come into contact with the person or animal. Hence the savage makes it a rule to shun the shadow of certain persons whom for various reasons he regards as sources of dangerous influence. Amongst the dangerous classes he commonly ranks mourners and women in general, but especially his mother-in-law. The Shuswap Indians think that the shadow of a mourner falling upon a person would make him sick. Amongst the Kurnai of Victoria novices at initiation were cautioned not to let a woman's shadow fall across them, as this would make them thin, lazy, and stupid. An Australian native is said to have once nearly died of fright because the shadow of his mother-in-law fell on his legs as he lay asleep under a tree. The awe and dread with which the untutored savage contemplates his mother-in-law are amongst the most familiar facts of anthropology. In the Yuin tribes of New South Wales the rule which forbade a man to hold any communication with his wife's mother was very strict. He might not look at her or even in her direction. It was a ground of divorce if his shadow happened to fall on his mother-in-law: in that case he had to leave his wife, and she returned to her parents. In New Britain* the native imagination fails to conceive the extent and nature of the calamities which would result from a man's accidentally speaking to his wife's mother; suicide of one or both would probably be the only course open to them. The most solemn form of oath a New Briton can take is, 'Sir, if I am not telling the truth, I hope I may shake hands with my mother-in-law.'

Nowhere, perhaps, does the equivalence of the shadow to the life or soul come out more clearly than in some customs practised to this day in South-eastern Europe. In modern Greece, when the foundation of a new building is being laid, it is the custom to kill a cock, a ram, or a lamb, and to let its blood flow on the foundation-stone, under which the animal is afterwards buried. The object of the sacrifice is to give strength and stability to the building. But sometimes, instead of killing an animal, the builder entices a man to the foundation-stone, secretly measures his body, or a part of it, or his shadow, and buries the measure under the foundation-stone; or he lays the foundation-stone upon the man's shadow. It is believed that the man will die within the year. The Roumanians of Transylvania think that he whose shadow is thus immured will die within forty days; so persons passing by a building which is in course of erection may hear a warning cry, 'Beware lest they take thy shadow!' Not long ago there were still shadow-traders whose business it was to provide architects with the shadows necessary for securing their walls. In these cases the measure of the shadow is looked on as equivalent to the shadow itself, and to bury it is to bury the life or soul of the man, who, deprived of it, must die. Thus the custom is a substitute for the old practice of immuring a living person in the walls, or crushing him under the foundation-stone of a new building, in order to give strength and durability to the structure, or more definitely in order that the angry ghost may haunt the place and guard it against the intrusion of enemies.

The soul sometimes supposed to be in the reflection.

As some peoples believe a man's soul to be in his shadow, so other (or the same) peoples believe it to be in his reflection in water or a mirror. Thus 'the Andamanese* do not regard their shadows but their reflections (in any mirror) as their souls'. When the Motumotu of New Guinea first saw their likenesses in a looking-glass, they thought that their reflections were their souls. In New Caledonia the old men are of opinion that a person's reflection in water or a mirror is his soul; but the younger men, taught by the Catholic priests, maintain that it is a reflection and nothing more, just like the reflection of palm-trees in the water. The reflection-soul, being external to the man, is exposed to much the same dangers as the shadow-soul. The Zulus will not look into a dark pool because they think there is a beast in it which will take away their reflections, so that they die. The Basutos say that crocodiles have the power of thus killing a man by dragging his reflection under water. When one of them dies suddenly and from no apparent cause, his relatives will allege that a crocodile must have taken his shadow some time when he crossed a stream. In Saddle Island, Melanesia, there is a pool 'into which if any one looks he dies; the malignant spirit takes hold upon his life by means of his reflection on the water'.

We can now understand why it was a maxim both in ancient India and ancient Greece not to look at one's reflection in water, and why the Greeks regarded it as an omen of death if a man dreamed of seeing himself so reflected. They feared that the water-spirits would drag the person's reflection or soul under water, leaving him soulless to perish. This was probably the origin of the classical story of the beautiful Narcissus, who languished and died through seeing his reflection in the water.

Further, we can now explain the widespread custom of covering up mirrors or turning them to the wall after a death has taken place in the house. It is feared that the soul, projected out of the person in the shape of his reflection in the mirror, may be carried off by the ghost of the departed, which is commonly supposed to linger about the house till the burial. The custom is thus exactly parallel to the Aru* custom of not sleeping in a house after a death for fear that the soul, projected out of the body in a dream, may meet the ghost and be carried off by it. The reason why sick people should not see themselves in a mirror, and why the mirror in a sick-room is therefore covered up, is also plain; in time of sickness, when the soul might take flight so easily, it is particularly dangerous to project it out of the body by means of the reflection in a mirror. The rule is therefore precisely parallel to the rule observed by some peoples of not allowing sick people to sleep; for in sleep the soul is projected out of the body, and there is always a risk that it may not return.

As with shadows and reflections, so with portraits; they are often believed to contain the soul of the person portrayed.

People who hold this belief are naturally loth to have their likenesses taken; for if the portrait is the soul, or at least a vital part of the person portrayed, whoever possesses the portrait will be able to exercise a fatal influence over the original of it. Thus the Esquimaux of Bering Strait believe that persons dealing in witchcraft have the power of stealing a person's shade, so that without it he will pine away and die. Once at a village on the lower Yukon River an explorer had set up his camera to get a picture of the people as they were moving about among their houses. While he was focussing the instrument, the headman of the village came up and insisted on peeping under the cloth. Being allowed to do so, he gazed intently for a minute at the moving figures on the ground glass, then suddenly withdrew his head and bawled at the top of his voice to the people, 'He has all of your shades in this box.' A panic ensued among the group, and in an instant they disappeared helter-skelter into their houses. The Tepehuanes of Mexico stood in mortal terror of the camera, and five days' persuasion was necessary to induce them to pose for it. When at last they consented, they looked like criminals about to be executed. They believed that by photographing people the artist could carry off their souls and devour them at his leisure moments. They said that, when the pictures reached his country, they would die or some other evil would befall them. When Dr Catat and some companions were exploring the Bara country on the west coast of Madagascar, the people suddenly became hostile. The day before the travellers, not without difficulty, had photographed the royal family, and now found themselves accused of taking the souls of the natives for the purpose of selling them when they returned to France. Denial was vain; in compliance with the custom of the country they were obliged to catch the souls, which were then put into a basket and ordered by Dr Catat to return to their respective owners.

Some villagers in Sikhim betrayed a lively horror and hid away whenever the lens of a camera, or 'the evil eye of the box' as they called it, was turned on them. They thought it took away their souls with their pictures, and so put it in the power of the owner of the pictures to cast spells on them, and they alleged that a photograph of the scenery blighted the landscape. Until the reign of the late King of Siam no Siamese coins were ever stamped with the image of the king, 'for at that time there was a strong prejudice against the making of portraits in any medium. Europeans who travel into the jungle have, even at the present time, only to point a camera at a crowd to procure its instant dispersion. When a copy of the face of a person is made and taken away from him, a portion of his life goes with the picture. Unless the sovereign had been blessed with the years of a Methuselah he could scarcely have permitted his life to be distributed in small pieces together with the coins of the realm.'

Beliefs of the same sort still linger in various parts of Europe. Not very many years ago some old women in the Greek island of Carpathus were very angry at having their likenesses drawn, thinking that in consequence they would pine and die. There are persons in the West of Scotland 'who refuse to have their likenesses taken lest it prove unlucky; and give as instances the cases of several of their friends who never had a day's health after being photographed.'

CHAPTER 12

TABOOS

i

Primitive conceptions of the soul helped to mould early kingships.

So much for the primitive conceptions of the soul and the dangers to which it is exposed. These conceptions are not limited to one people or country; with variations of detail they are found all over the world, and survive, as we have seen, in modern Europe. Beliefs so deep-seated and so widespread must necessarily have contributed to shape the mould in which the early kingship was cast. For if every person was at such pains to save his own soul from the perils which threatened it on so many sides, how much more carefully must *he* have been guarded upon whose life hung the welfare and even the existence of the whole people, and whom therefore it was the common interest of all to preserve? Therefore we should expect to find the king's life protected by a system of precautions or safeguards still more numerous and minute than those which in primitive society every man adopts for the safety of his own soul. Now in point of fact the life of the early kings is regulated, as we have seen and shall see more fully presently, by a very exact code of rules. May we not then conjecture that these rules are in fact the very safeguards which we should expect to find adopted for the protection of the king's life? An examination of the rules themselves confirms this conjecture. For from this it appears that some of the rules observed by the kings are identical with those observed by private persons out of regard for the safety of their souls; and even of those which seem peculiar to the king, many, if not all, are most readily explained on the hypothesis that they are nothing but safeguards or lifeguards of the king.

Tabooed acts: Taboos on intercourse with strangers.

As the object of the royal taboos is to isolate the king from all sources of danger, their general effect is to compel him to live in a state of seclusion, more or less complete, according to the number and stringency of the rules he observes. Now of all sources of danger none are more dreaded by the savage than magic and witchcraft, and he suspects all strangers of practising these black arts. To guard against the baneful influence exerted voluntarily or involuntarily by strangers is therefore an elementary dictate of savage prudence. Hence before strangers are allowed to enter a district, or at least before they are permitted to mingle freely with the inhabitants, certain ceremonies are often performed by the natives of the country for the purpose of disarming the strangers of their magical powers, of counteracting the baneful influence which is believed to emanate from them, or of disinfecting, so to speak, the tainted atmosphere by which they are supposed to be surrounded. Thus, in the island of Nanumea (South Pacific) strangers from ships or from other islands were not allowed to communicate with the people until they all, or a few as representatives of the rest, had been taken to each of the four temples in the island, and prayers offered that the god would avert any disease or treachery which these strangers might have brought with them. Meat offerings were also laid upon the altars, accompanied by songs and dances in honour of the god. While these ceremonies were going on, all the people except the priests and their attendants kept out of sight. Amongst the Ot Danoms of Borneo it is the custom that strangers entering the territory should pay to the natives a certain sum, which is spent in the sacrifice of buffaloes or pigs to the spirits of the land and water, in order to reconcile them to the presence of the strangers, and to induce them not to withdraw their favour from the people of the country, but to bless the rice-harvest, and so forth. The men of a certain district in Borneo, fearing to look upon a European traveller lest he should make them ill, warned their wives and children not to go near him. Those who could not restrain their curiosity killed fowls to appease the evil spirits and smeared themselves with the blood. 'More dreaded', says a traveller in Central Borneo, 'than the evil spirits of the neighbourhood are the evil spirits from a distance which accompany travellers. When a company from the middle Mahakam river visited me among the Blu-u Kayans in the year 1897, no woman showed herself outside her house without a burning bundle of *plehiding* bark, the stinking smoke of which drives away evil spirits.'

When Crevaux* was travelling in South America he entered a village of the Apalai Indians. A few moments after his arrival some of the Indians brought him a number of large black ants, of a species whose bite is painful, fastened on palm leaves. Then all the people of the village, without distinction of age or sex, presented themselves to him, and he had to sting them all with the ants on their faces, thighs, and other parts of their bodies. Sometimes, when he applied the ants too tenderly, they called out 'More! more!' and were not satisfied till their skin was thickly studded with tiny swellings like what might have been produced by whipping them with nettles. The object of this ceremony is made plain by the custom observed in Amboyna and Uliase* of sprinkling sick people with pungent spices, such as ginger and cloves, chewed fine, in order by the prickling sensation to drive away the demon of disease which may be clinging to their persons. It is probable that the same dread of strangers, rather than any desire to do them honour, is the motive of certain ceremonies which are sometimes observed at their reception, but of which the intention is not directly stated. In Afghanistan and in some parts of Persia the traveller, before he enters a village, is frequently received with a sacrifice of animal life or food, or of fire and incense. The Afghan Boundary Mission, in passing by villages in Afghanistan, was often met with fire and incense. Sometimes a tray of lighted embers is thrown under the hoofs of the traveller's horse, with the words, 'You are welcome.' On entering a village in Central Africa Emin Pasha was received with the sacrifice of two goats; their blood was sprinkled on the path and the chief stepped over the blood to greet Emin. Sometimes the dread of strangers and their magic is too great to allow of their reception on any terms. Thus when Speke arrived at a certain village, the natives shut their doors against him, 'because they had never before seen a white man nor the tin boxes that the men were carrying: "Who knows," they said, "but that these very boxes are the plundering Watuta transformed and come to kill us? You cannot be admitted." No persuasion could avail with them, and the party had to proceed to the next village.'

The fear thus entertained of alien visitors is often mutual. Entering a strange land the savage feels that he is treading enchanted ground, and he takes steps to guard against the demons that haunt it and the magical arts of its inhabitants. Thus on going to a strange land the Maoris performed certain ceremonies to make it 'common', lest it might have been previously 'sacred'. When Baron Miklucho-Maclay was approaching a village on the Maclay Coast of New Guinea, one of the natives who accompanied him broke a branch from a tree and going aside whispered to it for a while; then stepping up to each member of the party, one after another, he spat something upon his back and gave him some blows with the branch. Lastly, he went into the forest and buried the branch under withered leaves in the thickest part of the jungle. This ceremony was believed to protect the party against all treachery and danger in the village they were approaching. The idea probably was that the malignant influences were drawn off from the persons into the branch and buried with it in the depths of the forest. In Australia, when a strange tribe has been invited into a district and is approaching the encampment of the tribe which owns the land, 'the strangers carry lighted bark or burning sticks in their hands, for the purpose, they say, of clearing and purifying the air'.

Again, it is believed that a man who has been on a journey may have contracted some magic evil from the strangers with whom he has associated. Hence, on returning home, before he is readmitted to the society of his tribe and friends, he has to undergo certain purificatory ceremonies. Thus the Bechuanas 'cleanse or purify themselves after journeys by shaving their heads, etc., lest they should have contracted from strangers some evil by witchcraft or sorcery'. Two Hindoo ambassadors, who had been sent to England by a native prince and had returned to India, were considered to have so polluted themselves by contact with strangers that nothing but being born again could restore them to purity. 'For the purpose of regeneration it is directed to make an image of pure gold of the female power of nature, in the shape either of a woman or of a cow. In this statue the person to be regenerated is enclosed, and dragged through the usual channel. As a statue of pure gold and of proper dimensions would be too expensive, it is sufficient to make an image of the sacred *Yoni*, through which the person to be regenerated is to pass.' Such an image of pure gold was made at the prince's command, and his ambassadors were born again by being dragged through it.

When precautions like these are taken on behalf of the people in general against the malignant influence supposed to be exercised by strangers, it is no wonder that special measures are adopted to protect the king from the same insidious danger. In the middle ages the envoys who visited a Tartar Khan were obliged to pass between two fires before they were admitted to his presence, and the gifts they brought were also carried between the fires. The reason assigned for the custom was that the fire purged away any magic influence which the strangers might mean to exercise over the Khan. When subject chiefs come with their retinues to visit Kalamba (the most powerful chief of the Bashilange in the Congo Basin) for the first time or after being rebellious, they have to bathe, men and women together, in two brooks on two successive days, passing the nights under the open sky in the market-place. After the second bath they proceed, entirely naked, to the house of Kalamba, who makes a long white mark on the breast and forehead of each of them. Then they return to the market-place and dress, after which they undergo the pepper ordeal. Pepper is dropped into the eyes of each of them, and while this is being done the sufferer has to make a confession of all his sins, to answer all questions that may be put to him, and to take certain vows. This ends the ceremony, and the strangers are now free to take up their quarters in the town for as long as they choose to remain.

Tabooed acts: Taboos on eating and drinking.
In the opinion of savages the acts of eating and drinking are attended with special danger; for at these times the soul may escape from the mouth, or be extracted by the magic arts of an enemy present. Thus of the Bataks it is said that 'since the soul can leave the body, they always take care to prevent their soul from straying on occasions when they have most need of it. But it is only possible to prevent the soul from straying when one is in the house. At feasts one may find the whole house shut up, in order that the soul may stay and enjoy the good things set before it.' The Zafimanelo in Madagascar lock their doors when they eat, and hardly any one ever sees them eating. The Warua will not allow any one to see them eating and drinking, being doubly particular that no person of the opposite sex shall see them doing so. 'I had to pay a man to let me see him drink; I could not make a man let a woman see him drink.' When offered a drink they often ask that a cloth may be held up to hide them whilst drinking.

If these are the ordinary precautions taken by common people, the precautions taken by kings are extraordinary. The king of Loango may not be seen eating or drinking by man or beast under pain of death. A favourite dog having broken into the room where the king was dining, the king ordered it to be killed on the spot. Once the king's own son, a boy of twelve years old, inadvertently saw the king drink. Immediately the king ordered him to be finely apparelled and feasted, after which he commanded him to be cut in quarters, and carried about the city with a proclamation that he had seen the king drink. 'When the king has a mind to drink, he has a cup of wine brought; he that brings it has a bell in his hand, and as soon as he has delivered the cup to the king, he turns his face from him and rings the bell, on which all present fall down with their faces to the ground, and continue so till the king has drunk . . . His eating is much in the same style, for which he has a house on purpose, where his victuals are set upon a bensa or table: which he goes to, and shuts the door: when he has done, he knocks and comes out. So that none ever see the king eat or drink. For it is believed that if any one should, the king shall immediately die.' It is a capital offence to see the king of Dahomey at his meals. When he drinks in public, as he does on extraordinary occasions, he hides himself behind a curtain, or handkerchiefs are held up round his head, and all the people throw themselves with their faces to the earth.

Again, magic mischief may be wrought upon a man through the remains of the food he has partaken of, or the dishes out of which he has eaten. On the principles of sympathetic magic a real connexion continues to subsist between the food which a man has in his stomach and the refuse of it which he has left untouched, and hence by injuring the refuse you can simultaneously injure the eater. Among the Narrinyeri of South Australia every adult is constantly on the look-out for bones of beasts, birds, or fish, of which the flesh has been eaten by somebody, in order to construct a deadly charm out of them. Every one is therefore careful to burn the bones of the animals which he has eaten, lest they should fall into the hands of a sorcerer. In Tana, one of the New Hebrides, people bury or throw into the sea the leavings of their food, lest these should fall into the hands of the disease-makers. For if a disease-maker

[marginal note: Tabooed acts: Taboos on leaving food over.]

finds the remnants of a meal, say the skin of a banana, he picks it up and burns it slowly in the fire. As it burns, the person who ate the banana falls ill and sends to the disease-maker, offering him presents if he will stop burning the banana skin. In New Guinea the natives take the utmost care to destroy or conceal the husks and other remains of their food, lest these should be found by their enemies and used by them for the injury or destruction of the eaters. Hence they burn their leavings, throw them into the sea, or otherwise put them out of harm's way. From a like fear, no doubt, of sorcery, no one may touch the food which the king of Loango leaves upon his plate; it is buried in a hole in the ground. And no one may drink out of the king's vessel. In antiquity the Romans used immediately to break the shells of eggs and of snails which they had eaten, in order to prevent enemies from making magic with them. The common practice, still observed among us, of breaking egg-shells after the eggs have been eaten may very well have originated in the same superstition.

The superstitious fear of the magic that may be wrought on a man through the leavings of his food has had the beneficial effect of inducing many savages to destroy refuse which, if left to rot, might through its corruption have proved a real, not a merely imaginary, source of disease and death. Nor is it only the sanitary condition of a tribe which has benefited by this superstition; curiously enough the same baseless dread, the same false notion of causation, has indirectly strengthened the moral bonds of hospitality, honour, and good faith among men who entertain it. For it is obvious that no one who intends to harm a man by working magic on the refuse of his food will himself partake of that food, because if he did so he would, on the principles of sympathetic magic, suffer equally with his enemy from any injury done to the refuse. This is the idea which in primitive society lends sanctity to the bond produced by eating together,* by participation in the same food two men give, as it were, hostages for their good behaviour; each guarantees the other that he will devise no mischief against him, since, being physically united with him by the common food in their stomachs, any harm he might do to his fellow would recoil on his own head with precisely the same force with which it fell on the head of his victim. In strict logic, however, the sympathetic bond lasts only so long as the food is in the stomach of each of the parties. Hence the covenant formed by eating together is less solemn and durable than the covenant formed by transfusing the blood of the covenanting parties into each other's veins, for this transfusion seems to knit them together for life.

ii

We have seen that the Mikado's food was cooked every day in new pots and served up in new dishes; both pots and dishes were of common clay, in order that they might be broken or laid aside after they had been once used. They were generally broken, for it was believed that if any one else ate his food out of these sacred dishes, his mouth and throat would become swollen and inflamed. The same ill effect was thought to be experienced by any one who should wear the Mikado's clothes without his leave; he would have swellings and pains all over his body. In Fiji there is a special name (*kana lama*) for the disease supposed to be caused by eating out of a chief's dishes or wearing his clothes. 'The throat and body swell, and the impious person dies. I had a fine mat given to me by a man who durst not use it because Thakombau's eldest son had sat upon it. There was always a family or clan of commoners who were exempt from this danger. I was talking about this once to Thakombau. "Oh yes," said he. "Here, So-and-so! come and scratch my back." The man scratched; he was one of those who could do it with impunity.' The name of the men thus highly privileged was *Na nduka ni*, or the dirt of the chief.

In the evil effects thus supposed to follow upon the use of the vessels or clothes of the Mikado and a Fijian chief we see that other side of the god-man's character to which attention has been already called. The divine person is a source of danger as well as of blessing; he must not only be guarded, he must also be guarded against. His sacred organism, so delicate that a touch may disorder it, is also, as it were, electrically charged with a powerful magical or spiritual force which may discharge itself with fatal effect on whatever comes in contact with it. Accordingly the isolation of the man-god is quite as necessary for the safety of others as for his own. His magical virtue is in the strictest sense of the word contagious: his divinity is a fire,

Tabooed persons: Chiefs and kings tabooed.

which, under proper restraints, confers endless blessings, but, if rashly touched or allowed to break bounds, burns and destroys what it touches. Hence the disastrous effects supposed to attend a breach of taboo; the offender has thrust his hand into the divine fire, which shrivels up and consumes him on the spot.

For instance, it once happened that a New Zealand chief of high rank and great sanctity had left the remains of his dinner by the wayside. A slave, a stout, hungry fellow, coming up after the chief had gone, saw the unfinished dinner, and ate it up without asking questions. Hardly had he finished when he was informed by a horror-stricken spectator that the food of which he had eaten was the chief's. 'I knew the unfortunate delinquent well. He was remarkable for courage, and had signalised himself in the wars of the tribe,' but 'no sooner did he hear the fatal news than he was seized by the most extraordinary convulsions and cramp in the stomach, which never ceased till he died, about sundown the same day. He was a strong man, in the prime of life, and if any pakeha [European] freethinker should have said he was not killed by the *tapu* of the chief, which had been communicated to the food by contact, he would have been listened to with feelings of contempt for his ignorance and inability to understand plain and direct evidence.' This is not a solitary case. A Maori woman having eaten of some fruit, and being afterwards told that the fruit had been taken from a tabooed place, exclaimed that the spirit of the chief, whose sanctity had been thus profaned, would kill her. This was in the afternoon, and next day by twelve o'clock she was dead. A Maori chief's tinder-box was once the means of killing several persons; for, having been lost by him, and found by some men who used it to light their pipes, they died of fright on learning to whom it had belonged. So, too, the garments of a high New Zealand chief will kill any one else who wears them. A chief was observed by a missionary to throw down a precipice a blanket which he found too heavy to carry. Being asked by the missionary why he did not leave it on a tree for the use of a future traveller, the chief replied that 'it was the fear of its being taken by another which caused him to throw it where he did, for if it were worn, his tapu' (that is, his spiritual power communicated by contact to the blanket and through the blanket to the man) 'would kill the person'. For a similar reason a Maori chief would not blow a fire with his mouth; for his sacred breath would communicate its sanctity to the fire, which would pass it on to the pot on the fire, which would pass it on to the meat in the pot, which would pass it on to the man who ate the meat, which was in the pot, which stood on the fire, which was breathed on by the chief; so that the eater, infected by the chief's breath conveyed through these intermediaries, would surely die.

In general, we may say that the prohibition to use the vessels, garments, and so forth of certain persons, and the effects supposed to follow an infraction of the rule, are exactly the same whether the persons to whom the things belong are sacred or what we might call unclean and polluted. As the garments which have been touched by a sacred chief kill those who handle them, so do the things which have been touched by a menstruous woman. An Australian black-fellow, who discovered that his wife had lain on his blanket at her menstrual period, killed her and died of terror himself within a fortnight. Hence Australian women at these times are forbidden under pain of death to touch anything that men use, or even to walk on a path that any man frequents. They are also secluded at childbirth, and all vessels used by them during their seclusion are burned. In Uganda the pots which a woman touches, while the impurity of childbirth or of menstruation is on her, should be destroyed; spears and shields defiled by her touch are not destroyed but only purified.

Tabooed persons: Women tabooed at menstruation and childbirth.

Among many peoples similar restrictions are imposed on women in childbed and apparently for similar reasons; at such periods women are supposed to be in a dangerous condition which would infect any person or thing they might touch; hence they are put into quarantine until, with the recovery of their health and strength, the imaginary danger has passed away. Thus, in Tahiti a woman after childbirth was secluded for a fortnight or three weeks in a temporary hut erected on sacred ground; during the time of her seclusion she was debarred from touching provisions, and had to be fed by another. Further, if any one else touched the child at this period, he was subjected to the same restrictions as the mother until the ceremony of her purification had been performed. Similarly in the island of

Kadiak, off Alaska, a woman about to be delivered retires to a miserable low hovel built of reeds, where she must remain for twenty days after the birth of her child, whatever the season may be, and she is considered so unclean that no one will touch her, and food is reached to her on sticks. The Bribri Indians regard the pollution of childbed as much more dangerous even than that of menstruation. When a woman feels her time approaching, she informs her husband, who makes haste to build a hut for her in a lonely spot. There she must live alone, holding no converse with anybody save her mother or another woman. After her delivery the medicine-man purifies her by breathing on her and laying an animal, it matters not what, upon her. But even this ceremony only mitigates her uncleanness into a state considered to be equivalent to that of a menstruous woman; and for a full lunar month she must live apart from her housemates, observing the same rules with regard to eating and drinking as at her monthly periods. The case is still worse, the pollution is still more deadly, if she has had a miscarriage or has been delivered of a stillborn child. In that case she may not go near a living soul: the mere contact with things she has used is exceedingly dangerous: her food is handed to her at the end of a long stick. This lasts generally for three weeks, after which she may go home, subject only to the restrictions incident to an ordinary confinement.

Tabooed persons: Warriors tabooed.

Once more, warriors are conceived by the savage to move, so to say, in an atmosphere of spiritual danger which constrains them to practise a variety of superstitious observances quite different in their nature from those rational precautions which, as a matter of course, they adopt against foes of flesh and blood. The general effect of these observances is to place the warrior, both before and after victory, in the same state of seclusion or spiritual quarantine in which, for his own safety, primitive man puts his human gods and other dangerous characters. Thus when the Maoris went out on the war-path they were sacred or taboo in the highest degree, and they and their friends at home had to observe strictly many curious customs over and above the numerous taboos of ordinary life. They became, in the irreverent language of Europeans, who knew them in the old fighting days, 'tabooed an inch thick'; and as for the leader of the expedition, he was quite unapproachable. Similarly, when the Israelites marched forth to war they were bound by certain rules of ceremonial purity identical with rules observed by Maoris and Australian black-fellows on the war-path. The vessels they used were sacred, and they had to practise continence and a custom of personal cleanliness of which the original motive, if we may judge from the avowed motive of savages who conform to the same custom, was a fear lest the enemy should obtain the refuse of their persons, and thus be enabled to work their destruction by magic. Among some Indian tribes of North America a young warrior in his first campaign had to conform to certain customs, of which two were identical with the observances imposed by the same Indians on girls at their first menstruation: the vessels he ate and drank out of might be touched by no other person, and he was forbidden to scratch his head or any other part of his body with his fingers; if he could not help scratching himself, he had to do it with a stick. The latter rule, like the one which forbids a tabooed person to feed himself with his own fingers, seems to rest on the supposed sanctity or pollution, whichever we choose to call it, of the tabooed hands. Moreover, among these Indian tribes the men on the war-path had always to sleep at night with their faces turned towards their own country; however uneasy the posture, they might not change it. They might not sit upon the bare ground, nor wet their feet, nor walk on a beaten path if they could help it; when they had no choice but to walk on a path, they sought to counteract the ill effect of doing so by doctoring their legs with certain medicines or charms which they carried with them for the purpose. No member of the party was permitted to step over the legs, hands, or body of any other member who chanced to be sitting or lying on the ground; and it was equally forbidden to step over his blanket, gun, tomahawk, or anything that belonged to him. If this rule was inadvertently broken, it became the duty of the member whose person or property had been stepped over to knock the other member down, and it was similarly the duty of that other to be knocked down peaceably and without resistance.

In Windessi, Dutch New Guinea, when a party of head-hunters has been successful, and they are nearing home, they announce their approach and success by blowing on triton shells. Their canoes are also decked with branches. The faces of the men who have taken a head are blackened with charcoal. If several have taken part in killing the same victim, his head is divided among them. They always time their arrival so as to reach home in the early morning. They come rowing to the village with a great noise, and the women stand ready to dance in the verandahs of the houses. The canoes row past the *room sram* or house where the young men live; and as they pass, the murderers throw as many pointed sticks or bamboos at the wall or the roof as there were enemies killed. The day is spent very quietly. Now and then they drum or blow on the conch; at other times they beat the walls of the houses with loud shouts to drive away the ghosts of the slain. So the Yabim of New Guinea believe that the spirit of a murdered man pursues his murderer and seeks to do him a mischief. Hence they drive away the spirit with shouts and the beating of drums. When the Fijians had buried a man alive, as they often did, they used at nightfall to make a great uproar by means of bamboos, trumpet-shells, and so forth, for the purpose of frightening away his ghost, lest he should attempt to return to his old home. And to render his house unattractive to him they dismantled it and clothed it with everything that to their ideas seemed most repulsive. On the evening of the day on which they had tortured a prisoner to death, the American Indians were wont to run through the village with hideous yells, beating with sticks on the furniture, the walls, and the roofs of the huts to prevent the angry ghost of their victim from settling there and taking vengeance for the torments that his body had endured at their hands. 'Once,' says a traveller, 'on approaching in the night a village of Ottawas, I found all the inhabitants in confusion: they were all busily engaged in raising noises of the loudest and most inharmonious kind. Upon inquiry, I found that a battle had been lately fought between the Ottawas and the Kickapoos, and that the object of all this noise was to prevent the ghosts of the departed combatants from entering the village.'

Among the Natchez Indians of North America young braves who had taken their first scalps were obliged to observe certain rules of abstinence for six months. They might not sleep with their wives nor eat flesh; their only food was fish and hasty-pudding. If they broke these rules, they believed that the soul of the man they had killed would work their death by magic, that they would gain no more successes over the enemy, and that the least wound inflicted on them would prove mortal. When a Choctaw had killed an enemy and taken his scalp, he went into mourning for a month, during which he might not comb his hair, and if his head itched he might not scratch it except with a little stick which he wore fastened to his wrist for the purpose. This ceremonial mourning for the enemies they had slain was not uncommon among the North American Indians.

In savage society the hunter and the fisherman have often to observe rules of abstinence and to submit to ceremonies of purification of the same sort as those which are obligatory on the warrior and the manslayer; and though we cannot in all cases perceive the exact purpose which these rules and ceremonies are supposed to serve, we may with some probability assume that, just as the dread of the spirits of his enemies is the main motive for the seclusion and purification of the warrior who hopes to take or has already taken their lives, so the huntsman or fisherman who complies with similar customs is principally actuated by a fear of the spirits of the beasts, birds, or fish which he has killed or intends to kill.

Tabooed persons: Hunters tabooed.

While the savage respects, more or less, the souls of all animals, he treats with particular deference the spirits of such as are either especially useful to him or formidable on account of their size, strength, or ferocity. Thus the Indians of Nootka Sound prepared themselves for catching whales by observing a fast for a week, during which they ate very little, bathed in the water several times a day, sang, and rubbed their bodies, limbs, and faces with shells and bushes till they looked as if they had been severely torn with briars. They were likewise required to abstain from any commerce with their women for the like period, this last condition being considered indispensable to their success. A chief who failed to catch a whale has been known to attribute his failure to a breach of chastity on the part of his men. Rules of the same sort are, or were formerly, observed by Malagasy whalers. For eight days before they went to sea the crew of a whaler used to fast, abstaining from women and liquor, and confessing their most secret faults to each other; and if any man was found to have sinned deeply, he was forbidden to share in the expedition. In the island of Mabuiag continence was imposed on the people both before they went to hunt the dugong and while the turtles were pairing. The turtle-season lasts during parts of October and November; and if at that time unmarried persons had sexual intercourse with each other, it was believed that when the canoe approached the floating turtle, the male would separate from the female and both would dive down in different directions. So at Mowat in New Guinea men have no relation with women when the turtle are coupling, though there is considerable laxity of morals at other times. In Mirzapur,* when the seed of the silkworm is brought into the house, the Kol or Bhuiyar puts it in a place which has been carefully plastered with holy cow-dung to bring good luck. From that time the owner must be careful to avoid ceremonial impurity. He must give up cohabitation with his wife; he may not sleep on a bed, nor shave himself, nor cut his nails, nor anoint himself with oil, nor eat food cooked with butter, nor tell lies, nor do anything else that he deems wrong. He vows to Singarmati Devi that, if the worms are duly born, he will make her an offering. When the cocoons open and the worms appear, he assembles the women of the house and they sing the same song as at the birth of a baby, and red lead is smeared on the parting of the hair of all the married women of the neighbourhood. When the worms pair, rejoicings are made as at a marriage. Thus the silkworms are treated as far as possible like human beings. Hence the custom which prohibits the commerce of the sexes while the worms are hatching may be only an extension, by analogy, of the rule which is observed by many races, that the husband may not cohabit with his wife during pregnancy and lactation.

iii

The meaning of taboo.

Thus in primitive society the rules of ceremonial purity observed by divine kings, chiefs, and priests agree in many respects with the rules observed by homicides, women in childbed, girls at puberty, hunters and fishermen, and so on. To us these various classes of persons appear to differ totally in character and condition; some of them we should call holy, others we might pronounce unclean and polluted. But the savage makes no such moral distinction between them; the

conceptions of holiness and pollution are not yet differentiated
in his mind. To him the common feature of all these persons is
that they are dangerous and in danger, and the danger in which
they stand and to which they expose others is what we should
call spiritual or ghostly, and therefore imaginary. The danger,
however, is not less real because it is imaginary; imagination
acts upon man as really as does gravitation, and may kill him as
certainly as a dose of prussic acid. To seclude these persons
from the rest of the world so that the dreaded spiritual danger
shall neither reach them nor spread from them, is the object of
the taboos which they have to observe. These taboos act, so to
say, as electrical insulators to preserve the spiritual force with
which these persons are charged from suffering or inflicting
harm by contact with the outer world.

In the first place we may observe that the awful sanctity of
kings naturally leads to a prohibition to touch their sacred
persons. Thus it was unlawful to lay hands on the person of a
Spartan king: no one might touch the body of the king or queen
of Tahiti: it is forbidden to touch the person of the king of Siam
under pain of death; and no one may touch the king of
Cambodia, for any purpose whatever, without his express
command. In July 1874 the king was thrown from his carriage
and lay insensible on the ground, but not one of his suite dared
to touch him; a European coming to the spot carried the injured
monarch to his palace. Formerly no one might touch the king
of Corea; and if he deigned to touch a subject, the spot touched
became sacred, and the person thus honoured had to wear a
visible mark (generally a cord of red silk) for the rest of his life.
Above all, no iron might touch the king's body. In 1800 King
Tieng-tsong-tai-oang died of a tumour in the back, no one
dreaming of employing the lancet, which would probably have
saved his life. It is said that one king suffered terribly from an
abscess in the lip, till his physician called in a jester, whose
pranks made the king laugh heartily, and so the abscess burst.
Roman and Sabine priests might not be shaved with iron but
only with bronze razors or shears; and whenever an iron
graving-tool was brought into the sacred grove of the Arval
Brothers at Rome for the purpose of cutting an inscription in
stone, an expiatory sacrifice of a lamb and a pig must be offered,
which was repeated when the graving-tool was removed from

*Kings may
not be
touched.*

the grove. As a general rule iron might not be brought into Greek sanctuaries. In Crete sacrifices were offered to Menedemus without the use of iron, because the legend ran that Menedemus had been killed by an iron weapon in the Trojan war. The Archon of Plataea might not touch iron; but once a year, at the annual commemoration of the men who fell at the battle of Plataea, he was allowed to carry a sword wherewith to sacrifice a bull. To this day a Hottentot priest never uses an iron knife, but always a sharp splint of quartz, in sacrificing an animal or circumcising a lad. Amongst the Jews no iron tool was used in building the Temple at Jerusalem or in making an altar. The old wooden bridge (*Pons Sublicius*) at Rome, which was considered sacred, was made and had to be kept in repair without the use of iron or bronze. It was expressly provided by law that the temple of Jupiter Liber at Furfo might be repaired with iron tools. The council chamber at Cyzicus was constructed of wood without any iron nails, the beams being so arranged that they could be taken out and replaced.

Tabooed things: Iron tabooed.

This superstitious objection to iron perhaps dates from that early time in the history of society when iron was still a novelty, and as such was viewed by many with suspicion and dislike. For everything new is apt to excite the awe and dread of the savage. 'It is a curious superstition,' says a pioneer in Borneo, 'this of the Dusuns, to attribute anything—whether good or bad, lucky or unlucky—that happens to them to something novel which has arrived in their country. For instance, my living in Kindram has caused the intensely hot weather we have experienced of late.' The first introduction of iron ploughshares into Poland having been followed by a succession of bad harvests, the farmers attributed the badness of the crops to the iron ploughshares, and discarded them for the old wooden ones. To this day the primitive Baduwis of Java, who live chiefly by husbandry, will use no iron tools in tilling their fields.

There is a priestly king to the north of Zengwih in Burma, revered by the Sotih as the highest spiritual and temporal authority, into whose house no weapon or cutting instrument may be brought. This rule may perhaps be explained by a custom observed by various peoples after a death; they refrain from the use of sharp instruments so long as the ghost of the deceased is supposed to be near, lest they should wound it.

After a death the Roumanians of Transylvania are careful not to leave a knife lying with the sharp edge uppermost so long as the corpse remains in the house, 'or else the soul will be forced to ride on the blade'. For seven days after a death, the corpse being still in the house, the Chinese abstain from the use of knives and needles, and even of chopsticks, eating their food with their fingers. On the third, sixth, ninth, and fortieth days after the funeral the old Prussians and Lithuanians used to prepare a meal, to which, standing at the door, they invited the soul of the deceased. At these meals they sat silent round the table and used no knives, and the women who served up the food were also without knives. If any morsels fell from the table they were left lying there for the lonely souls that had no living relations or friends to feed them. When the meal was over the priest took a broom and swept the souls out of the house, saying, 'Dear souls, ye have eaten and drunk. Go forth, go forth.' We can now understand why no cutting instrument may be taken into the house of the Burmese pontiff. Like so many priestly kings, he is probably regarded as divine, and it is therefore right that his sacred spirit should not be exposed to the risk of being cut or wounded whenever it quits his body to hover invisible in the air or to fly on some distant mission.

We have seen that the Flamen Dialis was forbidden to touch or even name raw flesh. In the Pelew Islands when a raid has been made on a village and a head carried off, the relations of the slain man are tabooed and have to submit to certain observances in order to escape the wrath of his ghost. They are shut up in the house, touch no raw flesh, and chew betel over which an incantation has been uttered by the exorcist. After this the ghost of the slaughtered man goes away to the enemy's country in pursuit of his murderer. The taboo is probably based on the common belief that the soul or spirit of the animal is in the blood. As tabooed persons are believed to be in a perilous state—for example, the relations of the slain man are liable to the attacks of his indignant ghost—it is especially necessary to isolate them from contact with spirits; hence the prohibition to touch raw meat. But as usual the taboo is only the special enforcement of a general precept; in other words, its observance is particularly enjoined in circumstances which seem urgently to call for its application, but apart from such circumstances the

Tabooed things: Blood tabooed.

prohibition is also observed, though less strictly, as a common rule of life. Thus some of the Esthonians will not taste blood because they believe that it contains the animal's soul, which would enter the body of the person who tasted the blood. Some Indian tribes of North America, 'through a strong principle of religion, abstain in the strictest manner from eating the blood of any animal, as it contains the life and spirit of the beast'. Jewish hunters poured out the blood of the game they had killed and covered it up with dust. They would not taste the blood, believing that the soul or life of the animal was in the blood, or actually was the blood.

It is a common rule that royal blood may not be shed upon the ground. Hence when a king or one of his family is to be put to death a mode of execution is devised by which the royal blood shall not be spilt upon the earth. About the year 1688 the generalissimo of the army rebelled against the king of Siam and put him to death 'after the manner of royal criminals, or as princes of the blood are treated when convicted of capital crimes, which is by putting them into a large iron caldron, and pounding them to pieces with wooden pestles, because none of their royal blood must be spilt on the ground, it being, by their religion, thought great impiety to contaminate the divine blood by mixing it with earth'. When Kublai Khan defeated and took his uncle Nayan, who had rebelled against him, he caused Nayan to be put to death by being wrapt in a carpet and tossed to and fro till he died, 'because he would not have the blood of his Line Imperial spilt upon the ground or exposed in the eye of Heaven and before the Sun'. Friar Ricold mentions the Tartar maxim: 'One Khan will put another to death to get possession of the throne, but he takes great care that the blood be not spilt. For they say that it is highly improper that the blood of the Great Khan should be spilt upon the ground; so they cause the victim to be smothered somehow or other.' The like feeling prevails at the court of Burma, where a peculiar mode of execution without bloodshed is reserved for princes of the blood.

The reluctance to spill royal blood seems to be only a particular case of a general unwillingness to shed blood or at least to allow it to fall on the ground. Marco Polo tells us that in his day persons caught in the streets of Cambaluc (Peking) at unseasonable hours were arrested, and if found guilty of a misdemeanour were beaten with a stick. 'Under this punishment people sometimes die, but they adopt it in order to eschew bloodshed, for their *Bacsis* say that it is an evil thing to shed man's blood.' In West Sussex people believe that the ground on which human blood has been shed is accursed and will remain barren for ever. Among some primitive peoples, when the blood of a tribesman has to be spilt it is not suffered to fall upon the ground, but is received upon the bodies of his fellow-tribesmen. Thus in some Australian tribes boys who are being circumcised are laid on a platform, formed by the living bodies of the tribesmen; and when a boy's tooth is knocked out as an initiatory ceremony, he is seated on the shoulders of a man, on whose breast the blood flows and may not be wiped away. 'Also the Gauls used to drink their enemies' blood and paint themselves therewith. So also they write that the old Irish were wont; and so have I seen some of the Irish do, but not their enemies' but friends' blood, as, namely, at the execution of a notable traitor at Limerick, called Murrogh O'Brien, I saw an old woman, which was his foster-mother, take up his head whilst he was quartered and suck up all the blood that ran thereout, saying that the earth was not worthy to drink it, and therewith also steeped her face and breast and tore her hair, crying out and shrieking most terribly.'

The general explanation of the reluctance to shed blood on the ground is probably to be found in the belief that the soul is in the blood, and that therefore any ground on which it may fall necessarily becomes taboo or sacred. In New Zealand anything upon which even a drop of a high chief's blood chances to fall becomes taboo or sacred to him. For instance, a party of natives having come to visit a chief in a fine new canoe, the chief got into it, but in doing so a splinter entered his foot, and the blood trickled on the canoe, which at once became sacred to him. The owner jumped out, dragged the canoe ashore opposite the chief's house, and left it there. Again, a chief in entering a missionary's house knocked his head against a beam, and the blood flowed. The natives said that in former times the house would have belonged to the chief. As usually happens with taboos of universal application, the prohibition to spill the blood of a tribesman on the ground applies with peculiar stringency

to chiefs and kings, and is observed in their case long after it
has ceased to be observed in the case of others.

Tabooed
things: The
head tabooed.Many peoples regard the head as peculiarly sacred; the special
sanctity attributed to it is sometimes explained by a belief that
it contains a spirit which is very sensitive to injury or disrespect.
Thus the Yorubas hold that every man has three spiritual
inmates, of whom the first, called Olori, dwells in the head and
is the man's protector, guardian, and guide. Offerings are made
to this spirit, chiefly of fowls, and some of the blood mixed with
palm-oil is rubbed on the forehead. The Karens suppose that a
being called the *tso* resides in the upper part of the head, and
while it retains its seat no harm can befall the person from the
efforts of the seven *Kelahs*, or personified passions. 'But if
the *tso* becomes heedless or weak certain evil to the person is
the result. Hence the head is carefully attended to, and all
possible pains are taken to provide such dress and attire as will
be pleasing to the *tso*.' The Siamese think that a spirit called
khuan or *kwun* dwells in the human head, of which it is the
guardian spirit. The spirit must be carefully protected from
injury of every kind; hence the act of shaving or cutting the hair
is accompanied with many ceremonies. The *kwun* is very
sensitive on points of honour, and would feel mortally insulted
if the head in which he resides were touched by the hand of a
stranger. The Cambodians esteem it a grave offence to touch a
man's head; some of them will not enter a place where anything
whatever is suspended over their heads; and the meanest
Cambodian would never consent to live under an inhabited
room. Hence the houses are built of one storey only; and even
the Government respects the prejudice by never placing a
prisoner in the stocks under the floor of a house, though the
houses are raised high above the ground. The same superstition
exists amongst the Malays; for an early traveller reports that in
Java people 'wear nothing on their heads, and say that nothing
must be on their heads . . . and if any person were to put his
hand upon their head they would kill him; and they do not
build houses with storeys, in order that they may not walk over
each other's heads.'

No one was allowed to be over the head of the king of Tonga.
In Tahiti any one who stood over the king or queen, or passed
his hand over their heads, might be put to death. Until certain

rites were performed over it, a Tahitian infant was especially taboo; whatever touched the child's head, while it was in this state, became sacred and was deposited in a consecrated place railed in for the purpose at the child's house. If a branch of a tree touched the child's head, the tree was cut down; and if in its fall it injured another tree so as to penetrate the bark, that tree also was cut down as unclean and unfit for use. After the rites were performed these special taboos ceased; but the head of a Tahitian was always sacred, he never carried anything on it, and to touch it was an offence. So sacred was the head of a Maori chief that 'if he only touched it with his fingers, he was obliged immediately to apply them to his nose, and snuff up the sanctity which they had acquired by the touch, and thus restore it to the part from whence it was taken'. On account of the sacredness of his head a Maori chief 'could not blow the fire with his mouth, for the breath being sacred, communicated his sanctity to it, and a brand might be taken by a slave, or a man of another tribe, or the fire might be used for other purposes, such as cooking, and so cause his death'.

When the head was considered so sacred that it might not even be touched without grave offence, it is obvious that the cutting of the hair must have been a delicate and difficult operation. The difficulties and dangers which, on the primitive view, beset the operation are of two kinds. There is first the danger of disturbing the spirit of the head, which may be injured in the process and may revenge itself upon the person who molests him. Secondly, there is the difficulty of disposing of the shorn locks. For the savage believes that the sympathetic connexion which exists between himself and every part of his body continues to exist even after the physical connexion has been broken, and that therefore he will suffer from any harm that may befall the severed parts of his body, such as the clippings of his hair or the parings of his nails. Accordingly he takes care that these severed portions of himself shall not be left in places where they might either be exposed to accidental injury or fall into the hands of malicious persons who might work magic on them to his detriment or death. Such dangers are common to all, but sacred persons have more to fear from them than ordinary people, so the precautions taken by them are proportionately stringent. The simplest way of evading the

Tabooed things: Hair tabooed.

peril is not to cut the hair at all; and this is the expedient
adopted where the risk is thought to be more than usually great.
The Frankish kings were never allowed to crop their hair; from
their childhood upwards they had to keep it unshorn. To poll
the long locks that floated on their shoulders would have been
to renounce their right to the throne. When the wicked brothers
Clotaire and Childebert coveted the kingdom of their dead
brother Clodomir, they inveigled into their power their little
nephews, the two sons of Clodomir; and having done so, they
sent a messenger bearing scissors and a naked sword to the
children's grandmother, Queen Clotilde, at Paris. The envoy
showed the scissors and the sword to Clotilde, and bade her
choose whether the children should be shorn and live or remain
unshorn and die. The proud queen replied that if her grandchildren were not to come to the throne she would rather see
them dead than shorn. And murdered they were by their
ruthless uncle Clotaire with his own hand.* The king of
Ponape,* one of the Caroline Islands, must wear his hair long,
and so must his grandees.

But when it becomes necessary to crop the hair, measures are
taken to lessen the dangers which are supposed to attend the
operation. The chief of Namosi in Fiji always ate a man by way
of precaution when he had had his hair cut. 'There was a certain
clan that had to provide the victim, and they used to sit in
solemn council among themselves to choose him. It was a
sacrificial feast to avert evil from the chief.' Amongst the
Maoris many spells were uttered at hair-cutting; one, for
example, was spoken to consecrate the obsidian knife with
which the hair was cut; another was pronounced to avert the
thunder and lightning which hair-cutting was believed to cause.
'He who has had his hair cut is in immediate charge of the Atua
(spirit); he is removed from the contact and society of his family
and his tribe; he dare not touch his food himself; it is put into
his mouth by another person; nor can he for some days resume
his accustomed occupations or associate with his fellow-men.'
The person who cuts the hair is also tabooed; his hands having
been in contact with a sacred head, he may not touch food with
them or engage in any other employment; he is fed by another
person with food cooked over a sacred fire. He cannot be
released from the taboo before the following day, when he rubs

his hands with potato or fern root which has been cooked on a sacred fire; and this food having been taken to the head of the family in the female line and eaten by her, his hands are freed from the taboo. In some parts of New Zealand the most sacred day of the year was that appointed for hair-cutting; the people assembled in large numbers on that day from all the neighbourhood.

But even when the hair and nails have been safely cut, there remains the difficulty of disposing of them, for their owner believes himself liable to suffer from any harm that may befall them. The notion that a man may be bewitched by means of the clippings of his hair, the parings of his nails, or any other severed portion of his person is almost world-wide, and attested by evidence too ample, too familiar, and too tedious in its uniformity to be here analysed at length. The general idea on which the superstition rests is that of the sympathetic connexion supposed to persist between a person and everything that has once been part of his body or in any way closely related to him. A very few examples must suffice. They belong to that branch of sympathetic magic which may be called contagious. Dread of sorcery, we are told, formed one of the most salient characteristics of the Marquesan islanders in the old days. The sorcerer took some of the hair, spittle, or other bodily refuse of the man he wished to injure, wrapped it up in a leaf, and placed the packet in a bag woven of threads or fibres, which were knotted in an intricate way. The whole was then buried with certain rites, and thereupon the victim wasted away of a languishing sickness which lasted twenty days. His life, however, might be saved by discovering and digging up the buried hair, spittle, or what not; for as soon as this was done the power of the charm ceased. A Maori sorcerer intent on bewitching somebody sought to get a tress of his victim's hair, the parings of his nails, some of his spittle, or a shred of his garment. Having obtained the object, whatever it was, he chanted certain spells and curses over it in a falsetto voice and buried it in the ground. As the thing decayed, the person to whom it had belonged was supposed to waste away. When an Australian blackfellow wishes to get rid of his wife, he cuts off a lock of her hair in her sleep, ties it to his spear-thrower, and goes with it to a neighbouring tribe, where he gives it to a friend. His friend sticks the spear-thrower up every night before the camp fire, and when it falls down it is a sign that the wife is dead. The way in which the charm operates was explained to Dr Howitt by a Wirajuri man. 'You see,' he said, 'when a blackfellow doctor gets hold of something belonging to a man and roasts it with things, and sings over it, the fire catches hold of the smell of the man, and that settles the poor fellow.'

Often the clipped hair and nails are stowed away in any secret place, not necessarily in a temple or cemetery or at a tree, as in the cases already mentioned. Thus in Swabia you are recommended to deposit your clipped hair in some spot where neither sun nor moon can shine on it, for example in the earth or under a stone. In Danzig it is buried in a bag under the threshold. Sometimes the severed hair and nails are preserved, not to prevent them from falling into the hands of a magician, but that the owner may have them at the resurrection of the body, to which some races look forward. Thus the Incas of Peru 'took extreme care to preserve the nail-parings and the hairs that were shorn off or torn out with a comb; placing them in holes or niches in the walls; and if they fell out, any other Indian that saw them picked them up and put them in their places again. I very often asked different Indians, at various times, why they did this, in order to see what they would say, and they all replied in the same words saying, "Know that all persons who are born must return to life" (they have no word to express resuscitation), "and the souls must rise out of their tombs with all that belonged to their bodies. We, therefore, in order that we may not have to search for our hair and nails at a time when there will be much hurry and confusion, place them in one place, that they may be brought together more conveniently, and, whenever it is possible, we are also careful to spit in one place." ' Similarly the Turks never throw away the parings of their nails, but carefully stow them in cracks of the walls or of the boards, in the belief that they will be needed at the resurrection. The Armenians do not throw away their cut hair and nails and extracted teeth, but hide them in places that are esteemed holy, such as a crack in the church wall, a pillar of the house, or a hollow tree. They think that all these severed portions of themselves will be wanted at the resurrection, and that he who has not stowed them away in a safe place will have to hunt about for them on the great day. In the village of Drumconrath in Ireland there used to be some old women who, having ascertained from Scripture that the hairs of their heads were all numbered by the Almighty, expected to have to account for them at the day of judgment. In order to be able to do so they stuffed the severed hair away in the thatch of their cottages.

We have seen that among the many taboos which the Flamen Dialis at Rome had to observe, there was one that forbade him to have a knot on any part of his garments, and another that obliged him to wear no ring unless it were broken. In like manner Moslem pilgrims to Mecca are in a state of sanctity or taboo and may wear on their persons neither knots nor rings. These rules are probably of kindred significance, and may conveniently be considered together. To begin with knots, many people in different parts of the world entertain a strong objection to having any knot about their person at certain critical seasons, particularly childbirth, marriage, and death. Thus among the Saxons of Transylvania, when a woman is in travail all knots on her garments are united, because it is believed that this will facilitate her delivery, and with the same intention all the locks in the house, whether on doors or boxes, are unlocked. The Lapps think that a lying-in woman should have no knot on her garments, because a knot would have the effect of making the delivery difficult and painful. In the East Indies this superstition is extended to the whole time of pregnancy; the people believe that if a pregnant woman were to tie knots, or braid, or make anything fast, the child would thereby be constricted or the woman would herself be 'tied up' when her time came. Nay, some of them enforce the observance of the rule on the father as well as the mother of the unborn child. Among the Sea Dyaks neither of the parents may bind up anything with string or make anything fast during the wife's pregnancy. In the Toumbuluh tribe of North Celebes a ceremony is performed in the fourth or fifth month of a woman's pregnancy, and after it her husband is forbidden, among many other things, to tie any fast knots and to sit with his legs crossed over each other.

In all these cases the idea seems to be that the tying of a knot would, as they say in the East Indies, 'tie up' the woman, in

(margin note) Tabooed things: Knots and rings tabooed.

other words, impede and perhaps prevent her delivery, or delay her convalescence after the birth. On the principles of homoe-opathic or imitative magic the physical obstacle or impediment of a knot on a cord would create a corresponding obstacle or impediment in the body of the woman. That this is really the explanation of the rule appears from a custom observed by the Hos of West Africa at a difficult birth. When a woman is in hard labour and cannot bring forth, they call in a magician to her aid. He looks at her and says, 'The child is bound in the womb, that is why she cannot be delivered.' On the entreaties of her female relations he then promises to loose the bond so that she may bring forth. For that purpose he orders them to fetch a tough creeper from the forest, and with it he binds the hands and feet of the sufferer on her back. Then he takes a knife and calls out the woman's name, and when she answers he cuts through the creeper with a knife, saying, 'I cut through to-day thy bonds and thy child's bonds.' After that he chops up the creeper small, puts the bits in a vessel of water, and bathes the woman with the water. Here the cutting of the creeper with which the woman's hands and feet are bound is a simple piece of homoeopathic or imitative magic: by releasing her limbs from their bonds the magician imagines that he simultaneously releases the child in her womb from the trammels which impede its birth. The same train of thought underlies a practice observed by some peoples of opening all locks, doors, and so on, while a birth is taking place in the house. At such a time the Germans of Transylvania open all the locks, and the same thing is done also in Voigtland and Mecklenburg. In north-western Argyllshire superstitious people used to open every lock in the house at childbirth. In the island of Salsette near Bombay, when a woman is in hard labour, all locks of doors or drawers are opened with a key to facilitate her delivery. Among the Mande-lings of Sumatra the lids of all chests, boxes, pans, and so forth are opened; and if this does not produce the desired effect, the anxious husband has to strike the projecting ends of some of the house-beams in order to loosen them; for they think that 'everything must be open and loose to facilitate the delivery'. In Chittagong, when a woman cannot bring her child to the birth, the midwife gives orders to throw all doors and windows wide open, to uncork all bottles, to remove the bungs from all casks, to unloose the cows in the stall, the horses in the stable, the watchdog in his kennel, to set free sheep, fowls, ducks, and so forth. This universal liberty accorded to the animals and even to inanimate things is, according to the people, an infallible means of ensuring the woman's delivery and allowing the babe to be born. In the island of Saghalien,* when a woman is in labour, her husband undoes everything that can be undone. He loosens the plaits of his hair and the laces of his shoes. Then he unties whatever is tied in the house or its vicinity. In the courtyard he takes the axe out of the log in which it is stuck; he unfastens the boat, if it is moored to a tree, he withdraws the cartridges from his gun, and the arrows from his crossbow.

A Toumbuluh man* abstains not only from tying knots, but also from sitting with crossed legs during his wife's pregnancy. The train of thought is the same in both cases. Whether you cross threads in tying a knot, or only cross your legs in sitting at your ease, you are equally, on the principles of homoeopathic magic, crossing or thwarting the free course of things, and your action cannot but check and impede whatever may be going forward in your neighbourhood. Of this important truth the Romans were fully aware. To sit beside a pregnant woman or a patient under medical treatment with clasped hands, says the grave Pliny, is to cast a malignant spell over the person, and it is worse still if you nurse your leg or legs with your clasped hands, or lay one leg over the other. Such postures were regarded by the old Romans as a let and hindrance to business of every sort, and at a council of war or a meeting of magistrates, at prayers and sacrifices, no man was suffered to cross his legs or clasp his hands. The stock instance of the dreadful consequences that might flow from doing one or the other was that of Alcmena, who travailed with Hercules for seven days and seven nights, because the goddess Lucina sat in front of the house with clasped hands and crossed legs, and the child could not be born until the goddess had been beguiled into changing her attitude. It is a Bulgarian superstition that if a pregnant woman is in the habit of sitting with crossed legs, she will suffer much in childbed. In some parts of Bavaria, when conversation comes to a standstill and silence ensues, they say, 'Surely somebody has crossed his legs.'

The magical effect of knots in trammelling and obstructing human activity was believed to be manifested at marriage not less than at birth. During the Middle Ages, and down to the eighteenth century, it seems to have been commonly held in Europe that the consummation of marriage could be prevented by any one who, while the wedding ceremony was taking place, either locked a lock or tied a knot in a cord, and then threw the lock or the cord away. The lock or the knotted cord had to be flung into water; and until it had been found and unlocked, or untied, no real union of the married pair was possible. Hence it was a grave offence, not only to cast such a spell, but also to steal or make away with the material instrument of it, whether lock or knotted cord. In the year 1718 the parliament of Bordeaux sentenced some one to be burned alive for having spread desolation through a whole family by means of knotted cords; and in 1705 two persons were condemned to death in Scotland for stealing certain charmed knots which a woman had made, in order thereby to mar the wedded happiness of Spalding of Ashintilly. The belief in the efficacy of these charms appears to have lingered in the Highlands of Perthshire down to the end of the eighteenth century, for at that time it was still customary in the beautiful parish of Logierait, between the river Tummel and the river Tay, to unloose carefully every knot in the clothes of the bride and bridegroom before the celebration of the marriage ceremony. We meet with the same superstition and the same custom at the present day in Syria. The persons who help a Syrian bridegroom to don his wedding garments take care that no knot is tied on them and no button buttoned, for they believe that a button buttoned or a knot tied would put it within the power of his enemies to deprive him of his nuptial rights by magical means. The fear of such charms is diffused all over North Africa at the present day. To render a bridegroom impotent the enchanter has only to tie a knot in a handkerchief which he had previously placed quietly on some part of the bridegroom's body when he was mounted on horseback ready to fetch his bride: so long as the knot in the handkerchief remains tied, so long will the bridegroom remain powerless to consummate the marriage.

The maleficent power of knots may also be manifested in the infliction of sickness, disease, and all kinds of misfortune. Thus among the Hos of West Africa* a sorcerer will sometimes curse his enemy and tie a knot in a stalk of grass, saying, 'I have tied up So-and-so in this knot. May all evil light upon him! When he goes into the field, may a snake sting him! When he goes to the chase, may a ravening beast attack him! And when he steps into a river, may the water sweep him away! When it rains, may the lightning strike him! May evil nights be his!' It is believed that in the knot the sorcerer has bound up the life of his enemy. In the Koran there is an allusion to the mischief of 'those who puff into the knots', and an Arab commentator on the passage explains that the words refer to women who practise magic by tying knots in cords, and then blowing and spitting upon them. He goes on to relate how, once upon a time, a wicked Jew bewitched the prophet Mohammed himself by tying nine knots on a string, which he then hid in a well. So the prophet fell ill, and nobody knows what might have happened if the archangel Gabriel had not opportunely revealed to the holy man the place where the knotted cord was concealed. The trusty Ali soon fetched the baleful thing from the well; and the prophet recited over it certain charms, which were specially revealed to him for the purpose. At every verse of the charms a knot untied itself, and the prophet experienced a certain relief.

If knots are supposed to kill, they are also supposed to cure. This follows from the belief that to undo the knots which are causing sickness will bring the sufferer relief. But apart from this negative virtue of maleficent knots, there are certain beneficent knots to which a positive power of healing is ascribed. Pliny tells us that some folk cured diseases of the groin by taking a thread from a web, tying seven or nine knots on it, and then fastening it to the patient's groin; but to make the cure effectual it was necessary to name some widow as each knot was tied. O'Donovan describes a remedy for fever employed among the Turcomans. The enchanter takes some camel hair and spins it into a stout thread, droning a spell the while. Next he ties seven knots on the thread, blowing on each knot before he pulls it tight. This knotted thread is then worn as a bracelet on his wrist by the patient. Everyday one of the knots is untied and blown upon, and when the seventh knot is undone the whole thread is rolled up into a ball and thrown into a river, bearing away (as they imagine) the fever with it.

Again knots may be used by an enchantress to win a lover and attach him firmly to herself. Thus the love-sick maid in Virgil* seeks to draw Daphnis to her from the city by spells and by tying three knots on each of three strings of different colours. So an Arab maiden, who had lost her heart to a certain man, tried to gain his love and bind him to herself by tying knots in his whip; but her jealous rival undid the knots. On the same principle magic knots may be employed to stop a runaway. In Swazieland you may often see grass tied in knots at the side of the footpaths. Every one of these knots tells of a domestic tragedy. A wife has run away from her husband, and he and his friends have gone in pursuit, binding up the paths, as they call it, in this fashion to prevent the fugitive from doubling back over them. A net, from its affluence of knots, has always been considered in Russia very efficacious against sorcerers; hence in some places, when a bride is being dressed in her wedding attire, a fishing-net is flung over her to keep her out of harm's way. For a similar purpose the bridegroom and his companions are often girt with pieces of net, or at least with tight-drawn girdles, for before a wizard can begin to injure them he must undo all the knots in the net, or take off the girdles. But often a Russian amulet is merely a knotted thread. A skein of red wool wound about the arms and legs is thought to ward off agues and fevers; and nine skeins, fastened round a child's neck, are deemed a preservative against scarlatina. In the Tver Government a bag of a special kind is tied to the neck of the cow which walks before the rest of a herd, in order to keep off wolves; its force binds the maw of the ravening beast. On the same principle, a padlock is carried thrice round a herd of horses before they go afield in the spring, and the bearer locks and unlocks it as he goes, saying, 'I lock from my herd the mouths of the grey wolves with this steel lock.'

Knots and locks may serve to avert not only wizards and wolves but death itself. When they brought a woman to the stake at St Andrews in 1572 to burn her alive for a witch, they found on her a white cloth like a collar, with strings and many knots on the strings. They took it from her, sorely against her will, for she seemed to think that she could not die in the fire, if only the cloth with the knotted strings was on her. When it was taken away, she said, 'Now I have no hope of myself.' In many parts of England it is thought that a person cannot die so long as any locks are locked or bolts shot in the house. It is therefore a very common practice to undo all locks and bolts when the sufferer is plainly near his end, in order that his agony may not be unduly prolonged. For example, in the year 1863, at Taunton, a child lay sick of scarlatina and death seemed inevitable. 'A jury of matrons was, as it were, empanelled, and to prevent the child "dying hard" all the doors in the house, all the drawers, all the boxes, all the cupboards were thrown wide open, the keys taken out, and the body of the child placed under a beam, whereby a sure, certain, and easy passage into eternity could be secured.' Strange to say, the child declined to avail itself of the facilities for dying so obligingly placed at its disposal by the sagacity and experience of the British matrons of Taunton; it preferred to live rather than give up the ghost just then.

The rule which prescribes that at certain magical and religious ceremonies the hair should hang loose and the feet should be bare is probably based on the same fear of trammelling and impeding the action in hand, whatever it may be, by the presence of any knot or constriction, whether on the head or on the feet of the performer. A similar power to bind and hamper spiritual as well as bodily activities is ascribed by some people to rings. Thus in the island of Carpathus people never button the clothes they put upon a dead body and they are careful to remove all rings from it; 'for the spirit, they say, can even be detained in the little finger, and cannot rest'. Here it is plain that even if the soul is not definitely supposed to issue at death from the finger-tips, yet the ring is conceived to exercise a certain constrictive influence which detains and imprisons the immortal spirit in spite of its efforts to escape from the tabernacle of clay; in short the ring, like the knot, acts as a spiritual fetter. This may have been the reason of an ancient Greek maxim, attributed to Pythagoras, which forbade people to wear rings. Nobody might enter the ancient Arcadian sanctuary of the Mistress at Lycosura with a ring on his or her finger. Persons who consulted the oracle of Faunus had to be chaste, to eat no flesh, and to wear no rings.

On the other hand, the same constriction which hinders the egress of the soul may prevent the entrance of evil spirits; hence we find rings used as amulets against demons, witches, and ghosts. In the Tyrol it is said that a woman in childbed should never take off her wedding-ring, or spirits and witches will have power over her. Among the Lapps, the person who is about to place a corpse in the coffin receives from the husband, wife, or children of the deceased a brass ring, which he must wear fastened to his right arm until the corpse is safely deposited in the grave. The ring is believed to serve the person as an amulet against any harm which the ghost might do to him. How far the custom of wearing finger-rings may have been influenced by, or even have sprung from, a belief in their efficacy as amulets to keep the soul in the body, or demons out of it, is a question which seems worth considering. Here we are only concerned with the belief in so far as it seems to throw light on the rule that the Flamen Dialis might not wear a ring unless it were broken. Taken in conjunction with the rule which forbade him to have a knot on his garments, it points to a fear that the powerful spirit embodied in him might be trammelled and hampered in its goings-out and comings-in by such corporeal and spiritual fetters as rings and knots.

iv

Tabooed words: Personal names tabooed.

Unable to discriminate clearly between words and things, the savage commonly fancies that the link between a name and the person or thing denominated by it is not a mere arbitrary and ideal association, but a real and substantial bond which unites the two in such a way that magic may be wrought on a man just as easily through his name as through his hair, his nails, or any other material part of his person. In fact, primitive man regards his name as a vital portion of himself and takes care of it accordingly. Thus, for example; the North American Indian 'regards his name, not as a mere label, but as a distinct part of his personality, just as much as are his eyes or his teeth, and believes that injury will result as surely from the malicious handling of his name as from a wound inflicted on any part of his physical organism. This belief was found among the various tribes from the Atlantic to the Pacific, and has occasioned a number of curious regulations in regard to the concealment and change of names.' Some Esquimaux take new names when they are old, hoping thereby to get a new lease of life. The Tolampoos of Celebes believe that if you write a man's name down you can carry off his soul along with it. Many savages at the present day regard their names as vital parts of themselves, and therefore take great pains to conceal their real names, lest these should give to evil-disposed persons a handle by which to injure their owners.

Thus, we are told that the secrecy with which among the Australian aborigines personal names are often kept from general knowledge 'arises in great measure from the belief that an enemy, who knows your name, has in it something which he can use magically to your detriment'. Amongst the tribes of Central Australia every man, woman, and child has, besides a personal name which is in common use, a secret or sacred name which is bestowed by the older men upon him or her soon after birth, and which is known to none but the fully initiated members of the group. This secret name is never mentioned except upon the most solemn occasions; to utter it in the hearing of women or of men of another group would be a most serious breach of tribal custom, as serious as the most flagrant case of sacrilege among ourselves. When mentioned at all, the name is spoken only in a whisper, and not until the most elaborate precautions have been taken that it shall be heard by no one but members of the group. 'The native thinks that a stranger knowing his secret name would have special power to work him ill by means of magic.'

The same fear seems to have led to a custom of the same sort amongst the ancient Egyptians, whose comparatively high civilisation was strangely dashed and chequered with relics of the lowest savagery. Every Egyptian received two names, which were known respectively as the true name and the good name, or the great name and the little name; and while the good or little name was made public, the true or great name appears to have been carefully concealed. A Brahman child receives two names, one for common use, the other a secret name which none but his father and mother should know. The latter is only used at ceremonies such as marriage. The custom is intended to protect the person against magic, since a charm only becomes effectual in combination with the real name. Similarly, the natives of Nias believe that harm may be done to a person by the demons who hear his name pronounced. Hence the names of infants, who are especially exposed to the assaults of evil spirits, are never spoken; and often in haunted spots, such as the gloomy depths of the forest, the banks of a river, or beside a bubbling spring, men will abstain from calling each other by their names for a like reason.

The Indians of Chiloe* keep their names secret and do not like to have them uttered aloud; for they say that there are fairies or imps on the mainland or neighbouring islands who, if they knew folk's names, would do them an injury: but so long as they do not know the names, these mischievous sprites are powerless. The Araucanians will hardly ever tell a stranger their names because they fear that he would thereby acquire some supernatural power over themselves. Asked his name by a stranger, who is ignorant of their superstitions, an Araucanian* will answer, 'I have none.' When an Ojebway is asked his name, he will look at some bystander and ask him to answer. 'This reluctance arises from an impression they receive when young, that if they repeat their own names it will prevent their growth, and they will be small in stature. On account of this unwillingness to tell their names, many strangers have fancied that they either have no names or have forgotten them.'

In this last case no scruple seems to be felt about communicating a man's name to strangers, and no ill effects appear to be dreaded as a consequence of divulging it; harm is only done when a name is spoken by its owner. Why is this? and why in particular should a man be thought to stunt his growth by uttering his own name? We may conjecture that to savages who act and think thus a person's name only seems to be a part of himself when it is uttered with his own breath; uttered by the breath of others it has no vital connexion with him, and no harm can come to him through it. Whereas, so these primitive philosophers may have argued, when a man lets his own name pass his lips, he is parting with a living piece of himself, and if he persists in so reckless a course he must certainly end by dissipating his energy and shattering his constitution. Many a broken-down debauchee, many a feeble frame wasted with disease, may have been pointed out by these simple moralists to their awe-struck disciples as a fearful example of the fate that must sooner or later overtake the profligate who indulges immoderately in the seductive habit of mentioning his own name.

However we may explain it, the fact is certain that many a savage evinces the strongest reluctance to pronounce his own name, while at the same time he makes no objection at all to other people pronouncing it, and will even invite them to do so for him in order to satisfy the curiosity of an inquisitive stranger. Thus in some parts of Madagascar it is taboo for a person to tell his own name, but a slave or attendant will answer for him. The same curious inconsistency, as it may seem to us, is recorded of some tribes of American Indians. Thus we are told that 'the name of an American Indian is a sacred thing, not to be divulged by the owner himself without due consideration. One may ask a warrior of any tribe to give his name, and the question will be met with either a point-blank refusal or the more diplomatic evasion that he cannot understand what is wanted of him. The moment a friend approaches, the warrior first interrogated will whisper what is wanted, and the friend can tell the name, receiving a reciprocation of the courtesy from the other.' This general statement applies, for example, to the Indian tribes of British Columbia, as to whom it is said that 'one of their strangest prejudices, which appears to pervade all tribes alike, is a dislike to telling their names—thus you never get a man's right name from himself; but they will tell each other's names without hesitation'. In the whole of the East Indian Archipelago the etiquette is the same. As a general rule no one will utter his own name. To enquire, 'What is your name?' is a very indelicate question in native society. When in the course of administrative or judicial business a native is asked his name, instead of replying he will look at his comrade to indicate that he is to answer for him, or he will say straight out, 'Ask him.' The superstition is current all over the East Indies without exception, and it is found also among the Motu and Motumotu tribes, the Papuans of Finsch Haven in North New Guinea, the Nufoors of Dutch New Guinea, and the Melanesians of the Bismarck Archipelago. Among many tribes of South Africa men and women never mention their names if they can get any one else to do it for them, but they do not absolutely refuse when it cannot be avoided.

Sometimes the embargo laid on personal names is not permanent; it is conditional on circumstances, and when these change it ceases to operate. Thus when the Nandi men are away on a foray, nobody at home may pronounce the names of the absent warriors; they must be referred to as birds. Should a child so far forget itself as to mention one of the distant ones by name, the mother would rebuke it, saying, 'Don't talk of the birds who are in the heavens.' Among the Bangala of the Upper Congo, while a man is fishing and when he returns with his catch, his proper name is in abeyance and nobody may mention it. Whatever the fisherman's real name may be, he is called *mwele* without distinction. The reason is that the river is full of spirits, who, if they heard the fisherman's real name, might so work against him that he would catch little or nothing. Even when he has caught his fish and landed with them, the buyer must still not address him by his proper name, but must only call him *mwele*; for even then, if the spirits were to hear his proper name, they would either bear it in mind and serve him out another day, or they might so mar the fish he had caught that he would get very little for them. Hence the fisherman can extract heavy damages from anybody who mentions his name, or can compel the thoughtless speaker to relieve him of the fish at a good price so as to restore his luck. When the Sulka of New Britain are near the territory of their enemies the Gaktei, they take care not to mention them by their proper name, believing that were they to do so, their foes would attack and slay them. Hence in these circumstances they speak of the Gaktei as *o lapsiek*, that is, 'the rotten tree-trunks', and they imagine that by calling them that they make the limbs of their dreaded enemies ponderous and clumsy like logs. This example illustrates the extremely materialistic view which these savages take of the nature of words; they suppose that the mere utterance of an expression signifying clumsiness will homoeopathically affect with clumsiness the limbs of their distant foemen.

When it is deemed necessary that a man's real name should be kept secret, it is often customary, as we have seen, to call him by a surname or nickname. As distinguished from the real or primary names, these secondary names are apparently held to be no part of the man himself, so that they may be freely used and divulged to everybody without endangering his safety thereby. Sometimes in order to avoid the use of his own name a man will be called after his child. Thus we are informed that 'the Gippsland* blacks objected strongly to let any one outside the tribe know their names, lest their enemies, learning them, should make them vehicles of incantation, and so charm their lives away. As children were not thought to have enemies, they used to speak of a man as "the father, uncle, or cousin of So-and-so," naming a child; but on all occasions abstained from mentioning the name of a grown-up person.' The Alfoors of Poso in Celebes will not pronounce their own names. Among them, accordingly, if you wish to ascertain a person's name, you ought not to ask the man himself, but should enquire of others. But if this is impossible, for example, when there is no one else near, you should ask him his child's name, and then address him as the 'Father of So-and-so'. Nay, these Alfoors are shy of uttering the names even of children; so when a boy or girl has a nephew or niece, he or she is addressed as 'Uncle of So-and-so', or 'Aunt of So-and-so'. In pure Malay society, we are told, a man is never asked his name, and the custom of naming parents after their children is adopted only as a means of avoiding the use of the parents' own names. Among the land Dyaks children as they grow up are called, according to their sex, the father or mother of a child of their father's or mother's younger brother or sister, that is, they are called the father or mother of what we should call their first cousin. Among the Kukis and Zemis or Kacha Nagas of Assam parents drop their names after the birth of a child and are named Father and Mother of So-and-so. Childless couples go by the name of 'the childless father', 'the childless mother,' 'the father of no child', 'the mother of no child'. The widespread custom of naming a father after his child has sometimes been supposed to spring from a desire on the father's part to assert his paternity, apparently as a means of obtaining those rights over his children which had previously, under a system of mother-kin, been possessed by the mother. But this explanation does not account for the parallel custom of naming the mother after her child, which seems commonly to coexist with the practice of naming the father after the child. Still less, if possible, does it apply to the customs of calling childless couples the father and mother of children which do not exist, of naming people after their

younger brothers, and of designating children as the uncles and
aunts of So-and-so, or as the fathers and mothers of their first
cousins. But all these practices are explained in a simple and
natural way if we suppose that they originate in a reluctance to
utter the real names of persons addressed or directly referred
to. That reluctance is probably based partly on a fear of
attracting the notice of evil spirits, partly on a dread of
revealing the name to sorcerers, who would thereby obtain a
handle for injuring the owner of the name.

Tabooed
words:
Names of
relations
tabooed.

It might naturally be expected that the reserve so commonly
maintained with regard to personal names would be dropped or
at least relaxed among relations and friends. But the reverse of
this is often the case. It is precisely the persons most intimately
connected by blood and especially by marriage to whom the rule
applies with the greatest stringency. Such people are often
forbidden, not only to pronounce each other's names, but even
to utter ordinary words which resemble or have a single syllable
in common with these names. The persons who are thus
mutually debarred from mentioning each other's names are
especially husbands and wives, a man and his wife's parents,
and a woman and her husband's father. A Kirghiz woman dares
not pronounce the names of the older relations of her husband,
nor even use words which resemble them in sound. For
example, if one of these relations is called Shepherd, she may
not speak of sheep, but must call them 'the bleating ones'; if his
name is Lamb, she must refer to lambs as 'the young bleating
ones'. In Southern India wives believe that to tell their husband's name or to pronounce it even in a dream would bring
him to an untimely end. Among the Sea Dyaks a man may not
pronounce the name of his father-in-law or mother-in-law
without incurring the wrath of the spirits. And since he reckons
as his father-in-law and mother-in-law not only the father and
mother of his own wife, but also the fathers and mothers of his
brothers' wives and sisters' husbands, and likewise the fathers
and mothers of all his cousins, the number of tabooed names
may be very considerable and the opportunities of error correspondingly numerous. To make confusion worse confounded,
the names of persons are often the names of common things,
such as moon, bridge, barley, cobra, leopard; so that when any
of a man's many fathers-in-law and mothers-in-law are called

by such names, these common words may not pass his lips. Among the Alfoors of Minahassa, in Celebes, the custom is carried still further so as to forbid the use even of words which merely resemble the personal names in sound. It is especially the name of a father-in-law which is thus laid under an interdict. If he, for example, is called Kalala, his son-in-law may not speak of a horse by its common name *kawalo*; he must call it a 'riding-beast' (*sasakajan*). So among the Alfoors of the island of Buru* it is taboo to mention the names of parents and parents-in-law, or even to speak of common objects by words which resemble these names in sound. Thus, if your mother-in-law is called Dalu, which means 'betel,' you may not ask for betel by its ordinary name, you must ask for 'red mouth'; if you want betel-leaf, you may not say betel-leaf (*dalu 'mun*), you must say *karon fenna*. In the same island it is also taboo to mention the name of an elder brother in his presence. Transgressions of these rules are punished with fines. In Sunda* it is thought that a particular crop would be spoilt if a man were to mention the names of his father and mother.

In the western islands of Torres Straits* a man never mentioned the personal names of his father-in-law, mother-in-law, brother-in-law, and sister-in-law; and a woman was subject to the same restrictions. A brother-in-law might be spoken of as the husband or brother of some one whose name it was lawful to mention; and similarly a sister-in-law might be called the wife of So-and-so. If a man by chance used the personal name of his brother-in-law, he was ashamed and hung his head. His shame was only relieved when he had made a present as compensation to the man whose name he had taken in vain. The same compensation was made to a sister-in-law, a father-in-law, and a mother-in-law for the accidental mention of their names. Among the natives who inhabit the coast of the Gazelle Peninsula in New Britain to mention the name of a brother-in-law is the grossest possible affront you can offer to him; it is a crime punishable with death. In the Banks' Islands, Melanesia, the taboos laid on the names of persons connected by marriage are very strict. A man will not mention the name of his father-in-law, much less the name of his mother-in-law, nor may he name his wife's brother; but he may name his wife's sister—she is nothing to him. A woman may not name her father-in-law, nor on any account her son-in-law. Two people whose children have intermarried are also debarred from mentioning each other's names. And not only are all these persons forbidden to utter each other's names; they may not even pronounce ordinary words which chance to be either identical with these names or to have any syllables in common with them. Thus we hear of a native of these islands who might not use the common words for 'pig' and 'to die', because these words occurred in the polysyllabic name of his son-in-law; and we are told of another unfortunate who might not pronounce the everyday words for 'hand' and 'hot' on account of his wife's brother's name, and who was even debarred from mentioning the number 'one', because the word for 'one' formed part of the name of his wife's cousin.

The reluctance to mention the names or even syllables of the names of persons connected with the speaker by marriage can hardly be separated from the reluctance evinced by so many people to utter their own names or the names of the dead or of chiefs and kings; and if the reticence as to these latter names springs mainly from superstition, we may infer that the reticence as to the former has no better foundation. That the savage's unwillingness to mention his own name is based, at least in part, on a superstitious fear of the ill use that might be made of it by his foes, whether human or spiritual, has already been shown. It remains to examine the similar usage in regard to the names of the dead and of royal personages.

Tabooed words: Names of the dead tabooed.

The custom of abstaining from all mention of the names of the dead was observed in antiquity by the Albanians of the Caucasus, and at the present day it is in full force among many savage tribes. Among the aborigines of Victoria the dead were very rarely spoken of, and then never by their names; they were referred to in a subdued voice as 'the lost one' or 'the poor fellow that is no more'. To speak of them by name would, it was supposed, excite the malignity of Couit-gil, the spirit of the departed, which hovers on earth for a time before it departs for ever towards the setting sun. Of the tribes on the Lower Murray River we are told that when a person dies 'they carefully avoid mentioning his name; but if compelled to do so, they pronounce it in a very low whisper, so faint that they imagine the spirit cannot hear their voice'. Amongst the tribes of Central Australia no one may utter the name of the deceased during the period of mourning, unless it is absolutely necessary to do so, and then it is only done in a whisper for fear of disturbing and annoying the man's spirit which is walking about in ghostly form. If the ghost hears his name mentioned he concludes that his kinsfolk are not mourning for him properly; if their grief were genuine they could not bear to bandy his name about. Touched to the quick by their hard-hearted indifference, the indignant ghost will come and trouble them in dreams.

The same reluctance to utter the names of the dead appears to prevail among all the Indian tribes of America from Hudson's Bay Territory to Patagonia. Among the Goajiros of Colombia to mention the dead before his kinsmen is a dreadful offence, which is often punished with death; for if it happen on the *rancho* of the deceased, in presence of his nephew or uncle, they will assuredly kill the offender on the spot if they can. But if he escapes, the penalty resolves itself into a heavy fine, usually of two or more oxen.

A similar reluctance to mention the names of the dead is reported of peoples so widely separated from each other as the Samoyeds of Siberia and the Todas of Southern India; the Mongols of Tartary and the Tuaregs of the Sahara; the Ainos of Japan and the Akamba and Nandi of Eastern Africa; the Tinguianes of the Philippines and the inhabitants of the Nicobar Islands, of Borneo, of Madagascar, and of Tasmania. In all cases, even where it is not expressly stated, the fundamental reason for this avoidance is probably the fear of the ghost. That this is the real motive with the Tuaregs we are positively informed. They dread the return of the dead man's spirit, and do all they can to avoid it by shifting their camp after a death, ceasing for ever to pronounce the name of the departed, and eschewing everything that might be regarded as an evocation or recall of his soul. Hence they do not, like the Arabs, designate individuals by adding to their personal names the names of their fathers; they never speak of So-and-so, son of So-and-so; they give to every man a name which will live and die with him. So among some of the Victorian tribes in Australia personal names were rarely perpetuated, because the natives believed that any one who adopted the name of a deceased person would not live long; probably his ghostly namesake was supposed to come and fetch him away to the spirit-land.

The same fear of the ghost, which moves people to suppress his old name, naturally leads all persons who bear a similar name to exchange it for another, lest its utterance should attract the attention of the ghost, who cannot reasonably be expected to discriminate between all the different applications of the same name. Thus we are told that in the Adelaide and En-counter Bay tribes of South Australia the repugnance to men-tioning the names of those who have died lately is carried so far, that persons who bear the same name as the deceased abandon it, and either adopt temporary names or are known by any others that happen to belong to them. A similar custom prevails among some of the Queensland tribes; but the prohibition to use the names of the dead is not permanent, though it may last for many years. In some Australian tribes the change of name thus brought about is permanent; the old name is laid aside for ever, and the man is known by his new name for the rest of his life, or at least until he is obliged to change it again for a like reason. Among the North American Indians all persons, whether men or women, who bore the name of one who had just died were obliged to abandon it and to adopt other names, which was formally done at the first ceremony of mourning for the dead. In some tribes to the east of the Rocky Mountains this change of name lasted only during the season of mourning, but in other tribes on the Pacific Coast of North America it seems to have been permanent.

Sometimes by an extension of the same reasoning all the near relations of the deceased change their names, whatever they may happen to be, doubtless from a fear that the sound of the familiar names might lure back the vagrant spirit to its old home. Thus in some Victorian tribes the ordinary names of all the next of kin were disused during the period of mourning, and certain general terms, prescribed by custom, were substituted for them. To call a mourner by his own name was considered an insult to the departed, and often led to fighting and bloodshed. Among Indian tribes of North-western America near relations of the deceased often change their names 'under an impression that spirits will be attracted back to earth if they hear familiar names often repeated'. Among the Kiowa Indians the name of the dead is never spoken in the presence of the relatives, and on the death of any member of a family all the others take new names. This custom was noted by Raleigh's colonists on Roanoke Island more than three centuries ago. Among the Lengua Indians not only is a dead man's name never mentioned, but all the survivors change their names also. They say that Death has been among them and has carried off a list of the living, and that he will soon come back for more victims; hence in order to defeat his fell purpose they change their names, believing that on his return Death, though he has got them all on his list, will not be able to identify them under their new names, and will depart to pursue the search elsewhere. Nicobarese* mourners take new names in order to escape the unwelcome attentions of the ghost; and for the same purpose they disguise themselves by shaving their heads so that the ghost is unable to recognise them.

Further, when the name of the deceased happens to be that of some common object, such as an animal, or plant, or fire, or water, it is sometimes considered necessary to drop that word in ordinary speech and replace it by another. A custom of this sort, it is plain, may easily be a potent agent of change in language; for where it prevails to any considerable extent many words must constantly become obsolete and new ones spring up. And this tendency has been remarked by observers who have recorded the custom in Australia, America, and elsewhere.* For example, with regard to the Australian aborigines it has been noted that 'the dialects change with almost every tribe. Some tribes name their children after natural objects; and when the person so named dies, the word is never again mentioned; another word has therefore to be invented for the object after which the child was called.' The writer gives as an instance the case of a man whose name Karla signified 'fire'; when Karla died, a new word for fire had to be introduced. 'Hence,' adds the writer, 'the language is always changing.' Again, in the Encounter Bay tribe of South Australia, if a man of the name of Ngnke, which means 'water', were to die, the whole tribe would be obliged to use some other word to express water for a considerable time after his decease. The writer who records this custom surmises that it may explain the presence of a number of synonyms in the language of the tribe. This conjecture is confirmed by what we know of some Victorian tribes whose speech comprised a regular set of synonyms to be used instead of the common terms by all members of a tribe in times of mourning. For instance, if a man called Waa ('crow') departed this life, during the period of mourning for him nobody might call a crow a *waa*; everybody had to speak of the bird as a *narrapart*. When a person who rejoiced in the title of Ringtail Opossum (*weearn*) had gone the way of all flesh, his sorrowing relations and the tribe at large were bound for a time to refer to ringtail opossums by the more sonorous name of *manuungkuurt*. If the community were plunged in grief for the loss of a respected female who bore the honourable name of Turkey Bustard, the proper name for turkey bustards, which was *barrim barrim*, went out, and *tillit tilliitsh* came in. And so *mutatis mutandis* with the names of Black Cockatoo, Grey Duck, Gigantic Crane, Kangaroo, Eagle, Dingo, and the rest.

A similar custom used to be constantly transforming the language of the Abipones of Paraguay, amongst whom, however, a word once abolished seems never to have been revived. New words, says the missionary Dobrizhoffer, sprang up every year like mushrooms in a night, because all words that resembled the names of the dead were abolished by proclamation and others coined in their place. The mint of words was in the hands of the old women of the tribe, and whatever term they stamped with their approval and put in circulation was immediately accepted without a murmur by high and low alike, and spread like wildfire through every camp and settlement of the tribe. You would be astonished, says the same missionary, to see how meekly the whole nation acquiesces in the decision of a withered old hag, and how completely the old familiar words fall instantly out of use and are never repeated either through force of habit or forgetfulness. In the seven years that Dobrizhoffer spent among these Indians the native word for jaguar was changed thrice, and the words for crocodile, thorn, and the slaughter of cattle underwent similar though less varied vicissitudes. As a result of this habit, the vocabularies of the missionaries teemed with erasures, old words having constantly to be struck out as obsolete and new ones inserted in their place. In many tribes of British New Guinea the names of persons are also the names of common things. The people believe that if the name of a deceased person is pronounced, his spirit will return, and as they have no wish to see it back among them the mention of his name is tabooed and a new word is created to take its place, whenever the name happens to be a common term of the language. Consequently many words are permanently lost or revived with modified or new meanings. In the Nicobar Islands a similar practice has similarly affected the speech of the natives. 'A most singular custom', says Mr de Roepstorff, 'prevails among them which one would suppose must most effectually hinder the "making of history," or, at any rate, the transmission of historical narrative. By a strict rule, which has all the sanction of Nicobar superstition, no man's name may be mentioned after his death! To such a length is this carried that when, as very frequently happens, the man rejoiced in the name of "Fowl", "Hat", "Fire", "Road", etc., in its Nicobarese equivalent, the use of these words is carefully eschewed for the future, not only as being the personal designation of the deceased, but even as the names of the common things they represent; the words die out of the language, and either new vocables are coined to express the thing intended, or a substitute for the disused word is found in other Nicobarese dialects or in some foreign tongue. This extraordinary custom not only adds an element of instability to the language, but destroys the continuity of political life, and renders the record of past events precarious and vague, if not impossible.'

That a superstition which suppresses the names of the dead must cut at the very root of historical tradition has been remarked by other workers in this field. 'The Klamath* people', observes Mr A. S. Gatschet, 'possess no historic traditions going further back in time than a century, for the simple reason that there was a strict law prohibiting the mention of the person or acts of a deceased individual by *using his name*. This law was rigidly observed among the Californians no less than among the Oregonians, and on its transgression the death penalty could be inflicted. This is certainly enough to suppress all historical knowledge within a people. How can history be written without names?'

In many tribes, however, the power of this superstition to blot out the memory of the past is to some extent weakened and impaired by a natural tendency of the human mind. Time, which wears out the deepest impressions, inevitably dulls, if it does not wholly efface, the print left on the savage mind by the mystery and horror of death. Sooner or later, as the memory of his loved ones fades slowly away, he becomes more willing to speak of them, and thus their rude names may sometimes be rescued by the philosophie enquirer before they have vanished, like autumn leaves or winter snows, into the vast undistinguished limbo of the past. In some of the Victorian tribes the prohibition to mention the names of the dead remained in force only during the period of mourning; in the Port Lincoln tribe of South Australia it lasted many years. Among the Chinook Indians of North America 'custom forbids the mention of a dead man's name, at least till many years have elapsed after the bereavement'. Among the Puyallup Indians the observance of the taboo is relaxed after several years, when the mourners have forgotten their grief; and if the deceased was a famous warrior, one of his descendants, for instance a great-grandson, may be named after him. In this tribe the taboo is not much observed at any time except by the relations of the dead. Similarly the Jesuit missionary Lafitau tells us that the name of the departed and the similar names of the survivors were, so to say, buried with the corpse until, the poignancy of their grief being abated, it pleased the relations to 'lift up the tree and raise the dead'. By raising the dead they meant bestowing the name of the departed upon some one else, who thus became to all intents and purposes a reincarnation of the deceased, since on the principles of savage philosophy the name is a vital part, if not the soul, of the man.

Among the Lapps, when a woman was with child and near the time of her delivery, a deceased ancestor or relation used to appear to her in a dream and inform her what dead person was to be born again in her infant, and whose name the child was therefore to bear. If the woman had no such dream, it fell to the father or the relatives to determine the name by divination or by consulting a wizard. Among the Khonds* a birth is celebrated on the seventh day after the event by a feast given to the priest and to the whole village. To determine the child's name the priest drops grains of rice into a cup of water, naming with each grain a deceased ancestor. From the movements of the seed in the water, and from observations made on the person of the infant, he pronounces which of his progenitors has reappeared in him, and the child generally, at least among the northern tribes, receives the name of that ancestor. Among the Yorubas, soon after a child has been born, a priest of Ifa, the god of divination, appears on the scene to ascertain what ancestral soul has been reborn in the infant. As soon as this has been decided, the parents are told that the child must conform in all respects to the manner of life of the ancestor who now animates him or her, and if, as often happens, they profess ignorance, the priest supplies the necessary information. The child usually receives the name of the ancestor who has been born again in him.

When we see that in primitive society the names of mere commoners, whether alive or dead, are matters of such anxious care, we need not be surprised that great precautions should be taken to guard from harm the names of sacred kings and priests. Thus the name of the king of Dahomey is always kept secret, lest the knowledge of it should enable some evil-minded person to do him a mischief. The appellations by which the different kings of Dahomey have been known to Europeans are not their true names, but mere titles, or what the natives call 'strong names'. The natives seem to think that no harm comes of such titles being known, since they are not, like the birth-names, vitally connected with their owners. In the Galla kingdom of Ghera the birth-name of the sovereign may not be pronounced by a subject under pain of death, and common words which resemble it in sound are changed for others. Among the Bahima of Central Africa, when the king dies, his name is abolished from the language, and if his name was that of an animal, a new appellation must be found for the creature at once. For example, the king is often called a lion; hence at the death of a king named Lion a new name for lions in general has to be coined. In Siam it used to be difficult to ascertain the king's real name, since it was carefully kept secret from fear of sorcery; any one who mentioned it was clapped into gaol. The king might only be referred to under certain high-sounding titles, such as, 'the august', 'the perfect', 'the supreme', 'the great emperor', 'descendant of the angels', and so on. In Burma it was accounted an impiety of the deepest dye to mention the name of the reigning sovereign; Burmese subjects, even when they were far

Tabooed words: Names of kings and other sacred persons tabooed.

from their country, could not be prevailed upon to do so; after his accession to the throne the king was known by his royal titles only.

Among the Zulus no man will mention the name of the chief of his tribe or the names of the progenitors of the chief, so far as he can remember them; nor will he utter common words which coincide with or merely resemble in sound tabooed names. In the tribe of the Dwandwes there was a chief called Langa, which means the sun; hence the name of the sun was changed from *langa* to *gala*, and so remains to this day, though Langa died more than a hundred years ago. Again, in the Xnumayo tribe the word meaning 'to herd cattle' was changed from *alusa* or *ayusa* to *kagesa*, because u-Mayusi was the name of the chief. Besides these taboos, which were observed by each tribe separately, all the Zulu tribes united in tabooing the name of the king who reigned over the whole nation. Hence, for example, when Panda was king of Zululand, the word for 'a root of a tree', which is *impando*, was changed to *nxabo*. Again, the word for 'lies', or 'slander' was altered from *amacebo* to *amak-wata*, because *amacebo* contains a syllable of the name of the famous King Cetchwayo. These substitutions are not, however, carried so far by the men as by the women, who omit every sound even remotely resembling one that occurs in a tabooed name. At the king's kraal, indeed, it is sometimes difficult to understand the speech of the royal wives, as they treat in this fashion the names not only of the king and his forefathers, but even of his and their brothers back for generations. When to these tribal and national taboos we add those family taboos on the names of connexions by marriage which have been already described, we can easily understand how it comes about that in Zululand every tribe has words peculiar to itself, and that the women have a considerable vocabulary of their own. Members, too, of one family may be debarred from using words employed by those of another. The women of one kraal, for instance, may call a hyaena by its ordinary name; those of the next may use the common substitute; while in a third the substitute may also be unlawful and another term may have to be invented to supply its place. Hence the Zulu language at the present day almost presents the appearance of being a double one; indeed, for multitudes of things it possesses three or four synonyms, which through the blending of tribes are known all over Zululand.

In Madagascar a similar custom everywhere prevails and has resulted, as among the Zulus, in producing certain dialectic differences in the speech of the various tribes. There are no family names in Madagascar, and almost every personal name is drawn from the language of daily life and signifies some common object or action or quality, such as a bird, a beast, a tree, a plant, a colour, and so on. Now, whenever one of these common words forms the name or part of the name of the chief of the tribe, it becomes sacred and may no longer be used in its ordinary signification as the name of a tree, an insect, or what not. Hence a new name for the object must be invented to replace the one which has been discarded. It is easy to conceive what confusion and uncertainty may thus be introduced into a language when it is spoken by many little local tribes each ruled by a petty chief with his own sacred name. Yet there are tribes and people who submit to this tyranny of words as their fathers did before them from time immemorial. The inconvenient results of the custom are especially marked on the western coast of the island, where, on account of the large number of independent chieftains, the names of things, places, and rivers have suffered so many changes that confusion often arises, for when once common words have been banned by the chiefs the natives will not acknowledge to have ever known them in their old sense.

But it is not merely the names of living kings and chiefs which are tabooed in Madagascar; the names of dead sovereigns are equally under a ban, at least in some parts of the island. Thus among the Sakalavas, when a king has died, the nobles and people meet in council round the dead body and solemnly choose a new name by which the deceased monarch shall be henceforth known. After the new name has been adopted, the old name by which the king was known during his life becomes sacred and may not be pronounced under pain of death. Further, words in the common language which bear any resemblance to the forbidden name also become sacred and have to be replaced by others. Persons who uttered these forbidden words were looked on not only as grossly rude, but even as felons; they had committed a capital crime. However, these changes of vocabulary are confined to the district over which the deceased king reigned; in the neighbouring districts the old words continue to be employed in the old sense.

The sanctity attributed to the persons of chiefs in Polynesia naturally extended also to their names, which on the primitive view are hardly separable from the personality of their owners. Hence in Polynesia we find the same systematic prohibition to utter the names of chiefs or of common words resembling them which we have already met with in Zululand and Madagascar. Thus in New Zealand the name of a chief is held so sacred that, when it happens to be a common word, it may not be used in the language, and another has to be found to replace it. For example, a chief to the southward of East Cape bore the name of Maripi, which signified a knife, hence a new word (*nekra*) for knife was introduced, and the old one became obsolete. Elsewhere the word for water (*wai*) had to be changed, because it chanced to be the name of the chief, and would have been desecrated by being applied to the vulgar fluid as well as to his sacred person. This taboo naturally produced a plentiful crop of synonyms in the Maori language, and travellers newly arrived in the country were sometimes puzzled at finding the same things called by quite different names in neighbouring tribes. When a king comes to the throne in Tahiti, any words in the language that resemble his name in sound must be changed for others. In former times, if any man were so rash as to disregard this custom and to use the forbidden words, not only he but all his relations were immediately put to death. But the changes thus introduced were only temporary; on the death of the king the new words fell into disuse, and the original ones were revived.

v

General conclusion. Human gods, on whom the welfare of the community is believed to depend, are

It would be easy to extend the list of royal and priestly taboos, but the instances collected in the preceding pages may suffice as specimens. To conclude this part of our subject it only remains to state summarily the general conclusions to which our enquiries have thus far conducted us. We have seen that in savage or barbarous society there are often found men to whom the superstition of their fellows ascribes a controlling influence over the general course of nature. Such men are accordingly adored and treated as gods. Whether these human divinities also hold temporal sway over the lives and fortunes of their adorers, or whether their functions are purely spiritual and supernatural, in other words, whether they are kings as well as gods or only the latter, is a distinction which hardly concerns us here. Their supposed divinity is the essential fact with which we have to deal. In virtue of it they are a pledge and guarantee to their worshippers of the continuance and orderly succession of those physical phenomena upon which mankind depends for subsistence. Naturally, therefore, the life and health of such a god-man are matters of anxious concern to the people whose welfare and even existence are bound up with his; naturally he is constrained by them to conform to such rules as the wit of early man has devised for averting the ills to which flesh is heir, including the last ill, death. These rules, as an examination of them has shewn, are nothing but the maxims with which, on the primitive view, every man of common prudence must comply if he would live long in the land. But while in the case of ordinary men the observance of the rules is left to the choice of the individual, in the case of the god-man it is enforced under penalty of dismissal from his high station, or even of death. For his worshippers have far too great a stake in his life to allow him to play fast and loose with it. Therefore all the quaint superstitions, the old-world maxims, the venerable saws which the ingenuity of savage philosophers elaborated long ago, and which old women at chimney corners still impart as treasures of great price to their descendants gathered round the cottage fire on winter evenings—all these antique fancies clustered, all these cobwebs of the brain were spun about the path of the old king, the human god, who, immeshed in them like a fly in the toils of a spider, could hardly stir a limb for the threads of custom, 'light as air but strong as links of iron', that crossing and recrossing each other in an endless maze bound him fast within a network of observances from which death or deposition alone could release him.

obliged to observe many rules to ensure their own safety and that of their people.

Thus to students of the past the life of the old kings and priests teems with instruction. In it was summed up all that passed for wisdom when the world was young. It was the perfect pattern after which every man strove to shape his life; a

A study of these rules affords us an insight into

faultless model constructed with rigorous accuracy upon the lines laid down by a barbarous philosophy. Crude and false as that philosophy may seem to us, it would be unjust to deny it the merit of logical consistency. Starting from a conception of the vital principle as a tiny being or soul existing in, but distinct and separable from, the living being, it deduces for the practical guidance of life a system of rules which in general hangs well together and forms a fairly complete and harmonious whole. The flaw—and it is a fatal one—of the system lies not in its reasoning, but in its premises; in its conception of the nature of life, not in any irrelevancy of the conclusions which it draws from that conception. But to stigmatise these premises as ridiculous because we can easily detect their falseness, would be

ungrateful as well as unphilosophical. We stand upon the foundation reared by the generations that have gone before, and we can but dimly realise the painful and prolonged efforts which it has cost humanity to struggle up to the point, no very exalted one after all, which we have reached. Our gratitude is due to the nameless and forgotten toilers, whose patient thought and active exertions have largely made us what we are. The amount of new knowledge which one age, certainly which one man, can add to the common store is small, and it argues stupidity or dishonesty, besides ingratitude, to ignore the heap while vaunting the few grains which it may have been our privilege to add to it. There is indeed little danger at present of undervaluing the contributions which modern times and even classical antiquity have made to the general advancement of our race. But when we pass these limits, the case is different. Contempt and ridicule or abhorrence and denunciation are too often the only recognition vouchsafed to the savage and his ways. Yet of the benefactors whom we are bound thankfully to commemorate, many, perhaps most, were savages. For when all is said and done our resemblances to the savage are still far more numerous than our differences from him; and what we have in common with him, and deliberately retain as true and useful, we owe to our savage forefathers who slowly acquired by experience and transmitted to us by inheritance those seemingly fundamental ideas which we are apt to regard as original and intuitive. We are like heirs to a fortune which has been handed down for so many ages that the memory of those who built it up is lost, and its possessors for the time being regard it as having been an original and unalterable possession of their race since the beginning of the world. But reflection and enquiry should satisfy us that to our predecessors we are indebted for much of what we thought most our own, and that their errors were not wilful extravagances or the ravings of insanity, but simply hypotheses, justifiable as such at the time when they were propounded, but which a fuller experience has proved to be inadequate. It is only by the successive testing of hypotheses and rejection of the false that truth is at last elicited. After all, what we call truth is only the hypothesis which is found to work best. Therefore in reviewing the opinions and practices of ruder ages and races we shall do well to look with leniency upon their errors as inevitable slips made in the search for truth, and to give them the benefit of that indulgence which we ourselves may one day stand in need of: *cum excusatione itaque veteres audiendi sunt.**

BOOK II

KILLING THE GOD

CHAPTER 1

THE MORTALITY OF THE GODS

AT an early stage of his intellectual development man deems himself naturally immortal, and imagines that were it not for the baleful arts of sorcerers, who cut the vital thread prematurely short, he would live for ever. The illusion, so flattering to human wishes and hopes, is still current among many savage tribes at the present day, and it may be supposed to have prevailed universally in that Age of Magic which appears to have everywhere preceded the Age of Religion. But in time the sad truth of human mortality was borne in upon our primitive philosopher with a force of demonstration which no prejudice could resist and no sophistry dissemble. Among the manifold influences which combined to wring from him a reluctant assent to the necessity of death must be numbered the growing influence of religion, which by exposing the vanity of magic and of all the extravagant pretensions built on it gradually lowered man's proud and defiant attitude towards nature, and taught him to believe that there are mysteries in the universe which his feeble intellect can never fathom, and forces which his puny hands can never control. Thus more and more he learned to bow to the inevitable and to console himself for the brevity and the sorrows of life on earth by the hope of a blissful eternity hereafter. But if he reluctantly acknowledged the existence of beings at once superhuman and supernatural, he was as yet far from suspecting the width and the depth of the gulf which divided him from them. The gods with whom his imagination now peopled the darkness of the unknown were indeed admitted by him to be his superiors in knowledge and in power, in the joyous splendour of their life and in the length of its duration. But, though he knew it not, these glorious and awful beings were merely, like the spectre of the Brocken,* the reflections of his own diminutive personality exaggerated into gigantic proportions by distance and by the mists and clouds of ignorance upon which they were cast. Man in fact created gods

Mortality of savage gods.

in his own likeness and being himself mortal he naturally supposed his creatures to be in the same sad predicament. Thus the Greenlanders believed that a wind could kill their most powerful god, and that he would certainly die if he touched a dog. When they heard of the Christian God, they kept asking if he never died, and being informed that he did not, they were much surprised, and said that he must be a very great god indeed. In answer to the enquiries of Colonel Dodge, a North American Indian stated that the world was made by the Great Spirit. Being asked which Great Spirit he meant, the good one or the bad one, 'Oh, neither of *them*,' replied he, 'the Great Spirit that made the world is dead long ago. He could not possibly have lived as long as this.'* A tribe in the Philippine Islands told the Spanish conquerors that the grave of the Creator was upon the top of Mount Cabunian. Heitsi-eibib, a god or divine hero of the Hottentots, died several times and came to life again. His graves are generally to be met with in narrow defiles between mountains. When the Hottentots pass one of them, they throw a stone on it for good luck, sometimes muttering 'Give us plenty of cattle.' The grave of Zeus, the great god of Greece, was shewn to visitors in Crete as late as about the beginning of our era. The body of Dionysus was buried at Delphi beside the golden statue of Apollo, and his tomb bore the inscription, 'Here lies Dionysus dead, the son of Semele.' According to one account, Apollo himself was buried at Delphi; for Pythagoras is said to have carved an inscription on his tomb, setting forth how the god had been killed by the python and buried under the tripod. The ancient god Cronus was buried in Sicily, and the graves of Hermes, Aphrodite, and Ares were shewn in Hermopolis, Cyprus, and Thrace.

Mortality of Greek gods.

Mortality of Egyptian gods.

The great gods of Egypt themselves were not exempt from the common lot. They too grew old and died. For like men they were composed of body and soul, and like men were subject to all the passions and infirmities of the flesh. Their bodies, it is true, were fashioned of more ethereal mould, and lasted longer than ours, but they could not hold out for ever against the siege of time. Age converted their bones into silver, their flesh into gold, and their azure locks into lapis-lazuli. When their time came, they passed away from the cheerful world of the living to reign as dead gods over dead men in the melancholy world beyond the grave. Even their souls, like those of mankind, could only endure after death so long as their bodies held together; and hence it was as needful to preserve the corpses of the gods as the corpses of common folk, lest with the divine body the divine spirit should also come to an untimely end. At first their remains were laid to rest under the desert sands of the mountains, that the dryness of the soil and the purity of the air might protect them from putrefaction and decay. Hence one of the oldest titles of the Egyptian gods is 'they who are under the sands'. But when at a later time the discovery of the art of embalming gave a new lease of life to the souls of the dead by preserving their bodies for an indefinite time from corruption, the deities were permitted to share the benefit of an invention which held out to gods as well as to men a reasonable hope of immortality. Every province then had the tomb and mummy of its dead god. The mummy of Osiris was to be seen at Mendes; Thinis boasted of the mummy of Anhouri; and Heliopolis rejoiced in the possession of that of Toumou. But while their bodies lay swathed and bandaged here on earth in the tomb, their souls, if we may trust the Egyptian priests, shone as bright stars in the firmament. The soul of Isis sparkled in Sirius, the soul of Horus in Orion, and the soul of Typhon in the Great Bear. But the death of the god did not involve the extinction of his sacred stock; for he commonly had by his wife a son and heir, who on the demise of his divine parent succeeded to the full rank, power, and honours of the godhead. The high gods of Babylon also, though they appeared to their worshippers only in dreams and visions, were conceived to be human in their bodily shape, human in their passions, and human in their fate; for like men they were born into the world, and like men they loved and fought and died.

One of the most famous stories of the death of a god is told by Plutarch. It runs thus. In the reign of the emperor Tiberius a certain schoolmaster named Epitherses was sailing from Greece to Italy. The ship in which he had taken his passage was a merchantman and there were many other passengers on board. At evening, when they were off the Echinadian Islands, the wind died away, and the vessel drifted close in to the island of Paxos. Most of the passengers were awake and many were still drinking wine after dinner, when suddenly a voice hailed the

The death of the Great Pan.

ship from the island, calling upon Thamus. The crew and passengers were taken by surprise, for though there was an Egyptian pilot named Thamus on board, few knew him even by name. Twice the cry was repeated, but Thamus kept silence. However, at the third call he answered, and the voice from the shore, now louder than ever, said, 'When you are come to Palodes, announce that the Great Pan is dead.' Astonishment fell upon all, and they consulted whether it would be better to do the bidding of the voice or not. At last Thamus resolved that, if the wind held, he would pass the place in silence, but if it dropped when they were off Palodes he would give the message. Well, when they were come to Palodes, there was a great calm; so Thamus standing in the stern and looking towards the land cried out, as he had been bidden, 'The Great Pan is dead.' The words had hardly passed his lips when a loud sound of lamentation broke on their ears, as if a multitude were mourning. This strange story, vouched for by many on board, soon got wind at Rome, and Thamus was sent for and questioned by the emperor Tiberius himself, who caused enquiries to be made about the dead god.* In modern times, also, the annunciation of the death of the Great Pan has been much discussed and various explanations of it have been suggested. On the whole the simplest and most natural would seem to be that the deity whose sad end was thus mysteriously proclaimed and lamented was the Syrian god Tammuz or Adonis, whose death is known to have been annually bewailed by his followers both in Greece and in his native Syria. At Athens the solemnity fell at midsummer, and there is no improbability in the view that in a Greek island a band of worshippers of Tammuz should have been celebrating the death of their god with the customary passionate demonstrations of sorrow at the very time when a ship lay becalmed off the shore, and that in the stillness of the summer night the voices of lamentation should have been wafted with startling distinctness across the water and should have made on the minds of the listening passengers a deep and lasting impression. However that may be, stories of the same kind found currency in western Asia down to the Middle Ages. An Arab writer relates that in the year 1063 or 1064 AD, in the reign of the caliph Caiem, a rumour went abroad through Bagdad, which soon spread all over the province of Irac, that

Death of the King of the Jinn.

some Turks out hunting in the desert had seen a black tent, where many men and women were beating their faces and uttering loud cries, as it is the custom to do in the East when some one is dead. And among the cries they distinguished these words, 'The great King of the Jinn is dead, woe to this country!' In consequence of this a mysterious threat was circulated from Armenia to Chuzistan that every town which did not lament the dead King of the Jinn should utterly perish. Again, in the year 1203 or 1204 AD a fatal disease, which attacked the throat, raged in parts of Mosul and Irac, and it was divulged that a woman of the Jinn called Umm 'Uncūd or 'Mother of the Grape-cluster' had lost her son, and that all who did not lament for him would fall victims to the epidemic. So men and women sought to save themselves from death by assembling and beating their faces, while they cried out in a lamentable voice, 'O mother of the Grape-cluster, excuse us; the Grape-cluster is dead; we knew it not.'*

Death of Grape-cluster.

CHAPTER 2

THE KILLING OF THE DIVINE KING

Human gods are killed to prevent them from growing old and feeble.

IF the high gods, who dwell remote from the fret and fever of this earthly life, are yet believed to die at last, it is not to be expected that a god who lodges in a frail tabernacle of flesh should escape the same fate, though we hear of African kings who have imagined themselves immortal by virtue of their sorceries. Now primitive peoples, as we have seen, sometimes believe that their safety and even that of the world is bound up with the life of one of these god-men or human incarnations of the divinity. Naturally, therefore, they take the utmost care of his life, out of a regard for their own. But no amount of care and precaution will prevent the man-god from growing old and feeble and at last dying. His worshippers have to lay their account with this sad necessity and to meet it as best they can. The danger is a formidable one; for if the course of nature is dependent on the man-god's life, what catastrophes may not be expected from the gradual enfeeblement of his powers and their final extinction in death? There is only one way of averting these dangers. The man-god must be killed as soon as he shews symptoms that his powers are beginning to fail, and his soul must be transferred to a vigorous successor before it has been seriously impaired by the threatened decay. The advantages of thus putting the man-god to death instead of allowing him to die of old age and disease are, to the savage, obvious enough. For if the man-god dies what we call a natural death, it means, according to the savage, that his soul has either voluntarily departed from his body and refuses to return, or more commonly that it has been extracted, or at least detained in its wanderings, by a demon or sorcerer. In any of these cases the soul of the man-god is lost to his worshippers; and with it their prosperity is gone and their very existence endangered. Even if they could arrange to catch the soul of the dying god as it left his lips or his nostrils and so transfer it to a successor, this would not effect their purpose; for, dying of disease, his soul would necessarily leave his body in the last stage of weakness and exhaustion, and so enfeebled it would continue to drag out a languid, inert existence in any body to which it might be transferred. Whereas by slaying him his worshippers could, in the first place, make sure of catching his soul as it escaped and transferring it to a suitable successor; and, in the second place, by putting him to death before his natural force was abated, they would secure that the world should not fall into decay with the decay of the man-god. Every purpose, therefore, was answered, and all dangers averted by thus killing the man-god and transferring his soul, while yet at its prime, to a vigorous successor.

Some of the reasons for preferring a violent death to the slow death of old age or disease are obviously as applicable to common men as to the man-god. Thus the Mangaians* think that 'the spirits of those who die a natural death are excessively feeble and weak, as their bodies were at dissolution; whereas the spirits of those who are slain in battle are strong and vigorous, their bodies not having been reduced by disease'. The Barongo believe that in the world beyond the grave the spirits of their dead ancestors appear with the exact form and lineaments which their bodies exhibited at the moment of death; the spirits are young or old according as their bodies were young or old when they died; there are baby spirits who crawl about on all fours. The Lengua Indians of the Gran Chaco* are persuaded that the souls of the departed correspond exactly in form and characteristics to the bodies which they quitted at death; thus a tall man is tall, a short man is short, and a deformed man is deformed in the spirit-land, and the disembodied soul of a child remains a child, it never develops into an adult. Hence they burn the body of a murderer and scatter the ashes to the winds, thinking that this treatment will prevent his spirit from assuming human shape in the other world. So, too, the Naga tribes of Manipur hold that the ghost of a dead man is an exact image of the deceased as he was at the moment of death, with his scars, tattoo marks, mutilations, and all the rest. The Baganda think that the ghosts of men who were mutilated in life are mutilated in like manner after death; so to avoid that shame they will rather die with all their limbs than lose one by amputation and live. Hence, men sometimes prefer to kill themselves or to be

Preference for a violent death: the sick and old killed.

killed before they grow feeble, in order that in the future life their souls may start fresh and vigorous as they left their bodies, instead of decrepit and worn out with age and disease. Thus in Fiji, 'self-immolation is by no means rare, and they believe that as they leave this life, so they will remain ever after. This forms a powerful motive to escape from decrepitude, or from a crippled condition, by a voluntary death.' Or, as another observer of the Fijians puts it more fully, 'the custom of voluntary suicide on the part of the old men, which is among their most extraordinary usages, is also connected with their superstitions respecting a future life. They believe that persons enter upon the delights of their elysium with the same faculties, mental and physical, that they possess at the hour of death, in short, that the spiritual life commences where the corporeal existence terminates. With these views, it is natural that they should desire to pass through this change before their mental and bodily powers are so enfeebled by age as to deprive them of their capacity for enjoyment. To this motive must be added the contempt which attaches to physical weakness among a nation of warriors, and the wrongs and insults which await those who are no longer able to protect themselves. When therefore a man finds his strength declining with the advance of age, and feels that he will soon be unequal to discharge the duties of this life, and to partake in the pleasures of that which is to come, he calls together his relations, and tells them that he is now worn out and useless, that he sees they are all ashamed of him and that he has determined to be buried.' So on a day appointed they used to meet and bury him alive. In Vaté, one of the New Hebrides, the aged were buried alive at their own request. It was considered a disgrace to the family of an old chief if he was not buried alive. Of the Kamants, a Jewish tribe in Abyssinia, it is reported that 'they never let a person die a natural death, but that if any of their relatives is nearly expiring, the priest of the village is called to cut his throat; if this be omitted, they believe that the departed soul has not entered the mansions of the blessed'. The old Greek philosopher Heraclitus thought that the souls of those who die in battle are purer than the souls of those who die of disease.

Preference for a violent

Among the Chiriguanos, a tribe of South American Indians on the river Pilcomayo,* when a man was at the point of death his nearest relative used to break his spine by a blow of an axe, for they thought that to die a natural death was the greatest misfortune that could befall a man. Whenever a Payagua Indian of Paraguay, or a Guayana of south-eastern Brazil, grew weary of life, a feast was made, and amid the revelry and dancing the man was gummed and feathered with the plumage of many-coloured birds. A huge jar had been previously fixed in the ground to be ready for him; in this he was placed, the mouth of the jar was covered with a heavy lid of baked clay, the earth was heaped over it, and thus 'he went to his doom more joyful and gladsome than to his first nuptials'. Among the Koryaks of north-eastern Asia, when a man felt that his last hour was come, superstition formerly required that he should either kill himself or be killed by a friend, in order that he might escape the Evil One and deliver himself up to the Good God. Similarly among the Chukchees of the same region, when a man's strength fails and he is tired of life, he requests his son or other near relation to despatch him, indicating the manner of death he prefers to die. So, on a day appointed, his friends and neighbours assemble, and in their presence he is stabbed, strangled, or otherwise disposed of according to his directions. The turbulent Angamis are the most warlike and bloodthirsty of the wild head-hunting tribes in the valley of the Brahmapootra. Among them, when a warrior dies a natural death, his nearest male relative takes a spear and wounds the corpse by a blow on the head, in order that the man may be received with honour in the other world as one who has died in battle. The heathen Norsemen believed that only those who fell fighting were received by Odin in Valhalla; hence it appears to have been customary to wound the dying with a spear, in order to secure their admission to the happy land. The custom may have been a mitigation of a still older practice of slaughtering the sick. We know from Procopius that among the Heruli, a Teutonic tribe, the sick and old were regularly slain at their own request and then burned on a pyre.* The Wends used to kill their aged parents and other kinsfolk, and having killed them they boiled and ate their bodies; and the old folks preferred to die thus rather than to drag out a weary life of weakness and decrepitude.

ii

But it is with the death of the god-man—the divine king or priest—that we are here especially concerned. The mystic kings of Fire and Water in Cambodia are not allowed to die a natural death. Hence when one of them is seriously ill and the elders think that he cannot recover, they stab him to death. The people of Congo believed, as we have seen, that if their pontiff the Chitomé were to die a natural death, the world would perish, and the earth, which he alone sustained by his power and merit, would immediately be annihilated. Accordingly when he fell ill and seemed likely to die, the man who was destined to be his successor entered the pontiff's house with a rope or a club and strangled or clubbed him to death. A fuller account of this custom is given by an old Italian writer as follows: 'Let us pass to the death of the magicians, who often die a violent death, and that for the most part voluntarily. I shall speak only of the head of this crew, from whom his followers take example. He is called Ganga Chitomé, being reputed god of the earth. The first-fruits of all the crops are offered to him as his due, because they are thought to be produced by his power, and not by nature at the bidding of the Most High God. This power he boasts he can impart to others, when and to whom he pleases. He asserts that his body cannot die a natural death, and therefore when he knows he is near the end of his days, whether it is brought about by sickness or age, or whether he is deluded by the demon, he calls one of his disciples to whom he wishes to communicate his power, in order that he may succeed him. And having made him tie a noose to his neck he commands him to strangle him, or to knock him on the head with a great cudgel and kill him. His disciple obeys and sends him a martyr to the devil, to suffer torments with Lucifer in the flames for ever. This tragedy is enacted in public, in order that his successor may be manifested, who hath the power of fertilising the earth, the power having been imparted to him by the deceased; otherwise, so they say, the earth would remain barren, and the world would perish. Oh too great foolishness and palpable blindness of the gentiles, to enlighten the eye of whose mind there would be needed the very hand of Christ whereby he opened the bodily eyes of him that had been born blind! I know that in my time one of these magicians was cast into the sea, another into a river, a mother put to death with her son, and many more seized by our orders and banished.'* The Ethiopian kings of Meroe were worshipped as gods; but whenever the priests chose, they sent a messenger to the king, ordering him to die, and alleging an oracle of the gods as their authority for the command. This command the kings always obeyed down to the reign of Ergamenes, a contemporary of Ptolemy II., King of Egypt. Having received a Greek education which emancipated him from the superstitions of his countrymen, Ergamenes ventured to disregard the command of the priests, and, entering the Golden Temple with a body of soldiers, put the priests to the sword.* Ethiopian kings of Meroe.

Customs of the same sort appear to have prevailed in this region down to modern times. Thus we are told that in Fazoql, a district in the valley of the Blue Nile, to the west of Abyssinia, it was customary, as late as the middle of the nineteenth century, to hang a king who was no longer beloved. His relatives and ministers assembled round him, and announced that as he no longer pleased the men, the women, the asses, the oxen, and the fowls of the country, it was better he should die. Once on a time, when a king was unwilling to take the hint, his own wife and mother urged him so strongly not to disgrace himself by disregarding the custom, that he submitted to his fate and was strung up in the usual way. In some tribes of Fazoql the king had to administer justice daily under a certain tree. If from sickness or any other cause he was unable to discharge this duty for three whole days, he was hanged on the tree in a noose, which contained two razors so arranged that when the noose was drawn tight by the weight of the king's body they cut his throat. At Fazolglou an annual festival, which partook of the nature of a Saturnalia, was preceded by a formal trial of the king in front of his house. The judges were the chief men of the country. The king sat on his royal stool during the trial, surrounded by armed men, who were ready to carry out a sentence of death. A little way off a jackal and a dog were tied to a post. The conduct of the king during his year of office was discussed, complaints were heard, and if the verdict was unfavourable, the king was executed and his successor chosen from Kings of Fazoql on the Blue Nile.

among the members of his family. But if the monarch was
acquitted, the people at once paid their homage to him afresh,
and the dog or the jackal was killed in his stead. This custom
lasted down to the year 1837 or 1838, when king Yassin was
thus condemned and executed. His nephew Assusa was compelled under threats of death to succeed him in the office.
Afterwards it would seem that the death of the dog was
regularly accepted as a substitute for the death of the king. At
least this may be inferred from a later account of the Fazoql
practice, which runs thus: 'The meaning of another of their
customs is quite obscure. At a certain time of the year they have
a kind of carnival, where every one does what he likes best.
Four ministers of the king then bear him on an anqareb out of
his house to an open space of ground; a dog is fastened by a
long cord to one of the feet of the anqareb. The whole
population collects round the place, streaming in on every side.
They then throw darts and stones at the dog, till he is killed,
after which the king is again borne into his house.'

Shilluk cus-
tom of put-
ting divine
kings to
death.

A custom of putting their divine kings to death at the first
symptoms of infirmity or old age prevailed until lately, if indeed
it is even now extinct and not merely dormant, among the
Shilluk of the White Nile, and in recent years it has been
carefully investigated by Dr C. G. Seligmann, to whose researches I am indebted for the following detailed information
on the subject.* The Shilluk are a tribe or nation who inhabit
a long narrow fringe of territory on the western bank of the
White Nile from Kaka in the north to Lake No in the south, as
well as a strip on the eastern bank of the river, which stretches
from Fashoda to Taufikia and for some thirty-five miles up the
Sobat River. The country of the Shilluk is almost entirely in
grass, hence the principal wealth of the people consists in their
flocks and herds, but they also grow a considerable quantity of
the species of millet which is known as durra. But though the
Shilluk are mainly a pastoral people, they are not nomadic, but
live in many settled villages. The tribe at present numbers
about forty thousand souls, and is governed by a single king
(*ret*), whose residence is at Fashoda. His subjects take great care
of him, and hold him in much honour. In the old days his word
was law and he was not suffered to go forth to battle. At the
present day he still keeps up considerable state and exercises

much authority; his decisions on all matters brought before him are readily obeyed; and he never moves without a bodyguard of from twelve to twenty men. The reverence which the Shilluk pay to their king appears to arise chiefly from the conviction that he is a reincarnation of the spirit of Nyakang, the semi-divine hero who founded the dynasty and settled the tribe in their present territory, to which he is variously said to have conducted them either from the west or from the south.

The Shilluk kings supposed to be reincarnations of Nyakang, the semi-divine founder of the dynasty.

It is a fundamental article of the Shilluk creed that the spirit of the divine or semi-divine Nyakang is incarnate in the reigning king, who is accordingly himself invested to some extent with the character of a divinity. But while the Shilluk hold their kings in high, indeed religious reverence and take every precaution against their accidental death, nevertheless they cherish 'the conviction that the king must not be allowed to become ill or senile, lest with his diminishing vigour the cattle should sicken and fail to bear their increase, the crops should rot in the fields, and man, stricken with disease, should die in ever increasing numbers'. To prevent these calamities it used to be the regular custom with the Shilluk to put the king to death whenever he shewed signs of ill-health or failing strength. One of the fatal symptoms of decay was taken to be an incapacity to satisfy the sexual passions of his wives, of whom he has very many, distributed in a large number of houses at Fashoda. When this ominous weakness manifested itself, the wives reported it to the chiefs, who are popularly said to have intimated to the king his doom by spreading a white cloth over his face and knees as he lay slumbering in the heat of the sultry afternoon. Execution soon followed the sentence of death. A hut was specially built for the occasion: the king was led into it and lay down with his head resting on the lap of a nubile virgin: the door of the hut was then walled up; and the couple were left without food, water, or fire to die of hunger and suffocation. This was the old custom, but it was abolished some five generations ago on account of the excessive sufferings of one of the kings who perished in this way. He survived his companion for some days, and in the interval was so distressed by the stench of her putrefying body that he shouted to the people, whom he could hear moving outside, never again to let a king die in this prolonged and exquisite agony. After a time

Shilluk kings put to death when they shew signs of ill-health or failing strength.

his cries died away into silence; death had released him from his sufferings.

Shilluk kings formerly liable to be attacked and killed at any time by rival claimants to the throne.

From Dr Seligmann's enquiries it appears that not only was the Shilluk king liable to be killed with due ceremony at the first symptoms of incipient decay, but even while he was yet in the prime of health and strength he might be attacked at any time by a rival and have to defend his crown in a combat to the death. According to the common Shilluk tradition any son of a king had the right thus to fight the king in possession and, if he succeeded in killing him, to reign in his stead. As every king had a large harem and many sons, the number of possible candidates for the throne at any time may well have been not inconsiderable, and the reigning monarch must have carried his life in his hand. But the attack on him could only take place with any prospect of success at night; for during the day the king surrounded himself with his friends and bodyguards, and an aspirant to the throne could hardly hope to cut his way through them and strike home. It was otherwise at night. For then the guards were dismissed and the king was alone in his enclosure with his favourite wives, and there was no man near to defend him except a few herdsmen, whose huts stood a little way off. The hours of darkness were therefore the season of peril for the king. It is said that he used to pass them in constant watchfulness, prowling round his huts fully armed, peering into the blackest shadows, or himself standing silent and alert, like a sentinel on duty, in some dark corner. When at last his rival appeared, the fight would take place in grim silence, broken only by the clash of spears and shields, for it was a point of honour with the king not to call the herdsmen to his assistance.

Ceremonies at the accession of a Shilluk king.

An important part of the solemnities attending the accession of a Shilluk king appears to be intended to convey to the new monarch the divine spirit of Nyakang, which has been transmitted from the founder of the dynasty to all his successors on the throne. For this purpose a sacred four-legged stool and a mysterious object which bears the name of Nyakang himself are brought with much solemnity from the shrine of Nyakang at Akurwa to the small village of Kwom near Fashoda, where the king elect and the chiefs await their arrival. Then the image of Nyakang is placed on the stool; the king elect holds one leg of the stool and an important chief holds another. The king is surrounded by a crowd of princes and nobles, and near him stand two of his paternal aunts and two of his sisters. After that a bullock is killed and its flesh eaten by the men of certain families called *ororo*, who are said to be descended from the third of the Shilluk kings. Then the Akurwa men carry the image of Nyakang into the shrine, and the *ororo* men place the king elect on the sacred stool, where he remains seated for some time, apparently till sunset. When he rises, the Akurwa men carry the stool back into the shrine, and the king is escorted to three new huts, where he stays in seclusion for three days. On the fourth night he is conducted quietly, almost stealthily, to his royal residence at Fashoda, and next day he shews himself publicly to his subjects.

On the whole the theory and practice of the divine kings of the Shilluk correspond very nearly to the theory and practice of the priests of Nemi, the Kings of the Wood, if my view of the latter is correct. In both we see a series of divine kings on whose life the fertility of men, of cattle, and of vegetation is believed to depend, and who are put to death, whether in single combat or otherwise, in order that their divine spirit may be transmitted to their successors in full vigour, uncontaminated by the weakness and decay of sickness or old age, because any such degeneration on the part of the king would, in the opinion of his worshippers, entail a corresponding degeneration on mankind, on cattle, and on the crops. Parallel between the Shilluk kings and the King of the Wood at Nemi.

The Dinka* are a congeries of independent tribes in the valley of the White Nile, whose territory, lying mostly on the eastern bank of the river and stretching from the sixth to the twelfth degree of North Latitude, has been estimated to comprise between sixty and seventy thousand square miles. The nation embraces a number of independent tribes, and each tribe is mainly composed of the owners of cattle; for the Dinka are essentially a pastoral people, passionately devoted to the care of their numerous herds of oxen, though they also keep sheep and goats, and the women cultivate small quantities of millet (durra) and sesame. The tribes have no political union. Each village forms a separate community, pasturing its herds together in the same grass-land. With the change of the seasons the people migrate with their flocks and herds to and from the banks of the The Dinka of the Upper Nile.

Nile. It is in the season of the summer rains that the Dinka are most happy and prosperous. Then the cattle find sweet grass, plentiful water, coolness and shade in the forest; then the people subsist in comfort on the milk of their flocks and herds, supplementing it with the millet which they reap and the wild fruits which they gather in the forest; then they brew the native beer, then they marry and dance by night under the bright moon of the serene tropical sky. But in autumn a great change passes over the life of the community. When October has come, the rains are over, the grass of the pastures is eaten down or withered, the pools are dry; thirst compels the whole village, with its lowing herds and bleating flocks, to migrate to the neighbourhood of the river. Now begins a time of privation and suffering. There is no grass for the cattle save in some marshy spots, where the herdsman must fight his rivals in order to win a meagre supply of fodder for his starveling beasts. There is no milk for the people, no fruits on the trees, except a bitter sort of acorns, from which a miserable flour is ground to stay the pangs of hunger. The lean and famished natives are driven to fish in the river for the tubers of water-lilies, to grub in the earth for roots, to boil the leaves of trees, and as a last resource to drink the blood drawn from the necks of their wretched cattle. The gaunt appearance of the people at this season fills the beholder with horror. The herds are decimated by famine, but even more beasts perish by dysentery and other diseases when the first rains cause the fresh grass to sprout.

Dengdit, the Supreme Being of the Dinka.

It is no wonder that the rain, on which the Dinka are so manifestly dependent for their subsistence, should play a great part in their religion and superstition. They worship a supreme being whose name of Dengdit means literally Great Rain. It was he who created the world and established the present order of things, and it is he who sends down the rain from the 'rain-place', his home in the upper regions of the air. But

Totemism of the Dinka.

according to the Niel Dinka this great being was once incarnate in human form. Born of a woman, who descended from the sky, he became the ancestor of a clan which has the rain for its

Rain-makers among the Dinka.

totem. Perhaps without being unduly rash we may conjecture that the great god of the Dinka, who gives them the rain, was indeed, what tradition represents him as having been, a man among men, in fact a human rain-maker, whom at his death the superstition of his fellows promoted to the rank of a deity above the clouds. Be that as it may, the human rain-maker (*bain*) is a very important personage among the Dinka to this day; indeed the men in authority whom travellers dub chiefs or sheikhs are in fact the actual or potential rain-makers of the tribe or community. Each of them is believed to be animated by the spirit of a great rain-maker, which has come down to him through a succession of rain-makers; and in virtue of this inspiration a successful rain-maker enjoys very great power and is consulted on all important matters.

In spite, or rather in virtue, of the high honour in which he is held, no Dinka rain-maker is allowed to die a natural death of sickness or old age; for the Dinka believe that if such an untoward event were to happen, the tribe would suffer from disease and famine, and the herds would not yield their increase. So when a rain-maker feels that he is growing old and infirm, he tells his children that he wishes to die. Among the Agar Dinka a large grave is dug and the rain-maker lies down in it on his right side with his head resting on a skin. He is surrounded by his friends and relatives, including his younger children; but his elder children are not allowed to approach the grave lest in their grief and despair they should do themselves a bodily injury. For many hours, generally for more than a day, the rain-maker lies without eating or drinking. From time to time he speaks to the people, recalling the past history of the tribe, reminding them how he has ruled and advised them, and instructing them how they are to act in the future. Then, when he has concluded his admonition, he tells them that it is finished and bids them cover him up. So the earth is thrown down on him as he lies in the grave, and he soon dies of suffocation. Such, with minor variations, appears to be the regular end of the honourable career of a rain-maker in all the Dinka tribes.

It appears to have been a Zulu custom to put the king to death as soon as he began to have wrinkles or grey hairs. At least this seems implied in the following passage written by one who resided for some time at the court of the notorious Zulu tyrant Chaka, in the early part of the nineteenth century: 'The extraordinary violence of the king's rage with me was mainly occasioned by that absurd nostrum, the hair oil, with the notion

Dinka rain-makers not allowed to die a natural death.

Zulu kings put to death on the approach of old age.

of which Mr Farewell had impressed him as being a specific for removing all indications of age. From the first moment of his having heard that such a preparation was attainable, he evinced a solicitude to procure it, and on every occasion never forgot to remind us of his anxiety respecting it; more especially on our departure on the mission his injunctions were particularly directed to this object. It will be seen that it is one of the barbarous customs of the Zoolas in their choice or election of their kings that he must neither have wrinkles nor grey hairs, as they are both distinguishing marks of disqualification for becoming a monarch of a warlike people. It is also equally indispensable that their king should never exhibit those proofs of having become unfit and incompetent to reign; it is therefore important that they should conceal these indications so long as they possibly can. Chaka had become greatly apprehensive of the approach of grey hairs; which would at once be the signal for him to prepare to make his exit from this sublunary world, it being always followed by the death of the monarch.'* The writer to whom we are indebted for this instructive anecdote of the hair-oil omits to specify the mode in which a grey-haired and wrinkled Zulu chief used 'to make his exit from this sublunary world'; but on analogy we may conjecture that he did so by the simple and perfectly sufficient process of being knocked on the head.

Kings of Sofala put to death on account of bodily blemishes.

The custom of putting kings to death as soon as they suffered from any personal defect prevailed two centuries ago in the Caffre kingdom of Sofala, to the north of the present Zululand. We have seen that these kings of Sofala, each of whom bore the official name of Quiteve, were regarded as gods by their people, being entreated to give rain or sunshine, according as each might be wanted. Nevertheless a slight bodily blemish, such as the loss of a tooth, was considered a sufficient cause for putting one of these god-men to death, as we learn from the following passage of an old Portuguese historian: 'It was formerly the custom of the kings of this land to commit suicide by taking poison when any disaster or natural physical defect fell upon them, such as impotence, infectious disease, the loss of their front teeth, by which they were disfigured, or any other deformity or affliction. To put an end to such defects they killed themselves, saying that the king should be free from any blemish, and if not, it was better for his honour that he should die and seek another life where he would be made whole, for there everything was perfect. But the Quiteve who reigned when I was in those parts would not imitate his predecessors in this, being discreet and dreaded as he was; for having lost a front tooth he caused it to be proclaimed throughout the kingdom that all should be aware that he had lost a tooth and should recognise him when they saw him without it, and if his predecessors killed themselves for such things they were very foolish, and he would not do so; on the contrary, he would be very sorry when the time came for him to die a natural death, for his life was very necessary to preserve his kingdom and defend it from his enemies; and he recommended his successors to follow his example.'

According to the Book of Acaill and many other authorities no king who was afflicted with a personal blemish might reign over Ireland at Tara. Hence, when the great King Cormac Mac Art lost one eye by an accident, he at once abdicated. It is only natural, therefore, to suppose, especially with the other African examples before us, that any bodily defect or symptom of old age appearing on the person of the Ethiopian monarch was the signal for his execution. At a later time it is recorded that if the king of Ethiopia became maimed in any part of his body all his courtiers had to suffer the same mutilation. But this rule may perhaps have been instituted at the time when the custom of killing the king for any personal defect was abolished; instead of compelling the king to die because, for example, he had lost a tooth, all his subjects would be obliged to lose a tooth, and thus the invidious superiority of the subjects over the king would be cancelled. A rule of this sort is still observed in the same region at the court of the Sultans of Darfur.* When the Sultan coughs, every one makes the sound *ts ts* by striking the tongue against the root of the upper teeth; when he sneezes, the whole assembly utters a sound like the cry of the jeko; when he falls off his horse, all his followers must fall off likewise; if any one of them remains in the saddle, no matter how high his rank, he is laid on the ground and beaten. At the court of the king of Uganda in central Africa, when the king laughs, every one laughs; when he sneezes, every one sneezes; when he has a cold, every one pretends to have a cold; when he has his hair

Courtiers required to imitate their sovereign.

cut, so has everybody. At the court of Boni in Celebes it is a rule that whatever the king does all the courtiers must do. If he stands, they stand; if he sits, they sit; if he falls off his horse, they fall off their horses; if he bathes, they bathe, and passers-by must go into the water in the dress, good or bad, which they happen to have on. When the emperor of China laughs, the mandarins in attendance laugh also; when he stops laughing, they stop; when he is sad, their countenances are chopfallen; 'you would say that their faces are on springs, and that the emperor can touch the springs and set them in motion at pleasure'. But to return to the death of the divine king.

Many days' journey to the north-east of Abomey, the old capital of Dahomey, lies the kingdom of Eyeo. 'The Eyeos are governed by a king, no less absolute than the king of Dahomey, yet subject to a regulation of state, at once humiliating and extraordinary. When the people have conceived an opinion of his ill-government, which is sometimes insidiously infused into them by the artifice of his discontented ministers, they send a deputation to him with a present of parrots' eggs, as a mark of its authenticity, to represent to him that the burden of government must have so far fatigued him that they consider it full time for him to repose from his cares and indulge himself with a little sleep. He thanks his subjects for their attention to his ease, retires to his own apartment as if to sleep, and there gives directions to his women to strangle him. This is immediately executed, and his son quietly ascends the throne upon the usual terms of holding the reins of government no longer than whilst he merits the approbation of the people.' About the year 1774, a king of Eyeo, whom his ministers attempted to remove in the customary manner, positively refused to accept the proffered parrots' eggs at their hands, telling them that he had no mind to take a nap, but on the contrary was resolved to watch for the benefit of his subjects. The ministers, surprised and indignant at his recalcitrancy, raised a rebellion, but were defeated with great slaughter, and thus by his spirited conduct the king freed himself from the tyranny of his councillors and established a new precedent for the guidance of his successors. However, the old custom seems to have revived and persisted until late in the nineteenth century, for a Catholic missionary, writing in 1884, speaks of the practice as if it were still in vogue. Another

Kings of Eyeo put to death.

missionary, writing in 1881, thus describes the usage of the Egbas and the Yorubas* of west Africa: 'Among the customs of the country one of the most curious is unquestionably that of judging and punishing the king. Should he have earned the hatred of his people by exceeding his rights, one of his councillors, on whom the heavy duty is laid, requires of the prince that he shall "go to sleep," which means simply "take poison and die." If his courage fails him at the supreme moment, a friend renders him this last service, and quietly, without betraying the secret, they prepare the people for the news of the king's death. In Yoruba the thing is managed a little differently. When a son is born to the king of Oyo, they make a model of the infant's right foot in clay and keep it in the house of the elders (*ogboni*). If the king fails to observe the customs of the country, a messenger, without speaking a word, shews him his child's foot. The king knows what that means. He takes poison and goes to sleep.' The old Prussians acknowledged as their supreme lord a ruler who governed them in the name of the gods, and was known as God's Mouth (*Kirwaido*). When he felt himself weak and ill, if he wished to leave a good name behind him, he had a great heap made of thornbushes and straw, on which he mounted and delivered a long sermon to the people, exhorting them to serve the gods and promising to go to the gods and speak for the people. Then he took some of the perpetual fire which burned in front of the holy oak-tree, and lighting the pile with it burned himself to death.

Voluntary death by fire of the old Prussian Kirwaido.

We need not doubt the truth of this last tradition. Fanaticism or the mere love of notoriety has led men in other ages and other lands to court death in the flames. In antiquity the mountebank Peregrinus, after bidding for fame in the various characters of a Christian martyr, a shameless cynic, and a rebel against Rome, ended his disreputable and vainglorious career by publicly burning himself at the Olympic festival in the presence of a crowd of admirers and scoffers, among whom was the satirist Lucian.* Buddhist monks in China sometimes seek to attain Nirvana by the same method, the flame of their religious zeal being fanned by a belief that the merit of their death redounds to the good of the whole community, while the praises which are showered upon them in their lives, and the prospect

Voluntary deaths by fire.

Peregrinus at Olympia.

Buddhist monks in China.

of the honours and worship which await them after death, serve as additional incentives to suicide.

Religious suicides in Russia.

But the suicides by fire of Chinese Buddhists and Esquimaux sorcerers have been far surpassed by the frenzies of Christian fanaticism. In the seventeenth century the internal troubles of

Belief in the approaching end of the world.

their unhappy country, viewed in the dim light of prophecy, created a widespread belief among the Russian people that the end of the world was at hand, and that the reign of Antichrist was about to begin. We know from Scripture that the old serpent, which is the devil, has been or will be shut up under lock and key for a thousand years, and that the number of the Beast is six hundred and sixty-six. A simple mathematical calculation, based on these irrefragable data, pointed to the year one thousand six hundred and sixty-six as the date when the final consummation of all things and the arrival of the Beast in question might be confidently anticipated. When the year came and went and still, to the general surprise, the animal failed to put in an appearance, the calculations were revised, it was discovered that an error had crept into them, and the world was respited for another thirty-three years. But though opinions differed as to the precise date of the catastrophe, the pious were unanimous in their conviction of its proximity. Accordingly some of them ceased to till their fields, abandoned their houses, and on certain nights of the year expected the sound of the last trump in coffins which they took the precaution of closing, lest their senses, or what remained of them, should be overpowered

Epidemic of suicide.

by the awful vision of the Judgment Day. It would have been well if the delusion of their disordered intellects had stopped there. Unhappily in many cases it went much further, and suicide, universal suicide, was preached by fervent missionaries as the only means to escape the snares of Antichrist and to pass from the sins and sorrows of this fleeting world to the eternal joys of heaven. Whole communities hailed with enthusiasm the gospel of death, and hastened to put its precepts in practice. An

Suicide by starvation.

epidemic of suicide raged throughout northern and north-eastern Russia.

A Jewish Messiah.

As the Christians expected the arrival of Antichrist in the year 1666, so the Jews cheerfully anticipated the long-delayed advent of their Messiah in the same fateful year. A Jew of Smyrna, by name Sabatei-Sevi, availed himself of this general expectation to pose as the Messiah in person. He was greeted with enthusiasm. Jews from many parts of Europe hastened to pay their homage and, what was still better, their money to the future deliverer of his country, who in return parcelled out among them, with the greatest liberality, estates in the Holy Land which did not belong to him. But the alternative of death by impalement or conversion to Mohammedanism, which the Sultan submitted to his consideration, induced him to revise his theological opinions, and on looking into the matter more closely he discovered that his true mission in life was to preach the total abolition of the Jewish religion and the substitution for it of Islam.*

iii

In the cases hitherto described, the divine king or priest is suffered by his people to retain office until some outward defect, some visible symptom of failing health or advancing age, warns them that he is no longer equal to the discharge of his divine duties; but not until such symptoms have made their appearance is he put to death. Some peoples, however, appear to have thought it unsafe to wait for even the slightest symptom of decay and have preferred to kill the king while he was still in the full vigour of life. Accordingly, they have fixed a term beyond which he might not reign, and at the close of which he must die, the term fixed upon being short enough to exclude the probability of his degenerating physically in the interval. In some parts of southern India the period fixed was twelve years. Thus, according to an old traveller, in the province of Quila-care, about twenty leagues to the north-east of Cape Comorin, 'there is a Gentile house of prayer, in which there is an idol which they hold in great account, and every twelve years they celebrate a great feast to it, whither all the Gentiles go as to a jubilee. This temple possesses many lands and much revenue: it is a very great affair. This province has a king over it, who has not more than twelve years to reign from jubilee to jubilee. His manner of living is in this wise, that is to say: when the twelve years are completed, on the day of this feast there assemble together innumerable people, and much money is spent in giving food to Brahmans. The king has a wooden

Marginal notes:

Kings put to death after a fixed term.

Suicide of the kings of Quilacare at the end of a reign of twelve years.

scaffolding made, spread over with silken hangings: and on that day he goes to bathe at a tank with great ceremonies and sound of music, after that he comes to the idol and prays to it, and mounts on to the scaffolding, and there before all the people he takes some very sharp knives, and begins to cut off his nose, and then his ears, and his lips, and all his members, and as much flesh off himself as he can; and he throws it away very hurriedly until so much of his blood is spilled that he begins to faint, and then he cuts his throat himself. And he performs this sacrifice to the idol, and whoever desires to reign other twelve years and undertake this martyrdom for love of the idol, has to be present looking, on at this: and from that place they raise him up as king.'*

Custom of the kings of Calicut. The king of Calicut, on the Malabar coast, bears the title of Samorin or Samory, which in the native language is said to mean 'God on earth'. He 'pretends to be of a higher rank than the Brahmans, and to be inferior only to the invisible gods; a pretention that was acknowledged by his subjects, but which is held as absurd and abominable by the Brahmans, by whom he is only treated as a Sudra'. Formerly the Samorin had to cut his throat in public at the end of a twelve years' reign. But towards the end of the seventeenth century the rule had been modified as follows: 'Many strange customs were observed in this country in former times, and some very odd ones are still continued. It was an ancient custom for the Samorin to reign but twelve years, and no longer. If he died before his term was expired, it saved him a troublesome ceremony of cutting his own throat, on a publick scaffold erected for the purpose. He first made a feast for all his nobility and gentry, who are very numerous. After the feast he saluted his guests, and went on the scaffold, and very decently cut his own throat in the view of the assembly, and his body was, a little while after, burned with great pomp and ceremony, and the grandees elected a new Samorin. Whether that custom was a religious or a civil ceremony, I know not, but it is now laid aside. And a new custom is followed by the modern Samorins, that jubilee is proclaimed throughout his dominions, at the end of twelve years, and a tent is pitched for him in a spacious plain, and a great feast is celebrated for ten or twelve days, with mirth and jollity, guns firing night and day, so at the end of the feast any four of the guests that have a mind to gain a crown by a desperate action, in fighting their way through 30 or 40,000 of his guards, and kill the Samorin in his tent, he that kills him succeeds him in his empire. In anno 1695, one of those jubilees happened, and the tent pitched near Pennany, a seaport of his, about fifteen leagues to the southward of Calicut. There were but three men that would venture on that desperate action, who fell in, with sword and target, among the guard, and, after they had killed and wounded many, were themselves killed. One of the desperados had a nephew of fifteen or sixteen years of age, that kept close by his uncle in the attack on the guards, and, when he saw him fall, the youth got through the guards into the tent, and made a stroke at his Majesty's head, and had certainly despatched him if a large brass lamp which was burning over his head had not marred the blow; but, before he could make another, he was killed by the guards; and, I believe, the same Samorin reigns yet. I chanced to come that time along the coast and heard the guns for two or three days and nights successively.'

The English traveller, whose account I have quoted,* did not himself witness the festival he describes, though he heard the sound of the firing in the distance. Fortunately, exact records of these festivals and of the number of men who perished at them have been preserved in the archives of the royal family at Calicut. In the latter part of the nineteenth century they were examined by Mr W. Logan,* with the personal assistance of the reigning king, and from his work it is possible to gain an accurate conception both of the tragedy and of the scene where it was periodically enacted down to 1743, when the ceremony took place for the last time.

The festival at which the king of Calicut staked his crown and his life on the issue of battle was known as the *Maha Makham* or Great Sacrifice. It fell every twelfth year, when the planet Jupiter was in retrograde motion in the sign of the Crab, and it lasted twenty-eight days, culminating at the time of the eighth lunar asterism in the month of Makaram. As the date of the festival was determined by the position of Jupiter in the sky, and the interval between two festivals was twelve years, which is roughly Jupiter's period of revolution round the sun, we may conjecture that the splendid planet was supposed to be in a

The *Maha Makham* or Great Sacrifice at Calicut.

special sense the king's star and to rule his destiny, the period of its revolution in heaven corresponding to the period of his reign on earth. However that may be, the ceremony was observed with great pomp at the Tirunavayi temple, on the north bank of the Ponnani River. From the western gateway of the temple a perfectly straight road, hardly raised above the level of the surrounding rice-fields and shaded by a fine avenue, runs for half a mile to a high ridge with a precipitous bank, on which the outlines of three or four terraces can still be traced. On the topmost of these terraces the king took his stand on the eventful day. The view which it commands is a fine one. Across the flat expanse of the rice-fields, with the broad placid river winding through them, the eye ranges eastward to high table-lands, their lower slopes embowered in woods, while afar off looms the great chain of the western Ghauts, and in the furthest distance the Neilgherries or Blue Mountains, hardly distinguishable from the azure of the sky above.

The attack on the king.

But it was not to the distant prospect that the king's eyes naturally turned at this crisis of his fate. His attention was arrested by a spectacle nearer at hand. For all the plain below was alive with troops, their banners waving gaily in the sun, the white tents of their many camps standing sharply out against the green and gold of the rice-fields. Forty thousand fighting men or more were gathered there to defend the king. But if the plain swarmed with soldiers, the road that cuts across it from the temple to the king's stand was clear of them. Not a soul was stirring on it. Each side of the way was barred by palisades, and from the palisades on either hand a long hedge of spears, held by strong arms, projected into the empty road, their blades meeting in the middle and forming a glittering arch of steel. All was now ready. The king waved his sword. At the same moment a great chain of massy gold, enriched with bosses, was placed on an elephant at his side. That was the signal. On the instant a stir might be seen half a mile away at the gate of the temple. A group of swordsmen, decked with flowers and smeared with ashes, has stepped out from the crowd. They have just partaken of their last meal on earth, and they now receive the last blessings and farewells of their friends. A moment more and they are coming down the lane of spears, hewing and stabbing right and left at the spearmen, winding and turning and writhing among the blades as if they had no bones in their bodies. It is all in vain. One after the other they fall, some nearer the king, some further off, content to die, not for the shadow of a crown, but for the mere sake of approving their dauntless valour and swordsmanship to the world. On the last days of the festival the same magnificent display of gallantry, the same useless sacrifice of life was repeated again and again. Yet perhaps no sacrifice is wholly useless which proves that there are men who prefer honour to life.

When kings were bound to suffer death, whether at their own hands or at the hands of others, on the expiration of a fixed term of years, it was natural that they should seek to delegate the painful duty, along with some of the privileges of sovereignty, to a substitute who should suffer vicariously in their stead. This expedient appears to have been resorted to by some of the princes of Malabar. Thus we are informed by a native authority on that country that 'in some places all powers both executive and judicial were delegated for a fixed period to natives by the sovereign. This institution was styled *Thalavettiparothiam* or authority obtained by decapitation. *Parothiam* is the name of a supreme authority of those days. The name of the office is still preserved in the Cochin state, where the village headman is called a *Parathiakaran*. This *Thalavettiparothiam* was a terrible but interesting institution. It was an office tenable for five years during which its bearer was invested with supreme despotic powers within his jurisdiction. On the expiry of the five years the man's head was cut off and thrown up in the air amongst a large concourse of villagers, each of whom vied with the other in trying to catch it in its course down. He who succeeded was nominated to the post for the next five years.'* A similar delegation of the duty of dying for his country was perhaps practised by the Sultans of Java. At least such a custom would explain a strange scene which was witnessed at the court of one of these sultans by the famous traveller Ibn Batuta, a native of Tangier, who visited the East Indies in the first half of the fourteenth century. He says: 'During my audience with the Sultan I saw a man who held in his hand a knife like that used by a grape-gleaner. He placed it on his own neck and spoke for a long time in a language which I did not understand. After that he seized the knife with both hands at

Custom of
*Thalavettipa-
rothiam* in
Malabar.

Custom of
the Sultans
of Java.

once and cut his throat. His head fell to the ground, so sharp was the blade and so great the force with which he used it. I remained dumbfoundered at his behaviour, but the Sultan said to me, "Does any one do like that in your country?" I answered, "Never did I see such a thing." He smiled and replied, "These people are our slaves, and they kill themselves for love of us." Then he commanded that they should take away him who had slain himself and should burn him. The Sultan's officers, the grandees, the troops, and the common people attended the cremation.'

Pretence of putting the king's proxy to death.

When once kings, who had hitherto been bound to die a violent death at the end of a term of years, conceived the happy thought of dying by deputy in the persons of others, they would very naturally put it in practice; and accordingly we need not wonder at finding so popular an expedient, or traces of it, in many lands. Thus, for example, the Bhuiyas are an aboriginal race of north-eastern India, and one of their chief seats is Keonjhur. At the installation of a Rajah of Keonjhur a ceremony is observed which has been described as follows by an English officer who witnessed it: 'Then the sword, a very rusty old weapon, is placed in the Raja's hands, and one of the Bhuiyas, named Anand Kopat, comes before him, and kneeling sideways, the Raja touches him on the neck as if about to strike off his head, and it is said that in former days there was no fiction in this part of the ceremony. The family of the Kopat hold their lands on the condition that the victim when required shall be produced. Anand, however, hurriedly arose after the accolade and disappeared. He must not be seen for three days; then he presents himself again to the Raja as miraculously restored to life.' Here the custom of putting the king's proxy to death has dwindled, probably under English influence, to a mere pretence; but elsewhere it survives, or survived till recent times, in full force. Cassange, a native state in the interior of

Man killed at the installation of a king of Cassange.

Angola, is ruled by a king, who bears the title of Jaga. When a king is about to be installed in office, some of the chiefs are despatched to find a human victim, who may not be related by blood or marriage to the new monarch. When he comes to the king's camp, the victim is provided with everything he requires, and all his orders are obeyed as promptly as those of the sovereign. On the day of the ceremony the king takes his seat on a perforated iron stool, his chiefs, councillors, and the rest of the people forming a great circle round about him. Behind the king sits his principal wife, together with all his concubines. An iron gong, with two small bells attached to it, is then struck by an official, who continues to ring the bells during the ceremony. The victim is then introduced and placed in front of the king, but with his back towards him. Armed with a scimitar the king then cuts open the man's back, extracts his heart, and having taken a bite out of it, spits it out and gives it to be burned. The councillors meantime hold the victim's body so that the blood from the wound spouts against the king's breast and belly, and, pouring through the hole in the iron stool, is collected by the chiefs in their hands, who rub their breasts and beards with it, while they shout, 'Great is the king and the rites of the state!' After that the corpse is skinned, cut up, and cooked with the flesh of an ox, a dog, a hen, and some other animals. The meal thus prepared is served first to the king, then to the chiefs and councillors, and lastly to all the people assembled. Any man who refused to partake of it would be sold into slavery together with his family. The distinction with which the human victim is here treated before his execution suggests that he is a substitute for the king.

iv

There are some grounds for believing that the reign of many ancient Greek kings was limited to eight years, or at least that at the end of every period of eight years a new consecration, a fresh outpouring of the divine grace, was regarded as necessary in order to enable them to discharge their civil and religious duties. Thus it was a rule of the Spartan constitution that every eighth year the ephors should choose a clear and moonless night and sitting down observe the sky in silence. If during their vigil they saw a meteor or shooting star, they inferred that the king had sinned against the deity, and they suspended him from his functions until the Delphic or Olympic oracle should reinstate him in them.

At Babylon, within historical times, the tenure of the kingly office was in practice lifelong, yet in theory it would seem to have been merely annual. For every year at the festival of

Limited tenure of the kingship in ancient Greece.

The Spartan kings appear formerly to have held office for periods of eight years only.

Evidence of an annual tenure

of the king-
ship at Baby-
lon.

Zagmuk the king had to renew his power by seizing the hands
of the image of Marduk in his great temple of Esagil at Babylon.
Even when Babylon passed under the power of Assyria, the
monarchs of that country were expected to legalise their claim
to the throne every year by coming to Babylon and performing
the ancient ceremony at the New Year festival, and some of
them found the obligation so burdensome that rather than
discharge it they renounced the title of king altogether and
contented themselves with the humbler one of Governor. Fur-

Further, it
would seem
that in very
early times
the kings of
Babylon were
put to death
at the end of
a year's
reign.
The mock
king put to
death at the
festival of
the Sacaea
was probably
a substitute
for the real
king.

ther, it would appear that in remote times, though not within
the historical period, the kings of Babylon or their barbarous
predecessors forfeited not merely their crown but their life at
the end of a year's tenure of office. At least this is the
conclusion to which the following evidence seems to point.
According to the historian Berosus, who as a Babylonian priest
spoke with ample knowledge, there was annually celebrated in
Babylon a festival called the Sacaea. It began on the sixteenth
day of the month Lous, and lasted for five days. During these
five days masters and servants changed places, the servants
giving orders and the masters obeying them. A prisoner condemned to death was dressed in the king's robes, seated on the
king's throne, allowed to issue whatever commands he pleased,
to eat, drink, and enjoy himself, and to lie with the king's
concubines. But at the end of the five days he was stripped of
his royal robes, scourged, and hanged or impaled. During his
brief term of office he bore the title of Zoganes. This custom
might perhaps have been explained as merely a grim jest
perpetrated in a season of jollity at the expense of an unhappy
criminal. But one circumstance—the leave given to the mock
king to enjoy the king's concubines—is decisive against this
interpretation. Considering the jealous seclusion of an oriental
despot's harem we may be quite certain that permission to
invade it would never have been granted by the despot, least of
all to a condemned criminal, except for the very gravest cause.
This cause could hardly be other than that the condemned man
was about to die in the king's stead, and that to make the
substitution perfect it was necessary he should enjoy the full
rights of royalty during his brief reign. There is nothing
surprising in this substitution. The rule that the king must be
put to death either on the appearance of any symptom of bodily

decay or at the end of a fixed period is certainly one which, sooner or later, the kings would seek to abolish or modify. We have seen that in Ethiopia, Sofala, and Eyeo the rule was boldly set aside by enlightened monarchs; and that in Calicut the old custom of killing the king at the end of twelve years was changed into a permission granted to any one at the end of the twelve years' period to attack the king, and, in the event of killing him, to reign in his stead; though, as the king took care at these times to be surrounded by his guards, the permission was little more than a form. Another way of modifying the stern old rule is seen in the Babylonian custom just described. When the time drew near for the king to be put to death (in Babylon this appears to have been at the end of a single year's reign) he abdicated for a few days, during which a temporary king reigned and suffered in his stead. At first the temporary king may have been an innocent person, possibly a member of the king's own family; but with the growth of civilisation the sacrifice of an innocent person would be revolting to the public sentiment, and accordingly a condemned criminal would be invested with the brief and fatal sovereignty. In the sequel we shall find other examples of a dying criminal representing a dying god. For we must not forget that, as the case of the Shilluk kings clearly shews, the king is slain in his character of a god or a demigod, his death and resurrection, as the only means of perpetuating the divine life unimpaired, being deemed necessary for the salvation of his people and the world.

CHAPTER 3

TEMPORARY KINGS

Annual abdication of kings and their places temporarily taken by nominal sovereigns.

Temporary kings in Cambodia.

IN some places the modified form of the old custom of regicide which appears to have prevailed at Babylon has been further softened down. The king still abdicates annually for a short time and his place is filled by a more or less nominal sovereign; but at the close of his short reign the latter is no longer killed, though sometimes a mock execution still survives as a memorial of the time when he was actually put to death. To take examples. In the month of Méac (February) the king of Cambodia annually abdicated for three days. During this time he performed no act of authority, he did not touch the seals, he did not even receive the revenues which fell due. In his stead there reigned a temporary king called Sdach Méac, that is, King February. The office of temporary king was hereditary in a family distantly connected with the royal house, the sons succeeding the fathers and the younger brothers the elder brothers, just as in the succession to the real sovereignty. On a favourable day fixed by the astrologers the temporary king was conducted by the mandarins in triumphal procession. He rode one of the royal elephants, seated in the royal palanquin, and escorted by soldiers who, dressed in appropriate costumes, represented the neighbouring peoples of Siam, Annam, Laos, and so on. In place of the golden crown he wore a peaked white cap, and his regalia, instead of being of gold encrusted with diamonds, were of rough wood. After paying homage to the real king, from whom he received the sovereignty for three days, together with all the revenues accruing during that time (though this last custom has been omitted for some time), he moved in procession round the palace and through the streets of the capital. On the third day, after the usual procession, the temporary king gave orders that the elephants should trample under foot the 'mountain of rice', which was a scaffold of bamboo surrounded by sheaves of rice. The people gathered up the rice, each man taking home a little with him to secure a good harvest. Some of it was also taken to the king, who had it cooked and presented to the monks.

In Siam on the sixth day of the moon in the sixth month (the end of April) a temporary king is appointed, who for three days enjoys the royal prerogatives, the real king remaining shut up in his palace. This temporary king sends his numerous satellites in all directions to seize and confiscate whatever they can find in the bazaar and open shops; even the ships and junks which arrive in harbour during the three days are forfeited to him and must be redeemed. He goes to a field in the middle of the city, whither they bring a gilded plough drawn by gaily-decked oxen. After the plough has been anointed and the oxen rubbed with incense, the mock king traces nine furrows with the plough, followed by aged dames of the palace scattering the first seed of the season. As soon as the nine furrows are drawn, the crowd of spectators rushes in and scrambles for the seed which has just been sown, believing that, mixed with the seed-rice, it will ensure a plentiful crop. Then the oxen are unyoked, and rice, maize, sesame, sago, bananas, sugar-cane, melons, and so on, are set before them; whatever they eat first will, it is thought, be dear in the year following, though some people interpret the omen in the opposite sense. During this time the temporary king stands leaning against a tree with his right foot resting on his left knee. From standing thus on one foot he is popularly known as King Hop; but his official title is Phaya Phollathep, 'Lord of the Heavenly Hosts'. He is a sort of Minister of Agriculture; all disputes about fields, rice, and so forth, are referred to him. There is moreover another ceremony in which he personates the king. It takes place in the second month (which falls in the cold season) and lasts three days. He is conducted in procession to an open place opposite the Temple of the Brahmans, where there are a number of poles dressed like May-poles, upon which the Brahmans swing. All the while that they swing and dance, the Lord of the Heavenly Hosts has to stand on one foot upon a seat which is made of bricks plastered over, covered with a white cloth, and hung with tapestry. He is supported by a wooden frame with a gilt canopy, and two Brahmans stand one on each side of him. The dancing Brahmans carry buffalo horns with which they draw water from a large copper caldron and sprinkle it on the spectators; this is

Temporary kings in Siam in former days.

supposed to bring good luck, causing the people to dwell in peace and quiet, health and prosperity. The time during which the Lord of the Heavenly Hosts has to stand on one foot is about three hours. This is thought 'to prove the dispositions of the Devattas and spirits'. If he lets his foot down 'he is liable to forfeit his property and have his family enslaved by the king; as it is believed to be a bad omen, portending destruction to the state, and instability to the throne. But if he stand firm he is believed to have gained a victory over evil spirits, and he has moreover the privilege, ostensibly at least, of seizing any ship which may enter the harbour during these three days, and taking its contents, and also of entering any open shop in the town and carrying away what he chooses.'

Modern custom of temporary kings in Siam Such were the duties and privileges of the Siamese King Hop down to about the middle of the nineteenth century or later. Under the reign of the late enlightened monarch this quaint personage was to some extent both shorn of the glories and relieved of the burden of his office. He still watches, as of old, the Brahmans rushing through the air in a swing suspended between two tall masts, each some ninety feet high; but he is allowed to sit instead of stand, and, although public opinion still expects him to keep his right foot on his left knee during the whole of the ceremony, he would incur no legal penalty were he, to the great chagrin of the people, to put his weary foot to the ground. Other signs, too, tell of the invasion of the East by the ideas and civilisation of the West. The thoroughfares that lead to the scene of the performance are blocked with carriages: lamp-posts and telegraph posts, to which eager spectators cling like monkeys, rise above the dense crowd; and, while a tatter-demalion band of the old style, in gaudy garb of vermilion and yellow, bangs and tootles away on drums and trumpets of an antique pattern, the procession of barefooted soldiers in brilliant uniforms steps briskly along to the lively strains of a modern military band playing 'Marching through Georgia'.

Temporary kings in Samarcand and Upper Egypt. On the first day of the sixth month, which was regarded as the beginning of the year, the king and people of Samarcand used to put on new clothes and cut their hair and beards. Then they repaired to a forest near the capital where they shot arrows on horseback for seven days. On the last day the target was a gold coin, and he who hit it had the right to be king for one day. In Upper Egypt on the first day of the solar year by Coptic reckoning, that is, on the tenth of September, when the Nile has generally reached its highest point, the regular government is suspended for three days and every town chooses its own ruler. This temporary lord wears a sort of tall fool's cap and a long flaxen beard, and is enveloped in a strange mantle. With a wand of office in his hand and attended by men disguised as scribes, executioners, and so forth, he proceeds to the Governor's house. The latter allows himself to be deposed; and the mock king, mounting the throne, holds a tribunal, to the decisions of which even the governor and his officials must bow. After three days the mock king is condemned to death; the envelope or shell in which he was encased is committed to the flames, and from its ashes the Fellah creeps forth. The custom perhaps points to an old practice of burning a real king in grim earnest. In Uganda the brothers of the king used to be burned, because it was not lawful to shed the royal blood.

The Mohammedan students of Fez, in Morocco, are allowed to appoint a sultan of their own, who reigns for a few weeks, and is known as *Sulṭan t-tulba*, 'the Sultan of the Scribes'. This brief authority is put up for auction and knocked down to the highest bidder. It brings some substantial privileges with it, for the holder is freed from taxes thenceforward, and he has the right of asking a favour from the real sultan. That favour is seldom refused; it usually consists in the release of a prisoner. Moreover, the agents of the student-sultan levy fines on the shopkeepers and householders, against whom they trump up various humorous charges. The temporary sultan is surrounded with the pomp of a real court, and parades the streets in state with music and shouting, while a royal umbrella is held over his head. With the so-called fines and free-will offerings, to which the real sultan adds a liberal supply of provisions, the students have enough to furnish forth a magnificent banquet; and altogether they enjoy themselves thoroughly, indulging in all kinds of games and amusements. For the first seven days the mock sultan remains in the college; then he goes about a mile out of the town and encamps on the bank of the river, attended by the students and not a few of the citizens. On the seventh day of his stay outside the town he is visited by the real sultan, who grants him his request and gives him seven more days to

Temporary kings in Morocco.

reign, so that the reign of 'the Sultan of the Scribes' nominally lasts three weeks. But when six days of the last week have passed the mock sultan runs back to the town by night. This temporary sultanship always falls in spring, about the beginning of April. Its origin is said to have been as follows. When Mulai Rasheed II was fighting for the throne in 1664 or 1665, a certain Jew usurped the royal authority at Taza. But the rebellion was soon suppressed through the loyalty and devotion of the students. To effect their purpose they resorted to an ingenious stratagem. Forty of them caused themselves to be packed in chests which were sent as a present to the usurper. In the dead of night, while the unsuspecting Jew was slumbering peacefully among the packing-cases, the lids were stealthily raised, the brave forty crept forth, slew the usurper, and took possession of the city in the name of the real sultan, who, to mark his gratitude for the help thus rendered him in time of need, conferred on the students the right of annually appointing a sultan of their own. The narrative has all the air of a fiction devised to explain an old custom, of which the real meaning and origin had been forgotten.

Temporary king in Cornwall.

A custom of annually appointing a mock king for a single day was observed at Lostwithiel in Cornwall down to the sixteenth century. On 'little Easter Sunday' the freeholders of the town and manor assembled together, either in person or by their deputies, and one among them, as it fell to his lot by turn, gaily attired and gallantly mounted, with a crown on his head, a sceptre in his hand, and a sword borne before him, rode through the principal street to the church, dutifully attended by all the rest on horseback. The clergyman in his best robes received him at the churchyard stile and conducted him to hear divine service. On leaving the church he repaired, with the same pomp, to a house provided for his reception. Here a feast awaited him and his suite, and being set at the head of the table he was served on bended knees, with all the rites due to the estate of a prince. The ceremony ended with the dinner, and every man returned home.

Temporary kings at the beginning of a reign.

Sometimes the temporary king occupies the throne, not annually, but once for all at the beginning of each reign. Thus in the kingdom of Jambi, in Sumatra, it is the custom that at the beginning of a new reign a man of the people should occupy the throne and exercise the royal prerogatives for a single day. The origin of the custom is explained by a tradition that there were once five royal brothers, the four elder of whom all declined the throne on the ground of various bodily defects, leaving it to their youngest brother. But the eldest occupied the throne for one day, and reserved for his descendants a similar privilege at the beginning of every reign. Thus the office of temporary king is hereditary in a family akin to the royal house.

Some points about these temporary kings deserve to be specially noticed before we pass to the next branch of the evidence. In the first place, the Cambodian and Siamese examples shew clearly that it is especially the divine or magical functions of the king which are transferred to his temporary substitute. This appears from the belief that by keeping up his foot the temporary king of Siam gained a victory over the evil spirits, whereas by letting it down he imperilled the existence of the state. Again, the Cambodian ceremony of trampling down the 'mountain of rice', and the Siamese ceremony of opening the ploughing and sowing, are charms to produce a plentiful harvest, as appears from the belief that those who carry home some of the trampled rice, or of the seed sown, will thereby secure a good crop. Moreover, when the Siamese representative of the king is guiding the plough, the people watch him anxiously, not to see whether he drives a straight furrow, but to mark the exact point on his leg to which the skirt of his silken robe reaches; for on that is supposed to hang the state of the weather and the crops during the ensuing season. If the Lord of the Heavenly Hosts hitches up his garment above his knee, the weather will be wet and heavy rains will spoil the harvest. If he lets it trail to his ankle, a drought will be the consequence. But fine weather and heavy crops will follow if the hem of his robe hangs exactly half-way down the calf of his leg. So closely is the course of nature, and with it the weal or woe of the people, dependent on the minutest act or gesture of the king's representative. But the task of making the crops grow, thus deputed to the temporary kings, is one of the magical functions regularly supposed to be discharged by kings in primitive society. The rule that the mock king must stand on one foot upon a raised seat in the rice-field was perhaps originally meant as a charm to make the crop grow high; at least this was the object of a similar ceremony observed by the old Prussians. The tallest girl, standing on one foot upon a seat, with her lap full of cakes, a cup of brandy in her right hand and a piece of elm-bark or linden-bark in her left, prayed to the god Waizganthos that the flax might grow as high as she was standing. Then, after draining the cup, she had it refilled, and poured the brandy on the ground as an offering to Waizganthos, and threw down the cakes for his attendant sprites. If she remained steady on one foot throughout the ceremony, it was an omen that the flax crop would be good; but if she let her foot down, it was feared that the crop might fail. The same significance perhaps attaches to the swinging of the Brahmans, which the Lord of the Heavenly Hosts had formerly to witness standing on one foot. On the principles of homoeopathic or imitative magic it might be thought that the higher the priests swing the higher will grow the rice.

Temporary kings substituted in certain emergencies for Shahs of Persia.

In the foregoing cases the temporary king is appointed annually in accordance with a regular custom. But in other cases the appointment is made only to meet a special emergency, such as to relieve the real king from some actual or threatened evil by diverting it to a substitute, who takes his place on the throne for a short time. The history of Persia furnishes instances of such occasional substitutes for the Shah. Thus Shah Abbas the Great, the most eminent of all the kings of Persia, who reigned from 1586 to 1628 AD, being warned by his astrologers in the year 1591 that a serious danger impended over him, attempted to avert the omen by abdicating the throne and appointing a certain unbeliever named Yusoofee, probably a Christian, to reign in his stead. The substitute was accordingly crowned, and for three days, if we may trust the Persian historians, he enjoyed not only the name and the state but the power of the king. At the end of his brief reign he was put to death: the decree of the stars was fulfilled by this sacrifice; and Abbas, who reascended his throne in a most propitious hour, was promised by his astrologers a long and glorious reign.

CHAPTER 4

SACRIFICE OF THE KING'S SON

A POINT to notice about the temporary kings described in the foregoing chapter is that in two places (Cambodia and Jambi) they come of a stock which is believed to be akin to the royal family. If the view here taken of the origin of these temporary kingships is correct, we can easily understand why the king's substitute should sometimes be of the same race as the king. When the king first succeeded in getting the life of another accepted as a sacrifice instead of his own, he would have to shew that the death of that other would serve the purpose quite as well as his own would have done. Now it was as a god or demigod that the king had to die; therefore the substitute who died for him had to be invested, at least for the occasion, with the divine attributes of the king. This, as we have just seen, was certainly the case with the temporary kings of Siam and Cambodia; they were invested with the supernatural functions, which in an earlier stage of society were the special attributes of the king. But no one could so well represent the king in his divine character as his son, who might be supposed to share the divine afflatus of his father. No one, therefore, could so appropriately die for the king and, through him, for the whole people, as the king's son.

The temporary kings are sometimes related by blood to the real kings.

According to tradition, Aun or On, King of Sweden, sacrificed nine of his sons to Odin at Upsala in order that his own life might be spared. After he had sacrificed his second son he received from the god an answer that he should live so long as he gave him one of his sons every ninth year. When he had sacrificed his seventh son, he still lived, but was so feeble that he could not walk but had to be carried in a chair. Then he offered up his eighth son, and lived nine years more, lying in his bed. After that he sacrificed his ninth son, and lived another nine years, but so that he drank out of a horn like a weaned child. He now wished to sacrifice his only remaining son to Odin, but the Swedes would not allow him. So he died and was

Tradition of On, King of Sweden, and the sacrifice of his nine sons.

buried in a mound at Upsala. The poet Thiodolf told the king's history in verse:

'In Upsal's town the cruel king
Slaughtered his sons at Odin's shrine—
Slaughtered his sons with cruel knife,
To get from Odin length of life.
He lived until he had to turn
His toothless mouth to the deer's horn;
And he who shed his children's blood
Sucked through the ox's horn his food.
At length fell Death has tracked him down,
Slowly but sure, in Upsal's town.'

Tradition of King Athamas and his children.

In ancient Greece there seems to have been at least one kingly house of great antiquity of which the eldest sons were always liable to be sacrificed in room of their royal sires. When Xerxes was marching through Thessaly at the head of his mighty host to attack the Spartans at Thermopylae, he came to the town of Alus. Here he was shewn the sanctuary of Laphystian Zeus, about which his guides told him a strange tale. It ran somewhat as follows. Once upon a time the king of the country, by name Athamas, married a wife Nephele, and had by her a son called Phrixus and a daughter named Helle. Afterwards he took to himself a second wife called Ino, by whom he had two sons, Learchus and Melicertes. But his second wife was jealous of her step-children, Phrixus and Helle, and plotted their death. She went about very cunningly to compass her bad end. First of all she persuaded the women of the country to roast the seed corn secretly before it was committed to the ground. So next year no crops came up and the people died of famine. Then the king sent messengers to the oracle at Delphi to enquire the cause of the dearth. But the wicked step-mother bribed the messenger to give out as the answer of the god that the dearth would never cease till the children of Athamas by his first wife had been sacrificed to Zeus. When Athamas heard that, he sent for the children, who were with the sheep. But a ram with a fleece of gold opened his lips, and speaking with the voice of a man warned the children of their danger. So they mounted the ram and fled with him over land and sea. As they flew over the sea, the girl slipped from the animal's back, and falling into water was drowned. But her brother Phrixus was brought safe to the land of Colchis, where reigned a child of the Sun. Phrixus married the king's daughter, and she bore him a son Cytisorus. And there he sacrificed the ram with the golden fleece to Zeus the God of Flight; but some will have it that he sacrificed the animal to Laphystian Zeus. The golden fleece itself he gave to his wife's father, who nailed it to an oak tree, guarded by a sleepless dragon in a sacred grove of Ares. Meanwhile at home an oracle had commanded that King Athamas himself should be sacrificed as an expiatory offering for the whole country. So the people decked him with garlands like a victim and led him to the altar, where they were just about to sacrifice him when he was rescued either by his grandson Cytisorus, who arrived in the nick of time from Colchis, or by Hercules, who brought tidings that the king's son Phrixus was yet alive. Thus Athamas was saved, but afterwards he went mad, and mistaking his son Learchus for a wild beast shot him dead. Next he attempted the life of his remaining son Melicertes, but the child was rescued by his mother Ino, who ran and threw herself and him from a high rock into the sea. Mother and son were changed into marine divinities, and the son received special homage in the isle of Tenedos, where babes were sacrificed to him. Thus bereft of wife and children the unhappy Athamas quitted his country, and on enquiring of the oracle where he should dwell was told to take up his abode wherever he should be entertained by wild beasts. He fell in with a pack of wolves devouring sheep, and when they saw him they fled and left him the bleeding remnants of their prey. In this way the oracle was fulfilled. But because King Athamas had not been sacrificed as a sin-offering for the whole country, it was divinely decreed that the eldest male scion of his family in each generation should be sacrificed without fail, if ever he set foot in the town-hall, where the offerings were made to Laphystian Zeus by one of the house of Athamas. Many of the family, Xerxes was informed, had fled to foreign lands to escape this doom; but some of them had returned long afterwards, and being caught by the sentinels in the act of entering the town-hall were wreathed as victims, led forth in procession, and sacrificed.*

Male descendants of King Athamas liable to be sacrificed.

The suspicion that this barbarous custom by no means fell into disuse even in later days is strengthened by a case of human sacrifice which occurred in Plutarch's time at Orchomenus, a

Family of royal descent liable to be sacrificed at Orchomenus.

very ancient city of Boeotia, distant only a few miles across the plain from the historian's birthplace. Here dwelt a family of which the men went by the name of Psoloeis or 'Sooty', and the women by the name of Oleae or 'Destructive'. Every year at the festival of the Agrionia the priest of Dionysus pursued these women with a drawn sword, and if he overtook one of them he had the right to slay her. In Plutarch's lifetime the right was actually exercised by a priest Zoilus. Now the family thus liable to furnish at least one human victim every year was of royal descent, for they traced their lineage to Minyas, the famous old king of Orchomenus, the monarch of fabulous wealth, whose stately treasury, as it is called, still stands in ruins at the point where the long rocky hill of Orchomenus melts into the vast level expanse of the Copaic plain. Tradition ran that the king's three daughters long despised the other women of the country for yielding to the Bacchic frenzy, and sat at home in the king's house scornfully plying the distaff and the loom, while the rest, wreathed with flowers, their dishevelled locks streaming to the wind, roamed in ecstasy the barren mountains that rise above Orchomenus, making the solitude of the hills to echo to the wild music of cymbals and tambourines. But in time the divine fury infected even the royal damsels in their quiet chamber; they were seized with a fierce longing to partake of human flesh, and cast lots among themselves which should give up her child to furnish a cannibal feast. The lot fell on Leucippe, and she surrendered her son Hippasus, who was torn limb from limb by the three. From these misguided women sprang the Oleae and the Psoloeis, of whom the men were said to be so called because they wore sad-coloured raiment in token of their mourning and grief.*

Thessalian and Boeotian kings seem to have sacrificed their sons to Laphystian Zeus instead of themselves.

Now this practice of taking human victims from a family of royal descent at Orchomenus is all the more significant because Athamas himself is said to have reigned in the land of Orchomenus even before the time of Minyas, and because over against the city there rises Mount Laphystius, on which, as at Alus in Thessaly, there was a sanctuary of Laphystian Zeus, where, according to tradition, Athamas purposed to sacrifice his two children Phrixus and Helle. On the whole, comparing the traditions about Athamas with the custom that obtained with regard to his descendants in historical times, we may fairly infer that in Thessaly and probably in Boeotia there reigned of old a dynasty of which the kings were liable to be sacrificed for the good of the country to the god called Laphystian Zeus, but that they contrived to shift the fatal responsibility to their offspring, of whom the eldest son was regularly destined to the altar. As time went on, the cruel custom was so far mitigated that a ram was accepted as a vicarious sacrifice in room of the royal victim, provided always that the prince abstained from setting foot in the town-hall where the sacrifices were offered to Laphystian Zeus by one of his kinsmen. But if he were rash enough to enter the place of doom, to thrust himself wilfully, as it were, on the notice of the god who had good-naturedly winked at the substitution of a ram, the ancient obligation which had been suffered to lie in abeyance recovered all its force, and there was no help for it but he must die. The tradition which associated the sacrifice of the king or his children with a great dearth points clearly to the belief, so common among primitive folk, that the king is responsible for the weather and the crops, and that he may justly pay with his life for the inclemency of the one or the failure of the other. Athamas and his line, in short, appear to have united divine or magical with royal functions; and this view is strongly supported by the claims to divinity which Salmoneus, the brother of Athamas, is said to have set up. We have seen that this presumptuous mortal professed to be no other than Zeus himself, and to wield the thunder and lightning, of which he made a trumpery imitation by the help of tinkling kettles and blazing torches. If we may judge from analogy, his mock thunder and lightning were no mere scenic exhibition designed to deceive and impress the beholders; they were enchantments practised by the royal magician for the purpose of bringing about the celestial phenomena which they feebly mimicked.

Among the Semites of Western Asia the king, in a time of national danger, sometimes gave his own son to die as a sacrifice for the people. Thus Philo of Byblus, in his work on the Jews, says: 'It was an ancient custom in a crisis of great danger that the ruler of a city or nation should give his beloved son to die for the whole people, as a ransom offered to the avenging demons; and the children thus offered were slain with mystic rites. So Cronus, whom the Phoenicians call Israel, being king

Sacrifice of kings' sons among the Semites.

of the land and having an only-begotten son called Jeoud (for in the Phoenician tongue Jeoud signifies "only-begotten"), dressed him in royal robes and sacrificed him upon an altar in a time of war, when the country was in great danger from the enemy.' When the king of Moab was besieged by the Israelites and hard beset, he took his eldest son, who should have reigned in his stead, and offered him for a burnt offering on the wall.*

But amongst the Semites the practice of sacrificing their children was not confined to kings. In times of great calamity, such as pestilence, drought, or defeat in war, the Phoenicians used to sacrifice one of their dearest to Baal. 'Phoenician history', says an ancient writer, 'is full of such sacrifices.' The writer of a dialogue ascribed to Plato observes that the Carthaginians immolated human beings as if it were right and lawful to do so, and some of them, he adds, even sacrificed their own sons to Baal.* Among the Canaanites or aboriginal inhabitants of Palestine, whom the invading Israelites conquered but did not exterminate, the grisly custom of burning their children in honour of Baal or Moloch seems to have been regularly practised. To the best representatives of the Hebrew people, the authors of their noble literature, such rites were abhorrent, and they warned their fellow-countrymen against participating in them. 'When thou art come into the land which the Lord thy God giveth thee, thou shalt not learn to do after the abominations of those nations. There shall not be found with thee any one that maketh his son or his daughter to pass through the fire, one that useth divination, one that practiseth augury, or an enchanter, or a sorcerer, or a charmer, or a consulter with a familiar spirit, or a wizard, or a necromancer. For whosoever doeth these things is an abomination unto the Lord: and because of these abominations, the Lord thy God doth drive them out from before thee.' Again we read: 'And thou shalt not give any of thy seed to pass through the fire to Molech.'* Whatever effect these warnings may have had in the earlier days of Israelitish history, there is abundant evidence that in later times the Hebrews lapsed, or rather perhaps relapsed, into that congenial mire of superstition from which the higher spirits of the nation struggled—too often in vain—to rescue them. The Psalmist laments that his erring countrymen 'mingled them-

Sacrifice of children to Baal among the Semites.

Canaanite and Hebrew custom of burning children in honour of Baal or Moloch.

selves with the nations, and learned their works: and they served their idols; which became a snare unto them: yea, they sacrificed their sons and their daughters unto demons, and shed innocent blood, even the blood of their sons and of their daughters, whom they sacrificed unto the idols of Canaan; and the land was polluted with blood.'*

It would be interesting, though it might be fruitless, to enquire how far the Hebrew prophets and psalmists were right in their opinion that the Israelites learned these and other gloomy superstitions only through contact with the old inhabitants of the land, that the primitive purity of faith and morals which they brought with them from the free air of the desert was tainted and polluted by the grossness and corruption of the heathen in the fat land of Canaan. When we remember, however, that the Israelites were of the same Semitic stock as the population they conquered and professed to despise, and that the practice of human sacrifice is attested for many branches of the Semitic race, we shall, perhaps, incline to surmise that the chosen people may have brought with them into Palestine the seeds which afterwards sprang up and bore such ghastly fruit in the valley of Hinnom.

Did the Hebrews borrow the custom from the Canaanites?

We have still to ask which of their children the Semites picked out for sacrifice; for that a choice was made and some principle of selection followed, may be taken for granted. A people who burned all their children indiscriminately would soon extinguish themselves, and such an excess of piety is probably rare, if not unknown. In point of fact it seems, at least among the Hebrews, to have been only the firstborn child that was doomed to the flames. The prophet Micah asks, in a familiar passage, 'Wherewith shall I come before the Lord, and bow myself before the high God? shall I come before him with burnt offerings, with calves of a year old? Will the Lord be pleased with thousands of rams, or with ten thousands of rivers of oil? shall I give my firstborn for my transgression, the fruit of my body for the sin of my soul?' These were the questions which pious and doubting hearts were putting to themselves in the days of the prophet. The prophet's own answer is not doubtful. 'He hath shewed thee, O man, what is good; and what doth the Lord require of thee, but to do justly and to love mercy, and to walk humbly with thy God?'* It is a noble answer

Only the firstborn children were burned.

and one which only elect spirits in that or, perhaps, in any age have given.

But while morality ranges itself on the side of the prophet, it may be questioned whether history and precedent were not on the side of his adversaries. If the firstborn of men and cattle were alike sacred to God, and the firstborn of cattle were regularly sacrificed, while the firstborn of men were ransomed by a money payment, has not this last provision the appearance of being a later mitigation of an older and harsher custom which doomed firstborn children, like firstling lambs and calves and goats, to the altar or the fire? The suspicion is greatly strengthened by the remarkable tradition told to account for the sanctity of the firstborn. When Israel was in bondage in Egypt, so runs the tradition, God resolved to deliver them from captivity, and to lead them to the Promised Land. At dead of night he would pass through the land killing all the firstborn of the Egyptians, both man and beast; not one of them would be left alive in the morning. But the Israelites were warned of what was about to happen and told to keep indoors that night, and to put a mark on their houses, so that when he passed down the street on his errand of slaughter, God might know them at sight from the houses of the Egyptians and not turn in and massacre the wrong children and animals. All this was done. The massacre of Egyptian children and animals was successfully perpetrated and had the desired effect; and to commemorate this great triumph God ordained that all the firstborn of man and beast among the Israelites should be sacred to him ever afterwards, the edible animals to be sacrificed, and the uneatable, especially men and asses, to be ransomed by a substitute or by a pecuniary payment of so much a head. And a festival was to be celebrated every spring with rites exactly like those which were observed on the night of the great slaughter. The divine command was obeyed, and the festival thus instituted was the Passover.*

Originally
the firstborn
children
seem to have
been regular-
ly sacrificed:
their redemp-
tion was a

This was the origin, we are told, both of the sanctity of the firstborn and of the feast of the Passover. But when we are further told that the people whose firstborn were slaughtered on that occasion were not the Hebrews but their enemies, we are at once met by serious difficulties. Why, we may ask, should the Israelites kill the firstlings of their cattle for ever because God once killed those of the Egyptians? Here the reader may be reminded of another Hebrew tradition in which the sacrifice of the firstborn child is indicated still more clearly. Abraham, we are informed, was commanded by God to offer up his firstborn son Isaac as a burnt sacrifice, and was on the point of obeying the divine command, when God, content with this proof of his faith and obedience, substituted for the human victim a ram, which Abraham accordingly sacrificed instead of his son.* Putting the two traditions together and observing how exactly they dovetail into each other and into the later Hebrew practice of actually sacrificing the firstborn children* by fire to Baal or Moloch, we can hardly resist the conclusion that, before the practice of redeeming them was introduced, the Hebrews regularly sacrificed their firstborn children.

later mitigation of the rule.

The Borans, on the southern borders of Abyssinia, propitiate a sky-spirit called Wak by sacrificing their children and cattle to him. Among them when a man of any standing marries, he becomes a Raba, as it is called, and for a certain period after marriage, probably four to eight years, he must leave any children that are born to him to die in the bush. No Boran cares to contemplate the fearful calamities with which Wak would visit him if he failed to discharge this duty. After he ceases to be a Raba, a man is circumcised and becomes a Gudda. The sky-spirit has no claim on the children born after their father's circumcision, but they are sent away at a very early age to be reared by the Wata, a low caste of hunters. They remain with these people till they are grown up, and then return to their families. In this remarkable custom it would appear that the circumcision of the father is regarded as an atoning sacrifice which redeems the rest of his children from the spirit to whom they would otherwise belong. The obscure story told by the Israelites to explain the origin of circumcision seems also to suggest that the custom was supposed to save the life of the child by giving the deity a substitute for it.* Again, the Kerre, Banna, and Bashada, three tribes in the valley of the Omo River, to the south of Abyssinia, are in the habit of strangling their firstborn children and throwing the bodies away. The Kerre cast the bodies into the river Omo, where they are devoured by crocodiles; the other two tribes leave them in the forest to be eaten by the hyaenas. In Uganda if the firstborn child of a chief

Sacrifice of firstborn children among the Borans and other tribes to the south of Abyssinia.

Firstborn
male chil-
dren put to
death in
Uganda.
Sacrifice of
firstborn
children in
Europe and
America.

or any important person is a son, the midwife strangles it and
reports that the infant was still-born. 'This is done to ensure
the life of the father; if he has a son born first he will soon die,
and the child inherit all he has.' The heathen Russians often
sacrificed their firstborn to the god Perun. It is said that on
Mag Slacht or 'plain of prostrations', near the present village of
Ballymagauran, in the Country Cavan, there used to stand a
great idol called Cromm Cruach, covered with gold, to which
the ancient Irish sacrificed 'the firstlings of every issue and the
chief scions of every clan' in order to obtain plenty of corn,
honey, and milk. The Indians of Florida sacrificed their firstborn male children. An early Spanish historian of the conquest
of Peru, in describing the Indians of the Peruvian valleys
between San-Miguel and Caxamalca, records that 'they have
disgusting sacrifices and temples of idols which they hold in
great veneration; they offer them their most precious possessions. Every month they sacrifice their own children and smear
with the blood of the victims the face of the idols and the doors
of the temples.' In Puruha, a province of Quito, it used to be
customary to sacrifice the firstborn children to the gods. Their
remains were dried, enclosed in vessels of metal or stone, and
kept in the houses. The Ximanas and Cauxanas, two Indian
tribes in the upper valley of the Amazon, kill all their firstborn
children. If the firstborn is a girl, the Lengua Indians invariably
put it to death.

Different
motives may
have led to
the practice
of killing
firstborn.

    Thus it would seem that a custom of putting to death all
firstborn children has prevailed in many parts of the world.
What was the motive which led people to practise a custom
which to us seems at once so cruel and so foolish? It cannot
have been the purely prudential consideration of adjusting the
numbers of the tribe to the amount of the food-supply; for, in
the first place, savages do not take such thought for the morrow,
and, in the second place, if they did, they would be likely to kill
the later born children rather than the firstborn. The foregoing
evidence suggests that the custom may have been practised by
different peoples from different motives. In some cases the
death of the child appears to be definitely regarded as a
substitute for the death of the father, who obtains a new lease

A belief in
the rebirth of

of life by the sacrifice of his offspring. But in some cases it
would seem that the child has been killed, not so much as a

substitute for the father, as because it is supposed to endanger his life by absorbing his spiritual essence or vital energy. In fact, a belief in the transmigration or rebirth of souls has operated to produce a regular custom of infanticide, especially infanticide of the firstborn. At Whydah, on the Slave Coast of West Africa, where the doctrine of reincarnation is firmly held, it has happened that a child has been put to death because the fetish doctors declared it to be the king's father come to life again. The king naturally could not submit to be pushed from the throne by his predecessor in this fashion; so he compelled his supposed parent to return to the world of the dead from which he had very inopportunely effected his escape. The Hindoos are of opinion that a man is literally reborn in the person of his son. Thus in the *Laws of Manu* we read that 'the husband, after conception by his wife, becomes an embryo and is born again of her; for that is the wifehood of a wife, that he is born again by her'. Hence after the birth of a son the father is clearly in a very delicate position. Since he is his own son, can he himself, apart from his son, be said to exist? Does he not rather die in his own person as soon as he comes to life in the person of his son?

souls may in some cases have operated to produce infanticide, especially of the firstborn.

The Hindoos believe that a man is reborn in his son, while at the same time he dies in his own person.

Now to people who thus conceive the relation of father and son it is plain that fatherhood must appear a very dubious privilege; for if you die in begetting a son, can you be quite sure of coming to life again? His existence is at the best a menace to yours, and at the worst it may involve your extinction. The danger seems to lie especially in the birth of your first son; if only you can tide that over, you are, humanly speaking, safe. In fact, it comes to this, Are you to live? or is he? It is a painful dilemma. Parental affection urges you to die that he may live. Self-love whispers, 'Live and let him die. You are in the flower of your age. You adorn the circle in which you move. You are useful, nay, indispensable, to society. He is a mere babe. He never will be missed.' Such a train of thought, preposterous as it seems to us, might easily lead to a custom of killing the firstborn.

Painful dilemma of a father.

With the preceding evidence before us we may safely infer that a custom of allowing a king to kill his son, as a substitute or vicarious sacrifice for himself, would be in no way exceptional or surprising, at least in Semitic lands, where indeed

King's sons sacrificed instead of their fathers.

religion seems at one time to have recommended or enjoined every man, as a duty that he owed to his god, to take the life of his eldest son. And it would be entirely in accordance with analogy if, long after the barbarous custom had been dropped by others, it continued to be observed by kings, who remain in many respects the representatives of a vanished world, solitary pinnacles that topple over the rising waste of waters under which the past lies buried. We have seen that in Greece two families of royal descent remained liable to furnish human victims from their number down to a time when the rest of their fellow countrymen and countrywomen ran hardly more risk of being sacrificed than passengers in Cheapside at present run of being hurried into St Paul's or Bow Church and immolated on the altar. A final mitigation of the custom would be to substitute condemned criminals for innocent victims. Such a substitution is known to have taken place in the human sacrifices annually offered in Rhodes to Baal, and we have seen good grounds for believing that the criminal, who perished on the cross or the gallows at Babylon, died instead of the king in whose royal robes he had been allowed to masquerade for a few days.

Substitution of condemned criminals.

CHAPTER 5

THE KILLING OF THE TREE-SPIRIT

i

IT remains to ask what light the custom of killing the divine king or priest sheds upon the special subject of our enquiry. In an earlier part of this work we saw reason to suppose that the King of the Wood at Nemi was regarded as an incarnation of a tree-spirit or of the spirit of vegetation, and that as such he would be endowed, in the belief of his worshippers, with a magical power of making the trees to bear fruit, the crops to grow, and so on. His life must therefore have been held very precious by his worshippers, and was probably hedged in by a system of elaborate precautions or taboos like those by which, in so many places, the life of the man-god has been guarded against the malignant influence of demons and sorcerers. But we have seen that the very value attached to the life of the man-god necessitates his violent death as the only means of preserving it from the inevitable decay of age. The same reasoning would apply to the King of the Wood; he, too, had to be killed in order that the divine spirit, incarnate in him, might be transferred in its integrity to his successor. The rule that he held office till a stronger should slay him might be supposed to secure both the preservation of his divine life in full vigour and its transference to a suitable successor as soon as that vigour began to be impaired. For so long as he could maintain his position by the strong hand, it might be inferred that his natural force was not abated; whereas his defeat and death at the hands of another proved that his strength was beginning to fail and that it was time his divine life should be lodged in a less dilapidated tabernacle. This explanation of the rule that the King of the Wood had to be slain by his successor at least renders that rule perfectly intelligible. It is strongly supported by the theory and practice of the Shilluk, who put their divine king to death at the first signs of failing health, lest his decrepitude should entail a corresponding failure of vital energy on the corn, the cattle, and men. Moreover, it is

The single combat of the King of the Wood was probably a mitigation of an older custom of putting him to death at the end of a fixed term.

Killing the God

countenanced by the analogy of the Chitomé, upon whose life the existence of the world was supposed to hang, and who was therefore slain by his successor as soon as he showed signs of breaking up. Again, the terms on which in later times the King of Calicut held office are identical with those attached to the office of King of the Wood, except that whereas the former might be assailed by a candidate at any time, the King of Calicut might only be attacked once every twelve years. But as the leave granted to the King of Calicut to reign so long as he could defend himself against all comers was a mitigation of the old rule which set a fixed term to his life, so we may conjecture that the similar permission granted to the King of the Wood was a mitigation of an older custom of putting him to death at the end of a definite period. In both cases the new rule gave to the god-man, at least a chance for his life, which under the old rule was denied him; and people probably reconciled themselves to the change by reflecting that so long as the god-man could maintain himself by the sword against all assaults, there was no reason to apprehend that the fatal decay had set in.

Custom of killing the human representatives of the tree-spirit. The conjecture that the King of the Wood was formerly put to death at the expiry of a fixed term, without being allowed a chance for his life, will be confirmed if evidence can be adduced of a custom of periodically killing his counterparts, the human representatives of the tree-spirit, in Northern Europe. Now in point of fact such a custom has left unmistakable traces of itself in the rural festivals of the peasantry. To take examples.

At Niederpöring, in Lower Bavaria, the Whitsuntide representative of the tree-spirit—the *Pfingstl* as he was called—was clad from top to toe in leaves and flowers. On his head he wore a high pointed cap, the ends of which rested on his shoulders, only two holes being left in it for his eyes. The cap was covered with water-flowers and surmounted with a nosegay of peonies. The sleeves of his coat were also made of water-plants, and the rest of his body was enveloped in alder and hazel leaves. On each side of him marched a boy holding up one of the *Pfingstl's* arms. These two boys carried drawn swords, and so did most of the others who formed the procession. They stopped at every house where they hoped to receive a present; and the people, in hiding, soused the leaf-clad boy with water. All rejoiced when he was well drenched. Finally he waded into the brook up to his middle; whereupon one of the boys, standing on the bridge, pretended to cut off his head. At Wurmlingen, in Swabia, a score of young fellows dress themselves on Whit-Monday in white shirts and white trousers, with red scarves round their waists and swords hanging from the scarves. They ride on horseback into the wood, led by two trumpeters blowing their trumpets. In the wood they cut down leafy oak branches, in which they envelop from head to foot him who was the last of their number to ride out of the village. His legs, however, are encased separately, so that he may be able to mount his horse again. Further, they give him a long artificial neck, with an artificial head and a false face on the top of it. Then a May-tree is cut, generally an aspen or beech about ten feet high; and being decked with coloured handkerchiefs and ribbons it is entrusted to a special 'May-bearer'. The cavalcade then returns with music and song to the village. Amongst the personages who figure in the procession are a Moorish king with a sooty face and a crown on his head, a Dr Iron-Beard, a corporal, and an executioner. They halt on the village green, and each of the characters makes a speech in rhyme. The executioner announces that the leaf-clad man has been condemned to death, and cuts off his false head. Then the riders race to the May-tree, which has been set up a little way off. The first man who succeeds in wrenching it from the ground as he gallops past keeps it with all its decorations. The ceremony is observed every second or third year.

In Saxony and Thüringen there is a Whitsuntide ceremony called 'chasing the Wild Man out of the bush', or 'fetching the Wild Man out of the wood'. A young fellow is enveloped in leaves or moss and called the Wild Man. He hides in the wood and the other lads of the village go out to seek him. They find him, lead him captive out of the wood, and fire at him with blank muskets. He falls like dead to the ground, but a lad dressed as a doctor bleeds him, and he comes to life again. At this they rejoice, and, binding him fast on a waggon, take him to the village, where they tell all the people how they have caught the Wild Man. At every house they receive a gift. In the Erzgebirge the following custom was annually observed at Shrovetide about the beginning of the seventeenth century. Two men disguised as Wild Men, the one in brushwood and moss, the other in straw, were led about the streets, and at last taken to the market-place, where they were chased up and down, shot and stabbed. Before falling they reeled about with strange gestures and spirted blood on the people from bladders which they carried. When they were down, the huntsmen placed them on boards and carried them to the ale-house, the miners marching beside them and winding blasts on their mining tools as if they had taken a noble head of game. A very similar Shrovetide custom is still observed near Schluckenau in Bohemia. A man dressed up as a Wild Man is chased through several streets till he comes to a narrow lane across which a cord is stretched. He stumbles over the cord and, falling to the ground, is overtaken and caught by his pursuers. The executioner runs up and stabs with his sword a bladder filled with blood which the Wild Man wears round his body; so the Wild Man dies, while a stream of blood reddens the ground. Next day a straw-man, made up to look like the Wild Man, is placed on a litter, and, accompanied by a great crowd, is taken to a pool into which it is thrown by the executioner. The ceremony is called 'burying the Carnival'.

In Semic (Bohemia) the custom of beheading the King is observed on Whit-Monday. A troop of young people disguise themselves; each is girt with a girdle of bark and carries a wooden sword and a trumpet of willow-bark. The King wears a robe of tree-bark adorned with flowers, on his head is a crown of bark decked with flowers and branches, his feet are wound about with ferns, a mask hides his face, and for a sceptre he has a hawthorn switch in his hand. A lad leads him through the village by a rope fastened to his foot, while the rest dance about, blow their trumpets, and whistle. In every farmhouse the King is chased round the room, and one of the troop, amid much noise and outcry, strikes with his sword a blow on the King's robe of bark till it rings again. Then a gratuity is demanded. The ceremony of decapitation, which is here somewhat slurred over, is carried out with a greater semblance of reality in other parts of Bohemia. Thus in some villages of the Königgrätz district on Whit-Monday the girls assemble under one lime-tree and the young men under another, all dressed in their best and tricked out with ribbons. The young men twine a garland for the Queen, and the girls another for the King. When they have chosen the King and Queen they all go in procession two and two, to the ale-house, from the balcony of which the crier proclaims the names of the King and Queen. Both are then invested with the insignia of their office and are crowned with the garlands, while the music plays up. Then some one gets on a bench and accuses the King of various offences, such as ill-treating the cattle. The King appeals to witnesses and a trial ensues, at the close of which the judge, who carries a white wand as his badge of office, pronounces a verdict of 'Guilty' or 'Not guilty'. If the verdict is 'Guilty', the judge breaks his wand, the King kneels on a white cloth, all heads are bared, and a soldier sets three or four hats, one above the other, on his Majesty's head. The judge then pronounces the word 'Guilty' thrice in a loud voice, and orders the crier to behead the King. The crier obeys by striking off the King's hats with his wooden sword.

But perhaps, for our purpose, the most instructive of these mimic executions is the following Bohemian one. In some places of the Pilsen district (Bohemia) on Whit-Monday the King is dressed in bark, ornamented with flowers and ribbons; he wears a crown of gilt paper and rides a horse, which is also decked with flowers. Attended by a judge, an executioner, and other characters, and followed by a train of soldiers, all mounted, he rides to the village square, where a hut or arbour of green boughs has been erected under the May-trees, which are firs, freshly cut, peeled to the top, and dressed with flowers and ribbons. After the dames and maidens of the village have been criticised and a frog beheaded, the cavalcade rides to a place previously determined upon, in a straight, broad street. Here they draw up in two lines and the King takes to flight. He is given a short start and rides off at full speed, pursued by the whole troop. If they fail to catch him he remains King for another year, and his companions must pay his score at the ale-house in the evening. But if they overtake and catch him he is scourged with hazel rods or beaten with the wooden swords and compelled to dismount. Then the executioner asks, 'Shall I behead this King?' The answer is given, 'Behead him'; the executioner brandishes his axe, and with the words, 'One, two, three, let the King headless be!' he strikes off the King's crown. Amid the loud cries of the bystanders the King sinks to the ground; then he is laid on a bier and carried to the nearest farmhouse.

In most of the personages who are thus slain in mimicry it is impossible not to recognise representatives of the tree-spirit or spirit of vegetation, as he is supposed to manifest himself in spring. The bark, leaves, and flowers in which the actors are dressed, and the season of the year at which they appear, show that they belong to the same class as the Grass King, King of the May, Jack-in-the-Green, and other representatives of the vernal spirit of vegetation which we examined in an earlier part of this work. As if to remove any possible doubt on this head, we find that in two cases these slain men are brought into direct connexion with May-trees, which are the impersonal, as the May King, Grass King, and so forth, are the personal representatives of the tree-spirit. The drenching of the *Pfingstl* with water and his wading up to the middle into the brook are, therefore, no doubt rain-charms like those which have been already described.

But if these personages represent, as they certainly do, the spirit of vegetation in spring, the question arises, Why kill them? What is the object of slaying the spirit of vegetation at any time and above all in spring, when his services are most wanted? The only probable answer to this question seems to be given in the explanation already proposed of the custom of killing the divine king or priest. The divine life, incarnate in a material and mortal body, is liable to be tainted and corrupted by the weakness of the frail medium in which it is for a time enshrined; and if it is to be saved from the increasing enfeeblement which it must necessarily share with its human incarnation as he advances in years, it must be detached from him before, or at least as soon as, he exhibits signs of decay, in order to be transferred to a vigorous successor. This is done by killing the old representative of the god and conveying the divine spirit from him to a new incarnation. The killing of the god, that is, of his human incarnation, is therefore merely a necessary step to his revival or resurrection in a better form. Far from being an extinction of the divine spirit, it is only the beginning of a purer and stronger manifestation of it. If this explanation holds good of the custom of killing divine kings and priests in general, it is still more obviously applicable to the custom of annually

killing the representative of the tree-spirit or spirit of vegetation
in spring. For the decay of plant life in winter is readily
interpreted by primitive man as an enfeeblement of the spirit
of vegetation; the spirit has, he thinks, grown old and weak
and must therefore be renovated by being slain and brought
to life in a younger and fresher form. Thus the killing of the
representative of the tree-spirit in spring is regarded as a
means to promote and quicken the growth of vegetation. For
the killing of the tree-spirit is associated always (we must
suppose) implicitly, and sometimes explicitly also, with a revival or resurrection of him in a more youthful and vigorous
form. So in the Saxon and Thüringen custom, after the Wild
Man has been shot he is brought to life again by a doctor;
and in the Wurmlingen ceremony there figures a Dr Iron-
Beard, who probably once played a similar part. But of this
revival or resurrection of the god we shall have more to say
anon.

The points of similarity between these North European
personages and the subject of our enquiry—the King of the
Wood or priest of Nemi—are sufficiently striking. In these
northern maskers we see kings, whose dress of bark and leaves
along with the hut of green boughs and the fir-trees, under
which they hold their court, proclaim them unmistakably as,
like their Italian counterpart, Kings of the Wood. Like him they
die a violent death, but like him they may escape from it for a
time by their bodily strength and agility; for in several of these
northern customs the flight and pursuit of the king is a
prominent part of the ceremony, and in one case at least if the
king can outrun his pursuers he retains his life and his office
for another year. In this last case the king in fact holds office
on condition of running for his life once a year, just as the King
of Calicut in later times held office on condition of defending
his life against all comers once every twelve years, and just as
the priest of Nemi held office on condition of defending himself
against any assault at any time. In every one of these instances
the life of the god-man is prolonged on condition of his
showing, in a severe physical contest of fight or flight, that his
bodily strength is not decayed, and that, therefore, the violent
death, which sooner or later is inevitable, may for the present
be postponed. With regard to flight it is noticeable that flight

figured conspicuously both in the legend and in the practice of the King of the Wood. He had to be a runaway slave in memory of the flight of Orestes, the traditional founder of the worship; hence the Kings of the Wood are described by an ancient writer as 'both strong of hand and fleet of foot'. Perhaps if we knew the ritual of the Arician grove fully we might find that the king was allowed a chance for his life by flight, like his Bohemian brother. I have already conjectured that the annual flight of the priestly king at Rome (*regifugium*) was at first a flight of the same kind; in other words, that he was originally one of those divine kings who are either put to death after a fixed period or allowed to prove by the strong hand or the fleet foot that their divinity is vigorous and unimpaired. One more point of resemblance may be noted between the Italian King of the Wood and his northern counterparts. In Saxony and Thüringen the representative of the tree-spirit, after being killed, is brought to life again by a doctor. This is exactly what legend affirmed to have happened to the first King of the Wood at Nemi, Hippolytus or Virbius, who after he had been killed by his horses was restored to life by the physician Aesculapius. Such a legend tallies well with the theory that the slaying of the King of the Wood was only a step to his revival or resurrection in his successor.

ii

Burying the Carnival.

Thus far I have offered an explanation of the rule which required that the priest of Nemi should be slain by his successor. The explanation claims to be no more than probable; our scanty knowledge of the custom and of its history forbids it to be more. But its probability will be augmented in proportion to the extent to which the motives and modes of thought which it assumes can be proved to have operated in primitive society. Hitherto the god with whose death and resurrection we have been chiefly concerned has been the tree-god. But if I can show that the custom of killing the god and the belief in his resurrection originated, or at least existed, in the hunting and pastoral stage of society, when the slain god was an animal, and that it survived into the agricultural stage, when the slain god was the corn or a human being representing the corn, the probability of my explanation will have been considerably increased. This I shall attempt to do in the sequel, and in the course of the discussion I hope to clear up some obscurities which still remain, and to answer some objections which may have suggested themselves to the reader.

We start from the point at which we left off—the spring customs of European peasantry. Besides the ceremonies already described there are two kindred sets of observances in which the simulated death of a divine or supernatural being is a conspicuous feature. In one of them the being whose death is dramatically represented is a personification of the Carnival; in the other it is Death himself. The former ceremony falls naturally at the end of the Carnival, either on the last day of that merry season, namely Shrove Tuesday, or on the first day of Lent, namely Ash Wednesday. The date of the other ceremony—the Carrying or Driving out of Death, as it is commonly called—is not so uniformly fixed. Generally it is the fourth Sunday in Lent, which hence goes by the name of Dead Sunday; but in some places the celebration falls a week earlier, in others, as among the Czechs of Bohemia, a week later, while in certain German villages of Moravia it is held on the first Sunday after Easter. Perhaps, as has been suggested, the date may originally have been variable, depending on the appearance of the first swallow or some other herald of the spring. Some writers regard the ceremony as Slavonic in its origin. Grimm thought it was a festival of the New Year with the old Slavs, who began their year in March. We shall first take examples of the mimic death of the Carnival, which always falls before the other in the calendar.

At Frosinone, in Latium, about half-way between Rome and Naples, the dull monotony of life in a provincial Italian town is agreeably broken on the last day of the Carnival by the ancient festival known as the *Radica*. About four o'clock in the afternoon the town band, playing lively tunes and followed by a great crowd, proceeds to the Piazza del Plebiscito, where is the Sub-Prefecture as well as the rest of the Government buildings. Here, in the middle of the square, the eyes of the expectant multitude are greeted by the sight of an immense car decked with many-coloured festoons and drawn by four horses. Mounted on the car is a huge chair, on which sits enthroned the majestic figure of the Carnival, a man of stucco about nine feet high with a rubicund and smiling countenance. Enormous boots, a tin helmet like those which grace the heads of officers of the Italian marine, and a coat of many colours embellished with strange devices, adorn the outward man of this stately personage. His left hand rests on the arm of the chair, while with his right he gracefully salutes the crowd, being moved to this act of civility by a string which is pulled by a man who modestly shrinks from publicity under the mercy-seat. And now the crowd, surging excitedly round the car, gives vent to its feelings in wild cries of joy, gentle and simple being mixed up together and all dancing furiously the *Saltarello*. A special feature of the festival is that every one must carry in his hand what is called a *radica* ('root'), by which is meant a huge leaf of the aloe or rather the agave. Any one who ventured into the crowd without such a leaf would be unceremoniously hustled out of it, unless indeed he bore as a substitute a large cabbage at the end of a long stick or a bunch of grass curiously plaited. When the multitude, after a short turn, has escorted the slow-moving car to the gate of the Sub-Prefecture, they halt, and the car, jolting over the uneven ground, rumbles into the courtyard. A hush now falls on the crowd, their subdued voices sounding, according to the description of one who has heard them, like the murmur of a troubled sea. All eyes are turned anxiously to the door from which the Sub-Prefect himself and the other representatives of the majesty of the law are expected to issue and pay their homage to the hero of the hour. A few moments of suspense and then a storm of cheers and hand-clapping salutes the appearances of the dignitaries, as they file out and, descending the staircase, take their place in the procession. The hymn of the Carnival is now thundered out, after which, amid a deafening roar, aloe leaves and cabbages are whirled aloft and descend impartially on the heads of the just and the unjust, who lend fresh zest to the proceedings by engaging in a free fight. When these preliminaries have been concluded to the satisfaction of all concerned, the procession gets under way. The rear is brought up by a cart laden with barrels of wine and policemen, the latter engaged in the congenial task of serving out wine to all who ask for it, while a most internecine struggle, accompanied by a copious discharge of yells, blows, and blasphemy, goes on among the surging crowd at the cart's tail in their anxiety not to miss the glorious opportunity of intoxicating themselves at the public expense. Finally, after the procession has paraded the principal streets in this majestic manner, the effigy of Carnival is taken to the middle of a public square, stripped of his finery, laid on a pile of wood, and burnt amid the cries of the multitude, who thundering out once more the song of the Carnival fling their so-called 'roots' on the pyre and give themselves up without restraint to the pleasures of the dance.

A ceremony of the same sort is observed in Provence on Ash Wednesday. An effigy called Caramantran, whimsically attired, is drawn in a chariot or borne on a litter, accompanied by the populace in grotesque costumes, who carry gourds full of wine and drain them with all the marks, real or affected, of intoxication. At the head of the procession are some men disguised as judges and barristers, and a tall gaunt personage who masquerades as Lent; behind them follow young people mounted on miserable hacks and attired as mourners who pretend to bewail the fate that is in store for Caramantran. In the principal square the procession halts, the tribunal is constituted, and Caramantran placed at the bar. After a formal trial he is sentenced to death amid the groans of the mob: the barrister who defended him embraces his client for the last time: the officers of justice do their duty: the condemned is set with his back to a wall and hurried into eternity under a shower of stones. The sea or a river receives his mangled remains. Throughout nearly the whole of the Ardennes it was and still is customary on Ash Wednesday to burn an effigy which is supposed to represent the Carnival, while appropriate verses are sung round about the blazing figure. Very often an attempt is made to fashion the effigy in the likeness of the husband who is reputed to be least faithful to his wife of any in the village. As might perhaps have been anticipated, the distinction of being selected for portraiture under these painful circumstances has a slight tendency to breed domestic jars, especially when the portrait is burnt in front of the house of the gay deceiver whom it represents, while a powerful chorus of caterwauls, groans, and other melodious sounds bears public testimony to the opinion which his friends and neighbours entertain of his private virtues. In some villages

of the Ardennes a young man of flesh and blood, dressed up in
hay and straw, used to act the part of Shrove Tuesday (*Mardi
Gras*), as the personification of the Carnival is often called in
France after the last day of the period which he personates. He
was brought before a mock tribunal, and being condemned to
death was placed with his back to a wall, like a soldier at a
military execution, and fired at with blank cartridges. At
Vrigneaux-Bois one of these harmless buffoons, named Thierry,
was accidentally killed by a wad that had been left in a musket
of the firing-party. When poor Shrove Tuesday dropped under
the fire, the applause was loud and long, he did it so naturally;
but when he did not get up again, they ran to him and found
him a corpse. Since then there have been no more of these mock
executions in the Ardennes.

In Normandy on the evening of Ash Wednesday it used to be
the custom to hold a celebration called the Burial of Shrove
Tuesday. A squalid effigy scantily clothed in rags, a battered
old hat crushed down on his dirty face, his great round paunch
stuffed with straw, represented the disreputable old rake who,
after a long course of dissipation, was now about to suffer for
his sins. Hoisted on the shoulders of a sturdy fellow, who
pretended to stagger under the burden, this popular personification of the Carnival promenaded the streets for the last time
in a manner the reverse of triumphal. Preceded by a drummer
and accompanied by a jeering rabble, among whom the urchins
and all the tag-rag and bobtail of the town mustered in great
force, the figure was carried about by the flickering light of
torches to the discordant din of shovels and tongs, pots and
pans, horns and kettles, mingled with hootings, groans, and
hisses. From time to time the procession halted, and a champion of morality accused the broken-down old sinner of all the
excesses he had committed and for which he was now about to
be burned alive. The culprit, having nothing to urge in his own
defence, was thrown on a heap of straw, a torch was put to it,
and a great blaze shot up, to the delight of the children who
frisked round it screaming out some old popular verses about
the death of the Carnival. Sometimes the effigy was rolled down
the slope of a hill before being burnt. At Saint-Lô the ragged
effigy of Shrove Tuesday was followed by his widow, a big
burly lout dressed as a woman with a crape veil, who emitted

sounds of lamentation and woe in a stentorian voice. After being carried about the streets on a litter attended by a crowd of maskers, the figure was thrown into the River Vire. The final scene has been graphically described by Madame Octave Feuillet as she witnessed it in her childhood some sixty years ago. 'My parents invited friends to see, from the top of the tower of Jeanne Couillard, the funeral procession passing. It was there that, quaffing lemonade—the only refreshment allowed because of the fast—we witnessed at nightfall a spectacle of which I shall always preserve a lively recollection. At our feet flowed the Vire under its old stone bridge. On the middle of the bridge lay the figure of Shrove Tuesday on a litter of leaves, surrounded by scores of maskers dancing, singing, and carrying torches. Some of them in their motley costumes ran along the parapet like fiends. The rest, worn out with their revels, sat on the posts and dozed. Soon the dancing stopped, and some of the troop, seizing a torch, set fire to the effigy, after which they flung it into the river with redoubled shouts and clamour. The man of straw, soaked with resin, floated away burning down the stream of the Vire, lighting up with its funeral fires the woods on the bank and the battlements of the old castle in which Louis XI and Francis I had slept. When the last glimmer of the blazing phantom had vanished, like a falling star, at the end of the valley, every one withdrew, crowd and maskers alike, and we quitted the ramparts with our guests.'

iii

The ceremony of 'Carrying out Death' presents much the same features as 'Burying the Carnival'; except that the carrying out of Death is generally followed by a ceremony, or at least accompanied by a profession, of bringing in Summer, Spring, or Life. Thus in Middle Franken, a province of Bavaria, on the fourth Sunday in Lent, the village urchins used to make a straw effigy of Death, which they carried about with burlesque pomp through the streets, and afterwards burned with loud cries beyond the bounds. The Frankish custom is thus described by a writer of the sixteenth century: 'At Mid-Lent, the season when the church bids us rejoice, the young people of my native country make a straw image of Death, and fastening it to a pole

Carrying out Death.

carry it with shouts to the neighbouring villages. By some they
are kindly received, and after being refreshed with milk, peas,
and dried pears, the usual food of that season, are sent home
again. Others, however, treat them with anything but hospitality; for, looking on them as harbingers of misfortune, to wit
of death, they drive them from their boundaries with weapons
and insults.' In the villages near Erlangen, when the fourth
Sunday in Lent came round, the peasant girls used to dress
themselves in all their finery with flowers in their hair. Thus
attired they repaired to the neighbouring town, carrying puppets which were adorned with leaves and covered with white
cloths. These they took from house to house in pairs, stopping
at every door where they expected to receive something, and
singing a few lines in which they announced that it was
Mid-Lent and that they were about to throw Death into the
water. When they had collected some trifling gratuities they
went to the River Regnitz and flung the puppets representing
Death into the stream. This was done to ensure a fruitful and
prosperous year: further, it was considered a safeguard against
pestilence and sudden death. At Nuremberg girls of seven to
eighteen years of age go through the streets bearing a little open
coffin, in which is a doll hidden under a shroud. Others carry
a beech branch, with an apple fastened to it for a head, in an
open box. They sing, 'We carry Death into the water, it is well',
or 'We carry Death into the water, carry him in and out again'.
In some parts of Bavaria down to 1780 it was believed that a
fatal epidemic would ensue if the custom of 'Carrying out
Death' were not observed.

Ceremonies of the same sort are observed at Mid-Lent in
Silesia. Thus in many places the grown girls with the help of
the young men dress up a straw figure with women's clothes
and carry it out of the village towards the setting sun. At the
boundary they strip it of its clothes, tear it in pieces, and scatter
the fragments about the fields. This is called 'Burying Death'.
As they carry the image out, they sing that they are about to
bury Death under an oak, that he may depart from the people.
Sometimes the song runs that they are bearing Death over hill
and dale to return no more. In the Polish neighbourhood of
Gross-Strehlitz the puppet is called Goik. It is carried on
horseback and thrown into the nearest water. The people think

that the ceremony protects them from sickness of every sort in the coming year. In the districts of Wohlau and Guhrau the image of Death used to be thrown over the boundary of the next village. But as the neighbours feared to receive the ill-omened figure, they were on the look-out to repel it, and hard knocks were often exchanged between the two parties. In some Polish parts of Upper Silesia the effigy, representing an old woman, goes by the name of Marzana, the goddess of death. It is made in the house where the last death occurred, and is carried on a pole to the boundary of the village, where it is thrown into a pond or burnt. At Polkwitz the custom of 'Carrying out Death' fell into abeyance; but an outbreak of fatal sickness which followed the intermission of the ceremony induced the people to resume it.

The preceding evidence shows that the effigy of Death is often regarded with fear and treated with marks of hatred and abhorrence. Thus the anxiety of the villagers to transfer the figure from their own to their neighbours' land, and the reluctance of the latter to receive the ominous guest, are proof enough of the dread which it inspires. Further, in Lusatia and Silesia the puppet is sometimes made to look in at the window of a house, and it is believed that some one in the house will die within the year unless his life is redeemed by the payment of money. Again, after throwing the effigy away, the bearers sometimes run home lest Death should follow them, and if one of them falls in running, it is believed that he will die within the year. At Chrudim, in Bohemia, the figure of Death is made out of a cross, with a head and mask stuck at the top, and a shirt stretched out on it. On the fifth Sunday in Lent the boys take this effigy to the nearest brook or pool, and standing in a line throw it into the water. Then they all plunge in after it; but as soon as it is caught no one more may enter the water. The boy who did not enter the water or entered it last will die within the year, and he is obliged to carry the Death back to the village. The effigy is then burned. On the other hand, it is believed that no one will die within the year in the house out of which the figure of Death has been carried; and the village out of which Death has been driven is sometimes supposed to be protected against sickness and plague. In some villages of Austrian Silesia on the Saturday before Dead Sunday an effigy is made of old clothes, hay, and straw, for the purpose of driving Death out of the village. On Sunday the people armed with sticks and straps, assemble before the house where the figure is lodged. Four lads then draw the effigy by cords through the village amid exultant shouts, while all the others beat it with their sticks and straps. On reaching a field which belongs to a neighbouring village they lay down the figure, cudgel it soundly, and scatter the fragments over the field. The people believe that the village from which Death has been thus carried out will be safe from any infectious disease for the whole year.

iv

Bringing in Summer.

In the preceding ceremonies the return of Spring, Summer, or Life, as a sequel to the expulsion of Death, is only implied or at most announced. In the following ceremonies it is plainly enacted. Thus in some parts of Bohemia the effigy of Death is drowned by being thrown into the water at sunset; then the girls go out into the wood and cut down a young tree with a green crown, hang a doll dressed as a woman on it, deck the whole with green, red, and white ribbons, and march in procession with their *Lito* (Summer) into the village, collecting gifts and singing—

'Death swims in the water,   With yellow pancakes.
Spring comes to visit us,   We carried Death out of the village,
With eggs that are red,   We are carrying Summer into the village.'

In many Silesian villages the figure of Death, after being treated with respect, is stript of its clothes and flung with curses into the water, or torn to pieces in a field. Then the young folk repair to a wood, cut down a small fir-tree, peel the trunk, and deck it with festoons of evergreens, paper roses, painted egg-shells, motley bits of cloth, and so forth. The tree thus adorned is called Summer or May. Boys carry it from house to house singing appropriate songs and begging for presents. Among their songs is the following:

'We have carried Death out,   The Summer and the May,
We are bringing the dear Summer back,   And all the flowers gay.'

Sometimes they also bring back from the wood a prettily adorned figure, which goes by the name of Summer, May, or the Bride: in the Polish districts it is called Dziewanna, the goddess of spring.

At Eisenach on the fourth Sunday in Lent young people used to fasten a straw-man, representing Death, to a wheel, which they trundled to the top of a hill. Then setting fire to the figure they allowed it and the wheel to roll down the slope. Next they cut a tall fir-tree, tricked it out with ribbons, and set it up in the plain. The men then climbed the tree to fetch down the ribbons. In Upper Lusatia the figure of Death, made of straw and rags, is dressed in a veil furnished by the last bride and a shirt provided by the house in which the last death took place. Thus arrayed the figure is stuck on the end of a long pole and carried at full speed by the tallest and strongest girl, while the rest pelt the effigy with sticks and stones. Whoever hits it will be sure to live through the year. In this way Death is carried out of the village and thrown into the water or over the boundary of the next village. On their way home each one breaks a green branch and carries it gaily with him till he reaches the village, when he throws it away. Sometimes the young people of the next village, upon whose land the figure has been thrown, run after them and hurl it back, not wishing to have Death among them. Hence the two parties occasionally come to blows. In these cases Death is represented by the puppet which is thrown away, Summer or Life by the branches or trees which are brought back. But sometimes a new potency of life seems to be attributed to the image of Death itself, and by a kind of resurrection it becomes the instrument of the general revival. Thus in some parts of Lusatia women alone are concerned in carrying out Death, and suffer no male to meddle with it. Attired in mourning, which they wear the whole day, they make a puppet of straw, clothe it in a white shirt, and give it a broom in one hand and a scythe in the other. Singing songs and pursued by urchins throwing stones, they carry the puppet to the village boundary, where they tear it in pieces. Then they cut down a fine tree, hang the shirt on it, and carry it home singing.

In the Lusatian ceremony described above, the tree which is brought home after the destruction of the figure of Death is plainly equivalent to the trees or branches which, in the preceding customs, were brought back as representatives of

Summer or Life, after Death had been thrown away or destroyed. But the transference of the shirt worn by the effigy of Death to the tree clearly indicates that the tree is a kind of revivification, in a new form, of the destroyed effigy. These examples therefore suggest that the Death whose demolition is represented in these ceremonies cannot be regarded as the purely destructive agent which we understand by Death. If the tree which is brought back as an embodiment of the reviving vegetation of spring is clothed in the shirt worn by the Death which has just been destroyed, the object certainly cannot be to check and counteract the revival of vegetation: it can only be to foster and promote it. Therefore the being which has just been destroyed—the so-called Death—must be supposed to be endowed with a vivifying and quickening influence, which it can communicate to the vegetable and even the animal world.

Thus we may fairly conjecture that the names Carnival, Death, and Summer are comparatively late and inadequate expressions for the beings personified or embodied in the customs with which we have been dealing. The very abstractness of the names bespeaks a modern origin; for the personification of times and seasons like the Carnival and Summer, or of an abstract notion like death, is not primitive. But the ceremonies themselves bear the stamp of a dateless antiquity; therefore we can hardly help supposing that in their origin the ideas which they embodied were of a more simple and concrete order. The notion of a tree, perhaps of a particular kind of tree (for some savages have no word for tree in general), or even of an individual tree, is sufficiently concrete to supply a basis from which by a gradual process of generalisation the wider idea of a spirit of vegetation might be reached. But this general idea of vegetation would readily be confounded with the season in which it manifests itself; hence the substitution of Spring, Summer, or May for the tree-spirit or spirit of vegetation would be easy and natural. Again, the concrete notion of the dying tree or dying vegetation would by a similar process of generalisation glide into a notion of death in general; so that the practice of carrying out the dying or dead vegetation in spring, as a preliminary to its revival, would in time widen out into an attempt to banish Death in general from the village or district.

Sometimes in the popular customs of the peasantry the contrast between the dormant powers of vegetation in winter and their awakening vitality in spring takes the form of a dramatic contest between actors who play the parts respectively of Winter and Summer. Thus in the towns of Sweden on May Day two troops of young men on horseback used to meet as if for mortal combat. One of them was led by a representative of Winter clad in furs, who threw snowballs and ice in order to prolong the cold weather. The other troop was commanded by a representative of Summer covered with fresh leaves and flowers. In the sham fight which followed the party of Summer came off victorious, and the ceremony ended with a feast. Again, in the region of the middle Rhine, a representative of Summer clad in ivy combats a representative of Winter clad in straw or moss and finally gains a victory over him. The vanquished foe is thrown to the ground and stripped of his casing of straw, which is torn to pieces and scattered about, while the youthful comrades of the two champions sing a song to commemorate the defeat of Winter by Summer. Afterwards they carry about a summer garland or branch and collect gifts of eggs and bacon from house to house. Sometimes the champion who acts the part of Summer is dressed in leaves and flowers and wears a chaplet of flowers on his head. In the Palatinate this mimic conflict takes place on the fourth Sunday in Lent. All over Bavaria the same drama used to be acted on the same day, and it was still kept up in some places down to the middle of the nineteenth century or later. While Summer appeared clad all in green, decked with fluttering ribbons, and carrying a branch in blossom or a little tree hung with apples and pears, Winter was muffled up in cap and mantle of fur and bore in his hand a snow-shovel or a flail. Accompanied by their respective retinues dressed in corresponding attire, they went through all the streets of the village, halting before the houses and singing staves of old songs, for which they received presents of bread, eggs, and fruit. Finally, after a short struggle, Winter was beaten by Summer and ducked in the village well or driven out of the village with shouts and laughter into the forest.

At Goepfritz in Lower Austria, two men personating Summer and Winter used to go from house to house on Shrove Tuesday,

Battle of Summer and Winter.

and were everywhere welcomed by the children with great delight. The representative of Summer was clad in white and bore a sickle; his comrade, who played the part of Winter, had a fur cap on his head, his arms and legs were swathed in straw, and he carried a flail. In every house they sang verses alternately. At Drömling in Brunswick, down to the present time, the contest between Summer and Winter is acted every year at Whitsuntide by a troop of boys and a troop of girls. The boys rush singing, shouting, and ringing bells from house to house to drive Winter away; after them come the girls singing softly and led by a May Bride, all in bright dresses and decked with flowers and garlands to represent the genial advent of spring. Formerly the part of Winter was played by a straw-man which the boys carried with them; now it is acted by a real man in disguise.

Among the central Esquimaux of North America the contest between representatives of summer and winter, which in Europe has long degenerated into a mere dramatic performance, is still kept up as a magical ceremony of which the avowed intention is to influence the weather. In autumn, when storms announce the approach of the dismal Arctic winter, the Esquimaux divide themselves into two parties called respectively the ptarmigans and the ducks, the ptarmigans comprising all persons born in winter, and the ducks all persons born in summer. A long rope of sealskin is then stretched out, and each party laying hold of one end of it seeks by tugging with might and main to drag the other party over to its side. If the ptarmigans get the worst of it, then summer has won the game and fine weather may be expected to prevail through the winter.

v

Funeral of Kostrubonko, Kostroma, Kupalo, and Yarilo in Russia. In Russia funeral ceremonies like those of 'Burying the Carnival' and 'Carrying out Death' are celebrated under the names, not of Death or the Carnival, but of certain mythic figures, Kostrubonko, Kostroma, Kupalo, Lada, and Yarilo. These Russian ceremonies are observed both in spring and at midsummer. Thus 'in Little Russia it used to be the custom at Eastertide to celebrate the funeral of a being called Kostrubonko, the deity of the spring. A circle was formed of singers who moved slowly around a girl who lay on the ground as if dead, and as they went they sang:

> "Dead, dead is our Kostrubonko!
> Dead, dead is our dear one!"

until the girl suddenly sprang up, on which the chorus joyfully exclaimed:

> "Come to life, come to life has our Kostrubonko!
> Come to life, come to life has our dear one!" '*

On the Eve of St John (Midsummer Eve) a figure of Kupalo is made of straw and 'is dressed in woman's clothes, with a necklace and a floral crown. Then a tree is felled, and, after being decked with ribbons, is set up on some chosen spot. Near this tree, to which they give the name of Marena [Winter or Death], the straw figure is placed, together with a table, on which stand spirits and viands. Afterwards a bonfire is lit, and the young men and maidens jump over it in couples, carrying the figure with them. On the next day they strip the tree and the figure of their ornaments, and throw them both into a stream.' On St Peter's Day, the twenty-ninth of June, or on the following Sunday, 'the Funeral of Kostroma' or of Lada or of Yarilo is celebrated in Russia. In the Governments of Penza and Simbirsk the funeral used to be represented as follows. A bonfire was kindled on the twenty-eighth of June, and on the next day the maidens chose one of their number to play the part of Kostroma. Her companions saluted her with deep obeisances, placed her on a board, and carried her to the bank of a stream. There they bathed her in the water, while the oldest girl made a basket of lime-tree bark and beat it like a drum. Then they returned to the village and ended the day with processions, games, and dances. In the Murom district Kostroma was represented by a straw figure dressed in woman's clothes and flowers. This was laid in a trough and carried with songs to the bank of a lake or river. Here the crowd divided into two sides, of which the one attacked and the other defended the figure. At last the assailants gained the day, stripped the figure of its dress and ornaments, tore it in pieces, trod the straw of which it was made under foot, and flung it into the stream; while the defenders of the figure hid their faces in their hands and pretended to bewail the death of Kostroma. In the district of Kostroma the burial of Yarilo was celebrated on the twenty-ninth or thirtieth of June. The people chose an old man and gave him a small coffin containing a Priapus-like figure representing Yarilo. This he carried out of the town, followed by women chanting dirges and expressing by their gestures grief and despair. In the open fields a grave was dug, and into it the figure was lowered amid weeping and wailing, after which games and dances were begun, 'calling to mind, the funeral games celebrated in old times by the pagan Slavonians'. In Little Russia the figure of Yarilo was laid in a coffin and carried through the streets after sunset surrounded by drunken women, who kept repeating mournfully, 'He is dead! he is dead!' The men lifted and shook the figure as if they were trying to recall the dead man to life. Then they said to the women, 'Women, weep not. I know what is sweeter than honey.' But the women continued to lament and chant, as they do at funerals. 'Of what was he guilty? He was so good. He will arise no more. O how shall we part from thee? What is life without thee? Arise, if only for a brief hour. But he rises not, he rises not.' At last the Yarilo was buried in a grave.

These Russian customs are plainly of the same nature as those which in Austria and Germany are known as 'Carrying out Death'. Therefore if the interpretation here adopted of the latter is right, the Russian Kostrubonko, Yarilo, and the rest must also have been originally embodiments of the spirit of vegetation, and their death must have been regarded as a necessary preliminary to their revival. The revival as a sequel to the death is enacted in the first of the ceremonies described, the death and resurrection of Kostrubonko.

But while the death of vegetation appears to have been represented in all, and its revival in some, of these spring and midsummer ceremonies, there are features in some of them which can hardly be explained on this hypothesis alone. The solemn funeral, the lamentations, and the mourning attire, which often characterise these rites, are indeed appropriate at the death of the beneficent spirit of vegetation. But what shall we say of the glee with which the effigy is often carried out, of the sticks and stones with which it is assailed, and the taunts and curses which are hurled at it? What shall we say of the dread of the effigy evinced by the haste with which the bearers scamper home as soon as they have thrown it away, and by the belief that some one must soon die in any house into which it has looked? This dread might perhaps be explained by a belief that there is a certain infectiousness in the dead spirit of vegetation which renders its approach dangerous. But this explanation, besides being rather strained, does not cover the rejoicings which often attend the carrying out of Death. We must therefore recognise two distinct and seemingly opposite features in these ceremonies: on the one hand, sorrow for the death, and affection and respect for the dead; on the other hand, fear and hatred of the dead, and rejoicings at his death. How the former of these features is to be explained I have attempted to show: how the latter came to be so closely associated with the former is a question which I shall try to answer in the sequel.

vi

In the Kanagra district of India there is a custom observed by young girls in spring which closely resembles some of the European spring ceremonies just described. It is called the *Rali Ka melâ*, or fair of Ralî, the *Ralî* being a small painted earthen image of Siva or Pârvatî. The custom is in vogue all over the Kanagra district, and its celebration, which is entirely confined to young girls, lasts through most of Chet (March–April) up to the Sankrânt of Baisâkh (April). On a morning in March all the young girls of the village take small baskets of *dûb* grass and flowers to an appointed place, where they throw them in a heap. Round this heap they stand in a circle and sing. This goes on every day for ten days, till the heap of grass and flowers has reached a fair height. Then they cut in the jungle two branches, each with three prongs at one end, and place them, prongs downwards, over the heap of flowers, so as to make two tripods or pyramids. On the single uppermost points of these branches they get an image-maker to construct two clay images, one to represent Siva, and the other Pârvatî. The girls then divide themselves into two parties, one for Siva and one for Pârvatî, and marry the images in the usual way, leaving out no part of the ceremony. After the marriage they have a feast, the cost of

(margin note: Images of Siva and Pâr- vatî married, drowned, and mourned for in India.)

which is defrayed by contributions solicited from their parents. Then at the next Sankrânt (Baisâkh) they all go together to the river-side, throw the images into a deep pool, and weep over the place, as though they were performing funeral obsequies. The boys of the neighbourhood often tease them by diving after the images, bringing them up, and waving them about while the girls are crying over them. The object of the fair is said to be to secure a good husband.

That in this Indian ceremony the deities Siva and Pârvatî are conceived as spirits of vegetation seems to be proved by the placing of their images on branches over a heap of grass and flowers. Here, as often in European folk-custom, the divinities of vegetation are represented in duplicate, by plants and by puppets. The marriage of these Indian deities in spring corresponds to the European ceremonies in which the marriage of the vernal spirits of vegetation is represented by the King and Queen of May, the May Bride, Bridegroom of the May, and so forth. The throwing of the images into the water, and the mourning for them, are the equivalents of the European customs of throwing the dead spirit of vegetation under the name of Death, Yarilo, Kostroma, and the rest, into the water and lamenting over it. Again, in India, as often in Europe, the rite is performed exclusively by females. The notion that the ceremony helps to procure husbands for the girls can be explained by the quickening and fertilising influence which the spirit of vegetation is believed to exert upon the life of man as well as of plants.

The Magic Spring.

The general explanation which we have been led to adopt of these and many similar ceremonies is that they are, or were in their origin, magical rites intended to ensure the revival of nature in spring. The means by which they were supposed to effect this end were imitation and sympathy. Led astray by his ignorance of the true causes of things, primitive man believed that in order to produce the great phenomena of nature on which his life depended he had only to imitate them, and that immediately by a secret sympathy or mystic influence the little drama which he acted in forest glade or mountain dell, on desert plain or wind-swept shore, would be taken up and repeated by mightier actors on a vaster stage. He fancied that by masquerading in leaves and flowers he helped the bare earth to clothe herself with verdure, and that by playing the death and burial of winter he drove that gloomy season away, and made smooth the path for the footsteps of returning spring. We may smile at his vain endeavours if we please, but it was only by making a long series of experiments, of which some were almost inevitably doomed to failure, that man learned from experience the futility of some of his attempted methods and the fruitfulness of others. After all, magical ceremonies are nothing but experiments which have failed and which continue to be repeated merely because the operator is unaware of their failure. With the advance of knowledge these ceremonies either cease to be performed altogether or are kept up from force of habit long after the intention with which they were instituted has been forgotten. Thus fallen from their high estate, no longer regarded as solemn rites on the punctual performance of which the welfare and even the life of the community depend, they sink gradually to the level of simple pageants, mummeries, and pastimes, till in the final stage of degeneration they are wholly abandoned by older people, and, from having once been the most serious occupation of the sage, become at last the idle sport of children. It is in this final stage of decay that most of the old magical rites of our European forefathers linger on at the present day, and even from this their last retreat they are fast being swept away by the rising tide of those multitudinous forces, moral, intellectual, and social, which are bearing mankind onward to a new and unknown goal. We may feel some natural regret at the disappearance of quaint customs and picturesque ceremonies, which have preserved to an age often deemed dull and prosaic something of the flavour and freshness of the olden time, some breath of the springtime of the world; yet our regret will be lessened when we remember that these pretty pageants, these now innocent diversions, had their origin in ignorance and superstition; that if they are a record of human endeavour, they are also a monument of fruitless ingenuity, of wasted labour, and of blighted hopes; and that for all their gay trappings—their flowers, their ribbons, and their music—they partake far more of tragedy than of farce.

The interpretation which I have attempted to give of these ceremonies has been not a little confirmed by the discovery that the natives of Central Australia regularly practise magical ceremonies for the purpose of awakening the dormant energies of nature at the approach of what may be called the Australian spring.* Nowhere apparently are the alternations of the seasons more sudden and the contrasts between them more striking than in the deserts of Central Australia, where at the end of a long period of drought the sandy and stony wilderness, over which the silence and desolation of death appear to brood, is suddenly, after a few days of torrential rain, transformed into a landscape smiling with verdure and peopled with teeming multitudes of insects and lizards, of frogs and birds. The marvellous change which passes over the face of nature at such times has been compared even by European observers to the effect of magic; no wonder, then, that the savage should regard it as such in very deed. Now it is just when there is promise of the approach of a good season that the natives of Central Australia are wont especially to perform those magical ceremonies of which the avowed intention is to multiply the plants and animals they use as food. These ceremonies, therefore, present a close analogy to the spring customs of our European peasantry not only in the time of their celebration, but also in their aim; for we can hardly doubt that in instituting rites designed to assist the revival of plant life in spring our primitive forefathers were moved, not by any sentimental wish to smell at early violets, or pluck the rathe primrose, or watch yellow daffodils dancing in the breeze, but by the very practical consideration, certainly not formulated in abstract terms, that the life of man is inextricably bound up with that of plants, and that if they were to perish he could not survive. And as the faith of the Australian savage in the efficacy of his magic rites is confirmed by observing that their performance is invariably followed, sooner or later, by that increase of vegetable and animal life which it is their object to produce, so, we may suppose, it was with European savages in the olden time. The sight of the fresh green in brake and thicket, of vernal flowers blowing on mossy banks, of swallows arriving from the south, and of the sun mounting daily higher in the sky, would be welcomed by them as so many visible signs that their enchantments were indeed taking effect, and would inspire them with a cheerful confidence that

all was well with a world which they could thus mould to suit
their wishes. Only in autumn days, as summer slowly faded,
would their confidence again be dashed by doubts and mis-
givings at symptoms of decay, which told how vain were all
their efforts to stave off for ever the approach of winter and of
death.

CHAPTER 6

ADONIS

i

The changes of the seasons explained by the life and death of gods.

THE spectacle of the great changes which annually pass over the face of the earth has powerfully impressed the minds of men in all ages, and stirred them to meditate on the causes of transformations so vast and wonderful. Their curiosity has not been purely disinterested; for even the savage cannot fail to perceive how intimately his own life is bound up with the life of nature, and how the same processes which freeze the stream and strip the earth of vegetation menace him with extinction. At a certain stage of development men seem to have imagined that the means of averting the threatened calamity were in their own hands, and that they could hasten or retard the flight of the seasons by magic art. Accordingly they performed ceremonies and recited spells to make the rain to fall, the sun to shine, animals to multiply, and the fruits of the earth to grow. In course of time the slow advance of knowledge, which has dispelled so many cherished illusions, convinced at least the more thoughtful portion of mankind that the alternations of summer and winter, of spring and autumn, were not merely the result of their own magical rites, but that some deeper cause, some mightier power, was at work behind the shifting scenes of nature. They now pictured to themselves the growth and decay of vegetation, the birth and death of living creatures, as effects of the waxing or waning strength of divine beings, of gods and goddesses, who were born and died, who married and begot children, on the pattern of human life.

Magical ceremonies to revive the failing energies of the gods.

Thus the old magical theory of the seasons was displaced, or rather supplemented, by a religious theory. For although men now attributed the annual cycle of change primarily to corresponding changes in their deities, they still thought that by performing certain magical rites they could aid the god, who was the principle of life, in his struggle with the opposing principle of death. They imagined that they could recruit his failing energies and even raise him from the dead. The ceremonies which they observed for this purpose were in substance a dramatic representation of the natural processes which they wished to facilitate; for it is a familiar tenet of magic that you can produce any desired effect by merely imitating it. And as they now explained the fluctuations of growth and decay, of reproduction and dissolution, by the marriage, the death, and the rebirth or revival of the gods, their religious or rather magical dramas turned in great measure on these themes. They set forth the fruitful union of the powers of fertility, the sad death of one at least of the divine partners, and his joyful resurrection. Thus a religious theory was blended with a magical practice.

Of the changes which the seasons bring with them, the most striking within the temperate zone are those which affect vegetation. The influence of the seasons on animals, though great, is not nearly so manifest. Hence it is natural that in the magical dramas designed to dispel winter and bring back spring the emphasis should be laid on vegetation, and that trees and plants should figure in them more prominently than beasts and birds. Yet the two sides of life, the vegetable and the animal, were not dissociated in the minds of those who observed the ceremonies. Indeed they commonly believed that the tie between the animal and the vegetable world was even closer than it really is; hence they often combined the dramatic representation of reviving plants with a real or a dramatic union of the sexes for the purpose of furthering at the same time and by the same act the multiplication of fruits, of animals, and of men. To them the principle of life and fertility, whether animal or vegetable, was one and indivisible. To live and to cause to live, to eat food and to beget children, these were the primary wants of men in the past, and they will be the primary wants of men in the future so long as the world lasts. Other things may be added to enrich and beautify human life, but unless these wants are first satisfied, humanity itself must cease to exist. These two things, therefore, food and children, were what men chiefly sought to procure by the performance of magical rites for the regulation of the seasons.

Nowhere, apparently, have these rites been more widely and solemnly celebrated than in the lands which border the Eastern Mediterranean. Under the names of Osiris, Tammuz, Adonis,

The principles of animal and of vegetable life confused in these ceremonies.

Prevalence of these rites in Western Asia and Egypt.

and Attis, the peoples of Egypt and Western Asia represented the yearly decay and revival of life, especially of vegetable life, which they personified as a god who annually died and rose again from the dead. In name and detail the rites varied from place to place: in substance they were the same.

Tammuz or Adonis in Babylonia.

The worship of Adonis was practised by the Semitic peoples of Babylonia and Syria, and the Greeks borrowed it from them as early as the seventh century before Christ. The true name of the deity was Tammuz: the appellation of Adonis is merely the Semitic *Adon*, 'lord', a title of honour by which his worshippers addressed him. In the Hebrew text of the Old Testament the same name Adonai, originally perhaps Adoni, 'my lord', is often applied to Jehovah. But the Greeks through a misunderstanding converted the title of honour into a proper name. While Tammuz or his equivalent Adonis enjoyed a wide and lasting popularity among peoples of the Semitic stock, there are

His worship seems to have originated with the Sumerians.

grounds for thinking that his worship originated with a race of other blood and other speech, the Sumerians, who in the dawn of history inhabited the flat alluvial plain at the head of the Persian Gulf and created the civilization which was afterwards called Babylonian. In the religious literature of Babylonia Tammuz appears as the youthful spouse or lover of Ishtar, the great

Tammuz the lover of Ishtar.

mother goddess, the embodiment of the reproductive energies of nature. The references to their connexion with each other in

Descent of Ishtar to the nether world to recover Tammuz.

myth and ritual are both fragmentary and obscure, but we gather from them that every year Tammuz was believed to die, passing away from the cheerful earth to the gloomy subterranean world, and that every year his divine mistress journeyed in quest of him 'to the land from which there is no returning, to the house of darkness, where dust lies on door and bolt'. During her absence the passion of love ceased to operate: men and beasts alike forgot to reproduce their kinds: all life was threatened with extinction. So intimately bound up with the goddess were the sexual functions of the whole animal kingdom that without her presence they could not be discharged. A messenger of the great god Ea was accordingly despatched to rescue the goddess on whom so much depended. The stern queen of the infernal regions, Allatu or Eresh-Kigal by name, reluctantly allowed Ishtar to be sprinkled with the Water of Life and to depart, in company probably with her lover Tammuz, that the two might return together to the upper world, and that with their return all nature might revive.

Laments for the departed Tammuz are contained in several Babylonian hymns, which liken him to plants that quickly fade. He is

> 'A tamarisk that in the garden has drunk no water,
>   Whose crown in the field has brought forth no blossom.
> A willow that rejoiced not by the watercourse,
>   A willow whose roots were torn up.
> A herb that in the garden had drunk no water.'

His death appears to have been annually mourned, to the shrill music of flutes, by men and women about midsummer in the month named after him, the month of Tammuz. The dirges were seemingly chanted over an effigy of the dead god, which was washed with pure water, anointed with oil, and clad in a red robe, while the fumes of incense rose into the air, as if to stir his dormant senses by their pungent fragrance and wake him from the sleep of death. In one of these dirges, inscribed *Lament of the Flutes for Tammuz*, we seem still to hear the voices of the singers chanting the sad refrain and to catch, like far-away music, the wailing notes of the flutes:

> 'At his vanishing away she lifts up a lament,
>   "Oh my child!" at his vanishing away she lifts up a lament;
>   "My Damu!" at his vanishing away she lifts up a lament.
>   "My enchanter and priest!" at his vanishing away she lifts up a
>   lament,
> At the shining cedar, rooted in a spacious place,
>   In Eanna, above and below, she lifts up a lament.
> Like the lament that a house lifts up for its master, lifts she up a
>   lament,
>   Like the lament that a city lifts up for its lord, lifts she up a
>   lament.
> Her lament is the lament for a herb that grows not in the bed,
>   Her lament is the lament for the corn that grows not in the ear.
> Her chamber is a possession that brings not forth a possession,
>   A weary woman, a weary child, forspent.
> Her lament is for a great river, where no willows grow,
>   Her lament is for a field, where corn and herbs grow not.
> Her lament is for a pool, where fishes grow not.
>   Her lament is for a thicket of reeds, where no reeds grow.

Her lament is for woods, where tamarisks grow not.
Her lament is for a wilderness where no cypresses (?) grow.
Her lament is for the depth of a garden of trees, where honey and wine grow not.
Her lament is for meadows, where no plants grow.
Her lament is for a palace, where length of life grows not.'

Adonis in Greek mythology merely a reflection of the Oriental Tammuz.

The tragical story and the melancholy rites of Adonis are better known to us from the descriptions of Greek writers than from the fragments of Babylonian literature or the brief reference of the prophet Ezekiel, who saw the women of Jerusalem weeping for Tammuz at the north gate of the temple.* Mirrored in the glass of Greek mythology, the oriental deity appears as a comely youth beloved by Aphrodite. In his infancy the goddess hid him in a chest, which she gave in charge to Persephone, queen of the nether world. But when Persephone opened the chest and beheld the beauty of the babe, she refused to give him back to Aphrodite, though the goddess of love went down herself to hell to ransom her dear one from the power of the grave. The dispute between the two goddesses of love and death was settled by Zeus, who decreed that Adonis should abide with Persephone in the under world for one part of the year, and with Aphrodite in the upper world for another part. At last the fair youth was killed in hunting by a wild boar, or by the jealous Ares, who turned himself into the likeness of a boar in order to compass the death of his rival. Bitterly did Aphrodite lament her loved and lost Adonis. The strife between the divine rivals for the possession of Adonis appears to be depicted on an Etruscan mirror. The two goddesses, identified by inscriptions, are stationed on either side of Jupiter, who occupies the seat of judgment and lifts an admonitory finger as he looks sternly towards Persephone. Overcome with grief the goddess of love buries her face in her mantle, while her pertinacious rival, grasping a branch in one hand, points with the other at a closed coffer, which probably contains the youthful Adonis. In this form of the myth, the contest between Aphrodite and Persephone for the possession of Adonis clearly reflects the struggle between Ishtar and Allatu in the land of the dead, while the decision of Zeus that Adonis is to spend one part of the year under ground and another part above ground is merely a Greek version of the annual disappearance and reappearance of Tammuz.

ii

The myth of Adonis was localized and his rites celebrated with much solemnity at two places in Western Asia. One of these was Byblus on the coast of Syria, the other was Paphos in Cyprus. Both were great seats of the worship of Aphrodite, or rather of her Semitic counterpart, Astarte; and of both, if we accept the legends, Cinyras, the father of Adonis, was king. Of the two cities Byblus was the more ancient; indeed it claimed to be the oldest city in Phoenicia, and to have been founded in the early ages of the world by the great god El, whom Greeks and Romans identified with Cronus and Saturn respectively. However that may have been, in historical times it ranked as a holy place, the religious capital of the country, the Mecca or Jerusalem of the Phoenicians. The city stood on a height beside the sea, and contained a great sanctuary of Astarte, where in the midst of a spacious open court, surrounded by cloisters and approached from below by staircases, rose a tall cone or obelisk, the holy image of the goddess. In this sanctuary the rites of Adonis were celebrated. Indeed the whole city was sacred to him, and the river Nahr Ibrahim, which falls into the sea a little to the south of Byblus, bore in antiquity the name of Adonis. This was the kingdom of Cinyras. From the earliest to the latest times the city appears to have been ruled by kings, assisted perhaps by a senate or council of elders. The first of the kings of whom we have historical evidence was a certain Zekar-baal. He reigned about a century before Solomon; yet from that dim past his figure stands out strangely fresh and lifelike in the journal of an Egyptian merchant or official named Wen-Ammon, which has fortunately been preserved in a papyrus. This man spent some time with the king at Byblus, and received from him, in return for rich presents, a supply of timber felled in the forests of Lebanon. Another king of Byblus, who bore the name of Sibitti-baal, paid tribute to Tiglath-pileser III., king of Assyria, about the year 739 BC. Further, from an inscription of the fifth or fourth century before our era we learn that a king of Byblus, by name Yehaw-melech, son of Yehar-baal, and grandson of Adom-melech or Uri-melech, dedicated a pillared portico with a carved work of gold and a bronze altar to the

Worship of Adonis and Astarte at Byblus, the kingdom of Cinyras.

The kings of Byblus.

goddess, whom he worshipped under the name of Baalath Gebal, that is, the female Baal of Byblus.

Divinity of Semitic kings.

The names of these kings suggest that they claimed affinity with their god Baal or Moloch, for Moloch is only a corruption of *melech*, that is, 'king'. Such a claim at all events appears to have been put forward by many other Semitic kings. The early monarchs of Babylon were worshipped as gods in their lifetime. In like manner the kings of Byblus may have assumed the style of Adonis; for Adonis was simply the divine Adon or 'lord' of

Divinity of the Phoenician kings of Byblus and the Canaanite kings of Jerusalem.

the city, a title which hardly differs in sense from Baal ('master') and Melech ('king'). Some of the old Canaanite kings of Jerusalem appear to have played the part of Adonis in their lifetime, if we may judge from their names, Adoni-bezek and Adoni-zedek, which are divine rather than human titles. If the old priestly kings of Jerusalem regularly played the part of Adonis, we need not wonder that in later times the women of Jerusalem used to weep for Tammuz, that is, for Adonis, at the north gate of the temple. In doing so they may only have been continuing a custom which had been observed in the same place by the Canaanites long before the Hebrews invaded the land.

David as heir of the old sacred kings of Jerusalem.

If Jerusalem had been from of old the seat of a dynasty of spiritual potentates or Grand Lamas, who held the keys of heaven and were revered far and wide as kings and gods in one, we can easily understand why the upstart David chose it for the capital of the new kingdom which he had won for himself at the point of the sword. The central position and the natural strength of the virgin fortress need not have been the only or the principal inducements which decided the politic monarch to transfer his throne from Hebron to Jerusalem.* By serving himself heir to the ancient kings of the city he might reasonably hope to inherit their ghostly repute along with their broad acres, to wear their nimbus as well as their crown. The calm confidence with which the Jebusite inhabitants of that city awaited his attack, jeering at the besiegers from the battlements, may well have been born of a firm trust in the local deity rather than in the height and thickness of their grim old walls. Certainly the obstinacy with which in after ages the Jews defended the same place against the armies of Assyria and Rome sprang in large measure from a similar faith in the God of Zion.

But whether identified with Adonis or not, the Hebrew kings certainly seem to have been regarded as in a sense divine, as representing and to some extent embodying Jehovah on earth. For the king's throne was called the throne of Jehovah; and the application of the holy oil to his head was believed to impart to him directly a portion of the divine spirit. Hence he bore the title of Messiah, which with its Greek equivalent Christ means no more than 'the Anointed One'. Thus when David had cut off the skirt of Saul's robe in the darkness of a cave where he was in hiding, his heart smote him for having laid sacrilegious hands upon *Adoni Messiah Jehovah*, 'my Lord the Anointed of Jehovah'.

Like other divine or semi-divine rulers the Hebrew kings were apparently held answerable for famine and pestilence. When a dearth, caused perhaps by a failure of the winter rains, had visited the land for three years, King David inquired of the oracle, which discreetly laid the blame not on him but on his predecessor Saul. The dead king was indeed beyond the reach of punishment, but his sons were not. So David had seven of them sought out, and they were hanged before the Lord at the beginning of barley harvest in spring: and all the long summer the mother of two of the dead men sat under the gallows-tree, keeping off the jackals by night and the vultures by day, till with the autumn the blessed rain came at last to wet their dangling bodies and fertilize the barren earth once more. Then the bones of the dead were taken down from the gibbet and buried in the sepulchre of their fathers.* The season when these princes were put to death, at the beginning of barley harvest, and the length of time they hung on the gallows, seem to show that their execution was not a mere punishment, but that it partook of the nature of a rain-charm.

The Hebrew kings seem to have been held responsible for drought and famine.

In Israel the excess as well as the deficiency of rain seems to have been set down to the wrath of the deity. When the Jews returned to Jerusalem from the great captivity and assembled for the first time in the square before the ruined temple, it happened that the weather was very wet, and as the people sat shelterless and drenched in the piazza they trembled at their sin and at the rain. In all ages it has been the strength or the weakness of Israel to read the hand of God in the changing aspects of nature, and we need not wonder that at such a time

Excessive rain set down to the wrath of the deity.

and in so dismal a scene, with a lowering sky overhead, the blackened ruins of the temple before their eyes, and the steady drip of the rain over all, the returned exiles should have been oppressed with a double sense of their own guilt and of the divine anger. Perhaps, though they hardly knew it, memories of the bright sun, fat fields, and broad willow-fringed rivers of Babylon, which had been so long their home, lent a deeper shade of sadness to the austerity of the Judean landscape, with its gaunt grey hills stretching away, range beyond range, to the horizon, or dipping eastward to the far line of sombre blue which marks the sullen waters of the Dead Sea.

The Baal and his female Baalath the sources of all fertility.

But if Semitic kings in general and the kings of Byblus in particular often assumed the style of Baal or Adonis, it follows that they may have mated with the goddess, the Baalath or Astarte of the city. Certainly we hear of kings of Tyre and Sidon who were priests of Astarte. Now to the agricultural Semites the Baal or god of a land was the author of all its fertility; he it was who produced the corn, the wine, the figs, the oil, and the flax, by means of his quickening waters, which in the arid parts of the Semitic world are oftener springs, streams, and underground flow than the rains of heaven. Further, 'the life-giving power of the god was not limited to vegetative nature, but to him also was ascribed the increase of animal life, the multiplication of flocks and herds, and, not least, of the human inhabitants of the land. For the increase of animate nature is obviously conditioned, in the last resort, by the fertility of the soil, and primitive races, which have not learned to differentiate the various kinds of life with precision, think of animate as well as vegetable life as rooted in the earth and sprung from it.' In short, 'the Baal was conceived as the male principle of reproduction, the husband of the land which he fertilised.' So far, therefore, as the Semite personified the reproductive energies of nature as male and female, as a Baal and a Baalath, he appears to have identified the male power especially with water and the female especially with earth. On this view plants and trees, animals and men, are the offspring or children of the Baal and Baalath. If, then, at Byblus and elsewhere, the Semitic king was allowed, or rather required, to personate the god and marry the goddess, the intention of the custom can only have been to ensure the fertility of the land

Personation of the Baal by the king.

and the increase of men and cattle by means of homoeopathic magic. There is reason to think that a similar custom was observed from a similar motive in other parts of the ancient world, and particularly at Nemi, where both the male and the female powers, the Dianus and Diana, were in one aspect of their nature personifications of the life-giving waters.

The last king of Byblus bore the ancient name of Cinyras, and was beheaded by Pompey the Great for his tyrannous excesses. His legendary namesake Cinyras is said to have founded a sanctuary of Aphrodite, that is, of Astarte, at a place on Mount Lebanon, distant a day's journey from the capital. The spot was probably Aphaca, at the source of the river Adonis, half-way between Byblus and Baalbec; for at Aphaca there was a famous grove and sanctuary of Astarte which Constantine destroyed on account of the flagitious character of the worship. The site of the temple has been discovered by modern travellers near the village which still bears the name of Afka at the head of the wild, romantic, wooded gorge of the Adonis. The hamlet stands among groves of noble walnut-trees on the brink of the lyn. A little way off the river rushes from a cavern at the foot of a mighty amphitheatre of towering cliffs to plunge in a series of cascades into the awful depths of the glen. The deeper it descends, the ranker and denser grows the vegetation, which, sprouting from the crannies and fissures of the rocks, spreads a green veil over the roaring or murmuring stream in the tremendous chasm below. There is something delicious, almost intoxicating, in the freshness of these tumbling waters, in the sweetness and purity of the mountain air, in the vivid green of the vegetation. The temple, of which some massive hewn blocks and a fine column of Syenite granite still mark the site, occupied a terrace facing the source of the river and commanding a magnificent prospect. Across the foam and the roar of the waterfalls you look up to the cavern and away to the top of the sublime precipices above. So lofty is the cliff that the goats which creep along its ledges to browse on the bushes appear like ants to the spectator hundreds of feet below. Seaward the view is especially impressive when the sun floods the profound gorge with golden light, revealing all the fantastic buttresses and rounded towers of its mountain rampart, and falling softly on the varied green of the woods which clothe its depths. It was

Cinyras, king of Byblus.

Aphaca and the vale of the Adonis.

here that, according to the legend, Adonis met Aphrodite for the first or the last time, and here his mangled body was buried. A fairer scene could hardly be imagined for a story of tragic love and death. Yet, sequestered as the valley is and must always have been, it is not wholly deserted. A convent or a village may be observed here and there standing out against the sky on the top of some beetling crag, or clinging to the face of a nearly perpendicular cliff high above the foam and the din of the river; and at evening the lights that twinkle through the gloom betray the presence of human habitations on slopes which might seem inaccessible to man. In antiquity the whole of the lovely vale appears to have been dedicated to Adonis, and to this day it is haunted by his memory; for the heights which shut it in are crested at various points by ruined monuments of his worship, some of them overhanging dreadful abysses, down which it turns the head dizzy to look and see the eagles wheeling about their nests far below. One such monument exists at Ghineh. The face of a great rock, above a roughly hewn recess, is here carved with figures of Adonis and Aphrodite. He is portrayed with spear in rest, awaiting the attack of a bear, while she is seated in an attitude of sorrow.* Her grief-stricken figure may well be the mourning Aphrodite of the Lebanon described by Macrobius,* and the recess in the rock is perhaps her lover's tomb. Every year, in the belief of his worshippers, Adonis was wounded to death on the mountains, and every year the face of nature itself was dyed with his sacred blood. So year by year the Syrian damsels lamented his untimely fate,* while the red anemone, his flower, bloomed among the cedars of Lebanon, and the river ran red to the sea, fringing the winding shores of the blue Mediteranean, whenever the wind set inshore, with a sinuous band of crimson.

Monuments of Adonis.

iii

The island of Cyprus lies but one day's sail from the coast of Syria. Indeed, on fine summer evenings its mountains may be descried looming low and dark against the red fires of sunset. With its rich mines of copper and its forests of firs and stately cedars, the island naturally attracted a commercial and maritime people like the Phoenicians; while the abundance of its corn, its

Phoenician colonies in Cyprus.

wine, and its oil must have rendered it in their eyes a Land of Promise by comparison with the niggardly nature of their own rugged coast, hemmed in between the mountains and the sea. Accordingly they settled in Cyprus at a very early date and remained there long after the Greeks had also established themselves on its shores; for we know from inscriptions and coins that Phoenician kings reigned at Citium, the Chittim of the Hebrews, down to the time of Alexander the Great. Naturally the Semitic colonists brought their gods with them from the mother-land. They worshipped Baal of the Lebanon, who may well have been Adonis, and at Amathus on the south coast they instituted the rites of Adonis and Aphrodite, or rather Astarte. Here, as at Byblus, these rites resembled the Egyptian worship of Osiris so closely that some people even identified the Adonis of Amathus with Osiris.

But the great seat of the worship of Aphrodite and Adonis in Cyprus was Paphos on the south-western side of the island. Among the petty kingdoms into which Cyprus was divided from the earliest times until the end of the fourth century before our era Paphos must have ranked with the best. It is a land of hills and billowy ridges, diversified by fields and vineyards and intersected by rivers, which in the course of ages have carved for themselves beds of such tremendous depth that travelling in the interior is difficult and tedious. The lofty range of Mount Olympus (the modern Troodos), capped with snow the greater part of the year, screens Paphos from the northerly and easterly winds and cuts it off from the rest of the island. On the slopes of the range the last pine-woods of Cyprus linger, sheltering here and there monasteries in scenery not unworthy of the Apennines. The old city of Paphos occupied the summit of a hill about a mile from the sea; the newer city sprang up at the harbour some ten miles off. The sanctuary of Aphrodite at Old Paphos (the modern Kuklia) was one of the most celebrated shrines in the ancient world.

According to Herodotus, it was founded by Phoenician colonists from Ascalon; but it is possible that a native goddess of fertility was worshipped on the spot before the arrival of the Phoenicians, and that the newcomers identified her with their own Baalath or Astarte, whom she may have closely resembled. If two deities were thus fused in one, we may suppose that they

Margin notes:

Kingdom of Paphos.

Sanctuary of Aphrodite at Paphos.

The Aphrodite of Paphos a Phoenician or aboriginal deity.

were both varieties of that great goddess of motherhood and fertility whose worship appears to have been spread all over Western Asia from a very early time. The supposition is confirmed as well by the archaic shape of her image as by the licentious character of her rites; for both that shape and those rites were shared by her with other Asiatic deities. Her image was simply a white cone or pyramid.

It appears to have been customary to anoint the sacred cone with olive oil at a solemn festival, in which people from Lycia and Caria participated. To this day the old custom appears to survive at Paphos, for 'in honour of the Maid of Bethlehem the peasants of Kuklia anointed lately, and probably still anoint each year, the great corner-stones of the ruined Temple of the Paphian Goddess. As Aphrodite was supplicated once with cryptic rites, so is Mary entreated still by Moslems as well as Christians, with incantations and passings through perforated stones, to remove the curse of barrenness from Cypriote women, or increase the manhood of Cypriote men.' Thus the ancient worship of the goddess of fertility is continued under a different name. Even the name of the old goddess is retained in some parts of the island; for in more than one chapel the Cypriote peasants adore the mother of Christ under the title of Panaghia Aphroditessa.

In Cyprus it appears that before marriage all women were formerly obliged by custom to prostitute themselves to strangers at the sanctuary of the goddess, whether she went by the name of Aphrodite, Astarte, or what not. Similar customs prevailed in many parts of Western Asia. Whatever its motive, the practice was clearly regarded, not as an orgy of lust, but as a solemn religious duty performed in the service of that great Mother Goddess of Western Asia whose name varied, while her type remained constant, from place to place. Thus at Babylon every woman, whether rich or poor, had once in her life to submit to the embraces of a stranger at the temple of Mylitta, that is, of Ishtar or Astarte, and to dedicate to the goddess the wages earned by this sanctified harlotry. The sacred precinct was crowded with women waiting to observe the custom. Some of them had to wait there for years. At Heliopolis or Baalbec in Syria, famous for the imposing grandeur of its ruined temples, the custom of the country required that every maiden should

Her conical image.

Sacred prostitution in the worship of the Paphian Aphrodite and of other Asiatic goddesses.

prostitute herself to a stranger at the temple of Astarte, and matrons as well as maids testified their devotion to the goddess in the same manner. The emperor Constantine abolished the custom, destroyed the temple, and built a church in its stead. In Phoenician temples women prostituted themselves for hire in the service of religion, believing that by this conduct they propitiated the goddess and won her favour. 'It was a law of the Amorites, that she who was about to marry should sit in fornication seven days by the gate.' At Byblus the people shaved their heads in the annual mourning for Adonis. Women who refused to sacrifice their hair had to give themselves up to strangers on a certain day of the festival, and the money which they thus earned was devoted to the goddess. This custom may have been a mitigation of an older rule which at Byblus as elsewhere formerly compelled every woman without exception to sacrifice her virtue in the service of religion. I have already suggested a reason why the offering of a woman's hair was accepted as an equivalent for the surrender of her person.* We are told that in Lydia all girls were obliged to prostitute themselves in order to earn a dowry; but we may suspect that the real motive of the custom was devotion rather than economy. The suspicion is confirmed by a Greek inscription found at Tralles in Lydia, which proves that the practice of religious prostitution survived in that country as late as the second century of our era. It records of a certain woman, Aurelia Aemilia by name, not only that she herself served the god in the capacity of a harlot at his express command, but that her mother and other female ancestors had done the same before her; and the publicity of the record, engraved on a marble column which supported a votive offering, shows that no stain attached to such a life and such a parentage. In Armenia the noblest families dedicated their daughters to the service of the goddess Anaitis in her temple at Acilisena, where the damsels acted as prostitutes for a long time before they were given in marriage. Nobody scrupled to take one of these girls to wife when her period of service was over. Again, the goddess Ma was served by a multitude of sacred harlots at Comana in Pontus, and crowds of men and women flocked to her sanctuary from the neighbouring cities and country to attend the biennial festivals or to pay their vows to the goddess.

The Asiatic
Mother God-
dess a per-
sonification
of all the
reproductive
energies of
nature.

If we survey the whole of the evidence on this subject, some of which has still to be laid before the reader, we may conclude that a great Mother Goddess, the personification of all the reproductive energies of nature, was worshipped under different names but with a substantial similarity of myth and ritual by many peoples of Western Asia; that associated with her was a lover, or rather series of lovers, divine yet mortal, with whom she mated year by year, their commerce being deemed essential to the propagation of animals and plants, each in their several kind; and further, that the fabulous union of the divine pair was simulated and, as it were, multiplied on earth by the real, though temporary, union of the human sexes at the sanctuary of the goddess for the sake of thereby ensuring the fruitfulness of the ground and the increase of man and beast. And if the

Her worship
perhaps re-
flects a
period of sex-
ual commun-
ism.

conception of such a Mother Goddess dates, as seems probable, from a time when the institution of marriage was either unknown or at most barely tolerated as an immoral infringement of old communal rights, we can understand both why the goddess herself was regularly supposed to be at once unmarried and unchaste, and why her worshippers were obliged to imitate her more or less completely in these respects. For had she been a divine wife united to a divine husband, the natural counterpart of their union would have been the lawful marriage of men and women, and there would have been no need to resort to a system of prostitution or promiscuity in order to effect those purposes which, on the principles of homoeopathic magic, might in that case have been as well or better attained by the legitimate intercourse of the sexes in matrimony. Formerly, perhaps, every woman was obliged to submit at least once in her life to the exercise of those marital rights which at a still earlier period had theoretically belonged in permanence to all the males of the tribe. But in course of time, as the institution of individual marriage grew in favour, and the old communism fell more and more into discredit, the revival of the ancient practice even for a single occasion in a woman's life became ever more repugnant to the moral sense of the people, and accordingly they resorted to various expedients for evading in practice the obligation which they still acknowledged in theory. One of these evasions was to let the woman offer her hair instead of her person; another apparently was to substitute an obscene symbol for the obscene act. But while the majority of women thus contrived to observe the forms of religion without sacrificing their virtue, it was still thought necessary to the general welfare that a certain number of them should discharge the old obligation in the old way. These became prostitutes either for life or for a term of years at one of the temples: dedicated to the service of religion, they were invested with a sacred character, and their vocation, far from being deemed infamous, was probably long regarded by the laity as an exercise of more than common virtue, and rewarded with a tribute of mixed wonder, reverence, and pity, not unlike that which in some parts of the world is still paid to women who seek to honour their Creator in a different way by renouncing the natural functions of their sex and the tenderest relations of humanity. It is thus that the folly of mankind finds vent in opposite extremes alike harmful and deplorable.*

At Paphos the custom of religious prostitution is said to have been instituted by King Cinyras, and to have been practised by his daughters, the sisters of Adonis, who, having incurred the wrath of Aphrodite, mated with strangers and ended their days in Egypt. In this form of the tradition the wrath of Aphrodite is probably a feature added by a later authority, who could only regard conduct which shocked his own moral sense as a punishment inflicted by the goddess instead of as a sacrifice regularly enjoined by her on all her devotees. At all events the story indicates that the princesses of Paphos had to conform to the custom as well as women of humble birth. *(margin: The daughters of Cinyras.)*

Among the stories which were told of Cinyras, the ancestor of these priestly kings and the father of Adonis, there are some that deserve our attention. In the first place, he is said to have begotten his son Adonis in incestuous intercourse with his daughter Myrrha at a festival of the corn-goddess, at which women robed in white were wont to offer corn-wreaths as first-fruits of the harvest and to observe strict chastity for nine days.* Similar cases of incest with a daughter are reported of many ancient kings. It seems unlikely that such reports are without foundation, and perhaps equally improbable that they refer to mere fortuitous outbursts of unnatural lust. We may suspect that they are based on a practice actually observed for a definite reason in certain special circumstances. Now in *(margin: Incest of Cinyras with his daughter Myrrha, and birth of Adonis.)* *(margin: Legends of royal incest— a suggested explanation.)*

countries where the royal blood was traced through women only, and where consequently the king held office merely in virtue of his marriage with an hereditary princess, who was the real sovereign, it appears to have often happened that a prince married his own sister,* the princess royal, in order to obtain with her hand the crown which otherwise would have gone to another man, perhaps to a stranger. May not the same rule of descent have furnished a motive for incest with a daughter? For it seems a natural corollary from such a rule that the king was bound to vacate the throne on the death of his wife, the queen, since he occupied it only by virtue of his marriage with her. When that marriage terminated, his right to the throne terminated with it and passed at once to his daughter's husband. Hence if the king desired to reign after his wife's death, the only way in which he could legitimately continue to do so was by marrying his daughter, and thus prolonging through her the title which had formerly been his through her mother.

Cinyras is said to have been famed for his exquisite beauty and to have been wooed by Aphrodite herself. Thus it would appear, as scholars have already observed, that Cinyras was in a sense a duplicate of his handsome son Adonis, to whom the inflammable goddess also lost her heart. Further, these stories of the love of Aphrodite for two members of the royal house of Paphos can hardly be dissociated from the corresponding legend told of Pygmalion, the Phoenician king of Cyprus, who is said to have fallen in love with an image of Aphrodite and taken it to his bed.* When we consider that Pygmalion was the father-in-law of Cinyras, that the son of Cinyras was Adonis, and that all three, in successive generations, are said to have been concerned in a love-intrigue with Aphrodite, we can hardly help concluding that the early Phoenician kings of Paphos, or their sons, regularly claimed to be not merely the priests of the goddess but also her lovers, in other words, that in their official capacity they personated Adonis. At all events Adonis is said to have reigned in Cyprus, and it appears to be certain that the title of Adonis was regularly borne by the sons of all the Phoenician kings of the island. It is true that the title strictly signified no more than 'lord'; yet the legends which connect these Cyprian princes with the goddess of love make it probable that they claimed the divine nature as well as the human dignity of

Cinyras beloved by Aphrodite.

Pygmalion and Aphrodite.

The Phoenician kings of Cyprus or their sons appear to have been hereditary lovers of the goddess.

Adonis. The story of Pygmalion points to a ceremony of a sacred marriage in which the king wedded the image of Aphrodite, or rather of Astarte. If that was so, the tale was in a sense true, not of a single man only, but of a whole series of men, and it would be all the more likely to be told of Pygmalion, if that was a common name of Semitic kings in general, and of Cyprian kings in particular. Pygmalion, at all events, is known as the name of the famous king of Tyre from whom his sister Dido fled; and a king of Citium and Idalium in Cyprus, who reigned in the time of Alexander the Great, was also called Pygmalion, or rather Pumiyathon, the Phoenician name which the Greeks corrupted into Pygmalion. Further, it deserves to be noted that the names Pygmalion and Astarte occur together in a Punic inscription on a gold medallion which was found in a grave at Carthage; the characters of the inscription are of the earliest type. As the custom of religious prostitution at Paphos is said to have been founded by King Cinyras and observed by his daughters, we may surmise that the kings of Paphos played the part of the divine bridegroom in a less innocent rite than the form of marriage with a statue; in fact, that at certain festivals each of them had to mate with one or more of the sacred harlots of the temple, who played Astarte to his Adonis. If that was so, there is more truth than has commonly been supposed in the reproach cast by the Christian fathers that the Aphrodite worshipped by Cinyras was a common whore. The fruit of their union would rank as sons and daughters of the deity, and would in time become the parents of gods and goddesses, like their fathers and mothers before them. In this manner Paphos, and perhaps all sanctuaries of the great Asiatic goddess where sacred prostitution was practised, might be well stocked with human deities, the offspring of the divine king by his wives, concubines, and temple harlots. Any one of these might probably succeed his father on the throne or be sacrificed in his stead whenever stress of war or other grave junctures called, as they sometimes did, for the death of a royal victim. Such a tax, levied occasionally on the king's numerous progeny for the good of the country, would neither extinguish the divine stock nor break the father's heart, who divided his paternal affection among so many. At all events, if, as there seems reason to believe, Semitic kings were often regarded at

Sacred marriage of the kings of Paphos.

Sons and daughters, fathers and mothers of a god.

the same time as hereditary deities, it is easy to understand the frequency of Semitic personal names which imply that the bearers of them were the sons or daughters, the brothers or sisters, the fathers or mothers of a god. This interpretation is confirmed by a parallel Egyptian usage; for in Egypt, where the kings were worshipped as divine, the queen was called 'the wife of the god' or 'the mother of the god,' and the title 'father of the god' was borne not only by the king's real father but also by his father-in-law. Similarly, perhaps, among the Semites any man who sent his daughter to swell the royal harem may have been allowed to call himself 'the father of the god'.

Cinyras, like King David, a harper.

If we may judge by his name, the Semitic king who bore the name of Cinyras was, like King David, a harper; for the name of Cinyras is clearly connected with the Greek *cinyra*, 'a lyre', which in its turn comes from the Semitic *kinnor*, 'a lyre', the very word applied to the instrument on which David played before Saul. We shall probably not err in assuming that at Paphos as at Jerusalem the music of the lyre or harp was not a mere pastime designed to while away an idle hour, but formed part of the service of religion, the moving influence of its melodies being perhaps set down, like the effect of wine, to the direct inspiration of a deity. Certainly at Jerusalem the regular clergy of the temple prophesied to the music of harps, of psalteries, and of cymbals; and it appears that the irregular clergy also, as we may call the prophets, depended on some such stimulus for inducing the ecstatic state which they took for immediate converse with the divinity. Again, just as the cloud of melancholy which from time to time darkened the moody mind of Saul was viewed as an evil spirit from the Lord vexing him, so on the other hand the solemn strains of the harp, which soothed and composed his troubled thoughts, may well have seemed to the hag-ridden king the very voice of God or of his good angel whispering peace. Even in our own day a great religious writer, himself deeply sensitive to the witchery of music, has said that musical notes, with all their power to fire the blood and melt the heart, cannot be mere empty sounds and nothing more; no, they have escaped from some higher sphere, they are outpourings of eternal harmony, the voice of angels, the Magnificat of saints.* It is thus that the rude imaginings of primitive man are transfigured and his feeble lispings echoed

The use of music as a means of prophetic inspiration among the Hebrews.

The influence of music on religion.

with a rolling reverberation in the musical prose of Newman. Indeed the influence of music on the development of religion is a subject which would repay a sympathetic study. For we cannot doubt that this, the most intimate and affecting of all the arts, has done much to create as well as to express the religious emotions, thus modifying more or less deeply the fabric of belief to which at first sight it seems only to minister. The musician has done his part as well as the prophet and the thinker in the making of religion. Every faith has its appropriate music, and the difference between the creeds might almost be expressed in musical notation. The interval, for example, which divides the wild revels of Cybele from the stately ritual of the Catholic Church is measured by the gulf which severs the dissonant clash of cymbals and tambourines from the grave harmonies of Palestrina and Handel. A different spirit breathes in the difference of the music.

A constant feature in the myth of Adonis was his premature and violent death. If, then, the kings of Paphos regularly personated Adonis, we must ask whether they imitated their divine prototype in death as in life. Tradition varied as to the end of Cinyras. Some thought that he slew himself on discovering his incest with his daughter; others alleged that, like Marsyas, he was defeated by Apollo in a musical contest and put to death by the victor.* Yet he cannot strictly be said to have perished in the flower of his youth if he lived, as Anacreon averred, to the ripe age of one hundred and sixty.* If we must choose between the two stories, it is perhaps more likely that he died a violent death than that he survived to an age which surpassed that of Thomas Parr* by eight years, though it fell far short of the antediluvian standard. The life of eminent men in remote ages is exceedingly elastic and may be lengthened or shortened, in the interests of history, at the taste and fancy of the historian.

Traditions as to the death of Cinyras.

CHAPTER 7

SACRED PROSTITUTION

i

Sacred prostitution of Western Asia.

IN the preceding chapter we saw that a system of sacred prostitution was regularly carried on all over Western Asia, and that both in Phoenicia and in Cyprus the practice was specially associated with the worship of Adonis. As the explanation which I have adopted of the custom has been rejected in favour of another by writers whose opinions are entitled to be treated with respect,* I shall devote the present chapter to a further consideration of the subject, and shall attempt to gather, from a closer scrutiny and a wider survey of the field, such evidence as may set the custom and with it the worship of Adonis in a clearer light.

Sacred women in the Tamil temples of Southern India.

In India the dancing-girls dedicated to the service of the Tamil temples take the name of *deva-dasis*, 'servants or slaves of the gods', but in common parlance they are spoken of simply as harlots. Every Tamil temple of note in Southern India has its troop of these sacred women. Their official duties are to dance twice a day, morning and evening, in the temple, to fan the idol with Tibetan ox-tails, to dance and sing before it when it is borne in procession, and to carry the holy light called *Kúmbarti*. Inscriptions show that in AD 1004 the great temple of the Chola king Rajaraja at Tanjore had attached to it four hundred 'women of the temple', who lived at free quarters in the streets round about it and were allowed land free of taxes out of its endowment. From infancy they are trained to dance and sing. In order to obtain a safe delivery expectant mothers will often vow to dedicate their child, if she should prove to be a girl, to the service of God. Among the weavers of Tiru-kalli-kundram, a little town in the Madras Presidency, the eldest

Such women are sometimes married to the god and possessed by him.

daughter of every family is devoted to the temple. Girls thus made over to the deity are formally married, sometimes to the idol, sometimes to a sword, before they enter on their duties; from which it appears that they are often, if not regularly, regarded as the wives of the god.

Among the Kaikolans, a large caste of Tamil weavers who are spread all over Southern India, at least one girl in every family should be dedicated to the temple service. The ritual, as it is observed at the initiation of one of these girls in Coimbatore, includes 'a form of nuptial ceremony. The relations are invited for an auspicious day, and the maternal uncle, or his representative, ties a gold band on the girl's forehead, and, carrying her, places her on a plank before the assembled guests. A Brahman priest recites the *mantrams*, and prepares the sacred fire (*hōmam*). The uncle is presented with new cloths by the girl's mother. For the actual nuptials a rich Brahman, if possible, and, if not, a Brahman of more lowly status is invited. A Brahman is called in, as he is next in importance to, and the representative of the idol. It is said that, when the man who is to receive her first favours, joins the girl, a sword must be placed, at least for a few minutes, by her side.' When one of these dancing-girls dies, her body is covered with a new cloth which has been taken for the purpose from the idol, and flowers are supplied from the temple to which she belonged. No worship is performed in the temple until the last rites have been performed over her body, because the idol, being deemed her husband, is held to be in that state of ceremonial pollution common to human mourners which debars him from the offices of religion. In Mahratta such a female devotee is called Murli. Common folk believe that from time to time the shadow of the god falls on her and possesses her person. At such times the possessed woman rocks herself to and fro, and the people occasionally consult her as a soothsayer, laying money at her feet and accepting as an oracle the words of wisdom or folly that drop from her lips. Nor is the profession of a temple prostitute adopted only by girls. In Tulava, a district of Southern India, any woman of the four highest castes who wearies of her husband or, as a widow and therefore incapable of marriage, grows tired of celibacy, may go to a temple and eat of the rice offered to the idol. Thereupon, if she is a Brahman, she has the right to live either in the temple or outside of its precincts, as she pleases. If she decides to live in it, she gets a daily allowance of rice, and must sweep the temple, fan the idol, and confine her amours to the Brahmans. The male children of these women form a special class called Moylar, but are fond of assuming the title of Stanikas. As many of them as can find employment hang about the temple, sweeping the areas, sprinkling them with cow-dung, carrying torches before the gods, and doing other odd jobs. Some of them, debarred from these holy offices, are reduced to the painful necessity of earning their bread by honest work. The daughters are either brought up to live like their mothers or are given in marriage to the Stanikas. Brahman women who do not choose to live in the temples, and all the women of the three lower castes, cohabit with any man of pure descent, but they have to pay a fixed sum annually to the temple.

Among the Ewe peoples of West Africa the sacred prostitutes are regarded as the wives of the god.

Still more instructive for our present purpose are the West African customs. Among the Ewe-speaking peoples of the Slave Coast 'recruits for the priesthood are obtained in two ways, viz. by the affiliation of young persons, and by the direct consecration of adults. Young people of either sex dedicated or affiliated to a god are termed *kosio*, from *kono*, "unfruitful," because a child dedicated to a god passes into his service and is practically lost to his parents, and *si*, "to run away." As the females become the "wives" of the god to whom they are dedicated, the termination *si* in *vŏdu-si* [another name for these dedicated women], has been translated "wife" by some Europeans; but it is never used in the general acceptation of that term, being entirely restricted to persons consecrated to the gods. The chief business of the female *kosi* is prostitution, and in every town there is at least one institution in which the best-looking girls, between ten and twelve years of age, are received. Here they remain for three years, learning the chants and dances peculiar to the worship of the gods, and prostituting themselves to the priests and the inmates of the male seminaries; and at the termination of their novitiate they become public prostitutes. This condition, however, is not regarded as one for reproach; they are considered to be married to the god, and their excesses are supposed to be caused and directed by him. Properly speaking, their libertinage should be confined to the male worshippers at the temple of the god, but practically it is indiscriminate. Children who are born from such unions belong to the god.' These women are not allowed to marry since they are deemed the wives of a god.

Again, in this part of Africa 'the female *Kosio* of Dañh-gbi, or *Dañh-sio*, that is, the wives, priestesses, and temple prostitutes of Dañh-gbi, the python-god, have their own organization. Generally they live together in a group of houses or huts inclosed by a fence, and in these inclosures the novices undergo their three years of initiation. Most new members are obtained by the affiliation of young girls; but any woman whatever, married or single, slave or free, by publicly simulating possession, and uttering the conventional cries recognized as indicative of possession by the god, can at once join the body, and be admitted to the habitations of the order. The person of a woman who has joined in this manner is inviolable, and during the period of her novitiate she is forbidden, if single, to enter the house of her parents, and, if married, that of her husband. This inviolability, while it gives women opportunities of gratifying an illicit passion, at the same time serves occasionally to save the persecuted slave, or neglected wife, from the ill-treatment of the lord and master; for she has only to go through the conventional form of possession and an asylum is assured.' The python-god marries these women secretly in his temple, and they father their offspring on him; but it is the priests who consummate the union.

The human wives of the python-god.

For our purpose it is important to note that a close connexion is apparently supposed to exist between the fertility of the soil and the marriage of these women to the serpent. For the time when new brides are sought for the reptile-god is the season when the millet is beginning to sprout. Then the old priestesses, armed with clubs, run frantically through the streets shrieking like mad women and carrying off to be brides of the serpent any little girls between the ages of eight and twelve whom they may find outside of the houses. Pious people at such times will sometimes leave their daughters at their doors on purpose that they may have the honour of being dedicated to the god. The marriage of wives to the serpent-god is probably deemed necessary to enable him to discharge the important function of making the crops to grow and the cattle to multiply; for we read that these people 'invoke the snake in excessively wet, dry, or barren seasons; on all occasions relating to their government and the preservation of their cattle; or rather, in one word, in all necessities and difficulties, in which they do

Supposed connexion between the fertility of the soil and the marriage of women to the serpent.

not apply to their new batch of gods'.* Once in a bad season the Dutch factor Bosman found the King of Whydah in a great rage. His Majesty explained the reason of his discomposure by saying 'that that year he had sent much larger offerings to the snake-house than usual, in order to obtain a good crop; and that one of his vice-roys (whom he shewed me) had desired him afresh, in the name of the priests, who threatened a barren year, to send yet more. To which he answered that he did not intend to make any further offerings this year; and if the snake would not bestow a plentiful harvest on them, he might let it alone; for (said he) I cannot be more damaged thereby, the greatest part of my corn being already rotten in the field.'

Human wives of a snake-god among the Akikuyu.

The Akikuyu of British East Africa 'have a custom which reminds one of the West African python-god and his wives. At intervals of, I believe, several years the medicine-men order huts to be built for the purpose of worshipping a river snake. The snake-god requires wives, and women or more especially girls go to the huts. Here the union is consummated by the medicine-men. If the number of females who go to the huts voluntarily is not sufficient, girls are seized and dragged there. I believe the offspring of such a union is said to be fathered by God (Ngai): at any rate there are children in Kikuyu who are regarded as the children of God.'

Sacred men as well as women in West Africa: they are thought to be possessed by the deity.

Among the negroes of the Slave Coast there are, as we have seen, male *kosio* as well as female *kosio*; that is, there are dedicated men as well as dedicated women, priests as well as priestesses, and the ideas and customs in regard to them seem to be similar. Like the women, the men undergo a three years' novitiate, at the end of which each candidate has to prove that the god accepts him and finds him worthy of inspiration. Escorted by a party of priests he goes to a shrine and seats himself on a stool that belongs to the deity. The priests then anoint his head with a mystic decoction and invoke the god in a long and wild chorus. During the singing the youth, if he is acceptable to the deity, trembles violently, simulates convulsions, foams at the mouth, and dances in a frenzied style, sometimes for more than an hour. This is the proof that the god has taken possession of him. After that he has to remain in a temple without speaking for seven days and nights. At the end of that time, he is brought out, a priest opens his mouth to show that he may now use his tongue, a new name is given him, and he is fully ordained. Henceforth he is regarded as the priest and medium of the deity whom he serves, and the words which he utters in that morbid state of mental excitement which passes for divine inspiration, are accepted by the hearers as the very words of the god spoken by the mouth of the man. Any crime which a priest committed in a state of frenzy used to remain unpunished, no doubt because the act was thought to be the act of the god. But this benefit of clergy was so much abused that under King Gezo the law had to be altered; and although, while he is still possessed by the god, the inspired criminal is safe, he is now liable to punishment as soon as the divine spirit leaves him.

Among the Tshi-speaking peoples to the west, the customs and beliefs in regard to the dedicated men and dedicated women, the priests and priestesses, are very similar. These persons are believed to be from time to time possessed or inspired by the deity whom they serve; and in that state they are consulted as oracles. They work themselves up to the necessary pitch of excitement by dancing to the music of drums; each god has his special hymn, sung to a special beat of the drum, and accompanied by a special dance. It is while thus dancing to the drums that the priest or priestess lets fall the oracular words in a croaking or guttural voice which the hearers take to be the voice of the god. Hence dancing has an important place in the education of priests and priestesses; they are trained in it for months before they may perform in public. These mouthpieces of the deity are consulted in almost every concern of life and are handsomely paid for their services. 'Priests marry like any other members of the community, and purchase wives; but priestesses are never married, nor can any "head money" be paid for a priestess. The reason appears to be that a priestess belongs to the god she serves, and therefore cannot become the property of a man, as would be the case if she married one. This prohibition extends to marriage only, and a priestess is not debarred from sexual commerce. The children of a priest or priestess are not ordinarily educated for the priestly profession, one generation being usually passed over, and the grandchildren selected. Priestesses are ordinarily most licentious, and custom allows them to gratify their passions with any man who may

Similarly among the Tshi peoples of the Gold Coast there are sacred men and women, who are supposed to be inspired by the deity.

chance to take their fancy.'* The ranks of the hereditary priesthood are constantly recruited by persons who devote themselves or who are devoted by their relations or masters to the profession. Men, women, and even children can thus become members of the priesthood. If a mother has lost several of her children by death, she will not uncommonly vow to devote the next born to the service of the gods; for in this way she hopes to save the child's life. So when the child is born it is set apart for the priesthood, and on arriving at maturity generally fulfils the vow made by the mother and becomes a priest or priestess. At the ceremony of ordination the votary has to prove his or her vocation for the sacred life in the usual way by falling into or simulating convulsions, dancing frantically to the beat of drums, and speaking in a hoarse unnatural voice words which are deemed to be the utterance of the deity temporarily lodged in the body of the man or woman.

ii

In like manner the sacred prostitutes of Western Asia may have been viewed as possessed by the deity and married to the god.

Thus in Africa, and sometimes if not regularly in India, the sacred prostitutes attached to temples are regarded as the wives of the god, and their excesses are excused on the ground that the women are not themselves, but that they act under the influence of divine inspiration. This is in substance the explanation which I have given of the custom of sacred prostitution as it was practised in antiquity by the peoples of Western Asia. In their licentious intercourse at the temples the women, whether maidens or matrons or professional harlots, imitated the licentious conduct of a great goddess of fertility for the purpose of ensuring the fruitfulness of fields and trees, of man and beast; and in discharging this sacred and important function the women were probably supposed, like their West African sisters, to be actually possessed by the goddess.

Similarly the sacred men (*kedeshim*) of Western Asia may have been regarded as possessed by the deity and

As in West Africa the dedicated women have their counterpart in the dedicated men, so it was in Western Asia; for there the sacred men (*kedeshim*) clearly corresponded to the sacred women (*kedeshoth*), in other words, the sacred male slaves of the temples were the complement of the sacred female slaves. And as the characteristic feature of the dedicated men in West Africa is their supposed possession or inspiration by the deity, so we may conjecture was it with the sacred male slaves (the *kedeshim*) of Western Asia; they, too, may have been regarded as temporary or permanent embodiments of the deity, possessed from time to time by his divine spirit, acting in his name, and speaking with his voice. In like manner the Hebrew prophets were believed to be temporarily possessed and inspired by a divine spirit who spoke through them, just as a divine spirit is supposed by West African negroes to speak through the mouth of the dedicated men his priests. Indeed the points of resemblance between the prophets of Israel and West Africa are close and curious. The Hebrew prophets employed music in order to bring on the prophetic trance; they received the divine spirit through the application of a magic oil to their heads; they were apparently distinguished from common people by certain marks on the face; and they were consulted not merely in great national emergencies but in the ordinary affairs of everyday life, in which they were expected to give information and advice for a small fee. But while the prophets roved freely about the country, the *kedeshim* appear to have been regularly attached to a sanctuary; and among the duties which they performed at the shrines there were clearly some which revolted the conscience of men imbued with a purer morality. What these duties were, we may surmise partly from the behaviour of the sons of Eli to the women who came to the tabernacle,* partly from the beliefs and practices as to 'holy men' which survive to this day among the Syrian peasantry.

Of these 'holy men' we are told that 'so far as they are not impostors, they are men whom we would call insane, known among the Syrians as *mejnûn*, possessed by a *jinn* or spirit. They often go in filthy garments, or without clothing. Since they are regarded as intoxicated by deity, the most dignified men, and of the highest standing among the Moslems, submit to utter indecent language at their bidding without rebuke, and ignorant Moslem women do not shrink from their approach, because in their superstitious belief they attribute to them, as men possessed by God, a divine authority which they dare not resist. Such an attitude of compliance may be exceptional, but there are more than rumours of its existence. These "holy men" differ from the ordinary derwishes whom travellers so often see in Cairo, and from the ordinary madmen who are kept in fetters,

as acting and speaking in his name.

Resemblance of the Hebrew prophets to the sacred men of Western Africa.

'Holy men' in modern Syria.

so that they may not do injury to themselves and others. But their appearance, and the expressions regarding them, afford some illustrations of the popular estimate of ancient seers, or prophets, in the time of Hosea: "The prophet is a fool, the man that hath the spirit is mad";* and in the time of Jeremiah, the man who made himself a prophet was considered as good as a madman.' To complete the parallel these vagabonds 'are also believed to be possessed of prophetic power, so that they are able to foretell the future, and warn the people among whom they live of impending danger'.

The licence accorded to such 'holy men' may be explained by the desire of women for offspring.

We may conjecture that with women a powerful motive for submitting to the embraces of the 'holy men' is a hope of obtaining offspring by them. For in Syria it is still believed that even dead saints can beget children on barren women, who accordingly resort to their shrines in order to obtain the wish of their hearts. For example, at the Baths of Solomon in Northern Palestine, blasts of hot air escape from the ground; and one of them, named Abu Rabah, is a famous resort of childless wives who wish to satisfy their maternal longings. They let the hot air stream up over their bodies and really believe that children born to them after such a visit are begotten by the saint of the shrine. But the saint who enjoys the highest reputation in this respect is St George. He reveals himself at his shrines which are scattered all over the country; at each of them there is a tomb or the likeness of a tomb. The most celebrated of these sanctuaries is at Kalat el Hosn in Northern Syria. Barren women of all sects, including Moslems, resort to it. 'There are many natives who shrug their shoulders when this shrine is mentioned in connection with women. But it is doubtless true that many do not know what seems to be its true character, and who think that the most puissant saint, as they believe, in the world can give them sons.' 'But the true character of the place is beginning to be recognized, so that many Moslems have forbidden their wives to visit it.'

iii

Belief that men and women may

Customs like the foregoing may serve to explain the belief, which is not confined to Syria, that men and women may be in fact and not merely in metaphor the sons and daughters of a god; for these modern saints, whether Christian or Moslem, who father the children of Syrian mothers, are nothing but the old gods under a thin disguise. If in antiquity as at the present day Semitic women often repaired to shrines in order to have the reproach of barrenness removed from them—and the prayer of Hannah is a familiar example of the practice,* we could easily understand not only the tradition of the sons of God who begat children on the daughters of men, but also the exceedingly common occurrence of the divine titles in Hebrew names of human beings. Multitudes of men and women, in fact, whose mothers had resorted to holy places in order to procure offspring, would be regarded as the actual children of the god and would be named accordingly. Hence Hannah called her infant Samuel, which means 'name of God' or 'his name is God'; and probably she sincerely believed that the child was actually begotten in her womb by the deity. The dedication of such children to the service of God at the sanctuary was merely giving back the divine son to the divine father. Similarly in West Africa, when a woman has got a child at the shrine of Agbasia, the god who alone bestows offspring on women, she dedicates him or her as a sacred slave to the deity.

Thus in the Syrian beliefs and customs of to-day we probably have the clue to the religious prostitution practised in the very same regions in antiquity. Then as now women looked to the local god, the Baal or Adonis of old, the Abu Rabah or St George of to-day, to satisfy the natural craving of a woman's heart; and then as now, apparently, the part of the local god was played by sacred men, who in personating him may often have sincerely believed that they were acting under divine inspiration, and that the functions which they discharged were necessary for the fertility of the land as well as for the propagation of the human species. The purifying influence of Christianity and Mohammedanism has restricted such customs within narrow limits; even under Turkish rule they are now only carried on in holes and corners. Yet if the practice has dwindled, the principle which it embodies appears to be fundamentally the same; it is a desire for the continuance of the species, and a belief that an object so natural and legitimate can be accomplished by divine power manifesting itself in the bodies of men and women.

be the off-
spring of a
god.

The saints in
modern Syria
are the equi-
valents of the
ancient Baal
or Adonis.

Belief in the
physical
fatherhood of
God not con-
fined to
Syria.

Sons of the
serpent-god.

The belief in the physical fatherhood of God has not been
confined to Syria in ancient and modern times. Elsewhere many
men have been counted the sons of God in the most literal sense
of the word, being supposed to have been begotten by his holy
spirit in the wombs of mortal women. I shall merely illustrate
the creed by a few examples drawn from classical antiquity. Thus
in order to obtain offspring women used to resort to the great
sanctuary of Aesculapius, situated in a beautiful upland valley,
to which a path, winding through a long wooded gorge, leads
from the bay of Epidaurus. Here the women slept in the holy place
and were visited in dreams by a serpent; and the children to whom
they afterwards gave birth were believed to have been begotten
by the reptile. That the serpent was supposed to be the god himself
seems certain; for Aesculapius repeatedly appeared in the form
of a serpent,* and live serpents were kept and fed in his
sanctuaries for the healing of the sick, being no doubt regarded
as his incarnations. Hence the children born to women who had
thus visited a sanctuary of Aesculapius were probably fathered
on the serpent-god. Many celebrated men in classical antiquity
were thus promoted to the heavenly hierarchy by similar legends
of a miraculous birth. The famous Aratus of Sicyon was certainly
believed by his countrymen to be a son of Aesculapius; his mother
is said to have got him in intercourse with a serpent. Probably
she slept either in the shrine of Aesculapius at Sicyon, where a
figurine of her was shown seated on a serpent, or perhaps in the
more secluded sanctuary of the god at Titane, not many miles
off, where the sacred serpents crawled among ancient cypresses
on the hill-top which overlooks the narrow green valley of the
Asopus with the white turbid river rushing in its depths. There,
under the shadow of the cypresses, with the murmur of the
Asopus in her ears, the mother of Aratus may have conceived,
or fancied she conceived, the future deliverer of his country.
Again, the mother of Augustus is said to have got him by
intercourse with a serpent in a temple of Apollo; hence the
emperor was reputed to be the son of that god. Similar tales were
told of the Messenian hero Aristomenes, Alexander the Great,
and the elder Scipio: all of them were reported to have been
begotten by snakes. In the time of Herod a serpent, according
to Aelian, in like manner made love to a Judaean maid.* Can
the story be a distorted rumour of the parentage of Christ?

CHAPTER 8

THE RITUAL OF ADONIS

i

AT the festivals of Adonis, which were held in Western Asia and in Greek lands, the death of the god was annually mourned, with a bitter wailing, chiefly by women; images of him, dressed to resemble corpses, were carried out as to burial and then thrown into the sea or into springs; and in some places his revival was celebrated on the following day. But at different places the ceremonies varied somewhat in the manner and apparently also in the season of their celebration. At Alexandria images of Aphrodite and Adonis were displayed on two couches; beside them were set ripe fruits of all kinds, cakes, plants growing in flower-pots, and green bowers twined with anise. The marriage of the lovers was celebrated one day, and on the morrow women attired as mourners, with streaming hair and bared breasts, bore the image of the dead Adonis to the sea-shore and committed it to the waves. Yet they sorrowed not without hope, for they sang that the lost one would come back again. The date at which this Alexandrian ceremony was observed is not expressly stated; but from the mention of the ripe fruits it has been inferred that it took place in late summer. In the great Phoenician sanctuary of Astarte at Byblus the death of Adonis was annually mourned, to the shrill wailing notes of the flute, with weeping, lamentation, and beating of the breast; but next day he was believed to come to life again and ascend up to heaven in the presence of his worshippers. The disconsolate believers, left behind on earth, shaved their heads as the Egyptians did on the death of the divine bull Apis; women who could not bring themselves to sacrifice their beautiful tresses had to give themselves up to strangers on a certain day of the festival, and to dedicate to Astarte the wages of their shame.

This Phoenician festival appears to have been a vernal one, for its date was determined by the discoloration of the river Adonis, and this has been observed by modern travellers to occur in spring. At that season the red earth washed down from the mountains by the rain tinges the water of the river, and even the sea, for a great way with a blood-red hue, and the crimson stain was believed to be the blood of Adonis, annually wounded to death by the boar on Mount Lebanon. Again, the scarlet anemone is said to have sprung from the blood of Adonis, or to have been stained by it; and as the anemone blooms in Syria about Easter, this may be thought to show that the festival of Adonis, or at least one of his festivals, was held in spring. The name of the flower is probably derived from Naaman ('darling'), which seems to have been an epithet of Adonis. The Arabs still call the anemone 'wounds of the Naaman'. The red rose also was said to owe its hue to the same sad occasion; for Aphrodite, hastening to her wounded lover, trod on a bush of white roses; the cruel thorns tore her tender flesh, and her sacred blood dyed the white roses for ever red. It would be idle, perhaps, to lay much weight on evidence drawn from the calendar of flowers, and in particular to press an argument so fragile as the bloom of the rose. Yet so far as it counts at all, the tale which links the damask rose with the death of Adonis points to a summer rather than to a spring celebration of his passion. In Attica, certainly, the festival fell at the height of summer. For the fleet which Athens fitted out against Syracuse, and by the destruction of which her power was permanently crippled, sailed at midsummer, and by an ominous coincidence the sombre rites of Adonis were being celebrated at the very time. As the troops marched down to the harbour to embark, the streets through which they passed were lined with coffins and corpse-like effigies, and the air was rent with the noise of women wailing for the dead Adonis. The circumstance cast a gloom over the sailing of the most splendid armament that Athens ever sent to sea.* Many ages afterwards, when the Emperor Julian made his first entry into Antioch, he found in like manner the gay, the luxurious capital of the East plunged in mimic grief for the annual death of Adonis: and if he had any presentiment of coming evil, the voices of lamentation which struck upon his ear must have seemed to sound his knell.

The resemblance of these ceremonies to the Indian and European ceremonies which I have described elsewhere is obvious.* In particular, apart from the somewhat doubtful date of its celebration, the Alexandrian ceremony is almost identical

Margin notes:

The anemone and the red rose the flowers of Adonis.

Festivals of Adonis at Athens and Antioch.

Resemblance of these rites to Indian and European ceremonies.

with the Indian.* In both of them the marriage of two divine beings, whose affinity with vegetation seems indicated by the fresh plants with which they are surrounded, is celebrated in effigy, and the effigies are afterwards mourned over and thrown into the water. From the similarity of these customs to each other and to the spring and midsummer customs of modern Europe we should naturally expect that they all admit of a common explanation. Hence, if the explanation which I have adopted of the latter is correct, the ceremony of the death and resurrection of Adonis must also have been a dramatic representation of the decay and revival of plant life. The inference thus based on the resemblance of the customs is confirmed by the following features in the legend and ritual of Adonis. His affinity with vegetation comes out at once in the common story of his birth. He was said to have been born from a myrrh-tree, the bark of which bursting, after a ten months' gestation, allowed the lovely infant to come forth. According to some, a boar rent the bark with his tusk and so opened a passage for the babe. A faint rationalistic colour was given to the legend by saying that his mother was a woman named Myrrh, who had been turned into a myrrh-tree soon after she had conceived the child. The use of myrrh as incense at the festival of Adonis may have given rise to the fable. We have seen that incense was burnt at the corresponding Babylonian rites, just as it was burnt by the idolatrous Hebrews in honour of the Queen of Heaven, who was no other than Astarte. Again, the story that Adonis spent half, or according to others a third, of the year in the lower world and the rest of it in the upper world, is explained most simply and naturally by supposing that he represented vegetation, especially the corn, which lies buried in the earth half the year and reappears above ground the other half. Certainly of the annual phenomena of nature there is none which suggests so obviously the idea of death and resurrection as the disappearance and reappearance of vegetation in autumn and spring. Adonis has been taken for the sun;* but there is nothing in the sun's annual course within the temperate and tropical zones to suggest that he is dead for half or a third of the year and alive for the other half or two-thirds. He might, indeed, be conceived as weakened in winter, but dead he could not be thought to be; his daily reappearance contradicts the

The death and resurrection of Adonis a mythical expression for the annual decay and revival of plant life.

Adonis sometimes taken for the sun.

supposition. Within the Arctic Circle, where the sun annually disappears for a continuous period which varies from twenty-four hours to six months according to the latitude, his yearly death and resurrection would certainly be an obvious idea; but no one except the unfortunate astronomer Bailly* has maintained that the Adonis worship came from the Arctic regions. On the other hand, the annual death and revival of vegetation is a conception which readily presents itself to men in every stage of savagery and civilization; and the vastness of the scale on which this ever-recurring decay and regeneration takes place, together with man's intimate dependence on it for subsistence, combine to render it the most impressive annual occurrence in nature, at least within the temperate zones. It is no wonder that a phenomenon so important, so striking, and so universal should, by suggesting similar ideas, have given rise to similar rites in many lands. We may, therefore, accept as probable an explanation of the Adonis worship which accords so well with the facts of nature and with the analogy of similar rites in other lands. Moreover, the explanation is countenanced by a considerable body of opinion amongst the ancients themselves, who again and again interpreted the dying and reviving god as the reaped and sprouting grain.

The mourning for Adonis interpreted as a harvest rite.

It has been suggested by Father Lagrange* that the mourning for Adonis was essentially a harvest rite designed to propitiate the corn-god, who was then either perishing under the sickles of the reapers, or being trodden to death under the hoofs of the oxen on the threshing-floor. While the men slew him, the women wept crocodile tears at home to appease his natural indignation by a show of grief for his death. The theory fits in well with the dates of the festivals, which fell in spring or summer; for spring and summer, not autumn, are the seasons of the barley and wheat harvests in the lands which worshipped Adonis. Further, the hypothesis is confirmed by the practice of the Egyptian reapers, who lamented, calling upon Isis, when they cut the first corn; and it is recommended by the analogous customs of many hunting tribes, who testify great respect for the animals which they kill and eat.

But probably Adonis was a spirit of

Thus interpreted the death of Adonis is not the natural decay of vegetation in general under the summer heat or the winter cold; it is the violent destruction of the corn by man, who cuts it down on the field, stamps it to pieces on the threshing-floor, and grinds it to powder in the mill. That this was indeed the principal aspect in which Adonis presented himself in later times to the agricultural peoples of the Levant, may be admitted; but whether from the beginning he had been the corn and nothing but the corn, may be doubted. At an earlier period he may have been to the herdsman, above all, the tender herbage which sprouts after rain, offering rich pasture to the lean and hungry cattle. Earlier still he may have embodied the spirit of the nuts and berries which the autumn woods yield to the savage hunter and his squaw. And just as the husbandman must propitiate the spirit of the corn which he consumes, so the herdsman must appease the spirit of the grass and leaves which his cattle munch, and the hunter must soothe the spirit of the roots which he digs, and of the fruits which he gathers from the bough. In all cases the propitiation of the injured and angry sprite would naturally comprise elaborate excuses and apologies, accompanied by loud lamentations at his decease whenever, through some deplorable accident or necessity, he happened to be murdered as well as robbed. Only we must bear in mind that the savage hunter and herdsman of those early days had probably not yet attained to the abstract idea of vegetation in general; and that accordingly, so far as Adonis existed for them at all, he must have been the *Adon* or lord of each individual tree and plant rather than a personification of vegetable life as a whole. Thus there would be as many Adonises as there were trees and shrubs, and each of them might expect to receive satisfaction for any damage done to his person or property. And year by year, when the trees were deciduous, every Adonis would seem to bleed to death with the red leaves of autumn and to come to life again with the fresh green of spring.

fruits, edible roots, and grass before he became a spirit of the cultivated corn.

There is reason to think that in early times Adonis was sometimes personated by a living man who died a violent death in the character of the god. Further, there is evidence which goes to show that among the agricultural peoples of the Eastern Mediterranean, the corn-spirit, by whatever name he was known, was often represented, year by year, by human victims slain on the harvest-field. If that was so, it seems likely that the propitiation of the corn-spirit would tend to fuse to some extent with the worship of the dead. For the spirits of these victims

The propitiation of the corn-spirit may have fused with the worship of the dead.

might be thought to return to life in the ears which they had
fattened with their blood, and to die a second death at the
reaping of the corn. Now the ghosts of those who have perished
by violence are surly and apt to wreak their vengeance on their
slayers whenever an opportunity offers. Hence the attempt to
appease the souls of the slaughtered victims would naturally
blend, at least in the popular conception, with the attempt to
pacify the slain corn-spirit. And as the dead came back in the
sprouting corn, so they might be thought to return in the spring
flowers, waked from their long sleep by the soft vernal airs.
They had been laid to their rest under the sod. What more
natural than to imagine that the violets and the hyacinths, the
roses and the anemones, sprang from their dust, were empur-
pled or incarnadined by their blood, and contained some
portion of their spirit?

> 'I sometimes think that never blows so red
> The Rose as where some buried Caesar bled;
>   That every Hyacinth the Garden wears
> Dropt in her Lap from some once lovely Head.
>
> 'And this reviving Herb whose tender Green
> Fledges the River-Lip on which we lean—
>   Ah, lean upon it lightly, for who knows
> From what once lovely Lip it springs unseen?'*

In the summer after the battle of Landen, the most sangui-
nary battle of the seventeenth century in Europe, the earth,
saturated with the blood of twenty thousand slain, broke forth
into millions of poppies, and the traveller who passed that vast
sheet of scarlet might well fancy that the earth had indeed given
up her dead.* At Athens the great Commemoration of the Dead
fell in spring about the middle of March, when the early flowers
are in bloom. Then the dead were believed to rise from their
graves and go about the streets, vainly endeavouring to enter
the temples and the dwellings, which were barred against these
perturbed spirits with ropes, buckthorn, and pitch. The name
of the festival, according to the most obvious and natural
interpretation, means the Festival of Flowers, and the title
would fit well with the substance of the ceremonies if at that
season the poor ghosts were indeed thought to creep from the
narrow house with the opening flowers.* There may therefore
be a measure of truth in the theory of Renan, who saw in the

The festival
of the dead a
festival of
flowers.

Adonis worship a dreamy voluptuous cult of death, conceived not as the King of Terrors, but as an insidious enchanter who lures his victims to himself and lulls them into an eternal sleep. The infinite charm of nature in the Lebanon, he thought, lends itself to religious emotions of this sensuous, visionary sort, hovering vaguely between pain and pleasure, between slumber and tears. It would doubtless be a mistake to attribute to Syrian peasants the worship of a conception so purely abstract as that of death in general. Yet it may be true that in their simple minds the thought of the reviving spirit of vegetation was blent with the very concrete notion of the ghosts of the dead, who come to life again in spring days with the early flowers, with the tender green of the corn and the many-tinted blossoms of the trees. Thus their views of the death and resurrection of nature would be coloured by their views of the death and resurrection of man, by their personal sorrows and hopes and fears. In like manner we cannot doubt that Renan's theory of Adonis was itself deeply tinged by passionate memories, memories of the slumber akin to death which sealed his own eyes on the slopes of the Lebanon, memories of the sister who sleeps in the land of Adonis never again to wake with the anemones and the roses.*

ii

Perhaps the best proof that Adonis was a deity of vegetation, and especially of the corn, is furnished by the gardens of Adonis, as they were called. These were baskets or pots filled with earth, in which wheat, barley, lettuces, fennel, and various kinds of flowers were sown and tended for eight days, chiefly or exclusively by women. Fostered by the sun's heat, the plants shot up rapidly, but having no root they withered as rapidly away, and at the end of eight days were carried out with the images of the dead Adonis, and flung with them into the sea or into springs.

Pots of corn, herbs, and flowers, called the gardens of Adonis.

These gardens of Adonis are most naturally interpreted as representatives of Adonis or manifestations of his power; they represented him, true to his original nature, in vegetable form, while the images of him, with which they were carried out and cast into the water, portrayed him in his later human shape. All

These gardens of Adonis were charms to promote the growth of vegetation.

these Adonis ceremonies, if I am right, were originally intended as charms to promote the growth or revival of vegetation; and the principle by which they were supposed to produce this effect was homoeopathic or imitative magic. For ignorant people suppose that by mimicking the effect which they desire to produce they actually help to produce it; thus by sprinkling water they make rain, by lighting a fire they make sunshine, and so on. Similarly, by mimicking the growth of crops they hope to ensure a good harvest. The rapid growth of the wheat and barley in the gardens of Adonis was intended to make the corn shoot up; and the throwing of the gardens and of the images into the water was a charm to secure a due supply of fertilizing rain. The same, I take it, was the object of throwing the effigies of Death and the Carnival into water in the corresponding ceremonies of modern Europe.* Certainly the custom of drenching with water a leaf-clad person, who undoubtedly personifies vegetation, is still resorted to in Europe for the express purpose of producing rain. Similarly the custom of throwing water on the last corn cut at harvest, or on the person who brings it home (a custom observed in Germany and France, and till quite lately in England and Scotland), is in some places practised with the avowed intent to procure rain for the next year's crops. Thus in Wallachia and amongst the Roumanians in Transylvania, when a girl is bringing home a crown made of the last ears of corn cut at harvest, all who meet her hasten to throw water on her, and two farm-servants are placed at the door for the purpose; for they believe that if this were not done, the crops next year would perish from drought. At the spring ploughing in Prussia, when the ploughmen and sowers returned in the evening from their work in the fields, the farmer's wife and the servants used to splash water over them. The ploughmen and sowers retorted by seizing every one, throwing them into the pond, and ducking them under the water. The farmer's wife might claim exemption on payment of a forfeit, but every one else had to be ducked. By observing this custom they hoped to ensure a due supply of rain for the seed.

The opinion that the gardens of Adonis are essentially charms to promote the growth of vegetation, especially of the crops, and that they belong to the same class of customs as those spring and midsummer folk-customs of modern Europe which

Marginal notes:

The throwing of the 'gardens' into water was a rain-charm.

Parallel European customs of drenching the corn with water at harvest or sowing.

Gardens of Adonis among the Oraons and

I have described elsewhere, does not rest for its evidence merely on the intrinsic probability of the case. Fortunately we are able to show that gardens of Adonis (if we may use the expression in a general sense) are still planted, first, by a primitive race at their sowing season, and, second, by European peasants at midsummer. Amongst the Oraons and Mundas of Bengal, when the time comes for planting out the rice which has been grown in seed-beds, a party of young people of both sexes go to the forest and cut a young Karma-tree, or the branch of one. Bearing it in triumph they return dancing, singing, and beating drums, and plant it in the middle of the village dancing-ground. A sacrifice is offered to the tree; and next morning the youth of both sexes, linked arm-in-arm, dance in a great circle round the Karma-tree, which is decked with strips of coloured cloth and sham bracelets and necklets of plaited straw. As a preparation for the festival, the daughters of the headman of the village cultivate blades of barley in a peculiar way. The seed is sown in moist, sandy soil, mixed with turmeric, and the blades sprout and unfold of a pale-yellow or primrose colour. On the day of the festival the girls take up these blades and carry them in baskets to the dancing-ground, where, prostrating themselves reverentially, they place some of the plants before the Karma-tree. Finally, the Karma-tree is taken away and thrown into a stream or tank. The meaning of planting these barley blades and then presenting them to the Karma-tree is hardly open to question. Trees are supposed to exercise a quickening influence upon the growth of crops, and amongst the very people in question—the Mundas or Mundaris—'the grove deities are held responsible for the crops.' Therefore, when at the season for planting out the rice the Mundas bring in a tree and treat it with so much respect, their object can only be to foster thereby the growth of the rice which is about to be planted out; and the custom of causing barley blades to sprout rapidly and then presenting them to the tree must be intended to subserve the same purpose, perhaps by reminding the tree-spirit of his duty towards the crops, and stimulating his activity by this visible example of rapid vegetable growth. The throwing of the Karma-tree into the water is to be interpreted as a rain-charm. Whether the barley blades are also thrown into the water is not said; but if my interpretation of the custom is right, probably they are so.

A distinction between this Bengal custom and the Greek rites of Adonis is that in the former the tree-spirit appears in his original form as a tree; whereas in the Adonis worship he appears in human form, represented as a dead man, though his vegetable nature is indicated by the gardens of Adonis, which are, so to say, a secondary manifestation of his original power as a tree-spirit.

Gardens of Adonis in Rajputana.

Gardens of Adonis are cultivated also by the Hindoos, with the intention apparently of ensuring the fertility both of the earth and of mankind. Thus at Oodeypoor in Rajputana a festival is held 'in honour of Gouri, or Isani, the goddess of abundance, the Isis of Egypt, the Ceres of Greece'. The rites begin when the sun enters the sign of the Ram, the opening of the Hindoo year. An image of the goddess Gouri is made of earth, and a smaller one of her husband Iswara, and the two are placed together. A small trench is next dug, barley is sown in it, and the ground watered and heated artificially till the grain sprouts, when the women dance round it hand in hand, invoking the blessing of Gouri on their husbands. After that the young corn is taken up and distributed by the women to the men, who wear it in their turbans. In these rites the distribution of the barley shoots to the men, and the invocation of a blessing on their husbands by the wives, point clearly to the desire of offspring as one motive for observing the custom. The same motive probably explains the use of gardens of Adonis at the marriage of Brahmans in the Madras Presidency. Seeds of five or nine sorts are mixed and sown in earthen pots, which are made specially for the purpose and are filled with earth. Bride and bridegroom water the seeds both morning and evening for four days; and on the fifth day the seedlings are thrown, like the real gardens of Adonis, into a tank or river.

Gardens of Adonis on St John's Day in Sardinia.

In Sardinia the gardens of Adonis are still planted in connexion with the great Midsummer festival which bears the name of St John. At the end of March or on the first of April a young man of the village presents himself to a girl, and asks her to be his *comare* (gossip or sweetheart), offering to be her *compare*. The invitation is considered as an honour by the girl's family, and is gladly accepted. At the end of May the girl makes a pot of the bark of the cork-tree, fills it with earth, and sows a handful of wheat and barley in it. The pot being placed in the sun and often watered, the corn sprouts rapidly and has a good head by Midsummer Eve (St John's Eve, the twenty-third of June). Customs of the same sort are observed at the same season in Sicily. Pairs of boys and girls become gossips of St John on St John's Day by drawing each a hair from his or her head and performing various ceremonies over them. Thus they tie the hairs together and throw them up in the air, or exchange them over a potsherd, which they afterwards break in two, preserving each a fragment with pious care. The tie formed in the latter way is supposed to last for life.

Gardens of Adonis on St John's Day in Sicily.

In these midsummer customs of Sardinia and Sicily it is possible that St John has replaced Adonis. We have seen that the rites of Tammuz or Adonis were commonly celebrated about midsummer; according to Jerome, their date was June. And besides their date and their similarity in respect of the pots of herbs and corn, there is another point of affinity between the two festivals, the heathen and the Christian. In both of them water plays a prominent part. At his midsummer festival in Babylon the image of Tammuz, whose name is said to mean 'true son of the deep water', was bathed with pure water: at his summer festival in Alexandria the image of Adonis, with that of his divine mistress Aphrodite, was committed to the waves; and at the midsummer celebration in Greece the gardens of Adonis were thrown into the sea or into springs. Now a great feature of the midsummer festival associated with the name of St John is, or used to be, the custom of bathing in the sea, springs, rivers, or the dew on Midsummer Eve or the morning of Midsummer Day. Thus, for example, at Naples there is a church dedicated to St John the Baptist under the name of St John of the Sea (*S Giovan a mare*); and it was an old practice for men and women to bathe in the sea on St John's Eve, that is, on Midsummer Eve, believing that thus all their sins were washed away. In the Abruzzi water is still supposed to acquire certain marvellous and beneficent properties on St John's Night. They say that on that night the sun and moon bathe in the water. Hence many people take a bath in the sea or in a river at that season, especially at the moment of sunrise.

In these Sardinian and Sicilian ceremonies St John may have taken the place of Adonis.

Custom of bathing in water or washing in dew on the Eve or Day of St John (Midsummer Eve or Midsummer Day).

It may perhaps be suggested that this wide-spread custom of bathing in water or dew on Midsummer Eve or Midsummer

342 *Killing the God*

The custom of bathing at midsummer is pagan, not Christian, in its origin.

Day is purely Christian in origin, having been adopted as an appropriate mode of celebrating the day dedicated to the Baptist. But in point of fact the custom is older than Christianity, for it was denounced and forbidden as a heathen practice by Augustine,* and to this day it is practised at midsummer by the Mohammedan peoples of North Africa. We may conjecture that the Church, unable to put down this relic of paganism, followed its usual policy of accommodation by bestowing on the rite a Christian name and acquiescing, with a sigh, in its observance. And casting about for a saint to supplant a heathen patron of bathing, the Christian doctors could hardly have hit upon a more appropriate successor than St John the Baptist.

Old heathen festival of midsummer in Europe and the East.

But into whose shoes did the Baptist step? Was the displaced deity really Adonis, as the foregoing evidence seems to suggest? In Sardinia and Sicily it may have been so, for in these islands Semitic influence was certainly deep and probably lasting. The midsummer pastimes of Sardinian and Sicilian children may therefore be a direct continuation of the Carthaginian rites of Tammuz. Yet the midsummer festival seems too widely spread and too deeply rooted in Central and Northern Europe to allow us to trace it everywhere to an Oriental origin in general and to the cult of Adonis in particular. It has the air of a native of the soil rather than of an exotic imported from the East. We shall do better, therefore, to suppose that at a remote period similar modes of thought, based on similar needs, led men independently in many distant lands, from the North Sea to the Euphrates, to celebrate the summer solstice with rites which, while they differed in some things, yet agreed closely in others; that in historical times a wave of Oriental influence, starting perhaps from Babylonia, carried the Tammuz or Adonis form of the festival westward till it met with native forms of a similar festival; and that under pressure of the Roman civilization these different yet kindred festivals fused with each other and crystallized into a variety of shapes, which subsisted more or less separately side by side, till the Church, unable to suppress them altogether, stripped them so far as it could of their grosser features, and dexterously changing the names allowed them to pass muster as Christian.

Nor are these Sicilian and Calabrian customs the only Easter ceremonies which resemble the rites of Adonis. 'During the whole of Good Friday a waxen effigy of the dead Christ is exposed to view in the middle of the Greek churches and is covered with fervent kisses by the thronging crowd, while the whole church rings with melancholy, monotonous dirges. Late in the evening, when it has grown quite dark, this waxen image is carried by the priests into the street on a bier adorned with lemons, roses, jessamine, and other flowers, and there begins a grand procession of the multitude, who move in serried ranks, with slow and solemn step, through the whole town. Every man carries his taper and breaks out into doleful lamentation. At all the houses which the procession passes there are seated women with censers to fumigate the marching host. Thus the community solemnly buries its Christ as if he had just died. At last the waxen image is again deposited in the church, and the same lugubrious chants echo anew. These lamentations, accompanied by a strict fast, continue till midnight on Saturday. As the clock strikes twelve, the bishop appears and announces the glad tidings that "Christ is risen", to which the crowd replies, "He is risen indeed," and at once the whole city bursts into an uproar of joy, which finds vent in shrieks and shouts, in the endless discharge of carronades and muskets, and the explosion of fire-works of every sort. In the very same hour people plunge from the extremity of the fast into the enjoyment of the Easter lamb and neat wine.'*

Resemblance of the Easter ceremonies in the Greek Church to the rites of Adonis.

When we reflect how often the Church has skilfully contrived to plant the seeds of the new faith on the old stock of paganism, we may surmise that the Easter celebration of the dead and risen Christ was grafted upon a similar celebration of the dead and risen Adonis, which, as we have seen reason to believe, was celebrated in Syria at the same season. The type, created by Greek artists, of the sorrowful goddess with her dying lover in her arms, resembles and may have been the model of the *Pietà* of Christian art, the Virgin with the dead body of her divine Son in her lap, of which the most celebrated example is the one by Michael Angelo in St Peter's. That noble group, in which the living sorrow of the mother contrasts so wonderfully with the languor of death in the son, is one of the finest compositions in marble. Ancient Greek art

The Christian festival of Easter perhaps grafted on a festival of Adonis.

has bequeathed to us few works so beautiful, and none so pathetic.*

In this connexion a well-known statement of Jerome may not be without significance. He tells us that Bethlehem, the traditionary birthplace of the Lord, was shaded by a grove of that still older Syrian Lord, Adonis, and that where the infant Jesus had wept, the lover of Venus was bewailed.* Though he does not expressly say so, Jerome seems to have thought that the grove of Adonis had been planted by the heathen after the birth of Christ for the purpose of defiling the sacred spot. In this he may have been mistaken. If Adonis was indeed, as I have argued, the spirit of the corn, a more suitable name for his dwelling-place could hardly be found than Bethlehem, 'the House of Bread', and he may well have been worshipped there at his House of Bread long ages before the birth of Him who said, 'I am the bread of life.' Even on the hypothesis that Adonis followed rather than preceded Christ at Bethlehem, the choice of his sad figure to divert the allegiance of Christians from their Lord cannot but strike us as eminently appropriate when we remember the similarity of the rites which commemorated the death and resurrection of the two. One of the earliest seats of the worship of the new god was Antioch, and at Antioch, as we have seen, the death of the old god was annually celebrated with great solemnity. A circumstance which attended the entrance of Julian into the city at the time of the Adonis festival may perhaps throw some light on the date of its celebration. When the emperor drew near to the city he was received with public prayers as if he had been a god, and he marvelled at the voices of a great multitude who cried that the Star of Salvation had dawned upon them in the East. This may doubtless have been no more than a fulsome compliment paid by an obsequious Oriental crowd to the Roman emperor. But it is also possible that the rising of a bright star regularly gave the signal for the festival, and that as chance would have it the star emerged above the rim of the eastern horizon at the very moment of the emperor's approach. The coincidence, if it happened, could hardly fail to strike the imagination of a superstitious and excited multitude, who might thereupon hail the great man as the deity whose coming was announced by the sign in the heavens. Or the emperor may have mistaken for a greeting to himself the shouts which were addressed to the star. Now Astarte, the divine mistress of Adonis, was identified with the planet Venus, and her changes from a morning to an evening star were carefully noted by the Babylonian astronomers, who drew omens from her alternate appearance and disappearance. Hence we may conjecture that the festival of Adonis was regularly timed to coincide with the appearance of Venus as the Morning or Evening Star. But the star which the people of Antioch saluted at the festival was seen in the East; therefore, if it was indeed Venus, it can only have been the Morning Star. At Aphaca in Syria, where there was a famous temple of Astarte, the signal for the celebration of the rites was apparently given by the flashing of a meteor, which on a certain day fell like a star from the top of Mount Lebanon into the river Adonis. The meteor was thought to be Astarte herself, and its flight through the air might naturally be interpreted as the descent of the amorous goddess to the arms of her lover. At Antioch and elsewhere the appearance of the Morning Star on the day of the festival may in like manner have been hailed as the coming of the goddess of love to wake her dead leman from his earthy bed. If that were so, we may surmise that it was the Morning Star which guided the wise men of the East to Bethlehem, the hallowed spot which heard, in the language of Jerome, the weeping of the infant Christ and the lament for Adonis.

The Star of Bethlehem.

Attis the Phrygian counterpart of Adonis.

ANOTHER of those gods whose supposed death and resurrection struck such deep roots into the faith and ritual of Western Asia is Attis. He was to Phrygia* what Adonis was to Syria. Like Adonis, he appears to have been a god of vegetation, and his death and resurrection were annually mourned and rejoiced over at a festival in spring. The legends and rites of the two gods were so much alike that the ancients themselves sometimes identified them. Attis was said to have been a fair young shepherd or herdsman beloved by Cybele, the Mother of the Gods, a great Asiatic goddess of fertility, who had her chief home in Phrygia. Some held that Attis was her son. His birth, like that of many other heroes, is said to have been miraculous. His mother, Nana, was a virgin, who conceived by putting a ripe almond or a pomegranate in her bosom. Indeed in the Phrygian cosmogony an almond figured as the father of all things, perhaps because its delicate lilac blossom is one of the first heralds of the spring, appearing on the bare boughs before the leaves have opened. Two different accounts of the death of Attis were current. According to the one he was killed by a boar, like Adonis. According to the other he unmanned himself under a pine-tree, and bled to death on the spot. The latter is said to have been the local story told by the people of Pessinus, a great seat of the worship of Cybele, and the whole legend of which the story forms a part is stamped with a character of rudeness and savagery that speaks strongly for its antiquity. Both tales might claim the support of custom, or rather both were probably invented to explain certain customs observed by the worshippers. The story of the self-mutilation of Attis is clearly an attempt to account for the self-multilation of his priests, who regularly castrated themselves on entering the service of the goddess. The story of his death by the boar may have been told to explain why his worshippers, especially the people of Pessinus, abstained from eating swine. In like manner

His relation to Cybele.

His miraculous birth.

The death of Attis.

the worshippers of Adonis abstained from pork, because a boar had killed their god. After his death Attis is said to have been changed into a pine-tree.

The worship of the Phrygian Mother of the Gods was adopted by the Romans in 204 BC towards the close of their long struggle with Hannibal. For their drooping spirits had been opportunely cheered by a prophecy, alleged to be drawn from that convenient farrago of nonsense, the Sibylline Books, that the foreign invader would be driven from Italy if the great Oriental goddess were brought to Rome. Accordingly ambassadors were despatched to her sacred city Pessinus in Phrygia. The small black stone which embodied the mighty divinity was entrusted to them and conveyed to Rome, where it was received with great respect and installed in the temple of Victory on the Palatine Hill. It was the middle of April when the goddess arrived, and she went to work at once.* For the harvest that year was such as had not been seen for many a long day, and in the very next year Hannibal and his veterans embarked for Africa. As he looked his last on the coast of Italy, fading behind him in the distance, he could not foresee that Europe, which had repelled the arms, would yet yield to the gods, of the Orient. The vanguard of the conquerors had already encamped in the heart of Italy before the rearguard of the beaten army fell sullenly back from its shores.

We may conjecture, though we are not told, that the Mother of the Gods brought with her the worship of her youthful lover or son to her new home in the West. Certainly the Romans were familiar with the Galli, the emasculated priests of Attis, before the close of the Republic. These unsexed beings, in their Oriental costume, with little images suspended on their breasts, appear to have been a familiar sight in the streets of Rome, which they traversed in procession, carrying the image of the goddess and chanting their hymns to the music of cymbals and tambourines, flutes and horns, while the people, impressed by the fantastic show and moved by the wild strains, flung alms to them in abundance, and buried the image and its bearers under showers of roses. A further step was taken by the Emperor Claudius when he incorporated the Phrygian worship of the sacred tree, and with it probably the orgiastic rites of Attis, in the established religion of Rome. The great spring festival of

Worship of Cybele introduced into Rome in 204 BC.

Attis and his eunuch priests the Galli at Rome.

Cybele and Attis is best known to us in the form in which it was celebrated at Rome; but as we are informed that the Roman ceremonies were also Phrygian, we may assume that they differed hardly, if at all, from their Asiatic original. The order of the festival seems to have been as follows.

The spring festival of Cybele and Attis at Rome.

On the twenty-second day of March, a pine-tree was cut in the woods and brought into the sanctuary of Cybele, where it was treated as a great divinity. The duty of carrying the sacred tree was entrusted to a guild of Tree-bearers. The trunk was swathed like a corpse with woollen bands and decked with wreaths of violets, for violets were said to have sprung from the blood of Attis, as roses and anemones from the blood of Adonis; and the effigy of a young man, doubtless Attis himself, was tied to the middle of the stem. On the second day of the festival, the twenty-third of March, the chief ceremony seems to have been a blowing of trumpets. The third day, the twenty-fourth of March, was known as the Day of Blood: the Archigallus or high-priest drew blood from his arms and presented it as an offering. Nor was he alone in making this bloody sacrifice. Stirred by the wild barbaric music of clashing cymbals, rumbling drums, droning horns, and screaming flutes, the inferior clergy whirled about in the dance with waggling heads and streaming hair, until, rapt into a frenzy of excitement and insensible to pain, they gashed their bodies with potsherds or slashed them with knives in order to bespatter the altar and the sacred tree with their flowing blood. The ghastly rite probably formed part of the mourning for Attis and may have been intended to strengthen him for the resurrection. The Australian aborigines cut themselves in like manner over the graves of their friends for the purpose, perhaps, of enabling them to be born again. Further, we may conjecture, though we are not expressly told, that it was on the same Day of Blood and for the same purpose that the novices sacrificed their virility. Wrought up to the highest pitch of religious excitement they dashed the severed portions of themselves against the image of the cruel goddess. These broken instruments of fertility were afterwards reverently wrapt up and buried in the earth or in subterranean chambers sacred to Cybele, where, like the offering of blood, they may have been deemed instrumental in recalling Attis to life and hastening the general resurrection of nature, which was

The Day of Blood.

then bursting into leaf and blossom in the vernal sunshine. Some confirmation of this conjecture is furnished by the savage story that the mother of Attis conceived by putting in her bosom a pomegranate sprung from the severed genitals of a man-monster named Agdestis, a sort of double of Attis.

If there is any truth in this conjectural explanation of the custom, we can readily understand why other Asiatic goddesses of fertility were served in like manner by eunuch priests. These feminine deities required to receive from their male ministers, who personated the divine lovers, the means of discharging their beneficent functions: they had themselves to be impregnated by the life-giving energy before they could transmit it to the world. Goddesses thus ministered to by eunuch priests were the great Artemis of Ephesus and the great Syrian Astarte of Hierapolis,* whose sanctuary, frequented by swarms of pilgrims and enriched by the offerings of Assyria and Babylonia, of Arabia and Phoenicia, was perhaps in the days of its glory the most popular in the East. Now the unsexed priests of this Syrian goddess resembled those of Cybele so closely that some people took them to be the same. And the mode in which they dedicated themselves to the religious life was similar. The greatest festival of the year at Hierapolis fell at the beginning of spring, when multitudes thronged to the sanctuary from Syria and the regions round about. While the flutes played, the drums beat, and the eunuch priests slashed themselves with knives, the religious excitement gradually spread like a wave among the crowd of onlookers, and many a one did that which he little thought to do when he came as a holiday spectator to the festival. For man after man, his veins throbbing with the music, his eyes fascinated by the sight of the streaming blood, flung his garments from him, leaped forth with a shout, and seizing one of the swords which stood ready for the purpose, castrated himself on the spot. Then he ran through the city, holding the bloody pieces in his hand, till he threw them into one of the houses which he passed in his mad career. The household thus honoured had to furnish him with a suit of female attire and female ornaments, which he wore for the rest of his life. When the tumult of emotion had subsided, and the man had come to himself again, the irrevocable sacrifice must often have been followed by passionate sorrow and lifelong

Eunuch priests in the service of Asiatic goddesses.

regret. This revulsion of natural human feeling after the frenzies of a fanatical religion is powerfully depicted by Catullus in a celebrated poem.*

The sacrifice of virility.

The parallel of these Syrian devotees confirms the view that in the similar worship of Cybele the sacrifice of virility took place on the Day of Blood at the vernal rites of the goddess, when the violets, supposed to spring from the red drops of her wounded lover, were in bloom among the pines. Indeed the story that Attis unmanned himself under a pine-tree was clearly devised to explain why his priests did the same beside the sacred violet-wreathed tree at his festival. At all events, we can hardly doubt that the Day of Blood witnessed the mourning for Attis over an effigy of him which was afterwards buried. The image thus laid in the sepulchre was probably the same which had hung upon the tree. Throughout the period of mourning the worshippers fasted from bread, nominally because Cybele had done so in her grief for the death of Attis, but really perhaps for the same reason which induced the women of Harran to abstain from eating anything ground in a mill while they wept for Tammuz. To partake of bread or flour at such a season might have been deemed a wanton profanation of the bruised and broken body of the god. Or the fast may possibly have been a preparation for a sacramental meal.

The mourning for Attis.

The Festival of Joy (*Hilaria*) for the resurrection of Attis on March 25th.

But when night had fallen, the sorrow of the worshippers was turned to joy. For suddenly a light shone in the darkness: the tomb was opened: the god had risen from the dead; and as the priest touched the lips of the weeping mourners with balm, he softly whispered in their ears the glad tidings of salvation. The resurrection of the god was hailed by his disciples as a promise that they too would issue triumphant from the corruption of the grave. On the morrow, the twenty-fifth day of March, which was reckoned the vernal equinox, the divine resurrection was celebrated with a wild outburst of glee. At Rome, and probably elsewhere, the celebration took the form of a carnival. It was the Festival of Joy (*Hilaria*). A universal licence prevailed. Every man might say and do what he pleased. People went about the streets in disguise. No dignity was too high or too sacred for the humblest citizen to assume with impunity. In the reign of Commodus a band of conspirators thought to take advantage of the masquerade by dressing in the uniform of the Imperial

Guard, and so, mingling with the crowd of merrymakers, to get within stabbing distance of the emperor. But the plot miscarried. Even the stern Alexander Severus used to relax so far on the joyous day as to admit a pheasant to his frugal board. The next day, the twenty-sixth of March, was given to repose, which must have been much needed after the varied excitements and fatigues of the preceding days. Finally, the Roman festival closed on the twenty-seventh of March with a procession to the brook Almo. The silver image of the goddess, with its face of jagged black stone, sat in a wagon drawn by oxen. Preceded by the nobles walking barefoot, it moved slowly, to the loud music of pipes and tambourines, out by the Porta Capena, and so down to the banks of the Almo, which flows into the Tiber just below the walls of Rome. There the high-priest, robed in purple, washed the wagon, the image, and the other sacred objects in the water of the stream. On returning from their bath, the wain and the oxen were strewn with fresh spring flowers. All was mirth and gaiety. No one thought of the blood that had flowed so lately. Even the eunuch priests forgot their wounds.

The procession to the Almo.

Such, then, appears to have been the annual solemnization of the death and resurrection of Attis in spring. But besides these public rites, his worship is known to have comprised certain secret or mystic ceremonies, which probably aimed at bringing the worshipper, and especially the novice, into closer communication with his god. Our information as to the nature of these mysteries and the date of their celebration is unfortunately very scanty, but they seem to have included a sacramental meal and a baptism of blood. In the sacrament the novice became a partaker of the mysteries by eating out of a drum and drinking out of a cymbal, two instruments of music which figured prominently in the thrilling orchestra of Attis. The fast which accompanied the mourning for the dead god may perhaps have been designed to prepare the body of the communicant for the reception of the blessed sacrament by purging it of all that could defile by contact the sacred elements. In the baptism the devotee, crowned with gold and wreathed with fillets, descended into a pit, the mouth of which was covered with a wooden grating. A bull, adorned with garlands of flowers, its forehead glittering with gold leaf, was then driven on to the grating and

The mysteries of Attis.

The sacrament.

The baptism of blood.

there stabbed to death with a consecrated spear. Its hot reeking blood poured in torrents through the apertures, and was received with devout eagerness by the worshipper on every part of his person and garments, till he emerged from the pit, drenched, dripping, and scarlet from head to foot, to receive the homage, nay the adoration, of his fellows as one who had been born again to eternal life and had washed away his sins in the blood of the bull. For some time afterwards the fiction of a new birth was kept up by dieting him on milk like a new-born babe. The regeneration of the worshipper took place at the same time as the regeneration of his god, namely at the vernal equinox. At Rome the new birth and the remission of sins by the shedding of bull's blood appear to have been carried out above all at the sanctuary of the Phrygian goddess on the Vatican Hill, at or near the spot where the great basilica of St Peter's now stands; for many inscriptions relating to the rites were found when the church was being enlarged in 1608 or 1609. From the Vatican as a centre this barbarous system of superstition seems to have spread to other parts of the Roman empire. Inscriptions found in Gaul and Germany prove that provincial sanctuaries modelled their ritual on that of the Vatican. From the same source we learn that the testicles as well as the blood of the bull played an important part in the ceremonies. Probably they were regarded as a powerful charm to promote fertility and hasten the new birth.

The Vatican a centre of the worship of Attis.

CHAPTER 10

THE HANGED GOD

i

FROM inscriptions it appears that both at Pessinus and Rome the high-priest of Cybele regularly bore the name of Attis. It is therefore a reasonable conjecture that he played the part of his namesake, the legendary Attis, at the annual festival. We have seen that on the Day of Blood he drew blood from his arms, and this may have been an imitation of the self-inflicted death of Attis under the pine-tree. It is not inconsistent with this supposition that Attis was also represented at these ceremonies by an effigy; for instances can be shown in which the divine being is first represented by a living person and afterwards by an effigy, which is then burned or otherwise destroyed. Perhaps we may go a step farther and conjecture that this mimic killing of the priest, accompanied by a real effusion of his blood, was in Phrygia, as it has been elsewhere, a substitute for a human sacrifice which in earlier times was actually offered. We know from Strabo that the priests of Pessinus were at one time potentates as well as priests; they may, therefore, have belonged to that class of divine kings or popes whose duty it was to die each year for their people and the world. The name of Attis, it is true, does not occur among the names of the old kings of Phrygia, who seem to have borne the names of Midas and Gordias in alternate generations; but a very ancient inscription carved in the rock above a famous Phrygian monument, which is known as the Tomb of Midas, records that the monument was made for, or dedicated to, King Midas by a certain Ates, whose name is doubtless identical with Attis, and who, if not a king himself, may have been one of the royal family. It is worthy of note also that the name Atys, which, again, appears to be only another form of Attis, is recorded as that of an early king of Lydia; and that a son of Croesus, king of Lydia, not only bore the name Atys but was said to have been killed, while he was hunting a boar, by a member of the royal Phrygian family, who traced his lineage to King Midas and had fled to the court

The high priest of Attis bore the god's name and seems to have personated him.

The drawing of the high priest's blood may have been a substitute for putting him to death in the character of the god.

The name of Attis in the royal families of Phrygia and Lydia.

of Croesus because he had unwittingly slain his own brother. Scholars have recognized in this story of the death of Atys, son of Croesus, a mere double of the myth of Attis; and in view of the facts which have come before us in the present inquiry it is a remarkable circumstance that the myth of a slain god should be told of a king's son. May we conjecture that the Phrygian priests who bore the name of Attis and represented the god of that name were themselves members, perhaps the eldest sons, of the royal house, to whom their fathers, uncles, brothers, or other kinsmen deputed the honour of dying a violent death in the character of gods, while they reserved to themselves the duty of living, as long as nature allowed them, in the humbler character of kings? If this were so, the Phrygian dynasty of Midas may have presented a close parallel to the Greek dynasty of Athamas, in which the eldest sons seem to have been regularly destined to the altar. But it is also possible that the divine priests who bore the name of Attis may have belonged to that indigenous race which the Phrygians, on their irruption into Asia from Europe, appear to have found and conquered in the land afterwards known as Phrygia. On the latter hypothesis the priests may have represented an older and higher civilization than that of their barbarous conquerors. Be that as it may, the god they personated was a deity of vegetation whose divine life manifested itself especially in the pine-tree and the violets of spring; and if they died in the character of that divinity, they corresponded to the mummers who are still slain in mimicry by European peasants in spring, and to the priest who was slain long ago in grim earnest on the wooded shore of the Lake of Nemi.

The Phrygian priests of Attis may have been members of the royal family.

ii

The way in which the representatives of Attis were put to death is perhaps shown by the legend of Marsyas,

A reminiscence of the manner in which these old representatives of the deity were put to death is perhaps preserved in the famous story of Marsyas. He was said to be a Phrygian satyr or Silenus, according to others a shepherd or herdsman, who played sweetly on the flute. A friend of Cybele, he roamed the country with the disconsolate goddess to soothe her grief for the death of Attis. Vain of his skill, he challenged Apollo to a musical contest, he to play on the flute and Apollo on the lyre.

Being vanquished, Marsyas was tied up to a pine-tree and flayed or cut limb from limb either by the victorious Apollo or by a Scythian slave. His skin was shown at Celaenae in historical times. It hung at the foot of the citadel in a cave from which the river Marsyas rushed with an impetuous and noisy tide to join the Maeander. So the Adonis bursts full-born from the precipices of the Lebanon; so the blue river of Ibreez leaps in a crystal jet from the red rocks of the Taurus; so the stream, which now rumbles deep underground, used to gleam for a moment on its passage from darkness to darkness in the dim light of the Corycian cave. In all these copious fountains, with their glad promise of fertility and life, men of old saw the hand of God and worshipped him beside the rushing river with the music of its tumbling waters in their ears. At Celaenae, if we can trust tradition, the piper Marsyas, hanging in his cave, had a soul for harmony even in death; for it is said that at the sound of his native Phrygian melodies the skin of the dead satyr used to thrill, but that if the musician struck up an air in praise of Apollo it remained deaf and motionless.

who was hung on a pine-tree and flayed by Apollo.

In this Phrygian satyr, shepherd, or herdsman who enjoyed the friendship of Cybele, practised the music so characteristic of her rites, and died a violent death on her sacred tree, the pine, may we not detect a close resemblance to Attis, the favourite shepherd or herdsman of the goddess, who is himself described as a piper, is said to have perished under a pine-tree, and was annually represented by an effigy hung, like Marsyas, upon a pine? We may conjecture that in old days the priest who bore the name and played the part of Attis at the spring festival of Cybele was regularly hanged or otherwise slain upon the sacred tree, and that this barbarous custom was afterwards mitigated into the form in which it is known to us in later times, when the priest merely drew blood from his body under the tree and attached an effigy instead of himself to its trunk. In the holy grove at Upsala men and animals were sacrificed by being hanged upon the sacred trees. The human victims dedicated to Odin were regularly put to death by hanging or by a combination of hanging and stabbing, the man being strung up to a tree or a gallows and then wounded with a spear. Hence Odin was called the Lord of the Gallows or the God of the Hanged, and he is represented sitting under a gallows tree. Indeed he is said

Marsyas apparently a double of Attis.

The hanging and spearing of Odin and his human victims on sacred trees.

to have been sacrificed to himself in the ordinary way, as we learn from the weird verses of the *Havamal*, in which the god describes how he acquired his divine power by learning the magic runes:

> 'I know that I hung on the windy tree
> For nine whole nights,
> Wounded with the spear, dedicated to Odin,
> Myself to myself.'

The hanging and spearing of human victims among the Bagobos.

The Bagobos of Mindanao, one of the Philippine Islands, used annually to sacrifice human victims for the good of the crops in a similar way. Early in December, when the constellation Orion appeared at seven o'clock in the evening, the people knew that the time had come to clear their fields for sowing and to sacrifice a slave. The sacrifice was presented to certain powerful spirits as payment for the good year which the people had enjoyed, and to ensure the favour of the spirits for the coming season. The victim was led to a great tree in the forest; there he was tied with his back to the tree and his arms stretched high above his head, in the attitude in which ancient artists portrayed Marsyas hanging on the fatal tree. While he thus hung by the arms, he was slain by a spear thrust through his body at the level of the armpits. Afterwards the body was cut clean through the middle at the waist, and the upper part was apparently allowed to dangle for a little from the tree, while the under part wallowed in blood on the ground. The two portions were finally cast into a shallow trench beside the tree. Before this was done, anybody who wished might cut off a piece of flesh or a lock of hair from the corpse and carry it to the grave of some relation whose body was being consumed by a ghoul. Attracted by the fresh corpse, the ghoul would leave the mouldering old body in peace. These sacrifices have been offered by men now living.

The hanging of Artemis.

In Greece the great goddess Artemis herself appears to have been annually hanged in effigy in her sacred grove of Condylea among the Arcadian hills, and there accordingly she went by the name of the Hanged One. Indeed a trace of a similar rite may perhaps be detected even at Ephesus, the most famous of her sanctuaries, in the legend of a woman who hanged herself and was thereupon dressed by the compassionate goddess in her own divine garb and called by the name of Hecate. Similarly, at

Melite in Phthia, a story was told of a girl named Aspalis who hanged herself, but who appears to have been merely a form of Artemis. For after her death her body could not be found, but an image of her was discovered standing beside the image of Artemis, and the people bestowed on it the title of Hecaerge or Far-shooter, one of the regular epithets of the goddess. Every year the virgins sacrificed a young goat to the image by hanging it, because Aspalis was said to have hanged herself. The sacrifice may have been a substitute for hanging an image or a human representative of Artemis. Again, in Rhodes the fair Helen was worshipped under the title of Helen of the Tree, because the queen of the island had caused her handmaids, disguised as Furies, to string her up to a bough. That the Asiatic Greeks sacrificed animals in this fashion is proved by coins of Ilium, which represent an ox or cow hanging on a tree and stabbed with a knife by a man, who sits among the branches or on the animal's back. At Hierapolis also the victims were hung on trees before they were burnt. With these Greek and Scandinavian parallels before us we can hardly dismiss as wholly improbable the conjecture that in Phrygia a man-god may have hung year by year on the sacred but fatal tree. *The hanging of Helen.* *The hanging of animal victims.*

The tradition that Marsyas was flayed and that his skin was exhibited at Celaenae down to historical times may well reflect a ritual practice of flaying the dead god and hanging his skin upon the pine as a means of effecting his resurrection, and with it the revival of vegetation in spring. Similarly, in ancient Mexico the human victims who personated gods were often flayed and their bloody skins worn by men who appear to have represented the dead deities come to life again. When a Scythian king died, he was buried in a grave along with one of his concubines, his cup-bearer, cook, groom, lacquey, and messenger, who were all killed for the purpose, and a great barrow was heaped up over the grave. A year afterwards fifty of his servants and fifty of his best horses were strangled; and their bodies, having been disembowelled and cleaned out, were stuffed with chaff, sewn up, and set on scaffolds round about the barrow, every dead man bestriding a dead horse, which was bitted and bridled as in life. These strange horsemen were no doubt supposed to mount guard over the king. The setting up *Use of the skin of human victims to effect their resurrection.*

of their stuffed skins might be thought to ensure their ghostly resurrection.

The stuffed skin of the human representative of the Phrygian god may have been used for like purposes.

In like manner, if my conjecture is right, the man who represented the father-god of Phrygia used to be slain and his stuffed skin hung on the sacred pine in order that his spirit might work for the growth of the crops, the multiplication of animals, and the fertility of women. So at Athens an ox, which appears to have embodied the corn-spirit, was killed at an annual sacrifice, and its hide, stuffed with straw and sewn up, was afterwards set on its feet and yoked to a plough as if it were ploughing, apparently in order to represent, or rather to promote, the resurrection of the slain corn-spirit at the end of the threshing. This employment of the skins of divine animals for the purpose of ensuring the revival of the slaughtered divinity might be illustrated by other examples. Perhaps the hide of the bull which was killed to furnish the regenerating bath of blood in the rites of Attis may have been put to a similar use.

iii

Popularity of the worship of Cybele and Attis in the Roman Empire.

The worship of the Great Mother of the Gods and her lover or son was very popular under the Roman Empire. Inscriptions prove that the two received divine honours, separately or conjointly, not only in Italy, and especially at Rome, but also in the provinces, particularly in Africa, Spain, Portugal, France, Germany, and Bulgaria. Their worship survived the establishment of Christianity by Constantine; for Symmachus records the recurrence of the festival of the Great Mother, and in the days of Augustine her effeminate priests still paraded the streets and squares of Carthage with whitened faces, scented hair, and mincing gait, while, like the mendicant friars of the Middle Ages, they begged alms from the passers-by. In Greece, on the other hand, the bloody orgies of the Asiatic goddess and her consort appear to have found little favour. The barbarous and cruel character of the worship, with its frantic excesses, was doubtless repugnant to the good taste and humanity of the Greeks, who seem to have preferred the kindred but gentler rites of Adonis. Yet the same features which shocked and repelled the Greeks may have positively attracted the less refined Romans and barbarians of the West. The ecstatic frenzies, which were mistaken for divine inspiration, the mangling of the body, the theory of a new birth and the remission of sins through the shedding of blood, have all their origin in savagery, and they naturally appealed to peoples in whom the savage instincts were still strong. Their true character was indeed often disguised under a decent veil of allegorical or philosophical interpretation, which probably sufficed to impose upon the rapt and enthusiastic worshippers, reconciling even the more cultivated of them to things which otherwise must have filled them with horror and disgust.

The religion of the Great Mother, with its curious blending of crude savagery with spiritual aspirations, was only one of a multitude of similar Oriental faiths which in the later days of paganism spread over the Roman Empire, and by saturating the European peoples with alien ideals of life gradually undermined the whole fabric of ancient civilization. Greek and Roman society was built on the conception of the subordination of the individual to the community, of the citizen to the state; it set the safety of the commonwealth, as the supreme aim of conduct, above the safety of the individual whether in this world or in a world to come. Trained from infancy in this unselfish ideal, the citizens devoted their lives to the public service and were ready to lay them down for the common good; or if they shrank from the supreme sacrifice, it never occurred to them that they acted otherwise than basely in preferring their personal existence to the interests of their country. All this was changed by the spread of Oriental religions which inculcated the communion of the soul with God and its eternal salvation as the only objects worth living for, objects in comparison with which the prosperity and even the existence of the state sank into insignificance. The inevitable result of this selfish and immoral doctrine was to withdraw the devotee more and more from the public service, to concentrate his thoughts on his own spiritual emotions, and to breed in him a contempt for the present life which he regarded merely as a probation for a better and an eternal. The saint and the recluse, disdainful of earth and rapt in ecstatic contemplation of heaven, became in popular opinion the highest ideal of humanity, displacing the old ideal of the patriot and hero who, forgetful of self, lives and is ready to die for the good of his country. The earthly city seemed poor and

The spread of Oriental faiths over the Roman Empire contributed to undermine the fabric of Greek and Roman civilization by inculcating the salvation of the individual soul as the supreme aim of life.

contemptible to men whose eyes beheld the City of God coming in the clouds of heaven. Thus the centre of gravity, so to say, was shifted from the present to a future life, and however much the other world may have gained, there can be little doubt that this one lost heavily by the change. A general disintegration of the body politic set in. The ties of the state and the family were loosened: the structure of society tended to resolve itself into its individual elements and thereby to relapse into barbarism; for civilization is only possible through the active co-operation of the citizens and their willingness to subordinate their private interests to the common good. Men refused to defend their country and even to continue their kind. In their anxiety to save their own souls and the souls of others, they were content to leave the material world, which they identified with the principle of evil, to perish around them. This obsession lasted for a thousand years. The revival of Roman law, of the Aristotelian philosophy, of ancient art and literature at the close of the Middle Ages, marked the return of Europe to native ideals of life and conduct, to saner, manlier views of the world. The long halt in the march of civilization was over. The tide of Oriental invasion had turned at last. It is ebbing still.

Popularity of the worship of Mithra; its resemblance to Christianity and its rivalry with that religion. Among the gods of eastern origin who in the decline of the ancient world competed against each other for the allegiance of the West was the old Persian deity Mithra. The immense popularity of his worship is attested by the monuments illustrative of it which have been found scattered in profusion all over the Roman Empire. In respect both of doctrines and of rites the cult of Mithra appears to have presented many points of resemblance not only to the religion of the Mother of the Gods but also to Christianity. The similarity struck the Christian doctors themselves and was explained by them as a work of the devil, who sought to seduce the souls of men from the true faith by a false and insidious imitation of it. So to the Spanish conquerors of Mexico and Peru many of the native heathen rites appeared to be diabolical counterfeits of the Christian sacraments. With more probability the modern student of comparative religion traces such resemblances to the similar and independent workings of the mind of man in his sincere, if crude, attempts to fathom the secret of the universe, and to adjust his little life to its awful mysteries. However that may be, there can be no doubt that the Mithraic religion proved a formidable rival to Christianity, combining as it did a solemn ritual with aspirations after moral purity and a hope of immortality. Indeed the issue of the conflict between the two faiths appears for a time to have hung in the balance. An instructive relic of the long struggle is preserved in our festival of Christmas, which the Church seems to have borrowed directly from its heathen rival. In the Julian calendar the twenty-fifth of December was reckoned the winter solstice, and it was regarded as the Nativity of the Sun, because the day begins to lengthen and the power of the sun to increase from that turning-point of the year. The ritual of the nativity, as it appears to have been celebrated in Syria and Egypt, was remarkable. The celebrants retired into certain inner shrines, from which at midnight they issued with a loud cry, 'The Virgin has brought forth! The light is waxing!' The Egyptians even represented the new-born sun by the image of an infant which on his birthday, the winter solstice, they brought forth and exhibited to his worshippers. No doubt the Virgin who thus conceived and bore a son on the twenty-fifth of December was the great Oriental goddess whom the Semites called the Heavenly Virgin or simply the Heavenly Goddess; in Semitic lands she was a form of Astarte. Now Mithra was regularly identified by his worshippers with the Sun, the Unconquered Sun, as they called him; hence his nativity also fell on the twenty-fifth of December. The Gospels say nothing as to the day of Christ's birth, and accordingly the early Church did not celebrate it. In time, however, the Christians of Egypt came to regard the sixth of January as the date of the Nativity, and the custom of commemorating the birth of the Saviour on that day gradually spread until by the fourth century it was universally established in the East. But at the end of the third or the beginning of the fourth century the Western Church, which had never recognized the sixth of January as the day of the Nativity, adopted the twenty-fifth of December as the true date, and in time its decision was accepted also by the Eastern Church. At Antioch the change was not introduced till about the year 375 AD.

What considerations led the ecclesiastical authorities to institute the festival of Christmas? The motives for the innovation are stated with great frankness by a Syrian writer, himself a

The festival of Christmas borrowed by the Church from the religion of Mithra.

Motives for the institution of Christmas.

Christian. 'The reason', he tells us, 'why the fathers transferred the celebration of the sixth of January to the twenty-fifth of December was this. It was a custom of the heathen to celebrate on the same twenty-fifth of December the birthday of the Sun, at which they kindled lights in token of festivity. In these solemnities and festivities the Christians also took part. Accordingly when the doctors of the Church perceived that the Christians had a leaning to this festival, they took counsel and resolved that the true Nativity should be solemnized on that day and the festival of the Epiphany on the sixth of January. Accordingly, along with this custom, the practice has prevailed of kindling fires till the sixth.' The heathen origin of Christmas is plainly hinted at, if not tacitly admitted, by Augustine when he exhorts his Christian brethren not to celebrate that solemn day like the heathen on account of the sun, but on account of him who made the sun. In like manner Leo the Great rebuked the pestilent belief that Christmas was solemnized because of the birth of the new sun, as it was called, and not because of the nativity of Christ.

The Easter celebration of the death and resurrection of Christ appears to have been assimilated to the celebration of the death and resurrection of Attis, which was held at Rome at the same season.

Thus it appears that the Christian Church chose to celebrate the birthday of its Founder on the twenty-fifth of December in order to transfer the devotion of the heathen from the Sun to him who was called the Sun of Righteousness. If that was so, there can be no intrinsic improbability in the conjecture that motives of the same sort may have led the ecclesiastical authorities to assimilate the Easter festival of the death and resurrection of their Lord to the festival of the death and resurrection of another Asiatic god which fell at the same season. Now the Easter rites still observed in Greece, Sicily, and Southern Italy bear in some respects a striking resemblance to the rites of Adonis, and I have suggested that the Church may have consciously adapted the new festival to its heathen predecessor for the sake of winning souls to Christ. But this adaptation probably took place in the Greek-speaking rather than in the Latin-speaking parts of the ancient world; for the worship of Adonis, while it flourished among the Greeks, appears to have made little impression on Rome and the West. Certainly it never formed part of the official Roman religion. The place which it might have taken in the affections of the vulgar was already occupied by the similar but more barbarous worship of Attis and the Great Mother. Now the death and resurrection of Attis were officially celebrated at Rome on the twenty-fourth and twenty-fifth of March, the latter being regarded as the spring equinox, and therefore as the most appropriate day for the revival of a god of vegetation who had been dead or sleeping throughout the winter. But according to an ancient and widespread tradition Christ suffered on the twenty-fifth of March, and accordingly some Christians regularly celebrated the Crucifixion on that day without any regard to the state of the moon. This custom was certainly observed in Phrygia, Cappadocia, and Gaul, and there seem to be grounds for thinking that at one time it was followed also in Rome. Thus the tradition which placed the death of Christ on the twenty-fifth of March was ancient and deeply rooted. It is all the more remarkable because astronomical considerations prove that it can have had no historical foundation. The inference appears to be inevitable that the passion of Christ must have been arbitrarily referred to that date in order to harmonize with an older festival of the spring equinox. But the resurrection of Attis, who combined in himself the characters of the divine Father and the divine Son, was officially celebrated at Rome on the same day. When we remember that the festival of St George in April has replaced the ancient pagan festival of the Parilia; that the festival of St John the Baptist in June has succeeded to a heathen Midsummer festival of water; that the festival of the Assumption of the Virgin in August has ousted the festival of Diana; that the feast of All Souls in November is a continuation of an old heathen feast of the dead; and that the Nativity of Christ himself was assigned to the winter solstice in December because that day was deemed the Nativity of the Sun; we can hardly be thought rash or unreasonable in conjecturing that the other cardinal festival of the Christian Church—the solemnization of Easter—may have been in like manner, and from like motives of edification, adapted to a similar celebration of the Phrygian god Attis at the vernal equinox.

Heathen festivals displaced by Christian.

In point of fact it appears from the testimony of an anonymous Christian, who wrote in the fourth century of our era, that Christians and pagans alike were struck by the remarkable coincidence between the death and resurrection of their respective deities, and that the coincidence formed a theme of bitter

Different theories by which pagans and Christians explained the coincidence.

controversy between the adherents of the rival religions, the pagans contending that the resurrection of Christ was a spurious imitation of the resurrection of Attis, and the Christians asserting with equal warmth that the resurrection of Attis was a diabolical counterfeit of the resurrection of Christ. In these unseemly bickerings the heathen took what to a superficial observer might seem strong ground by arguing that their god was the older and therefore presumably the original, not the counterfeit, since as a general rule an original is older than its copy. This feeble argument the Christians easily rebutted. They admitted, indeed, that in point of time Christ was the junior deity, but they triumphantly demonstrated his real seniority by falling back on the subtlety of Satan, who on so important an occasion had surpassed himself by inverting the usual order of nature.

Compromise of Christianity with paganism.

Taken altogether, the coincidences of the Christian with the heathen festivals are too close and too numerous to be accidental. They mark the compromise which the Church in the hour of its triumph was compelled to make with its vanquished yet still dangerous rivals. The inflexible Protestantism of the primitive missionaries, with their fiery denunciations of heathendom, had been exchanged for the supple policy, the easy tolerance, the comprehensive charity of shrewd ecclesiastics, who clearly perceived that if Christianity was to conquer the world it could do so only by relaxing the too rigid principles of its Founder, by widening a little the narrow gate which leads to salvation. In

Parallel with Buddhism.

this respect an instructive parallel might be drawn between the history of Christianity and the history of Buddhism. Both systems were in their origin essentially ethical reforms born of the generous ardour, the lofty aspirations, the tender compassion of their noble Founders, two of those beautiful spirits who appear at rare intervals on earth like beings come from a better world to support and guide our weak and erring nature. Both preached moral virtue as the means of accomplishing what they regarded as the supreme object of life, the eternal salvation of the individual soul, though by a curious antithesis the one sought that salvation in a blissful eternity, the other in a final release from suffering, in annihilation. But the austere ideals of sanctity which they inculcated were too deeply opposed not only to the frailties but to the natural instincts of humanity ever

to be carried out in practice by more than a small number of
disciples, who consistently renounced the ties of the family and
the state in order to work out their own salvation in the still
seclusion of the cloister. If such faiths were to be nominally
accepted by whole nations or even by the world, it was essential
that they should first be modified or transformed so as to accord
in some measure with the prejudices, the passions, the superstitions of the vulgar. This process of accommodation was carried
out in after ages by followers who, made of less ethereal stuff
than their masters, were for that reason the better fitted to
mediate between them and the common herd. Thus as time
went on, the two religions, in exact proportion to their growing
popularity, absorbed more and more of those baser elements
which they had been instituted for the very purpose of suppressing. Such spiritual decadences are inevitable. The world
cannot live at the level of its great men. Yet it would be unfair
to the generality of our kind to ascribe wholly to their intellectual and moral weakness the gradual divergence of Buddhism
and Christianity from their primitive patterns. For it should
never be forgotten that by their glorification of poverty and
celibacy both these religions struck straight at the root not
merely of civil society but of human existence. The blow was
parried by the wisdom or the folly of the vast majority of
mankind, who refused to purchase a chance of saving their souls
with the certainty of extinguishing the species.

Osiris the Egyptian counter part of Adonis and Attis.

IN ancient Egypt the god whose death and resurrection were annually celebrated with alternate sorrow and joy was Osiris, the most popular of all Egyptian deities; and there are good grounds for classing him in one of his aspects with Adonis and Attis as a personification of the great yearly vicissitudes of nature, especially of the corn. But the immense vogue which he enjoyed for many ages induced his devoted worshippers to heap upon him the attributes and powers of many other gods; so that it is not always easy to strip him, so to say, of his borrowed plumes and to restore them to their proper owners.

The myth of Osiris.

The story of Osiris is told in a connected form only by Plutarch,* whose narrative has been confirmed and to some extent amplified in modern times by the evidence of the monuments. The tragic tale runs thus:

Osiris a son of the earth-god and the sky-goddess.

Osiris was the offspring of an intrigue between the earth-god Seb (Keb or Geb, as the name is sometimes transliterated) and the sky-goddess Nut. The Greeks identified his parents with their own deities Cronus and Rhea. When the sun-god Ra perceived that his wife Nut had been unfaithful to him, he declared with a curse that she should be delivered of the child in no month and no year. But the goddess had another lover, the god Thoth or Hermes, as the Greeks called him, and he playing at draughts with the moon won from her a seventy-second part of every day, and having compounded five whole days out of these parts he added them to the Egyptian year of three hundred and sixty days. This was the mythical origin of the five supplementary days which the Egyptians annually inserted at the end of every year in order to establish a harmony between lunar and solar time. On these five days, regarded as outside the year of twelve months, the curse of the sun-god did not rest, and accordingly Osiris was born on the first of them. At his nativity a voice rang out proclaiming that the Lord of All had come into the world. Some say that a certain Pamyles heard a voice from the temple at Thebes bidding him announce with a shout that a great king, the beneficent Osiris, was born. But Osiris was not the only child of his mother. On the second of the supplementary days she gave birth to the elder Horus, on the third to the god Set, whom the Greeks called Typhon, on the fourth to the goddess Isis, and on the fifth to the goddess Nephthys. Afterwards Set married his sister Nephthys, and Osiris married his sister Isis.

Reigning as a king on earth, Osiris reclaimed the Egyptians from savagery, gave them laws, and taught them to worship the gods. Before his time the Egyptians had been cannibals. But Isis, the sister and wife of Osiris, discovered wheat and barley growing wild, and Osiris introduced the cultivation of these grains amongst his people, who forthwith abandoned cannibalism and took kindly to a corn diet. Moreover, Osiris is said to have been the first to gather fruit from trees, to train the vine to poles, and to tread the grapes. Eager to communicate these beneficent discoveries to all mankind, he committed the whole government of Egypt to his wife Isis, and travelled over the world, diffusing the blessings of civilization and agriculture wherever he went. In countries where a harsh climate or niggardly soil forbade the cultivation of the vine, he taught the inhabitants to console themselves for the want of wine by brewing beer from barley. Loaded with the wealth that had been showered upon him by grateful nations, he returned to Egypt, and on account of the benefits he had conferred on mankind he was unanimously hailed and worshipped as a deity. But his brother Set (whom the Greeks called Typhon) with seventy-two others plotted against him. Having taken the measure of his good brother's body by stealth, the bad brother Typhon fashioned and highly decorated a coffer of the same size, and once when they were all drinking and making merry he brought in the coffer and jestingly promised to give it to the one whom it should fit exactly. Well, they all tried one after the other, but it fitted none of them. Last of all Osiris stepped into it and lay down. On that the conspirators ran and slammed the lid down on him, nailed it fast, soldered it with molten lead, and flung the coffer into the Nile. This happened on the seventeenth day of the month Athyr, when the sun is in the sign of the Scorpion, and in the eight-and-twentieth year of the

Osiris intro-
duces the cul-
tivation of
corn and of
the vine.

His violent
death.

reign or the life of Osiris. When Isis heard of it she sheared off a lock of her hair, put on mourning attire, and wandered disconsolately up and down, seeking the body.

By the advice of the god of wisdom she took refuge in the papyrus swamps of the Delta. Seven scorpions accompanied her in her flight. One evening when she was weary she came to the house of a woman, who, alarmed at the sight of the scorpions, shut the door in her face. Then one of the scorpions crept under the door and stung the child of the woman that he died. But when Isis heard the mother's lamentation, her heart was touched, and she laid her hands on the child and uttered her powerful spells; so the poison was driven out of the child and he lived. Afterwards Isis herself gave birth to a son in the swamps. She had conceived him while she fluttered in the form of a hawk over the corpse of her dead husband. The infant was the younger Horus, who in his youth bore the name of Harpocrates, that is, the child Horus. Him Buto, the goddess of the north, hid from the wrath of his wicked uncle Set. Yet she could not guard him from all mishap; for one day when Isis came to her little son's hiding-place she found him stretched lifeless and rigid on the ground: a scorpion had stung him. Then Isis prayed to the sun-god Ra for help. The god hearkened to her and staid his bark in the sky, and sent down Thoth to teach her the spell by which she might restore her son to life. She uttered the words of power, and straightway the poison flowed from the body of Horus, air passed into him, and he lived. Then Thoth ascended up into the sky and took his place once more in the bark of the sun, and the bright pomp passed onward jubilant.

Meantime the coffer containing the body of Osiris had floated down the river and away out to sea, till at last it drifted ashore at Byblus, on the coast of Syria. Here a fine *erica*-tree shot up suddenly and enclosed the chest in its trunk. The king of the country, admiring the growth of the tree, had it cut down and made into a pillar of his house; but he did not know that the coffer with the dead Osiris was in it. Word of this came to Isis and she journeyed to Byblus, and sat down by the well, in humble guise, her face wet with tears. To none would she speak till the king's handmaidens came, and them she greeted kindly, and braided their hair, and breathed on them from her own

divine body a wondrous perfume. But when the queen beheld
the braids of her handmaidens' hair and smelt the sweet smell
that emanated from them, she sent for the stranger woman and
took her into her house and made her the nurse of her child.
But Isis gave the babe her finger instead of her breast to suck,
and at night she began to burn all that was mortal of him away,
while she herself in the likeness of a swallow fluttered round
the pillar that contained her dead brother, twittering mournfully. But the queen spied what she was doing and shrieked out
when she saw her child in flames, and thereby she hindered him
from becoming immortal. Then the goddess revealed herself
and begged for the pillar of the roof, and they gave it her, and
she cut the coffer out of it, and fell upon it and embraced it and
lamented so loud that the younger of the king's children died
of fright on the spot. But the trunk of the tree she wrapped in
fine linen, and poured ointment on it, and gave it to the king
and queen, and the wood stands in a temple of Isis and is
worshipped by the people of Byblus to this day. And Isis put
the coffer in a boat and took the eldest of the king's children
with her and sailed away. As soon as they were alone, she
opened the chest, and laying her face on the face of her brother
she kissed him and wept. But the child came behind her softly
and saw what she was about, and she turned and looked at him
in anger, and the child could not bear her look and died; but
some say that it was not so, but that he fell into the sea and was
drowned. It is he whom the Egyptians sing of at their banquets
under the name of Maneros. But Isis put the coffer by and went
to see her son Horus at the city of Buto, and Typhon found the
coffer as he was hunting a boar one night by the light of a full
moon. And he knew the body, and rent it into fourteen pieces,
and scattered them abroad. But Isis sailed up and down the
marshes in a shallop made of papyrus, looking for the pieces;
and that is why when people sail in shallops made of papyrus,
the crocodiles do not hurt them, for they fear or respect the
goddess. And that is the reason, too, why there are many graves
of Osiris in Egypt, for she buried each limb as she found it. But
others will have it that she buried an image of him in every city,
pretending it was his body, in order that Osiris might be
worshipped in many places, and that if Typhon searched for the
real grave he might not be able to find it. However, the genital

The body of
Osiris dis-
membered
by Typhon,
and the
pieces re-
covered by
Isis.

member of Osiris had been eaten by the fishes, so Isis made an image of it instead, and the image is used by the Egyptians at their festivals to this day. 'Isis', writes the historian Diodorus Siculus, 'recovered all the parts of the body except the genitals; and because she wished that her husband's grave should be unknown and honoured by all who dwell in the land of Egypt, she resorted to the following device. She moulded human images out of wax and spices, corresponding to the stature of Osiris, round each one of the parts of his body. Then she called in the priests according to their families and took an oath of them all that they would reveal to no man the trust she was about to repose in them. So to each of them privately she said that to them alone she entrusted the burial of the body, and reminding them of the benefits they had received she exhorted them to bury the body in their own land and to honour Osiris as a god. She also besought them to dedicate one of the animals of their country, whichever they chose, and to honour it in life as they had formerly honoured Osiris, and when it died to grant it obsequies like his. And because she would encourage the priests in their own interest to bestow the aforesaid honours, she gave them a third part of the land to be used by them in the service and worship of the gods. Accordingly it is said that the priests, mindful of the benefits of Osiris, desirous of gratifying the queen, and moved by the prospect of gain, carried out all the injunctions of Isis. Wherefore to this day each of the priests imagines that Osiris is buried in his country, and they honour the beasts that were consecrated in the beginning, and when the animals die the priests renew at their burial the mourning for Osiris. But the sacred bulls, the one called Apis and the other Mnevis, were dedicated to Osiris, and it was ordained that they should be worshipped as gods in common by all the Egyptians; since these animals above all others had helped the discoverers of corn in sowing the seed and procuring the universal benefits of agriculture.'*

Diodorus Siculus on the burial of Osiris.

Such is the myth or legend of Osiris, as told by Greek writers and eked out by more or less fragmentary notices or allusions in native Egyptian literature. A long inscription in the temple at Denderah has preserved a list of the god's graves, and other texts mention the parts of his body which were treasured as holy relics in each of the sanctuaries. Thus his heart was at

The various members of Osiris treasured as relics in various parts of Egypt.

Athribis, his backbone at Busiris, his neck at Letopolis, and his head at Memphis. As often happens in such cases, some of his divine limbs were miraculously multiplied. His head, for example, was at Abydos as well as at Memphis, and his legs, which were remarkably numerous, would have sufficed for several ordinary mortals. In this respect, however, Osiris was nothing to St Denys, of whom no less than seven heads, all equally genuine, are extant.

According to native Egyptian accounts, which supplement that of Plutarch, when Isis had found the corpse of her husband Osiris, she and her sister Nephthys sat down beside it and uttered a lament which in after ages became the type of all Egyptian lamentations for the dead. 'Come to thy house,' they wailed, 'Come to thy house. O god On! come to thy house, thou who hast no foes. O fair youth, come to thy house, that thou mayest see me. I am thy sister, whom thou lovest; thou shalt not part from me. O fair boy, come to thy house. . . . I see thee not, yet doth my heart yearn after thee and mine eyes desire thee. Come to her who loves thee, who loves thee, Unnefer, thou blessed one! Come to thy sister, come to thy wife, to thy wife, thou whose heart stands still. Come to thy housewife. I am thy sister by the same mother, thou shalt not be far from me. Gods and men have turned their faces towards thee and weep for thee together . . . I call after thee and weep, so that my cry is heard to heaven, but thou hearest not my voice; yet am I thy sister, whom thou didst love on earth; thou didst love none but me, my brother! my brother!' This lament for the fair youth cut off in his prime reminds us of the laments for Adonis.

Osiris mourned by Isis and Nephthys.

The lamentations of the two sad sisters were not in vain. In pity for her sorrow the sun-god Ra sent down from heaven the jackal-headed god Anubis, who, with the aid of Isis and Nephthys, of Thoth and Horus, pieced together the broken body of the murdered god, swathed it in linen bandages, and observed all the other rites which the Egyptians were wont to perform over the bodies of the departed. Then Isis fanned the cold clay with her wings: Osiris revived, and thenceforth reigned as king over the dead in the other world. There he bore the titles of Lord of the Underworld, Lord of Eternity, Ruler of the Dead. There, too, in the great Hall of the Two Truths, assisted by forty-two assessors, one from each of the principal

Being brought to life again, Osiris reigns as king and judge of the dead in the other world.

districts of Egypt, he presided as judge at the trial of the souls of the departed, who made their solemn confession before him, and, their heart having been weighed in the balance of justice, received the reward of virtue in a life eternal or the appropriate punishment of their sins.

In the resurrection of Osiris the Egyptians saw a pledge of their own immortality.

In the resurrection of Osiris the Egyptians saw the pledge of a life everlasting for themselves beyond the grave. They believed that every man would live eternally in the other world if only his surviving friends did for his body what the gods had done for the body of Osiris. Hence the ceremonies observed by the Egyptians over the human dead were an exact copy of those which Anubis, Horus, and the rest had performed over the dead god. 'At every burial there was enacted a representation of the divine mystery which had been performed of old over Osiris, when his son, his sisters, his friends were gathered round his mangled remains and succeeded by their spells and manipulations in converting his broken body into the first mummy, which they afterwards reanimated and furnished with the means of entering on a new individual life beyond the grave. The mummy of the deceased was Osiris; the professional female mourners were his two sisters Isis and Nephthys; Anubis, Horus, all the gods of the Osirian legend gathered about the corpse.'

Every dead Egyptian identified with Osiris.

Thus every dead Egyptian was identified with Osiris and bore his name. From the Middle Kingdom onwards it was the regular practice to address the deceased as 'Osiris So-and-So', as if he were the god himself, and to add the standing epithet 'true of speech', because true speech was characteristic of Osiris. The thousands of inscribed and pictured tombs that have been opened in the valley of the Nile prove that the mystery of the resurrection was performed for the benefit of every dead Egyptian; as Osiris died and rose again from the dead, so all men hoped to arise like him from death to life eternal.

Combat between Set and Horus, the brother and the son of Osiris, for the crown of Egypt.

If we may trust Egyptian legend, the trials and contests of the royal house did not cease with the restoration of Osiris to life and his elevation to the rank of presiding deity in the world of the dead. When Horus the younger, the son of Osiris and Isis, was grown to man's estate, the ghost of his royal and murdered father appeared to him and urged him, like another Hamlet, to avenge the foul unnatural murder upon his wicked uncle. Thus encouraged, the youth attacked the miscreant. The combat was terrific and lasted many days. Horus lost an eye in the conflict and Set suffered a still more serious mutilation. At last Thoth parted the combatants and healed their wounds; the eye of Horus he restored by spitting on it. According to one account the great battle was fought on the twenty-sixth day of the month of Thoth. Foiled in open war, the artful uncle now took the law of his virtuous nephew. He brought a suit of bastardy against Horus, hoping thus to rob him of his inheritance and to get possession of it himself. The case was tried before the supreme court of the gods in the great hall at Heliopolis. Thoth, the god of wisdom, pleaded the cause of Osiris, and the august judges decided that 'the word of Osiris was true'. Moreover, they pronounced Horus to be the true-begotten son of his father. So that prince assumed the crown and mounted the throne of the lamented Osiris.

These legends of a contest for the throne of Egypt may perhaps contain a reminiscence of real dynastical struggles which attended an attempt to change the right of succession from the female to the male line. For under a rule of female kinship the heir to the throne is either the late king's brother, or the son of the late king's sister, while under a rule of male kinship the heir to the throne is the late king's son. In the legend of Osiris the rival heirs are Set and Horus, Set being the late king's brother, and Horus the late king's son; though Horus indeed united both claims to the crown, being the son of the king's sister as well as of the king. A similar attempt to shift the line of succession seems to have given rise to similar contests at Rome.

The legend of their contest may be a reminiscence of dynastic struggles.

The legend recorded by Plutarch which associated the dead Osiris with Byblus in Phoenicia is doubtless late and probably untrustworthy. It may have been suggested by the resemblance which the worship of the Egyptian Osiris bore to the worship of the Phoenician Adonis in that city. But it is possible that the story has no deeper foundation than a verbal misunderstanding. For Byblus is not only the name of a city, it is the Greek word for papyrus; and as Isis is said after the death of Osiris to have taken refuge in the papyrus swamps of the Delta, where she gave birth to and reared her son Horus, a Greek writer may

The association of Osiris with Byblus.

perhaps have confused the plant with the city of the same name. However that may have been, the association of Osiris with Adonis at Byblus gave rise to a curious tale. It is said that every year the people beyond the rivers of Ethiopia used to write a letter to the women of Byblus informing them that the lost and lamented Adonis was found. This letter they enclosed in an earthen pot, which they sealed and sent floating down the river to the sea. The waves carried the pot to Byblus, where every year it arrived at the time when the Syrian women were weeping for their dead Lord. The pot was taken up from the water and opened: the letter was read; and the weeping women dried their tears, because the lost Adonis was found.

CHAPTER 12

FEASTS OF ALL SOULS

BUT we have still to consider the Osirian festivals of the official calendar, so far as these are described by Greek writers or recorded on the monuments.

Herodotus tells us that the grave of Osiris was at Sais in Lower Egypt, and that there was a lake there upon which the sufferings of the god were displayed as a mystery by night. This commemoration of the divine passion was held once a year: the people mourned and beat their breasts at it to testify their sorrow for the death of the god; and an image of a cow, made of gilt wood with a golden sun between its horns, was carried out of the chamber in which it stood the rest of the year. The cow no doubt represented Isis herself, for cows were sacred to her, and she was regularly depicted with the horns of a cow on her head, or even as a woman with the head of a cow. It is probable that the carrying out of her cow-shaped image symbolized the goddess searching for the dead body of Osiris; for this was the native Egyptian interpretation of a similar ceremony observed in Plutarch's time about the winter solstice, when the gilt cow was carried seven times round the temple. A great feature of the festival was the nocturnal illumination. People fastened rows of oil-lamps to the outside of their houses, and the lamps burned all night long. The custom was not confined to Sais, but was observed throughout the whole of Egypt.

This universal illumination of the houses on one night of the year suggests that the festival may have been a commemoration not merely of the dead Osiris but of the dead in general, in other words, that it may have been a night of All Souls. For it is a widespread belief that the souls of the dead revisit their old homes on one night of the year; and on that solemn occasion people prepare for the reception of the ghosts by laying out food for them to eat, and lighting lamps to guide them on their dark road from and to the grave. The following instances will illustrate the custom.

The sufferings of Osiris displayed as a mystery at Sais.

The illumination of houses throughout Egypt on the night of the festival suggests that the rite was a Feast of All Souls.

The Esquimaux of St Michael and the lower Yukon River in
Alaska hold a festival of the dead every year at the end of
November or the beginning of December, as well as a greater
festival at intervals of several years. At these seasons, food,
drink, and clothes are provided for the returning ghosts in the
kashim or clubhouse of the village, which is illuminated with oil

The lighting
of the lamps
for the dead.

lamps. Every man or woman who wishes to honour a dead
friend sets up a lamp on a stand in front of the place which the
deceased used to occupy in the clubhouse. These lamps, filled
with seal oil, are kept burning day and night till the festival is
over. They are believed to light the shades on their return to
their old home and back again to the land of the dead. If any
one fails to put up a lamp in the clubhouse and to keep it
burning, the shade whom he or she desires to honour could not
find its way to the place and so would miss the feast. On the
eve of the festival the nearest male relation goes to the grave
and summons the ghost by planting there a small model of a
seal spear or of a wooden dish, according as the deceased was a
man or a woman. The badges of the dead are marked on these
implements. When all is ready, the ghosts gather in the fire-pit
under the clubhouse, and ascending through the floor at the
proper moment take possession of the bodies of their namesakes, to whom the offerings of food, drink, and clothing are
made for the benefit of the dead. Thus each shade obtains the
supplies he needs in the other world. After the songs of
invitation to the dead have been sung, the givers of the feast
take a small portion of food from every dish and cast it down
as an offering to the shades; then each pours a little water on
the floor so that it runs through the cracks. In this way they
believe that the spiritual essence of all the food and water is
conveyed to the souls. The remainder of the food is afterwards
distributed among the people present, who eat of it heartily.
Then with songs and dances the feast comes to an end, and the
ghosts are dismissed to their own place.

The Indians of California used to observe annual ceremonies
of mourning for the dead, at some of which the souls of the
departed were represented by living persons. Ten or more men
would prepare themselves to play the part of the ghosts by
fasting for several days, especially by abstaining from flesh.
Disguised with paint and soot, adorned with feathers and

grasses, they danced and sang in the village or rushed about in the forest by night with burning torches in their hands. After a time they presented themselves to the relations of the deceased, who looked upon these maskers as in very truth their departed friends and received them accordingly with an outburst of lamentation, the old women scratching their own faces and smiting their breasts with stones in token of mourning. These masquerades were generally held in February. During their continuance a strict fast was observed in the village.

The Miztecs of Mexico believed that the souls of the dead came back in the twelfth month of every year, which corresponded to our November. On this day of All Souls the houses were decked out to welcome the spirits. Jars of food and drink were set on a table in the principal room, and the family went forth with torches to meet the ghosts and invite them to enter. Then returning themselves to the house they knelt around the table, and with eyes bent on the ground prayed the souls to accept of the offerings and to procure the blessings of the gods upon the family. Thus they remained on bended knees and with downcast eyes till the morning, not daring to look at the table lest they should offend the spirits by spying on them at their meal. With the first beams of the sun they rose, glad at heart. The jars of food which had been presented to the dead were given to the poor or deposited in a secret place.

Annual festival of the dead among the Miztecs of Mexico.

Again, the natives of Sumba,* an East Indian island, celebrate a New Year's festival, which is at the same time a festival of the dead. The graves are in the middle of the village, and at a given moment all the people repair to them and raise a loud weeping and wailing. Then after indulging for a short time in the national pastimes they disperse to their houses, and every family calls upon its dead to come back. The ghosts are believed to hear and accept the invitation. Accordingly betel and areca nuts are set out for them. Victims, too, are sacrificed in front of every house, and their hearts and livers are offered with rice to the dead. After a decent interval these portions are distributed amongst the living, who consume them and banquet gaily on flesh and rice, a rare event in their frugal lives. Then they play, dance, and sing to their heart's content, and the festival which began so lugubriously ends by being the merriest of the year. A little before daybreak the invisible guests take their departure.

Annual festival of the dead in Sumba.

All the people turn out of their houses to escort them a little way. Holding in one hand the half of a coco-nut, which contains a small packet of provisions for the dead, and in the other hand a piece of smouldering wood, they march in procession, singing a drawling song to the accompaniment of a gong and waving the lighted brands in time to the music. So they move through the darkness till with the last words of the song they throw away the coco-nuts and the brands in the direction of the spirit-land, leaving the ghosts to wend their way thither, while they themselves return to the village.

Festival of the dead among the Sea Dyaks of Borneo. The Sea Dyaks of Borneo celebrate a great festival in honour of the dead at irregular intervals, it may be one or more years after the death of a particular person. All who have died since the last feast was held, and have not yet been honoured by such a celebration, are remembered at this time; hence the number of persons commemorated may be great, especially if many years have elapsed since the last commemoration service. On the eve of the feast the women take bamboo splints and fashion out of them little models of various useful articles, and these models are hung over the graves for the use of the dead in the other world. The dead arrive in a boat from the other world; for living Dyaks generally travel by river, from which it necessarily follows that Dyak ghosts do so likewise. The ship in which the ghostly visitors voyage to the land of the living is not much to look at, being in appearance nothing but a tiny boat made out of a bamboo which has been used to cook rice. Even this is not set floating on the river but is simply thrown away under the house. Yet through the incantations uttered by the professional wailing-woman the bark is wafted away to the spirit world and is there converted into a large war-canoe. Gladly the ghosts embark and sail away as soon as the final summons comes. It always comes in the evening, for it is then that the wailer begins to croon her mournful ditties; but the way is so long that the spirits do not arrive in the house till the day is breaking. To refresh them after their weary journey a bamboo full of rice-spirit awaits them; and this they partake of by deputy, for a brave old man, who does not fear the face of ghosts, quaffs the beverage in their stead amid the joyful shouts of the spectators. On the morning after the feast the living pay the last offices of respect to the dead. Monuments made of ironwood, the little bamboo articles, and food of all kinds are set upon the graves. In consideration of these gifts the ghosts now relinquish all claims on their surviving relatives, and henceforth earn their own living by the sweat of their brow. Before they take their final departure they come to eat and drink in the house for the last time.

Thus the Dyak festival of the dead is not an annual welcome accorded to all the souls of ancestors; it is a propitiatory ceremony designed to secure once for all the eternal welfare of the recently departed, or at least to prevent their ghosts from returning to infest and importune the living. The same is perhaps the intention of the 'soul departure' (*Kathi Kasham*) festival which the Tangkul Nagas of Manipur, in Assam, celebrate every year about the end of January. At this great feast the dead are represented by living men, chosen on the ground of their likeness to the departed, who are decked with ornaments and treated as if they were in truth the deceased persons come to life again. In that character they dance together in the large open space of the village, they are fed by the female relations, and they go from house to house, receiving presents of cloth. The festival lasts ten days, but the great day is the ninth. Huge torches of pinewood are made ready to be used that evening when darkness has fallen. The time of departure of the dead is at hand. Their living representatives are treated to a last meal in the houses, and they distribute farewell presents to the sorrowing kinsfolk, who have come to bid them good-bye. When the sun has set, a procession is formed. At the head of it march men holding aloft the flaring, sputtering torches. Then follow the elders armed and in martial array, and behind them stalk the representatives of the dead, with the relations of the departed crowding and trooping about them. Slowly and mournfully the sad procession moves, with loud lamentations, through the darkness to a spot at the north end of the village which is overshadowed by a great tree. The light of the torches is to guide the souls of the dead to their place of rest; the warlike array of the elders is to guard them from the perils and dangers of the way. At the village boundary the procession stops and the torch-bearers throw down their torches. At the same moment the spirits of the dead are believed to pass into the dying flambeaux and in that guise to depart to the far country.

Annual festival of the dead among the Nagas of Manipur.

There is therefore no further need for their living representatives, who are accordingly stripped of all their finery on the spot. When the people return home, each family is careful to light a pine torch and set it burning on a stone in the house just inside the front door; this they do as a precaution to prevent their own souls from following the spirits of the dead to the other world. The expense of thus despatching the dead to their long home is very great; when the head of a family dies, debts may be incurred and rice-fields and houses sold to defray the cost of carriage. Thus the living impoverish themselves in order to enrich the dead.

Annual festival of the dead in Cambodia.

The great festival of the dead in Cambodia takes place on the last day of the month Phatrabot (September–October), but ever since the moon began to wane everybody has been busy preparing for it. In every house cakes and sweetmeats are set out, candles burn, incense sticks smoke, and the whole is offered to the ancestral shades with an invocation which is thrice repeated: 'O all you our ancestors who are departed, deign to come and eat what we have prepared for you, and to bless your posterity and make it happy.' Fifteen days afterwards many little boats are made of bark and filled with rice, cakes, small coins, smoking incense sticks, and lighted candles. At evening these are set floating on the river, and the souls of the dead embark in them to return to their own place. The living now bid them farewell. 'Go to the lands,' they say, 'go to the fields you inhabit, to the mountains, under the stones which are your abodes. Go away! return! In due time your sons and your grandsons will think of you. Then you will return, you will return, you will return.' The river is now covered with twinkling points of fire. But the current soon bears them away, and as they vanish one by one in the darkness the souls depart with them to the far country.

Feast of All Souls in Brittany and other parts of France.

Similar beliefs as to the annual return of the dead survive to this day in many parts of Europe and find expression in similar customs. The day of the dead or of All Souls, as we call it, is commonly the second of November. Thus in Lower Brittany the souls of the departed come to visit the living on the eve of that day. After vespers are over, the priests and choir walk in procession, 'the procession of the charnel-house', chanting a weird dirge in the Breton tongue. Then the people go home, gather round the fire, and talk of the departed. The housewife covers the kitchen table with a white cloth, sets out cider, curds, and hot pancakes on it, and retires with the family to rest. The fire on the hearth is kept up by a huge log known as 'the log of the dead' (*kef ann Anaon*). Soon doleful voices outside in the darkness break the stillness of night. It is the 'singers of death' who go about the streets waking the sleepers by a wild and melancholy song, in which they remind the living in their comfortable beds to pray for the poor souls in pain. All that night the dead warm themselves at the hearth and feast on the viands prepared for them. Sometimes the awe-struck listeners hear the stools creaking in the kitchen, or the dead leaves outside rustling under the ghostly footsteps. In the Vosges Mountains on All Souls' Eve the solemn sound of the church bells invites good Christians to pray for the repose of the dead. While the bells are ringing, it is customary in some families to uncover the beds and open the windows, doubtless in order to let the poor souls enter and rest. No one that evening would dare to remain deaf to the appeal of the bells. The prayers are prolonged to a late hour of the night. When the last *De profundis* has been uttered, the head of the family gently covers up the beds, sprinkles them with holy water, and shuts the windows. In some villages fire is kept up on the hearth and a basket of nuts is placed beside it for the use of the ghosts.

In Bruges, Dinant, and other towns of Belgium holy candles burn all night in the houses on the Eve of All Souls, and the bells toll till midnight, or even till morning. People, too, often set lighted candles on the graves. At Scherpenheuvel the houses are illuminated, and the people walk in procession carrying lighted candles in their hands. A very common custom in Belgium is to eat 'soul-cakes' or 'soul-bread' on the eve or the day of All Souls. The eating of them is believed to benefit the dead in some way. Perhaps originally, as among the Esquimaux of Alaska to this day, the ghosts were thought to enter into the bodies of their relatives and so to share the victuals which the survivors consumed. Similarly at festivals in honour of the dead in Northern India it is customary to feed Brahmans, and the food which these holy men partake of is believed to pass to the deceased and to refresh their languid spirits. The same idea of eating and drinking by proxy may perhaps partly explain many

Feast of All Souls in Belgium.

other funeral feasts. Be that as it may, at Dixmude and elsewhere in Belgium they say that you deliver a soul from Purgatory for every cake you eat. At Antwerp they give a local colour to the soul-cakes by baking them with plenty of saffron, the deep yellow tinge being suggestive of the flames of Purgatory. People in Antwerp at the same season are careful not to slam doors or windows for fear of hurting the ghosts.

Soul-cakes
and All
Souls' Day
in Southern
Germany.

The custom of baking soul-cakes, sometimes called simply 'souls', on All Souls' Day is widespread in Southern Germany and Austria; everywhere, we may assume, the cakes were originally intended for the benefit of the hungry dead, though they are often eaten by the living. In the Upper Palatinate people throw food into the fire on All Souls' Day for the poor souls, set lights on the table for them, and pray on bended knees for their repose. On the graves, too, lights are kindled, vessels of holy water placed, and food deposited for the refreshment of the souls. All over the Upper Palatinate on All Souls' Day it is also customary to bake special cakes of fine bread and distribute them to the poor, who eat them perhaps as the deputies of the dead.

Feast of All
Souls in the
Tyrol.

In the Tyrol the beliefs and customs are similar. There, too, 'soul-lights', that is, lamps filled with lard or butter are lighted and placed on the hearth on All Souls' Eve in order that poor souls, escaped from the fires of Purgatory, may smear the melted grease on their burns and so alleviate their pangs. Some people also leave milk and dough-nuts for them on the table all night. The graves also are illuminated with wax candles and decked with such a profusion of flowers that you might think it was springtime. In the Italian Tyrol it is customary to give bread or money to the poor on All Souls' Day; in the Val di Ledro children threaten to dirty the doors of houses if they do not get the usual dole. Some rich people treat the poor to bean-soup on that day. Others put pitchers full of water in the kitchen on All Souls' night that the poor souls may slake their thirst. In Baden it is still customary to deck the graves with flowers and lights on All Saints' Day and All Souls' Day. The lights are sometimes kindled in hollow turnips, on the sides of which inscriptions are carved and shine out in the darkness. If any child steals a turnip-lantern or anything else from a grave, the indignant ghost who has been robbed appears to the thief

Feast of All
Souls in
Baden.

the same night and reclaims his stolen property. A relic of the old custom of feeding the dead survives in the practice of giving soul-cakes to godchildren.

On All Saints' Day, the first of November, shops and streets in the Abruzzi are filled with candles, which people buy in order to kindle them in the evening on the graves of their relations. For all the dead come to visit their homes that night, the Eve of All Souls, and they need lights to show them the way. For their use, too, lights are kept burning in the houses all night. Before people go to sleep they place on the table a lighted lamp or candle and a frugal meal of bread and water. The dead issue from their graves and stalk in procession through every street of the village. You can see them if you stand at a cross-road with your chin resting on a forked stick. First pass the souls of the good, and then the souls of the murdered and the damned. Once, they say, a man was thus peeping at the ghastly procession. The good souls told him he had better go home. He did not, and when he saw the tail of the procession he died of fright. *Feast of All Souls in the Abruzzi.*

In our own country the old belief in the annual return of the dead long lingered in the custom of baking 'soul-cakes' and eating them or distributing them to the poor on All Souls' Day. Peasant girls used to go from farmhouse to farmhouse on that day, singing, *Soul-cakes on All-Souls Day in England.*

> 'Soul, soul, for a soul cake,
> Pray you, good mistress, a soul cake.'

In Shropshire down to the seventeenth century it was customary on All Souls' Day to set on the table a high heap of soul-cakes, and most visitors to the house took one of them. The antiquary John Aubrey, who records the custom, mentions also the appropriate verses:

> 'A soul-cake, a soul-cake,
> Have mercy on all Christen soules for a soule-cake.'

A comparison of these European customs with the similar heathen rites can leave no room for doubt that the nominally Christian feast of All Souls is nothing but an old pagan festival of the dead which the Church, unable or unwilling to suppress, resolved from motives of policy to connive at. But whence did *The nominally Christian feast of All Souls on Nov. 2 appears to be*

an old Celtic
festival of
the dead
adopted by
the Church
in 998 AD.

it borrow the practice of solemnizing the festival on that particular day, the second of November? In order to answer this question we should observe, first, that celebrations of this sort are often held at the beginning of a New Year, and, second, that the peoples of North–Western Europe, the Celts and the Teutons, appear to have dated the beginning of their year from the beginning of winter, the Celts reckoning it from the first of November and the Teutons from the first of October. The difference of reckoning may be due to a difference of climate, the home of the Teutons in Central and Northern Europe being a region where winter sets in earlier than on the more temperate and humid coasts of the Atlantic, the home of the Celts. These considerations suggest that the festival of All Souls on the second of November originated with the Celts, and spread from them to the rest of the European peoples, who, while they preserved their old feasts of the dead practically unchanged, may have transferred them to the second of November. This conjecture is supported by what we know of the ecclesiastical institution, or rather recognition, of the festival. For that recognition was first accorded at the end of the tenth century in France, a Celtic country, from which the Church festival gradually spread over Europe. It was Odilo, abbot of the great Benedictine monastery of Clugny, who initiated the change in 998 AD by ordering that in all the monasteries over which he ruled, a solemn mass should be celebrated on the second of November for all the dead who sleep in Christ. The example thus set was followed by other religious houses, and the bishops, one after another, introduced the new celebration into their dioceses. Thus the festival of All Souls gradually established itself throughout Christendom, though in fact the Church has never formally sanctioned it by a general edict nor attached much weight to its observance. Indeed, when objections were raised to the festival at the Reformation, the ecclesiastical authorities seemed ready to abandon it. These facts are explained very simply by the theory that an old Celtic commemoration of the dead lingered in France down to the end of the tenth century, and was then, as a measure of policy and a concession to ineradicable paganism, at last incorporated in the Catholic ritual. The consciousness of the heathen origin of the practice would naturally prevent the supreme authorities from

Institution of
the Feast of
All Souls by
the Abbot of
Clugny.

insisting strongly on its observance. They appear rightly to have regarded it as an outpost which they could surrender to the forces of rationalism without endangering the citadel of the faith.

Perhaps we may go a step further and explain in like manner the origin of the feast of All Saints on the first of November. For the analogy of similar customs elsewhere would lead us to suppose that the old Celtic festival of the dead was held on the Celtic New Year's Day, that is, on the first, not the second, of November. May not then the institution of the feast of All Saints on that day have been the first attempt of the Church to give a colour of Christianity to the ancient heathen rite by substituting the saints for the souls of the dead as the true object of worship? The facts of history seem to countenance this hypothesis. For the feast of All Saints was instituted in France and Germany by order of the Emperor Lewis the Pious in 835 AD, that is, about a hundred and sixty years before the introduction of the feast of All Souls. The innovation was made by the advice of the pope, Gregory IV, whose motive may well have been that of suppressing an old pagan custom which was still notoriously practised in France and Germany. The idea, however, was not a novel one, for the testimony of Bede proves that in Britain, another Celtic country, the feast of All Saints on the first of November was already celebrated in the eighth century. We may conjecture that this attempt to divert the devotion of the faithful from the souls of the dead to the saints proved a failure, and that finally the Church reluctantly decided to sanction the popular superstition by frankly admitting a feast of All Souls into the calendar. But it could not assign the new, or rather the old, festival to the old day, the first of November, since that was already occupied by the feast of All Saints. Accordingly it placed the mass for the dead on the next day, the second of November. On this theory the feasts of All Saints and of All Souls mark two successive efforts of the Catholic Church to eradicate an old heathen festival of the dead. Both efforts failed. 'In all Catholic countries the day of All Souls has preserved the serious character of a festival of the dead which no worldly gaieties are allowed to disturb. It is then the sacred duty of the survivors to visit the graves of their loved ones in the churchyard, to deck them with flowers and lights,

The feast of All Saints on Nov. 1 seems also to have displaced a heathen festival of the dead.

and to utter a devout prayer—a pious custom with which in cities like Paris and Vienna even the gay and frivolous comply for the sake of appearance, if not to satisfy an impulse of the heart.'*

CHAPTER 13

ISIS

THE original meaning of the goddess Isis is more difficult to determine than that of her brother and husband Osiris. Her attributes and epithets were so numerous that in the hieroglyphics she is called 'the many-named', 'the thousand-named', and in Greek inscriptions 'the myriad-named'.

Multifarious attributes of Isis.

In her character of a goddess of fecundity Isis answered to the great mother goddesses of Asia, though she differed from them in the chastity and fidelity of her conjugal life; for while they were unmarried and dissolute, she had a husband and was a true wife to him as well as an affectionate mother to their son. Hence her beautiful Madonna-like figure reflects a more refined state of society and of morals than the coarse, sensual, cruel fingers of Astarte, Anaitis, Cybele, and the rest of that crew. A clear trace, indeed, of an ethical standard very different from our own lingers in her double relation of sister and wife to Osiris; but in most other respects she is rather late than primitive, the full-blown flower rather than the seed of a long religious development. The attributes ascribed to her were too various to be all her own. They were graces borrowed from many lesser deities, sweets rifled from a thousand humbler plants to feed the honey of her superb efflorescence. Yet in her complex nature it is perhaps still possible to detect the original nucleus round which by a slow process of accretion the other elements gathered. For if her brother and husband Osiris was in one of his aspects the corn-god, as we have seen reason to believe, she must surely have been the corn-goddess. There are at least some grounds for thinking so. For if we may trust Diodorus Siculus, whose authority appears to have been the Egyptian historian Manetho, the discovery of wheat and barley was attributed to Isis, and at her festivals stalks of these grains were carried in procession to commemorate the boon she had conferred on men. A further detail is added by Augustine. He says that Isis made the discovery of barley at the moment when she was

How Isis resembled yet differed from the Mother Goddesses of Asia.

Isis perhaps originally a goddess of the corn.

sacrificing to the common ancestors of her husband and herself, all of whom had been kings, and that she showed the newly discovered ears of barley to Osiris and his councillor Thoth or Mercury, as Roman writers called him. That is why, adds Augustine, they identify Isis with Ceres.* Further, at harvest-time, when the Egyptian reapers had cut the first stalks, they laid them down and beat their breasts, wailing and calling upon Isis. Amongst the epithets by which Isis is designated in the inscriptions are 'Creatress of green things', 'Green goddess, whose green colour is like unto the greenness of the earth', 'Lady of Bread', 'Lady of Beer', 'Lady of Abundance'. According to Brugsch she is 'not only the creatress of the fresh verdure of vegetation which covers the earth, but is actually the green corn-field itself, which is personified as a goddess'. This is confirmed by her epithet *Sochit* or *Sochet*, meaning 'a corn-field', a sense which the word still retains in Coptic. The Greeks conceived of Isis as a corn-goddess, for they identified her with Demeter. In a Greek epigram she is described as 'she who has given birth to the fruits of the earth', and 'the mother of the ears of corn'; and in a hymn composed in her honour she speaks of herself as 'queen of the wheat-field', and is described as 'charged with the care of the fruitful furrow's wheat-rich path'. Accordingly, Greek or Roman artists often represented her with ears of corn on her head or in her hand.

Refinement and spiritualization of Isis in later times the popularity of her worship in the Roman empire.

Such, we may suppose, was Isis in the olden time, a rustic Corn-Mother adored with uncouth rites by Egyptian swains. But the homely features of the clownish goddess could hardly be traced in the refined, the saintly form which, spiritualized by ages of religious evolution, she presented to her worshippers of after days as the true wife, the tender mother, the beneficent queen of nature, encircled with the nimbus of moral purity, of immemorial and mysterious sanctity. Thus chastened and trans-figured she won many hearts far beyond the boundaries of her native land. In that welter of religions which accompanied the decline of national life in antiquity her worship was one of the most popular at Rome and throughout the empire. Some of the Roman emperors themselves were openly addicted to it. And however the religion of Isis may, like any other, have been often worn as a cloak by men and women of loose life, her rites appear on the whole to have been honourably distinguished by a dignity and composure, a solemnity and decorum well fitted to soothe the troubled mind, to ease the burdened heart. They appealed therefore to gentle spirits, and above all to women, whom the bloody and licentious rites of other Oriental goddesses only shocked and repelled. We need not wonder, then, that in a period of decadence, when traditional faiths were shaken, when systems clashed, when men's minds were disquieted, when the fabric of empire itself, once deemed eternal, began to show ominous rents and fissures, the serene figure of Isis with her spiritual calm, her gracious promise of immortality, should have appeared to many like a star in a stormy sky, and should have roused in their breasts a rapture of devotion not unlike that which was paid in the Middle Ages to the Virgin Mary. Indeed her stately ritual, with its shaven and tonsured priests, its matins and vespers, its tinkling music, its baptism and aspersions of holy water, its solemn processions, its jewelled images of the Mother of God, presented many points of similarity to the pomps and ceremonies of Catholicism. The resemblance need not be purely accidental. Ancient Egypt may have contributed its share to the gorgeous symbolism of the Catholic Church as well as to the pale abstractions of her theology. Certainly in art the figure of Isis suckling the infant Horus is so like that of the Madonna and child that it has sometimes received the adoration of ignorant Christians. And to Isis in her later character of patroness of mariners the Virgin Mary perhaps owes her beautiful epithet of *Stella Maris*, 'Star of the Sea', under which she is adored by tempest-tossed sailors. The attributes of a marine deity may have been bestowed on Isis by the sea-faring Greeks of Alexandria. They are quite foreign to her original character and to the habits of the Egyptians, who had no love of the sea. On this hypothesis Sirius, the bright star of Isis, which on July mornings rises from the glassy waves of the eastern Mediterranean, a harbinger of halcyon weather to mariners, was the true *Stella Maris*, 'the Star of the Sea'.

Resemblance of Isis to the Madonna.

CHAPTER 14

MOTHER-KIN AND MOTHER GODDESSES

Essential
similarity of
Adonis,
Attis, and
Osiris.

WE have now concluded our inquiry into the nature and
worship of the three Oriental deities Adonis, Attis, and Osiris.
The substantial similarity of their mythical character justifies us
in treating of them together. All three apparently embodied the
powers of fertility in general and of vegetation in particular. All
three were believed to have died and risen again from the dead;
and the divine death and resurrection of all three were dramatically represented at annual festivals, which their worshippers
celebrated with alternate transports of sorrow and joy, of
weeping and exultation. The natural phenomena thus mythically conceived and mythically represented were the great changes
of the seasons, especially the most striking and impressive of all,
the decay and revival of vegetation; and the intention of the
sacred dramas was to refresh and strengthen, by sympathetic
magic, the failing energies of nature, in order that the trees
should bear fruit, that the corn should ripen, that men and
animals should reproduce their kinds.

The super-
iority of the
goddesses as-
sociated with
Adonis,
Attis, and
Osiris points
to a system
of mother-
kin.

But the three gods did not stand by themselves. The mythical
personification of nature, of which all three were in at least one
aspect the products, required that each of them should be
coupled with a goddess, and in each case it appears that
originally the goddess was a more powerful and important
personage than the god. At all events it is always the god rather
than the goddess who comes to a sad end, and whose death is
annually mourned. Thus, whereas Osiris was slain by Typhon,
his divine spouse Isis survived and brought him to life again.
This feature of the myth seems to indicate that in the beginning
Isis was, what Astarte and Cybele always continued to be, the
stronger divinity of the pair. Now the superiority thus assigned
to the goddess over the god is most naturally explained as the
result of a social system in which maternity counted for more
than paternity, descent being traced and property handed down
through women rather than through men. At all events this

explanation cannot be deemed intrinsically improbable if we can show that the supposed cause has produced the very same effect among existing peoples, about whose institutions we possess accurate information. This I will now endeavour to do.

The social system which traces descent and transmits property through the mother alone may be called mother-kin,* while the converse system which traces descent and transmits property through the father alone may be called father-kin. A good example of the influence which mother-kin may exert on religion is furnished by the Khasis of Assam. Like the ancient Egyptians and the Semites of Syria and Mesopotamia, the Khasis live in settled villages and maintain themselves chiefly by the cultivation of the ground; yet 'their social organization presents one of the most perfect examples still surviving of matriarchal institutions, carried out with a logic and thoroughness which, to those accustomed to regard the status and authority of the father as the foundation of society, are exceedingly remarkable. Not only is the mother the head and source, and only bond of union, of the family: in the most primitive part of the hills, the Synteng country, she is the only owner of real property, and through her alone is inheritance transmitted. The father has no kinship with his children, who belong to their mother's clan; what he earns goes to his own matriarchal stock, and at his death his bones are deposited in the cromlech of his mother's kin. In Jowai he neither lives nor eats in his wife's house, but visits it only after dark. In the veneration of ancestors, which is the foundation of the tribal piety, the primal ancestress (*Ka lāwbei*) and her brother are the only persons regarded. The flat memorial stones set up to perpetuate the memory of the dead are called after the woman who represents the clan (*māw kynthei*), and the standing stones ranged behind them are dedicated to the male kinsmen on the mother's side. In harmony with this scheme of ancestor worship, the other spirits to whom propitiation is offered are mainly female, though here male personages also figure. The powers of sickness and death are all female, and these are those most frequently worshipped. The two protectors of the household are goddesses, though with them is also revered the first father of the clan, U *Thāwlang*. Priestesses assist at all sacrifices, and the male officiants are only their deputies; in one important

Mother-kin and father-kin.

The Khasis of Assam have mother-kin, and among them goddesses predominate over gods and priestesses over priests.

state, Khyrim, the High Priestess and actual head of the State is a woman, who combines in her person sacerdotal and regal functions.'*

Again, the Pelew Islanders have mother-kin, and the deities of their clans are all goddesses.

Another instance of the same cause producing the same effect may be drawn from the institutions of the Pelew Islanders,* which have been described by an accurate observer long resident in the islands. These people, who form a branch of the Micronesian stock, are divided into a series of exogamous families or clans with descent in the female line, so that, as usually happens under such a system, a man's heirs are not his own children but the children of his sister or of his maternal aunt. Every family or clan traces its descent from a woman, the common mother of the whole kin, and accordingly the members of the clan worship a goddess, not a god. These families or clans, with female descent and a worship of goddesses rather than of gods, are grouped together in villages, each village comprising about a score of clans and forming with its lands a petty independent state. Every such village-state has its special deity or deities, generally a god and a goddess. But these political deities of the villages are said to be directly derived from the domestic deities of the families or clans, from which it seems to follow that among these people gods are historically later than goddesses and have been developed out of them. The late origin of the gods as compared with the goddesses is further indicated by the nature of their names.

This preference for goddesses is to be explained by the importance of women in the social system of the Pelew Islanders.

This preference for goddesses over gods in the clans of the Pelew Islanders has been explained, no doubt rightly, by the high importance of women in the social system of the people. For the existence of the clan depends entirely on the life of the women, not at all upon the life of the men. If the women survive, it is no matter though every man of the clan should perish; for the women will, as usual, marry men of another clan, and their offspring will inherit their mother's clan, thereby prolonging its existence. Whereas if the women of the clan all die out, the clan necessarily becomes extinct, even though every man of it should survive; for the men must, as usual, marry women of another clan, and their offspring will inherit their mothers' clan, not the clan of their fathers, which accordingly, with the death of the fathers, is wiped out from the community.

Thus the present, or at least the recent, state of society and religion in the Pelew Islands presents some interesting parallels to the social and religious condition of Western Asia and Egypt in early days, if the conclusions reached in this work are correct. In both regions we see a society based on mother-kin developing a religion in which goddesses of the clan originally occupied the foremost place, though in later times, as the clans coalesced into states, the old goddesses have been rivalled and to some extent supplanted by the new male gods of the enlarged pantheon. But in the religion of the Pelew Islanders, as in that of the Khasis and the ancient Egyptians, the balance of power has never wholly shifted from the female to the male line, because society has never passed from mother-kin to father-kin. And in the Pelew Islands as in the ancient East we see the tide of political power running strongly in the direction of theocracy, the people resigning the conduct of affairs into the hands of men who claimed to rule them in the name of the gods. In the Pelew Islands such men might have developed into divine kings like those of Babylon and Egypt, if the natural course of evolution had not been cut short by the intervention of Europe.

Parallel between the Pelew Islands of to-day and the religious and social state of Western Asia and Egypt in antiquity.

The evidence of the Khasis and the Pelew Islanders, two peoples very remote and very different from each other, suffices to prove that the influence which mother-kin may exert on religion is real and deep. But in order to dissipate misapprehensions, which appear to be rife on this subject, it may be well to remind or inform the reader that the ancient and widespread custom of tracing descent and inheriting property through the mother alone does not by any means imply that the government of the tribes which observe the custom is in the hands of women; in short, it should always be borne in mind that mother-kin does not mean mother-rule. On the contrary, the practice of mother-kin prevails most extensively amongst the lowest savages, with whom woman, instead of being the ruler of man, is always his drudge and often little better than his slave. Indeed, so far is the system from implying any social superiority of women that it probably took its rise from what we should regard as their deepest degradation, to wit, from a state of society in which the relations of the sexes were so loose and vague that children could not be fathered on any particular man.

Mother-kin does not imply that the government is in the hands of women.

The inheritance of property, especially of landed property, through the mother certainly tends to raise the social importance of women, but this tendency is never carried so far as to subordinate men politically to women.

When we pass from the purely savage state to that higher plane of culture in which the accumulation of property, and especially of landed property, has become a powerful instrument of social and political influence, we naturally find that wherever the ancient preference for the female line of descent has been retained, it tends to increase the importance and enhance the dignity of woman; and her aggrandizement is most marked in princely families, where she either herself holds royal authority as well as private property, or at least transmits them both to her consort or her children. But this social advance of women has never been carried so far as to place men as a whole in a position of political subordination to them. Even where the system of mother-kin in regard to descent and property has prevailed most fully, the actual government has generally, if not invariably, remained in the hands of men. Exceptions have no doubt occurred; women have occasionally arisen who by sheer force of character have swayed for a time the destinies of their people. But such exceptions are rare and their effects transitory; they do not affect the truth of the general rule that human society has been governed in the past and, human nature remaining the same, is likely to be governed in the future, mainly by masculine force and masculine intelligence.

Thus while the Khasis and Pelew Islanders have mother-kin, they are governed by men, not by women.

To this rule the Khasis, with their elaborate system of mother-kin, form no exception. For among them, while landed property is both transmitted through women and held by women alone, political power is transmitted indeed through women, but is held by men; in other words, the Khasi tribes are, with a single exception, governed by kings, not by queens. And even in the one tribe, which is nominally ruled by women, the real power is delegated by the reigning queen or High Priestess to her son, her nephew, or a more distant male relation. In all the other tribes the kingship may be held by a woman only on the failure of all male heirs in the female line. So far is mother-kin from implying mother-rule. A Khasi king inherits power in right of his mother, but he exercises it in his own. Similarly the Pelew Islanders, in spite of their system of mother-kin, are governed by chiefs, not by chieftainesses. It is true that there are chieftainesses, and that they indirectly exercise much influence; but their direct authority is limited to the affairs of women, especially to the administration of the women's clubs or associations, which answer to the clubs or associations of the men. And to take another example, the Melanesians, like the Khasis and the Pelew Islanders, have the system of mother-kin, being similarly divided into exogamous clans with descent in the female line; 'but it must be understood that the mother is in no way the head of the family. The house of the family is the father's, the garden is his, the rule and government are his.'

We may safely assume that the practice has been the same among all the many peoples who have retained the ancient system of mother-kin under a monarchical constitution. In Africa, for example, the chieftainship or kingship often descends in the female line, but it is men, not women, who inherit it. The theory of a gynaecocracy is in truth a dream of visionaries and pedants. And equally chimerical is the idea that the predominance of goddesses under a system of mother-kin like that of the Khasis is a creation of the female mind. If women ever created gods, they would be more likely to give them masculine than feminine features. In point of fact the great religious ideals which have permanently impressed themselves on the world seem always to have been a product of the male imagination. Men make gods and women worship them.* The combination of ancestor-worship with mother-kin furnishes a simple and sufficient explanation of the superiority of goddesses over gods in a state of society where these conditions prevail. Men naturally assign the first place in their devotions to the ancestress from whom they trace their descent.

The theory of a gynaeco-cracy and of the predominance of the female imagination in religion is an idle dream.

CHAPTER 15

DIONYSUS

Death and resurrection of Oriental gods of vegetation. The Dying and Reviving god of vegetation in ancient Greece.

IN the preceding chapters we saw that in antiquity the civilised nations of western Asia and Egypt pictured to themselves the changes of the seasons, and particularly the annual growth and decay of vegetation, as episodes in the life of gods, whose mournful death and happy resurrection they celebrated with dramatic rites of alternate lamentation and rejoicing. But if the celebration was in form dramatic, it was in substance magical; that is to say, it was intended, on the principles of sympathetic magic, to ensure the vernal regeneration of plants and the multiplication of animals, which had seemed to be menaced by the inroads of winter. In the ancient world, however, such ideas and such rites were by no means confined to the Oriental peoples of Babylon and Syria, of Phrygia and Egypt; they were not a product peculiar to the religious mysticism of the dreamy East, but were shared by the races of livelier fancy and more mercurial temperament who inhabited the shores and islands of the Aegean.

Dionysus, the god of the vine, originally a Thracian deity.

The god Dionysus or Bacchus is best known to us as a personification of the vine and of the exhilaration produced by the juice of the grape. His ecstatic worship, characterised by wild dances, thrilling music, and tipsy excess, appears to have originated among the rude tribes of Thrace, who were notoriously addicted to drunkenness. The resemblance which his story and his ceremonies present to those of Osiris have led some enquirers both in ancient and modern times to hold that Dionysus was merely a disguised Osiris, imported directly from Egypt into Greece. But the great preponderance of evidence points to his Thracian origin, and the similarity of the two worships is sufficiently explained by the similarity of the ideas and customs on which they were founded.

Dionysus a god of trees, especially of fruit-trees.

While the vine with its clusters was the most characteristic manifestation of Dionysus, he was also a god of trees in general. Thus we are told that almost all the Greeks sacrificed to

'Dionysus of the tree'. In Boeotia one of his titles was 'Dionysus in the tree'. His image was often merely an upright post, without arms, but draped in a mantle, with a bearded mask to represent the head, and with leafy boughs projecting from the head or body to shew the nature of the deity.

Further, there are indications, few but significant, that Dionysus was conceived as a deity of agriculture and the corn. He is spoken of as himself doing the work of a husbandman: he is reported to have been the first to yoke oxen to the plough, which before had been dragged by hand alone; and some people found in this tradition the clue to the bovine shape in which, as we shall see, the god was often supposed to present himself to his worshippers. Thus guiding the ploughshare and scattering the seed as he went, Dionysus is said to have eased the labour of the husbandman. Further, we are told that in the land of the Bisaltae, a Thracian tribe, there was a great and fair sanctuary of Dionysus, where at his festival a bright light shone forth at night as a token of an abundant harvest vouchsafed by the deity; but if the crops were to fail that year, the mystic light was not seen, darkness brooded over the sanctuary as at other times. Moreover, among the emblems of Dionysus was the winnowing-fan, that is the large open shovel-shaped basket, which down to modern times has been used by farmers to separate the grain from the chaff by tossing the corn in the air. This simple agricultural instrument figured in the mystic rites of Dionysus; indeed the god is traditionally said to have been placed at birth in a winnowing-fan as in a cradle: in art he is represented as an infant so cradled; and from these traditions and representations he derived the epithet of *Liknites*, that is, 'He of the Winnowing-fan'.

Dionysus was believed to have died a violent death, but to have been brought to life again; and his sufferings, death, and resurrection were enacted in his sacred rites. His tragic story is thus told by the poet Nonnus. Zeus in the form of a serpent visited Persephone, and she bore him Zagreus, that is, Dionysus, a horned infant. Scarcely was he born, when the babe mounted the throne of his father Zeus and mimicked the great god by brandishing the lightning in his tiny hand. But he did not occupy the throne long; for the treacherous Titans, their faces whitened with chalk, attacked him with knives while he

Dionysus as a god of agriculture and the corn.

The winnowing-fan as an emblem of Dionysus.

Myth of the death and resurrection of Dionysus.

was looking at himself in a mirror. For a time he evaded their assaults by turning himself into various shapes, assuming the likeness successively of Zeus and Cronus, of a young man, of a lion, a horse, and a serpent. Finally, in the form of a bull, he was cut to pieces by the murderous knives of his enemies. His Cretan myth, as related by Firmicus Maternus,* ran thus. He was said to have been the bastard son of Jupiter, a Cretan king. Going abroad, Jupiter transferred the throne and sceptre to the youthful Dionysus, but, knowing that his wife Juno cherished a jealous dislike of the child, he entrusted Dionysus to the care of guards upon whose fidelity he believed he could rely. Juno, however, bribed the guards, and amusing the child with rattles and a cunningly-wrought looking-glass lured him into an ambush, where her satellites, the Titans, rushed upon him, cut him limb from limb, boiled his body with various herbs, and ate it. But his sister Minerva, who had shared in the deed, kept his heart and gave it to Jupiter on his return, revealing to him the whole history of the crime. In his rage, Jupiter put the Titans to death by torture, and, to soothe his grief for the loss of his son, made an image in which he enclosed the child's heart, and then built a temple in his honour. In this version a Euhemeristic* turn has been given to the myth by representing Jupiter and Juno (Zeus and Hera) as a king and queen of Crete. The guards referred to are the mythical Curetes who danced a war-dance round the infant Dionysus, as they are said to have done round the infant Zeus. Very noteworthy is the legend, recorded both by Nonnus and Firmicus, that in his infancy Dionysus occupied for a short time the throne of his father Zeus. So Proclus tells us that 'Dionysus was the last king of the gods appointed by Zeus. For his father set him on the kingly throne, and placed in his hand, the sceptre, and made him king of all the gods of the world.' Such traditions point to a custom of temporarily investing the king's son with the royal dignity as a preliminary to sacrificing him instead of his father.

Legend that the infant Dionysus occupied for a short time the throne of his father Zeus.

Turning from the myth to the ritual, we find that the Cretans celebrated a biennial festival at which the passion of Dionysus was represented in every detail. All that he had done or suffered in his last moments was enacted before the eyes of his worshippers, who tore a live bull to pieces with their teeth and roamed the woods with frantic shouts. In front of them was carried a

Death and resurrection of Dionysus represented in his rites.

casket supposed to contain the sacred heart of Dionysus, and to the wild music of flutes and cymbals they mimicked the rattles by which the infant god had been lured to his doom. Where the resurrection formed part of the myth, it also was acted at the rites, and it even appears that a general doctrine of resurrection, or at least of immortality, was inculcated on the worshippers; for Plutarch, writing to console his wife on the death of their infant daughter, comforts her with the thought of the immortality of the soul as taught by tradition and revealed in the mysteries of Dionysus.*

A feature in the mythical character of Dionysus, which at first sight appears inconsistent with his nature as a deity of vegetation, is that he was often conceived and represented in animal shape, especially in the form, or at least with the horns, of a bull. Thus he is spoken of as 'cow-born', 'bull', 'bull-shaped', 'bull-faced', 'bull-browed', 'bull-horned', 'horn-bearing', 'two-horned', 'horned'. He was believed to appear, at least occasionally, as a bull. His images were often, as at Cyzicus, made in bull shape, or with bull horns; and he was painted with horns. Types of the horned Dionysus are found amongst the surviving monuments of antiquity. On one statuette he appears clad in a bull's hide, the head, horns, and hoofs hanging down behind. Again, he is represented as a child with clusters of grapes round his brow, and a calf's head, with sprouting horns, attached to the back of his head. On a red-figured vase the god is portrayed as a calf-headed child seated on a woman's lap. The people of Cynaetha in north-western Arcadia held a festival of Dionysus in winter, when men, who had greased their bodies with oil for the occasion, used to pick out a bull from the herd and carry it to the sanctuary of the god. Dionysus was supposed to inspire their choice of the particular bull, which probably represented the deity himself; for at his festivals he was believed to appear in bull form. The women of Elis hailed him as a bull, and prayed him to come with his bull's foot. They sang, 'Come hither, Dionysus, to thy holy temple by the sea; come with the Graces to thy temple, rushing with thy bull's foot, O goodly bull, O goodly bull!' The Bacchanals of Thrace wore horns in imitation of their god. The rending and devouring of live bulls and calves appear to have been a regular feature of the Dionysiac rites.* When we consider the practice of portraying the god

Dionysus represented in the form of a bull.

as a bull or with some of the features of the animal, the belief that he appeared in bull form to his worshippers at the sacred rites, and the legend that in bull form he had been torn in pieces, we cannot doubt that in rending and devouring a live bull at his festival the worshippers of Dionysus believed themselves to be killing the god, eating his flesh, and drinking his blood.

Dionysus as a goat.

Another animal whose form Dionysus assumed was the goat. One of his names was 'Kid'. At Athens and at Hermion he was worshipped under the title of 'the one of the Black Goatskin', and a legend ran that on a certain occasion he had appeared clad in the skin from which he took the title. In the wine-growing district of Phlius, where in autumn the plain is still thickly mantled with the red and golden foliage of the fading vines, there stood of old a bronze image of a goat, which the husbandmen plastered with gold-leaf as a means of protecting their vines against blight. The image probably represented the vine-god himself. To save him from the wrath of Hera, his father Zeus changed the youthful Dionysus into a kid; and when the gods fled to Egypt to escape the fury of Typhon, Dionysus was turned into a goat. Hence when his worshippers rent in pieces a live goat and devoured it raw, they must have believed that they were eating the body and blood of the god.

Live goats rent and devoured by his worshippers.

Later misinterpretations of the custom of killing a god in animal form.

The custom of killing a god in animal form, which we shall examine more in detail further on, belongs to a very early stage of human culture, and is apt in later times to be misunderstood. The advance of thought tends to strip the old animal and plant gods of their bestial and vegetable husk, and to leave their human attributes (which are always the kernel of the conception) as the final and sole residuum. In other words, animal and plant gods tend to become purely anthropomorphic. When they have become wholly or nearly so, the animals and plants which were at first the deities themselves, still retain a vague and ill-understood connexion with the anthropomorphic gods who have been developed out of them. The origin of the relationship between the deity and the animal or plant having been forgotten, various stories are invented to explain it. These explanations may follow one of two lines according as they are based on the habitual or on the exceptional treatment of the sacred animal or plant. The sacred animal was habitually spared, and only exceptionally slain; and accordingly the myth might be devised to explain either why it was spared or why it was killed. Devised for the former purpose, the myth would tell of some service rendered to the deity by the animal; devised for the latter purpose, the myth would tell of some injury inflicted by the animal on the god. The reason given for sacrificing goats to Dionysus exemplifies a myth of the latter sort. They were sacrificed to him, it was said, because they injured the vine. Now the goat, as we have seen, was originally an embodiment of the god himself. But when the god had divested himself of his animal character and had become essentially anthropomorphic, the killing of the goat in his worship came to be regarded no longer as a slaying of the deity himself, but as a sacrifice offered to him; and since some reason had to be assigned why the goat in particular should be sacrificed, it was alleged that this was a punishment inflicted on the goat for injuring the vine, the object of the god's especial care. Thus we have the strange spectacle of a god sacrificed to himself on the ground that he is his own enemy. And as the deity is supposed to partake of the victim offered to him, it follows that, when the victim is the god's old self, the god eats of his own flesh. Hence the goat-god Dionysus is represented as eating raw goat's blood; and the bull-god Dionysus is called 'eater of bulls'. On the analogy of these instances we may conjecture that wherever a deity is described as the eater of a particular animal, the animal in question was originally nothing but the deity himself.

It remains to mention that in some places, instead of an animal, a human being was torn in pieces at the rites of Dionysus. This was the practice in Chios and Tenedos; and at Potniae in Boeotia the tradition ran that it had been formerly the custom to sacrifice to the goat-smiting Dionysus a child, for whom a goat was afterwards substituted. At Orchomenus, as we have seen, the human victim was taken from the women of an old royal family. As the slain bull or goat represented the slain god, so, we may suppose, the human victim also represented him.

The legends of the deaths of Pentheus and Lycurgus,* two kings who are said to have been torn to pieces, the one by Bacchanals, the other by horses, for their opposition to the rites of Dionysus, may be, as I have already suggested, distorted

The legendary deaths of Pentheus and Lycurgus

reminiscences of a custom of sacrificing divine kings in the character of Dionysus and of dispersing the fragments of their broken bodies over the fields for the purpose of fertilising them. In regard to Lycurgus, king of the Thracian tribe of the Edonians, it is expressly said that his subjects at the bidding of an oracle caused him to be rent in pieces by horses for the purpose of restoring the fertility of the ground after a period of barrenness and dearth. There is no improbability in the tradition. We have seen that in Africa and other parts of the world kings or chiefs have often been put to death by their people for similar reasons. Further, it is significant that King Lycurgus is said to have slain his own son Dryas with an axe in a fit of madness, mistaking him for a vine-branch. Have we not in this tradition a reminiscence of a custom of sacrificing the king's son in place of the father?

The theory that in prehistoric times Greek and Thracian kings or their sons may have been dismembered in the character of the vine-god or the corn-god for the purpose of fertilising the earth or quickening the vines has received of late years some confirmation from the discovery that down to the present time in Thrace, the original home of Dionysus, a drama is still annually performed which reproduces with remarkable fidelity some of the most striking traits in the Dionysiac myth and ritual.*

The drama, which may reasonably be regarded as a direct descendant of the Dionysiac rites, is annually performed at the Carnival in all the Christian villages which cluster round Viza, the ancient Bizya, a town of Thrace situated about midway between Adrianople and Constantinople. In antiquity the city was the capital of the Thracian tribe of the Asti; the kings had their palace there, probably in the acropolis, of which some fine walls are still standing. Inscriptions preserved in the modern town record the names of some of these old kings. The date of the celebration is Cheese Monday, as it is locally called, which is the Monday of the last week of Carnival. The principal parts in the drama are taken by two men disguised in goatskins. Each of them wears a headdress made of a complete goatskin, which is stuffed so as to rise a foot or more like a shako over his head, while the skin falls over the face, forming a mask with holes cut for the eyes and mouth. One of the two skin-clad actors carries

Marginal notes:

may be reminiscences of a custom of sacrificing divine kings in the character of Dionysus.

Survival of Dionysiac rites among the modern Thracian peasantry.

Drama annually performed at the Carnival in the villages round Viza, an old Thracian capital.

The actors in the drama.

a bow and the other a wooden effigy of the male organ of generation. Both these actors must be married men. Two unmarried boys dressed as girls and sometimes called brides also take part in the play; and a man disguised as an old woman in rags carries a mock baby in a basket; the brat is supposed to be a seven-months' child born out of wedlock and begotten by an unknown father. The basket in which the hopeful infant is paraded bears the ancient name of the winnowing-fan (*likni*, contracted from *liknon*) and the babe itself receives the very title. 'He of the Winnowing-fan' (*Liknites*) which in antiquity was applied to Dionysus. Two other actors, clad in rags with blackened faces and armed with stout saplings, play the parts of a gypsy-man and his wife; others personate policemen armed with swords and whips; and the troupe is completed by a man who discourses music on a bagpipe.

Such are the masqueraders. The morning of the day on which they perform their little drama is spent by them going from door to door collecting bread, eggs, or money. At every door the two skin-clad maskers knock, the boys disguised as girls dance, and the gypsy man and wife enact an obscene pantomime on the straw-heap before the house. When every house in the village has been thus visited, the troop takes up position on the open space before the village church, where the whole population has already mustered to witness the performance. After a dance hand in hand, in which all the actors take part, the two skin-clad maskers withdraw and leave the field to the gypsies, who now pretend to forge a ploughshare, the man making believe to hammer the share and his wife to work the bellows. At this point the old woman's baby is supposed to grow up at a great pace, to develop a huge appetite for meat and drink, and to clamour for a wife. One of the skin-clad men now pursues one of the two pretended brides, and a mock marriage is celebrated between the couple. After these nuptials have been performed with a parody of a real wedding, the mock bridegroom is shot by his comrade with the bow and falls down on his face like dead. His slayer thereupon feigns to skin him with a knife; but the dead man's wife laments over her deceased husband with loud cries, throwing herself across his prostrate body. In this lamentation the slayer himself and all the other actors join in: a Christian funeral service is burlesqued; and the

The ceremonies include the forging of a ploughshare, a mock marriage, and a pretence of death and resurrection.

pretended corpse is lifted up as if to be carried to the grave. At this point, however, the dead man disconcerts the preparations for his burial by suddenly coming to life again and getting up. So ends the drama of death and resurrection.

Analogy of these modern Thracian ceremonies to the ancient rites of Dionysus.

In these ceremonies, still annually held at and near an old capital of Thracian kings, the points of similarity to the ritual of the ancient Thracian deity Dionysus are sufficiently obvious. The goatskins in which the principal actors are disguised remind us of the identification of Dionysus with a goat: the infant, cradled in a winnowing-fan and taking its name from the implement, answers exactly to the traditions and the monuments which represent the infant Dionysus as similarly cradled and similarly named: the pretence that the baby is a seven-months' child born out of wedlock and begotten by an unknown father tallies precisely with the legend that Dionysus was born prematurely in the seventh month as the offspring of an intrigue between a mortal woman and a mysterious divine father: the same coarse symbol of reproductive energy which characterised the ancient ritual of Dionysus figures conspicuously in the modern drama: and the simulated slaughter and resurrection of the same goatskin-clad actor may be compared with the traditional slaughter and resurrection of the god himself.

CHAPTER 16

DEMETER AND PERSEPHONE

DIONYSUS was not the only Greek deity whose tragic story and ritual appear to reflect the decay and revival of vegetation. In another form and with a different application the old tale reappears in the myth of Demeter and Persephone. Substantially their myth is identical with the Syrian one of Aphrodite (Astarte) and Adonis, the Phrygian one of Cybele and Attis, and the Egyptian one of Isis and Osiris. In the Greek fable, as in its Asiatic and Egyptian counterparts, a goddess mourns the loss of a loved one, who personifies the vegetation, more especially the corn, which dies in winter to revive in spring; only whereas the Oriental imagination figured the loved and lost one as a dead lover or a dead husband lamented by his leman or his wife, Greek fancy embodied the same idea in the tenderer and purer form of a dead daughter bewailed by her sorrowing mother.

Demeter and Persephone as Greek personifications of the decay and revival of vegetation.

The oldest literary document which narrates the myth of Demeter and Persephone is the beautiful Homeric *Hymn to Demeter*, which critics assign to the seventh century before our era. The object of the poem is to explain the origin of the Eleusinian mysteries,* and the complete silence of the poet as to Athens and the Athenians, who in after ages took a conspicuous part in the festival, renders it probable that the hymn was composed in the far off time when Eleusis was still a petty independent state, and before the stately procession of the Mysteries had begun to defile, in bright September days, over the low chain of barren rocky hills which divides the flat Eleusinian cornland from the more spacious olive-clad expanse of the Athenian plain. Be that as it may, the hymn reveals to us the conception which the writer entertained of the character and functions of the two goddesses: their natural shapes stand out sharply enough under the thin veil of poetical imagery. The youthful Persephone, so runs the tale, was gathering roses and lilies, crocuses and violets, hyacinths and narcissuses in a lush meadow, when the earth gaped and Pluto, lord of the Dead,

The Homeric Hymn to Demeter.

The rape of Persephone.

issuing from the abyss carried her off on his golden car to be his bride and queen in the gloomy subterranean world. Her sorrowing mother Demeter, with her yellow tresses veiled in a dark mourning mantle, sought her over land and sea, and learning from the Sun her daughter's fate she withdrew in high dudgeon from the gods and took up her abode at Eleusis, where she presented herself to the king's daughters in the guise of an old woman, sitting sadly under the shadow of an olive tree beside the Maiden's Well, to which the damsels had come to draw water in bronze pitchers for their father's house. In her wrath at her bereavement the goddess suffered not the seed to grow in the earth but kept it hidden under ground, and she vowed that never would she set foot on Olympus and never would she let the corn sprout till her lost daughter should be restored to her. Vainly the oxen dragged the ploughs to and fro in the fields; vainly the sower dropped the barley seed in the brown furrows; nothing came up from the parched and crumbling soil. Even the Rarian plain near Eleusis, which was wont to wave with yellow harvests, lay bare and fallow. Mankind would have perished of hunger and the gods would have been robbed of the sacrifices which were their due, if Zeus in alarm had not commanded Pluto to disgorge his prey, to restore his bride Persephone to her mother Demeter. The grim lord of the Dead smiled and obeyed, but before he sent back his queen to the upper air on a golden car, he gave her the seed of a pomegranate to eat, which ensured that she would return to him. But Zeus stipulated that henceforth Persephone should spend two thirds of every year with her mother and the gods in the upper world and one third of the year with her husband in the nether world, from which she was to return year by year when the earth was gay with spring flowers. Gladly the daughter then returned to the sunshine, gladly her mother received her and fell upon her neck; and in her joy at recovering the lost one Demeter made the corn to sprout from the clods of the ploughed fields and all the broad earth to be heavy with leaves and blossoms. And straightway she went and shewed this happy sight to the princes of Eleusis, to Triptolemus, Eumolpus, Diocles, and to the king Celeus himself, and moreover she revealed to them her sacred rites and mysteries. Blessed, says the poet, is the mortal man who has seen these things, but he

The wrath of Demeter.

The return of Persephone.

who has had no share of them in life will never be happy in death when he has descended into the darkness of the grave. So the two goddesses departed to dwell in bliss with the gods on Olympus; and the bard ends the hymn with a pious prayer to Demeter and Persephone that they would be pleased to grant him a livelihood in return for his song.

It has been generally recognised, and indeed it seems scarcely open to doubt, that the main theme which the poet set before himself in composing this hymn was to describe the traditional foundation of the Eleusinian mysteries by the goddess Demeter. The whole poem leads up to the transformation scene in which the bare leafless expanse of the Eleusinian plain is suddenly turned, at the will of the goddess, into a vast sheet of ruddy corn; the beneficent deity takes the princes of Eleusis, shews them what she has done, teaches them her mystic rites, and vanishes with her daughter to heaven. The revelation of the mysteries is the triumphal close of the piece. This conclusion is confirmed by a more minute examination of the poem, which proves that the poet has given, not merely a general account of the foundation of the mysteries, but also in more or less veiled language mythical explanations of the origin of particular rites which we have good reason to believe formed essential features of the festival. Amongst the rites as to which the poet thus drops significant hints are the preliminary fast of the candidates for initiation, the torchlight procession, the all-night vigil, the sitting of the candidates, veiled and in silence, on stools covered with sheepskins, the use of scurrilous language, the breaking of ribald jests, and the solemn communion with the divinity by participation in a draught of barley-water from a holy chalice.

The aim of the Homeric *Hymn to Demeter* is to explain the traditional foundation of the Eleusinian mysteries by Demeter.

But there is yet another and a deeper secret of the mysteries which the author of the poem appears to have divulged under cover of his narrative. He tells us how, as soon as she had transformed the barren brown expanse of the Eleusinian plain into a field of golden grain, she gladdened the eyes of Triptolemus and the other Eleusinian princes by shewing them the growing or standing corn. When we compare this part of the story with the statement of a Christian writer of the second century, Hippolytus, that the very heart of the mysteries consisted in shewing to the initiated a reaped ear of corn, we can hardly doubt that the poet of the hymn was well acquainted

Revelation of a reaped ear of corn the crowning act of the mysteries.

with this solemn rite, and that he deliberately intended to explain its origin in precisely the same way as he explained other rites of the mysteries, namely by representing Demeter as having set the example of performing the ceremony in her own person. Thus myth and ritual mutually explain and confirm each other. The poet of the seventh century before our era gives us the myth—he could not without sacrilege have revealed the ritual: the Christian father reveals the ritual, and his revelation accords perfectly with the veiled hint of the old poet. On the whole, then, we may, with many modern scholars, confidently accept the statement of the learned Christian father Clement of Alexandria, that the myth of Demeter and Persephone was acted as a sacred drama in the mysteries of Eleusis.

Demeter and Persephone personifications of the corn.

But if the myth was acted as a part, perhaps as the principal part, of the most famous and solemn religious rites of ancient Greece, we have still to enquire, What was, after all, stripped of later accretions, the original kernel of the myth which appears to later ages surrounded and transfigured by an aureole of awe and mystery, lit up by some of the most brilliant rays of Grecian literature and art? If we follow the indications given by our oldest literary authority on the subject, the author of the Homeric *Hymn to Demeter*, the riddle is not hard to read; the figures of the two goddesses, the mother and the daughter, resolve themselves into personifications of the corn. At least this appears to be fairly certain for the daughter Persephone.

Persephone the seed sown in autumn and sprouting in spring.

The goddess who spends three or, according to another version of the myth, six months of every year with the dead under ground and the remainder of the year with the living above ground; in whose absence the barley seed is hidden in the earth and the fields lie bare and fallow; on whose return in spring to the upper world the corn shoots up from the clods and the earth is heavy with leaves and blossoms—this goddess can surely be nothing else than a mythical embodiment of the vegetation, and particularly of the corn, which is buried under the soil for some months of every winter and comes to life again, as from the grave, in the sprouting cornstalks and the opening flowers and foliage of every spring. No other reason-

Demeter the old corn of last year.

able and probable explanation of Persephone seems possible. And if the daughter goddess was a personification of the young corn of the present year, may not the mother goddess be a personification of the old corn of last year, which has given birth to the new crops?

The Sicilians celebrated the festival of Demeter at the beginning of the sowing, and the festival of Persephone at the harvest. This proves that they associated, if they did not identify, the Mother Goddess with the seed-corn and the Daughter Goddess with the ripe ears.

Could any association or identification be more easy and obvious to people who personified the processes of nature under the form of anthropomorphic deities? As the seed brings forth the ripe ear, so the Corn Mother Demeter gave birth to the Corn Daughter Persephone. It is true that difficulties arise when we attempt to analyse this seemingly simple conception. How, for example, are we to divide exactly the two persons of the divinity? At what precise moment does the seed cease to be the Corn Mother and begin to burgeon out into the Corn Daughter? And how far can we identify the material substance of the barley and wheat with the divine bodies of the Two Goddesses? Questions of this sort probably gave little concern to the sturdy swains who ploughed, sowed, and reaped the fat fields of Sicily. We cannot imagine that their night's rest was disturbed by uneasy meditations on these knotty problems. It would hardly be strange if the muzzy mind of the Sicilian bumpkin, who looked with blind devotion to the Two Goddesses for his daily bread, totally failed to distinguish Demeter from the seed and Persephone from the ripe sheaves, and if he accepted implicitly the doctrine of the real presence of the divinities in the corn without discriminating too curiously between the material and the spiritual properties of the barley or the wheat. And if he had been closely questioned by a rigid logician as to the exact distinction to be drawn between the two persons of the godhead who together represented for him the annual vicissitudes of the cereals, Hodge might have scratched his head and confessed that it puzzled him to say where precisely, the one goddess ended and the other began, or why the seed buried in the ground should figure at one time as the dead daughter Persephone descending into the nether world, and at another as the living Mother Demeter about to give birth to next year's crop. Theological subtleties like these have posed longer heads than are commonly to be found on bucolic shoulders.

Difficulty of distinguishing between Demeter and Persephone as personifications of different aspects of the corn.

Belief in
ancient and
modern
times that
the corn-
crops de-
pend on
possession
of an image
of Demeter.

How deeply implanted in the mind of the ancient Greeks was this faith in Demeter as goddess of the corn may be judged by the circumstance that the faith actually persisted among their Christian descendants at her old sanctuary of Eleusis down to the beginning of the nineteenth century. For when the English traveller Dodwell revisited Eleusis, the inhabitants lamented to him the loss of a colossal image of Demeter, which was carried off by Clarke in 1802 and presented to the University of Cambridge, where it still remains.* 'In my first journey to Greece', says Dodwell, 'this protecting deity was in its full glory, situated in the centre of a threshing-floor, amongst the ruins of her temple. The villagers were impressed with a persuasion that their rich harvests were the effect of her bounty, and since her removal, their abundance, as they assured me, has disappeared.' Thus we see the Corn Goddess Demeter standing on the threshing-floor of Eleusis and dispensing corn to her worshippers in the nineteenth century of the Christian era, precisely as her image stood and dispensed corn to her worshippers on the threshing-floor of Cos in the days of Theocritus. And just as the people of Eleusis last century attributed the diminution of their harvests to the loss of the image of Demeter, so in antiquity the Sicilians, a corn-growing people devoted to the worship of the two Corn Goddesses, lamented that the crops of many towns had perished because the unscrupulous Roman governor Verres had impiously carried off the image of Demeter from her famous temple at Henna. Could we ask for a clearer proof that Demeter was indeed the goddess of the corn than this belief, held by the Greeks down to modern times, that the corn-crops depended on her presence and bounty and perished when her image was removed?

CHAPTER 17

WOMAN'S PART IN PRIMITIVE AGRICULTURE

IF Demeter was indeed a personification of the corn, it is natural to ask, why did the Greeks personify the corn as a goddess rather than a god? why did they ascribe the origin of agriculture to a female rather than to a male power? They conceived the spirit of the vine as masculine; why did they conceive the spirit of the barley and wheat as feminine? To this it has been answered that the personification of the corn as feminine, or at all events the ascription of the discovery of agriculture to a goddess, was suggested by the prominent part which women take in primitive agriculture.*

Theory that the personification of corn as feminine was suggested by the part played by women in primitive agriculture.

Before the invention of the plough, which can hardly be worked without resort to the labour of men, it was and still is customary in many parts of the world to break up the soil for cultivation with hoes, and among not a few savage peoples to this day the task of hoeing the ground and sowing the seed devolves mainly or entirely upon the women, while the men take little or no part in cultivation beyond clearing the land by felling the forest trees and burning the fallen timber and brushwood which encumber the soil. Thus, for example, among the Zulus, 'when a piece of land has been selected for cultivation, the task of clearing it belongs to the men. If the ground be much encumbered, this becomes a laborious undertaking, for their axe is very small, and when a large tree has to be encountered, they can only lop the branches; fire is employed when it is needful to remove the trunk. The reader will therefore not be surprised that the people usually avoid bushland, though they seem to be aware of its superior fertility. As a general rule the men take no further share in the labour of cultivation; and, as the site chosen is seldom much encumbered and frequently bears nothing but grass, their part of the work is very slight. The women are the real labourers; for (except in some particular cases) the entire business of digging, planting, and weeding devolves on them; and, if we regard the assagai and

Among many savage tribes the labour of hoeing the ground and sowing the seed devolves on women.

Agricultural work done by women among the Zulus and other tribes of South Africa.

shield as symbolical of the man, the hoe may be looked upon as emblematic of the woman . . . With this rude and heavy instrument the woman digs, plants, and weeds her garden.' A special term of contempt is applied to any Zulu man, who, deprived of the services of his wife and family, is compelled by hard necessity to handle the hoe himself. Similarly among the Baronga of Delagoa Bay, 'when the rains begin to fall, sometimes as early as September but generally later, they hasten to sow. With her hoe in her hands, the mistress of the field walks with little steps; every time she lifts a clod of earth well broken up, and in the hole thus made she plants three or four grains of maize and covers them up.' Among the Barotsé, who cultivate millet, maize, and peas to a small extent and in a rudimentary fashion, women alone are occupied with the field-work, and their only implement is a spade or hoe. Of the Matabelé we are told that 'most of the hard work is performed by the women; the whole of the cultivation is done by them.' Among the Awemba, to the west of Lake Tanganyika, the bulk of the work in the plantations falls on the women; in particular the men refuse to hoe the ground. They have a saying, 'Is not each male child born for the axe and each female child for the hoe?'

Chastity required in the sowers of seed.

The natives of the Tanganyika plateau 'cultivate the banana, and have a curious custom connected with it. No man is permitted to sow; but when the hole is prepared a little girl is carried to the spot on a man's shoulders. She first throws into the hole a sherd of broken pottery, and then scatters the seed over it.' The reason of the latter practice has been explained by more recent observers. 'Young children, it may here be noted, are often employed to administer drugs, remedies, even the Poison Ordeal, and to sow the first seeds. Such acts, the natives say, must be performed by chaste and innocent hands, lest a contaminated touch should destroy the potency of the medicine or of the seedlings planted. It used to be a very common sight upon the islands of Lake Bangweolo to watch how a Bisa woman would solve the problem of her own moral unfitness by carrying her baby-girl to the banana-plot, and inserting seedlings in the tiny hands for dropping into the holes already prepared.' Similarly among the people of the Lower Congo 'women must remain chaste while planting pumpkin and calabash seeds, they are not allowed to touch any pig-meat, and they must wash their hands before touching the seeds. If a woman does not observe all these rules, she must not plant the seeds, or the crop will be bad; she may make the holes, and her baby girl, or another who has obeyed the restrictions, can drop in the seeds and cover them over.'

Of the Caffres of South Africa in general we read that agriculture is 'mainly the work of the women, for in olden days the men were occupied in hunting and fighting. The women do but scratch the land with hoes, sometimes using long-handled instruments, as in Zululand, and sometimes short-handled ones, as above the Zambesi. When the ground is thus prepared, the women scatter the seed, throwing it over the soil quite at random. They know the time to sow by the position of the constellations, chiefly by that of the Pleiades. They date their new year from the time they can see this constellation just before sunrise.' In Basutoland, where the women also till the fields, though the lands of chiefs are dug and sowed by men, an attempt is made to determine the time of sowing by observation of the moon, but the people generally find themselves out in their reckoning, and after much dispute are forced to fall back upon the state of the weather and of vegetation as better evidence of the season of sowing. Intelligent chiefs rectify the calendar at the summer solstice, which they call the summer-house of the sun.

Among the Nandi of British East Africa 'the rough work of clearing the bush for plantations is performed by the men, after which nearly all work in connexion with them is done by the women. The men, however, assist in sowing the seed, and in harvesting some of the crops.' The Baganda of Central Africa subsist chiefly on bananas, and among them 'the garden and its cultivation have always been the woman's department. Princesses and peasant women alike looked upon cultivation as their special work; the garden with its produce was essentially the wife's domain, and she would under no circumstances allow her husband to do any digging or sowing in it. No woman would remain with a man who did not give her a garden and a hoe to dig it with; if these were denied her, she would seek an early opportunity to escape from her husband and return to her relations to complain of her treatment, and to obtain justice or a divorce. When a man married he sought a plot of land for his

Woman's part in agriculture among the Caffres of South Africa in general.

Agricultural work done by women among the Nandi and other tribes of Central and Western Africa.

Agricultural work of women among the Baganda.

wife in order that she might settle to work and provide food for the household.' In Kiziba, a district immediately to the south of Uganda, the tilling of the soil is exclusively the work of the women. They turn up the soil with hoes, make holes in the ground with digging-sticks or their fingers, and drop a few seeds into each hole. Among the Niam-Niam of Central Africa 'the men most studiously devote themselves to their hunting, and leave the culture of the soil to be carried on exclusively by the women'; and among the Monbuttoo of the same region in like manner, 'whilst the women attend to the tillage of the soil and the gathering of the harvest, the men, unless they are absent either for war or hunting, spend the entire day in idleness'. As to the Bangala of the Upper Congo we read that 'large farms were made around the towns. The men did the clearing of the bush, felling the trees, and cutting down the undergrowth; the women worked with them, heaping up the grass and brushwood ready for burning, and helping generally. As a rule the women did the hoeing, planting, and weeding, but the men did not so despise this work as never to do it.' In this tribe 'the food belonged to the woman who cultivated the farm, and while she supplied her husband with the vegetable food, he had to supply the fish and meat and share them with his wife or wives.' Amongst the Tofoke, a tribe of the Congo State on the equator, all the field labour, except the clearing away of the forest, is performed by the women. They dig the soil with a hoe and plant maize and manioc. A field is used only once. So with the Ba-Mbala, a Bantu tribe between the rivers Inzia and Kwilu, the men clear the ground for cultivation, but all the rest of the work of tillage falls to the women, whose only tool is an iron hoe. Fresh ground is cleared for cultivation every year. The Mpongwe of the Gaboon, in West Africa, cultivate manioc (cassava), maize, yams, plantains, sweet potatoes, and ground nuts. When new clearings have to be made in the forest, the men cut down and burn the trees, and the women put in the crop. The only tool they use is a dibble, with which they turn up a sod, put in a seed, and cover it.

Agricultural work of women on the Congo.

Among some peoples of the Indian Archipelago, after the land has been cleared for cultivation by the men, the work of planting and sowing is divided between men and women, the men digging holes in the ground with pointed sticks, and the

Division of agricultural work between men and women

women following them, putting the seeds or shoots into the holes, and then huddling the earth over them; for savages seldom sow broadcast, they laboriously dig holes and insert the seed in them. This division of agricultural labour between the sexes is adopted by various tribes of Celebes, Ceram, Borneo, Nias, and New Guinea. Sometimes the custom of entrusting the sowing of the seed to women appears to be influenced by superstitious as well as economic considerations. Thus among the Indians of the Orinoco, who with an infinitude of pains cleared the jungle for cultivation by cutting down the forest trees with their stone axes, burning the fallen lumber, and breaking up the ground with wooden instruments hardened in the fire, the task of sowing the maize and planting the roots was performed by the women alone; and when the Spanish missionaries expostulated with the men for not helping their wives in this toilsome duty, they received for answer that as women knew how to conceive seed and bear children, so the seeds and roots planted by them bore fruit far more abundantly than if they had been planted by male hands.

in the Indian Archipelago.

Even among savages who have not yet learned to cultivate any plants the task of collecting the edible seeds and digging up the edible roots of wild plants appears to devolve mainly on women, while the men contribute their share to the common food supply by hunting and fishing, for which their superior strength, agility, and courage especially qualify them. For example, among the Indians of California, who were entirely ignorant of agriculture, the general division of labour between the sexes in the search for food was that the men killed the game and caught the salmon, while the women dug the roots and brought in most of the vegetable food, though the men helped them to gather acorns, nuts, and berries. Among the Indians of San Juan Capistrano in California, while the men passed their time in fowling, fishing, dancing, and lounging, 'the women were obliged to gather seeds in the fields, prepare them for cooking, and to perform all the meanest offices, as well as the most laborious. It was painful in the extreme, to behold them, with their infants hanging upon their shoulders, groping about in search of herbs or seeds, and exposed, as they frequently were to the inclemency of the weather.'

Among savages who have not learned to till the ground the task of collecting the vegetable food in the form of wild seeds and roots generally devolves on women. Examples furnished by the Californian Indians.

The digging
of the earth
for wild
fruits may
have led to
the origin of
agriculture.

In these customs observed by savages who are totally ignorant of agriculture we may perhaps detect some of the steps by which mankind have advanced from the enjoyment of the wild fruits of the earth to the systematic cultivation of plants. For an effect of digging up the earth in the search for roots has probably been in many cases to enrich and fertilise the soil and so to increase the crop of roots or herbs; and such an increase would naturally attract the natives in larger numbers and enable them to subsist for longer periods on the spot without being compelled by the speedy exhaustion of the crop to shift their quarters and wander away in search of fresh supplies. Moreover, the winnowing of the seeds on ground which had thus been turned up by the digging-sticks of the women would naturally contribute to the same result. For though savages at the level of the Californian Indians and the aborigines of Australia have no idea of using seeds for any purpose but that of immediate consumption, and it has never occurred to them to incur a temporary loss for the sake of a future gain by sowing them in the ground, yet it is almost certain that in the process of winnowing the seeds as a preparation for eating them many of the grains must have escaped and, being wafted by the wind, have fallen on the upturned soil and borne fruit. Thus by the operations of turning up the ground and winnowing the seed, though neither operation aimed at anything beyond satisfying the immediate pangs of hunger, savage man or rather savage woman was unconsciously preparing for the whole community a future and more abundant store of food, which would enable them to multiply and to abandon the old migratory and wasteful manner of life for a more settled and economic mode of existence. So curiously sometimes does man, aiming his shafts at a near but petty mark, hit a greater and more distant target.

On the whole, then, it appears highly probable that as a consequence of a certain natural division of labour between the sexes women have contributed more than men towards the greatest advance in economic history, namely, the transition from a nomadic to a settled life, from a natural to an artificial basis of subsistence.

CHAPTER 18

THE CORN-MOTHER AND CORN-MAIDEN

i

IT has been argued by W. Mannhardt* that the first part of Demeter's name is derived from an alleged Cretan word *deai*, 'barley', and that accordingly Demeter means neither more nor less than 'Barley-mother' or 'Corn-mother'; for the root of the word seems to have been applied to different kinds of grain by different branches of the Aryans. As Crete appears to have been one of the most ancient seats of the worship of Demeter, it would not be surprising if her name were of Cretan origin. But the etymology is open to serious objections, and it is safer therefore to lay no stress on it. Be that as it may, we have found independent reasons for identifying Demeter as the Corn-mother, and of the two species of corn associated with her in Greek religion, namely barley and wheat, the barley has perhaps the better claim to be her original element; for not only would it seem to have been the staple food of the Greeks in the Homeric age, but there are grounds for believing that it is one of the oldest, if not the very oldest, cereal cultivated by the Aryan race. Certainly the use of barley in the religious ritual of the ancient Hindoos as well as of the ancient Greeks furnishes a strong argument in favour of the great antiquity of its cultivation, which is known to have been practised by the lake-dwellers of the Stone Age in Europe. *(margin: Suggested derivation of the name Demeter.)*

Analogies to the Corn-mother or Barley-mother of ancient Greece have been collected in great abundance by W. Mannhardt from the folk-lore of modern Europe. In Germany the corn is very commonly personified under the name of the Corn-mother. Thus in spring, when the corn waves in the wind, the peasants say, 'There comes the Corn-mother', or 'The Corn-mother is running over the field', or 'The Corn-mother is going through the corn.' When children wish to go into the fields to pull the blue corn-flowers or the red poppies, they are told not to do so, because the Corn-mother is sitting in the corn and will catch them. Or again she is called, according to the *(margin: The Corn-mother among the Germans and the Slavs.)*

crop, the Rye-mother or the Pea-mother, and children are warned against straying in the rye or among the peas by threats of the Rye-mother or the Pea-mother. In Norway also the Pea-mother is said to sit among the peas. Similar expressions are current among the Slavs. The Poles and Czechs warn children against the Corn-mother who sits in the corn. Or they call her the old Corn-woman, and say that she sits in the corn and strangles the children who tread it down. The Lithuanians say, 'The Old Rye-woman sits in the corn.' Again the Corn-mother is believed to make the crop grow. Thus in the neighbourhood of Magdeburg it is sometimes said, 'It will be a good year for flax; the Flax-mother has been seen.' At Dinkels-bühl, in Bavaria, down to the latter part of the nineteenth century, people believed that when the crops on a particular farm compared unfavourably with those of the neighbourhood, the reason was that the Corn-mother had punished the farmer for his sins. In a village of Styria it is said that the Corn-mother, in the shape of a female puppet made out of the last sheaf of corn and dressed in white, may be seen at midnight in the corn-fields, which she fertilises by passing through them; but if she is angry with a farmer, she withers up all his corn.

The Corn-mother in the last sheaf. Further, the Corn-mother plays an important part in harvest customs. She is believed to be present in the handful of corn which is left standing last on the field; and with the cutting of this last handful she is caught, or driven away, or killed. In the first of these cases, the last sheaf is carried joyfully home and honoured as a divine being. It is placed in the barn, and at threshing the corn-spirit appears again. In the Hanoverian district of Hadeln the reapers stand round the last sheaf and beat it with sticks in order to drive the Corn-mother out of it. They call to each other, 'There she is! hit her! Take care she doesn't catch you!' The beating goes on till the grain is completely threshed out; then the Corn-mother is believed to be driven away. In the neighbourhood of Danzig the person who cuts the last ears of corn makes them into a doll, which is called the Corn-mother or the Old Woman and is brought home on the last waggon. In some parts of Holstein the last sheaf is dressed in woman's clothes and called the Corn-mother. It is carried home on the last waggon, and then thoroughly drenched with water. The drenching with water is doubtless a rain-charm. In the district of Bruck in Styria the last sheaf, called the Corn-mother, is made up into the shape of a woman by the oldest married woman in the village, of an age from fifty to fifty-five years. The finest ears are plucked out of it and made into a wreath, which, twined with flowers, is carried on her head by the prettiest girl of the village to the farmer or squire, while the Corn-mother is laid down in the barn to keep off the mice. In other villages of the same district the Corn-mother, at the close of harvest, is carried by two lads at the top of a pole. They march behind the girl who wears the wreath to the squire's house, and while he receives the wreath and hangs it up in the hall, the Corn-mother is placed on the top of a pile of wood, where she is the centre of the harvest supper and dance. Afterwards she is hung up in the barn and remains there till the threshing is over. The man who gives the last stroke at threshing is called the son of the Corn-mother; he is tied up in the Corn-mother, beaten, and carried through the village. The wreath is dedicated in church on the following Sunday; and on Easter Eve the grain is rubbed out of it by a seven-years-old girl and scattered amongst the young corn. At Christmas the straw of the wreath is placed in the manger to make the cattle thrive. Here the fertilising power of the Corn-mother is plainly brought out by scattering the seed taken from her body (for the wreath is made out of the Corn-mother) among the new corn; and her influence over animal life is indicated by placing the straw in the manger. At Westerhüsen, in Saxony, the last corn cut is made in the shape of a woman decked with ribbons and cloth. It is fastened to a pole and brought home on the last waggon. One of the people in the waggon keeps waving the pole, so that the figure moves as if alive. It is placed on the threshing-floor, and stays there till the threshing is done. Amongst the Slavs also the last sheaf is known as the Rye-mother, the Wheat-mother, the Oats-mother, the Barley-mother, and so on, according to the crop. In the district of Tarnow, Galicia, the wreath made out of the last stalks is called the Wheat-mother, Rye-mother, or Pea-mother. It is placed on a girl's head and kept till spring, when some of the grain is mixed with the seed-corn. Here again the fertilising power of the Corn-mother is indicated. In France, also, in the neighbourhood of Auxerre, the last sheaf goes by the name of the Mother

Fertilising power of the Corn-mother.

The Corn-mother in the last sheaf among the Slavs and in France.

of the Wheat, Mother of the Barley, Mother of the Rye, or
Mother of the Oats. They leave it standing in the field till the
last waggon is about to wend homewards. Then they make a
puppet out of it, dress it with clothes belonging to the farmer,
and adorn it with a crown and a blue or white scarf. A branch
of a tree is stuck in the breast of the puppet, which is now called
the Ceres. At the dance in the evening the Ceres is set in the
middle of the floor, and the reaper who reaped fastest dances
round it with the prettiest girl for his partner. After the dance
a pyre is made. All the girls, each wearing a wreath, strip the
puppet, pull it to pieces, and place it on the pyre, along with
the flowers with which it was adorned. Then the girl who was
the first to finish reaping sets fire to the pile, and all pray that
Ceres may give a fruitful year. Here, as Mannhardt observes,
the old custom has remained intact, though the name Ceres is
a bit of schoolmaster's learning. In Upper Brittany the last sheaf
is always made into human shape; but if the farmer is a married
man, it is made double and consists of a little corn-puppet
placed inside of a large one. This is called the Mother-sheaf. It
is delivered to the farmer's wife, who unties it and gives
drink-money in return.

The Grand-
mother in
the last sheaf.   Sometimes the last sheaf is called the Grandmother, and is
adorned with flowers, ribbons, and a woman's apron. In East
Prussia, at the rye or wheat harvest, the reapers call out to the
woman who binds the last sheaf, 'You are getting the Old
Grandmother.' In the neighbourhood of Magdeburg the men
and women servants strive who shall get the last sheaf, called
the Grandmother. Whoever gets it will be married in the next
year, but his or her spouse will be old; if a girl gets it, she will
marry a widower; if a man gets it, he will marry an old crone.
In Silesia the Grandmother—a huge bundle made up of three
or four sheaves by the person who tied the last sheaf—was
formerly fashioned into a rude likeness of the human form. In
the neighbourhood of Belfast the last sheaf sometimes goes
by the name of the Granny. It is not cut in the usual way, but
all the reapers throw their sickles at it and try to bring it down.
It is plaited and kept till the (next ?) autumn. Whoever gets it
will marry in the course of the year.

The Corn-
queen and   In Russia also the last sheaf is often shaped and dressed as a
woman, and carried with dance and song to the farmhouse. Out

of the last sheaf the Bulgarians make a doll which they call the
Corn-queen or Corn-mother; it is dressed in a woman's shirt,
carried round the village, and then thrown into the river in
order to secure plenty of rain and dew for the next year's crop.
Or it is burned and the ashes strewn on the fields, doubtless to
fertilise them. The name Queen, as applied to the last sheaf, has
its analogies in central and northern Europe. Thus, in the
Salzburg district of Austria, at the end of the harvest a great
procession takes place, in which a Queen of the Corn-ears
(*Ährenkönigin*) is drawn along in a little carriage by young
fellows. The custom of the Harvest Queen appears to have been
common in England. Brand quotes from Hutchinson's *History
of Northumberland* the following: 'I have seen, in some places,
an image apparelled in great finery, crowned with flowers, a
sheaf of corn placed under her arm, and a scycle in her hand,
carried out of the village in the morning of the conclusive
reaping day, with music and much clamour of the reapers, into
the field, where it stands fixed on a pole all day, and when the
reaping is done, is brought home in like manner. This they call
the Harvest Queen, and it represents the Roman Ceres.'* Again,
the traveller Dr E. D. Clarke tells us that 'even in the town of
Cambridge, and centre of our University, such curious remains
of antient customs may be noticed, in different seasons of the
year, which pass without observation. The custom of blowing
horns upon the first of May (Old Style) is derived from a
festival in honour of Diana. At the *Hawkie*, as it is called, or
Harvest Home, I have seen a clown dressed in woman's clothes,
having his face painted, his head decorated with ears of corn,
and bearing about him other symbols of Ceres, carried in a
waggon, with great pomp and loud shouts, through the streets,
the horses being covered with white sheets: and when I inquired
the meaning of the ceremony, was answered by the people that
they were drawing the Morgay (MHTHP TH) or Harvest
Queen.'* Milton must have been familiar with the custom of the
Harvest Queen, for in *Paradise Lost* he says:

> 'Adam the while
> Waiting desirous her return, had wove
> Of choicest flow'rs a garland to adorn
> Her tresses, and her rural labours crown,
> As reapers oft are wont their harvest-queen.'*

In these customs the spirit of the ripe corn is regarded as old, or at least as of mature age. But in other cases the corn-spirit is conceived as young. Thus at Saldern, near Wolfenbuttel, when the rye has been reaped, three sheaves are tied together with a rope so as to make a puppet with the corn ears for a head. This puppet is called the Maiden or the Corn-maiden (*Kornjunfer*). Sometimes the corn-spirit is conceived as a child who is separated from its mother by the stroke of the sickle. This last view appears in the Polish custom of calling out to the man who cuts the last handful of corn, 'You have cut the navel-string.' In some districts of West Prussia the figure made out of the last sheaf is called the Bastard, and a boy is wrapt up in it. The woman who binds the last sheaf and represents the Corn-mother is told that she is about to be brought to bed; she cries like a woman in travail, and an old woman in the character of grandmother acts as midwife. At last a cry is raised that the child is born; whereupon the boy who is tied up in the sheaf whimpers and squalls like an infant. The grandmother wraps a sack, in imitation of swaddling bands, round the pretended baby, who is carried joyfully to the barn, lest he should catch cold in the open air. In other parts of North Germany the last sheaf, or the puppet made out of it, is called the Child, the Harvest-Child, and so on, and they call out to the woman who binds the last sheaf, 'you are getting the child.'

The last corn
cut called the
Maiden in
the High-
lands of
Scotland.

In some parts of the Highlands of Scotland the last handful of corn that is cut by the reapers on any particular farm is called the Maiden, or in Gaelic *Maidhdeanbuain*, literally 'the shorn Maiden'. Superstitions attach to the winning of the Maiden. If it is got by a young person, they think it an omen that he or she will be married before another harvest. For that or other reasons there is a strife between the reapers as to who shall get the Maiden, and they resort to various stratagems for the purpose of securing it. One of them, for example, will often leave a handful of corn uncut and cover it up with earth to hide it from the other reapers, till all the rest of the corn on the field is cut down. Several may try to play the same trick, and the one who is coolest and holds out longest obtains the coveted distinction. When it has been cut, the Maiden is dressed with ribbons into a sort of doll and affixed to a wall of the farmhouse. In the north of Scotland the Maiden is carefully preserved till Yule morning, when it is divided among the cattle 'to make them thrive all the year round'. In the island of Mull and some parts of the mainland of Argyleshire the last handful of corn cut is called the Maiden (*Maighdean-Bhuana*). Near Ardrishaig, in Argyleshire, the Maiden is made up in a fanciful three-cornered shape, decorated with ribbons, and hung from a nail on the wall.

A somewhat maturer but still youthful age is assigned to the corn-spirit by the appellations of Bride, Oats-bride, and Wheat-bride, which in Germany are sometimes bestowed both on the last sheaf and on the woman who binds it. At wheat-harvest near Müglitz, in Moravia, a small portion of the wheat is left standing after all the rest has been reaped. This remnant is then cut, amid the rejoicing of the reapers, by a young girl who wears a wreath of wheaten ears on her head and goes by the name of the Wheat-bride. It is supposed that she will be a real bride that same year. In the upland valley of Alpach, in North Tyrol, the person who brings the last sheaf into the granary is said to have the Wheat-bride or the Rye-bride according to the crop, and is received with great demonstrations of respect and rejoicing. The people of the farm go out to meet him, bells are rung, and refreshments offered to him on a tray. In Austrian Silesia a girl is chosen to be the Wheat-bride, and much honour is paid to her at the harvest-festival. Near Roslin and Stonehaven, in Scotland, the last handful of corn cut 'got the name of "the bride," and she was placed over the *bress* or chimney-piece; she had a ribbon tied below her numerous *ears*, and another round her waist'. *The corn-spirit as a bride.*

Sometimes the idea implied by the name of Bride is worked out more fully by representing the productive powers of vegetation as bride and bridegroom. Thus in the Vorharz an Oats-man and an Oats-woman, swathed in straw, dance at the harvest feast. In South Saxony an Oats-bridegroom and an Oats-bride figure together at the harvest celebration. The Oats-bridegroom is a man completely wrapt in oats-straw; the Oats-bride is a man dressed in woman's clothes, but not wrapt in straw. They are drawn in a waggon to the ale-house, where the dance takes place. At the beginning of the dance the dancers pluck the bunches of oats one by one from the Oats-bride-groom, while he struggles to keep them, till at last he is *The corn-spirit as Bride and Bridegroom.*

completely stript of them and stands bare, exposed to the laughter and jests of the company. In Austrian Silesia the ceremony of 'the Wheat-bride' is celebrated by the young people at the end of the harvest. The woman who bound the last sheaf plays the part of the Wheat-bride, wearing the harvest-crown of wheat ears and flowers on her head. Thus adorned, standing beside her Bridegroom in a waggon and attended by bridesmaids, she is drawn by a pair of oxen, in full imitation of a marriage procession, to the tavern where the dancing is kept up till morning.

The corn-spirit in the double form of the Old Wife and the Maiden simultaneously at harvest in the Highlands of Scotland.

In these last instances the corn-spirit is personified in double form as male and female. But sometimes the spirit appears in a double female form as both old and young, corresponding exactly to the Greek Demeter and Persephone, if my interpretation of these goddesses is right. We have seen that in Scotland, especially among the Gaelic-speaking population, the last corn cut is sometimes called the Old Wife and sometimes the Maiden. Now there are parts of Scotland in which both an Old Wife (*Cailleach*) and a Maiden are cut at harvest. The accounts of this custom are not quite clear and consistent. The

In these customs the Old Wife represents the old corn of last year, and the Maiden the new corn of this year.

general rule seems to be that, where both a Maiden and an Old Wife (*Cailleach*) are fashioned out of the reaped corn at harvest, the Maiden is always made out of the last stalks left standing, and is kept by the farmer on whose land it was cut; while the Old Wife is made out of other stalks, sometimes out of the first stalks cut, and is regularly passed on to a laggard farmer who happens to be still reaping after his brisker neighbour has cut all his corn. Thus while each farmer keeps his own Maiden, as the embodiment of the young and fruitful spirit of the corn, he passes on the Old Wife as soon as he can to a neighbour, and so the old lady may make the round of all the farms in the district before she finds a place in which to lay her venerable head. The farmer with whom she finally takes up her abode is of course the one who has been the last of all the countryside to finish reaping his crops, and thus the distinction of entertaining her is rather an invidious one. If the Old Wife represents the corn-spirit of the past year, as she probably does wherever she is contrasted with and opposed to a Maiden, it is natural enough that her faded charms should have less attractions for the husbandman than the buxom form of her daughter, who may be expected to become in her turn the mother of the golden grain when the revolving year has brought round another autumn. The same desire to get rid of the effete Mother of the Corn by palming her off on other people comes out clearly in some of the customs observed at the close of threshing, particularly in the practice of passing on a hideous straw puppet to a neighbour farmer who is still threshing his corn.

The harvest customs just described are strikingly analogous to the spring customs which we reviewed in the first part of this work. (1) As in the spring customs the tree-spirit is represented both by a tree and by a person, so in the harvest customs the corn-spirit is represented both by the last sheaf and by the person who cuts or binds or threshes it. The equivalence of the person to the sheaf is shewn by giving him or her the same name as the sheaf; by wrapping him or her in it; and by the rule observed in some places, that when the sheaf is called the Mother, it must be made up into human shape by the oldest married woman, but that when it is called the Maiden, it must be cut by the youngest girl. Here the age of the personal representative of the corn-spirit corresponds with that of the supposed age of the corn-spirit. (2) Again, the same fertilising influence which the tree-spirit is supposed to exert over vegetation, cattle, and even women is ascribed to the corn-spirit. Thus, its supposed influence on vegetation is shewn by the practice of taking some of the grain of the last sheaf (in which the corn-spirit is regularly supposed to be present), and scattering it among the young corn in spring or mixing it with the seed-corn. Its influence on animals is shewn by giving the last sheaf to a mare in foal, to a cow in calf, and to horses at the first ploughing. Lastly, its influence on women is indicated by the custom of delivering the Mother-sheaf, made into the likeness of a pregnant woman, to the farmer's wife; by the belief that the woman who binds the last sheaf will have a child next year; perhaps, too, by the idea that the person who gets it will soon be married.

Analogy of the harvest customs to the spring customs of Europe.

Plainly, therefore, these spring and harvest customs are based on the same ancient modes of thought, and form parts of the same primitive heathendom, which was doubtless practised by our forefathers long before the dawn of history. Amongst the marks of a primitive ritual we may note the following:

The spring and harvest customs of Europe are parts of a primitive heathen ritual.

1. No special class of persons is set apart for the performance of the rites; in other words, there are no priests. The rites may be performed by any one, as occasion demands.

2. No special places are set apart for the performance of the rites; in other words, there are no temples. The rites may be performed anywhere, as occasion demands.

3. Spirits, not gods, are recognised. (*a*) As distinguished from gods, spirits are restricted in their operations to definite departments of nature. Their names are general, not proper. Their attributes are generic, rather than individual; in other words, there is an indefinite number of spirits of each class, and the individuals of a class are all much alike; they have no definitely marked individuality; no accepted traditions are current as to their origin, life, adventures, and character. (*b*) On the other hand gods, as distinguished from spirits, are not restricted to definite departments of nature. It is true that there is generally some one department over which they preside as their special province; but they are not rigorously confined to it; they can exert their power for good or evil in many other spheres of nature and life. Again, they bear individual or proper names, such as Demeter, Persephone, Dionysus; and their individual characters and histories are fixed by current myths and the representations of art.

4. The rites are magical rather than propitiatory. In other words, the desired objects are attained, not by propitiating the favour of divine beings through sacrifice, prayer, and praise, but by ceremonies which, as I have already explained, are believed to influence the course of nature directly through a physical sympathy or resemblance between the rite and the effect which it is the intention of the rite to produce.

Reasons for
regarding the
spring and
harvest cus-
toms of mod-
ern Europe
as a primit-
ive ritual.

Judged by these tests, the spring and harvest customs of our European peasantry deserve to rank as primitive. For no special class of persons and no special places are set exclusively apart for their performance; they may be performed by any one, master or man, mistress or maid, boy or girl; they are practised, not in temples or churches, but in the woods and meadows, beside brooks, in barns, on harvest fields and cottage floors. The supernatural beings whose existence is taken for granted in them are spirits rather than deities: their functions are limited to certain well-defined departments of nature: their names are general, like the Barley-mother, the Old Woman, the Maiden, not proper names like Demeter, Persephone, Dionysus. Their generic attributes are known, but their individual histories and characters are not the subject of myths. For they exist in classes rather than as individuals, and the members of each class are indistinguishable. For example, every farm has its Corn-mother, or its Old Woman, or its Maiden; but every Corn-mother is much like every other Corn-mother, and so with the Old Women and Maidens. Lastly, in these harvest, as in the spring customs, the ritual is magical rather than propitiatory. This is shewn by throwing the Corn-mother into the river in order to secure rain and dew for the crops; by making the Old Woman heavy in order to get a heavy crop next year; by strewing grain from the last sheaf amongst the young crops in spring; and by giving the last sheaf to the cattle to make them thrive.

ii

European peoples, ancient and modern, have not been singular in personifying the corn as a mother goddess. The same simple idea has suggested itself to other agricultural races in distant parts of the world, and has been applied by them to other indigenous cereals than barley and wheat. If Europe has its Wheat-mother and its Barley-mother, America has its Maize-mother and the East Indies their Rice-mother.

The Corn-mother in many lands.

We have seen that among European peoples it is a common custom to keep the plaited corn-stalks of the last sheaf, or the puppet which is formed out of them, in the farm-house from harvest to harvest. The intention no doubt is, or rather originally was, by preserving the representative of the corn-spirit to maintain the spirit itself in life and activity throughout the year, in order that the corn may grow and the crops be good. This interpretation of the custom is at all events rendered highly probable by a similar custom observed by the ancient Peruvians, and thus described by the old Spanish historian Acosta: 'They take a certain portion of the most fruitful of the maize that grows in their farms, the which they put in a certain granary which they do call *Pirua*, with certain ceremonies, watching three nights; they put this maize in the richest garments they have, and being thus wrapped and dressed, they worship this

The Maize-mother among the Peruvian Indians.

Pirua, and hold it in great veneration, saying it is the mother of the maize of their inheritances, and that by this means the maize augments and is preserved. In this month [the sixth month, answering to May] they make a particular sacrifice, and the witches demand of this *Pirua* if it hath strength sufficient to continue until the next year; and if it answers no, then they carry this maize to the farm to burn, whence they brought it, according to every man's power; then they make another *Pirua*, with the same ceremonies, saying that they renew it, to the end the seed of maize may not perish, and if it answers that it hath force sufficient to last longer, they leave it until the next year. This foolish vanity continueth to this day, and it is very common amongst the Indians to have these *Piruas*.'*

In this description of the custom there seems to be some error. Probably it was the dressed-up bunch of maize, not the granary (*Pirua*), which was worshipped by the Peruvians and regarded as the Mother of the Maize. This is confirmed by what we know of the Peruvian custom from another source. The Peruvians, we are told, believed all useful plants to be animated by a divine being who causes their growth. According to the particular plant, these divine beings were called the Maize-mother (*Zara-mama*), the Quinoa-mother (*Quinoa-mama*), the Coca-mother (*Coca-mama*), and the Potato-mother (*Axo-mama*). Figures of these divine mothers were made respectively of ears of maize and leaves of the quinoa and coca plants; they were dressed in women's clothes and worshipped. Thus the Maize-mother was represented by a puppet made of stalks of maize dressed in full female attire; and the Indians believed that 'as mother, it had the power of producing and giving birth to much maize'. Probably, therefore, Acosta misunderstood his inform-ant, and the Mother of the Maize which he describes was not the granary (*Pirua*), but the bunch of maize dressed in rich vestments. The Peruvian Mother of the Maize, like the harvest-Maiden at Balquhidder, was kept for a year in order that by her means the corn might grow and multiply. But lest her strength might not suffice to last till the next harvest, she was asked in the course of the year how she felt, and if she answered that she felt weak, she was burned and a fresh Mother of the Maize made, 'to the end the seed of maize may not perish'. Here, it may be observed, we have a strong confirmation of the expla-

The Maize-mother, the Quinoa-mother, the Coca-mother, and the Pota-to-mother among the Peruvian Indians.

nation already given of the custom of killing the god, both periodically and occasionally. The Mother of the Maize was allowed, as a rule, to live through a year, that being the period during which her strength might reasonably be supposed to last unimpaired; but on any symptom of her strength failing she was put to death, and a fresh and vigorous Mother of the Maize took her place, lest the maize which depended on her for its existence should languish and decay.

Hardly less clearly does the same train of thought come out in the harvest customs formerly observed by the Zapotecs of Mexico. At harvest the priests, attended by the nobles and people, went in procession to the maize fields, where they picked out the largest and finest sheaf. This they took with great ceremony to the town or village, and placed it in the temple upon an altar adorned with wild flowers. After sacrificing to the harvest god, the priests carefully wrapped up the sheaf in fine linen and kept it till seed-time. Then the priests and nobles met again at the temple, one of them bringing the skin of a wild beast, elaborately ornamented, in which the linen cloth containing the sheaf was enveloped. The sheaf was then carried once more in procession to the field from which it had been taken. Here a small cavity or subterranean chamber had been prepared, in which the precious sheaf was deposited, wrapt in its various envelopes. After sacrifice had been offered to the gods of the fields for an abundant crop the chamber was closed and covered over with earth. Immediately thereafter the sowing began. Finally, when the time of harvest drew near, the buried sheaf was solemnly disinterred by the priests, who distributed the grain to all who asked for it. The packets of grain so distributed were carefully preserved as talismans till the harvest. In these ceremonies, which continued to be annually celebrated long after the Spanish conquest, the intention of keeping the finest sheaf buried in the maize field from seed-time to harvest was undoubtedly to quicken the growth of the maize.

Customs of the ancient Mexicans at the maize-harvest.

The Corn-mother of our European peasants has her match in the Rice-mother of the Minangkabauers of Sumatra. The Minangkabauers definitely attribute a soul to rice, and will sometimes assert that rice pounded in the usual way tastes better than rice ground in a mill, because in the mill the body

The Rice-mother among the Minangkabauers of Sumatra.

of the rice was so bruised and battered that the soul has fled from it. Like the Javanese they think that the rice is under the special guardianship of a female spirit called Saning Sari, who is conceived as so closely knit up with the plant that the rice often goes by her name, as with the Romans the corn might be called Ceres. In particular Saning Sari is represented by certain stalks or grains called *indoea padi*, that is, literally, 'Mother of Rice', a name that is often given to the guardian spirit herself. This so-called Mother of Rice is the occasion of a number of ceremonies observed at the planting and harvesting of the rice as well as during its preservation in the barn. When the seed of the rice is about to be sown in the nursery or bedding-out ground, where under the wet system of cultivation it is regularly allowed to sprout before being transplanted to the fields, the best grains are picked out to form the Rice-mother. These are then sown in the middle of the bed, and the common seed is planted round about them. The state of the Rice-mother is supposed to exert the greatest influence on the growth of the rice; if she droops or pines away, the harvest will be bad in consequence. The woman who sows the Rice-mother in the nursery lets her hair hang loose and afterwards bathes, as a means of ensuring an abundant harvest. When the time comes to transplant the rice from the nursery to the field, the Rice-mother receives a special place either in the middle or in a corner of the field, and a prayer or charm is uttered as follows: 'Saning Sari, may a measure of rice come from a stalk of rice and a basketful from a root; may you be frightened neither by lightning nor by passers-by! Sunshine make you glad; with the storm may you be at peace; and may rain serve to wash your face!' While the rice is growing, the particular plant which was thus treated as the Rice-mother is lost sight of; but before harvest another Rice-mother is found. When the crop is ripe for cutting, the oldest woman of the family or a sorcerer goes out to look for her. The first stalks seen to bend under a passing breeze are the Rice-mother, and they are tied together but not cut until the first-fruits of the field have been carried home to serve as a festal meal for the family and their friends, nay even for the domestic animals; since it is Saning Sari's pleasure that the beasts also should partake of her good gifts. After the meal has been eaten, the Rice-mother is fetched home by persons in gay attire, who carry her very carefully under an umbrella in a neatly worked bag to the barn, where a place in the middle is assigned to her. Every one believes that she takes care of the rice in the barn and even multiplies it not uncommonly.

Once more, the European custom of representing the corn-spirit in the double form of bride and bridegroom has its parallel in a ceremony observed at the rice-harvest in Java. Before the reapers begin to cut the rice, the priest or sorcerer picks out a number of ears of rice, which are tied together, smeared with ointment, and adorned with flowers. Thus decked out, the ears are called the *padi-pĕngantèn*, that is, the Rice-bride and the Rice-bridegroom; their wedding feast is celebrated, and the cutting of the rice begins immediately afterwards. Later on, when the rice is being got in, a bridal chamber is partitioned off in the barn, and furnished with a new mat, a lamp, and all kinds of toilet articles. Sheaves of rice, to represent the wedding guests, are placed beside the Rice-bride and the Rice-bridegroom. Not till this has been done may the whole harvest be housed in the barn. And for the first forty days after the rice has been housed, no one may enter the barn, for fear of disturbing the newly-wedded pair.

The Rice-bride and the Rice-bride-groom at harvest in Java.

Another account of the Javanese custom runs as follows. When the rice at harvest is to be brought home, two handfuls of common unhusked rice (paddy) are tied together into a sheaf, and two handfuls of a special kind of rice (*kleefrijst*) are tied up into another sheaf; then the two sheaves are fastened together in a bundle which goes by the name of 'the bridal pair' (*pĕngantenan*). The special rice is the bridegroom, the common rice is the bride. At the barn 'the bridal pair' is received on a winnowing-fan by a wizard, who removes them from the fan and lays them on the floor with a couch of *kloewih* leaves under them 'in order that the rice may increase', and beside them he places a *kĕmiri* nut, tamarind pips, and a top and string as playthings with which the young couple may divert themselves. The bride is called Emboq Sri and the bridegroom Sadana, and the wizard addresses them by name, saying: 'Emboq Sri and Sadana, I have now brought you home and I have prepared a place for you. May you sleep agreeably in this agreeable place! Emboq Sri and Sadana, you have been received

Another account of the Javanese custom.

by So-and-So (the owner), let So-and-So lead a life free from care. May Emboq Sri's luck continue in this very agreeable place!'

iii

The Greeks may have started with the personification of the corn as a single goddess, and the conception of a second goddess may have been a later development.

On looking over the harvest customs which have been passed under review, it may be noticed that they involve two distinct conceptions of the corn-spirit. For whereas in some of the customs the corn-spirit is treated as immanent in the corn, in others it is regarded as external to it. Thus when a particular sheaf is called by the name of the corn-spirit, and is dressed in clothes and handled with reverence, the spirit is clearly regarded as immanent in the corn. But when the spirit is said to make the crops grow by passing through them, or to blight the grain of those against whom she has a grudge, she is apparently conceived as distinct from, though exercising power over, the corn. Conceived in the latter way the corn-spirit is in a fair way to become a deity of the corn, if she has not become so already. Of these two conceptions, that of the corn-spirit as immanent in the corn is doubtless the older, since the view of nature as animated by indwelling spirits appears to have generally preceded the view of it as controlled by external deities; to put it shortly, animism precedes deism. In the harvest customs of our European peasantry the corn-spirit seems to be conceived now as immanent in the corn and now as external to it. In Greek mythology, on the other hand, Demeter is viewed rather as the deity of the corn than as the spirit immanent in it. The process of thought which leads to the change from the one mode of conception to the other is anthropomorphism, or the gradual investment of the immanent spirits with more and more of the attributes of humanity. As men emerge from savagery the tendency to humanise their divinities gains strength; and the more human these become the wider is the breach which severs them from the natural objects of which they were at first merely the animating spirits or souls. But in the progress upwards from savagery men of the same generation do not march abreast; and though the new anthropomorphic gods may satisfy the religious wants of the more developed intelligences, the backward members of the community will cling by preference to the old

Duplication of deities as a consequence of the anthropomorphic tendency.

animistic notions. Now when the spirit of any natural object such as the corn has been invested with human qualities, detached from the object, and converted into a deity controlling it, the object itself is, by the withdrawal of its spirit, left inanimate; it becomes, so to say, a spiritual vacuum. But the popular fancy, intolerant of such a vacuum, in other words, unable to conceive anything as inanimate, immediately creates a fresh mythical being, with which it peoples the vacant object. Thus the same natural object comes to be represented in mythology by two distinct beings: first by the old spirit now separated from it and raised to the rank of a deity; second, by the new spirit, freshly created by the popular fancy to supply the place vacated by the old spirit on its elevation to a higher sphere. For example, in Japanese religion the solar character of Ama-terasu, the great goddess of the Sun, has become obscured, and accordingly the people have personified the sun afresh under the name of *Nichi-rin sama*, 'sun-wheeling personage', and *O tentō sama*, 'august-heaven-path-personage'; to the lower class of Japanese at the present day, especially to women and children, *O tentō sama* is the actual sun, sexless, mythless, and unencumbered by any formal worship, yet looked up to as a moral being who rewards the good, punishes the wicked, and enforces oaths made in his name. In such cases the problem for mythology is, having got two distinct personifications of the same object, what to do with them? How are their relations to each other to be adjusted, and room found for both in the mythological system? When the old spirit or new deity is conceived as creating or producing the object in question, the problem is easily solved. Since the object is believed to be produced by the old spirit, and animated by the new one, the latter, as the soul of the object, must also owe its existence to the former; thus the old spirit will stand to the new one as producer to produced, that is, in mythology, as parent to child, and if both spirits are conceived as female, their relation will be that of mother and daughter. In this way, starting from a single personification of the corn as female, mythic fancy might in time reach a double personification of it as mother and daughter. It would be very rash to affirm that this was the way in which the myth of Demeter and Persephone actually took shape; but it seems a legitimate conjecture that the reduplication of deities,

Example of such duplication in Japan, where there are two distinct deities of the sun.

Perhaps the Greek personification of the corn as a mother and a daughter

(Demeter and Persephone) is a case of such a mythical duplication.

of which Demeter and Persephone furnish an example, may sometimes have arisen in the way indicated. For example, among the pairs of deities dealt with in a former part of this work, it has been shewn that there are grounds for regarding both Isis and her companion god Osiris as personifications of the corn. On the hypothesis just suggested, Isis would be the old corn-spirit, and Osiris would be the newer one, whose relationship to the old spirit was variously explained as that of brother, husband, and son; for of course mythology would always be free to account for the coexistence of the two divinities in more ways than one. It must not, however, be forgotten that this proposed explanation of such pairs of deities as Demeter and Persephone or Isis and Osiris is purely conjectural, and is only given for what it is worth.

CHAPTER 19

LITYERSES

i

AN attempt has been made to shew that in the Corn-mother and Harvest-maiden of Northern Europe we have the prototypes of Demeter and Persephone. But an essential feature is still wanting to complete the resemblance. A leading incident in the Greek myth is the death and resurrection of Persephone; it is this incident which, coupled with the nature of the goddess as a deity of vegetation, links the myth with the cults of Adonis, Attis, Osiris, and Dionysus; and it is in virtue of this incident that the myth finds a place in our discussion of the Dying God. It remains, therefore, to see whether the conception of the annual death and resurrection of a god, which figures so prominently in these great Greek and Oriental worships, has not also its origin or its analogy in the rustic rites observed by reapers and vine-dressers amongst the corn-shocks and the vines.

> Death and resurrection a leading incident in the myth of Persephone, as in the myths of Adonis, Attis, Osiris, and Dionysus.

Our general ignorance of the popular superstitions and customs of the ancients has already been confessed. But the obscurity which thus hangs over the first beginnings of ancient religion is fortunately dissipated to some extent in the present case. The worships of Osiris, Adonis, and Attis had their respective seats, as we have seen, in Egypt, Syria, and Phrygia; and in each of these countries certain harvest and vintage customs are known to have been observed, the resemblance of which to each other and to the national rites struck the ancients themselves, and, compared with the harvest customs of modern peasants and barbarians, seems to throw some light on the origin of the rites in question.

> Popular harvest and vintage customs in ancient Egypt, Syria, and Phrygia.

It has been already mentioned, on the authority of Diodorus, that in ancient Egypt the reapers were wont to lament over the first sheaf cut, invoking Isis as the goddess to whom they owed the discovery of corn.* To the plaintive song or cry sung or uttered by Egyptian reapers the Greeks gave the name of Maneros, and explained the name by a story that Maneros, the

> Maneros, a plaintive song of Egyptian reapers.

only son of the first Egyptian king, invented agriculture, and, dying an untimely death, was thus lamented by the people. It appears, however, that the name Maneros is due to a misunderstanding of the formula *mââ-ne-hra*, 'Come to the house', which has been discovered in various Egyptian writings, for example in the dirge of Isis in the Book of the Dead. Hence we may suppose that the cry *mââ-ne-hra* was chanted by the reapers over the cut corn as a dirge for the death of the corn-spirit (Isis or Osiris) and a prayer for its return.

Linus or Ailinus, a plaintive song sung at the vintage in Phoenicia.

In Phoenicia and Western Asia a plaintive song, like that chanted by the Egyptian corn-reapers, was sung at the vintage and probably (to judge by analogy) also at harvest. This Phoenician song was called by the Greeks Linus or Ailinus and explained, like Maneros, as a lament for the death of a youth named Linus. According to one story Linus was brought up by a shepherd, but torn to pieces by his dogs. But, like Maneros, the name Linus or Ailinus appears to have originated in a verbal misunderstanding, and to be nothing more than the cry *ai lanu*, that is 'Woe to us', which the Phoenicians probably uttered in mourning for Adonis; at least Sappho seems to have regarded Adonis and Linus as equivalent.

Lityerses, a song sung at reaping and threshing in Phrygia. Legend of Lityerses.

In Phrygia the corresponding song, sung by harvesters both at reaping and at threshing, was called Lityerses. According to one story, Lityerses was a bastard son of Midas, King of Phrygia, and dwelt at Celaenae. He used to reap the corn, and had an enormous appetite. When a stranger happened to enter the cornfield or to pass by it, Lityerses gave him plenty to eat and drink, then took him to the corn-fields on the banks of the Maeander and compelled him to reap along with him. Lastly, it was his custom to wrap the stranger in a sheaf, cut off his head with a sickle, and carry away his body, swathed in the corn stalks. But at last Hercules* undertook to reap with him, cut off his head with the sickle, and threw his body into the river. As Hercules is reported to have slain Lityerses in the same way that Lityerses slew others (as Theseus treated Sinis and Sciron), we may infer that Lityerses used to throw the bodies of his victims into the river. According to another version of the story, Lityerses, a son of Midas, was wont to challenge people to a reaping match with him, and if he vanquished them he used to thrash them; but one day he met with a stronger reaper, who slew him.

There are some grounds for supposing that in these stories of Lityerses we have the description of a Phrygian harvest custom in accordance with which certain persons, especially strangers passing the harvest field, were regularly regarded as embodiments of the corn-spirit, and as such were seized by the reapers, wrapt in sheaves, and beheaded, their bodies, bound up in the corn-stalks, being afterwards thrown into water as a rain-charm. The grounds for this supposition are, first, the resemblance of the Lityerses story to the harvest customs of European peasantry, and, second, the frequency of human sacrifices offered by savage races to promote the fertility of the fields. We will examine these grounds successively, beginning with the former.

The story of Lityerses seems to reflect an old Phrygian harvest custom of killing strangers as embodiments of the corn-spirit.

We have seen that in modern Europe the person who cuts or binds or threshes the last sheaf is often exposed to rough treatment at the hands of his fellow-labourers. For example, he is bound up in the last sheaf, and, thus encased, is carried or carted about, beaten, drenched with water, thrown on a dung-hill, and so forth. Or, if he is spared this horseplay, he is at least the subject of ridicule or is thought to be destined to suffer some misfortune in the course of the year. Hence the harvesters are naturally reluctant to give the last cut at reaping or the last stroke at threshing or to bind the last sheaf, and towards the close of the work this reluctance produces an emulation among the labourers, each striving to finish his task as fast as possible, in order that he may escape the invidious distinction of being last. For example, in the neighbourhood of Danzig, when the winter corn is cut and mostly bound up in sheaves, the portion which still remains to be bound is divided amongst the women binders, each of whom receives a swath of equal length to bind. A crowd of reapers, children, and idlers gather round to witness the contest, and at the word, 'Seize the Old Man', the women fall to work, all binding their allotted swaths as hard as they can. The spectators watch them narrowly, and the woman who cannot keep pace with the rest and consequently binds the last sheaf has to carry the Old Man (that is, the last sheaf made up in the form of a man) to the farmhouse and deliver it to the farmer with the words, 'Here I bring you the Old Man.' At the supper which follows, the Old Man is placed at the table and receives an abundant portion of food, which, as he cannot eat it, falls to the share of the woman who carried him. Afterwards

Contests among reapers, binders, and threshers in order not to be the last at their work.

the Old Man is placed in the yard and all the people dance round him. Or the woman who bound the last sheaf dances for a good while with the Old Man, while the rest form a ring round them; afterwards they all, one after the other, dance a single round with him. Further, the woman who bound the last sheaf goes herself by the name of the Old Man till the next harvest, and is often mocked with the cry, 'Here comes the Old Man.' In the Mittelmark district of Prussia, when the rye has been reaped, and the last sheaves are about to be tied up, the binders stand in two rows facing each other, every woman with her sheaf and her straw rope before her. At a given signal they all tie up their sheaves, and the one who is the last to finish is ridiculed by the rest. Not only so, but her sheaf is made up into human shape and called the Old Man, and she must carry it home to the farmyard, where the harvesters dance in a circle round her and it. Then they take the Old Man to the farmer and deliver it to him with the words, 'We bring the Old Man to the Master. He may keep him till he gets a new one.' After that the Old Man is set up against a tree, where he remains for a long time, the butt of many jests. At Aschbach in Bavaria, when the reaping is nearly finished, the reapers say, 'Now, we will drive out the Old Man.' Each of them sets himself to reap a patch of corn as fast as he can; he who cuts the last handful or the last stalk is greeted by the rest with an exulting cry, 'You have the Old Man.' Sometimes a black mask is fastened on the reaper's face and he is dressed in woman's clothes; or if the reaper is a woman, she is dressed in man's clothes. A dance follows. At the supper the Old Man gets twice as large a portion of food as the others. The proceedings are similar at threshing; the person who gives the last stroke is said to have the Old Man. At the supper given to the threshers he has to eat out of the cream-ladle and to drink a great deal. Moreover, he is quizzed and teased in all sorts of ways till he frees himself from further annoyance by treating the others to brandy or beer.

The corn-spirit supposed to be killed at reaping or threshing.

Passing to the second point of comparison between the Lityerses story and European harvest customs, we have now to see that in the latter the corn-spirit is often believed to be killed at reaping or threshing. In the Romsdal and other parts of Norway, when the haymaking is over, the people say that 'the Old Hay-man has been killed'. In some parts of Bavaria the man who gives the last stroke at threshing is said to have killed the Corn-man, the Oats-man, or the Wheat-man, according to the crop. In the Canton of Tillot, in Lothringen, at threshing the last corn the men keep time with their flails, calling out as they thresh, 'We are killing the Old Woman! We are killing the Old Woman!' If there is an old woman in the house she is warned to save herself, or she will be struck dead. Near Ragnit, in Lithuania, the last handful of corn is left standing by itself, with the words, 'The Old Woman (*Boba*) is sitting in there.' Then a young reaper whets his scythe, and, with a strong sweep, cuts down the handful. It is now said of him that 'he has cut off the Boba's head'; and he receives a gratuity from the farmer and a jugful of water over his head from the farmer's wife. According to another account, every Lithuanian reaper makes haste to finish his task; for the Old Rye-woman lives in the last stalks, and whoever cuts the last stalks kills the Old Rye-woman, and by killing her he brings trouble on himself. In Wilkischken, in the district of Tilsit, the man who cuts the last corn goes by the name of 'the killer of the Rye-woman'. In Lithuania, again, the corn-spirit is believed to be killed at threshing as well as at reaping. When only a single pile of corn remains to be threshed, all the threshers suddenly step back a few paces, as if at the word of command. Then they fall to work, plying their flails with the utmost rapidity and vehemence, till they come to the last bundle. Upon this they fling themselves with almost frantic fury, straining every nerve, and raining blows on it till the word 'Halt!' rings out sharply from the leader. The man whose flail is the last to fall after the command to stop has been given is immediately surrounded by all the rest, crying out that 'he has struck the Old Rye-woman dead'. He has to expiate the deed by treating them to brandy; and, like the man who cuts the last corn, he is known as 'the killer of the Old Rye-woman'. Sometimes in Lithuania the slain corn-spirit was represented by a puppet. Thus a female figure was made out of corn-stalks, dressed in clothes, and placed on the threshing-floor, under the heap of corn which was to be threshed last. Whoever thereafter gave the last stroke at threshing 'struck the Old Woman dead'. We have already met with examples of burning the figure which represents the corn-spirit. In the East Riding of Yorkshire a custom called 'burning the

Old Witch' is observed on the last day of harvest. A small sheaf of corn is burnt on the field in a fire of stubble; peas are parched at the fire and eaten with a liberal allowance of ale; and the lads and lasses romp about the flames and amuse themselves by blackening each other's faces. Sometimes, again, the corn-spirit is represented by a man, who lies down under the last corn; it is threshed upon his body, and the people say that 'the Old Man is being beaten to death'. We saw that sometimes the farmer's wife is thrust, together with the last sheaf, under the threshing-machine, as if to thresh her, and that afterwards a pretence is made of winnowing her. At Volders, in the Tyrol, husks of corn are stuck behind the neck of the man who gives the last stroke at threshing, and he is throttled with a straw garland. If he is tall, it is believed that the corn will be tall next year. Then he is tied on a bundle and flung into the river. In Carinthia, the thresher who gave the last stroke, and the person who untied the last sheaf on the threshing-floor, are bound hand and foot with straw bands, and crowns of straw are placed on their heads. Then they are tied, face to face, on a sledge, dragged through the village, and flung into a brook. The custom of throwing the representative of the corn-spirit into a stream, like that of drenching him with water, is, as usual, a rain-charm.

Corn-spirit represented by a man, who is threshed.

Thus far the representatives of the corn-spirit have generally been the man or woman who cuts, binds, or threshes the last corn. We now come to the cases in which the corn-spirit is represented either by a stranger passing the harvest-field (as in the Lityerses tale), or by a visitor entering it for the first time. All over Germany it is customary for the reapers or threshers to lay hold of passing strangers and bind them with a rope made of corn-stalks, till they pay a forfeit; and when the farmer himself or one of his guests enters the field or the threshing-floor for the first time, he is treated in the same way. Sometimes the rope is only tied round his arm or his feet or his neck. But sometimes he is regularly swathed in corn. Thus at Solör in Norway, whoever enters the field, be he the master or a stranger, is tied up in a sheaf and must pay a ransom. In the neighbourhood of Soest, when the farmer visits the flax-pullers for the first time, he is completely enveloped in flax. Passers-by are also surrounded by the women, tied up in flax, and

Corn-spirit represented by a stranger or a visitor to the harvest-field, who is treated accordingly.

compelled to stand brandy. At Nördlingen strangers are caught
with straw ropes and tied up in a sheaf till they pay a forfeit.
Among the Germans of Haselberg, in West Bohemia, as soon as
a farmer had given the last corn to be threshed on the
threshing-floor, he was swathed in it and had to redeem himself
by a present of cakes. In Anhalt, when the proprietor or one of
his family, the steward, or even a stranger enters the harvest-
field for the first time after the reaping has begun, the wife of
the chief reaper ties a rope twisted of corn-ears, or a nosegay
made of corn-ears and flowers, to his arm, and he is obliged to
ransom himself by the payment of a fine. In the canton of
Putanges, in Normandy, a pretence of tying up the owner of the
land in the last sheaf of wheat is still practised, or at least was
still practised some quarter of a century ago. The task falls to
the women alone. They throw themselves on the proprietor,
seize him by the arms, the legs, and the body, throw him to the
ground, and stretch him on the last sheaf. Then a show is made
of binding him, and the conditions to be observed at the
harvest-supper are dictated to him. When he has accepted
them, he is released and allowed to get up.

Ceremonies of a somewhat similar kind are performed by the
Tarahumare Indians of Mexico not only at harvest but also at
hoeing and ploughing. 'When the work of hoeing and weeding
is finished, the workers seize the master of the field, and, tying
his arms crosswise behind him, load all the implements, that is
to say, the hoes, upon his back, fastening them with ropes.
Then they form two single columns, the landlord in the middle
between them, and all facing the house. Thus they start
homeward. Simultaneously the two men at the heads of the
columns begin to run rapidly forward some thirty yards, cross
each other, then turn back, run along the two columns, cross
each other again at the rear and take their places each at the end
of his row. As they pass each other ahead and in the rear of the
columns they beat their mouths with the hollow of their hands
and yell. As soon as they reach their places at the foot, the next
pair in front of the columns starts off, running in the same way,
and thus pair after pair performs the tour, the procession all the
time advancing toward the house. A short distance in front of
it they come to a halt, and are met by two young men who carry
red handkerchiefs tied to sticks like flags. The father of the

Ceremonies of the Tarahumare Indians at hoeing, ploughing and harvest.

family, still tied up and loaded with the hoes, steps forward alone and kneels down in front of his house-door. The flag-bearers wave their banners over him, and the women of the household come out and kneel on their left knees, first toward the east, and after a little while toward each of the other cardinal points, west, south, and north. In conclusion the flags are waved in front of the house. The father then rises and the people untie him, whereupon he first salutes the women with the usual greeting, "*Kwīra!*" or "*Kwirevá!*" Now they all go into the house, and the man makes a short speech thanking them all for the assistance they have given him, for how could he have gotten through his work without them? They have provided him with a year's life (that is, with the wherewithal to sustain it), and now he is going to give them tesvino. He gives a drinking-gourd full to each one in the assembly, and appoints one man among them to distribute more to all. The same ceremony is performed after the ploughing and after the harvesting. On the first occasion the tied man may be made to carry the yoke of the oxen, on the second he does not carry anything.'

Pretence made by the reapers of killing some one with their scythes.

The evidence adduced above suffices to prove that, like the ancient Lityerses, modern European reapers have been wont to lay hold of a passing stranger and tie him up in a sheaf. It is not to be expected that they should complete the parallel by cutting off his head; but if they do not take such a strong step, their language and gestures are at least indicative of a desire to do so. For instance, in Mecklenburg on the first day of reaping, if the master or mistress or a stranger enters the field, or merely passes by it, all the mowers face towards him and sharpen their scythes, clashing their whet-stones against them in unison, as if they were making ready to mow. Then the woman who leads the mowers steps up to him and ties a band round his left arm. He must ransom himself by payment of a forfeit. Near Ratzeburg, when the master or other person of mark enters the field or passes by it, all the harvesters stop work and march towards him in a body, the men with their scythes in front. On meeting him they form up in line, men and women. The men stick the poles of their scythes in the ground, as they do in whetting them; then they take off their caps and hang them on the scythes, while their leader stands forward and makes a speech.

When he has done, they all whet their scythes in measured time very loudly, after which they put on their caps. Two of the women binders then come forward; one of them ties the master or stranger (as the case may be) with corn-ears or with a silken band; the other delivers a rhyming address. In some parts of Pomerania every passer-by is stopped, his way being barred with a corn-rope. The reapers form a circle round him and sharpen their scythes, while their leader says:

> 'The men are ready,
> The scythes are bent,
> The corn is great and small,
> The gentleman must be mowed.'

Thus in these harvest-customs of modern Europe the person who cuts, binds, or threshes the last corn is treated as an embodiment of the corn-spirit by being wrapt up in sheaves, killed in mimicry by agricultural implements, and thrown into the water. These coincidences with the Lityerses story seem to prove that the latter is a genuine description of an old Phrygian harvest-custom. But since in the modern parallels the killing of the personal representative of the corn-spirit is necessarily omitted or at most enacted only in mimicry, it is desirable to shew that in rude society human beings have been commonly killed as an agricultural ceremony to promote the fertility of the fields. The following examples will make this plain.

Killing of the personal representative of the corn-spirit.

ii

The Indians of Guayaquil, in Ecuador, used to sacrifice human blood and the hearts of men when they sowed their fields. The people of Cañar (now Cuenca in Ecuador) used to sacrifice a hundred children annually at harvest. The kings of Quito, the Incas of Peru, and for a long time the Spaniards were unable to suppress the bloody rite. At a Mexican harvest-festival, when the first-fruits of the season were offered to the sun, a criminal was placed between two immense stones, balanced opposite each other, and was crushed by them as they fell together. His remains were buried, and a feast and dance followed. This sacrifice was known as 'the meeting of the stones'. 'Tlaloc was worshipped in Mexico as the god of the thunder and the storm

Human sacrifices for the crops in South and Central America.

which precedes the fertilising rain; elsewhere his wife Xochiquetzal, who at Tlaxcallan was called Matlalcuéyé or the Lady of the Blue Petticoats, shared these honours, and it was to her that many countries in Central America particularly paid their devotions. Every year, at the time when the cobs of the still green and milky maize are about to coagulate and ripen, they used to sacrifice to the goddess four young girls, chosen among the noblest families of the country; they were decked out in festal attire, crowned with flowers, and conveyed in rich palanquins to the brink of the hallowed waters, where the sacrifice was to be offered. The priests, clad in long floating robes, their heads encircled with feather crowns, marched in front of the litters carrying censers with burning incense. The town of Elopango, celebrated for its temple, was near the lake of the same name, the etymology of which refers to the sheaves of tender maize (*elotl*, "sheaf of tender maize"). It was dedicated to the goddess Xochiquetzal, to whom the young victims were offered by being hurled from the top of a rock into the abyss. At the moment of consummating this inhuman rite, the priests addressed themselves in turn to the four virgins in order to banish the fear of death from their minds. They drew for them a bright picture of the delights they were about to enjoy in the company of the gods, and advised them not to forget the earth which they had left behind, but to entreat the divinity, to whom they despatched them, to bless the forthcoming harvest.' We have seen that the ancient Mexicans also sacrificed human beings at all the various stages in the growth of the maize, the age of the victims corresponding to the age of the corn; for they sacrificed new-born babes at sowing, older children when the grain had sprouted, and so on till it was fully ripe, when they sacrificed old men. No doubt the correspondence between the ages of the victims and the state of the corn was supposed to enhance the efficacy of the sacrifice.

Human sacrifices for the crops in Africa.

At Lagos it was the custom annually to impale a young girl alive soon after the spring equinox in order to secure good crops. Along with her were sacrificed sheep and goats, which, with yams, heads of maize, and plantains, were hung on stakes on each side of her. The victims were bred up for the purpose in the king's seraglio, and their minds had been so powerfully wrought upon by the fetish men that they went cheerfully to

their fate. A similar sacrifice used to be annually offered at
Benin. The Marimos, a Bechuana tribe, sacrifice a human being
for the crops. The victim chosen is generally a short, stout man.
He is seized by violence or intoxicated and taken to the fields,
where he is killed amongst the wheat to serve as 'seed' (so they
phrase it). After his blood has coagulated in the sun, it is
burned along with the frontal bone, the flesh attached to it, and
the brain; the ashes are then scattered over the ground to
fertilise it. The rest of the body is eaten. The Wamegi of the
Usagara hills in German East Africa used to offer human
sacrifices of a peculiar kind once a year about the time of
harvest, which was also the time of sowing; for the Wamegi
have two crops annually, one in September and one in February.
The festival was usually held in September or October. The
victim was a girl who had attained the age of puberty. She was
taken to a hill where the festival was to be celebrated, and there
she was crushed to death between two branches. The sacrifice
was not performed in the fields, and my informant could not
ascertain its object, but we may conjecture that it was to ensure
good crops in the following year.

The Shans of Indo-China still believe in the efficacy of
human sacrifice to procure a good harvest, though they act on
the belief less than some other tribes of this region. Their
practice now is to poison somebody at the state festival, which
is generally held at some time between March and May. Among
the Lhota Naga, one of the many savage tribes who inhabit the
deep rugged labyrinthine glens which wind into the mountains
from the rich valley of Brahmapootra,* it used to be a common
custom to chop off the heads, hands, and feet of people they
met with, and then to stick up the severed extremities in their
fields to ensure a good crop of grain. They bore no ill-will
whatever to the persons upon whom they operated in this
unceremonious fashion. Once they flayed a boy alive, carved
him in pieces, and distributed the flesh among all the villagers,
who put it into their corn-bins to avert bad luck and ensure
plentiful crops of grain. The Angami, another tribe of the same
region, used also to relieve casual passers-by of their heads,
hands, and feet, with the same excellent intention. The hill
tribe Kudulu, near Vizagapatam in the Madras Presidency,
offered human sacrifices to the god Jankari for the purpose of

Human sacrifices for the crops among the Shans of Indo-China and the Nagas and other tribes of India.

obtaining good crops. The ceremony was generally performed on the Sunday before or after the Pongal feast. For the most part the victim was purchased, and until the time for the sacrifice came he was free to wander about the village, to eat and drink what he liked, and even to lie with any woman he met. On the appointed day he was carried before the idol drunk; and when one of the villagers had cut a hole in his stomach and smeared the blood on the idol, the crowds from the neighbouring villages rushed upon him and hacked him to pieces. All who were fortunate enough to secure morsels of his flesh carried them away and presented them to their village idols. The Gonds of India, a Dravidian race, kidnapped Brahman boys, and kept them as victims to be sacrificed on various occasions. At sowing and reaping, after a triumphal procession, one of the lads was slain by being punctured with a poisoned arrow. His blood was then sprinkled over the ploughed field or the ripe crop, and his flesh was devoured. The Oraons or Uraons of Chota Nagpur worship a goddess called Anna Kuari, who can give good crops and make a man rich, but to induce her to do so it is necessary to offer human sacrifices. In spite of the vigilance of the British Government these sacrifices are said to be still secretly perpetrated. The victims are poor waifs and strays whose disappearance attracts no notice. April and May are the months when the catchpoles are out on the prowl. At that time strangers will not go about the country alone, and parents will not let their children enter the jungle or herd the cattle. When a catchpole has found a victim, he cuts his throat and carries away the upper part of the ring finger and the nose. The goddess takes up her abode in the house of any man who has offered her a sacrifice, and from that time his fields yield a double harvest. The form she assumes in the house is that of a small child. When the householder brings in his unhusked rice, he takes the goddess and rolls her over the heap to double its size. But she soon grows restless and can only be pacified with the blood of fresh human victims.

iii

Human representative of

To return now to the Lityerses story. It has been shewn that in rude society human beings have been commonly killed to promote the growth of the crops. There is therefore no improbability in the supposition that they may once have been killed for a like purpose in Phrygia and Europe; and when Phrygian legend and European folk-custom, closely agreeing with each other, point to the conclusion that men were so slain, we are bound, provisionally at least, to accept the conclusion. Further, both the Lityerses story and European harvest-customs agree in indicating that the victim was put to death as a representative of the corn-spirit, and this indication is in harmony with the view which some savages appear to take of the victim slain to make the crops flourish. On the whole, then, we may fairly suppose that both in Phrygia and in Europe the representative of the corn-spirit was annually killed upon the harvest-field. Grounds have been already shewn for believing that similarly in Europe the representative of the tree-spirit was annually slain. The proofs of these two remarkable and closely analogous customs are entirely independent of each other. Their coincidence seems to furnish fresh presumption in favour of both.

the corn-spirit slain on the harvest-field.

To the question, How was the representative of the corn-spirit chosen? one answer has been already given. Both the Lityerses story and European folk-custom shew that passing strangers were regarded as manifestations of the corn-spirit escaping from the cut or threshed corn, and as such were seized and slain. But this is not the only answer which the evidence suggests. According to the Phrygian legend the victims of Lityerses were not simply passing strangers, but persons whom he had vanquished in a reaping contest and afterwards wrapt up in corn-sheaves and beheaded. This suggests that the representative of the corn-spirit may have been selected by means of a competition on the harvest-field, in which the vanquished competitor was compelled to accept the fatal honour. The supposition is countenanced by European harvest-customs. Now, since it is in the character of representative of the corn-spirit that the thresher of the last corn is slain in mimicry, and since the same representative character attaches (as we have seen) to the cutter and binder as well as to the thresher of the last corn, and since the same repugnance is evinced by harvesters to be last in any one of these labours, we may conjecture that a pretence has been commonly made of killing the reaper and binder as well as the thresher of the last corn, and that in

The victim who represented the corn-spirit may have been a passing stranger or the reaper, binder, or thresher of the last corn.

ancient times this killing was actually carried out. This conjecture is corroborated by the common superstition that whoever cuts the last corn must die soon. Sometimes it is thought that the person who binds the last sheaf on the field will die in the course of next year. The reason for fixing on the reaper, binder, or thresher of the last corn as the representative of the corn-spirit may be this. The corn-spirit is supposed to lurk as long as he can in the corn, retreating before the reapers, the binders, and the threshers at their work. But when he is forcibly expelled from his refuge in the last corn cut or the last sheaf bound or the last grain threshed, he necessarily assumes some other form than that of the corn-stalks which had hitherto been his garment or body. And what form can the expelled corn-spirit assume more naturally than that of the person who stands nearest to the corn from which he (the corn-spirit) has just been expelled? But the person in question is necessarily the reaper, binder, or thresher of the last corn. He or she, therefore, is seized and treated as the corn-spirit himself.

Perhaps the victim annually sacrificed in the character of the corn-spirit may have been the king himself.

Thus the person who was killed on the harvest-field as the representative of the corn-spirit may have been either a passing stranger or the harvester who was last at reaping, binding, or threshing. But there is a third possibility, to which ancient legend and modern folk-custom alike point. Lityerses not only put strangers to death; he was himself slain, and apparently in the same way as he had slain others, namely, by being wrapt in a corn-sheaf, beheaded, and cast into the river; and it is implied that this happened to Lityerses on his own land. Similarly in modern harvest-customs the pretence of killing appears to be carried out quite as often on the person of the master (farmer or squire) as on that of strangers. Now when we remember that Lityerses was said to have been a son of the King of Phrygia, and that in one account he is himself called a king, and when we combine with this the tradition that he was put to death, apparently as a representative of the corn-spirit, we are led to conjecture that we have here another trace of the custom of annually slaying one of those divine or priestly kings who are known to have held ghostly sway in many parts of Western Asia and particularly in Phrygia. The custom appears, as we have seen, to have been so far modified in places that the king's son was slain in the king's stead. Of the custom thus modified the story of Lityerses would be, in one version at least, a reminiscence.

Turning now to the relation of the Phrygian Lityerses to the Phrygian Attis, it may be remembered that at Pessinus—the seat of a priestly kingship—the high-priest appears to have been annually slain in the character of Attis, a god of vegetation, and that Attis was described by an ancient authority as 'a reaped ear of corn'. Thus Attis, as an embodiment of the corn-spirit, annually slain in the person of his representative, might be thought to be ultimately identical with Lityerses, the latter being simply the rustic prototype out of which the state religion of Attis was developed. It may have been so; but, on the other hand, the analogy of European folk-custom warns us that amongst the same people two distinct deities of vegetation may have their separate personal representatives, both of whom are slain in the character of gods at different times of the year. For in Europe, as we have seen, it appears that one man was commonly slain in the character of the tree-spirit in spring, and another in the character of the corn-spirit in autumn. It may have been so in Phrygia also. Attis was especially a tree-god, and his connexion with corn may have been only such an extension of the power of a tree-spirit as is indicated in customs like the Harvest-May. Again, the representative of Attis appears to have been slain in spring; whereas Lityerses must have been slain in summer or autumn, according to the time of the harvest in Phrygia. On the whole, then, while we are not justified in regarding Lityerses as the prototype of Attis, the two may be regarded as parallel products of the same religious idea, and may have stood to each other as in Europe the Old Man of harvest stands to the Wild Man, the Leaf Man, and so forth, of spring. Both were spirits or deities of vegetation, and the personal representatives of both were annually slain. But whereas the Attis worship became elevated into the dignity of a State religion and spread to Italy, the rites of Lityerses seem never to have passed the limits of their native Phrygia, and always retained their character of rustic ceremonies performed by peasants on the harvest-field.

There is a good deal more evidence that in Egypt the slain corn-spirit—the dead Osiris—was represented by a human victim, whom the reapers slew on the harvest-field, mourning

Relation of Lityerses to Attis: both may have been originally corn-spirits, or the one a corn-spirit and the other a tree-spirit.

Human representatives both of Lityerses and Attis annually slain.

The corn-spirit in Egypt

his death in a dirge, to which the Greeks, through a verbal misunderstanding, gave the name of Maneros. For the legend of Busiris seems to preserve a reminiscence of human sacrifices once offered by the Egyptians in connexion with the worship of Osiris. Busiris was said to have been an Egyptian king who sacrificed all strangers on the altar of Zeus. The origin of the custom was traced to a dearth which afflicted the land of Egypt for nine years. A Cyprian seer informed Busiris that the dearth would cease if a man were annually sacrificed to Zeus. So Busiris instituted the sacrifice. But when Hercules came to Egypt, and was being dragged to the altar to be sacrificed, he burst his bonds and slew Busiris and his son. Here then is a legend that in Egypt a human victim was annually sacrificed to prevent the failure of the crops, and a belief is implied that an omission of the sacrifice would have entailed a recurrence of that infertility which it was the object of the sacrifice to prevent. So the Pawnees believed that an omission of the human sacrifice at planting would have been followed by a total failure of their crops. The name Busiris was in reality the name of a city, *pe-Asar*, 'the house of Osiris,' the city being so called because it contained the grave of Osiris. Indeed some high modern authorities believe that Busiris was the original home of Osiris, from which his worship spread to other parts of Egypt. The human sacrifices were said to have been offered at his grave, and the victims were red-haired men, whose ashes were scattered abroad by means of winnowing-fans. This tradition of human sacrifices offered at the tomb of Osiris is confirmed by the evidence of the monuments; for 'we find in the temple of Dendereh a human figure with a hare's head and pierced with knives, tied to a stake before Osiris Khenti-Amentiu, and Horus is shown in a Ptolemaic sculpture at Karnak killing a bound hare-headed figure before the bier of Osiris, who is represented in the form of Harpocrates. That these figures are really human beings with the head of an animal fastened on is proved by another sculpture at Dendereh, where a kneeling man has the hawk's head and wings over his head and shoulders, and in another place a priest has the jackal's head on his shoulders, his own head appearing through the disguise. Besides, Diodorus tells us that the Egyptian kings in former times had worn on their heads the fore-part of a lion, or of a bull, or of a dragon, showing that this method of disguise or transformation was a well-known custom.'

In the light of the foregoing discussion the Egyptian tradition of Busiris admits of a consistent and fairly probable explanation. Osiris, the corn-spirit, was annually represented at harvest by a stranger, whose red hair made him a suitable representative of the ripe corn. This man, in his representative character, was slain on the harvest-field, and mourned by the reapers, who prayed at the same time that the corn-spirit might revive and return (*mââ-ne-rha*, Maneros) with renewed vigour in the following year. Finally, the victim, or some part of him, was burned, and the ashes scattered by winnowing-fans over the fields to fertilise them. The Romans sacrificed red-haired puppies in spring to avert the supposed blighting influence of the Dog-star, believing that the crops would thus grow ripe and ruddy. The heathen of Harran offered to the sun, moon, and planets human victims who were chosen on the ground of their supposed resemblance to the heavenly bodies to which they were sacrificed; for example, the priests, clothed in red and smeared with blood, offered a red-haired, red-cheeked man to 'the red planet Mars' in a temple which was painted red and draped with red hangings. These and the like cases of assimilating the victim to the god, or to the natural phenomenon which he represents, are based ultimately on the principle of homoeopathic or imitative magic, the notion being that the object aimed at will be most readily attained by means of a sacrifice which resembles the effect that it is designed to bring about.

Assimilation of human victims to the corn which they represent.

Thus, if I am right, the key to the mysteries of Osiris is furnished by the melancholy cry of the Egyptian reapers, which down to Roman times could be heard year after year sounding across the fields, announcing the death of the corn-spirit, the rustic prototype of Osiris. Similar cries, as we have seen, were also heard on all the harvest-fields of Western Asia. By the ancients they are spoken of as songs; but to judge from the analysis of the names Linus and Maneros, they probably consisted only of a few words uttered in a prolonged musical note which could be heard for a great distance. Such sonorous and long-drawn cries, raised by a number of strong voices in concert, must have had a striking effect, and could hardly fail

The key to the mysteries of Osiris furnished by the lamentations of the reapers for the annual death of the corn-spirit.

to arrest the attention of any wayfarer who happened to be within hearing. The sounds, repeated again and again, could probably be distinguished with tolerable ease even at a distance; but to a Greek traveller in Asia or Egypt the foreign words would commonly convey no meaning, and he might take them, not unnaturally, for the name of some one upon whom the reapers were calling.

'Crying the neck' at harvest in Devonshire.

Down to recent times Devonshire reapers uttered cries of the same sort, and performed on the field a ceremony exactly analogous to that in which, if I am not mistaken, the rites of Osiris originated. The cry and the ceremony are thus described by an observer who wrote in the first half of the nineteenth century. 'After the wheat is all cut, on most farms in the north of Devon, the harvest people have a custom of "crying the neck." I believe that this practice is seldom omitted on any large farm in that part of the country. It is done in this way. An old man, or some one else well acquainted with the ceremonies used on the occasion (when the labourers are reaping the last field of wheat), goes round to the shocks and sheaves, and picks out a little bundle of all the best ears he can find; this bundle he ties up very neat and trim, and plats and arranges the straws very tastefully. This is called "the neck" of wheat, or wheaten-ears. After the field is cut out, and the pitcher once more circulated, the reapers, binders, and the women stand round in a circle. The person with "the neck" stands in the centre, grasping it with both his hands. He first stoops and holds it near the ground, and all the men forming the ring take off their hats, stooping and holding them with both hands towards the ground. They then all begin at once in a very prolonged and harmonious tone to cry "The neck!" at the same time slowly raising themselves upright, and elevating their arms and hats above their heads; the person with "the neck" also raising it on high. This is done three times. They then change their cry to "Wee yen!"—"Way yen!"—which they sound in the same prolonged and slow manner as before, with singular harmony and effect, three times. This last cry is accompanied by the same movements of the body and arms as in crying "the neck" ... After having thus repeated "the neck" three times, and "wee yen," or "way yen" as often, they all burst out into a kind of loud and joyous laugh, flinging up their hats and caps into the air, capering about and perhaps kissing the girls. One of them then gets "the neck" and runs as hard as he can down to the farmhouse, where the dairymaid, or one of the young female domestics, stands at the door prepared with a pail of water. If he who holds "the neck" can manage to get into the house, in any way unseen, or openly, by any other way than the door at which the girl stands with the pail of water, then he may lawfully kiss her; but, if otherwise, he is regularly soused with the contents of the bucket. On a fine still autumn evening the "crying of the neck" has a wonderful effect at a distance, far finer than that of the Turkish muezzin, which Lord Byron eulogises so much, and which he says is preferable to all the bells in Christendom.'*

In the foregoing customs a particular bunch of ears, generally the last left standing, is conceived as the neck of the corn-spirit, who is consequently beheaded when the bunch is cut down. Similarly in Shropshire the name 'neck', or 'the gander's neck', used to be commonly given to the last handful of ears left standing in the middle of the field when all the rest of the corn was cut. It was plaited together, and the reapers, standing ten or twenty paces off, threw their sickles at it. Whoever cut it through was said to have cut off the gander's neck. The 'neck' was taken to the farmer's wife, who was supposed to keep it in the house for good luck till the next harvest came round. Near Trèves, the man who reaps the last standing corn 'cuts the goat's neck off'. At Faslane, on the Gareloch (Dumbartonshire), the last handful of standing corn was sometimes called the 'head'. At Aurich, in East Friesland, the man who reaps the last corn 'cuts the hare's tail off'. In mowing down the last corner of a field French reapers sometimes call out, 'We have the cat by the tail'. In Bresse (Bourgogne) the last sheaf represented the fox. Beside it a score of ears were left standing to form the tail, and each reaper, going back some paces, threw his sickle at it. He who succeeded in severing it 'cut off the fox's tail', and a cry of '*You cou cou!*' was raised in his honour. These examples leave no room to doubt the meaning of the Devonshire and Cornish expression 'the neck', as applied to the last sheaf. The corn-spirit is conceived in human or animal form, and the last standing corn is part of its body—its neck, its head, or its tail. Sometimes, as we have seen, the last corn is regarded as the

Cutting 'the neck' in Shropshire.

Why the last corn cut is called 'the neck.'

navel-string. Lastly, the Devonshire custom of drenching with
water the person who brings in 'the neck' is a rain-charm, such
as we have had many examples of.

CHAPTER 20

THE CORN-SPIRIT AS AN ANIMAL

i

IN some of the examples which I have cited to establish the meaning of the term 'neck' as applied to the last sheaf, the corn-spirit appears in animal form as a gander, a goat, a hare, a cat, and a fox. This introduces us to a new aspect of the corn-spirit, which we must now examine. By doing so we shall not only have fresh examples of killing the god, but may hope also to clear up some points which remain obscure in the myths and worship of Adonis, Attis, Osiris, Dionysus, Demeter, and Virbius.

Animal embodiments of the corn-spirit.

Amongst the many animals whose forms the corn-spirit is supposed to take are the wolf, dog, hare, fox, cock, goose, quail, cat, goat, cow (ox, bull), pig, and horse. In one or other of these shapes the corn-spirit is often believed to be present in the corn, and to be caught or killed in the last sheaf. As the corn is being cut the animal flees before the reapers, and if a reaper is taken ill on the field, he is supposed to have stumbled unwittingly on the corn-spirit, who has thus punished the profane intruder. It is said 'The Rye-wolf has got hold of him', 'The Harvest-goat has given him a push.' The person who cuts the last corn or binds the last sheaf gets the name of the animal, as the Rye-wolf, the Rye-sow, the Oats-goat, and so forth, and retains the name sometimes for a year. Also the animal is frequently represented by a puppet made out of the last sheaf or of wood, flowers, and so on, which is carried home amid rejoicings on the last harvest-waggon. Even where the last sheaf is not made up in animal shape, it is often called the Rye-wolf, the Hare, Goat, and so forth. Generally each kind of crop is supposed to have its special animal, which is caught in the last sheaf, and called the Rye-wolf, the Barley-wolf, the Oats-wolf, the Pea-wolf, or the Potato-wolf, according to the crop; but sometimes the figure of the animal is only made up once for all at getting in the last crop of the whole harvest. Sometimes the creature is believed to be killed by the last stroke of the sickle or scythe. But oftener it is thought to live so long as there is corn still unthreshed, and to be caught in the last sheaf threshed. Hence the man who gives the last stroke with the flail is told that he has got the Corn-sow, the Threshing-dog, or the like. When the threshing is finished, a puppet is made in the form of the animal, and this is carried by the thresher of the last sheaf to a neighbouring farm, where the threshing is still going on. This again shows that the corn-spirit is believed to live wherever the corn is still being threshed. Sometimes the thresher of the last sheaf himself represents the animal; and if the people of the next farm, who are still threshing, catch him, they treat him like the animal he represents, by shutting him up in the pig-sty, calling him with the cries commonly addressed to pigs, and so forth. These general statements will now be illustrated by examples.

The corn-spirit as a wolf or dog. We begin with the corn-spirit conceived as a wolf or a dog. This conception is common in France, Germany, and Slavonic countries. Thus, when the wind sets the corn in wave-like motion the peasants often say, 'The Wolf is going over, or through, the corn,' 'The Rye-wolf is rushing over the field', 'The Wolf is in the corn', 'The mad Dog is in the corn', 'The big Dog is there.' When children wish to go into the corn-fields to pluck ears or gather the blue corn-flowers, they are warned not to do so, for 'The big Dog sits in the corn', or 'The Wolf sits, in the corn, and will tear you in pieces', 'The Wolf will eat you.' The wolf against whom the children are warned is not a common wolf, for he is often spoken of as the Corn-wolf, Rye-wolf, or the like; thus they say, 'The Rye-wolf will come and eat you up, children', 'The Rye-wolf will carry you off', and so forth. Still he has all the outward appearance of a wolf. For in the neighbourhood of Feilenhof (East Prussia), when a wolf was seen running through a field, the peasants used to watch whether he carried his tail in the air or dragged it on the ground. If he dragged it on the ground, they went after him, and thanked him for bringing them a blessing, and even set tit-bits before him. But if he carried his tail high, they cursed him and tried to kill him. Here the wolf is the corn-spirit whose fertilising power is in his tail.

Both dog and wolf appear as embodiments of the corn-spirit in harvest-customs. Thus in some parts of Silesia the person who cuts or binds the last sheaf is called the Wheat-dog or the

Peas-pug. But it is in the harvest-customs of the north-east of France that the idea of the Corn-dog comes out most clearly. Thus when a harvester, through sickness, weariness, or laziness, cannot or will not keep up with the reaper in front of him, they say, 'The White Dog passed near him,' 'He has the White Bitch', or 'The White Bitch has bitten him.' In the Vosges the Harvest-May is called the 'Dog of the harvest', and the person who cuts the last handful of hay or wheat is said to 'kill the Dog'. About Lons-le-Saulnier, in the Jura, the last sheaf is called the Bitch. In the neighbourhood of Verdun the regular expression for finishing the reaping is, 'They are going to kill the Dog'; and at Epinal they say, according to the crop, 'We will kill the Wheat-dog, or the Rye-dog, or the Potato-dog.' In Lorraine it is said of the man who cuts the last corn, 'He is killing the Dog of the harvest.' At Dux, in the Tyrol, the man who gives the last stroke at threshing is said to 'strike down the Dog'; and at Ahnebergen, near Stade, he is called, according to the crop, Corn-pug, Rye-pug, Wheat-pug.

So with the wolf. In Silesia, when the reapers gather round the last patch of standing corn to reap it they are said to be about 'to catch the Wolf'. In various parts of Mecklenburg, where the belief in the Corn-wolf is particularly prevalent, every one fears to cut the last corn, because they say that the Wolf is sitting in it; hence every reaper exerts himself to the utmost in order not to be the last, and every woman similarly fears to bind the last sheaf because 'the Wolf is in it'. So both among the reapers and the binders there is a competition not to be the last to finish. And in Germany generally it appears to be a common saying that 'the Wolf sits in the last sheaf'. In some places they call out to the reaper, 'Beware of the Wolf'; or they say, 'He is chasing the Wolf out of the corn.' In Mecklenburg the last bunch of standing corn is itself commonly called the Wolf, and the man who reaps it 'has the Wolf', the animal being described as the Rye-wolf, the Wheat-wolf, the Barley-wolf, and so on according to the particular crop. The reaper of the last corn is himself called Wolf or the Rye-wolf, if the crop is rye, and in many parts of Mecklenburg he has to support the character by pretending to bite the other harvesters or by howling like a wolf. The last sheaf of corn is also called the Wolf or the Rye-wolf or the Oats-wolf according to the crop, and of the woman who binds it they say, 'The Wolf is biting her', 'She has the Wolf', 'She must fetch the Wolf' (out of the corn). Moreover, she herself is called Wolf; they cry out to her, 'Thou art the Wolf', and she has to bear the name for a whole year; sometimes, according to the crop, she is called the Rye-wolf or the Potato-wolf. In the island of Rügen not only is the woman who binds the last sheaf called Wolf, but when she comes home she bites the lady of the house and the stewardess, for which she receives a large piece of meat. Yet nobody likes to be the Wolf. The same woman may be Rye-wolf, Wheat-wolf, and Oats-wolf, if she happens to bind the last sheaf of rye, wheat, and oats. At Buir, in the district of Cologne, it was formerly the custom to give to the last sheaf the shape of a wolf. It was kept in the barn till all the corn was threshed. Then it was brought to the farmer and he had to sprinkle it with beer or brandy. At Brunshaupten in Mecklenburg the young woman who bound the last sheaf of wheat used to take a handful of stalks out of it and make 'the Wheat-wolf' with them; it was the figure of a wolf about two feet long and half a foot high, the legs of the animal being represented by stiff stalks and its tail and mane by wheat-ears. This Wheat-wolf she carried back at the head of the harvesters to the village, where it was set up on a high place in the parlour of the farm and remained there for a long time. In many places the sheaf called the Wolf is made up in human form and dressed in clothes. This indicates a confusion of ideas between the corn-spirit conceived in human and in animal form. Generally the Wolf is brought home on the last waggon with joyful cries. Hence the last waggon-load itself receives the name of the Wolf.

Again, the Wolf is supposed to hide himself amongst the cut corn in the granary, until he is driven out of the last bundle by the strokes of the flail. Hence at Wanzleben, near Magdeburg, after the threshing the peasants go in procession, leading by a chain a man who is enveloped in the threshed-out straw and is called the Wolf. He represents the corn-spirit who has been caught escaping from the threshed corn. In the district of Treves it is believed that the Corn-wolf is killed at threshing. The men thresh the last sheaf till it is reduced to chopped straw. In this way they think that the Corn-wolf, who was lurking in the last sheaf, has been certainly killed.

In France also the Corn-wolf appears at harvest. Thus they call out to the reaper of the last corn, 'You will catch the Wolf.' Near Chambéry they form a ring round the last standing corn, and cry, 'The Wolf is in there.' In Finistère, when the reaping draws near an end, the harvesters cry, 'There is the Wolf; we will catch him.' Each takes a swath to reap, and he who finishes first calls out, 'I've caught the Wolf.' In Guyenne, when the last corn has been reaped, they lead a wether all round the field. It is called 'the Wolf of the field.' Its horns are decked with a wreath of flowers and corn-ears, and its neck and body are also encircled with garlands and ribbons. All the reapers march, singing, behind it. Then it is killed on the field. In this part of France the last sheaf is called the *conjoulage*, which, in the patois, means a wether. Hence the killing of the wether represents the death of the corn-spirit, considered as present in the last sheaf; but two different conceptions of the corn-spirit—as a wolf and as a wether—are mixed up together.

Sometimes it appears to be thought that the Wolf, caught in the last corn, lives during the winter in the farmhouse, ready to renew his activity as corn-spirit in the spring. Hence at midwinter, when the lengthening days begin to herald the approach of spring, the Wolf makes his appearance once more. In Poland a man, with a wolf's skin thrown over his head, is led about at Christmas; or a stuffed wolf is carried about by persons who collect money. There are facts which point to an old custom of leading about a man enveloped in leaves and called the Wolf, while his conductors collected money.

Another form which the corn-spirit often assumes is that of a cock. In Austria children are warned against straying in the corn-fields, because the Corn-cock sits there, and will peck their eyes out. In North Germany they say that 'the Cock sits in the last sheaf'; and at cutting the last corn the reapers cry, 'Now we will chase out the Cock.' When it is cut they say, 'We have caught the Cock.' At Braller, in Transylvania, when the reapers come to the last patch of corn, they cry, 'Here we shall catch the Cock.' At Fürstenwalde, when the last sheaf is about to be bound, the master releases a cock, which he has brought in a basket, and lets it run over the field. All the harvesters chase it till they catch it. Elsewhere the harvesters all try to seize the last corn cut; he who succeeds in grasping it must

The corn-spirit as a cock.

crow, and is called Cock. Among the Wends it is or used to be customary for the farmer to hide a live cock under the last sheaf as it lay on the field; and when the corn was being gathered up, the harvester who lighted upon this sheaf had a right to keep the cock, provided he could catch it. This formed the close of the harvest-festival and was known as 'the Cock-catching', and the beer which was served out to the reapers at this time went by the name of 'Cock-beer'. The last sheaf is called Cock, Cock-sheaf, Harvest-cock, Harvest-hen, Autumn-hen. A distinction is made between a Wheat-cock, Bean-cock, and so on, according to the crop. At Wünschensuhl, in Thüringen, the last sheaf is made into the shape of a cock, and called the Harvest-cock. A figure of a cock, made of wood, pasteboard, ears of corn, or flowers, is borne in front of the harvest-waggon, especially in Westphalia, where the cock carries in his beak fruits of the earth of all kinds. Sometimes the image of the cock is fastened to the top of a May-tree on the last harvest-waggon. Elsewhere a live cock, or a figure of one, is attached to a harvest-crown and carried on a pole. In Galicia and elsewhere this live cock is fastened to the garland of corn-ears or flowers, which the leader of the women-reapers carries on her head as she marches in front of the harvest procession. In Silesia a live cock is presented to the master on a plate. The harvest-supper is called Harvest-cock, Stubble-cock, etc., and a chief dish at it, at least in some places, is a cock. If a waggoner upsets a harvest-waggon, it is said that 'he has spilt the Harvest cock', and he loses the cock, that is, the harvest-supper. The harvest-waggon, with the figure of the cock on it, is driven round the farmhouse before it is taken to the barn. Then the cock is nailed over or at the side of the house-door, or on the gable, and remains there till next harvest. In East Friesland the person who gives the last stroke at threshing is called the Clucking-hen, and grain is strewed before him as if he were a hen.

Again, the corn-spirit is killed in the form of a cock. In parts of Germany, Hungary, Poland, and Picardy the reapers place a live cock in the corn which is to be cut last, and chase it over the field, or bury it up to the neck in the ground; afterwards they strike off its head with a sickle or scythe. In many parts of Westphalia, when the harvesters bring the wooden cock to the farmer, he gives them a live cock, which they kill with whips or sticks, or behead with an old sword, or throw into the barn to the girls, or give to the mistress to cook. If the harvest-cock has not been spilt—that is, if no waggon has been upset—the harvesters have the right to kill the farmyard cock by throwing stones at it or beheading it. Where this custom has fallen into disuse, it is still common for the farmer's wife to make cockie-leekie for the harvesters, and to show them the head of the cock which has been killed for the soup. In the neighbourhood of Klausenburg, Transylvania, a cock is buried on the harvest-field in the earth, so that only its head appears. A young man then takes a scythe and cuts off the cock's head at a single sweep. If he fails to do this, he is called the Red Cock for a whole year, and people fear that next year's crop will be bad. Near Udvarhely, in Transylvania, a live cock is bound up in the last sheaf and killed with a spit. It is then skinned. The flesh is thrown away, but the skin and feathers are kept till next year; and in spring the grain from the last sheaf is mixed with the feathers of the cock and scattered on the field which is to be tilled. Nothing could set in a clearer light the identification of the cock with the spirit of the corn. By being tied up in the last sheaf and killed, the cock is identified with the corn, and its death with the cutting of the corn. By keeping its feathers till spring, then mixing them with the seed-corn taken from the very sheaf in which the bird had been bound, and scattering the feathers together with the seed over the field, the identity of the bird with the corn is again emphasised, and its quickening and fertilising power, as an embodiment of the corn-spirit, is intimated in the plainest manner. Thus the corn-spirit, in the form of a cock, is killed at harvest, but rises to fresh life and activity in spring. Again, the equivalence of the cock to the corn is expressed, hardly less plainly, in the custom of burying the bird in the ground, and cutting off its head (like the ears of corn) with the scythe.

Another common embodiment of the corn-spirit is the hare. In Galloway the reaping of the last standing corn is called 'cutting the Hare'. The mode of cutting it is as follows. When the rest of the corn has been reaped, a handful is left standing to form the Hare. It is divided into three parts and plaited, and the ears are tied in a knot. The reapers then retire a few yards and each throws his or her sickle in turn at the Hare to cut it

The corn-spirit as a hare.

down. It must be cut below the knot, and the reapers continue to throw their sickles at it, one after the other, until one of them succeeds in severing the stalks below the knot. The Hare is then carried home and given to a maidservant in the kitchen, who places it over the kitchen-door on the inside. Sometimes the Hare used to be thus kept till the next harvest. In the parish of Minnigaff, when the Hare was cut, the unmarried reapers ran home with all speed, and the one who arrived first was the first to be married. In Germany also one of the names for the last sheaf is the Hare. Thus in some parts of Anhalt, when the corn has been reaped and only a few stalks are left standing, they say, 'The Hare will soon come', or the reapers cry to each other, 'Look how the Hare comes jumping out'. In East Prussia they say that the Hare sits in the last patch of standing corn, and must be chased out by the last reaper. The reapers hurry with their work, each being anxious not to have 'to chase out the Hare'; for the man who does so, that is, who cuts the last corn, is much laughed at. At Aurich, as we have seen, an expression for cutting the last corn is 'to cut off the Hare's tail'. 'He is killing the Hare' is commonly said of the man who cuts the last corn in Germany, Sweden, Holland, France, and Italy. In Norway the man who is thus said to 'kill the Hare' must give 'hare's blood' in the form of brandy to his fellows to drink. In Lesbos, when the reapers are at work in two neighbouring fields, each party tries to finish first in order to drive the Hare into their neighbour's field; the reapers who succeed in doing so believe that next year the crop will be better. A small sheaf of corn is made up and kept beside the holy picture till next harvest.

The corn-spirit as a cat. Again, the corn-spirit sometimes takes the form of a cat. Near Kiel children are warned not to go into the corn-fields because 'the Cat sits there'. In the Eisenach Oberland they are told 'The Corn-cat will come and fetch you', 'The Corn-cat goes in the corn'. In some parts of Silesia at mowing the last corn they say, 'The Cat is caught'; and at threshing, the man who gives the last stroke is called the Cat. In the neighbourhood of Lyons the last sheaf and the harvest-supper are both called the Cat. About Vesoul when they cut the last corn they say, 'We have the Cat by the tail.' At Briançon, in Dauphiné, at the beginning of reaping, a cat is decked out with ribbons, flowers, and ears of corn. It is called the Cat of the ball-skin (*le chat de peau de balle*). If a reaper is wounded at his work, they make the cat lick the wound. At the close of the reaping the cat is again decked out with ribbons and ears of corn; then they dance and make merry. When the dance is over the girls solemnly strip the cat of its finery. At Grüneberg, in Silesia, the reaper who cuts the last corn goes by the name of the Tom-cat. He is enveloped in rye-stalks and green withes, and is furnished with a long plaited tail. Sometimes as a companion he has a man similarly dressed, who is called the (female) Cat. Their duty is to run after people whom they see and to beat them with a long stick. Near Amiens the expression for finishing the harvest is, 'They are going to kill the Cat'; and when the last corn is cut they kill a cat in the farmyard. At threshing, in some parts of France, a live cat is placed under the last bundle of corn to be threshed, and is struck dead with the flails. Then on Sunday it is roasted and eaten as a holiday dish. In the Vosges Mountains the close of haymaking or harvest is called 'catching the cat', 'killing the dog', or more rarely 'catching the hare'. The cat, the dog, or the hare is said to be fat or lean according as the crop is good or bad. The man who cuts the last handful of hay or of wheat is said to catch the cat or the hare or to kill the dog.

Further, the corn-spirit often appears in the form of a goat. In some parts of Prussia, when the corn bends before the wind, they say, 'The Goats are chasing each other'. 'The wind is driving the Goats through the corn', 'The Goats are browsing there', and they expect a very good harvest. Again they say, 'The Oats-goat is sitting in the oats-field', 'The Corn-goat is sitting in the rye-field.' Children are warned not to go into the corn-fields to pluck the blue corn-flowers, or amongst the beans to pluck pods, because the Rye-goat, the Corn-goat, the Oats-goat, or the Bean-goat is sitting or lying there, and will carry them away or kill them'. When a harvester is taken sick or lags behind his fellows at their work, they call out, 'The Harvest-goat has pushed him', 'He has been pushed by the Corn-goat.' In the neighbourhood of Braunsberg (East Prussia) at binding the oats every harvester makes haste 'lest the Corn-goat push him'. At Oefoten, in Norway, each reaper has his allotted patch to reap. When a reaper in the middle has not finished reaping his piece after his neighbours have finished theirs, they say of

The corn-spirit as a goat.

him, 'He remains on the island.' And if the laggard is a man, they imitate the cry with which they call a he-goat; if a woman, the cry with which they call a she-goat. Near Straubing, in Lower Bavaria, it is said of the man who cuts the last corn that 'he has the Corn-goat, or the Wheat-goat, or the Oats-goat', according to the crop. Moreover, two horns are set up on the last heap of corn, and it is called 'the horned Goat'. At Kreutzburg, East Prussia, they call out to the woman who is binding the last sheaf, 'The Goat is sitting in the sheaf.' At Gablingen, in Swabia, when the last field of oats upon a farm is being reaped, the reapers carve a goat out of wood. Ears of oats are inserted in its nostrils and mouth, and it is adorned with garlands of flowers. It is set up on the field and called the Oats-goat. When the reaping approaches an end, each reaper hastens to finish his piece first; he who is the last to finish gets the Oats-goat. Again, the last sheaf is itself called the Goat. Thus, in the valley of the Wiesent, Bavaria, the last sheaf bound on the field is called the Goat, and they have a proverb, 'The field must bear a goat.' At Spachbrücken, in Hesse, the last handful of corn which is cut is called the Goat, and the man who cuts it is much ridiculed. At Dürrenbüchig and about Mosbach in Baden the last sheaf is also called the Goat. Sometimes the last sheaf is made up in the form of a goat, and they say, 'The Goat is sitting in it.' Again, the person who cuts or binds the last sheaf is called the Goat. Thus, in parts of Mecklenburg they call out, to the woman who binds the last sheaf, 'You are the Harvest-goat.' Near Uelzen, in Hanover, the harvest festival begins with 'the bringing of the Harvest-goat'; that is, the woman who bound the last sheaf is wrapt in straw, crowned with a harvest-wreath, and brought in a wheel-barrow to the village, where a round dance takes place. About Lune-burg, also, the woman who binds the last corn is decked with a crown of corn-ears and is called the Corn-goat. At Münzesheim in Baden the reaper who cuts the last handful of corn or oats is called the Corn-goat or the Oats-goat. In the Canton St Gall, Switzerland, the person who cuts the last handful of corn on the field, or drives the last harvest-waggon to the barn, is called the Corn-goat or the Rye-goat, or simply the Goat. In the Canton Thurgau he is called Corn-goat; like a goat he has a bell hung round his neck, is led in triumph, and drenched with liquor. In parts of Styria, also, the man who cuts the last corn is called Corn-goat, Oats-goat, or the like. As a rule, the man who thus gets the name of Corn-goat has to bear it a whole year till the next harvest.

According to one view, the corn-spirit, who has been caught in the form of a goat or otherwise, lives in the farmhouse or barn over winter. Thus, each farm has its own embodiment of the corn-spirit. But, according to another view, the corn-spirit is the genius or deity, not of the corn of one farm only, but of all the corn. Hence when the corn on one farm is all cut, he flees to another where there is still corn left standing. This idea is brought out in a harvest-custom which was formerly observed in Skye. The farmer who first finished reaping sent a man or woman with a sheaf to a neighbouring farmer who had not finished; the latter in his turn, when he had finished, sent on the sheaf to his neighbour who was still reaping; and so the sheaf made the round of the farms till all the corn was cut. The sheaf was called the *goabbir bhacagh*, that is, the Cripple Goat. The custom appears not to be extinct at the present day, for it was reported from Skye not very many years ago. The corn-spirit was probably thus represented as lame because he had been crippled by the cutting of the corn. Sometimes the old woman who brings home the last sheaf must limp on one foot.

But sometimes the corn-spirit, in the form of a goat, is believed to be slain on the harvest-field by the sickle or scythe. Thus, in the neighbourhood of Bernkastel, on the Moselle, the reapers determine by lot the order in which they shall follow each other. The first is called the fore-reaper, the last the tail-bearer. If a reaper overtakes the man in front he reaps past him, bending round so as to leave the slower reaper in a patch by himself. This patch is called the Goat; and the man for whom 'the Goat is cut' in this way, is laughed and jeered at by his fellows for the rest of the day. When the tail-bearer cuts the last ears of corn, it is said, 'He is cutting the Goat's neck off.' In the neighbourhood of Grenoble, before the end of the reaping, a live goat is adorned with flowers and ribbons and allowed to run about the field. The reapers chase it and try to catch it. When it is caught, the farmer's wife holds it fast while the farmer cuts off its head. The goat's flesh serves to furnish the harvest-supper. A piece of the flesh is pickled and kept till the next harvest, when another goat is killed. Then all the harvesters eat of the flesh. On the same day the skin of the goat is made into a cloak, which the farmer, who works with his men, must always wear at harvest-time if rain or bad weather sets in. But if a reaper gets pains in his back, the farmer gives him the goat-skin to wear. The reason for this seems to be that the pains in the back, being inflicted by the corn-spirit, can also be healed by it. Similarly, we saw that elsewhere, when a reaper is wounded at reaping, a cat, as the representative of the corn-spirit, is made to lick the wound. Esthonian reapers in the island of Mon think that the man who cuts the first ears of corn at harvest will get pains in his back, probably because the corn-spirit is believed to resent especially the first wound; and, in order to escape pains in the back, Saxon reapers in Transylvania gird their loins with the first handful of ears which they cut. Here, again, the corn-spirit is applied to for healing or protection, but in his original vegetable form, not in the form of a goat or a cat.

Further, the corn-spirit under the form of a goat is sometimes conceived as lurking among the cut corn in the barn, till he is driven from it by the threshing-flail. Thus in Baden the last sheaf to be threshed is called the Corn-goat, the Spelt-goat, or the Oats-goat according to the kind of grain. Again, near Marktl, in Upper Bavaria, the sheaves are called Straw-goats or simply Goats. They are laid in a great heap on the open field and threshed by two rows of men standing opposite each other, who, as they ply their flails, sing a song in which they say that they see the Straw-goat amongst the corn-stalks. The last Goat, that is, the last sheaf, is adorned with a wreath of violets and other flowers and with cakes strung together. It is placed right in the middle of the heap. Some of the threshers rush at it and tear the best of it out; others lay on with their flails so recklessly that heads are sometimes broken. At Oberinntal, in the Tyrol, the last thresher is called Goat. So at Haselberg, in West Bohemia, the man who gives the last stroke at threshing oats is called the Oats-goat. At Tettnang, in Würtemburg, the thresher who gives the last stroke to the last bundle of corn before it is turned goes by the name of the He-goat, and it is said, 'He has driven the He-goat away.' The person who, after the bundle has been turned, gives the last stroke of all, is called the She-goat.

In this custom it is implied that the corn is inhabited by a pair of corn-spirits, male and female.

Further, the corn-spirit, captured in the form of a goat at threshing, is passed on to a neighbour whose threshing is not yet finished. In Franche Comté, as soon as the threshing is over, the young people set up a straw figure of a goat on the farmyard of a neighbour who is still threshing. He must give them wine or money in return. At Ellwangen, in Würtemburg, the effigy of a goat is made out of the last bundle of corn at threshing; four sticks form its legs, and two its horns. The man who gives the last stroke with the flail must carry the Goat to the barn of a neighbour who is still threshing and throw it down on the floor; if he is caught in the act, they tie the Goat on his back. A similar custom is observed at Indersdorf, in Upper Bavaria; the man who throws the straw Goat into the neighbour's barn imitates the bleating of a goat; if they catch him, they blacken his face and tie the Goat on his back. At Saverne, in Alsace, when a farmer is a week or more behind his neighbours with his threshing, they set a real stuffed goat or fox before his door.

Sometimes the spirit of the corn in goat form is believed to be killed at threshing. In the district of Traunstein, Upper Bavaria, they think that the Oats-goat is in the last sheaf of oats. He is represented by an old rake set up on end, with an old pot for a head. The children are then told to kill the Oats-goat.

Another form which the corn-spirit often assumes is that of a bull, cow, or ox. When the wind sweeps over the corn they say at Conitz, in West Prussia, 'The Steer is running in the corn'; when the corn is thick and strong in one spot, they say in some parts of East Prussia, 'The Bull is lying in the corn.' When a harvester has overstrained and lamed himself, they, say in the Graudenz district of West Prussia, 'The Bull pushed him'; in Lorraine they say, 'He has the Bull'. The meaning of both expressions is that he has unwittingly lighted upon the divine corn-spirit, who has punished the profane intruder with lameness. So near Chambéry when a reaper wounds himself with his sickle, it is said that he has 'the wound of the Ox'. In the district of Bunzlau (Silesia) the last sheaf is sometimes made into the shape of a horned ox, stuffed with tow and wrapt in corn-ears. This figure is called the Old Man. In some parts of Bohemia the last sheaf is made up in human form and called the

The corn-spirit as a bull, cow, or ox.

Buffalo-bull. These cases show a confusion of the human with the animal shape of the corn-spirit. The confusion is like that of killing a wether under the name of a wolf. All over Swabia the last bundle of corn on the field is called the Cow; the man who cuts the last ears 'has the Cow', and is himself called Cow or Barley-cow or Oats-cow, according to the crop; at the harvest-supper he gets a nosegay of flowers and corn-ears and a more liberal allowance of drink than the rest. But he is teased and laughed at; so no one likes to be the Cow. The Cow was sometimes represented by the figure of a woman made out of ears of corn and corn-flowers. It was carried to the farmhouse by the man who had cut the last handful of corn. The children ran after him and the neighbours turned out to laugh at him, till the farmer took the Cow from him. Here again the confusion between the human and the animal form of the corn-spirit is apparent. In various parts of Switzerland the reaper who cuts the last ears of corn is called Wheat-cow, Corn-cow, Oats-cow, or Corn-steer, and is the butt of many a joke. On the other hand, in the district of Rosenheim, Upper Bavaria, when a farmer is later of getting in his harvest than his neighbours, they set up on his land a Straw-bull, as it is called. This is a gigantic figure of a bull made of stubble on a framework of wood and adorned with flowers and leaves. Attached to it is a label on which are scrawled doggerel verses in ridicule of the man on whose land the Straw-bull is set up.

Again, the corn-spirit in the form of a bull or ox is killed on the harvest-field at the close of the reaping. At Pouilly, near Dijon, when the last ears of corn are about to be cut, an ox adorned with ribbons, flowers, and ears of corn is led all round the field, followed by the whole troop of reapers dancing. Then a man disguised as the Devil cuts the last ears of corn and immediately slaughters the ox. Part of the flesh of the animal is eaten at the harvest-supper; part is pickled and kept till the first day of sowing in spring. At Pont à Mousson and elsewhere on the evening of the last day of reaping, a calf adorned with flowers and ears of corn is led thrice round the farmyard, being allured by a bait or driven by men with sticks, or conducted by the farmer's wife with a rope. The calf chosen for this ceremony is the calf which was born first on the farm in the spring of the year. It is followed by all the reapers with their tools. Then it is allowed to run free; the reapers chase it, and whoever catches it is called King of the Calf. Lastly, it is solemnly killed; at Lunéville the man who acts as butcher is the Jewish merchant of the village.

Sometimes again the corn-spirit hides himself amongst the cut corn in the barn to reappear in bull or cow form at threshing. Thus at Wurmlingen, in Thüringen, the man who gives the last stroke at threshing is called the Cow, or rather the Barley-cow, Oats-cow, Peas-cow, or the like, according to the crop. He is entirely enveloped in straw; his head is surmounted by sticks in imitation of horns, and two lads lead him by ropes to the well to drink. On the way thither he must low like a cow, and for a long time afterwards he goes by the name of the Cow. At Obermedlingen, in Swabia, when the threshing draws near an end, each man is careful to avoid giving the last stroke. He who does give it 'gets the Cow', which is a straw figure dressed in an old ragged petticoat, hood, and stockings. It is tied on his back with a straw-rope; his face is blackened, and being bound with straw-ropes to a wheelbarrow he is wheeled round the village. Here, again, we meet with that confusion between the human and animal shape of the corn-spirit which we have noted in other customs. In Canton Schaffhausen the man who threshes the last corn is called the Cow; in Canton Thurgau, the Corn-bull; in Canton Zurich, the Thresher-cow. In the last-mentioned district he is wrapt in straw and bound to one of the trees in the orchard. At Arad, in Hungary, the man who gives the last stroke at threshing is enveloped in straw and a cow's hide with the horns attached to it. At Pessnitz, in the district of Dresden, the man who gives the last stroke with the flail is called Bull. He must make a straw-man and set it up before a neighbour's window. Here, apparently, as in so many cases, the corn-spirit is passed on to a neighbour who has not finished threshing. So at Herbrechtingen, in Thüringen, the effigy of a ragged old woman is flung into the barn of the farmer who is last with his threshing. The man who throws it in cries, 'There is the Cow for you.' If the threshers catch him they detain him over night and punish him by keeping him from the harvest-supper. In these latter customs the confusion between the human and the animal shape of the corn-spirit meets us again.

Further, the corn-spirit in bull form is sometimes believed to be killed at threshing. At Auxerre, in threshing the last bundle of corn, they call out twelve times, 'We are killing the Bull.' In the neighbourhood of Bordeaux, where a butcher kills an ox on the field immediately after the close of the reaping, it is said of the man who gives the last stroke at threshing that 'he has killed the Bull'. At Chambéry the last sheaf is called the sheaf of the Young Ox, and a race takes place to it in which all the reapers join. When the last stroke is given at threshing they say that 'the Ox is killed'; and immediately thereupon a real ox is slaughtered by the reaper who cut the last corn. The flesh of the ox is eaten by the threshers at supper.

We have seen that sometimes the young corn-spirit, whose task it is to quicken the corn of the coming year, is believed to be born as a Corn-baby on the harvest-field. Similarly in Berry the young corn-spirit is sometimes supposed to be born on the field in calf form; for when a binder has not rope enough to bind all the corn in sheaves, he puts aside the wheat that remains over and imitates the lowing of a cow. The meaning is that 'the sheaf has given birth to a calf'. In Puy-de-Dôme when a binder cannot keep up with the reaper whom he or she follows, they say 'He (or she) is giving birth to the Calf.' In some parts of Prussia, in similar circumstances, they call out to the woman, 'The Bull is coming', and imitate the bellowing of a bull. In these cases the woman is conceived as the Corn-cow or old corn-spirit, while the supposed calf is the Corn-calf or young corn-spirit. In some parts of Austria a mythical calf (*Muhkälbchen*) is believed to be seen amongst the sprouting corn in spring and to push the children; when the corn waves in the wind they say, 'The Calf is going about.' Clearly, as Mannhardt observes, this calf of the spring-time is the same animal which is afterwards believed to be killed at reaping.

The corn-spirit as a horse or mare. Sometimes the corn-spirit appears in the shape of a horse or mare. Between Kalw and Stuttgart, when the corn bends before the wind, they say, 'There runs the Horse.' At Bohlingen, near Radolfzell in Baden, the last sheaf of oats is called the Oats-stallion. In Hertfordshire, at the end of the reaping, there is or used to be observed a ceremony called 'crying the Mare'. The last blades of corn left standing on the field are tied together and called the Mare. The reapers stand at a distance and throw their sickles at it; he who cuts it through 'has the prize, with acclamations and good cheer'. After it is cut the reapers cry thrice with a loud voice, 'I have her!' Others answer thrice, 'What have you?'—'A Mare! a Mare! a Mare!'—'Whose is she?' is next asked thrice. 'A. B.'s' naming the owner thrice. 'Whither will you send her?'—'To C. D.,' naming some neighbour who has not reaped all his corn. In this custom the corn-spirit in the form of a mare is passed on from a farm where the corn is all cut to another farm where it is still standing, and where therefore the corn-spirit may be supposed naturally to take refuge. In Shropshire the custom is similar. The farmer who finishes his harvest last, and who therefore cannot send the Mare to any one else, is said 'to keep her all winter'. The mocking offer of the Mare to a laggard neighbour was sometimes responded to by a mocking acceptance of her help. Thus an old man told an inquirer, 'While we wun at supper, a mon cumm'd wi' a autar [halter] to fatch her away.' At one place a real mare used to be sent, but the man who rode her was subjected to some rough treatment at the farmhouse to which he paid his unwelcome visit.

In the neighbourhood of Lille the idea of the corn-spirit in horse form is clearly preserved. When a harvester grows weary at his work, it is said, 'He has the fatigue of the Horse.' The first sheaf, called the 'Cross of the Horse', is placed on a cross of boxwood in the barn, and the youngest horse on the farm must tread on it. The reapers dance round the last blades of corn, crying, 'See the remains of the Horse.' The sheaf made out of these last blades is given to the youngest horse of the parish (*commune*) to eat. This youngest horse of the parish clearly represents, as Mannhardt says, the corn-spirit of the following year, the Corn-foal, which absorbs the spirit of the old Corn-horse by eating the last corn cut; for, as usual, the old corn-spirit takes his final refuge in the last sheaf. The thresher of the last sheaf is said to 'beat the Horse'.

The last animal embodiment of the corn-spirit which we shall notice is the pig (boar or sow). In Thüringen, when the wind sets the young corn in motion, they sometimes say, 'The Boar is rushing through the corn.' Amongst the Esthonians of the island of Oesel the last sheaf is called the Rye-boar, and the man who gets it is saluted with a cry of 'You have the Rye-boar on

The corn-spirit as a pig.

your back!' In reply he strikes up a song, in which he prays for plenty. At Kohlerwinkel, near Augsburg, at the close of the harvest, the last bunch of standing corn is cut down, stalk by stalk, by all the reapers in turn. He who cuts the last stalk 'gets the Sow', and is laughed at. In other Swabian villages also the man who cuts the last corn 'has the Sow', or 'has the Rye-sow'. At Bohlingen, near Radolfzell in Baden, the last sheaf is called the Rye-sow or the Wheat-sow, according to the crop; and at Röhrenbach in Baden the person who brings the last armful for the last sheaf is called the Corn-sow or the Oats-sow. At Friedingen, in Swabia, the thresher who gives the last stroke is called Sow—Barley-sow, Corn-sow, or the like, according to the crop. At Onstmettingen the man who gives the last stroke at threshing 'has the Sow'; he is often bound up in a sheaf and dragged by a rope along the ground. And, generally, in Swabia the man who gives the last stroke with the flail is called Sow. He may, however, rid himself of this invidious distinction by passing on to a neighbour the straw-rope, which is the badge of his position as Sow. So he goes to a house and throws the straw-rope into it, crying, 'There, I bring you the Sow.' All the inmates give chase; and if they catch him they beat him, shut him up for several hours in the pig-sty, and oblige him to take the 'Sow' away again. In various parts of Upper Bavaria the man who gives the last stroke at threshing must 'carry the Pig'—that is, either a straw effigy of a pig or merely a bundle of straw-ropes. This he carries to a neighbouring farm where the threshing is not finished, and throws it into the barn. If the threshers catch him they handle him roughly, beating him, blackening or dirtying his face, throwing him into filth, binding the Sow on his back, and so on; if the bearer of the Sow is a woman they cut off her hair. At the harvest supper or dinner the man who 'carried the Pig' gets one or more dumplings made in the form of pigs. When the dumplings are served up by the maid-servant, all the people at table cry 'Süz, süz, süz!' that being the cry used in calling pigs. Sometimes after dinner the man who 'carried the Pig' has his face blackened, and is set on a cart and drawn round the village by his fellows, followed by a crowd crying 'Süz, süz, süz!' as if they were calling swine. Sometimes, after being wheeled round the village, he is flung on the dunghill.

Again, the corn-spirit in the form of a pig plays his part at sowing-time as well as at harvest. At Neuautz, in Courland, when barley is sown for the first time in the year, the farmer's wife boils the chine of a pig along with the tail, and brings it to the sower on the field. He eats of it, but cuts off the tail and sticks it in the field; it is believed that the ears of corn will then grow as long as the tail. Here the pig is the corn-spirit, whose fertilising power is sometimes supposed to lie especially in his tail. As a pig he is put in the ground at sowing-time, and as a pig he reappears amongst the ripe corn at harvest. For amongst the neighbouring Esthonians, as we have seen, the last sheaf is called the Rye-boar. Somewhat similar customs are observed in Germany. In the Salza district, near Meiningen, a certain bone in the pig is called 'the Jew on the winnowing-fan'. The flesh of this bone is boiled on Shrove Tuesday, but the bone is put amongst the ashes which the neighbours exchange as presents on St Peter's Day (the twenty-second of February), and then mix with the seed-corn. In the whole of Hesse, Meiningen, and other districts, people eat pea-soup with dried pig-ribs on Ash Wednesday or Candlemas. The ribs are then collected and hung in the room till sowing-time, when they are inserted in the sown field or in the seed-bag amongst the flax seed. This is thought to be an infallible specific against earth-fleas and moles, and to cause the flax to grow well and tall.

But the idea of the corn-spirit as embodied in pig form is nowhere more clearly expressed than in the Scandinavian custom of the Yule Boar. In Sweden and Denmark at Yule (Christmas) it is the custom to bake a loaf in the form of a boar-pig. This is called the Yule Boar. The corn of the last sheaf is often used to make it. All through Yule the Yule Boar stands on the table. Often it is kept till the sowing-time in spring, when part of it is mixed with the seed-corn and part given to the ploughman and plough-horses or plough-oxen to eat, in the expectation of a good harvest. In this custom the corn-spirit, immanent in the last sheaf, appears at midwinter in the form of a boar made from the corn of the last sheaf; and his quickening influence on the corn is shown by mixing part of the Yule Boar with the seed-corn, and giving part of it to the ploughman and his cattle to eat. Similarly we saw that the

Corn-wolf makes his appearance at mid-winter, the time when the year begins to verge towards spring. Formerly a real boar was sacrificed at Christmas, and apparently also a man in the character of the Yule Boar. This, at least, may perhaps be inferred from a Christmas custom still observed in Sweden. A man is wrapt up in a skin, and carries a wisp of straw in his mouth, so that the projecting straws look like the bristles of a boar. A knife is brought, and an old woman, with her face blackened, pretends to sacrifice him.

On Christmas Eve in some parts of the Esthonian island of Oesel they bake a long cake with the two ends turned up. It is called the Christmas Boar, and stands on the table till the morning of New Year's Day, when it is distributed among the cattle. In other parts of the island the Christmas Boar is not a cake but a little pig born in March, which the housewife fattens secretly, often without the knowledge of the other members of the family. On Christmas Eve the little pig is secretly killed, then roasted in the oven, and set on the table standing on all-fours, where it remains in this posture for several days. In other parts of the island, again, though the Christmas cake has neither the name nor the shape of a boar, it is kept till the New Year, when half of it is divided among all the members and all the quadrupeds of the family. The other half of the cake is kept till sowing-time comes round, when it is similarly distributed in the morning among human beings and beasts. In other parts of Esthonia, again, the Christmas Boar, as it is called, is baked of the first rye cut at harvest; it has a conical shape and a cross is impressed on it with a pig's bone or a key, or three dints are made in it with a buckle or a piece of charcoal. It stands with a light beside it on the table all through the festal season. On New Year's Day and Epiphany, before sunrise, a little of the cake is crumbled with salt and given to the cattle. The rest is kept till the day when the cattle are driven out to pasture for the first time in spring. It is then put in the herdsman's bag, and at evening is divided among the cattle to guard them from magic and harm. In some places the Christmas Boar is partaken of by farm-servants and cattle at the time of the barley sowing, for the purpose of thereby producing a heavier crop.

ii

So much for the animal embodiments of the corn-spirit as they are presented to us in the folk-customs of Northern Europe. These customs bring out clearly the sacramental character of the harvest-supper. The corn-spirit is conceived as embodied in an animal; this divine animal is slain, and its flesh and blood are partaken of by the harvesters. Thus, the cock, the hare, the cat, the goat, and the ox are eaten sacramentally by the harvesters, and the pig is eaten sacramentally by ploughmen in spring. Again, as a substitute for the real flesh of the divine being, bread or dumplings are made in his image and eaten sacramentally; thus, pig-shaped dumplings are eaten by the harvesters, and loaves made in boar-shape (the Yule Boar) are eaten in spring by the ploughman and his cattle.

Sacramental character of the harvest-supper.

The reader has probably remarked the complete parallelism between the conceptions of the corn-spirit in human and in animal form. The parallel may be here briefly resumed. When the corn waves in the wind it is said either that the Corn-mother or that the Corn-wolf, etc., is passing through the corn. Children are warned against straying in corn-fields either because the Corn-mother or because the Corn-wolf, etc., is there. In the last corn cut or the last sheaf threshed either the Corn-mother or the Corn-wolf, etc., is supposed to be present. The last sheaf is itself called either the Corn-mother or the Corn-wolf, etc., and is made up in the shape either of a woman or of a wolf, etc. The person who cuts, binds, or threshes the last sheaf is called either the Old Woman or the Wolf, etc., according to the name bestowed on the sheaf itself. As in some places a sheaf made in human form and called the Maiden, the Mother of the Maize, etc., is kept from one harvest to the next in order to secure a continuance of the corn-spirit's blessing, so in some places the Harvest-cock and in others the flesh of the goat is kept for a similar purpose from one harvest to the next. As in some places the grain taken from the Corn-mother is mixed with the seed-corn in spring to make the crop abundant, so in some places the feathers of the cock, and in Sweden the Yule Boar, are kept till spring and mixed with the seed-corn for a like purpose. As part of the Corn-mother or Maiden is given

Parallelism between the conceptions of the corn-spirit in human and animal forms.

to the cattle at Christmas or to the horses at the first ploughing, so part of the Yule Boar is given to the ploughing horses or oxen in spring. Lastly, the death of the corn-spirit is represented by killing or pretending to kill either his human or his animal representative; and the worshippers partake sacramentally either of the actual body and blood of the representative of the divinity, or of bread made in his likeness.

Other animal forms assumed by the corn-spirit are the fox, stag, roe, sheep, bear, ass, mouse, quail, stork, swan, and kite. If it is asked why the corn-spirit should be thought to appear in the form of an animal and of so many different animals, we may reply that to primitive man the simple appearance of an animal or bird among the corn is probably enough to suggest a mysterious link between the creature and the corn; and when we remember that in the old days, before fields were fenced in, all kinds of animals must have been free to roam over them, we need not wonder that the corn-spirit should have been identified even with large animals like the horse and cow, which nowadays could not, except by a rare accident, be found straying in an English corn-field. This explanation applies with peculiar force to the very common case in which the animal embodiment of the corn-spirit is believed to lurk in the last standing corn. For at harvest a number of wild animals, such as hares, rabbits, and partridges, are commonly driven by the progress of the reaping into the last patch of standing corn, and make their escape from it as it is being cut down. So regularly does this happen that reapers and others often stand round the last patch of corn armed with sticks or guns, with which they kill the animals as they dart out of their last refuge among the stalks. Now, primitive man, to whom magical changes of shape seem perfectly credible, finds it most natural that the spirit of the corn, driven from his home in the ripe grain, should make his escape in the form of the animal which is seen to rush out of the last patch of corn as it falls under the scythe of the reaper. Thus the identification of the corn-spirit with an animal is analogous to the identification of him with a passing stranger. As the sudden appearance of a stranger near the harvest-field or threshing-floor is, to the primitive mind, enough to identify him as the spirit of the corn escaping from the cut or threshed corn, so the sudden appearance of an animal issuing from the cut corn is enough to identify it with the corn-spirit escaping from his ruined home. The two identifications are so analogous that they can hardly be dissociated in any attempt to explain them. Those who look to some other principle than the one here suggested for the explanation of the latter identification are bound to show that their theory covers the former identification also.

iii

However we may explain it, the fact remains that in peasant folk-lore the corn-spirit is very commonly conceived and represented in animal form. May not this fact explain the relation in which certain animals stood to the ancient deities of vegetation, Dionysus, Demeter, Adonis, Attis, and Osiris?

Ancient deities of vegetation as animals.

To begin with Dionysus. We have seen that he was represented sometimes as a goat and sometimes as a bull. As a goat he can hardly be separated from the minor divinities, the Pans, Satyrs, and Silenuses, all of whom are closely associated with him and are represented more or less completely in the form of goats. Thus, Pan was regularly portrayed in sculpture and painting with the face and legs of a goat. The Satyrs were depicted with pointed goat-ears, and sometimes with sprouting horns and short tails. They were sometimes spoken of simply as goats; and in the drama their parts were played by men dressed in goatskins. Silenus is represented in art clad in a goatskin. Further, the Fauns, the Italian counterpart of the Greek Pans and Satyrs, are described as being half goats, with goat-feet and goat-horns. Again, all these minor goat-formed divinities partake more or less clearly of the character of woodland deities. Thus, Pan was called by the Arcadians the Lord of the Wood. The Silenuses kept company with the tree-nymphs. The Fauns are expressly designated as woodland deities; and their character as such is still further brought out by their association, or even identification, with Silvanus and the Silvanuses, who, as their name of itself indicates, are spirits of the woods. Lastly, the association of the Satyrs with the Silenuses, Fauns, and Silvanuses proves that the Satyrs also were woodland deities. These goat-formed spirits of the woods have their counterparts in the folk-lore of Northern Europe. Thus, the Russian wood-spirits, called *Ljeschie* (from *ljes*, 'wood'), are believed to appear partly in human shape, but with the horns, ears, and legs of goats. The *Ljeschi* can alter his stature at pleasure; when he walks in the wood he is as tall as the trees; when he walks in the meadows he is no higher than the grass. Some of the *Ljeschie* are spirits of the corn as well as of the wood; before harvest they are as tall as the corn-stalks, but after it they shrink to the height of the stubble. This brings out—what we have remarked before—the close connexion between tree-spirits and corn-spirits, and shows how easily the former may melt into the latter. Similarly the Fauns, though wood-spirits, were believed to foster the growth of the crops. We have already seen how often the corn-spirit is represented in folk-custom as a goat. On the whole, then, as Mannhardt argues, the Pans, Satyrs, and Fauns perhaps belong to a widely diffused class of wood-spirits conceived in goat-form. The fondness of goats for straying in woods and nibbling the bark of trees, to which indeed they are most destructive, is an obvious and perhaps sufficient reason why wood-spirits should so often be supposed to take the form of goats. The inconsistency of a god of vegetation subsisting upon the vegetation which he personifies is not one to strike the primitive mind. Such inconsistencies arise when the deity, ceasing to be immanent in the vegetation, comes to be regarded as its owner or lord; for the idea of owning the vegetation naturally leads to that of subsisting on it. Sometimes the corn-spirit, originally conceived as immanent in the corn, afterwards comes to be regarded as its owner, who lives on it and is reduced to poverty and want by being deprived of it. Hence he is often known as 'the Poor Man' or 'the Poor Woman'. Occasionally the last sheaf is left standing on the field for 'the Poor Old Woman' or for 'the Old Rye-woman'.

Thus the representation of wood-spirits in the form of goats appears to be both widespread and, to the primitive mind, natural. Therefore when we find, as we have done, that Dionysus—a tree-god—is sometimes represented in goat-form, we can hardly avoid concluding that this representation is simply a part of his proper character as a tree-god and is not to be explained by the fusion of two distinct and independent worships, in one of which he originally appeared as a tree-god and in the other as a goat.

Dionysus was also figured, as we have seen, in the shape of a bull. After what has gone before we are naturally led to expect that his bull form must have been only another expression for his character as a deity of vegetation, especially as the bull is a common embodiment of the corn-spirit in Northern Europe; and the close association of Dionysus with Demeter and Persephone in the mysteries of Eleusis shows that he had at least strong agricultural affinities.

The probability of this view will be somewhat increased if it can be shown that in other rites than those of Dionysus the ancients slew an ox as a representative of the spirit of vegetation. This they appear to have done in the Athenian sacrifice known as 'the murder of the ox' (*bouphonia*).* It took place about the end of June or beginning of July, that is, about the time when the threshing is nearly over in Attica. According to tradition the sacrifice was instituted to procure a cessation of drought and dearth which had afflicted the land. The ritual was as follows. Barley mixed with wheat, or cakes made of them, were laid upon the bronze altar of Zeus Polieus on the Acropolis. Oxen were driven round the altar, and the ox which went up to the altar and ate the offering on it was sacrificed. The axe and knife with which the beast was slain had been previously wetted with water brought by maidens called 'water-carriers'. The weapons were then sharpened and handed to the butchers, one of whom felled the ox with the axe and another cut its throat with the knife. As soon as he had felled the ox, the former threw the axe from him and fled; and the man who cut the beast's throat apparently imitated his example. Meantime the ox was skinned and all present partook of its flesh. Then the hide was stuffed with straw and sewed up; next the stuffed animal was set on its feet and yoked to a plough as if it were ploughing. A trial then took place in an ancient law-court presided over by the King (as he was called) to determine who had murdered the ox. The maidens who had brought the water accused the men who had sharpened the axe and knife; the men who had sharpened the axe and knife blamed the men who had handed these implements to the butchers; the men who had handed the implements to the butchers blamed the butchers; and the butchers laid the blame on the axe and knife, which were accordingly found guilty, condemned, and cast into the sea.

The bouphonia, an Athenian sacrifice of an ox to Zeus Polieus.

The name of this sacrifice—'the *murder* of the ox'—the pains taken by each person who had a hand in the slaughter to lay the blame on some one else, together with the formal trial and punishment of the axe or knife or both, prove that the ox was here regarded not merely as a victim offered to a god, but as itself a sacred creature, the slaughter of which was sacrilege or murder. This is borne out by a statement of Varro that to kill an ox was formerly a capital crime in Attica. The mode of selecting the victim suggests that the ox which tasted the corn was viewed as the corn-deity taking possession of his own. This interpretation is supported by the following custom. In Beauce, in the district of Orleans, on the twenty-fourth or twenty-fifth of April they make a straw man called 'the great *mondard*'. For they say that the old *mondard* is now dead and it is necessary to make a new one. The straw man is carried in solemn procession up and down the village and at last is placed upon the oldest apple-tree. There he remains till the apples are gathered, when he is taken down and thrown into the water, or he is burned and his ashes cast into water. But the person who plucks the first fruit from the tree succeeds to the title of 'the great *mondard*'. Here the straw figure, called 'the great *mondard*' and placed on the oldest apple-tree in spring, represents the spirit of the tree, who, dead in winter, revives when the apple-blossoms appear on the boughs. Thus the person who plucks the first fruit from the tree and thereby receives the name of 'the great *mondard*' must be regarded as a representative of the tree-spirit. Primitive peoples are usually reluctant to taste the annual first-fruits of any crop, until some ceremony has been performed which makes it safe and pious for them to do so. The reason of this reluctance appears to be a belief that the first-fruits either belong to or actually contain a divinity. Therefore when a man or animal is seen boldly to appropriate the sacred first-fruits, he or it is naturally regarded as the divinity himself in human or animal form taking possession of his own. The time of the Athenian sacrifice, which fell about the close of the threshing, suggests that the wheat and barley laid upon the altar were a harvest offering; and the sacramental character of the subsequent repast—all partaking of the flesh of the divine animal—would make it parallel to the harvest-suppers of modern Europe, in which, as we have seen, the flesh of the animal which stands for the corn-spirit is eaten by the harvesters. Again, the tradition that the sacrifice was instituted in order to put an end to drought and famine is in favour of taking it as a harvest festival. The resurrection of the corn-spirit, enacted by setting up the stuffed ox and yoking it to the plough, may be compared with the resurrection of the tree-spirit in the person of his representative, the Wild Man.

The ox appears as a representative of the corn-spirit in other parts of the world. At Great Bassam, in Guinea,* two oxen are slain annually to procure a good harvest. If the sacrifice is to be effectual, it is necessary that the oxen should weep. So all the women of the village sit in front of the beasts, chanting, 'The ox will weep; yes, he will weep!' From time to time one of the women walks round the beasts, throwing manioc meal or palm wine upon them, especially into their eyes. When tears roll down from the eyes of the oxen, the people dance, singing, 'The ox weeps! the ox weeps!' Then two men seize the tails of the beasts and cut them off at one blow. It is believed that a great misfortune will happen in the course of the year if the tails are not severed at one blow. The oxen are afterwards killed, and their flesh is eaten by the chiefs. Here the tears of the oxen, like those of the human victims amongst the Khonds and the Aztecs, are probably a rain-charm. We have already seen that the virtue of the corn-spirit, embodied in animal form, is sometimes supposed to reside in the tail, and that the last handful of corn is sometimes conceived as the tail of the corn-spirit. In the Mithraic religion this conception is graphic-ally set forth in some of the numerous sculptures which represent Mithras kneeling on the back of a bull and plunging a knife into its flank; for on certain of these monuments the tail of the bull ends in three stalks of corn, and in one of them corn-stalks instead of blood are seen issuing from the wound inflicted by the knife. Such representations certainly suggest that the bull, whose sacrifice appears to have formed a leading feature in the Mithraic ritual, was conceived, in one at least of its aspects, as an incarnation of the corn-spirit.

Still more clearly does the ox appear as a personification of the corn-spirit in a ceremony which is observed in all the provinces and districts of China to welcome the approach of spring. On the first day of spring, usually on the third or fourth of February, which is also the beginning of the Chinese New Year, the governor or prefect of the city goes in procession to the east gate of the city, and sacrifices to the Divine Husbandman, who is represented with a bull's head on the body of a man. A large effigy of an ox, cow, or buffalo has been prepared for the occasion, and stands outside of the east gate, with agricultural implements beside it. The figure is made of differently-coloured pieces of paper pasted on a framework either by a blind man or according to the directions of a necromancer. The colours of the paper prognosticate the character of the coming year; if red prevails, there will be many fires; if white, there will be floods and rain; and so with the other colours. The mandarins walk slowly round the ox, beating it severely at each step with rods of various hues. It is filled with five kinds of grain, which pour forth when the effigy is broken by the blows of the rods. The paper fragments are then set on fire, and a scramble takes place for the burning fragments, because the people believe that whoever gets one of them is sure to be fortunate throughout the year. A live buffalo is next killed, and its flesh is divided among the mandarins. According to one account, the effigy of the ox is made of clay, and, after being beaten by the governor, is stoned by the people till they break it in pieces, 'from which they expect an abundant year'. Here the corn-spirit appears to be plainly represented by the corn-filled ox, whose fragments may therefore be supposed to bring fertility with them.

On the whole we may perhaps conclude that both as a goat and as a bull Dionysus was essentially a god of vegetation. The Chinese and European customs which I have cited may perhaps shed light on the custom of rending a live bull or goat at the rites of Dionysus. The animal was torn in fragments, as the Khond victim was cut in pieces, in order that the worshippers might each secure a portion of the life-giving and fertilising influence of the god. The flesh was eaten raw as a sacrament, and we may conjecture that some of it was taken home to be buried in the fields, or otherwise employed so as to convey to the fruits of the earth the quickening influence of the god of vegetation. The resurrection of Dionysus, related in his myth, may have been enacted in his rites by stuffing and setting up the slain ox, as was done at the Athenian *bouphonia*.

iv

Passing next to the corn-goddess Demeter, and remembering that in European folk-lore the pig is a common embodiment of the corn-spirit, we may now ask whether the pig, which was so closely associated with Demeter, may not have been originally the goddess herself in animal form? The pig was sacred to her; in art she was portrayed carrying or accompanied by a pig; and the pig was regularly sacrificed in her mysteries, the reason assigned being that the pig injures the corn and is therefore an enemy of the goddess. But after an animal has been conceived as a god, or a god as an animal, it sometimes happens, as we have seen, that the god sloughs off his animal form and becomes purely anthropomorphic; and that then the animal, which at first had been slain in the character of the god, comes to be viewed as a victim offered to the god on the ground of its hostility to the deity; in short, the god is sacrificed to himself on the ground that he is his own enemy. This happened to Dionysus, and it may have happened to Demeter also. And in fact the rites of one of her festivals, the Thesmophoria,* bear out the view that originally the pig was an embodiment of the corn-goddess herself, either Demeter or her daughter and double Persephone. The Attic Thesmophoria was an autumn festival, celebrated by women alone in October, and appears to have represented with mourning rites the descent of Persephone (or Demeter) into the lower world, and with joy her return from the dead. Hence the name Descent or Ascent variously applied to the first, and the name *Kalligeneia* (fair-born) applied to the third day of the festival. Now it was customary at the Thesmophoria to throw pigs, cakes of dough, and branches of pine-trees into 'the chasms of Demeter and Persephone', which appear to have been sacred caverns or vaults. In these caverns or vaults there were said to be serpents, which guarded the caverns and consumed most of the flesh of the pigs and dough-cakes which were thrown in. Afterwards—apparently at the next annual festival—the decayed remains of the pigs, the cakes, and the pine-branches were fetched by women called 'drawers', who, after observing rules of ceremonial purity for three days, descended into the caverns, and, frightening away the serpents

Demeter, the pig and the horse.

by clapping their hands, brought up the remains and placed them on the altar. Whoever got a piece of the decayed flesh and cakes, and sowed it with the seed-corn in his field, was believed to be sure of a good crop.

To explain the rude and ancient ritual of the Thesmophoria the following legend was told. At the moment when Pluto carried off Persephone, a swineherd called Eubuleus chanced to be herding his swine on the spot, and his herd was engulfed in the chasm down which Pluto vanished with Persephone. Accordingly at the Thesmophoria pigs were annually thrown into caverns to commemorate the disappearance of the swine of Eubuleus. It follows from this that the casting of the pigs into the vaults at the Thesmophoria formed part of the dramatic representation of Persephone's descent into the lower world; and as no image of Persephone appears to have been thrown in, we may infer that the descent of the pigs was not so much an accompaniment of her descent as the descent itself, in short, that the pigs were Persephone. Afterwards when Persephone or Demeter (for the two are equivalent) took on human form, a reason had to be found for the custom of throwing pigs into caverns at her festival; and this was done by saying that when Pluto carried off Persephone there happened to be some swine browsing near, which were swallowed up along with her. The story is obviously a forced and awkward attempt to bridge over the gulf between the old conception of the corn-spirit as a pig and the new conception of her as an anthropomorphic goddess. A trace of the older conception survived in the legend that when the sad mother was searching for traces of the vanished Persephone the footprints of the lost one were obliterated by the footprints of a pig; originally, we may conjecture, the footprints of the pig were the footprints of Persephone and of Demeter herself. A consciousness of the intimate connexion of the pig with the corn lurks in the legend that the swineherd Eubuleus was a brother of Triptolemus, to whom Demeter first imparted the secret of the corn. Indeed, according to one version of the story, Eubuleus himself received, jointly with his brother Triptolemus, the gift of the corn from Demeter as a reward for revealing to her the fate of Persephone. Further, it is to be noted that at the Thesmophoria the women appear to have eaten swine's flesh. The meal, if I am right, must have been a solemn sacrament or communion, the worshippers partaking of the body of the god.

As thus explained, the Thesmophoria has its analogies in the folk-customs of Northern Europe which have been already described. Just as at the Thesmophoria—an autumn festival in honour of the corn-goddess—swine's flesh was partly eaten, partly kept in caverns till the following year, when it was taken up to be sown with the seed-corn in the fields for the purpose of securing a good crop; so in the neighbourhood of Grenoble the goat killed on the harvest-field is partly eaten at the harvest-supper, partly pickled and kept till the next harvest; so at Pouilly the ox killed on the harvest-field is partly eaten by the harvesters, partly pickled and kept till the first day of sowing in spring, probably to be then mixed with the seed, or eaten by the ploughmen, or both; so at Udvarhely the feathers of the cock which is killed in the last sheaf at harvest are kept till spring, and then sown with the seed on the field; so in Hesse and Meiningen the flesh of pigs is eaten on Ash Wednesday or Candlemas, and the bones are kept till sowing-time, when they are put into the field sown or mixed with the seed in the bag; so, lastly, the corn from the last sheaf is kept till Christmas, made into the Yule Boar, and afterwards broken and mixed with the seed-corn at sowing in spring. Thus, to put it generally, the corn-spirit is killed in animal form in autumn; part of his flesh is eaten as a sacrament by his worshippers; and part of it is kept till next sowing-time or harvest as a pledge and security for the continuance or renewal of the corn-spirit's energies.

If persons of fastidious taste should object that the Greeks never could have conceived Demeter and Persephone to be embodied in the form of pigs, it may be answered that in the cave of Phigalia in Arcadia the Black Demeter was portrayed with the head and mane of a horse on the body of a woman. Between the portrait of a goddess as a pig, and the portrait of her as a woman with a horse's head, there is little to choose in respect of barbarism. The legend told of the Phigalian Demeter indicates that the horse was one of the animal forms assumed in ancient Greece, as in modern Europe, by the corn-spirit. It was said that in her search for her daughter, Demeter assumed the form of a mare to escape the addresses of Poseidon, and that, offended at his importunity, she withdrew in dudgeon to a cave

not far from Phigalia in the highlands of Western Arcadia.
There, robed in black, she tarried so long that the fruits of the
earth were perishing, and mankind would have died of famine
if Pan had not soothed the angry goddess and persuaded her to
quit the cave. In memory of this event, the Phigalians set up an
image of the Black Demeter in the cave; it represented a woman
dressed in a long robe, with the head and mane of a horse. The
Black Demeter, in whose absence the fruits of the earth perish,
is plainly a mythical expression for the bare wintry earth
stripped of its summer mantle of green.

v

Attis,
Adonis, and
the pig.

Passing now to Attis and Adonis, we may note a few facts
which seem to show that these deities of vegetation had also,
like other deities of the same class, their animal embodiments.
The worshippers of Attis abstained from eating the flesh of
swine. This appears to indicate that the pig was regarded as
an embodiment of Attis. And the legend that Attis was killed
by a boar points in the same direction. For after the examples
of the goat Dionysus and the pig Demeter it may almost be
laid down as a rule that an animal which is said to have
injured a god was originally the god himself. Perhaps the cry of
'Hyes Attes! Hyes Attes!' which was raised by the worshippers
of Attis may be neither more nor less than 'Pig Attis! Pig
Attis!'—*hyes* being possibly a Phrygian form of the Greek *hys*,
'a pig'.

In regard to Adonis, his connexion with the boar was not
always explained by the story that he had been killed by the
animal. According to another story, a boar rent with his tusk
the bark of the tree in which the infant Adonis was born.
According to yet another story, he perished at the hands of
Hephaestus on Mount Lebanon while he was hunting wild
boars. These variations in the legend serve to show that, while
the connexion of the boar with Adonis was certain, the reason
of the connexion was not understood, and that consequently
different stories were devised to explain it. Certainly the pig
ranked as a sacred animal among the Syrians. At the great
religious metropolis of Hierapolis on the Euphrates pigs were
neither sacrificed nor eaten, and if a man touched a pig he was

unclean for the rest of the day. Some people said this was because the pigs were unclean; others said it was because the pigs were sacred. This difference of opinion points to a hazy state of religious thought in which the ideas of sanctity and uncleanness are not yet sharply distinguished, both being blent in a sort of vaporous solution to which we give the name of taboo. It is quite consistent with this that the pig should have been held to be an embodiment of the divine Adonis, and the analogies of Dionysus and Demeter make it probable that the story of the hostility of the animal to the god was only a late misapprehension of the old view of the god as embodied in a pig. The rule that pigs were not sacrificed or eaten by worshippers of Attis and presumably of Adonis does not exclude the possibility that in these rituals the pig was slain on solemn occasions as a representative of the god and consumed sacramentally by the worshippers. Indeed, the sacramental killing and eating of an animal implies that the animal is sacred, and that, as a general rule, it is spared.

The attitude of the Jews to the pig was as ambiguous as that of the heathen Syrians towards the same animal. The Greeks could not decide whether the Jews worshipped swine or abominated them. On the one hand they might not eat swine; but on the other hand they might not kill them. And if the former rule speaks for the uncleanness, the latter speaks still more strongly for the sanctity of the animal. For whereas both rules may, and one rule must, be explained on the supposition that the pig was sacred; neither rule must, and one rule cannot, be explained on the supposition that the pig was unclean. If, therefore, we prefer the former supposition, we must conclude that, originally at least, the pig was revered rather than abhorred by the Israelites. We are confirmed in this opinion by observing that down to the time of Isaiah some of the Jews used to meet secretly in gardens to eat the flesh of swine and mice as a religious rite. Doubtless this was a very ancient ceremony, dating from a time when both the pig and the mouse were venerated as divine, and when their flesh was partaken of sacramentally on rare and solemn occasions as the body and blood of gods. And in general it may perhaps be said that all so-called unclean animals were originally sacred; the reason for not eating them was that they were divine.

vi

In ancient Egypt, within historical times, the pig occupied the same dubious position as in Syria and Palestine, though at first sight its uncleanness is more prominent than its sanctity. The Egyptians are generally said by Greek writers to have abhorred the pig as a foul and loathsome animal. If a man so much as touched a pig in passing, he stepped into the river with all his clothes on, to wash off the taint. To drink pig's milk was believed to cause leprosy to the drinker. Swineherds, though natives of Egypt, were forbidden to enter any temple, and they were the only men who were thus excluded. No one would give his daughter in marriage to a swineherd, or marry a swineherd's daughter; the swineherds married among themselves. Yet once a year the Egyptians sacrificed pigs to the moon and to Osiris, and not only sacrificed them, but ate of their flesh, though on any other day of the year they would neither sacrifice them nor taste of their flesh. Those who were too poor to offer a pig on this day baked cakes of dough, and offered them instead. This can hardly be explained except by the supposition that the pig was a sacred animal which was eaten sacramentally by his worshippers once a year.

The view that in Egypt the pig was sacred is borne out by the very facts which, to moderns, might seem to prove the contrary. Thus the Egyptians thought, as we have seen, that to drink pig's milk produced leprosy. But exactly analogous views are held by savages about the animals and plants which they deem most sacred. Thus in the island of Wetar (between New Guinea and Celebes) people believe themselves to be variously descended from wild pigs, serpents, crocodiles, turtles, dogs, and eels; a man may not eat an animal of the kind from which he is descended; if he does so, he will become a leper, and go mad. Amongst the Omaha Indians of North America men whose totem is the elk believe that if they ate the flesh of the male elk they would break out in boils and white spots in different parts of their bodies. In the same tribe men whose totem is the red maize think that if they ate red maize they would have running sores all round their mouths. The Bush negroes of Surinam, who practise totemism, believe that if they ate the *capiaï* (an animal like a pig) it would give them leprosy; perhaps the *capiaï* is one of their totems. The Syrians, in antiquity, who esteemed fish sacred, thought that if they ate fish their bodies would break out in ulcers, and their feet and stomach would swell up. The Chasas of Orissa believe that if they were to injure their totemic animal they would be attacked by leprosy and their line would die out. These examples prove that the eating of a sacred animal is often believed to produce leprosy or other skin-diseases; so far, therefore, they support the view that the pig must have been sacred in Egypt, since the effect of drinking its milk was believed to be leprosy.

Again, the rule that, after touching a pig, a man had to wash himself and his clothes, also favours the view of the sanctity of the pig. For it is a common belief that the effect of contact with a sacred object must be removed, by washing or otherwise, before a man is free to mingle with his fellows. Thus the Jews wash their hands after reading the sacred scriptures. Before coming forth from the tabernacle after the sin-offering the high priest had to wash himself, and put off the garments which he had worn in the holy place. It was a rule of Greek ritual that, in offering an expiatory sacrifice, the sacrificer should not touch the sacrifice, and that, after the offering was made, he must wash his body and his clothes in a river or spring before he could enter a city or his own house. The Polynesians felt strongly the need of ridding themselves of the sacred contagion, if it may be so called, which they caught by touching sacred objects. Various ceremonies were performed for the purpose of removing this contagion. We have seen, for example, how in Tonga a man who happened to touch a sacred chief, or anything personally belonging to him, had to perform a certain ceremony before he could feed himself with his hands; otherwise it was believed that he would swell up and die, or at least be afflicted with scrofula or some other disease. We have seen, too, what fatal effects are supposed to follow, and do actually follow, from contact with a sacred object in New Zealand. In short, primitive man believes that what is sacred is dangerous; it is pervaded by a sort of electrical sanctity which communicates a shock to, even if it does not kill, whatever comes in contact with it. Hence the savage is unwilling to touch or even to see that which he deems peculiarly holy. Thus Bechuanas, of the Crocodile clan, think it 'hateful and unlucky' to meet or see a crocodile; the sight is thought to cause inflammation of the eyes. Yet the crocodile is their most sacred object; they call it their father, swear by it, and celebrate it in their festivals. The goat is the sacred animal of the Madenassana Bushmen; yet 'to look upon it would be to render the man for the time impure, as well as to cause him undefined uneasiness'. The Elk clan, among the Omaha Indians, believe that even to touch the male elk would be followed by an eruption of boils and white spots on the body. Members of the Reptile clan in the same tribe think that if one of them touches or smells a snake it will make his hair white. In Samoa people whose god was a butterfly believed that if they caught a butterfly it would strike them dead. Again, in Samoa the reddish-seared leaves of the banana-tree were commonly used as plates for handing food; but if any member of the Wild Pigeon family had used banana leaves for this purpose, it was supposed that he would suffer from rheumatic swellings or an eruption all over the body like chicken-pox. The Mori clan of the Bhils in Central India worship the peacock as their totem and make offerings of grain to it; yet members of the clan believe that were they even to set foot on the tracks of a peacock they would afterwards suffer from some disease, and if a woman sees a peacock she must veil her face and look away. Thus the primitive mind seems to conceive of holiness as a sort of dangerous virus, which a prudent man will shun as far as possible, and of which, if he should chance to be infected by it, he will carefully disinfect himself by some form of ceremonial purification.

In the light of these parallels the beliefs and customs of the Egyptians touching the pig are probably to be explained as based upon an opinion of the extreme sanctity rather than of the extreme uncleanness of the animal; or rather, to put it more correctly, they imply that the animal was looked on, not simply as a filthy and disgusting creature, but as a being endowed with high supernatural powers, and that as such it was regarded with that primitive sentiment of religious awe and fear in which the feelings of reverence and abhorrence are almost equally blended. The ancients themselves seem to have been aware that there was another side to the horror with which swine seemed to inspire the Egyptians. For the Greek astronomer and mathematician

Eudoxus, who resided fourteen months in Egypt and conversed with the priests, was of opinion that the Egyptians spared the pig, not out of abhorrence, but from a regard to its utility in agriculture; for, according to him, when the Nile had subsided, herds of swine were turned loose over the fields to tread the seed down into the moist earth. But when a being is thus the object of mixed and implicitly contradictory feelings, he may be said to occupy a position of unstable equilibrium. In course of time one of the contradictory feelings is likely to prevail over the other, and according as the feeling which finally predominates is that of reverence or abhorrence, the being who is the object of it will rise into a god or sink into a devil. The latter, on the whole, was the fate of the pig in Egypt. For in historical times the fear and horror of the pig seem certainly to have outweighed the reverence and worship of which he may once have been the object, and of which, even in his fallen state, he never quite lost trace. He came to be looked on as an embodiment of Set or Typhon, the Egyptian devil and enemy of Osiris. For it was in the shape of a black pig that Typhon injured the eye of the god Horus, who burned him and instituted the sacrifice of the pig, the sun-god Ra having declared the beast abominable. Again, the story that Typhon was hunting a boar when he discovered and mangled the body of Osiris, and that this was the reason why pigs were sacrificed once a year, is clearly a modernised version of an older story that Osiris, like Adonis and Attis, was slain or mangled by a boar, or by Typhon in the form of a boar. Thus, the annual sacrifice of a pig to Osiris might naturally be interpreted as vengeance inflicted on the hostile animal that had slain or mangled the god. But, in the first place, when an animal is thus killed as a solemn sacrifice once and once only in the year, it generally or always means that the animal is divine, that he is spared and respected the rest of the year as a god and slain, when he is slain, also in the character of a god. In the second place, the examples of Dionysus and Demeter, if not of Attis and Adonis, have taught us that the animal which is sacrificed to a god on the ground that he is the god's enemy may have been, and probably was, originally the god himself. Therefore, the annual sacrifice of a pig to Osiris, coupled with the alleged hostility of the animal to the god, tends to show, first, that originally the pig was a god, and, second, that he was Osiris. At a later age, when Osiris became anthropomorphic and his original relation to the pig had been forgotten, the animal was first distinguished from him, and afterwards opposed as an enemy to him by mythologists who could think of no reason for killing a beast in connexion with the worship of a god except that the beast was the god's enemy; or, as Plutarch puts it, not that which is dear to the gods, but that which is the contrary, is fit to be sacrified. At this later stage the havoc which a wild boar notoriously makes amongst the corn would supply a plausible reason for regarding him as the foe of the corn-spirit, though originally, if I am right, the very freedom with which the boar ranged at will through the corn led people to identify him with the corn-spirit, to whom he was afterwards opposed as an enemy.

The view which identifies the pig with Osiris derives not a little support from the sacrifice of pigs to him on the very day on which, according to tradition, Osiris himself was killed; for thus the killing of the pig was the annual representation of the killing of Osiris, just as the throwing of the pigs into the caverns at the Thesmophoria was an annual representation of the descent of Persephone into the lower world; and both customs are parallel to the European practice of killing a goat, cock, and so forth, at harvest as a representative of the corn-spirit.

Again, the theory that the pig, originally Osiris himself, afterwards came to be regarded as an embodiment of his enemy Typhon, is supported by the similar relation of red-haired men and red oxen to Typhon. For in regard to the red-haired men who were burned and whose ashes were scattered with winnowing-fans, we have seen fair grounds for believing that originally, like the red-haired puppies killed at Rome in spring, they were representatives of the corn-spirit himself, that is, of Osiris, and were slain for the express purpose of making the corn turn red or golden. Yet at a later time these men were explained to be representatives, not of Osiris, but of his enemy Typhon, and the killing of them was regarded as an act of vengeance inflicted on the enemy of the god. Similarly, the red oxen sacrificed by the Egyptians were said to be offered on the ground of their resemblance to Typhon; though it is more likely that originally they were slain on the ground of their resemblance to the corn-spirit Osiris. We have seen that the ox is a common representative of the corn-spirit and is slain as such on the harvest-field.

Osiris was regularly identified with the bull Apis of Memphis and the bull Mnevis of Heliopolis. But it is hard to say whether these bulls were embodiments of him as the corn-spirit, as the red oxen appear to have been, or whether they were not in origin entirely distinct deities who came to be fused with Osiris at a later time. The universality of the worship of these two bulls seems to put them on a different footing from the ordinary sacred animals whose worships were purely local. But whatever the original relation of Apis to Osiris may have been, there is one fact about the former which ought not to be passed over in a disquisition on the custom of killing a god. Although the bull Apis was worshipped as a god with much pomp and profound reverence, he was not suffered to live beyond a certain length of time which was prescribed by the sacred books, and on the expiry of which he was drowned in a holy spring. The limit, according to Plutarch, was twenty-five years; but it cannot always have been enforced, for the tombs of the Apis bulls have been discovered in modern times, and from the inscriptions on them it appears that in the twenty-second dynasty two of the holy steers lived more than twenty-six years.

vii

We are now in a position to hazard a conjecture as to the meaning of the tradition that Virbius, the first of the divine Kings of the Wood at Aricia, had been killed in the character of Hippolytus by horses. Having found, first, that spirits of the corn are not infrequently represented in the form of horses; and, second, that the animal which in later legends is said to have injured the god was sometimes originally the god himself, we may conjecture that the horses by which Virbius or Hippolytus was said to have been slain were really embodiments of him as a deity of vegetation. The myth that he had been killed by horses was probably invented to explain certain features in his worship, amongst others the custom of excluding horses from his sacred grove. For myth changes while custom remains constant; men continue to do what their fathers did before them, though the reasons on which their fathers acted have

Virbius and the horse.

been long forgotten. The history of religion is a long attempt to reconcile old custom with new reason, to find a sound theory for an absurd practice. In the case before us we may be sure that the myth is more modern than the custom and by no means represents the original reason for excluding horses from the grove. From their exclusion it might be inferred that horses could not be the sacred animals or embodiment or embodiments of the god of the grove. But the inference would be rash. The goat was at one time a sacred animal or embodiment of Athena, as may be inferred from the practice of representing the goddess clad in a goat-skin (*aegis*). Yet the goat was neither sacrificed to her as a rule, nor allowed to enter her great sanctuary, the Acropolis at Athens. The reason alleged for this was that the goat injured the olive, the sacred tree of Athena. So far, therefore, the relation of the goat to Athena is parallel to the relation of the horse to Virbius, both animals being excluded from the sanctuary on the ground of injury done by them to the god. But from Varro we learn that there was an exception to the rule which excluded the goat from the Acropolis. Once a year, he says, the goat was driven on to the Acropolis for a necessary sacrifice. Now, as has been remarked before, when an animal is sacrificed once and once only in the year, it is probably slain, not as a victim offered to the god, but as a representative of the god himself. Therefore we may infer that if a goat was sacrificed on the Acropolis once a year, it was sacrificed in the character of Athena herself; and it may be conjectured that the skin of the sacrificed animal was placed on the statue of the goddess and formed the *aegis*, which would thus be renewed annually. Similarly at Thebes in Egypt rams were sacred and were not sacrificed. But on one day in the year a ram was killed, and its skin was placed on the statue of the god Ammon. Now, if we knew the ritual of the Arician grove better, we might find that the rule of excluding horses from it, like the rule of excluding goats from the Acropolis at Athens, was subject to an annual exception, a horse being once a year taken into the grove and sacrificed as an embodiment of the god Virbius. By the usual misunderstanding the horse thus killed would come in time to be regarded as an enemy offered up in sacrifice to the god whom he had injured, like the pig which was sacrificed to Demeter and Osiris or the goat which was sacrificed to Dionysus, and possibly to Athena. It is so easy for a writer to record a rule without noticing an exception that we need not wonder at finding the rule of the Arician grove recorded without any mention of an exception such as I suppose. If we had had only the statements of Athenaeus and Pliny, we should have known only the rule which forbade the sacrifice of goats to Athena and excluded them from the Acropolis, without being aware of the important exception which the fortunate preservation of Varro's work has revealed to us.

The conjecture that once a year a horse may have been sacrificed in the Arician grove as a representative of the deity of the grove derives some support from the similar sacrifice of a horse which took place once a year at Rome. On the fifteenth of October in each year a chariot-race was run on the Field of Mars. Stabbed with a spear, the right-hand horse of the victorious team was then sacrificed to Mars for the purpose of ensuring good crops, and its head was cut off and adorned with a string of loaves. Thereupon the inhabitants of two wards—the Sacred Way and the Subura—contended with each other who should get the head. If the people of the Sacred Way got it, they fastened it to a wall of the king's house; if the people of the Subura got it, they fastened it to the Mamilian tower. The horse's tail was cut off and carried to the king's house with such speed that the blood dripped on the hearth of the house. Further, it appears that the blood of the horse was caught and preserved till the twenty-first of April, when the Vestal Virgins mixed it with the blood of the unborn calves which had been sacrificed six days before. The mixture was then distributed to shepherds, and used by them for fumigating their flocks.

Annual sacrifice of a horse at Rome in October.

In this ceremony the decoration of the horse's head with a string of loaves, and the alleged object of the sacrifice, namely, to procure a good harvest, seem to indicate that the horse was killed as one of those animal representatives of the corn-spirit of which we have found so many examples. The custom of cutting off the horse's tail is like the African custom of cutting off the tails of the oxen and sacrificing them to obtain a good crop. In both the Roman and the African custom the animal apparently stands for the corn-spirit, and its fructifying power is supposed to reside especially in its tail. The latter idea occurs, as we have seen, in European folk-lore. Again, the practice of fumigating the cattle in spring with the blood of the horse may be compared with the practice of giving the Old Wife, the Maiden, or the *clyack* sheaf as fodder to the horses in spring or the cattle at Christmas, and giving the Yule Boar to the ploughing oxen or horses to eat in spring. All these usages aim at ensuring the blessing of the corn-spirit on the homestead and its inmates and storing it up for another year.

Archaic character of the sacrifice and its analogies in the harvest customs of Northern Europe.

The Roman sacrifice of the October horse, as it was called, carries us back to the early days when the Subura, afterwards a low and squalid quarter of the great metropolis, was still a separate village, whose inhabitants engaged in a friendly contest on the harvest-field with their neighbours of Rome, then a little rural town. The Field of Mars on which the ceremony took place lay beside the Tiber, and formed part of the king's domain down to the abolition of the monarchy. For tradition ran that at the time when the last of the kings was driven from Rome the corn stood ripe for the sickle on the crown lands beside the river; but no one would eat the accursed grain and it was flung into the river in such heaps that, the water being low with the summer heat, it formed the nucleus of an island. The horse sacrifice was thus an old autumn custom observed upon the king's corn-fields at the end of the harvest. The tail and blood of the horse, as the chief parts of the corn-spirit's representative, were taken to the king's house and kept there; just as in Germany the harvest-cock is nailed on the gable or over the door of the farmhouse; and as the last sheaf, in the form of the Maiden, is carried home and kept over the fireplace in the Highlands of Scotland. Thus the blessing of the corn-spirit was brought to the king's house and hearth and, through them, to the community of which he was the head. Similarly in the spring and autumn customs of Northern Europe the Maypole is sometimes set up in front of the house of the mayor or burgomaster, and the last sheaf at harvest is brought to him as the head of the village. But while the tail and blood fell to the king, the neighbouring village of the Subura, which no doubt once had a similar ceremony of its own, was gratified by being allowed to compete for the prize of the horse's head. The Mamilian tower, to which the Suburans nailed the horse's head when they succeeded in carrying it off, appears to have been a peel-tower or keep of the old Mamilian family, the magnates of the village. The ceremony thus performed on the king's fields and at his house on behalf of the whole town and of the neighbouring village presupposes a time when each township performed a similar ceremony on its own fields. In the rural districts of Latium the villages may have continued to observe the custom, each on its own land, long after the Roman hamlets had merged their separate harvest-homes in the common celebration on the king's lands. There is no intrinsic improbability in the supposition that the sacred grove of Aricia, like the Field of Mars at Rome, may have been the scene of a common harvest celebration, at which a horse was sacrificed with the same rude rites on behalf of the neighbouring villages. The horse would represent the fructifying spirit both of the tree and of the corn, for the two ideas melt into each other, as we see in customs like the Harvest-May.

Custom of eating the new corn sacramentally as the body of the corn-spirit.

WE have now seen that the corn-spirit is represented sometimes in human, sometimes in animal form, and that in both cases he is killed in the person of his representative and eaten sacramentally. To find examples of actually killing the human representative of the corn-spirit we had naturally to go to savage races; but the harvest-suppers of our European peasants have furnished unmistakable examples of the sacramental eating of animals as representatives of the corn-spirit. But further, as might have been anticipated, the new corn is itself eaten

Loaves baked of the new corn in human shape and eaten.

sacramentally, that is, as the body of the corn-spirit. In Wermland, Sweden, the farmer's wife uses the grain of the last sheaf to bake a loaf in the shape of a little girl; this loaf is divided amongst the whole household and eaten by them. Here the loaf represents the corn-spirit conceived as a maiden; just as in Scotland the corn-spirit is similarly conceived and represented by the last sheaf made up in the form of a woman and bearing the name of the Maiden. As usual, the corn-spirit is believed to reside in the last sheaf; and to eat a loaf made from the last sheaf is, therefore, to eat the corn-spirit itself. Similarly at La Palisse, in France, a man made of dough is hung upon the fir-tree which is carried on the last harvest-waggon. The tree and the dough-man are taken to the mayor's house and kept there till the vintage is over. Then the close of the harvest is celebrated by a feast at which the mayor breaks the dough-man in pieces and gives the pieces to the people to eat.

Old Lithuanian ritual at eating the new corn.

In these examples the corn-spirit is represented and eaten in human shape. In other cases, though the new corn is not baked in loaves of human shape, still the solemn ceremonies with which it is eaten suffice to indicate that it is partaken of sacramentally, that is, as the body of the corn-spirit. For example, the following ceremonies used to be observed by Lithuanian peasants at eating the new corn. About the time of the autumn sowing, when all the corn had been got in and the threshing had begun, each farmer held a festival called Sabarios, that is, 'the mixing or throwing together'. He took nine good handfuls of each kind of crop—wheat, barley, oats, flax, beans, lentils, and the rest; and each handful he divided into three parts. The twenty-seven portions of each grain were then thrown on a heap and all mixed up together. The grain used had to be that which was first threshed and winnowed and which had been set aside and kept for this purpose. A part of the grain thus mixed was employed to bake little loaves, one for each of the household; the rest was mixed with more barley or oats and made into beer. The first beer brewed from this mixture was for the drinking of the farmer, his wife, and children; the second brew was for the servants. The beer being ready, the farmer chose an evening when no stranger was expected. Then he knelt down before the barrel of beer, drew a jugful of the liquor and poured it on the bung of the barrel, saying, 'O fruitful earth, make rye and barley and all kinds of corn to flourish.' Next he took the jug to the parlour, where his wife and children awaited him. On the floor of the parlour lay bound a black or white or speckled (not a red) cock and a hen of the same colour and of the same brood, which must have been hatched within the year. Then the farmer knelt down, with the jug in his hand, and thanked God for the harvest and prayed for a good crop next year. Next all lifted up their hands and said, 'O God, and thou, O earth, we give you this cock and hen as a free-will offering.' With that the farmer killed the fowls with the blows of a wooden spoon, for he might not cut their heads off. After the first prayer and after killing each of the birds he poured out a third of the beer. Then his wife boiled the fowls in a new pot which had never been used before. After that, a bushel was set, bottom upwards, on the floor, and on it were placed the little loaves mentioned above and the boiled fowls. Next the new beer was fetched, together with a ladle and three mugs, none of which was used except on this occasion. When the farmer had ladled the beer into the mugs, the family knelt down round the bushel. The father then uttered a prayer and drank off the three mugs of beer. The rest followed his example. Then the loaves and the flesh of the fowls were eaten, after which the beer went round again, till every one had emptied each of the three mugs nine times. None of the food should remain over; but if anything did happen to be left, it was consumed next morning with the same ceremonies. The bones were given to the dog to eat; if he did not eat them all up, the remains were buried under the dung in the cattle-stall. This ceremony was observed at the beginning of December. On the day on which it took place no bad word might be spoken.

Modern European ceremonies at eating the new corn or new potatoes.

Such was the custom about two hundred years or more ago. At the present day in Lithuania, when new potatoes or loaves made from the new corn are being eaten, all the people at table pull each other's hair. The meaning of this last custom is obscure, but a similar custom was certainly observed by the heathen Lithuanians at their solemn sacrifices. Many of the Esthonians of the island of Oesel will not eat bread baked of the new corn till they have first taken a bite at a piece of iron. The iron is here plainly a charm, intended to render harmless the spirit that is in the corn. In Sutherlandshire at the present day, when the new potatoes are dug all the family must taste them, otherwise 'the spirits in them [the potatoes] take offence, and the potatoes would not keep'. In one part of Yorkshire it is still customary for the clergyman to cut the first corn; and my informant believes that the corn so cut is used to make the communion bread. If the latter part of the custom is correctly reported (and analogy is all in its favour), it shews how the Christian communion has absorbed within itself a sacrament which is doubtless far older than Christianity.

Ceremony of the heathen Cheremiss at eating the new corn.

Among the heathen Cheremiss on the left bank of the Volga, when the first bread baked from the new corn is to be eaten, the villagers assemble in the house of the oldest inhabitant, the eastern door is opened, and all pray with their faces towards it. Then the sorcerer or priest gives to each of them a mug of beer, which they drain; next he cuts and hands to every person a morsel of the loaf, which they partake of. Finally, the young people go to the elders and bowing down to the earth before them say, 'We pray God that you may live, and that God may let us pray next year for new corn.' The rest of the day is passed in mirth and dancing. The whole ceremony, observes the writer who has described it, looks almost like a caricature of the Eucharist. According to another account, each Cheremiss householder on this occasion, after bathing, places some of each kind of grain, together with malt, cakes, and drink, in a vessel, which he holds up to the sun, at the same time thanking the gods for the good things which they have bestowed upon him. But this part of the ceremony is a sacrifice rather than a sacrament of the new corn.

The Aino* or Ainu of Japan are said to distinguish various kinds of millet as male and female respectively, and these kinds, taken together, are called 'the divine husband and wife cereal' (*Umurek haru kamui*). 'Therefore before millet is pounded and made into cakes for general eating, the old men have a few made for themselves first to worship. When they are ready they pray to them very earnestly and say:—"O thou cereal deity, we worship thee. Thou hast grown very well this year, and thy flavour will be sweet. Thou art good. The goddess of fire will be glad, and we also shall rejoice greatly. O thou god, O thou divine cereal, do thou nourish the people. I now partake of thee. I worship thee and give thee thanks." After having thus prayed, they, the worshippers, take a cake and eat it, and from this time the people may all partake of the new millet. And so with many gestures of homage and words of prayer this kind of food is dedicated to the well-being of the Ainu. No doubt the cereal offering is regarded as a tribute paid to god, but that god is no other than the seed itself; and it is only a god in so far as it is beneficial to the human body.'

Ceremony of the Aino at eating the new millet.

Amongst the Burghers or Badagas, a tribe of the Neilgherry Hills in Southern India, the first handful of seed is sown and the first sheaf reaped by a Curumbar—a man of a different tribe, the members of which the Burghers regard as sorcerers. The grain contained in the first sheaf 'is that day reduced to meal, made into cakes, and, being offered as a first-fruit oblation, is, together with the remainder of the sacrificed animal, partaken of by the Burgher and the whole of his family, as the meat of a federal offering and sacrifice'. Amongst the Coorgs of Southern India the man who is to cut the first sheaf of rice at harvest is chosen by an astrologer. At sunset the whole household takes a hot bath and then goes to the rice-field, where the chosen reaper cuts an armful of rice with a new sickle, and distributes two or more stalks to all present. Then all return to the threshing-floor. A bundle of leaves is adorned with a stalk of rice and fastened to the post in the centre of the threshing-floor. Enough of the new rice is now threshed,

Ceremonies observed at eating the new rice in India.

cleaned, and ground to provide flour for the dough-cakes which each member of the household is to eat. Then they go to the door of the house, where the mistress washes the feet of the sheaf-cutter, and presents to him, and after him to all the rest, a brass vessel full of milk, honey, and sugar, from which each person takes a draught. Next the man who cut the sheaf kneads a cake of rice-meal, plantains, milk, honey, seven new rice corns, seven pieces of coco-nut, and so on. Every one receives a little of this cake on an Ashvatha leaf, and eats it. The ceremony is then over and the sheaf-cutter mixes with the company. When he was engaged in cutting the rice no one might touch him. Among the Hindoos of Southern India the eating of the new rice is the occasion of a family festival called Pongol. The new rice is boiled in a new pot on a fire which is kindled at noon on the day when, according to Hindoo astrologers, the sun enters the tropic of Capricorn. The boiling of the pot is watched with great anxiety by the whole family, for as the milk boils, so will the coming year be. If the milk boils rapidly, the year will be prosperous; but it will be the reverse if the milk boils slowly. Some of the new boiled rice is offered to the image of Ganesa; then every one partakes of it. In some parts of Northern India the festival of the new crop is known as *Navan*, that is 'new grain'. When the crop is ripe, the owner takes the omens, goes to the field, plucks five or six ears of barley in the spring crop and one of the millets in the autumn harvest. This is brought home, parched, and mixed with coarse sugar, butter, and curds. Some of it is thrown on the fire in the name of the village gods and deceased ancestors; the rest is eaten by the family. At Gilgit, in the Hindoo Koosh, before wheat-harvest begins, a member of every household gathers a handful of ears of corn secretly at dusk. A few of the ears are hung up over the door of the house, and the rest are roasted next morning, and eaten steeped in milk. The day is spent in rejoicings, and next morning the harvest begins.

Ceremonies observed by the Chams at ploughing, sowing, reaping, and eating the new rice.

The Chams of Binh-Thuan, in Indo-China, may not reap the rice-harvest until they have offered the first-fruits to Po-Nagar, the goddess of agriculture, and have consumed them sacramentally. These first-fruits are gathered from certain sacred fields called *Hamou-Klêk-Laoa* or 'fields of secret tillage', which are both sown and reaped with peculiar ceremonies. Apparently the tilling of the earth is considered a crime which must be perpetrated secretly and afterwards atoned for. On a lucky day in June, at the first cock-crow, two men lead the buffaloes and the plough to the sacred field, round which they draw three furrows in profound silence and then retire. Afterwards at dawn the owner of the land comes lounging by, as if by the merest chance. At sight of the furrows he stops, pretends to be much surprised, and cries out, 'Who has been secretly ploughing my field this night?' Hastening home, he kills a kid or some fowls, cooks the victuals, and prepares five quids of betel, some candles, a flask of oil, and lustral water of three different sorts. With these offerings and the plough drawn by the buffaloes, he returns to the field, where he lights the candles and spreading out the victuals worships Po-Nagar and the other deities, saying: 'I know not who has secretly ploughed my field this night. Pardon, ye gods, those who have done this wrong. Accept these offerings. Bless us. Suffer us to proceed with this work.' Then, speaking in the name of the deities, he gives the reassuring answer, 'All right. Plough away!' With the lustral water he washes or sprinkles the buffaloes, the yoke, and the plough. The oil serves to anoint the plough and to pour libations on the ground. The five quids of betel are buried in the field. Thereupon the owner sows a handful of rice on the three furrows that have been traced, and eats the victuals with his people. After all these rites have been duly performed, he may plough and sow his land as he likes. When the rice has grown high enough in this 'field of secret tillage' to hide pigeons, offerings of ducks, eggs, and fowls are made to the deities; and fresh offerings, which generally consist of five plates of rice, two boiled fowls, a bottle of spirits, and five quids of betel, are made to Po-Nagar and the rest at the time when the rice is in bloom. Finally, when the rice in 'the field of secret tillage' is ripe, it has to be reaped before any of the rest. Offerings of food, such as boiled fowls, plates of rice, cakes, and so forth, are spread out on the field; a candle is lit, and a priest or, in his absence, the owner prays to the guardian deities to come and partake of the food set before them. After that the owner of the land cuts three stalks of rice with a sickle in the middle of the field, then he cuts three handfuls at the side, and places the whole in a napkin. These are the first-fruits offered to Po-Nagar, the goddess of agriculture. On being taken home the rice from the three handfuls is husked, pounded in a mortar, and presented to the goddess with these words: 'Taste, O goddess, these first-fruits which have just been reaped.' This rice is afterwards eaten, while the straw and husks are burned. Having eaten the first-fruits of the rice, the owner takes the three stalks cut in the middle of the field, passes them through the smoke of the precious eagle-wood, and hangs them up in his house, where they remain till the next sowing-time comes round. The grain from these three stalks will form the seed of the three furrows in 'the field of secret tillage'. Not till these ceremonies have been performed is the proprietor at liberty to reap the rest of that field and all the others.

Ceremony at eating the new yams at Onitsha on the Niger.

The ceremony of eating the new yams at Onitsha,* on the Niger, is thus described: 'Each headman brought out six yams, and cut down young branches of palm-leaves and placed them before his gate, roasted three of the yams, and got some kola-nuts and fish. After the yam is roasted, the *Libia*, or country doctor, takes the yam, scrapes it into a sort of meal, and divides it into halves; he then takes one piece, and places it on the lips of the person who is going to eat the new yam. The eater then blows up the steam from the hot yam, and afterwards pokes the whole into his mouth, and says, "I thank God for being permitted to eat the new yam"; he then begins to chew it heartily, with fish likewise.'

The sacrament of first-fruits sometimes combined with a sacrifice of them to gods or spirits.

In some of the festivals which we have examined, as in the Cheremiss and Cham ceremonies, the sacrament of first-fruits is combined with a sacrifice or presentation of them to gods or spirits, and in course of time the sacrifice of first-fruits tends to throw the sacrament into the shade, if not to supersede it. The mere fact of offering the first-fruits to the gods or spirits comes now to be thought a sufficient preparation for eating the new corn; the higher powers having received their share, man is free to enjoy the rest. This mode of viewing the new fruits implies that they are regarded no longer as themselves instinct with divine life, but merely as a gift bestowed by the gods upon man, who is bound to express his gratitude and homage to his divine benefactors by returning to them a portion of their bounty. More examples of the sacrifice, as distinct from sacrament,* of first-fruits will be given presently.

ii

The custom of eating bread sacramentally as the body of a god was practised by the Aztecs before the discovery and conquest of Mexico by the Spaniards. Twice a year, in May and December, an image of the great Mexican god Huitzilopochtli or Vitzilipuztli was made of dough, then broken in pieces, and solemnly eaten by his worshippers. The May ceremony is thus described by the historian Acosta: 'The Mexicans in the month of May made their principal feast to their god Vitzilipuztli, and two days before this feast, the virgins whereof I have spoken (the which were shut up and secluded in the same temple and were as it were religious women) did mingle a quantity of the seed of beets with roasted maize, and then they did mould it with honey, making an idol of that paste in bigness like to that of wood, putting instead of eyes grains of green glass, of blue or white; and for teeth grains of maize set forth with all the ornament and furniture that I have said. This being finished, all the noblemen came and brought it an exquisite and rich garment, like unto that of the idol, wherewith they did attire it. Being thus clad and deckt, they did set it in an azured chair and in a litter to carry it on their shoulders. The morning of this feast being come, an hour before day all the maidens came forth attired in white, with new ornaments, the which that day were called the Sisters of their god Vitzilipuztli, they came crowned with garlands of maize roasted and parched, being like unto azahar or the flower or orange; and about their necks they had great chains of the same, which went bauldrickwise under their left arm. Their cheeks were dyed with vermilion, their arms from the elbow to the wrist were covered with red parrots' feathers.' Young men, dressed in red robes and crowned like the virgins with maize, then carried the idol in its litter to the foot of the great pyramid-shaped temple, up the steep and narrow steps of which it was drawn to the music of flutes, trumpets, cornets, and drums. 'While they mounted up the idol all the people stood in the court with much reverence and fear. Being mounted to the top, and that they had placed it in a little lodge of roses which they held ready, presently came the young men, which strewed many flowers of sundry kinds, wherewith they

Aztec custom of eating sacramentally a dough image of the god Huitzilopochtli or Vitzilipuztli as a mode of communion with the deity.

filled the temple both within and without. This done, all the virgins came out of their convent, bringing pieces of paste compounded of beets and roasted maize, which was of the same paste whereof their idol was made and compounded, and they were of the fashion of great bones. They delivered them to the young men, who carried them up and laid them at the idol's feet, wherewith they filled the whole place that it could receive no more. They called these morsels of paste the flesh and bones of Vitzilipuztli. Having laid abroad these bones, presently came all the ancients of the temple, priests, Levites, and all the rest of the ministers, according to their dignities and antiquities (for herein there was a strict order amongst them) one after another, with their veils of diverse colours and works, every one according to his dignity and office, having garlands upon their heads and chains of flowers about their necks; after them came their gods and goddesses whom they worshipped, of diverse figures, attired in the same livery; then putting themselves in order about those morsels and pieces of paste, they used certain ceremonies with singing and dancing. By means whereof they were blessed and consecrated for the flesh and bones of this idol. This ceremony and blessing (whereby they were taken for the flesh and bones of the idol) being ended, they honoured those pieces in the same sort as their god.

'Then come forth the sacrificers, who began the sacrifice of men in the manner as hath been spoken, and that day they did sacrifice a greater number than at any other time, for that it was the most solemn feast they observed. The sacrifices being ended, all the young men and maids came out of the temple attired as before, and being placed in order and rank, one directly against another, they danced by drums, the which sounded in praise of the feast, and of the idol which they did celebrate. To which song all the most ancient and greatest noblemen did answer dancing about them, making a great circle, as their use is, the young men and maids remaining always in the midst. All the city came to this goodly spectacle, and there was a commandment very strictly observed throughout all the land, that the day of the feast of the idol of Vitzilipuztli they should eat no other meat but this paste, with honey, whereof the idol was made. And this should be eaten at the point of day, and they should drink no water nor any other thing till after noon: they held it for an ill sign, yea, for sacrilege to do the contrary: but after the ceremonies ended, it was lawful for them to eat anything. During the time of this ceremony they hid the water from their little children, admonishing all such as had the use of reason not to drink any water; which, if they did, the anger of God would come upon them, and they should die, which they did observe very carefully and strictly. The ceremonies, dancing, and sacrifice ended, they went to unclothe themselves, and the priests and superiors of the temple took the idol of paste, which they spoiled of all the ornaments it had, and made many pieces, as well of the idol itself as of the truncheons which they consecrated, and then they gave them to the people in manner of a communion, beginning with the greater, and continuing unto the rest, both men, women, and little children, who received it with such tears, fear, and reverence as it was an admirable thing, saying that they did eat the flesh and bones of God, wherewith they were grieved. Such as had any sick folks demanded thereof for them, and carried it with great reverence and veneration.'*

From this interesting passage we learn that the ancient Mexicans, even before the arrival of Christian missionaries, were fully acquainted with the theological doctrine of transubstantiation* and acted upon it in the solemn rites of their religion. They believed that by consecrating bread their priests could turn it into the very body of their god, so that all who thereupon partook of the consecrated bread entered into a mystic communion with the deity by receiving a portion of his divine substance into themselves. The doctrine of transubstantiation, or the magical conversion of bread into flesh, was also familiar to the Aryans of ancient India long before the spread and even the rise of Christianity. The Brahmans taught that the rice-cakes offered in sacrifice were substitutes for human beings, and that they were actually converted into the real bodies of men by the manipulation of the priest. We read that 'when it (the rice-cake) still consists of rice-meal, it is the hair. When he pours water on it, it becomes skin. When he mixes it, it becomes flesh: for then it becomes consistent; and consistent also is the flesh. When it is baked, it becomes bone: for then it becomes somewhat hard; and hard is the bone. And when he is about to take it off (the fire) and sprinkles it with butter, he changes it

The doctrine of transubstantiation or the magical conversion of bread into flesh recognised by the ancient Aztecs and Brahmans.

into marrow. This is the completeness which they call the fivefold animal sacrifice.' These remarkable tranformations, daily wrought by the priest, on the rice-wafer, were, however, nothing at all to those which the gods themselves accomplished when they first instituted the rite. For the horse and the ox which they sacrificed became a *bos gaurus* and a gayal respectively; the sheep was turned into a camel; and the goat was converted into a remarkable species of deer, enriched with eight legs, which slew lions and elephants. On the whole it would seem that neither the ancient Hindoos nor the ancient Mexicans had much to learn from the most refined mysteries of Catholic theology.

The sacred food not to be defiled by contact with common food.

Now, too, we can perfectly understand why on the day of their solemn communion with the deity the Mexicans refused to eat any other food than the consecrated bread which they revered as the very flesh and bones of their God, and why up till noon they might drink nothing at all, not even water. They feared no doubt to defile the portion of God in their stomachs by contact with common things. A similar pious fear led the Creek and Seminole Indians, as we saw, to adopt the more thoroughgoing expedient of rinsing out their insides by a strong purgative before they dared to partake of the sacrament of first-fruits. We can now also conjecture the reason why Zulu boys, after eating the flesh of the black bull at the feast of first-fruits, are forbidden to drink anything till the next day.

Aztec custom of killing the god Huitzilopochtli in effigy and eating him afterwards.

At the festival of the winter solstice in December the Aztecs killed their god Huitzilopochtli in effigy first and ate him afterwards. As a preparation for this solemn ceremony an image of the deity in the likeness of a man was fashioned out of seeds of various sorts, which were kneaded into a dough with the blood of children. The bones of the god were represented by pieces of acacia wood. This image was placed on the chief altar of the temple, and on the day of the festival the king offered incense to it. Early next day it was taken down and set on its feet in a great hall. Then a priest, who bore the name and acted the part of the god Quetzalcoatl, took a flint-tipped dart and hurled it into the breast of the dough-image, piercing it through and through. This was called 'killing the god Huitzilopochtli so that his body might be eaten.' One of the priests cut out the heart of the image and gave it to the king to eat. The rest of the image was divided into minute pieces, of which every man great and small, down to the male children in the cradle, received one to eat. But no woman might taste a morsel. The ceremony was called *teoqualo*, that is, 'god is eaten'.

The custom of entering into communion with a god by eating of his effigy survived till lately among the Huichol Indians of Mexico. In a narrow valley, at the foot of a beetling crag of red rock, they have a small thatched temple of the God of fire, and here down to recent years stood a small image of the deity in human form roughly carved out of solidified volcanic ash. The idol was very dirty and smeared with blood, and in his right side was a hole, which owed its existence to the piety and devotion of his worshippers. For they believed that the power of healing and a knowledge of mysteries could be acquired by eating a little of the god's holy body, and accordingly shamans, or medicine-men, who desired to lay in a stock of these accomplishments, so useful in the exercise of their profession, were wont to repair to the temple, where, having deposited an offering of food or a votive bowl, they scraped off with their finger-nails some particles of the god's body and swallowed them. After engaging in this form of communion with the deity they had to abstain from salt and from all carnal converse with their wives for five months. Again, the Malas, a caste of pariahs in Southern India, communicate with the goddess Sunkalamma by eating her effigy. The communion takes place at marriage. An image of the goddess in the form of a truncated cone is made out of rice and green gram cooked together, and it is decorated with a nose jewel, garlands, and other religious symbols. Offerings of rice, frankincense, camphor, and a coco-nut are then made to the image, and a ram or he-goat is sacrificed. After the sacrifice has been presented, all the persons assembled prostrate themselves in silence before the image, then they break it in pieces, and distributing the pieces among themselves they swallow them. In this way they are, no doubt, believed to absorb the divine essence of the goddess whose broken body has just passed into their stomachs. In Europe the Catholic Church has resorted to similar means for enabling the pious to enjoy the ineffable privilege of eating the persons of the Infant God and his Mother. For this purpose images of the Madonna are printed on some soluble and harmless substance and sold in sheets like postage stamps. The worshipper buys as many of

Communion with a god by eating of his effigy among the Huichol Indians of Mexico and the Malas of Southern India.

Catholic custom of eating effigies of the Madonna.

these sacred emblems as he has occasion for, and affixing one or more of them to his food swallows the bolus. The practice is not confined to the poor and ignorant. In his youth Count von Hoensbroech and his devout mother used thus to consume portions of God and his Mother with their meals.*

iii

Loaves called *Maniæ* baked at Aricia.

Woollen effigies dedicated at Rome to Mania, the Mother or Grandmother of Ghosts, at the Compitalia.

We are now able to suggest an explanation of the proverb 'There are many Manii at Aricia.'* Certain loaves made in the shape of men were called by the Romans *maniæ*, and it appears that this kind of loaf was especially made at Aricia. Now, Mania, the name of one of these loaves, was also the name of the Mother or Grandmother of Ghosts, to whom woollen effigies of men and women were dedicated at the festival of the Compitalia. These effigies were hung at the doors of all the houses in Rome; one effigy was hung up for every free person in the house, and one effigy, of a different kind, for every slave. The reason was that on this day the ghosts of the dead were believed to be going about, and it was hoped that, either out of good nature or through simple inadvertence, they would carry off the effigies at the door instead of the living people in the house. According to tradition, these woollen figures were sub-

The loaves at Aricia perhaps sacramental bread made in the likeness of the King of the Wood.

stitutes for a former custom of sacrificing human beings. Upon data so fragmentary and uncertain, it is impossible to build with confidence; but it seems worth suggesting that the loaves in human form, which appear to have been baked at Aricia, were sacramental bread, and that in the old days, when the divine King of the Wood was annually slain, loaves were made in his image, like the paste figures of the gods in Mexico, India, and Europe, and were eaten sacramentally by his worshippers. The Mexican sacraments in honour of Huitzilopochtli were also accompanied by the sacrifice of human victims. The tradition that the founder of the sacred grove at Aricia was a man named Manius, from whom many Manii were descended, would thus be an etymological myth invented to explain the name *maniæ* as applied to these sacramental loaves. A dim recollection of the original connexion of the loaves with human sacrifices may perhaps be traced in the story that the effigies dedicated to Mania at the Compitalia were substitutes for human victims.

CHAPTER 22

THE FLESH DIET

THE practice of killing a god has now been traced amongst peoples who have reached the agricultural stage of society. We have seen that the spirit of the corn, or of other cultivated plants, is commonly represented either in human or in animal form, and that in some places a custom has prevailed of killing annually either the human or the animal representative of the god. One reason for thus killing the corn-spirit in the person of his representative has been given implicitly in an earlier part of this work: we may suppose that the intention was to guard him or her (for the corn-spirit is often feminine) from the enfeeblement of old age by transferring the spirit, while still hale and hearty, to the person of a youthful and vigorous successor. Apart from the desirability of renewing his divine energies, the death of the corn-spirit may have been deemed inevitable under the sickles or the knives of the reapers, and his worshippers may accordingly have felt bound to acquiesce in the sad necessity. But, further, we have found a widespread custom of eating the god sacramentally, either in the shape of the man or animal who represents the god, or in the shape of bread made in human or animal form. The reasons for thus partaking of the body of the god are, from the primitive standpoint, simple enough. The savage commonly believes that by eating the flesh of an animal or man he acquires not only the physical, but even the moral and intellectual qualities which were characteristic of that animal or man; so when the creature is deemed divine, our simple savage naturally expects to absorb a portion of its divinity along with its material substance. It may be well to illustrate by instances this common faith in the acquisition of virtues or vices of many kinds through the medium of animal food, even when there is no pretence that the viands consist of the body or blood of a god. The doctrine forms part of the widely ramified system of sympathetic or homoeopathic magic.

Custom of killing and eating the corn-spirit sacramentally.

Belief of the savage that by eating an animal or man he acquires the qualities of that animal or man.

Thus, for example, the Creeks, Cherokee, and kindred tribes of North American Indians 'believe that nature is possest of such a property, as to transfuse into men and animals the qualities, either of the food they use, or of those objects that are presented to their senses; he who feeds on venison is, according to their physical system, swifter and more sagacious than the man who lives on the flesh of the clumsy bear, or helpless dunghill fowls, the slow-footed tame cattle, or the heavy wallowing swine. This is the reason that several of their old men recommend, and say, that formerly their greatest chieftains observed a constant rule in their diet, and seldom ate of any animal of a gross quality, or heavy motion of body, fancying it conveyed a dullness through the whole system, and disabled them from exerting themselves with proper vigour in their martial, civil, and religious duties.' The Zaparo Indians of Ecuador 'will, unless from necessity, in most cases not eat any heavy meats, such as tapir and peccary, but confine themselves to birds, monkeys, deer, fish, etc., principally because they argue that the heavier meats make them unwieldy, like the animals who supply the flesh, impeding their agility, and unfitting them for the chase.' Similarly some of the Brazilian Indians would eat no beast, bird, or fish that ran, flew, or swam slowly, lest by partaking of its flesh they should lose their agility and be unable to escape from their enemies. The Caribs abstained from the flesh of pigs lest it should cause them to have small eyes like pigs; and they refused to partake of tortoises from a fear that if they did so they would become heavy and stupid like the animal. Among the Fans of West Africa men in the prime of life never eat tortoises for a similar reason; they imagine that if they did so, their vigour and fleetness of foot would be gone. But old men may eat tortoises freely, because having already lost the power of running they can take no harm from the flesh of the slow-footed creature. Some of the Chiriguanos of eastern Bolivia would not touch the flesh of the vicuña, because they imagined that if they ate it they would become woolly like the vicuña. On the other hand the Abipones of Paraguay ate the flesh of jaguars in order to acquire the courage of the beast; indeed the number of jaguars which they consumed for this object is said to have been very great, and with a like intent they eagerly devoured the flesh of bulls, stags, boars, and ant-bears, being persuaded that by frequently partaking of such food they increased their strength, activity, and courage. On the other hand they all abhorred the thought of eating hens, eggs, sheep, fish, and tortoises, because they believed that these tender viands begot sloth and listlessness in their bodies and cowardice in their minds. The Thompson Indians of British Columbia would not eat the heart of the fool-hen, nor would they allow their dogs to devour the bird, lest they should grow foolish like the bird.

When a Wagogo man of German East Africa kills a lion, he eats the heart in order to become brave like a lion; but he thinks that to eat the heart of a hen would make him timid. Among the Ja-luo, a tribe of Nilotic negroes, young men eat the flesh of leopards in order to make themselves fierce in war. The flesh of the lion and also that of the spotted leopard are sometimes cooked and eaten by native warriors in South-Eastern Africa, who hope thereby to become as brave as lions. When a Zulu army assembles to go forth to battle, the warriors eat slices of meat which is smeared with a powder made of the dried flesh of various animals, such as the leopard, lion, elephant, snakes, and so on; for thus it is thought that the soldiers will acquire the bravery and other warlike qualities of these animals. Sometimes if a Zulu has killed a wild beast, for instance a leopard, he will give his children the blood to drink, and will roast the heart for them to eat, expecting that they will thus grow up brave and daring men. But others say that this is dangerous, because it is apt to produce courage without prudence, and to make a man rush heedlessly on his death. Among the Wabondei of Eastern Africa the heart of a lion or leopard is eaten with the intention of making the eater strong and brave. In British Central Africa aspirants after courage consume the flesh and especially the hearts of lions, while lecherous persons eat the testicles of goats. Among the Suk of British East Africa the fat and heart of a lion are sometimes given to children to eat in order that they may become strong; but they are not allowed to know what they are eating. Arab women in North Africa give their male children a piece of a lion's heart to eat to make them fearless. The flesh of an elephant is thought by the Ewe-speaking peoples of West Africa to make the eater strong. Before they go forth to fight, Wajagga warriors drink a magical potion, which often consists of shavings of the horn and hide of a rhinoceros mixed with beer; this is supposed to impart to them the strength and force of the animal. When a serious disease has attacked a Zulu kraal, the medicine-man takes the bone of a very old dog, or the bone of an old cow, bull, or other very old animal, and administers it to the healthy as well as to the sick people, in order that they may live to be as old as the animal of whose bone they have partaken. So to restore the aged Aeson to youth, the witch Medea infused into his veins a decoction of the liver of the long-lived deer and the head of a crow that had outlived nine generations of men.* In antiquity the flesh of deer and crows was eaten for other purposes than that of prolonging life. As deer were supposed not to suffer from fever, some women used to taste venison every morning, and it is said that in consequence they lived to a great age without ever being attacked by a fever; only the venison lost all its virtue if the animal had been killed by more blows than one. Again, ancient diviners sought to imbue themselves with the spirit of prophecy by swallowing vital portions of birds and beasts of omen; for example, they thought that by eating the hearts of crows or moles or hawks they took into their bodies, along with the flesh, the prophetic soul of the creature.

Ancient beliefs as to the homoeopathic magic of the flesh of animals.

Beliefs of the Dyaks and Aino as to the homoeopathic magic of the flesh of animals.

Among the Dyaks of North-West Borneo young men and warriors may not eat venison, because it would make them as timid as deer; but the women and very old men are free to eat it. However, among the Kayans of the same region, who share the same view as to the ill effect of eating venison, men will partake of the dangerous viand provided it is cooked in the open air, for then the timid spirit of the animal is supposed to escape at once into the jungle and not to enter into the eater. The Aino of Japan think that the otter is a very forgetful animal, and they often call a person with a bad memory an 'otter head'. On the other hand they believe that the heart of the water-ousel is exceedingly wise, and that in speech the bird is most eloquent. Therefore whenever he is killed, he should be at once torn open and his heart wrenched out and swallowed before it has time to grow cold or suffer damage of any kind. If a man swallows it thus, he will become very fluent and wise, and will be able to argue down all his adversaries. In Northern India people fancy that if you eat the eyeballs of an owl you will be able like an owl to see in the dark.

Again, the flesh and blood of dead men are commonly eaten and drunk to inspire bravery, wisdom, or other qualities for which the men themselves were remarkable, or which are supposed to have their special seat in the particular part eaten. Thus among the mountain tribes of South-Eastern Africa there are ceremonies by which the youths are formed into guilds or lodges, and among the rites of initiation there is one which is intended to infuse courage, intelligence, and other qualities into the novices. Whenever an enemy who has behaved with conspicuous bravery is killed, his liver, which is considered the seat of valour; his ears, which are supposed to be the seat of intelligence; the skin of his forehead, which is regarded as the seat of perseverance; his testicles, which are held to be the seat of strength, and other members, which are viewed as the seat of other virtues, are cut from his body and baked to cinders. The ashes are carefully kept in the horn of a bull, and, during the ceremonies observed at circumcision, are mixed with other ingredients into a kind of paste, which is administered by the tribal priest to the youths. By this means the strength, valour, intelligence, and other virtues of the slain are believed to be imparted to the eaters. When Basutos of the mountains have killed a very brave foe, they immediately cut out his heart and eat it, because this is supposed to give them his courage and strength in battle. At the close of the war the man who has slain such a foe is called before the chief and gets from the doctor a medicine which he chews with his food. The third day after this he must wash his body in running water, and at the expiry of ten days he may return to his wives and children. So an Ovambo warrior in battle will tear out the heart of his slain foe in the belief that by eating it he can acquire the bravery of the dead man. A similar belief and practice prevail among some of the tribes of British Central Africa, notably among the Angoni. These tribes also mutilate the dead and reduce the severed parts to ashes. Afterwards the ashes are stirred into a broth or gruel, 'which must be "lapped" up with the hand and thrown into the mouth, but not eaten as ordinary food is taken, to give the soldiers courage, perseverance, fortitude, strategy, patience and wisdom'. In former times whenever a Nandi warrior killed an

The flesh and blood, but especially the hearts, of dead men eaten or drunk for the sake of acquiring the good qualities of the dead.

enemy he used to eat a morsel of the dead man's heart to make himself brave. The Wagogo of German East Africa do the same thing for the same purpose. When Sir Charles M'Carthy was killed by the Ashantees in 1824, it is said that his heart was devoured by the chiefs of the Ashantee army, who hoped by this means to imbibe his courage. His flesh was dried and parcelled out among the lower officers for the same purpose, and his bones were long kept at Coomassie as national fetishes.* Among the Yoruba the priests of Ogun, the war-god, usually take out the hearts of human victims, which are then dried, crumbled to powder, mixed with rum, and sold to aspirants after courage, who swallow the mixture in the belief that they thereby absorb the manly virtue of which the heart is supposed to be the seat.

Other parts than the heart are eaten for the purpose of acquiring the virtues of the deceased.

But while the human heart is thus commonly eaten for the sake of imbuing the eater with the qualities of its original owner, it is not, as we have already seen, the only part of the body which is consumed for this purpose. Thus in New Caledonia the victors in a fight used to eat the bodies of the slain, 'not, as might be supposed, from a taste for human flesh, but in order to assimilate part of the bravery which the deceased was supposed to possess'. Among the tribes about Maryborough in Queensland, when a man was killed in a ceremonial fight, it was customary for his friends to skin and eat him, in order that his warlike virtues might pass into the eaters. Warriors of the Theddora and Ngarigo tribes in South-Eastern Australia used to eat the hands and feet of their slain enemies, believing that in this way they acquired some of the qualities and courage of the dead. In the Dieri tribe of Central Australia, when a man had been condemned and killed by a properly constituted party of executioners, the weapons with which the deed was done were washed in a small wooden vessel, and the bloody mixture was administered to all the slayers in a prescribed manner, while they lay down on their backs and the elders poured it into their mouths. This was believed to give them double strength, courage, and great nerve for any future enterprise. The Kamilaroi of New South Wales ate the liver as well as the heart of a brave man to get his courage. In Tonquin also there is a popular superstition that the liver of a brave man makes brave any who partake of it. Hence when a Catholic missionary was beheaded in Tonquin in 1837, the executioner cut out the liver of his victim and ate part of it, while a soldier attempted to devour another part of it raw. With a like intent the Chinese swallow the bile of notorious bandits who have been executed. The Dyaks of Sarawak used to eat the palms of the hands and the flesh of the knees of the slain in order to steady their own hands and strengthen their own knees. The Tolalaki, notorious head-hunters of Central Celebes, drink the blood and eat the brains of their victims that they may become brave. The Italones of the Philippine Islands drink the blood of their slain enemies, and eat part of the back of their heads and of their entrails raw to acquire their courage. For the same reason the Efugaos, another tribe of the Philippines, suck the brains of their foes. The notorious Zulu chief Matuana drank the gall of thirty chiefs, whose people he had destroyed, in the belief that it would make him strong. It is a Zulu fancy that by eating the centre of the forehead and the eyebrow of an enemy they acquire the power of looking steadfastly at a foe. In Tud or Warrior Island, Torres Straits, men would drink the sweat of renowned warriors, and eat the scrapings from their finger-nails which had become coated and sodden with human blood. This was done 'to make strong and like stone; no afraid'. In Nagir, another island of Torres Straits, in order to infuse courage into boys a warrior used to take the eye and tongue of a man whom he had killed, and after mincing them and mixing them with his urine he administered the compound to the boy, who received it with shut eyes and open mouth seated between the warrior's legs. Before every warlike expedition the people of Minahassa in Celebes used to take the locks of hair of a slain foe and dabble them in boiling water to extract the courage; this infusion of bravery was then drunk by the warriors. In New Zealand 'the chief was an *atua* [god], but there were powerful and powerless gods; each naturally sought to make himself one of the former; the plan therefore adopted was to incorporate the spirits of others with their own; thus, when a warrior slew a chief, he immediately gouged out his eyes and swallowed them, the *atua tonga*, or divinity, being supposed to reside in that organ; thus he not only killed the body, but also possessed himself of the soul of his enemy, and consequently the more chiefs he slew the greater did his divinity become.'

Savages
sometimes
seek to form
a covenant of
friendship
with their
dead foes by
drinking
their blood.

Strange as it may seem to us, one motive which induces a savage warrior to eat the flesh or drink the blood of the foe whom he has slain appears to be a wish to form an indissoluble covenant of friendship and brotherhood with his victim. For it is a widespread belief among savages that by transfusing a little of their blood into each other's bodies two men become kinsmen and allies; the same blood now circulating in the veins of both, neither can injure the other without at the same time injuring himself; the two have therefore given each other the strongest bond, the best possible hostages, for their good behaviour. Acting on this theory, the primitive warrior seeks to convert his slain foe into the firmest of friends by imbibing the dead man's blood or swallowing his flesh. That at all events appears to be the idea at the root of the following customs. When an Arawak Indian of British Guiana has murdered another, he repairs on the third night to the grave of his victim, and pressing a pointed stick through the corpse he licks off and swallows any blood that he finds adhering to the stick. For he believes that if he did not taste his victim's blood, he would go mad and die; whereas by swallowing the blood he averts any ill consequences that might flow to him from the murder. The belief and practice of the Nandi are similar: 'To the present day, when a person of another tribe has been slain by a Nandi, the blood must be carefully washed off the spear or sword into a cup made of grass, and drunk by the slayer. If this is not done it is thought that the man will become frenzied.' So among the tribes of the Lower Niger 'it is customary and necessary for the executioner to lick the blood that is on the blade'; moreover, 'the custom of licking the blood off the blade of a sword by which a man has been killed in war is common to all these tribes, and the explanation given me by the Ibo, which is generally accepted, is, that if this was not done, the act of killing would so affect the strikers as to cause them to run amok among their own people; because the sight and smell of blood render them absolutely senseless as well as regardless of all consequences. And this licking the blood is the only sure remedy, and the only way in which they can recover themselves.' Among the Shans executioners believe that they would soon fall ill and die if they did not taste the blood of their victims.

Another mode of entering into communion with the dead by means of their bodily relics is to grind their bones to powder or to burn them to ashes, and then to swallow the powder or the ashes mixed with food or drink. This method of absorbing the virtues or appropriating the souls of deceased kinsfolk has been practised by a number of Indian tribes of South America. Thus the Tarianas, Tucanos, and other tribes in the valley of the Amazon, about a month after the funeral, disinter the corpse, which is then much decomposed, and put it in a great pan or oven over the fire till all the volatile parts are driven off with a most horrible stench, leaving only a black carbonaceous paste. This paste is then pounded into a fine powder, and being mixed in several large vats of the native beer, the liquor is drunk by the assembled company until all is consumed. They believe that thus the virtues of the deceased are transmitted to the drinkers. Similarly among the Xomanas and Passes of the Rio Negro and Japura River in Brazil, it was customary to burn the bones of the dead and mingle the ashes in their drink; 'for they fancied, that by this means they received into their own bodies the spirits of their deceased friends'. We may suppose that a similar motive underlies the custom wherever it has been observed by the Indians of South America, even when this particular motive is not expressly alleged by our authorities. For example, the Retoroños, Pechuyos, and Guarayos of eastern Bolivia 'manifested their feeling for the dead by a remarkable custom: when the body had mouldered they dug up the bones, reduced them to powder, and mingling it with maize, composed a sort of cake, which they considered it the strongest mark of friendship to offer and partake. Some of the first missionaries were regaled with this family bread, before they knew what they were eating.' Again, in the province of Coro, in north-western Venezuela, when a chief died, they lamented him in the night, celebrating his actions; then they parched his body at the fire, and reducing it to powder drank it up in their liquor, deeming this act the highest honour they could pay him. The Tauaré Indians of the Rio Enivra burn their dead, keep their ashes in hollow reeds, and eat a portion of the ashes with every meal. So in antiquity Artemisia expressed her love and grief for her dead husband Mausolus by powdering his ashes and drinking them in water.

Communion with the dead by swallowing their ashes.

The savage custom of eating a god.

It is now easy to understand why a savage should desire to partake of the flesh of an animal or man whom he regards as divine. By eating the body of the god he shares in the god's attributes and powers. And when the god is a corn-god, the corn is his proper body; when he is a vine-god, the juice of the grape is his blood; and so by eating the bread and drinking the wine the worshipper partakes of the real body and blood of his god. Thus the drinking of wine in the rites of a vine-god like Dionysus is not an act of revelry, it is a solemn sacrament. Yet a time comes when reasonable men find it hard to understand how any one in his senses can suppose that by eating bread or drinking wine he consumes the body or blood of a deity. 'When we call corn Ceres and wine Bacchus,' says Cicero, 'we use a common figure of speech; but do you imagine that anybody is so insane as to believe that the thing he feeds upon is a god?'* In writing thus the Roman philosopher little foresaw that in Rome itself, and in the countries which have derived their creed from her, the belief which he here stigmatises as insane was destined to persist for thousands of years, as a cardinal doctrine of religion, among peoples who pride themselves on their religious enlightenment by comparison with the blind superstitions of pagan antiquity. So little can even the greatest minds of one generation foresee the devious track which the religious faith of mankind will pursue in after ages.

Cicero on transubstantiation.

CHAPTER 23

KILLING THE DIVINE ANIMAL

i

IN the preceding chapters we saw that many communities which have progressed so far as to subsist mainly by agriculture have been in the habit of killing and eating their farinaceous deities either in their proper form of corn, rice, and so forth, or in the borrowed shapes of animals and men. It remains to shew that hunting and pastoral tribes, as well as agricultural peoples, have been in the habit of killing the beings whom they worship. Our first example is drawn from the Indians of California, who living in a fertile country under a serene and temperate sky, nevertheless rank near the bottom of the savage scale. Where a stretch of iron-bound coast breaks the long line of level sands that receive the rollers of the Pacific, there stood in former days, not far from the brink of the great cliffs, the white mission-house of San Juan Capistrano. Among the monks who here exercised over a handful of wretched Indians the austere discipline of Catholic Spain, there was a certain Father Geronimo Boscana who has bequeathed to us a precious record of the customs and superstitions of his savage flock. Thus he tells us that the Acagchemem tribe adored the great buzzard, and that once a year they celebrated a great festival called *Panes* or bird-feast in its honour. The day selected for the festival was made known to the public on the evening before its celebration and preparations were at once made for the erection of a special temple (*vanquech*), which seems to have been a circular or oval enclosure of stakes with the stuffed skin of a coyote or prairie-wolf set up on a hurdle to represent the god Chinigchinich. When the temple was ready, the bird was carried into it in solemn procession and laid on an altar erected for the purpose. Then all the young women, whether married or single, began to run to and fro, as if distracted, some in one direction and some in another, while the elders of both sexes remained silent spectators of the scene, and the captains, tricked out in paint and feathers, danced round their adored bird. These ceremonies

Hunting and pastoral tribes as well as agricultural peoples, have been in the habit of killing and eating the beings whom they worship. The Californian Indians used solemnly to kill the great buzzard which they adored; but they believed that though they slew it annually, it always came to life again.

being concluded, they seized upon the bird and carried it to the principal temple, all the assembly uniting in the grand display, and the captains dancing and singing at the head of the procession. Arrived at the temple, they killed the bird without losing a drop of its blood. The skin was removed entire and preserved with the feathers as a relic or for the purpose of making the festal garment or *paelt*. The carcase was buried in a hole in the temple, and the old women gathered round the grave weeping and moaning bitterly, while they threw various kinds of seeds or pieces of food on it, crying out, 'Why did you run away? Would you not have been better with us? you would have made *pinole* (a kind of gruel) as we do, and if you had not run away, you would not have become a *Panes*,' and so on. When this ceremony was concluded, the dancing was resumed and kept up for three days and nights. They said that the *Panes* was a woman who had run off to the mountains and there been changed into a bird by the god Chinigchinich. They believed that though they sacrificed the bird annually, she came to life again and returned to her home in the mountains. Moreover they thought that 'as often as the bird was killed, it became multiplied; because every year all the different Capitanes celebrated the same feast of *Panes*, and were firm in the opinion that the birds sacrificed were but one and the same female'.

Perhaps they hoped by the sacrifice of the individual bird to preserve the species.

The unity in multiplicity thus postulated by the Californians is very noticeable and helps to explain their motive for killing the divine bird. The notion of the life of a species as distinct from that of an individual, easy and obvious as it seems to us, appears to be one which the Californian savage cannot grasp. He is unable to conceive the life of the species otherwise than as an individual life, and therefore as exposed to the same dangers and calamities which menace and finally destroy the life of the individual. Apparently he imagines that a species left to itself will grow old and die like an individual, and that therefore some step must be taken to save from extinction the particular species which he regards as divine. The only means he can think of to avert the catastrophe is to kill a member of the species in whose veins the tide of life is still running strong, and has not yet stagnated among the fens of old age. The life thus diverted from one channel will flow, he fancies, more freshly and freely in a new one; in other words, the slain animal will revive and enter on a new term of life with all the spring and energy of youth.

The Thebans and all other Egyptians who worshipped the Theban god Ammon held rams to be sacred, and would not sacrifice them. But once a year at the festival of Ammon they killed a ram, skinned it, and clothed the image of the god in the skin. Then they mourned over the ram and buried it in a sacred tomb. The custom was explained by a story that Zeus had once exhibited himself to Hercules clad in the fleece and wearing the head of a ram.* Of course the ram in this case was simply the beast-god of Thebes, as the wolf was the beast-god of Lycopolis, and the goat was the beast-god of Mendes. In other words, the ram was Ammon himself. On the monuments, it is true, Ammon appears in semi-human form with the body of a man and the head of a ram. But this only shews that he was in the usual chrysalis state through which beast-gods regularly pass before they emerge as full-blown anthropomorphic gods. The ram, therefore, was killed, not as a sacrifice to Ammon, but as the god himself, whose identity with the beast is plainly shewn by the custom of clothing his image in the skin of the slain ram. The reason for thus killing the ram-god annually may have been that which I have assigned for the general custom of killing a god and for the special Californian custom of killing the divine buzzard. As applied to Egypt, this explanation is supported by the analogy of the bull-god Apis, who was not suffered to outlive a certain term of years.* The intention of thus putting a limit to the life of the human god was, as I have argued, to secure him from the weakness and frailty of age. The same reasoning would explain the custom—probably an older one—of putting the beast-god to death annually, as was done with the ram of Thebes.

One point in the Theban ritual—the application of the skin to the image of the god—deserves particular attention. If the god was at first the living ram, his representation by an image must have originated later. But how did it originate? One answer to this question is perhaps furnished by the practice of preserving the skin of the animal which is slain as divine. The Californians, as we have seen, preserved the skin of the buzzard; and the skin of the goat, which is killed on the harvest-field as a representative of the corn-spirit, is kept for various supersti-

Ancient Egyptian sacrifice of a ram at the festival of Ammon.

Use of the skin of the sacrificed animal.

tious purposes. The skin in fact was kept as a token or memorial of the god, or rather as containing in it a part of the divine life, and it had only to be stuffed or stretched upon a frame to become a regular image of him. At first an image of this kind would be renewed annually, the new image being provided by the skin of the slain animal. But from annual images to permanent images the transition is easy. We have seen that the older custom of cutting a new May-tree every year was superseded by the practice of maintaining a permanent May-pole, which was, however, annually decked with fresh leaves and flowers, and even surmounted each year by a fresh young tree.* Similarly when the stuffed skin, as a representative of the god, was replaced by a permanent image of him in wood, stone, or metal, the permanent image was annually clad in the fresh skin of the slain animal. When this stage had been reached, the custom of killing the ram came naturally to be interpreted as a sacrifice offered to the image, and was explained by a story like that of Ammon and Hercules.

ii

Ambiguous attitude of the Aino towards the bear.

Doubt also hangs at first sight over the meaning of the bear-sacrifice offered by the Aino or Ainu, a people who are found in the Japanese island of Yezo or Yesso, as well as in Saghalien and the southern of the Kurile Islands. It is not quite easy to define the attitude of the Aino towards the bear. On the one hand they give it the name of *kamui* or 'god'; but as they apply the same word to strangers, it may mean no more than a being supposed to be endowed with superhuman, or at all events extraordinary, powers. Again, it is said that 'the bear is their chief divinity'; 'in the religion of the Aino the bear plays a chief part'; 'amongst the animals it is especially the bear which receives an idolatrous veneration'; 'they worship it after their fashion'; 'there is no doubt that this wild beast inspires more of the feeling which prompts worship than the inanimate forces of nature, and the Aino may be distinguished as bear-worshippers'. Yet, on the other hand, they kill the bear whenever they can; 'in bygone years the Ainu considered bear-hunting the most manly and useful way in which a person could possibly spend his time'; 'the men spend the autumn, winter, and spring in hunting deer and bears. Part of their tribute or taxes is paid in skins, and they subsist on the dried meat'; bear's flesh is indeed one of their staple foods; they eat it both fresh and salted; and the skins of bears furnish them with clothing. In fact, the worship of which writers on this subject speak appears to be paid chiefly to the dead animal. Thus, although they kill a bear whenever they can, 'in the process of dissecting the carcass they endeavour to conciliate the deity, whose representative they have slain, by making elaborate obeisances and deprecatory salutations'; 'when a bear has been killed the Ainu sit down and admire it, make their salaams to it, worship it, and offer presents of *inao*'; 'when a bear is trapped or wounded by an arrow, the hunters go through an apologetic or propitiatory ceremony'. The skulls of slain bears receive a place of honour in their huts, or are set up on sacred posts outside the huts, and are treated with much respect: libations of millet beer, and of *sake*, an intoxicating liquor, are offered to them; and they are addressed as 'divine preservers' (*akoshiratki kamui*), or 'precious divinities'. The skulls of foxes are also fastened to the sacred posts outside the huts; they are regarded as charms against evil spirits, and are consulted as oracles. Yet it is expressly said, 'The live fox is revered just as little as the bear; rather they avoid it as much as possible, considering it a wily animal.' The bear can hardly, therefore, be described as a sacred animal of the Aino, nor yet as a totem; for they do not call themselves bears, and they kill and eat the animal freely. However, they have a legend of a woman who had a son by a bear; and many of them who dwell in the mountains pride themselves on being descended from a bear. Such people are called 'Descendants of the bear' (*Kimun Kamui sanikiri*), and in the pride of their heart they will say, 'As for me, I am a child of the god of the mountains; I am descended from the divine one who rules in the mountains,' meaning by 'the god of the mountains' no other than the bear. It is therefore possible that, as our principal authority, the Revd J. Batchelor,* believes, the bear may have been the totem of an Aino clan; but even if that were so it would not explain the respect shewn for the animal by the whole Aino people.

But it is the bear-festival of the Aino which concerns us here. Towards the end of winter a bear cub is caught and brought

Aino custom of catching a bear cub,

rearing it for
several years,
and killing it
at a solemn
festival.

into the village. If it is very small, it is suckled by an Aino woman, but should there be no woman able to suckle it, the little animal is fed from the hand or the mouth. If it cries loudly and long for its mother, as it is apt to do, its owner will take it to his bosom and let it sleep with him for a few nights, thus dispelling its fears and sense of loneliness. During the day it plays about in the hut with the children and is treated with great affection. But when the cub grows big enough to pain people by hugging or scratching them, he is shut up in a strong wooden cage, where he stays generally for two or three years, fed on fish and millet porridge, till it is time for him to be killed and eaten. But 'it is a peculiarly striking fact that the young bear is not kept merely to furnish a good meal; rather he is regarded and honoured as a fetish, or even as a sort of higher being'. In Yezo the festival is generally celebrated in September or October. Before it takes place the Aino apologise to their gods, alleging that they have treated the bear kindly as long as they could, now they can feed him no longer, and are obliged to kill him. A man who gives a bear-feast invites his relations and friends; in a small village nearly the whole community takes part in the feast; indeed, guests from distant villages are invited and generally come, allured by the prospect of getting drunk for nothing. The form of invitation runs somewhat as follows: 'I, so and so, am about to sacrifice the dear little divine thing who resides among the mountains. My friends and masters, come ye to the feast; we will then unite in the great pleasure of sending the god away. Come.' When all the people are assembled in front of the cage, an orator chosen for the purpose addresses the bear and tells it that they are about to send it forth to its ancestors. He craves pardon for what they are about to do to it, hopes it will not be angry, and comforts it by assuring the animal that many of the sacred whittled sticks (*inao*) and plenty of cakes and wine will be sent with it on the long journey. One speech of this sort which Mr Batchelor heard ran as follows: 'O thou divine one, thou wast sent into the world for us to hunt. O thou precious little divinity, we worship thee; pray hear our prayer. We have nourished thee and brought thee up with a deal of pains and trouble, all because we love thee so. Now, as thou hast grown big, we are about to send thee to thy father and mother. When thou comest to them please speak well of us, and

tell them how kind we have been; please come to us again and we will sacrifice thee.' Having been secured with ropes, the bear is then let out of the cage and assailed with a shower of blunt arrows in order to rouse it to fury. When it has spent itself in vain struggles, it is tied up to a stake, gagged and strangled, its neck being placed between two poles, which are then violently compressed, all the people eagerly helping to squeeze the animal to death. An arrow is also discharged into the beast's heart by a good marksman, but so as not to shed blood, for they think that it would be very unlucky if any of the blood were to drip on the ground. However, the men sometimes drink the warm blood of the bear 'that the courage and other virtues it possesses may pass into them'; and sometimes they besmear themselves and their clothes with the blood in order to ensure success in hunting. When the animal has been strangled to death, it is skinned and its head is cut off and set in the east window of the house, where a piece of its own flesh is placed under its snout, together with a cup of its own meat boiled, some millet dumplings, and dried fish. Prayers are then addressed to the dead animal; amongst other things it is sometimes invited, after going away to its father and mother, to return into the world in order that it may again be reared for sacrifice. When the bear is supposed to have finished eating its own flesh, the man who presides at the feast takes the cup containing the boiled meat, salutes it, and divides the contents between all the company present: every person, young and old alike, must taste a little. The cup is called 'the cup of offering' because it has just been offered to the dead bear. When the rest of the flesh has been cooked, it is shared out in like manner among all the people, everybody partaking of at least a morsel; not to partake of the feast would be equivalent to excommunication, it would be to place the recreant outside the pale of Aino fellowship.

The Aino of Saghalien rear bear cubs and kill them with similar ceremonies. We are told that they do not look upon the bear as a god but only as a messenger whom they despatch with various commissions to the god of the forest. The animal is kept for about two years in a cage, and then killed at a festival, which always takes place in winter and at night. The day before the sacrifice is devoted to lamentation, old women relieving each other in the duty of weeping and groaning in front of the bear's

The custom of rearing and killing bears among the Aino of Saghalien.

cage. Then about the middle of the night or very early in the
morning an orator makes a long speech to the beast, reminding
him how they have taken care of him, and fed him well, and
bathed him in the river, and made him warm and comfortable.
'Now', he proceeds, 'we are holding a great festival in your
honour. Be not afraid. We will not hurt you. We will only kill
you and send you to the god of the forest who loves you. We
are about to offer you a good dinner, the best you have ever
eaten among us, and we will all weep for you together. The
Aino who will kill you is the best shot among us. There he is,
he weeps and asks your forgiveness; you will feel almost
nothing, it will be done so quickly. We cannot feed you always,
as you will understand. We have done enough for you; it is now
your turn to sacrifice yourself for us. You will ask God to send
us, for the winter, plenty of otters and sables, and for the
summer, seals and fish in abundance. Do not forget our
messages, we love you much, and our children will never forget
you.' When the bear has partaken of his last meal amid the
general emotion of the spectators, the old women weeping
afresh and the men uttering stifled cries, he is strapped, not
without difficulty and danger, and being let out of the cage is
led on leash or dragged, according to the state of his temper,
thrice round his cage, then round his master's house, and lastly
round the house of the orator. Thereupon he is tied up to a tree,
which is decked with sacred whittled sticks (*inao*) of the usual
sort; and the orator again addresses him in a long harangue,
which sometimes lasts till the day is beginning to break.
'Remember,' he cries, 'remember! I remind you of your whole
life and of the services we have rendered you. It is now for you
to do your duty. Do not forget what I have asked of you. You
will tell the gods to give us riches, that our hunters may return
from the forest laden with rare furs and animals good to eat;
that our fishers may find troops of seals on the shore and in the
sea, and that their nets may crack under the weight of the fish.
We have no hope but in you. The evil spirits laugh at us, and
too often they are unfavourable and malignant to us, but they
will bow before you. We have given you food and joy and
health; now we kill you in order that you may in return send
riches to us and to our children.' To this discourse the bear,
more and more surly and agitated, listens without conviction;

round and round the tree he paces and howls lamentably, till, just as the first beams of the rising sun light up the scene, an archer speeds an arrow to his heart. No sooner has he done so, than the marksman throws away his bow and flings himself on the ground, and the old men and women do the same, weeping and sobbing. Then they offer the dead beast a repast of rice and wild potatoes, and having spoken to him in terms of pity and thanked him for what he has done and suffered, they cut off his head and paws and keep them as sacred things. A banquet on the flesh and blood of the bear follows. Women were formerly excluded from it, but now they share with the men. The blood is drunk warm by all present; the flesh is boiled, custom forbids it to be roasted. And as the relics of the bear may not enter the house by the door, and Aino houses in Saghalien have no windows, a man gets up on the roof and lets the flesh, the head, and the skin down through the smoke-hole. Rice and wild potatoes are then offered to the head, and a pipe, tobacco, and matches are considerately placed beside it. Custom requires that the guests should eat up the whole animal before they depart: the use of salt and pepper at the meal is forbidden; and no morsel of the flesh may be given to the dogs. When the banquet is over, the head is carried away into the depth of the forest and deposited on a heap of bears' skulls, the bleached and mouldering relics of similar festivals in the past.

The Gilyaks, a Tunguzian people of Eastern Siberia, hold a bear-festival of the same sort once a year in January. 'The bear is the object of the most refined solicitude of an entire village and plays the chief part in their religious ceremonies.' An old she-bear is shot and her cub is reared, but not suckled, in the village. When the bear is big enough he is taken from his cage and dragged through the village. But first they lead him to the bank of the river, for this is believed to ensure abundance of fish to each family. He is then taken into every house in the village, where fish, brandy, and so forth are offered to him. Some people prostrate themselves before the beast. His entrance into a house is supposed to bring a blessing; and if he snuffs at the food offered to him, this also is a blessing. Nevertheless they tease and worry, poke and tickle the animal continually, so that he is surly and snappish. After being thus taken to every house, he is tied to a peg and shot dead with

Bear-festivals of the Gilyaks.

arrows. His head is then cut off, decked with shavings, and placed on the table where the feast is set out. Here they beg pardon of the beast and worship him. Then his flesh is roasted and eaten in special vessels of wood finely carved. They do not eat the flesh raw nor drink the blood, as the Aino do. The brain and entrails are eaten last; and the skull, still decked with shavings, is placed on a tree near the house. Then the people sing and both sexes dance in ranks, as bears.

Similar respect shewn by the Aino for the eagles and hawks which they keep in cages and kill.

Again, the Aino keep eagles in cages, worship them as divinities, and ask them to defend the people from evil. Yet they offer the bird in sacrifice, and when they are about to do so they pray to him, saying: 'O precious divinity, O thou divine bird, pray listen to my words. Thou dost not belong to this world, for thy home is with the Creator and his golden eagles. This being so, I present thee with these *inao* and cakes and other precious things. Do thou ride upon the *inao* and ascend to thy home in the glorious heavens. When thou arrivest, assemble the deities of thy own kind together and thank them for us for having governed the world. Do thou come again, I beseech thee, and rule over us. O my precious one, go thou quietly.' Once more, the Aino revere hawks, keep them in cages, and offer them in sacrifice. At the time of killing one of them the following prayer should be addressed to the bird: 'O divine hawk, thou art an expert hunter, please cause thy cleverness to descend on me.' If a hawk is well treated in captivity and prayed to after this fashion when he is about to be killed, he will surely send help to the hunter.

Advantages which the Aino hopes to reap from slaughtering the worshipful animals.

Thus the Aino hopes to profit in various ways by slaughtering the creatures, which, nevertheless, he treats as divine. He expects them to carry messages for him to their kindred or to the gods in the upper world; he hopes to partake of their virtues by imbibing parts of their bodies or in other ways; and apparently he looks forward to their bodily resurrection in this world, which will enable him again to catch and kill them, and again to reap all the benefits which he has already derived from their slaughter. For in the prayers addressed to the worshipful bear and the worshipful eagle before they are knocked on the head the creatures are invited to come again, which seems clearly to point to a faith in their future resurrection. If any doubt could exist on this head, it would be dispelled by the evidence of Mr Batchelor, who tells us that the Aino 'are firmly convinced that the spirits of birds and animals killed in hunting or offered in sacrifice come and live again upon the earth clothed with a body; and they believe, further, that they appear here for the special benefit of men, particularly Ainu hunters.' The Aino, Mr Batchelor tells us, 'confessedly slays and eats the beast that another may come in its place and be treated in like manner'; and at the time of sacrificing the creatures 'prayers are said to them which form a request that they will come again and furnish viands for another feast, as if it were an honour to them to be thus killed and eaten, and a pleasure as well. Indeed such is the people's idea.' These last observations, as the context shews, refer especially to the sacrifice of bears.

Thus among the benefits which the Aino anticipates from the slaughter of the worshipful animals not the least substantial is that of gorging himself on their flesh and blood, both on the present and on many a similar occasion hereafter; and that pleasing prospect again is derived from his firm faith in the spiritual immortality and bodily resurrection of the dead animals. A like faith is shared by many savage hunters in many parts of the world and has given rise to a variety of quaint customs, some of which will be described presently. Meantime it is not unimportant to observe that the solemn festivals at which the Aino, the Gilyaks, and other tribes slaughter the tame caged bears with demonstrations of respect and sorrow, are probably nothing but an extension or glorification of similar rites which the hunter performs over any wild bear which he chances to kill in the forest. Indeed with regard to the Gilyaks we are expressly informed that this is the case. If we would understand the meaning of the Gilyak ritual, says Mr Sternberg, 'we must above all remember that the bear-festivals are not, as is usually but falsely assumed, celebrated only at the killing of a house-bear but are held on every occasion when a Gilyak succeeds in slaughtering a bear in the chase. It is true that in such cases the festival assumes less imposing dimensions, but in its essence it remains the same. When the head and skin of a bear killed in the forest are brought into the village, they are accorded a triumphal reception with music and solemn ceremonial ... Hence the great winter festival is only an extension of the rite which is observed at the slaughter of every bear.'

The bear-festivals of these tribes are probably nothing but an extension of the similar rites which the hunter performs over any wild bear which he kills in the forest.

The apparent
contradiction
in the beha-
viour of
these tribes
to bears is
not so great
as it seems
to us at first
sight. Savage
logic.

Thus the apparent contradiction in the practice of these tribes, who venerate and almost deify the animals which they habitually hunt, kill, and eat, is not so flagrant as at first sight it appears to us: the people have reasons, and some very practical reasons, for acting as they do. For the savage is by no means so illogical and unpractical as to superficial observers he is apt to seem; he has thought deeply on the questions which immediately concern him, he reasons about them, and though his conclusions often diverge very widely from ours, we ought not to deny him the credit of patient and prolonged meditation on some fundamental problems of human existence. In the present case, if he treats bears in general as creatures wholly subservient to human needs and yet singles out certain individuals of the species for homage which almost amounts to deification, we must not hastily set him down as irrational and inconsistent, but must endeavour to place ourselves at his point of view, to see things as he sees them, and to divest ourselves of the prepossessions which tinge so deeply our own views of the world. If we do so, we shall probably discover that, however absurd his conduct may appear to us, the savage nevertheless generally acts on a train of reasoning which seems to him in harmony with the facts of his limited experience. I shall attempt to shew that the solemn ceremonial of the bear-festival among the Ainos and other tribes of north-eastern Asia is only a particularly striking example of the respect which on the principles of his rude philosophy the savage habitually pays to the animals which he kills and eats.

iii

The savage
believes that
animals, like
men, are en-
dowed with
souls which
survive the
death of
their bodies.

The explanation of life by the theory of an indwelling and practically immortal soul is one which the savage does not confine to human beings but extends to the animate creation in general. In so doing he is more liberal and perhaps more logical than the civilised man, who commonly denies to animals that privilege of immortality which he claims for himself. The savage is not so proud; he commonly believes that animals are endowed with feelings and intelligence like those of men, and that, like men, they possess souls which survive the death of their bodies either to wander about as disembodied spirits or to be born again in animal form. Thus, for example, we are told that the Indian of Guiana does not see 'any sharp line of distinction, such as we see, between man and other animals, between one kind of animal and another, or between animals—man included—and inanimate objects. On the contrary, to the Indian, all objects, animate and inanimate, seem exactly of the same nature except that they differ in the accident of bodily form. Every object in the whole world is a being, consisting of a body and spirit, and differs from every other object in no respect except that of bodily form, and in the greater or less degree of brute power and brute cunning consequent on the difference of bodily form and bodily habits.' Similarly we read that 'in Cherokee mythology, as in that of Indian tribes generally, there is no essential difference between men and animals. In the primal genesis period they seem to be completely undifferentiated, and we find all creatures alike living and working together in harmony and mutual helpfulness until man, by his aggressiveness and disregard for the rights of the others, provokes their hostility, when insects, birds, fishes, reptiles, and fourfooted beasts join forces against him. Henceforth their lives are apart, but the difference is always one of degree only.'

The American Indians draw no sharp distinction between animals and men.

Thus to the savage, who regards all living creatures as practically on a footing of equality with man, the act of killing and eating an animal must wear a very different aspect from that which the same act presents to us, who regard the intelligence of animals as far inferior to our own and deny them the possession of immortal souls. Hence on the principles of his rude philosophy the primitive hunter who slays an animal believes himself exposed to the vengeance either of its disembodied spirit or of all the other animals of the same species, whom he considers as knit together, like men, by the ties of kin and the obligations of the blood feud, and therefore as bound to resent the injury done to one of their number. Accordingly the savage makes it a rule to spare the life of those animals which he has no pressing motive for killing, at least such fierce and dangerous animals as are likely to exact a bloody vengeance for the slaughter of one of their kind.

Hence the savage attempts to propitiate the animals which he kills and the other members of the species.

The natives of Madagascar never kill a crocodile 'except in retaliation for one of their friends who has been destroyed by a crocodile. They believe that the wanton destruction of one of

Crocodiles respected in Madagascar.

these reptiles will be followed by the loss, of human life, in accordance with the principle of *lex talionis*.' The people who live near the lake Itasy in Madagascar make a yearly proclamation to the crocodiles, announcing that they will revenge the death of some of their friends by killing as many crocodiles in return, and warning all well-disposed crocodiles to keep out of the way, as they have no quarrel with them, but only with their evil-minded relations who have taken human life. Various tribes of Madagascar believe themselves to be descended from crocodiles, and accordingly they view the scaly reptile as, to all intents and purposes, a man and a brother. If one of the animals should so far forget himself as to devour one of his human kinsfolk, the chief of the tribe, or in his absence an old man familiar with the tribal customs, repairs at the head of the people to the edge of the water, and summons the family of the culprit to deliver him up to the arm of justice. A hook is then baited and cast into the river or lake. Next day the guilty brother, or one of his family, is dragged ashore, and after his crime has been clearly brought home to him by a strict interrogation, he is sentenced to death and executed. The claims of justice being thus satisfied and the majesty of the law fully vindicated, the deceased crocodile is lamented and buried like a kinsman; a mound is raised over his relics and a stone marks the place of his head. The Malagasy, indeed, regard the crocodile with superstitious veneration as the king of the waters and supreme in his own element. When they are about to cross a river they pronounce a solemn oath, or enter into an engagement to acknowledge his sovereignty over the waters. An aged native has been known to covenant with the crocodiles for nearly half an hour before plunging into the stream. After that he lifted up his voice and addressed the animal, urging him to do him no harm, since he had never hurt the crocodile; assuring him that he had never made war on any of his fellows, but on the contrary had always entertained the highest veneration for him; and adding that if he wantonly attacked him, vengeance would follow sooner or later; while if the crocodile devoured him, his relations and all his race would declare war against the beast. This harangue occupied another quarter of an hour, after which the orator dashed fearlessly into the stream.

No consideration will induce a Sumatran to catch or wound a tiger except in self-defence or immediately after a tiger has destroyed a friend or relation. When a European has set traps for tigers, the people of the neighbourhood have been known to go by night to the place and explain to the animals that the traps are not set by them nor with their consent. If it is necessary to kill a tiger which has wrought much harm in the village, the Minangkabauers of Sumatra try to catch him alive in order to beg for his forgiveness before despatching him, and in ordinary life they will not speak evil of him or do anything that might displease him. For example, they will not use a path that has been untrodden for more than a year, because the tiger has chosen that path for himself, and would deem it a mark of disrespect were any one else to use it. Again, persons journeying by night will not walk one behind the other, nor keep looking about them, for the tiger would think that this betrayed fear of him, and his feelings would be hurt by the suspicion. Neither will they travel bareheaded, for that also would be disrespectful to the tiger; nor will they knock off the glowing end of a firebrand, for the flying sparks are like the tiger's glistering eyes, and he would treat this as an attempt to mimic him. The population of Mandeling, a district on the west coast of Sumatra, is divided into clans, one of which claims to be descended from a tiger. It is believed that the animal will not attack or rend the members of this clan, because they are his kinsmen. When members of the clan come upon the tracks of a tiger, they enclose them with three little sticks as a mark of homage; and when a tiger has been shot, the women of the clan are bound to offer betel to the dead beast. The Battas of Sumatra seldom kill a tiger except from motives of revenge, observing the rule an eye for an eye and a tooth for a tooth, or, as they express it, 'He who owes gold must pay in gold; he who owes breath (that is, life) must pay with breath.' Nor can the beast be attacked without some ceremony; only weapons that have proved themselves able to kill may be used for the purpose. When the tiger has been killed, they bring the carcase to the village, set offerings before it, and burn incense over it, praying the spirit of the tiger to quit its material envelope and enter the incense pot. As soon as the soul may be supposed to have complied with this request, a speaker explains to the

Tigers respected in Sumatra.

Ceremonies at killing tigers in Sumatra and Bengal.

spirits in general the reasons for killing the tiger, and begs them to set forth these reasons to the departed soul of the beast, lest the latter should be angry and the people should suffer in consequence. Then they dance round the dead body of the tiger till they can dance no longer, after which they skin the carcase and bury it. The inhabitants of the hills near Rajamahall, in Bengal, believe that if any man kills a tiger without divine orders, either he or one of his relations will be devoured by a tiger. Hence they are very averse to killing a tiger, unless one of their kinsfolk has been carried off by one of the beasts. In that case they go out for the purpose of hunting and slaying a tiger; and when they have succeeded they lay their bows and arrows on the carcase and invoke God, declaring that they slew the animal in retaliation for the loss of a kinsman. Vengeance having been thus taken, they swear not to attack another tiger except under similar provocation. The natives of Cochin China have a great respect for the tiger, whom they regard as a terrible divinity. Yet they set traps for him and leave no stone unturned to catch him. Once he is ensnared, they offer him their excuses and condolences for the painful position in which he finds himself.

Ceremonies observed in Kiziba at the killing of a snake.

In Kiziba, a district of Central Africa, to the west of Lake Victoria Nyanza, if a woman accidentally kills a snake with her hoe while she is working in the field, she hastens in great agitation to the snake-priest and hands him over the hoe, together with two strings of cowries and an ox-hide, begging him to appease the angry spirit of the slain serpent. In this application she is accompanied and supported by all the villagers, who share her fears and anxiety. Accordingly the priest beats his drum as a sign that no woman of the village is to work in the fields till further notice. Next he wraps the dead serpent in a piece of the ox-hide and buries it solemnly. On the following day he performs a ceremony of purification for the slaughter of the reptile. He compounds a medicine out of the guts of a leopard or hyaena and earth or mud dissolved in water, and with this mixture he disinfects all the houses in the village, beginning with the house of the woman who killed the serpent. Next he proceeds to the fields, where all the women of the village have collected their hoes. These he purifies by dipping them in the fluid and then twirling them about so as to make the drops of water fly off. From that moment the danger incurred by the slaughter of the reptile is averted. The spirit of the serpent is appeased, and the women may resume their usual labours in the fields.

When the Kwakiutl Indians of British Columbia have slain a wolf they lay the carcase on a blanket and take out the heart, of which every person who helped to kill the beast must eat four morsels. Then they wail over the body, saying, 'Woe! our great friend!' After that they cover the carcase with a blanket and bury it. A bow or gun that killed a wolf is regarded as unlucky, and the owner gives it away. These Indians believe that the slaying of a wolf produces a scarcity of game. When the Tinneh Indians of Central Alaska have killed a wolf or a wolverine, the carcase is brought into the camp or village with great pomp. The people go forth to meet it, saying, 'The chief is coming.' Then the body is carried into a hut and propped up in a sitting posture; and the medicine-man spreads before it a copious banquet, to which every family in the village has contributed of its best. When the dead animal is supposed to have satisfied his hunger, the men consume the remains of the feast, but no woman is allowed to participate in what has been thus offered to the wolf or the wolverine. No ordinary Cherokee dares to kill a wolf, if he can possibly help it; for he believes that the kindred of the slain beast would surely avenge its death, and that the weapon with which the deed had been done would be quite useless for the future, unless it were cleaned and exorcised by a medicine-man. However, certain persons who know the proper rites of atonement for such a crime can kill wolves with impunity, and they are sometimes hired to do so by people who have suffered from the raids of the wolves on their cattle or fish-traps. The professional wolf-killer prays to the animal whom he has bereaved of life, and seeks to avert the vengeance of the other wolves by laying the blame of the slaughter on the people of another settlement. To purify the gun which has perpetrated the murder, he unscrews the barrel, inserts into it seven small sour-wood rods which have been heated in the fire, and then allows the barrel and its contents to lie in a running stream till morning. When the Chuckchees of north-eastern Siberia have killed a wolf, they hold a festival, at which they cry, 'Wolf, be not angry with us. It was not we who killed you,

Ceremonies observed by the North American Indians and others at the killing of a wolf.

it was the Russians who destroyed you.' In ancient Athens any man who killed a wolf had to bury it by subscription.

But the savage clearly cannot afford to spare all animals. He must either eat some of them or starve, and when the question thus comes to be whether he or the animal must perish, he is forced to overcome his superstitious scruples and take the life of the beast. At the same time he does all he can to appease his victims and their kinsfolk. Even in the act of killing them he testifies his respect for them, endeavours to excuse or even conceal his share in procuring their death, and promises that their remains will be honourably treated. By thus robbing death of its terrors he hopes to reconcile his victims to their fate and to induce their fellows to come and be killed also. For example, it was a principle with the Kamtchatkans never to kill a land or sea animal without first making excuses to it and begging that the animal would not take it ill. Also they offered it cedar-nuts and so forth, to make it think that it was not a victim but a guest at a feast. They believed that this hindered other animals of the same species from growing shy. For instance, after they had killed a bear and feasted on its flesh, the host would bring the bear's head before the company, wrap it in grass, and present it with a variety of trifles. Then he would lay the blame of the bear's death on the Russians, and bid the beast wreak his wrath upon them. Also he would ask the bear to inform the other bears how well he had been treated, that they too might come without fear. Seals, sea-lions, and other animals were treated by the Kamtchatkans with the same ceremonious respect. Moreover, they used to insert sprigs of a plant resembling bear's wort in the mouths of the animals they killed; after which they would exhort the grinning skulls to have no fear but to go and tell it to their fellows, that they also might come and be caught and so partake of this splendid hospitality. When the Ostiaks have hunted and killed a bear, they cut off its head and hang it on a tree. Then they gather round in a circle and pay it divine honours. Next they run towards the carcase uttering lamentations and saying, 'Who killed you? It was the Russians. Who cut off your head? It was a Russian axe. Who skinned you? It was a knife made by a Russian.' They explain, too, that the feathers which sped the arrow on its flight came from the wing of a strange bird, and that they did nothing but let the arrow go.

Apologies offered by savages to the animals which they are obliged to kill.

Propitiation of slain bears by Kamtchatkans, Ostiaks and Koryak.

They do all this because they believe that the wandering ghost of the slain bear would attack them on the first opportunity, if they did not thus appease it. Or they stuff the skin of the slain bear with hay; and after celebrating their victory with songs of mockery and insult, after spitting on and kicking it, they set it up on its hind legs, 'and then, for a considerable time, they bestow on it all the veneration due to a guardian god'. When a party of Koryak have killed a bear or a wolf, they skin the beast and dress one of themselves in the skin. Then they dance round the skin-clad man, saying that it was not they who killed the animal, but some one else, generally a Russian. When they kill a fox they skin it, wrap the body in grass, and bid him go tell his companions how hospitably he has been received, and how he has received a new cloak instead of his old one.

The Baganda greatly fear the ghosts of buffaloes which they have killed, and they always appease these dangerous spirits. On no account will they bring the head of a slain buffalo into a village or into a garden of plantains: they always eat the flesh of the head in the open country. Afterwards they place the skull in a small hut built for the purpose, where they pour out beer as an offering and pray to the ghost to stay where he is and not to harm them. Oddly enough the Baganda also dread the ghosts of sheep, which they believe would haunt and kill the butcher if they saw him give the fatal stroke. Hence when a man is about to slaughter a sheep, he gets another man to divert its attention, and coming up behind the unsuspecting animal he stuns it with the blow of an axe-handle; then, before it can recover consciousness, he adroitly cuts its throat. In this way the ghost of the sheep is bamboozled and will not haunt the butcher. Moreover, when a sheep dies in a house, the housewife may not say bluntly to her husband, 'The sheep is dead', or its ghost, touched to the quick, would certainly make her fall ill and might even kill her. She must put a finer point on the painful truth by saying, 'I am unable to untie such and such a sheep.' Her husband understands her, but the ghost of the animal does not, or at all events he does not resent so delicate an allusion to its melancholy decease. Even the ghost of a fowl may haunt a Muganda woman and make her ill, if she has accidentally killed it with her hoe and flung away the body in the long grass instead of carrying it to her husband and confessing her fault.

Propitiation of slain buffaloes and sheep in Uganda.

When the inhabitants of the Isle of St Mary, to the north of Madagascar, go a-whaling, they single out the young whales for attack and 'humbly beg the mother's pardon, stating the necessity that drives them to kill her progeny, and requesting that she will be pleased to go below while the deed is doing, that her maternal feelings may not be outraged by witnessing what must cause her so much uneasiness'. An Ajumba hunter having killed a female hippopotamus on Lake Azyingo in West Africa, the animal was decapitated and its quarters and bowels removed. Then the hunter, naked, stepped into the hollow of the ribs, and kneeling down in the bloody pool washed his whole body with the blood and excretions of the animal, while he prayed to the soul of the hippopotamus not to bear him a grudge for having killed her and so blighted her hopes of future maternity; and he further entreated the ghost not to stir up other hippopotamuses to avenge her death by butting at and capsizing his canoe. The ounce, a leopard-like creature, is dreaded for its depredations by the Indians of Brazil. When they have caught one of these animals in a snare, they kill it and carry the body home to the village. There the women deck the carcase with feathers of many colours, put bracelets on its legs, and weep over it, saying, 'I pray thee not to take vengeance on our little ones for having been caught and killed through thine own ignorance. For it was not we who deceived thee, it was thyself. Our husbands only set the trap to catch animals that are good to eat: they never thought to take thee in it. Therefore, let not thy soul counsel thy fellows to avenge thy death on our little ones!' When the Yuracares Indians of Bolivia have killed great apes in their tropical forests, they bring the bodies home, set them out in a row on palm leaves with their heads all looking one way, sprinkle them with chicha, and say, 'We love you, since we have brought you home.' They imagine that the performance of this ceremony is very gratifying to the other apes in the woods. Before they leave a temporary camp in the forest, where they have killed a tapir and dried the meat on a babracot,* the Indians of Guiana invariably destroy this babracot, saying that should a tapir passing that way find traces of the slaughter of one of his kind, he would come by night on the next occasion when Indians slept at that place, and, taking a man, would babracot him in revenge.

When a Blackfoot Indian has caught eagles in a trap and killed them, he takes them home to a special lodge, called the eagles' lodge, which has been prepared for their reception outside of the camp. Here he sets the birds in a row on the ground, and propping up their heads on a stick, puts a piece of dried meat in each of their mouths in order that the spirits of the dead eagles may go and tell the other eagles how well they are being treated by the Indians. So when Indian hunters of the Orinoco region have killed an animal, they open its mouth and pour into it a few drops of the liquor they generally carry with them, in order that the soul of the dead beast may inform its fellows of the welcome it has met with, and that they too, cheered by the prospect of the same kind reception, may come with alacrity to be killed. A Cherokee hunter who has killed an eagle stands over the dead bird and prays it not to avenge itself on his tribe, because it is not he but a Spaniard who has done the cruel deed. When a Teton Indian is on a journey and he meets a grey spider or a spider with yellow legs, he kills it, because some evil would befall him if he did not. But he is very careful not to let the spider know that he kills it, for if the spider knew, his soul would go and tell the other spiders, and one of them would be sure to avenge the death of his relation. So in crushing the insect, the Indian says, 'O Grandfather Spider, the Thunder-beings kill you.' And the spider is crushed at once and believes what is told him. His soul probably runs and tells the other spiders that the Thunder-beings have killed him; but no harm comes of that. For what can grey or yellow-legged spiders do to the Thunder-beings?

Propitiation of dead eagles.

Deceiving the ghosts of spiders.

But it is not merely dangerous creatures with whom the savage desires to keep on good terms. It is true that the respect which he pays to wild beasts is in some measure proportioned to their strength and ferocity. Thus the savage Stiens of Cambodia, believing that all animals have souls which roam about after their death, beg an animal's pardon when they kill it, lest its soul should come and torment them. Also they offer it sacrifices, but these sacrifices are proportioned to the size and strength of the animal. The ceremonies observed at the death of an elephant are conducted with much pomp and last seven days. Similar distinctions are drawn by North American Indians. 'The bear, the buffalo, and the beaver are manidos

The ceremonies of propitiation offered to slain animals vary with the more or less dangerous character of the creature.

[divinities] which furnish food. The bear is formidable, and good to eat. They render ceremonies to him, begging him to allow himself to be eaten, although they know he has no fancy for it. We kill you, but you are not annihilated. His head and paws are objects of homage . . . Other animals are treated similarly from similar reasons . . . Many of the animal manidos, not being dangerous, are often treated with contempt—the terrapin, the weasel, polecat, etc.' The distinction is instructive. Animals which are feared, or are good to eat, or both, are treated with ceremonious respect; those which are neither formidable nor good to eat are despised. We have had examples of reverence paid to animals which are both feared and eaten. It remains to prove that similar respect is shewn to animals which, without being feared, are either eaten or valued for their skins.

When Siberian sable-hunters have caught a sable, no one is allowed to see it, and they think that if good or evil be spoken of the captured sable no more sables will be caught. A hunter has been known to express his belief that the sables could hear what was said of them as far off as Moscow. He said that the chief reason why the sable hunt was now so unproductive was that some live sables had been sent to Moscow. There they had been viewed with astonishment as strange animals, and the sables cannot abide that. Another, though minor, cause of the diminished take of sables was, he alleged, that the world is now much worse than it used to be, so that nowadays a hunter will sometimes hide the sable which he has got instead of putting it into the common stock. This also, said he, the sables cannot abide. A Russian traveller happening once to enter a Gilyak hut in the absence of the owner, observed a freshly killed sable hanging on the wall. Seeing him look at it, the housewife in consternation hastened to muffle the animal in a fur cap, after which it was taken down, wrapt in birch bark, and put away out of sight. Despite the high price he offered for it, the traveller's efforts to buy the animal were unavailing. It was bad enough, they told him, that he, a stranger, had seen the dead sable in its skin, but far worse consequences for the future catch of sables would follow if they were to sell him the animal entire. Alaskan hunters preserve the bones of sables and beavers out of reach of the dogs for a year and then bury them carefully, 'lest the spirits who look after the beavers and sables should consider that they

Animals which, without being feared, are valued for their flesh or their skin, are also treated with respect.

Respect shewn to dead sables.

Bones of sables and beavers kept out of reach of dogs, lest

are regarded with contempt, and hence no more should be killed or trapped'. The Shuswap Indians of British Columbia think that if they did not throw beaver-bones into the river, the beavers would not go into the traps any more, and that the same thing would happen were a dog to eat the flesh or gnaw the bone of a beaver. Carrier Indians who have trapped martens or beavers take care to keep them from the dogs; for if a dog were to touch these animals the Indians believe that the other martens or beavers would not suffer themselves to be caught. A missionary who fell in with an old Carrier Indian asked him what luck he had in the chase. 'Oh, don't speak to me about it,' replied the Indian; 'there are beavers in plenty. I caught one myself immediately after my arrival here, but unluckily a dog got hold of it. You know that after that it has been impossible for me to catch another.' 'Nonsense,' said the missionary; 'set your traps as if nothing had happened, and you will see.' 'That would be useless,' answered the Indian in a tone of despair, 'quite useless. You don't know the ways of the beaver. If a dog merely touches a beaver, all the other beavers are angry at the owner of the dog and always keep away from his traps.'

The elan, deer, and elk were treated by the American Indians with the same punctilious respect, and for the same reason. Their bones might not be given to the dogs nor thrown into the fire, nor might their fat be dropped upon the fire, because the souls of the dead animals were believed to see what was done to their bodies and to tell it to the other beasts, living and dead. Hence, if their bodies were ill-used, the animals of that species would not allow themselves to be taken, neither in this world nor in the world to come. The houses of the Indians of Honduras were encumbered with the bones of deer, the Indians believing that if they threw the bones away, the other deer could not be taken. Among the Chiquites of Paraguay a sick man would be asked by the medicine-man whether he had not thrown away some of the flesh of the deer or turtle, and if he answered yes, the medicine-man would say, 'That is what is killing you. The soul of the deer or turtle has entered into your body to avenge the wrong you did it.' Before the Tzentales of Southern Mexico and the Kekchis of Guatemala venture to skin a deer which they have killed, they lift up its head and burn copal before it as an offering; otherwise a certain being named

the spirits of the dead animals should be offended.

Deer, elk, and elan treated by the American Indians with ceremonious respect.

Tzultacca would be angry and send them no more game. Cherokee hunters ask pardon of the deer they kill. If they failed to do so, they think that the Little Deer, the chief of the deer tribe, who can never die or be wounded, would track the hunter to his home by the blood-drops on the ground and would put the spirit of rheumatism into him. Sometimes the hunter, on starting for home, lights a fire in the trail behind him to prevent the Little Deer from pursuing him. Before they went out to hunt for deer, antelope, or elk the Apaches used to resort to sacred caves, where the medicine-men propitiated with prayer and sacrifice the animal gods whose progeny they intended to destroy.

Porcupines, turtles, and mice treated by American Indians with ceremonious respect.

Indians of the Lower Fraser River regard the porcupine as their elder brother. Hence when a hunter kills one of these creatures he asks his elder brother's pardon and does not eat of the flesh till the next day. The Sioux will not stick an awl or needle into a turtle, for they are sure that, if they were to do so, the turtle would punish them at some future time. Some of the North American Indians believed that each sort of animal had its patron or genius who watched over and preserved it. An Indian girl having once picked up a dead mouse, her father snatched the little creature from her and tenderly caressed and fondled it. Being asked why he did so, he said that it was to appease the genius of mice, in order that he might not torment his daughter for eating the mouse. With that he handed the mouse to the girl and she ate it.

Dead foxes, turtles, deer, and pigs treated with ceremonious respect.

When the Koryak have killed a fox, they take the body home and lay it down near the fire, saying, 'Let the guest warm himself. When he feels warm, we will free him from his overcoat.' So when the frozen carcase is thawed, they skin it and wrap long strips of grass round about it. Then the animal's mouth is filled with fish-roe, and the mistress of the house gashes the flesh and puts more roe or dried meat into the gashes, making believe that the gashes are the fox's pockets, which she thus fills with provisions. Then the carcase is carried out of the house, and the people say, 'Go and tell your friends that it is good to visit yonder house. "Instead of my old coat, they gave me a new one still warmer and with longer hair. I have eaten my fill, and had my pockets well stored. You, too, go and visit them."' The natives think that if they neglected to observe this ceremonial they would have no luck in hunting foxes. When a Ewe hunter of Togoland has killed an antelope of a particular kind (*Antilope leucoryx*), he erects an enclosure of branches, within which he places the lower jawbones of all the animals he has shot. Then he pours palm-wine and sprinkles meal on the bones, saying, 'Ye lower jawbones of beasts, ye are now come home. Here is food, here is drink. Therefore lead your comrades (that is, the living beasts of the forest) hither also.'

The Lengua Indians of the Gran Chaco love to hunt the ostrich, but when they have killed one of these birds and are bringing home the carcase to the village, they take steps to outwit the resentful ghost of their victim. They think that when the first natural shock of death is passed, the ghost of the ostrich pulls himself together and makes after his body. Acting on this sage calculation, the Indians pluck feathers from the breast of the bird and strew them at intervals along the track. At every bunch of feathers the ghost stops to consider, 'Is this the whole of my body or only a part of it?' The doubt gives him pause, and when at last he has made up his mind fully at all the bunches, and has further wasted valuable time by the zigzag course which he invariably pursues in going from one to another, the hunters are safe at home, and the bilked ghost may stalk in vain round about the village, which he is too timid to enter. *(margin: Ghost of ostrich outwitted.)*

The preceding review of customs observed by savages for the conciliation and multiplication of animals which they hunt and kill, is fitted to impress us with a lively sense of the unquestioning faith which primitive man reposes in the immortality of the lower creatures. He appears to assume as an axiom too obvious to be disputed that beasts, birds, and fishes have souls like his own, which survive the death of their bodies and can be reborn in other bodies to be again killed and eaten by the hunter. The whole series of customs described in the foregoing pages—customs which are apt to strike the civilised reader as quaint and absurd—rests on this fundamental assumption. A consideration of them suggests a doubt whether the current explanation of the savage belief in human immortality is adequate to account for all the facts. That belief is commonly deduced from a primitive theory of dreams. The savage, it is said, fails to distinguish the *(margin: Unquestioning faith of savages in the immortality of animals.)* *(margin: The savage faith in human immortality is commonly supposed to)*

be deduced
from a primit-
ive theory of
dreams.

visions of sleep from the realities of waking life, and accordingly
when he has dreamed of his dead friends he necessarily concludes that they have not wholly perished, but that their spirits
continue to exist in some place and some form, though in the
ordinary course of events they elude the perceptions of his
senses. On this theory the conceptions, whether gross or
refined, whether repulsive or beautiful, which savages and
perhaps civilised men have formed of the state of the departed,
would seem to be no more than elaborate hypotheses constructed to account for appearances in dreams; these towering
structures, for all their radiant or gloomy grandeur, for all the
massy strength and solidity with which they present themselves
to the imagination of many, may turn out on inspection to be
mere visionary castles built of clouds and vapour, which a
breath of reason suffices to melt into air.

But can a
theory of
dreams ac-
count for the
savage belief
in the immor-
tality of
animals?

But even if we grant for the sake of argument that this theory
offers a ready explanation of the widespread belief in human
immortality, it is less easy to see how the theory accounts for
the corresponding belief of so many races in the immortality of
the lower animals. In his dreams the savage recognises the
images of his departed friends by those familiar traits of feature,
voice, and gesture which characterised them in life. But can we
suppose that he recognises dead beasts, birds, and fishes in like
manner? that their images come before him in sleep with all the
particular features, the minute individual differences, which
distinguished them in life from their fellows, so that when he
sees them he can say to himself, for example, 'This is the very
tiger that I speared yesterday; his carcase is dead, but his spirit
must be still alive'; or, 'That is the very salmon I caught and
ate this morning; I certainly killed his body, but clearly I have
not succeeded in destroying his soul'? No doubt it is possible
that the savage has arrived at his theory of animal immortality
by some such process of reasoning, but the supposition seems
at least more far-fetched and improbable than in the case of
human immortality. And if we admit the insufficiency of the
explanation in the one case, we seem bound to admit it, though
perhaps in a less degree, in the other case also. In short, we
conclude that the theory of dreams appears to be hardly enough
by itself to account for the widespread belief in the immortality
of men and animals; dreams have probably done much to

confirm that belief, but would they suffice to originate it? We may reasonably doubt it.

Accordingly we are driven to cast about for some more adequate explanation of this prevalent and deeply rooted persuasion. In search of such an explanation perhaps we need go no further than the sense of life which every man feels in his own breast. We have seen that to the savage death presents itself not as a natural necessity but as a lamentable accident or crime that cuts short an existence which, but for it, might have lasted for ever. Thus arguing apparently from his own sensations he conceives of life as an indestructible kind of energy, which when it disappears in one form must necessarily reappear in another, though in the new form it need not be immediately perceptible by us; in other words, he infers that death does not destroy the vital principle nor even the conscious personality, but that it merely transforms both of them into other shapes, which are not the less real because they commonly elude the evidence of our senses. If I am right in thus interpreting the thought of primitive man, the savage view of the nature of life singularly resembles the modern scientific doctrine of the conservation of energy. According to that doctrine, no material energy ever perishes or is even diminished; when it seems to suffer diminution or extinction, all that happens is that a portion or the whole of it has been transmuted into other shapes which, though qualitatively different from, are quantitatively equivalent to, the energy in its original form. In short, if we listen to science, nothing in the physical world is ever lost, but all things are perpetually changing: the sum of energy in the universe is constant and invariable, though it undergoes ceaseless transformations. A similar theory of the indestructibility of energy is implicitly applied by the savage to explain the phenomena of life and death, and logically enough he does not limit the application to human beings but extends it to the lower animals. Therein he shews himself a better reasoner than his civilised brother, who commonly embraces with avidity the doctrine of human immortality but rejects with scorn, as derogatory to human dignity, the idea that animals have immortal souls. And when he attempts to confirm his own cherished belief in a life after death by appealing to similar beliefs among savages and inferring from them a natural instinct of immortality,

Apparently the savage conceives life as an indestructible form of energy.

Analogy of the conception to the modern scientific conception of the conservation of energy.

it is well to remind him that, if he stands by that appeal, he must, like the savage, consistently extend the privilege of immortality to the despised lower animals; for surely it is improper for him to pick and choose his evidence so as to suit his prepossessions, accepting those parts of the savage creed which tally with his own and rejecting those which do not. On logical and scientific grounds he seems bound to believe either more or less: he must hold that men and animals are alike immortal or that neither of them is so.

iv

The ambiguous behaviour of the Aino towards bears explained.

We are now perhaps in a position to understand the ambiguous behaviour of the Aino towards the bear. It has been shewn that the sharp line of demarcation which we draw between mankind and the lower animals does not exist for the savage. To him many of the other animals appear as his equals or even his superiors, not merely in brute force but in intelligence; and if choice or necessity leads him to take their lives, he feels bound, out of regard to his own safety, to do it in a way which will be as inoffensive as possible not merely to the living animal, but to its departed spirit and to all the other animals of the same species, which would resent an affront put upon one of their kind much as a tribe of savages would revenge an injury or insult offered to a tribesman. We have seen that among the many devices by which the savage seeks to atone for the wrong done by him to his animal victims one is to shew marked deference to a few chosen individuals of the species, for such behaviour is apparently regarded as entitling him to exterminate with impunity all the rest of the species upon which he can lay hands. This principle perhaps explains the attitude, at first sight puzzling and contradictory, of the Aino towards the bear. The flesh and skin of the bear regularly afford them food and clothing; but since the bear is an intelligent and powerful animal, it is necessary to offer some satisfaction or atonement to the bear species for the loss which it sustains in the death of so many of its members. This satisfaction or atonement is made by rearing young bears, treating them, so long as they live, with respect, and killing them with extraordinary marks of sorrow and devotion. So the other bears are appeased, and do not resent the slaughter of their kind by attacking the slayers or deserting the country, which would deprive the Aino of one of their means of subsistence.

Thus the primitive worship of animals assumes two forms, which are in some respects the converse of each other. On the one hand, animals are worshipped, and are therefore neither killed nor eaten. On the other hand, animals are worshipped because they are habitually killed and eaten. In both forms of worship the animal is revered on account of some benefit, positive or negative, which the savage hopes to receive from it. In the former worship the benefit comes either in the positive form of protection, advice, and help which the animal affords the man, or in the negative one of abstinence from injuries which it is in the power of the animal to inflict. In the latter worship the benefit takes the material form of the animal's flesh and skin. The two forms of worship are in some measure antithetical: in the one, the animal is not eaten because it is revered; in the other, it is revered because it is eaten.

Two forms of the worship of animals.

Corresponding to the two distinct types of animal worship, there are two distinct types of the custom of killing the animal god. On the one hand, when the revered animal is habitually spared, it is nevertheless killed—and sometimes eaten—on rare and solemn occasions. Examples of this custom have been already given and an explanation of them offered.* On the other hand, when the revered animal is habitually killed, the slaughter of any one of the species involves the killing of the god, and is atoned for on the spot by apologies and sacrifices, especially when the animal is a powerful and dangerous one; and, in addition to this ordinary and everyday atonement, there is a special annual atonement, at which a select individual of the species is slain with extraordinary marks of respect and devotion. Clearly the two types of sacramental killing—the Egyptian and the Aino types, as we may call them for distinction—are liable to be confounded by an observer; and, before we can say to which type any particular example belongs, it is necessary to ascertain whether the animal sacramentally slain belongs to a species which is habitually spared, or to one which is habitually killed by the tribe. In the former case the example belongs to the Egyptian type of sacrament, in the latter to the Aino type.

Two types of animal sacrament, the Egyptian and the Aino type.

v

The form of communion in which the sacred animal is taken from house to house, that all may enjoy a share of its divine influence, has been exemplified by the Gilyak custom of promenading the bear through the village before it is slain. Ceremonies closely analogous have survived in Europe into recent times, and doubtless date from a very primitive paganism. The best-known example is the 'hunting of the wren'.

By many European peoples—the ancient Greeks and Romans, the modern Italians, Spaniards, French, Germans, Dutch, Danes, Swedes, English, and Welsh—the wren has been designated the king, the little king, the king of birds, the hedge king, and so forth, and has been reckoned amongst those birds which it is extremely unlucky to kill. In England it is supposed that if any one kills a wren or harries its nest, he will infallibly break a bone or meet with some dreadful misfortune within the year; sometimes it is thought that the cows will give bloody milk. In Scotland the wren is called 'the Lady of Heaven's hen', and boys say:

> 'Malisons, malisons, mair than ten,
> That harry the Ladye of Heaven's hen!'*

At Saint Donan, in Brittany, people believe that if children touch the young wrens in the nest, they will suffer from the fire of St Lawrence, that is, from pimples on the face, legs, and so on. In other parts of France it is thought that if a person kills a wren or harries its nest, his house will be struck by lightning, or that the fingers with which he did the deed will shrivel up and drop off, or at least be maimed, or that his cattle will suffer in their feet.

Notwithstanding such beliefs, the custom of annually killing the wren has prevailed widely both in this country and in France. In the Isle of Man down to the eighteenth century the custom was observed on Christmas Eve or rather Christmas morning. On the twenty-fourth of December, towards evening, all the servants got a holiday; they did not go to bed all night, but rambled about till the bells rang in all the churches at midnight. When prayers were over, they went to hunt the wren,

and having found one of these birds they killed it and fastened
it to the top of a long pole with its wings extended. Thus they
carried it in procession to every house chanting the following
rhyme:

> 'We hunted the wren for Robin the Bobbin,
> We hunted the wren for Jack of the Can,
> We hunted the wren for Robin the Bobbin,
> We hunted the wren for every one.'

When they had gone from house to house and collected all the
money they could, they laid the wren on a bier and carried it
in procession to the parish churchyard, where they made a
grave and buried it 'with the utmost solemnity, singing dirges
over her in the Manks language, which they call her knell; after
which Christmas begins'. The burial over, the company outside
the churchyard formed a circle and danced to music. About the
middle of the nineteenth century the burial of the wren took
place in the Isle of Man on St Stephen's Day (the twenty-sixth
of December). Boys went from door to door with a wren
suspended by the legs in the centre of two hoops, which crossed
each other at right angles and were decorated with evergreens
and ribbons. The bearers sang certain lines in which reference
was made to boiling and eating the bird. If at the close of the
song they received a small coin, they gave in return a feather of
the wren; so that before the end of the day the bird often hung
almost featherless. The wren was then buried, no longer in the
churchyard, but on the seashore or in some waste place. The
feathers distributed were preserved with religious care, it being
believed that every feather was an effectual preservative from
shipwreck for a year, and a fisherman would have been thought
very foolhardy who had not one of them. Even to the present
time, in the twentieth century, the custom is generally observed, at least in name, on St Stephen's Day, throughout the
Isle of Man.

In the 'hunting of the wren' there is nothing to shew that the
customs in question have any relation to agriculture. So far as
appears, they may date from a time before the invention of
husbandry when animals were revered as divine in themselves,
not merely as divine because they embodied the corn-spirit; and
the analogy of the Gilyak procession of the bear is in favour of

Processions of men disguised as animals, in which the animal seems to represent the corn-spirit.

assigning the corresponding European customs to this very early date. On the other hand, there are certain European processions of animals, or of men disguised as animals, which may perhaps be purely agricultural in their origin; in other words, the animals which figure in them may have been from the first nothing but representatives of the corn-spirit conceived in animal shape. Thus, for example, in country districts of Bohemia it is, or used to be, customary during the last days of the Carnival for young men to go about in procession from house to house collecting gratuities. Usually a man or boy is swathed from head to foot in pease-straw and wrapt round in straw-ropes: thus attired he goes by the name of the Shrovetide or Carnival Bear (*Fastnachtsbär*) and is led from house to house to the accompaniment of music and singing. In every house he dances with the girls, the maids, and the housewife herself, and drinks to the health of the good man, the good wife, and the girls. In some parts of Bohemia the straw-clad man in these Shrovetide processions is called, not the Bear, but the Oats-goat, and he wears horns on his head to give point to the name. These different names and disguises indicate that in some places the corn-spirit is conceived as a bear and in others as a goat. Many examples of the conception of the corn-spirit as a goat have already been cited; the conception of him as a bear seems to be less common. In the neighbourhood of Gniewkowo, in Prussian Lithuania, the two ideas are combined, for on Twelfth Day a man wrapt in pease-straw to represent a Bear and another wrapt in oats-straw to represent a Goat go together about the village; they imitate the actions of the two animals and perform dances, for which they receive a present in every house. At Marburg in Steiermark the corn-spirit figures now as a wolf and now as a bear. The man who gave the last stroke at threshing is called the Wolf. All the other men flee from the barn, and wait till the Wolf comes forth; whereupon they pounce on him, wrap him in straw to resemble a wolf, and so lead him about the village. He keeps the name of Wolf till Christmas, when he is wrapt in a goat's skin and led from house to house as a Pease-bear at the end of a rope. In this custom the dressing of the mummer in a goat's skin seems to mark him out as the representative of a goat; so that here the mythical fancy of the people apparently hesitates between a goat, a bear, and a

The Shrovetide Bear in Bohemia.

The Oats-goat, the Pease-bear, etc.

wolf as the proper embodiment of the corn-spirit. In Scandinavia the conception of the spirit as a goat who appears at Christmas (*Julbuck*) appears to be common. Thus, for example, in Bergslagshärad (Sweden) it used to be customary at Christmas to lead about a man completely wrapt in corn-straw and wearing a goat's horns on his head: he personated the Yule goat. In some parts of Sweden a regular feature of the little Christmas drama is a pretence of slaughtering the Yule-goat, who, however, comes to life again. The actor, hidden by a coverlet made of skins and wearing a pair of formidable horns, is led into the room by two men, who make believe to slaughter him, while they sing verses referring to the mantles of various colours, red, blue, white, and yellow, which they laid on him, one after the other. At the conclusion of the song, the Yule-goat, after feigning death, jumps up and skips about to the amusement of the spectators.

The Yule-goat in Sweden.

In England a custom like some of the preceding still prevails at Whittlesey in Cambridgeshire on the Tuesday after Plough Monday, as I learn from an obliging communication of Professor G. C. Moore Smith of Sheffield University. He writes: 'When I was at Whittlesey yesterday I had the pleasure of meeting a "Straw-bear," if not two, in the street. I had not been at Whittlesey on the day for nearly forty years, and feared the custom had died out. In my boyhood the Straw-bear was a man completely swathed in straw, led by a string by another and made to dance in front of people's houses, in return for which money was expected. This always took place on the Tuesday following Plough-Monday. Yesterday the Straw-bear was a boy, and I saw no dancing. Otherwise there was no change.'

The Straw-bear at Whittlesey.

A comparison of this English custom with the similar Continental customs which have been described above, raises a presumption that the Straw-bear, who is thus led about from house to house, represents the corn-spirit bestowing his blessing on every homestead in the village. This interpretation is strongly confirmed by the date at which the ceremony takes place. For the date is the day after Plough Monday, and it can hardly be doubted that the old popular celebration of Plough Monday has a direct reference to agriculture. Plough Monday is the first Monday of January after Twelfth Day. On that day it used to be the custom in various parts of England for a band

The ceremonies of Plough Monday in England.

of sturdy swains to drag a gaily decorated plough from house to house and village to village, collecting contributions which were afterwards spent in rustic revelry at a tavern. The men who drew the plough were called Plough Bullocks; they wore their shirts over their coats, and bunches of ribbons flaunted from their hats and persons. Among them there was always one who personated a much bedizened old woman called Bessy; under his gown he formerly had a bullock's tail fastened to him behind, but this appendage was afterwards discarded. He skipped, danced and cut capers, and carried a money-box soliciting contributions from the onlookers.

Such rites no doubt date from a remote antiquity.

These rites no doubt date from an extremely early age in the history of agriculture. They are probably far older than Christianity, older even than those highly developed forms of Greek religion with which ancient writers and artists have made us familiar, but which have been for so many centuries a thing of the past. Thus it happens that, while the fine flower of the religious consciousness in myth, ritual, and art is fleeting and evanescent, its simpler forms are comparatively stable and permanent, being rooted deep in those principles of common minds which bid fair to outlive all the splendid but transient creations of genius. It may be that the elaborate theologies, the solemn rites, the stately temples, which now attract the reverence or the wonder of mankind, are destined themselves to pass away like 'all Olympus' faded hierarchy', and that simple folk will still cherish the simple faiths of their nameless and dateless forefathers, will still believe in witches and fairies, in ghosts and hobgoblins, will still mumble the old spells and make the old magic passes, when the muezzin shall have ceased to call the faithful to prayer from the minarets of St Sophia, and when the worshippers shall gather no more in the long-drawn aisles of Nôtre Dame and under the dome of St Peter's.

BOOK III

THE SCAPEGOAT

CHAPTER 1

THE TRANSFERENCE OF EVIL

i

IN the preceding parts of this work we have traced the practice of killing a god among peoples in the hunting, pastoral, and agricultural stages of society; and I have attempted to explain the motives which led men to adopt so curious a custom. One aspect of the custom still remains to be noticed. The accumulated misfortunes and sins of the whole people are sometimes laid upon the dying god, who is supposed to bear them away for ever, leaving the people innocent and happy. The notion that we can transfer our guilt and sufferings to some other being who will bear them for us is familiar to the savage mind. It arises from a very obvious confusion between the physical and the mental, between the material and the immaterial. Because it is possible to shift a load of wood, stones, or what not, from our own back to the back of another, the savage fancies that it is equally possible to shift the burden of his pains and sorrows to another, who will suffer them in his stead. Upon this idea he acts, and the result is an endless number of very unamiable devices for palming off upon some one else the trouble which a man shrinks from bearing himself. In short, the principle of vicarious suffering is commonly understood and practised by races who stand on a low level of social and intellectual culture. In the following pages I shall illustrate the theory and the practice as they are found among savages in all their naked simplicity, undisguised by the refinements of metaphysics and the subtleties of theology.

The principle of vicarious suffering.

The devices to which the cunning and selfish savage resorts for the sake of easing himself at the expense of his neighbour are manifold; only a few typical examples out of a multitude can be cited. At the outset it is to be observed that the evil of which a man seeks to rid himself need not be transferred to a person; it may equally well be transferred to an animal or a thing, though in the last case the thing is often only a vehicle to convey the trouble to the first person who touches it. In some

Transference of evil to things.

of the East Indian islands they think that epilepsy can be cured by striking the patient on the face with the leaves of certain trees and then throwing them away. The disease is believed to have passed into the leaves, and to have been thrown away with them. In the Warramunga and Tjingilli tribes of Central Australia men who suffered from headache have often been seen wearing women's head-rings. 'This was connected with the belief that the pain in the head would pass into the rings, and that then it could be thrown away with them into the bush, and so got rid of effectually. The natives have a very firm belief in the efficacy of this treatment. In the same way when a man suffers from internal pain, usually brought on by overeating, his wife's head-rings are placed on his stomach; the evil magic which is causing all the trouble passes into them, and they are then thrown away into the bushes, where the magic is supposed to leave them. After a time they are searched for by the woman, who brings them back, and again wears them in the ordinary way'. Among the Sihanaka of Madagascar, when a man is very sick, his relatives are sometimes bidden by the diviner to cast out the evil by means of a variety of things, such as a stick of a particular sort of tree, a rag, a pinch of earth from an ant's nest, a little money, or what not. Whatever they may be, they are brought to the patient's house and held by a man near the door, while an exorcist stands in the house and pronounces the formula necessary for casting out the disease. When he has done, the things are thrown away in a southward direction, and all the people in the house, including the sick man, if he has strength enough, shake their loose robes and spit towards the door in order to expedite the departure of the malady. When an Atkhan of the Aleutian Islands had committed a grave sin and desired to unburden himself of his guilt, he proceeded as follows. Having chosen a time when the sun was clear and unclouded, he picked up certain weeds and carried them about his person. Then he laid them down, and calling the sun to witness, cast his sins upon them, after which, having eased his heart of all that weighed upon it, he threw the weeds into the fire, and fancied that thus he cleansed himself of his guilt. In Vedic times a younger brother who married before his elder brother was thought to have sinned in so doing, but there was a ceremony by which he could purge himself of his sin. Fetters

Evils swept away by rivers.

of reed-grass were laid on him in token of his guilt, and when they had been washed and sprinkled they were flung into a foaming torrent, which swept them away, while the evil was bidden to vanish with the foam of the stream. The Matse negroes of Togoland think that the river Awo has power to carry away the sorrows of mankind. So when one of their friends has died, and their hearts are heavy, they go to the river with leaves of the raphia palm tied round their necks and drums in their hands. Standing on the bank they beat the drums and cast the leaves into the stream. As the leaves float away out of sight to the sound of the rippling water and the roll of the drums, they fancy that their sorrow too is lifted from them. Similarly, the ancient Greeks imagined that the pangs of love might be healed by bathing in the river Selemnus.* The Indians of Peru sought to purify themselves from their sins by plunging their heads in a river; they said that the river washed their sins away.

An Arab cure for melancholy or madness caused by love is to put a dish of water on the sufferer's head, drop melted lead into it, and then bury the lead in an open field; thus the mischief that was in the man goes away. Amongst the Miotse of China, when the eldest son of the house attains the age of seven years, a ceremony called 'driving away the devil' takes place. The father makes a kite of straw and lets it fly away in the desert, bearing away all evil with it. When an Indian of Santiago Tepehuacan is ill, he will sometimes attempt to rid himself of the malady by baking thrice seven cakes; of these he places seven in the top of the highest pine-tree of the forest, seven he lays at the foot of the tree, and seven he casts into a well, with the water of which he then washes himself. By this means he transfers the sickness to the water of the well and so is made whole. The Baganda believed that plague was caused by the god Kaumpuli, who resided in a deep hole in his temple. To prevent him from escaping and devastating the country, they battened him down in the hole by covering the top with plantain-stems and piling wild-cat-skins over them; there was nothing like wild-cat-skins to keep him down, so hundreds of wild cats were hunted and killed every year to supply the necessary skins. However, sometimes in spite of these precautions the god contrived to escape, and then the people died. When a garden

Transference of evil to things.

or house was plague-stricken, the priests purified it by transferring the disease to a plantain-tree and then carrying away the tree to a piece of waste land. The way in which they effected the transference of the disease was this. They first made a number of little shields and spears out of plantain fibre and reeds and placed them at intervals along the path leading from the garden to the main road. A young plantain-tree, about to bear fruit, was then cut down, the stem was laid in the path leading to one of the plague-stricken huts, and it was speared with not less than twenty reed spears, which were left sticking in it, while some of the plantain-fibre shields were also fastened to it. This tree was then carried down the path to the waste land and left there. It went by the name of the Scapegoat (*kyonzire*). To make quite sure that the plague, after being thus deposited in the wilderness, should not return by the way it went, the priests raised an arch, covered with barkcloth, over the path at the point where it diverged from the main road. This arch was thought to interpose an insurmountable barrier to the return of the plague.

Dyak transference of evil to things.

Dyak priestesses expel ill-luck from a house by hewing and slashing the air in every corner of it with wooden swords, which they afterwards wash in the river, to let the ill-luck float away down stream. Sometimes they sweep misfortune out of the house with brooms made of the leaves of certain plants and sprinkled with rice-water and blood. Having swept it clean out of every room and into a toy-house made of bamboo, they set the little house with its load of bad luck adrift on the river. The current carries it away out to sea, where it shifts its baleful cargo to a certain kettle-shaped ship, which floats in mid-ocean and receives in its capacious hold all the ills that flesh is heir to. Well would it be with mankind if the evils remained for ever tossing far away on the billows; but, alas, they are dispersed from the ship to the four winds, and settle again, and yet again, on the weary Dyak world. On Dyak rivers you may see many of the miniature houses, laden with manifold misfortunes, bobbing up and down on the current, or sticking fast in the thickets that line the banks.

Evils transferred to other persons

These examples illustrate the purely beneficent side of the transference of evil; they shew how men seek to alleviate human sufferings by diverting them to material objects, which are then thrown away or otherwise disposed of so as to render them *through the* innocuous. Often, however, the transference of evil to a material *medium of things.* object is only a step towards foisting it upon a living person. This is the maleficent side of such transferences. It is exemplified in the following cases. To cure toothache some of the Australian blacks apply a heated spear-thrower to the cheek. The spear-thrower is then cast away, and the toothache goes with it in the shape of a black stone called *karriitch*. Stones of this kind are found in old mounds and sandhills. They are carefully collected and thrown in the direction of enemies in order to give them toothache. In Mirzapur a mode of transferring disease is to fill a pot with flowers and rice and bury it in a pathway covered up with a flat stone. Whoever touches this is supposed to contract the disease. The practice is called *chalauwa*, or 'passing on' the malady. This sort of thing goes on daily in Upper India. Often while walking of a morning in the bazaar you will see a little pile of earth adorned with flowers in the middle of the road. Such a pile usually contains some scabs or scales from the body of a smallpox patient, which are placed there in the hope that some one may touch them, and by catching the disease may relieve the sufferer. The Bahima, a pastoral people of the Uganda Protectorate, often suffer from deep-seated abscesses: 'their cure for this is to transfer the disease to some other person by obtaining herbs from the medicine-man, rubbing them over the place where the swelling is, and burying them in the road where people continually pass; the first person who steps over these buried herbs contracts the disease, and the original patient recovers.' The practice of the Wagogo of German East Africa is similar. When a man is ill, the native doctor will take him to a cross-road, where he prepares his medicines, uttering at the same time the incantations which are necessary to give the drugs their medical virtue. Part of the dose is then administered to the patient, and part is buried under a pot turned upside down at the cross-road. It is hoped that somebody will step over the pot, and catching the disease, which lurks in the pot, will thereby relieve the original sufferer. A variation of this cure is to plaster some of the medicine, or a little of the patient's blood, on a wooden peg and to drive the peg into a tree; any one who passes the tree and is so imprudent as to draw out the peg, will carry away with it the disease.

Evils trans-
ferred to
human
beings in
India and
elsewhere.

Again, men sometimes play the part of scapegoat by diverting to themselves the evils that threaten others. An ancient Hindoo ritual describes how the pangs of thirst may be transferred from a sick man to another. The operator seats the pair on branches, back to back, the sufferer with his face to the east, and the whole man with his face to the west. Then he stirs some gruel in a vessel placed on the patient's head and hands the stir-about to the other man to drink. In this way he transfers the pangs of thirst from the thirsty soul to the other, who obligingly receives them in his stead. There is a painful Telugu remedy for a fever: it is to embrace a bald-headed Brahman widow at the earliest streak of dawn. By doing so you get rid of the fever, and no doubt (though this is not expressly affirmed) you at the same time transfer it to the bald-headed widow. When a Cingalese is dangerously ill, and the physicians can do nothing, a devil-dancer is called in, who by making offerings to the devils, and dancing in the masks appropriate to them, conjures these demons of disease, one after the other, out of the sick man's body and into his own. Having thus successfully extracted the cause of the malady, the artful dancer lies down on a bier, and shamming death, is carried to an open place outside the village. Here, being left to himself, he soon comes to life again, and hastens back to claim his reward. In 1590 a Scotch witch of the name of Agnes Sampson was convicted of curing a certain Robert Kers of a disease 'laid upon him by a westland warlock when he was at Dumfries, whilk sickness she took upon herself, and kept the same with great groaning and torment till the morn, at whilk time there was a great din heard in the house'. The noise was made by the witch in her efforts to shift the disease, by means of clothes, from herself to a cat or dog. Unfortunately the attempt partly miscarried. The disease missed the animal and hit Alexander Douglas of Dalkeith, who dwined and died of it, while the original patient, Robert Kers, was made whole. The Dyaks believe that certain men possess in themselves the power of neutralizing bad omens. So, when evil omens have alarmed a farmer for the safety of his crops, he takes a small portion of his farm produce to one of these wise men, who eats it raw for a small consideration, 'and thereby appropriates to himself the evil omen, which in him becomes innocuous, and thus delivers the other from the ban of the *pemali* or taboo'.

'In one part of New Zealand an expiation for sin was felt to be necessary; a service was performed over an individual, by which all the sins of the tribe were supposed to be transferred to him, a fern stalk was previously tied to his person, with which he jumped into the river, and there unbinding, allowed it to float away to the sea, bearing their sins with it.' In great emergencies the sins of the Rajah of Manipur used to be transferred to somebody else, usually to a criminal, who earned his pardon by his vicarious sufferings. To effect the transference the Rajah and his wife, clad in fine robes, bathed on a scaffold erected in the bazaar, while the criminal crouched beneath it. With the water which dripped from them on him their sins also were washed away and fell on the human scapegoat. To complete the transference the Rajah and his wife made over their fine robes to their substitute, while they themselves, clad in new raiment, mixed with the people till evening. But at the close of the day they entered into retreat and remained in seclusion for about a week, during which they were esteemed sacred or tabooed. Further, in Manipur 'they have a noteworthy system of keeping count of the years. Each year is named after some man, who—for a consideration—undertakes to bear the fortune good or bad of the year. If the year be good, if there be no pestilence and a good harvest, he gets presents from all sorts of people, and I remember hearing that in 1898, when the cholera was at its worst, a deputation came to the Political Agent and asked him to punish the name-giver, as it was obvious that he was responsible for the epidemic. In former times he would have got into trouble.' The nomination of the eponym, or man who is to give his name to the year, takes place at a festival called *Chirouba*, which falls about the middle of April. It is the priests who nominate the eponym, after comparing his horoscope with that of the Rajah and of the State generally. The retiring official, who gave his name to the past year, addresses his successor as follows: 'My friend, I bore and took away all evil spirits and sins from the Rajah and his people during the last year. Do thou likewise from to-morrow until the next *Chirouba*.' Then the incoming official, who is to give his name to the New Year, addresses the Rajah in these words: 'O son of heaven, Ruler of the Kings, great and ancient Lord, Incarnation of God, the great Lord

Sins and mis-fortunes transferred to human scapegoats in New Zealand and Manipur.

Annual eponyms in Manipur.

Pakhangba, Master of the bright Sun, Lord of the Plain and Despot of the Hills, whose kingdom is from the hills on the east to the mountains on the west, the old year perishes, the new cometh. New is the sun of the new year, and bright as the new sun shalt thou be, and mild withal as the moon. May thy beauty and thy strength grow with the growth of the new year. From to-day will I bear on my head all thy sins, diseases, misfortunes, shame, mischief, all that is aimed in battle against thee, all that threatens thee, all that is bad and hurtful for thee and thy kingdom.' For these important services the eponym or vicar receives from the Rajah a number of gifts, including a basket of salt, and his grateful country rewards his self-sacrific-

Eponymous magistrates as public scapegoats.

ing devotion by bestowing many privileges on him. Elsewhere, perhaps, if we knew more about the matter, we might find that eponymous magistrates who give their names to the year have been similarly regarded as public scapegoats, who bore on their devoted heads the misfortunes, the sins, and the sorrows of the whole people.

Indian story of the transference of sins to a holy man.

In the *Jataka*, or collection of Indian stories which narrate the many transmigrations of the Buddha, there is an instructive tale, which sets forth how sins and misfortunes can be transferred by means of spittle to a holy ascetic. A lady of easy virtue, we are told, had lost the favour of King Dandaki and bethought herself how she could recover it. As she walked in the park revolving these things in her mind, she spied a devout ascetic named Kisavaccha. A thought struck her. 'Surely,' said she to herself, 'this must be Ill Luck. I will get rid of my sin on his person and then go and bathe.' No sooner said than done. Chewing her toothpick, she collected a large clot of spittle in her mouth with which she beslavered the matted locks of the venerable man, and having hurled her toothpick at his head into the bargain she departed with a mind at peace and bathed. The stratagem was entirely successful; for the king took her into his good graces again. Not long after it chanced that the king deposed his domestic chaplain from his office. Naturally chagrined at this loss of royal favour, the clergyman repaired to the king's light o' love and enquired how she had contrived to recapture the monarch's affection. She told him frankly how she had got rid of her sin and emerged without a stain on her character by simply spitting on the head of Ill Luck in the royal park. The chaplain took the hint, and hastening to the park bespattered in like manner the sacred locks of the holy man; and in consequence he was soon reinstated in office. It would have been well if the thing had stopped there, but unfortunately it did not. By and by it happened that there was a disturbance on the king's frontier, and the king put himself at the head of his army to go forth and fight. An unhappy idea occurred to his domestic chaplain. Elated by the success of the expedient which had restored him to royal favour, he asked the king, 'Sire, do you wish for victory or defeat?' 'Why for victory, of course,' replied the king. 'Then you take my advice,' said the chaplain; 'just go and spit on the head of Ill Luck, who dwells in the royal park; you will thus transfer all your sin to his person.' It seemed to the king a capital idea and he improved on it by proposing that the whole army should accompany him and get rid of their sins in like manner. They all did so, beginning with the king, and the state of the holy man's head when they had all done is something frightful to contemplate. But even this was not the worst. For after the king had gone, up came the commander-in-chief and seeing the sad plight of the pious ascetic, he took pity on him and had his poor bedabbled hair thoroughly washed. The fatal consequences of this kindly-meant but most injudicious shampoo may easily be anticipated. The sins which had been transferred with the saliva to the person of the devotee were now restored to their respective owners; and to punish them for their guilt fire fell from heaven and destroyed the whole kingdom for sixty leagues round about.

A less harmless way of relieving an army from guilt or misfortune used in former times to be actually practised by the Baganda. When an army had returned from war, and the gods warned the king by their oracles that some evil had attached itself to the soldiers, it was customary to pick out a woman slave from the captives, together with a cow, a goat, a fowl, and a dog from the booty, and to send them back under a strong guard to the borders of the country from which they had come. There their limbs were broken and they were left to die; for they were too crippled to crawl back to Uganda. In order to ensure the transference of the evil to these substitutes, bunches of grass were rubbed over the people and cattle and then tied to the victims. After that the army was pronounced clean and was

Transference of evils to human scape-goats in Uganda.

allowed to return to the capital. A similar mode of transferring evil to human and animal victims was practised by the Baganda whenever the gods warned the king that his hereditary foes the Banyoro were working magic against him and his people.

In Travancore, when a rajah is near his end, they seek out a holy Brahman, who consents to take upon himself the sins of the dying man in consideration of the sum of ten thousand rupees. Thus prepared to immolate himself on the altar of duty as a vicarious sacrifice for sin, the saint is introduced into the chamber of death, and closely embraces the dying rajah, saying to him, 'O King, I undertake to bear all your sins and diseases. May your Highness live long and reign happily.' Having thus, with a noble devotion, taken to himself the sins of the sufferer, and likewise the rupees, he is sent away from the country and never more allowed to return.

In Tahiti, where the bodies of chiefs and persons of rank were embalmed and preserved above ground in special sheds or houses erected for them, a priest was employed at the funeral rites who bore the title of the 'corpse-praying priest'. His office was singular. When the house for the dead had been prepared, and the corpse placed on the platform or bier, the priest ordered a hole to be made in the floor, near the foot of the platform. Over this he prayed to the god by whom it was supposed that the soul of the deceased had been called away. The purport of his prayer was that all the dead man's sins, especially the one for which his soul had been required of him, might be deposited there that they might not attach in any degree to the survivors, and that the anger of the god might be appeased. He next addressed the corpse, usually saying, 'With you let the guilt now remain.' The pillar or post of the corpse, as it was called, was then planted in the hole, and the hole filled up. As soon as the ceremony of depositing the sins in the hole was over, all who had touched the body or the garments of the deceased, which were buried or destroyed, fled precipitately into the sea, to cleanse themselves from the pollution which they had contracted by touching the corpse. They also cast into the sea the garments they had worn while they were performing the last offices to the dead. Having finished their ablutions, they gathered a few pieces of coral from the bottom of the sea, and returning with them to the house addressed the corpse, saying,

'With you may the pollution be.' So saying they threw down the coral on the top of the hole which had been dug to receive the sins and the defilement of the dead. In this instance the sins of the departed, as well as the pollution which the primitive mind commonly associates with death, are not borne by a living person, but buried in a hole. Yet the fundamental idea—that of the transference of sins—is the same whether the vehicle or receptacle destined to catch and draw off the evil be a person, an animal, or a thing, is for the purpose in hand a matter of little moment.

ii

The public attempts to expel the accumulated ills of a whole community may be divided into two classes, according as the expelled evils are immaterial and invisible or are embodied in a material vehicle or scapegoat. The former may be called the direct or immediate expulsion of evils; the latter the indirect or mediate expulsion, or the expulsion by scapegoat. We begin with examples of the former.

The Solomon Islanders of Bougainville Straits believe that epidemics are always, or nearly always, caused by evil spirits; and accordingly when the people of a village have been suffering generally from colds, they have been known to blow conch-shells, beat tins, shout, and knock on the houses for the purpose of expelling the demons and so curing their colds. When cholera has broken out in a Burmese village the able-bodied men scramble on the roofs and lay about them with bamboos and billets of wood, while all the rest of the population, old and young, stand below and thump drums, blow trumpets, yell, scream, beat floors, walls, tin pans, everything to make a din. This uproar, repeated on three successive nights, is thought to be very effective in driving away the cholera demons. The Shans of Kengtung, a province of Upper Burma, imagine that epidemics are brought about by the prowling ghosts of wicked men, such as thieves and murderers, who cannot rest but go about doing all the harm they can to the living. Hence when sickness is rife, the people take steps to expel these dangerous spirits. The Buddhist priests exert themselves actively in the beneficent enterprise. They assemble in a

Demons of sickness expelled in the Solomon Islands.

Demons of sickness expelled in Burma.

body at the Town Court and read the scriptures. Guns are fired and processions march to the city gates, by which the fiends are supposed to take their departure. There small trays of food are left for them, but the larger offerings are deposited in the middle of the town. When smallpox first appeared amongst the Kumis of South-Eastern India, they thought it was a devil come from Aracan. The villages were placed in a state of siege, no one being allowed to leave or enter them. A monkey was killed by being dashed on the ground, and its body was hung at the village gate. Its blood, mixed with small river pebbles, was sprinkled on the houses, the threshold of every house was swept with the monkey's tail, and the fiend was adjured to depart. During the hot summer cholera is endemic in Southern China, and from time to time, when the mortality is great, vigorous attempts are made to expel the demons who do all the mischief. For this salutary purpose processions parade the streets by night; images of the gods are borne in them, torches waved, gongs beaten, guns fired, crackers popped, swords brandished, demon-dispelling trumpets blown, and priests in full canonicals trot up and down jingling handbells, winding blasts on buffalo horns, and reciting exorcisms. Sometimes the deities are represented in these processions by living men, who are believed to be possessed by the divine spirit. Such a man-god may be seen naked to the waist with his dishevelled hair streaming down his back; long daggers are stuck in his cheeks and arms, so that the blood drips from them. In his hand he carries a two-edged sword, with which he deals doughty blows at the invisible foes in the air; but sometimes he inflicts bloody wounds on his own back with the weapon or with a ball which is studded with long sharp nails. Other inspired men are carried in armchairs, of which the seat, back, arms, and foot-rest are set with nails or composed of rows of parallel sword-blades, that cut into the flesh of the wretches seated on them: others are stretched at full length on beds of nails. For hours these bleeding votaries are carried about the city. Again, it is not uncommon to see in the procession a medium or man-god with a thick needle thrust through his tongue. His bloody spittle drips on sheets of paper, which the crowd eagerly scrambles for, knowing that with the blood they have absorbed the devil-dispelling power inherent in the man-god. The bloody papers, pasted on the lintel, walls, or

Demons of sickness expelled in India and China.

beds of a house or on the bodies of the family, are supposed to afford complete protection against cholera. Such are the methods by which in Southern China the demons of disease are banished the city.

In Japan the old-fashioned method of staying an epidemic is to expel the demon of the plague from every house into which he has entered. The treatment begins with the house in which the malady has appeared in the mildest form. First of all a Shinto priest makes a preliminary visit to the sick-room and extracts from the demon a promise that he will depart with him at his next visit. The day after he comes again, and, seating himself near the patient, beseeches the evil spirit to come away with him. Meanwhile red rice, which is used only on special occasions, has been placed at the sufferer's head, a closed litter made of pine boughs has been brought in, and four men equipped with flags or weapons have taken post in the four corners of the room to prevent the demon from seeking refuge there. All are silent but the priest. The prayer being over, the sick man's pillow is hastily thrown into the litter, and the priest cries, 'All right now!' At that the bearers double with it into the street, the people within and without beat the air with swords, sticks, or anything that comes to hand, while others assist in the cure by banging away at drums and gongs. A procession is now formed in which only men take part, some of them carrying banners, others provided with a drum, a bell, a flute, a horn, and all of them wearing fillets and horns of twisted straw to keep the demon away from themselves. As the procession starts an old man chants, 'What god are you bearing away?' To which the others respond in chorus, 'The god of the pest we are bearing away!' Then to the music of the drum, the bell, the flute, and the horn the litter is borne through the streets. During its passage all the people in the town who are not taking part in the ceremony remain indoors, every house along the route of the procession is carefully closed, and at the crossroads swordsmen are stationed, who guard the street by hewing the air to right and left with their blades, lest the demon should escape by that way. The litter is thus carried to a retired spot between two towns and left there, while all who escorted it thither run away. Only the priest remains behind for half an hour to complete the exorcism and the cure. The bearers of the

Demons of sickness expelled in Japan.

litter spend the night praying in a temple. Next day they return home, but not until they have plunged into a cold bath in the open air to prevent the demon from following them. The same litter serves to convey the evil spirit from every house in the town.

Flight from the demons of sickness.

Sometimes, instead of chasing the demon of disease from their homes, savages prefer to leave him in peaceable possession, while they themselves take to flight and attempt to prevent him from following in their tracks. Thus when the Patagonians were attacked by smallpox, which they attributed to the machinations of an evil spirit, they used to abandon their sick and flee, slashing the air with their weapons and throwing water about in order to keep off the dreadful pursuer; and when after several days' march they reached a place where they hoped to be beyond his reach, they used by way of precaution to plant all their cutting weapons with the sharp edges turned towards the quarter from which they had come, as if they were repelling a charge of cavalry. Similarly, when the Lules or Tonocotes Indians of the Gran Chaco were attacked by an epidemic, they regularly sought to evade it by flight, but in so doing they always followed a sinuous, not a straight, course; because they said that when the disease made after them he would be so exhausted by the turnings and windings of the route that he would never be able to come up with them. When the Indians of New Mexico were decimated by smallpox or other infectious disease, they used to shift their quarters every day, retreating into the most sequestered parts of the mountains and choosing the thorniest thickets they could find, in the hope that the smallpox would be too afraid of scratching himself on the thorns to follow them. When some Chins on a visit to Rangoon were attacked by cholera, they went about with drawn swords to scare away the demon, and they spent the day hiding under bushes so that he might not be able to find them.

The periodic expulsion of evils.

The expulsion of evils, from being occasional, tends to become periodic. It comes to be thought desirable to have a general riddance of evil spirits at fixed times, usually once a year, in order that the people may make a fresh start in life, freed from all the malignant influences which have been long accumulating about them. Some of the Australian blacks annually expelled the ghosts of the dead from their territory. The

Annual expulsion of

ceremony was witnessed by the Revd W. Ridley on the banks ghosts in Australia. of the River Barwan. 'A chorus of twenty, old and young, were singing and beating time with boomerangs . . . Suddenly, from under a sheet of bark darted a man with his body whitened by pipeclay, his head and face coloured with lines of red and yellow, and a tuft of feathers fixed by means of a stick two feet above the crown of his head. He stood twenty minutes perfectly still, gazing upwards. An aboriginal who stood by told me he was looking for the ghosts of dead men. At last he began to move very slowly, and soon rushed to and fro at full speed, flourishing a branch as if to drive away some foes invisible to us. When I thought this pantomime must be almost over, ten more, similarly adorned, suddenly appeared from behind the trees, and the whole party joined in a brisk conflict with their mysterious assailants . . . At last, after some rapid evolutions in which they put forth all their strength, they rested from the exciting toil which they had kept up all night and for some hours after sunrise; they seemed satisfied that the ghosts were driven away for twelve months. They were performing the same ceremony at every station along the river, and I am told it is an annual custom.'

Certain seasons of the year mark themselves naturally out as Annual expulsion of Tuña among the Esquimaux of Alaska. appropriate moments for a general expulsion of devils. Such a moment occurs towards the close of an Arctic winter, when the sun reappears on the horizon after an absence of weeks or months. Accordingly, at Point Barrow, the most northerly extremity of Alaska, and nearly of America, the Esquimaux choose the moment of the sun's reappearance to hunt the mischievous spirit Tuña from every house. The ceremony was witnessed by the members of the United States Polar Expedition, who wintered at Point Barrow. A fire was built in front of the council-house, and an old woman was posted at the entrance to every house. The men gathered round the council-house, while the young women and girls drove the spirits out of every house with their knives, stabbing viciously under the bunk and deer-skins, and calling upon Tuña to be gone. When they thought he had been driven out of every hole and corner, they thrust him down through the hole in the floor and chased him into the open air with loud cries and frantic gestures. Meanwhile the old woman at the entrance of the house made passes with a long knife in the air to keep him from returning. Each

party drove the spirit towards the fire and invited him to go into
it. All were by this time drawn up in a semicircle round the fire,
when several of the leading men made specific charges against
the spirit; and each after his speech brushed his clothes violently, calling on the spirit to leave him and go into the fire. Two
men now stepped forward with rifles loaded with blank cartridges, while a third brought a vessel of urine and flung it on the
flames. At the same time one of the men fired a shot into the
fire; and as the cloud of steam rose it received the other shot,
which was supposed to finish Tuña for the time being.

Annual expul-   In late autumn, when storms rage over the land and break the
sion of   icy fetters by which the frozen sea is as yet but slightly bound,
Sedna among
the Esqui-   when the loosened floes are driven against each other and break
maux of Baf-   with loud crashes, and when the cakes of ice are piled in wild
fin Land.   disorder one upon another, the Esquimaux of Baffin Land fancy
they hear the voices of the spirits who people the mischief-laden
air. Then the ghosts of the dead knock wildly at the huts, which
they cannot enter, and woe to the hapless wight whom they
catch; he soon sickens and dies. Then the phantom of a huge
hairless dog pursues the real dogs, which expire in convulsions
and cramps at sight of him. All the countless spirits of evil are
abroad, striving to bring sickness and death, foul weather and
failure in hunting on the Esquimaux. Most dreaded of all these
spectral visitants are Sedna, mistress of the nether world, and
her father, to whose share dead Esquimaux fall. While the other
spirits fill the air and the water, she rises from under ground.
It is then a busy season for the wizards. In every house you may
hear them singing and praying, while they conjure the spirits,
seated in a mystic gloom at the back of the hut, which is dimly
lit by a lamp burning low. The hardest task of all is to drive
away Sedna, and this is reserved for the most powerful enchanter. A rope is coiled on the floor of a large hut in such a
way as to leave a small opening at the top, which represents the
breathing hole of a seal. Two enchanters stand beside it, one of
them grasping a spear as if he were watching a seal-hole in
winter, the other holding the harpoon-line. A third sorcerer sits
at the back of the hut chanting a magic song to lure Sedna to
the spot. Now she is heard approaching under the floor of the
hut, breathing heavily; now she emerges at the hole; now she is
harpooned and sinks away in angry haste, dragging the harpoon

with her, while the two men hold on to the line with all their might. The struggle is severe, but at last by a desperate wrench she tears herself away and returns to her dwelling in Adlivun. When the harpoon is drawn up out of the hole it is found to be splashed with blood, which the enchanters proudly exhibit as a proof of their prowess. Thus Sedna and the other evil spirits are at last driven away, and next day a great festival is celebrated by old and young in honour of the event. But they must still be cautious, for the wounded Sedna is furious and will seize any one she may find outside of his hut; so they all wear amulets on the top of their hoods to protect themselves against her. These amulets consist of pieces of the first garments that they wore after birth.

The Koryaks of the Taigonos Peninsula, in north-eastern Asia, celebrate annually a festival after the winter solstice. Rich men invite all their neighbours to the festival, offer a sacrifice to 'The-One-on-High', and slaughter many reindeer for their guests. If there is a shaman present he goes all round the interior of the house, beating the drum and driving away the demons (*kalau*). He searches all the people in the house, and if he finds a demon's arrow sticking in the body of one of them, he pulls it out, though naturally the arrow is invisible to common eyes. In this way he protects them against disease and death. If there is no shaman present, the demons may be expelled by the host or by a woman skilled in incantations.

Annual expulsion of demons among the Koryaks.

The negroes of Guinea annually banish the devil from all their towns with much ceremony at a time set apart for the purpose. At Axim, on the Gold Coast, this annual expulsion is preceded by a feast of eight days, during which mirth and jollity, skipping, dancing, and singing prevail, and 'a perfect lampooning liberty is allowed, and scandal so highly exalted, that they may freely sing of all the faults, villanies, and frauds of their superiors as well as inferiors, without punishment, or so much as the least interruption'. On the eighth day they hunt out the devil with a dismal cry, running after him and pelting him with sticks, stones, and whatever comes to hand. When they have driven him far enough out of the town, they all return. In this way he is expelled from more than a hundred towns at the same time. To make sure that he does not return to their houses, the women wash and scour all their wooden and

Annual expulsion of demons among the negroes of Guinea.

earthen vessels, 'to free them from all uncleanness and the devil'. A later writer tells us that 'on the Gold Coast there are stated occasions, when the people turn out *en masse* (generally at night) with clubs and torches to drive away the evil spirits from their towns. At a given signal, the whole community start up, commence a most hideous howling, beat about in every nook and corner of their dwellings, then rush into the streets, with their torches and clubs, like so many frantic maniacs, beat the air, and scream at the top of their voices, until some one announces the departure of the spirits through some gate of the town, when they are pursued several miles into the woods, and warned not to come back. After this the people breathe easier, sleep more quietly, have better health, and the town is once more cheered by an abundance of food.'

Annual expul-
sion of de-
mons at
Cape Coast
Castle.

At Cape Coast Castle, on the Gold Coast, the ceremony was witnessed on the ninth of October 1844 by an Englishman, who has described it as follows: 'To-night the annual custom of driving the evil spirit, Abonsam, out of the town has taken place. As soon as the eight o'clock gun fired in the fort the people began firing muskets in their houses, turning all their furniture out of doors, beating about in every corner of the rooms with sticks, etc., and screaming as loudly as possible, in order to frighten the devil. Being driven out of the houses, as they imagine, they sallied forth into the streets, throwing lighted torches about, shouting, screaming, beating sticks together, rattling old pans, making the most horrid noise, in order to drive him out of the town into the sea. The custom is preceded by four weeks' dead silence; no gun is allowed to be fired, no drum to be beaten, no palaver to be made between man and man. If, during these weeks, two natives should disagree and make a noise in the town, they are immediately taken before the king and fined heavily. If a dog or pig, sheep or goat be found at large in the street, it may be killed, or taken by anyone, the former owner not being allowed to demand any compensation. This silence is designed to deceive Abonsam, that, being off his guard, he may be taken by surprise, and frightened out of the place. If anyone die during the silence, his relatives are not allowed to weep until the four weeks have been completed.'

Annual
expulsion

In Central Europe it was apparently on Walpurgis Night, the Eve of May Day, above all other times that the baleful powers of the witches were exerted to the fullest extent; nothing therefore could be more natural than that men should be on their guard against them at that season, and that, not content with merely standing on their defence, they should boldly have sought to carry the war into the enemy's quarters by attacking and forcibly expelling the uncanny crew. Amongst the weapons with which they fought their invisible adversaries in these grim encounters were holy water, the fumes of incense or other combustibles, and loud noises of all kinds, particularly the clashing of metal instruments, amongst which the ringing of church bells was perhaps the most effectual. Some of these strong measures are still in use among the peasantry, or were so down to recent years, and there seems no reason to suppose that their magical virtue has been at all impaired by lapse of time. In the Tyrol, as in other places, the expulsion of the powers of evil at, this season goes by the name of 'Burning out the Witches'. It takes place on May Day, but people have been busy with their preparations for days before. On a Thursday at midnight bundles are made up of resinous splinters, black and red spotted hemlock, caperspurge, rosemary, and twigs of the sloe. These are kept and burned on May Day by men who must first have received plenary absolution from the Church. On the last three days of April all the houses are cleansed and fumigated with juniper berries and rue. On May Day, when the evening bell has rung and the twilight is falling, the ceremony of 'Burning out the Witches' begins. Men and boys make a racket with whips, bells, pots, and pans; the women carry censers; the dogs are unchained and run barking and yelping about. As soon as the church bells begin to ring, the bundles of twigs, fastened on poles, are set on fire and the incense is ignited. Then all the house-bells and dinner-bells are rung, pots and pans are clashed, dogs bark, every one must make a noise. And amid this hubbub all scream at the pitch of their voices,

> 'Witch flee, flee from here,
> Or it will go ill with thee.'

Then they run seven times round the houses, the yards, and the village. So the witches are smoked out of their lurking-places and driven away.

of witches on Walpurgis Night (the Eve of May Day).

Annual expulsion of witches on May Day in the Tyrol.

The custom of expelling the witches on Walpurgis Night is still, or was down to thirty or forty years ago, observed in many parts of Bavaria and among the Germans of Bohemia. Thus in the Böhmerwald Mountains, which divide Bavaria from Bohemia, all the young fellows of the village assemble after sunset on some height, especially at a crossroad, and crack whips for a while in unison with all their strength. This drives away the witches; for so far as the sound of the whips is heard, these maleficent beings can do no harm. The peasants believe firmly in the efficacy of this remedy. A yokel will tell his sons to be sure to crack their whips loudly and hit the witches hard; and to give more sting to every blow the whip-lashes are knotted. On returning to the village the lads often sing songs and collect contributions of eggs, lard, bread, and butter. In some places, while the young fellows are cracking their whips, the herdsmen wind their horns, and the long-drawn notes, heard far-off in the silence of night, are very effectual for banning the witches. In other places, again, the youth blow upon so-called shawms made of peeled willow-wood in front of every house, especially in front of such houses as are suspected of harbouring a witch.

In Voigtland, a bleak mountainous region of Central Germany bordering on the Frankenwald Mountains, the belief in witchcraft is still widely spread. The time when the witches are particularly dreaded is Walpurgis Night, but they play their pranks also on Midsummer Eve, St Thomas's Eve, and Christmas Eve. On these days they try to make their way into a neighbour's house and to borrow or steal something from it; and woe betide the man in whose house they have succeeded in their nefarious errand! It is on Walpurgis Night and Midsummer Eve that they ride through the air astride of pitchforks and churndashers. They also bewitch the cattle; so to protect the poor beasts from their hellish machinations the people on these days chalk up three crosses on the doors of the cattle-stalls or hang up St John's wort, marjoram, and so forth. Very often, too, the village youth turn out in a body and drive the witches away with the cracking of whips, the firing of guns, and the waving of burning besoms through the air, not to mention shouts and noises of all sorts. Such customs appear to be observed generally in Thüringen, of which Voigtland is a part. The people think that the blows of the whip actually fall on the witches hovering unseen in the air, and that so far as the cracking of the whips is heard, the crops will be good and nothing will be struck by lightning, no doubt because the witches have been banished by the sound.

iii

Oftener, however, the expelled demons are not represented at all, but are understood to be present invisibly in the material and visible vehicle which conveys them away. The vehicle which conveys away the demons may be of various kinds. A common one is a little ship or boat. Thus, in the southern district of the island of Ceram, when a whole village suffers from sickness, a small ship is made and filled with rice, tobacco, eggs, and so forth, which have been contributed by all the people. A little sail is hoisted on the ship. When all is ready, a man calls out in a very loud voice, 'O all ye sicknesses, ye smallpoxes, agues, measles, etc., who have visited us so long and wasted us so sorely, but who now cease to plague us, we have made ready this ship for you and we have furnished you with provender sufficient for the voyage. Ye shall have no lack of food nor of betel-leaves nor of areca nuts nor of tobacco. Depart, and sail away from us directly; never come near us again; but go to a land which is far from here. Let all the tides and winds waft you speedily thither, and so convey you thither that for the time to come we may live sound and well, and that we may never see the sun rise on you again.' Then ten or twelve men carry the vessel to the shore, and let it drift away with the land-breeze, feeling convinced that they are free from sickness for ever, or at least till the next time. If sickness attacks them again, they are sure it is not the same sickness, but a different one, which in due time they dismiss in the same manner. When the demon-laden bark is lost to sight, the bearers return to the village, whereupon a man cries out, 'The sicknesses are now gone, vanished, expelled, and sailed away.' At this all the people come running out of their houses, passing the word from one to the other with great joy, beating on gongs and on tinkling instruments.

At Sucla-Tirtha, in India, an earthen pot containing the accumulated sins of the people is (annually?) set adrift on the

[margin note] Demons of sickness expelled in a small ship in Ceram.

Annual
expulsion of
embodied
evils in
India, China,
and Corea.

river. Legend says that the custom originated with a wicked priest who, after atoning for his guilt by a course of austerities and expiatory ceremonies, was directed to sail upon the river in a boat with white sails. If the white sails turned black, it would be a sign that his sins were forgiven him. They did so, and he joyfully allowed the boat to drift with his sins to sea. Amongst many of the aboriginal tribes of China, a great festival is celebrated in the third month of every year. It is held by way of a general rejoicing over what the people believe to be a total annihilation of the ills of the past twelve months. The destruction is supposed to be effected in the following way. A large earthenware jar filled with gunpowder, stones, and bits of iron is buried in the earth. A train of gunpowder, communicating with the jar, is then laid; and a match being applied, the jar and its contents are blown up. The stones and bits of iron represent the ills and disasters of the past year, and the dispersion of them by the explosion is believed to remove the ills and disasters themselves. The festival is attended with much revelling and drunkenness. On New Year's Day people in Corea seek to rid themselves of all their distresses by painting images on paper, writing against them their troubles of body or mind, and afterwards giving the papers to a boy to burn. Another method of effecting the same object at the same season is to make rude dolls of straw, stuff them with a few copper coins, and throw them into the street. Whoever picks up such an effigy gets all the troubles and thereby relieves the original sufferer. Again, on the fourteenth day of the first month the Coreans fly paper kites inscribed with a wish that all the ills of the year may fly away

Annual ex-
pulsion or
destruction
of demons
embodied
in images
in Tibet.

with them. Mr George Bogle,* the English envoy sent to Tibet by Warren Hastings, witnessed the celebration of the Tibetan New Year's Day at Teshu Lumbo, the capital of the Teshu Lama. Monks walked in procession round the court to the music of cymbals, tabors, trumpets, hautboys and drums. Then others, clad in masquerade dress and wearing masks which represented the heads of animals, mostly wild beasts, danced with antic motions. 'After this, the figure of a man, chalked upon paper, was laid upon the ground. Many strange ceremonies, which to me who did not understand them appeared whimsical, were performed about it; and a great fire being kindled in a corner of the court, it was at length held over it, and being formed of combustibles, vanished with much smoke and explosion. I was told it was a figure of the devil.'

At Old Calabar on the coast of Guinea, the devils and ghosts are, or used to be, publicly expelled once in two years. Among the spirits thus driven from their haunts are the souls of all the people who died since the last lustration of the town. About three weeks or a month before the expulsion, which according to one account takes place in the month of November, rude effigies representing men and animals, such as crocodiles, leopards, elephants, bullocks, and birds, are made of wicker-work or wood, and being hung with strips of cloth and bedizened with gew-gaws, are set before the door of every house. About three o'clock in the morning of the day appointed for the ceremony the whole population turns out into the streets, and proceeds with a deafening uproar and in a state of the wildest excitement to drive all lurking devils and ghosts into the effigies, in order that they may be banished with them from the abodes of men. For this purpose bands of people roam through the streets knocking on doors, firing guns, beating drums, blowing on horns, ringing bells, clattering pots and pans, shouting and hallooing with might and main, in short making all the noise it is possible for them to raise. The hubbub goes on till the approach of dawn, when it gradually subsides and ceases altogether at sunrise. By this time the houses have been thoroughly swept, and all the frightened spirits are supposed to have huddled into the effigies or their fluttering drapery. In these wicker figures are also deposited the sweepings of the houses and the ashes of yesterday's fires. Then the demon-laden images are hastily snatched up, carried in tumultuous procession down to the brink of the river, and thrown into the water to the tuck of drums. The ebb-tide bears them away seaward, and thus the town is swept clean of ghosts and devils for another two years. This biennial expulsion of spirits goes by the name of *Ndok*, and the effigies by which it is effected are called *Nabikem* or *Nabikim*.*

The scapegoat by means of which the accumulated ills of a whole year are publicly expelled is sometimes an animal. On one day of the year the Bhotiyas of Juhar, in the Western Himalayas, take a dog, intoxicate him with spirits and bhang or hemp, and having fed him with sweetmeats, lead him round the

Biennial expulsion of demons embodied in effigies at Old Calabar.

Annual expulsion of evils in an animal scapegoat among the Garos of Assam.

village and let him loose. They then chase and kill him with sticks and stones, and believe that, when they have done so, no

Dogs as
scapegoats in
India, Scot-
land and
America.

disease or misfortune will visit the village during the year. In some parts of Breadalbane it was formerly the custom on New Year's Day to take a dog to the door, give him a bit of bread, and drive him out, saying, 'Get away, you dog! Whatever death of men or loss of cattle would happen in this house to the end of the present year, may it all light on your head!' It appears that the white dogs annually sacrificed by the Iroquois at their New Year Festival are, or have been, regarded as scapegoats. According to Mr J. V. H. Clark, who witnessed the ceremony in January 1841, on the first day of the festival all the fires in the village were extinguished, the ashes scattered to the winds, and a new fire kindled with flint and steel. On a subsequent day, men dressed in fantastic costumes went round the village, gathering the sins of the people. When the morning of the last day of the festival was come, two white dogs, decorated with red paint, wampum, feathers, and ribbons, were led out. They were soon strangled, and hung on a ladder. Firing and yelling succeeded, and half an hour later the animals were taken into a house, 'where the people's sins were transferred to them.' The carcases were afterwards burnt on a pyre of wood. According to the Revd Mr Kirkland, who wrote in the eighteenth century, the ashes of the pyre upon which one of the white dogs was burnt were carried through the village and sprinkled at the door of every house. On the Day of Atonement, which was the tenth day of the seventh month, the Jewish high-priest laid both

The Jewish
scapegoat.

his hands on the head of a live goat, confessed over it all the iniquities of the Children of Israel, and, having thereby transferred the sins of the people to the beast, sent it away into the wilderness.*

Human
scapegoats
formerly put
to death
every year in
Africa.

The scapegoat upon whom the sins of the people are periodically laid, may also be a human being.

Among the Yoruba negroes of West Africa 'the human victim chosen for sacrifice, and who may be either a free-born or a slave, a person of noble or wealthy parentage, or one of humble birth, is, after he has been chosen and marked out for the purpose, called an *Oluwo*. He is always well fed and nourished and supplied with whatever he should desire during the period of his confinement. When the occasion arrives for him to be sacrificed and offered up, he is commonly led about and paraded through the streets of the town or city of the Sovereign who would sacrifice him for the well-being of his government and of every family and individual under it, in order that he might carry off the sin, guilt, misfortune and death of all without exception. Ashes and chalk would be employed to hide his identity by the one being freely thrown over his head, and his face painted with the latter, whilst individuals would often rush out of their houses to lay their hands upon him that they might thus transfer to him their sin, guilt, trouble, and death. This parading done, he is taken through a temporary sacred shed of palm and other tree branches, and especially of the former, the Igbodu and to its first division, where many persons might follow him, and through a second where only the chiefs and other very important persons might escort and accompany him to, and to a third where only the Babalawo [priest] and his official assistant, the Ajigbona, are permitted to enter with him. Here, after he himself has given out or started his last song, which is to be taken up by the large assembly of people who will have been waiting to hear his last word or his last groan, his head is taken off and his blood offered to the gods. The announcement of his last word or his last groan heard and taken up by the people, would be a signal for joy, gladness, and thanks giving, and for drum beating and dancing, as an expression of their gratification because their sacrifice has been accepted, the divine wrath is appeased, and the prospect of prosperity or increased prosperity assured.'*

Sometimes the scapegoat is a divine animal. The people of Malabar share the Hindoo reverence for the cow, to kill and eat which 'they esteem to be a crime as heinous as homicide or wilful murder.' Nevertheless the 'Bramans transfer the sins of the people into one or more Cows, which are then carry'd away, both the Cows and the Sins wherewith these Beasts are charged, to what place the Braman shall appoint.' When the ancient Egyptians sacrificed a bull, they invoked upon its head all the evils that might otherwise befall themselves and the land of Egypt, and thereupon they either sold the bull's head to the Greeks or cast it into the river. Now, it cannot be said that in the times known to us the Egyptians worshipped bulls in general, for they seem to have commonly killed and eaten them.

Divine animals as scapegoats in India and ancient Egypt.

But a good many circumstances point to the conclusion that originally all cattle, bulls as well as cows, were held sacred by the Egyptians. For not only were all cows esteemed holy by them and never sacrificed, but even bulls might not be sacrificed unless they had certain natural marks; a priest examined every bull before it was sacrificed; if it had the proper marks, he put his seal on the animal in token that it might be sacrificed; and if a man sacrificed a bull which had not been sealed, he was put to death. Moreover, the worship of the black bulls Apis and Mnevis, especially the former, played an important part in Egyptian religion; all bulls that died a natural death were carefully buried in the suburbs of the cities, and their bones were afterwards collected from all parts of Egypt and interred in a single spot; and at the sacrifice of a bull in the great rites of Isis all the worshippers beat their breasts and mourned. On the whole, then, we are perhaps entitled to infer that bulls were originally, as cows were always, esteemed sacred by the Egyptians, and that the slain bull upon whose head they laid the misfortunes of the people was once a divine scapegoat.

Divine men as scapegoats among the Gonds of India and the Albanians of the Caucasus.

Lastly, the scapegoat may be a divine man. Thus, in November the Gonds of India worship Ghansyam Deo, the protector of the crops, and at the festival the god himself is said to descend on the head of one of the worshippers, who is suddenly seized with a kind of fit and, after staggering about, rushes off into the jungle, where it is believed that, if left to himself, he would die mad. However, they bring him back, but he does not recover his senses for one or two days. The people think that one man is thus singled out as a scapegoat for the sins of the rest of the village. In the temple of the Moon the Albanians of the Eastern Caucasus kept a number of sacred slaves, of whom many were inspired and prophesied. When one of these men exhibited more than usual symptoms of inspiration or insanity, and wandered solitary up and down the woods, like the Gond in the jungle, the high priest had him bound with a sacred chain and maintained him in luxury for a year. At the end of the year he was anointed with unguents and led forth to be sacrificed. A man whose business it was to slay these human victims and to whom practice had given dexterity, advanced from the crowd and thrust a sacred spear into the victim's side, piercing his heart. From the manner in which the slain man fell, omens were drawn as to the welfare of the commonwealth. Then the body was carried to a certain spot where all the people stood upon it as a purificatory ceremony. This last circumstance clearly indicates that the sins of the people were transferred to the victim, just as the Jewish priest transferred the sins of the people to the scapegoat by laying his hands on the animal's head; and since the man was believed to be possessed by the divine spirit, we have here an undoubted example of a mangod slain to take away the sins and misfortunes of the people.

In Tibet the ceremony of the scapegoat presents some remarkable features. The Tibetan new year begins with the new moon which appears about the fifteenth of February. For twenty-three days afterwards the government of Lhasa, the capital, is taken out of the hands of the ordinary rulers and entrusted to the monk of the Debang monastery who offers to pay the highest sum for the privilege. The successful bidder is called the Jalno, and he announces his accession to power in person, going through the streets of Lhasa with a silver stick in his hand. Monks from all the neighbouring monasteries and temples assemble to pay him homage. The Jalno exercises his authority in the most arbitrary manner for his own benefit, as all the fines which he exacts are his by purchase. The profit he makes is about ten times the amount of the purchase money. His men go about the streets in order to discover any conduct on the part of the inhabitants that can be found fault with. Every house in Lhasa is taxed at this time, and the slightest offence is punished with unsparing rigour by fines. This severity of the Jalno drives all working classes out of the city till the twenty-three days are over. But if the laity go out, the clergy come in. All the Buddhist monasteries of the country for miles round about open their gates and disgorge their inmates. All the roads that lead down into Lhasa from the neighbouring mountains are full of monks hurrying to the capital, some on foot, some on horseback, some riding asses or lowing oxen, all carrying their prayer-books and culinary utensils. In such multitudes do they come that the streets and squares of the city are encumbered with their swarms, and incarnadined with their red cloaks. The disorder and confusion are indescribable. Bands of the holy men traverse the streets chanting prayers or uttering wild cries. They meet, they jostle, they quarrel, they fight;

Annual human scapegoats in Tibet.

The Jalno, the temporary ruler of Lhasa.

bloody noses, black eyes, and broken heads are freely given and received. All day long, too, from before the peep of dawn till after darkness has fallen, these red-cloaked monks hold services in the dim incense-laden air of the great Machindranath temple, the cathedral of Lhasa; and thither they crowd thrice a day to receive their doles of tea and soup and money. The cathedral is a vast building, standing in the centre of the city, and surrounded by bazaars and shops. The idols in it are richly inlaid with gold and precious stones.

The Jalno and the King of the Years. Twenty-four days after the Jalno has ceased to have authority, he assumes it again, and for ten days acts in the same arbitrary manner as before. On the first of the ten days the priests again assemble at the cathedral, pray to the gods to prevent sickness and other evils among the people, 'and, as a peace-offering, sacrifice one man. The man is not killed purposely, but the ceremony he undergoes often proves fatal. Grain is thrown against his head, and his face is painted half white, half black.' Thus grotesquely disguised, and carrying a coat of skin on his arm, he is called the King of the Years, and sits daily in the market-place, where he helps himself to whatever he likes and goes about shaking a black yak's tail over the people, who thus transfer their bad luck to him. On the tenth day, all the troops in Lhasa march to the great temple and form in line before it. The King of the Years is brought forth from the temple and receives small donations from the assembled multitude. He then ridicules the Jalno, saying to him, 'What we perceive through the five senses is no illusion. All you teach is untrue,' and the like. The Jalno, who represents the Grand Lama for the time being, contests these heretical opinions; the dispute waxes warm, and at last both agree to decide the questions at issue by a cast of the dice, the Jalno offering to change places with the scapegoat should the throw be against him. If the King of the Years wins, much evil is prognosticated; but if the Jalno wins, there is great rejoicing, for it proves that his adversary has been accepted by the gods as a victim to bear all the sins of the people of Lhasa. Fortune, however, always favours the Jalno, who throws sixes with unvarying success, while his opponent turns up only ones. Nor is this so extraordinary as at first sight it might appear; for the Jalno's dice are marked with nothing but sixes and his adversary's with nothing but ones. When he sees the finger of Providence thus plainly pointed against him, the King of the Years is terrified and flees away upon a white horse, with a white dog, a white bird, salt, and so forth, which have all been provided for him by the government. His face is still painted half white and half black, and he still wears his leathern coat. The whole populace pursues him, hooting, yelling, and firing blank shots in volleys after him. Thus driven out of the city, he is detained for seven days in the great chamber of horrors at the Samyas monastery, surrounded by monstrous and terrific images of devils and skins of huge serpents and wild beasts. Thence he goes away into the mountains of Chetang, where he has to remain an outcast for several months or a year in a narrow den. If he dies before the time is out, the people say it is an auspicious omen; but if he survives, he may return to Lhasa and play the part of scapegoat over again the following year.

Expulsion of the King of the Years.

This quaint ceremonial, still annually observed in the secluded capital of Buddhism—the Rome of Asia—is interesting because it exhibits, in a clearly marked religious stratification, a series of divine redeemers themselves redeemed, of vicarious sacrifices vicariously atoned for, of gods undergoing a process of fossilization, who, while they retain the privileges, have disburdened themselves of the pains and penalties of divinity. In the Jalno we may without undue straining discern a successor of those temporary kings, those mortal gods, who purchase a short lease of power and glory at the price of their lives. That he is the temporary substitute of the Grand Lama is certain; that he is, or was once, liable to act as scapegoat for the people is made nearly certain by his offer to change places with the real scapegoat—the King of the Years—if the arbitrament of the dice should go against him. It is true that the conditions under which the question is now put to the hazard have reduced the offer to an idle form. But such forms are no mere mushroom growths, springing up of themselves in a night. If they are now lifeless formalities, empty husks devoid of significance, we may be sure that they once had a life and a meaning; if at the present day they are blind alleys leading nowhere, we may be certain that in former days they were paths that led somewhere, if only to death. That death was the goal to which of old the Tibetan scapegoat passed after his brief period of licence in the

The Grand Lama, the Jalno, and the King of the Years in their relations to each other.

Probability that of old the Tibetan scapegoat was put to death as a substitute for the Grand Lama.

market-place, is a conjecture that has much to commend it. Analogy suggests it; the blank shots fired after him, the statement that the ceremony often proves fatal, the belief that his death is a happy omen, all confirm it. We need not wonder then that the Jalno, after paying so dear to act as deputy-deity for a few weeks, should have preferred to die by deputy rather than in his own person when his time was up. The painful but necessary duty was accordingly laid on some poor devil, some social outcast, some wretch with whom the world had gone hard, who readily agreed to throw away his life at the end of a few days if only he might have his fling in the meantime. For observe that while the time allowed to the original deputy—the Jalno—was measured by weeks, the time allowed to the deputy's deputy was cut down to days, ten days according to one authority, seven days according to another. So short a rope was doubtless thought a long enough tether for so black or sickly a sheep; so few sands in the hour-glass, slipping so fast away, sufficed for one who had wasted so many precious years. Hence in the jack-pudding who now masquerades with motley countenance in the market-place of Lhasa, sweeping up misfortune with a black yak's tail, we may fairly see the substitute of a substitute, the vicar of a vicar, the proxy on whose back the heavy burden was laid when it had been lifted from nobler shoulders. But the clue, if we have followed it aright, does not stop at the Jalno; it leads straight back to the pope of Lhasa himself, the Grand Lama, of whom the Jalno is merely the temporary vicar. The analogy of many customs in many lands points to the conclusion that, if this human divinity stoops to resign his ghostly power for a time into the hands of a substitute, it is, or rather was once, for no other reason than that the substitute might die in his stead. Thus through the mist of ages unillumined by the lamp of history, the tragic figure of the pope of Buddhism—God's vicar on earth for Asia—looms dim and sad as the man-god who bore his people's sorrows, the Good Shepherd who laid down his life for the sheep.

iv

The foregoing survey of the custom of publicly expelling the accumulated evils of a village or town or country suggests a few general observations.

In the first place, it will not be disputed that what I have called the immediate and the mediate expulsions of evil are identical in intention; in other words, that whether the evils are conceived of as invisible or as embodied in a material form, is a circumstance entirely subordinate to the main object of the ceremony, which is simply to effect a total clearance of all the ills that have been infesting a people. If any link were wanting to connect the two kinds of expulsion, it would be furnished by such a practice as that of sending the evils away in a litter or a boat. For here, on the one hand, the evils are invisible and intangible; and, on the other hand, there is a visible and tangible vehicle to convey them away. And a scapegoat is nothing more than such a vehicle.

On scapegoats in general.

In the second place, when a general clearance of evils is resorted to periodically, the interval between the celebrations of the ceremony is commonly a year, and the time of year when the ceremony takes place usually coincides with some well-marked change of season, such as the beginning or end of winter in the arctic and temperate zones, and the beginning or end of the rainy season in the tropics. The increased mortality which such climatic changes are apt to produce, especially amongst ill-fed, ill-clothed, and ill-housed savages, is set down by primitive man to the agency of demons, who must accordingly be expelled. Hence, in the tropical regions of New Britain and Peru, the devils are or were driven out at the beginning of the rainy season; hence, on the dreary coasts of Baffin Land, they are banished at the approach of the bitter arctic winter. When a tribe has taken to husbandry, the time for the general expulsion of devils is naturally made to agree with one of the great epochs of the agricultural year, as sowing, or harvest; but, as these epochs themselves naturally coincide with changes of season, it does not follow that the transition from the hunting or pastoral to the agricultural life involves any alteration in the time of celebrating this great annual rite. But, at whatever season of the year it is held, the general expulsion of devils commonly marks the beginning of the new year. For, before entering on a new year, people are anxious to rid themselves of the troubles that have harassed them in the past; hence it comes about that in so many communities the beginning of the new year is inaugurated with a solemn and public banishment of evil spirits.

In the third place, it is to be observed that this public and periodic expulsion of devils is commonly preceded or followed by a period of general license, during which the ordinary restraints of society are thrown aside, and all offences, short of the gravest, are allowed to pass unpunished. The extraordinary relaxation of all ordinary rules of conduct on such occasions is doubtless to be explained by the general clearance of evils which precedes or follows it. On the one hand, when a general riddance of evil and absolution from all sin is in immediate prospect, men are encouraged to give the rein to their passions, trusting that the coming ceremony will wipe out the score which they are running up so fast. On the other hand, when the ceremony has just taken place, men's minds are freed from the oppressive sense, under which they generally labour, of an atmosphere surcharged with devils; and in the first revulsion of joy they overleap the limits commonly imposed by custom and morality. When the ceremony takes place at harvest-time, the elation of feeling which it excites is further stimulated by the state of physical wellbeing produced by an abundant supply of food.

Fourthly, the employment of a divine man or animal as a scapegoat is especially to be noted; indeed, we are here directly concerned with the custom of banishing evils only in so far as these evils are believed to be transferred to a god who is afterwards slain. For, as has already been pointed out, the custom of killing a god dates from so early a period of human history that in later ages, even when the custom continues to be practised, it is liable to be misinterpreted. The divine character of the animal or man is forgotten, and he comes to be regarded merely as an ordinary victim. This is especially likely to be the case when it is a divine man who is killed. For when a nation becomes civilised, if it does not drop human sacrifices altogether, it at least selects as victims only such wretches as would be put to death at any rate. Thus the killing of a god may sometimes come to be confounded with the execution of a criminal.

If we ask why a dying god should be chosen to take upon himself and carry away the sins and sorrows of the people, it may be suggested that in the practice of using the divinity as a scapegoat we have a combination of two customs which were at one time distinct and independent. On the one hand we have seen that it has been customary to kill the human or animal god in order to save his divine life from being weakened by the inroads of age. On the other hand we have seen that it has been customary to have a general expulsion of evils and sins once a year. Now, if it occurred to people to combine these two customs, the result would be the employment of the dying god as a scapegoat. He was killed, not originally to take away sin, but to save the divine life from the degeneracy of old age; but, since he had to be killed at any rate, people may have thought that they might as well seize the opportunity to lay upon him the burden of their sufferings and sins, in order that he might bear it away with him to the unknown world beyond the grave.

The use of the divinity as a scapegoat clears up the ambiguity which, as we saw, appears to hang about the European folk-custom of 'carrying out Death.' Grounds have been shown for believing that in this ceremony the so-called Death was originally the spirit of vegetation, who was annually slain in spring, in order that he might come to life again with all the vigour of youth. But, as I pointed out, there are certain features in the ceremony which are not explicable on this hypothesis alone. Such are the marks of joy with which the effigy of Death is carried out to be buried or burnt, and the fear and abhorrence of it manifested by the bearers. But these features become at once intelligible if we suppose that the Death was not merely the dying god of vegetation, but also a public scapegoat, upon whom were laid all the evils that had afflicted the people during the past year. Joy on such an occasion is natural and appropriate; and if the dying god appears to be the object of that fear and abhorrence which are properly due not to himself, but to the sins and misfortunes with which he is laden, this arises merely from the difficulty of distinguishing, or at least of marking the distinction, between the bearer and the burden.

When the burden is of a baleful character, the bearer of it will be feared and shunned just as much as if he were himself instinct with those dangerous properties of which, as it happens, he is only the vehicle. Similarly we have seen that disease-laden and sin-laden boats are dreaded and shunned by East Indian peoples. Again, the view that in these popular customs the Death is a scapegoat as well as a representative of the divine spirit of vegetation derives some support from the circumstance that its expulsion is always celebrated in spring and chiefly by Slavonic peoples. For the Slavonic year began in spring; and thus, in one of its aspects, the ceremony of 'carrying out Death' would be an example of the widespread custom of expelling the accumulated evils of the old year before entering on a new one.

CHAPTER 2

ANCIENT SCAPEGOATS

i

WE are now prepared to notice the use of the human scapegoat in classical antiquity. Every year on the fourteenth of March a man clad in skins was led in procession through the streets of Rome, beaten with long white rods, and driven out of the city. He was called Mamurius Veturius, that is, 'the old Mars,' and as the ceremony took place on the day preceding the first full moon of the old Roman year (which began on the first of March), the skin-clad man must have represented the Mars of the past year, who was driven out at the beginning of a new one. Now Mars was originally not a god of war but of vegetation. For it was to Mars that the Roman husbandman prayed for the prosperity of his corn and his vines, his fruit-trees and his copses; it was to Mars that the priestly college of the Arval Brothers, whose business it was to sacrifice for the growth of the crops, addressed their petitions almost exclusively; and it was to Mars, as we saw,* that a horse was sacrificed in October to secure an abundant harvest. Moreover, it was to Mars, under his title of 'Mars of the woods' (*Mars Silvanus*), that farmers offered sacrifice for the welfare of their cattle. Once more, the consecration of the vernal month of March to Mars seems to point him out as the deity of the sprouting vegetation. Thus the Roman custom of expelling the old Mars at the beginning of the new year in spring is identical with the Slavonic custom of 'carrying out Death', if the view here taken of the latter custom is correct. The similarity of the Roman and Slavonic customs has been already remarked by scholars, who appear, however, to have taken Mamurius Veturius and the corresponding figures in the Slavonic ceremonies to be representatives of the old year rather than of the old god of vegetation. It is possible that ceremonies of this kind may have come to be thus interpreted in later times even by the people who practised them. But the personification of a period of time is too abstract an idea to be primitive. However, in the Roman, as in the Slavonic, ceremony,

Annual expulsion of 'the Old Mars' in the month of March in ancient Rome.

the representative of the god appears to have been treated not only as a deity of vegetation but also as a scapegoat. His expulsion implies this; for there is no reason why the god of vegetation, as such, should be expelled the city. But it is otherwise if he is also a scapegoat; it then becomes necessary to drive him beyond the boundaries, that he may carry his sorrowful burden away to other lands. And, in fact, Mamurius Veturius appears to have been driven away to the land of the Oscans, the enemies of Rome.

'The Old Mars' seems to have been beaten by the Salii, the dancing priests of Mars.

The blows with which the 'old Mars' was expelled the city seem to have been administered by the dancing priests of Mars, the Salii. At least we know that in their songs these priests made mention of Mamurius Veturius; and we are told that on a day dedicated to him they beat a hide with rods. It is therefore highly probably that the hide which they drubbed on that day was the one worn by the representative of the deity whose name they simultaneously chanted. Thus on the fourteenth day of March every year Rome witnessed the curious spectacle of the human incarnation of a god chased by the god's own priests with blows from the city. The rite becomes at least intelligible on the theory that the man so beaten and expelled stood for the outworn deity of vegetation, who had to be replaced by a fresh and vigorous young divinity at the beginning of a New Year, when everywhere around in field and meadow, in wood and thicket the vernal flowers, the sprouting grass, and the opening buds and blossoms testified to the stirring of new life in nature after the long torpor and stagnation of winter. The dancing priests of the god derived their name of Salii from the leaps or dances which they were bound to execute as a solemn religious ceremony every year in the Comitium, the centre of Roman political life. Twice a year, in the spring month of March and the autumn month of October, they discharged this sacred duty; and as they did so they invoked Saturn, the Roman god of sowing. As the Romans sowed the corn both in spring and autumn, and as down to the present time in Europe superstitious rustics are wont to dance and leap high in spring for the purpose of making the crops grow high, we may conjecture that the leaps and dances performed by the Salii, the priests of the old Italian god of vegetation, were similarly supposed to quicken the growth of the corn by homoeopathic or imitative

The dances of the Salii in spring and autumn were perhaps intended to quicken the growth of the corn sown at these seasons.

magic. The Salii were not limited to Rome; similar colleges of dancing priests are known to have existed in many towns of ancient Italy; everywhere, we may conjecture, they were supposed to contribute to the fertility of the earth by their leaps and dances. Nor was the martial equipment of the Salii so alien to this peaceful function as a modern reader might naturally suppose. Each of them wore on his head a peaked helmet of bronze, and at his side a sword; on his left arm he carried a shield of a peculiar shape, and in his right hand he wielded a staff with which he smote on the shield till it rang again. Such weapons in priestly hands may be turned against spiritual foes; in the preceding pages we have met with many examples of the use of material arms to rout the host of demons who oppress the imagination of primitive man, and we have seen that the clash and clangour of metal is often deemed particularly effective in putting these baleful beings to flight. May it not have been so with the martial priests of Mars? We know that they paraded the city for days together in a regular order, taking up their quarters for the night at a different place each day; and as they went they danced in triple time, singing and clashing on their shields and taking their time from a fugleman, who skipped and postured at their head. We may conjecture that in so doing they were supposed to be expelling the powers of evil which had accumulated during the preceding year or six months, and which the people pictured to themselves in the form of demons lurking in the houses, temples, and the other edifices of the city. In savage communities such tumultuous and noisy processions often parade the village for a similar purpose. Similarly, we have seen that among the Iroquois men in fantastic costume used to go about collecting the sins of the people as a preliminary to transferring them to the scapegoat dogs; and we have met with many examples of armed men rushing about the streets and houses to drive out demons and evils of all kinds. Why should it not have been so also in ancient Rome? The religion of the old Romans is full of relics of savagery.

The armed processions of the Salii may have been intended to rout out and expel the demons lurking in the city.

If there is any truth in this conjecture, we may suppose that, as priests of a god who manifested his power in the vegetation of spring, the Salii turned their attention above all to the demons of blight and infertility, who might be thought by their

The demons expelled by the Salii may have been above all the

demons of
blight and in-
fertility. This
conjecture is
supported by
analogous
ceremonies
performed by
savages for
the purpose
of driving off
the demons
that would
harm the
crops.

maleficent activity to counteract the genial influence of the
kindly god and to endanger the farmer's prospects in the
coming summer or winter. Thus, at the time of sowing
the Khonds drive out the 'evil spirits, spoilers of the seed' from
every house in the village, the expulsion being effected by
young men who beat each other and strike the air violently
with long sticks. If I am right in connecting the vernal and
the autumnal processions of the Salii with the vernal and the
autumnal sowing, the analogy between the Khond and the
Roman customs would be very close. In West Africa the fields
of the King of Whydah, according to an old French traveller,
'are hoed and sowed before any of his subjects has leave to hoe
and sow a foot of his own lands. These labours are performed
thrice a year. The chiefs lead their people before the king's
palace at daybreak, and there they sing and dance for a full
quarter of an hour. Half of these people are armed as in a day
of battle, the other half have only their farm tools. They go all
together singing and dancing to the scene of their labours, and
there, keeping time to the sound of the instruments, they work
with such speed and neatness that it is a pleasure to behold. At
the end of the day they return and dance before the king's
palace. This exercise refreshes them and does them more good
than all the repose they could take.'* From this account we
might infer that the dancing was merely a recreation of the
field-labourers, and that the music of the band had no other
object than to animate them in their work by enabling them to
ply their mattocks in time to its stirring strains. But this
inference, though it seems to have been drawn by the traveller
who has furnished the account, would probably be erroneous.
For if half of the men were armed as for war, what were they
doing in the fields all the time that the others were digging? A
clue to unravel the mystery is furnished by the description
which a later French traveller gives of a similar scene witnessed
by him near Timbo in French Guinea. He saw some natives at
work preparing the ground for sowing. 'It is a very curious
spectacle: fifty or sixty blacks in a line, with bent backs, are
smiting the earth simultaneously with their little iron tools,
which gleam in the sun. Ten paces in front of them, marching
backwards, the women sing a well marked air, clapping their
hands as for a dance, and the hoes keep time to the song.

Between the workers and the singers a man runs and dances, crouching on his hams like a clown, while he whirls about his musket and performs other manœuvres with it. Two others dance, also pirouetting and smiting the earth here and there with their little hoe. All that is necessary for exorcising the spirits and causing the grain to sprout.' Here, while the song of the women gives the time to the strokes of the hoes, the dances and other antics of the armed man and his colleagues are intended to exorcise or ward off the spirits who might interfere with the diggers and so prevent the grain from sprouting.

Again, an old traveller in southern India tells us that 'the men of Calicut, when they wish to sow rice, observe this practice. First, they plough the land with oxen as we do, and when they sow the rice in the field they have all the instruments of the city continually sounding and making merry. They also have ten or twelve men clothed like devils, and these unite in making great rejoicing with the players on the instruments, in order that the devil may make that rice very productive.' We may suspect that the noisy music is played and the mummers cut their capers for the purpose rather of repelling demons than of inducing them to favour the growth of the rice. However, where our information is so scanty it would be rash to dogmatize. Perhaps the old traveller was right in thinking that the mummers personated devils. Among the Kayans of Central Borneo men disguised in wooden masks and great masses of green foliage certainly play the part of demons for the purpose of promoting the growth of the rice just before the seed is committed to the ground; and it is notable that among the performances which they give on this occasion are war dances. Again, among the Kaua and Kobeua Indians of North-Western Brazil masked men who represent spirits or demons of fertility perform dances or rather pantomimes for the purpose of stimulating the growth of plants, quickening the wombs of women, and promoting the multiplication of animals.

In the Austrian provinces of Salzburg and Tyrol bands of mummers wearing grotesque masks, with bells jingling on their persons, and carrying long sticks or poles in their hands, used formerly to run and leap about on certain days of the year for the purpose of procuring good crops. They were called *Perchten*,* a name derived from Perchta, Berchta, or Percht, a

Dances of masked men in India, Borneo, and South America to promote the growth of the crops.

Dances of mummers called Perchten in Austria for the good of the crops.

The mythical old woman called Perchta.

mythical old woman, whether goddess or elf, who is well known all over South Germany; Mrs Perchta (*Frau Perchta*), as they call her, is to be met with in Elsace, Swabia, Bavaria, Austria, and Switzerland, but nowhere, perhaps, so commonly as in Salzburg and the Tyrol. In the Tyrol she appears as a little old woman with a very wrinkled face, bright lively eyes, and a long hooked nose; her hair is dishevelled, her garments tattered and torn. She goes about especially during the twelve days from Christmas to Twelfth Night (Epiphany), above all on the Eve of Twelfth Night, which is often called Perchta's Day. Many precautions must be observed during these mystic days in order not to incur her displeasure, for she is mischievous to man and beast. On the Eve of Twelfth Night everybody should eat pancakes baked of meal and milk or water. If anybody does not do so, old Mrs Perchta comes and slits up his stomach, takes out the other food, fills up the vacuity so created with a tangled skein and bricks, and then sews up the orifice neatly, using, singularly enough, a ploughshare for a needle and an iron chain for thread. In other or the same places she does the same thing to anybody who does not eat herrings and dumplings on Twelfth Night. Some say that she rides on the storm like the Wild Huntsman, followed by a boisterous noisy pack, and carrying off people into far countries. Yet withal old Mrs Perchta has her redeeming qualities. Good children who spin diligently and learn their lessons she rewards with nuts and sugar plums. It has even been affirmed that she makes the ploughed land fruitful and causes the cattle to thrive.

The running and leaping of the *Perchten* mummers on Twelfth Night.

The processions of maskers who took their name of *Perchten* from this quaint creation of the popular fancy were known as *Perchten*-running or *Perchten*-leaping from the runs and leaps which the men took in their wild headlong course through the streets and over the fields. They appear to have been held in all the Alpine regions of Germany, but are best known to us in the Tyrol and Salzburg.

The Ugly *Perchten* in Salzburg.

In the province of Salzburg the *Perchten* mummers are also divided into two sets, the Beautiful *Perchten* and the Ugly *Perchten*. The Ugly *Perchten* are properly speaking twelve young men dressed in black sheepskins and wearing hoods of badger-skins and grotesque wooden masks, which represent either coarse human features with long teeth and horns, or else the features of fabulous animals with beaks and bristles or movable jaws. They all carry bells, both large and small, fastened to broad leathern girdles. The procession was headed by a man with a big drum, and after him came lads bearing huge torches and lanterns fastened to tall poles; for in Salzburg or some parts of it these mummers played their pranks by night. Behind the torch-bearers came two Fools, a male and a female, the latter acted by a lad in woman's clothes. The male Fool carried a sausage-like roll, with which he struck at all women or girls of his acquaintance when they shewed themselves at the open doors or windows. Along with the *Perchten* themselves went a train of young fellows cracking whips, blowing horns, or jingling bells. The ways might be miry and the night pitch dark, but with flaring lights the procession swept rapidly by, the men leaping along with the help of their long sticks and waking the echoes of the slumbering valley by their loud uproar. From time to time they stopped at a farm, danced and cut their capers before the house, for which they were rewarded by presents of food and strong drink; to offer them money would have been an insult. By midnight the performance came to an end, and the tired maskers dispersed to their homes.

Unlike their Ugly namesakes, who seem now to be extinct, the Beautiful *Perchten* still parade from time to time among the peasantry of the Salzburg highlands; but the intervals between their appearances are irregular, varying from four to seven years or more. Unlike the Ugly *Perchten*, they wear no masks and appear in full daylight, always on Perchta's Day (Twelfth Night, the sixth of January) and the two following Sundays. They are attended by a train of followers who make a great din with bells, whips, pipes, horns, rattles, and chains. Amongst them one or two clowns, clothed in white and wearing tall pointed hats of white felt with many jingling bells attached to them, play a conspicuous part. They carry each a sausage-shaped roll stuffed with tow, and with this instrument they strike lightly such women and girls among the spectators as they desire particularly to favour. Another attendant carries the effigy of a baby in swaddling bands, made of linen rags, and fastened to a string; this effigy he throws at women and girls and then pulls back again, but he does this only to women and girls whom he respects and to whom he wishes well. At

St Johann the *Perchten* carry drawn swords; each is attended by a lad dressed as a woman; and they are followed by men clad in black sheepskins, wearing the masks of devils, and holding chains in their hands.

These masquerades originally intended both to stimulate vegetation in spring and to expel demons.

Surveying these masquerades and processions, as they have been or still are celebrated in modern Europe, we may say in general that they appear to have been originally intended both to stimulate the growth of vegetation in spring and to expel the demoniac or other evil influences which were thought to have accumulated during the preceding winter or year; and that these two motives of stimulation and expulsion, blended and perhaps confused together, appear to explain the quaint costumes of the mummers, the multitudinous noises which they make, and the blows which they direct either at invisible foes or at the visible and tangible persons of their fellows. In the latter case the beating may be supposed to serve as a means of forcibly freeing the sufferers from the demons or other evil things that cling to them unseen.

Application of these conclusions to the expulsion of 'the Old Mars' in ancient Rome.

To apply these conclusions to the Roman custom of expelling Mamurius Veturius or 'the Old Mars' every year in spring, we may say that they lend some support to the theory which sees in 'the Old Mars' the outworn deity of vegetation driven away to make room, either for a younger and more vigorous personification of vernal life, or perhaps for the return of the same deity refreshed and renovated by the treatment to which he had been subjected, and particularly by the vigorous application of the rod to his sacred person. For, as we shall see presently, King Solomon was by no means singular in his opinion of the refreshing influence of a sound thrashing. So far as 'the Old Mars' was supposed to carry away with him the accumulated weaknesses and other evils of the past year, so far would he serve as a public scapegoat, like the effigy in the Slavonic custom of 'Carrying out Death', which appears not only to represent the vegetation-spirit of the past year, but also to act as a scapegoat, carrying away with it a heavy load of suffering, misfortune, and death.

ii

Human scapegoats in

The ancient Greeks were also familiar with the use of a human scapegoat. In Plutarch's native town of Chaeronea a ceremony of this kind was performed by the chief magistrate at the Town Hall, and by each householder at his own home. It was called the 'expulsion of hunger'. A slave was beaten with rods of the *agnus castus*, and turned out of doors with the words, 'Out with hunger, and in with wealth and health.' When Plutarch held the office of chief magistrate of his native town he performed this ceremony at the Town Hall, and he has recorded the discussion to which the custom afterwards gave rise.* _{ancient Greece. The 'Expulsion of Hunger' at Chaeronea.}

But in civilized Greece the custom of the scapegoat took darker forms than the innocent rite over which the amiable and pious Plutarch presided. Whenever Marseilles, one of the busiest and most brilliant of Greek colonies, was ravaged by a plague, a man of the poorer classes used to offer himself as a scapegoat. For a whole year he was maintained at the public expense, being fed on choice and pure food. At the expiry of the year he was dressed in sacred garments, decked with holy branches, and led through the whole city, while prayers were uttered that all the evils of the people might fall on his head. He was then cast out of the city or stoned to death by the people outside of the walls.* _{Human scapegoats at Marseilles.} The Athenians regularly maintained a number of degraded and useless beings at the public expense; and when any calamity, such as plague, drought, or famine, befell the city, they sacrificed two of these outcasts as scapegoats. One of the victims was sacrificed for the men and the other for the women. The former wore round his neck a string of black, the latter a string of white figs. Sometimes, it seems, the victim slain on behalf of the women was a woman. They were led about the city and then sacrificed, apparently by being stoned to death outside the city.* But such sacrifices were not confined to extraordinary occasions of public calamity; it appears that every year, at the festival of the Thargelia in May, two victims, one for the men and one for the women, were led out of Athens and stoned to death. _{Human scapegoats put to death at Athens.} The city of Abdera in Thrace was publicly purified once a year, and one of the burghers, set apart for the purpose, was stoned to death as a scapegoat or vicarious sacrifice for the life of all the others; six days before his execution he was excommunicated, 'in order that he alone might bear the sins of all the people'. _{Human scapegoats annually stoned to death at Abdera.}

From the Lover's Leap, a white bluff at the southern end of their island, the Leucadians used annually to hurl a criminal

Annual
human scape-
goats in Leu-
cadia.

into the sea as a scapegoat. But to lighten his fall they fastened live birds and feathers to him, and a flotilla of small boats waited below to catch him and convey him beyond the boundary. Probably these humane precautions were a mitigation of an earlier custom of flinging the scapegoat into the sea to drown. The Leucadian ceremony took place at the time of a sacrifice to Apollo, who had a temple or sanctuary on the spot. Elsewhere it was customary to cast a young man every year into the sea, with the prayer, 'Be thou our offscouring.' This ceremony was supposed to rid the people of the evils by which they were beset, or according to a somewhat different interpretation it redeemed them by paying the debt they owed to the sea-god.

Human scape-
goats an-
nually put to
death at the
festival of
the Thargelia
in Asia
Minor.

As practised by the Greeks of Asia Minor in the sixth century before our era, the custom of the scapegoat was as follows. When a city suffered from plague, famine, or other public calamity, an ugly or deformed person was chosen to take upon himself all the evils which afflicted the community. He was brought to a suitable place, where dried figs, a barley loaf, and cheese were put into his hand. These he ate. Then he was beaten seven times upon his genital organs with squills and branches of the wild fig and other wild trees, while the flutes played a particular tune. Afterwards he was burned on a pyre built of the wood of forest trees; and his ashes were cast into the sea. A similar custom appears to have been annually celebrated by the Asiatic Greeks at the harvest festival of the Thargelia.

Mannhardt's
interpreta-
tion of the
custom of
beating the
human scape-
goat on the
genitals: it
was intended
to free his re-
productive
energies
from any re-
straint laid
on them by
demoniacal
or other ma-
lignant
agency.

In the ritual just described the scourging of the victim with squills, branches of the wild fig, and so forth, cannot have been intended to aggravate his sufferings, otherwise any stick would have been good enough to beat him with. The true meaning of this part of the ceremony has been explained by W. Mannhardt. He points out that the ancients attributed to squills a magical power of averting evil influences, and that accordingly they hung them up at the doors of their houses and made use of them in purificatory rites. Hence the Arcadian custom of whipping the image of Pan with squills at a festival, or whenever the hunters returned empty-handed,* must have been meant, not to punish the god, but to purify him from the harmful influences which were impeding him in the exercise of his divine functions as a god who should supply the hunter with game. Similarly the object of beating the human scapegoat on the genital organs with squills and so on, must have been to release his reproductive energies from any restraint or spell under which they might be laid by demoniacal or other malignant agency; and as the Thargelia at which he was annually sacrificed was an early harvest festival celebrated in May, we must recognize in him a representative of the creative and fertilizing god of vegetation. The representative of the god was annually slain for the purpose I have indicated, that of maintaining the divine life in perpetual vigour, untainted by the weakness of age; and before he was put to death it was not unnatural to stimulate his reproductive powers in order that these might be transmitted in full activity to his successor, the new god or new embodiment of the old god, who was doubtless supposed immediately to take the place of the one slain. Similar reasoning would lead to a similar treatment of the scapegoat on special occasions, such as drought or famine. If the crops did not answer to the expectation of the husbandman, this would be attributed to some failure in the generative powers of the god whose function it was to produce the fruits of the earth. It might be thought that he was under a spell or was growing old and feeble. Accordingly he was slain in the person of his representative, with all the ceremonies already described, in order that, born young again, he might infuse his own youthful vigour into the stagnant energies of nature. On the same principle we can understand why Mamurius Veturius was beaten with rods, why the slave at the Chaeronean ceremony was beaten with the *agnus castus* (a tree to which magical properties were ascribed), why the effigy of Death in some parts of Europe is assailed with sticks and stones, and why at Babylon the criminal who played the god was scourged before he was crucified.* The purpose of the scourging was not to intensify the agony of the divine sufferer, but on the contrary to dispel any malignant influences by which at the supreme moment he might conceivably be beset.

Thus far I have assumed that the human victims at the Thargelia represented the spirits of vegetation in general, but it has been well remarked by Mr W. R. Paton that these poor wretches seem to have masqueraded as the spirits of fig-trees in particular. He points out that the process of caprification, as it

W. R. Paton's view that the human scapegoats at the Thargelia

personated
the spirits of
fig-trees, and
that the cere-
mony was a
magical rite
for the fertili-
zation of fig-
trees, being
copied from
the process
of caprifica-
tion.

is called, that is, the artificial fertilization of the cultivated fig-trees by hanging strings of wild figs among the boughs, takes place in Greece and Asia Minor in June about a month after the date of the Thargelia, and he suggests that the hanging of the black and white figs round the necks of the two human victims, one of whom represented the men and the other the women, may have been a direct imitation of the process of caprification designed, on the principle of imitative magic, to assist the fertilization of the fig-trees. And since caprification is in fact a marriage of the male fig-tree with the female fig-tree, Mr Paton further supposes that the loves of the trees may, on the same principle of imitative magic, have been simulated by a mock or even a real marriage between the two human victims, one of whom appears sometimes to have been a woman. On this view the practice of beating the human victims on their genitals with branches of wild fig-trees and with squills was a charm intended to stimulate the generative powers of the man and woman who for the time being personated the male and the female fig-trees respectively, and who by their union in marriage, whether real or pretended, were believed to help the trees to bear fruit.

This theory
is confirmed
by a compari-
son with the
Roman rites
of the *Nonae
Caprotinae*.

The theory is ingenious and attractive; and to some extent it is borne out by the Roman celebration of the *Nonae Caprotinae*. For on the *Nonae Caprotinae*, the seventh of July, the female slaves, in the attire of free women, feasted under a wild fig-tree, cut a rod from the tree, beat each other, perhaps with the rod, and offered the milky juice of the tree to the goddess Juno Caprotina, whose surname seems to point her out as the goddess of the wild fig-tree (*caprificus*). Here the rites performed in July by women under the wild fig-tree, which the ancients rightly regarded as a male and employed to fertilize the cultivated female fig-tree, can hardly be dissociated from the caprification or artificial marriage of the fig-trees which, according to Columella, was best performed in July; and if the blows which the women gave each other on this occasion were administered, as seems highly probable, by the rod which they cut from the wild fig-tree, the parallel between the Roman and the Greek ceremony would be still closer; since the Greeks, as we saw, beat the genitals of the human victims with branches of wild fig-trees. It is true that the human sacrifices, which formed so prominent a feature in the Greek celebration of the Thargelia, do not figure in the Roman celebration of the *Nonae Caprotinae* within historical times; yet a trace of them may perhaps be detected in the tradition that Romulus himself mysteriously disappeared on that very day in the midst of a tremendous thunder-storm, while he was reviewing his army outside the walls of Rome at the Goat's Marsh ('*ad Caprae paludem*'), a name which suggests that the place was not far distant from the wild fig-tree or the goat-fig (*caprificus*), as the Romans called it, where the slave women performed their curious ceremonies. The legend that he was cut in pieces by the patricians, who carried away the morsels of his body under their robes and buried them in the earth, exactly describes the treatment which the Khonds used to accord to the bodies of the human victims for the purpose of fertilizing their fields. Can the king have played at Rome the same fatal part in the fertilization of fig-trees which, if Mr Paton is right, was played in Greece by the male victim? The traditionary time, place, and manner of his death all suggest it. So many coincidences between the Greek and Roman ceremonies and traditions can hardly be wholly accidental; and accordingly I incline to think that there may well be an element of truth in Mr Paton's theory, though it must be confessed that the ancient writers who describe the Greek custom appear to regard it merely as a purification of the city and not at all as a mode of fertilizing fig-trees. In similar ceremonies, which combine the elements of purification and fertilization, the notion of purification apparently tends gradually to overshadow the notion of fertilization in the minds of those who practise the rites. It seems to have been so in the case of the annual expulsion of Mamurius Veturius from ancient Rome and in the parallel processions of the *Perchten* in modern Europe; it may have been so also in the case of the human sacrifices at the Thargelia.

The interpretation which I have adopted of the custom of beating the human scapegoat with certain plants is supported by many analogies. We have already met with examples of a practice of beating sick people with the leaves of certain plants or with branches in order to rid them of noxious influences. Some of the Dravidian tribes of Northern India, who attribute epilepsy, hysteria, and similar maladies to demoniacal possession,

Beating as a mode of dispelling evil influences.

endeavour to cure the sufferer by thrashing him soundly with a sacred iron chain, which is believed to have the effect of immediately expelling the demon. When a herd of camels refuses to drink, the Arabs will sometimes beat the male beasts on the back to drive away the jinn who are riding them and frightening the females.

Beating people with instruments which possess and impart special virtues.

Sometimes, in the opinion of those who resort to it, the effect of a beating is not merely the negative one of dispelling demoniac or other baneful influences; it confers positive benefits by virtue of certain useful properties supposed to inhere in the instrument with which the beating is administered. Thus among the Kai of German New Guinea, when a man wishes to make his banana shoots bear fruit quickly, he beats them with a stick cut from a banana-tree which has already borne fruit. Here it is obvious that fruitfulness is believed to inhere in a stick cut from a fruitful tree and to be imparted by contact to the young banana plants. Similarly in New Caledonia a man will beat his taro plants lightly with a branch, saying as he does so, 'I beat this taro that it may grow,' after which he plants the branch in the ground at the end of the field. Among the Indians of Brazil at the mouth of the Amazon, when a man wishes to increase the size of his generative organ, he strikes it with the fruit of a white aquatic plant called an *aninga*, which grows luxuriantly on the banks of the river. The fruit, which is inedible, resembles a banana, and is clearly chosen for this purpose on account of its shape. The ceremony should be performed three days before or after the new moon. In the county of Bekes, in Hungary, barren women are fertilized by being struck with a stick which has first been used to separate pairing dogs. Here a fertilizing virtue is clearly supposed to be inherent in the stick and to be conveyed by contact to the women. The Toradjas of Central Celebes think that the plant *Dracaena terminalis* has a strong soul, because when it is lopped, it soon grows up again. Hence when a man is ill, his friends will sometimes beat him on the crown of the head with *Dracaena* leaves in order to strengthen his weak soul with the strong soul of the plant. At Mowat in British New Guinea small boys are beaten lightly with sticks during December 'to make them grow strong and hardy.'

These analogies, accordingly, support the interpretation which, following my predecessors W. Mannhardt and Mr W. R. Paton,

I have given of the beating inflicted on the human victims at the Greek harvest festival of the Thargelia. That beating, being administered to the generative organs of the victims by fresh green plants and branches, is most naturally explained as a charm to increase the reproductive energies of the men or women either by communicating to them the fruitfulness of the plants and branches, or by ridding them of maleficent influences; and this interpretation is confirmed by the observation that the two victims represented the two sexes, one of them standing for the men in general and the other for the women. The season of the year when the ceremony was performed, namely the time of the corn harvest, tallies well with the theory that the rite had an agricultural significance. Further, that it was above all intended to fertilize the fig-trees is strongly suggested by the strings of black and white figs which were hung round the necks of the victims, as well as by the blows which were given their genital organs with the branches of a wild fig-tree; since this procedure closely resembles the procedure which ancient and modern husbandmen in Greek lands have regularly resorted to for the purpose of actually fertilizing their fig-trees. When we remember what an important part the artificial fertilization of the date palm-tree appears to have played of old not only in the husbandry but in the religion of Mesopotamia, there seems no reason to doubt that the artificial fertilization of the fig-tree may in like manner have vindicated for itself a place in the solemn ritual of Greek religion.

Hence the custom of beating the human victims at the Thargelia with fig-branches and squills was probably a charm to increase their reproductive energies.

If these considerations are just, we must apparently conclude that while the human victims at the Thargelia certainly appear in later classical times to have figured chiefly as public scape-goats, who carried away with them the sins, misfortunes, and sorrows of the whole people, at an earlier time they may have been looked on as embodiments of vegetation, perhaps of the corn but particularly of the fig-trees; and that the beating which they received and the death which they died were intended primarily to brace and refresh the powers of vegetation then beginning to droop and languish under the torrid heat of the Greek summer.

Hence the human victims at the Thargelia may have primarily represented spirits of vegetation.

The view here taken of the Greek scapegoat, if it is correct, obviates an objection which might otherwise be brought against the main argument of this book. To the theory that the priest

Parallel be-
tween the
human sacri-
fices at the
Thargelia
and the
bloody ritual
of the Ari-
cian Grove.

of Aricia was slain as a representative of the spirit of the grove, it might have been objected that such a custom has no analogy in classical antiquity. But reasons have now been given for believing that the human being periodically and occasionally slain by the Asiatic Greeks was regularly treated as an embodiment of a divinity of vegetation. Probably the persons whom the Athenians kept to be sacrificed were similarly treated as divine. That they were social outcasts did not matter. On the primitive view a man is not chosen to be the mouth-piece or embodiment of a god on account of his high moral qualities or social rank. The divine afflatus descends equally on the good and the bad, the lofty and the lowly. If then the civilized Greeks of Asia and Athens habitually sacrificed men whom they regarded as incarnate gods, there can be no inherent improbability in the supposition that at the dawn of history a similar custom was observed by the semi-barbarous Latins in the Arician Grove.

CHAPTER 3

KILLING THE GOD IN MEXICO

BY no people does the custom of sacrificing the human repres- The custom
entative of a god appear to have been observed so commonly of sacrificing
and with so much solemnity as by the Aztecs of ancient Mexico. human repre-
With the ritual of these remarkable sacrifices we are well the gods
acquainted, for it has been fully described by the Spaniards who among the
conquered Mexico in the sixteenth century, and whose curiosity Mexico.
was naturally excited by the discovery in this distant region of
a barbarous and cruel religion which presented many curious
points of analogy to the doctrine and ritual of their own church.
'They took a captive', says the Jesuit Acosta, 'such as they
thought good; and afore they did sacrifice him unto their idols,
they gave him the name of the idol, to whom he should be
sacrificed, and apparelled him with the same ornaments like
their idol, saying, that he did represent the same idol. And
during the time that this representation lasted, which was for a
year in some feasts, in others six months, and in others less,
they reverenced and worshipped him in the same manner as the
proper idol; and in the meantime he did eat, drink, and was
merry. When he went through the streets, the people came
forth to worship him, and every one brought him an alms, with
children and sick folks, that he might cure them, and bless
them, suffering him to do all things at his pleasure, only he was
accompanied with ten or twelve men lest he should fly. And he
(to the end he might be reverenced as he passed) sometimes
sounded upon a small flute, that the people might prepare to
worship him. The feast being come, and he grown fat, they
killed him, opened him, and ate him, making a solemn sacrifice
of him.'*

This general description of the custom may now be illustrated Sacrifice of a
by particular examples. Thus at the festival called Toxcatl, the man in the
greatest festival of the Mexican year, a young man was annually character of
sacrificed in the character of Tezcatlipoca, 'the god of gods', the great god
after having been maintained and worshipped as that great deity Tezcatlipoca
at the festival

in person for a whole year. According to the old Franciscan monk Sahagun, our best authority on the Aztec religion, the sacrifice of the human god fell at Easter or a few days later, so that, if he is right, it would correspond in date as well as in character to the Christian festival of the death and resurrection of the Redeemer. More exactly he tells us that the sacrifice took place on the first day of the fifth Aztec month, which according to him began on the twenty-third or twenty-seventh day of April.

At this festival the great god died in the person of one human representative and came to life again in the person of another, who was destined to enjoy the fatal honour of divinity for a year and to perish, like all his predecessors, at the end of it. The young man singled out for this high dignity was carefully chosen from among the captives on the ground of his personal beauty. He had to be of unblemished body, slim as a reed and straight as a pillar, neither too tall nor too short. If through high living he grew too fat, he was obliged to reduce himself by drinking salt water. And in order that he might behave in his lofty station with becoming grace and dignity he was carefully trained to comport himself like a gentleman of the first quality, to speak correctly and elegantly, to play the flute, to smoke cigars and to snuff at flowers with a dandified air. He was honourably lodged in the temple where the nobles waited on him and paid him homage, bringing him meat and serving like a prince. The king himself saw to it that he was apparelled in gorgeous attire, 'for already he esteemed him as a god'. Eagle down was gummed to his head and white cock's feathers were stuck in his hair, which drooped to his girdle. A wreath of flowers like roasted maize crowned his brows, and a garland of the same flowers passed over his shoulders and under his arm-pits. Golden ornaments hung from his nose, golden armlets adorned his arms, golden bells jingled on his legs at every step he took; earrings of turquoise dangled from his ears, bracelets of turquoise bedecked his wrists; necklaces of shells encircled his neck and depended on his breast; he wore a mantle of network, and round his middle a rich waist-cloth. When this bejewelled exquisite lounged through the streets playing on his flute, puffing at a cigar, and smelling at a nosegay, the people whom he met threw themselves on the earth before him and prayed to him with sighs and tears, taking up the dust in their hands and putting it in their mouths in token of the deepest humiliation and subjection. Women came forth with children in their arms and presented them to him, saluting him as a god. For 'he passed for our Lord God; the people acknowledged him as the Lord'. All who thus worshipped him on his passage he saluted gravely and courteously. Lest he should flee, he was everywhere attended by a guard of eight pages in the royal livery, four of them with shaven crowns like the palace-slaves, and four of them with the flowing locks of warriors; and if he contrived to escape, the captain of the guard had to take his place as the representative of the god and to die in his stead. Twenty days before he was to die, his costume was changed, and four damsels, delicately nurtured and bearing the names of four goddesses—the Goddess of Flowers, the Goddess of the Young Maize, the Goddess 'Our Mother among the Water', and the Goddess of Salt—were given him to be his brides, and with them he consorted. During the last five days divine honours were showered on the destined victim. The king remained in his palace while the whole court went after the human god. Solemn banquets and dances followed each other in regular succession and at appointed places. On the last day the young man, attended by his wives and pages, embarked in a canoe covered with a royal canopy and was ferried across the lake to a spot where a little hill rose from the edge of the water. It was called the Mountain of Parting, because here his wives bade him a last farewell. Then, accompanied only by his pages, he repaired to a small and lonely temple by the wayside. Like the Mexican temples in general, it was built in the form of a pyramid; and as the young man ascended the stairs he broke at every step one of the flutes on which he had played in the days of his glory. On reaching the summit he was seized and held down by the priests on his back upon a block of stone, while one of them cut open his breast, thrust his hand into the wound, and wrenching out his heart held it up in sacrifice to the sun. The body of the dead god was not, like the bodies of common victims, sent rolling down the steps of the temple, but was carried down to the foot, where the head was cut off and spitted on a pike. Such was the regular end of the man who personated the greatest god of the Mexican pantheon.

The manner of the sacrifice.

Sacrifice of a man in the character of the great Mexican god Vitzilopochtli (Huitzilopochtli) in the month of May.

But he was not the only man who played the part of a god and was sacrificed as such in the month of May. The great god Vitzilopochtli or Huitzilopochtli was also worshipped at the same season. An image of him was made out of dough in human shape, arrayed in all the ornaments of the deity, and set up in his temple. But the god had also his living representative in the person of a young man, who, like the human representative of Tezcatlipoca, personated the divinity for a whole year and was sacrificed at the end. In the month of May it was the duty of the divine man, destined so soon to die, to lead the dances which formed a conspicuous feature of the festivities. Courtiers and warriors, old and young, danced in winding figures, holding each other by the hand; and with them danced young women, who had taken a vow to dance with roasted maize. On their heads these damsels wore crowns of roasted maize; festoons of maize hung from their shoulders and crossed on their breasts; their faces were painted, and their arms and legs were covered with red feathers. Dancing in this attire the damsels were said to hold the god Vitzilopochtli in their arms; but they conducted themselves with the utmost gravity and decorum. So they danced till nightfall. Next morning they danced again, and in the course of the day the man who represented the god Vitzilopochtli was put to death. He had the privilege of choosing the hour when he was to die. When the fatal moment drew near, they clothed him in a curious dress of paper painted all over with black circles; on his head they clapped a paper mitre decked with eagle feathers and nodding plumes, among which was fastened a blood-stained obsidian knife. Thus attired, with golden bells jingling at his ankles, he led the dance at all the balls of the festival, and thus attired he went to his death. The priests seized him, stretched him out gripped him tight, cut out his heart, and held it up to the sun. His head was severed from the trunk and spiked beside the head of the other human god, who had been sacrificed not long before.

Sacrifice of a man in the character of the great Mexican god Quetzalcoatl in the month of February.

In Cholula, a wealthy trading city of Mexico, the merchants worshipped a god named Quetzalcoatl. His image, set upon a richly decorated altar or pedestal in a spacious temple, had the body of a man but the head of a bird, with a red beak surmounted by a crest, the face dyed yellow, with a black band running from the eyes to below the beak, and the tongue lolling out. On its head was a paper mitre painted black, white, and red; on its neck a large golden jewel in the shape of butterfly wings; about its body a feather mantle, black, red, and white; golden socks and golden sandals encased its legs and feet. In the right hand the image wielded a wooden instrument like a sickle, and in the left a buckler covered with the black and white plumage of sea-birds. The festival of this god was celebrated on the third day of February. Forty days before the festival 'the merchants bought a slave well proportioned, without any fault or blemish, either of sickness or of hurt, whom they did attire with the ornaments of the idol, that he might represent it forty days. Before his clothing they did cleanse him, washing him twice in a lake, which they called the lake of the gods; and being purified, they attired him like the idol. During these forty days, he was much respected for his sake whom he represented. By night they did imprison him (as hath been said) lest he should fly, and in the morning they took him out of prison, setting him upon an eminent place, where they served him, giving him exquisite meats to eat. After he had eaten, they put a chain of flowers about his neck, and many nosegays in his hands. He had a well-appointed guard, with much people to accompany him. When he went through the city, he went dancing and singing through all the streets, that he might be known for the resemblance of their god, and when he began to sing, the women and little children came forth of their houses to salute him, and to offer unto him as to their god. Two old men of the ancients of the temple came unto him nine days before the feast, and humbling themselves before him, they said with a low and submissive voice, "Sir, you must understand that nine days hence the exercise of dancing and singing doth end, and thou must then die"; and then he must answer, "In a good hour." They call this ceremony *Neyòlo Maxilt Ileztli*, which is to say, the advertisement; and when they did thus advertise him, they took very careful heed whether he were sad, or if he danced as joyfully as he was accustomed, the which if he did not as cheerfully as they desired, they made a foolish superstition in this manner. They presently took the sacrifizing razors, the which they washed and cleansed from the blood of men which remained of the former sacrifices. Of this washing they made a drink mingled with another liquor made of cacao, giving it him to drink; they said that this would make him forget what had been said unto him, and would make him in a manner insensible, returning to his former dancing and mirth. They said, moreover, that he would offer himself cheerfully to death, being enchanted with this drink. The cause why they sought to take from him this heaviness, was, for that they held it for an ill augury, and a fore-telling of some great harm. The day of the feast being come, after they had done him much honour, sung, and given him incense, the sacrificers took him about midnight and did sacrifice him, as hath been said, offering his heart unto the Moon, the which they did afterwards cast against the idol, letting the body fall to the bottom of the stairs of the temple, where such as had offered him took him up, which were the merchants, whose feast it was. Then having carried him into the chiefest man's house amongst them, the body was drest with diverse sauces, to celebrate (at the break of day) the banquet and dinner of the feast, having first bid the idol good morrow, with a small dance, which they made whilst the day did break, and that they prepared the sacrifice. Then did all the merchants assemble at this banquet, especially those which made it a trafick to buy and sell slaves, who were bound every year to offer one, for the resemblance of their god. This idol was one of the most honoured in all the land; and therefore the temple where he was, was of great authority.'

Sacrifice of a woman in the character of the Mexican Goddess of Salt in the month of June.

The honour of living for a short time in the character of a god and dying a violent death in the same capacity was not restricted to men in Mexico; women were allowed, or rather compelled, to enjoy the glory and to share the doom as representatives of goddesses. Thus in the seventh month of their year, which corresponded roughly to June, the Aztecs celebrated a festival in honour of Huixtocihuatl, the Goddess of Salt. She was said to be a sister of the Rain Gods, but having quarrelled with them she was banished and driven to take up her abode in the salt water. Being of an ingenious turn of mind, she invented the process of extracting salt by means of pans; hence she was worshipped by all salt-makers as their patron goddess. Her garments were yellow; on her head she wore a mitre surmounted by bunches of waving green plumes, which shone with greenish iridescent hues in the sun. Her robe and petticoats were embroidered with patterns simulating the waves of the sea. Golden ear-rings in the form of flowers dangled at her ears; golden bells jingled at her ankles. In one hand she carried a round shield painted with the leaves of a certain plant and adorned with drooping fringes of parrots' feathers; in the other hand she carried a stout baton ending in a knob and bedecked with paper, artificial flowers, and feathers. For ten days before her festival a woman personated the goddess and wore her gorgeous costume. It was her duty during these days to lead the dances which at this season were danced by the women and girls of the salt-makers. They danced, young, old, and children, in a ring, all holding a cord, their heads crowned with garlands of a fragrant flower (*Artemisia laciniata*) and singing airs in a shrill soprano. In the middle of the ring danced the woman who represented the goddess, with her golden bells jingling at every step, brandishing her shield, and marking the time of the dance and song with her baton. On the last day, the eve of the festival, she had to dance all night without resting till break of day, when she was to die. Old women supported her in the weary task, and they all danced together, arm in arm. With her, too, danced the slaves who were to die with her in the morning. When the hour was come, they led her, still personating the goddess, up the steps of the temple of Tlaloc, followed by the doomed captives. Arrived at the summit of the pyramid, the butchery began with the captives, while the woman stood looking on. Her turn being come, they threw her on her back on the block, and while five men held her down and two others compressed her throat with a billet of wood or the sword of a sword-fish to prevent her from screaming, the priest cut open her breast with his knife, and thrusting his hand into the wound tore out her heart and flung it into a bowl. When all was over, the salt-makers who had witnessed the sacrifice went home to drink and make merry.

Again, in the eighth month of the Mexican year, which answered to the latter end of June and the early part of July, the Aztecs sacrificed a woman who personated Xilonen, the goddess of the young maize-cobs (*xilotl*). The festival at which the sacrifice took place was held on the tenth day of the month about the time when the maize is nearly ripe, and when fibres shooting forth from the green ear shew that the grain is fully formed. For eight days before the festival men and women, clad

Sacrifice of a woman in the character of the Mexican Goddess of the Young Maize about Midsummer.

in rich garments and decked with jewels, danced and sang together in the courts of the temples, which were brilliantly illuminated for the purpose. Rows of tall braziers sent up a flickering blaze, and torchbearers held aloft huge torches of pinewood. Some of the dancers themselves carried heavy torches, which flared and spluttered as they danced. The dances began at sundown and lasted till about nine o'clock. None but tried and distinguished warriors might take part in them. The women wore their long hair hanging loose on their back and shoulders, in order that the tassels of the maize might likewise grow long and loose, for the more tassels the more grain in the ear. Men and women danced holding each other by the hand or with their arms round each other's waists, marking time exactly with their feet to the music of the drums and moving out and in among the flaming braziers and torches. The dances were strictly decorous. If any man was detected making love to one of the women dancers, he was publicly disgraced, severely punished, and never allowed to dance and sing in public again. On the eve of the festival the woman who was to die in the character of the Goddess of the Young Maize was arrayed in the rich robes and splendid jewels of the divinity whom she personated. The upper part of her face was painted red and the lower part yellow, probably to assimilate her to the ruddy and orange hues of the ripe maize. Her legs and arms were covered with red feathers. She wore a paper crown decked with a bunch of feathers; necklaces of gems and gold encircled her neck; her garments were embroidered with quaint figures; her shoes were striped with red. In her left hand she held a round shield, in her right a crimson baton. Thus arrayed, she was led by other women to offer incense in four different places. All the rest of the night she and they danced and sang in front of the temple of the goddess Xilonen, whose living image she was supposed to be. In the morning the nobles danced a solemn dance by themselves, leaning, or making believe to lean, on stalks of maize. The women, pranked with garlands and festoons of yellow flowers, danced also by themselves along with the victim. Among the priests the one who was to act as executioner wore a fine bunch of feathers on his back. Another shook a rattle before the doomed woman as she mounted up the steps of the temple of Cinteotl, the Goddess of the Maize. On reaching the summit she was seized by a priest, who threw her on his back, while the sacrificer severed her head from her body, tore out her heart, and threw it in a saucer. When this sacrifice had been performed in honour of Xilonen, the Goddess of the Young Maize, the people were free to eat the green ears of maize and the bread that was baked of it. No one would have dared to eat of these things before the sacrifice.

Again, in the seventeenth month of the Mexican year, which corresponded to the latter part of December and the early part of January, the Aztecs sacrificed a woman, who personated the goddess Ilamatecutli or Tonan, which means 'Our Mother'. Her festival fell on Christmas Day, the twenty-fifth of December. The image of the goddess wore a two-faced mask with large mouths and protruding eyes. The woman who represented her was dressed in white robes and shod with white sandals. Over her white mantle she wore a leathern jerkin, the lower edge of which was cut into a fringe of straps, and to the end of each strap was fastened a small shell. As she walked, the shells clashed together and made a noise which was heard afar off. The upper half of her face was painted yellow and the lower half black; and she wore a wig. In her hand she carried a round whitewashed shield decorated in the middle with a circle of eagle feathers, while white heron plumes, ending in eagle feathers, drooped from it. Thus arrayed and personating the goddess, the woman danced alone to music played by old men, and as she danced she sighed and wept at the thought of the death that was so near. At noon or a little later the dance ceased; and when the sun was declining in the west, they led her up the long ascent to the summit of Huitzilopochtli's temple. Behind her marched the priests clad in the trappings of all the gods, with masks on their faces. One of them wore the costume and the mask of the goddess Ilamatecutli, whom the victim also represented. On reaching the lofty platform which crowned the pyramidal temple, they slew her in the usual fashion, wrenched out her heart, and cut off her head. The dripping head was given to the priest who wore the costume and mask of the goddess and waving it up and down he danced round the platform, followed by all the other priests in the attire and masks of the gods. When the dance had lasted a certain time, the leader gave the signal, and they all trooped down the long

Sacrifice of a woman in the character of the Mexican goddess 'Our Mother' on Christmas Day.

flight of stairs to disrobe themselves and deposit the masks and costumes in the chapels where they were usually kept. Next day the people indulged in a certain pastime. Men and boys furnished themselves with little bags or nets stuffed with paper, flowers of galingale, or green leaves of maize, which they tied to strings, and used them as instruments to strike any girl or woman they might meet in the streets. Sometimes three or four urchins would gather round one girl, beating her till she cried; but some shrewd wenches went about that day armed with sticks, with which they retaliated smartly on their assailants. It was a penal offence to put stones or anything else that could hurt in the bags.

Sacrifice of a woman in the character of the Mexican goddess the Mother of the Gods at the end of August or beginning of September.

In the preceding custom, what are we to make of the sacrifice of a woman, who personated the goddess, by a man who also wore the costume and mask of the goddess, and who immediately after the sacrifice danced with the bleeding head of the victim? Perhaps the intention of the strange rite was to represent the resurrection of the slain goddess in the person of the priest who wore her costume and mask and dangled the severed head of her slaughtered representative. If that was so, it would explain another and still ghastlier rite, in which the Mexicans seem to have set forth the doctrine of the divine resurrection. This was to skin the slain woman who had personated the goddess and then to clothe in the bloody skin a man, who pranced about in it, as if he were the dead woman or rather goddess come to life again. Thus in the eleventh Mexican month, which corresponded to the latter part of August and the early part of September, they celebrated a festival in honour of a goddess called the Mother of the Gods (*Teteo innan*) or Our Ancestress (*Toci*), or the Heart of the Earth, and they sacrificed a woman clad in the costume and ornaments of the goddess. She was a slave bought for the purpose by the guilds of physicians, surgeons, blood-letters, midwives, and fortune-tellers, who particularly worshipped this deity. When the poor wretch came forth decked in all the trappings of the goddess, the people, we are told, looked on her as equivalent to the Mother of the Gods herself and paid her as much honour and reverence as if she had indeed been that great divinity. For eight days they danced silently in four rows, if dance it could be called in which the dancers scarcely stirred their legs and bodies, but contented themselves with moving their hands, in which they held branches of blossoms, up and down in time to the tuck of drum. These dances began in the afternoon and lasted till the sun went down. No one might speak during their performance; only some lively youths mimicked by a booming murmur of the lips the rub-a-dub of the drums. When the dances were over, the medical women, young and old, divided themselves into two parties and engaged in a sham fight before the woman who acted the part of the Mother of the Gods. This they did to divert her and keep her from being sad and shedding tears; for if she wept, they deemed it an omen that many men would die in battle and many women in childbed. The fight between the women consisted in throwing balls of moss, leaves, or flowers at each other; and she who personated the goddess led one of the parties to the attack. These mock battles lasted four days.

After that they led the woman who was to die to the market-place, that she might bid it farewell; and by way of doing so she scattered the flour of maize wherever she went. The priests then attended her to a building near the temple in which she was to be sacrificed. The knowledge of her doom was kept from her as far as possible. The medical women and the midwives comforted her, saying, 'Be not cast down, sweetheart; this night thou shalt sleep with the king; therefore rejoice.' Then they put on her the ornaments of the goddess, and at midnight led her to the temple where she was to die. On the passage not a word was spoken, not a cough was heard; crowds were gathered to see her pass, but all kept a profound silence. Arrived at the summit of the temple she was hoisted on to the back of one priest, while another adroitly cut off her head. The body, still warm, was skinned, and a tall robust young man clothed himself in the bleeding skin and so became in turn a living image of the goddess. One of the woman's thighs was flayed separately, and the skin carried to another temple, where a young man put it over his face as a mask and so personated the maize-goddess Cinteotl, daughter of the Mother of the Gods. Meantime the other, clad in the rest of the woman's skin, hurried down the steps of the temple. The nobles and warriors fled before him, carrying blood-stained besoms of couchgrass, but turned to look back at him from time to time and smote upon their shields as if to bid him come on. He followed hard after them

The farewell to the market.

The skin of the sacrificed woman flayed and worn by a man who personated the goddess.

and all who saw that flight and pursuit quaked with fear. On arriving at the foot of the temple of Huitzilopochtli, the man who wore the skin of the dead woman and personated the Mother of the Gods, lifted up his arms and stood like a cross before the image of the god; this action he repeated four times. Then he joined the man who personated the maize-goddess Cinteotl, and together they went slowly to the temple of the Mother of the Gods, where the woman had been sacrificed. All this time it was night. Next morning at break of day the man who personated the Mother of the Gods took up his post on the highest point of the temple; there they decked him in all the gorgeous trappings of the goddess and set a splendid crown on his head. Then the captives were set in a row before him, and arrayed in all his finery he slaughtered four of them with his own hand: the rest he left to be butchered by the priests. A variety of ceremonies and dances followed. Amongst others, the blood of the human victims was collected in a bowl and set before the man who personated the Mother of the Gods. He dipped his finger into the blood and then sucked his bloody finger; and when he had sucked it he bowed his head and uttered a dolorous groan, whereat the Indians believed the earth itself shook and trembled, as did all who heard it. Finally the skin of the slain woman and the skin of her thigh were carried away and deposited separately at two towers, one of which stood on the border of the enemy's country.

Young girl chosen to personate the Mexican Goddess of the Maize, Chicomecohuatl.

This remarkable festival in honour of the Mother of the Gods is said to have been immediately preceded by a similar festival in honour of the Maize Goddess Chicomecohuatl. The image of this goddess was of wood and represented her as a girl of about twelve years of age wearing feminine ornaments painted in gay colours. On her head was a pasteboard mitre; her long hair fell on her shoulders; in her ears she had golden earrings; round her neck she wore a necklace of golden maize-cobs strung on a blue ribbon, and in her hands she held the likeness of maize-cobs made of feathers and garnished with gold. Her festival, which was observed throughout the whole country with great devotion on the fifteenth day of September, was preceded by a strict fast of seven days, during which old and young, sick and whole, ate nothing but broken victuals and dry bread and drank nothing but water, and did penance by drawing blood from their ears.

The blood so drawn was kept in vessels, which were not scoured, so that a dry crust formed over it. On the day before the fast began the people ate and drank to their heart's content, and they sanctified a woman to represent Atlatatonan, the Goddess of Lepers, dressing her up in an appropriate costume. When the fast was over, the high priest of the temple of Tlaloc sacrificed the woman in the usual way by tearing out her heart and holding it up as an offering to the sun. Her body, with all the robes and ornaments she had worn, was cast into a well or vault in the temple, and along with the corpse were thrown in all the plates and dishes out of which the people had eaten, and all the mats on which they had sat or slept during the fast, as if, says the historian, they had been infected with the plague of leprosy. After that the people were free to eat bread, salt, and tomatoes; and immediately after the sacrifice of the woman who personated the Goddess of Leprosy they sanctified a young slave girl of twelve or thirteen years, the prettiest they could find, to represent the Maize Goddess Chicomecohuatl. They invested her with the ornaments of the goddess, putting the mitre on her head and the maize-cobs round her neck and in her hands, and fastening a green feather upright on the crown of her head to imitate an ear of maize. This they did, we are told, in order to signify that the maize was almost ripe at the time of the festival, but because it was still tender they chose a girl of tender years to play the part of the Maize Goddess. The whole long day they led the poor child in all her finery, with the green plume nodding on her head, from house to house dancing merrily to cheer people after the dulness and privations of the fast.

In the evening all the people assembled at the temple, the courts of which they lit up by a multitude of lanterns and candles. There they passed the night without sleeping, and at midnight, while the trumpets, flutes, and horns discoursed solemn music, a portable framework or palanquin was brought forth, bedecked with festoons of maize-cobs and peppers and filled with seeds of all sorts. This the bearers set down at the door of the chamber in which the wooden image of the goddess stood. Now the chamber was adorned and wreathed, both outside and inside, with wreaths of maize-cobs, peppers, pumpkins, roses, and seeds of every kind, a wonder to behold; the

Adoration of the girl who personated the Goddess of the Maize.

whole floor was covered deep with these verdant offerings of the pious. When the music ceased, a solemn procession came forth of priests and dignitaries, with flaring lights and smoking censers, leading in their midst the girl who played the part of the goddess. Then they made her mount the framework, where she stood upright on the maize and peppers and pumpkins with which it was strewed, her hands resting on two bannisters to keep her from falling. Then the priests swung the smoking censers round her; the music struck up again, and while it played, a great dignitary of the temple suddenly stepped up to her with a razor in his hand and adroitly shore off the green feather she wore on her head, together with the hair in which it was fastened, snipping the lock off by the root. The feather and the hair he then presented to the wooden image of the goddess with great solemnity and elaborate ceremonies, weeping and giving her thanks for the fruits of the earth and the abundant crops which she had bestowed on the people that year; and as he wept and prayed, all the people, standing in the courts of the temple, wept and prayed with him. When that ceremony was over, the girl descended from the framework and was escorted to the place where she was to spend the rest of the night. But all the people kept watch in the courts of the temple by the light of torches till break of day.

The girl who personated the Goddess of the Maize carried in procession and worshipped with offerings of human blood.

The morning being come, and the courts of the temple being still crowded by the multitude, who would have deemed it sacrilege to quit the precincts, the priests again brought forth the damsel attired in the costume of the goddess, with the mitre on her head and the cobs of maize about her neck. Again she mounted the portable framework or palanquin and stood on it, supporting herself by her hands on the bannisters. Then the elders of the temple lifted it on their shoulders, and while some swung burning censers and others played on instruments or sang, they carried it in procession through the great courtyard to the hall of the god Huitzilopochtli and then back to the chamber, where stood the wooden image of the Maize Goddess, whom the girl personated. There they caused the damsel to descend from the palanquin and to stand on the heaps of corn and vegetables that had been spread in profusion on the floor of the sacred chamber. While she stood there all the elders and nobles came in a line, one behind the other, carrying the saucers of dry and clotted blood which they had drawn from their ears by way of penance during the seven days' fast. One by one they squatted on their haunches before her, which was the equivalent of falling on their knees with us, and scraping the crust of blood from the saucer cast it down before her as an offering in return for the benefits which she, as the embodiment of the Maize Goddess, had conferred upon them. When the men had thus humbly offered their blood to the human representative of the goddess, the women, forming a long line, did so likewise, each of them dropping on her hams before the girl and scraping her blood from the saucer. The ceremony lasted a long time, for great and small, young and old, all without exception had to pass before the incarnate deity and make their offering. When it was over, the people returned home with glad hearts to feast on flesh and viands of every sort as merrily, we are told, as good Christians at Easter partake of meat and other carnal mercies after the long abstinence of Lent. And when they had eaten and drunk their fill and rested after the night watch, they returned quite refreshed to the temple to see the end of the festival. And the end of the festival was this. The multitude being assembled, the priests solemnly incensed the girl who personated the goddess; then they threw her on her back on the heap of corn and seeds, cut off her head, caught the gushing blood in a tub, and sprinkled the blood on the wooden image of the goddess, the walls of the chamber, and the offerings of corn, peppers, pumpkins, seeds, and vegetables which cumbered the floor. After that they flayed the headless trunk, and one of the priests made shift to squeeze himself into the bloody skin. Having done so they clad him in all the robes which the girl had worn; they put the mitre on his head, the necklace of golden maize-cobs about his neck, the maize-cobs of feathers and gold in his hands; and thus arrayed they led him forth in public, all of them dancing to the tuck of drum, while he acted as fugleman, skipping and posturing at the head of the procession as briskly as he could be expected to do, incommoded as he was by the tight and clammy skin of the girl and by her clothes, which must have been much too small for a grown man.

In the foregoing custom the identification of the young girl with the Maize Goddess appears to be complete. The golden maize cobs which she wore round her neck, the artificial maize

The human representative of the Maize Goddess put to death on a heap of corn and her skin flayed and worn by a priest.

Identification of the human victim with

cobs which she carried in her hands, the green feather which was stuck in her hair in imitation (we are told) of a green ear of maize, all set her forth as a personification of the corn-spirit; and we are expressly informed that she was specially chosen as a young girl to represent the young maize, which at the time of the festival had not yet fully ripened. Further, her identification with the corn and the corn-goddess was clearly announced by making her stand on the heaps of maize and there receive the homage and blood-offerings of the whole people, who thereby returned her thanks for the benefits which in her character of a divinity she was supposed to have conferred upon them. Once more, the practice of beheading her on a heap of corn and seeds and sprinkling her blood, not only on the image of the Maize Goddess, but on the piles of maize, peppers, pumpkins, seeds, and vegetables, can seemingly have had no other object but to quicken and strengthen the crops of corn and the fruits of the earth in general by infusing into their representatives the blood of the Corn Goddess herself.

The resurrec-
tion of the
Maize God-
dess set forth
by the wear-
ing of the
skin of her
human repre-
sentative.

Lastly, the concluding act of the sacred drama, in which the body of the dead Maize Goddess was flayed and her skin worn, together with all her sacred insignia, by a man who danced before the people in this grim attire, seems to be best explained on the hypothesis that it was intended to ensure that the divine death should be immediately followed by the divine resurrection. If that was so, we may infer with some degree of probability that the practice of killing a human representative of a deity has commonly, perhaps always, been regarded merely as a means of perpetuating the divine energies in the fulness of youthful vigour, untainted by the weakness and frailty of age, from which they must have suffered if the deity had been allowed to die a natural death.

Xipe, the
Flayed God,
and the Mexi-
can festival
of the
Flaying of
Men.

This interpretation of the Mexican custom of flaying human beings and permitting or requiring other persons to parade publicly in the skins of the victims may perhaps be confirmed by a consideration of the festival at which this strange rite was observed on the largest scale, and which accordingly went by the name of the Festival of the Flaying of Men (*Tlacaxipeualiztli*). It was celebrated in the second month of the Aztec year, which corresponded to the last days of February and the early part of March. The exact day of the festival was the twentieth of March, according to one pious chronicler, who notes with unction that the bloody rite fell only one day later than the feast which Holy Church solemnizes in honour of the glorious St Joseph. The god whom the Aztecs worshipped in this strange fashion was named Xipe, 'the Flayed One', or Totec, 'Our Lord'. On this occasion he also bore the solemn name of Youallauan, 'He who drinks in the Night'. His image was of stone and represented him in human form with his mouth open as if in the act of speaking; his body was painted yellow on the one side and drab on the other; he wore the skin of a flayed man over his own, with the hands of the victim dangling at his wrists. On his head he had a hood of various colours, and about his loins a green petticoat reaching to his knees with a fringe of small shells. In his two hands he grasped a rattle like the head of a poppy with the seeds in it; while on his left arm he supported a yellow shield with a red rim. At his festival the Mexicans killed all the prisoners they had taken in war, men, women, and children. The number of the victims was very great. A Spanish historian of the sixteenth century estimated that in Mexico more people used to be sacrificed on the altar than died a natural death. All who were sacrificed to Xipe, 'the Flayed God', were themselves flayed, and men who had made a special vow to the god put on the skins of the human victims and went about the city in that guise for twenty days, being everywhere welcomed and revered as living images of the deity. Forty days before the festival, according to the historian Duran, they chose a man to personate the god, clothed him in all the insignia of the divinity, and led him about in public, doing him as much reverence all these days as if he had really been what he pretended to be. Moreover, every parish of the capital did the same; each of them had its own temple and appointed its own human representative of the deity, who received the homage and worship of the parishioners for the forty days.

On the day of the festival these mortal gods and all the other prisoners, with the exception of a few who were reserved for a different death, were killed in the usual way. The scene of the slaughter was the platform on the summit of the god Huitzilopochtli's temple. Some of the poor wretches fainted when they came to the foot of the steps and had to be dragged up the long staircase by the hair of their heads. Arrived at the summit they

The human shambles.

were slaughtered one by one on the sacrificial stone by the high priest, who cut open their breasts, tore out their hearts, and held them up to the sun, in order to feed the great luminary with these bleeding relics. Then the bodies were sent rolling down the staircase, clattering and turning over and over like gourds as they bumped from step to step till they reached the bottom. There they were received by other priests, or rather human butchers, who with a dexterity acquired by practice slit the back of each body from the nape of the neck to the heels and peeled off the whole skin in a single piece as neatly as if it had been a sheepskin. The skinless body was then fetched away by its owner, that is, by the man who had captured the prisoner in war. He took it home with him, carved it, sent one of the thighs to the king, and other joints to friends, or invited them to come and feast on the carcase in his house. The skins of the human victims were also a perquisite of their captors, and were lent or hired out by them to men who had made a vow of going about clad in the hides for twenty days. Such men clothed in the reeking skins of the butchered prisoners were called Xixipeme or Tototectin after the god Xipe or Totec, whose living image they were esteemed and whose costume they wore. Among the devotees who bound themselves to this pious exercise were persons who suffered from loathsome skin diseases, such as smallpox, abscesses, and the itch; and among them there was a fair sprinkling of debauchees, who had drunk themselves nearly blind and hoped to recover the use of their precious eyes by parading for a month in this curious mantle. Thus arrayed, they went from house to house throughout the city, entering everywhere and asking alms for the love of God. On entering a house each of these reverend palmers was made to sit on a heap of leaves; festoons of maize and wreaths of flowers were placed round his body; and he was given wine to drink and cakes to eat. And when a mother saw one of these filthy but sanctified ruffians passing along the street, she would run to him with her infant and put it in his arms that he might bless it, which he did with unction, receiving an alms from the happy mother in return. The earnings of these begging-friars on their rounds were sometimes considerable, for the rich people rewarded them handsomely. Whatever they were, the collectors paid them in to the owners of the skins, who thus

The holy beggars clad in the skins of the flayed human victims.

made a profit by hiring out these valuable articles of property. Every night the wearers of the skins deposited them in the temple and fetched them again next morning when they set out on their rounds. At the end of the twenty days the skins were dry, hard, shrivelled and shrunken, and they smelt so villainously that people held their noses when they met the holy beggars arrayed in their fetid mantles. The time being come to rid themselves of these encumbrances, the devotees walked in solemn procession, wearing the rotten skins and stinking like dead dogs, to the temple called Yopico, where they stripped themselves of the hides and plunged them into a tub or vat, after which they washed and scrubbed themselves thoroughly, while their friends smacked their bare bodies loudly with wet hands in order to squeeze out the human grease with which they were saturated. Finally, the skins were solemnly buried, as holy relics, in a vault of the temple. The burial service was accompanied by chanting and attended by the whole people; and when it was over, one of the high dignitaries preached a sermon to the assembled congregation, in which he dwelt with pathetic eloquence on the meanness and misery of human existence and exhorted his hearers to lead a sober and quiet life, to cultivate the virtues of reverence, modesty, humility and obedience, to be kind and charitable to the poor and to strangers; he warned them against the sins of robbery, fornication, adultery, and covetousness; and kindling with the glow of his oratory, he passionately admonished, entreated, and implored all who heard him to choose the good and shun the evil, drawing a dreadful picture of the ills that would overtake the wicked here and hereafter, while he painted in alluring colours the bliss in store for the righteous and the rewards they might expect to receive at the hands of the deity in the life to come.

While most of the men who masqueraded in the skins of the human victims appear to have personated the Flayed God Xipe, whose name they bore in the form Xixipeme, others assumed the ornaments and bore the names of other Mexican deities, such as Huitzilopochtli and Quetzalcoatl; the ceremony of investing them with the skins and the insignia of divinity was called *netcotoquiliztli*, which means 'to think themselves gods'. Amongst the gods thus personated was Totec. His human representative wore, over the skin of the flayed man, all the

Various Mexican gods personated by the men clad in the skins of the human victims.

splendid trappings of the deity. On his head was placed a curious crown decorated with rich feathers. A golden crescent dangled from his nose, golden earrings from his ears, and a necklace of hammered gold encircled his neck. His feet were shod in red shoes decorated with quail's feathers; his loins were begirt with a petticoat of gorgeous plumage; and on his back three small paper flags fluttered and rustled in the wind. In his left hand he carried a golden shield and in his right a rattle, which he shook and rattled as he walked with a majestic dancing step. Seats were always prepared for this human god; and when he sat down, they offered him a paste made of uncooked maize-flour. Also they presented to him little bunches of cobs of maize chosen from the seed-corn; and he received as offerings the first fruits and the first flowers of the season.

Men roasted alive as images of the Fire-god. In the eighteenth and last month of their year, which fell in January, the Mexicans held a festival in honour of the god of fire. Every fourth year the festival was celebrated on a grand scale by the sacrifice of a great many men and women, husbands and wives, who were dressed in the trappings of the fire-god and regarded as his living images. Bound hand and foot, they were thrown alive into a great furnace, and after roasting in it for a little were raked out of the fire before they were dead in order to allow the priest to cut the hearts out of their scorched, blistered, and still writhing bodies in the usual way. The intention of the sacrifice probably was to maintain the Fire-god in full vigour, lest he should grow decrepit or even die of old age, and mankind should thus be deprived of his valuable services. This important object was attained by feeding the fire with live men and women, who thus as it were poured a fresh stock of vital energy into the veins of the Fire-god and perhaps of his wife also. But they had to be raked out of the flames before they were dead; for clearly it would never do to let them die in the fire, else the Fire-god whom they personated would die also. For the same reason their hearts had to be torn from their bodies while they were still palpitating; what use could the Fire-god make of human hearts that were burnt to cinders?

Women flayed in honour of the Fire-god and their skins This was the ordinary mode of sacrificing the human representatives of the Fire-god every fourth year. But in Quauhtitlan, a city distant four leagues from the city of Mexico, the custom was different. On the eve of the festival two women were beheaded on the altar of the temple and afterwards flayed, faces and all, and their thigh bones extracted. Next morning two men of high rank clothed themselves in the skins, including the skins of the women's faces, which they put over their own; and thus arrayed and carrying in their hands the thigh bones of the victims they came down the steps of the temple roaring like wild beasts. A vast crowd of people had assembled to witness the spectacle, and when they saw the two men coming down the steps in the dripping skins, brandishing the bones, and bellowing like beasts, they were filled with fear and said, 'There come our gods!' Arrived at the foot of the staircase these human gods engaged in a dance, which they kept up for the rest of the day, never divesting themselves of the bloody skins till the festival was over.

worn by men who personated gods.

The theory that the custom of wearing the skin of a flayed man or woman and personating a god in that costume is intended to represent the resurrection of the deity derives some support from the class of persons who made a vow to masquerade in the skins. They were, as we have seen, especially men who suffered from diseases of the skin and the eyes: they hoped, we are told, by wearing the skins to be cured of their ailments, and the old Spanish monk who records the belief adds dryly that some were cured and some were not. We may conjecture that by donning the skins of men who had acted the part of gods they expected to slough off their own diseased old skins and to acquire new and healthy skins, like those of the deities. This notion may have been suggested to them by the observation of certain animals, such as serpents and lizards, which seem to renew their youth by casting their skins and appear refreshed and renovated in new integuments. That many savages have noticed such transformations in the animal world is proved by the tales which some of them tell to account for the origin of death among mankind. For example, the Arawaks of British Guiana say that man was created by a good being whom they call Kururumany. Once on a time this kindly creator came to earth to see how his creature man was getting on. But men were so ungrateful that they tried to kill their Maker. Hence he took from them the gift of immortality and bestowed it upon animals that change their skins, such as snakes, lizards, and beetles. Again, the Tamanachiers, an Indian tribe of the Orinoco, tell

The personation of a god by a man wearing the skin of a human victim is probably intended to represent and ensure the resurrection of the deity.

The idea of resurrection from the dead is suggested by the observation of snakes and other creatures that cast their skins.

how the creator kindly intended to make men immortal by telling them that they should change their skins. He meant to say that by so doing they should renew their youth like serpents and beetles. But the glad tidings were received with such incredulity by an old woman that the creator in a huff changed his tune and said very curtly, 'Ye shall die.'

In Annam they say that Ngoc hoang sent a messenger from heaven to inform men that when they reached old age they should change their skins and live for ever, but that when serpents grew old, they must die. Unfortunately for the human race the message was perverted in the transmission, so that men do not change their skins and are therefore mortal, whereas serpents do cast their old skins and accordingly live for ever. According to the natives of Nias the personage who was charged by the creator with the duty of putting the last touches to man broke his fast on bananas instead of on river-crabs, as he should have done; for had he only eaten river-crabs, men would have changed their skins like crabs, and like crabs would have never died. But the serpents, wiser in their generation than men, ate the crabs, and that is why they too are immortal. Stories of the same sort are current among the Melanesians. Thus the natives of the Gazelle Peninsula in New Britain account for the origin of death by a tale very like that told in Annam. The Good Spirit, they say, loved men and wished to make them immortal, but he hated serpents and wished to kill them. So he despatched his brother to mankind with this cheering message: 'Go to men and take them the secret of immortality. Tell them to cast their skin every year. So will they be protected from death, for their life will be constantly renewed. But tell the serpents that they must henceforth die.' Through the carelessness or treachery of the messenger this message was reversed; so that now, as we all know, men die and serpents live for ever by annually casting their skins. Again, if we can trust the traditions of the Banks' Islanders and New Hebrideans, there was a time when men did really cast their skins and renew their youth. The melancholy change to mortality was brought about by an old woman, who most unfortunately resumed her old cast-off skin to please an infant, which squalled at seeing her in her new integument. The Gallas of East Africa say that God sent a certain bird (*holawaka*, 'the sheep of God') to tell men that they would not die, but that when they grew old they would slough their skins and so renew their youth. But the bird foolishly or maliciously delivered the message to serpents instead of to men, and that is why ever since men have been mortal and serpents immortal. For that evil deed God punished the bird with a painful malady from which it suffers to this day, and it sits on the tops of trees and moans and wails perpetually.

Thus it appears that some peoples have not only observed the curious transformations which certain animals undergo, but have imagined that by means of such transformations the animals periodically renew their youth and live for ever. From such observations and fancies it is an easy step to the conclusion that man might similarly take a fresh lease of life and renew the lease indefinitely, if only he could contrive like the animals to get a new skin. This desirable object the Mexicans apparently sought to accomplish by flaying men and wearing their bleeding skins like garments thrown over their own. By so doing persons who suffered from cutaneous diseases hoped to acquire a new and healthy skin; and by so doing the priests attempted not merely to revive the gods whom they had just slain in the persons of their human representatives, but also to restore to their wasting and decaying frames all the vigour and energy of youth.

Hence the Mexicans apparently thought that they could renew their own skins by putting on those of other people.

The rites described in the preceding pages suffice to prove that human sacrifices of the sort I suppose to have prevailed at Aricia were, as a matter of fact, systematically offered on a large scale by a people whose level of culture was probably not inferior, if indeed it was not distinctly superior, to that occupied by the Italian races at the early period to which the origin of the Arician priesthood must be referred. The positive and indubitable evidence of the prevalence of such sacrifices in one part of the world may reasonably be allowed to strengthen the probability of their prevalence in places for which the evidence is less full and trustworthy. Taken all together, the facts which we have passed in review seem to shew that the custom of killing men whom their worshippers regard as divine has prevailed in many parts of the world. But to clinch the argument, it is clearly desirable to prove that the custom of putting to death a human representative of a god was known and practised in ancient Italy elsewhere than in the Arician Grove. This proof I now propose to adduce.

General conclusion: the custom of putting human beings to death in the character of gods has prevailed in many parts of the world.

CHAPTER 4

THE SATURNALIA

i

Annual
periods of
license.

IN an earlier part of this book we saw that many peoples have
been used to observe an annual period of license, when the
customary restraints of law and morality are thrown aside, when
the whole population give themselves up to extravagant mirth
and jollity, and when the darker passions find a vent which
would never be allowed them in the more staid and sober course
of ordinary life. Such outbursts of the pent-up forces of human
nature, too often degenerating into wild orgies of lust and
crime, occur most commonly at the end of the year, and are
frequently associated, as I have had occasion to point out, with
one or other of the agricultural seasons, especially with the time
of sowing or of harvest. Now, of all these periods of license the
one which is best known and which in modern languages has
given its name to the rest, is the Saturnalia. This famous festival
fell in December, the last month of the Roman year, and was
popularly supposed to commemorate the merry reign of Saturn,
the god of sowing and of husbandry, who lived on earth long
ago as a righteous and beneficent king of Italy, drew the rude
and scattered dwellers on the mountains together, taught them
to till the ground, gave them laws, and ruled in peace. His reign
was the fabled Golden Age: the earth brought forth abundantly:
no sound of war or discord troubled the happy world: no baleful
love of lucre worked like poison in the blood of the industrious
and contented peasantry. Slavery and private property were
alike unknown: all men had all things in common. At last the
good god, the kindly king, vanished suddenly; but his memory
was cherished to distant ages, shrines were reared in his honour,
and many hills and high places in Italy bore his name. Yet the
bright tradition of his reign was crossed by a dark shadow: his
altars are said to have been stained with the blood of human
victims, for whom a more merciful age afterwards substituted
effigies.* Of this gloomy side of the god's religion there is little
or no trace in the descriptions which ancient writers have left

The Roman
Saturnalia.

us of the Saturnalia. Feasting and revelry and all the mad pursuit of pleasure are the features that seem to have especially marked this carnival of antiquity, as it went on for seven days in the streets and public squares and houses of ancient Rome from the seventeenth to the twenty-third of December.

But no feature of the festival is more remarkable, nothing in it seems to have struck the ancients themselves more than the license granted to slaves at this time. The distinction between the free and the servile classes was temporarily abolished. The slave might rail at his master, intoxicate himself like his betters, sit down at table with them, and not even a word of reproof would be administered to him for conduct which at any other season might have been punished with stripes, imprisonment, or death. Nay, more, masters actually changed places with their slaves and waited on them at table; and not till the serf had done eating and drinking was the board cleared and dinner set for his master. So far was this inversion of ranks carried, that each household became for a time a mimic republic in which the high offices of state were discharged by the slaves, who gave their orders and laid down the law as if they were indeed invested with all the dignity of the consulship, the praetorship, and the bench. Like the pale reflection of power thus accorded to bondsmen at the Saturnalia was the mock kingship for which freemen cast lots at the same season. The person on whom the lot fell enjoyed the title of king, and issued commands of a playful and ludicrous nature to his temporary subjects. One of them he might order to mix the wine, another to drink, another to sing, another to dance, another to speak in his own dispraise, another to carry a flute-girl on his back round the house.

Now, when we remember that the liberty allowed to slaves at this festive season was supposed to be an imitation of the state of society in Saturn's time, and that in general the Saturnalia passed for nothing more or less than a temporary revival or restoration of the reign of that merry monarch, we are tempted to surmise that the mock king who presided over the revels may have originally represented Saturn himself. The conjecture is strongly confirmed, if not established, by a very curious and interesting account of the way in which the Saturnalia was celebrated by the Roman soldiers stationed on the Danube in the reign of Maximian and Diocletian. The account is preserved

The license granted to slaves at the Saturnalia.

The mock King of the Saturnalia.

Personation of Saturn at the Saturnalia by a soldier who afterwards suffered death.

in a narrative of the martyrdom of St Dasius, which was unearthed from a Greek manuscript in the Paris library, and published by Professor Franz Cumont of Ghent.* Two briefer descriptions of the event and of the custom are contained in manuscripts at Milan and Berlin; one of them had already seen the light in an obscure volume printed at Urbino in 1727, but its importance for the history of the Roman religion, both ancient and modern, appears to have been overlooked until Professor Cumont drew the attention of scholars to all three narratives by publishing them together some years ago. According to these narratives, which have all the appearance of being authentic, and of which the longest is probably based on official documents, the Roman soldiers at Durostorum* in Lower Moesia celebrated the Saturnalia year by year in the following manner. Thirty days before the festival they chose by lot from amongst themselves a young and handsome man, who was then clothed in royal attire to resemble Saturn. Thus arrayed and attended by a multitude of soldiers he went about in public with full license to indulge his passions and to taste of every pleasure, however base and shameful. But if his reign was merry, it was short and ended tragically; for when the thirty days were up and the festival of Saturn had come, he cut his own throat on the altar of the god whom he personated. In the year AD 303 the lot fell upon the Christian soldier Dasius, but he refused to play the part of the heathen god and soil his last days by debauchery. The threats and arguments of his commanding officer Bassus failed to shake his constancy, and accordingly he was beheaded, as the Christian martyrologist records with minute accuracy, at Durostorum by the soldier John on Friday the twentieth day of November, being the twenty-fourth day of the moon, at the fourth hour.

The sarcophagus of St Dasius, the martyr on whom the lot fell to play the part of Saturn.

Since this narrative was published by Professor Cumont, its historical character, which had been doubted or denied, has received strong confirmation from an interesting discovery. In the crypt of the cathedral which crowns the promontory of Ancona* there is preserved, among other remarkable antiquities, a white marble sarcophagus bearing a Greek inscription, in characters of the age of Justinian, to the following effect: 'Here lies the holy martyr Dasius, brought from Durostorum.' The sarcophagus was transferred to the crypt of the cathedral in 1848 from the church of San Pellegrino, under the high altar of which, as we learn from a Latin inscription let into the masonry, the martyr's bones still repose with those of two other saints. How long the sarcophagus was deposited in the church of San Pellegrino, we do not know; but it is recorded to have been there in the year 1650. We may suppose that the saint's relics were transferred for safety to Ancona at some time in the troubled centuries which followed his martyrdom, when Moesia was occupied and ravaged by successive hordes of barbarian invaders. At all events it appears certain from the independent and mutually confirmatory evidence of the martyrology and the monuments that Dasius was no mythical saint, but a real man, who suffered death for his faith at Durostorum in one of the early centuries of the Christian era. Finding the narrative of the nameless martyrologist thus established as to the principal fact recorded, namely, the martyrdom of St Dasius, we may reasonably accept his testimony as to the manner and cause of the martyrdom, all the more because his narrative is precise, circumstantial, and entirely free from the miraculous element. Accordingly I conclude that the account which he gives of the celebration of the Saturnalia among the Roman soldiers is trustworthy.

This account sets in a new and lurid light the office of the King of the Saturnalia, the ancient Lord of Misrule, who presided over the winter revels at Rome in the time of Horace and of Tacitus. It seems to prove that his business had not always been that of a mere harlequin or merry-andrew whose only care was that the revelry should run high and the fun grow fast and furious, while the fire blazed and crackled on the hearth, while the streets swarmed with festive crowds, and through the clear frosty air, far away to the north, Soracte shewed his coronal of snow. When we compare this comic monarch of the gay, the civilized metropolis with his grim counterpart of the rude camp on the Danube, and when we remember the long array of similar figures, ludicrous yet tragic, who in other ages and in other lands, wearing mock crowns and wrapped in sceptred palls, have played their little pranks for a few brief hours or days, then passed before their time to a violent death, we can hardly doubt that in the King of the Saturnalia at Rome, as he is depicted by classical writers, we see

The mock King of the Saturnalia may have been the degenerate successor of a series of temporary kings who personated Saturn at the Saturnalia and were put to death in the character of the god.

only a feeble emasculated copy of that original, whose strong features have been fortunately preserved for us by the obscure author of the *Martyrdom of St Dasius*. In other words, the martyrologist's account of the Saturnalia agrees so closely with the accounts of similar rites elsewhere, which could not possibly have been known to him, that the substantial accuracy of his description may be regarded as established; and further, since the custom of putting a mock king to death as a representative of a god cannot have grown out of a practice of appointing him to preside over a holiday revel, whereas the reverse may very well have happened, we are justified in assuming that in an earlier and more barbarous age it was the universal practice in ancient Italy, wherever the worship of Saturn prevailed, to choose a man who played the part and enjoyed all the traditionary privileges of Saturn for a season, and then died, whether by his own or another's hand, whether by the knife or the fire or on the gallows-tree, in the character of the good god who gave his life for the world. In Rome itself and other great towns the growth of civilization had probably mitigated this cruel custom long before the Augustan age, and transformed it into the innocent shape it wears in the writings of the few classical writers who bestow a passing notice on the holiday King of the Saturnalia. But in remoter districts the older and sterner practice may long have survived; and even if after the unification of Italy the barbarous usage was suppressed by the Roman government, the memory of it would be handed down by the peasants and would tend from time to time, as still happens with the lowest forms of superstition among ourselves, to lead to a recrudescence of the practice, especially among the rude soldiery on the outskirts of the empire over whom the once iron hand of Rome was beginning to relax its grasp.

ii

The modern
Carnivals is
perhaps the
equivalent of
the ancient
Saturnalia.

The resemblance between the Saturnalia of ancient and the Carnival of modern Italy has often been remarked; but in the light of all the facts that have come before us, we may well ask whether the resemblance does not amount to identity. We have seen that in Italy, Spain, and France, that is, in the countries where the influence of Rome has been deepest and most lasting, a conspicuous feature of the Carnival is a burlesque figure personifying the festive season, which after a short career of glory and dissipation is publicly shot, burnt, or otherwise destroyed, to the feigned grief or genuine delight of the populace. If the view here suggested of the Carnival is correct, this grotesque personage is no other than a direct successor of the old King of the Saturnalia, the master of the revels, the real man who personated Saturn and, when the revels were over, suffered a real death in his assumed character.

As the Carnival is always held on the last three days before the beginning of Lent, its date shifts somewhat from year to year, but it invariably falls either in February or March. Hence it does not coincide with the date of the Saturnalia, which within historical times seems to have been always celebrated in December even in the old days, before Caesar's reform of the calendar, when the Roman year ended with February instead of December. Yet if the Saturnalia, like many other seasons of license, was originally celebrated as a sort of public purification at the end of the old year or the beginning of the new one, it may at a still more remote period, when the Roman year began with March,* have been regularly held either in February or March and therefore at approximately the same date as the modern Carnival. So strong and persistent are the conservative instincts of the peasantry in respect to old custom, that it would be no matter for surprise if, in rural districts of Italy, the ancient festival continued to be celebrated at the ancient time long after the official celebration of the Saturnalia in the towns had been shifted from February to December. Latin Christianity, which struck at the root of official or civic paganism, has always been tolerant of its rustic cousins, the popular festivals and ceremonies which, unaffected by political and religious revolutions, by the passing of empires and of gods, have been carried on by the people with but little change from time immemorial, and represent in fact the original stock from which the state religions of classical antiquity were comparatively late offshoots. Thus it may very well have come about that while the new faith stamped out the Saturnalia in the towns, it suffered the original festival, disguised by a difference of date, to linger unmolested in the country; and so the old feast of Saturn, under the modern name of the Carnival, has

The modern Carnival is perhaps the equivalent of the ancient Saturnalia.

reconquered the cities, and goes on merrily under the eye and with the sanction of the Catholic Church.

The opinion that the Saturnalia originally fell in February or the beginning of March receives some support from the circumstance that the festival of the Matronalia, at which mistresses feasted their slaves just as masters did theirs at the Saturnalia, always continued to be held on the first of March, even when the Roman year began with January.* It is further not a little recommended by the consideration that this date would be eminently appropriate for the festival of Saturn, the old Italian god of sowing and planting. It has always been a puzzle to explain why such a festival should have been held at midwinter; but on the present hypothesis the mystery vanishes. With the Italian farmer February and March were the great season of the spring sowing and planting; nothing could be more natural than that the husbandman should inaugurate the season with the worship of the deity to whom he ascribed the function of quickening the seed. It is no small confirmation of this theory that the last day of the Carnival, namely Shrove Tuesday, is still, or was down to recent times, the customary season in Central Europe for promoting the growth of the crops by means of leaps and dances. The custom fits in very well with the view which derives the Carnival from an old festival of sowing such as the Saturnalia probably was in its origin. Further, the orgiastic character of the festival is readily explained by the help of facts which met us in a former part of our investigation. We have seen that between the sower and the seed there is commonly supposed to exist a sympathetic connexion of such a nature that his conduct directly affects and can promote or retard the growth of the crops. What wonder then if the simple husbandman imagined that by cramming his belly, by swilling and guzzling just before he proceeded to sow his fields, he thereby imparted additional vigour to the seed?

But while his crude philosophy may thus have painted gluttony and intoxication in the agreeable colours of duties which he owed to himself, to his family, and to the commonwealth, it is possible that the zest with which he acquitted himself of his obligations may have been whetted by a less comfortable reflection. In modern times the indulgence of the Carnival is immediately followed by the abstinence of Lent; and

The Saturnalia may have originally fallen at the end of February, which would be an appropriate time for a festival of sowing.

The Lenten fast in spring may be an old heathen period of abstinence intended to promote the growth of the seed.

if the Carnival is the direct descendant of the Saturnalia, may not Lent in like manner be merely the continuation, under a thin disguise, of a period of temperance which was annually observed, from superstitious motives, by Italian farmers long before the Christian era? Direct evidence of this, so far as I am aware, is not forthcoming; but we have seen that a practice of abstinence from fleshly lusts has been observed by various peoples as a sympathetic charm to foster the growth of the seed;* and such an observance would be an appropriate sequel to the Saturnalia, if that festival was indeed, as I conjecture it to have been, originally held in spring as a religious or magical preparation for sowing and planting. When we consider how widely diffused is the belief in the sympathetic influence which human conduct, and especially the intercourse of the sexes, exerts on the fruits of the earth, we may be allowed to conjecture that the Lenten fast, with the rule of continence which is recommended, if not strictly enjoined, by the Catholic and Coptic churches during that season, was in its origin intended, not so much to commemorate the sufferings of a dying god, as to foster the growth of the seed, which in the bleak days of early spring the husbandman commits with anxious care and misgiving to the bosom of the naked earth. Ecclesiastical historians have been puzzled to say why after much hesitation and great diversity of usage in different places the Christian church finally adopted forty days as the proper period for the mournful celebration of Lent. Perhaps in coming to this decision the authorities were guided, as so often, by a regard for an existing pagan celebration of similar character and duration which they hoped by a change of name to convert into a Christian solemnity. Such a heathen Lent they may have found to hand in the rites of Persephone, the Greek goddess of the corn, whose image, carved out of a tree, was annually brought into the cities and mourned for forty nights, after which it was burned. The time of year when these lamentations took place is not mentioned by the old Christian writer who records them; but they would fall most appropriately at the season when the seed was sown or, in mythical language, when the corn-goddess was buried, which in ancient Italy, as we saw, was done above all in the months of February and March. We know that at the time of the autumnal sowing Greek women

Autumnal
rites of
mourning
and fasting
for the sake
of the seed.

held a sad and serious festival because the Corn-goddess Perse-phone or the Maiden, as they called her, then went down into the earth with the sown grain, and Demeter fondly mourned her daughter's absence; hence in sympathy with the sorrowful mother the women likewise mourned and observed a solemn fast and abstained from the marriage bed. It is reasonable, therefore, to suppose that they practised similar rules of mourning and abstinence for a like reason at the time of the spring sowing, and that the ancient ritual survives in the modern Lent, which preserves the memory of the *Mater Dolorosa*, though it has substituted a dead Son for a dead Daughter.

The
Buddhist
Lent.

Be that as it may, it is worthy of note that in Burma a similar fast, which English writers call the Buddhist Lent, is observed for three months every year while the ploughing and sowing of the fields go forward; and the custom is believed to be far older than Buddhism, which has merely given it a superficial tinge like the veneer of Christianity which, if I am right, has overlaid an old heathen observance in Lent. This Burmese Lent, we are told, covers the rainy season from the full moon of July to the full moon of October. 'This is the time to plough, this is the time to sow; on the villagers' exertions in these months depends all their maintenance for the rest of the year. Every man, every woman, every child, has hard work of some kind or another. And so, what with the difficulties of travelling, what with the work there is to do, and what with the custom of Lent, every one stays at home. It is the time for prayer, for fasting, for improving the soul. Many men during these months will live even as the monks live, will eat but before midday, will abstain from tobacco. There are no plays during Lent, and there are no marriages. It is the time for preparing the land for the crop; it is the time for preparing the soul for eternity. The congregations on the Sundays will be far greater at this time than at any other; there will be more thought of the serious things of life.'*

iii

Inversion of
social ranks
at ancient
Greek fest-
ivals held in

Beyond the limits of Italy festivals of the same general character as the Saturnalia appear to have been held over a considerable area of the ancient world. A characteristic feature of the Saturnalia, as we saw, was an inversion of social ranks, masters changing places with their slaves and waiting upon them, while slaves were indulged with a semblance not merely of freedom but even of power and office. In various parts of Greece the same hollow show of granting liberty to slaves was made at certain festivals. Thus at a Cretan festival of Hermes the servants feasted and their masters waited upon them. In the month of Geraestius the Troezenians observed a certain solemnity lasting many days, on one of which the slaves played at dice with the citizens and were treated to a banquet by their lords. The Thessalians held a great festival called Peloria, which Baton of Sinope identified with the Saturnalia, and of which the antiquity is vouched for by a tradition that it originated with the Pelasgians. At this festival sacrifices were offered to Pelorian Zeus, tables splendidly adorned were set out, all strangers were invited to the feast, all prisoners released, and the slaves sat down to the banquet, enjoyed full freedom of speech, and were served by their masters.

Crete, Troezen, and Thessaly.

But the Greek festival which appears to have corresponded most closely to the Italian Saturnalia was the Cronia or festival of Cronus, a god whose barbarous myth and cruel ritual clearly belong to a very early stratum of Greek religion, and who was by the unanimous voice of antiquity identified with Saturn. We are told that his festival was celebrated in most parts of Greece, but especially at Athens, where the old god and his wife Rhea had a shrine near the stately, but far more modern, temple of Olympian Zeus. A joyous feast, at which masters and slaves sat down together, formed a leading feature of the solemnity. At Athens the festival fell in the height of summer, on the twelfth day of the month Hecatombaeon, formerly called the month of Cronus, which answered nearly to July; and tradition ran that Cecrops, the first king of Attica, had founded an altar in honour of Cronus and Rhea, and had ordained that master and man should share a common meal when the harvest was got in. Yet there are indications that at Athens the Cronia may once have been a spring festival. For a cake with twelve knobs, which perhaps referred to the twelve months of the year, was offered to Cronus by the Athenians on the fifteenth day of the month Elaphebolion, which corresponded roughly to March, and there are traces of a license accorded to slaves at the Dionysiac festival of the opening of the wine-jars, which fell on the

The Greek festival of the Cronia compared to the Roman Saturnalia.

The Olympian Cronia held at the spring equinox.

eleventh day of the preceding month Anthesterion. At Olympia the festival of Cronus undoubtedly occurred in spring; for here a low but steep hill, now covered with a tangled growth of dark holly-oaks and firs, was sacred to him, and on its top certain magistrates, who bore the title of kings, offered sacrifice to the old god at the vernal equinox in the Elean month Elaphius.

In this last ceremony, which probably went on year by year long before the upstart Zeus had a temple built for himself at the foot of the hill, there are two points of special interest, first the date of the ceremony, and second the title of the celebrants. First, as to the date, the spring equinox, or the twenty-first of March, must have fallen so near the fifteenth day of the Athenian month Elaphebolion, that we may fairly ask whether the Athenian custom of offering a cake to Cronus on that day The magistrates called Kings who celebrated the Cronia at Olympia may have personated King Cronus himself. may not also have been an equinoctial ceremony. In the second place, the title of kings borne by the magistrates who sacrificed to Cronus renders it probable that, like magistrates with similar high-sounding titles elsewhere in republican Greece, they were the lineal descendants of sacred kings whom the superstition of their subjects invested with the attributes of divinity. If that was so, it would be natural enough that one of these nominal kings should pose as the god Cronus in person. For, like his Italian counterpart Saturn, the Greek Cronus was believed to have been a king who reigned in heaven or on earth during the blissful Golden Age, when men passed their days like gods without toil or sorrow, when life was a long round of festivity, and death came like sleep, sudden but gentle, announced by none of his sad forerunners, the ailments and infirmities of age. Thus the analogy of the Olympian Cronia, probably one of the oldest of Greek festivals, to the Italian Saturnalia would be very close if originally, as I conjecture, the Saturnalia fell in spring and Saturn was personated at it, as we have good reason to Perhaps the man who annually personated King Cronus was put to death. believe, by a man dressed as a king. May we go a step further and suppose that, just as the man who acted King Saturn at the Saturnalia was formerly slain in that character, so one of the kings who celebrated the Cronia at Olympia not only played the part of Cronus, but was sacrificed, as god and victim in one, on the top of the hill? Cronus certainly bore a sinister reputation in antiquity. He passed for an unnatural parent who had devoured his own offspring, and he was regularly identified by the Greeks with the cruel Semitic Baals who delighted in the sacrifice of human victims, especially of children. A legend which savours strongly of infant sacrifice is reported of a shrine that stood at the very foot of the god's own hill at Olympia; and a quite unambiguous story was told of the sacrifice of a babe to Lycaean Zeus on Mount Lycaeus in Arcadia, where the worship of Zeus was probably nothing but a continuation, under a new name, of the old worship of Cronus, and where human victims appear to have been regularly offered down to the Christian era. The Rhodians annually sacrificed a man to Cronus in the month Metageitnion; at a later time they kept a condemned criminal in prison till the festival of the Cronia was come, then led him forth outside the gates, made him drunk with wine, and cut his throat. With the parallel of the Saturnalia before our eyes, we may surmise that the victim who thus ended his life in a state of intoxication at the Cronia perhaps personated King Cronus himself, the god who reigned in the happy days of old when men had nothing to do but to eat and drink and make merry. At least the Rhodian custom lends some countenance to the conjecture that formerly a human victim may have figured at the sacrifice which the so-called kings offered to Cronus on his hill at Olympia. In this connexion it is to be remembered that we have already found well-attested examples of a custom of sacrificing the scions of royal houses in ancient Greece.* If the god to whom, or perhaps rather in whose character, the princes were sacrificed, was Cronus, it would be natural that the Greeks of a later age should identify him with Baal or Moloch, to whom in like manner Semitic kings offered up their children. The Laphystian Zeus of Thessaly and Boeotia, whom tradition associated with these human sacrifices, was probably, like the Lycaean Zeus of Arcadia, nothing but the aboriginal deity, commonly known as Cronus, whose gloomy rites the Greek invaders suffered the priests of the vanquished race to continue after the ancient manner, while they quieted their scruples of conscience or satisfied their pride as conquerors by investing the bloodthirsty old savage with the name, if not with the character, of their own milder deity, the humane and gracious Zeus.

A man annually sacrificed to Cronus at the Cronia in Rhodes.

iv

The Babylo-
nian festival
of the Sacaea.
When we pass from Europe to western Asia, from ancient
Greece to ancient Babylon and the regions where Babylonian
influence penetrated, we are still met with festivals which bear
the closest resemblance to the oldest form of the Italian
Saturnalia. The reader may remember the festival of the Sacaea,
on which I had occasion to touch in an earlier part of this
work.* It was held at Babylon during five days of the month
Lous, beginning with the sixteenth day of the month. During
its continuance, just as at the Saturnalia, masters and servants
changed places, the servants issuing orders and the masters
obeying them; and in each house one of the servants, dressed as
a king and bearing the title of Zoganes, bore rule over the
household. Further, just as at the Saturnalia in its original form
a man was dressed as King Saturn in royal robes, allowed to
indulge his passions and caprices to the full, and then put to
death, so at the Sacaea a condemned prisoner, who probably
also bore for the time being the title of Zoganes, was arrayed in
the king's attire and suffered to play the despot, to use the
king's concubines, and to give himself up to feasting and
debauchery without restraint, only however in the end to be
stript of his borrowed finery, scourged, and hanged or crucified.* From Strabo we learn that this Asiatic counterpart of the
Saturnalia was celebrated in Asia Minor wherever the worship
of the Persian goddess Anaitis had established itself. He describes it as a Bacchic orgy, at which the revellers were
disguised as Scythians, and men and women drank and dallied
together by day and night.

The Sacaea
by some
identified
with Zakmuk
or Zagmuk,
the Babylo-
nian festival
of the New
Year, which
was held
about the
spring equi-
nox in March.
As the worship of Anaitis, though of Persian origin, appears
to have been deeply leavened with coarse elements which it
derived from the religion of Babylon, we may perhaps regard
Mesopotamia as the original home from which the Sacaean
festival spread westward into other parts of Asia Minor. Now
the Sacaean festival, described by the Babylonian priest Berosus
in the first book of his history of Babylon, has been plausibly
identified with the great Babylonian festival of the New Year
called Zakmuk, Zagmuk, Zakmuku, or Zagmuku, which has
become known to us in recent times through inscriptions. The

Babylonian year began with the spring month of Nisan, which seems to have covered the second half of March and the first half of April. Thus the New Year festival, which occupied at least the first eleven days of Nisan, probably included the spring equinox. It was held in honour of Marduk or Merodach, the chief god of Babylon, whose great temple of Esagila in the city formed the religious centre of the solemnity. For here, in a splendid chamber of the vast edifice, all the gods were believed to assemble at this season under the presidency of Marduk for the purpose of determining the fates for the new year, especially the fate of the king's life. On this occasion the king of Babylon was bound annually to renew his regal power by grasping the hands of the image of Marduk in his temple, as if to signify that he received the kingdom directly from the deity and was unable without the divine assistance and authority to retain it for more than a year. Unless he thus formally reinstated himself on the throne once a year, the king ceased to reign legitimately. When Babylonia was conquered by Assyria, the Assyrian monarchs themselves used to come to Babylon and perform the ceremony of grasping the god's hands in order to establish by this solemn act their title to the kingdom which they had won for themselves by the sword; until they had done so, they were not recognized as kings by their Babylonian subjects. Some of them indeed found the ceremony either so burdensome or so humiliating to their pride as conquerors, that rather than perform it they renounced the title of king of Babylon altogether and contented themselves with the more modest title of regent. Another notable feature of the Babylonian festival of the New Year appears to have been a ceremonial marriage of the god Marduk; for in a hymn relating to the solemnity it is said of the deity that 'he hastened to his bridal'. The festival was of hoar antiquity, for it was known to Gudea, an old king of Southern Babylonia who flourished between two and three thousand years before the beginning of our era, and it is mentioned in an early account of the Great Flood. At a much later period it is repeatedly referred to by King Nebuchadnezzar and his successors. Nebuchadnezzar records how he built of bricks and bitumen a chapel or altar, 'a thing of joy and rejoicing', for the great festival of Marduk, the lord of the gods; and we read of the rich and

Annual renewal of the king of Babylon's power at the Zakmuk festival.

abundant offerings which were made by the high priest at this time.

Unfortunately the notices of this Babylonian festival of the New Year which have come down to us deal chiefly with its mythical aspect and throw little light on the mode of its celebration. Hence its identity with the Sacaea must remain for the present a more or less probable hypothesis. In favour of the hypothesis may be alleged in the first place the resemblance of the names Sacaea and Zoganes to Zakmuk or Zagmuku, if that was the real pronunciation of the name, and in the second place the very significant statement that the fate of the king's life was supposed to be determined by the gods, under the presidency of Marduk, at the Zakmuk or New Year's festival. When we remember that the central feature of the Sacaea appears to have been the saving of the king's life for another year by the vicarious sacrifice of a criminal on the cross or the gallows, we can understand that the season was a critical one for the king, and that it may well have been regarded as determining his fate for the ensuing twelve months. The annual ceremony of renewing the king's power by contact with the god's image, which formed a leading feature of the Zakmuk festival, would be very appropriately performed immediately after the execution or sacrifice of the temporary king who died in the room of the real monarch.

A fresh and powerful argument in favour of the identity of the two festivals is furnished by the connexion which has been traced between both of them and the Jewish feast of Purim. There are good grounds for believing that Purim was unknown to the Jews until after the exile, and that they learned to observe it during their captivity in the East The festival is first mentioned in the book of Esther,* which by the majority of critics is assigned to the fourth or third century BC, and which certainly cannot be older than the Persian period, since the scene of the narrative is laid in Susa at the court of a Persian king Ahasuerus, whose name appears to be the Hebrew equivalent of Xerxes. The next reference to Purim occurs in the second book of Maccabees, a work written probably about the beginning of our era. Thus from the absence of all notice of Purim in the older books of the Bible, we may fairly conclude that the festival was instituted or imported at a comparatively late date among the Jews. The same conclusion is supported by the book of Esther itself, which was manifestly written to explain the origin of the feast and to suggest motives for its observance. For, according to the author of the book, the festival was established to commemorate the deliverance of the Jews from a great danger which threatened them in Persia under the reign of King Xerxes. Thus the opinion of modern scholars that the feast of Purim, as celebrated by the Jews, was of late date and oriental origin, is borne out by the tradition of the Jews themselves. An examination of that tradition and the mode of celebrating the feast renders it probable that Purim is nothing but a more or less disguised form of the Babylonian festival of the Sacaea or Zakmuk.

In the first place, the feast of Purim was and is held on the fourteenth and fifteenth days of Adar, the last month of the Jewish year, which corresponds roughly to March. Thus the date agrees nearly, though not exactly, with the date of the Babylonian Zakmuk, which fell a fortnight later in the early days of the following month Nisan. If the links which bind Purim to Zakmuk are reasonably strong, the chain of evidence which connects the Jewish festival with the Sacaea is much stronger. Nor is this surprising when we remember that, while the popular mode of celebrating Zakmuk is unknown, we possess important and trustworthy details as to the manner of holding the Sacaea. We have seen that the Sacaea was a wild Bacchanalian revel at which men and women disguised themselves and drank and played together in a fashion that was more gay than modest. Now this is, or used to be, precisely the nature of Purim. The two days of the festival, according to the author of the book of Esther, were to be kept for ever as 'days of feasting and gladness, and of sending portions one to another, and gifts to the poor.'* And this joyous character the festival seems always to have retained. The author of a tract in the Talmud lays it down as a rule that at the feast of Purim every Jew is bound to drink until he cannot distinguish between the words 'Cursed be Haman' and 'Blessed be Mordecai'; and he tells how on one occasion a certain Rabba drank so deep at Purim that he murdered a rabbi without knowing what he was about. Indeed Purim has been described as the Jewish Bacchanalia, and we are told that at this season everything is lawful

The Jewish festival of Purim seems to be derived from the Babylonian festival of Zakmuk. Connexion of Purim with the Sacaea.

The joyous nature of Purim.

which can contribute to the mirth and gaiety of the festival. Writers of the seventeenth century assert that during the two days, and especially on the evening of the second day, the Jews did nothing but feast and drink to repletion, play, dance, sing, and make merry; in particular they disguised themselves, men and women exchanging clothes, and thus attired ran about like mad, in open defiance of the Mosaic law, which expressly forbids men to dress as women and women as men. Among the Jews of Frankfort, who inhabited the squalid but quaint and picturesque old street known as the Judengasse, which many of us still remember, the revelry at Purim ran as high as ever in the eighteenth century. The gluttony and intoxication began punctually at three o'clock in the afternoon of the first day and went on until the whole community seemed to have taken leave of their senses. They ate and drank, they frolicked and cut capers, they reeled and staggered about, they shrieked, yelled, stamped, clattered, and broke each other's heads with wooden hammers till the blood flowed. On the evening of the first day the women were allowed, as a special favour, to open their latticed window and look into the men's synagogue, because the great deliverance of the Jews from their enemies in the time of King Ahasuerus was said to have been effected by a woman. A feature of the festival which should not be overlooked was the acting of the story of Esther as a comedy, in which Esther, Ahasuerus, Haman, Mordecai, and others played their parts after a fashion that sometimes degenerated from farce into ribaldry. Thus on the whole we may take it that Purim has always been a Saturnalia, and therefore corresponds in character to the Sacaea as that festival has been described for us by Strabo.

The origin of Purim according to the book of Esther.

But further, when we examine the narrative which professes to account for the institution of Purim, we discover in it not only the strongest traces of Babylonian origin, but also certain singular analogies to those very features of the Sacaean festival with which we are here more immediately concerned. The book of Esther turns upon the fortunes of two men, the vizier Haman and the despised Jew Mordecai, at the court of a Persian king. Mordecai, we are told, had given mortal offence to the vizier, who accordingly prepares a tall gallows on which he hopes to see his enemy hanged, while he himself expects to receive the highest mark of the king's favour by being allowed to wear the royal crown and the royal robes, and thus attired to parade the streets mounted on the king's own horse and attended by one of the noblest princes, who should proclaim to the multitude his temporary exaltation and glory. But the artful intrigues of the wicked vizier miscarried and resulted in precisely the opposite of what he had hoped and expected; for the royal honours which he had looked for fell to his rival Mordecai, and he himself was hanged on the gallows which he had made ready for his foe. In this story we seem to detect a reminiscence, more or less confused, of the Zoganes of the Sacaea, in other words, of the custom of investing a private man with the insignia of royalty for a few days and then putting him to death on the gallows or the cross. It is true that in the narrative the part of the Zoganes is divided between two actors, one of whom hopes to play the king but is hanged instead, while the other acts the royal part and escapes the gallows to which he was destined by his enemy. But this bisection, so to say, of the Zoganes may have been deliberately invented by the Jewish author of the book of Esther for the sake of setting the origin of Purim, which it was his purpose to explain, in a light that should reflect glory on his own nation. Or, perhaps more probably, it points back to a custom of appointing two mock kings at the Sacaea, one of whom was put to death at the end of the festival, while the other was allowed to go free, at least for a time. We shall be the more inclined to adopt the latter hypothesis when we observe that corresponding to the two rival aspirants to the temporary kingship there appear in the Jewish narrative two rival queens, Vashti and Esther, one of whom succeeds to the high estate from which the other has fallen. Further, it is to be noted that Mordecai, the successful candidate for the mock kingship, and Esther, the successful candidate for the queenship, are linked together by close ties both of interest and blood, the two being said to be cousins. This suggests that in the original story or the original custom there may have figured two pairs of kings and queens, of whom one pair is represented in the Jewish narrative by Mordecai and Esther and the other by Haman and Vashti.

The rival pairs Mordecai and Esther on the one side, Haman and Vashti on the other.

If we are right in tracing the origin of Purim to the Babylonian Sacaea and in finding the counterpart of the Zoganes in Haman and Mordecai, it would appear that the Zoganes during

The mock king of the Sacaea seems

his five days of office personated not merely a king but a god,
whether that god was the Babylonian Marduk or some other
deity not yet identified. The union of the divine and royal
characters in a single person is so common that we need not be
surprised at meeting with it in ancient Babylon. And the view
that the mock king of the Sacaea died as a god on the cross or
the gallows is no novelty. The acute and learned Movers long
ago observed that 'we should be overlooking the religious
significance of oriental festivals and the connexion of the Sacaea
with the worship of Anaitis, if we were to treat as a mere jest
the custom of disguising a slave as a king. We may take it for
certain that with the royal dignity the king of the Sacaea
assumed also the character of an oriental ruler as representative of the divinity, and that when he took his pleasure
among the women of the king's harem, he played the part of
Sandan or Sardanapalus himself. For according to ancient
oriental ideas the use of the king's concubines constituted a
claim to the throne, and we know from Dio that the five-days'
king received full power over the harem. Perhaps he began his
reign by publicly cohabiting with the king's concubines, just as
Absalom went in to his father's concubines in a tent spread on
the roof of the palace before all Israel, for the purpose of
thereby making known and strengthening his claim to the
throne.'*

The mock
king of the
Sacaea may
have mated
with a
woman who
played the
part of a god-
dess,
whether An-
aitis, Astarte,
or Semiramis.

Whatever may be thought of this latter conjecture, there can
be no doubt that Movers is right in laying great stress both on
the permission given to the mock king to invade the real king's
harem, and on the intimate connexion of the Sacaea with the
worship of Anaitis. That connexion is vouched for by Strabo,
and when we consider that in Strabo's time the cult of the old
Persian goddess Anaitis was thoroughly saturated with Babylonian elements and had practically merged in the sensual worship
of the Babylonian Ishtar or Astarte, we shall incline to view
with favour Movers's further conjecture, that a female slave
may have been appointed to play the divine queen to the part
of the divine king supported by the Zoganes, and that reminiscences of such a queen have survived in the myth or legend of
Semiramis. According to tradition, Semiramis was a fair court-
esan beloved by the king of Assyria, who took her to wife. She
won the king's heart so far that she persuaded him to yield up

to her the kingdom for five days, and having assumed the sceptre and the royal robes she made a great banquet on the first day, but on the second day she shut up her husband in prison or put him to death and thenceforward reigned alone. Taken with Strabo's evidence as to the association of the Sacaea with the worship of Anaitis, this tradition seems clearly to point to a custom of giving the Zoganes, during his five days' reign, a queen who represented the goddess Anaitis or Semiramis or Astarte, in short the great Asiatic goddess of love and fertility, by whatever name she was called. For that in Eastern legend Semiramis was a real queen of Assyria, who had absorbed many of the attributes of the goddess Astarte, appears to be established by the researches of modern scholars. The identity of Anaitis and the mythical Semiramis is clearly proved by the circumstance that the great sanctuary of Anaitis at Zela* in Pontus was actually built upon a mound of Semiramis; probably the old worship of the Semitic goddess always continued there even after her Semitic name of Semiramis or Astarte had been exchanged for the Persian name of Anaitis, perhaps in obedience to a decree of the Persian king Artaxerxes II, who first spread the worship of Anaitis in the west of Asia. It is highly significant, not only that the Sacaean festival was annually held at this ancient seat of the worship of Semiramis or Astarte; but further, that the whole city of Zela was formerly inhabited by sacred slaves and harlots, ruled over by a supreme pontiff, who administered it as a sanctuary rather than as a city. Formerly, we may suppose, this priestly king himself died a violent death at the Sacaea in the character of the divine lover of Semiramis, while the part of the goddess was played by one of the sacred prostitutes. The probability of this is greatly strengthened by the existence of the so-called mound of Semiramis under the sanctuary. For the mounds of Semiramis, which were pointed out all over Western Asia, were said to have been the graves of her lovers whom she buried alive. The tradition ran that the great and lustful queen Semiramis, fearing to contract a lawful marriage lest her husband should deprive her of power, admitted to her bed the handsomest of her soldiers, only, however, to destroy them all afterwards. Now this tradition is one of the surest indications of the identity of the mythical Semiramis with the Babylonian goddess Ishtar or Astarte. For the

Identity of the mythical Semiramis with Astarte.

The lovers of Semiramis and Ishtar (Astarte).

famous Babylonian epic which recounts the deeds of the hero Gilgamesh tells how, when he clothed himself in royal robes and put his crown on his head, the goddess Ishtar was smitten with love of him and wooed him to be her mate. But Gilgamesh rejected her insidious advances, for he knew the sad fate that had overtaken all her lovers, and he reproached the cruel goddess, saying:

'Tammuz, the lover of thy youth,
Thou causest to weep every year.
The bright-coloured *allallu* bird thou didst love.
Thou didst crush him and break his pinions.
In the woods he stands and laments, "O my pinions!"
Thou didst love the lion of perfect strength,
Seven and seven times thou didst dig pit-falls for him.
Thou didst love the horse that joyed in the fray,
With whip and spur and lash thou didst urge him on.
Thou didst force him on for seven double hours,
Thou didst force him on when wearied and thirsty;
His mother the goddess Silili thou madest weep.
Thou didst also love a shepherd of the flock,
Who continually poured out for thee the libation,
And daily slaughtered kids for thee;
But thou didst smite him, and didst change him into a wolf,
So that his own sheep-boys hunted him,
And his own hounds tore him to pieces.'

The hero also tells the miserable end of a gardener in the service of the goddess's father. The hapless swain had once been honoured with the love of the goddess, but when she tired of him she changed him into a cripple so that he could not rise from his bed. Therefore Gilgamesh fears to share the fate of all her former lovers and spurns her proffered favours. But it is not merely that the myth of Ishtar thus tallies with the legend of Semiramis; the worship of the goddess was marked by a profligacy which has found its echo in the loose character ascribed by tradition to the queen. Inscriptions, which confirm and supplement the evidence of Herodotus, inform us that Ishtar was served by harlots of three different classes all dedicated to her worship. Indeed, there is reason to think that these women personated the goddess herself, since one of the names given to them is applied also to her.

The sacred harlots of Ishtar.

Thus we can hardly doubt that the mythical Semiramis is substantially a form of Ishtar or Astarte, the great Semitic goddess of love and fertility; and if this is so, we may assume with at least a fair degree of probability that the high pontiff of Zela or his deputy, who played the king of the Sacaea at the sanctuary of Semiramis, perished as one of the unhappy lovers of the goddess, perhaps as Tammuz, whom she caused 'to weep every year'. When he had run his brief meteoric career of pleasure and glory, his bones would be laid in the great mound which covered the mouldering remains of many mortal gods, his predecessors, whom the goddess had honoured with her fatal love.

The myth of Ishtar (Astarte) and her lovers acted at the Sacaea in Zela.

Here then at the great sanctuary of the goddess in Zela it appears that her myth was regularly translated into action; the story of her love and the death of her divine lover was performed year by year as a sort of mystery-play by men and women who lived for a season and sometimes died in the character of the visionary beings whom they personated. The intention of these sacred dramas,* we may be sure, was neither to amuse nor to instruct an idle audience, and as little were they designed to gratify the actors, to whose baser passions they gave the reins for a time. They were solemn rites which mimicked the doings of divine beings, because man fancied that by such mimicry he was able to arrogate to himself the divine functions and to exercise them for the good of his fellows. The operations of nature, to his thinking, were carried on by mythical personages very like himself; and if he could only assimilate himself to them completely he would be able to wield all their powers. This is probably the original motive of most religious dramas or mysteries among rude peoples. The dramas are played, the mysteries are performed, not to teach the spectators the doctrines of their creed, still less to entertain them, but for the purpose of bringing about those natural effects which they represent in mythical disguise; in a word, they are magical ceremonies and their mode of operation is mimicry or sympathy. We shall probably not err in assuming that many myths, which we now know only as myths, had once their counterpart in magic; in other words, that they used to be acted as a means of producing in fact the events which they describe in figurative language. Ceremonies often die out while myths survive, and

Such sacred dramas are magical rites intended to influence the course of nature.

thus we are left to infer the dead ceremony from the living myth. If myths are, in a sense, the reflections or shadows of men cast upon the clouds, we may say that these reflections continue to be visible in the sky and to inform us of the doings of the men who cast them, long after the men themselves are not only beyond our range of vision but sunk beneath the horizon.

Magical intention of sacred dramas and masked dances among savages.

The principle of mimicry is implanted so deep in human nature and has exerted so far-reaching an influence on the development of religion as well as of the arts that it may be well, even at the cost of a short digression, to illustrate by example some of the modes in which primitive man has attempted to apply it to the satisfaction of his wants by means of religious or magical dramas. For it seems probable that the masked dances and ceremonies, which have played a great part in the social life of savages in many quarters of the world, were primarily designed to subserve practical purposes rather than simply to stir the emotions of the spectators and to while away the languor and tedium of idle hours. The actors sought to draw down blessings on the community by mimicking certain powerful superhuman beings and in their assumed character working those beneficent miracles which in the capacity of mere men they would have confessed themselves powerless to effect. In fact the aim of these elementary dramas, which contain in germ the tragedy and comedy of civilized nations, was the acquisition of superhuman power for the public good. That this is the real intention of at least many of these dramatic performances will appear from the following accounts.

Masked dances among the Indians of North-West America.

A conspicuous feature in the social life of the Indian tribes of North-Western America are the elaborate masked dances or pantomimes in which the actors personate spirits or legendary animals. Most of them appear designed to bring before the eyes of the people the guardian spirits of the clans. 'Owing to the fact that these spirits are hereditary, their gifts are always contained in the legend detailing their acquisition by the ancestor of a clan. The principal gifts in these tales are the magic harpoon which insures success in sea-otter hunting; the death bringer which, when pointed against enemies, kills them; the water of life which resuscitates the dead; the burning fire which, when pointed against an object, burns it; and a dance, a song, and cries which are peculiar to the spirit. The gift of this dance means that the protégé of the spirit is to perform the same dances which have been shown to him. In these dances he personates the spirit. He wears his mask and his ornaments. Thus the dance must be considered a dramatic performance of the myth relating to the acquisition of the spirit, and shows to the people that the performer by his visit to the spirit has obtained his powers and desires. When nowadays a spirit appears to a young Indian, he gives him the same dance, and the youth also returns from the initiation filled with the powers and desires of the spirit. He authenticates his initiation by his dance in the same way as his mythical ancestor did. The obtaining of the magical gifts from these spirits is called *lokoala*, while the person who has obtained them becomes *naualaku*, supernatural, which is also the quality of the spirit himself. The ornaments of all these spirits are described as made of cedar bark, which is dyed red in the juice of alder bark. They appear to their devotees only in winter, and therefore the dances are also performed only in winter.' In some of the dances the performers imitate animals, and the explanation which the Indians give of these dances is that 'the ceremonial was instituted at the time when men had still the form of animals; before the transformer had put everything into its present shape. The present ceremonial is a repetition of the ceremonial performed by the man animals or, as we may say, a dramatization of the myth. Therefore the people who do not represent spirits, represent these animals.'*

The Monumbo of German New Guinea perform masked dances in which the dancers personate supernatural beings or animals, such as kangaroos, dogs, and cassowaries. They consecrate the masks by fumigating them with the smoke of a certain creeper, and believe that by doing so they put life into them. Accordingly they afterwards treat the masks with respect, talk to them as if they were alive, and refuse to part with them to Europeans. Certain of the masks they even regard as guardian spirits and appeal to them for fine weather, help in the chase or in war, and so forth. Every clan owns some masks and the head man of the clan makes all the arrangements for a masquerade. The dances are accompanied by songs of which the words are unintelligible even to the natives themselves. Again, the Kayans

Masked dances of the Monumbo in German New Guinea.

Masked dances of the Kayans of Borneo.

of Central Borneo perform masked dances for the purpose of ensuring abundant crops of rice. The actors personate demons, wearing grotesque masks on their faces, their bodies swathed in cumbrous masses of green leaves. 'In accordance with their belief that the spirits are more powerful than men, the Kayans assume that when they imitate the form of spirits and play their part, they acquire superhuman power. Hence just as their spirits can fetch back the souls of men, so they imagine that they can lure to themselves the souls of the rice.'

Dramatic performances of the Sea Dyaks of Borneo, in which the actor personates a god.

When the Sea Dyaks of Borneo have taken a human head, they hold a Head-feast (*Gawè Pala*) in honour of the war-god or bird-chief Singalang Burong, who lives far away above the sky. At this festival a long liturgy called *mengap* is chanted, the god is invoked, and is believed to be present in the person of an actor, who poses as the deity and blesses the people in his name. 'But the invocation is not made by the human performer in the manner of a prayer direct to this great being; it takes the form of a story, setting forth how the mythical hero Kling or Klieng made a head-feast and fetched Singalang Burong to it. This Kling, about whom there are many fables, is a spirit, and is supposed to live somewhere or other not far from mankind, and to be able to confer benefits upon them. The Dyak performer or performers then, as they walk up and down the long verandah of the house singing the *mengap*, in reality describe Kling's *Gawè Pala* [head-feast], and how Singalang Burong was invited and came. In thought the Dyaks identify themselves with Kling, and the resultant signification is that the recitation of this story is an invocation to Singalang Burong, who is supposed to come not to Kling's house only, but to the actual Dyak house where the feast is celebrated; and he is received by a particular ceremony, and is offered food or sacrifice.' At the close of the ceremony 'the performer goes along the house, beginning with the head man, touches each person in it, and pronounces an invocation upon him. In this he is supposed to personate Singalang Burong and his sons-in-law, who are believed to be the real actors. Singalang Burong himself *nenjangs* the headmen, and his sons-in-law, the birds, bless the rest. The touch of the human performer, and the accompanying invocation are thought to effect a communication between these bird-spirits from the skies and each individual being. The great bird-chief and his dependants come from above to give men their charms and their blessings. Upon the men the performer invokes physical strength and bravery in war; and upon the women luck with paddy, cleverness in Dyak feminine accomplishments, and beauty in form and complexion.'*

Thus the dramatic performances of these primitive peoples are in fact religious or oftener perhaps magical ceremonies, and the songs or recitations which accompany them are spells or incantations, though the real character of both is apt to be overlooked by civilized man, accustomed as he is to see in the drama nothing more than an agreeable pastime or at best a vehicle of moral instruction. Yet if we could trace the drama of the civilized nations back to its origin, we might find that it had its roots in magical or religious ideas like those which still mould and direct the masked dances of many savages. Certainly the Athenians in the heyday of their brilliant civilization retained a lively sense of the religious import of dramatic performances; for they associated them directly with the worship of Dionysus and allowed them to be enacted only during the festivals of the god. In India, also, the drama appears to have been developed out of religious dances or pantomimes, in which the actors recited the deeds and played the parts of national gods and heroes. Hence it is at least a legitimate hypothesis that the criminal, who masqueraded as a king and perished in that character at the Bacchanalian festival of the Sacaea, was only one of a company of actors, who figured on that occasion in a sacred drama of which the substance has been preserved to us in the book of Esther.

Religious or magical origin of the drama.

When once we perceive that the gods and goddesses, the heroes and heroines of mythology have been represented officially, so to say, by a long succession of living men and women who bore the names and were supposed to exercise the functions of these fabulous creatures, we have attained a point of vantage from which it seems possible to propose terms of peace between two rival schools of mythologists who have been waging fierce war on each other for ages. On the one hand it has been argued that mythical beings are nothing but personifications of natural objects and natural processes; on the other hand, it has been maintained that they are nothing but notable men and women who in their lifetime, for one reason or

The representation of mythical beings by living men and women may furnish a common ground where two rival schools of mythology can meet and be reconciled.

another, made a great impression on their fellows, but whose doings have been distorted and exaggerated by a false and credulous tradition. These two views, it is now easy to see, are not so mutually exclusive as their supporters have imagined. The personages about whom all the marvels of mythology have been told may have been real human beings, as the Euhemerists allege; and yet they may have been at the same time personifications of natural objects or processes, as the adversaries of Euhemerism assert. The doctrine of incarnation supplies the missing link that was needed to unite the two seemingly inconsistent theories. If the powers of nature or a certain department of nature be conceived as personified in a deity, and that deity can become incarnate in a man or woman, it is obvious that the incarnate deity is at the same time a real human being and a personification of nature. To take the instance with which we are here concerned, Semiramis may have been the great Semitic goddess of love, Ishtar or Astarte, and yet she may be supposed to have been incarnate in a woman or even in a series of real women, whether queens or harlots, whose memory survives in ancient history. Saturn, again, may have been the god of sowing and planting, and yet may have been represented on earth by a succession or dynasty of sacred kings, whose gay but short lives may have contributed to build up the legend of the Golden Age. The longer the series of such human divinities, the greater, obviously, the chance of their myth or legend surviving; and when moreover a deity of a uniform type was represented, whether under the same name or not, over a great extent of country by many local dynasties of divine men or women, it is clear that the stories about him would tend still further to persist and be stereotyped.

The conclusions which we have reached in regard to the legend of Semiramis and her lovers probably holds good of all the similar tales that were current in antiquity throughout the East; in particular, it may be assumed to apply to the myths of Aphrodite and Adonis in Syria, of Cybele and Attis in Phrygia, and of Isis and Osiris in Egypt. If we could trace these stories back to their origin, we might find that in every case a human couple acted year by year the parts of the loving goddess and the dying god. We know that down to Roman times Attis was personated by priests who bore his name; and if within the period of which we have knowledge the dead Attis and the dead Adonis were represented only by effigies, we may surmise that it had not always been so, and that in both cases the dead god was once represented by a dead man. Further, the license accorded to the man who played the dying god at the Sacaea speaks strongly in favour of the hypothesis that before the incarnate deity was put to a public death he was in all cases allowed, or rather required, to enjoy the embraces of a woman who played the goddess of love. The reason for such an enforced union of the human god and goddess is not hard to divine. If primitive man believes that the growth of the crops can be stimulated by the intercourse of common men and women, what showers of blessings will he not anticipate from the commerce of a pair whom his fancy invests with all the dignity and powers of deities of fertility?

Thus the theory of Movers, that at the Sacaea the Zoganes represented a god and paired with a woman who personated a goddess, turns out to rest on deeper and wider foundations than that able scholar was aware of. He thought that the divine couple who figured by deputy at the ceremony were Semiramis and Sandan or Sardanapalus. It now appears that he was substantially right as to the goddess; but we have still to enquire into the god. There seems to be no doubt that the name Sardanapalus is only the Greek way of representing Ashurbanipal, the name of the greatest and nearly the last king of Assyria. But the records of the real monarch which have come to light within recent years give little support to the fables that attached to his name in classical tradition. For they prove that, far from being the effeminate weakling he seemed to the Greeks of a later age, he was a warlike and enlightened monarch, who carried the arms of Assyria to distant lands and fostered at home the growth of science and letters. Still, though the historical reality of King Ashurbanipal is as well attested as that of Alexander or Charlemagne, it would be no wonder if myths gathered, like clouds, round the great figure that loomed large in the stormy sunset of Assyrian glory. Now the two features that stand out most prominently in the legends of Sardanapalus are his extravagant debauchery and his violent death in the flames of a great pyre, on which he burned himself and his concubines to save them from falling into the hands of his

Sardanapalus and Ashurbanipal.

The legendary death of Sardanapalus in the fire.

victorious enemies.* It is said that the womanish king, with painted face and arrayed in female attire, passed his days in the seclusion of the harem, spinning purple wool among his concubines and wallowing in sensual delights; and that in the epitaph which he caused to be carved on his tomb he recorded that all the days of his life he ate and drank and toyed, remembering that life is short and full of trouble, that fortune is uncertain, and that others would soon enjoy the good things which he must leave behind. These traits bear little resemblance to the portrait of Ashurbanipal either in life or in death; for after a brilliant career of conquest the Assyrian king died in old age, at the height of human ambition, with peace at home and triumph abroad, the admiration of his subjects and the terror of his foes. But if the traditional characteristics of Sardanapalus harmonize but ill with what we know of the real monarch of that name, they fit well enough with all that we know or can conjecture of the mock kings who led a short life and a merry during the revelry of the Sacaea, the Asiatic equivalent of the Saturnalia. We can hardly doubt that for the most part such men, with death staring them in the face at the end of a few days, sought to drown care and deaden fear by plunging madly into all the fleeting joys that still offered themselves under the sun. When their brief pleasures and sharp sufferings were over, and their bones or ashes mingled with the dust, what more natural that on their tomb—those mounds in which the people saw, not untruly, the graves of the lovers of Semiramis—there should be carved some such lines as those which tradition placed in the mouth of the great Assyrian king, to remind the heedless passer-by of the shortness and vanity of life?

v

Traces of human sacrifice in the Jewish festival of Purim: effigies of Haman burnt.

If the Jewish festival of Purim was, as I have attempted to shew, directly descended either from the Sacaea or from some other Semitic festival, of which the central feature was the sacrifice of a man in the character of a god, we should expect to find traces of human sacrifice lingering about it in one or other of those mitigated forms to which I have just referred. This expectation is fully borne out by the facts. For from an early time it has been customary with the Jews at the feast of Purim to burn or otherwise destroy effigies of Haman. The practice was well known under the Roman empire, for in the year 408 AD the emperors Honorius and Theodosius issued a decree commanding the governors of the provinces to take care that the Jews should not burn effigies of Haman on a cross at one of their festivals. We learn from the decree that the custom gave great offence to the Christians, who regarded it as a blasphemous parody of the central mystery of their own religion, little suspecting that it was nothing but a continuation, in a milder form, of a rite that had probably been celebrated in the East long ages before the birth of Christ. The Arab historian Albîrûnî, who wrote in the year 1000 AD, informs us that at Purim the Jews of his time rejoiced greatly over the death of Haman, and that they made figures which they beat and burned, 'imitating the burning of Haman'. Hence one name for the festival was Hâmân-Sûr. Another Arabic writer, Makrîzî, who died in 1442 AD, says that at the feast of Purim, which fell on the fifteenth day of the month Adar, some of the Jews used to make effigies of Haman which they first played with and then threw into the fire. During the Middle Ages the Italian Jews celebrated Purim in a lively fashion which has been compared by their own historians to that of the Carnival. The children used to range themselves in rows opposite each other and pelt one another with nuts, while grown-up people rode on horseback through the streets with pine branches in their hands or blew trumpets and made merry round a puppet representing Haman, which was set on a platform or scaffold and then solemnly burnt on a pyre. In the eighteenth century the Jews of Frankfort used at Purim to make pyramids of thin wax candles, which they set on fire; also they fashioned images of Haman and his wife out of candles and burned them on the reading-desk in the synagogue.

Now, when we consider the close correspondence in character as well as in date between the Jewish Purim and the Christian Carnival, and remember further that the effigy of Carnival, which is now destroyed at this merry season, had probably its prototype in a living man who was put to a violent death in the character of Saturn at the Saturnalia, analogy of itself would suggest that in former times the Jews, like the Babylonians, from whom they appear to have derived their Purim, may at one

Accusations of ritual murder brought against the Jews.

time have burned, hanged, or crucified a real man in the character of Haman. Into this troubled arena I prefer not to enter; I will only observe that, so far as I have looked into the alleged cases, and these are reported in sufficient detail, the majority of the victims are said to have met their fate in spring,

Mitigation of
human sacri-
fice by the
substitution
of a criminal
for the victim.

often in the week before Easter. But between the stage when human sacrifice goes on unabashed in the light of common day, and the stage when it has been driven out of sight into dark holes and corners, there intervenes a period during which the custom is slowly dwindling away under the growing light of knowledge and philanthropy. In this middle period many subterfuges are resorted to for the sake of preserving the old ritual in a form which will not offend the new morality. A common and successful device is to consummate the sacrifice on the person of a malefactor, whose death at the altar or elsewhere is little likely to excite pity or indignation, since it partakes of the character of a punishment, and people recognize that if the miscreant had not been dealt with by the priest, it would have been needful in the public interest to hand him over to the executioner. It seems therefore by no means impossible that the Jews, in borrowing the Sacaea from Babylon under the new name of Purim, should have borrowed along with it the custom of putting to death a malefactor who, after masquerading as Mordecai in a crown and royal robe, was hanged or crucified in the character of Haman.

At the Sacaean festival, if I am right, a man, who personated a god or hero of the type of Tammuz or Adonis, enjoyed the favours of a woman, probably a sacred harlot, who represented the great Semitic goddess Ishtar or Astarte; and after he had thus done his part towards securing, by means of sympathetic magic, the revival of plant life in spring, he was put to death. We may suppose that the death of this divine man was mourned over by his worshippers, and especially by women, in much the same fashion as the women of Jerusalem wept for Tammuz at the gate of the temple, and as Syrian damsels mourned the dead Adonis, while the river ran red with his blood. Such rites appear, in fact, to have been common all over Western Asia; the particular name of the dying god varied in different places, but in substance the ritual was the same. Fundamentally, the custom was a religious or rather magical ceremony intended to ensure the revival and reproduction of life in spring.

Now, if this interpretation of the Sacaea is correct, it is obvious that one important feature of the ceremony is wanting in the brief notices of the festival that have come down to us. The death of the man-god at the festival is recorded, but nothing is said of his resurrection. Yet if he really personated a being of the Adonis or Attis type, we may feel pretty sure that his dramatic death was followed at a shorter or longer interval by his dramatic revival, just as at the festivals of Attis and Adonis the resurrection of the dead god quickly succeeded to his mimic death. Here, however, a difficulty presents itself. At the Sacaea the man-god died a real, not a mere mimic death; and in ordinary life the resurrection even of a man-god is at least not an everyday occurrence. What was to be done? The man, or rather the god, was undoubtedly dead. How was he to come to life again? Obviously the best, if not the only way, was to set another and living man to support the character of the reviving god, and we may conjecture that this was done. We may suppose that the insignia of royalty which had adorned the dead man were transferred to his successor, who, arrayed in them, would be presented to his rejoicing worshippers as their god come to life again; and by his side would probably be displayed a woman in the character of his divine consort, the goddess Ishtar or Astarte. In favour of this hypothesis it may be observed that it at once furnishes a clear and intelligible explanation of a remarkable feature in the book of Esther which has not yet, so far as I am aware, been adequately elucidated; I mean that apparent duplication of the principal characters to which I have already directed the reader's attention. If I am right, Haman represents the temporary king or mortal god who was put to death at the Sacaea; and his rival Mordecai represents the other temporary king who, on the death of his predecessor, was invested with his royal insignia, and exhibited to the people as the god come to life again. Similarly Vashti, the deposed queen in the narrative, corresponds to the woman who played the part of queen and goddess to the first mock king, the Haman; and her successful rival, Esther or Ishtar, answers to the woman who figured as the divine consort of the second mock king, the Mordecai or Marduk.

The resurrection of the dead god perhaps represented by a living man who afterwards died in earnest in the character of the god.

This would explain the apparent duplication of the principal characters in the book of Esther. Haman and Vashti would represent the gods dying, while Mordecai and Esther would represent the gods rising from the dead.

The Persian setting of the book of Esther.

The Persian setting, in which the Hebrew author of the book of Esther has framed his highly-coloured picture, naturally suggests that the Jews derived their feast of Purim not directly from the old Babylonians, but from their Persian conquerors. Even if this could be demonstrated, it would in no way invalidate the theory that Purim originated in the Babylonian festival of the Sacaea, since we know that the Sacaea was celebrated by the Persians. Hence it becomes worth while to enquire whether in the Persian religion we can detect any traces of a festival akin to the Sacaea or Purim. Here Lagarde has shewn the way by directing attention to the old Persian cere-

The Persian ceremony of the 'Ride of the Beardless One' in spring.

mony known as the 'Ride of the Beardless One'.* This was a rite performed both in Persia and Babylonia at the beginning of spring, on the first day of the first month, which in the most ancient Persian calendar corresponded to March, so that the date of the ceremony agrees with that of the Babylonian New Year festival of Zakmuk. A beardless and, if possible, one-eyed buffoon was set naked on an ass, a horse, or a mule, and conducted in a sort of mock triumph through the streets of the city. In one hand he held a crow and in the other a fan, with which he fanned himself, complaining of the heat, while the people pelted him with ice and snow and drenched him with cold water. He stopped at the doors of the rich, and if they did not give him what he asked for, he befouled their garments with mud or a mixture of red ochre and water, which he carried in an earthenware pot. If a shopkeeper hesitated a moment to respond to his demands, the importunate beggar had the right to confiscate all the goods in the shop; so the tradesmen who saw him bearing down on them, not unnaturally hastened to anticipate his wants by contributing of their substance before he could board them. Everything that he thus collected from break of day to the time of morning prayers belonged to the king or governor of the city; but everything that he laid hands on between the first and the second hour of prayer he kept for himself. After the second prayers he disappeared, and if the people caught him later in the day they were free to beat him to their heart's content.

The 'Beardless One' in the Persian

Now in this harlequin, who rode through the streets attended by all the king's men, and levying contributions which went either to the royal treasury or to the pocket of the collector, we recognise the familiar features of the mock or temporary king, who is invested for a short time with the pomp and privileges of royalty for reasons which have been already explained. The abrupt disappearance of the Persian clown at a certain hour of the day, coupled with the leave given to the populace to thrash him if they found him afterwards, points plainly enough to the harder fate that probably awaited him in former days, when he paid with his life for his brief tenure of a kingly crown. The resemblance between his burlesque progress and that of Mordecai through the streets of Susa is obvious; though the Jewish author of Esther has depicted in brighter colours the pomp of his hero 'in royal apparel of blue and white, and with a great crown of gold, and with a robe of fine linen and purple', riding the king's own charger, and led through the city by one of the king's most noble princes. In the present instance the purpose of the 'Ride of the Beardless One' at the beginning of spring is sufficiently obvious; it was meant to hasten the departure of winter and the approach of summer. On the principles of homoeopathic or imitative magic, which is little more than an elaborate system of make-believe, you can make the weather warm by pretending that it is so; or if you cannot, you may be sure that there is some person wiser than yourself who can. Such a wizard, in the estimation of the Persians, was the beardless one-eyed man who went through the performance I have described; and no doubt his physical defects were believed to contribute in some occult manner to the success of the rite. The ceremony was thus the oriental equivalent of those popular European customs which celebrate the advent of spring by representing in a dramatic form the expulsion or defeat of winter by the victorious summer. But whereas in Europe the two rival seasons are often, if not regularly, personated by two actors or two effigies, in Persia a single actor sufficed. Whether he definitely represented winter or summer is not quite clear; but his pretence of suffering from heat and his final disappearance suggest that, if he personified either of the seasons, it was the departing winter rather than the coming summer.

If there is any truth in the connexion thus traced between Purim and the 'Ride of the Beardless One', we are now in a position finally to unmask the leading personages in the book of Esther. I have attempted to shew that Haman and Vashti are

ceremony is apparently the degenerate successor of a temporary king.

The opposition of Haman and Vashti to Mordecai

and Esther
seems to be a
contrast be-
tween the an-
nual death of
nature in
winter and
its revival in
spring.

little more than doubles of Mordecai and Esther, who in turn
conceal under a thin disguise the features of Marduk and Ishtar,
the great god and goddess of Babylon. But why, the reader may
ask, should the divine pair be thus duplicated and the two pairs
set in opposition to each other? The answer is suggested by the
popular European celebrations of spring to which I have just
adverted. If my interpretation of these customs is right, the
contrast between the summer and winter, or between the life
and death, which figure in effigy or in the persons of living
representatives at the spring ceremonies of our peasantry, is
fundamentally a contrast between the dying or dead vegetation
of the old and the sprouting vegetation of the new year—a
contrast which would lose nothing of its point when, as in
ancient Rome and Babylon and Persia, the beginning of spring
was also the beginning of the new year. In these and in all the
ceremonies we have been examining the antagonism is not
between powers of a different order, but between the same
power viewed in different aspects as old and young; it is, in
short, nothing but the eternal and pathetic contrast between
youth and age. And as the power or spirit of vegetation is
represented in religious ritual and popular custom by a human
pair, whether they be called Ishtar and Tammuz, or Venus and
Adonis, or the Queen and King of May, so we may expect to
find the old decrepit spirit of the past year personated by one
pair, and the fresh young spirit of the new year by another.
This, if my hypothesis is right, is the ultimate explanation of
the struggle between Haman and Vashti on the one side, and
their doubles Mordecai and Esther on the other. In the last
analysis both pairs stood for the powers that make for the
fertility of plants and perhaps also of animals; but the one pair
embodied the failing energies of the past, and the other the
vigorous and growing energies of the coming year. Both powers,
on my hypothesis, were personified not merely in myth, but in
custom; for year by year a human couple undertook to quicken
the life of nature by a union in which, as in a microcosm, the
loves of tree and plant, of herb and flower, of bird and beast
were supposed in some mystic fashion to be summed up.
Originally, we may conjecture, such couples exercised their
functions for a whole year, on the conclusion of which the male
partner—the divine king—was put to death; but in historical

times it seems that, as a rule, the human god—the Saturn, Zoganes, Tammuz, or whatever he was called—enjoyed his divine privileges, and discharged his divine duties only for a short part of the year. This curtailment of his reign on earth was probably introduced at the time when the old hereditary divinities or deified kings contrived to shift the most painful part of their duties to a substitute, whether that substitute was a son or a slave or a malefactor. Having to die as a king, it was necessary that the substitute should also live as a king for a season; but the real monarch would naturally restrict within the narrowest limits both of time and of power a reign which, so long as it lasted, necessarily encroached upon and indeed superseded his own. What became of the divine king's female partner, the human goddess who shared his bed and transmitted his beneficent energies to the rest of nature, we cannot say. So far as I am aware, there is little or no evidence that she like him suffered death when her primary function was discharged. The nature of maternity suggests an obvious reason for sparing her a little longer, till that mysterious law, which links together woman's life with the changing aspects of the nightly sky, had been fulfilled by the birth of an infant god, who should in his turn, reared perhaps by her tender care, grow up to live and die for the world.

CHAPTER 5

THE CRUCIFIXION OF CHRIST

The mockery
of Christ
compared to
the mockery
of the King
of the Satur-
nalia.

AN eminent scholar has recently pointed out the remarkable
resemblance between the treatment of Christ by the Roman
soldiers at Jerusalem and the treatment of the mock king of the
Saturnalia by the Roman soldiers at Durostorum; and he would
explain the similarity by supposing that the soldiers ridiculed
the claims of Christ to a divine kingdom by arraying him in the
familiar garb of old King Saturn, whose quaint person figured
so prominently at the winter revels.* Even if the theory should
prove to be right, we can hardly suppose that Christ played the
part of the regular Saturn of the year, since at the beginning of
our era the Saturnalia fell at midwinter, whereas Christ was
crucified at the Passover in spring. There is, indeed, as I have
pointed out, some reason to think that when the Roman year
began in March the Saturnalia was held in spring, and that in
remote districts the festival always continued to be celebrated
at the ancient date. If the Roman garrison of Jerusalem con-
formed to the old fashion in this respect, it seems not quite
impossible that their celebration of the Saturnalia may have
coincided with the Passover; and that thus Christ, as a condemned criminal, may have been given up to them to make
sport with as the Saturn of the year. But on the other hand it
is rather unlikely that the officers, as representatives of the
State, would have allowed their men to hold the festival at any
but the official date; even in the distant town of Durostorum
we saw that the Roman soldiers celebrated the Saturnalia in
December. Thus if the legionaries at Jerusalem really intended
to mock Christ by treating him like the burlesque king of the
Saturnalia, they probably did so only by way of a jest which was
in more senses than one unseasonable.

The mockery
of Christ
compared to
the mockery

But closely as the passion of Christ resembles the treatment
of the mock king of the Saturnalia, it resembles still more
closely the treatment of the mock king of the Sacaea. The
description of the mockery by St Matthew is the fullest. It runs

thus: 'Then released he Barabbas unto them: and when he had
scourged Jesus, he delivered him to be crucified. Then the
soldiers of the governor took Jesus into the common hall, and
gathered unto him the whole band of soldiers. And they
stripped him, and put on him a scarlet robe. And when they
had platted a crown of thorns, they put it upon his head, and a
reed in his right hand: and they bowed the knee before him, and
mocked him, saying, Hail, King of the Jews! And they spit upon
him, and took the reed, and smote him on the head. And after
that they had mocked him, they took the robe off from him, and
put his own raiment on him, and led him away to crucify him.'*
Compare with this the treatment of the mock king of the
Sacaea, as it is described by Dio Chrysostom: 'They take one of
the prisoners condemned to death and seat him upon the king's
throne, and give him the king's raiment, and let him lord it and
drink and run riot and use the king's concubines during these
days, and no man prevents him from doing just what he likes.
But afterwards they strip and scourge and crucify him.'* Now
it is quite possible that this remarkable resemblance is after all
a mere coincidence, and that Christ was executed in the
ordinary way as a common malefactor; but on the other hand
there are so many scattered hints and indications of something
unusual, so many broken lines seemingly converging towards
the cross on Calvary, that it is worth while to follow them up
and see where they lead us. In attempting to draw these
fragmentary data together, to bridge the chasms, and to restore
the shattered whole, we must beware of mistaking hypothesis
for the facts which it only professes to cement; yet even if our
hypothesis should be thought to bear a somewhat undue proportion to the facts, the excess may perhaps be overlooked in
consideration of the obscurity and the importance of the
enquiry.

We have seen reason to think that the Jewish festival of Purim
is a continuation, under a changed name, of the Babylonian
Sacaea, and that in celebrating it by the destruction of an effigy
of Haman the modern Jews have kept up a reminiscence of the
ancient custom of crucifying or hanging a man in the character
of a god at the festival. Is it not possible that at an earlier time
they may, like the Babylonians themselves, have regularly
compelled a condemned criminal to play the tragic part, and

perished in that character.

that Christ thus perished in the character of Haman? The resemblance between the hanged Haman and the crucified Christ struck the early Christians themselves; and whenever the Jews destroyed an effigy of Haman they were accused by their Christian neighbours of deriding the most sacred mystery of the new faith. It is probable that on this painful subject the Christians were too sensitive; remembering the manner of their Founder's death it was natural that they should wince at any pointed allusion to a cross, a gallows, or a public execution, even when the shaft was not aimed at them. An objection to supposing that Christ died as the Haman of the year is that according to the Gospel narrative the crucifixion occurred at the Passover, on the fourteenth day of the month Nisan, whereas the feast of Purim, at which the hanging of Haman would naturally take place, fell exactly a month earlier, namely, on the fourteenth day of the month Adar. I have no wish to blink or extenuate the serious nature of the difficulty arising from this discrepancy of dates, but I would suggest some considerations which may make us hesitate to decide that the discrepancy is fatal. In the first place, it is possible, though perhaps not probable, that Christian tradition shifted the date of the crucifixion by a month in order to make the great sacrifice of the Lamb of God coincide with that annual sacrifice of the Passover lamb which in the belief of pious hearts had so long foreshadowed it and was thenceforth to cease. Instances of gentle pressure brought to bear, for purposes of edification, on stubborn facts are perhaps not wholly unknown in the annals of religion. But the express testimony of history is never to be lightly set aside; and in the investigation of its problems a solution which assumes the veracity and accuracy of the historian is, on an even balance of probabilities, always to be preferred to one which impugns them both. Now in the present case we have seen reason to think that the Babylonian New Year festival, of which Purim was a continuation, did fall in Nisan at or near the time of the Passover, and that when the Jews borrowed the festival they altered the date from Nisan to Adar in order to prevent the new feast from clashing with the old Passover. A reminiscence of the original date of Purim perhaps survives in the statement in the book of Esther that Haman caused *pur* or lots to be cast before him from the month of

But the Passover, at which Christ was crucified, fell a month after Purim.

Nisan onward. It thus seems not impossible that occasionally, for some special reason, the Jews should have celebrated the feast of Purim, or at least the death of Haman, at or about the time of the Passover. But there is another possibility which, remote and fanciful as it may appear, deserves at least to be mentioned. The mock king of the Saturnalia was allowed a period of license of thirty days before he was put to death. If we could suppose that in like manner the Jews spared the human representative of Haman for one month from Purim, the date of his execution would fall exactly on the Passover. Which, if any, of these conjectural solutions of the difficulty is the true one, I will not undertake to say. I am fully conscious of the doubt and uncertainty that hang round the whole subject; and if in this and what follows I throw out some hints and suggestions, it is more in the hope of stimulating and directing further enquiry than with any expectation of reaching definite conclusions.

Perhaps the annual Haman, like the annual Saturn, was allowed a month's license before being put to death.

It may be objected that the mockery of Christ was done, not by the Jews, but by the Roman soldiers, who knew and cared nothing about Haman; how then can we suppose that the purple or scarlet robe, the sceptre of reed, and the crown of thorns, which the soldiers thrust upon Christ, were the regular insignia of the Haman of the year? To this we may reply, in the first place, that even if the legions stationed in Syria were not recruited in the country, they may have contracted some of the native superstitions and have fallen in with the local customs. This is not an idle conjecture. We know that the third legion during its stay in Syria learned the Syrian custom of saluting the rising sun, and that this formal salute, performed by the whole regiment as one man at a critical moment of the great battle of Bedriacum, actually helped to turn the scale when the fortune of empire hung trembling in the balance. But it is not necessary to suppose that the garrison of Jerusalem really shared the beliefs and prejudices of the mob whom they overawed; soldiers everywhere are ready to go with a crowd bent on sport, without asking any curious questions as to the history or quality of the entertainment, and we should probably do the humanity of Roman soldiers too much honour if we imagined that they would be deterred by any qualm of conscience from joining in the pastime, which is still so popular, of baiting a Jew to death.

The part taken by the soldiers in the mockery of Christ.

But in the second place it should be observed that, according to one of the Evangelists, it was not the soldiers of Pilate who mocked Jesus, but the soldiers of Herod,* and we may fairly assume that Herod's guards were Jews.

The theory that Christ died, not as a malefactor, but in the character of Haman helps to explain both Pilate's reluctance to put him to death, and it also explains the remarkable superscription on the cross.

The hypothesis that the crucifixion with all its cruel mockery was not a punishment specially devised for Christ, but was merely the fate that annually befell the malefactor who played Haman, appears to go some way towards relieving the Gospel narrative of certain difficulties which otherwise beset it. If, as we read in the Gospels, Pilate was really anxious to save the innocent man whose fine bearing seems to have struck him, what was to hinder him from doing so? He had the power of life and death; why should he not have exercised it on the side of mercy, if his own judgment inclined that way? His reluctant acquiescence in the importunate demand of the rabble becomes easier to understand if we assume that custom obliged him annually at this season to give up to them a prisoner on whom they might play their cruel pranks. On this assumption Pilate had no power to prevent the sacrifice; the most he could do was to choose the victim.

Again, consider the remarkable statement of the Evangelists that Pilate set up over the cross a superscription stating that the man who hung on it was king of the Jews. Is it likely that in the reign of Tiberius a Roman governor, with the fear of the jealous and suspicious old emperor before his eyes, would have ventured, even in mockery, to blazon forth a seditious claim of this sort unless it were the regular formula employed on such occasions, recognized by custom, and therefore not liable to be misconstrued into treason by the malignity of informers and the fears of a tyrant?

But if the tragedy of the ill-fated aspirant after royal honours was annually enacted at Jerusalem by a prisoner who perished on the cross, it becomes probable that the part of his successful rival was also played by another actor who paraded in the same kingly trappings but did not share the same fate. If Jesus was the Haman of the year, where was the Mordecai? Perhaps we may find him in Barabbas.

The part of Mordecai in the annual

We are told by the Evangelists that at the feast which witnessed the crucifixion of Christ it was the custom for the Roman governor to release one prisoner, whomsoever the

people desired, and that Pilate, convinced of the innocence of
Jesus, attempted to persuade the multitude to choose him as the
man who should go free. But, hounded on by the priests and
elders who had marked out Jesus for destruction, the rabble
would not hear of this, and clamoured for the blood of Jesus,
while they demanded the release of a certain miscreant, by name
Barabbas, who lay in gaol for murder and sedition. Accordingly
Pilate had to give way: Christ was crucified and Barabbas set at
liberty. Now what, we may ask, was the reason for setting free
a prisoner at this festival? In the absence of positive information, we may conjecture that the gaol-bird whose cage was
thrown open at this time had to purchase his freedom by
performing some service from which decent people would
shrink. Such a service may very well have been that of going
about the streets, rigged out in tawdry splendour with a tinsel
crown on his head and a sham sceptre in his hand, preceded and
followed by all the tag-rag and bobtail of the town hooting,
jeering, and breaking coarse jests at his expense, while some
pretended to salaam his mock majesty, and others belaboured
the donkey on which he rode. It was in this fashion, probably,
that in Persia the beardless and one-eyed man made his undig-
nified progress through the town, to the delight of ragamuffins
and the terror of shopkeepers, whose goods he unceremoniously
confiscated if they did not hasten to lay their peace-offerings at
his feet. So, perhaps, the ruffian Barabbas, when his irons were
knocked off and the prison door had grated on its hinges to let
him forth, tasted the first sweets of liberty in this public
manner, even if he was not suffered, like his one-eyed brother,
to make raids with impunity on the stalls of the merchants and
the tables of the money-changers. A curious confirmation of
this conjecture is supplied by a passage in the writings of Philo
the Jew,* who lived at Alexandria in the time of Christ. He tells
us that when Agrippa, the grandson of Herod, had received the
crown of Judea from Caligula at Rome, the new king passed
through Alexandria on his way to his own country. The
disorderly populace of that great city, animated by a hearty
dislike of his nation, seized the opportunity of venting their
spite by publicly defaming and ridiculing the Jewish monarch.
Among other things they laid hold of a certain harmless lunatic
named Carabas, who used to roam the streets stark naked, the

(marginal notes)

drama in which Christ died as Haman may have been played by Barabbas.

The mock King Carabas in Egypt.

butt and laughing-stock of urchins and idlers. This poor wretch they set up in a public place, clapped a paper crown on his head, thrust a broken reed into his hand by way of a sceptre, and having huddled a mat instead of a royal robe about his naked body, and surrounded him with a guard of bludgeonmen, they did obeisance to him as to a king and made a show of taking his opinion on questions of law and policy. To point the jest unmistakably at the Syrian king Agrippa, the bystanders raised cries of 'Marin! Marin!' which they understood to be the Syrian word for 'lord'. This mockery of the Jewish king closely resembles the mockery of Christ; and the joke, such as it was, would receive a keener edge if we could suppose that the riff-raff of Alexandria were familiar with the Jewish practice of setting up a sham king on certain occasions, and that they meant by implication to ridicule the real King Agrippa by comparing him to his holiday counterfeit. May we go a step further and conjecture that one at least of the titles of the mock king of the Jews was regularly Barabbas? The poor imbecile who masqueraded in a paper crown at Alexandria was probably a Jew, otherwise the jest would have lost much of its point; and his name, according to the Greek manuscripts of Philo, was Carabas. But Carabas is meaningless in Hebrew, whereas Barabbas is a regularly formed Hebrew word meaning 'Son of the Father'. The palaeographic difference between the two forms is slight, and perhaps we shall hardly be deemed very rash if we conjecture that in the passage in question Philo himself wrote Barabbas, which a Greek copyist, ignorant of Hebrew, afterwards corrupted into Carabas. If this were granted, we should still have to assume that both Philo and the authors of the Gospels fell into the mistake of treating as the name of an individual what in fact was a title of office.

Thus the hypothesis which, with great diffidence, I would put forward for consideration is this. It was customary, we may suppose, with the Jews at Purim, or perhaps occasionally at Passover, to employ two prisoners to act the parts respectively of Haman and Mordecai in the passion-play which formed a central feature of the festival. Both men paraded for a short time in the insignia of royalty, but their fates were different; for while at the end of the performance the one who played Haman was hanged or crucified, the one who personated Mordecai and

Hypothesis that every spring at Purim or Passover the Jews paraded two prisoners in the characters of Haman and Mordecai, of whom one

bore in popular parlance the title of Barabbas was allowed to go free. Pilate, perceiving the trumpery nature of the charges brought against Jesus, tried to persuade the Jews to let him play the part of Barabbas, which would have saved his life; but the merciful attempt failed and Jesus perished on the cross in the character of Haman. The description of his last triumphal ride into Jerusalem reads almost like an echo of that brilliant progress through the streets of Susa which Haman aspired to and Mordecai accomplished; and the account of the raid which he immediately afterwards made upon the stalls of the hucksters and money-changers in the temple, may raise a question whether we have not here a trace of those arbitrary rights over property which it has been customary on such occasions to accord to the temporary king.

If it be asked why one of these temporary kings should bear the remarkable title of Barabbas or 'Son of the Father', I can only surmise that the title may perhaps be a relic of the time when the real king, the deified man, used to redeem his own life by deputing his son to reign for a short time and to die in his stead. We have seen that the custom of sacrificing the son for the father was common, if not universal, among Semitic peoples; and if we are right in our interpretation of the Passover, that festival—the traditional date of the crucifixion—was the very season when the dreadful sacrifice of the first-born was consummated. Hence Barabbas or the 'Son of the Father' would be a natural enough title for the man or child who reigned and died as a substitute for his royal sire. Even in later times, when the father provided a less precious substitute than his own offspring, it would be quite in accordance with the formal conservatism of religion that the old title should be retained after it had ceased to be appropriate; indeed the efficacy of the sacrifice might be thought to require and justify the pious fiction that the substitute was the very son of that divine father who should have died, but who preferred to live, for the good of his people. If in the time of Christ, as I have conjectured, the title of Barabbas or Son of the Father was bestowed on the Mordecai, the mock king who lived, rather than on the Haman, the mock king who died at the festival, this distinction can hardly have been original; for at first, we may suppose, the same man served in both capacities at different

[margin note:] was put to death and the other released.

[margin note:] Barabbas ('Son of the Father') may have been the regular title of the prisoner who was released in the character of Mordecai.

times, as the Mordecai of one year and the Haman of the next. The two characters, as I have attempted to shew, are probably nothing but two different aspects of the same deity considered at one time as dead and at another as risen; hence the human being who personated the risen god would in due time, after he had enjoyed his divine honours for a season, act the dead god by dying in good earnest in his own person; for it would be unreasonable to expect of the ordinary man-god that he should play the two parts in the reverse order by dying first and coming to life afterwards. In both parts the substitute would still be, whether in sober fact or in pious fiction, the Barabbas or Son of that divine Father who generously gave his own son to die for the world.

The theory that Christ was put to death, not as a criminal, but as the annual representative of a god, whose counterparts were well known all over Western Asia, may help to explain his early deification and the rapid spread of his worship.

To conclude this speculation I venture to urge in its favour that it seems to shed fresh light on some of the causes which contributed to the remarkably rapid diffusion of Christianity in Asia Minor. We know from a famous letter of the younger Pliny addressed to the Emperor Trajan in the year 112 AD that by the beginning of our era, less than a hundred years after the Founder's death, Christianity had made such strides in Bithynia and Pontus that not only cities but villages and rural districts were affected by it, and that multitudes of both sexes and of every age and every rank professed its tenets; indeed things had gone so far that the temples were almost deserted, the sacred rites of the public religion discontinued, and hardly a purchaser could be found for the sacrificial victims.* It is obvious, therefore, that the new faith had elements in it which appealed powerfully to the Asiatic mind. What these elements were, the present investigation has perhaps to some extent disclosed. We have seen that the conception of the dying and risen god was no new one in these regions. All over Western Asia from time immemorial the mournful death and happy resurrection of a divine being appear to have been annually celebrated with alternate rites of bitter lamentation and exultant joy; and through the veil which mythic fancy has woven round this tragic figure we can still detect the features of those great yearly changes in earth and sky which, under all distinctions of race and religion, must always touch the natural human heart with alternate emotions of gladness and regret, because they exhibit on the vastest scale open to our observation the mysterious struggle between life and death. But man has not always been willing to watch passively this momentous conflict; he has felt that he has too great a stake in its issue to stand by with folded hands while it is being fought out; he has taken sides against the forces of death and decay—has flung into the trembling scale all the weight of his puny person, and has exulted in his fancied strength when the great balance has slowly inclined towards the side of life, little knowing that for all his strenuous efforts he can as little stir that balance by a hair's-breadth as can the primrose on a mossy bank in spring or the dead leaf blown by the chilly breath of autumn. Nowhere do these efforts, vain and pitiful, yet pathetic, appear to have been made more persistently and systematically than in Western Asia. In name they varied from place to place, but in substance they were all alike. A man, whom the fond imagination of his worshippers invested with the attributes of a god, gave his life for the life of the world; after infusing from his own body a fresh current of vital energy into the stagnant veins of nature, he was cut off from among the living before his failing strength should initiate a universal decay, and his place was taken by another who played, like all his predecessors, the ever-recurring drama of the divine resurrection and death. Such a drama, if our interpretation of it is right, was the original story of Esther and Mordecai or, to give them their older names, of Ishtar and Marduk. It was played in Babylonia, and from Babylonia the returning captives brought it to Judaea, where it was acted, rather as an historical than a mythical piece, by players who, having to die in grim earnest on a cross or gallows, were naturally drawn rather from the gaol than the green-room. A chain of causes which, because we cannot follow them, might in the loose language of daily life be called an accident, determined that the part of the dying god in this annual play should be thrust upon Jesus of Nazareth, whom the enemies he had made in high places by his outspoken strictures were resolved to put out of the way. They succeeded in ridding themselves of the popular and troublesome preacher; but the very step by which they fancied they had simultaneously stamped out his revolutionary doctrines contributed more than anything else they could have done to scatter them broadcast not only over Judaea but over Asia; for it impressed upon what had been hitherto mainly an ethical mission the character of a divine revelation culminating in the passion and death of the incarnate Son of a heavenly Father. In this form the story of the life and death of Jesus exerted an influence which it could never have had if the great teacher had died, as is commonly supposed, the death of a vulgar malefactor. It shed round the cross on Calvary a halo of divinity which multitudes saw and worshipped afar off; the blow struck on Golgotha set a thousand expectant strings vibrating in unison wherever men had heard the old, old story of the dying and risen god. Every year, as another spring bloomed and another autumn faded across the earth, the field had been ploughed and sown and borne fruit of a kind till it received that seed which was destined to spring up and overshadow the world. In the great army of martyrs who in many ages and in many lands, not in Asia only, have died a cruel death in the character of gods, the devout Christian will doubtless discern types and forerunners of the coming Saviour— stars that heralded in the morning sky the advent of the Sun of Righteousness—earthen vessels wherein it pleased the divine wisdom to set before hungering souls the bread of heaven. The sceptic, on the other hand, with equal confidence, will reduce Jesus of Nazareth to the level of a multitude of other victims of a barbarous superstition, and will see in him no more than a moral teacher, whom the fortunate accident of his execution invested with the crown, not merely of a martyr, but of a god. The divergence between these views is wide and deep. Which of them is the truer and will in the end prevail? Time will decide the question of prevalence, if not of truth. Yet we would fain believe that in this and in all things the old maxim will hold good—*Magna est veritas et praevalebit.**

BOOK IV

THE GOLDEN BOUGH

CHAPTER 1

BETWEEN HEAVEN AND EARTH

i

WE have travelled far since we turned our backs on Nemi and set forth in quest of the secret of the Golden Bough. We now enter on the last stage of our journey. The reader may remember that at the outset two questions were proposed: Why had the priest of Aricia to slay his predecessor? And why, before doing so, had he to pluck the Golden Bough? Of these two questions the first has now been answered. The priest of Aricia, if I am right, was one of those sacred kings or human divinities on whose life the welfare of the community and even the course of nature in general are believed to be intimately dependent. It does not appear that the subjects or worshippers of such a spiritual potentate form to themselves any very clear notion of the exact relationship in which they stand to him; probably their ideas on the point are vague and fluctuating, and we should err if we attempted to define the relationship with logical precision. All that the people know, or rather imagine, is that somehow they themselves, their cattle, and their crops are mysteriously bound up with their divine king, so that according as he is well or ill the community is healthy or sickly, the flocks and herds thrive or languish with disease, and the fields yield an abundant or a scanty harvest. The worst evil which they can conceive of is the natural death of their ruler, whether he succumb to sickness or old age, for in the opinion of his followers such a death would entail the most disastrous consequences on themselves and their possessions; fatal epidemics would sweep away man and beast, the earth would refuse her increase, nay the very frame of nature itself might be dissolved. To guard against these catastrophes it is necessary to put the king to death while he is still in the full bloom of his divine manhood, in order that his sacred life, transmitted in unabated force to his successor, may renew its youth, and thus by successive transmissions through a perpetual line of vigorous incarnations may remain eternally fresh and young, a pledge

The priest of Aricia and the Golden Bough.

and security that men and animals shall in like manner renew their youth by a perpetual succession of generations, and that seedtime and harvest, and summer and winter, and rain and sunshine shall never fail. That, if my conjecture is right, was why the priest of Aricia, the King of the Wood at Nemi, had regularly to perish by the sword of his successor. But we have still to ask, What was the Golden Bough? and why had each candidate for the Arician priesthood to pluck it before he could slay the priest?

It will be well to begin by noticing two of those rules or taboos by which, as we have seen, the life of divine kings or priests is regulated. The first of the rules is that the divine personage may not touch the ground with his foot. This rule was observed by the supreme pontiff of the Zapotecs in Mexico; he profaned his sanctity if he so much as touched the ground with his foot. Montezuma, emperor of Mexico, never set foot on the ground; he was always carried on the shoulders of noblemen, and if he lighted anywhere they laid rich tapestry for him to walk upon. For the Mikado of Japan to touch the ground with his foot was a shameful degradation; indeed, in the sixteenth century, it was enough to deprive him of his office. Outside his palace he was carried on men's shoulders; within it he walked on exquisitely wrought mats. The king and queen of Tahiti might not touch the ground anywhere but within their hereditary domains; for the ground on which they trod became sacred. In travelling from place to place they were carried on the shoulders of sacred men. They were always accompanied by several pairs of these sanctified attendants; and when it became necessary to change their bearers, the king and queen vaulted on to the shoulders of their new bearers without letting their feet touch the ground. It was an evil omen if the king of Dosuma touched the ground, and he had to perform an expiatory ceremony. Within his palace the king of Persia walked on carpets on which no one else might tread; outside of it he was never seen on foot but only in a chariot or on horseback. In old days the king of Siam never set foot upon the earth, but was carried on a throne of gold from place to place. Formerly neither the kings of Uganda, nor their mothers, nor their queens might walk on foot outside of the spacious enclosures in which they lived. Whenever they went forth they were carried

What was the Golden Bough?

Sacred kings and priests forbidden to touch the ground with their feet.

on the shoulders of men of the Buffalo clan, several of whom accompanied any of these royal personages on a journey and took it in turn to bear the burden. The king sat astride the bearer's neck with a leg over each shoulder and his feet tucked under the bearer's arms. When one of these royal carriers grew tired he shot the king on to the shoulders of a second man without allowing the royal feet to touch the ground. In this way they went at a great pace and travelled long distances in a day, when the king was on a journey. The bearers had a special hut in the king's enclosure in order to be at hand the moment they were wanted. Among the Ibo people about Awka, in Southern Nigeria, the priest of the Earth has to observe many taboos; for example, he may not see a corpse, and if he meets one on the road he must hide his eyes with his wristlet. He must abstain from many foods, such as eggs, birds of all sorts, mutton, dog, bush-buck, and so forth. He may neither wear nor touch a mask, and no masked man may enter his house. If a dog enters his house, it is killed and thrown out. As priest of the Earth he may not sit on the bare ground, nor eat things that have fallen on the ground, nor may earth be thrown at him. According to ancient Brahmanic ritual a king at his inauguration trod on a tiger's skin and a golden plate; he was shod with shoes of boar's skin, and so long as he lived thereafter he might not stand on the earth with his bare feet.

But besides persons who are permanently sacred or tabooed and are therefore permanently forbidden to touch the ground with their feet, there are others who enjoy the character of sanctity or taboo only on certain occasions, and to whom accordingly the prohibition in question only applies at the definite seasons during which they exhale the odour of sanctity. Thus among the Kayans or Bahaus of Central Borneo, while the priestesses are engaged in the performance of certain rites they may not step on the ground, and boards are laid for them to tread on. At a funeral ceremony observed by night among the Michemis, a Tibetan tribe near the northern frontier of Assam, a priest fantastically bedecked with tiger's teeth, many-coloured plumes, bells, and shells, executed a wild dance for the purpose of exorcising the evil spirits; then all fires were extinguished and a new light was struck by a man suspended by his feet from a beam in the ceiling; 'he did not touch the ground', we are

Certain persons on certain occasions forbidden to touch the ground with their feet.

told, 'in order to indicate that the light came from heaven.'
Again, newly born infants are strongly tabooed; accordingly in
Loango they are not allowed to touch the earth. Among the
Iluvans of Malabar the bridegroom on his wedding-day is
bathed by seven young men and then carried or walks on planks
from the bathing-place to the marriage booth; he may not touch
the ground with his feet. With the Dyaks of Landak and Tajan,
two districts of Dutch Borneo, it is a custom that for a certain
time after marriage neither bride nor bridegroom may tread on
the earth. Warriors, again, on the war-path are surrounded, so
to say, by an atmosphere of taboo; hence some Indians of North
America might not sit on the bare ground the whole time they
were out on a warlike expedition. In Laos the hunting of
elephants gives rise to many taboos; one of them is that the
chief hunter may not touch the earth with his foot. Accordingly,
when he alights from his elephant, the others spread a carpet of
leaves for him to step upon. German wiseacres recommended
that when witches were led to the block or the stake, they
should not be allowed to touch the bare earth, and a reason
suggested for the rule was that if they touched the earth they
might make themselves invisible and so escape. The sagacious
author* of *The Striped-petticoat Philosophy* in the eighteenth
century ridicules the idea as mere silly talk. He admits, indeed,
that the women were conveyed to the place of execution in
carts; but he denies that there is any deep significance in the
cart, and he is prepared to maintain this view by a chemical
analysis of the timber of which the cart was built. To clinch his
argument he appeals to plain matter of fact and his own
personal experience. Not a single instance, he assures us with
apparent satisfaction, can be produced of a witch who escaped
the axe or the fire in this fashion. 'I have myself', says he, 'in
my youth seen divers witches burned, some at Arnstadt, some
at Ilmenau, some at Schwenda, a noble village between Arnstadt
and Ilmenau, and some of them were pardoned and beheaded
before being burned. They were laid on the earth in the place
of execution and beheaded like any other poor sinner; whereas
if they could have escaped by touching the earth, not one of
them would have failed to do so'.

Apparently holiness, magical virtue, taboo, or whatever we
may call that mysterious quality which is supposed to pervade

sacred or tabooed persons, is conceived by the primitive philosopher as a physical substance or fluid, with which the sacred man is charged just as a Leyden jar* is charged with electricity; and exactly as the electricity in the jar can be discharged by contact with a good conductor, so the holiness or magical virtue in the man can be discharged and drained away by contact with the earth, which on this theory serves as an excellent conductor for the magical fluid. Hence in order to preserve the charge from running to waste, the sacred or tabooed personage must be carefully prevented from touching the ground; in electrical language he must be insulated, if he is not to be emptied of the precious substance or fluid with which he, as a vial, is filled to the brim. And in many cases apparently the insulation of the tabooed person is recommended as a precaution not merely for his own sake but for the sake of others; for since the virtue of holiness or taboo is, so to say, a powerful explosive which the smallest touch may detonate, it is necessary in the interest of the general safety to keep it within narrow bounds, lest breaking out it should blast, blight, and destroy whatever it comes into contact with.

Sacred or tabooed persons apparently thought to be charged with a mysterious virtue like a fluid, which will run to waste or explode if it touches the ground.

ii

The second rule to be here noted is that the sun may not shine upon the divine person. This rule was observed both by the Mikado and by the pontiff of the Zapotecs. The latter 'was looked upon as a god whom the earth was not worthy to hold, nor the sun to shine upon'. The Japanese would not allow that the Mikado should expose his sacred person to the open air, and the sun was not thought worthy to shine on his head. The Indians of Granada, in South America, 'kept those who were to be rulers or commanders, whether men or women, locked up for several years when they were children, some of them seven years, and this so close that they were not to see the sun, for if they should happen to see it they forfeited their lordship, eating certain sorts of food appointed; and those who were their keepers at certain times went into their retreat or prison and scourged them severely.' Thus, for example, the heir to the throne of Bogota, who was not the son but the sister's son of the king, had to undergo a rigorous training from his infancy:

Sacred persons not allowed to see the sun.

he lived in complete retirement in a temple, where he might not
see the sun nor eat salt nor converse with a woman: he was
surrounded by guards who observed his conduct and noted all
his actions: if he broke a single one of the rules laid down for
him, he was deemed infamous and forfeited all his rights to the
throne. So, too, the heir to the kingdom of Sogamoso, before
succeeding to the crown, had to fast for seven years in the
temple, being shut up in the dark and not allowed to see the
sun or light. The prince who was to become Inca of Peru had
to fast for a month without seeing light. On the day when a
Brahman student of the Veda took a bath, to signify that the
time of his studentship was at an end, he entered a cow-shed
before sunrise, hung over the door a skin with the hair inside,
and sat there; on that day the sun should not shine upon him.

Tabooed persons not allowed to see the sun.

　　Again, women after childbirth and their offspring are more or
less tabooed all the world over; hence in Corea the rays of the
sun are rigidly excluded from both mother and child for a
period of twenty-one or a hundred days, according to their
rank, after the birth has taken place. Among some of the tribes
on the north-west coast of New Guinea a woman may not leave
the house for months after childbirth. When she does go out,
she must cover her head with a hood or mat; for if the sun were
to shine upon her, it is thought that one of her male relations
would die. Again, mourners are everywhere taboo; accordingly
in mourning the Ainos of Japan wear peculiar caps in order that
the sun may not shine upon their heads. During a solemn fast
of three days the Indians of Costa Rica eat no salt, speak as little
as possible, light no fires, and stay strictly indoors, or if they go
out during the day they carefully cover themselves from the
light of the sun, believing that exposure to the sun's rays would
turn them black.

Certain persons forbidden to see fire.

On Yule Night it has been customary in parts
of Sweden from time immemorial to go on pilgrimage, whereby
people learn many secret things and know what is to happen in
the coming year. As a preparation for this pilgrimage, 'some
secrete themselves for three days previously in a dark cellar, so
as to be shut out altogether from the light of heaven. Others
retire at an early hour of the preceding morning to some
out-of-the-way place, such as a hay-loft, where they bury
themselves in the hay, that they may neither see nor hear any
living creature; and here they remain, in silence and fasting,

until after sundown; whilst there are those who think it sufficient if they rigidly abstain from food on the day before commencing their wanderings. During this period of probation a man ought not to see fire, but should this have happened, he must strike a light with flint and steel, whereby the evil that would otherwise have ensued will be obviated.' During the sixteen days that a Pima Indian is undergoing purification for killing an Apache he may not see a blazing fire.

Acarnanian peasants* tell of a handsome prince called Sunless, who would die if he saw the sun. So he lived in an underground palace on the site of the ancient Oeniadae, but at night he came forth and crossed the river to visit a famous enchantress who dwelt in a castle on the further bank. She was loth to part with him every night long before the sun was up, and as he turned a deaf ear to all her entreaties to linger, she hit upon the device of cutting the throats of all the cocks in the neighbourhood. So the prince, whose ear had learned to expect the shrill clarion of the birds as the signal of the growing light, tarried too long, and hardly had he reached the ford when the sun rose over the Aetolian mountains, and its fatal beams fell on him before he could regain his dark abode.

The story of Prince Sunless.

CHAPTER 2

THE SECLUSION OF GIRLS

i

Girls at puberty forbidden to touch the ground and to see the sun.

Now it is remarkable that the foregoing two rules—not to touch the ground and not to see the sun—are observed either separately or conjointly by girls at puberty in many parts of the world. Thus amongst the negroes of Loango girls at puberty are confined in separate huts, and they may not touch the ground with any part of their bare body. Among the Zulus and kindred tribes of South Africa, when the first signs of puberty shew themselves 'while a girl is walking, gathering wood, or working in the field, she runs to the river and hides herself among the reeds for the day, so as not to be seen by men. She covers her head carefully with her blanket that the sun may not shine on it and shrivel her up into a withered skeleton, as would result from exposure to the sun's beams. After dark she returns to her home and is secluded' in a hut for some time. During her seclusion, which lasts for about a fortnight, neither she nor the girls who wait upon her may drink any milk, lest the cattle should die. And should she be overtaken by the first flow while she is in the fields, she must, after hiding in the bush, scrupulously avoid all pathways in returning home. Similarly, among the Baganda, when a girl menstruated for the first time she was secluded and not allowed to handle food; and at the end of her seclusion the kinsman with whom she was staying (for among the Baganda young people did not reside with their parents) was obliged to jump over his wife, which with the Baganda is regarded as equivalent to having intercourse with her. Should the girl happen to be living near her parents at the moment when she attained to puberty, she was expected on her recovery to inform them of the fact, whereupon her father jumped over her mother. Were this custom omitted, the Baganda thought that the girl would never have children or that they would die in infancy. Thus the pretence of sexual intercourse between the parents or other relatives of the girl was a magical ceremony to ensure her fertility. It is significant that among the

Seclusion of girls at puberty among the Baganda.

Baganda the first menstruation was often called a marriage, and the girl was spoken of as a bride. These terms so applied point to a belief like that of the Siamese, that a girl's first menstruation results from her defloration by one of a host of aerial spirits, and that the wound thus inflicted is repeated afterwards every month by the same ghostly agency. For a like reason, probably, the Baganda imagine that a woman who does not menstruate exerts a malign influence on gardens and makes them barren if she works in them. For not being herself fertilized by a spirit, how can she fertilize the garden?

Among the Amambwe, Winamwanga, Alungu, and other tribes of the great plateau to the west of Lake Tanganyika,[*] 'when a young girl knows that she has attained puberty, she forthwith leaves her mother's hut, and hides herself in the long grass near the village, covering her face with a cloth and weeping bitterly. Towards sunset one of the older women—who, as directress of the ceremonies, is called *nachimbusa*—follows her, places a cooking-pot by the cross-roads, and boils therein a concoction of various herbs, with which she anoints the neophyte. At nightfall the girl is carried on the old woman's back to her mother's hut. When the customary period of a few days has elapsed, she is allowed to cook again, after first whitewashing the floor of the hut. But, by the following month, the preparations for her initiation are complete. The novice must remain in her hut throughout the whole period of initiation, and is carefully guarded by the old women, who accompany her whenever she leaves her quarters, veiling her head with a native cloth. The ceremonies last for at least one month.' During this period of seclusion, drumming and songs are kept up within the mother's hut by the village women, and no male, except, it is said, the father of twins, is allowed to enter. The directress of the rites and the older women instruct the young girl as to the elementary facts of life, the duties of marriage, and the rules of conduct, decorum, and hospitality to be observed by a married woman. Amongst other things the damsel must submit to a series of tests such as leaping over fences, thrusting her head into a collar made of thorns, and so on. The lessons which she receives are illustrated by mud figures of animals and of the common objects of domestic life. Moreover, the directress of studies embellishes the walls of the hut with rude

Seclusion of girls at puberty among the tribes of the Tanganyika plateau.

pictures, each with its special significance and song, which must be understood and learned by the girl. In the foregoing account the rule that a damsel at puberty may neither see the sun nor touch the ground seems implied by the statement that on the first discovery of her condition she hides in long grass and is carried home after sunset on the back of an old woman.

Seclusion of girls at puberty in New Ireland.

In New Ireland* girls are confined for four or five years in small cages, being kept in the dark and not allowed to set foot on the ground. The custom has been thus described by an eye-witness. 'I heard from a teacher about some strange custom connected with some of the young girls here, so I asked the chief to take me to the house where they were. The house was about twenty-five feet in length, and stood in a reed and bamboo enclosure, across the entrance to which a bundle of dried grass was suspended to show that it was strictly "*tabu*." Inside the house were three conical structures about seven or eight feet in height, and about ten or twelve feet in circumference at the bottom, and for about four feet from the ground, at which point they tapered off to a point at the top. These cages were made of the broad leaves of the pandanus-tree, sewn quite close together so that no light and little or no air could enter. On one side of each is an opening which is closed by a double door of plaited cocoa-nut tree and pandanus-tree leaves. About three feet from the ground there is a stage of bamboos which forms the floor. In each of these cages we were told there was a young woman confined, each of whom had to remain for at least four or five years, without ever being allowed to go outside the house. I could scarcely credit the story when I heard it; the whole thing seemed too horrible to be true. I spoke to the chief, and told him that I wished to see the inside of the cages, and also to see the girls that I might make them a present of a few beads. He told me that it was "*tabu*," forbidden for any men but their own relations to look at them; but I suppose the promised beads acted as an inducement, and so he sent away for some old lady who had charge, and who alone is allowed to open the doors. While we were waiting we could hear the girls talking to the chief in a querulous way as if objecting to something or expressing their fears. The old woman came at length and certainly she did not seem a very pleasant jailor or guardian; nor did she seem to favour the request of the chief to allow us to see the girls, as she regarded us with anything but pleasant looks. However, she had to undo the door when the chief told her to do so, and then the girls peeped out at us, and, when told to do so, they held out their hands for the beads. I, however, purposely sat at some distance away and merely held out the beads to them, as I wished to draw them quite outside, that I might inspect the inside of the cages. This desire of mine gave rise to another difficulty, as these girls were not allowed to put their feet to the ground all the time they were confined in these places. However, they wished to get the beads, and so the old lady had to go outside and collect a lot of pieces of wood and bamboo, which she placed on the ground, and then going to one of the girls, she helped her down and held her hand as she stepped from one piece of wood to another until she came near enough to get the beads I held out to her. I then went to inspect the inside of the cage out of which she had come, but could scarcely put my head inside of it, the atmosphere was so hot and stifling. It was clean and contained nothing but a few short lengths of bamboo for holding water. There was only room for the girl to sit or lie down in a crouched position on the bamboo platform, and when the doors are shut it must be nearly or quite dark inside. The girls are never allowed to come out except once a day to bathe in a dish or wooden bowl placed close to each cage. They say that they perspire profusely. They are placed in these stifling cages when quite young, and must remain there until they are young women, when they are taken out and have each a great marriage feast provided for them. One of them was about fourteen or fifteen years old, and the chief told us that she had been there for five years, but would soon be taken out now. The other two were about eight and ten years old, and they have to stay there for several years longer.'*

Among the Ot Danoms of Borneo girls at the age of eight or ten years are shut up in a little room or cell of the house, and cut off from all intercourse with the world for a long time. The cell, like the rest of the house, is raised on piles above the ground, and is lit by a single small window opening on a lonely place, so that the girl is in almost total darkness. She may not leave the room on any pretext whatever, not even for the most necessary purposes. None of her family may see her all the time she is shut up, but a single slave woman is appointed to wait on her. During her lonely confinement, which often lasts seven years, the girl occupies herself in weaving mats or with other handiwork. Her bodily growth is stunted by the long want of exercise, and when, on attaining womanhood, she is brought out, her complexion is pale and wax-like. She is now shewn the sun, the earth, the water, the trees, and the flowers, as if she were newly born.

Seclusion of girls at puberty among the Guaranis, Chiriguanos, and Lengua Indians of South America.

When symptoms of puberty appeared on a girl for the first time, the Guaranis of Southern Brazil, on the borders of Paraguay, used to sew her up in her hammock, leaving only a small opening in it to allow her to breathe. In this condition, wrapt up and shrouded like a corpse, she was kept for two or three days or so long as the symptoms lasted, and during this time she had to observe a most rigorous fast. After that she was entrusted to a matron, who cut the girl's hair and enjoined her to abstain most strictly from eating flesh of any kind until her hair should be grown long enough to hide her ears. Meanwhile the diviners drew omens of her future character from the various birds or animals that flew past or crossed her path. If they saw a parrot, they would say she was a chatterbox; if an owl, she was lazy and useless for domestic labours, and so on. In similar circumstances the Chiriguanos of south-eastern Bolivia hoisted the girl in her hammock to the roof, where she stayed for a month: the second month the hammock was let half-way down from the roof; and in the third month old women, armed with sticks, entered the hut and ran about striking everything they met, saying they were hunting the snake that had wounded the girl. The Lengua Indians of the Paraguayan Chaco under similar circumstances hang the girl in her hammock from the roof of the house, but they leave her there only three days and nights, during which they give her nothing to eat but a little Paraguay tea or boiled maize. Only her mother or grandmother has access to her; nobody else approaches or speaks to her. If she is obliged to leave the hammock for a little, her friends take great care to prevent her from touching the *Boyrusu*, which is an imaginary serpent that would swallow her up. She must also be very careful not to set foot on the droppings of fowls or animals, else she would suffer from sores on the throat and breast. On the third day they let her down from the hammock, cut her hair, and make her sit in a corner of the room with her face turned to the wall. She may speak to nobody, and must abstain from flesh and fish. These rigorous observances she must practise for nearly a year. Many girls die or are injured for life in consequence of the hardships they endure at this time. Their only occupations during their seclusion are spinning and weaving.

Among the Yuracares, an Indian tribe of Bolivia, at the eastern foot of the Andes, when a girl perceives the signs of puberty, she informs her parents. The mother weeps and the father constructs a little hut of palm leaves near the house. In this cabin he shuts up his daughter so that she cannot see the light, and there she remains fasting rigorously for four days. Meantime the mother, assisted by the women of the neighbourhood, has brewed a large quantity of the native intoxicant called *chicha*, and poured it into wooden troughs and palm leaves. On the morning of the fourth day, three hours before the dawn, the girl's father, having arrayed himself in his savage finery, summons all his neighbours with loud cries. The damsel is seated on a stone, and every guest in turn cuts off a lock of her hair, and running away hides it in the hollow trunk of a tree in the depths of the forest. When they have all done so and seated themselves again gravely in the circle, the girl offers to each of them a calabash full of very strong *chicha*. Before the wassailing begins, the various fathers perform a curious operation on the arms of their sons, who are seated beside them. The operator takes a very sharp bone of an ape, rubs it with a pungent spice, and then pinching up the skin of his son's arm he pierces it with the bone through and through, as a surgeon might introduce a seton. This operation he repeats till the young man's arm is riddled with holes at regular intervals from the shoulder to the wrist. Almost all who take part in the festival are covered with these wounds, which the Indians call *culucute*. Having thus prepared themselves to spend a happy day, they drink, play on flutes, sing and dance till evening. Rain, thunder, and lightning, should they befall, have no effect in damping the general enjoyment or preventing its continuance till after the sun has set. The motive for perforating the arms of the young men is to make them skilful hunters; at each perforation the sufferer is cheered by the promise of another sort of game or fish which the surgical operation will infallibly procure for him. The same

Seclusion of girls at puberty among the Yuracares of Bolivia.

operation is performed on the arms and legs of the girls, in order that they may be brave and strong; even the dogs are operated on with the intention of making them run down the game better. For five or six months afterwards the damsel must cover her head with bark and refrain from speaking to men. The Yuracares think that if they did not submit a young girl to this severe ordeal, her children would afterwards perish by accidents of various kinds, such as the sting of a serpent, the bite of a jaguar, the fall of a tree, the wound of an arrow, or what not.

Seclusion of girls at puberty among the Indians of the Gran Chaco.

Among the Matacos or Mataguayos, an Indian tribe of the Gran Chaco, a girl at puberty has to remain in seclusion for some time. She lies covered up with branches or other things in a corner of the hut, seeing no one and speaking to no one, and during this time she may eat neither flesh nor fish. Meantime a man beats a drum in front of the house. Similarly among the Tobas, another Indian tribe of the same region, when a chief's daughter has just attained to womanhood, she is shut up for two or three days in the house, all the men of the tribe scour the country to bring in game and fish for a feast, and a Mataco Indian is engaged to drum, sing, and dance in front of the house without cessation, day and night, till the festival is over. As the merry-making lasts for two or three weeks, the exhaustion of the musician at the end of it may be readily conceived. Meat and drink are supplied to him on the spot where he pays his laborious court to the Muses. The proceed-

Seclusion of girls at puberty among the Indians of Brazil.

ings wind up with a saturnalia and a drunken debauch. Among the Yaguas, an Indian tribe of the Upper Amazon, a girl at puberty is shut up for three months in a lonely hut in the forest, where her mother brings her food daily. When a girl of the Peguenches tribe perceives in herself the first signs of woman-hood, she is secluded by her mother in a corner of the hut screened off with blankets, and is warned not to lift up her eyes on any man. Next day, very early in the morning and again after sunset, she is taken out by two women and made to run till she is tired; in the interval she is again secluded in her corner. On the following day she lays three packets of wool beside the path near the house to signify that she is now a woman. Among the Passes, Mauhes, and other tribes of Brazil the young woman in similar circumstances is hung in her hammock from the roof and has to fast there for a month or as long as she can hold out.

One of the early settlers in Brazil, about the middle of the sixteenth century, has described the severe ordeal which damsels at puberty had to undergo among the Indians on the south-east coast of that country, near what is now Rio de Janeiro. When a girl had reached this critical period of life, her hair was burned or shaved off close to the head. Then she was placed on a flat stone and cut with the tooth of an animal from the shoulders all down the back, till she ran with blood. Next the ashes of a wild gourd were rubbed into the wounds; the girl was bound hand and foot, and hung in a hammock, being enveloped in it so closely that no one could see her. Here she had to stay for three days without eating or drinking. When the three days were over, she stepped out of the hammock upon the flat stone, for her feet might not touch the ground. If she had a call of nature, a female relation took the girl on her back and carried her out, taking with her a live coal to prevent evil influences from entering the girl's body. Being replaced in her hammock, she was now allowed to get some flour, boiled roots, and water, but might not taste salt or flesh. Thus she continued to the end of the first monthly period, at the expiry of which she was gashed on the breast and belly as well as all down the back. During the second month she still stayed in her hammock, but her rule of abstinence was less rigid, and she was allowed to spin. The third month she was blackened with a certain pigment and began to go about as usual.

Amongst the Macusis of British Guiana, when a girl shews the first signs of puberty, she is hung in a hammock at the highest point of the hut. For the first few days she may not leave the hammock by day, but at night she must come down, light a fire, and spend the night beside it, else she would break out in sores on her neck, throat, and other parts of her body. So long as the symptoms are at their height, she must fast rigorously. When they have abated, she may come down and take up her abode in a little compartment that is made for her in the darkest corner of the hut. In the morning she may cook her food, but it must be at a separate fire and in a vessel of her own. After about ten days the magician comes and undoes the spell by muttering charms and breathing on her and on the more valuable of the things with which she has come in contact. The pots and drinking-vessels which she used are broken and

Seclusion of girls at puberty among the Indians of Guiana.

Custom of
beating the
girls and of
causing them
to be stung
by ants.

the fragments buried. After her first bath, the girl must submit
to be beaten by her mother with thin rods without uttering a
cry. At the end of the second period she is again beaten, but
not afterwards. She is now 'clean', and can mix again with
people. Other Indians of Guiana, after keeping the girl in her
hammock at the top of the hut for a month, expose her to
certain large ants, whose bite is very painful. Sometimes, in
addition to being stung with ants, the sufferer has to fast day
and night so long as she remains slung up on high in her
hammock, so that when she comes down she is reduced to a
skeleton. The intention of stinging her with ants is said to be
to make her strong to bear the burden of maternity. Amongst
the Uaupes of Brazil a girl at puberty is secluded in the house
for a month, and allowed only a small quantity of bread and
water. Then she is taken out into the midst of her relations and
friends, each of whom gives her four or five blows with pieces
of *sipo* (an elastic climber), till she falls senseless or dead. If she
recovers, the operation is repeated four times at intervals of six
hours, and it is considered an offence to the parents not to
strike hard. Meantime, pots of meats and fish have been made
ready; the *sipos* are dipped into them and then given to the girl
to lick, who is now considered a marriageable woman.

Custom in
South Amer-
ica of caus-
ing young
men to be
stung with
ants as an in-
itiatory rite.

In such cases
the beating
or stinging
was origin-
ally a purifi-
cation; at a
later time it
is interpreted
as a test of
courage and
endurance.

The custom of stinging the girl at such times with ants or
beating her with rods is intended, we may be sure, not as a
punishment or a test of endurance, but as a purification, the
object being to drive away the malignant influences with which
a girl in this condition is believed to be beset and enveloped. In
like manner it is probable that beating or scourging as a
religious or ceremonial rite was originally a mode of purification. It was meant to wipe off and drive away a dangerous
contagion, whether personified as demoniacal or not, which was
supposed to be adhering physically, though invisibly, to the
body of the sufferer. The pain inflicted on the person beaten
was no more the object of the beating than it is of a surgical
operation with us; it was a necessary accident, that was all. In
later times such customs were interpreted otherwise, and the
pain, from being an accident, became the prime object of the
ceremony, which was now regarded either as a test of endurance
imposed upon persons at critical epochs of life, or as a mortification of the flesh well pleasing to the god. But asceticism, under

any shape or form, is never primitive. The savage, it is true, in certain circumstances will voluntarily subject himself to pains and privations which appear to us wholly needless; but he never acts thus unless he believes that some solid temporal advantage is to be gained by so doing. Pain for the sake of pain, whether as a moral discipline in this life or as a means of winning a glorious immortality hereafter, is not an object which he sets himself deliberately to pursue.

In Cambodia a girl at puberty is put to bed under a mosquito curtain, where she should stay a hundred days. Usually, however, four, five, ten, or twenty days are thought enough; and even this, in a hot climate and under the close meshes of the curtain, is sufficiently trying. According to another account, a Cambodian maiden at puberty is said to 'enter into the shade'. During her retirement, which, according to the rank and position of her family, may last any time from a few days to several years, she has to observe a number of rules, such as not to be seen by a strange man, not to eat flesh or fish, and so on. She goes nowhere, not even to the pagoda. But this state of seclusion is discontinued during eclipses; at such times she goes forth and pays her devotions to the monster who is supposed to cause eclipses by catching the heavenly bodies between his teeth. This permission to break her rule of retirement and appear abroad during an eclipse seems to shew how literally the injunction is interpreted which forbids maidens entering on womanhood to look upon the sun.

Seclusion of girls at puberty in Cambodia.

ii

A superstition so widely diffused as this might be expected to leave traces in legends and folk-tales. And it has done so. In a Danish story we read of a princess who was fated to be carried off by a warlock if ever the sun shone on her before she had passed her thirtieth year; so the king her father kept her shut up in the palace, and had all the windows on the east, south, and west sides blocked up, lest a sunbeam should fall on his darling child, and he should thus lose her for ever. Only at evening, when the sun was down, might she walk for a little in the beautiful garden of the castle. In time a prince came a-wooing, followed by a train of gorgeous knights and squires

Traces of the seclusion of girls at puberty in folk-tales. Danish story of the girl who might not see the sun.

on horses all ablaze with gold and silver. The king said the
prince might have his daughter to wife on condition that he
would not carry her away to his home till she was thirty years
old but would live with her in the castle, where the windows
looked out only to the north. The prince agreed, so married
they were. The bride was only fifteen, and fifteen more long
weary years must pass before she might step out of the gloomy
donjon, breathe the fresh air, and see the sun. But she and her
gallant young bridegroom loved each other and they were
happy. Often they sat hand in hand at the window looking out
to the north and talked of what they would do when they were
free. Still it was a little dull to look out always at the same
window and to see nothing but the castle woods, and the distant
hills, and the clouds drifting silently over them. Well, one day
it happened that all the people in the castle had gone away to a
neighbouring castle to witness a tournament and other gaieties,
and the two young folks were left as usual all alone at the
window looking out to the north. They sat silent for a time
gazing away to the hills. It was a grey sad day, the sky was
overcast, and the weather seemed to draw to rain. At last the
prince said, 'There will be no sunshine to-day. What if we were
to drive over and join the rest at the tournament?' His young
wife gladly consented, for she longed to see more of the world
than those eternal green woods and those eternal blue hills,
which were all she ever saw from the window. So the horses
were put into the coach, and it rattled up to the door, and in
they got and away they drove. At first all went well. The clouds
hung low over the woods, the wind sighed in the trees, a
drearier day you could hardly imagine. So they joined the rest
at the other castle and took their seats to watch the jousting in
the lists. So intent were they in watching the gay spectacle of
the prancing steeds, the fluttering pennons, and the glittering
armour of the knights, that they failed to mark the change, the
fatal change, in the weather. For the wind was rising and had
begun to disperse the clouds, and suddenly the sun broke
through, and the glory of it fell like an aureole on the young
wife, and at once she vanished away. No sooner did her
husband miss her from his side than he, too, mysteriously
disappeared. The tournament broke up in confusion, the bereft
father hastened home, and shut himself up in the dark castle

from which the light of life had departed. The green woods and
the blue hills could still be seen from the window that looked
to the north, but the young faces that had gazed out of it so
wistfully were gone, as it seemed, for ever.*

A Tyrolese story tells how it was the doom of a lovely maiden
with golden hair to be transported into the belly of a whale if
ever a sunbeam fell on her. Hearing of the fame of her beauty
the king of the country sent for her to be his bride, and her
brother drove the fair damsel to the palace in a carefully closed
coach, himself sitting on the box and handling the reins. On the
way they overtook two hideous witches, who pretended they
were weary and begged for a lift in the coach. At first the
brother refused to take them in, but his tender-hearted sister
entreated him to have compassion on the two poor footsore
women; for you may easily imagine that she was not acquainted
with their true character. So down he got rather surlily from
the box, opened the coach door, and in the two witches stepped,
laughing in their sleeves. But no sooner had the brother
mounted the box and whipped up the horses, than one of the
two wicked witches bored a hole in the closed coach. A sunbeam
at once shot through the hole and fell on the fair damsel. So she
vanished from the coach and was spirited away into the belly of
a whale in the neighbouring sea. You can imagine the consternation of the king, when the coach door opened and instead of his
blooming bride out bounced two hideous hags!

In a modern Greek folk-tale the Fates predict that in her
fifteenth year a princess must be careful not to let the sun shine
on her, for if this were to happen she would be turned into a
lizard. In another modern Greek tale the Sun bestows a
daughter upon a childless woman on condition of taking the
child back to himself when she is twelve years old. So, when
the child was twelve, the mother closed the doors and windows,
and stopped up all the chinks and crannies, to prevent the Sun
from coming to fetch away her daughter. But she forgot to stop
up the key-hole, and a sunbeam streamed through it and carried
off the girl. In a Sicilian story a seer foretells that a king will
have a daughter who, in her fourteenth year, will conceive a
child by the Sun. So, when the child was born, the king shut
her up in a lonely tower which had no window, lest a sunbeam
should fall on her. When she was nearly fourteen years old, it

Tyrolese
story of the
girl who
might not
see the sun.

Modern
Greek stories
of the maid
who might
not see the
sun.

happened that her parents sent her a piece of roasted kid, in which she found a sharp bone. With this bone she scraped a hole in the wall, and a sunbeam shot through the hole and got her with child.

The story of Danaë and its parallel in a Kirghiz legend.

The old Greek story of Danaë,* who was confined by her father in a subterranean chamber or a brazen tower, but impregnated by Zeus, who reached her in the shape of a shower of gold, perhaps belongs to the same class of tales. It has its counterpart in the legend which the Kirghiz of Siberia tell of their ancestry. A certain Khan had a fair daughter, whom he kept in a dark iron house, that no man might see her. An old woman tended her; and when the girl was grown to maidenhood she asked the old woman, 'Where do you go so often?' 'My child,' said the old dame, 'there is a bright world. In that bright world your father and mother live, and all sorts of people live there. That is where I go.' The maiden said, 'Good mother, I will tell nobody, but shew me that bright world.' So the old woman took the girl out of the iron house. But when she saw the bright world, the girl tottered and fainted; and the eye of God fell upon her, and she conceived. Her angry father put her in a golden chest and sent her floating away (fairy gold can float in fairyland) over the wide sea. The shower of gold in the Greek story, and the eye of God in the Kirghiz legend, probably stand for sunlight and the sun.

iii

The reason for the seclusion of women at puberty is the dread of menstruous blood.

The motive for the restraints so commonly imposed on girls at puberty is the deeply ingrained dread which primitive man universally entertains of menstruous blood. He fears it at all times but especially on its first appearance; hence the restrictions under which women lie at their first menstruation are usually more stringent than those which they have to observe at any subsequent recurrence of the mysterious flow.

Dread and seclusion of menstruous women among the aborigines of Australia.

Thus in the Encounter Bay tribe of South Australia there is, or used to be, a 'superstition which obliges a woman to separate herself from the camp at the time of her monthly illness, when, if a young man or boy should approach, she calls out, and he immediately makes a circuit to avoid her. If she is neglectful upon this point, she exposes herself to scolding, and sometimes to severe beating by her husband or nearest relation, because the boys are told from their infancy, that if they see the blood they will early become grey-headed, and their strength will fail prematurely.' And of the South Australian aborigines in general we read that there is a 'custom requiring all boys and un-initiated young men to sleep at some distance from the huts of the adults, and to remove altogether away in the morning as soon as daylight dawns, and the natives begin to move about. This is to prevent their seeing the women, some of whom may be menstruating; and if looked upon by the young males, it is supposed that dire results will follow.' And amongst these tribes women in their courses 'are not allowed to eat fish of any kind, or to go near the water at all; it being one of their superstitions, that if a female, in that state, goes near the water, no success can be expected by the men in fishing.' Similarly, among the natives of the Murray River, menstruous women 'were not allowed to go near water for fear of frightening the fish. They were also not allowed to eat them, for the same reason. A woman during such periods would never cross the river in a canoe, or even fetch water for the camp. It was sufficient for her to say, *Thama*, to ensure her husband getting the water himself.' The Dieri of Central Australia believe that if women at these times were to eat fish or bathe in a river, the fish would all die and the water would dry up. In this tribe a mark made with red ochre round a woman's mouth indicates that she has her courses; no one would offer fish to such a woman. The Arunta of Central Australia forbid menstruous women to gather the *irriakura* bulbs, which form a staple article of diet for both men and women. They believe that were a woman to break this rule, the supply of bulbs would fail.

Among most tribes of North American Indians the custom was that women in their courses retired from the camp or the village and lived during the time of their uncleanness in special huts or shelters which were appropriated to their use. There they dwelt apart, eating and sleeping by themselves, warming themselves at their own fires, and strictly abstaining from all communications with men, who shunned them just as if they were stricken with the plague. No article of furniture used in these menstrual huts might be used in any other, not even the flint and steel with which in the old days the fires were kindled.

[margin note] Dread and seclusion of menstruous women among the Indians of North America.

No one would borrow a light from a woman in her seclusion. If a white man in his ignorance asked to light his pipe at her fire, she would refuse to grant the request, telling him that it would make his nose bleed and his head ache, and that he would fall sick in consequence.

Customs and beliefs of the Carrier Indians in regard to menstruous women.

Among the Carriers,* as soon as a girl has experienced the first flow of the menses which in the female constitution are a natural discharge, her father believed himself under the obligation of atoning for her supposedly sinful condition by a small impromptu distribution of clothes among the natives. This periodical state of women was considered as one of legal impurity fateful both to the man who happened to have any intercourse, however indirect, with her, and to the woman herself who failed in scrupulously observing all the rites prescribed by ancient usage for persons in her condition.

Seclusion of Carrier girls at puberty.

'Upon entering into that stage of her life, the maiden was immediately sequestered from company, even that of her parents, and compelled to dwell in a small branch hut by herself away from beaten paths and the gaze of passers-by. As she was supposed to exercise malefic influence on any man who might inadvertently glance at her, she had to wear a sort of head-dress combining in itself the purposes of a veil, a bonnet, and a mantlet. It was made of tanned skin, its forepart was shaped like a long fringe completely hiding from view the face and breasts; then it formed on the head a close-fitting cap or bonnet, and finally fell in a broad band almost to the heels. This head-dress was made and publicly placed on her head by a paternal aunt, who received at once some present from the girl's father. When, three or four years later, the period of sequestration ceased, only this same aunt had the right to take off her niece's ceremonial head-dress. Furthermore, the girl's fingers, wrists, and legs at the ankles and immediately below the knees, were encircled with ornamental rings and bracelets of sinew intended as a protection against the malign influences she was supposed to be possessed with. To a belt girding her waist were suspended two bone implements called respectively *Tsoenkuz* (bone tube) and *Tsiltsoet* (head scratcher). The former was a hollowed swan bone to drink with, any other mode of drinking being unlawful to her. The latter was fork-like and was called into requisition whenever she wanted to scratch her head—immediate contact of the fingers with the head being reputed injurious to her health. While thus secluded, she was called *asta*, that is "interred alive" in Carrier, and she had to submit to a rigorous fast and abstinence. Her only allowed food consisted of dried fish boiled in a small bark vessel which nobody else must touch, and she had to abstain especially from meat of any kind, as well as fresh fish. Nor was this all she had to endure; even her contact, however remote, with these two articles of diet was so dreaded that she could not cross the public paths or trails, or the tracks of animals. Whenever absolute necessity constrained her to go beyond such spots, she had to be packed or carried over them lest she should contaminate the game or meat which had passed that way, or had been brought over these paths; and also for the sake of self-preservation against tabooed, and consequently to her, deleterious food. In the same way she was never allowed to wade in streams or lakes, for fear of causing death to the fish.'

'It was also a prescription of the ancient ritual code for females during this primary condition to eat as little as possible, and to remain lying down, especially in course of each monthly flow, not only as a natural consequence of the prolonged fast and resulting weakness; but chiefly as an exhibition of a becoming penitential spirit which was believed to be rewarded by long life and continual good health in after years. These mortifications or seclusion did not last less than three or four years.'

The philosophic student of human nature will observe, or learn, without surprise that ideas thus deeply ingrained in the savage mind reappear at a more advanced stage of society in those elaborate codes which have been drawn up for the guidance of certain peoples by lawgivers who claim to have derived the rules they inculcate from the direct inspiration of the deity. However we may explain it, the resemblance which exists between the earliest official utterances of the deity and the ideas of savages is unquestionably close and remarkable; whether it be, as some suppose, that God communed face to face with man in those early days, or, as others maintain, that man mistook his wild and wandering thoughts for a revelation from heaven. Be that as it may, certain it is that the natural uncleanness of woman at her monthly periods is a conception

Similar rules of seclusion enjoined on menstruous women in ancient Hindoo, Persian, and Hebrew codes.

which has occurred, or been revealed, with singular unanimity to several ancient legislators. The Hindoo lawgiver Manu,* who professed to have received his institutes from the creator Brahman, informs us that the wisdom, the energy, the strength, the sight, and the vitality of a man who approaches a woman in her courses will utterly perish; whereas, if he avoids her, his wisdom, energy, strength, sight, and vitality will all increase. The Persian lawgiver Zoroaster, who, if we can take his word for it, derived his code from the mouth of the supreme being Ahura Mazda, devoted special attention to the subject. According to him, the menstrous flow, at least in its abnormal manifestations, is a work of Ahriman, or the devil. Therefore, so long as it lasts, a woman 'is unclean and possessed of the demon; she must be kept confined, apart from the faithful whom her touch would defile, and from the fire which her very look would injure; she is not allowed to eat as much as she wishes, as the strength she might acquire would accrue to the fiends. Her food is not given her from hand to hand, but is passed to her from a distance, in a long leaden spoon.' The Hebrew lawgiver Moses,* whose divine legation is as little open to question as that of Manu and Zoroaster, treats the subject at still greater length; but I must leave to the reader the task of comparing the inspired ordinances on this head with the merely human regulations of the Carrier Indians which they so closely resemble.

Superstitions as to menstruous women in ancient and modern Europe. In the oldest existing cyclopaedia—the *Natural History* of Pliny—the list of dangers apprehended from menstruation is longer than any furnished by mere barbarians. According to Pliny, the touch of a menstruous woman turned wine to vinegar, blighted crops, killed seedlings, blasted gardens, brought down the fruit from trees, dimmed mirrors, blunted razors, rusted iron and brass (especially at the waning of the moon), killed bees, or at least drove them from their hives, caused mares to miscarry, and so forth.* Similarly, in various parts of Europe, it is still believed that if a woman in her courses enters a brewery the beer will turn sour; if she touches beer, wine, vinegar, or milk, it will go bad; if she makes jam, it will not keep; if she mounts a mare, it will miscarry; if she touches buds, they will wither; if she climbs a cherry tree, it will die. In Brunswick people think that if a menstruous woman assists at the killing of a pig, the pork will putrefy. In the Greek island of Calymnos a woman at such times may not go to the well to draw water, nor cross a running stream, nor enter the sea. Her presence in a boat is said to raise storms.

Thus the object of secluding women at menstruation is to neutralize the dangerous influences which are supposed to emanate from them at such times. That the danger is believed to be especially great at the first menstruation appears from the unusual precautions taken to isolate girls at this crisis. Two of these precautions have been illustrated above, namely, the rules that the girl may not touch the ground nor see the sun. The general effect of these rules is to keep her suspended, so to say, between heaven and earth. Whether enveloped in her hammock and slung up to the roof, as in South America, or raised above the ground in a dark and narrow cage, as in New Ireland, she may be considered to be out of the way of doing mischief, since, being shut off both from the earth and from the sun, she can poison neither of these great sources of life by her deadly contagion. In short, she is rendered harmless by being, in electrical language, insulated. But the precautions thus taken to isolate or insulate the girl are dictated by a regard for her own safety as well as for the safety of others. For it is thought that she herself would suffer if she were to neglect the prescribed regimen. Thus Zulu girls believe that they would shrivel to skeletons if the sun were to shine on them at puberty, and in some Brazilian tribes the young women think that a transgression of the rules would entail sores on the neck and throat. In short, the girl is viewed as charged with a powerful force which, if not kept within bounds, may prove destructive both to herself and to all with whom she comes in contact. To repress this force within the limits necessary for the safety of all concerned is the object of the taboos in question.

The inten-
tion of se-
cluding
menstruous
women is to
neutralize
the danger-
ous influ-
ences which
are thought
to emanate
from them in
that condi-
tion.
Suspension
between
heaven and
earth.

The same explanation applies to the observance of the same rules by divine kings and priests. The uncleanness, as it is called, of girls at puberty and the sanctity of holy men do not, to the primitive mind, differ materially from each other. They are only different manifestations of the same mysterious energy which, like energy in general, is in itself neither good nor bad, but becomes beneficent or maleficent according to its application. Accordingly, if, like girls at puberty, divine personages

The same ex-
planation ap-
plies to the
similar rules
of seclusion
observed by
divine kings
and priests.

may neither touch the ground nor see the sun, the reason is, on the one hand, a fear lest their divinity might, at contact with earth or heaven, discharge itself with fatal violence on either; and, on the other hand, an apprehension that the divine being, thus drained of his ethereal virtue, might thereby be incapacitated for the future performance of those magical functions, upon the proper discharge of which the safety of the people and even of the world is believed to hang. Thus the rules in question are intended to preserve the life of the divine person and with it the life of his subjects and worshippers. Nowhere, it is thought, can his precious yet dangerous life be at once so safe and so harmless as when it is neither in heaven nor in earth, but, as far as possible, suspended between the two.

Suspension between heaven and earth.

In legends and folk-tales, which reflect the ideas of earlier ages, we find this suspension between heaven and earth attributed to beings who have been endowed with the coveted yet burdensome gift of immortality. The wizened remains of the deathless Sibyl are said to have been preserved in a jar or urn which hung in a temple of Apollo at Cumae; and when a group of merry children, tired, perhaps, of playing in the sunny streets, sought the shade of the temple and amused themselves by gathering underneath the familiar jar and calling out, 'Sibyl, what do you wish?' a hollow voice, like an echo, used to answer from the urn, 'I wish to die.'* A story, taken down from the lips of a German peasant at Thomsdorf, relates that once upon a time there was a girl in London who wished to live for ever, so they say:

Stories of immortality attained by suspension between heaven and earth.

> 'London, London is a fine town.
> A maiden prayed to live for ever.'

And still she lives and hangs in a basket in a church, and every St John's Day, about the hour of noon, she eats a roll of bread. Another German story tells of a lady who resided at Danzig and was so rich and so blest with all that life can give that she wished to live always. So when she came to her latter end, she did not really die but only looked like dead, and very soon they found her in a hollow of a pillar in the church, half standing and half sitting, motionless. She stirred never a limb, but they saw quite plainly that she was alive, and she sits there down to this blessed day. Every New Year's Day the sacristan comes and

puts a morsel of the holy bread in her mouth, and that is all she
has to live on. Long, long has she rued her fatal wish who set
this transient life above the eternal joys of heaven. A third
German story tells of a noble damsel who cherished the same
foolish wish for immortality. So they put her in a basket and
hung her up in a church, and there she hangs and never dies,
though many a year has come and gone since they put her there.
But every year on a certain day they give her a roll, and she eats
it and cries out, 'For ever! for ever! for ever!' And when she has
so cried she falls silent again till the same time next year, and
so it will go on for ever and for ever. A fourth story, taken down
near Oldenburg in Holstein, tells of a jolly dame that ate and
drank and lived right merrily and had all that heart could
desire, and she wished to live always. For the first hundred
years all went well, but after that she began to shrink and
shrivel up, till at last she could neither walk nor stand nor eat
nor drink. But die she could not. At first they fed her as if she
were a little child, but when she grew smaller and smaller they
put her in a glass bottle and hung her up in the church. And
there she still hangs, in the church of St Mary, at Lübeck. She
is as small as a mouse, but once a year she stirs.

CHAPTER 3

BALDER'S FIRES

How Balder, the good and beautiful god, was done to death by a stroke of the mistletoe.

A DEITY whose life might in a sense be said to be neither in heaven nor on earth but between the two, was the Norse Balder, the good and beautiful god, the son of the great god Odin, and himself the wisest, mildest, best beloved of all the immortals. The story of his death, as it is told in the younger or prose *Edda*,* runs thus. Once on a time Balder dreamed heavy dreams which seemed to forebode his death. Thereupon the gods held a council and resolved to make him secure against every danger. So the goddess Frigg took an oath from fire and water, iron and all metals, stones and earth, from trees, sicknesses and poisons, and from all four-footed beasts, birds, and creeping things, that they would not hurt Balder. When this was done Balder was deemed invulnerable; so the gods amused themselves by setting him in their midst, while some shot at him, others hewed at him, and others threw stones at him. But whatever they did, nothing could hurt him; and at this they were all glad. Only Loki, the mischief-maker, was displeased, and he went in the guise of an old woman to Frigg, who told him that the weapons of the gods could not wound Balder, since she had made them all swear not to hurt him. Then Loki asked, 'Have all things sworn to spare Balder?' She answered, 'East of Walhalla grows a plant called mistletoe; it seemed to me too young to swear.' So Loki went and pulled the mistletoe and took it to the assembly of the gods. There he found the blind god Hother standing at the outside of the circle. Loki asked him, 'Why do you not shoot at Balder?' Hother answered, 'Because I do not see where he stands; besides I have no weapon.' Then said Loki, 'Do like the rest and shew Balder honour, as they all do. I will shew you where he stands, and do you shoot at him with this twig.' Hother took the mistletoe and threw it at Balder, as Loki directed him. The mistletoe struck Balder and pierced him through and through, and he fell down dead. And that was the greatest misfortune that ever befell gods and men. For a while the gods stood speechless, then they lifted up their voices and wept bitterly. They took Balder's body and brought it to the sea-shore. There stood Balder's ship; it was called Ringhorn, and was the hugest of all ships. The gods wished to launch the ship and to burn Balder's body on it, but the ship would not stir. So they sent for a giantess called Hyrrockin. She came riding on a wolf and gave the ship such a push that fire flashed from the rollers and all the earth shook. Then Balder's body was taken and placed on the funeral pile upon his ship. When his wife Nanna saw that, her heart burst for sorrow and she died. So she was laid on the funeral pile with her husband, and fire was put to it. Balder's horse, too, with all its trappings, was burned on the pile.

In the older or poetic *Edda* the tragic tale of Balder is hinted at rather than told at length. Among the visions which the Norse Sibyl sees and describes in the weird prophecy known as the *Voluspa* is one of the fatal mistletoe. 'I behold', says she, 'Fate looming for Balder, Woden's son, the bloody victim. There stands the Mistletoe slender and delicate, blooming high above the ground. Out of this shoot, so slender to look on, there shall grow a harmful fateful shaft. Hod shall shoot it, but Frigga in Fen-hall shall weep over the woe of Wal-hall.' Yet looking far into the future the Sibyl sees a brighter vision of a new heaven and a new earth, where the fields unsown shall yield their increase and all sorrows shall be healed; then Balder will come back to dwell in Odin's mansions of bliss, in a hall brighter than the sun, shingled with gold, where the righteous shall live in joy for ever more.

Tale of Balder in the older Edda.

Writing about the end of the twelfth century, the old Danish historian Saxo Grammaticus tells the story of Balder in a form which professes to be historical. According to him, Balder and Hother were rival suitors for the hand of Nanna, daughter of Gewar, King of Norway. Now Balder was a demigod and common steel could not wound his sacred body. The two rivals encountered each other in a terrific battle, and though Odin and Thor and the rest of the gods fought for Balder, yet was he defeated and fled away, and Hother married the princess. Nevertheless Balder took heart of grace and again met Hother in a stricken field. But he fared even worse than before; for Hother dealt him a deadly wound with a magic sword, which

The story of Balder as related by Saxo Grammaticus.

he had received from Miming, the Satyr of the woods; and after lingering three days in pain Balder died of his hurt and was buried with royal honours in a barrow.

Whether he was a real or merely a mythical personage, Balder was worshipped in Norway. On one of the bays of the beautiful Sogne Fiord, which penetrates far into the depths of the solemn Norwegian mountains, with their sombre pine-forests and their lofty cascades dissolving into spray before they reach the dark water of the fiord far below, Balder had a great sanctuary. It was called Balder's Grove. A palisade enclosed the hallowed ground, and within it stood a spacious temple with the images of many gods, but none of them was worshipped with such devotion as Balder. So great was the awe with which the heathen regarded the place that no man might harm another there, nor steal his cattle, nor defile himself with women. But women cared for the images of the gods in the temple; they warmed them at the fire, anointed them with oil, and dried them with cloths.

It might be rash to affirm that the romantic figure of Balder was nothing but a creation of the mythical fancy, a radiant phantom conjured up as by a wizard's wand to glitter for a time against the gloomy background of the stern Norwegian landscape. It may be so; yet it is also possible that the myth was founded on the tradition of a hero, popular and beloved in his lifetime, who long survived in the memory of the people, gathering more and more of the marvellous about him as he passed from generation to generation of story-tellers. At all events it is worth while to observe that a somewhat similar story is told of another national hero, who may well have been a real man. In his great poem, *The Epic of Kings*, which is founded on Persian traditions, the poet Firdusi tells us that in the combat between Rustem and Isfendiyar the arrows of the former did no harm to his adversary, 'because Zerdusht had charmed his body against all dangers, so that it was like unto brass'. But Simurgh, the bird of God, shewed Rustem the way he should follow in order to vanquish his redoubtable foe. He rode after her, and they halted not till they came to the sea-shore. There she led him into a garden, where grew a tamarisk, tall and strong, and the roots thereof were in the ground, but the branches pierced even unto the sky. Then the bird of God bade Rustem break from the tree a branch that was long and slender, and fashion it into an arrow, and she said, 'Only through his eyes can Isfendiyar be wounded. If, therefore, thou wouldst slay him, direct this arrow unto his forehead, and verily it shall not miss its aim.' Rustem did as he was bid; and when next he fought with Isfendiyar, he shot the arrow at him, and it pierced his eye, and he died. Great was the mourning for Isfendiyar. For the space of one year men ceased not to lament for him, and for many years they shed bitter tears for that arrow, and they said, 'The glory of Iran hath been laid low.'

Whatever may be thought of an historical kernel underlying a mythical husk in the legend of Balder, the details of the story suggest that it belongs to that class of myths which have been dramatized in ritual, or, to put it otherwise, which have been performed as magical ceremonies for the sake of producing those natural effects which they describe in figurative language. A myth is never so graphic and precise in its details as when it is, so to speak, the book of the words which are spoken and acted by the performers of the sacred rite. That the Norse story of Balder was a myth of this sort will become probable if we can prove that ceremonies resembling the incidents in the tale have been performed by Norsemen and other European peoples. Now the main incidents in the tale are two—first, the pulling of the mistletoe, and second, the death and burning of the god; and both of them may perhaps be found to have had their counterparts in yearly rites observed, whether separately or conjointly, by people in various parts of Europe. We shall begin with the annual festivals of fire and shall reserve the pulling of the mistletoe for consideration later on.

The myth of Balder was perhaps acted as a magical ceremony. The two chief incidents of the myth, namely the pulling of the mistletoe and the death and burning of the god, have perhaps their counterparts in popular ritual.

ii

All over Europe the peasants have been accustomed from time immemorial to kindle bonfires on certain days of the year, and to dance round or leap over them. Customs of this kind can be traced back on historical evidence to the Middle Ages, and their analogy to similar customs observed in antiquity goes with strong internal evidence to prove that their origin must be sought in a period long prior to the spread of Christianity. Indeed the earliest proof of their observance in Northern

European custom of kindling bonfires on certain days of the year, dancing round them and leaping over them.

Effigies are
sometimes
burnt in the
fires.

Europe is furnished by the attempts made by Christian synods in the eighth century to put them down as heathenish rites. Not uncommonly effigies are burned in these fires, or a pretence is made of burning a living person in them; and there are grounds for believing that anciently human beings were actually burned on these occasions. A general survey of the customs in question will bring out the traces of human sacrifice, and will serve at the same time to throw light on their meaning.

Custom of
kindling bon-
fires on the
first Sunday
in Lent in
the Belgian
Ardennes.

The custom of kindling bonfires on the first Sunday in Lent has prevailed in Belgium, the north of France, and many parts of Germany. Thus in the Belgian Ardennes for a week or a fortnight before the 'day of the great fire', as it is called, children go about from farm to farm collecting fuel. At Grand Halleux any one who refuses their request is pursued next day by the children, who try to blacken his face with the ashes of the extinct fire. When the day has come, they cut down bushes, especially juniper and broom, and in the evening great bonfires blaze on all the heights. It is a common saying that seven bonfires should be seen if the village is to be safe from conflagrations. If the Meuse happens to be frozen hard at the time, bonfires are lit also on the ice. At Grand Halleux they set up a pole called *makral*, or 'the witch', in the midst of the pile, and the fire is kindled by the man who was last married in the village. In the neighbourhood of Morlanwelz a straw man is burnt in the fire. Young people and children dance and sing round the bonfires, and leap over the embers to secure good crops or a happy marriage within the year, or as a means of guarding themselves against colic.

Bonfires on
the first Sun-
day of Lent
in Germany
and Austria.

In Germany, Austria, and Switzerland at the same season similar customs have prevailed. Thus in the Eifel Mountains, Rhenish Prussia, on the first Sunday in Lent young people used to collect straw and brushwood from house to house. These they carried to an eminence and piled up round a tall, slim beech-tree, to which a piece of wood was fastened at right angles to form a cross. The structure was known as the 'hut' or 'castle'. Fire was set to it and the young people marched round the blazing 'castle' bareheaded, each carrying a lighted torch and praying aloud. Sometimes a straw-man was burned in the 'hut'. People observed the direction in which the smoke blew from the fire. If it blew towards the corn-fields, it was a sign that the harvest would be abundant. On the same day, in some parts of the Eifel, a great wheel was made of straw and dragged by three horses to the top of a hill. Thither the village boys marched at nightfall, set fire to the wheel, and sent it rolling down the slope. Two lads followed it with levers to set it in motion again, in case it should anywhere meet with a check. At Oberstattfeld the wheel had to be provided by the young man who was last married. About Echternach in Luxemburg the same ceremony is called 'burning the witch'; while it is going on, the older men ascend the heights and observe what wind is blowing, for that is the wind which will prevail the whole year. At Voralberg in the Tyrol, on the first Sunday in Lent, a slender young fir-tree is surrounded with a pile of straw and firewood. To the top of the tree is fastened a human figure called the 'witch', made of old clothes and stuffed with gunpowder. At night the whole is set on fire and boys and girls dance round it, swinging torches and singing rhymes in which the words, 'corn in the winnowing-basket, the plough in the earth' may be distinguished. In Swabia on the first Sunday in Lent a figure called the 'witch' or the 'old wife' or 'winter's grandmother' is made up of clothes and fastened to a pole. This is stuck in the middle of a pile of wood, to which fire is applied. While the 'witch' is burning, the young people throw blazing discs into the air. The discs are thin round pieces of wood, a few inches in diameter, with notched edges to imitate the rays of the sun or stars. They have a hole in the middle, by which they are attached to the end of a wand. Before the disc is thrown it is set on fire, the wand is swung to and fro, and the impetus thus communicated to the disc is augmented by dashing the rod sharply against a sloping board. The burning disc is thus thrown off, and mounting high into the air, describes a long fiery curve before it reaches the ground.

> 'Burning the witch.'

> Burning discs thrown into the air.

It seems hardly possible to separate from these bonfires, kindled on the first Sunday in Lent, the fires in which, about the same season, the effigy called Death is burned as part of the ceremony of 'carrying out Death'.* At Spachendorf, in Austrian Silesia, on the morning of Rupert's Day (Shrove Tuesday?), a straw-man, dressed in a fur coat and a fur cap, is laid in a hole outside the village and there burned, and that while it is blazing every one seeks to snatch a fragment of it, which he fastens to

> Connexion of these bonfires with the custom of 'carrying out Death.'

a branch of the highest tree in his garden or buries in his field, believing that this will make the crops to grow better. The ceremony is known as the 'burying of Death'. Even when the straw-man is not designated as Death, the meaning of the observance is probably the same; for the name Death, as I have tried to shew, does not express the original intention of the ceremony. At Cobern in the Eifel Mountains the lads make up a straw-man on Shrove Tuesday. The effigy is formally tried and accused of having perpetrated all the thefts that have been committed in the neighbourhood throughout the year. Being condemned to death, the straw-man is led through the village, shot, and burned upon a pyre. They dance round the blazing pile, and the last bride must leap over it. In Oldenburg on the evening of Shrove Tuesday people used to make long bundles of straw, which they set on fire, and then ran about the fields waving them, shrieking, and singing wild songs. Finally they burned a straw-man on the field. In the district of Düsseldorf the straw-man burned on Shrove Tuesday was made of an unthreshed sheaf of corn. On the first Monday after the spring equinox the urchins of Zurich drag a straw-man on a little cart through the streets, while at the same time the girls carry about a May-tree. When vespers ring, the straw-man is burned. In the district of Aachen on Ash Wednesday a man used to be encased in peas-straw and taken to an appointed place. Here he slipped quietly out of his straw casing, which was then burned, the children thinking that it was the man who was being burned. In the Val di Ledro (Tyrol) on the last day of the Carnival a figure is made up of straw and brushwood and then burned. The figure is called the Old Woman, and the ceremony 'burning the Old Woman'.

Effigies burnt on Shrove Tuesday.

Fire-festivals on Easter Eve. Custom in Catholic countries of kindling a holy new fire at the church on Easter Saturday;

Another occasion on which these fire-festivals are held is Easter Eve, the Saturday before Easter Sunday. On that day it has been customary in Catholic countries to extinguish all the lights in the churches, and then to make a new fire, sometimes with flint and steel, sometimes with a burning-glass. At this fire is lit the great Paschal or Easter candle, which is then used to rekindle all the extinguished lights in the church. In many parts of Germany a bonfire is also kindled, by means of the new fire, on some open space near the church. It is consecrated, and the people bring sticks of oak, walnut, and beech, which they char in the fire, and then take home with them. Some of these marvellous properties ascribed to the embers of the fire. charred sticks are thereupon burned at home in a newly-kindled fire, with a prayer that God will preserve the homestead from fire, lightning, and hail. Thus every house receives 'new fire'. Some of the sticks are kept throughout the year and laid on the hearth-fire during heavy thunder-storms to prevent the house from being struck by lightning, or they are inserted in the roof with the like intention. Others are placed in the fields, gardens, and meadows, with a prayer that God will keep them from blight and hail. Such fields and gardens are thought to thrive more than others; the corn and the plants that grow in them are not beaten down by hail, nor devoured by mice, vermin, and beetles; no witch harms them, and the ears of corn stand close and full. The charred sticks are also applied to the plough. The ashes of the Easter bonfire, together with the ashes of the consecrated palm-branches, are mixed with the seed at sowing. A wooden figure called Judas is sometimes burned in the The burning of Judas. consecrated bonfire, and even where this custom has been abolished the bonfire itself in some places goes by the name of 'the burning of Judas'.

In Florence the ceremony of kindling the new fire on Easter The new fire on Easter Saturday at Florence. Eve is peculiar. The holy flame is elicited from certain flints which are said to have been brought by a member of the Pazzi family from the Holy Land. They are kept in the church of the Holy Apostles on the Piazza del Limbo, and on the morning of Easter Saturday the prior strikes fire from them and lights a candle from the new flame. The burning candle is then carried in solemn procession by the clergy and members of the municipality to the high altar in the cathedral. A vast crowd has meanwhile assembled in the cathedral and the neighbouring square to witness the ceremony; amongst the spectators are many peasants drawn from the surrounding country, for it is commonly believed that on the success or failure of the ceremony depends the fate of the crops for the year. Outside the door of the cathedral stands a festal car drawn by two fine white oxen with gilded horns. The body of the car is loaded with a pyramid of squibs and crackers and is connected by a wire with a pillar set up in front of the high altar. The wire extends down the middle of the nave at a height of about six feet from the ground. Beneath it a clear passage is left, the spectators being ranged on either side and crowding the vast interior from wall to wall. When all is ready, High Mass is celebrated, and precisely at noon, when the first words of the *Gloria* are being chanted, the sacred fire is applied to the pillar, which like the car is wreathed with fireworks. A moment more and a fiery dove comes flying down the nave, with a hissing sound and a sputter of sparks, between the two hedges of eager spectators. If all goes well, the bird pursues its course along the wire and out at the door, and in another moment a prolonged series of fizzes, pops and bangs announces to the excited crowd in the cathedral that the fireworks on the car are going off. Great is the joy accordingly, especially among the bumpkins, who are now sure of an abundant harvest. But if, as sometimes happens, the dove stops short in its career and fizzles out, revealing itself as a stuffed bird with a packet of squibs tied to its tail, great is the consternation, and deep the curses that issue from between the set teeth of the clodhoppers, who now give up the harvest for lost. Formerly the unskilful mechanician who was responsible for the failure would have been clapped into gaol; but nowadays he is thought sufficiently punished by the storm of public indignation and the loss of his pay. The disaster is announced by placards posted about the streets in the evening; and next morning the newspapers are full of gloomy prognostications.

The new fire on Easter Saturday in the Church of the Holy Sepulchre at Jerusalem.

But usages of this sort are not confined to the Latin Church; they are common to the Greek Church also. Every year on the Saturday before Easter Sunday a new fire is miraculously kindled at the Holy Sepulchre in Jerusalem. It descends from heaven and ignites the candles which the patriarch holds in his hands, while with closed eyes he wrestles in prayer all alone in the chapel of the Angel. The worshippers meanwhile wait anxiously in the body of the church, and great are their transports of joy when at one of the windows of the chapel, which had been all dark a minute before, there suddenly appears the hand of an angel, or of the partriarch, holding a lighted taper. This is the sacred new fire; it is passed out to the expectant believers, and the desperate struggle which ensues among them to get a share of its blessed influence is only terminated by the intervention of the Turkish soldiery, who restore peace and order by hustling the whole multitude impartially out of the church. In days gone by many lives were often lost in these holy scrimmages. For example, in the year 1834, the famous Ibrahim Pasha witnessed the frantic scene from one of the galleries, and, being moved with compassion at the sight, descended with a few guards into the arena in the chimerical hope of restoring peace and order among the contending Christians. He contrived to force his way into the midst of the dense crowd, but there the heat and pressure were so great that he fainted away; a body of soldiers, seeing his danger, charged straight into the throng and carried him out of it in their arms, trampling under foot the dying and dead in their passage. Nearly two hundred people were killed that day in the church. The fortunate survivors on these occasions who succeeded in obtaining a portion of the coveted fire applied it freely to their faces, their beards, and their garments. The theory was that the fire, being miraculous, could only bless and not burn them; but the practical results of the experiment were often disappointing, for while the blessings were more or less dubious, there could be no doubt whatever about the burns. The history of the miracle has been carefully investigated by a Jesuit father. The conclusions at which he arrives are that the miracle was a miracle indeed so long as the Catholics had the management of it; but that since it fell into the hands of the heretics it has been nothing but a barefaced trick and imposture.* Many people will be disposed to agree with the latter conclusion who might hesitate to accept the former.

At Athens the new fire is kindled in the cathedral at midnight on Holy Saturday. A dense crowd with unlit candles in their hands fills the square in front of the cathedral; the king, the archbishop, and the highest dignitaries of the church, arrayed in their gorgeous robes, occupy a platform; and at the exact moment of the resurrection the bells ring out, and the whole square bursts as by magic into a blaze of light. Theoretically all the candles are lit from the sacred new fire in the cathedral, but practically it may be suspected that the matches which bear the name of Lucifer have some share in the sudden illumination.* Effigies of Judas used to be burned at Athens on Easter Saturday, but the custom has been forbidden by the Government. However, firing goes on more or less continuously all over the city both on Easter Saturday and Easter Sunday, and the cartridges used on this occasion are not always blank. The

The new fire and the burning of Judas on Easter Saturday in Greece.

shots are aimed at Judas, but sometimes they miss him and hit other people. Outside of Athens the practice of burning Judas in effigy still survives in some places. For example, in Cos a straw image of the traitor is made on Easter Day, and after being hung up and shot at it is burned. A similar custom appears to prevail at Thebes; it used to be observed by the Macedonian peasantry, and it is still kept up at Therapia, a fashionable summer resort of Constantinople.

In spite of the thin cloak of Christianity thrown over these customs by representing the new fire as an emblem of Christ and the figure burned in it as an effigy of Judas, we can hardly doubt that both practices are of pagan origin. Neither of them has the authority of Christ or of his disciples; but both of them have abundant analogies in popular custom and superstition.

iii

In the central Highlands of Scotland bonfires, known as the Beltane fires, were formerly kindled with great ceremony on the first of May, and the traces of human sacrifices at them were particularly clear and unequivocal. The custom of lighting the bonfires lasted in various places far into the eighteenth century, and the descriptions of the ceremony by writers of that period present such a curious and interesting picture of ancient heathendom surviving in our own country that I will reproduce them in the words of their authors. The fullest of the descriptions, so far as I know, is the one bequeathed to us by John Ramsay, laird of Ochtertyre, near Crieff, the patron of Burns and the friend of Sir Walter Scott. From his voluminous manuscripts, written in the last quarter of the eighteenth century, a selection was published in the latter part of the nineteenth century. The following account of Beltane is extracted from a chapter dealing with Highland superstitions. Ramsay says: 'But the most considerable of the Druidical festivals is that of Beltane, or May-day, which was lately observed in some parts of the Highlands with extraordinary ceremonies. Of later years it is chiefly attended to by young people, persons advanced in years considering it as inconsistent with their gravity to give it any countenance. Yet a number of circumstances relative to it may be collected from tradition, or the conversation of very old people, who witnessed this feast in their youth, when the ancient rites were better observed.

'This festival is called in Gaelic *Beal-tene—i.e.*, the fire of Bel ... Like the other public worship of the Druids, the Beltane feast seems to have been performed on hills or eminences. They thought it degrading to him whose temple is the universe, to suppose that he would dwell in any house made with hands. Their sacrifices were therefore offered in the open air, frequently upon the tops of hills, where they were presented with the grandest views of nature, and were nearest the seat of warmth and order. And, according to tradition, such was the manner of celebrating this festival in the Highlands within the last hundred years. But since the decline of superstition, it has been celebrated by the people of each hamlet on some hill or rising ground around which their cattle were pasturing. Thither the young folks repaired in the morning, and cut a trench, on the summit of which a seat of turf was formed for the company. And in the middle a pile of wood or other fuel was placed, which of old they kindled with *tein-eigin—i.e.*, forced-fire or *need-fire*. Although, for many years past, they have been contented with common fire, yet we shall now describe the process, because it will hereafter appear that recourse is still had to the *tein-eigin* upon extraordinary emergencies.

Need-fire.

'The night before, all the fires in the country were carefully extinguished, and next morning the materials for exciting this sacred fire were prepared. The most primitive method seems to be that which was used in the islands of Skye, Mull, and Tiree. A well-seasoned plank of oak was procured, in the midst of which a hole was bored. A wimble of the same timber was then applied, the end of which they fitted to the hole. But in some parts of the mainland the machinery was different. They used a frame of green wood, of a square form, in the centre of which was an axle-tree. In some places three times three persons, in others three times nine, were required for turning round by turns the axle-tree or wimble. If any of them had been guilty of murder, adultery, theft, or other atrocious crime, it was imagined either that the fire would not kindle, or that it would be devoid of its usual virtue. So soon as any sparks were emitted by means of the violent friction, they applied a species of agaric which grows on old birch-trees, and is very combustible. This

Need-fire
kindled by
the friction
of oak wood.

fire had the appearance of being immediately derived from heaven, and manifold were the virtues ascribed to it. They esteemed it a preservative against witchcraft, and a sovereign remedy against malignant diseases, both in the human species and in cattle; and by it the strongest poisons were supposed to have their nature changed.

The Beltane cake and the Beltane carline (*cailleach*).

'After kindling the bonfire with the *tein-eigin* the company prepared their victuals. And as soon as they had finished their meal, they amused themselves a while in singing and dancing round the fire. Towards the close of the entertainment, the person who officiated as master of the feast produced a large cake baked with eggs and scalloped round the edge, called *am bonnach beal-tine*—i.e., the Beltane cake. It was divided into a number of pieces, and distributed in great form to the company. There was one particular piece which whoever got was called *cailleach beal-tine*—i.e., the Beltane *carline*, a term of great reproach. Upon his being known, part of the company laid hold of him and made a show of putting him into the fire; but the majority interposing, he was rescued. And in some places they laid him flat on the ground, making as if they would quarter him. Afterwards, he was pelted with egg-shells, and retained the odious appellation during the whole year. And while the feast was fresh in people's memory, they affected to speak of the *cailleach beal-tine* as dead.

Local differences in the Beltane cakes.

'This festival was longest observed in the interior Highlands, for towards the west coast the traces of it are faintest. In Glenorchy and Lorne, a large cake is made on that day, which they consume in the house; and in Mull it has a large hole in the middle, through which each of the cows in the fold is milked. In Tiree it is of a triangular form. The more elderly people remember when this festival was celebrated without-doors with some solemnity in both these islands. There are at present no vestiges of it in Skye or the Long Island, the inhabitants of which have substituted the *connach Micheil* or St Michael's cake. It is made at Michaelmas with milk and oatmeal, and some eggs are sprinkled on its surface. Part of it is sent to the neighbours.

Evidence of two fires at Beltane.

'It is probable that at the original Beltane festival there were two fires kindled near one another. When any person is in a critical dilemma, pressed on each side by unsurmountable difficulties, the Highlanders have a proverb, *The e' eada anda theine bealtuin*—*i.e.*, he is between the two Beltane fires. There are in several parts small round hills, which, it is like, owe their present names to such solemn uses. One of the highest and most central in Icolmkil is called *Cnoch-nan-ainneal*—*i.e.*, the hill of the fires. There is another of the same name near the kirk of Balquhidder; and at Killin there is a round green eminence which seems to have been raised by art. It is called *Tom-nan-ainneal*—*i.e.*, the eminence of the fires. Around it there are the remains of a circular wall about two feet high. On the top a stone stands upon end. According to the tradition of the inhabitants, it was a place of Druidical worship; and it was afterwards pitched on as the most venerable spot for holding courts of justice for the country of Breadalbane. The earth of this eminence is still thought to be possessed of some healing virtue, for when cattle are observed to be diseased some of it is sent for, which is rubbed on the part affected.'*

Thomas Pennant, who travelled in Perthshire in the year 1769, tells us that 'on the first of May, the herdsmen of every village hold their Bel-tien, a rural sacrifice. They cut a square trench on the ground, leaving the turf in the middle; on that they make a fire of wood, on which they dress a large caudle of eggs, butter, oatmeal and milk; and bring besides the ingredients of the caudle, plenty of beer and whisky; for each of the company must contribute something. The rites begin with spilling some of the caudle on the ground, by way of libation: on that every one takes a cake of oatmeal, upon which are raised nine square knobs, each dedicated to some particular being, the supposed preserver of their flocks and herds, or to some particular animal, the real destroyer of them: each person then turns his face to the fire, breaks off a knob, and flinging it over his shoulders, says, "This I give to thee, preserve thou my horses; this to thee, preserve thou my sheep; and so on." After that, they use the same ceremony to the noxious animals: "This I give to thee, O fox! spare thou my lambs; this to thee, O hooded crow! this to thee, O eagle!" When the ceremony is over, they dine on the caudle; and after the feast is finished, what is left is hid by two persons deputed for that purpose; but on the next Sunday they re-assemble, and finish the reliques of the first entertainment.'*

Pennant's description of the Beltane fires and cakes in Perthshire.

In the Hebrides 'the Beltane bannock is smaller than that
made at St Michael's, but is made in the same way; it is no
longer made in Uist, but Father Allan remembers seeing his
grandmother make one about twenty-five years ago. There was
also a cheese made, generally on the first of May, which was
kept to the next Beltane as a sort of charm against the
bewitching of milk-produce. The Beltane customs seem to have
been the same as elsewhere. Every fire was put out and a large
one lit on the top of the hill, and the cattle driven round it
sunwards (*dessil*), to keep off murrain all the year. Each man
would take home fire wherewith to kindle his own.'

In Wales also the custom of lighting Beltane fires at the
beginning of May used to be observed, but the day on which
they were kindled varied from the Eve of May Day to the third
of May. The flame was sometimes elicited by the friction of two
pieces of oak, as appears from the following description. 'The
fire was done in this way. Nine men would turn their pockets
inside out, and see that every piece of money and all metals
were off their persons. Then the men went into the nearest
woods, and collected sticks of nine different kinds of trees.
These were carried to the spot where the fire had to be built.
There a circle was cut in the sod, and the sticks were set
crosswise. All around the circle the people stood and watched
the proceedings. One of the men would then take two bits of
oak, and rub them together until a flame was kindled. This was
applied to the sticks, and soon a large fire was made. Sometimes
two fires were set up side by side. These fires, whether one or
two, were called *coelcerth* or bonfire. Round cakes of oatmeal
and brown meal were split in four, and placed in a small
flour-bag, and everybody present had to pick out a portion. The
last bit in the bag fell to the lot of the bag-holder. Each person
who chanced to pick up a piece of brown-meal cake was
compelled to leap three times over the flames, or to run thrice
between the two fires, by which means the people thought they
were sure of a plentiful harvest. Shouts and screams of those
who had to face the ordeal could be heard ever so far, and
those who chanced to pick the oatmeal portions sang and
danced and clapped their hands in approval, as the holders of
the brown bits leaped three times over the flames, or ran three
times between the two fires. As a rule, no danger attended these

curious celebrations, but occasionally somebody's clothes caught fire, which was quickly put out. The greatest fire of the year was the eve of May, or May first, second, or third. The Midsummer Eve fire was more for the harvest. Very often a fire was built on the eve of November. The high ground near the Castle Ditches at Llantwit Major, in the Vale of Glamorgan, was a familiar spot for the Beltane on May third and on Midsummer Eve . . . Sometimes the Beltane fire was lighted by the flames produced by stone instead of wood friction. Charred logs and faggots used in the May Beltane were carefully preserved and from them the next fire was lighted. May fires were always started with old faggots of the previous year, and midsummer from those of the last summer. It was unlucky to build a midsummer fire from May faggots. People carried the ashes left after these fires to their homes, and a charred brand was not only effectual against pestilence, but magical in its use. A few of the ashes placed in a person's shoes protected the wearer from any great sorrow or woe.'

The first of May is a great popular festival in the more midland and southern parts of Sweden. On the eve of the festival, huge bonfires, which should be lighted by striking two flints together, blaze on all the hills and knolls. Every large hamlet has its own fire, round which the young people dance in a ring. The old folk notice whether the flames incline to the north or to the south. In the former case, the spring will be cold and backward; in the latter, it will be mild and genial. Similarly, in Bohemia, on the eve of May Day, young people kindle fires on hills and eminences, at crossways, and in pastures, and dance round them. They leap over the glowing embers or even through the flames. The ceremony is called 'burning the witches'. In some places an effigy representing a witch used to be burnt in the bonfire. We have to remember that the eve of May Day is the notorious Walpurgis Night, when the witches are everywhere speeding unseen through the air on their hellish errands. On this witching night children in Voigtland also light bonfires on the heights and leap over them. Moreover, they wave burning brooms or toss them into the air. So far as the light of the bonfire reaches, so far will a blessing rest on the fields. The kindling of the fires on Walpurgis Night is called 'driving away the witches'. The custom of kindling fires on the

Fires on the Eve of May Day in Sweden.

Fires on the Eve of May Day in Austria and Saxony for the purpose of burning the witches.

eve of May Day (Walpurgis Night) for the purpose of burning the witches is, or used to be, widespread in the Tyrol, Moravia, Saxony and Silesia.

iv

The great season for fire-festivals in Europe is the summer solstice, Midsummer Eve or Midsummer Day, which the church has dedicated to St John the Baptist.

But the season at which these fire-festivals have been mostly generally held all over Europe is the summer solstice, that is Midsummer Eve (the twenty-third of June) or Midsummer Day (the twenty-fourth of June). A faint tinge of Christianity has been given to them by naming Midsummer Day after St John the Baptist, but we cannot doubt that the celebration dates from a time long before the beginning of our era. The summer solstice, or Midsummer Day, is the great turning-point in the sun's career, when, after climbing higher and higher day by day in the sky, the luminary stops and thenceforth retraces his steps down the heavenly road. Such a moment could not but be regarded with anxiety by primitive man so soon as he began to observe and ponder the courses of the great lights across the celestial vault; and having still to learn his own powerlessness in face of the vast cyclic changes of nature, he may have fancied that he could help the sun in his seeming decline—could prop his failing steps and rekindle the sinking flame of the red lamp in his feeble hand. In some such thoughts as these the midsummer festivals of our European peasantry may perhaps have taken their rise. Whatever their origin, they have prevailed all over this quarter of the globe, from Ireland on the west to Russia on the east, and from Norway and Sweden on the north to Spain and Greece on the

The bonfires, the torches, and the burning wheels of the festival.

south. According to a mediæval writer, the three great features of the midsummer celebration were the bonfires, the procession with torches round the fields, and the custom of rolling a wheel. He tells us that boys burned bones and filth of various kinds to make a foul smoke, and that the smoke drove away certain noxious dragons which at this time, excited by the summer heat, copulated in the air and poisoned the wells and rivers by dropping their seed into them; and he explains the custom of trundling a wheel to mean that the sun, having now reached the highest point in the ecliptic, begins thenceforward to descend.

A good general account of the midsummer customs, together with some of the reasons popularly alleged for observing them, is given by Thomas Kirchmeyer, a writer of the sixteenth century, in his poem *The Popish Kingdome*:

'Then doth the joyfull feast of John the Baptist take his turne,
When bonfiers great with loftie flame, in every towne doe burne;
And yong men round about with maides, doe daunce in every streete,
With garlands wrought of Motherwort, or else with Vervain sweete,
And many other flowres faire, with Violets in their handes,
Whereas they all do fondly thinke, that whosoever standes,
And thorow the flowres beholds the flame, his eyes shall feele no paine.
When thus till night they daunced have, they through the fire amaine
With striving mindes doe runne, and all their hearbes they cast therin,
And then with wordes devout and prayers, they solemnely begin,
Desiring God that all their illes may there consumed bee,
Whereby they thinke through all that yeare from Agues to be free.
Some others get a rotten wheele, all worne and cast aside,
Which covered round about with strawe, and tow, they closely hide:
And caryed to some mountaines top, being all with fire light,
They hurle it downe with violence, when darke appeares the night:
Resembling much the Sunne, that from the heavens downe should fal,
A straunge and monstrous sight it seemes, and fearfull to them all:
But they suppose their mischiefes all are likewise throwne to hell,
And that from harmes and daungers now, in safetie here they dwell.'*

From these general descriptions, which to some extent still hold good, or did so till lately, we see that the main features of the midsummer fire-festival resemble those which we have found to characterize the vernal festivals of fire. The similarity of the two sets of ceremonies will plainly appear from the following examples.

Down at least to the middle of the nineteenth century the midsummer fires used to blaze all over Upper Bavaria. They were kindled especially on the mountains, but also far and wide in the lowlands, and we are told that in the darkness and stillness of night the moving groups, lit up by the flickering glow of the flames, presented an impressive spectacle. In some places the people shewed their sense of the sanctity of the fires by using for fuel the trees past which the gay procession had defiled, with fluttering banners, on Corpus Christi Day. In others the children collected the firewood from door to door on the eve of the festival, singing their request for fuel at every

Cattle driven
through the
fire.

The new fire.

Omens of
the harvest
drawn from
the fires.

Burning
discs thrown
into the air.

The Mid-
summer fires
in Sweden.

house in doggerel verse. Cattle were driven through the fire to cure the sick animals and to guard such as were sound against plague and harm of every kind throughout the year. Many a householder on that day put out the fire on the domestic hearth and rekindled it by means of a brand taken from the midsummer bonfire. The people judged of the height to which the flax would grow in the year by the height to which the flames of the bonfire rose; and whoever leaped over the burning pile was sure not to suffer from backache in reaping the corn at harvest. But it was especially the practice for lovers to spring over the fire hand in hand, and the way in which each couple made the leap was the subject of many a jest and many a superstition.* In one district the custom of kindling the bonfires was combined with that of lighting wooden discs and hurling them in the air after the manner which prevails at some of the spring festivals. In many parts of Bavaria it was believed that the flax would grow as high as the young people leaped over the fire. In others the old folk used to plant three charred sticks from the bonfire in the fields, believing that this would make the flax grow tall. Elsewhere an extinguished brand was put in the roof of the house to protect it against fire. In the towns about Würzburg the bonfires used to be kindled in the market-places, and the young people who jumped over them wore garlands of flowers, especially of mugwort and vervain, and carried sprigs of larkspur in their hands. They thought that such as looked at the fire holding a bit of larkspur before their face would be troubled by no malady of the eyes throughout the year. Further, it was customary at Würzburg, in the sixteenth century, for the bishop's followers to throw burning discs of wood into the air from a mountain which overhangs the town. The discs were discharged by means of flexible rods, and in their flight through the darkness presented the appearance of fiery dragons.

In Sweden the Eve of St John (St Hans) is the most joyous night of the whole year. Throughout some parts of the country, especially in the provinces of Bohus and Scania and in districts bordering on Norway, it is celebrated by the frequent discharge of firearms and by huge bonfires, formerly called Balder's Balefires (*Balder's Bålar*), which are kindled at dusk on hills and eminences and throw a glare of light over the surrounding landscape. The people dance round the fires and leap over or through them. In parts of Norrland on St John's Eve the bonfires are lit at the cross-roads. The fuel consists of nine different sorts of wood, and the spectators cast into the flames a kind of toad-stool (*Bäran*) in order to counteract the power of the Trolls and other evil spirits, who are believed to be abroad that night; for at that mystic season the mountains open and from their cavernous depths the uncanny crew pours forth to dance and disport themselves for a time. The peasants believe that should any of the Trolls be in the vicinity they will shew themselves; and if an animal, for example a he or she goat, happens to be seen near the blazing, crackling pile, the peasants are firmly persuaded that it is no other than the Evil One in person. Further, it deserves to be remarked that in Sweden St John's Eve is a festival of water as well as of fire; for certain holy springs are then supposed to be endowed with wonderful medicinal virtues, and many sick people resort to them for the healing of their infirmities.

In Brittany, apparently, the custom of the Midsummer bonfires is kept up to this day. Thus in Lower Brittany every town and every village still lights its *tantad* or bonfire on St John's Night. When the flames have died down, the whole assembly kneels round about the bonfire and an old man prays aloud. Then they all rise and march thrice round the fire; at the third turn they stop and every one picks up a pebble and throws it on the burning pile. After that they disperse. In Finistère the bonfires of St John's Day are kindled by preference in an open space near a chapel of St John; but if there is no such chapel, they are lighted in the square facing the parish church and in some districts at cross-roads. Everybody brings fuel for the fire, it may be a faggot, a log, a branch, or an armful of gorse. When the vespers are over, the parish priest sets a light to the pile. All heads are bared, prayers recited, and hymns sung. Then the dancing begins. The young folk skip round the blazing pile and leap over it, when the flames have died down. If anybody makes a false step and falls or rolls in the hot embers, he or she is greeted with hoots and retires abashed from the circle of dancers. Brands are carried home from the bonfire to protect the houses against lightning, conflagrations, and certain maladies and spells. The precious talisman is carefully kept in a cupboard till St John's Day of the following year. At Quimper, and in the district of Léon, chairs used to be placed round the midsummer bonfire, that the souls of the dead might sit on them and warm themselves at the blaze. At Brest on this day thousands of people used to assemble on the ramparts towards evening and brandish lighted torches, which they swung in circles or flung by hundreds into the air. The closing of the town gates put an end to the spectacle, and the lights might be seen dispersing in all directions like wandering will-o'-the-wisps. In Upper Brittany the materials for the midsummer bonfires, which generally consist of bundles of furze and heath, are furnished by voluntary contributions, and piled on the tops of hills round poles, each of which is surmounted by a nosegay or a crown. This nosegay or crown is generally provided by a man named John or a woman named Jean, and it is always a John or a Jean who puts a light to the bonfire. While the fire is blazing the people dance and sing round it, and when the flames have subsided they leap over the glowing embers. Charred sticks from the bonfire are thrown into wells to improve the water, and they are also taken home as a protection against thunder. To make them thoroughly effective, however, against thunder and lightning you should keep them near your bed, between a bit of a Twelfth Night cake and a sprig of boxwood which has been blessed on Palm Sunday. Flowers from the nosegay or crown which overhung the fire are accounted charms against disease and pain, both bodily and spiritual; hence girls hang them at their breast by a thread of scarlet wool. In many parishes of Brittany the priest used to go in procession with the crucifix and kindle the bonfire with his own hands; and farmers were wont to drive their flocks and herds through the fire in order to preserve them from sickness till midsummer of the following year. Also it was believed that every girl who danced round nine of the bonfires would marry within the year.

Uses made of the charred sticks and flowers.

The Midsummer fires in Normandy.

In Normandy the midsummer fires have now almost disappeared, at least in the district known as the Bocage, but they used to shine on every hill. They were commonly made by piling brushwood, broom, and ferns about a tall tree, which was decorated with a crown of moss and sometimes with flowers. While they burned, people danced and sang round them, and young folk leaped over the flames or the glowing ashes. In the valley of the Orne the custom was to kindle the bonfire just at the moment when the sun was about to dip below the horizon; and the peasants drove their cattle through the fires to protect them against witchcraft, especially against the spells of witches and wizards who attempted to steal the milk and butter. At Jumièges in Normandy, down to the first half of the nineteenth century, the midsummer festival was marked by certain singular features which bore the stamp of a very high antiquity. Every year, on the twenty-third of June, the Eve of St John, the Brotherhood of the Green Wolf chose a new chief or master, who had always to be taken from the hamlet of Conihout. On being elected, the new head of the brotherhood assumed the title of the Green Wolf, and donned a peculiar costume consisting of a long green mantle and a very tall green hat of a conical shape and without a brim. Thus arrayed he stalked solemnly at the head of the brothers, chanting the hymn of St John, the crucifix and holy banner leading the way, to a place called Chouquet. Here the procession was met by the priest, precentors, and choir, who conducted the brotherhood to the parish church. After hearing mass the company adjourned to the house of the Green Wolf, where a simple repast, such as is required by the church on fast-days, was served up to them. Then they danced before the door till it was time to light the bonfire. Night being come, the fire was kindled to the sound of hand-bells by a young man and a young woman, both decked with flowers. As the flames rose, the *Te Deum* was sung, and a villager thundered out a parody in the Norman dialect of the hymn *ut queant laxis*. Meantime the Green Wolf and his brothers, with their hoods down on their shoulders and holding each other by the hand, ran round the fire after the man who had been chosen to be the Green Wolf of the following year. Though only the first and the last man of the chain had a hand free, their business was to surround and seize thrice the future Green Wolf, who in his efforts to escape belaboured the brothers with a long wand which he carried. When at last they succeeded in catching him they carried him to the burning pile and made as if they would throw him on it. This ceremony over, they returned to the house of the Green Wolf, where a supper, still of the most meagre fare, was set before them. Up till midnight a sort of religious solemnity prevailed. No unbecoming word might fall from the lips of any of the company,

The fires as a protection against witchcraft.

The Brotherhood of the Green Wolf at Jumièges.

Pretence of throwing the Green Wolf into the fire.

and a censor, armed with a hand-bell, was appointed to mark and punish instantly any infraction of the rule. But at the stroke of twelve all this was changed. Constraint gave way to license; pious hymns were replaced by Bacchanalian ditties, and the shrill quavering notes of the village fiddle hardly rose above the roar of voices that went up from the merry brotherhood of the Green Wolf. Next day, the twenty-fourth of June or Midsummer Day, was celebrated by the same personages with the same noisy gaiety. One of the ceremonies consisted in parading, to the sound of musketry, an enormous loaf of consecrated bread, which, rising in tiers, was surmounted by a pyramid of verdure adorned with ribbons. After that the holy handbells, deposited on the step of the altar, were entrusted as insignia of office to the man who was to be the Green Wolf next year.

Lady Wilde's account of the Midsummer fires in Ireland.

Lady Wilde's* account of the midsummer festival in Ireland is picturesque and probably correct in substance, although she does not cite her authorities. As it contains some interesting features which are not noticed by the other writers on Ireland whom I have consulted, I will quote the greater part of it in full. 'In ancient times', she says, 'the sacred fire was lighted with great ceremony on Midsummer Eve; and on that night all the people of the adjacent country kept fixed watch on the western promontory of Howth, and the moment the first flash was seen from that spot the fact of ignition was announced with wild cries and cheers repeated from village to village, when all the local fires began to blaze, and Ireland was circled by a cordon of flame rising up from every hill. Then the dance and song began round every fire, and the wild hurrahs filled the air with the most frantic revelry. Many of these ancient customs are still continued, and the fires are still lighted on St John's Eve on every hill in Ireland. When the fire has burned down to a red glow the young men strip to the waist and leap over or through the flames; this is done backwards and forwards several times, and he who braves the greatest blaze is considered the victor over the powers of evil, and is greeted with tremendous applause. When the fire burns still lower, the young girls leap the flame, and those who leap clean over three times back and forward will be certain of a speedy marriage and good luck in after-life, with many children. The married women then walk through the lines of the burning embers; and when the fire is nearly burnt and trampled down, the yearling cattle are driven through the hot ashes, and their back is singed with a lighted hazel twig. These rods are kept safely afterwards, being considered of immense power to drive the cattle to and from the watering places. As the fire diminishes the shouting grows fainter, and the song and the dance commence; while professional story-tellers narrate tales of fairy-land, or of the good old times long ago, when the kings and princes of Ireland dwelt amongst their own people, and there was food to eat and wine to drink for all comers to the feast at the king's house. When the crowd at length separate, every one carries home a brand from the fire, and great virtue is attached to the lighted *brone* which is safely carried to the house without breaking or falling to the ground. Many contests also arise amongst the young men; for whoever enters his house first with the sacred fire brings the good luck of the year with him.'

The custom of kindling bonfires on Midsummer Day or on Midsummer Eve is widely spread among the Mohammedan peoples of North Africa, particularly in Morocco and Algeria; it is common both to the Berbers and to many of the Arabs or Arabic-speaking tribes. In these countries Midsummer Day (the twenty-fourth of June, Old Style) is called *l'ánṣăra*. The fires are lit in the courtyards, at cross-roads, in the fields, and sometimes on the threshing-floors. Plants which in burning give out a thick smoke and an aromatic smell are much sought after for fuel on these occasions; among the plants used for the purpose are giant-fennel, thyme, rue, chervil-seed, camomile, geranium, and penny-royal. People expose themselves, and especially their children, to the smoke, and drive it towards the orchards and the crops. Also they leap across the fires; in some places everybody ought to repeat the leap seven times. Moreover they take burning brands from the fires and carry them through the houses in order to fumigate them. They pass things through the fire, and bring the sick into contact with it, while they utter prayers for their recovery. The ashes of the bonfires are also reputed to possess beneficial properties; hence in some places people rub their hair or their bodies with them. For example, the Andjra mountaineers of Morocco kindle large fires in open places of their villages on Midsummer Day. Men,

The Midsummer fires among the Mohammedans of Morocco and Algeria.

women, and children jump over the flames or the glowing embers, believing that by so doing they rid themselves of all misfortune which may be clinging to them; they imagine, also, that such leaps cure the sick and procure offspring for childless couples.

The Midsummer festival in North Africa is probably older than Mohammedanism.

The celebration of a midsummer festival by Mohammedan peoples is particularly remarkable, because the Mohammedan calendar, being purely lunar and uncorrected by intercalation, necessarily takes no note of festivals which occupy fixed points in the solar year; all strictly Mohammedan feasts, being pinned to the moon, slide gradually with that luminary through the whole period of the earth's revolution about the sun. This fact of itself seems to prove that among the Mohammedan peoples of Northern Africa, as among the Christian peoples of Europe, the midsummer festival is quite independent of the religion which the people publicly profess, and is a relic of a far older paganism.

v

The coincidence of the Midsummer festival with the summer solstice implies that the founders of the festival regulated their calendar by observation of the sun.

From the foregoing survey we may infer that among the heathen forefathers of the European peoples the most popular and widespread fire-festival of the year was the great celebration of Midsummer Eve or Midsummer Day. The coincidence of the festival with the summer solstice can hardly be accidental. Rather we must suppose that our pagan ancestors purposely timed the ceremony of fire on earth to coincide with the arrival of the sun at the highest point of his course in the sky. If that was so, it follows that the old founders of the midsummer rites had observed the solstices or turning-points of the sun's apparent path in the sky, and that they accordingly regulated their festal calendar to some extent by astronomical considerations.

On the other hand the Celts divided their year, not by the solstices, but by the beginning of summer (the first of May) and

But while this may be regarded as fairly certain for what we may call the aborigines throughout a large part of the continent, it appears not to have been true of the Celtic peoples who inhabited the Land's End of Europe, the islands and promontories that stretch out into the Atlantic ocean on the North-West. The principal fire-festivals of the Celts, which have survived, though in a restricted area and with diminished pomp, to modern times and even to our own day, were seemingly timed without any reference to the position of the sun in the heaven. They were two in number, and fell at an interval of six months, one being celebrated on the eve of May Day and the other on Allhallow Even or Hallowe'en, as it is now commonly called, that is, on the thirty-first of October, the day preceding All Saints' or Allhallows' Day. These dates coincide with none of the four great hinges on which the solar year revolves, to wit, the solstices and the equinoxes. Nor do they agree with the principal seasons of the agricultural year, the sowing in spring and the reaping in autumn. For when May Day comes, the seed has long been committed to the earth; and when November opens, the harvest has long been reaped and garnered, the fields lie bare, the fruit-trees are stripped, and even the yellow leaves are fast fluttering to the ground. Yet the first of May and the first of November mark turning-points of the year in Europe; the one ushers in the genial heat and the rich vegetation of summer, the other heralds, if it does not share, the cold and barrenness of winter. Now these particular points of the year, as has been well pointed out by a learned and ingenious writer,* while they are of comparatively little moment to the European husbandman, do deeply concern the European herdsman; for it is on the approach of summer that he drives his cattle out into the open to crop the fresh grass, and it is on the approach of winter that he leads them back to the safety and shelter of the stall. Accordingly it seems not improbable that the Celtic bisection of the year into two halves at the beginning of May and the beginning of November dates from a time when the Celts were mainly a pastoral people, dependent for their subsistence on their herds, and when accordingly the great epochs of the year for them were the days on which the cattle went forth from the homestead in early summer and returned to it again in early winter.

the beginning of winter (the first of November).

The division seems to have been neither astronomical nor agricultural but pastoral, being determined by the times when cattle are driven to and from their summer pasture.

Of the two feasts Hallowe'en was perhaps of old the more important, since the Celts would seem to have dated the beginning of the year from it rather than from Beltane.* In the Isle of Man, one of the fortresses in which the Celtic language and lore longest held out against the siege of the Saxon invaders, the first of November, Old Style, has been regarded as New Year's day down to recent times. Thus Manx mummers used to go round on Hallowe'en (Old Style), singing, in the

Hallowe'en (the evening of October 31st) seems to have marked the beginning of the Celtic year.

Manx language, a sort of Hogmanay song which began 'To-night is New Year's Night, *Hogunnaa!*' One of Sir John Rhys's Manx informants, an old man of sixty-seven, 'had been a farm servant from the age of sixteen till he was twenty-six to the same man, near Regaby, in the parish of Andreas, and he remembers his master and a near neighbour of his discussing the term New Year's Day as applied to the first of November, and explaining to the younger men that it had always been so in old times. In fact, it seemed to him natural enough, as all tenure of land ends at that time, and as all servant men begin their service then.' In ancient Ireland, as we saw, a new fire used to be kindled every year on Hallowe'en or the Eve of Samhain, and from this sacred flame all the fires in Ireland were rekindled. Such a custom points strongly to Samhain or All Saints' Day (the first of November) as New Year's Day; since the annual kindling of a new fire takes place most naturally at the beginning of the year, in order that the blessed influence of the fresh fire may last throughout the whole period of twelve months. Another confirmation of the view that the Celts dated their year from the first of November is furnished by the manifold modes of divination which, as we shall see presently, were commonly resorted to by Celtic peoples on Hallowe'en for the purpose of ascertaining their destiny, especially their fortune in the coming year; for when could these devices for prying into the future be more reasonably put in practice than at the beginning of the year? As a season of omens and auguries Hallowe'en seems to have far surpassed Beltane in the imagination of the Celts; from which we may with some probability infer that they reckoned their year from Hallowe'en rather than Beltane. Another circumstance of great moment which points to the same conclusion is the association of the dead with Hallowe'en. Not only among the Celts but throughout Europe, Hallowe'en, the night which marks the transition from autumn to winter, seems to have been of old the time of year when the souls of the departed were supposed to revisit their old homes in order to warm themselves by the fire and to comfort themselves with the good cheer provided for them in the kitchen or the parlour by their affectionate kinsfolk. It was, perhaps, a natural thought that the approach of winter should drive the poor shivering hungry ghosts from the bare fields and

The many forms of divination resorted to at Hallowe'en are appropriate to the beginning of a New Year.

Hallowe'en also a festival of the dead.

the leafless woodlands to the shelter of the cottage with its familiar fireside. Did not the lowing kine then troop back from the summer pastures in the forests and on the hills to be fed and cared for in the stalls, while the bleak winds whistled among the swaying boughs and the snow drifts deepened in the hollows? and could the good-man and the good-wife deny to the spirits of their dead the welcome which they gave to the cows?

But it is not only the souls of the departed who are supposed to be hovering unseen on the day 'when autumn to winter resigns the pale year'. Witches then speed on their errands of mischief, some sweeping through the air on besoms, others galloping along the roads on tabby-cats, which for that evening are turned into coal-black steeds. The fairies, too, are all let loose, and hobgoblins of every sort roam freely about. In South Uist and Eriskay there is a saying:

> 'Hallowe'en will come, will come,
> Witchcraft [or divination] will be set agoing,
> Fairies will be at full speed,
> Running in every pass.
> Avoid the road, children, children.'*

But while a glamour of mystery and awe has always clung to Hallowe'en in the minds of the Celtic peasantry, the popular celebration of the festival has been, at least in modern times, by no means of a prevailingly gloomy cast; on the contrary it has been attended by picturesque features and merry pastimes, which rendered it the gayest night of all the year. Amongst the things which in the Highlands of Scotland contributed to invest the festival with a romantic beauty were the bonfires which used to blaze at frequent intervals on the heights. 'On the last day of autumn children gathered ferns, tar-barrels, the long thin stalks called *gàinisg*, and everything suitable for a bonfire. These were placed in a heap on some eminence near the house, and in the evening set fire to. The fires were called *Samhnagan*. There was one for each house, and it was an object of ambition who should have the biggest. Whole districts were brilliant with bonfires, and their glare across a Highland loch, and from many eminences, formed an exceedingly picturesque scene.' Like the Beltane fires on the first of May, the Hallowe'en bonfires seem to have been kindled most commonly in the Perthshire Highlands. In the parish of Callander, which includes the now

Hallowe'en
fires in the
parishes of
Callander
and Logierait.

famous pass of the Trossachs opening out on the winding and
wooded shores of the lovely Loch Katrine, the Hallowe'en
bonfires were still kindled down to near the end of the
eighteenth century. When the fire had died down, the ashes
were carefully collected in the form of a circle, and a stone was
put in, near the circumference, for every person of the several

Divination
from stones.

families interested in the bonfire. Next morning, if any of these
stones was found to be displaced or injured, the people made
sure that the person represented by it was *fey** or devoted, and
that he could not live twelve months from that day.

Divination at
Hallowe'en
in Queen's
County.

In Queen's County, Ireland, down to the latter part of the
nineteenth century children practised various of these rites of
divination on Hallowe'en. Girls went out into the garden
blindfold and pulled up cabbages: if the cabbage was well
grown, the girl would have a handsome husband, but if it had
a crooked stalk, the future spouse would be a stingy old man.
Nuts, again, were placed in pairs on the bar of the fire, and
from their behaviour omens were drawn of the fate in love and
marriage of the couple whom they represented. Lead, also, was
melted and allowed to drop into a tub of cold water, and from
the shapes which it assumed in the water predictions were made
to the children of their future destiny. Again, apples were
bobbed for in a tub of water and brought up with the teeth; or
a stick was hung from a hook with an apple at one end and a
candle at the other, and the stick being made to revolve you
made a bite at the apple and sometimes got a mouthful of candle

Divination at
Hallowe'en
in County
Leitrim.

instead. In County Leitrim, also, down to near the end of the
nineteenth century various forms of divination were practised
at Hallowe'en. Girls ascertained the character of their future
husbands by the help of cabbages just as in Queen's County.
Again, if a girl found a branch of a briar-thorn which had bent
over and grown into the ground so as to form a loop, she would
creep through the loop thrice late in the evening in the devil's
name, then cut the briar and put it under her pillow, all without
speaking a word. Then she would lay her head on the pillow
and dream of the man she was to marry. Boys, also, would
dream in like manner of love and marriage at Hallowe'en, if
only they would gather ten leaves of ivy without speaking,
throw away one, and put the other nine under their pillow.
Again, divination was practised by means of a cake called

barm-breac, in which a nut and a ring were baked. Whoever got the ring would be married first; whoever got the nut would marry a widow or a widower; but if the nut were an empty shell, he or she would remain unwed. Again, a girl would take a clue of worsted, go to a lime kiln in the gloaming, and throw the clew into the kiln in the devil's name, while she held fast the other end of the thread. Then she would rewind the thread and ask, 'Who holds my clue?' and the name of her future husband would come up from the depth of the kiln. Another way was to take a rake, go to a rick and walk round it nine times, saying, 'I rake this rick in the devil's name.' At the ninth time the wraith of your destined partner for life would come and take the rake out of your hand. Once more, before the company separated for the night, they would rake the ashes smooth on the hearth, and search them next morning for tracks, from which they judged whether anybody should come to the house, or leave it, or die in it before another year was out. In County Roscommon, which borders on County Leitrim, a cake is made in nearly every house on Hallowe'en, and a ring, a coin, a sloe, and a chip of wood are put into it. Whoever gets the coin will be rich; whoever gets the ring will be married first; whoever gets the chip of wood, which stands for a coffin, will die first; and whoever gets the sloe will live longest, because the fairies blight the sloes in the hedges on Hallowe'en, so that the sloe in the cake will be the last of the year. Again, on the same mystic evening girls take nine grains of oats in their mouths, and going out without speaking walk about till they hear a man's name pronounced; it will be the name of their future husband. In County Roscommon, too, on Hallowe'en there is the usual dipping in water for apples or sixpences, and the usual bites at a revolving apple and tallow candle.

Divination at Hallowe'en in County Roscommon.

In the Isle of Man also, another Celtic country, Hallowe'en was celebrated down to modern times by the kindling of fires, accompanied with all the usual ceremonies designed to prevent the baneful influence of fairies and witches.

Hallowe'en fires in the Isle of Man.

vi

If the heathen of ancient Europe celebrated, as we have good reason to believe, the season of Midsummer with a great festival of fire, of which the traces have survived in many places down to our own time, it is natural to suppose that they should have observed with similar rites the corresponding season of Midwinter; for Midsummer and Midwinter, or, in more technical language, the summer solstice and the winter solstice, are the two great turning-points in the sun's apparent course through the sky, and from the standpoint of primitive man nothing might seem more appropriate than to kindle fires on earth at the two moments when the fire and heat of the great luminary in heaven begin to wane or to wax. In this way the savage philosopher, to whose meditations on the nature of things we owe many ancient customs and ceremonies, might easily imagine that he helped the labouring sun to relight his dying lamp, or at all events to blow up the flame into a brighter blaze. Certain it is that the winter solstice, which the ancients erroneously assigned to the twenty-fifth of December, was celebrated in antiquity as the Birthday of the Sun, and that festal lights or

Christmas
the continua-
tion of an
old heathen
festival of
the sun.

fires were kindled on this joyful occasion. Our Christmas festival is nothing but a continuation under a Christian name of this old solar festivity; for the ecclesiastical authorities saw fit, about the end of the third or the beginning of the fourth century, arbitrarily to transfer the nativity of Christ from the sixth of January to the twenty-fifth of December, for the purpose of diverting to their Lord the worship which the heathen had hitherto paid on that day to the sun.

The Yule log
is the Mid-
winter
counterpart
of the Mid-
summer bon-
fire.

In modern Christendom the ancient fire-festival of the winter solstice appears to survive, or to have survived down to recent years, in the old custom of the Yule log, clog, or block, as it was variously called in England. The custom was widespread in Europe, but seems to have flourished especially in England, France, and among the South Slavs; at least the fullest accounts of the custom come from these quarters. That the Yule log was only the winter counterpart of the Midsummer bonfire, kindled within doors instead of in the open air on account of the cold and inclement weather of the season, was pointed out long ago by our English antiquary John Brand;* and the view is supported by the many quaint superstitions attaching to the Yule log, superstitions which have no apparent connexion with Christianity but carry their heathen origin plainly stamped upon them. But while the two solstitial celebrations were both festivals of fire, the necessity or desirability of holding the winter celebration within doors lent it the character of a private or domestic festivity, which contrasts strongly with the publicity of the summer celebration, at which the people gathered on some open space or conspicuous height, kindled a huge bonfire in common, and danced and made merry round it together.

Among the Germans the custom of the Yule log is known to have been observed in the eleventh century; for in the year 1184 the parish priest of Ahlen, in Münsterland, spoke of 'bringing a tree to kindle the festal fire at the Lord's Nativity'. Down to about the middle of the nineteenth century the old rite was kept up in some parts of central Germany, as we learn from an account of it given by a contemporary writer. After mentioning the custom of feeding the cattle and shaking the fruit-trees on Christmas night, to make them bear fruit, he goes on as follows: 'Other customs pointing back to the far-off times of heathendom may still be met with among the old-fashioned peasants of the mountain regions. Such is in the valleys of the Sieg and Lahn the practice of laying a new log as a foundation of the hearth. A heavy block of oak-wood, generally a stump grubbed up from the ground, is fitted either into the floor of the hearth, or into a niche made for the purpose in the wall under the hook on which the kettle hangs. When the fire on the hearth glows, this block of wood glows too, but it is so placed that it is hardly reduced to ashes within a year. When the new foundation is laid, the remains of the old block are carefully taken out, ground to powder, and strewed over the fields during the Twelve Nights. This, so people fancied, promotes the fruitfulness of the year's crops.' In some parts of the Eifel Mountains, to the west of Coblentz, a log of wood called the *Christbrand* used to be placed on the hearth on Christmas Eve; and the charred remains of it on Twelfth Night were put in the cornbin to keep the mice from devouring the corn. At Weidenhausen and Girkshausen, in Westphalia, the practice was to withdraw the Yule log (*Christbrand*) from the fire so soon as it was slightly charred; it was then kept carefully to be replaced on the fire whenever a thunder-storm broke, because the people believed that lightning would not strike a house in which the Yule log was smouldering. In some villages near Berleburg in Westphalia the old

The Yule log in Germany.

custom was to tie up the Yule log in the last sheaf cut at harvest. On Christmas Eve the peasantry of the Oberland, in Meiningen, a province of Central Germany, used to put a great block of wood called the *Christklotz* on the fire before they went to bed; it should burn all night, and the charred remains were believed to guard the house for the whole year against the risk of fire, burglary, and other misfortunes. The Yule log seems to be known only in the French-speaking parts of Switzerland, where it goes by the usual French name of *Bûche de Noël*. In the Jura mountains of the canton of Bern, while the log is burning on the hearth the people sing a blessing over it as follows:

'May the log burn!
May all good come in!
May the women have children
And the sheep lambs!
White bread for every one
And the vat full of wine!'

The embers of the Yule log were kept carefully, for they were believed to be a protection against lightning.

It is remarkable how common the belief appears to have been that the remains of the Yule log, if kept throughout the year, had power to protect the house against fire and especially against lightning. As the Yule log was frequently of oak, it seems possible that this belief may be a relic of the old Aryan creed which associated the oak-tree with the god of thunder. Whether the curative and fertilizing virtues ascribed to the ashes of the Yule log, which are supposed to heal cattle as well as men, to enable cows to calve, and to promote the fruitfulness of the earth, may not be derived from the same ancient source, is a question which deserves to be considered.

Thus far we have regarded only the private or domestic celebration of the fire-festival at midwinter. The public celebration of such rites at that season of the year appears to have been rare and exceptional in Central and Northern Europe. However, some instances are on record. Thus at Schweina, in Thuringia, down to the second half of the nineteenth century, the young people used to kindle a great bonfire on the Antonius Mountain every year on Christmas Eve. Neither the civil nor the eccle-

Margin notes:

The Yule log in Switzerland.

Belief that the Yule log protects against fire and lightning.

Public celebrations of the fire-festival at Midwinter. The bon-fire on Christmas Eve at Schweina in Thuringia.

siastical authorities were able to suppress the celebration; nor could the cold, rain, and snow of the season damp or chill the enthusiasm of the celebrants. For some time before Christmas the young men and boys were busy building a foundation for the bonfire on the top of the mountain, where the oldest church of the village used to stand. The foundation consisted of a pyramidal structure composed of stones, turf, and moss. When Christmas Eve came round, a strong pole, with bundles of brushwood tied to it, was erected on the pyramid. The young folk also provided themselves with poles to which old brooms or faggots of shavings were attached. These were to serve as torches. When the evening grew dark and the church bells rang to service, the troop of lads ascended the mountain; and soon from the top the glare of the bonfire lit up the darkness, and the sound of a hymn broke the stillness of night. In a circle round the great fire lesser fires were kindled; and last of all the lads ran about swinging their lighted torches, till these twinkling points of fire, moving down the mountain-side, went out one by one in the darkness. At midnight the bells rang out from the church tower, mingled with the blast of borus and the sound of singing. Feasting and revelry were kept up throughout the night, and in the morning young and old went to early mass to be edified by hearing of the light eternal.

In Lerwick, the capital of the Shetland Islands, 'on Christmas Eve, the fourth of January,—for the old style is still observed— the children go *a guizing*, that is to say, they disguising themselves in the most fantastic and gaudy costumes, parade the streets, and infest the houses and shops, begging for the wherewithal to carry on their Christmas amusements. One o'clock on Yule morning having struck, the young men turn out in large numbers, dressed in the coarsest of garments, and, at the double-quick march, drag huge tar barrels through the town, shouting and cheering as they go, or blowing loud blasts with their "louder horns." The tar barrel simply consists of several—say from four to eight—tubs filled with tar and chips, placed on a platform of wood. It is dragged by means of a chain, to which scores of jubilant youths readily yoke themselves. They have recently been described by the worthy burgh officer

Procession with burning tar-barrels on Christmas Eve (Old Style) at Lerwick.

of Lerwick as "fiery chariots, the effect of which is truly grand and terrific." In a Christmas morning the dark streets of Lerwick are generally lighted up by the bright glare, and its atmosphere blackened by the dense smoke of six or eight tar barrels in succession. On the appearance of daybreak, at six a.m., the morning revellers put off their coarse garments—well begrimed by this time—and in their turn become guizards. They assume every imaginable form of costume—those of soldiers, sailors, highlanders, Spanish chevaliers, etc. Thus disguised, they either go in pairs, as man and wife, or in larger groups, and proceed to call on their friends, to wish them the compliments of the season. Formerly, these adolescent guizards used to seat themselves in crates, and accompanied by fiddlers, were dragged through the town.'

The Persians used to celebrate a festival of fire called *Sada* or *Saza* at the winter solstice. On the longest night of the year they kindled bonfires everywhere, and kings and princes tied dry grass to the feet of birds and animals, set fire to the grass, and then let the birds and beasts fly or run blazing through the air or over the fields and mountains, so that the whole air and earth appeared to be on fire.

vii

The fire-festivals hiterto described are all celebrated periodically at certain stated times of the year. But besides these regularly recurring celebrations the peasants in many parts of Europe have been wont from time immemorial to resort to a ritual of fire at irregular intervals in seasons of distress and calamity, above all when their cattle were attacked by epidemic disease. No account of the popular European fire-festivals would be complete without some notice of these remarkable rites, which have all the greater claim on our attention because they may perhaps be regarded as the source and origin of all the other fire-festivals; certainly they must date from a very remote antiquity. The general name by which they are known among the Teutonic peoples is need-fire.

The history of the need-fire can be traced back to the early Middle Ages; for in the reign of Pippin, King of the Franks, the practice of kindling need-fires was denounced as a heathen superstition by a synod of prelates and nobles held under the presidency of Boniface, Archbishop of Mainz. The method of kindling the need-fire is described as follows by a writer towards the end of the seventeenth century: 'When an evil plague has broken out among the cattle, large and small, and the herds have thereby suffered great ravages, the peasants resolve to light a need-fire. On a day appointed there must be no single flame in any house nor on any hearth. From every house a quantity of straw and water and underwood must be brought forth; then a strong oaken pole is fixed firmly in the earth, a hole is bored in it, and a wooden winch, well smeared with pitch and tar, is inserted in the hole and turned round forcibly till great heat and then fire is generated. The fire so produced is caught in fuel and fed with straw, heath, and underwood till it bursts out into a regular need-fire, which must then be somewhat spread out between walls or fences, and the cattle and horses driven through it twice or thrice with sticks and whips. Others set up two posts, each with a hole in it, and insert a winch, along with old greasy rags, in the holes. Others use a thick rope, collect nine kinds of wood, and keep them in violent motion till fire leaps forth. Perhaps there may be other ways of generating or kindling this fire, but they are all directed simply at the cure of the cattle. After passing twice or thrice through the fire the cattle are driven to their stalls or to pasture, and the heap of wood that had been collected is destroyed, but in some places every householder must take with him a brand, extinguish it in a washing-tub or trough, and put it in the manger where the cattle are fed, where it must lie for some time. The poles that were used to make the need-fire, together with the wood that was employed as a winch, are sometimes burned with the rest of the fuel, sometimes carefully preserved after the cattle have been thrice driven through the flames.'*

In the summer of 1828 there was much sickness among the pigs and the cows of Eddesse, a village near Meinersen, in the south of Hanover. When all ordinary measures to arrest the malady failed, the farmers met in solemn conclave on the village green and determined that next morning there should be a need-fire. Thereupon the head man of the village sent word from house to house that on the following day nobody should kindle a fire before sunrise, and that everybody should stand by

Marginal notes:
Method of kindling the need-fire.

The mode of kindling the need-fire in Hanover.

ready to drive out the cattle. The same afternoon all the necessary preparations were made for giving effect to the decision of the collective wisdom. A narrow street was enclosed with planks, and the village carpenter set to work at the machinery for kindling the fire. He took two posts of oak wood, bored a hole about three inches deep and broad in each, and set the two poles up facing each other at a distance of about two feet. Then he fitted a roller of oak wood into the two holes of the posts, so that it formed a cross-piece between them. About two o'clock next morning every householder brought a bundle of straw and brushwood and laid it down across the street in a prescribed order. The sturdiest swains who could be found were chosen to make the need-fire. For this purpose a long hempen rope was wound twice round the oaken roller in the oaken posts: the pivots were well smeared with pitch and tar: a bundle of tow and other tinder was laid close at hand, and all was ready. The stalwart clodhoppers now seized the two ends of the rope and went to work with a will. Puffs of smoke soon issued from the sockets, but to the consternation of the bystanders not a spark of fire could be elicited. Some people openly declared their suspicion that some rascal had not put out the fire in his house, when suddenly the tinder burst into flame. The cloud passed away from all faces; the fire was applied to the heaps of fuel, and when the flames had somewhat died down, the herds were forcibly driven through the fire, first the pigs, next the cows, and last of all the horses. The herdsmen then drove the beasts to pasture, and persons whose faith in the efficacy of the need-fire was particularly robust carried home brands.

The use of the need-fire a relic of a time when all fires were kindled by the friction of wood.

Thus it appears that in many parts of Europe it has been customary to kindle fire by the friction of wood for the purpose of curing or preventing the spread of disease, particularly among cattle. The mode of striking a light by rubbing two dry sticks against each other is the one to which all over the world savages have most commonly resorted for the sake of providing themselves with fire; and we can scarcely doubt that the practice of kindling the need-fire in this primitive fashion is merely a survival from the time when our savage forefathers lit all their fires in that way. Nothing is so conservative of old customs as religious or magical ritual, which invests these relics of the past with an atmosphere of mysterious virtue and sanctity. To the educated mind it seems obvious that a fire which a man kindles with the sweat of his brow by laboriously rubbing one stick against each other can possess neither more nor less virtue than one which he has struck in a moment by the friction of a lucifer match; but to the ignorant and superstitious this truth is far from apparent, and accordingly they take infinite pains to do in a roundabout way what they might have done directly with the greatest ease, and what, even when it is done, is of no use whatever for the purpose in hand. A vast proportion of the labour which mankind has expended throughout the ages has been no better spent; it has been like the stone of Sisyphus eternally rolled up hill only to revolve eternally down again, or like the water poured for ever by the Danaids into broken pitchers which it could never fill.

The curious notion that the need-fire cannot kindle if any other fire remains alight in the neighbourhood seems to imply that fire is conceived as a unity which is broken up into fractions and consequently weakened in exact proportion to the number of places where it burns; hence in order to obtain it at full strength you must light it only at a single point, for then the flame will burst out with a concentrated energy derived from the tributary fires which burned on all the extinguished hearths of the country. So in a modern city if all the gas were turned off simultaneously at all the burners but one, the flame would no doubt blaze at that one burner with a fierceness such as no single burner could shew when all are burning at the same time. The analogy may help us to understand the process of reasoning which leads the peasantry to insist on the extinction of all common fires when the need-fire is about to be kindled. Perhaps, too, it may partly explain that ceremonial extinction of all old fires on other occasions which is often required by custom as a preliminary to the lighting of a new and sacred fire. We have seen that in the Highlands of Scotland all common fires were extinguished on the Eve of May-day as a preparation for kindling the Beltane bonfire by friction next morning; and no doubt the reason for the extinction was the same as in the case of the need-fire. Indeed we may assume with a fair degree of probability that the need-fire was the parent of the periodic fire-festivals; at first invoked only at irregular intervals to cure

The belief that the need-fire cannot kindle if any other fire remains alight in the neighbourhood.

certain evils as they occurred, the powerful virtue of fire was afterwards employed at regular intervals to prevent the occurrence of the same evils as well as to remedy such as had actually arisen.

viii

At some of the fire-festivals the pretence of burning live persons in the fires points to a former custom of human sacrifice.

In the popular customs connected with the fire-festivals of Europe there are certain features which appear to point to a former practice of human sacrifice. We have seen reasons for believing that in Europe living persons have often acted as representatives of the tree-spirit and corn-spirit and have suffered death as such. There is no reason, therefore, why they should not have been burned, if any special advantages were likely to be attained by putting them to death in that way. The consideration of human suffering is not one which enters into the calculations of primitive man. Now, in the fire-festivals which we are discussing, the pretence of burning people is sometimes carried so far that it seems reasonable to regard it as a mitigated survival of an older custom of actually burning them. Thus in Aachen, as we saw, the man clad in peas-straw acts so cleverly that the children really believe he is being burned. Similarly at the Beltane fires in Scotland the pretended victim was seized, and a show made of throwing him into the flames, and for some time afterwards people affected to speak of him as dead. At Wolfeck, in Austria, on Midsummer Day, a boy completely clad in green fir branches goes from house to house, accompanied by a noisy crew, collecting wood for the bonfire. As he gets the wood he sings:

'Forest trees I want,
No sour milk for me,
But beer and wine,
So can the wood-man be jolly and gay.'*

In some parts of Bavaria, also, the boys who go from house to house collecting fuel for the midsummer bonfire envelop one of their number from head to foot in green branches of firs, and lead him by a rope through the whole village. At Moosheim, in Würtemberg, the festival of St John's Fire usually lasted for fourteen days, ending on the second Sunday after Midsummer

Day. On this last day the bonfire was left in charge of the children, while the older people retired to a wood. Here they encased a young fellow in leaves and twigs, who, thus disguised, went to the fire, scattered it, and trod it out. All the people present fled at the sight of him.

But it seems possible to go farther than this. Of human sacrifices offered on these occasions the most unequivocal traces, as we have seen, are those which, about a hundred years ago, still lingered at the Beltane fires in the Highlands of Scotland, that is, among a Celtic people who, situated in a remote corner of Europe and almost completely isolated from foreign influence, had till then conserved their old heathenism better perhaps than any other people in the West of Europe. It is significant, therefore, that human sacrifices by fire are known, on unquestionable evidence, to have been systematically practised by the Celts. The earliest description of these sacrifices has been bequeathed to us by Julius Caesar.* As conqueror of the hitherto independent Celts of Gaul, Caesar had ample opportunity of observing the national Celtic religion and manners, while these were still fresh and crisp from the native mint and had not yet been fused in the melting-pot of Roman civilization. With his own notes Caesar appears to have incorporated the observations of a Greek explorer, by name Posidonius, who travelled in Gaul about fifty years before Caesar carried the Roman arms to the English Channel. The Greek geographer Strabo and the historian Diodorus seem also to have derived their descriptions of the Celtic sacrifices from the work of Posidonius, but independently of each other, and of Caesar, for each of the three derivative accounts contain some details which are not to be found in either of the others. By combining them, therefore, we can restore the original account of Posidonius with some probability, and thus obtain a picture of the sacrifices offered by the Celts of Gaul at the close of the second century before our era. The following seem to have been the main outlines of the custom. Condemned criminals were reserved by the Celts in order to be sacrificed to the gods at a great festival which took place once in every five years. The more there were of such victims, the greater was believed to be the fertility of the land. If there were not enough criminals to furnish victims, captives taken in war were immolated to supply

Human sacrifices by fire among the ancient Gauls.

the deficiency. When the time came the victims were sacrificed by the Druids or priests. Some they shot down with arrows, some they impaled, and some they burned alive in the following manner. Colossal images of wicker-work or of wood and grass were constructed; these were filled with live men, cattle, and animals of other kinds; fire was then applied to the images, and they were burned with their living contents.*

Men and animals enclosed in great wicker-work images and burnt alive.

Such were the great festivals held once every five years. But besides these quinquennial festivals, celebrated on so grand a scale, and with, apparently, so large an expenditure of human life, it seems reasonable to suppose that festivals of the same sort, only on a lesser scale, were held annually, and that from these annual festivals are lineally descended some at least of the fire-festivals which, with their traces of human sacrifices, are still celebrated year by year in many parts of Europe. The gigantic images constructed of osiers or covered with grass in which the Druids enclosed their victims remind us of the leafy framework in which the human representative of the tree-spirit is still so often encased. Hence, seeing that the fertility of the land was apparently supposed to depend upon the due performance of these sacrifices, Mannhardt interpreted the Celtic victims, cased in osiers and grass, as representatives of the tree-spirit or spirit of vegetation.

As the fertility of the land was supposed to depend on these sacrifices, Mannhardt interpreted the victims as representatives of tree-spirits or spirits of vegetation.

These wicker giants of the Druids seem to have had till lately their representatives at the spring and midsummer festivals of modern Europe. Most towns and even villages of Brabant and Flanders have, or used to have, similar wicker giants which were annually led about to the delight of the populace, who loved these grotesque figures, spoke of them with patriotic enthusiasm, and never wearied of gazing at them. The name by which the giants went was Reuzes, and a special song called the Reuze song was sung in the Flemish dialect while they were making their triumphal progress through the streets. The most celebrated of these monstrous effigies were those of Antwerp and Wetteren. At Ypres a whole family of giants contributed to the public hilarity at the Carnival. At Cassel and Hazebrouch, in the French department of Nord, the giants made their annual appearance on Shrove Tuesday. At Antwerp the giant was so big that no gate in the city was large enough to let him go through; hence he could not visit his brother giants in neigh-

Wicker-work giants in Brabant and Flanders.

bouring towns, as the other Belgian giants used to do on solemn occasions. He was designed in 1534 by Peter van Aelst, painter to the Emperor Charles the Fifth, and is still preserved with other colossal figures in a large hall at Antwerp. At Ath, in the Belgian province of Hainaut, the popular procession of the giants took place annually in August down to the year 1869 at least. For three days the colossal effigies of Goliath and his wife, of Samson and an Archer (*Tirant*), together with a two-headed eagle, were led about the streets on the shoulders of twenty bearers concealed under the flowing drapery of the giants, to the great delight of the townspeople and a crowd of strangers who assembled to witness the pageant. The custom can be traced back by documentary evidence to the middle of the fifteenth century; but it appears that the practice of giving Goliath a wife dates only from the year 1715. Their nuptials were solemnized every year on the eve of the festival in the church of St Julien, whither the two huge figures were escorted by the magistrates in procession.

Thus it appears that the sacrificial rites of the Celts of ancient Gaul can be traced in the popular festivals of modern Europe. Naturally it is in France, or rather in the wider area comprised within the limits of ancient Gaul, that these rites have left the clearest traces in the customs of burning giants of wicker-work and animals enclosed in wicker-work or baskets. These customs, it will have been remarked, are generally observed at or about midsummer. From this we may infer that the original rites of which these are the degenerate successors were solemnized at midsummer. This inference harmonizes with the conclusion suggested by a general survey of European folk-custom, that the midsummer festival must on the whole have been the most widely diffused and the most solemn of all the yearly festivals celebrated by the primitive Aryans in Europe. At the same time we must bear in mind that among the British Celts the chief fire-festivals of the year appear certainly to have been those of Beltane (May Day) and Hallowe'en (the last day of October); and this suggests a doubt whether the Celts of Gaul also may not have celebrated their principal rites of fire, including their burnt sacrifices of men and animals, at the beginning of May or the beginning of November rather than at Midsummer.

Thus the sacrificial rites of the ancient Gauls have their counterparts in the popular festivals of modern Europe.

The men, women, and animals burnt at these festivals were perhaps thought to be witches or wizards in disguise.

We have still to ask, What is the meaning of such sacrifices? Why were men and animals burnt to death at these festivals? If we are right in interpreting the modern European fire-festivals as attempts to break the power of witchcraft by burning or banning the witches and warlocks,* it seems to follow that we must explain the human sacrifices of the Celts in the same manner; that is, we must suppose that the men whom the Druids burnt in wicker-work images were condemned to death on the ground that they were witches or wizards, and that the mode of execution by fire was chosen because, as we have seen, burning alive is deemed the surest mode of getting rid of these noxious and dangerous beings. The same explanation would apply to the cattle and wild animals of many kinds which the Celts burned along with the men. They, too, we may conjecture, were supposed to be either under the spell of witchcraft or actually to be the witches and wizards, who had transformed themselves into animals for the purpose of prosecuting their infernal plots against the welfare of their fellow creatures. This conjecture is confirmed by the observation that the victims most commonly burned in modern bonfires have been cats, and that cats are precisely the animals into which, with the possible exception of hares, witches were most usually supposed to transform themselves. Serpents and foxes used sometimes to be burnt in the midsummer fires; and Welsh and German witches are reported to have assumed the form both of foxes and serpents. In short, when we remember the great variety of animals whose forms witches can assume at pleasure, it seems easy on this hypothesis to account for the variety of living creatures that have been burnt at festivals both in ancient Gaul and modern Europe; all these victims, we may surmise, were doomed to the flames, not because they were animals, but because they were believed to be witches who had taken the shape of animals for their nefarious purposes. One advantage of explaining the ancient Celtic sacrifices in this way is that it introduces, as it were, a harmony and consistency into the treatment which Europe has meted out to witches from the earliest times down to about two centuries ago, when the growing influence of rationalism discredited the belief in witchcraft and put a stop to the custom of burning witches. On this view the Christian Church in its dealings with the black art merely carried out the traditional policy of Druidism, and it might be a nice question to decide which of the two, in pursuance of that policy, exterminated the larger number of innocent men and women. Be that as it may, we can now perhaps understand why the Druids believed that the more persons they sentenced to death, the greater would be the fertility of the land. To a modern reader the connexion at first sight may not be obvious between the activity of the hangman and the productivity of the earth. But a little reflection may satisfy him that when the criminals who perish at the stake or on the gallows are witches, whose delight it is to blight the crops of the farmer or to lay them low under storms of hail, the execution of these wretches is really calculated to ensure an abundant harvest by removing one of the principal causes which paralyse the efforts and blast the hopes of the husbandman.

Relation of
the fire-fest-
ivals to the
myth of
Balder.

THE reader may remember that the preceding account of fire-festivals was suggested by the myth of the Norse god Balder, who is said to have been slain by a branch of mistletoe and burnt in a great fire. We have now to enquire how far the customs which have been passed in review help to shed light on the myth. In this enquiry it may be convenient to begin with the mistletoe, the instrument of Balder's death.

Veneration
of the
Druids for
the mistletoe.

From time immemorial the mistletoe has been the object of superstitious veneration in Europe. It was worshipped by the Druids, as we learn from a famous passage of Pliny. After enumerating the different kinds of mistletoe, he proceeds: 'In treating of this subject, the admiration in which the mistletoe is held throughout Gaul ought not to pass unnoticed. The Druids, for so they call their wizards, esteem nothing more sacred than the mistletoe and the tree on which it grows, provided only that the tree is an oak. But apart from this they choose oak-woods for their sacred groves and perform no sacred rites without oak-leaves; so that the very name of Druids may be regarded as a Greek appellation derived from their worship of the oak. For they believe that whatever grows on these trees is sent from heaven, and is a sign that the tree has been chosen by the god himself. The mistletoe is very rarely to be met with; but when it is found, they gather it with solemn ceremony. This they do above all on the sixth day of the moon, from whence they date the beginnings of their months, of their years, and of their thirty years' cycle, because by the sixth day the moon has plenty of vigour and has not run half its course. After due preparations have been made for a sacrifice and a feast under the tree, they hail it as the universal healer and bring to the spot two white bulls, whose horns have never been bound before. A priest clad in a white robe climbs the tree and with a golden sickle cuts the mistletoe, which is caught in a white cloth. Then they sacrifice the victims, praying that God may make his own gift to prosper with those upon whom he has bestowed it. They believe that a potion prepared from mistletoe will make barren animal to bring forth, and that the plant is a remedy against all poison. So much of men's religion is commonly concerned with trifles.'*

In another passage Pliny tells us that in medicine the mistletoe which grows on an oak was esteemed the most efficacious, and that its efficacy was by some superstitious people supposed to be increased if the plant was gathered on the first day of the moon without the use of iron, and if when gathered it was not allowed to touch the earth; oak-mistletoe thus obtained was deemed a cure for epilepsy; carried about by women it assisted them to conceive; and it healed ulcers most effectually, if only the sufferer chewed a piece of the plant and laid another piece on the sore. Yet, again, he says that mistletoe was supposed, like vinegar and an egg, to be an excellent means of extinguishing a fire.

Medical and magical virtues ascribed to mistletoe in ancient Italy.

If in these latter passages Pliny refers, as he apparently does, to the beliefs current among his contemporaries in Italy, it will follow that the Druids and the Italians were to some extent agreed as to the valuable properties possessed by mistletoe which grows on an oak; both of them deemed it an effectual remedy for a number of ailments, and both of them ascribed to it a quickening virtue, the Druids believing that a potion prepared from mistletoe would fertilize barren cattle, and the Italians holding that a piece of mistletoe carried about by a woman would help her to conceive a child. Further, both peoples thought that if the plant were to exert its medicinal properties it must be gathered in a certain way and at a certain time. It might not be cut with iron, hence the Druids cut it with gold; and it might not touch the earth, hence the Druids caught it in a white cloth. In choosing the time for gathering the plant, both peoples were determined by observation of the moon; only they differed as to the particular day of the moon, the Italians preferring the first, and the Druids the sixth.

Agreement between the Druids and the ancient Italians as to the valuable properties of mistletoe.

But the favourite time would seem to be Midsummer Eve or Midsummer Day. We have seen that both in France and Sweden special virtues are ascribed to mistletoe gathered at Midsummer. The rule in Sweden is that 'mistletoe must be cut on the night of Midsummer Eve when sun and moon stand in the sign of their might'. Again, in Wales it was believed that a sprig of mistletoe gathered on St John's Eve (Midsummer Eve), or at any time before the berries appeared, would induce dreams of omen, both good and bad, if it were placed under the pillow of the sleeper. Thus mistletoe is one of the many plants whose magical or medicinal virtues are believed to culminate with the culmination of the sun on the longest day of the year. Hence it seems reasonable to conjecture that in the eyes of the Druids, also, who revered the plant so highly, the sacred mistletoe may have acquired a double portion of its mystic qualities at the solstice in June, and that accordingly they may have regularly cut it with solemn ceremony on Midsummer Eve.

The two main incidents of Balder's myth, namely the pulling of the mistletoe and the lighting of the bonfire, are reproduced in the great Midsummer celebration of Scandinavia.

Be that as it may, certain it is that the mistletoe, the instrument of Balder's death, has been regularly gathered for the sake of its mystic qualities on Midsummer Eve in Scandinavia, Balder's home. The plant is found commonly growing on pear-trees, oaks, and other trees in thick damp woods throughout the more temperate parts of Sweden. Thus one of the two main incidents of Balder's myth is reproduced in the great midsummer festival of Scandinavia. But the other main incident of the myth, the burning of Balder's body on a pyre, has also its counterpart in the bonfires which still blaze, or blazed till lately, in Denmark, Norway, and Sweden on Midsummer Eve. It does not appear, indeed, that any effigy is burned in these bonfires; but the burning of an effigy is a feature which might easily drop out after its meaning was forgotten. And the name of Balder's balefires (*Balder's Bălar*), by which these midsummer fires were formerly known in Sweden, puts their connexion with Balder beyond the reach of doubt, and makes it probable that in former times either a living representative or an effigy of Balder was annually burned in them. Midsummer was the season sacred to Balder, and the Swedish poet Tegner, in placing the burning of Balder at midsummer, may very well have followed an old tradition that the summer solstice was the time when the good god came to his untimely end.

Hence the myth of Balder was probably the explanation

Thus it has been shewn that the leading incidents of the Balder myth have their counterparts in those fire-festivals of our European peasantry which undoubtedly date from a time long prior to the introduction of Christianity. The pretence of throwing the victim chosen by lot into the Beltane fire, and the similar treatment of the man, the future Green Wolf, at the midsummer bonfire in Normandy,* may naturally be interpreted as traces of an older custom of actually burning human beings on these occasions; and the green dress of the Green Wolf, coupled with the leafy envelope of the young fellow who trod out the midsummer fire at Moosheim, seems to hint that the persons who perished at these festivals did so in the character of tree-spirits or deities of vegetation. From all this we may reasonably infer that in the Balder myth on the one hand, and the fire-festivals and custom of gathering mistletoe on the other hand, we have, as it were, the two broken and dissevered halves of an original whole. In other words, we may assume with some degree of probability that the myth of Balder's death was not merely a myth, that is, a description of physical phenomena in imagery borrowed from human life, but that it was at the same time the story which people told to explain why they annually burned a human representative of the god and cut the mistletoe with solemn ceremony. If I am right, the story of Balder's tragic end formed, so to say, the text of the sacred drama which was acted year by year as a magical rite to cause the sun to shine, trees to grow, crops to thrive, and to guard man and beast from the baleful arts of fairies and trolls, of witches and warlocks. The tale belonged, in short, to that class of nature myths which are meant to be supplemented by ritual; here, as so often, myth stood to magic in the relation of theory to practice.

given of a similar rite.

But if the victims—the human Balders—who died by fire, whether in spring or at midsummer, were put to death as living embodiments of tree-spirits or deities of vegetation, it would seem that Balder himself must have been a tree-spirit or deity of vegetation. It becomes desirable, therefore, to determine, if we can, the particular kind of tree or trees, of which a personal representative was burned at the fire-festivals. For we may be quite sure that it was not as a representative of vegetation in general that the victim suffered death. The idea of vegetation in general is too abstract to be primitive. Most probably the victim at first represented a particular kind of sacred tree. Now of all European trees none has such claims as the oak to be considered as pre-eminently the sacred tree of the Aryans. Its

If a human representative of a tree-spirit was burned in the bonfires, what kind of tree did he represent?

The oak the principal sacred tree of the Aryans.

worship is attested for all the great branches of the Aryan stock in Europe. According to Grimm, the oak ranked first among the holy trees of the Germans. It is certainly known to have been adored by them in the age of heathendom, and traces of its worship have survived in various parts of Germany almost to the present day. Among the ancient Italians the oak was sacred above all other trees. We may certainly conclude that this tree was venerated by the Aryans in common before the dispersion; and that their primitive home must have lain in a land which was clothed with forests of oak.

Hence the tree represented by the human victim who was burnt at the fire-festivals was probably the oak.

Now, considering the primitive character and remarkable similarity of the fire-festivals observed by all the branches of the Aryan race in Europe, we may infer that these festivals form part of the common stock of religious observances which the various peoples carried with them in their wanderings from their old home. But, if I am right, an essential feature of those primitive fire-festivals was the burning of a man who represented the tree-spirit. In view, then, of the place occupied by the oak in the religion of the Aryans, the presumption is that the tree so represented at the fire-festivals must originally have been the oak. Now it is sometimes required that the need-fire, or other sacred fire, should be made by the friction of a particular kind of wood; and when the kind of wood is prescribed, whether among Celts, Germans, or Slavs, that wood appears to be generally the oak. Now, if the sacred fire was regularly kindled by the friction of oak-wood, we may infer that originally the fire was also fed with the same material. In point of fact, it appears that the perpetual fire of Vesta at Rome was fed with oak-wood. At the Boeotian festival of the Daedala, the analogy of which to the spring and midsummer festivals of modern Europe has been already pointed out,* the great feature was the felling and burning of an oak. The general conclusion is, that at those periodic or occasional ceremonies the ancient Aryans both kindled and fed the fire with the sacred oak-wood.

If the human victims burnt at the fire-festival represented the oak, the reason for

But if at these solemn rites the fire was regularly made of oak-wood, it follows that any man who was burned in it as a personification of the tree-spirit could have represented no tree but the oak. The sacred oak was thus burned in duplicate; the wood of the tree was consumed in the fire, and along with it was consumed a living man as a personification of the oak-spirit. The conclusion thus drawn for the European Aryans in general is confirmed in its special application to the Scandinavians by the relation in which amongst them the mistletoe appears to have stood to the burning of the victim in the midsummer fire. We have seen that among Scandinavians it has been customary to gather the mistletoe at midsummer. But so far as appears on the face of this custom, there is nothing to connect it with the midsummer fires in which human victims or effigies of them were burned. Even if the fire, as seems probable, was originally always made with oak-wood, why should it have been necessary to pull the mistletoe? The last link between the midsummer customs of gathering the mistletoe and lighting the bonfires is supplied by Balder's myth, which can hardly be disjoined from the customs in question. The myth suggests that a vital connexion may once have been believed to subsist between the mistletoe and the human representative of the oak who was burned in the fire. According to the myth, Balder could be killed by nothing in heaven or earth except the mistletoe; and so long as the mistletoe remained on the oak, he was not only immortal but invulnerable. Now, if we suppose that Balder was the oak, the origin of the myth becomes intelligible. The mistletoe was viewed as the seat of life of the oak, and so long as it was uninjured nothing could kill or even wound the oak. The conception of the mistletoe as the seat of life of the oak would naturally be suggested to primitive people by the observation that while the oak is deciduous, the mistletoe which grows on it is evergreen. In winter the sight of its fresh foliage among the bare branches must have been hailed by the worshippers of the tree as a sign that the divine life which had ceased to animate the branches yet survived in the mistletoe, as the heart of a sleeper still beats when his body is motionless. Hence when the god had to be killed—when the sacred tree had to be burnt—it was necessary to begin by breaking of the mistletoe. For so long as the mistletoe remained intact, the oak (so people might think) was invulnerable; all the blows of their knives and axes would glance harmless from its surface. But once tear from the oak its sacred heart—the mistletoe—and the tree nodded to its fall. And when in later times the spirit of the oak came to be represented by a living man, it was logically necessary to suppose that, like the tree he personated, he could

[side note:] pulling the mistletoe may have been a belief that the life of the oak was in the mistletoe, and that the tree could not perish either by fire or water so long as the mistletoe remained intact among its boughs

neither be killed nor wounded so long as the mistletoe remained uninjured. The pulling of the mistletoe was thus at once the signal and the cause of his death.

Conception of a being whose life is outside himself.

But since the idea of a being whose life is thus, in a sense, outside himself, must be strange to many readers, and has, indeed, not yet been recognized in its full bearing on primitive superstition, it will be worth while to illustrate it by examples drawn both from story and custom. The result will be to shew that, in assuming this idea as the explanation of Balder's relation to the mistletoe, I assume a principle which is deeply engraved on the mind of primitive man.

ii

Belief that a man's soul may be deposited for safety in a secure place outside his body, and that so long as it remains there intact he himself is invulnerable and immortal.

In a former part of this work we saw that, in the opinion of primitive people, the soul may temporarily absent itself from the body without causing death.* Such temporary absences of the soul are often believed to involve considerable risk, since the wandering soul is liable to a variety of mishaps at the hands of enemies, and so forth. But there is another aspect to this power of disengaging the soul from the body. If only the safety of the soul can be ensured during its absence, there is no reason why the soul should not continue absent for an indefinite time; indeed a man may, on a pure calculation of personal safety, desire that his soul should never return to his body. Unable to conceive of life abstractly as a 'permanent possibility of sensation' or a 'continuous adjustment of internal arrangements to external relations', the savage thinks of it as a concrete material thing of a definite bulk, capable of being seen and handled, kept in a box or jar, and liable to be bruised, fractured, or smashed in pieces. It is not needful that the life, so conceived, should be in the man; it may be absent from his body and still continue to animate him by virtue of a sort of sympathy or action at a distance. So long as this object which he calls his life or soul remains unharmed, the man is well; if it is injured, he suffers; if it is destroyed, he dies. Or, to put it otherwise, when a man is ill or dies, the fact is explained by saying that the material object called his life or soul, whether it be in his body or out of it, has either sustained injury or been destroyed. But there may be circumstances in which, if the life or soul remains in the man, it stands a greater chance of sustaining injury than if it were stowed away in some safe and secret place. Accordingly, in such circumstances, primitive man takes his soul out of his body and deposits it for security in some snug spot, intending to replace it in his body when the danger is past. Or if he should discover some place of absolute security, he may be content to leave his soul there permanently. The advantage of this is that, so long as the soul remains unharmed in the place where he has deposited it, the man himself is immortal; nothing can kill his body, since his life is not in it.

Evidence of this primitive belief is furnished by a class of folk-tales of which the Norse story of 'The giant who had no heart in his body' is perhaps the best-known example. Stories of this kind are widely diffused over the world, and from their number and the variety of incident and of details in which the leading idea is embodied, we may infer that the conception of an external soul is one which has had a powerful hold on the minds of men at an early stage of history. *This belief is illustrated by folk-tales told by many peoples.*

In the first place, the story of the external soul is told, in various forms, by all Aryan peoples from Hindoostan to the Hebrides. A very common form of it is this: A warlock, giant, or other fairyland being is invulnerable and immortal because he keeps his soul hidden far away in some secret place; but a fair princess, whom he holds enthralled in his enchanted castle, wiles his secret from him and reveals it to the hero, who seeks out the warlock's soul, heart, life, or death (as it is variously called), and, by destroying it, simultaneously kills the warlock. *Stories of an external soul common among Aryan peoples.* Thus a Hindoo story tells how a magician called Punchkin held a queen captive for twelve years, and would fain marry her, but she would not have him. At last the queen's son came to rescue her, and the two plotted together to kill Punchkin. So the queen spoke the magician fair, and pretended that she had at last made up her mind to marry him. 'And do tell me,' she said, 'are you quite immortal? Can death never touch you? And are you too great an enchanter ever to feel human suffering?' 'It is true', he said, 'that I am not as others. Far, far away, hundreds of thousands of miles from this, there lies a desolate country covered with thick jungle. In the midst of the jungle grows a circle of palm trees, and in the centre of the circle stand six chattees full of water, piled one above another: below the sixth *The external soul in Hindoo stories. Punchkin and the parrot.*

chattee is a small cage, which contains a little green parrot;—on the life of the parrot depends my life;—and if the parrot is killed I must die. It is, however,' he added, 'impossible that the parrot should sustain any injury, both on account of the inaccessibility of the country, and because, by my appointment, many thousand genii surround the palm trees, and kill all who approach the place.' But the queen's young son overcame all difficulties, and got possession of the parrot. He brought it to the door of the magician's palace, and began playing with it. Punchkin, the magician, saw him, and, coming out, tried to persuade the boy to give him the parrot. 'Give me my parrot!' cried Punchkin. Then the boy took hold of the parrot and tore off one of his wings; and as he did so the magician's right arm fell off. Punchkin then stretched out his left arm, crying, 'Give me my parrot!' The prince pulled off the parrot's second wing, and, the magician's left arm tumbled off. 'Give me my parrot!' cried he, and fell on his knees. The prince pulled off the parrot's right leg, the magician's right leg fell off; the prince pulled off the parrot's left leg, down fell the magician's left. Nothing remained of him except the trunk and the head; but still he rolled his eyes, and cried, 'Give me my parrot!' 'Take your parrot, then,' cried the boy; and with that he wrung the bird's neck, and threw it at the magician; and, as he did so, Punchkin's head twisted round, and, with a fearful groan, he died!*

The external soul in a Siamese or Cambodian story.

In a Siamese or Cambodian story, probably derived from India, we are told that Thossakan or Ravana, the King of Ceylon, was able by magic art to take his soul out of his body and leave it in a box at home, while he went to the wars. Thus he was invulnerable in battle. When he was about to give battle to Rama, he deposited his soul with a hermit called Fire-eye, who was to keep it safe for him. So in the fight Rama was astounded to see that his arrows struck the king without wounding him. But one of Rama's allies, knowing the secret of the king's invulnerability, transformed himself by magic into the likeness of the king, and going to the hermit asked back his soul. On receiving it he soared up into the air and flew to Rama, brandishing the box and squeezing it so hard that all the breath left the King of Ceylon's body, and he died. In a Bengalee story a prince going into a far country planted with his own hands a tree in the courtyard of his father's palace, and said to his parents, 'This tree is my life. When you see the tree green and fresh, then know that it is well with me; when you see the tree fade in some parts, then know that I am in an ill case; and when you see the whole tree fade, then know that I am dead and gone.' In another Indian tale a prince, setting forth on his travels, left behind him a barley plant, with instructions that it should be carefully tended and watched; for if it flourished, he would be alive and well, but if it drooped, then some mischance was about to happen to him. And so it fell out. For the prince was beheaded, and as his head rolled off, the barley plant snapped in two and the ear of barley fell to the ground. In the legend of the origin of Gilgit there figures a fairy king whose soul is in the snows and who can only perish by fire. Indian stories of a tree and a barley plant that were life-tokens.

In Greek tales, ancient and modern, the idea of an external soul is not uncommon. When Meleager* was seven days old, the Fates appeared to his mother and told her that Meleager would die when the brand which was blazing on the hearth had burnt down. So his mother snatched the brand from the fire and kept it in a box. But in after-years, being enraged at her son for slaying her brothers, she burnt the brand in the fire and Meleager expired in agonies, as if flames were preying on his vitals. Again, Nisus King of Megara had a purple or golden hair on the middle of his head, and it was fated that whenever the hair was pulled out the king should die. When Megara was besieged by the Cretans, the king's daughter Scylla fell in love with Minos, their king, and pulled out the fatal hair from her father's head. So he died. Similarly Poseidon made Pterelaus immortal by giving him a golden hair on his head. But when Taphos, the home of Pterelaus, was besieged by Amphitryo, the daughter of Pterelaus fell in love with Amphitryo and killed her father by plucking out the golden hair with which his life was bound up. In a modern Greek folk-tale a man's strength lies in three golden hairs on his head. When his mother pulls them out, he grows weak and timid and is slain by his enemies. The external soul in Greek stories. Meleager and the firebrand. Nisus and his purple or golden hair. Pterelaus and his golden hair. Modern Greek parallels.

Ancient Italian legend furnishes a close parallel to the Greek story of Meleager. Silvia, the young wife of Septimius Marcellus, had a child by the god Mars. The god gave her a spear, with which he said that the fate of the child would be bound up. When the boy grew up he quarrelled with his maternal The external soul in Italian stories. Silvia's son.

uncles and slew them. So in revenge his mother burned the spear on which his life depended.* In one of the stories of the *Pentamerone* a certain queen has a twin brother, a dragon. The astrologers declared at her birth that she would live just as long as the dragon and no longer, the death of the one involving the death of the other. If the dragon were killed, the only way to restore the queen to life would be to smear her temples, breast, pulses, and nostrils with the blood of the dragon.

An Italian tale sets forth how a great cloud, which was really a fairy, used to receive a young girl as tribute every year from a certain city; and the inhabitants had to give the girls up, for if they did not, the cloud would throw things at them and kill them all. One year it fell to the lot of the king's daughter to be handed over to the cloud, and they took her in procession, to the roll of muffled drums, and attended by her weeping father and mother, to the top of a mountain, and left her sitting in a chair there all alone. Then the fairy cloud came down on the top of the mountain, set the princess in her lap, and began to suck her blood out of her little finger; for it was on the blood of girls that this wicked fairy lived. When the poor princess was faint with the loss of blood and lay like a log, the cloud carried her away up to her fairy palace in the sky. But a brave youth had seen all that happened from behind a bush, and no sooner did the fairy spirit away the princess to her palace than he turned himself into an eagle and flew after them. He lighted on a tree just outside the palace, and looking in at the window he beheld a room full of young girls all in bed; for these were the victims of former years whom the fairy cloud had half killed by sucking their blood; yet they called her mamma. When the fairy went away and left the girls, the brave young man had food drawn up for them by ropes, and he told them to ask the fairy how she might be killed and what was to become of them when she died. It was a delicate question, but the fairy answered it, saying, 'I shall never die.' However, when the girls pressed her, she took them out on a terrace and said, 'Do you see that mountain far off there? On that mountain is a tigress with seven heads. If you wish me to die, a lion must fight that tigress and tear off all seven of her heads. In her body is an egg, and if any one hits me with it in the middle of my forehead, I shall die; but if that egg falls into my hands, the tigress will come to life again, resume her seven heads, and I shall live.' When the young girls heard this they pretended to be glad and said, 'Good! certainly our mamma can never die,' but naturally they were discouraged. However, when she went away again, they told it all to the young man, and he bade them have no fear. Away he went to the mountain, turned himself into a lion, and fought the tigress. Meantime the fairy came home, saying, 'Alas! I feel ill!' For six days the fight went on, the young man tearing off one of the tigress's heads each day, and each day the strength of the fairy kept ebbing away. Then after allowing himself two days' rest the hero tore off the seventh head and secured the egg, but not till it had rolled into the sea and been brought back to him by a friendly dog-fish. When he returned to the fairy with the egg in his hand, she begged and prayed him to give it her, but he made her first restore the young girls to health and send them away in handsome carriages. When she had done so, he struck her on the forehead with the egg, and she fell down dead.

Stories of the same sort are current among Slavonic peoples. In some of them, as in the biblical story of Samson and Delilah, the warlock is questioned by a treacherous woman as to the place where his strength resides or his life or death is stowed away; and his suspicions being roused by her curiosity, he at first puts her off with false answers, but is at last beguiled into telling her the truth, thereby incurring his doom through her treachery. Thus a Russian story tells how a certain warlock called Kashtshei or Koshchei the Deathless carried off a princess and kept her prisoner in his golden castle. However, a prince made up to her one day as she was walking alone and disconsolate in the castle garden, and cheered by the prospect of escaping with him she went to the warlock and coaxed him with false and flattering words, saying, 'My dearest friend, tell me, I pray you, will you never die?' 'Certainly not,' says he. 'Well,' says she, 'and where is your death? is it in your dwelling?' 'To be sure it is,' says he, 'it is in the broom under the threshold.' Thereupon the princess seized the broom and threw it on the fire, but although the broom burned, the deathless Koshchei remained alive; indeed not so much as a hair of him was singed. Balked in her first attempt, the artful hussy pouted and said, 'You do not love me true, for you have not

The external soul in Slavonic stories.

Russian story of Koshchei the Deathless, whose death was in an egg.

told me where your death is; yet I am not angry, but love you with all my heart.' With these fawning words she besought the warlock to tell her truly where his death was. So he laughed and said, 'Why do you wish to know? Well then, out of love I will tell you where it lies. In a certain field there stand three green oaks, and under the roots of the largest oak is a worm, and if ever this worm is found and crushed, that instant I shall die.' When the princess heard these words, she went straight to her lover and told him all; and he searched till he found the oaks and dug up the worm and crushed it. Then he hurried to the warlock's castle, but only to learn from the princess that the warlock was still alive. Then she fell to wheedling and coaxing Koshchei once more, and this time, overcome by her wiles, he opened his heart to her and told her the truth. 'My death,' said he, 'is far from here and hard to find, on the wide ocean. In that sea is an island, and on the island there grows a green oak, and beneath the oak is an iron chest, and in the chest is a small basket, and in the basket is a hare, and in the hare is a duck, and in the duck is an egg; and he who finds the egg and breaks it, kills me at the same time.' The prince naturally procured the fateful egg and with it in his hands he confronted the deathless warlock. The monster would have killed him, but the prince began to squeeze the egg. At that the warlock shrieked with pain, and turning to the false princess, who stood by smirking and smiling, 'Was it not out of love for you,' said he, 'that I told you where my death was? And is this the return you make to me?' With that he grabbed at his sword, which hung from a peg on the wall; but before he could reach it, the prince had crushed the egg, and sure enough the deathless warlock found his death at the same moment.

Other versions of the story of Koshchei the Deathless.

In another version of the same story, when the cunning warlock deceives the traitress by telling her that his death is in the broom, she gilds the broom, and at supper the warlock sees it shining under the threshold and asks her sharply, 'What's that?' 'Oh,' says she, 'you see how I honour you.' 'Simpleton!' says he, 'I was joking. My death is out there fastened to the oak fence.' So next day when the warlock was out, the prince came and gilded the whole fence; and in the evening when the warlock was at supper he looked out of the window and saw the fence glittering like gold. 'And pray what may that be?' said he to the princess. 'You see,' said she, 'how I respect you. If you are dear to me, dear too is your death. That is why I have gilded the fence in which your death resides.' The speech pleased the warlock, and in the fulness of his heart he revealed to her the fatal secret of the egg. When the prince, with the help of some friendly animals, obtained possession of the egg, he put it in his bosom and repaired to the warlock's house. The warlock himself was sitting at the window in a very gloomy frame of mind; and when the prince appeared and shewed him the egg, the light grew dim in the warlock's eyes and he became all of a sudden very meek and mild. But when the prince began to play with the egg and to throw it from one hand to the other, the deathless Koshchei staggered from one corner of the room to the other, and when the prince broke the egg, Koshchei the Deathless fell down and died. 'In one of the descriptions of Koshchei's death, he is said to be killed by a blow on the forehead inflicted by the mysterious egg—that last link in the magic chain by which his life is darkly bound. In another version of the same story, but told of a snake, the fatal blow is struck by a small stone found in the yolk of an egg, which is inside a duck, which is inside a hare, which is inside a stone, which is on an island.' In another Russian story the death of an enchantress is in a blue rose-tree in a blue forest. Prince Ivan uproots the rose-tree, whereupon the enchantress straightway sickens. He brings the rose-tree to her house and finds her at the point of death. Then he throws it into the cellar, crying, 'Behold her death!' and at once the whole building shakes, 'and becomes an island, on which are people who had been sitting in Hell, and who offer up thanks to Prince Ivan.' In another Russian story a prince is grievously tormented by a witch who has got hold of his heart, and keeps it seething in a magic cauldron.

Death in the blue rose-tree.

In a Bohemian tale a warlock's strength lies in an egg which is in a duck, which is in a stag, which is under a tree. A seer finds the egg and sucks it. Then the warlock grows as weak as a child, 'for all his strength had passed into the seer.' A Servian story relates how a certain warlock called True Steel carried off a prince's wife and kept her shut up in his cave. But the prince contrived to get speech of her and told her that she must persuade True Steel to reveal to her where his strength lay. So

The external soul in Bohemian and Servian stories.

True Steel, whose strength was in a bird.

when True Steel came home, the prince's wife said to him, 'Tell me, now, where is your great strength?' He answered, 'My wife, my strength is in my sword.' Then she began to pray and turned to his sword. When True Steel saw that, he laughed and said, 'O foolish woman! my strength is not in my sword, but in my bow and arrows.' Then she turned towards the bow and arrows and prayed. But True Steel said, 'I see, my wife, you have a clever teacher who has taught you to find out where my strength lies. I could almost say that your husband is living, and it is he who teaches you.' But she assured him that nobody had taught her. When she found he had deceived her again, she waited for some days and then asked him again about the secret of his strength. He answered, 'Since you think so much of my strength, I will tell you truly where it is. Far away from here there is a very high mountain; in the mountain there is a fox; in the fox there is a heart; in the heart there is a bird, and in this bird is my strength. It is no easy task, however, to catch the fox, for she can transform herself into a multitude of creatures.' So next day, when True Steel went forth from the cave, the prince came and learned from his wife the true secret of the warlock's strength. So away he hied to the mountain, and there, though the fox, or rather the vixen, turned herself into various shapes, he managed with the help of certain friendly eagles, falcons, and dragons, to catch and kill her. Then he took out the fox's heart, and out of the heart he took the bird and burned it in a great fire. At that very moment True Steel fell down dead.

The external soul in Arabian stories. The jinnee and the sparrow.

In the *Arabian Nights* we read how Seyf el-Mulook, after wandering for four months over mountains and hills and deserts, came to a lofty palace in which he found the lovely daughter of the King of India sitting alone on a golden couch in a hall spread with silken carpets. She tells him that she is held captive by a jinnee, who had swooped down on her and carried her off while she was disporting herself with her female slaves in a tank in the great garden of her father the king. Seyf el-Mulook then offers to smite the jinnee with the sword and slay him. 'But', she replied, 'thou canst not slay him unless thou kill his soul.' 'And in what place', said he, 'is his soul?' She answered, 'I asked him respecting it many times; but he would not confess to me its place. It happened, however, that I urged

him, one day, and he was enraged against me, and said to me,
"How often wilt thou ask me respecting my soul? What is the
reason of thy question respecting my soul?" So I answered
him, "O Ḥátim, there remaineth to me no one but thee,
excepting God; and I, as long as I live, would not cease to hold
thy soul in my embrace; and if I do not take care of thy soul,
and put it in the midst of my eye, how can I live after thee? If
I knew thy soul, I would take care of it as of my right eye." And
thereupon he said to me, "When I was born, the astrologers
declared that the destruction of my soul would be effected by
the hand of one of the sons of the human kings. I therefore took
my soul, and put it into the crop of a sparrow, and I imprisoned
the sparrow in a little box, and put this into another small
box, and this I put within seven other small boxes, and I put
these within seven chests, and the chests I put into a coffer of
marble within the verge of this circumambient ocean; for this
part is remote from the countries of mankind, and none of
mankind can gain access to it." ' But Seyf el-Mulook got
possession of the sparrow and strangled it, and the jinnee fell
upon the ground a heap of black ashes.

In a Mongolian story the hero Joro gets the better of his
enemy the lama Tschoridong in the following way. The lama,
who is an enchanter, sends out his soul in the form of a wasp
to sting Joro's eyes. But Joro catches the wasp in his hand, and
by alternately shutting and opening his hand he causes the lama
alternately to lose and recover consciousness. In a Tartar poem
two youths cut open the body of an old witch and tear out her
bowels, but all to no purpose, she still lives. On being asked
where her soul is, she answers that it is in the middle of her
shoe-sole in the form of a seven-headed speckled snake. So one
of the youths slices her shoe-sole with his sword, takes out the
speckled snake, and cuts off its seven heads. Then the witch
dies. Another Tartar poem describes how the hero Kartaga
grappled with the Swan-woman. Long they wrestled. Moons
waxed and waned and still they wrestled; years came and went,
and still the struggle went on. But the piebald horse and the
black horse knew that the Swan-woman's soul was not in her.
Under the black earth flow nine seas; where the seas meet and
form one, the sea comes to the surface of the earth. At the
mouth of the nine seas rises a rock of copper; it rises to the

*The external
soul in a
Mongolian
story and
Tartar poems.*

surface of the ground, it rises up between heaven and earth, this rock of copper. At the foot of the copper rock is a black chest, in the black chest is a golden casket, and in the golden casket is the soul of the Swan-woman. Seven little birds are the soul of the Swan-woman; if the birds are killed the Swan-woman will die straightway. So the horses ran to the foot of the copper rock, opened the black chest, and brought back the golden casket. Then the piebald horse turned himself into a bald-headed man, opened the golden casket, and cut off the heads of the seven birds. So the Swan-woman died.

The external
soul in a
Chinese story.

A modern Chinese story tells how an habitual criminal used to take his soul out of his own body for the purpose of evading the righteous punishment of his crimes. This bad man lived in Khien (Kwei-cheu), and the sentences that had been passed on him formed a pile as high as a hill. The mandarins had flogged him to death with sticks and flung his mangled corpse into the river, but three days afterwards the scoundrel got his soul back again, and on the fifth day he resumed his career of villainy as if nothing had happened. The thing occurred again and again, till at last it reached the ears of the Governor of the province, who flew into a violent passion and proposed to the Governor-General to have the rascal beheaded. And beheaded he was; but in three days the wretch was alive again with no trace of decapitation about him except a slender red thread round his neck. And now, like a giant refreshed, he began a fresh series of enormities. He even went so far as to beat his own mother. This was more than she could bear, and she brought the matter before the magistrate. She produced in court a vase and said, 'In this vase my refractory son has hidden his soul. Whenever he was conscious of having committed a serious crime, or a misdeed of the most heinous kind, he remained at home, took his soul out of his body, purified it, and put it in the vase. Then the authorities only punished or executed his body of flesh and blood, and not his soul. With his soul, refined by a long process, he then cured his freshly mutilated body, which thus became able in three days to recommence in the old way. Now, however, his crimes have reached a climax, for he has beaten me, an old woman, and I cannot bear it. I pray you, smash this vase, and scatter his soul by fanning it away with a windwheel; and if then you castigate his body anew, it is probable that bad son of mine will really die.' The mandarin took the hint. He had the rogue cudgelled to death, and when they examined the corpse they found that decay had set in within ten days.

A Hausa story from Northern Nigeria runs thus. A certain man and his wife had four daughters born to them in succession, but every one of the baby girls mysteriously disappeared on the day when she was to be weaned; so the parents fell under the suspicion of having devoured them. Last of all there was born to them a son, who to avoid accidents was left to wean himself. One day, as he grew up, the son received a magic lotion from an old woman, who told him to rub his eyes with it. He did so, and immediately he saw a large house and entering it he found his eldest sister married to a bull. She bade him welcome and so did her husband the bull; and when he went away, the bull very kindly presented him with a lock of his hair as a keepsake. In like manner the lad discovered his other three sisters, who were living in wedlock with a ram, a dog, and a hawk respectively. All of them welcomed him and from the ram, the dog, and the hawk he received tokens of regard in the shape of hair or feathers. Then he returned home and told his parents of his adventure and how he had found his sisters alive and married. Next day he went to a far city, where he made love to the Queen and persuaded her to plot with him against the life of the King her husband. So she coaxed the King to shew his affection for her by 'taking his own life, and joining it to her'. The unsuspecting husband, as usual, fell into the trap set for him by his treacherous wife. He confided to her the secret of his life. 'My life', said he, 'is behind the city, behind the city in a thicket. In this thicket there is a lake; in the lake is a rock; in the rock is a gazelle; in the gazelle is a dove; and in the dove is a small box.' The Queen divulged the secret to her lover, who kindled a fire behind the city and threw into it the hair and feathers which he had received from the friendly animals, his brothers-in-law. Immediately the animals themselves appeared and readily gave their help in the enterprise. The bull drank up the lake; the ram broke up the rock; the dog caught the gazelle; the hawk captured the dove. So the youth extracted the precious box from the dove and repaired to the palace, where he found the King already dead. His Majesty had been ailing from the moment when the young man left the city, and he

The external soul in a Hausa story. The king whose life was in a box.

The helpful animals.

grew steadily worse with every fresh success of the adventurer who was to supplant him. So the hero became King and married the false Queen; and his sisters' husbands were changed from animals into men and received subordinate posts in the government. The hero's parents, too, came to live in the city over which he reigned.

The Kwakiutl Indians of British Columbia tell of an ogress, who could not be killed because her life was in a hemlock branch. A brave boy met her in the woods, smashed her head with a stone, scattered her brains, broke her bones, and threw them into the water. Then, thinking he had disposed of the ogress, he went into her house. There he saw a woman rooted to the floor, who warned him, saying, 'Now do not stay long. I know that you have tried to kill the ogress. It is the fourth time that somebody has tried to kill her. She never dies; she has nearly come to life. There in that covered hemlock branch is her life. Go there, and as soon as you see her enter, shoot her life. Then she will be dead.' Hardly had she finished speaking when sure enough in came the ogress, singing as she walked:

> 'I have the magical treasure,
> I have the supernatural power,
> I can return to life.'

Such was her song. But the boy shot at her life, and she fell dead to the floor.

iii

Thus the idea that the soul may be deposited for a longer or shorter time in some place of security outside the body, or at all events in the hair, is found in the popular tales of many races. It remains to shew that the idea is not a mere figment devised to adorn a tale, but is a real article of primitive faith, which has given rise to a corresponding set of customs.

We have seen that in the tales the hero, as a preparation for battle, sometimes removes his soul from his body, in order that his body may be invulnerable and immortal in the combat. With a like intention the savage removes his soul from his body on various occasions of real or imaginary peril. Thus among the people of Minahassa in Celebes, when a family moves into a

[Marginal notes:]

The ogress whose life was in a hemlock branch.

The external soul in folk-custom.

The soul removed from the body as a precaution in seasons of danger.

new house, a priest collects the souls of the whole family in a bag, and afterwards restores them to their owners, because the moment of entering a new house is supposed to be fraught with supernatural danger. In Southern Celebes, when a woman is brought to bed, the messenger who fetches the doctor or the midwife always carries with him something made of iron, such as a chopping-knife, which he delivers to the doctor. The doctor must keep the thing in his house till the confinement is over, when he gives it back, receiving a fixed sum of money for doing so. The chopping-knife, or whatever it is, represents the woman's soul, which at this critical time is believed to be safer out of her body than in it. Hence the doctor must take great care of the object; for were it lost, the woman's soul would assuredly, they think, be lost with it.

The natives of Amboyna used to think that their strength was in their hair and would desert them if it were shorn. A criminal under torture in a Dutch Court of that island persisted in denying his guilt till his hair was cut off, when he immediately confessed. One man, who was tried for murder, endured without flinching the utmost ingenuity of his torturers till he saw the surgeon standing with a pair of shears. On asking what this was for, and being told that it was to cut his hair, he begged they would not do it, and made a clean breast. In subsequent cases, when torture failed to wring a confession from a prisoner, the Dutch authorities made a practice of cutting off his hair. In Ceram it is still believed that if young people have their hair cut they will be weakened and enervated thereby.

Here in Europe it used to be thought that the maleficent powers of witches and wizards resided in their hair, and that nothing could make any impression on these miscreants so long as they kept their hair on. Hence in France it was customary to shave the whole bodies of persons charged with sorcery before handing them over to the torturer. Millaeus witnessed the torture of some persons at Toulouse, from whom no confession could be wrung until they were stripped and completely shaven, when they readily acknowledged the truth of the charge. A woman also, who apparently led a pious life, was put to the torture on suspicion of witchcraft, and bore her agonies with incredible constancy, until complete depilation drove her to admit her guilt. The noted inquisitor Sprenger contented himself with shaving the head of the suspected witch or wizard; but his more thoroughgoing colleague Cumanus shaved the whole bodies of forty-one women before committing them all to the flames. He had high authority for this rigorous scrutiny, since Satan himself, in a sermon preached from the pulpit of North Berwick church, comforted his many servants by assuring them that no harm could befall them 'sa lang as their hair wes on, and sould newir latt ane teir fall fra thair ene'. Similarly in Bastar, a province of India, 'if a man is adjudged guilty of witchcraft, he is beaten by the crowd, his hair is shaved, the hair being supposed to constitute his power of mischief, his front teeth are knocked out, in order, it is said, to prevent him from muttering incantations . . . Women suspected of sorcery have to undergo the same ordeal; if found guilty, the same punishment is awarded, and after being shaved, their hair is attached to a tree in some public place.' So among the Bhils of India, when a woman was convicted of witchcraft and had been subjected to various forms of persuasion, such as hanging head downwards from a tree and having pepper put into her eyes, a lock of hair was cut from her head and buried in the ground, 'that the last link between her and her former powers of mischief might be broken'. In like manner among the Aztecs of Mexico, when wizards and witches 'had done their evil deeds, and the time came to put an end to their detestable life, some one laid hold of them and cropped the hair on the crown of their heads, which took from them all their power of sorcery and enchantment, and then it was that by death they put an end to their odious existence'.

Life of a person supposed to be bound up with that of a tree or plant.

Further it has been shewn that in folk-tales the life of a person is sometimes so bound up with the life of a plant that the withering of the plant will immediately follow or be followed by the death of the person. Similarly among the natives of the Pennefather River in Queensland, when a visitor has made himself very agreeable and taken his departure, an effigy of him about three or four feet long is cut on some soft tree, such as the *Canarium australasicum*, so as to face in the direction taken by the popular stranger. Afterwards from observing the state of the tree the natives infer the corresponding state of their absent friend, whose illness or death are apparently supposed to be portended by the fall of the leaves or of the tree. In Uganda, when a new royal enclosure with its numerous houses was built for a new king, barkcloth trees used to be planted at the main entrance by priests of each principal deity and offerings were laid under each tree for its particular god. Thenceforth 'the trees were carefully guarded and tended, because it was believed that as they grew and flourished, so the king's life and power would increase'. Among the M'Bengas in Western Africa, about the Gaboon, when two children are born on the same day, the people plant two trees of the same kind and dance round them. The life of each of the children is believed to be bound up with the life of one of the trees; and if the tree dies or is thrown down, they are sure that the child will soon die. In Sierra Leone also it is customary at the birth of a child to plant a shoot of a *malep*-tree, and they think that the tree will grow with the child and be its god. If a tree which has been thus planted withers away, the people consult a sorcerer on the subject. Among the Wajagga of German East Africa, when a child is born, it is usual to plant a cultivated plant of some sort behind the house. The plant is thenceforth carefully tended, for they believe that were it to wither away the child would die. When the navel-string drops from the infant, it is buried under the plant. The species of birth-plant varies with the clan; members of one clan, for example, plant a particular sort of banana, members of another clan plant a sugar-cane, and so on. Among the Swahili of East Africa, when a child is born, the afterbirth and navel-string are buried in the courtyard and a mark is made on the spot. Seven days afterwards, the hair of the child is shaved and deposited, along with the clippings of its nails, in the same place. Then over all these relics of the infant's person a coco-nut is planted. As the tree grows up from the nut, the child likes to point it out to his playfellows and tell them, 'This coco-nut palm is my navel.' In planting the coco-nut the parents say, 'May God cause our child to grow up, that he or she may one day enjoy the coco-nut milk of the tree which we plant here.' Though it is not expressly affirmed, we may perhaps assume that such a birth-tree is supposed to stand in a sympathetic relation with the life of the person. In the Cameroons, also, the life of a person is believed to be sympathetically bound up with that of a tree. The chief of Old Town in Calabar kept his soul in a sacred grove near a spring of water.

Birth-trees in Africa.

When some Europeans, in frolic or ignorance, cut down part of the grove, the spirit was most indignant and threatened the perpetrators of the deed, according to the king, with all manner of evil. Among the Fans of the French Congo, when a chief's son is born, the remains of the navel-string are buried under a sacred fig-tree, and 'thenceforth great importance is attached to the growth of the tree; it is strictly forbidden to touch it. Any attempt on the tree would be considered as an attack on the human being himself.' Among the Boloki of the Upper Congo a family has a plant with red leaves (called *nkungu*) for its totem. When a woman of the family is with child for the first time, one of the totemic plants is planted near the hearth outside the house and is never destroyed, otherwise it is believed that the child would be born thin and weak and would remain puny and sickly. 'The healthy life of the children and family is bound up with the healthiness and life of the totem tree as respected and preserved by the family.' Among the Baganda of Central Africa a child's afterbirth was called the second child and was believed to be animated by a spirit, which at once became a ghost. The afterbirth was usually buried at the root of a banana tree, and afterwards the tree was carefully guarded by old women, who prevented any one from going near it; they tied ropes of fibre from tree to tree to isolate it, and all the child's excretions were thrown into this enclosure. When the fruit ripened, it was cut by the old woman in charge. The reason for guarding the tree thus carefully was a belief that if any stranger were to eat of the fruit of the tree or to drink beer brewed from it, he would carry off with him the ghost of the child's afterbirth, which had been buried at the root of the banana-tree, and the living child would then die in order to follow its twin ghost. Whereas a grandparent of the child, by eating the fruit or drinking the beer, averted this catastrophe and ensured the health of the child. Among the Wakondyo, at the north-western corner of Lake Albert Nyanza, it is customary to bury the afterbirth at the foot of a young banana-tree, and the fruit of this particular tree may be eaten by no one but the woman who assisted at the birth. The reason for the custom is not mentioned, but probably, as among the Baganda, the life of the child is supposed to be bound up with the life of the tree, since the afterbirth, regarded as a spiritual double of the infant, has been buried at the root of the tree.

In the midst of the 'Forbidden City' at Peking there is a tiny private garden, where the emperors of the now fallen Manchu dynasty used to take the air and refresh themselves after the cares of state. In accordance with Chinese taste the garden is a labyrinth of artificial rockeries, waterfalls, grottoes, and kiosks, in which everything is as unlike nature as art can make it. The trees in particular (*Arbor vitae*), the principal ornament of the garden, exhibit the last refinement of the gardener's skill, being clipped and distorted into a variety of grotesque shapes. Only one of the trees remained intact and had been spared these deformations for centuries. Far from being stunted by the axe or the shears, the tree was carefully tended and encouraged to shoot up to its full height. 'It was the "Life-tree of the Dynasty", and according to legend the prosperity or fall of the present dynasty went hand in hand with the welfare or death of the tree. Certainly, if we accept the tradition, the days of the present reigning house must be numbered, for all the care and attention lavished on the tree have been for some years in vain. A glance at our illustration shews the tree as it still surpasses all its fellows in height and size; but it owes its pre-eminence only to the many artificial props which hold it up. In reality the "Life-tree of the Dynasty" is dying, and might fall over night, if one of its artificial props were suddenly to give way. For the superstitious Chinese—and superstitious they certainly are—it is a very, very evil omen.' Some twelve years have passed since this passage was written, and in the interval the omen has been fulfilled—the Manchu dynasty has fallen. We may conjecture that the old tree in the quaint old garden has fallen too. So vain are all human efforts to arrest the decay of royal houses by underpropping trees on which nature herself has passed a sentence of death.

At Rome in the ancient sanctuary of Quirinus there grew two old myrtle-trees, one named the Patrician and the other the Plebeian. For many years, so long as the patricians were in the ascendant, their myrtle-tree flourished and spread its branches abroad, while the myrtle of the plebeians was shrivelled and shrunken; but from the time of the Marsian war, when the power of the nobles declined, their myrtle in like manner drooped and withered, whereas that of the popular party held up its head and grew strong. Thrice when Vespasia was with

The Life-tree of the Manchu dynasty.

The myrtle-trees of the patricians and plebeians at Rome.

The oak of the Vespasian family.

child, an old oak in the garden of the Flavian family near Rome suddenly put forth branches. The first branch was puny and soon withered away, and the girl who was born accordingly died within the year; the second branch was long and sturdy; and the third was like a tree. So on the third occasion the happy father reported to his mother that a future emperor was born to her as a grandchild. The old lady only laughed to think that at her age she should keep her wits about her, while her son had lost his; yet the omen of the oak came true, for the grandson was afterwards the emperor Vespasian.

Belief in a sympathetic relation between a man and an animal such that the fate of the one depends on that of the other.

But in practice, as in folk-tales, it is not merely with inanimate objects and plants that a person is occasionally believed to be united by a bond of physical sympathy. The same bond, it is supposed, may exist between a man and an animal, so that the welfare of the one depends on the welfare of the other, and when the animal dies the man dies also. The analogy between the custom and the tales is all the closer because in both of them the power of thus removing the soul from the body and stowing it away in an animal is often a special privilege of wizards and witches. Thus the Yakuts of Siberia

The external souls of Yakut shamans in animals.

believe that every shaman or wizard keeps his soul, or one of his souls, incarnate in an animal which is carefully concealed from all the world. 'Nobody can find my external soul,' said one famous wizard, 'it lies hidden far away in the stony mountains of Edzhigansk.' Only once a year, when the last snows melt and the earth turns black, do these external souls of wizards appear in the shape of animals among the dwellings of men. They wander everywhere, yet none but wizards can see them. The strong ones sweep roaring and noisily along, the weak steal about quietly and furtively. Often they fight, and then the wizard whose external soul is beaten, falls ill or dies. The weakest and most cowardly wizards are they whose souls are incarnate in the shape of dogs, for the dog gives his human double no peace, but gnaws his heart and tears his body. The most powerful wizards are they whose external souls have the shape of stallions, elks, black bears, eagles, or boars. Again, the Samoyeds of the Turukhinsk region hold that every shaman has a familiar spirit in the shape of a boar, which he leads about by a magic belt. On the death of the boar the shaman himself dies; and stories are told of battles between wizards, who send their spirits to fight before they encounter each other in person. In Yorkshire witches are thought to stand in such peculiarly close relations to hares, that if a particular hare is killed or wounded, a certain witch will at the same moment be killed or receive a hurt in her body exactly corresponding to the wound in the hare. However, this fancy is probably a case of the general European belief that witches have the power of temporarily transforming themselves into certain animals, particularly hares and cats, and that any hurts inflicted on such transformed animals are felt by the witches who are concealed in the animals. But the notion that a person can temporarily transform himself into an animal differs from the notion that he can deposit his soul for a longer or shorter period in an animal, while he himself retains the human form; though in the cloudy mind of the peasant and the savage the two ideas may not always be sharply distinguished. The Malays believe that 'the soul of a person may pass into another person or into an animal, or rather that such a mysterious relation can arise between the two that the fate of the one is wholly dependent on that of the other'.

Sympathetic relation between witches and hares.

Among the Melanesians of Mota, one of the New Hebrides islands, the conception of an external soul is carried out in the practice of daily life. The Mota word for soul is *atai*. 'The use of the word *atai* in Mota seems properly and originally to have been to signify something peculiarly and intimately connected with a person and sacred to him, something that he has set his fancy upon when he has seen it in what has seemed to him a wonderful manner, or some one has shewn it to him as such. Whatever the thing might be the man believed it to be the reflection of his own personality; he and his *atai* flourished, suffered, lived, and died together. But the word must not be supposed to have been borrowed from this use and applied secondarily to describe the soul; the word carries a sense with it which is applicable alike to that second self, the visible object so mysteriously connected with the man, and to this invisible second self which we call the soul. There is another Mota word, *tamaniu*, which has almost if not quite the same meaning as *atai* has when it describes something animate or inanimate which a man has come to believe to have an existence intimately connected with his own. The word *tamaniu* may be taken to be

Melanesian conception of the *tamaniu*, a person's external soul lodged in an animal or other object.

properly "likeness", and the noun form of the adverb *tama*, as, like. It was not every one in Mota who had his *tamaniu*; only some men fancied that they had this relation to a lizard, a snake, or it might be a stone; sometimes the thing was sought for and found by drinking the infusion of certain leaves and heaping together the dregs; then whatever living thing was first seen in or upon the heap was the *tamaniu*. It was watched but not fed or worshipped; the natives believed that it came at call, and that the life of the man was bound up with the life of his *tamaniu*, if a living thing, or with its safety; should it die, or if not living get broken or be lost, the man would die. Hence in case of sickness they would send to see if the *tamaniu* was safe and well. This word has never been used apparently for the soul in Mota; but in Aurora in the New Hebrides it is the accepted equivalent. It is well worth observing that both the *atai* and the *tamaniu*, and it may be added the Motlav *talegi*, is something which has a substantial existence of its own, as when a snake or stone is a man's *atai* or *tamaniu*; a soul then when called by these names is conceived of as something in a way substantial.'

From this account, which we owe to the careful and accurate researches of the Revd Dr Codrington, we gather that while every person in Mota has a second self or external soul in a visible object called an *atai*, only some people have, it may be, a second external soul in another visible object called a *tamaniu*. We may conjecture that persons who have a *tamaniu* in addition to an *atai* are more than usually anxious as to the state of their soul, and that they seek to put it in perfect security by what we may call a system of double insurance, calculating that if one of their external souls should die or be broken, they themselves may still survive by virtue of the survival of the other. Be that as it may, the *tamaniu* discharges two functions, one of them defensive and the other offensive. On the one hand, so long as it lives or remains unbroken, it preserves its owner in life; and on the other hand it helps him to injure his enemies. In its offensive character, if the *tamaniu* happens to be an eel, it will bite its owner's enemy; if it is a shark, it will swallow him. In its defensive character, the state of the *tamaniu* is a symptom or life-token of the state of the man; hence when he is ill he will visit and examine it, or if he cannot go himself he will send another to inspect it and report. In either case the man turns the animal, if animal it be, carefully over in order to see what is the matter with it; should something be found sticking to its skin, it is removed, and through the relief thus afforded to the creature the sick man recovers. But if the animal should be found dying, it is an omen of death for the man; for whenever it dies he dies also.

The theory of an external soul deposited in an animal appears to be very prevalent in West Africa, particularly in Nigeria, the Cameroons, and the Gaboon. In the latter part of the nineteenth century two English missionaries, established at San Salvador, the capital of the King of Congo, asked the natives repeatedly whether any of them had seen the strange, big, East African goat which Stanley had given to a chief at Stanley Pool in 1877. But their enquiries were fruitless; no native would admit that he had seen the goat. Some years afterwards the missionaries discovered why they could obtain no reply to their enquiry. All the people, it turned out, imagined that the missionaries believed the spirit of the King of Salvador to be contained in the goat, and that they wished to obtain possession of the animal in order to exercise an evil influence on his majesty. The belief from the standpoint of the Congo savages was natural enough, since in that region some chiefs regularly link their fate to that of an animal. Thus the Chief Bankwa of Ndolo, on the Moeko River, had conferred this honour on a certain hippopotamus of the neighbourhood, at which he would allow nobody to shoot. At the village of Ongek, in the Gaboon, a French missionary* slept in the hut of an old Fan chief. Awakened about two in the morning by a rustling of dry leaves, he lit a torch, when to his horror he perceived a huge black serpent of the most dangerous sort, coiled in a corner, with head erect, shining eyes, and hissing jaws, ready to dart at him. Instinctively he seized his gun and pointed it at the reptile, when suddenly his arm was struck up, the torch was extinguished, and the voice of the old chief said, 'Don't fire! don't fire! I beg of you. In killing the serpent, it is me that you would kill. Fear nothing. The serpent is my *elangela*.' So saying he flung himself on his knees beside the reptile, put his arms about it, and clasped it to his breast. The serpent received his caresses quietly, manifesting neither anger nor fear, and the chief carried it off and laid it down beside him in another hut, exhorting the missionary to have no

The theory of an external soul lodged in an animal is very prevalent in West Africa.

The soul of a chief in a hippopotamus or a black snake.

Belief of the
Fans that
every wiz-
ard unites
his life to
that of a
wild animal
by a rite of
blood
brother-
hood.

fear and never to speak of the subject. His curiosity being excited by this adventure, the missionary, Father Trilles, pursued his enquiries and ascertained that among the Fans of the Gaboon every wizard is believed at initiation to unite his life with that of some particular wild animal by a rite of blood-brotherhood; he draws blood from the ear of the animal and from his own arm, and inoculates the animal with his own blood, and himself with the blood of the beast. Henceforth such an intimate union is established between the two that the death of the one entails the death of the other. The alliance is thought to bring to the wizard or sorcerer a great accession of power, which he can turn to his advantage in various ways. In the first place, like the warlock in the fairy tales who has deposited his life outside of himself in some safe place, the Fan wizard now deems himself invulnerable. Moreover, the animal with which he has exchanged blood has become his familiar, and will obey any orders he may choose to give it; so he makes use of it to injure and kill his enemies. For that reason the creature with whom he establishes the relation of blood-brotherhood is never a tame or domestic animal, but always a ferocious and dangerous wild beast, such as a leopard, a black serpent, a crocodile, a hippopotamus, a wild boar, or a vulture. Of all these creatures the leopard is by far the commonest familiar of Fan wizards, and next to it comes the black serpent; the vulture is the rarest. Witches as well as wizards have their familiars; but the animals with which the lives of women are thus bound up generally differ from those to which men commit their external souls. A witch never has a panther for her familiar, but often a venomous species of serpent, sometimes a horned viper, sometimes a black serpent, sometimes a green one that lives in banana-trees; or it may be a vulture, an owl, or other bird of night. In every case the beast or bird with which the witch or wizard has contracted this mystic alliance is an individual, never a species; and when the individual animal dies the alliance is naturally at an end, since the death of the animal is supposed to entail the death of the man.

Belief of
the Ibos in
external
human souls
which

A similar belief in the external souls of living people is entertained by the Ibos. They think that a man's spirit can quit his body for a time during life and take up its abode in an animal. This is called *ishi anu*, 'to turn animal'. A man who wishes to acquire this power procures a certain drug from a wise man and mixes it with his food. After that his soul goes out and enters into the animal. If it should happen that the animal is killed while the man's soul is lodged in it, the man dies; and if the animal be wounded, the man's body will presently be covered with boils. This belief instigates to many deeds of darkness; for a sly rogue will sometimes surreptitiously administer the magical drug to his enemy in his food, and having thus smuggled the other's soul into an animal will destroy the creature, and with it the man whose soul is lodged in it. A like belief is reported to prevail among the tribes of the Obubura Hill district on the Cross River in Southern Nigeria. Once when Mr Partridge's canoe-men wished to catch fish near a town of the Assiga tribe, the people objected, saying, 'Our souls live in those fish, and if you kill them we shall die.'

The negroes of Calabar, at the mouth of the Niger, believe that every person has four souls, one of which always lives outside of his or her body in the form of a wild beast in the forest. This external soul, or bush soul, as Miss Kingsley calls it, may be almost any animal, for example, a leopard, a fish, or a tortoise; but it is never a domestic animal and never a plant. Unless he is gifted with second sight, a man cannot see his own bush soul, but a diviner will often tell him what sort of creature his bush soul is, and after that the man will be careful not to kill any animal of that species, and will strongly object to any one else doing so. A man and his sons have usually the same sort of animals for their bush souls, and so with a mother and her daughters. But sometimes all the children of a family take after the bush soul of their father; for example, if his external soul is a leopard, all his sons and daughters will have leopards for their external souls. And on the other hand, sometimes they all take after their mother; for instance, if her external soul is a tortoise, all the external souls of her sons and daughters will be tortoises too. So intimately bound up is the life of the man with that of the animal which he regards as his external or bush soul, that the death or injury of the animal necessarily entails the death or injury of the man. And, conversely, when the man dies, his bush soul can no longer find a place of rest, but goes mad and rushes into the fire or charges people and is knocked on the head, and that is an end of it. When a person is sick, the

(marginal notes)
are lodged in animals.

Belief of the negroes of Calabar that every person has an external or bush soul lodged in a wild beast.

diviner will sometimes tell him that his bush soul is angry at being neglected; thereupon the patient will make an offering to the offended spirit and deposit it in a tiny hut in the forest at the spot where the animal, which is his external soul, was last seen. If the bush soul is appeased, the patient recovers; but if it is not, he dies. Yet the foolish bush soul does not understand that in injuring the man it injures itself, and that it cannot long survive his decease.

The conception of an external soul lodged in an animal occurs among the Indians of Central America, some of whom call such a soul a *nagual*.

Amongst the Zapotecs of Central America, when a woman was about to be confined, her relations assembled in the hut, and began to draw on the floor figures of different animals, rubbing each one out as soon as it was completed. This went on till the moment of birth, and the figure that then remained sketched upon the ground was called the child's *tona* or second self. 'When the child grew old enough, he procured the animal that represented him and took care of it, as it was believed that health and existence were bound up with that of the animal's, in fact that the death of both would occur simultaneously', or rather that when the animal died the man would die too. Among the Indians of Guatemala and Honduras the *nagual* or *naual* is 'that animate or inanimate object, generally an animal, which stands in a parallel relation to a particular man, so that the weal and woe of the man depend on the fate of the *nagual*'. According to an old writer, many Indians of Guatemala 'are deluded by the devil to believe that their life dependeth upon the life of such and such a beast (which they take unto them as their familiar spirit), and think that when that beast dieth they must die; when he is chased, their hearts pant; when he is faint, they are faint; nay, it happeneth that by the devil's delusion they appear in the shape of that beast (which commonly by their choice is a buck, or doe, a lion, or tigre, or dog, or eagle) and in that shape have been shot at and wounded.' Herrera's account of the way in which the Indians of Honduras acquired their *naguals*, runs thus: 'The devil deluded them, appearing in the shape of a lion or a tiger, or a coyte, a beast like a wolf, or in the shape of an alligator, a snake, or a bird, that province abounding in creatures of prey, which they called *naguales*, signifying keepers or guardians, and when the bird died the Indian that was in league with him died also, which often happened and was looked upon as infallible. The manner of

contracting this alliance was thus. The Indian repaired to the
river, wood, hill, or most obscure place, where he called upon
the devils by such names as he thought fit, talked to the rivers,
rocks, or woods, said he went to weep that he might have the
same his predecessors had, carrying a cock or a dog to sacrifice.
In that melancholy fit he fell asleep, and either in a dream or
waking saw some one of the aforesaid birds or other creatures,
whom he entreated to grant him profit in salt, cacao, or any
other commodity, drawing blood from his own tongue, ears, and
other parts of his body, making his contract at the same time
with the said creature, the which either in a dream or waking
told him, "Such a day you shall go abroad asporting, and I will
be the first bird or other animal you shall meet, and will be your
nagual and companion at all times." Whereupon such friendship
was contracted between them, that when one of them died the
other did not survive, and they fancied that he who had no
nagual could not be rich.' The Indians were persuaded that the
death of their *nagual* would entail their own. Legend affirms
that in the first battles with the Spaniards on the plateau of
Quetzaltenango the *naguals* of the Indian chiefs fought in the
form of serpents. The *nagual* of the highest chief was especially
conspicuous, because it had the form of a great bird, resplend-
ent in green plumage. The Spanish general Pedro de Alvarado
killed the bird with his lance, and at the same moment the
Indian chief fell dead to the ground.

In many tribes of South-Eastern Australia each sex used to
regard a particular species of animals in the same way that a
Central American Indian regarded his *nagual*, but with this
difference, that whereas the Indian apparently knew the individual animal with which his life was bound up, the Australians
only knew that each of their lives was bound up with some one
animal of the species, but they could not say with which. The
result naturally was that every man spared and protected all the
animals of the species with which the lives of the men were
bound up; and every woman spared and protected all the
animals of the species with which the lives of the women were
bound up; because no one knew but that the death of any
animal of the respective species might entail his or her own; just
as the killing of the green bird was immediately followed by the
death of the Indian chief, and the killing of the parrot by

In some
tribes of
South-East-
ern Australia
the lives of
the two sexes
are thought
to be bound
up with the
lives of the
two different
kinds of an-
imals, as bats
and owls.

the death of Punchkin in the fairy tale. Thus, for example, the Wotjobaluk tribe of South-Eastern Australia 'held that "the life of Ngŭnŭngŭnŭt (the Bat) is the life of a man, and the life of Yártatgŭrk (the Nightjar) is the life of a woman", and that when either of these creatures is killed the life of some man or of some woman is shortened. In such a case every man or every woman in the camp feared that he or she might be the victim, and from this cause great fights arose in this tribe. I learn that in these fights, men on one side and women on the other, it was not at all certain which would be victorious, for at times the women gave the men a severe drubbing with their yamsticks, while often women were injured or killed by spears.' The Wotjobaluk said that the bat was the man's 'brother' and that the nightjar was his 'wife'. The particular species of animals with which the lives of the sexes were believed to be respectively bound up varied somewhat from tribe to tribe. Thus whereas among the Wotjobaluk the bat was the animal of the men, at Gunbower Creek on the Lower Murray the bat seems to have been the animal of the women, for the natives would not kill it for the reason that 'if it was killed, one of their lubras [women] would be sure to die in consequence'. In the Kurnai tribe of Gippsland the emu-wren (*Stipiturus malachurus*) was the 'man's brother' and the superb warbler (*Malurus cyaneus*) was the 'woman's sister'; at the initiation of young men into the tribal mysteries the name of the emu-wren was invoked over the novices for the purpose of infusing manly virtue into them. Among the Yuin on the south-eastern coast of Australia, the 'woman's sister' was the tree-creeper (*Climacteris scandens*), and the men had both the bat and the emu-wren for their 'brothers'. In the Kulin nation each sex had a pair of 'brothers' and 'sisters'; the men had the bat and the emu-wren for their 'brothers', and the women had the superb warbler and the small nightjar for their 'sisters'. It is notable that in South-Eastern Australia the animals thus associated with the lives of men and women were generally flying creatures, either birds or bats. However, in the Port Lincoln tribe of South Australia the man's 'brother' and the woman's 'sister' seem to have been identified with the male and female respectively of a species of lizard; for we read that 'a small kind of lizard, the male of which is called *ibirri*, and the female *waka*, is said to have divided the sexes in the human species; an event that would appear not to be much approved of by the natives, since either sex has a mortal hatred against the opposite sex of these little animals, the men always destroying the *waka* and the women the *ibirri*.' But whatever the particular sorts of creature with which the lives of men and women were believed to be bound up, the belief itself and the fights to which it gave rise are known to have prevailed over a large part of South-Eastern Australia, and probably they extended much farther. The belief was a very serious one, and so consequently were the fights which sprang from it. Thus among some tribes of Victoria 'the common bat belongs to the men, who protect it against injury, even to the half-killing of their wives for its sake. The fern owl, or large goatsucker, belongs to the women, and, although a bird of evil omen, creating terror at night by its cry, it is jealously protected by them. If a man kills one, they are as much enraged as if it was one of their children, and will strike him with their long poles.'

The jealous protection thus afforded by Australian men and women to bats and owls respectively (for bats and owls seem to be the creatures usually allotted to the two sexes) is not based upon purely selfish considerations. For each man believes that not only his own life but the lives of his father, brothers, sons, and so on are bound up with the lives of particular bats, and that therefore in protecting the bat species he is protecting the lives of all his male relations as well as his own. Similarly, each woman believes that the lives of her mother, sisters, daughters, and so forth, equally with her own, are bound up with the lives of particular owls, and that in guarding the owl species she is guarding the lives of all her female relations besides her own. Now, when men's lives are thus supposed to be contained in certain animals, it is obvious that the animals can hardly be distinguished from the men, or the men from the animals. If my brother John's life is in a bat, then, on the one hand, the bat is my brother as well as John; and, on the other hand, John is in a sense a bat, since his life is in a bat. Similarly, if my sister Mary's life is in an owl, then the owl is my sister and Mary is an owl. This is a natural enough conclusion, and the Australians have not failed to draw it. When the bat is the man's animal, it is called his brother; and when the owl is the woman's animal, it is called her sister. And conversely a man addresses a woman

Bats regarded as the brothers of men, and owls as the sisters of women.

as an owl, and she addresses him as a bat. So with the other animals allotted to the sexes respectively in other tribes. For example, among the Kurnai all emu-wrens were 'brothers' of the men, and all the men were emu-wrens; all superb warblers were 'sisters' of the women, and all the women were superb warblers.

CHAPTER 5

DEATH AND RESURRECTION

i

BUT when a savage names himself after an animal, calls it his brother, and refuses to kill it, the animal is said to be his totem. Accordingly in the tribes of South-Eastern Australia which we have been considering the bat and the owl, the emu-wren and the superb warbler, may properly be described as totems of the sexes. But the assignation of a totem to a sex is comparatively rare, and has hitherto been discovered nowhere but in Australia. Far more commonly the totem is appropriated not to a sex, but to a clan, and is hereditary either in the male or female line. The relation of an individual to the clan totem does not differ in kind from his relation to the sex totem; he will not kill it, he speaks of it as his brother, and he calls himself by its name. Now if the relations are similar, the explanation which holds good of the one ought equally to hold good of the other. Therefore the reason why a clan revere a particular species of animals or plants (for the clan totem may be a plant) and call themselves after it, would seem to be a belief that the life of each individual of the clan is bound up with some one animal or plant of the species, and that his or her death would be the consequence of killing that particular animal, or destroying that particular plant. This explanation of totemism squares very well with Sir George Grey's definition of a totem or *kobong* in Western Australia. He says: 'A certain mysterious connection exists between a family and its *kobong*, so that a member of the family will never kill an animal of the species to which his *kobong* belongs, should he find it asleep; indeed he always kills it reluctantly, and never without affording it a chance to escape. This arises from the family belief that some one individual of the species is their nearest friend, to kill whom would be a great crime, and to be carefully avoided. Similarly, a native who has a vegetable for his *kobong* may not gather it under certain circumstances, and at a particular period of the year.'* Here it will be observed that though each man spares all the animals or

Sex totems and clan totems may both be based on the notion that men and women keep their external souls in their totems, whether these are animals, plants, or what not.

plants of the species, they are not all equally precious to him; far from it, out of the whole species there is only one which is specially dear to him; but as he does not know which the dear one is, he is obliged to spare them all from fear of injuring the one. Again, this explanation of the clan totem harmonizes with the supposed effect of killing one of the totem species. 'One day one of the blacks killed a crow. Three or four days afterwards a Boortwa (crow) [*i.e.* a man of the Crow clan] named Larry died. He had been ailing for some days, but the killing of his *wingong* [totem] hastened his death.' Here the killing of the crow caused the death of a man of the Crow clan, exactly as, in the case of the sex-totems, the killing of a bat causes the death

of a Bat-man or the killing of an owl causes the death of an Owl-woman. Similarly, the killing of his *nagual* causes the death of a Central American Indian, the killing of his bush soul causes the death of a Calabar negro, the killing of his *tamaniu* causes the death of a Banks Islander, and the killing of the animal in which his life is stowed away causes the death of the giant or warlock in the fairy tale.

Thus it appears that the story of 'The giant who had no heart in his body' may perhaps furnish the key to the relation which is supposed to subsist between a man and his totem. The totem, on this theory, is simply the receptacle in which a man keeps his life, as Punchkin kept his life in a parrot.*

ii

This view of totemism throws light on a class of religious rites of which no adequate explanation, so far as I am aware, has yet been offered. Amongst many savage tribes, especially such as are known to practise totemism, it is customary for lads at puberty to undergo certain initiatory rites, of which one of the commonest is a pretence of killing the lad and bringing him to life again. Such rites become intelligible if we suppose that their substance consists in extracting the youth's soul in order to transfer it to his totem. For the extraction of his soul would naturally be supposed to kill the youth or at least to throw him into a death-like trance, which the savage hardly distinguishes from death. His recovery would then be attributed either to the gradual recovery of his system from the violent shock which it had received, or, more probably, to the infusion into him of fresh life drawn from the totem. Thus the essence of these initiatory rites, so far as they consist in a simulation of death and resurrection, would be an exchange of life or souls between the man and his totem. The primitive belief in the possibility of such an exchange of souls comes clearly out in the story of the Basque hunter who affirmed that he had been killed by a bear, but that the bear had, after killing him, breathed its own soul into him, so that the bear's body was now dead, but he himself was a bear, being animated by the bear's soul. This revival of the dead hunter as a bear is exactly analogous to what, on the theory here suggested, is supposed to take place in the ceremony of killing a lad at puberty and bringing him to life again. The lad dies as a man and comes to life again as an animal; the animal's soul is now in him, and his human soul is in the animal. With good right, therefore, does he call himself a Bear or a Wolf, etc., according to his totem; and with good right does he treat the bears or the wolves, etc., as his brethren, since in these animals are lodged the souls of himself and his kindred.

Among the tribes settled on the southern coast of New South Wales, of which the Coast Murring tribe may be regarded as typical, the drama of resurrection from the dead was exhibited in a graphic form to the novices at initiation. Before they were privileged to witness this edifying spectacle they had been raised to the dignity of manhood by an old man, who promoted them to their new status by the simple process of knocking a tooth out of the mouth of each with the help of a wooden chisel and hammer. The ceremony of the resurrection has been described for us in detail by an eye-witness, the late Dr A. W. Howitt, one of the best authorities on the customs of the Australian aborigines. The scene selected for the sacred drama was the bottom of a deep valley, where a sluggish stream wound through a bed of tall sharp-edged sedge. Though the hour was between ten and eleven o'clock in the morning, the sun had but just peeped over the mountains which enclosed the valley like a wall on the east; and while the upper slopes, clothed with a forest of tall rowan trees, looked warm and bright in sunshine, which shot between the grey stems and under the light feathery foliage of the trees, all the bottom of the dell was still in deep

A drama of resurrection from the dead used to be shewn to novices at initiation in some tribes of New South Wales. Dr Howitt's description of the scene.

shadow and dank with the moisture of the night's rain. While the novices rested and warmed themselves at a crackling fire, the initiated men laid their heads together, prepared a stock of decorations made of stringy bark, and dug a grave. There was some discussion as to the shape of the grave, but the man who was to be buried in it decided the question by declaring that he would be laid in it on his back at full length. He was a man of the eagle-hawk totem and belonged to the tribal subdivision called Yibai. So while two men under his directions were digging the grave with sticks in the friable granitic soil, he superintended the costume of the other actors in the drama. Sheets of bark were beaten out into fleeces of stringy fibre, and in these garments six performers were clothed from head to foot so that not even a glimpse could be obtained of their faces. Four of them were tied together by a cord which was fastened to the back of their heads, and each of them carried two pieces of bark in his hands. The other two walked free, but hobbled along bent double and supporting their tottery steps on staves to mark the weight of years; for they played the part of two medicine-men of venerable age and great magical power. By this time the grave was ready, and the eagle-hawk man stretched himself in it at full length on a bed of leaves, his head resting on a rolled-up blanket, just as if he were a corpse. In his two hands, crossed on his chest, he held the stem of a young tree (*Persoonia linearis*), which had been pulled up by the roots and now stood planted on his chest, so that the top of it rose several feet above the level of the ground. A light covering of dried sticks filled the grave, and dead leaves, tufts of grass, and small plants were artistically arranged over them so as to complete the illusion. All being now ready, the novices were led by their sisters' husbands to the grave and placed in a row beside it, while a singer, perched on the trunk of a fallen tree at the head of the grave, crooned a melancholy ditty, the song of Yibai. Though the words of the song consisted merely of a monotonous repetition of the words *Burrin-burrin Yibai*, that is, Stringy-bark Yibai, they were understood to refer to the eagle-hawk totem, as well as to the tribal subdivision of the buried man. Then to the slow, plaintive but well-marked air of the song the actors began to move forward, winding among the trees, logs, and rocks. On came the four disguised men, stepping in time to

The seeming dead man in the grave.

the music, swaying from side to side, and clashing their bark clappers together at every step, while beside them hobbled the two old men keeping a little aloof to mark their superior dignity. They represented a party of medicine-men, guided by two reverend seniors, who had come on pilgrimage to the grave of a brother medicine-man, him of the eagle-hawk totem, who lay buried here in the lonely valley, now illumined by the warm rays of the sun; for by this time the morning was wearing on to noon. When the little procession, chanting an invocation to Daramulun, had defiled from among the rocks and trees into the open, it drew up on the side of the grave opposite to the novices, the two old men taking up a position in the rear of the dancers. For some time the dance and song went on till the tree that seemed to grow from the grave began to quiver. 'Look there!' cried the sisters' husbands to the novices, pointing to the trembling leaves. As they looked, the tree quivered more and more, then was violently agitated and fell to the ground, while amid the excited dancing of the dancers and the chanting of the tuneful choir the supposed dead man spurned from him the superincumbent mass of sticks and leaves, and springing to his feet danced his magic dance in the grave itself, and exhibited in his mouth the magic substances which he was supposed to have received from Daramulun in person.

The resurrection from the grave.

In certain districts of Viti Levu, the largest of the Fijian Islands, the drama of death and resurrection used to be acted with much solemnity before the eyes of young men at initiation. The ceremonies were performed in certain sacred precincts of oblong shape, enclosed by low walls or rows of stones but open to the sky. In these open-air temples of the dead the ceremony of initiating young men was performed as a rule every year at the end of October or the beginning of November, which was the commencement of the Fijian New Year; hence the novices who were initiated at that season went by the name of *Vilavou* or New Year's Men. The exact time for celebrating the rite was determined by the flowering of the *ndrala* tree (*Erythrina*); but it roughly coincided with the New Year of the Tahitians and Hawaiians, who dated the commencement of the year by observation of the Pleiades. The highlanders of Fiji, who alone celebrated these rites, did not trouble their heads about the stars. As a preparation for the solemnity the heads of the

The drama of death and resurrection used to be enacted before young men at initiation in some parts of Fiji.

Description of the rite.

novices were shaved and their beards, if they had any, were carefully eradicated. On four successive days they went in procession to the temple and there deposited in the Holy of Holies their offerings of cloth and weapons to the ancestral spirits. But on the fifth and great day of the festival, when they again entered the sacred ground, they beheld a sight which froze their souls with horror. Stretched on the ground was a row of dead or seemingly dead and murdered men, their bodies cut open and covered with blood, their entrails protruding. At the further end sat the High Priest, regarding them with a stony glare, and to reach him the trembling novices had to crawl on hands and knees over the ghastly blood-bedabbled corpses that lay between. Having done so they drew up in a line before him. Suddenly he blurted out a piercing yell, at which the counterfeit dead men started to their feet and ran down to the river to cleanse themselves from the blood and guts of pigs with which they were beslobbered. The High Priest now unbent his starched dignity, and skipping from side to side cried in stridulous tones, 'Where are the people of my enclosure? Are they gone to Tonga Levu? Are they gone to the deep sea?' He was soon answered by a deep-mouthed chant, and back from the river marched the dead men come to life, clean, fresh, and garlanded, swaying their bodies in time to the music of their solemn hymn. They took their places in front of the novices and a religious silence ensued. Such was the drama of death and resurrection.

The Akikuyu of East Africa 'have a curious custom which requires that every boy just before circumcision must be born again. The mother stands up with the boy crouching at her feet; she pretends to go through all the labour pains, and the boy on being reborn cries like a babe and is washed. He lives on milk for some days afterwards.' A fuller description of the ceremony was given by a member of the Kikuyu tribe as follows: 'A day is appointed, any time of year, by father and mother. If the father is dead another elder is called in to act as proxy in his stead, or if the mother is not living another woman to act in her place. Any woman thus acting as representative is looked upon in future by the boy as his own mother. A goat or sheep is killed in the afternoon by any one, usually not by the father, and the stomach and intestines reserved. The ceremony begins in the evening. A piece of skin is cut in a circle, and passed over one

The mimic death.

The mimic resurrection.

Ritual of the new birth among the Akikuyu of British East Africa.

shoulder of the candidate and under the other arm. The stomach of the goat is similarly treated and passed over the other shoulder and under the other arm. All the boy's ornaments are removed, but not his clothes. No men are allowed inside the hut, but women are present. The mother sits on a hide on the floor with the boy between her knees. The sheep's gut is passed round the woman and brought in front of the boy. The woman groans as in labour, another woman cuts the gut, and the boy imitates the cry of a new-born infant. The women present all applaud, and afterwards the assistant and the mother wash the boy. That night the boy sleeps in the same hut as the mother.' Here the cutting of the sheep's gut, which unites the mother to the boy, is clearly an imitation of severing the navel string. Nor is it boys alone who are born again among the Akikuyu. 'Girls go through the rite of second birth as well as boys. It is sometimes administered to infants. At one time the new birth was combined with circumcision, and so the ceremony admitted to the privileges and religious rites of the tribe. Afterwards trouble took place on account of mere boys wishing to take their place alongside of the young men and maintaining they were justified in doing so. The old men then settled the matter by separating the two. Unless the new birth has been administered the individual is not in a position to be admitted to circumcision, which is the outward sign of admittance to the nation. Any who have not gone through the rite cannot inherit property, nor take any part in the religious rites of the country.' For example, a man who has not been born again is disqualified for carrying his dying father out into the wilds and for disposing of his body after death. The new birth seems to take place usually about the tenth year, but the age varies with the ability of the father to provide a goat, whose guts are necessary to enable the boy or girl to be born again in due form.

Among the Indians of Virginia, an initiatory ceremony, called *Huskanaw*, took place every sixteen or twenty years, or oftener, as the young men happened to grow up. The youths were kept in solitary confinement in the woods for several months, receiving no food but an infusion of some intoxicating roots, so that they went raving mad, and continued in this state eighteen or twenty days. 'Upon this occasion it is pretended that these poor creatures drink so much of the water of Lethe that they

Rites of initiation among the Indians of Virginia: pretence of the novices that they have forgotten their former life.

perfectly lose the remembrance of all former things, even of their parents, their treasure, and their language. When the doctors find that they have drunk sufficiently of the Wysoccan (so they call this mad potion), they gradually restore them to their senses again by lessening the intoxication of their diet; but before they are perfectly well they bring them back into their towns, while they are still wild and crazy through the violence of the medicine. After this they are very fearful of discovering anything of their former remembrance; for if such a thing should happen to any of them, they must immediately be *Huskanaw'd* again; and the second time the usage is so severe that seldom any one escapes with life. Thus they must pretend to have forgot the very use of their tongues, so as not to be able to speak, nor understand anything that is spoken, till they learn it again. Now, whether this be real or counterfeit, I don't know; but certain it is that they will not for some time take notice of anybody nor anything with which they were before acquainted, being still under the guard of their keepers, who constantly wait upon them everywhere till they have learnt all things perfectly over again. Thus they unlive their former lives, and commence men by forgetting that they ever have been boys.'*

The motive for attempting to deposit the soul in a safe place outside of the body at puberty may have been a fear of the dangers which, according to primitive notions, attend the union of the sexes.

Thus, on the theory here suggested, wherever totemism is found, and wherever a pretence is made of killing and bringing to life again the novice at initiation, there may exist or have existed not only a belief in the possibility of permanently depositing the soul in some external object—animal, plant, or what not—but an actual intention of so doing. If the question is put, why do men desire to deposit their life outside their bodies? the answer can only be that, like the giant in the fairy tale, they think it safer to do so than to carry it about with them, just as people deposit their money with a banker rather than carry it on their persons. We have seen that at critical periods the life or soul is sometimes temporarily stowed away in a safe place till the danger is past. But institutions like totemism are not resorted to merely on special occasions of danger; they are systems into which every one, or at least every male, is obliged to be initiated at a certain period of life. Now the period of life at which initiation takes place is regularly puberty; and this fact suggests that the special danger which totemism and systems like it are intended to obviate is supposed not to arise till sexual maturity has been attained, in fact, that the danger apprehended is believed to attend the relation of the sexes to each other. It would be easy to prove by a long array of facts that the sexual relation is associated in the primitive mind with many serious perils; but the exact nature of the danger apprehended is still obscure.* We may hope that a more exact acquaintance with savage modes of thought will in time disclose this central mystery of primitive society, and will thereby furnish the clue, not only to totemism, but to the origin of the marriage system.

CHAPTER 6

THE GOLDEN BOUGH

i

Balder's life
or death in
the mistletoe.

THUS the view that Balder's life was in the mistletoe is entirely in harmony with primitive modes of thought. It may indeed sound like a contradiction that, if his life was in the mistletoe, he should nevertheless have been killed by a blow from the plant. But when a person's life is conceived as embodied in a particular object, with the existence of which his own existence is inseparably bound up, and the destruction of which involves his own, the object in question may be regarded and spoken of indifferently as his life or his death, as happens in the fairy tales. Hence if a man's death is in an object, it is perfectly natural that he should be killed by a blow from it. In the fairy tales Koshchei the Deathless is killed by a blow from the egg or the stone in which his life or death is secreted; the ogres burst when a certain grain of sand—doubtless containing their life or death—is carried over their heads; the magician dies when the stone in which his life or death is contained is put under his pillow; and the Tartar hero is warned that he may be killed by the golden arrow or golden sword in which his soul has been stowed away.

The view
that the mis-
tletoe con-
tained the
life of the
oak may have
been sug-
gested by the
position of
the parasite
among the
boughs.

The idea that the life of the oak was in the mistletoe was probably suggested, as I have said, by the observation that in winter the mistletoe growing on the oak remains green while the oak itself is leafless. But the position of the plant—growing not from the ground but from the trunk or branches of the tree—might confirm this idea. Primitive man might think that, like himself, the oak-spirit had sought to deposit his life in some safe place, and for this purpose had pitched on the mistletoe, which, being in a sense neither on earth nor in heaven, might be supposed to be fairly out of harm's way. In the first chapter we saw that primitive man seeks to preserve the life of his human divinities by keeping them poised between earth and heaven, as the place where they are least likely to be assailed by the dangers that encompass the life of man on earth. We can therefore understand why it has been a rule both of ancient and of modern folk-medicine that the mistletoe should not be allowed to touch the ground; were it to touch the ground, its healing virtue would be gone.

Again, the view that the mistletoe owes its mystic character partly to its not growing on the ground is confirmed by a parallel superstition about the mountain-ash or rowan-tree. In Jutland a rowan that is found growing out of the top of another tree is esteemed 'exceedingly effective against witchcraft: since it does not grow on the ground witches have no power over it; if it is to have its full effect it must be cut on Ascension Day.' Hence it is placed over doors to prevent the ingress of witches. In Sweden and Norway, also, magical properties are ascribed to a 'flying-rowan' (*flögrönn*), that is to a rowan which is found growing not in the ordinary fashion on the ground but on another tree, or on a roof, or in a cleft of the rock, where it has sprouted from seed scattered by birds. They say that a man who is out in the dark should have a bit of 'flying-rowan' with him to chew; else he runs a risk of being bewitched and of being unable to stir from the spot. A Norwegian story relates how once on a time a Troll so bewitched some men who were ploughing in a field that they could not drive a straight furrow; only one of the ploughmen was able to resist the enchantment because by good luck his plough was made out of a 'flying-rowan'. In Sweden, too, the 'flying-rowan' is used to make the divining rod, which discovers hidden treasures. This useful art has nowadays unfortunately been almost forgotten, but three hundred years ago it was in full bloom, as we gather from the following contemporary account. 'If in the woods or elsewhere, on old walls or on high mountains or rocks you perceive a rowan-tree (*runn*) which has sprung from a seed that a bird has dropped from its bill, you must either knock or break off that rod or tree in the twilight between the third day and the night after Ladyday. But you must take care that neither iron nor steel touches it and that in carrying it home you do not let it fall on the ground. Then place it under the roof on a spot under which you have laid various metals, and you will soon be surprised to see how that rod under the roof gradually bends in the direction of the metals. When your rod has sat there in the same spot for fourteen days or more, you take a knife or an awl,

Analogous superstitions attaching to a parasitic rowan.

which has been stroked with a magnet, and with it you slit the
bark on all sides, and pour or drop the blood of a cock (best of
all the blood from the comb of a cock which is all of one colour)
on the said slits in the bark; and when the blood has dried, the
rod is ready and will give public proof of the efficacy of its
marvellous properties.' Just as in Scandinavia the parasitic
rowan is deemed a counter-charm to sorcery, so in Germany the
parasitic mistletoe is still commonly considered a protection
against witchcraft, and in Sweden, as we saw, the mistletoe
which is gathered on Midsummer Eve is attached to the ceiling
of the house, the horse's stall or the cow's crib, in the belief that
this renders the Troll powerless to injure man or beast.

The Golden Bough seems to have been a glorified mistletoe. It is not a new opinion that the Golden Bough was the
mistletoe. True, Virgil does not identify but only compares it
with mistletoe.* But this may be only a poetical device to cast
a mystic glamour over the humble plant. Or, more probably, his
description was based on a popular superstition that at certain
times the mistletoe blazed out into a supernatural golden glory.
The poet tells how two doves, guiding Aeneas to the gloomy
vale in whose depth grew the Golden Bough, alighted upon a
tree, 'whence shone a flickering gleam of gold. As in the woods
in winter cold the mistletoe—a plant not native to its tree—is
green with fresh leaves and twines its yellow berries about the
boles; such seemed upon the shady holm-oak the leafy gold, so
rustled in the gentle breeze the golden leaf.'* Here Virgil
definitely describes the Golden Bough as growing on a holm-
oak, and compares it with the mistletoe. The inference is almost
inevitable that the Golden Bough was nothing but the mistletoe
seen through the haze of poetry or of popular superstition.

If the Golden Bough was the mistletoe, the King of the Wood at Nemi may have personated an oak spirit and perished in an oak fire. Now grounds have been shewn for believing that the priest
of the Arician grove—the King of the Wood—personified the
tree on which grew the Golden Bough. Hence if that tree was
the oak, the King of the Wood must have been a personification
of the oak-spirit. It is, therefore, easy to understand why, before
he could be slain, it was necessary to break the Golden Bough.
As an oak-spirit, his life or death was in the mistletoe on the
oak, and so long as the mistletoe remained intact, he, like
Balder, could not die. To slay him, therefore, it was necessary
to break the mistletoe, and probably, as in the case of Balder,
to throw it at him. And to complete the parallel, it is only

necessary to suppose that the King of the Wood was formerly burned, dead or alive, at the midsummer fire festival which, as we have seen, was annually celebrated in the Arician grove.* The perpetual fire which burned in the grove, like the perpetual fire which burned in the temple of Vesta at Rome was probably fed with the sacred oak-wood; and thus it would be in a great fire of oak that the King of the Wood formerly met his end. At a later time, as I have suggested, his annual tenure of office was lengthened or shortened, as the case might be, by the rule which allowed him to live so long as he could prove his divine right by the strong hand. But he only escaped the fire to fall by the sword.

Thus it seems that at a remote age in the heart of Italy, beside the sweet Lake of Nemi, the same fiery tragedy was annually enacted which Italian merchants and soldiers were afterwards to witness among their rude kindred, the Celts of Gaul, and which, if the Roman eagles had ever swooped on Norway, might have been found repeated with little difference among the barbarous Aryans of the North. The rite was probably an essential feature in the ancient Aryan worship of the oak.

A similar tragedy may have been enacted over the human representative of Balder in Norway.

It only remains to ask, Why was the mistletoe called the Golden Bough? The whitish-yellow of the mistletoe berries is hardly enough to account for the name, for Virgil says that the bough was altogether golden, stem as well as leaves. Perhaps the name may be derived from the rich golden yellow which a bough of mistletoe assumes when it has been cut and kept for some months; the bright tint is not confined to the leaves, but spreads to the stalks as well, so that the whole branch appears to be indeed a Golden Bough. Breton peasants hang up great bunches of mistletoe in front of their cottages, and in the month of June these bunches are conspicuous for the bright golden tinge of their foliage. In some parts of Brittany, especially about Morbihan, branches of mistletoe are hung over the doors of stables and byres to protect the horses and cattle, probably against witchcraft.

The name of the Golden Bough may have been applied to the mistletoe on account of the golden tinge which the plant assumes in withering.

The yellow colour of the withered bough may partly explain why the mistletoe has been sometimes supposed to possess the property of disclosing treasures in the earth; for on the principles of homoeopathic magic there is a natural affinity between a yellow bough and yellow gold. This suggestion is confirmed

The yellow hue of withered mistletoe may partly explain why

by the analogy of the marvellous properties popularly ascribed
to the mythical fern-seed or fern-bloom. Now it is a property
of this mythical fern-seed that whoever has it, or will ascend a
mountain holding it in his hand on Midsummer Eve, will
discover a vein of gold or will see the treasures of the earth
shining with a bluish flame. In Russia they say that if you
succeed in catching the wondrous bloom of the fern at midnight
on Midsummer Eve, you have only to throw it up into the air,
and it will fall like a star on the very spot where a treasure lies
hidden. In Brittany treasure-seekers gather fern-seed at midnight on Midsummer Eve, and keep it till Palm Sunday of the
following year; then they strew the seed on ground where they
think a treasure is concealed. Sometimes the fern-seed is

supposed to bloom on Christmas night, and whoever catches it
will become very rich. In Styria they say that by gathering
fern-seed on Christmas night you can force the devil to bring
you a bag of money.

Thus, on the principle of like by like, fern-seed is supposed
to discover gold because it is itself golden; and for a similar
reason it enriches its possessor with an unfailing supply of gold.
But while the fern-seed is described as golden, it is equally
described as glowing and fiery. Hence, when we consider that
two great days for gathering the fabulous seed are Midsummer
Eve and Christmas—that is, the two solstices (for Christmas is
nothing but an old heathen celebration of the winter solstice)—
we are led to regard the fiery aspect of the fern-seed as primary,
and its golden aspect as secondary and derivative. Fern-seed, in
fact, would seem to be an emanation of the sun's fire at the two
turning-points of its course, the summer and winter solstices.
This view is confirmed by a German story in which a hunter is
said to have procured fern-seed by shooting at the sun on
Midsummer Day at noon; three drops of blood fell down, which
he caught in a white cloth, and these blood-drops were the
fern-seed. Here the blood is clearly the blood of the sun, from
which the fern-seed is thus directly derived. Thus it may be
taken as probable that fern-seed is golden, because it is believed
to be an emanation of the sun's golden fire.

Now, like fern-seed, the mistletoe is gathered either at
Midsummer or Christmas—that is, at the summer and winter
solstices—and, like fern-seed, it is supposed to possess the

power of revealing treasures in the earth. On Midsummer Eve people in Sweden make divining-rods of mistletoe, or of four different kinds of wood one of which must be mistletoe. The treasure-seeker places the rod on the ground after sun-down, and when it rests directly over treasure, the rod begins to move as if it were alive. Now, if the mistletoe discovers gold, it must be in its character of the Golden Bough; and if it is gathered at the solstices, must not the Golden Bough, like the golden fern-seed, be an emanation of the sun's fire? The question cannot be answered with a simple affirmative. We have seen that the old Aryans perhaps kindled the solstitial and other ceremonial fires in part as sun-charms, that is, with the intention of supplying the sun with fresh fire; and as these fires were usually made by the friction or combustion of oak-wood, it may have appeared to the ancient Aryan that the sun was periodically recruited from the fire which resided in the sacred oak. In other words, the oak may have seemed to him the original storehouse or reservoir of the fire which was from time to time drawn out to feed the sun. But if the life of the oak was conceived to be in the mistletoe, the mistletoe must on that view have contained the seed or germ of the fire which was elicited by friction from the wood of the oak. Thus, instead of saying that the mistletoe was an emanation of the sun's fire, it might be more correct to say that the sun's fire was regarded as an emanation of the mistletoe.

gathered at solstices (Midsummer and Christ-mas) and is supposed to reveal treas-ures in the earth; per-haps, there-fore, it too is deemed an emanation of the sun's golden fire.

These considerations may partially explain why Virgil makes Aeneas carry a glorified bough of mistletoe with him on his descent into the gloomy subterranean world. The poet describes how at the very gates of hell there stretched a vast and gloomy wood, and how the hero, following the flight of two doves that lured him on, wandered into the depths of the immemorial forest till he saw afar off through the shadows of the trees the flickering light of the Golden Bough illuminating the matted boughs overhead. If the mistletoe, as a yellow withered bough in the sad autumn woods, was conceived to contain the seed of fire, what better companion could a forlorn wanderer in the nether shades take with him than a bough that would be a lamp to his feet as well as a rod and staff to his hands? Armed with it he might boldly confront the dreadful spectres that would cross his path on his adventurous journey. Hence when Aeneas,

Aeneas and the Golden Bough.

emerging from the forest, comes to the banks of Styx, winding slow with sluggish stream through the infernal marsh, and the surely ferryman refuses him passage in his boat, he has but to draw the Golden Bough from his bosom and hold it up, and straightway the blusterer quails at the sight and meekly receives the hero into his crazy bark, which sinks deep in the water under the unusual weight of the living man. There is some reason to suppose that when Orpheus in like manner descended alive to hell to rescue the soul of his dead wife Eurydice from the shades, he carried with him a willow bough to serve as a passport on his journey to and from the land of the dead. Again, on an ancient sarcophagus, which exhibits in sculptured relief the parting of Adonis from Aphrodite, the hapless youth, reclining in the lap of his leman, holds a branch, which has been taken to signify that he, too, by the help of the mystic bough, might yet be brought back from the gates of death to life and love.

Orpheus and the willow.

Now, too, we can conjecture why Virbius at Nemi came to be confounded with the sun. If Virbius was, as I have tried to shew, a tree-spirit, he must have been the spirit of the oak on which grew the Golden Bough; for tradition represented him as the first of the Kings of the Wood. As an oak-spirit he must have been supposed periodically to rekindle the sun's fire, and might therefore easily be confounded with the sun itself. Similarly we can explain why Balder, an oak-spirit, was described as 'so fair of face and so shining that a light went forth from him', and why he should have been so often taken to be the sun. And in general we may say that in primitive society, when the only known way of making fire is by the friction of wood, the savage must necessarily conceive of fire as a property stored away, like sap or juice, in trees, from which he has laboriously to extract it. The Senal Indians of California 'profess to believe that the whole world was once a globe of fire, whence that element passed up into the trees, and now comes out whenever two pieces of wood are rubbed together'. Similarly the Maidu Indians of California hold that 'the earth was primarily a globe of molten matter, and from that the principle of fire ascended through the roots into the trunk and branches of trees, whence the Indians can extract it by means of their drill'. In Namoluk, one of the Caroline Islands, they say that

Trees thought by the savage to be the seat of fire because he elicits it by friction from their wood.

the art of making fire was taught men by the gods. Olofaet, the cunning master of flames, gave fire to the bird *mwi* and bade him carry it to earth in his bill. So the bird flew from tree to tree and stored away the slumbering force of the fire in the wood, from which men can elicit it by friction. In the ancient Vedic hymns of India the fire-god Agni 'is spoken of as born in wood, as the embryo of plants, or as distributed in plants. He is also said to have entered into all plants or to strive after them. When he is called the embryo of trees or of trees as well as plants, there may be a side-glance at the fire produced in forests by the friction of the boughs of trees.' In some Australian languages the words for wood and fire are said to be the same.

A tree which has been struck by lightning is naturally regarded by the savage as charged with a double or triple portion of fire; for has he not seen the mighty flash enter into the trunk with his own eyes? Hence perhaps we may explain some of the many superstitious beliefs concerning trees that have been struck by lightning. When the Thompson Indians of British Columbia wished to set fire to the houses of their enemies, they shot at them arrows which were either made from a tree that had been struck by lightning or had splinters of such wood attached to them. Perhaps they conceived such trees as reservoirs of heat, and imagined that by using them up they would exhaust the supply and thus lower the temperature of the atmosphere. Wendish peasants of Saxony similarly refuse to burn in their stoves the wood of trees that have been struck by lightning; but the reason they give for their refusal is different. They say that with such fuel the house would be burnt down. In like manner the Thonga of South Africa will not use such wood as fuel nor warm themselves at a fire which has been kindled with it; but what danger they apprehend from the wood we are not told. On the contrary, when lightning sets fire to a tree, the Winamwanga of Northern Rhodesia put out all the fires in the village and plaster the fireplaces afresh, while the head men convey the lightning-kindled fire to the chief, who prays over it. The chief then sends out the new fire to all his villages, and the villagers reward his messengers for the boon. This shews that they look upon fire kindled by lightning with reverence, and the reverence is intelligible, for they speak of thunder and lightning as God himself coming down to earth.

(margin note) Trees that have been struck by lightning are deemed by the savage to be charged with a double portion of fire.

Similarly the Maidu Indians of California believe that a Great Man created the world and all its inhabitants, and that lightning is nothing but the Great Man himself descending swiftly out of heaven and rending the trees with his flaming arm.

It is a plausible theory that the reverence which the ancient peoples of Europe paid to the oak, and the connexion which they traced between the tree and their sky-god, were derived from the much greater frequency with which the oak appears to be struck by lightning than any other tree of our European forests. However we may explain it, whether by the easier passage of electricity through oakwood than through any other timber, or in some other way, the fact itself may well have attracted the notice of our rude forefathers, who dwelt in the vast forests which then covered a large part of Europe; and they might naturally account for it in their simple religious way by supposing that the great sky-god, whom they worshipped and whose awful voice they heard in the roll of thunder, loved the oak above all the trees of the wood and often descended into it from the murky cloud in a flash of lightning, leaving a token of his presence or of his passage in the riven and blackened trunk and the blasted foliage. Such trees would thenceforth be encircled by a nimbus of glory as the visible seats of the thundering sky-god. Certain it is that, like some savages, both Greeks and Romans identified their great god of the sky and of the oak with the lightning flash which struck the ground; and they regularly enclosed such a stricken spot and treated it thereafter as sacred. It is not rash to suppose that the ancestors of the Celts and Germans in the forests of Central Europe paid a like respect for like reasons to a blasted oak.

If there is any truth in this conjecture, the real reason why the Druids worshipped a mistletoe-bearing oak above all other trees of the forest was a belief that every such oak had not only been struck by lightning but bore among its branches a visible emanation of the celestial fire; so that in cutting the mistletoe with mystic rites they were securing for themselves all the magical properties of a thunderbolt. If that was so, we must apparently conclude that the mistletoe was deemed an emanation of the lightning rather than, as I have thus far argued, of the midsummer sun. Perhaps, indeed, we might combine the two seemingly divergent views by supposing that in the old

Aryan creed the mistletoe descended from the sun on Midsummer Day in a flash of lightning. Whether on mythical principles the two interpretations can really be reconciled with each other or not, I will not presume to say; but even should they prove to be discrepant, the inconsistency need not have prevented our rude forefathers from embracing both of them at the same time with an equal fervour of conviction; for like the great majority of mankind the savage is above being hidebound by the trammels of a pedantic logic. In attempting to track his devious thought through the jungle of crass ignorance and blind fear, we must always remember that we are treading enchanted ground, and must beware of taking for solid realities the cloudy shapes that cross our path or hover and gibber at us through the gloom. We can never completely replace ourselves at the standpoint of primitive man, see things with his eyes, and feel our hearts beat with the emotions that stirred his. All our theories concerning him and his ways must therefore fall far short of certainty; the utmost we can aspire to in such matters is a reasonable degree of probability.

To conclude these enquiries we may say that if Balder was indeed, as I have conjectured, a personification of a mistletoe-bearing oak, his death by a blow of the mistletoe might on the new theory be explained as a death by a stroke of lightning. So long as the mistletoe, in which the flame of the lightning smouldered, was suffered to remain among the boughs, so long no harm could befall the good and kindly god of the oak, who kept his life stowed away for safety between earth and heaven in the mysterious parasite; but when once that seat of his life, or of his death, was torn from the branch and hurled at the trunk, the tree fell—the god died—smitten by a thunderbolt. *Hence the stroke of mistletoe that killed Balder may have been a stroke of lightning.*

And what we have said of Balder in the oak forests of Scandinavia may perhaps, with all due diffidence in a question so obscure and uncertain, be applied to the priest of Diana, the King of the Wood, at Aricia in the oak forests of Italy. He may have personated in flesh and blood the great Italian god of the sky, Jupiter, who had kindly come down from heaven in the lightning flash to dwell among men in the mistletoe—the thunder-besom—the Golden Bough—growing on the sacred oak beside the still waters of the lake of Nemi. If that was so, we need not wonder that the priest guarded with drawn sword the *The King of the Wood and the Golden Bough.*

mystic bough which contained the god's life and his own. The goddess whom he served and married was herself, if I am right, no other than the Queen of Heaven, the true wife of the sky-god. For she, too, loved the solitude of the woods and the lonely hills, and sailing overhead on clear nights in the likeness of the silver moon she looked down with pleasure on her own fair image reflected on the calm, the burnished surface of the lake, Diana's Mirror.

ii

Looking back at the end of the journey.

We are at the end of our enquiry, but as often happens in the search after truth, if we have answered one question, we have raised many more; if we have followed one track home, we have had to pass by others that opened off it and led, or seemed to lead, to far other goals than the sacred grove at Nemi. Some of these paths we have followed a little way; others, if fortune should be kind, the writer and the reader may one day pursue together. For the present we have journeyed far enough together, and it is time to part. Yet before we do so, we may well ask ourselves whether there is not some more general conclusion, some lesson, if possible, of hope and encouragement, to be drawn from the melancholy record of human error and folly which has engaged our attention.

The movement of human thought in the past from magic to religion.

If then we consider, on the one hand, the essential similarity of man's chief wants everywhere and at all times, and on the other hand, the wide difference between the means he has adopted to satisfy them in different ages, we shall perhaps be disposed to conclude that the movement of the higher thought, so far as we can trace it, has on the whole been from magic through religion to science. In magic man depends on his own strength to meet the difficulties and dangers that beset him on every side. He believes in a certain established order of nature on which he can surely count, and which he can manipulate for his own ends. When he discovers his mistake, when he recognizes sadly that both the order of nature which he had assumed and the control which he had believed himself to exercise over it were purely imaginary, he ceases to rely on his own intelligence and his own unaided efforts, and throws himself humbly on the mercy of certain great invisible beings behind the veil of nature, to whom he now ascribes all those far-reaching powers which he once arrogated to himself. Thus in the acuter minds magic is gradually superseded by religion, which explains the succession of natural phenomena as regulated by the will, the passion, or the caprice of spiritual beings like man in kind, though vastly superior to him in power.

But as time goes on this explanation in its turn proves to be unsatisfactory. For it assumes that the succession of natural events is not determined by immutable laws, but is to some extent variable and irregular, and this assumption is not borne out by closer observation. On the contrary, the more we scrutinize that succession the more we are struck by the rigid uniformity, the punctual precision with which, wherever we can follow them, the operations of nature are carried on. Every great advance in knowledge has extended the sphere of order and correspondingly restricted the sphere of apparent disorder in the world, till now we are ready to anticipate that even in regions where chance and confusion appear still to reign, a fuller knowledge would everywhere reduce the seeming chaos to cosmos. Thus the keener minds, still pressing forward to a deeper solution of the mysteries of the universe, come to reject the religious theory of nature as inadequate, and to revert in a measure to the older standpoint of magic by postulating explicitly, what in magic had only been implicitly assumed, to wit, an inflexible regularity in the order of natural events, which, if carefully observed, enables us to foresee their course with certainty and to act accordingly. In short, religion, regarded as an explanation of nature, is displaced by science. *The movement of thought from religion to science.*

But while science has this much in common with magic that both rest on a faith in order as the underlying principle of all things, readers of this work will hardly need to be reminded that the order presupposed by magic differs widely from that which forms the basis of science. The difference flows naturally from the different modes in which the two orders have been reached. For whereas the order on which magic reckons is merely an extension, by false analogy, of the order in which ideas present themselves to our minds, the order laid down by science is derived from patient and exact observation of the phenomena themselves. The abundance, the solidity, and the splendour of the results already achieved by science are well *Contrast between the views of natural order postulated by magic and by science respectively.*

fitted to inspire us with a cheerful confidence in the soundness of its method. Here at last, after groping about in the dark for countless ages, man has hit upon a clue to the labyrinth, a golden key that opens many locks in the treasury of nature. It is probably not too much to say that the hope of progress—moral and intellectual as well as material—in the future is bound up with the fortunes of science, and that every obstacle placed in the way of scientific discovery is a wrong to humanity.

The scientific theory of the world not necessarily final. Yet the history of thought should warn us against concluding that because the scientific theory of the world is the best that has yet been formulated, it is necessarily complete and final. We must remember that at bottom the generalizations of science or, in common parlance, the laws of nature are merely hypotheses devised to explain that ever-shifting phantasmagoria of thought which we dignify with the high-sounding names of the world and the universe. In the last analysis magic, religion, and science are nothing but theories of thought; and as science has supplanted its predecessors, so it may hereafter be itself superseded by some more perfect hypothesis, perhaps by some totally different way of looking at the phenomena—of registering the shadows on the screen—of which we in this generation can form no idea. The advance of knowledge is an infinite progression towards a goal that for ever recedes. We need not murmur at the endless pursuit:

> 'Fatti non foste a viver come bruti
> Ma per seguir virtute e conoscenza.'*

The shadow across the path. Great things will come of that pursuit, though we may not enjoy them. Brighter stars will rise on some voyager of the future—some great Ulysses of the realms of thought—than shine on us. The dreams of magic may one day be the waking realities of science. But a dark shadow lies athwart the far end of this fair prospect. For however vast the increase of knowledge and of power which the future may have in store for man, he can scarcely hope to stay the sweep of those great forces which seem to be making silently but relentlessly for the destruction of all this starry universe in which our earth swims as a speck or mote. In the ages to come man may be able to predict, perhaps even to control, the wayward courses of the winds and clouds, but hardly will his puny hands have strength to speed afresh our slackening planet in its orbit or rekindle the dying fire of the sun.* Yet the philosopher who trembles at the idea of such distant catastrophes may console himself by reflecting that these gloomy apprehensions, like the earth and the sun themselves, are only parts of that unsubstantial world which thought has conjured up out of the void, and that the phantoms which the subtle enchantress has evoked to-day she may ban to-morrow. They too, like so much that to common eyes seems solid, may melt into air, into thin air.*

Without dipping so far into the future, we may illustrate the course which thought has hitherto run by likening it to a web woven of three different threads—the black thread of magic, the red thread of religion, and the white thread of science, if under science we may include those simple truths, drawn from observation of nature, of which men in all ages have possessed a store. Could we then survey the web of thought from the beginning, we should probably perceive it to be at first a chequer of black and white, a patchwork of true and false notions, hardly tinged as yet by the red thread of religion. But carry your eye further along the fabric and you will remark that, while the black and white chequer still runs through it, there rests on the middle portion of the web, where religion has entered most deeply into its texture, a dark crimson stain, which shades off insensibly into a lighter tint as the white thread of science is woven more and more into the tissue. To a web thus chequered and stained, thus shot with threads of diverse hues, but gradually changing colour the farther it is unrolled, the state of modern thought, with all its divergent aims and conflicting tendencies, may be compared. Will the great movement which for centuries has been slowly altering the complexion of thought be continued in the near future? or will a reaction set in which may arrest progress and even undo much that has been done? To keep up our parable, what will be the colour of the web which the Fates are now weaving on the humming loom of time? will it be white or red? We cannot tell. A faint glimmering light illumines the backward portion of the web. Clouds and thick darkness hide the other end.

The web of thought.

iii

Nemi at even-
ing: the *Ave
Maria* bell.

Our long voyage of discovery is over and our bark has drooped her weary sails in port at last. Once more we take the road to Nemi. It is evening, and as we climb the long slope of the Appian Way up to the Alban Hills, we look back and see the sky aflame with sunset, its golden glory resting like the aureole of a dying saint over Rome and touching with a crest of fire the dome of St Peter's. The sight once seen can never be forgotten, but we turn from it and pursue our way darkling along the mountain side, till we come to Nemi and look down on the lake in its deep hollow, now fast disappearing in the evening shadows. The place has changed but little since Diana received the homage of her worshippers in the sacred grove. The temple of the sylvan goddess, indeed, has vanished and the King of the Wood no longer stands sentinel over the Golden Bough. But Nemi's woods are still green, and as the sunset fades above them in the west, there comes to us, borne on the swell of the wind the sound of the church bells of Rome ringing the Angelus.* *Ave Maria!* Sweet and solemn they chime out from the distant city and die lingeringly away across the wide Campagnan marshes. *Le roi est mort, vive le roi! Ave Maria!*

EXPLANATORY NOTES

In the following notes successive editions of *The Golden Bough* are abbreviated thus: GB1: the first (two-volume) edition of 1890; GB2: the second (three-volume) edition of 1900; GB3 the third (twelve-volume) edition of 1906–15; GBA: the abridgement of 1922. Within the third edition the volume numbers and titles are these: i, *The Magic Art and the Evolution of Kings* (vol. i); ii, *The Magic Art and the Evolution of Kings* (vol. ii); iii, *Taboo and the Perils of the Soul*; iv, *The Dying God*; v, *Adonis, Attis, Osiris* (vol. i); vi, *Adonis, Attis, Osiris* (vol. ii); vii, *Spirits of the Corn and of the Wild* (vol. i); viii, *Spirits of the Corn and of the Wild* (vol. ii); ix, *The Scapegoat*; x, *Balder the Beautiful* (vol. i); xi, *Balder the Beautiful* (vol. ii).

BOOK I: THE KING OF THE WOOD

Chapter 1: The King of the Wood (GB3 i. 1–43).

9   *Who. . . . woodlands wild*: when Frazer first drafted these lines in 1890 he had seen neither Turner's picture nor the lakeside scene at Nemi. Nemi he first visited in the winter of 1900, shortly after completing GB2. And for much of his life Turner's painting was on loan from the National Gallery in London to the National Gallery in Dublin. Frazer had, however, seen it in reproductions, which did not prevent him from making one incidental blunder, since it is not Lake Nemi, twelve miles to the south-east of Rome, that it depicts but the legendary Lake Avernus. The painting now hangs in the Clore extension of the Tate Gallery in London.

10   *the sanctuary*: the site was excavated in 1885 by Sir John Savile Lumley, then British Ambassador in Rome. Frazer's reading of the account of the dig in *The Athenaeum* was one of the incidents that sparked off his interest in the cult and thereby inspired his book. Savile's and Frazer's interpretations of the nature and functions of the shrine have persistently been challenged. See *The Making of the Golden Bough*, 2–12. The site was covered in immediately after the investigations, and now lies beneath strawberry plantations.

11   *Here Caligula . . . lake*: Caligula's barges were later discovered and placed on display, only to be blown up in 1944 in a fit of pique by the retreating German army. The resulting rubble is now housed in two long warehouse structures by the lakeside.

12–13   *The strange . . . Nemi*: this passage, adopted unchanged from GB1 i. 3, is a fine résumé of Frazer's understanding of the comparative method and his aims in deploying it in this book.

         I begin . . . combat: Orestes had sought sanctuary in Tauris after his sacrilegious murder of his mother Clytemnestra in revenge for her murder of

Agamemnon, his father. Clytemnestra's excuse was that Agamemnon had earlier caused their daughter Iphigenia to be slaughtered on the sacrifical block in Aulis to secure fair winds for the Trojan expedition. But when Orestes arrived in Tauris he found his sister installed as high priestess of the shrine of Diana Taurica, and together they escaped from the Crimea to Italy, where according to one version of the legend they then set up the Arician cult. For the murder of Agamemnon the source is Aeschylus' *Agamemnon*. For Orestes's revenge, his *Choephoroe* and the *Electras* of Sophocles and Euripides. For the miraculous translation of Iphigenia to Tauris from the sacrifical block, see the disputed end to Euripides's *Iphigenia in Aulis*. None of these Greek sources, however, mention the escape of brother and sister to Italy, for which the lone source is Servius's fourth-century commentary on Virgil's *Aeneid*, vi. 136. It is Virgil, in the line thus commented on, who describes the golden bough '*ramus . . . aureus*', though Servius alone connects this bough with the priest of Nemi. It is Servius too, as we shall see, who alone alludes to the possibility of a sacred marriage within the grove. The Greek traveller is Pausanias whose *Description of Greece* Frazer translated and edited in 1898. On Pausanias, ii. 27. 4, which mentions the connection of Hippolytus with the Arician cult, Frazer's commentary simply reads: 'I have suggested an explanation of this custom in *The Golden Bough*' (Pausanias's *Description of Greece*, vol. iii, p. 251).

14   *Fifteenth of August*: this is the first of Frazer's meticulous placed, and subversive, associations of pagan festivals with the feasts of the Christian Church. The purport is to suggest the presence of something close to what we know as syncretism, the symbiosis of one religious system upon another, earlier one. Eventually Frazer's identifications covered most of the Christian calendar. See below Book 2, chap: 10.

    Ovid . . . water: Ovid, *Fasti*, iii. 273 ff. But the outlet no longer exists.

    the love of women: the best-known source for Hippolytus's spurning of women is Euripides's *Hippolytus*, 10–19, 1092 ff. Frazer's hunch is that Virbius, an ancient Italian sylvan deity, was none other than Hippolytus in disguise or rather, more probably, that when the deities of the Greeks installed themselves in Italy, Hippolytus attached himself to an already-existing sylvan figure. The Roman religion was hence syncretic upon the Greek.

15   *some foreign ritual*: an early statement of a principle which was to become, especially in GB3, fundamental to the thinking behind *The Golden Bough*. Rather than ritual enshrining myth as had commonly been thought, Frazer's theory is that myth developed as a way of explaining and justifying ritual, which in turn acted upon philosophical assumptions deeply embedded within the mind. Frazer's views on the order of these phases was apt to waver, but in essence it remained constant: philosophy–ritual–myth.

17 *Adonis is the most familar type*: Adonis was the Greek sobriquet for the Semitic God Tammuz, annually mourned on his autumnal demise by the goddess Ishtar. In the Greek myth she became Aphrodite, and in the Roman Venus. For Frazer's treatment of this cult see Book II, Chap. 6 and 8 below.

at his manly sports: in Euripides's play Hippolytus appears framed between the shrines of Artemis, goddess of the chase and of chastity, and Aphrodite, the goddess of physical love. The source for the shrine of 'peeping Aphrodite' is again Pausanias, ii, 32. 3.

18 *Byblus*: a Phoenician city on what is now the coast of Lebanon dedicated to the worship of Astarte and Tammuz. For a description of the site, see below, Book II, Chap. 6.

19 *Ephesus . . . worship*: Diana of the Ephesians was the subject of a famous diatribe by St Paul which caused a riot among the silversmiths who provided trinkets for her shrine. See Acts 19: 24–8. Within the shrine her torso was covered by multiple protuberances which most have interpreted as breasts, though eggs and even bull's testicles have been suggested.

Chapter 2: Priestly Kings (GB3 i. 44–51).

23 *Zela and Pessinus*: Zela was a theodicy or priestly state in Upper Asia Minor in which the hard agricultural labour was performed by hiero-dules attached to the temple of Anaitis. Pessinus was a centre for the worship of Cybele, the Phrygian mother-goddess, in what is now southern Turkey.

the Gallas: an Ethiopian people.

the Matabeles: a southern African people occupying a large tract of what is now Zimbabwe.

Chapter 3: Magic and Religion (incorporates two chapters from GB3 i.: 'Sympathetic Magic', pp. 52–219, and 'Magic and Religion', pp. 220–43).

27 'the association of ideas': a term first employed by John Locke in his *Essay Concerning Human Understanding* (1689). But it was David Hume, in his *Treatise of Human Nature* (1739–40), who first systematically applied the phrase to the epistemology of belief, including religious belief. For Hume there was no *necessary* connection between events. The belief in cause and effect was to be explained by the frequent concurrence of events which thereafter came to be linked in the mind through their contiguity (that is adjacency in space or in time) or else resemblance. The more frequent was the concurrence, the more firmly grounded was the belief.

28 *Homoeopathic Magic . . . Contagious Magic*: It will be seen that these are merely the magical application of Hume's laws of resemblance and continuity. (See previous note). In GB1 these twin facets of sympathetic magic

are not distinguished. The distinction between them in 1900 was one of the salient features of GB2.

28 *an Ojebway Indian ... he does so*: a fictional instance of such malevolent homoeopathic use of images, pre-dating *The Golden Bough* by some twelve years, occurs in Thomas Hardy's *The Return of the Native* (1878) in which an effigy of Eustacia Vye is melted down, upon which she promptly drowns. By 1890 Frazer had already noted: 'If it is wished to kill a person an image of him is taken and then destroyed; and it is believed that through a certain physical sympathy between the person and the image, the man feels the injuries done to the image as if they were done to his own body, and that when it is destroyed he must instantaneously perish' (GB1 i. 9). When in the year of the book's publication Hardy read these remarks, his reaction was one of delighted recognition, commenting in his journal on the remarkable parity between the superstitions and customs of 'a remote Asiatic and a Dorset labourer'. See *Sir James Frazer and the Literary Imagination*, p. v.

31 *Nowhere ... Central Australia*: the instances cited in this paragraph are taken from Spencer and Gillen's *Native Tribes of Central Australia* (1899), in which the authors had described a series of so-called *intichiuma* ceremonies performed in the spring in order to fertilize the natural life of the outback. The principal effect of Spencer and Gillen's revelations on Frazer was to cause him drastically to revise his ideas concerning totemism. Previously he had thought of an individual's totem as his 'external soul' (see below, Book I, Chap. 11 and Book IV, Chaps. 4 and 5); he now came to view totems collectively as the focus of annual sacraments intended to secure the food supply. A secondary effect was to clarify in his mind the particular force of homoeopathic as distinct from contagious magic.

35 *A modern advocate ... savage*: a side-thrust this at the Society for Psychical Research, which throughout the 1890s had been attempting to place telepathy on a scientific footing. For Frazer by contrast, telepathy belonged to the magical rather than to the scientific phase of mankind's development. It is the 'modern advocate' who is out of step with history.

36 *Among ... Gold Coast*: the Tschi- (or Twi-) speaking peoples constitute a large section of the ethnic and linguistic grouping collectively known as the Akan, stretching from the far west of what is now Ghana across to the Akwapim Ridge to the north of its capital Accra. Among the Akan the most powerful segment, in Frazer's time as now, were the Ashanti (or as he spells them, Ashantee) residing in the forest zone around Kumasi.

38 *The late ... Howitt*: Dr A. W. Howitt (1830–1908) was one of Frazer's earliest informants on the customs and observances of aboriginal Australians. In recognition of this fact Frazer wrote a moving obituary tribute to him later collected in *The Gorgon's Head* (1927). The incident here in

question appears in Howitt's article 'On some Australian Beliefs' in the *Journal of the Anthropological Institute*, xiii (1884), 456 f.

the Basutos: the Basutos inhabit a substantial mountainous territory to the north of Cape Province, between the Orange Free State and Natal.

40 *Caroline Islands*: in the Pacific Ocean, due north of Papua New Guinea.

Kei islanders: the Kei Islands lie to the south-west of Papua New Guinea.

41 *Thus . . . alleviated*: Pliny, *Naturalis Historia*, xxviii. 36.

It is constantly . . . generation: Francis Bacon, *Natural History*, cent. x, para. 998. The superstition discussed by Bacon seems to have been common knowledge in the seventeenth century since, as Frazer's footnote informs us, in Act v, Scene 1 of Dryden's *The Tempest* 'Ariel directs Prospero to anoint the sword which wounded Hippolito, and to wrap it up close from the air'. Dryden, *Works*, ed. Walter Scott (London, 1808), iii. 191.

42 *Thus in Suffolk . . . animal*: F. N. Webb, in *Folklore*, xvi (1905), 337.

48 *Osiris*: the Egyptian god of the dead, interpreted by Frazer in GB3 vi. (*Adonis, Attis, Osiris*, vol. ii) as a corn spirit. See Book Two, Chap. 10 below.

49 *generally known as mana*: the Maori concept of *mana* was something of a thorn in Frazer's flesh since it was conceived of as a source of energy which was both supernatural and yet harnessed by the individual mind as a medium of human agency. It was thus arguably both magical and religious. As such it played a significant role in the thinking of later ritualists who, while following Frazer's general line, were keen to dissent from its details. See especially Jane Ellen Harrison, *Themis* (Cambridge, 1912), 67–8, 74–6, 84–9, 137–8, 154–5, 156–7, 160–5. R. H. Codrington's remarks occur in *The Melanesians* (Oxford, 1891), 191 ff.

51 *might be the petition*: a memorable re-enactment of the Mass of the Holy Spirit is enacted in Barbey d'Aurevilly's novel *L'Ensorcelée*, set in early nineteenth-century Normandy.

52 *as to whom we possess accurate information*: see Frazer's *Totemism and Exogamy*, i. 41 ff. The notion that the aborigines, being the oldest-surviving people on earth, occupied a stage of cultural development in which magic was unadulterated by religion, was mandatory for ethnographers of Frazer's generation, but has since been discounted.

54 *Quod semper, quod ubique, quod ab omnibus*: 'Always, everywhere, and by all.'

a witch in Ireland: not many years before Frazer wrote these lines a young woman was indeed burned alive in Clonmel in the West of Ireland by her husband, who thought that she had been bewitched. See 'The Witch-burning at Clonmel', *Folklore*, vi (1895), 373–4.

55   *treading in a narrow circle*: the discovery of the ineptitude of magic, and consequent reliance upon divine power, was later dubbed by R. S. Marrett 'the birth of humility'.

57   *In la sua volontade è nostra pace*: Dante: *Paradiso*, iii. 85. 'In His Will is our peace.'

Chapter 4: Human Gods (GB3 i. 373–421).

62   *the Sandwich Islands*: another name for the Hawaiian Islands.

65   *the Marquesas*: in Northern Polynesia.

67   *The Mashona . . . away*: the Mashonas and the Matabele are two neighbouring peoples in what is now Zimbabwe.

    The Baganda: a Ugandan people with an ancient and established kingship, on whom Frazer's main informant was the missionary Revd John Roscoe, whom he interviewed in Cambridge on 6 August 1897, continuing to correspond until Roscoe's death. The Baganda monarchy was suppressed in 1966 and restored in 1993.

68   *The . . . Loango*: a people in present-day Zaïre.

    Mombasa: on the coast of Kenya.

69   *law-book of Manu*: *The Laws of Manu* are one of the oldest-surviving Brahminical codes. They had been the object of some interest in Europe ever since Sir Henry Sumner Maine had written about them in *Ancient Law* (1861).

70   *Cardinal Manning* (1808–92): Roman Catholic Primate of All England. He was famous for his aquiline and haughty good looks.

71   *the Albigenses*: or Albigensians, an heretical Christian sect who flourished in the south of France in the early Middle Ages.

Chapter 5: Departmental Kings of Nature (GB3 ii. 1–6).

Chapter 6: The Worship of Trees (incorporates GB3 ii. Chap. 9 ('The Worship of Trees'), pp. 7–58 and Chap. 10 ('Relicts of Tree-worship in Modern Europe'), pp. 59–96).

83   *natural woods*: J. Grimm, *Deutsche Mythologie*, i. 53 ff., where he also attributes to early tree worship the eventual evolution of the Gothic style of church architecture.

Chapter 7: The Sacred Marriage (incorporates GB3 Chap. 11 ('The Influence of the Sexes upon Vegetation'), pp. 97–119 and Chap. 12 ('The Sacred Marriage'), pp. 120–70).

99   *Manipur*: in the extreme east of India in the state of Assam, very close to the Burmese border.

103 *plants, animals, and women*: *Oedipos Tyrannos*, 22 ff., 95 ff. According to Creon, who is reporting the verdict of the oracle at Delphi, the crops, the flocks, herds, and pregnant women are all being blighted because of a dread pollution, a *miasma*, which infects the land. We subsequently discover that one of the causes of this pollution is Oedipus's unwitting cohabitation with his mother Jocasta.

105 *Milton*: Frazer's cited source for Milton's praise of chastity is the 'Apology for Smectymnus' in the Complete Edition of the *Historical, Political, and Miscellaneous Works of John Milton* (London, 1738), but he might as well have cited *Comus*, 420–7:

> 'Tis chastity, my brother, chastity:
> She that has that, is clad in compleat steel,
> And like a quiver'd Nymph with Arrows keen
> May trace huge Forests, and unharbour'd Heaths,
> Infamous Hills, and sandy perilous wildes,
> Where through the sacred rayes of Chastity,
> No savage fierce, Bandite, or mountaneer,
> Will dare to soyl her Virgin purity . . .

The first brother's wording here implicitly compares the lady subjected in the masque to the cunning wiles of the seducer Comus, to Diana, though in Chapter 1 of his book Frazer has already argued for her as a goddess of fertility.

106 *freedom and truth*: notice how subtly seductive is Frazer's argument here, implicitly equating sexual forbearance, which the Victorians liked to think that they rated highly, with its seeming opposite, profligacy. For Frazer's later elision of the modes of life of prostitutes and of nuns, see Book II Chap. 6 below.

110 *an application of hemlock*: a cue for one of Frazer's famously lugubrious footnotes: 'In antiquity it was believed that an anointment or plaster of hemlock applied to the genital organs prevented them from discharging their function. Dr J. B. Bradbury, Downing Professor of Medicine in the University of Cambridge, informs me that the belief is correct' (GB3 ii. 139).

would otherwise have perished: The 'antiquary' is once again Pausanias (ix. 3).

Chapter 8: The Kings of Rome (GB3 ii. 171–94, where it is entitled 'The Kings of Rome and Alba').

117 *Is this . . . think it so*: Ovid, *Tristia*, iii. 31 ff. Frazer's own translation, partly echoing Hamlet, I. v. 41.

119 *in the altar of the sky*: the Capitoline Hill in ancient times housed the temples both of Jupiter and of Juno. The site of Juno's temple is now crowned by the church of Sta Maria d'Aracoeli. It was while

wandering around the aisles of this church that, on 15 October 1764, Gibbon conceived the idea of writing his *History of the Decline and Fall of the Roman Empire*.

Chapter 9: The Succession to the Kingdom (GB3 ii. 266–323, where it is entitled 'The Succession to the Kingdom in Ancient Latium').

122   *To put it ... through men*: Beena marriage had been a subject of investigation by Frazer's fellow Scot J. F. M'Lennan, who had regarded it as one of the principal pieces of evidence for the practice of polyandry in the ancient world. In *Primitive Marriage* (1865) he had distinguished between two different types of polyandry in Ceylon: *deega* polyandry, in which the wife takes up residence with the husband(s) and *beena* polyandry in which the husband(s) take up residence with the wife. *Beena* marriage was hence a sort of exogamous matrilocal union. Since it was polyandrous, the paternity of the children could never be certain, and descent was therefore traced through the female line. Mother-kin as it became known, or matriliny as we now prefer to call it, had famously been investigated in 1861 by the Swiss jurist Jacob Bachofen in his work *Das Mutterecht*, but Frazer's own speculations spring fully armed from the forehead of M'Lennan, whom he had read while still a student for the bar.

125   *Now this ... West Africa*: the Twi-speaking kingdom of Ashanti occupies the inner, forested zone of what is now Ghana. Among the Ashanti, as amongst other peoples of the Akan group, traces of matrilinear organization may be found even now. For the Ashanti Frazer's source was T. E. Bowdich's *Mission from Cape Coast to Ashanti* (new edn., 1873), but readers may now turn to the works of Frazer's correspondent and protégé Colonel R. S. Rattray.

127   *Saxo Grammaticus ... throne*: *Historia Danica*, iv. Grammaticus too is one of our earliest sources for the Hamlet legend. For the union of Clytemnestra and Aegisthus, see Aeschylus's *Agamemnon*.

128   *Bede ... male line*: Bede, *Historia ecclesiastica gentis Anglorum*, ii, 1. 7.

      These traditions ... among the Kirghiz: the Kirghiz are a pastoral people in Turkestan. It was one of M'Lennan's principal contentions that in early pre-Islamic societies, where female infanticide had made girls scarce, brides were often captured in whirlwind raids on neighbouring clans. But in *Studies in Ancient History* (1886) he initiates the idea of the bride-race, in support of which he cites the Kirghiz together with the Koryak and Malay instances here cited. The Koryak are a non-Slavonic people in the extreme east of Russia.

130   *On the twenty-fourth day ... Forum*: this custom, as Frazer's wording acknowledges, gives an entirely fresh slant to the American expression (first cited in 1826 OED) 'to run for office'. Frazer's sources for the

regifugium are Ovid, *Fasti*, ii. 685 ff. and Plutarch *Quaestiones Romanae*, 63. The *Fasti* is a poetic almanac of the principal festivals of the Roman year which Ovid wrote while in exile in Tomis on the Black Sea in a vain attempt to regain official favour and, with it, re-entry into Rome. Later, in 1929, Frazer was to translate and edit the *Fasti* in several volumes, but in the the meantime it is one of his chief quarries for Roman custom.

133   *the Banyoro*: (or sometimes Bunyoro), neighbours and ancient rivals of the Baganda in Uganda, for whom see note to p. 67 above. As time went on, Frazer's dependency on African evidence to endorse his main case concerning the kingship became increasingly marked. See especially *The Aftermath*, 315, 324, etc.

  Charles the Second: Pepys's Diary for 23 April, 1661: 'And three times the King-at-armes went to the three open places on the scaffold and proclaimed that if any one should show any reason why Ch. Steward should not be King of England, that he should speak.' But Pepys does not mention the gauntlet. Not did he wait to hear the result, since 'I had so great a list to pisse'. *The Diary of Samuel Pepys* (London: G. Bell and Sons Ltd., 1970), ii. 84.

Chapter 10: The Burden of Royalty (GB3 iii. 1–25).

134   *The Mikado*: the title 'Mikado' is from Japanese *mi* (sublime) and *kado* (door), and is the title by which the Japanese used to refer to their emperor when in the presence of Europeans, apparently through analogy with the 'Sublime Porte' of the Ottomans. Gilbert and Sullivan's opera had been first performed at the Savoy Theatre on 14 March 1885.

136   *The following description . . . new vessels*: both accounts of the Mikado's miraculous incarceration are from John Pinkerton's *General Collection of Voyages and Travels* (London, 1808–14), one of Frazer's earlier sources for divine kingship far and wide and one to which, from 1888 on, as his notebooks show, he assiduously applied himself (subsequently referred to as 'Pinkerton'). They are Kaempfer's 'Account of Japan' (Pinkerton, ii. 716 ff.), and Coron's 'Account of Japan' (Pinkerton, vii. 613). Another source was *Descriptio regni Japoniae et Siam* (Cambridge, 1673) by B. Varentius, whose *Geographia Generalis* had earlier been issued in a revised edition by Isaac Newton (Cambridge, 1672).

  Cape Padron: in present-day Angola.

  Togo . . . West Africa: until 1918 Togo (adjoining modern Ghana to the east) was a German possession.

140   *. . . of the Slave Coast*: more strictly, of the Gold Coast. The Ewes (pronounced 'e-vays') occupy the extreme south-eastern portion of what is now Ghana, beyond the Volta river, and spreading over into Togo.

142–3   *The life of the kings ... wine*: Diodorus Siculus, *Bibliotheca*, i. 70.

146   *in Cambodia ... successors*: see Book I, Chapter 5 above.

147   *The Mikados ... tycoons*: the notion that authority in Japan was divided
        between sacred and secular rulers once more goes back to Frazer's Euro-
        pean sources. Kaempfer, trans. Scheuchzer (Glasgow, 1906) iii, ii: 'In
        spiritual affairs they are under the absolute jurisdiction of the Mikado';
        'The secular monarch professes the religion of his fore-fathers, and pays his
        duty once a year to the Mikado.' 'Tycoon' was the title by which the
        Shogun was introduced to foreigners. The first recorded usage of the term
        in the sense of a business magnate is 1861.

148   *Tonquin*: or Tonkin in present-day Vietnam. Source: Richard's 'History of
        Tonquin' in Pinkerton ix. 744 ff.

149   *the Getae*: a people from Thrace in northern Greece who by the fourth
        century BC had migrated northwards to settle in the vicinity of the
        Carpathian Mountains in modern Romania. They were sometimes confused
        with the Goths. Source: Strabo's *Geographia*, vii. 3. 5.

150   *two powers in a single king*: the apparent source for this farrago of nonsense
        (what one may well ask is 'the true negro culture'?) was Mary Kingsley,
        with whom Frazer discussed the matter of the division of the kingship on
        1 June 1897. (The conversation is recorded in Frazer's notebook 'M' in the
        British Library collection Add Ms. 45, 450.) She later expanded her ideas
        in *The Journal of the Anthropological Institute*, xxix (1899), 61 ff.

151   *Porto Novo*: in the extreme south-east corner of Dahomey, virtually on the
        Nigerian border.

Chapter 11: The Perils of the Soul (GB3 iii. Chap. 2, pp. 26–100).

154   *a European missionary*: R. Salvado, *Mémoires historiques sur l'Australie*
        (Paris, 1854), 162. The missionary is not named. Frazer's footnote reads:
        'In this edifying catechism there is little to choose between the savagery of
        the white man and the savagery of the black.'

        The Hurons: a pre-Columbian people inhabiting what is now the southern
        part of Quebec, on the northern shores of Lake Huron.

        Nias: an island to the east of Sumatra.

        Haida: a people of the Queen Charlotte Islands off the coast of British
        Columbia.

157   *The Karens*: the 'Red Karens' are a people from Borneo, sometimes
        referred to as the 'Karennis'.

158   *Karo-Bataks*: sometimes referred to as the Battas, a people from Sumatra.

        Amoy: or Szeming, a settlement on the coast of Fukien in eastern China
        immediately opposite Taiwan.

159 *Danger Island*: one of the Cook Islands in the southern Pacific, about half-way between Tonga and Tahiti.

160 *The island of Wetar*: or Weta, one of the Indonesian group, off the north-east coast of Timor.

The Banks Islands: in the New Hebrides group mid-way between Australia and Fiji.

161 *New Britain*: lies in the Bismarck Archipelago off the north coast of New Guinea. Frazer does not comment on the state of affairs in old Britain.

162 *The Andamanese*: the Andaman Islands, now an Indian possession, lie between the Bay of Bengal and the Andaman Sea opposite the coast of southern Burma.

163 *Aru*: the Aru Islands lie in the Arufura Sea between south-west New Guinea and Australia's Northern Territory.

Chapter 12: Taboos (incorporates GB3 iii. Chap. 3 ('Tabooed Acts'), pp. 101–30; Chap. 4 ('Tabooed Persons'), pp. 131–223; Chap. 5 ('Tabooed Things'), pp. 223–317; Chap. 6 ('Tabooed Words'), pp. 318–418; and Chap. 7 ('Our Debt to the Savage'), pp. 419–22).

167 *Crevaux*: J. Crevaux, *Voyages dans l'Amerique du Sud* (Paris: 1883), 300.

168 *Amboyna and Uliase*: two islands lying on the equator in the Moluccan Sea to the north of Celebes.

172 *eating together*: the argument here is cognate with that in *Pysche's Task* (1909), where Frazer is concerned to stress the advantages of superstition as the foundation of civilized convention.

180 *Mirzapur*: in Uttar Pradesh in north-east India, to the south of the border with Nepal.

188 *with his own hand*: the anecdote relates to an episode in the history of the Franks (Gregory de Tours, *Histoire ecclesiastique des Francs*, trad. M. Guizot (Paris 1874) iii. 18).

Ponape: in the north-east corner of the Caroline Islands, a group in Micronesia in the western Pacific Ocean.

193 *the island of Saghalien*: more usually known as Sakhalin, a Russian possession just above Hokkaido in the north of Japan.

A Toumbuluh man: the Toumbuluh are a people of Celebes.

195 *the Hos of West Africa*: in fact, of what was then the Gold Coast and is now Ghana. The Hos live to the east of the Volta river in the east of the country, and may be considered a sub-group of the Ewes.

196 *the love-sick maid in Virgil*: *Eclogues* 8.

200 *The Indians of Chiloe*: an island off the coast of southern Chile.

200 *an Araucanian*: the Araucanians are a pre-Columbian people of Chile.

203 *Gippsland*: in Victoria, Australia.

205 *the island of Buru*: in Indonesia, about 300 miles to the east of Celebes.

   Sunda: the Sunda Strait lies between Sumatra and Java.

   Torres Straits: the Torres Straits lie at the extreme upper end of Australia, beyond the tip of Cape York Peninsula in Queensland. They were the destination of a famous ethnographic expedition in 1898, which Frazer was invited to accompany. He thought seriously about it but declined, preferring to continue in his role of 'comparative anthropologist' at home.

209 *Nicobarese*: the Nicobar Islands are an Indian possession between the Bay of Bengal and the Andaman Sea, about 300 miles to the west of Malaysia.

   ... America and elsewhere: this observation proved useful when in the 1930s Claude Lévi-Strauss examined such shifts of language among pre-Columbian Brazilian peoples. Lévi-Strauss's account of such linguistic transformation in works such as *La Pensée sauvage* in the 1960s had a profound influence on French Structuralist anthropology.

211 *The Klamath*: a pre-Columbian people in what is now Oregon.

212 *The Khonds*: hail from India.

219 *cum excusatione itaque veteres audiendi sunt*: 'With such a plea the ancestors are meet to be heard.'

BOOK II: KILLING THE GOD

Chapter 1: The Mortality of the Gods (GB3 iv. 1–8).

223 *the spectre of the Brocken*: a phenomenon sometimes experienced when climbing in high mountains as a result of which the observer's shadow appears fantastically distorted and enlarged on the mists swirling around the peak opposite. It was first observed on the 3,747 foot-high Brocken of the Harz range in Saxony, and had been described with some vividness by James Hogg in *The Private Memoirs and Confessions of a Justified Sinner* (1824), in which George Colwan sees the giant apparition on the early morning vapours surrounding the summit of Arthur's Seat in Edinburgh (The World's Classics, 1981, p. 41).

224 *In answer . . . this*: A. I. Dodge, *Our Wild Indians* (Hartford, Conn., 1886), 112.

226 *enquiries to be made about the dead god*: Plutarch, *De defectu oracularum*, 17. The point presumably is that the crew mistook the god's name for that of one of their own number.

227 *O mother . . . knew it not*: William Robertson Smith, *The Religion of the Semites* (London, 1890), 412, 414. Smith, not surprisingly, thought that the ancient Iraquis were mourning the grapes.

Chapter 2: The Killing of the Divine King (GB3 iv. 9–119).

229 *the Mangaians*: inhabitants of the Cook Islands of the Southern Pacific.

the Gran Chaco: this runs between northern Argentina and southern Paraguay.

230 *the river Pilcomayo*: rising in the Andes in western Bolivia, the Pilcomayo empties into the River Paraguay.

231 *then burned on a pyre*: Procopius, *De Bello Gothico*, ii. 14. The Wends were another ancient Teutonic tribe.

233 *Let us pass... banished*: G. Merolla, *Relazione del viaggio nel regno di Congo*, quoted in Pinkerton, xvi. 228.

put the priests to the sword: Meroe was the capital of the ancient Nilotic kingdom of Napata, between present-day Merowe and Atbara in northern Sudan. The information, which proved influential in Frazer's thinking, comes from Strabo, xvii. 2.3.

234 *Dr Seligmann... the subject*: in 1911 Charles Seligmann, who was later to form one of the cluster of anthropologists who gathered round the rising star of Malonowski at the London School of Economics, was engaged in research among the Shilluk and the Dinka of the White Nile. He sent Frazer the typescript of an unpublished work entitled 'The Divine Kings of the Shilluk', large portions of which Frazer incorporated, with due acknowledgement, into his text. The passages concerned seemed to represent a clinching vindication of the theory of the Nemi priesthood, but it ought to all fairness to be added that Seligmann had previously read *The Golden Bough*, and that his account of the unfortunate *ret*'s defence of his throne by moonlight is shot through with Frazer's lyrical cadences. The relevant paragraphs in Seligmann's work are set out in *Anthologia Anthropologica*, i. 509 ff.

237 *The Dinka*: for a later, very different account of the Dinka, see E. E. Evans-Pritchard, *The Dinka* (Oxford, 1940). But Evans-Pritchard had very little faith either in Seligmann's or in Frazer's theories.

240 *The extraordinary violence... death of the monarch*: Nathaniel Isaacs, *Travels and Adventures in Eastern Africa* (London, 1836), i. 295 ff.

241 *the Sultans of Darfur*: Darfur is in eastern Sudan. Its metropolis is El Fascher.

243 *The Egbas and the Yorubas*: the Egbas are in fact a subgroup of the Yoruba, a numerous people who inhabit a large part of south-western Nigeria. The Egbas are centred in Abeokuta, a town about 80 miles to the north of Lagos and 80 miles to the south-east of Ibadan. Oyo, another Yoruba town, lies approximately 60 miles to the north-east of Ibadan.

the satirist Lucian: Lucian *De morte Peregrini*, from which cynical account Frazer adopts his tone.

245 *As the Christians ... Islam*: the unsurprising source for this piece of anti-religious propaganda is Voltaire, *Essai sur les Mœurs*, iii. 142–5.

246 *There is a Gentile house ... up as king*: Frazer read of this harrowing instance of self-dismemberment in Duarte Barbosa, *A Description of the Coasts of East Africa and the Malabar in the Beginning of the Sixteenth Century* (London: The Hakluyt Society, 1866), 172 ff.

247 *The English traveller, whose account I have quoted*: in fact a Scottish visitor, one Alexander Hamilton who, after several years knocking around the far East, returned and dedicated his *New Account of the East Indies* to his laird. It was Frazer's reading of Hamilton's account of the contest for the throne of Malabar in Pinkerton, viii. 374, that set him on the trail of *The Golden Bough*. See *The Making of the Golden Bough*, 50–2.

Mr W. Logan: William Logan, *Malabar* (Madras, 1887), i. 162–9. Logan was a district officer in Malabar.

249 *In ... five years*: T. K. Gopal Parickhar, *Madras and its Folk* (Madras: 1900), 120 f.

Chapter 3: Temporary Kings (GB3 iv. 148–59).

Chapter 4: The Sacrifice of the King's Son (GB3 iv. 160–95).

263 *... and sacrificed*: Herodotus, vii. 197, and others.

264 *In Plutarch's ... grief*: Plutarch, *Quaestiones Graecae* 38; Ovid. *Metamorphoses*, iv. 1 f.

266 *... offering on the wall*: 2 Kings 3: 27.

... sons to Baal: Plato, *Minos*. This dialogue is now thought definitely to be spurious.

When thou are come ... Molech: Deuteronomy 18: 9–12 and Leviticus 18: 21, both in the Revised Version, as are the following.

267 *... polluted with blood*: Psalms 106: 35–8.

... humbly with thy God: Micah 6: 6–8.

268 *... was the Passover*: Exodus 11–13: 16. Numbers 3: 13; 8: 17.

269 *instead of his son*: Genesis 22: 1–13.

... their firstborn children: bearing in mind the unflattering impression given of a callous deity, and the extreme offence likely to be caused by Frazer's conclusions to Jew and Christian alike, it is not surprising that none of this appears in the 1922 abridgement.

a substitute for it: Exodus 4: 24–6.

Chapter 5: Killing the Tree-Spirit (GB3 iv. 215–71).

293 *Come to life, Kostrubonko*: readers will notice a similarity between the mock rite here described and that enacted, in somewhat grimmer earnest, in

Stravinsky's ballet *Le Sacre du printemps* (1913). As a matter of fact Stravinsky seems to have had just these springtime festivities in mind. According to his friend and collaborator Nicholas Roerich, the scenario concerned a sacrifice to Yarilo. See Eric White, *Stravinsky* (London: Faber, 1966) and Peter L. Carracciolo, 'Carnivals of Mass Murder', in *Sir James Frazer and the Literary Imagination*, 226, n. 13.

298 *Australian spring*: the ceremonies were known as *intichiuma* ceremonies and had been discovered by Baldwin Spencer and Francis Gillen, whose description of them in *The Native Tribes of Central Australia* (Macmillan, 1899) had a galvanizing effect upon Frazer's thinking in the lead-up to the writing of GB2.

Chapter 6: Adonis (incorporates GB3 v. Chap. 1 ('The Myth of Adonis'), pp. 3–12; Chap. 2 ('Adonis in Syria'), pp. 13–30; and Chap. 3 ('Adonis in Cyprus'), pp. 31–56).

304 *at the north gate of the temple*: Ezekiel 8: 14.

306 *from Hebron to Jerusalem*: David reigned for seven years in Hebron, followed by thirty-three in Jerusalem. Frazer's argument here is that, coming from the same Semitic stock as the native Canaanites, David sought by moving his capital to appropriate the divine aura enjoyed by original rulers of the city.

307 *sepulchre of their fathers*: 2 Samuel 21: 1–14.

310 *in an attitude of sorrow*: the impression of the rock-hewn monument of Ghineh, like much in Frazer's account of the Phoenician sites, is derived from Ernest Renan's *Mission de Phénicie* (Paris: 1864). Renan had visited the Lebanon in the 1860s, and there is much in the religious nostaligia of this French scholar and apostate that throughout permeates Frazer's description of Syria. Frazer had not, needless to say, visited these sites himself.

described by Macrobius: Macrobius, *Saturnalia*, i. 23. 5.

his untimely fate: Lucian, *De dea Syria*, 8.

313 *of her person*: see Book I, Chap. 1 above.

315 *alike harmful and deplorable*: the equating here of the lives of prostitutes and nuns is one of Frazer's boldest strokes. It stems, however, quite logically from his earlier point about sexuality as a force that may be expended for the public weal either though expression or abstinence.

for nine days: Ovid, *Metamorphoses* x. 298 ff.

316 *married his own sister*: as did the Pharaohs of Egypt. The custom was first given the explanation Frazer here offers by M'Lennan in his *The Patriarchal Theory* (London, 1885).

316 *taken it to his bed*: thus at least in the oldest version of the story as
     recounted by Clement of Alexandria. For Pygmalion as sculptor who falls
     in love with his own creation (and hence by derivation for Shaw's Professor
     Higgins), we have to turn to Ovid, *Metamorphoses* x. 243–97.

318 *the Magnificat of saints*: the 'great religious writer' who so praised the
     power of music was John Henry Newman in *Sermons Preached before the
     University of Oxford*, no. xv. For all that, it was said of Frazer by even so
     close an ally as his wife, that his sense of musical pitch was so poor that
     when the strains of *Rule Britannia!* broke over the aisles of the Albert Hall,
     he had physically to be restrained from standing up.

319 *put to death by the victor*: see Book II, Chap. 9 below.

     one hundred and sixty: cited by Pliny in his *Naturalis Historia*, vii. 154.

     Thomas Parr: died in 1635 in the reign of Charles I, and was reputed to
     have lived in the reigns of nine previous monarchs, and to have survived
     for 152 years.

**Chapter 7: Sacred Prostitution (GB3 v. 57–109, where it is entitled
'Sacred Men and Women').**

320 *writers whose opinions are entitled to be treated with respect*: the alternative
     theory which Frazer devotes the next few pages of GB3 to demolishing is
     that sacred prostitution was in essence 'a purely secular and precautionary
     practice of destroying a bride's virginity before handing her over to her
     husband in order that the bridegroom's intercourse should be safe from a
     peril that is much dreaded by men in a certain stage of culture'. We might
     add that, if so, it was a comparatively late stage. That intercourse might
     itself be dangerous was a phobia that much preoccupied Frazer at an early
     point in his career (see *The Making of the Golden Bough*, 74–9). He had
     noted, for example, that in the case of widows danger was to be ap-
     prehended from the ghost of the deceased husband. The Koryaks thus used
     to insist that a widow give herself to an unknown third party before she
     married. But in the backwoods of Kamchatka outsiders are exceptionally
     rare; it therefore behoved the woman to avail herself of the slightest
     opportunity to perform her customary obligation. Occasionally there was an
     extreme dearth of strangers and hence a backlog of widows who were prone
     to throw themselves at any passer-by, as the Second Bering Expedition
     discovered to its delight when, in a condition of extreme need, they arrived
     in the wilds of Kamchatka in 1729. (Frazer himself, it must be noted,
     married a widow.) Later Frazer seems to have felt that the danger inhered
     in the menstrual blood (see below Book IV, Chapter 2). He then, however,
     dropped the theory altogether, so that the section here omitted is in the
     nature of a recantation. I have simply passed on to Frazer's examples.

324 *invoke . . . of gods*: W. Bosman, 'Description of the Gold Coast of Guinea',
     in Pinkerton, xvi. 494.

326 *take their fancy*: A. B. Ellis, *The Tschi-speaking Peoples of the Gold Coast of West Africa* (London, 1887), 120–38.

327 *to the tabernacle*: 1 Samuel 2: 22—'Now Eli was very old, and heard all that his sons did unto Israel; and how they lay with the women that assembled at the door of the tabernacle of the congregation.'

328 *... the spirit is mad*: Hosea 9: 7.

329 *example of the practice*: 1 Samuel 2. Hannah was praying for offspring, but Eli thought that she was drunk.

330 *in the form of a serpent*: Pausanias, ii. 10. 3; ii. 23. 7. Another explanation for this common observation is that the snake embodied the spirit of the dead. See Jane Ellen Harrison, *Prolegomena to the Study of Greek Religion* (Cambridge, 1903), 342–3.

... to a Judaean maid: Aelion, *De natura animalium*, vi. 17.

Chapter 8: The Ritual of Adonis (incorporates GB3 v. Chap. 9 ('The Ritual of Adonis'), pp. 223–35 and Chap. 10 ('The Gardens of Adonis'), pp. 236–59).

332 *Athens ever sent to sea*: Plutarch, *Alcibiades*, 18; ibid. *Nicias*, 13. 'The date of the sailing', adds Frazer in his footnote 'is given by Thucydides (vi. 30) who, with his habitual contempt for the customs of his countrymen, disdains to notice the coincidence.'

... elsewhere is obvious: see Book II, Chap. 5 above.

333 *with the Indian*: the marriage of Siva and Pârvatî described pp. 295–6 above.

... taken for the sun: a lone side-swipe this at the solar school of mythology, whose principal exponenent in the 1870s and 1880s had been Friedrich Max Müller. The solarists held that all myths were nothing but descriptions of the path of the sun, either diurnal or else annual, but alas had no more luck with their theory than did George Eliot's Mr Casaubon in *Middlemarch* with his forlorn 'Key to All Mythologies'.

334 *the unfortunate astronomer Bailly*: Bailly's progress to the scaffold had been memorably described by Carlyle in *The French Revolution*, book v, Chap. 2. The day was 19 November 1793 and bitterly chill; 'The guillotine is taken down, though with hands numbed by the sleety drizzle; it is carried to the river-side; is there set up again with slow numbness; pulse after pulse counting itself out in the old man's weary heart. For hours long; amid the curses, and the bitter frost-rain, "Bailly, thou tremblest!" said one. "*Mon ami*, it is for cold," said Bailly, "c'est de froid" ' (Oxford: The World's Classics, 1989), 341. Despite this, in his *Letters sur l'Origine des Sciences* (London and Paris, 1777) Bailly had wanted to position the zone of Adonis close to the North Pole.

Father Lagrange: M J. Lagrange, *Études sur les religions semitiques* (Paris, 1905), 305 ff.

336 *I sometimes think . . . unseen*: The *Rubáiyát of Omar Khayyám*, in the Fitz-gerald translation.

given up her dead: T. B. Macaulay, *History of England*, vol. iv, chap. xx (London, 1855), 410.

The name of the festival . . . flowers: the title of the festival was the *Anthesteria*. That it was at once a floral and a memorial festival had been suggested by Jane Ellen Harrison in her *Prolegomena to the Study of Greek Religion* (Cambridge, 1903), 32 ff.

337 *with the anemones and the roses*: in 1861 Ernest Renan visited the Holy Land to conduct the preliminary researches for his *Vie de Jésus*. His companion on this trip had been his sister Henriette. Whilst visiting Mount Lebanon both had succumbed to malaria, and when he eventually awoke from his coma at Amschidt on 20 September it was to learn that Henriette had died. Renan's later tear-soaked evocation of the Phoenician sites is in his *Mission de Phénicie* (1864).

338 *ceremonies of modern Europe*: see Book II, Chap. 5 above.

342 *. . . by Augustine*: Augustine, quoted in Jacob Grimm, *Deutsche Mythologie* (Berlin, 1875–8), i. 490.

. . . Easter lamb and neat wine: Frazer is following the German folklorist C. Wachsmuth is his description of the Greek rite. For a later description of the same, see Book IV, Chap. 3 below. It was Frazer's contention that the Greek Easter festivities were likely to have been erected on the foundation of Adonis worship which, as he has already demonstrated, had struck deep roots in the Aegean. The Roman rite, he thought, was more likely to reflect the worship of Attis. Again, see Book II, Chap. 10 below.

344 *That noble group . . . pathetic*: this is only one of the works of Western art which Frazer might have called in evidence. Shakespeare's *Venus and Adonis* was perhaps a shade too obvious. But, bearing in mind his theme, it is strange that he nowhere alludes to the 'Garden of Adonis' sequence from Spenser's *The Faerie Queene*, III. vi. As Graham Hough remarks, 'the theme is cosmological. The garden is mythologically the place where Venus meets Adonis; and it is also the garden of generation where all living things are reformed after they have disintegrated.' Graham Hough, *A Preface to the Faerie Queene* (London: Duckworth, 1962), 176.

In this connexion . . . bewailed: Jerome, *Epistolae*, lviii. 3.

Chapter 9: Attis (GB3 v. 263–76, there entitled 'The Myth and Ritual of Attis').

346 *Phrygia*: a district of ancient Asia Minor covering approximately Anatolia in modern Turkey.

347 *she went to work at once*: Livy, xxix. chaps. 10, 11, and 14.

349 *Hierapolis*: one of the most important religious sites in the ancient world, Hierapolis was situated near the banks of the River Euphrates some distance to the east of Aleppo in modern Syria.

350 *depicted . . . poem*: Catullus' *Attis* had been translated by Grant Allen, with an accompanying anthropological commentary, in 1892.

Chapter 10: The Hanged God (incorporates GB3 v. Chap. 4 ('Human Representatives of Attis'), pp. 285–7; Chap. 5 ('The Hanged God'), pp. 288–97; and Chap. 6 ('Oriental Religions in the West'), pp. 298–312).

Chapter 11: Osiris (GB3 vi. Chap. 1 ('The Myth of Osiris'), pp. 3–23).

366 *by Plutarch*: Plutarch's, *Isis and Osiris* is the source of the myth, though not of the interpretation. It was Plutarch's contention that 'Osiris' was the name of a god which had subsequently, and through mistaken identity, come to attach itself to the corn. It was Frazer's opinion, by contrast, that the name originally signified the cut corn, or rather the spirit of the cut corn, and then became that of a god. The disagreement is fundamental to Frazer's method. For Osiris as the spirit of the corn see Book II, Chap. 19 and 20 below. It is also Plutarch who informs us about the annual pig sacrifice to Osiris, though none of the ancients seem to have been quite clear about the nature of the god.

370 *Isis . . . agriculture*: Diodorus Siculus, i. 21, 5–11.

Chapter 12: Feasts of All Souls (incorporates the first half of GB3 vi. Chap. 4 ('The Official Festivals of Osiris'), pp. 49–95).

377 *Sumba*: in the Java group, about 200 miles east of Bali.

386 *impulse of the heart*: J. J. Herzog and C. F. Pitt, *Real-Encyclopädie für protestantische Theologie und Kirche* (Leipzig, 1883), i. 304.

Chapter 13: Isis (GB3 vi. 115–19).

388 *Isis with Ceres*: Augustine, *De civitate dei*, viii. 27.

Chapter 14: Mother-Kin and Mother-Goddesses (GB3 vi. 201–18).

391 *mother-kin*: in previous editions Frazer had employed Bachofen's term 'mother-right', in accordance with the widely entertained fallacy that descent through the mother conferred actual political power upon women. Of this error the present chapter is by way of being a recantation. We now more usually speak of 'matriliny'.

392 *their social organization . . . regal functions*: Sir Charles Lyall, in his introduction to P. T. R. Gurdon, *The Khasis* (London, 1907), pp. xxiii ff.

  the Pelew Islanders: the Pelew (or Pelaw) islands lie approximately 600 miles due east of the Philippines.

395 *Men make Gods and women worship them*: quoted in Simone de Beauvoir, *Le Deuxième sexe* (Paris: Gallimard, 1949), I: Les Faits et les mythes, 127–8.

Chapter 15: Dionysus (GB3 vii. 1–29).

398 *His myth . . . Maternus*: Firmicus Maternus, *De errore profanum religionum*, 6. A fourth-century convert to Christianity, Firmicus railed against the devices of the heathen, thus serving as an invaluable informant on the very customs he was so concerned to condemn.

Euhemeristic: Euhemerism is the belief that all the gods were at one time or another great men who have subsequently been deified. It was first propounded by Euhemerus of Messina in the third century AD in his *Sacred History*.

399 *Plutarch . . . Dionysus*: Plutarch, *Consolatio ad uxorem*, 10.

The rending . . . rites: see esp. Euripides *The Bacchae*, 735 ff.

401 *Pentheus and Lycurgus*: Pentheus was a ruler of Thebes who attempted to repress the Dionysian cult, being rewarded for his pains by being torn limb from limb by his mother Agave, who had succumbed to it. Lycurgus was a son of Dryas who drove Dionysus into the sea and was subsequently blinded. There is a remarkable symmetry in the Theban myth, since three of the grandsons of Cadmus, the founder of the city, were supposed to have been torn asunder: Dionysus (whose mother was Semele); Actaeon (whose mother was Autonoe); and Pentheus. Actaeon, it will be remembered, spied upon Artemis bathing and was torn to shreds by her hounds. Such unfortunates are not rare in myth or legend; for them we commonly reserve the epithet 'sparagmatic' after *sparagmos* (Greek), a rending.

402 *Dionysiac myth and ritual*: the Thracian rite had been written up by D. M. Hawkins in the *Journal of Hellenic Studies* in 1906. It was taken up and transformed into the centre-piece of a theory of magical drama by William Ridgeway in his *The Origin of Attic Theatre* (Cambridge, 1910)

Chapter 16: Demeter and Persephone (GB3 vii. 35–91).

405 *Eleusinian mysteries*: Eleusis is a Greek village at the head of the Saronic Gulf approximately 30 miles to the west of Athens. In ancient times, when it was joined to the city by a sacred way, it was the centre of a religious cult secret to its devotees. The focus of this cult was the annual performance of a mystical drama which it is Frazer's purpose in this chapter to explore.

410 *where it still remains*: originally kept in the old University Library in Cambridge, this has since been transferred to the Fitzwilliam Museum. The draperies are still clearly visible, as is the 'cista' of harvest offerings she carried on her head, even if the arms that once held it in position have gone and the face is indecipherable with age. Dodwell, alas, was a mite over-credulous when talking to the local farmers, since the colossus has long

been recognized as one of a pair of Caryatids from the sanctuary, the other of which is held in the museum at Eleusis. It has even been suggested (by Svornos in 1914) that the two statues represent daughters of a Roman visitor to the shrine, one Appius Claudius Pulcher. These later extrapolations do not, however, detract from the validity of Frazer's point about the deep pull exercised by superstition on the minds of the peasantry, for whom by 1902 she had *become* Demeter. See Ludwig Budde and Ricard Nicholls, *A Catalogue of the Greek and Roman Sculpture in the Fitzwilliam Museum, Cambridge* (Cambridge University Press for the Fitzwilliam Museum, 1967), plate 25 and pp. 46–9.

Chapter 17: Woman's Part in Primitive Agriculture (GB3 vii).

411   *prominent part . . . agriculture*: by F. B. Jevons in his *Introduction to the History of Religion* (London, 1896). Frazer's pursuit of this particular hare represents a rare foray into the functionalist viewpoint favoured by his anthropological successors.

Chapter 18: Corn-Mother and Corn-Maiden (incorporates GB3 vii. Chap. 5 ('The Corn-Mother and Maiden in Northern Europe'), pp. 131–70; and Chap. 6 ('The Corn-Mother in Many Lands'), pp. 171–213).

417   'W. Mannhardt': From the very first the German folklorist Wilhelm Mannhardt had been one of Frazer's main sources of information on the agricultural customs of the European peasantry. The reference here is to his *Mythologische Forschungen* (Strasbourg, 1884), pp. 292 ff.

421   *. . . the Roman Ceres*: Hutchinson, *History of Northumberland*, quoted in J. Brand, *Popular Antiquities of Great Britain* (London, 1883–4), ii. 20.

     even in the town . . . Harvest Queen: E. D. Clarke, *Travels in Various Countries of Europe, Asia, and Africa* (London, 1813), 229.

     Adam the while . . . harvest-queen: *Paradise Lost*, ix. 838–42. Adam's harvest-queen, needless to say, is Eve.

428   *. . . have these Piruas*: J. de Acosta, *Natural and Moral History of the Indies*, bk. v, chap. 28, consulted by Frazer in a translation issued by the Hakluyt Society in 1880.

Chapter 19: Lityerses (GB3 vii. 214–99).

435   *It has been . . . corn*: See above, Book II, Chap. 13.

436   *Hercules*: the principal classical source for this legend is a play, *Daphnis*, by the third-century tragedian Sositheus. Hercules' feat was no part of the famous Twelve Labours but performed later while enslaved to Omphale, queen of Lydia. The sequel is narrated by Robert Graves in his *The Greek Myths*: 'At Celaenae lived Lityerses the farmer, the bastard son of King Minos, who would offer hospitality to wayfarers but force them to compete

with him in reaping the harvest. If their strength flagged, he would whip them at evening, when he had won the contest, would behead them and conceal their bodies in sheaves, chanting lugubriously as he did so. Heracles visited Celaenae in order to rescue the shepherd Daphnis, a son of Hermes who, after searching throughout the world for his beloved Pimplea, carried off by pirates, had at last found her among the slave-girls of Lityerses. Daphnis was challenged to the reaping contest, but Heracles taking his place out-reaped Lityerses, whom he decapitated with a sickle, throwing the trunk into the river Maeander. Not only did Daphnis win back Pimplea, but Heracles gave her Lityerses's palace as a dowry. In honour of Lityerses, Phrygian reapers sing a harvest dirge closely resembling that raised in honour of Maneros, son, of the first Egyptian king, who also died on the harvest field' (ii. 164). Frazer's and Graves's further sources are the Scholiast on Theocritus x; Photius's *Lexicon*; 'Suidas'; and Heyschius. In his interpretation of the myth Frazer religiously follows Mannhardt, whose *Mythologische Forschungen* was an application of the Lityerses legend to European harvest customs.

445 *Brahmapootra*: (Brahmaputra) along the Himalayan fringes of Assam, in the extreme east of India.

453 *After the wheat . . . Christendom*: from W. Hone's *Everyday Book*, published in London in the early part of the nineteenth century.

Chapter 20: The Corn-Spirit as an Animal (incorporates GB3 vii. Chap. 8 ('The Corn-Spirit as An Animal'), pp. 270–305 and GB3 viii. Chap. 9 ('Ancient Deities of Vegetation As Animals'), pp. 1–47).

479 *Bouphonia*: Pausanias, i. 24. 4., and Porphyry, *De abstentitia*, ii. 29 f. Porphyry's is one of the earliest treatises that we possess on the subject of vegetarianism. His point is that even the gods are natural vegetarians, since the ox is drawn to the oat-cake. Frazer's construction of the ritual, as it will be seen, is quite otherwise. For two completely different interpretations of the cult, see Jane Ellen Harrison, *Prolegomena to Greek Religion*, 111–33 and her *Themis*, 142–50.

481 *in Guinea*: actually in the Ivory Coast, of which Grand Bassam is the old capital, about 30 miles to the east of the present capital of Abidjan.

483 *the Thesmophoria*: in ancient Greek a *thesmos* is a law or a settled custom. During the annual autumn festival Demeter was honoured under the sobriquet Demeter Thesmophoros, or Demeter the Bearer of Laws. All of which suggests that at one level the festival had to do with the settlement of social habit consequent upon the establishment of stable, agrarian communities.

Chapter 21: Eating the God (GB3 vii. 48–108).

501 *The Aino*: a Mongolian people from the northern Japanese island of Hokkaido.

504 *the new yams at Onitsha*: for which custom, see Chinua Achebe's novel *Arrow of God* (Heinemann, 1964), in which the priest refuses to eat the new yams, thus holding up the entire procession of the agricultural year.

    sacrifice, as distinct from sacrament: the distinction here derives from Christian eucharistic theology. In the Lord's Supper or the Mass the elements—the bread and the wine—are brought up to the altar before the Consecration and offered to the deity. After the consecration they then become (according to the Catholic viewpoint at least) imbued with the presence of Christ, who is thus imbibed sacramentally. The offering is a sacrifice; the communion itself a sacrament. Frazer provided examples of the 'sacrifice of the first fruits' in a later chapter (GB3 viii. 109–37), which here, as in 1922, has been omitted.

507 *Then come . . . veneration*: J. de Acosta, *Natural and Moral History of the Indies* (London: The Hakluyt Society, 1880), bk. v, chap. 24.

    transubstantiation: the doctrine that, at the climax of the Mass, the bread and the wine turn physically into the Body and Blood of Christ, is central to Catholic theology. Frazer's point here is that the ideas and processes on which the doctrine are based are pre-Christian, and magical.

510 *. . . with their meals*: Frazer's footnote: ' "Graf Paul von Hoensbroech", *14 Jahre Jesuit* (Leipzig, 1909–1910), i. 25 *ff*. The practice was officially sanctioned by a decree of the Inquisition, 29th July 1903.'

    . . . many Manii at Aricia: see above, Book I, Chap. 1, p. 16.

Chapter 22: The Flesh Diet (GB3 viii. Chap. 12, where it is entitled 'Homoeopathic Magic of A Flesh Diet'. The whole chapter then is a working example of the second of Frazer's two types of magic. See above, Book I, Chap. 3.)

514 *nine generations of men*: according to Ovid in his *Metamporphoses*, vii. 271 ff.

516 *. . . as national fetishes*: Revd J. L. Wilson, *Western Africa* (London: 1856), 167 ff. This, for once, is true.

520 *when we . . . god*: Cicero, *De natura deorum*, iii. 16.

Chapter 23: Killing the Divine Animal (incorporates GB3 viii. Chap. 13 ('Killing the Divine Animal'), pp. 169–203; Chap. 14 ('The Propitiation of Wild Animals by Hunters'); and Chap. 17 ('Types of Animal Sacrament'), pp. 310–35).

523 *head of a ram*: Herodotus, i. 42. It was common practice for the Greeks to appropriate Egyptian gods into their pantheon. Thus in Herodotus's account Ammon (or Ammun) becomes Zeus. In Greek statuary Ammon frequently appears as Zeus with the addition of ram's horns.

523   ... *a certain term of years*: Apis had been central to William Robertson
      Smith's interpretation of sacrifice, from which Frazer dissented. Herodotus
      (ii. 153) had said that the Apis bull, which was worshipped under the title
      'the Renewal of Ptah's Life' at Memphis (about 10 miles south of Cairo)
      was sacrificed amid great signs of weeping and then his body imbibed. In
      his *Religion of the Semites* (London, 1890), 283, Smith took this to mean
      that the worshippers regarded the bull as a totem, that is one of the circle
      of kindred, and that they were therefore mourning one of their number. But
      Frazer, who distrusted Smith's theory of totemic sacrifice, had contributed
      another piece of information from Plutarch: that each bull was only
      permitted to live for twenty-five years, which Frazer took to be the limit of
      its active life. Therefore, he argued, the sacrifice was a way of releasing the
      pent-up spirit of the bull from one, worn-out incarnation, and letting it flow
      into another, fresher one.

524   *We have seen ... tree*: see above, Book I, Chap. 6.

525   *Revd J. Batchelor*: Revd J. Batchelor, *The Ainu and Their Folklore* (London,
      1901). But Frazer had earlier information on the Ainu whose bear- festival
      became, from GB1 on, one major strand in his distinction between two
      principal kinds of animal sacrament, the other being typified by the Ammon
      and Apis sacrifices in Egypt above cited.

540   *a babracot*: an elementary barbecue.

549   ... *explanation of them offered*: see above, pp. 521 ff.

550   *Malisons ... hen!*: quoted by Christopher Okibgo in 'Limits', *Labyrinths
      with Path of Thunder* (London: Heinemann, 1971), 24, where it is applied
      to the rapine of traditional Igbo shrines by the British.

BOOK III: THE SCAPEGOAT

Chapter 1: The Transference of Evil (GB3 ix. 1–71).

559   *Selemnus*: small river in Achaia which empties into the narrows between
      the Gulfs of Patras and Corinth. It is alluded to by Pausanias, vii. 23. 3. In
      his commentary to his translation Frazer writes: 'The Selemnus is probably
      the stream which comes down from the village of Kastritza and joins the
      sea a little to the east of Cape Rhium' (*Pausanius's Description of Greece*, vol.
      iv. p. 158).

578   *George Bogle*: Frazer's maternal great-great-grandfather. His account of his
      adventures had been published by Frazer's family while James was still an
      undergraduate at Cambridge, under the title *Narratives of the Mission of
      George Bogle to Tibet and of the Journey of Thomas Manning to Llasa*, ed. by
      Charles L. Markham (London, 1876).

579   *At old Calabar ... Nabikim*: The rite is described by Mary Kingsley, in
      Travels in West Africa (London, 1897), p. 495. Calabar is an old Efik

settlement on the congeries of creeks that lie between the Nigerian and Cameroonian borders.

580 *sent it away into the wilderness*: Leviticus 16, the Authorized Version's translation of which is the source for the English word 'scapegoat'. But the English translators were working from the Vulgate, where Saint Jerome's *caper emissarius* is in fact a mistranslation of the demon Azazel, to whom the Hebrew says the goat is expelled. The mistranslation, however, has got into various European tongues, as French *bouc émissaire*, and so on.

581 *Among the Yoruba . . . assured*: the ultimate source here is one of Frazer's few African informants, Bishop James Johnson. The Yorubas were very early evangelized. A ritual of this kind would seem to lie behind Wole Soyinka's play *The Strong Breed*, set in Western Nigeria in the 1960s, in which a stranger, 'Eman', is forced to play the part of a scapegoat, ending his life on a tree.

Chapter 2: Ancient Scapegoats (GB3 ix. 229–74, entitled 'Human Scapegoats in Classical Antiquity').

591 *to Mars, as we saw*: in Book II, Chap. 20, pp. 495–7.

594 *are hoed . . . take*: Labat, *Voyage du Chevalier Des Marchais en Guinée Isles voisines, et à Cayenne* (Amsterdam, 1731), ii. 80.

595 *they were called Perchten*: the view taken of the Perchten dancers here is somewhat indebted to Mrs Frazer's researches in dancing. See Lilly Grove (Mrs J. G. Frazer), *Dancing* (London, 1889). It should be fairly obvious that the author has in mind an implied analogy with English Morris dancers. See, for example, his footnote to GB1 ii. 210–11: 'The salii were said to have been founded by Morrius, King of the Veii (Servius on Virgil, *Aen.* viii, 285). Morrius seems to be etymologically the same with Mamurius or Mars. Can the English Morris (in *Morris* dancers) be the same?'

599 *afterwards gave rise*: Plutarch, *Quaestiones conviviales*, vi. 8.

outside of the walls: our information here comes from Servius who is commenting on the odd use of the word *sacra* in Virgil, *Aeneid*, iii. 57, a usage that drives it close to the sense 'taboo'. But Servius himself concedes that he is drawing on Petronius, one of the fragments of whose lost *Satyricon* had furnished him with the facts.

They were led . . . city: they were called *pharmakoi* (compare our 'pharmacist'); indeed, it is from Heyschius's definition of that word in his lexicon that our knowledge of the annual Athenian purge is derived.

600 *the Arcadian custom . . . empty-handed*: from Theocritus's *Idylls*, vii. 106 ff.

601 *scourged before he was crucified*: see above, pp. 251–3, and below, p. 642.

Chapter 3: Killing the God in Mexico (GB3 ix. 275–305. In GBA this is transposed, appearing after, rather than before, the discussion of the Saturnalia).

607 *... a solemn sacrifice of him*: J. de Acosta, *The Natural and Moral History of the Indies* (London: The Hakluyt Society, 1880), ii. 323. This translation was first published in 1604, making it almost contemporaneous with the King James's version of the Bible to whose account of the Crucifixion its cadences seem to ally it. The affinity can only, however, be the result of the stylistics of the period, though Acosta's account is itself alert to the Biblical parallels.

Chapter 4: The Saturnalia. This represents Parts 1, 3, 4, and the opening phases of Part 5 of the vast Chapter 8 of GB3 ix: 'The Saturnalia and Kindred Festivals' (pp. 306–411).

630 *his altars ... effigies*: our fullest account of the seven days of the festival is in Macrobius's *Saturnalia*, a late Roman pseudo-Platonic dialogue or rather symposium that takes place during the celebrations. It is from Macrobius that the dark hints concerning former human sacrifice are culled. But Frazer also draws on Lucian's *Saturnalia*.

632 *Franz Cumont of Ghent*: in 'Les Actes de S. Dasius', *Analecta Bollandiana*, xvi (1897), 5–16.

Durostorum: situated on the Danube near the town of Silistra in what is now Bulgaria.

Ancona: on the Adriatic coast of Italy.

635 *Roman year began with March*: a dim recollection of an original ten-month year is retained in the names of the last four months in our calendar, since September, October, November, and December are not for us, as they at one time must have been for the Romans, the seventh, eighth, ninth, and tenth months. The usual way of accounting for this is that in early Italian communities the period of time that we call January and February must have been esteemed as vacant, a sort of agricultural hibernation, since the ground was then too hard to till and farming work was thus thought impossible. If that is the case, the old year may very well have begun in March. For the execution of the Carnival, see above, pp. 280 ff.

636 *The opinion ... January*: Macrobius, *Saturnalia*, i. 12. 7.

637 *foster the growth of the seed*: see above, Book I, Chap. 7.

638 *This ... life*: H. Fielding, *The Soul of the People* (London, 1898), 172 ff.

641 *we have ... Greece*: see Book II, Chap. 4 above.

642 *earlier part of the work*: see Book II, Chap. 2 above, pp. 251–3.

hanged or crucified: the uncertainty in Frazer's past participle here relates to one of the few documents we have which describes the Sacaea in any detail. In Dio Chrysostom's fourth dialogue there is an argument between Diogenes and Alexander the Great. Diogenes is upbraiding Alexander for his lack of humility. Would it not be more seemly for him to adopt the dress of the servant? Why, even the Babylonians do this, paying obeisance to a condemned criminal—evidently the Zoganes—who is permitted to rule the roost for several days before being stripped and 'strung up'. The last verb—*ekremāsan*—is exceedingly ambigous, since it could also mean 'crucified'. It would be highly convenient for Frazer's general argument if it did so, but as it is the ambiguity remains, and Frazer can do nothing but acknowledge it.

644   *in the book of Esther*: Esther 9: 20, 26.

645   *days of feasting . . . poor*: Esther 10: 22.

648   *we should . . . throne*: F. C. Movers, *Die Phoenizier* (Bonn, 1841), i. 490 ff. Dio is the Church Father, St Dio Chrysostom.

649   *Zela*: see note to p. 23 above.

651   *these sacred dramas*: the passage which follows is the fountainhead of the ritualistic view of drama which held sway in academic circles roughly from 1900 (the year of the publication of GB2) until the 1920s. Ripples from it can be felt even today, in the theatrical as much as in the academic world. It was taken up with alacrity by the school of thinkers we now know as the Cambridge ritualists: Jane Ellen Harrison; Frank Cornford; William Ridgeway; A. B. Cooke. Briefly, Gilbert Murray was also affected. All of these, at one time or another, were deeply influenced by the view that the ancient Greek dramas must be regarded as in essence forms of magical ritual intended to orchestrate, or else to imitate, the courses of the natural world. A famous, or perhaps notorious—certainly an influential—instance of this is the 'excursus' on Attic tragedy which in 1910 Gilbert Murray contributed to Jane Harrison's *Themis*, interpreting all Greek tragedy, however unlikely, as a retelling of the story of the *Eniautos-daimon* or year spirit. By 1913 Murray could confidently describe this as the 'orthodox view of the origin of tragedy. The year Daimon waxes proud and is slain by his enemy, who becomes thereby a murderer and must in turn perish at the hands of the expected avenger, who is at the same time the wronged one re-arisen' (*Euripides and His Age*, Home University library, 1911, 61–7). There is a rather lurid version of this sequence of events, too, in *The White Goddess* by Robert Graves, who was inclined to the view that such a rivalry-plot must underlie not only all drama but all poetry as well. The whole view has recently been exploded, not least by Oliver Taplin in his *Greek Tragedy in Action* (Oxford, 1985). It is, however, unfair to regard Frazer as the progenitor of the view in its more extreme form. As the present passage makes clear, his view was this: rituals are performed so as to influence the course of the seasons; the performers at such rites re-enact ancient roles to

which names are attached corresponding eventually to supposed deities. Thus Anaitis is the name given to all those who once performed her part in the sacred rite; the same might be said of Adonis, Dionysus, and so on. To the original order of events (philosophy–ritual–myth) must therefore be added another term, so that the complete sequence runs like this: philosophy–ritual–drama–myth. In this view, myth is not so much the plot of the drama as a story told by the spectators in order to explain it; and the names of the parts refer to a whole procession of actors or actresses who at some time or another have played them. As I have said, 'it was as if at the end of a very long run of *Coriolanus* the critics started referring to Coriolanus when they meant Laurence Oliver' (*The Making of the Golden Bough*, 165). But Frazer nowhere says that all drama is like this (though all ritual might be), and he nowhere brings in scripted dramas to lend credence to his case. Would that his followers had been quite so scrupulous.

653 *The ceremonials... animals*: Franz Boas, 'The Social Organization of the Secret Societies of the Kwakiutl Indians', *Report of the United States National Museum for 1895* (Washington, 1897), 396, 420.

655 *The performer... complexion*: Revd J. Perha, 'Mengap, the Song of the Dyak Sea Feast', *Journal of the Straits Branch of the Royal Asiatic Society*, no 2, pp. 123, 134.

658 *Now... victorious enemies*: for which view of the man, see Byron's poetic drama *Sardanapalus*.

662 *Here... Beardless One*: Lagarde's article on the 'Purim' appeared in a journal published in Gottingen in 1887.

Chapter 5: The Crucifixion of Christ (GB2 ii. 186–98; GB3 ix. 412–23). (On its appearance in GB2 it was violently attacked by Andrew Lang in the *Fortnightly Review*, lxix (1901), 650–62, whereupon Frazer took umbrage and placed it in an apologetic appendix to GB3. In GBA it disappears altogether. The transposition of the previous chapter is an evident and hasty attempt to fill the resulting gap in the architecture of the work.)

666 *An eminent scholar... winter revels*: P. Wendland in his article 'Jesus as Saturn-King', which appeared in the journal *Hermes*, xxxiii (1898), 175–9.

667 *... to crucify him*: Matthew 27: 26–31.

and crucify him: Dio Chrysostom, in his fourth dialogue. See note to p. 642 above.

670 *the soldiers of Herod*: Luke 23: 2.

671 *Philo the Jew*: Philo Judaeus, *Adversus Flaccum*, ed. Th. Mangoy (London: 1742), 520–32.

674 *for the sacrificial victims*: Pliny, *Epistolae*, x. 96.

676 *Magna est veritas et praevalebit*: 'Great is the truth, and shall prevail.'
Quoted by Thomas Brooks (1608–80) in *The Crown and Glory of Christianity* (1662), 407. Brooks was remembering, or rather half-remembering, the Vulgate translation of the apocryphal Third Book of Esdras, 4: 41, which, however, has 'Magna est veritas et praevalet' ('Great is the truth, and doth prevail').

BOOK IV: THE GOLDEN BOUGH

Chapter 1: Between Heaven and Earth (GB3 x. 1–21).

682 *The sagacious author*: *Die gestriegelte Rockenphilosophie* or 'The Striped-petticoat philosophy' was an anonymous anti-feminist tract published in Chemnitz in 1759.

683 *Leyden jar*: an hermetically sealed electrical condenser, invented in Leyden in 1745–6.

685 *Acarnanian peasants*: ancient inhabitants of the area of western central Greece due south of the Gulf of Amvrakia.

Chapter 2: The Seclusion of Girls (GB3 x. 22–100, where it is entitled 'The Seclusion of Girls at Puberty').

687 *to the west of Lake Tanganyika*: that is, in present-day Zaïre.

688 *New Ireland*: in the north-eastern corner of the Bismark Archipelago to the east of the New Guinea group.

689 *I heard ... longer*: the Revd G. Brown, quoted by the Revd B. Danks, 'Marriage Customs in the New Guinea Group', *Journal of the Anthropological Institute*, xviii (1889), 284 f.

697 *... as it seemed, for ever*: Svend Grundvig, *Danische Volks-marken*, trans. A. Strodtmann (Leipzig, 1879), 199 ff. sqq.

698 *Greek story of Danaë*: Pausanias, ii. 43. 7. Apollodorus, *Bibliotheca*, ii. 4. 1 (with Frazer's notes to his edition of each). Danaë was the daughter of Ancrisius, king of Argos, who was told by the oracle that her son would kill him. He therefore confined Danaë in a locked tower; but Zeus, her lover, turned himself into a shower of gold and so succeeded in visiting her. Their son Perseus later killed Ancrisius accidentally in a discus-throwing competition. In Pausanias's time visitors to Argos were shown the tower. There was, however, some confusion as to the exact nature of her prison. As Frazer says in his note to Pausanias: 'Pausanias describes Danaë's prison as a bronze chamber above a subterranean structure. Apollodorus (ii, 41), with whom Sophocles (944 ff.) seems to agree, describes it as a large brazen underground chamber. Horace (Odes, ii. 16. i.) speaks of it as a brazen tower' (*Pausanias's Description of Greece*, vol. iii. p. 205). In Sophocles it is to Danaë that Antigone is compared when she is about to be incarcerated by Creon.

700 *Carriers*: a pre-Columbian people from the Dené group distinguished by
      the fact that their widows, rather than bury their husbands, carried their
      charred bones around with them.

702 *Manu*: see above, note to p. 69 *The Laws of Manu* had been memorably
      translated by G. Buhler in Max Müller's *Sacred Books of the East*, vol. xxv
      (Oxford, 1886), where the proscriptions concerning menstrous women
      appear on p. 135.

      The Hebrew lawgiver Moses: in Leviticus 15: 19–33.

      According to Pliny . . . so forth: Pliny, *Naturalis Historia*, vii.

704 *I wish to die*: Petronius, *Satyricon*, 48. The anecdote occurs during the
      dinner of Trimalchio, at which the *nouveau riche* host is boasting of his
      travels and wordly acquaintance. But the story rebounds against him,
      serving simply to demonstrate his ignorance, since the Cumaean sybil was
      well known to be suspended, not as he says '*in ampulla*' (in an urn), but in
      a basket. The passage is deployed with like satyric intent as an epigraph to
      T. S. Eliot's *The Waste Land* (1922).

**Chapter 3: Balder's Fires (incorporates GB3 x. Chap. 3 ('The Myth of
Balder'), pp. 101–5; Chap. 4 ('The Fire Festivals of Europe'), pp. 106–327;
and GB3 xi. Chap. 7 ('The Burning of Human Beings in Fires'), p. 21–44).**

706 *younger or prose Edda*: the Edda is one of the oldest surviving Norse
      sagas, read by Frazer in K. Simrock's German-language edition of 1882. Saxo
      Grammaticus also tells the story of Balder, as for the late Victorians had John
      Rhys in *Celtic Heathendom* (London and Edinburgh, 1888). But Balder had
      possessed a huge symbolic significance for the British ever since 1855, when
      Matthew Arnold in his poem *Balder Dead* had evoked the burning of his
      corpse-laden ship as it floats on a fjord fitfully lit, as it seemed, by the dying
      embers of all of the gods. This passage should be read out against the ebbing
      strains of Wagner's *Götterdämmerung*, as the kingdom of the gods goes up in
      flames. The intention is not all that dissimilar.

711 *carrying out Death*: see above, Book II, Chap. 5.

715 *bare-faced trick and imposture*: the progenitor of this libel was Father
      S. Aboujust SJ, in 'Le feu du Saint-Sepulcre', *Les Missions Catholiques*, viii
      (1876), 165–8.

      sudden illumination: Frazer had witnessed this ceremony while on the first of
      his Greek tours in the spring of 1890. It is described in his notebook for 13
      April and was subsequently written up for *Folklore*, i (1890), 275. In GB3 x.
      130 his footnote runs: 'Having been honoured, like other strangers, with a
      place on the platform, I did not myself detect the presence of Lucifer at work
      among the multitude below; I merely suspected his insidious presence.'

719 *This festival . . . affected*: *Scotland and Scotsmen in the Eighteenth Century*,
      from the MSS of John Ramsay, Esq. of Ochertyre, edited by Alexander

Allardyce (Edinburgh and London: 1888), ii. 439–45. Frazer comments: 'The etymology of the word Beltane is obscure; the popular derivation of the first part from the Phoenician Baal is absurd.'

on the first of May . . . entertainment: Thomas Pennant's 'Tour of Scotland', in Pinkerton, iii. 49.

723   *Then doth . . . they dwell*: *The Popish Kingdom or reigne of Antichrist*, written in Latin verse by Thomas Naogeorgus and Englyshed by Barnaby Googe, 1570, edited by R. C. Hope (London, 1880), p. 54 verso.

724   *But it was . . . surperstition*: compare leaping of lovers over an open bonfire in Michael Tippett's opera *The Midsummer Marriage* (1946–52). It was Tippett's reading of GB3, a full set of which he had possessed since 1925, that 'opened my eyes to the ritual origins of theatre, affecting conclusively the ways I was later to conceive of opera'. *The Twentieth Century Blues* (London: Hutchinson, 1991), 19.

728   *Lady Wilde*: Oscar Wilde's mother, the redoubtable Speranza, in *Ancient Legends, Myths, Charms and Superstitions of Ireland* (London, 1887), a work of recourse for Lady Gregory among others, as for W. B. Yeats and the whole Irish cultural renaissance. The passage occurs in her first volume, p. 214.

731   *a learned and ingenious writer*: this turns out to be E. K. Chambers, in his *The Mediaeval Stage* (Oxford, 1903), i. 110 ff.

Of . . . Beltane: see Book II, Chap. 12 above.

733   *Hallowe'en . . . children*: A. Goodrich-Freyer, 'More Folklore from the Hebrides', *Folklore*, xiii (1902), 53.

734   *fey*: that is (in Scots), doomed, or with a look of death hanging about him.

736   *John Brand*: the aptly named Dr Brand was author of *Popular Antiquities from Great Britain* (London, 1882–3), where, on p. 471 of volume I, he states: 'I am pretty confident that the Yule block will be found, in its first use, to have been only a counterpart to the Midsummer fires, made within doors because of the cold weather at this winter solstice, as those in the hot season, at the summer one, are kindled in the open air'.

741   *When an evil . . . flames*: Joh. Ruskius, quoted by J. Grimm in his *Deutsche Mythologie*, i. 502.

744   *Forest . . . gay*: cited by Mannhardt in his *Der Baumkultus der Germanen und ihrer Nachbarstamme* (Berlin, 1875).

745   *Julius Caesar*: in *De Bello Gallico*, vi. 15.

746   *living contents*: a particularly sinister re-enactment of this custom is portrayed in Anthony Shaffer's film *The Wicker Man* (1973), in which a young policeman is lured to a cliff-top in the Highlands and then burned alive in a wicker cage.

748   This is the view of the matter taken in GB3. Previously, Frazer had been
      inclined to view fire-festivals as sun charms.

**Chapter 4: The External Soul (incorporates GB3 xi. Chap. 9 ('Balder and
the Misteltoe'), pp. 76–94; Chap. 10 ('The External Soul in Folk-Tales'),
pp. 95–152; and sections 1–3 of Chap. 11 ('The External Soul in
Folk-Custom'), pp. 153–218).**

751   *In treating ... trifles*: Pliny, *Naturalis Historia*, xvi. 249 ff. This passage
      was the occasion for Frazer's most celebrated scholarly *faux pas*. The
      prominence which midsummer celebrations possess through these closing
      phases of the work was originally the result of his mistranslating Pliny's
      phrase 'omnia sexta luna' as 'in the sixth month', that is, in June. The
      mistranslation occurs in GB1 ii. 285, and as soon as it was published the
      Oxford classicist Warde Fowler wrote to tell him that the phrase could only
      mean 'on the sixth day of every month'. With that Frazer's theory, and his
      self-assurance, collapsed. When he realized that he had founded a whole
      plank of his argument on a misprision he had a fit of panic, wrote to *The
      Athenaeum* confessing his error, and even tried to resign from Trinity. But
      H. Montagu Butler, then master of the college, handed back his letter of
      resignation with a weary smile, saying, after Luther, 'pecca fortiter' ('sin
      more strongly'). And the theory of the midsummer fires lived to fight
      another day, if under a slightly different banner. It is arguable, for all that,
      that Balder as a prop for these closing stages of the work never quite
      recovers.

753   *bonfire in Normandy*: see above, pp. 746–8.

754   *At ... pointed out*: see Book I, Chap. 7 above.

756   *... without causing death*: see above, Book I, Chap. 11 *passim*.

758   *with a fearful groan, he died*: the tale was published by Frazer's friend, the
      amateur folklorist Edward Clodd, in the *Folk-lore Journal*, ii (1884),
      288–303. See also Clodd's *Myths and Dreams* (London, 1885), 188–98.

759   *Meleager*: the story of Meleager, like those of Nisus and Pterelaus below,
      is culled from Apollodorus' *Bibliotheca*, which Frazer edited and translated
      in 1921. The Meleager legend occurs at 1. 8, the Nisus legend at iii. 15. 8,
      and the Pterelaus legend at ii. 4. 5, and 7.

760   *on which his life depended*: Plutarch, *Parallela*, 26.

777   *a French Missionary*: Father H. Trilles, 'Chez les Fans', *Les Missions
      Catholiques*, xxx (1898), 322.

**Chapter 5: Death and Resurrection (incorporates sections 4 and 5 of GB3
xi. 218–78).**

785   *A certain ... year*: (Sir) George Grey, *Journals of Two Expeditions of
      Discovery in North-West and Western Australia* (London: 1841), ii. 228 f.

786 *The totem ... parrot*: this represents the first of Frazer's three successive theories of totemism, the so-called Depository Theory, first outlined in GB1 ii. 338–9. Since articulating it, Frazer had passed through a Sacramental Theory which he had temporarily embraced under the influence of Baldwin Spencer's work on the aborigines. According to this theory, the members of the totemic clan occasionally reasserted their union with the totem by devouring it in a sacramental feast. The totem, therefore, was precisely that which, once a year, they did eat. This theory is most notably expressed in GB2, but by GB3 Frazer had passed on to yet another theory, the so-called Conceptional Theory of totemism, according to which totems were assigned according to the traditional site closest to which the mother was passing when she first felt the child quicken in her womb. The first theory (in which, to be honest, Frazer had already lost faith) is here retained because it is needed to support the next phase of the argument.

792 *Upon this occasion ... boys*: Robert Beverley, *History of Virginia* (London, 1722), 177 ff.

793 *obscure*: see note to p. 320 above.

Chapter 6: The Golden Bough (incorporates GB3 xi. Chap. 12 ('The Golden Bough'), pp. 279–303 and Chap. 13 ('Farewell to Nemi'), pp. 304–9).

796 *Virgil ... compares it with mistletoe*: it may well be thought that at this point Frazer gives the game away. Poets do not habitually compare objects to themselves.

   whence shone ... leaf: Virgil, *Aeneid*, vi. 203 ff.

797 *annually celebrated ... grove*: Actually an August festival. For this and for the perpetual fire in the sanctuary, see Book I, Chap. 1 above.

806 *Fatte ... conoscenza*: 'You were not made to live like beasts but to pursue virtue and understanding'. Dante, *Inferno* xxvi. ll. 119–20. Ulysses' 'picciol oration' to his shipmates urging them beyond the Straits of Gibraltar in search of knowledge. The quotation epitomizes Frazer's ambiguous feelings concerning the scientific enterprise for, as my friend, Dr Ralph Pite of Corpus Christi College writes (letter of 16 July 1993) 'the speech is persuasive, the aspirations admirable, the consequence fatal'.

807 *rekindle the dying fire of the sun*: according to William Thomson, Lord Kelvin, at whose feet Frazer had studied physics at the University of Glasgow in the early 1870s, the sun's life, and hence that of the solar system, was limited by the amount of heat that it could generate. The universe was like an immense fire gradually going cold. The pessimism induced by this, the Second Law of Thermodynamics, cast, a pall over Frazer's essential progressivism, and not only his. In his footnote he cites

a letter of Charles Darwin: 'To think of the progress of millions of years, with every continent swarming with good and enlightened men, all ending in this, and with probably no fresh start until this our planetary system has been again converted into red-hot gas. *Sic transit gloria mundi* with a vengeance.' (Frances Darwin (ed.), *More Letters of Charles Darwin* (London: 1903), i. 260 f.)

into air, into thin air: Frazer is half-quoting *The Tempest* IV. iv. 149–59:

> Our revels now are ended. These our actors,
> As I foretold you, were all spirits and
> All melted into air, into thin air;
> And, like the baseless fabric of this vision,
> The cloud-capp'd towers, the gorgeous palaces,
> The solemn temples, the great globe itself,
> Yea, all which it inherit, shall dissolve
> And, like this insubstantial pageant faded,
> Leave not a rack behind. We are such stuff
> As dreams are made on, and our little life
> Is rounded with a sleep.

The corollary of this allusion is that Frazer himself is Prospero who, deeper than ever plummet sound, is about to drown his book.

808 *ringing the Angelus*: shortly after GB1 was published, it was pointed out to Frazer that the bells of St Peter's are inaudible from Nemi. He refused to change the reference, answering that in imagination he heard them still. The real reason is that the closing paragraph contains a coded reference once more to Renan, in which that arch-rationalist took it upon himself to reprove the all-too-barren intellectualism of the German theologian, Ludwig Feuerbach. Frazer quotes the reproof, a caveat aimed at his own speculations, in *Folklore in the Old Testament* (iii. 453–4), and we may as well end with it: 'Ah, if seated on the ruins of the Palatine or the Coelian Mount, he had heard the sounds of the eternal bells lingering and dying over the deserted hills where Rome once was . . . [he] would not thus have cast reproach on one half of human poetry, not cried aloud as if he would repel from him the phantom of Iscariot!'

INDEX

The Oxford World's Classics Website

www.worldsclassics.co.uk

- Browse the full range of Oxford World's Classics online

- Sign up for our monthly e-alert to receive information on new titles

- Read extracts from the Introductions

- Listen to our editors and translators talk about the world's greatest literature with our Oxford World's Classics audio guides

- Join the conversation, follow us on Twitter at OWC_Oxford

- Teachers and lecturers can order inspection copies quickly and simply via our website

www.worldsclassics.co.uk

American Literature

British and Irish Literature

Children's Literature

Classics and Ancient Literature

Colonial Literature

Eastern Literature

European Literature

Gothic Literature

History

Medieval Literature

Oxford English Drama

Poetry

Philosophy

Politics

Religion

The Oxford Shakespeare

A complete list of Oxford World's Classics, including Authors in Context, Oxford English Drama, and the Oxford Shakespeare, is available in the UK from the Marketing Services Department, Oxford University Press, Great Clarendon Street, Oxford OX2 6DP, or visit the website at www.oup.com/uk/worldsclassics.

In the USA, visit www.oup.com/us/owc for a complete title list.

Oxford World's Classics are available from all good bookshops. In case of difficulty, customers in the UK should contact Oxford University Press Bookshop, 116 High Street, Oxford OX1 4BR.

A SELECTION OF OXFORD WORLD'S CLASSICS

THOMAS AQUINAS	Selected Philosophical Writings
FRANCIS BACON	The Essays
WALTER BAGEHOT	The English Constitution
GEORGE BERKELEY	Principles of Human Knowledge and Three Dialogues
EDMUND BURKE	A Philosophical Enquiry into the Origin of Our Ideas of the Sublime and Beautiful Reflections on the Revolution in France
CONFUCIUS	The Analects
ÉMILE DURKHEIM	The Elementary Forms of Religious Life
FRIEDRICH ENGELS	The Condition of the Working Class in England
JAMES GEORGE FRAZER	The Golden Bough
SIGMUND FREUD	The Interpretation of Dreams
THOMAS HOBBES	Human Nature and De Corpore Politico Leviathan
JOHN HUME	Selected Essays
NICCOLO MACHIAVELLI	The Prince
THOMAS MALTHUS	An Essay on the Principle of Population
KARL MARX	Capital The Communist Manifesto
J. S. MILL	On Liberty and Other Essays Principles of Political Economy and Chapters on Socialism
FRIEDRICH NIETZSCHE	Beyond Good and Evil The Birth of Tragedy On the Genealogy of Morals Twilight of the Idols

THOMAS PAINE	**Rights of Man, Common Sense, and Other Political Writings**
JEAN-JACQUES ROUSSEAU	**The Social Contract** **Discourse on the Origin of Inequality**
ADAM SMITH	**An Inquiry into the Nature and Causes of the Wealth of Nations**
MARY WOLLSTONECRAFT	**A Vindication of the Rights of Woman**